ACPL, Laramie, WY   11/2016
000400679471
Stone, Katherine,
A new collection of three complete novel
Pieces: 1

D0193265

ALBANY COUNTY
PUBLIC LIBRARY
Serving the Laramie Plains since 1887

Laramie, Wyoming 82070

PRESENTED BY

A Friend

THREE COMPLETE NOVELS

KATHERINE STONE

A New Collection of Three Complete Novels

KATHERINE STONE

PROMISES

RAINBOWS

TWINS

WINGS BOOKS
New York • Avenel, New Jersey

WITHDRAWN

ALBANY COUNTY
PUBLIC LIBRARY
LARAMIE, WYOMING

This omnibus was originally published in separate volumes under the titles:

Promises, copyright © 1993 by Katherine Stone
Rainbows, copyright © 1992 by Katherine Stone
Twins, copyright © 1989 by Katherine Stone

All rights reserved.

This edition contains the complete and unabridged texts of the original editions. They have been completely reset for this volume.

This 1995 edition is published by Wings Books, distributed by Random House Value Publishing, Inc., 40 Engelhard Avenue, Avenel, New Jersey 07001, by arrangement with Zebra Books, an imprint of Kensington Publishing Corp.

Random House
New York • Toronto • London • Sydney • Auckland

Printed and bound in the United States of America

Library of Congress Cataloging-in-Publication Data

Stone, Katherine, 1949–
   [Novels. Selections]
   A new collection of three complete novels / Katherine Stone.
     p. cm.
   Contents: Promises—Rainbows—Twins.
   ISBN 0-517-11840-8
   1. Man-woman relationships—United States—Fiction. 2. Women physicians—United States—Fiction. 3. Sisters—United States—Fiction. 4. Twins—United States—Fiction. 5. Love stories, American. I. Title.
PS3569.T64134A6 1995
813'.54—dc20

94-29800
CIP

8 7 6 5 4 3 2 1

Contents

———◆———

PART ONE

CHAPTER ONE

*D*r. Elizabeth Jennings abandoned all hope of fur-
ther sleep shortly before dawn. She had been awake for almost two hours, far too
excited—and anxious—to drift back to the tranquility of dreams. Today Elizabeth
was going to assist Dr. Nicholas Chase with the transplantation of a small portion
of a young mother's healthy liver to her infant daughter's diseased one. If everything went well, and it would because of Nick's immense talent, both mother and
daughter would have a long life of health and love ahead of them.

Today's surgery wouldn't be the world's first living donor liver transplantation—that monumental surgery had been done twenty-one months before—but it
would be the first such operation performed in San Francisco, and the first also in
which Elizabeth would participate. The surgery wasn't new to Nick, of course. He
had been a member of the surgical team in Chicago on that historic day in November 1989, and he had since become a leading expert on the lifesaving operation.
Now, in just a few hours, Nick was going to introduce the extraordinary technique
to his own surgical team at Pacific Heights Medical Center as well as to other Bay
Area transplant surgeons who had been specially invited to observe the delicate
and difficult surgery from the amphitheater above the operating room. Only one
surgeon would be in the operating room with Nick, assisting him . . .

How Elizabeth wished she could believe that she had been handpicked by Nick
because he valued her surgical skill, the decisive agility of her slender fingers combined with her unshakable calm in the OR, but she had no proof whatsoever that
the great Nicholas Chase thought she had any surgical aptitude at all. He hadn't
chosen her to be the second member of his two-member team, after all, he had
simply inherited her.

Elizabeth was already on the faculty of the medical center's prestigious Department of Surgery when Nick arrived. She had been recruited because of her expertise in trauma, and once there, because the center's organ transplantation program
was expanding, the transplant service chief had convinced her to become trained
in that surgical subspecialty as well. Elizabeth had just completed that training
when, eight months ago, Nick had arrived to become the new transplant service
chief—and he had inherited her as his assistant, the person designated to work
most closely with him, the other half of his two-person team.

Dr. Elizabeth Jennings was beneath Dr. Nicholas Chase in academic rank, of
course. Nick was eight years her senior both in age and in surgical experience. But
she was a good surgeon, perhaps even a gifted one. Still, with Nick she felt uncertain, as if he were uncertain of her, unsure of what to do with her and strangely
wary. He was always polite to her, a cool formal politeness that kept a vast distance
between them despite the intimacy of the work they did together.

Somewhere in that cool wary distance, and all its uneasy silences, was Nick privately wishing that she had followed his predecessor—and her mentor—to Boston, so that he would have been free to recruit someone new, someone he really wanted, a choice not a legacy? Had Nick awakened early today, too, the peacefulness of his sleep disrupted by the smoldering displeasure that it would be she who would be assisting him with today's momentous surgery?

It was that anxiety, that tormenting worry amid the excitement she felt about the day that lay ahead, that finally drove Elizabeth from her bed. She would banish that worry, she decided, with hot tea and the splendor of daybreak over San Francisco Bay. Elizabeth had a view of that splendor, of all the magnificent and ever-changing dramas of sea and sky, from the living room of her Pacific Heights apartment. The worry would vanish with the golden dawn, she would force it to; and then she would focus all the energy and attention of her bright mind on the extraordinary task that lay ahead—mentally reviewing the scientific papers she had read, the diagrams she had memorized, the words Nick himself had said, as recently as last night, about the intricate technique, the precise timing, the potential catastrophes.

Elizabeth made tea then settled into a cozy chair in the living room and gazed outside. The tormenting worry about Nick would be conquered by the pale yellow rays of morning. But it was night still, the darkest hour before dawn, and she simply permitted all the thoughts and worries about him to surface, narrowing her luminous emerald eyes as if hoping to see them more clearly. But there was no clarity.

There were only the dark shadows cast by the dark, handsome, mysterious Dr. Chase.

Nick was the best surgeon Elizabeth had ever known. Everyone at the medical center knew that about Nick. Just as everyone seemed to know about his affairs with the hospital's most beautiful women. Nick's affairs were short-lived—and mysterious, occurring in darkness, breathless rendezvous of pleasure and passion that began at midnight and always ended before dawn. Dr. Nicholas Chase didn't seduce with romantic candlelight dinners, he didn't need to, nor apparently was there ever much meaningful conversation, just enough words from Nick to make it abundantly clear that he was not interested in love.

Elizabeth did not want to hear about Nick's love . . . sex . . . life. She did not want to learn that even his immense talent as a surgeon was eclipsed by his extraordinary expertise as a lover. But since the devastatingly sexy black-haired, blue-eyed doctor and his affairs were a favorite topic of conversation at the hospital, it was virtually impossible not to unwittingly overhear. And more than once, astonishingly, one of Nick's women had actually come to her, seeking her advice, as if she would have some special insight into his mysteries and secrets. She was Nick's partner after all, his shadow, his sidekick. Surely in the long emotional hours that she and Nick spent together, saving lives and losing them, he would have confided some truths about himself. Elizabeth would never have revealed such truths had she known them, but of course she knew nothing. Even in the most emotional times, there had been only politeness from Nick—and distance and silence.

Elizabeth did not want to know about Nick's affairs. But she did: his breathtaking sensuality, his talent for pleasure, the reckless abandon of his passion—and yet the surprising care he took to be certain that the intimacy was safe, for all the new reasons—and for the oldest reason of all.

Nicholas Chase did not want to become a father, his beautiful women all agreed. Not that he would *be* a father of course, they added knowingly, predicting with absolute certainty that Nick would wash his hands of that responsibility as thoroughly as he scrubbed before a case in the OR.

That's not true! Elizabeth protested silently whenever she heard the confident pronouncement. If Nick fathered a child, he would be very responsible. She was sure of it. And she was sure, too, that the man who was such a good doctor, so caring and so compassionate with his patients, would be a wonderful and loving father.

Elizabeth defended Nick in silence, in her heart, in the same heart that ached whenever she inadvertently stumbled into a discussion about him. Did Nick know that such discussions took place? she wondered. Would it bother him if he did? Elizabeth hoped it would. It was so private, and it should have been so special. The women with whom Nick shared himself didn't want him, not really, not for keeps. They knew how dangerous he was, how wild and restless, how intense and demanding, how undeserving of their trust much less their love. Nick's lovers didn't want Nick, and Nick didn't want them—except for the night-cloaked moments of pleasure about which Elizabeth hated hearing so much.

Why would Nick give himself away so freely? Why would he devalue himself that way? It was as if he didn't believe there was anything important or special about him, as if he didn't matter at all. Nicholas Chase mattered very much to Elizabeth Jennings, even though it was painfully obvious that the feeling wasn't mutual.

Elizabeth had wondered in the beginning if it was possible that Nick actually felt threatened by her. Her remarkable academic and career successes rivaled his own stunning accomplishments at her age; and she, like he, had chosen to become expert in both trauma and transplantation surgery. Was Nick threatened by her accomplishments and her talent? Or was he simply annoyed by her boldly calm and competent invasion of the sacrosanct male domain of the operating room?

Neither, Elizabeth was forced to realize. Nick was neither threatened nor annoyed. It was the nineties, after all, and Nicholas Chase was a modern man, not a chauvinist. By night, yes, he had meaningless affairs with women doctors; but that was by mutual consent, an enthusiastic choice to share passion and nothing else. And by day, in the hospital, he consulted those same women physicians, wanting their medical opinions, listening with uncondescending interest to what they said and then daring to both agree and disagree.

It wasn't that Nick disliked women physicians. It was just, quite simply, that he didn't like *her*. The dark blue eyes that flirted with every other woman with such effortlessness that the seduction seemed almost instinctive had never been anything but subdued and solemn with her. Subdued and solemn and sometimes— when they were alone and Nick was so lost in thought that he seemed to have forgotten she was there—Elizabeth caught glimpses of powerful currents swirling beneath the sensual calm, flickers of secret and turbulent emotions in the ocean blue depths. What she saw, what she believed she saw, was pain, uncertainty, and a sadness as dark and deep as the blue itself.

She had to be mistaken. Nick was confident, arrogant even, and deservedly so, both personally and professionally. Confident and arrogant, alluring and dangerous—not anguished, not uncertain, not sad. It had to be an optical illusion created by his tall, dark, handsome shadow and further blurred by her own emotions about him . . .

"Hopeless," Elizabeth whispered to the night-black sky that was now beginning to yield to the pale yellow rays of morning. A soft smile touched her lips as she realized the word she whispered was, like the awakening dawn, a glimmer of light and truth. Her relationship—*relationship?*—with Nick was hopeless. Of course stunningly gorgeous Nicholas Chase would never find stunningly wholesome Elizabeth Jennings desirable. But she wished, oh how she wished, that he would like her.

"Completely hopeless," she repeated softly as she left the coziness of the chair to make a second cup of tea, one to last until the sky was bright gold and it was time to shower and dress before making the two-minute walk from her apartment to the medical center.

While waiting for the water to heat, Elizabeth gazed thoughtfully at the mug her hands had found in the predawn darkness. It was her favorite, a festive scene of brightly colored balloons floating amid swirls of confetti and personalized with the exuberant command, emblazoned in brilliant fuschia: ELIZABETH! CELEBRATE!!

The mug had been one of two gifts given to her by her best friend in celebration of her twenty-first birthday. Larisa's other gift had been a bottle of Courvoisier. "Because, Liz," she had announced, her voice solemn but her eyes sparkling as she spoke the nickname no one else ever had, "you're twenty-one years old now. You have to at least *taste* alcohol!" Even then both Elizabeth and Larisa had known that of the two gifts the mug would get the most use. And indeed now, nine years later, the bottle of vintage cognac remained almost full—and the mug was still Elizabeth's favorite.

Elizabeth sighed softly as she looked at the mug and remembered that twenty-first birthday . . . and the triumphant years that had followed for both of them . . . and the three years that had elapsed since she had last heard from Larisa. No, that was wrong. It had been three years since Elizabeth had mailed her last letter to her best friend, but it had been three and a half years since Larisa had last communicated with her. Elizabeth very much missed the letters punctuated with exclamation points and smiling—and frowning—faces; and she missed even more the latenight phone calls that had stopped even before the letters but had once been an effortless flow of quietly shared secrets and dreams interspersed with soft cascades of merry, and so uncomplicated, laughter.

As Elizabeth poured the hot tea water into the mug and thought about the uncomplicated laughter, she imagined a scene between her best friend and the man who had so complicated her own life. Even Nick, a connoisseur of beautiful women, would be dazzled by Larisa's beauty. Even he would be captivated by the brilliant blue eyes that would appraise him with provocative boldness.

Larisa's appraisal of Nick would be unhurried, a leisurely and pleasurable perusal, and when at last she was finished, she would tell him with unblushing candor that she approved of his rich coal black hair and his seductive dark blue eyes and the proud strength of his sculpted features and the devastating sexiness of his lazy smile.

"Well, Nick, you are indeed as advertised—really quite gorgeous," she would say. Then, after Nick had, with silent eloquence, returned the compliment in kind, she would continue, "I have some questions for you, Doctor. Most of them are Elizabeth's questions, but I do have one of my own, which I'll save for last. So, let's see. What are you, confident and arrogant, or uncertain and sad? You look confident and arrogant to me—and very dangerous. But even though I see only seduction, Liz has told me that sometimes she has seen pain. And I can't simply discount her impressions, you see, because her instincts about people are usually pure gold. Although, admittedly, she is so generous that she has been known to find good where no one else can . . ." Larisa's focus would drift for a moment, from her search for the real Nicholas Chase to thoughts of her friend—her own relentless teasing that Elizabeth always saw the best in people, and her immense pride in her generous friend for doing so.

Then she would concentrate once again on Nick, and still seeing for herself only the arrogant confidence of a stunningly handsome man, she would demand,

"What is the story with these meaningless affairs that occur only in darkness? Oh, don't get me wrong. I don't care that they're meaningless. But what is this prince of midnight nonsense? A ploy to add more danger, more romance, more drama? You don't need the extra theatrics, Doctor Chase. In broad daylight, in the harshest of lights, I am quite certain that you could seduce." Larisa would smile radiantly at the inscrutable blue eyes and when it became abundantly clear that they were going to remain inscrutable to her forever, she would give a resigned sigh and say, "Well. I can tell that even if there is some deep secret anguish you aren't going to reveal it to me. So, let me ask my question."

The provocative teasing would leave Larisa's voice then and her beautiful face would become thoughtful as she asked with quiet bewilderment, "Why don't you like my friend?" And then, in the long silence that would surely follow, her eyes would flash with anger and when she spoke again it would be with icy indignation, "How *dare* you not like Elizabeth!"

Elizabeth gave a soft shake of her dark brown curls at the image of Larisa, free-spirited and provocative, irreverent and bold, fiercely loyal and mother-bear protective. That was the Larisa who had been randomly assigned to be her freshman roommate at Berkeley. It had been the frisky trick of some wily computer, matching—*mismatching*—glamorous and sophisticated Larisa Locksley with naive and unglamorous Elizabeth Jennings. But they had become best friends throughout the three years each had spent in college and best friends after despite the continent of separation and divergence of life-styles that occurred when Larisa had moved to New York to become a top fashion model and Elizabeth had remained in San Francisco to attend medical school.

And when, six years ago, Larisa had joyfully announced her engagement to the very handsome and staggeringly wealthy thirty-year-old Julian Chancellor, and had wanted her best friend to be her maid of honor, the June wedding had been arranged to accommodate Elizabeth's rigorous on-call schedule as a surgery resident at the grueling and prestigious program at Parkland in Dallas. With careful planning she had been able to get away for twenty-four hours, arriving in New York just in time for the rehearsal dinner at La Côte Basque in Manhattan and leaving the Southampton Club on Long Island the following afternoon just moments after the bride and groom themselves had bid adieu to their wedding guests. The twenty-four hours had been a festive whirl of dazzle and elegance, crescendoing to the picture-perfect garden wedding—and yet Elizabeth had returned to Dallas with a feeling of sadness, an ominous and unshakable impression that Larisa's vibrant spirit had seemed a little subdued.

Elizabeth didn't see Larisa again. But for the next three years there were phone calls and letters, and with each ensuing one the impression became even stronger: her bright, funny, outrageous and courageous friend was fading. During college Elizabeth had always sensed that despite the many secrets Larisa had shared with her, there were important ones that she hadn't—and Elizabeth had never pushed. Were there new secrets now? she wondered as she felt Larisa fading. Secrets that Larisa either could not or would not share?

Elizabeth respected Larisa's privacy. She only offered her support and her friendship. But still Larisa withdrew. The phone calls stopped, and the letters became shorter as the gaps between them became longer. Finally, when four of her letters to Larisa went unanswered over a six-month period, Elizabeth herself stopped writing, not out of pique, but because it was so obvious that Larisa no longer wanted to continue the correspondence.

Maybe Larisa hasn't faded, Elizabeth told herself. Maybe it is simply time for our surprising friendship to fade. The thought saddened Elizabeth, but not nearly as much as the image of a faded Larisa did.

Although she had never actually said so, Elizabeth knew that the childhood of which Larisa had so rarely spoken could not have been a happy one. And she wanted happiness for her best friend. Happiness—and love. For as long as Elizabeth had known her, there had been men in Larisa's life, but until Julian the relationships had always been fleeting. Larisa had kept them that way, ending them quickly but never cruelly, always genuinely surprised when even the most gentle rejection had caused rage, as if she believed that the man had never really wanted her, only her astonishing beauty.

"Julian loves me for me," Larisa had confessed to Elizabeth shortly before her fairy-tale wedding, a soft confession of disbelief and joy.

Elizabeth had been so thrilled for Larisa, and so very eager to meet the man who had brought her friend such happiness at last. But when she met the handsome and powerful Julian Chancellor, Elizabeth had been swept by a strange uneasiness. She hadn't been able to free herself of it, nor had she been able to clearly define it. All she knew was that when she met Julian the invisible rose-colored glasses, about which Larisa had always teased her, had been quite firmly in place, and she had been prepared, as always, to see only the very best. But even though Elizabeth could not define what she had seen, and most surely had never communicated her uneasiness to Larisa, there was something about Julian Chancellor that had sent shivers of ice through her.

Then—and still.

Elizabeth melted the icy shivers now by curling her fingers around the warm mug and smiling at the brilliant fuschia command.

Celebrate, Larisa, she commanded silently in return. I hope that I was very wrong about Julian. I hope that he has given you all the wonderful love and happiness that you deserve and that at this very moment, as you are awakening a continent away in your penthouse in Manhattan, your heart is overflowing with joy . . .

Chapter Two

Manhattan
August 1991

*E*ight-thirty, read the Lalique crystal clock beside the bed. Far below the Fifth Avenue penthouse, Manhattan was awake and already very hot and humid beneath the glaring August sun.

Eight-thirty! Larisa was seized with panic as the realization settled. At three, when she had been certain that Julian had truly gone, she had crawled to the bathroom and taken a long, hot, necessary shower. She had wanted to leave then, but she had been far too weak, far too dizzy. She had needed to lie down again, just for a few moments, just a brief rest . . .

But she had fallen asleep, and now five precious hours had passed, and what if Julian was putting his key into the front door lock at this very moment? What if he was closer even than that, his footsteps softly muted by the plush carpet?

Julian won't return, Larisa bravely told her racing heart. He won't return until this evening, as usual. As usual . . . as if nothing had happened. He will spend today negotiating new multimillion-dollar deals, and perhaps negotiating the recapture of whatever real estate deal it was that he had lost yesterday—a loss which had triggered such violence and such rage.

Julian won't return, Larisa assured herself bravely. But still, I have to get up and pack and leave—*now*.

In the wonderful dreams Larisa had dreamed during the past five hours, both her body and spirit had been strong, not damaged, and together they had already taken her very far away. But those were dreams, wonderful dreams, and she was awake now, still in the penthouse where Julian might return, still needing to leave.

As she became more wakeful, the courageous woman in her dreams seemed to vanish and the bright light of day exposed the wonderful dreams for what they had actually been: impossible ones. How could she possibly leave him? She was bound to him, wasn't she, tightly and forever? Oh, yes, the chains that bound her to Julian were quite invisible, but they were also very real—terribly, painfully real. Julian owned her, all of her, her heart, her spirit, her body, her destiny. Larisa knew exactly what Julian owned, what he possessed and controlled, because his possessions were gifts of love and trust that she herself had given him; and she knew exactly how much he owned—*everything*—because it was she who had given him everything she had to give.

The invisible chains were all that were necessary to imprison the invisible woman she had become. She was without any substance whatsoever, lighter than air, floating, floating. Larisa's mind floated now, blurred by the vicious blows to her head, and in a moment she would float back to those wonderful courageous dreams . . .

No! The cry came from very deep within her, from some resilient place that didn't belong to Julian because all this time it had been hidden even from her. The voice continued with nurturing calm, *You can sleep later. But right now you must get up. You must act out the scenes you have so carefully rehearsed in your dreams. Right now!*

Larisa obeyed the voice. Too quickly, she realized as the room began to whirl violently when she sat up. But the whirling was more than simply a too hasty change of position. It was part of her, inside her. Inside her head because of the blows? Or inside the slender abdomen that screamed in silent pain, as if in horrified witness to hidden pools of blood? Whatever its source, Larisa realized that the whirling was going to travel with her on her journey. She spent a few moments getting used to it, accepting it. When she finally stood, she wobbled again, and waited again, adjusting. Then, when the whirling was under her control, even though it hadn't abated, she simply willed herself to become the brave woman about whom she had dreamed.

Larisa moved slowly, conserving energy, but she moved decisively, too, reliving the scenes that had already been so successfully enacted in her dreams. She needed to dress elegantly. She was the ravishingly beautiful wife of billionaire Julian Chancellor, after all, and it was essential that anyone who happened to see her as she made her escape not ever guess that anything was amiss. She needed a summer travel outfit, and she had many, but today there were other requirements as well. Today whatever she wore had to conceal the purple bruises on her snow-white limbs and it had to drape softly, loosely, on her ravaged body. Larisa selected a long-sleeved teal silk blouse and matching silk harem pants, accessorized, at least until she was far away from eyes that might recognize her, by a gold chain belt around her slender aching waist.

The outfit was fine, elegant and concealing, but what about her beautiful recognizable face? Would she be able to wear her trademark hairstyle, her magnificent red-gold hair swept off her face and twisted into a lustrous knot atop her head? That was the hairstyle Manhattan had come to expect. For the past six years the luxuriant fire-kissed golden mane for which she had been so famous during her modeling days had been hidden entirely from public view, allowed to flow freely only for Julian. He had insisted on it.

Would it be possible for her to fully expose her face today as always? Larisa wondered as she approached the mirror with trepidation, so very fearful of what she might see—or might not see. Eighteen years ago, after the first time she had been brutally betrayed, whenever she had looked into a mirror, she had seen nothing. Where her face should have been, there had been no image at all, only a blurry oval shadow. The facelessness then had lasted for almost four years, and even when she had finally been able to see her reflection again, what Larisa had seen was only an extraordinarily beautiful mask, a ravishing disguise that would enable her to move through the world with an aura of glittering confidence despite her true uncertainty and fear. The remarkable face, the exquisite masquerade, had made Larisa Locksley rich and famous. And it had made Julian Chancellor want to own her. And sometime in the past year or two—or maybe three or even four—there had been days when Larisa would look into a mirror and see again only the blurry oval shadow.

As a teenager, Larisa had been unable to conquer the shadowy facelessness. She had never even wanted to. But in the past few years, she had learned of necessity how to force her image to come into view. That was what she did now, watching her face surface from the dark depths, cringing when she first saw her eyes, so haunted and hopeless, then resolutely leaving them to begin the careful search for bruises.

There were swollen lumps on both sides of her head, warm, tender gravestones that marked the death of her love. But those lumps were beneath her golden-red hair. No one would notice them.

And her face itself? It was quite undamaged—except for the haunted hopeless blue. Julian had been terribly careful not to damage his most prized possession. Larisa trembled at the thought and its hideous meaning. Had Julian really known what he was doing? Had there actually been thought and control in his rage? She didn't know, didn't want to know. She only knew that she was grateful that her face had been spared his brutal violence.

Grateful? Yes, because it meant she could leave today. And there was more gratitude—to whoever it was who had tricked Julian out of the property he had obviously wanted so desperately and lost. Larisa had known nothing about the real estate deal, and still didn't, except that apparently clever and devious Julian, himself a master of trickery, had been outdone, and that had enraged him, and somehow, inexplicably and irrationally, he had shifted all the blame of his defeat to her. The blame, the rage . . . and the punishment. He had punished her with words first, a vicious assault that left her heart in a thousand weeping pieces, and then he had punished her further, physically, mercilessly ignoring her terrified pleas and finally possessing her against her will—as if she had no will, as if she was his to own, to harm, to control, to destroy.

She *was* his, a gift of love from her to him, because she had loved him, and had needed his love, and because she had so desperately needed to believe that she had been right to trust him. She had acceded to Julian's every wish, his every whim, betraying herself in the process, somehow convincing herself that each demand was merely a romantic request of love. She had abandoned the modeling career she had loved—yes, willingly!—because Julian had wanted her to be available to him and his insatiable desire for her at all times. He had wanted her to abandon even more, everything that had come before him: her career, her friends, all ties with her past. Was it a romantic request, a wish for her life and her happiness to begin with their love? Or a blue-blooded request, the *Mayflower* descendant wanting to erase forever the memory of his bride's decidedly underprivileged lineage? Or was the request simply a controlling demand, wanting all invisible bonds to bind her to him and him alone?

Larisa had convinced herself that Julian's requests were romantic ones. Without hesitation she had abandoned her career and the friends she had made during her years as a model . . . and finally, three and a half years ago, she had even abandoned the only friend who had ever really mattered. Had she really severed her relationship with Elizabeth to please Julian? Or had it been in truth because something deep inside her hadn't wanted her best friend to know what had become of her, what she herself had *allowed* to happen to her?

Julian took, and Larisa gave, giving herself away, betraying her own heart and spirit with each new gift, dying a little more every day—and yet resolutely denying the truth because her need to believe in his love was so great. She might have lived—and died—with Julian forever. But after last night . . .

She had been raped once before, when she was twelve. On that distant night of terror there had been no one to protect her from the violence or to rescue her from the anguish of its aftermath. When Julian raped her last night, he had raped once again the innocent little girl who dwelled within her still. Despite her pleas, Larisa had been unable to protect either herself or the fragile child inside against Julian's violence. But now, gently yet firmly guided by the strong and courageous woman of her dreams, she was going to rescue them both from further anguish and harm.

Larisa was grateful to whoever it was who had tricked Julian and unmasked his brutal rage.

Because now she knew all about Julian and his love.

Now she could deny the truth no longer.

Larisa felt as if she were moving in slow motion through a whirling world of pain and fear. The pain was constant, a fiery legacy of Julian's venom, but the fear came in terrifying waves, crashing with each new sound, however slight, and lasting until the sound—the traffic far below, the air conditioner exhaling its cool air to offset the oppressive heat—was identified as being not Julian.

For a brief hopeful moment, Larisa wondered if Julian might be relieved if he returned and discovered she was leaving. *No*, the answer came swiftly, carried by yet another crashing wave of fear. Julian would be enraged. And the rage she had witnessed last night, when he had simply lost a piece of property he had wanted to add to his already vast empire, would be trivial compared to his rage at the loss of his wife.

Move more quickly! she urged her weak and whirling body.

She was dressed now and looked presentable, elegant. She needed only to pack and get whatever money she could find in Julian's desk. Neither would take long. Quickly and without sentimentality, she put an assortment of designer clothes in her suitcase, leaving room on top for the few items of clothing that were important to her, the few comfortable and treasured friends she had kept hidden from Julian.

Hidden? her mind echoed. Shouldn't that have been a clue? Doesn't hiding things from your husband seem like a marriage with problems?

She had hidden such trivial things: her well-worn, much beloved jeans from college, a blue sweatshirt with BERKELEY emblazoned in gold, the tattered cotton bathrobe and nightgown she had worn when she and Elizabeth stayed up all night sharing secrets and dreams. The clothes were rags, but they were the only friends from her past that still survived.

After the college clothes were packed, there was still a little room left in the suitcase. On impulse, or perhaps it had already been planned in her dreams, Larisa retrieved the long gown of flowing white silk—hidden also—from a far corner of her closet. She had loved the gown the moment she had seen it. So romantic, she had thought. So innocent, so pure, its delicate pearl and silver beads glistening like dewdrops on roses. How eager she had been to show her romantic discovery to Julian. How perfect it was, she had thought, for the enchanted evening before their fairy-tale wedding.

But Julian hadn't liked the beautiful gown. He had already decided what she would wear that night, a designer gown that tastefully yet undeniably celebrated the perfect body that would soon be his, provocative and luscious, not innocent and pure. Julian had wanted Larisa to wear his choice, and of course she had. But what if, on the eve of their wedding, she had said no? Would Julian have forced the issue? Might she have known the truth even then?

Larisa had hidden her college clothes and the never-worn gown from Julian for six years. Had he discovered those treasures of her past, he might have been annoyed, contemptuous of her silly sentimentality. But, she thought as she removed four small pink packets from their hiding place between layers of silk and satin in her dresser drawer, if Julian knew I had these . . .

A shiver of ice passed through her as she stared at the birth-control pills, the tiny reminders of such foolish hope and such shattering loss. How she had wanted children, his children, *their* children. How joyful, how hopeful she had been when the gynecologist she had consulted four months before her wedding—because she had known she must—had told her, "Yes, there is definitely very significant damage to the Fallopian tubes, but it's virtually impossible to predict to what extent that damage will affect your fertility. I have personally cared for women with similar tubal damage who have had totally normal pregnancies." Her past, that long ago night of terror, would not come back to haunt her, Larisa had told herself. She would have normal pregnancies, and she and Julian would have babies conceived in the greatest of love and raised by parents who would love and protect and cherish them—as parents should.

Larisa never told Julian that she was trying to get pregnant. She had wanted to surprise him, believing he would be thrilled, imagining the joy on his handsome face at the wonderful news. And she had hidden her own sadness from him as month after month—and then year after year—she failed to conceive.

After five years, the diagnosis seemed quite secure: she was infertile. There might be surgical and *in vitro* techniques that could be tried, of course, but it seemed very certain that she would never become pregnant without such sophisticated intervention. There was no reason whatsoever for her to use birth control.

But that was what she did, beginning nine months ago, because that was when something deep inside told her, warned her, that it would be disastrous to start a family with Julian. He wasn't ready, *they* weren't ready, to be the kind of parents she wanted for their babies. It would have been a miracle for her to conceive after five years of trying unsuccessfully—and Larisa had no reason to believe in miracles—but nonetheless she began taking birth-control pills to prevent the miracle she had once wanted with all her heart.

And when, six months ago, for the first time in their marriage Julian had told her he wanted children and wanted her to begin trying to get pregnant right away, she had agreed without protest—and each day, without fail, she had continued to take a pill from the carefully hidden pink packets.

He would kill me if he found these, Larisa thought with terrifying confidence as she put the pink packets in the suitcase on top of the lovingly folded white silk gown. She would finish the current cycle of pills, she decided, to make certain that last night's violence hadn't created a physical bond to Julian in addition to the invisible ones. Then she would throw the rest of the packets away. It was impossible to imagine ever making love again, and even if that impossible day ever came, she knew she didn't really need contraception.

Larisa closed the suitcase, her packing complete, then left the bedroom in search of the cash she would need to make her escape. She was married to one of the richest men in America, but she had no credit cards, no checkbook, no access to any money at all beyond what Julian kept in his desk in the penthouse's elegant wood-paneled library.

Larisa had been financially independent—until Julian. He had wanted to take care of her as no one had ever wanted to before, providing everything for her, freeing her from such trivialities as bills and checking accounts. And she had allowed Julian to provide everything, believing the romantic illusion of freedom, when in fact she was a prisoner, a pampered princess in a most luxurious prison, trapped by the decisions she herself had made in the name of love.

She hadn't felt trapped until now. Just her signature—Mrs. Julian Chancellor—could buy her a fortune in clothes or gems in any boutique in Manhattan, or a gourmet meal drenched in Dom Perignon at Le Cirque or La Côte; and there had always been enough cash, far more than she had ever needed, in the desk drawer. Julian liked to carry cash, to bestow lavish tips or pay outright for extravagant meals when he felt like it. The amounts of money he routinely carried, hundreds or even thousands of dollars, would be quite substantial for most men, but they were virtually spare change for a billionaire.

Still, at first, Julian had resisted the idea of leaving money for Larisa. Her name—the name that proved she was his wife—was surely all she would ever need to get whatever she wanted. But what if I want to leave a cash tip? she had asked. Or what if I want to buy a warm pretzel smothered in mustard from a corner vendor? Or what if, she had whispered softly, I want to surprise you with new sexy lingerie? That's a surprise I want to share with you, Julian, not with your accountant!

Julian had acceded to Larisa's wish on this one small point. She was to help herself to the money in his desk, he told her. And over the years she had, to leave tips and buy pretzels and presents—and to pay for her birth-control pills.

Now Larisa needed the money from Julian's desk to help her escape from him.

But what if Julian had taken it all with him when he left last night? Well . . . she did have a contingency plan. She would pawn the flawless eight-carat diamond engagement ring she wore. The plan was workable, but terrifying. It would necessarily involve others in the scandal of their failed marriage and blue-blooded Julian Chancellor hated the taint of scandal almost as much as he hated losing things he wanted.

Larisa sighed a soft breath of relief as she opened the desk drawer and saw the neat stack of bills—twenties, fifties, hundreds. She took the entire stack, her slender fingers flipping through it as she returned to the bedroom to get her suitcase, and even more relief pulsed through her as she realized the amount: four thousand three hundred and fifty. She would be able to get very far away.

Before leaving the bedroom, Larisa removed the magnificent diamond engagement ring, a Chancellor family heirloom, as well as her gold and diamond wedding band. She put the rings and her set of keys on the antique bureau nearest Julian's dressing room. She had no intention of leaving a note. The rings, the keys, the still-open door to her closet would send an eloquent message that she had gone.

After moving the suitcase from the bedroom to the penthouse's marble foyer, Larisa placed a call to the building's bellman. Mrs. Julian Chancellor did not carry her own suitcase to the curb, not even when she was making her desperate escape. When the bellman arrived, he took the suitcase without question or comment. Like all the staff of the luxury apartment building, he was discreet, carefully trained never to initiate a personal conversation, not even a polite query about her destination. There was nothing unusual about her leaving alone for a trip, of course. She often answered Julian's impulsive summons to join him in Paris or London or Rome, and sometimes, when he was away, she would go by herself to the sanctuary of one of the world's most tranquil spas.

Nothing unusual, but still Larisa's heart quivered. What if Julian had left instructions to be notified immediately if his wife even tried to leave the building today?

Paranoia! she told herself, although the quivering didn't abate.

When they reached the street level, the bellman offered to call one of the fleet of limousines always available to the Chancellors.

"Oh, no, thank you," Larisa answered with an easy gracious smile as her blue eyes fell gratefully on an already waiting taxi. "A cab will be just fine."

"Air France, please," Larisa told the cab driver as they neared Kennedy. Later, if anyone wanted to know, the driver would recall that he had driven Mrs. Julian Chancellor to the Air France terminal, presumably to catch the Concorde to Paris.

With painful yet forcefully confident strides, Larisa carried her suitcase into the terminal, past the check-in counters and into a nearby restroom. Once there, she removed the golden pins that secured her famous topknot, freeing the silky mane of golden-red hair to tumble halfway down her back and softly veil her beautiful face. Next she unclasped the gold belt, transforming her outfit from sleek to baggy. Then she stood in front of the mirror and forced her image to come into focus. She no longer looked liked stylish and elegant Larisa Chancellor. She looked like what she was, a weary traveler.

Far too weary, she realized, to carry out the next phase of her plan, to catch the shuttle bus to the United terminal and take the first available flight to anywhere. Far too weary . . . and so weak . . . and, despite the oppressive heat of the day, so terribly cold.

Her ever-weakening body urged her to lie down on the tile floor, here and now, and simply close her eyes and float off to her wonderful dreams. Larisa fought the almost overwhelming urge with terrifying images of what would happen if she succumbed to it. She would be found and rushed by ambulance to Memorial Hospital in Manhattan. Someone would call Julian, to gently notify him of the brutal assault on his beautiful wife that had apparently occurred at the airport, and after that there would be even more violence.

Fueled more by sheer fear than by any strength left in her fragile body, Larisa walked back outside and boarded the first motel courtesy van that appeared. During her years as a top fashion model, when her famous name and face were recognized around the world, Larisa had often traveled under assumed names, embellished by the appropriate foreign accents. Then it had been a game, amusing and without significant consequence if the charade failed, but it wasn't a game now. It was absolutely necessary that the motel clerk not identify her. Her soft French accent and halting English had to convince him that she was indeed Chantal Chandon, a possibly beautiful Frenchwoman hidden behind sunglasses and a shimmering red and gold curtain of hair who was probably meeting a lover for a clandestine affair. Whether the clerk was convinced or simply totally disinterested, Larisa didn't know; but, after paying him in full in cash for one night's lodging, she left to find her room with the wonderfully comforting impression that he would forget all about her the moment she was out of his sight.

Then she was in the room. First she threw the deadbolt lock that would protect her from intrusion from the outside world. Next she turned off the air-conditioning, because she was so cold, shivering now; and then, after exchanging the elegant teal silk for her beloved tattered nightgown, she curled in a tight ball beneath the covers of the bed. Soon, she told herself, very soon there would be warmth. Without air-conditioning, the small room would rapidly acquire and hold the humid heat of the steamy August day.

The warmth did come quickly, and as it enveloped her, Larisa allowed herself at last to drift to the memories of the wonderful dreams in which she was already safe and strong and far away. This is as far as I can get today, she reminded herself gently. And maybe this is already too far, she realized as she felt the dramatic effect of the sultry air on her body. The heat was making her even weaker—and so very dizzy even though she was lying down. Maybe she would die here, a warm, safe, peaceful death. Or maybe when she didn't leave the room as promised tomorrow, someone would break through the deadbolt lock and discover that her unconscious and battered body still had a little life, and she would be rushed to the care of a trauma surgeon.

The thought wasn't as terrifying now as it had been earlier, because now the trauma surgeon had a face: the lovely face of her best friend, her only true friend ever, the friend she had abandoned. A soft smile touched Larisa's lips as her mind filled with distant images of Elizabeth. There they were, Liz and Lara, walking around campus together, Elizabeth raving about the magnificence of the sky even if it was gray and scowling, or marveling at the delicate fragrance of the flowers they passed even though all that anyone else could detect were the city scents of pollution and fumes. That was Elizabeth, seeing the silver lining in the darkest of clouds, finding the perfume amid the heavy breath of diesel. Happy, joyous, optimistic—and quite oblivious to the grim realities. Larisa hadn't been oblivious, of course. Long before college she had known that most dark clouds didn't have silver linings, and that sometimes the most delicate of flowers died because there was no one who cared enough to rescue them.

Even at age eighteen Larisa hadn't been oblivious to the realities of clouds and flowers, nor had she been oblivious to the eyes that had followed the two of them on their journeys around Berkeley. The stares she herself had drawn had always been filled with unconcealed desire, lustful, possessive, wanting her extraordinary beauty and yet somehow contemptuous of it. And the stares Elizabeth had drawn? People of all ages and both sexes had simply smiled at her. She was everyone's long-lost sister or daughter, happily returning to them at last, a boundless source of warmth and comfort and joy.

How comforting it would be to be a patient in Elizabeth's gentle care. Larisa thought of herself in that role now, a trauma victim presenting herself to Elizabeth's emergency room. The intelligent emerald eyes would offer a warm greeting of welcome, and then the delicate but confident hands of the talented seamstress would gently examine the ravaged body that lay before her. And when Elizabeth had finished her gentle and careful exam, she would say with quiet yet reassuring candor, "I think you may have internal injuries, Lara. I'll need to operate to repair the damage."

"All right," Larisa would answer. "But, Liz, what about the other trauma, to my heart and my soul?"

"I'll help you with that trauma too, Lara. I promise I will."

As Larisa drifted off to sleep, or perhaps to death, she imagined a distant time when she would awaken again and call her best friend. Elizabeth should be in San Francisco now. At least, that had been her plan in the last unanswered letter Larisa had received three years ago. As soon as she completed her chief residency in trauma surgery in Dallas she would join the faculty of Pacific Heights Medical Center. There had been other news in that letter, personal not professional—a cardiologist who Elizabeth had been dating for several months. "It's possible," Elizabeth had written, "—and only *possible*, Lara!—that he will follow me to San Francisco."

Had Elizabeth's cardiologist followed her to the City by the Bay? Larisa wondered. Had Elizabeth truly fallen in love at last? Did those gentle and accomplished surgeon's hands now wear a gold wedding band? That was all Elizabeth would choose to wear, Larisa was certain of it. Elizabeth would wear a plain gold band, a simple yet compelling symbol of the deepest commitment and love—not the glittering jewels Larisa had worn, symbols of nothing, dazzling illusions that were decorative only . . . as she herself had always been.

CHAPTER THREE

"*Is* little Molly all right?"

"How is Mary Ann?"

Variations of those two questions greeted Pacific Heights Medical Center's transplant team as they entered the hospital's largest conference room to meet with members of the news media shortly after the completion of the historic transplant surgery. The largest conference room was necessary. The Bay Area's news corps had assembled in full force to learn what had happened to the sunny infant Molly and her brave mother Mary Ann, both of whom had become well known and much beloved by the reading and viewing public in the weeks preceding the surgery.

The press conference had been partially scripted in advance. The center's director of public relations would make the opening remarks—a brief summary of the surgical technique, a reminder that this was the *first* such surgery to be performed in San Francisco, an overall introduction of the entire transplant team, and a few specific introductions as well. After the opening remarks and introductions, the director would turn the podium over to Nick to answer specific questions about the surgery.

The director realized at once that if he wanted to have the journalists' attention for what was essentially but importantly a public relations promo, he needed to give them the good news first. So he began, "Both Molly and Mary Ann are fine. In a moment I'll let Doctor Chase give you the details, but first I would like to draw your attention to the packet of information you each have received . . ."

Elizabeth listened vaguely to the director, so that she would be ready to smile on cue when he introduced her; but mostly, her heart still racing with exhilaration, she thought about the surgery. It had all gone so well. There had been virtually no words exchanged between herself and Nick—none had been necessary, of course, because he had explained the procedure with such clarity beforehand—so they had operated in silence . . . and it had been a perfectly choreographed dance of their talented hands, moving together in graceful harmony, without a falter, without a single false step . . .

"The surgery was performed by Doctors Elizabeth Jennings and Nicholas Chase. Doctor Jennings is an associate professor of surgery with training in trauma as well as transplantation surgery."

It was time for Elizabeth to smile. And somehow she did, even though her racing heart almost stopped. The director should have said, "The surgery was performed by Doctor Nicholas Chase *with assistance from* Doctor Elizabeth Jennings." True, Nick had permitted her to do far more of the intricate suturing than she had ever dared imagine he would. In fact, it was she who had placed almost all of the tiny critical stitches that bound Mary Ann's tissue to Molly's. Was it silent—and thrilling—proof of Nick's confidence in her after all? she had wondered for a brief hopeful moment. No, she had reminded herself swiftly. Nick had simply been doing his job, fulfilling his teaching responsibilities to his junior faculty and making very certain that all members of his transplant team—be they chosen or inherited—knew the techniques perfectly, so that PHMC could become the major West Coast transplant center Nick wanted it to be.

Nick was the maestro, and she was his pupil, and just as she had been celebrating their magnificent dance, her mind spinning in pirouettes of pure joy, the memory of the breathtaking performance had been abruptly undermined—during its curtain call!—by this indisputable *faux pas*. She had been remembering the silent grace, marveling still at the wondrous harmony of their hands, thinking about operating with him again and again, and now . . .

Now the director had given the master and the novice equal billing.

Was Nick infuriated by the mistake? It seemed so careless, and so surprising. Surely Nick had read over the words the director would speak at the press conference. Had he just checked for technical accuracy, not imagining there would be such a breech in surgical protocol?

The bright lights of the television cameras moved quickly from her face to Nick's. He smiled as he was introduced, his sexy half smile, and it was absolutely impossible to tell from his expression if he was angered, or perhaps even enraged, by the director's extraordinary blunder—just as it was absolutely impossible to detect anything but polite calm in the voice that addressed the press a few moments later.

"The surgery on both mother and daughter was uneventful," Nick began. "There were no intraoperative complications whatsoever."

"Now what, Doctor?"

"Now the vigil begins, especially for Molly. There are the usual postoperative concerns, notably bleeding, for both of them, but for Molly there are the immunologic and physiologic issues as well. She has been given immunosuppressive therapy to minimize the risk of rejection of the transplant, but the question remains: Will her immune system accept the transplanted tissue? And, if so, will the new liver become functional?"

The press conference lasted thirty minutes. The reporters wanted all the remarkable details about the surgery, and they also wanted as much footage as possible of the handsome surgeon—his long-lashed dark blue eyes, his tousled coal-black hair, the patch of bare chest that was now so tantalizingly revealed by the deep V in his royal blue surgical scrubs. They all knew that their viewers had fallen in love with the sexy surgeon who had been interviewed during the weeks preceding the historic surgery, the Dr. Nicholas Chase who wore a crisp white coat over a starched shirt and conservative tie. But now the cameras captured an even better, even more enticing image of him . . . a wild and alluring image that made the inevitable and compelling mental transition from operating room to bedroom almost effortless.

Following the press conference, Elizabeth and Nick made rounds on Mary Ann in the surgery ICU, and Molly in the pediatric ICU, and their patients on the wards, and then Mary Ann again, and then Molly. Mother and daughter were rock steady, vital signs normal and postop lab values all excellent.

"Well," Nick said when he and Elizabeth had finished rounds and were standing in the nurses' station in the pediatric ICU. "I think I'll go get changed."

Nick's words were not, Elizabeth knew, an invitation to walk with him down the three flights of stairs to the surgical dressing rooms. Nor, she knew, would she answer by boldly announcing that she would accompany him—even though it was an opportune time for her to change, too. Opportune, because everything was under control, but not essential, because she was on call tonight and could change at any time—and Nick was doubtless getting ready to leave.

Dr. Nicholas Chase wasn't officially on call tonight, but he would expect Elizabeth to page him immediately if even the slightest problem arose. Page, not telephone, because although Nick had given her his unlisted home phone number, he had told her that he would have his pager with him at all times. He preferred, apparently, to be summoned by the soft beep of a pager rather than the harsh ring of a telephone; and he preferred, apparently, to be able to return the page when he chose, rather than being forced to answer the ringing intrusion at an inconvenient moment. Nick always answered Elizabeth's pages promptly, even in the middle of the night; and she was quite happy that she had never needed to dial the phone number he had given her. The pager seemed less personal, less intimate, even if the only privacy she was invading was a sound sleep.

Now Nick was going to change, and she needed to change too, and with any other surgeon with whom she had accomplished so much, such a flawless surgery, such a wonderful outcome so far, Elizabeth would have simply announced that she would walk with him. And they would have talked, allowing their exhilaration to surface, just a little, sharing the triumph and quietly confessing to the feelings of immense relief and gratitude they both felt. But if she accompanied Nick now, Elizabeth knew there would be only silence. Polite silence, yes, and perhaps an awkward smile or two, but silence nonetheless. Nick would be silent as always, and she would be too, because as effortlessly as she found words for the rest of the world, it seemed quite impossible for her to ever find precisely the right ones to speak to him.

"I think I'll go to the ward," she murmured finally, realizing as she spoke that once again she had not found the right words. She had no reason to go to the ward. She and Nick had just finished rounding there, and both knew perfectly well that all their patients were quite stable and that there were no worrisome loose ends whatsoever.

"Okay," he replied, his voice polite, solemn, and not questioning. "I'll see you later."

Halfway across the ICU, Nick's long graceful strides came to an abrupt halt, his path purposefully, teasingly blocked by Sara, the beautiful British pediatric anesthesiologist who had done the anesthesia for Molly. Elizabeth didn't hear their words, but she saw that there was animated conversation, not awkward silence, an effortless flow embellished by provocative smiles and flirtatious eyes. And when they parted, Nick to change, and Sara to do the final postanesthesia check on Molly, the smiles lingered, perhaps in anticipation of a midnight rendezvous to celebrate.

Once Nick finally disappeared beyond the double doors that separated the ICU from the rest of the hospital, Elizabeth began her walk toward the same doors. Where are you going? she asked herself. You don't really need to go to the ward, remember? That was just a flimsy excuse. Everything is under control now, a momentary calm in the center of what may be a nighttime of never-ending storms. You really should be walking to the dressing rooms with Nick, thinking of intelligent and insightful things to say to him—and saying them.

Elizabeth felt a little lost. There were rarely moments in the hospital when she had nothing to do. Surely there was something, just a ten-minute task until Nick was safely in the men's dressing room and she could sneak into the women's. As her mind searched, she was suddenly rescued by the soft insistent ring of her beeper. The calm was over. She was needed. Good.

"An outside call, Doctor Jennings," the page operator told her when she answered her page. Then, addressing the caller, the operator said, "I have Doctor Jennings on the line now. Go ahead, please."

"Elizabeth? I didn't realize they'd actually get you . . . I only asked if you were on the staff . . . I was just going to leave a message if they said yes." The words had come in a rush, and now Larisa stopped, breathless and whirling as flames of fire blazed inside her.

"Larisa?" Elizabeth spoke with soft, hopeful surprise to the faraway voice. The voice was a mere shadow of the once so vibrant one, and Elizabeth was swept with worry at its frailty; but she forced the worry from her own voice, filling it with warmth and welcome, and repeated, "Larisa? Is that you?"

"Yes." Larisa was curled beneath the covers in the motel room, very cold still despite the ambient heat and her own fiery pain. But at the gentle welcome in Elizabeth's voice a wave of true warmth washed through her. She clutched the receiver, the lifeline to that wonderful and hopeful warmth, even tighter in her pale white hands. "It's me. A voice from the past. Hi."

"*Hi.* This is so amazing. I was thinking about you today." Thinking about you, worrying about you, hoping that my worries were without substance. "Talk to me."

"You can talk now? You don't have any trauma cases at the moment?"

Except for me? Except for the friend who has been such a terrible friend, but who, because you are so generous, you seem to have instantly forgiven.

"No, well, as a matter of fact, tonight I'm on call for the transplant service."

"I thought you'd trained in trauma."

"I did, and I take trauma call too." Elizabeth laughed softly. "Long story."

"But as always you're doing twice as much as even the most supernormal human being could do," Larisa said, her frail voice gaining strength as it filled with fondness and pride for her remarkable friend. "I haven't forgotten your double major in biology and chemistry in college. Your reason then, as I recall, was that both were so interesting and challenging that you simply couldn't choose one over the other."

"It's the same with trauma and transplant," Elizabeth admitted. After a moment she added with quiet reverence, "Today, Lara, I got to assist with a living donor liver transplant. We transplanted tissue from a mother about our age to her eight-month-old daughter."

"Oh, Liz," Larisa replied with matching wonder. "And . . . ?"

"And so far they both are fine. It's really an extraordinary surgery. However, don't let me get going on the miracles of transplantation surgery or we'll never talk about you."

I don't care if we never talk about me, Larisa thought as she clutched the receiver even tighter and curled more deeply into the so very comforting faraway warmth. "I want to hear all about the miracles of transplantation—and all about you."

"Then before we sign off tonight we'll arrange a time for one of our famous all-night talks, but for now that's me in a nutshell. Trauma and transplant, and still quite unmarried."

"The cardiologist from Dallas?"

"That lingered, long distance, for almost two years. About eight months ago, we decided it just wasn't meant to be." Eight months ago . . . when Nicholas Chase arrived. Clamping down firmly on the frisky thought, Elizabeth added breezily, "So, I'm not involved with anyone now, completely devoted to my career."

"And your family?" Larisa prompted, knowing that soon, too soon, the conversation would shift to her . . . and wanting to linger as long as possible in the happy, accomplished, and so wonderfully *non*sordid life of her best friend. "Your parents and Mark?"

"They're all fine. My parents are finally taking the sabbatical they've been talking about for years. They left last week for London and will be there until next June. And Mark's with a very good law firm here in the city. He's fine, and Wendy's fine, and their girls are wonderful, nine and eleven already, happy and healthy. So, that's it. Everybody's fine," Elizabeth said with finality. Then, continuing gently, she urged, "Now, tell me about you, Lara. Something's happened, hasn't it?"

"Yes," she admitted softly as a war raged inside her. It was a battle of warmth and ice—the safe wonderful warmth of her best friend . . . and the terrifyingly dangerous icy memories of the man she had married. Speaking bravely to the warmth, she confessed, "I left Julian today, Liz. He's probably realizing just about now that I'm gone."

"And you're not going back," Elizabeth said with quiet calm, a statement, not a question. You're not going back to the man who claimed to have loved you but who somehow caused your wonderful vibrant spirit to fade away.

"No," Larisa agreed, her voice not nearly as confident as her friend's. She had come this far in her impossible dream of escape, but the invisible chains were there still, reminding her that she was owned, not by herself but by another, and reminding her, too, that even though they had slackened briefly, permitting her to indulge in this fantasy of escape, soon they would constrict again, more tightly than ever, a suffocating punishment for her courageous folly. *No. I own myself! Yes, I did betray myself once. I gave Julian everything he wanted of me, even parts of myself that I should have known to protect and cherish. But I will never betray myself again. Please let me have a chance to prove that!*

"Lara?"

"No," she repeated quietly. "I'm not ever going back to Julian."

"Good. So, where are you now?"

"In a motel at JFK."

"Planning to take the first flight in the morning to San Francisco, I hope."

"Oh, I—"

"Actually, if you get a flight that is due in tomorrow night, like about eight, barring an emergency I should be able to meet you. I have a very spacious apartment, including a large second bedroom that is completely unused. Admittedly, it's not decorated, but it does have a perfectly good bed, and even a dresser and a chair, and it's yours for as long as you want it."

"Oh," Larisa whispered. "That sounds so good to me."

"It sounds good to me, too. So *come.*"

"Okay," Larisa said to her friend. And then, speaking also to the invisible chains and icy memories, she added bravely, "I will."

"Terrific. If you want to take an earlier flight, to get out of New York as soon as possible, the apartment has a doorman on duty at all times so I can easily arrange to have him let you in."

"No," Larisa answered swiftly, wondering if even by tomorrow afternoon she would be strong enough for a six-hour flight. *I will be strong enough by then,* she promised herself. *I will be.* "Arriving about eight tomorrow night will be fine—perfect."

"Okay, well, let's see. Call me back when you know the flight information. If I'm tied up, you can leave a message with the page operator. And, in case we don't talk again, and on the off chance that I'm not at the gate when you arrive, just call here from the airport. The page operator will know why I'm delayed and she'll have all the details of a contingency plan. Okay?"

"Yes, okay. And Liz? Thank you."

"Of course!"

"Oh, and I don't think he will, I imagine he thinks you're still in Dallas"— *unless he read the letters you wrote me*—"but if Julian calls—"

"Don't worry. I'll tell him I haven't heard from you for over three years."

CHAPTER FOUR

$\mathcal{B}$y five-thirty Friday afternoon, Elizabeth was finishing her last progress note of the day. Molly and Mary Ann both continued to be remarkably stable, as did the patients on the ward. Elizabeth knew how well they were all doing because she had spent most of last night and today watching them, checking on them over and over again, troubleshooting small problems so that they would never grow into large ones.

As an attending physician, Elizabeth was expected to take call from home, not at the hospital. There were residents, fellows, and a Code Blue team in the hospital at all times, after all, not to mention the fact that she could get to the center's ICUs and ER as quickly from her own apartment as she could from some parts of the gigantic medical complex. But still, unless there was a compelling reason for her to be at home, Elizabeth usually spent most of her on-call nights at the hospital, as she had last night, just in case.

She had returned to her apartment at dawn to shower and change, and to give the apartment a quick once-over-lightly in case she didn't have a chance to later in the day. But now it was only five-thirty, and Larisa wasn't arriving until eight-fifteen, so she had plenty of time to buy flowers, and run the vacuum she hadn't run at daybreak, and give everything a final dust and polish.

Lots of flowers, she decided, smiling softly as she closed the metal cover of the chart, the last progress note of the day now complete.

"Elizabeth?"

Her smile vanished at the sound of his voice, and her entire body went on alert, as it always did when she was with him, muscles tense, stomach churning, heart racing. She was sitting on a stool in the nurses' station, and he was standing, towering above her. With any other man, Elizabeth would have remained seated and simply looked up to greet him, her emerald eyes sparkling with warmth and welcome. And, she well knew, with any other woman, Nick would have casually leaned toward her, a dark blue greeting of pure seduction.

But he wasn't any man, so Elizabeth stood at attention.

And she wasn't any woman, so Nick backed away a little as she stood, creating more space, more distance, between them.

"Yes, Nick?"

"Something . . . important . . . has come up, Elizabeth," he began haltingly. "I wondered if it would be possible for you to take call for me tonight?"

Was he trying to charm her at long last, filling the sensuous dark blue with sheepish apology at his surprising last-minute imposition? Elizabeth saw apology in Nick's eyes, but not a flicker of charm. In fact, what she saw, what she believed she saw, was almost heart-stopping worry—and fear. Another optical illusion surely, but still she answered, "Oh, sure, of course I can."

"It's more than just covering transplant, Elizabeth. I'm on second call tonight for trauma as well. If it's not convenient, I can see if Bill or Ed can cover."

"No, it's fine, Nick, really."

"Thank you," he said quietly, the immense relief obvious in his troubled eyes. "I really appreciate this, Elizabeth. You're scheduled to be on on Sunday, aren't you? Why don't I take call for you then?"

"That's not really a fair trade for you, Nick. I'm on first call for trauma on Sunday and it's a weekend."

"I consider it more than fair. Okay?"

"Okay," she said, agreeing only because she sensed his sudden restlessness. He was obviously very eager to leave, but he wanted to settle the trade with her first. "That's fine, Nick. I'll notify paging of the changes."

"All right." His eyes met hers and for a moment the restlessness vanished and there was pure gratitude; and there was something else, dark and intense, a deep and powerful current that she couldn't identify but which made her tremble . . . and which somehow touched his voice with exquisite softness as he said, "Thank you, Elizabeth."

"You're welcome, Nick."

Elizabeth remained standing at attention as she watched Nick disappear along the linoleum corridor, his long strides taking him swiftly toward whatever, *whoever*, was so important that he had made the surprising request. Had Nicholas Chase finally found a lover for whom he truly cared? A beautiful woman who was so important to him that when she requested an entire evening with him, a romantic candlelight dinner in prelude to their late-night hours of breathless passion, Nick had instantly complied? Yes, apparently he had found such a woman, Elizabeth decided. And, she thought, whoever she was, Nick obviously cared about her very deeply.

After Nick had vanished from her sight, Elizabeth sighed softly and settled once again onto the stool. She needed to notify paging of the changes in the on-call schedule—and also to tell the page operator that she was expecting a call from Larisa later on. Elizabeth might be scrubbed in the OR when Larisa's plane landed, or she might be at the apartment arranging flowers, but one thing was certain: she wouldn't be at the gate to greet her friend when she arrived. Second call for trauma meant that she had to be within minutes of the hospital at all times.

You really are a bastard, Nicholas Chase. The thought came with a rush of anger but without a flicker of surprise. Dr. Stephen Sheridan was quite confident of his assessment of his colleague. The trouble was that Elizabeth didn't share the sentiment. Which was why, when Stephen walked into the nurses' station just in time to overhear the exchange between Elizabeth and Nick, he hadn't intervened. And which was why now, even though Nick had gone and Elizabeth was making a phone call, Stephen still hadn't approached her.

He needed to be a little more calm. He needed to remember the necessary truce that he and Elizabeth had declared on the subject of Nick.

The truce was necessary to preserve the friendship that was so important to both of them, a friendship that had begun years before, when Elizabeth had been a fourth-year medical student and Stephen had been her attending physician on the oncology service. He had heard about her even before meeting her, the star student who was nice in addition to being brilliant; and Elizabeth had heard, too, in advance about him, the stunningly handsome heir to the Sheridan publishing fortune who had chosen to dedicate his life to the mysteries and challenges of medicine instead of to the luxuries and pleasures to which his vast wealth had given him carte blanche from the moment of his birth. Stephen had known before he ever met Elizabeth Jennings that the faculty considered her the most promising student they had seen in years; and Elizabeth had known before she ever met Stephen Sheridan that everyone believed that eventually he would conquer the obstacles that remained in the quest for the cure for cancer.

Stephen and Elizabeth had met during attending rounds; and later that night, while she had been roaming the oncology ward, keeping vigil over her—their—patients, just in case, she had run into him, having left his nearby laboratory to do the same thing. And they had talked, as colleagues, not as student and teacher, sharing their passion for science, musing together about the mysteries yet to be unraveled and the problems yet to be solved.

They had talked often during that month, late at night; and a few months later Elizabeth left for her surgical residency in Dallas; and she and Stephen didn't see each other again until she returned to PHMC five years later. Then they simply picked up where they had left off, running into each other on the wards late at night and talking for hours about the exciting challenges of their chosen careers. It was Stephen who had been most encouraging in her decision to pursue the specialty training in transplantation surgery. Dual specialties were often complementary, he had offered, citing his own dual training in immunology and oncology. And besides, he had added, since he was one of the two immunologists who managed the immunosuppressive therapy for the transplant recipients, if she became a transplant surgeon, they would be caring for patients together again.

At some point, the late-night conversations between Dr. Elizabeth Jennings and Dr. Stephen Sheridan shifted from professional to personal—a transition that was so seamless and so welcome that they both simply acknowledged it with gentle smiles. And now Elizabeth and Stephen were respected colleagues; and they worked together to care for such precious young lives as that of Molly, for whom Elizabeth had expertly placed the precise stitches and for whom Stephen had with matching precision and expertise selected doses of immunosuppression carefully balanced to help without causing harm; and they were very good friends.

Stephen felt protective of her, and he very much wanted to shield Elizabeth from the hurt and uncertainty caused by Nicholas Chase, but it was impossible. Every time he even casually alluded to one of Nick's flaws, not the least of which was the way Nick treated *her*, Elizabeth bristled and leapt immediately to Nick's defense. So they had declared a necessary truce on the topic of the blue-eyed surgeon.

But no white flags were unfurled inside Stephen now as he watched Elizabeth make the call to the page operator. No white flags, just pure anger. Nick was taking advantage of her kindness! True, although Stephen himself knew that Larisa was arriving this evening—Elizabeth had told him when she stopped by his research lab at midnight last night—Nick undoubtedly didn't. Nor did Nick know how worried Elizabeth was about her friend, how fragile she had thought Larisa sounded, how eager she was to be at the airport to greet her.

Now Nick had undermined that plan. Not on purpose, admittedly, but Nick's arrogant selfishness angered Stephen nonetheless. Nick had known Elizabeth would agree to cover for him, because even a man as self-absorbed as Nicholas Chase had surely noticed how much lovely Elizabeth Jennings cared about him. Nick noticed it, and cruelly dismissed it, until he needed her help, as he apparently did tonight . . . then he simply used Elizabeth's caring about him to his own advantage.

Such a bastard, Stephen thought, not feeling any more calm at all, but crossing to Elizabeth nonetheless because her phone call was completed.

"Hello there."

For the second time in just a few minutes, Elizabeth recognized the familiar male voice coming from overhead. But this time, the voice triggered welcome, not heart-racing wariness, and this time she simply swiveled on the stool and smiled as she looked up into the long-lashed dark brown eyes of her very handsome friend. Stephen was the hospital's *other* tall, dark, and sexy thirty-eight-year-old bachelor. Both men sent powerfully compelling messages of intelligence and sensuality; but if Nicholas Chase was a blue-eyed panther, restless and wild, untamed and untamable, Stephen Sheridan was an elegant thoroughbred, sleek and stylish and with the most impeccable of bloodlines.

"Hello there," Elizabeth echoed. Then, tilting her head inquisitively, she added, "You look worried."

"I was thinking about the administration of LKC I'm giving tonight."

LKC was Stephen's creation, an innovative immunotherapy that combined interleukin-2 with activated killer cells, not a cure yet, not *the* cure, but the most major advance to date in the war against cancer. Infusions of LKC were always anticipated with a mixture of solemnity and hope. Lethal anaphylaxis could occur at any time during the infusion, but even the fear of that catastrophic complication was offset by the therapy's extraordinary potential benefit. For some reason Stephen seemed unusually worried about the dose of LKC he would administer this evening.

"Is there something particularly problematic about this evening's infusion, Stephen?"

"Not the infusion, just the timing. We're scheduled to begin at seven, and it will take about three and a half hours, during which time I can't leave the patient's bedside."

Elizabeth looked at her friend with surprise. She knew all this. "And?"

"And Larisa's plane is due at eight-fifteen."

"And you overheard my conversation with Nick and know that I can't meet her so you're trying to figure how you can." Elizabeth's smile sparkled as she asked, "Did anyone ever tell you that you're an awfully nice man?"

"You're the one who's nice—far too nice." Stephen added quietly, "You could have told him no, you know."

"Well." Elizabeth shrugged. "It seemed very important, whatever it was."

"So was meeting Larisa at the airport. You told me she sounded very fragile."

"Yes, she did, and I had hoped to have been able to be at the airport to meet her. But we have a contingency plan. She can take a cab to the apartment and maybe it will be so quiet tonight that I'll be there when she arrives. You can't reschedule the infusion, Stephen," Elizabeth added quietly, even though "won't" would have been a more correct word than "can't." Stephen could reschedule, but Elizabeth knew that he wouldn't; and neither she nor Larisa would have wanted him to. It would be too unfair, too emotionally difficult for the patient for whom Stephen's wonder therapy could mean either a dramatic prolongation of life—or a dramatic death despite the fact that Stephen would be at his bedside, ready to leap into action, and the Code Blue team would be nearby and on alert.

"I would if I could."

"I know you would, Stephen. Thank you."

"For the record, in the interest of at least noting events as they happen, you have to admit that it was an incredible imposition for Nick to have asked you to cover for him at the last minute."

"He probably guessed I wouldn't have any major conflicts, even though it's a Friday night," Elizabeth said thoughtfully. Then, as she saw sudden anger on Stephen's handsome face in response to her honest—and not the least bit self-deprecating—observation, her eyes danced merrily and she added lightly, "Stephen! It's true, after all. If Larisa hadn't called out of the blue, I wouldn't have had any conflicts tonight."

"Well, again for the record—are you paying attention, Elizabeth?—Nick did not ask you to cover because it's Friday night and he figured that you would be available."

"Oh, no?"

"No. Whatever else the man is, and we won't get into that at the moment, Nicholas Chase is *not* an idiot. He knows very well that you're the best surgeon in San Francisco—and parts east."

Elizabeth's beautiful emerald eyes filled with gentle fondness for her very good friend as she laughed softly and said, "Dream on, Doctor!"

CHAPTER FIVE

"Nick," Margaret whispered with obvious relief when Nick appeared in the kitchen of his—their—Pacific Heights home. A warm smile briefly brightened Margaret's youthful seventy-four-year-old face, but it lapsed quickly back to the expression of worry that matched the worry Nick had heard in her voice when she had called to urge him to come home, soon, if he possibly could. "I'm so glad you were able to get away."

Margaret Reilly was not an alarmist. Although she had been unable ever to have children of her own, as much as she had wanted them, Margaret knew children, especially sick ones, very well. For fifty years of her life, she had been a pediatric nurse. During her long career, she had worked in all possible settings—well-baby clinic, and inpatient ward, and emergency room, and intensive care—and she had seen children of all ages and in all extremes of sickness and health. And tonight Margaret saw in the glassy blue eyes of the precious little boy who was in her charge something that truly terrified her.

It was as if Justin had given up hope.

"How is he?" Nick asked. His own eyes, the same dark blue as the young glassy ones, were filled, too, with terror.

"He's the same as when I called you, Nick. I was just about to try some more ginger ale. I haven't been able to get him to drink anything and his temp is still very high. I haven't given him aspirin, of course, because even though it seems like the same summer virus that the other neighborhood children have . . ." Margaret didn't finish the worry. She didn't need to utter aloud the concern that Justin might have a chicken pox prodrome, in which case aspirin could be dangerous, perhaps even lethal. She and Nick both knew all too well about Reye Syndrome and all the other diseases that could come without warning and steal beloved children from their families. Margaret looked at Nick's worried blue eyes and felt his restlessness. He wanted to hear her experienced assessment, but mostly he wanted to dash upstairs to the bedroom that was closest to his own. "Go ahead, Nick. I'll get the ginger ale and join you."

Justin was a small motionless mound beneath the patchwork quilt that had been lovingly made for him by Margaret. *So still.* That was what Margaret had said when she had called, "He's so quiet, Nick, and so still." As Nick neared his son's bed, he saw a second small motionless mound beneath the quilt: Mr. Bear. Once that fluffy friend had been as big as Justin, bigger even, but as Justin had grown—healthy and happy and oh so quickly!—Mr. Bear had become smaller. But he was still very much loved by the little boy, and he was cradled now, clutched tightly, in Justin's small arms.

Nick knelt beside the bed and gazed for a moment at the flushed face of his four-year-old son. Justin's eyes were closed, but he wasn't asleep, only very still. Gently, so gently, Nick touched a cool loving hand to his son's hot forehead and whispered, "Jussie?"

The dark blue eyes that Justin had inherited from his father fluttered open, unfocused at first and disbelieving. And then, as he focused on the eyes that gazed at him with such love, his small arms released their clutch of Mr. Bear and extended with an eagerness that was almost desperation to Nick.

"Daddy!"

Nick curled Justin's small hot body close to his own and gently kissed the fever-dampened silky golden hair as he asked, "How's my little boy? Are you sick?"

Justin nodded against Nick's caressing lips and curled even closer to his father. Nick closed his eyes briefly, an emotional moment of silent gratitude and relief. He would examine his son very carefully, but the young blue eyes were alive now, and when Nick finally opened his own eyes and saw a relieved and smiling Margaret, he knew it was as she had said, just an innocuous summer virus.

But there was more, what Margaret hadn't said but what they both knew: it was just an innocuous summer virus, but it was complicated by ancient fears for which Nick would never forgive himself.

"I love you, Jussie," Nick whispered. "I missed you. Did it seem like I'd been away for a long time? Yes? Well, I kissed you goodbye this morning, but you were still asleep, so you don't remember."

"He just needed his daddy," Margaret said softly. Justin loved her and trusted her, but tonight, because he was sick, he had needed the most important person in his life—his father.

"I guess so," Nick agreed quietly, astonished that he could mean so much to anyone, least of all this precious little boy.

"Can you stay long, Nick?" Margaret asked before withdrawing to give Nick and Justin privacy.

"I can stay all night. Elizabeth agreed to take call for me."

The mysterious Elizabeth, Margaret mused thoughtfully, with a motherly mixture of fondness and curiosity. There was always such softness in Nick's voice when he spoke of her. And, a month ago, when Margaret had finally decided to simply ask him quite bluntly what Elizabeth was like, Nick had replied quietly and without hesitation, "She's remarkable." Margaret had been very tempted to drop by the hospital to meet the remarkable Elizabeth, or even to suggest that Nick invite her to dinner sometime. But she did neither, because she knew how determined Nick was to keep the important truth of his personal life—the existence of his beloved son—completely separate and private from his work. Margaret had hoped to at least catch a glimpse of Elizabeth Jennings on the television coverage of yesterday's press conference. But on every channel, the producers had all made the same editorial decision: to show as much footage as possible of the tousled black hair and seductive dark blue eyes of Nicholas Chase.

So Margaret was left simply to wonder about the woman surgeon with whom Nick spent so much of his life and about whom he spoke so often—probably far more often than he realized—and always with such softness.

"That was very nice of her," Margaret said finally.

"Yes it was," Nick agreed quietly. "If something comes up with Molly or Mary Ann, she'll page me of course, but I don't expect either of them to have problems. Which means that I don't have to go anywhere. I can stay right here all night long."

Right here was exactly where Nick planned to stay, all night long, holding Justin, reassuring his little boy that he was loved, so very loved, and that he would never be abandoned again.

Justin wouldn't remember the first six months of his life, not consciously, and sometimes, because Justin seemed so happy and well adjusted, Nick allowed himself the luxury of believing that the wounds of those first six months were magically healed, without any scars whatsoever. But Justin's stillness tonight, his bewildered fear, proved that there were scars still in his small heart, a deep terrifying memory of the time in his young life when he had not been loved . . .

"You—we—are going to have a baby." Glenna's eyes flashed triumphantly as she made the shattering announcement. "So, Doctor Nicholas Chase, now try telling me that our relationship is over."

"Why?" Nick asked with quiet horror. "Why would you do this to yourself, to us, and most of all to an innocent child? Tell me why, Glenna. Please."

"Don't you think we'll make a nice happy family, Nick?"

"We aren't happy together now, Glenna," Nick reminded her solemnly. "We never will be."

"Oh, Nicky," Glenna purred. "We fight. We say cruel and hurtful things to each other. But maybe this mock hatred is really just denial of how much we love each other."

"We don't love each other, Glenna."

Nick knew about himself that he was incapable of love, and the many women with whom he had been involved had always seemed to know that, too. They were drawn to him by his looks, his wildness, his dangerous yet compelling sensuality, but a deep instinct inevitably warned them to play only—and never to care—and certainly never to expect nor want more from him than the talented caresses of his eyes, his lips, his hands, and his body. Women seemed to know neither to want nor expect Nick's heart. They seemed to sense, quite correctly, that it wasn't worth having.

Until Glenna, all the women in Nick's life had been smart enough to stay emotionally very far away. Glenna should have known to stay far away, because Nick's relationship with her had been even more cold and uncaring than most. But instead, she had obviously quite intentionally chosen to create a permanent bond between them. Some deep flaw in her, perhaps as deep and self-destructive as his own flaws, had compelled her to this terribly selfish act.

What was it that she wanted? Nick wondered. Not love, obviously. Money and prestige, perhaps? The luxuries that would be hers as the wife of a rich and famous surgeon? Yes, he thought. That was probably it. But at what cost to herself, to all of them?

"I know for a fact that I have no business being a parent, Glenna." With quiet sadness for the innocent new life that was growing inside her, Nick added, "And I'm not sure that you do."

"Thank you for your confidence," Glenna bristled. Then, raising her beautiful chin, she announced defiantly, "I am having this baby, Nick."

"I'm not asking you not to. I'm just telling you that I don't think that it is in anyone's best interest—not yours, not mine, and certainly not the baby's—for me to be part of its life."

"Maybe not. But, Nick, you owe it to your unborn baby to at least try."

Nick and Glenna weren't in love, and didn't really even like each other, and yet they married. The marriage lasted just long enough for Justin to be born to parents who were legally married and to be given Nick's last name. According to the courts, the marriage of Nicholas and Glenna Chase lasted five months. But, in fact, they only lived together for the first two, after which time Glenna angrily accepted defeat.

"You didn't want it to work, you bastard!"

"I couldn't make it work, Glenna, and neither could you."

"And what about the baby?" Glenna asked. Then, answering her own question, her voice filled with icy warning, "I want it to have all the privileges that are its due as the child of a wealthy and successful surgeon."

"All right," Nick agreed softly, as his mind cried silently, but what about love? If he gave Glenna all the money she wanted, would she love the innocent life she carried?

She claimed that she desperately wanted the baby, and claimed, too, that she already loved it deeply. Nick prayed that that was true. He knew, without a flicker of doubt, that even given Glenna's selfishness, the baby would be far better off with her than with him. He had no illusions whatsoever about his own ability—inability—to love. It would be best for his unborn child if the only role he ever played in its life would be to provide money. And that was what was agreed. Glenna would have custody, and she and the baby would receive the lion's share of Nick's earnings until the child was an adult. The divorce settlement was agreed upon before the baby's birth and would be signed and filed promptly thereafter.

Assuming, Nick decided privately, that the baby is even mine.

Justin Chase was born in the Chicago hospital where Nick was a surgeon and where until their marriage Glenna had been a nurse. Glenna had quit working the day they married, but she had kept in close touch with her friends at the hospital, bitterly revealing to them in sordid detail the disintegration of her relationship with Nick. By the time Justin was born, anyone on the staff who cared to listen had heard all about Nick's crimes, his broken promises, his cruel indifference to Glenna, his cavalier disregard for his unborn child. The assault was one-sided—Nick endured the unconcealed glowers and offered no defense—but even with rebuttal Glenna's version would have been believed without question. Nick had a long history of stormy romances. Glenna, it seemed, was simply his latest victim. Glenna *and* the unborn baby.

Only Margaret Reilly staunchly defended Nick. Then the head nurse in the hospital's pediatric ICU, Margaret had known Nick since shortly after his arrival at the hospital as a surgery intern over ten years before. It was her husband Edward, a gifted pediatric surgeon, who had actually met Nick first—and who had immediately recognized in the taciturn young intern a surgical gift similar to his own.

Edward and Margaret Reilly had spent the first half of their forty-five-year marriage hoping for a family. But the small lives on which Edward operated and for whom Margaret so lovingly cared were the only children they were ever to have. Then Nick arrived, and without knowing it, and certainly without willing it, he tugged at their generous and loving heartstrings. He was so bright, so sensitive, so talented—and yet so troubled, so self-destructive, so obviously without any respect for himself whatsoever. Edward and Margaret each spent long emotional hours working side by side with Nick, Edward in the OR, Margaret in the ICU, and both would have quite happily welcomed him as a son. But he was withdrawn, and the Reillys themselves were both quiet and unassuming, and it wasn't until tragedy struck that it became apparent that they had reached him after all.

On that snowy November night, during evening postop rounds, Dr. Edward Reilly suffered a fatal heart attack. It was Nick who caught him as he collapsed, and Nick who held him so gently, comforting him as a loving son would comfort his beloved father. And it was because of Nick that in the moments before he lost consciousness, Edward felt great happiness and peace.

The Code Blue team arrived swiftly, and everything was done correctly, but it was not possible to save Edward's life. Nick held his lifeless body again, after he died, and then, because she needed to be told in person by someone who cared deeply about both of them, Nick drove through the snowstorm to the Reilly home in Winnetka to tell Margaret. He held her as she cried, and even though she never saw them, there were tears in Nick's eyes, too.

In the five years between Edward's death and the birth of Nick's son, the relationship between Margaret and Nick appeared unchanged from what it had always been. They were colleagues, working together to save small lives, nothing more. But there was more, a deep silent bond, a caring that compelled Margaret to staunchly defend Nick against his many critics and to go to him to tell him personally when Justin was born.

Margaret found him in his office.

"A healthy little boy, Nick," she said gently.

"I'm glad he's healthy, Margaret." *I hope he will be happy.*

"Are you going to see him?"

"No."

"Nick . . ."

"There's really no point. It would serve no purpose whatsoever." Nick's solemn dark blue eyes were resolute and unyielding. They had to be, because he could tell that Margaret was about to tell him what she thought: that he should see his son, that he should be a father to him, that he would be a *good* father.

Their eyes met for a long silent moment, and it was only when Margaret saw flickers of fear that she finally relented.

"Okay, Nick," she said quietly.

"Thank you," he answered with matching quiet. Then he asked, "Will you do something for me, Margaret? Will you get some of his blood for tissue typing?"

"Do you think he might not be yours?"

"I just want to be sure."

"All right," Margaret agreed. She knew Glenna, and she knew that with Glenna anything was possible. She found herself hoping that the newborn infant wasn't Nick's after all, hoping that he could be spared the guilt that she knew would torment him always.

"Maybe you could just arrange to have them take a little extra when they're getting the routine bloodwork . . ."

"You don't want to have him stuck unnecessarily."

"I have no wish to hurt that little boy, Margaret." Nick held up his hands to stop the words he knew he would hear, the gentle plea for him to be the father he knew so well he could not be.

"I know that you don't, Nick."

Nick had a sample of Justin's blood and one of his own run in the highly specialized immunology lab that provided detailed tissue typing data for the transplantation program. The match was astonishing, a genetic similarity that was a transplant surgeon's dream. If ever his son needed a blood transfusion, or a new kidney, or a bone marrow transplantation . . .

Nick made certain that his attorney communicated that important bit of information to Glenna's attorney. Some day, perhaps, there might be a time when Justin would benefit from his genetic similarity to his father. It was a remote possibility, and obviously one that, for Justin's sake, Nick hoped would never come to pass, but it was the only silver lining he could find in the astonishing match. Mostly, the remarkable genetic similarity made him very sad. He would not wish his own genetic makeup on anyone, especially not an innocent child. Even though he was protecting his son by staying far away from him, had he unwittingly given him a genetic inheritance that would destine Justin to live with the same demons that had plagued Nick for his entire life?

No, Nick told himself. Surely environment played a role. Glenna didn't drink, had no drug dependencies whatsoever, and she would have all the wealth and luxury that were so clearly important to her. She didn't need to work, which meant she could be at home with Justin, loving him, making him feel safe and wanted, giving him a boyhood so different from the loveless and so very silent childhood Nick himself had lived. The silence of Nick's childhood had had many facets, sometimes brooding, sometimes demanding, sometimes filled with such anger that it would finally explode in a vicious burst of condemnation. The silence had been multifaceted, but never once, not in all the years Nick had lived with his perfectionistic alcoholic father, had the silence been peaceful.

Nick had made brave solemn promises to himself that he would not become his father, nor would he make the mistakes his father had made. But Nick was very much like the father he loathed, and now he had repeated the greatest and most grievous mistake his father had ever made: he had had a son.

But Justin's life would be different.

It already was different.

Because Justin would never know the dark moods, nor the screaming nightmares, nor the relentless perfectionism of his own alcoholic father.

Love him, Glenna, Nick pleaded with silent desperation as he stared at the lab data that proved without a doubt that Justin was his. Make him feel safe and happy and loved. And please, *please*, don't ever doom him to the terrifying monsters that lurk in the many sounds of silence.

"I need to see you." Glenna didn't bother to identify herself. She knew Nick would recognize her voice; and he did, even though it had been over six months ago, shortly before Justin's birth, since he had last heard it. He had sent the large monthly checks to her without fail, in fact usually ahead of schedule, but still her voice sounded ominous, filled with censure and warning.

"All right," he agreed quietly. "I should be through here by seven this evening and have the weekend off. Tell me when and where."

"Your apartment at eight tonight."

Nick reached his Lake Shore Drive apartment thirty minutes before Glenna was due to arrive. It gave him enough time to shower and change—for himself not for her—and as well to pour the first glass of what would be a weekend of Scotch. Since he wasn't on call, he would spend the entire time drinking, in silent solitude, stopping early enough Sunday evening that his brilliant mind and talented hands would be clear and steady when he returned to the hospital on Monday. Dr. Nicholas Chase was never, ever, intoxicated when he was responsible for patients, either at the hospital or on call at home. He never had been, nor would he ever be. And he was rarely, never, sober when he was responsible only for himself.

Most people would not have known when Nick wasn't sober. Not since his teens had he ever appeared to be drunk. What they would have noticed was simply that he was withdrawn; and had they been able to penetrate the brooding silence and somehow convinced him to explain why he drank, Nick would have told them the truth: to numb the pain, to forget the memories, to escape the nightmares that haunted him even in the brightest light of day.

Nick drank, whenever it was safe for him to do so, whenever the only person on earth to whom he was accountable was himself.

The intercom buzzed at eight P.M., and Glenna was announced by the building's security guard. As he waited for the elevator to carry her the twenty-four floors to his apartment, Nick swallowed half of the full glass of Scotch that he had just poured. It was a lot of alcohol, swallowed quickly, but it had virtually no effect. His tolerance to alcohol was very high. He would need much much more to even begin his most necessary escape from pain.

Which meant that the images Nick saw when he opened the apartment door were very clear, very vivid—and terribly painful: Glenna's expensive new clothes, her flashing defiant eyes, the bulging canvas bag slung over her shoulder, the blond-haired infant propped against her hip and held firmly in a position that faced him away from her instead of being nestled gently, protectively, against her.

"He's yours now," she announced harshly, accusingly, as if everything that had happened had been Nick's idea and Nick's fault. "I can't take care of him anymore."

Nick saw the truth of Glenna's words in her eyes. There was defiance there, but frailty too. Perhaps she had tried to love her baby and failed. Or perhaps she hadn't really tried at all. It hardly mattered. What mattered was that it was painfully clear that the role of loving mother was simply too much for her. Maybe Glenna had expected the baby to provide whatever it was she so desperately needed, to magically fill an emptiness inside her, just as she had expected Nick to fill that same void. But the baby, Nick's baby, had failed her—just as Nick himself had—and Glenna obviously bitterly blamed the small infant for that failure, just as she had bitterly blamed his father.

Nick looked at Glenna for a moment, long enough to realize what had happened. Then his gaze was powerfully drawn to the small bundle held firmly against her hip. Justin was very still, very quiet, as Nick himself often became—as he made himself become with alcohol. And, like an alcohol-numbed Nick, Justin simply stared into space, his eyes unfocused and unseeing. As Nick gazed at his son's profile, Justin turned toward him, his dark blue eyes bewildered and empty, but not searching. He seemed to know that there was no reason to search, that there was nothing out there: no laughter, no love, no joy.

Nick didn't make a conscious decision to move, but suddenly he reached for the little boy . . . and then Justin was in his arms, curled tightly against his chest, quiet still, bewildered still, but making no move to twirl to see his mother, no squirming effort to free himself from the grasp of the stranger who held him so closely that his small ears could hear the thundering pounding of the stranger's angry heart.

Once free of Justin, Glenna removed the canvas bag from her shoulder. "The rest of his things and his crib are in the lobby. The security guard helped me unload everything, so you might want to tip him. I haven't been compensated enough yet for the last six months of caring for your baby, Nick. I'm planning to leave Chicago, so I'll need money for the move and to support me while I look for a new job. My attorney—"

"Get out."

"I mean it, Nick," Glenna countered bravely, although her voice wavered as she met his icy blue eyes. "I tried, but you didn't give me enough. I needed more."

"I mean it, too, Glenna," Nick said with controlled rage. "Get out. Now."

For a very long time, Nick just held his son, unable to speak, unable to stop the tears that spilled from his own eyes. Tears had flooded his eyes only once as an adult, the night Edward Reilly died. And before that? Nick didn't remember. Surely he had cried as a small boy, until he finally understood that tears didn't drown the fear or the sadness or the pain.

Nick cried now, and when the warm surprising wetness on Justin's golden head made him look up at his father, Nick whispered softly, "Hello, little Justin. I'm your daddy."

I'm your daddy, and oh, my Justin, what great damage have I unwittingly done to you? I truly believed that it was best for you to be with her, so much better than being with me.

If his son could have chosen his parents, Nick thought, he most assuredly would have chosen neither himself nor Glenna. But Justin couldn't choose, and now there were no options left for him, and the realization filled Nick with sadness and fear. People entrusted their lives to Dr. Nicholas Chase, of course, and for the hours and days that they were in his care, Nick never betrayed that immense trust. And the care he gave those patients? He had on occasion heard himself described as sensitive and compassionate, but Nick believed that the only care he truly gave his patients was technical—the agile artistry of his talented hands, the compulsiveness of his bright perfectionistic mind—and not, not ever, emotional.

The little life cradled in his arms, the small human being who had already been so badly wounded, desperately needed all the emotional care he could get. Justin needed love, and all Nick could do was make a solemn vow.

I will be the best father that I possibly can be, I promise you. I will never abandon you again, Justin, and I will try, oh, how I will try . . .

Nick held his son all that night, and all the next day, and all the next night, and all the next day, never breaking the physical bond, not for a moment. And he talked to his son, speaking with a softness that his voice had never held before, reassuring the small quiet life and confessing truths about his own childhood that he had never before spoken aloud.

At midnight Friday, Nick thought, just maybe, there was the faintest glimmer of life in the dark blue eyes that had been staring at him. Six hours later, when Justin awakened from where he had slept all night—curled against Nick's chest while Nick remained awake and watchful—he greeted his father with a look of surprise, but not fear, and after a moment his small hands reached up tentatively and patted Nick's unshaven face. On Saturday afternoon, Justin smiled, just a little, just enough to flood Nick's eyes with tears of joy, even though he knew how very fragile it was and that perhaps there had already been damage that could never be undone. And on Sunday, as Nick bathed him, as they bathed together, Justin laughed, a few surprised notes, rusty and uncertain, but the most wonderful sound Nick had ever heard.

Glenna had brought Justin's belongings—food, blankets, clothes, diapers, crib . . . but no toys. Nick's apartment was now cluttered with those symbols of his son, but the apartment still seemed sterile and colorless, the way Nick always kept it for himself, a place to be silent and numb. But there would be no silence here ever again. And no numbness, either, Nick thought as he poured out the never touched second half of the glass of Scotch that he had begun to drink moments before Glenna arrived. He would never drink again—not as long as he was responsible for this fragile, innocent, wounded little life.

After their bath and Justin's lunch on Sunday, Nick took Justin to the Water Tower, Michigan Avenue's famous shopping complex, located just a few blocks from Nick's lakeside apartment. He bought many brightly colored mobiles, blocks, and balls, and one big soft brown thing—because Justin's blue eyes had fallen on it the moment they walked into the store and had kept returning to it—Mr. Bear. Mr. Bear was the last purchase Nick could make if he was to carry his son and all the toys, and it was time to return to the apartment anyway because it was late Sunday afternoon and beginning at dawn tomorrow, Nick had patients who were even now, on the eve of their operations, counting on his talent and expertise.

It was time for Nick to make the call he had been planning to make since late Friday night.

If he had ever asked for help in his entire life, Nick didn't remember when it had been. But he must have asked at one time, long ago, perhaps in the same silent anguished way that his son was asking now. His own pleas, his own silent screams of loneliness and fear had gone unanswered. Justin's would not, not anymore.

As Nick thought about the call he would make to ask for help for himself and his son, he was amazed at how easy it felt . . . because of who she was, because she was so generous and so kind. He had called her several times in the two months since her mandatory retirement at age seventy that they had both tried to fight. The conversations had been awkward, even though she had talked cheerfully about the things she might do: buy a condo in Florida, perhaps, or take a cruise around the world. She had lots of money, of course. She and Edward could have retired long ago, but they had both chosen to work because they had loved it—because they had both loved caring for the children.

The conversations in the past two months had been awkward, and now Nick was calling to ask for her help, and he had never asked for anyone's help before . . . but the call didn't feel awkward at all.

"Hello, Margaret, it's Nick. I have some news."

"Oh?" Then, because she heard such tenderness in his voice, she offered quietly, "It sounds like good news."

"Justin is with me, Margaret. He's going to live with me from now on." Nick fought a rush of emotion, then continued solemnly, "It was a mistake to let him live with Glenna. He's in a shell, a protective shell . . ."

"You'll lure him out of it, Nick. I'm sure you will. And I will do whatever I can. I mean that. Anything."

"Well . . . I have to go to work tomorrow. I don't want to leave him, but I have to. I have a lot of vacation time that I can take, but it will be a couple of weeks before I can clear my schedule. Anyway, I've spent the weekend just being with him, instead of trying to find someone to look after him while I'm at work."

"Because you already knew you had someone. I would love to take care of Justin, Nick, and I will for as long as he needs me . . ."

Justin needed them both—the loving seventy-year-old woman who had always wanted a child and the father who had always doubted his own ability to love and yet meant everything to his son. Together, Nick and Margaret helped the damaged and neglected infant become a sunny toddler and then a happy, well-adjusted little boy. It didn't happen overnight, and for a very long time, Nick and Margaret had feared the deep wounds would never heal.

Margaret was with Justin almost constantly and Nick was with him as much as possible. When Nick had to be away—at work, and later, when he and Margaret agreed that it was emotionally safe for Justin, on the trips he made to share his unique expertise with other surgeons—Justin still heard his voice. Nick called home often, and even before Justin himself could speak, he recognized his father's voice and was reassured and comforted by it.

As a boy, Nick had never been touched, neither in love nor in anger. In the middle of the night, when he had awakened with nightmares and the vicious monsters of his dreams had come alive, he had trembled in the terrifying darkness, wanting to scream aloud but afraid to shatter the inviolate silence, waiting instead to be devoured. Nick touched his own son, gentle caresses of reassurance and love, and at night when Justin slept, Nick sat beside his crib, wakeful and watching, prepared to comfort the moment the small blue eyes opened. In the beginning, there were nights when Justin did awaken and was instantly greeted by his father's soft words and gentle touch; but eventually Justin slept all night long, his golden lashes fluttering occasionally with dreams that brought soft smiles to his lips, not troubled frowns to his small brow.

Justin slept peacefully, blissfully, unlike his father whose sleep had been tormented by nightmares forever. Nick's nightmares and the childhood memories that had given rise to them were so interwoven that the real and imagined had long since become irrevocably blurred. Had he really been the one to discover his mother's lifeless body? In his bloody nightmares of agonizing helplessness and horror, he had been the one. And had she really slashed her wrists so deeply and so savagely that her death was a swift and absolute certainty? Had she really needed to find such desperate and irreversible escape from her small son? *That*, the reason she had killed herself, had been mercilessly carved into his young heart. Even before her pale lifeless body had been taken away forever, his father had first spoken the words he would speak over and over and over again: "Look what you made her do, Nicholas. *Look.*"

The belief that his mother's death had been his fault, that there was something so unworthy and unlovable about him that she had killed herself to get away from him, became a fundamental truth of Nick's life. But as he held his own son, loving Justin so much, Nick knew that a little boy—he had only been three at the time— could not have driven his mother to suicide. She obviously had been plagued by her own demons, just as Nick was plagued by his, but hers had been so strong, so painful and so powerful, that she had even abandoned her baby.

It was impossible for Nick to imagine abandoning Justin, no matter how strong or painful or powerful his own demons became. He would live with them, as he always had, but now, without the numbing escape of alcohol, his badly injured heart would be exposed at all times, its wounds raw and weeping. Nick's demons weren't vanquished by his immense love for his son. In fact, the pain was worse than ever before, because now he was more aware than ever of the unspeakable harms that had been so willfully done to him as a child.

The pain was worse and so were the nightmares and Nick needed to find new ways to escape and to numb. At first, in the middle of the night, while Justin and Margaret were sleeping and he himself was driven gasping from sleep, Nick would run. He ran as fast as he could for as far as he could, until every cell in his strong lean body screamed with exhaustion and the physical pain surpassed the emotional . . . and then, to make the most welcome escape last a little longer, he would run even farther.

Eventually, Nick found other forms of physical release as well, satiating the gnawing sexual hungers of his strong healthy body with late-night forays into passion and pleasure. He was more careful than ever neither to harm nor mislead the women with whom he shared his sensual talents; but still, he knew, he was regarded as cruel, cavalier, and dangerous. He *was* dangerous, of course. Already once in the name of love he had caused great harm . . .

As Justin stirred in his arms now, the memory of the great harm he had so unwittingly caused his son came rushing back. Nick had allowed himself to believe that his happy and well-adjusted son had magically and totally recovered from the first six months of his life. But today had proven that the wounds were still there, buried very deep in his small heart. They had been exposed by the virus that had made him sick and vulnerable, and his dark blue eyes had been so terrifyingly bewildered, just as they had been the first time Nick had ever seen him. Bewildered, and so fearful of abandonment.

I will never abandon you, my precious Justin, Nick vowed silently as he gently kissed his sleeping son's golden hair. And I will try so very hard never again to cause harm.

Nick wanted to harm no one, not ever, and most assuredly not someone he loved. His love for Justin had come as a wondrous surprise, a magical gift of joy that was far more than he deserved, and it had not occurred to Nick that he would ever love anyone but his son.

But now he did. And, he knew, she cared about him too. Far too much. Elizabeth didn't seem to know that she deserved someone much better than he, someone whose heart was whole not wounded—a heart that smiled with radiant joy, as hers did, not screamed with pain, like his.

It was a constant battle for Nick to prevent himself from becoming lost in the beautiful and so welcoming emerald eyes . . . and to stop his arms from gently drawing her lovely body close to his . . . and to forbid his lips from confessing to her all his secret truths . . . and to vanquish from his damaged heart the foolish yet so wondrous wish that with her the impossible could be possible after all.

It was a constant battle, but it was a battle that Nick always won. Because he loved her. Because he knew with absolute certainty that it was best for Elizabeth if he stayed very far away.

PART TWO

CHAPTER SIX

*E*lizabeth was scrubbed in the OR when Larisa called the hospital from the airport at eight-thirty. The page operator was expecting her call and pleasantly relayed the messages from Elizabeth—the address to her apartment, the assurance that the building's doorman was expecting her, and the hope that she herself would be home shortly after ten.

Forty-five minutes later Larisa was alone in her friend's apartment, and the anxiety that had traveled with her since the moment she emerged from the motel room at Kennedy magically vanished. She had made it. She was here, in this bright cheerful apartment, and she felt so safe—at last.

Her bedroom was, as Elizabeth had warned, quite undecorated, except for its spectacular view of downtown San Francisco and the bay beyond—and except for an elegant pale pink rose that rested gently on a pillow on the bed. The bed . . . throughout the transcontinental flight Larisa had promised her dizzy and aching body that as soon as she reached her destination she would lie down. But now the relief at having successfully made the long journey gave her a brave and euphoric burst of energy.

Besides, she thought, Elizabeth will be home soon.

Larisa left her bedroom in search of the kitchen, to heat some water for tea. En route she paused briefly at the open door of Elizabeth's bedroom. The room was a mirror image of hers, but its views were toward the west—to the medical center and ocean and sunset—whereas her easterly views were of city and sunrise and bay. On the floor were neat stacks of medical journals and scientific papers-in-progress, and the walls were adorned with framed photographs of happiness and hope—a sailboat skimming across a sapphire sea, rainbows appearing through a sky of storm clouds, a forest dressed in the white laciness of freshly fallen snow.

So very Liz, Larisa thought as she left Elizabeth's bedroom and crossed the living room to the kitchen.

Her plans to heat the water were preempted the moment Larisa saw the flowers. There were a great many of them, a bountiful bouquet of fragrance and color. Their stems were soaking in the sink and on the nearby counter were scissors, sugar, and an assortment of vases—from Lalique crystal and Lenox china to a handcrafted pottery pitcher and an empty wine carafe. Elizabeth had obviously been in the process of arranging the flowers when she had been called back to the hospital.

Smiling softly, Larisa approached the sink full of flowers and began the creative task herself.

Which was where she was still, filling the final vase, when Elizabeth arrived home twenty minutes later. The sound of the running tap water prevented Larisa from hearing Elizabeth come in the front door, so Elizabeth's first glimpse of her friend was of Larisa's back, the glittering golden red mane that fell halfway to her waist, the once-familiar baggy jeans and Berkeley sweatshirt, the ballerina-graceful movements of her arms and hands as she placed the flowers in the vase just so.

When Elizabeth finally spoke, she did so very softly, not wanting to startle.

"Lara?"

But when Larisa turned and Elizabeth truly saw her best friend, it was she who was startled. For over six years she had worried that Larisa's wonderful vibrant spirit had begun to fade—and now it seemed as if even more of her friend had faded. She and Larisa were exactly the same height, but now Larisa seemed smaller, and so frail, a delicate porcelain doll paradoxically clothed in a sweatshirt and jeans. Porcelain? No, Elizabeth realized. The once creamy richness was gone from Larisa's skin. It was snow-white now and almost translucent, a gossamer thin covering over her fragile body.

Elizabeth gazed at her, suspended for a moment between her impulse to rush to her as her friend and her concern as a well-trained trauma surgeon about the cause of the extreme pallor and frailty. Friendship triumphed—at least for now.

"Welcome!" she said, embellishing her warmly enthusiastic greeting with a gentle hug.

"Thank you," Larisa whispered. Elizabeth's hug was very gentle, as if she knew she might break, and Larisa had seen the flickers of emerald worry in her friend's intelligent eyes. So she said as brightly, as lightly, as possible, "I know I look like death. This has all been a bit of an ordeal."

"You're awfully pale, Lara."

"Too much stress, too little sleep, and no sun," Larisa explained with a shrug. It was, at least, a partial truth. After a moment she confessed softly, a pure and happy truth, "But I'm already better, Liz, just being here."

"I'm very glad you're here," Elizabeth answered, deciding to push no further now, and forced to let the subject drop anyway because her best friend's attention was suddenly focused on *her*.

For several moments Larisa simply stared. She was gazing at the same Elizabeth, of course—fresh and natural and so wonderfully radiant. But the lovely girl-next-door look was gone, replaced by a softly feminine and alluringly womanly beauty. The rich dark brown hair that had always curled naturally and luxuriantly—albeit randomly—was styled now, rich and luxuriant still, but swept into magnificent lustrous swirls; and the wide clear emerald eyes, always so luminous and sparkling, were subtly enhanced now, luminous and sparkling still, but intriguing, bewitching, hypnotic; and even though Elizabeth was dressed simply, the lines of the dress were elegant and the fabric was the color of fire, not the brown or blue she had always worn before.

"*I* may look like death," Larisa began finally, her own beautiful bright blue eyes suddenly alive and sparkling. "But you, Elizabeth Jennings, look positively glamorous."

"I don't know about glamorous . . . but maybe a little better. I gave myself a New Year's makeover." Her resolution to look as good as she possibly could *did* coincide with the new year—but in truth the more pertinent coincidence was the scheduled arrival of the new transplant service chief, Dr. Nicholas Chase, on January fifteenth. Elizabeth had already met Nick, when he had interviewed for the position in early December. He had been touring the medical center, and she had been emerging from the operating room, having operated all night, rumpled and tousled—and so very aware of how bedraggled she must have looked to the appraising dark blue eyes. "There's a wonderful place in Union Square called 'Sydney's, Of

Course.' It's a combination clothing boutique and salon, so you can simply walk in and have a complete fashion overhaul—clothes, hair, makeup, the works. Which is what I did."

"Well, you look absolutely terrific." Impulsively reaching to touch a rich dark brown swirl, Larisa added softly, "Those curls."

"Attributable to an interested and creative hair stylist—and, of course, the magic of mousse," Elizabeth explained with a smile, even though her heart ached with renewed worry because the hand that had fondly touched her exuberant but stylish curls had been so pale and trembling. Smiling still, she suggested gently, "Why don't we sit, Lara? I've been on my feet for hours. I'll just put on some water for tea and we can plop down right here amid all these beautifully arranged flowers."

Without waiting for Larisa's concurrence, Elizabeth put her suggestion into action, filling the tea kettle and gesturing for her friend to sit at the small kitchen table.

"That's a very nice dress," Larisa said when they both had mugs of tea and were seated. "The color is really wonderful on you."

"I remember a very dear friend subtly suggesting for years that I might try brighter colors." Elizabeth smiled at the very good friend and then continued, "This dress, in fact my entire new revised wardrobe, is thanks to a woman at Sydney's named Christine. She's like you, Lara. She has a remarkable eye for color and fashion and style that I've just never had."

"I'm not exactly a fashion plate at the moment, although I do love this old outfit."

"So do I, and I have an identical one in my bedroom. Someday we may have to put on our matching outfits and prowl around the old alma mater and reminisce. This weekend's out, I'm afraid, because even though after tonight I won't be officially on call again until Monday, I want to stay fairly close by, because of the liver transplantation we just did."

"It's fine with me to stay right here and drink tea in this cozy apartment."

"And stay up all night talking, like the good old days?"

"That sounds wonderful. I guess it's pretty obvious from my outfit that I'm already regressing." Larisa sighed and admitted softly, "I suppose what I'd really like to do is go back about ten years and start all over again."

"Ten years? Would you really want to undo your modeling career?"

"No. I did love modeling. But if I could just have another shot at the last six . . ." Larisa looked at her sympathetic friend and confessed quietly, "I'm too tired to talk about Julian tonight. Let's stick to happier topics, okay? Like how terrific you look."

"And how I'm on call!" Elizabeth said with a soft laugh as she rose to answer the suddenly ringing telephone.

The call was from the hospital, but it was Stephen, not the ER. The LKC infusion had been completed without incident, and now, having been accepted by the patient's immune system, the new warrior cells were hard at work in his body, waging their valiant battle against the tumor—and Stephen was calling to see if Larisa had arrived.

"Yes, she's here, safe and sound," Elizabeth answered, smiling at Larisa even as she wondered at the truth of her own words. Was Larisa safe? And sound? "We're in the kitchen, surrounded by flowers, drinking tea."

When Elizabeth's brief conversation was over she explained, "That was Stephen Sheridan. He's an immunologist at the center, and a good friend. I hope you don't mind that I told him you were coming. I know he won't tell anyone."

"No, I don't mind." Then, remembering the warmth and familiarity in Elizabeth's voice as she had spoken with Stephen, Larisa smiled and prompted boldly, "A good friend?"

"A very good friend. Stephen is a very nice man."

Nice, Larisa mused. Elizabeth had always attracted nice men—nice, kind, generous, as Elizabeth herself was. And the men *she* had always attracted? They had never been nice. Like Julian, they had always wanted to possess her, to conquer and control her. Were there two entirely different kinds of men on earth? Larisa wondered. And was it her destiny to forever attract the ones who were cruel, and unkind, and selfish?

"Is Stephen married, Liz?"

"No, Mademoiselle Matchmaker, but he is involved."

Eager to hear all about Elizabeth's life—and Elizabeth's friends—Larisa pressed with genuine interest, "With who?"

"Her name is Madolyn Mitchell. She's an anchorwoman for one of the local stations. *The* anchorwoman, actually. She does the newscasts on weeknights at five and eleven and commands something like seventy percent of the audience."

"It sounds as if she could move on to a bigger market than local television."

"She's planning to. In fact she's in the midst of discussions about a network position in New York right now."

"Would Stephen move to New York with her?"

"Oh." Elizabeth frowned thoughtfully. "I don't know. I don't think so."

"It sounds as if you don't think he should."

"Oh, well, I don't know." Elizabeth shrugged. She and Stephen had had many honest conversations about their love lives—and the fact that despite careful searches neither had ever found a compelling love—and in the almost six months that Stephen had been dating Madolyn, he hadn't amended that fact. "I guess I've never thought Madolyn was right for Stephen—not that I have anyone else in mind!—but I suppose the truth is that she may be exactly the kind of woman he needs. She's almost as dedicated to her career as Stephen is to his, and maybe someone who doesn't expect too much of him and isn't too great a distraction for him would be best."

"I still get the distinct impression that you simply don't think Madolyn's the right woman for your very good friend. And you're probably right, Liz," Larisa affirmed with quiet confidence. "You're pretty good at being able to tell who would make your friends happy—or unhappy." Larisa paused briefly then asked, "You never really liked Julian, did you?"

"I barely knew him, Lara."

"I know, but still . . ." Larisa wanted to know what it was that Elizabeth had seen so quickly in Julian and that she herself had missed seeing for so very long. She wanted to know how Elizabeth spotted the nice men, and the not so nice ones, and if perhaps her friend could share that wisdom with her. But asking those questions now would lead to topics that she was far too tired to discuss.

The telephone rang and Larisa smiled as, for the second time tonight, a possible discussion of Julian was saved by the bell.

This time the call was from the emergency room. Elizabeth was needed. The first-call trauma attending was scrubbed in OR with a gunshot wound to the chest, and they had just received word that a badly injured victim from an MVA—motor vehicle accident—was en route.

"You'd better go!" Larisa exclaimed after Elizabeth had hung up and explained the call.

"The ambulance is still twenty minutes away and I can get to the hospital in less than two. But this will probably keep me busy for the rest of the night. I have to make rounds on the transplant service in the morning, so you won't see me again until at least noon."

"At which time you'll need to crash."

"I might take a brief nap, but I'll be fine. I actually have an appointment with Christine at Sydney's at five tomorrow. Four weeks from tomorrow there's going to be a black-tie ball at the Fairmont celebrating the groundbreaking for the new Immunology Institute—of which Stephen will be the director—and I need a formal gown." Elizabeth tilted her dark brown head and added, "Four weeks from tomorrow is also September fourteenth."

"Your thirty-first birthday!"

"Yes—which is all the more reason for me to try to look as good as possible that night. Would you like to come to Sydney's with me? Or are you planning to keep a lower profile than that?"

"I'm recognized in Manhattan, in certain exclusive boutiques and restaurants, but I can't imagine anyone here would recognize me. Aristocratic Julian always thought it was incredibly crass, incredibly *nouveau riche*, to have our photographs taken for society pages of magazines or newspapers, and it's been over six years since I last modeled."

"Not that any of the pictures taken of you as a model ever really looked like you."

"You didn't think so?" Larisa asked, surprised. "I know the look changed from photograph to photograph—changes in hair and makeup and camera angle—but I always thought there was a similarity between them."

"The photographs were similar, but I never saw one that I thought was really you—the *real* you."

The real me, Larisa thought with a shiver. Of course there had never been such a shot. Or if there had, the photographer who had taken it would have promptly destroyed the negative, wanting no record of the embarrassing fact that he had actually made the ever-dazzling ever-confident supermodel Larisa Locksley look vulnerable and afraid.

"Well, anyway," Larisa continued hurriedly after an uneasy moment. "Even if someone happened to recognize me, it wouldn't be a problem. Only Julian knows that I'm missing and he wouldn't tell a soul. He absolutely hates scandal, even the whisper of it. If he needs to explain my absence, he'll say I'm off at a spa somewhere."

"Good. So, you can come to Sydney's with me. I'm eager for you to see the boutique and to meet Christine."

"Me too."

"I'd better go. Make yourself at home and get a good night's sleep. Tomorrow, after we've gone to Sydney's, we can talk about Julian . . . if you want to." Elizabeth saw both hope and apprehension on Larisa's pale beautiful face at the suggestion. Once the young Liz and Lara had shared their secrets and their dreams, trusting each other without question. On impulse, Elizabeth offered a secret of her own, "And tomorrow I'll tell you about Nick."

"Nick?" Larisa smiled. *"Nick?"*

"I don't know why I said that! There's really nothing." *Nothing and everything.*

"Great." Larisa laughed softly, a joyous giggle that felt quite rusty, because it had been so very long, but which also felt quite wonderful. "I can't wait to hear every meaningless detail!"

CHAPTER SEVEN

It's as if she knows how weak I am, Larisa thought as Elizabeth drove to the valet parking in front of Sydney's instead of searching for a more distant parking place. She was weak still, despite a wonderfully deep and dreamless sleep, and the embers of pain that smoldered in her abdomen threatened to burst into flames. But she had wanted to accompany Elizabeth to Sydney's, had been determined to.

"The grand entrance," Elizabeth explained with an easy smile as she slowed the car to a gentle stop.

Their car doors were gallantly opened by two valets, and in just a few short steps they were inside Sydney's. And it was, Larisa decided, like being in a magnificent garden of fragrance and fabric. The intoxicating fragrance came from hundreds of roses artfully arranged in elaborate crystal vases, and the wonderful clothes were arranged as beautifully as the flowers in bright colorful bouquets of elegance and style. There were mirrors in this lush garden, and a sparkling fountain, and glittering crystal chandeliers. Champagne and cappuccino were served in the atrium and romantic songs of love softly filled the rose-fragrant air.

Sydney's, Of Course was very busy on this Saturday afternoon, and yet the boutique had been so brilliantly designed that there was a feeling of endless spaciousness and intimate privacy.

"This is wonderful," Larisa said after a few moments of silent admiration.

"Wait until you see the dressing rooms. They're very large and totally private. Each one is actually two rooms—one for changing and one for viewing. The viewing room has realistic mirrors and lighting as well as comfortable sofas for guests, such as yourself, to wait between showings. I just need to check with the receptionist to see what room we're in. Christine's probably already there arranging the gowns she has preselected."

"This is very good," Larisa murmured appreciatively. "Someone was really thinking when this place was created. Sydney, I suppose."

The dressing room was on the second floor, and yes, the receptionist confirmed, Christine would be there when they arrived. As she followed Elizabeth toward the wide circular staircase that swept up to the second floor, Larisa felt a clutch of fear. Her energy had held as they had wandered slowly among the bouquets of clothes and roses, but could she really climb the stairs? There was an all-glass elevator beyond a sparkling fountain, but . . .

It's only one flight, Larisa told herself. I can make it. If I become breathless halfway up, I can always stop on the pretext of wanting to gaze back at the colorful panorama of the first floor.

Halfway up, as she was thinking about doing just that, Larisa was rescued by the sudden appearance of a violet-eyed raven-haired beauty who was descending the stairs as she and Elizabeth were climbing up.

"Elizabeth!"

"Hello, Madolyn," Elizabeth greeted warmly. After a brief hesitation, she said, "Madolyn, I'd like you to meet Larisa. Larisa, this is Madolyn."

To protect Larisa's privacy, Elizabeth had purposefully omitted last names from the introduction. But, Larisa knew, this *had* to be the Madolyn with whom Stephen Sheridan was involved. She had a star quality about her, and a face that surely loved the camera. As she and the anchorwoman exchanged polite hellos, Larisa felt herself being scrutinized. Madolyn didn't seem to recognize her specifically, but she obviously identified her in general—a stunningly beautiful woman who was by definition some sort of competition. Larisa felt the heat of Madolyn's stare as the remarkable violet eyes searched intently for some indisputable defect in the dazzle, some flaw that made Larisa less beautiful and less desirable than she. Larisa was used to such appraisals, and the smoldering hostility that invariably accompanied the discovery that there were no defects or flaws—no physical ones that is.

Why are you looking at *me?* Larisa wondered. I'm no threat to you at all. If you want something to worry about, worry about the obviously very close and very important friendship between Stephen and Elizabeth.

"You're leaving Sydney's empty-handed, Madolyn?" Elizabeth asked after several moments of tense and highly charged silence.

"It only looks that way," Madolyn said, shifting her gaze from Larisa to Elizabeth and obviously relaxing as she did so. She gushed breathlessly, "Actually, I've just spent the last hour selecting fabric for the gown Christine is making for me for the Fairmont ball. She designed it herself—with my input of course—and it's going to be *wonderful*. I wanted something very special because it will be such a special night for Stephen. Promise not to tell him, Elizabeth? I want it to be a big surprise."

"I won't tell him, Madolyn."

"Good, thanks. Well, I have to go. Stephen and I are meeting at the Cliff House at six. Nice to have met you . . ." Madolyn paused for just a fraction of a second, just long enough to give the unmistakable impression that her bright and impeccably trained journalistic mind had not bothered to remember Larisa's name. Then she added sweetly, "Larisa."

As Madolyn continued down the staircase, Larisa and Elizabeth walked up the remaining half flight. Larisa's energy had been rejuvenated by the brief rest as well as by the instinctive rush of adrenaline released by Madolyn's intense scrutiny. Still, she waited to speak again until they had reached the top of the stairs and were walking toward the designated dressing room.

"So, that was Madolyn," she said with a sly smile. Then smiling more broadly, she asked, "Remember when we were in college and you actually believed that if you couldn't say something nice about someone you shouldn't say anything at all? You always found something nice to say, of course, and I spent three years having to lock my lips." Larisa's delicate fingers duplicated the gesture she had made so often in college, the twisting motion of turning a key to keep her lips from speaking aloud whatever clever but not so nice thought danced in her mind. "I can tell you still subscribe to that code, Elizabeth Jennings."

"Not really. Not *always*," Elizabeth told the sparkling blue eyes that now sent a challenge: No? Then prove it! "Okay, I admit, I'm not crazy about Madolyn. Okay, okay, I'll say it: Stephen could do much better. There!" Elizabeth laughed softly, then became thoughtful as she added quietly, "I remember that in college you pretended that you could always think of something not nice to say about virtually everyone—but the truth was that you were the first to rush to the defense of anyone who needed defending."

"Well, I think Madolyn can defend herself quite admirably."

"Agreed. I do, however, think that it's very nice that she's having Christine design a gown for her. I think that's something that Christine will enjoy doing very much."

"I'm quite sure Madolyn is doing it for Madolyn, not for Christine. However," Larisa added fondly, "the search for—and discovery of!—the silver lining has been duly noted."

"Thank you." Elizabeth tilted her dark luxuriant curls in acknowledgment, then predicted seriously, "You're going to like Christine, Lara. She's the kind of person who you would have instantly rushed to defend in college."

In fact Larisa *had* instantly rushed to defend Christine in college.

"Larisa?" Christine asked as soon as Larisa and Elizabeth entered the private dressing room.

"Yes." Larisa smiled warmly, reassuringly, at the very pretty woman who had greeted her with soft surprise and shy uncertainty. Christine's involvement in fashion made it quite likely that she of all people in San Francisco might recognize Larisa as the once-famous high-fashion model. But Christine's quiet greeting had seemed more personal than professional. "I'm sorry, Christine, have we met?"

"I'm not sure we ever actually introduced ourselves, but twelve years ago, when we were both freshmen at Berkeley, you once helped me very much—far more than you realized at the time." Now it was Larisa's turn to look surprised, and a little uncertain, and Christine's turn to warmly reassure, "Maybe you won't remember the incident at all, but, if you don't mind, I'd like to tell you my memory of it."

"Okay."

"Well . . . there was a design seminar taught by a man named David Andrews."

David Andrews, Elizabeth's mind echoed silently. The name was quite familiar to her, but it was a familiarity that was far more recent than twelve years ago. Could it possibly be the *same* David Andrews?

"David Andrews," Larisa murmured after a moment, echoing aloud the name that spun silently in Elizabeth's mind. David Andrews had been a campus legend. Twenty years older than the average college freshman, the very sexy art professor nonetheless had a steady stream of young women determined to seduce him. But he stayed very far away from his students, a restraint that only made him all the more desirable: sexy *and* ethical, the perfect romantic hero, nobly depriving himself of the passion he most surely wanted because propriety mandated it. As Larisa thought about it now, a far more likely explanation for David Andrews's restraint seemed obvious: what possible interest could a gorgeous thirty-eight-year-old man have had in giggling eighteen-year-old girls? "Yes, I remember him. He was supposed to be a sensational teacher, but also incredibly sexy, which was why there was always such competition to get into his design seminars. Only one of the seminars was even open to freshmen and you had to show up bright and early in the art department office on registration day to have any hope of getting in."

David Andrews's name had triggered distant memories, and now as Larisa looked closely at Christine even more memories flooded back. Christine's glittering spun-gold hair had been very long then, waist length, a shimmering golden veil that had concealed all of her pretty face—except for her remarkable lavender eyes.

The dazzling golden hair was shorter now—and knotted into a sedate chignon—but the luminous eyes were the same. Smiling now at those eyes, Larisa said, "We were both there, in the art department office, waiting to sign up for the seminar."

"Yes, that's right," Christine said, obviously pleased that Larisa had remembered. "There were six of us waiting, and as we waited the other girls shared their reasons for wanting to take the seminar—basically because of David, of how attractive he was. But that wasn't your reason. You wanted to take the seminar because you were going to be a top fashion model and you wanted to learn all you could about color and design."

"And then one of the other girls asked you for your reason," Larisa said quietly, now vividly remembering the scene. There had been such apprehension as Christine had steeled herself for the scorn of the others. She was so obviously shy, so decidedly *un*glamorous in the drab clothes she wore. She was no more the other girls' image of a future fashion designer than she was the image of someone who would have had designs on the handsome teacher. Christine had been apprehensive, fearful even. But, nonetheless her expression had filled with shy yet proud defiance as she had made her startling pronouncement. "And you said that you were going to be a fashion designer."

"Yes," Christine replied softly, grateful still after all these years for what Larisa had done next—and so swiftly that there hadn't been even a heartbeat of stunned awkward silence. "And you said that you hoped that one day you would have the opportunity to model my designs. That was so nice of you to say, Larisa. And then a few minutes later, when we were told that there were only five places available in the seminar, you withdrew your name so that I could get in."

"And you took the seminar, and now, according to what we just heard from Madolyn Mitchell, you're designing beautiful evening gowns."

"I took the seminar, and now I'm designing at least one gown, which I hope will be beautiful." Christine paused and then said softly, "But the most important thing that happened because of what you did that morning was that I met and married David."

"Did you? Good for you." Good for David, Larisa added silently, feeling sudden respect for the man she had known only by rumor. David Andrews had effortlessly resisted the provocative advances of all the giggling eighteen-year-olds. But he had been unable to resist the shy and proud—and so serious—Christine. "I remember hearing that he had gotten married. No one really knew any details."

"No. We had to be very careful, because he was a teacher and I was his student. We actually saw each other only in class while I was in his seminar, but we both knew. When the course was over, David asked me if I would mind not enrolling for a second term." She added softly, "And then he asked me if I would marry him."

"How romantic." Larisa looked then from Christine to Elizabeth. She expected a knowing smile from her always optimistic friend at the fairy-tale romance; but there was no smile on Elizabeth's serious face and her emerald eyes were strangely distant, troubled even. After a confused moment, Larisa turned back to Christine, and as her gaze drifted from the smiling lavender eyes to the gold wedding band on Christine's delicate hand, Larisa herself offered the happy ending she had expected Elizabeth to provide, "And it's been wonderful."

"We had eleven wonderful years," Christine agreed quietly. A frown clouded her lovely face. "David died a year ago."

"Oh, no. Christine, I'm so sorry."

"It's okay, Larisa," Christine assured swiftly. "I'm the one who brought it up—

and I *wanted* to. I've always hoped that there would be a day when I would see you again and be able to thank you for your kindness to me that morning. It meant so much. I was terribly shy then, and it was so nice of you to leap to my defense. And when you withdrew your name so that I could get into the seminar . . . well, it's because of your kindness that I met David. I think it's an amazing coincidence that you and Elizabeth are friends."

There is another coincidence, Elizabeth thought as she silently struggled with that coincidence and her decision about whether or not to reveal it. She hadn't been specifically involved in the care of David Andrews, but she had known a great deal about the talented artist who had been inexplicably stricken with liver cancer. David had been the first recipient of LKC. Having failed conventional chemotherapy, he had been literally dying when the decision had been made to try Stephen's new and innovative immunotherapy; and with that revolutionary therapy, David had lived, quality life, for another year.

Everyone at the medical center—and oncologists around the world—knew about the dramatic scientific breakthrough. But that was pure science, without a patient's name attached. Elizabeth had learned David's name from Stephen; and during that final year of David's life she had heard it often, because Stephen had shared with her both the hope and the sadness he had felt for his patient—and for his courageous young wife. But if Stephen had ever referred to Mrs. David Andrews by her first name, Elizabeth didn't remember it; and even had she known that Christine's last name was Andrews, she doubted that she would have made the connection.

Christine knew of Elizabeth's friendship with Stephen, as well as of Madolyn's intimate relationship with him, and yet she had said nothing about her own connection to him. Christine had chosen not to mention the coincidence, and that was obviously her choice to make.

But now Elizabeth had her own choice to make, and she decided that she felt uncomfortable keeping silent.

"Your husband was a patient of Stephen Sheridan's, wasn't he?"

"Yes," Christine answered. She turned to Elizabeth, and said, "I didn't realize that you had known David, Elizabeth."

"I didn't know him. I only knew of him—through Stephen." Elizabeth drew a soft breath and, her voice gently apologetic, explained, "Sometimes it's necessary, emotionally necessary, for doctors to talk to each other about patients, even if they aren't both actually involved in that patient's care."

"I don't mind that he talked to you about David," Christine assured quietly. "I know how dedicated he is, and how much he cares, and how wonderfully he cared for David. I suppose I should have asked if you knew about David, but I guess it just seemed less . . . complicated . . . not to. No one at Sydney's knows anything about him. I started working here a month after his death and—"

"And it's very private," Elizabeth said softly. "And it will stay that way."

"Thank you."

After a long but not awkward silence, during which the three women exchanged smiles of understanding and trust, Larisa finally enthused, "I'm so impressed with the outfits you've put together for Elizabeth, Christine. I can't wait to see the gowns you've selected for the ball."

"They're in the changing room. I think there are several that will look wonderful on you, Elizabeth, but if you don't agree, I'd be very happy to design something for you, too . . ."

* * *

It was quickly apparent that it would not be necessary for Christine to design an evening gown for Elizabeth. Every gown she had selected did, in fact, look quite wonderful. As they discussed which was the best of the best, the most ravishing and glamorous, the thoughtful analysis was liberally sprinkled with the fond smiles and gentle teases of friendship.

Eventually they reached a consensus: the coral silk chiffon. The bright, rich color was absolutely perfect for Elizabeth, Christine and Larisa agreed. And, they concurred, the gown's long elegant lines artfully accentuated her long and elegant figure.

Larisa herself had a strong sense of style and color, but she saw in Christine a true gift: the appreciation of what looked best coupled with the creative flair to make it look even better. As she sat on the sofa in the salon's private viewing area watching Christine's lavender eyes focus intently on the issue of which shoes best accessorized the gown, Larisa thought about what she had said to Christine on that long-ago morning in the art department at Berkeley—the hope that one day she would have the opportunity to model one of Christine's designs.

Larisa knew it was a hope that would never come true. Christine might become a famous designer, of course. She was only thirty, after all, and so clearly gifted. But Larisa knew that her own modeling days were over. Even though the world had enjoyed watching supermodels Christie Brinkley, Lauren Hutton, and Cheryl Tiegs age beautifully, Larisa Locksley had been out of the public eye for over six years. No one was bonded to her, and the contrast between the woman she had been six years ago and the woman she was now would be too harsh.

The problem wasn't her body. When strong and healthy, her shape was still as sleek and provocative as ever. Julian had insisted on it. No, Larisa knew, the problem was her eyes. Before Julian, she had been able to make the brilliant blue glow with hope and joy. She had learned the radiant look from Elizabeth, for whom it was entirely authentic, a happy and optimistic vision of the bountiful promises of life. Her best friend's luminous emerald eyes sparkled still, but Larisa knew that she could no longer mimic the joyous look. Her own eyes had seen far too much now, and they sent messages over which she had no control . . . haunted messages of hopelessness . . . of dreams shattered and love betrayed.

CHAPTER EIGHT

The day was still warm and sunny when Elizabeth and Larisa emerged from Sydney's. As they stood in the late afternoon sunshine awaiting the arrival of Elizabeth's car, Elizabeth asked her friend what she would like to do with the glorious summer evening that lay ahead. A picnic supper in Ghirardelli's waterfront park perhaps? Or seafood salad on Fisherman's Wharf? Or a leisurely stroll along Pacific Beach at sunset?

I can't do any of those things, Larisa thought. Her now exhausted body trembled with weakness and the embers in her abdomen had become a fire that threatened to rage out of control. Instead of Ghirardelli or the wharf or the beach, perhaps she should ask Elizabeth to take her to the medical center to determine the extent of her trauma, to see if there had been life-threatening injuries to vital organs other than the one of which she was already fully aware: her heart.

No, Larisa told herself. She was fatigued now, wobbly and in pain, but overall she had been better today than yesterday, and tomorrow she would be even better still, and on Monday, while Elizabeth was at work, she would walk to the nearby pharmacy to buy iron and vitamins. And, by next weekend, she would be able to accompany Elizabeth to their once-favorite haunts.

But not now.

"Aren't you tired, Liz?" she asked softly. "You were up all night and you only had a short nap."

Elizabeth looked thoughtfully at the friend who had always before been the one with unlimited energy. Despite the pale whiteness of her once rich creamy skin, in the dressing salon at Sydney's Larisa had seemed almost like her old self—funny, clever, and lively. But, Elizabeth realized now as she looked closely at the strain on Larisa's beautiful face, the glimpse of Larisa-past had come at great expense.

"Are you okay, Lara? I know you've been under a great deal of stress . . . but I wonder if there's something more." Elizabeth tilted her head and guessed gently, "Pregnancy, maybe?"

"I'm definitely not pregnant. And I am okay." *I will be okay.* "I'm just tired, Liz, that's all."

The beautiful strained face sent a message of courage—and of fear—and Elizabeth respected her friend's obvious wish that she push no further. So she simply smiled and confessed, "Well, I'm tired, too, in a cozy sort of way. Why don't we just pick up some food on the way home, change into our bathrobes, and talk until we fall asleep?"

In college, Elizabeth and Larisa had shared their secrets, their wishes, and their dreams. Now, as they sat in the living room of Elizabeth's apartment and watched the golden splendor of the sun as it fell into the Pacific, they remembered that time of sharing . . . and they remembered the dreams.

From the very beginning, Elizabeth's dream had been to become a doctor. When Larisa had pressed for more parts to the dream, eighteen-year-old Elizabeth had confessed that yes, she did want to fall in love someday, and yes, she wanted to get married and have children. Larisa took the simple facts of Elizabeth's dream and embellished with enthusiasm fueled by the heartfelt conviction that everything her generous and optimistic friend dreamed for herself *should* come true.

"You had me living in a charming white-and-yellow house surrounded by white-and-yellow roses and a picket fence," Elizabeth said as she recalled vividly the richly textured portrait Larisa had painted of her future. "I was going to have an office in the house—so I could be a doctor, a wife, and a mother all at once—and while I was doing all that, you would be gallavanting around the world, modeling the latest fashions and having a never-ending series of glamorous, amorous adventures."

"Glamorous, amorous," Larisa echoed quietly. She had known so clearly in college that she would never fall in love. She believed in love and romance for Elizabeth, of course, but never, not ever, for herself. There would be men in the glamorous life she would lead as a high-fashion model, handsome and dashing men with whom she would share grand adventures, but there would never be love. That had been her plan. Now she thought, I should have stayed with that plan. "And every so often I'd come visit you and dazzle your children with discreetly edited versions of my adventures. And eventually, when there had been enough adventures, I'd come to stay, probably forever, and simply sit on your veranda sipping lemonade amid the roses and writing my best-selling memoirs."

"We never exactly decided where that charming house was, did we?" Elizabeth asked. "Somewhere pastoral and folksy, a perfect place for raising children, but with virtual instant access to every advance modern medicine had to offer."

"Of course! And it had lots of snow in winter, for sleigh rides and ice-skating and twinkling lights of Christmas, but in summer, when I was sipping lemonade and writing my steamy memoirs, it was the South at its most hot and sultry." Larisa shrugged softly. The lovely place she had so enthusiastically envisioned for them in which to share their dreams didn't exist. And the dreams themselves? She had become the model she had dreamed of becoming. And Elizabeth had become the gifted surgeon. But what about the other parts of Elizabeth's dream? Larisa tilted her head thoughtfully and asked quietly, "Have you ever fallen in love?"

"I guess not. Whatever falling in love is." Elizabeth smiled, and then confessed, "I've wondered if it's actually happened and I just didn't realize it because I was expecting so much—too much, some impossible fantasy. I've always told myself, no, when it happens, when you really fall in love, you'll know. It will be so compelling—and so wonderful—that there will be no doubt."

"Isn't it strange, Liz? Of the two of us, you were the only one who truly believed in love. And yet somehow I convinced myself that I had found my fairy-tale prince. The real truth is that Julian found me. He'd seen my photographs and wanted to meet me. I knew that at the time—and I suppose I should have known that I was just another trophy for him—but I allowed myself the foolish delusion that he loved me for me." A frown saddened her beautiful pale face. "I'm not sure he ever really did."

"Marriage can begin with great love and still falter, Lara."

"Yes, well, it definitely faltered. Or maybe I was the one who faltered," she added quietly. "Maybe Julian did love me at one time and I somehow disappointed him."

"I doubt that."

"I have to accept at least half the responsibility for the failure of my marriage. And I do, even though I'm not yet sure exactly what it was I did wrong." *I gave him everything I had to give—and it was too much of myself to have given away—and yet still it was not enough for him.* Larisa sighed. "I guess it's pretty obvious that it's too soon for me to talk about this coherently. It's all still a confusing blur. But one thing isn't confused." Her worried blue eyes met the sympathetic emerald ones, and drawing strength from Elizabeth's strength, she vowed solemnly, "I'm not going back to him."

"Good." Elizabeth smiled and suggested gently, "I think maybe the sooner the marriage is officially over, the easier it will be for you to go on."

Larisa shuddered involuntarily as she remembered Julian's violent rage over the simple loss of a piece of real estate. After a moment she said, "I'm not sure that Julian will ever give me a divorce, Liz. He hates to lose anything that he believes should belong to him."

"Julian doesn't have a choice about giving you a divorce, Lara. If you want a divorce, you can have it. The choice is yours as much as Julian's."

Choice. The word echoed in Larisa's mind like the most rare and wonderful of delicacies. Choice hadn't been a part of her life for the past six years, despite her world of riches and luxury. Even leaving Julian hadn't truly been a choice, only the deepest instinct for survival compelled by the anguished cry of an innocent girl who had been brutally betrayed once again.

"Julian is very powerful. He'll get the best attorneys. It may be very difficult for me even to find someone who is willing to do battle with him."

"You already have someone," Elizabeth countered. Her expression became thoughtful and her voice filled with sisterly confidence and pride as she elaborated, "You have my brother."

"Mark? He's doing divorce law?"

"Yes. It began by accident when the divorce attorney in his law firm left unexpectedly, in the midst of a very bitter action. Mark was asked to fill in, and it turned out that he had a remarkably calming effect, managing to guide even that acrimonious divorce to an almost harmonious dissolution. As a result, he's now handling all the firm's divorce cases."

"It doesn't surprise me that Mark does it well," Larisa said. *Harmony and fairness are Jennings family traits.* "But doesn't he find it distasteful? Divorce is such a failure."

"I think Mark finds it challenging and rewarding to help make what is such an emotionally difficult situation as painless as possible."

"Just like what you do with dying patients."

"Oh, well, I don't know. Anyway, Mark has become a little famous in legal circles for his success with divorce cases. He's handled some of San Francisco's biggest and most difficult ones. He's also handled a few in Hollywood, ones in which no one even knew the divorce was happening until the press agents quietly announced that it was a done thing. Mark believes very strongly that divorce should be private. He refuses to take cases in which either party wants publicity—newspaper headlines, Larry King, Phil Donahue, that sort of thing—and you've already told me that Julian hates even the whisper of scandal." Elizabeth smiled triumphantly. "So Mark is the perfect choice."

Mark. Larisa had met him only moments after she had met Elizabeth. Mark, then a third-year law student at Hastings, had been the protective older brother, showing up in his little sister's dormitory room to make sure everything was all right, including her new roommate. Larisa's reaction to handsome and confident Mark Jennings had been her reaction to all men: a wariness that had manifested itself as haughty contempt. In fact, Larisa had trusted no one then—neither men nor women. She had learned to trust her warm and generous roommate, of course, and eventually she had even been friendly to the older brother who was so protective of Elizabeth—a protectiveness that would have extended to Larisa had she permitted it to. But Larisa wouldn't allow Mark to protect her, and there had always remained a little distance and uncertainty between them. Mark didn't really approve of her, Larisa had decided. She was far too wild, too provocative, and too brazen for his innocent little sister.

Larisa knew that Julian and his attorneys would say whatever was necessary to persuade her attorney that a divorce was simply out of the question. Did she want Mark, who already disapproved of her, to hear the lies she knew they would speak? That her obviously erratic and emotional behavior was perhaps best explained by her addiction to cocaine? Or that she was sexually wanton and had had numerous extramarital affairs? Mark would tell her what Julian had said, and then she would have to confess to him that at the center of each lie there was in fact a little bit of truth. Yes, she would tell him, on occasion she *had* used cocaine; and she might even add that although she hated using the drug, there were times when it made everything much easier. But she would be far too ashamed to admit to Mark that she had only used the illicit snow-white powder when Julian had forced her to, because she had had too little will—and far too much of a wish to please him, *to have him love her*—to ever say no to him.

And her sexual wantonness? Larisa had satisfied Julian's every sexual whim, and more and more he had insisted that cocaine become part of their lovemaking, and she had perhaps been wanton with him. But she had never had an affair, never even considered it. Julian had had affairs, many of them. She might confess that to Mark, another admission of her own failure, but she would never be able to tell him or anyone about the last night with Julian. She was far too ashamed to admit that greatest failure of all—the betrayal of herself, the giving away of herself until there had been so little left, so little respect or value or worth that Julian hadn't hesitated to possess her violently and against her will.

Larisa had no doubt that Mark Jennings had a gift for serenely handling even the messiest of divorces. She could even imagine him being quite undaunted by Julian and his slick and powerful attorneys. But did she really want Mark to know about her foolish romanticism, her terrible mistakes, her unspeakable shame?

"Mark will be deeply offended if you don't at least talk to him," Elizabeth said as if in response to Larisa's silent question. "Even if you decide not to have him represent you, you should trust him to give you good advice."

"I *do* trust him. It's just that this is all so sordid."

"He'll want to help," Elizabeth countered firmly. Then, with a note of finality, she added, "So. That's settled. We'll call him at home tomorrow morning and set up an appointment for sometime this week."

"Okay," Larisa agreed as she thought, I'm so needy. I always have been. And Elizabeth and Mark have always been so willing to give. Someday, maybe, please, I'll be able to repay them for their kindness. "Thank you."

"You're welcome!" Elizabeth smiled and added sympathetically, "I know there's a lot about what happened with Julian that's still just pure emotion. You want it all to make sense, and maybe someday it will. But, Lara, maybe it won't. I'm not sure feelings can be wrapped up in neat little packages. Sometimes relationships simply fail no matter how much you care or how hard you try to make them work."

As Larisa saw the gentle sadness in Elizabeth's emerald eyes and heard a wistful softness in her friend's voice that she had never heard before, she realized that Elizabeth's gentle words of wisdom were very personal. But, as far as Larisa knew, none of Elizabeth's relationships had ever failed. They had just faded, gradually losing brilliance like the sun falling from the sky. True, as might accompany the final adieu to the warmth and goodness of a glorious summer day, there had sometimes been a gentle sadness, a wistful regret that the golden sunshine couldn't last forever—but there had never been a sense of failure.

Until now.

After a moment Larisa guessed, "Are you talking about Nick?"

"Oh! No." Elizabeth frowned thoughtfully before confessing quietly, "Well, maybe I am. My relationship with Nick has been a failure, but it's not a grand love affair gone awry. The truth is that Nicholas Chase has never even liked me."

"If Nicholas Chase, whoever he is, doesn't like you, then there's something fatally wrong with him."

"No. There's nothing wrong with Nick."

"And there's nothing wrong with you," Larisa reminded fondly. "So, tell me about him."

"Okay." Elizabeth drew a breath and then began, "He's a gifted surgeon, the most talented I've ever known, and he is also a wonderfully sensitive and compassionate physician. But . . . he and I just don't connect. We never have. In the past eight months I've probably spent more hours with Nick than I've spent with any other man. We've been together, literally, for up to thirty-six hours at a time, working together, saving lives and losing them. With anyone else there would be something personal, an acknowledgment at least of the emotion of what we're doing."

"And the ice man won't talk about his emotions?"

"Not with me. Nick and I don't talk at all, unless it's a necessary conversation about one of our patients."

"But you're so easy to talk to! You're always so interested and open, and you always have such cheerful things to say."

"Thanks. But with Nick I feel very uncomfortable. Every time I think of something light and cheerful that I could say, I decide against it for fear that he would consider it silly or foolish."

"I don't get it, Lizzie," Larisa said. "The man sounds perfectly awful."

"But he isn't awful, Lara, that's the point. And with everyone else, he's very charming and personable."

"Then there's a piece missing, something you haven't told me. Everyone likes you." Larisa hesitated a moment, then suggested, "Maybe he's secretly in love with you."

"Oh, no." Elizabeth's cheeks flushed pink. "I can assure you that he's not."

"I think you'd better tell me all about Doctor Nicholas Chase—from the beginning."

Larisa listened in intent and interested silence as Elizabeth recapped the past eight months: how Nick had inherited her, his too-talked about midnight affairs with the hospital's most beautiful women, the emotional distance he had kept from her from the very beginning, and her secret worry that Nick didn't respect her as a surgeon and wished that she would simply disappear. . . .

"But he has to know that you're an excellent surgeon—because you are! You've had enough people tell you that over the years and surely it's something that you know yourself."

"Yes. I am a good surgeon," Elizabeth admitted quietly. "I do know that. My patients do very well, but . . ."

"But because of this Nick character, you're beginning to doubt yourself." Larisa's own self-esteem had been very fragile for a very long time and with very good reason. And even though it had been terribly painful when her delicate and precarious self-worth had been so brutally shattered by Julian, it made sense. It was even, somehow, all right. But it was not all right for someone to shake the confidence of the lovely and so worthy Elizabeth Jennings. "Don't ever doubt yourself, Liz."

"I'm trying to resist doing just that," Elizabeth said, smiling gratefully at the mother-bear protectiveness of her friend. "I'm trying to be scientific and analytical about the situation, but the truth is I've actually been thinking about looking for a job somewhere else."

"But you love San Francisco! Not only is it your home, but you're at a prestigious institution, doing trauma *and* transplantation, both of which are obviously very exciting and challenging for you."

"True, all true. The most important truth, though, is that the very best part of what I'm doing is having the chance to work with Nick. He's so talented, and I'm learning so much from him, but with each passing day the awkwardness I feel and the conspicuous absence of our relationship becomes all the more obvious." Elizabeth paused. Then murmuring almost to herself, she admitted, "It's just very difficult."

I can see how difficult this is for you, Larisa thought. You really care about this ice man, don't you? Oh, Liz, have you fallen in love at long last?

As Larisa's blue eyes left her friend's lovely, troubled face and gazed outside to the dazzling glitter of San Francisco at night, she wondered, Nicholas Chase, whoever you are, how crazy can you be?

CHAPTER NINE

"*You're* going to operate?" the surgery resident asked incredulously, regretting his honest, startled question the moment his eyes met Nick's. "I mean . . . it seems . . . don't the lab data we have—the X rays and scans—indicate such massive tissue injury that there's no hope?"

Nick's icy glare relented slightly at the resident's uneasiness. He was an excellent resident, hard-working and careful, and he was also probably absolutely right: there was very little hope, probably none, for the four-year-old boy who only an hour ago had been happily playing in the safe sanctuary of his own front yard. The warm tranquility of the sunny morning—and the promise of the young sunny life—had been irrevocably shattered as a drunk driver had spun his car out of control and into the yard. Because of its reputation for the treatment of pediatric trauma, the badly injured little boy had been rushed to Pacific Heights Medical Center. The driver of the car, almost certainly lethally injured, too, had been taken to San Francisco General.

"You may well be right," Nick admitted to the resident. "You probably are. But I'm going to operate."

Nick hesitated a moment, not debating his decision to give the small boy every possible chance to live, but debating whether or not to involve Elizabeth in what was virtually destined to be a tragedy without a silver lining. They would almost certainly open the small abdomen and find irreparable harm, far beyond the limits of modern medicine to save. Why involve Elizabeth in that unspeakable sadness and loss? The answer came quickly: Because if there is a chance to save this precious and innocent young life, I need her delicate talented fingers, her calm resolute courage, and the radiant hopefulness of her lovely emerald eyes.

"You don't really need to get involved," Nick told the resident. "Just Doctor Jennings and I will scrub, if she's available. Would you mind paging her for me to see if she's free while I get the consent from Danny's parents?"

*   *   *

Elizabeth was on the pediatric ward when the page from ER came. She was just completing the discharge orders for Molly, who was going home a remarkable seven days after her transplantation surgery. Mary Ann had been discharged four days earlier, although she had been in the hospital almost continually ever since, watching her infant daughter grow stronger and healthier each day. Elizabeth frowned briefly as she dialed the number displayed on her pager. She wasn't on trauma call today.

But Nick was, the resident said when she answered the page. And he wondered if she would be available to operate with him—right away—on a critically injured child. Yes, of course, she told the resident. She would be down in just a few moments.

As she neared the emergency room, Elizabeth caught sight of Nick. He was in one of the private waiting rooms that had been specifically designed for families of the most critically injured and were a discreet distance from the noise and chaos of the general waiting area. Facing Nick, listening intently to his words, was an obviously anxious and distraught young couple. The little boy's parents, Elizabeth assumed as she quietly joined them in the small room.

Usually when she and Nick operated on a trauma patient, Elizabeth established rapport with the family while Nick saw to the last-minute details. He would always meet the family before the surgery, of course, but usually long after she had. This time it was Nick who was with the family . . . and it was Nick who spoke the honest and extraordinary words that Elizabeth overheard as she neared.

"I don't want to give you any false hope. The chances of saving Danny's life are very small, perhaps even nonexistent. But I want to operate, to be absolutely certain that there is nothing that can be done."

"You'll do the surgery yourself, Doctor Chase?" Danny's father asked with fragile hope. He recognized Nick, of course, the famous transplant surgeon who had so recently performed the miraculous life-saving surgery on little Molly.

"Yes." Nick turned to Elizabeth then and added, "And this is Doctor Jennings. She'll be operating with me."

"You operated on Mary Ann and Molly, too, didn't you?" Danny's mother asked, recognizing Elizabeth's name but not her face because the photographic coverage had been only of Nick.

"Yes." Elizabeth smiled warmly, instinctively wanting to reassure but feeling a bit awkward because what Nick had told them was so terribly far from reassuring. But, she thought, there was one point on which she could authentically reassure: with Nicholas Chase as their son's surgeon, Danny was in the best hands on earth.

The best hands. Nick's strong, lean fingers worked with graceful—yet almost frantic—agility to stop the bleeding, and Elizabeth's delicate fingers joined the frenzied dance, moving in perfect wordless harmony with Nick's. But for the first time in all the times that she and Nick had operated together, Elizabeth wondered what they were doing. True, more than once, she had been with Nick when his talented fingers had saved a life that had seemed almost beyond hope. But for Danny there was so obviously no hope at all. There had been far too much destruction to his small body.

Once Elizabeth had overheard Nick talking about the possibility of emergency organ transplantation in cases of severe trauma. It was a thrilling idea, one which she had often wondered about as well, an exciting and innovative concept that she and Nick might have talked about—if they talked. But even if donor organs were available to them, to Danny, right this minute, and even if they decided to try the avant-garde therapy, Elizabeth knew that still this little boy could not be saved.

Nick didn't have any surgical advances to offer Danny. He had only his immense talent and whatever it was deep inside that filled his intense dark blue eyes with such torment and compelled him to fight desperately to save this young life. Nick was a noble warrior valiantly fighting a battle that he could not win. But, Elizabeth knew, Nick would not view his valiant fight as either noble or heroic— only as a devastating defeat. And she could not shake the ominous impression that when Danny died something within Nick would die too.

Why are you doing this, Nick? she wanted to cry. Even you can't save him. And if you can't, no one can. Stop, please, before you destroy yourself!

Elizabeth would never say such words aloud in the operating room. She, like Nick, always operated as if her patients were wide-awake and quite able to hear all words, and sense all emotions and all fears. Elizabeth didn't speak the words, and her skillful delicate hands helped Nick and Danny without faltering.

It was Nick who finally broke the silence. And when he did, his voice was very soft and very calm, so that if somehow Danny could hear, he would feel neither alarm nor fear.

"It's time to close."

Nick spoke the words with reassuring calm, but his blue eyes were filled with excruciating anguish; and as he closed the young skin with such tender care, there was apology, too, in the tormented blue depths.

While the anesthesiologist and scrub nurse were getting Danny ready to be moved to the nearby recovery room, Elizabeth and Nick left the operating suite, as was customary, to give instructions to the nursing staff in recovery in advance of the patient's arrival.

This time there were very special instructions. Nick gave them to Stephanie, a beautiful woman who knew him well—at least intimately.

"Danny isn't going to live much longer, Steph," Nick told her. "I want you to find a quiet and private place for him—not dark, just quiet and private. And I want his parents to be with him if they want to be. I'll talk to them. If it's too difficult for them to be with him when he dies, then I'll be with him. If they do decide they can be here, you need to know that I'll be waiting in the surgery lounge. I'm counting on you to let me know right away when you think they need me."

"Okay, Nick," Stephanie answered solemnly as she gently touched his taut bare forearm. "You can count on me."

"Good. Thank you."

As Elizabeth and Nick walked in silence from recovery to the room where Danny's parents were waiting, she thought about how effortlessly Stephanie had touched him. It hadn't been a gesture of intimacy, just one of understanding and empathy, the kind of warm touch Elizabeth herself might have offered any other man who was so obviously as troubled as Nick. She and Nick *had* touched today, of course, as they always did when they operated, the necessary touches of the intricate surgery they performed together. Usually when their fingers touched, Nick's felt quite warm, symbols of the fiery heat and smoldering sensuality that blazed within him.

But today there had been no warmth at all in the long talented fingers with which her own had danced with graceful precision. Today Elizabeth had felt only ice . . . and she sensed such tension in the strong lean body of the warrior who fought so valiantly beside her.

When they reached Danny's parents, it was Nick who spoke. He hadn't given them false hope before the surgery, and now he simply told them more truths.

"Danny is alive still, but he's not going to live much longer," Nick said quietly. And then, even more quietly, he added, "I'm so sorry."

"Can we see him?"

"Of course you can. He won't regain consciousness, but that doesn't mean he won't be able to hear your words and know that you're with him. So, if you can, don't let him hear your fear, only your love, only your happiness that he's your little boy." Emotion stopped Nick's voice. After a moment he added with exquisite gentleness, "Maybe that's impossible for you to do."

"No," Danny's mother answered. "We can do it. We *will.*"

"Yes," his father agreed. His eyes flooded with tears, but his voice, like his wife's, was resolved to be strong for their son for as long as Danny needed their strength. "We will. And thank you, Doctor Chase. We know that you tried and that you cared."

When Nick had told Stephanie that he would be waiting in the surgery lounge, he had said "I" not "we." But Elizabeth accompanied him to the lounge anyway. True, Danny's parents clearly looked more to Nick than to her, but Danny was her patient too. And, even if Danny's parents didn't need her, Elizabeth wanted to be available for Nick in case he did.

In case Nick *needed* her? The foolishness of the thought became quickly and abundantly clear. Nick was withdrawn, completely lost in his own thoughts, neither knowing nor caring that she was there. As Elizabeth watched the unrelenting torment in his dark blue eyes, she felt helplessness—and anger. Anger was such an unfamiliar emotion for her, and this anger was so unfocused. It was an ache, imprisoned deep inside, in her heart, and it paced with restless power, wanting to scream—and needing to escape. With any other surgeon, even if it was someone she barely knew or liked, after an emotionally devastating surgery such as this, they would have talked. They would have tried to make sense of the senseless and expressed at the very least their shared anger at the whim of fate that had so swiftly and violently taken a little boy's life.

But not with Nick.

Was that why she was angry? Because Nick was shutting her out? Or was she angry at herself for her own lack of courage in simply reaching out to him? She was angry with both herself and Nick, she decided. And yet, when she finally articulated the anger, the target was neither of them, but instead the tragedy itself and its real perpetrator. The tragedy that had befallen Danny had not, of course, been a whim of fate. It had been the irresponsible act of an adult human being against an innocent little child.

"How can people drink and drive? Hasn't that lesson been learned yet?" she demanded, her voice quiet yet impassioned. She wanted to talk to Nick, to draw him out, but when his blue eyes lifted to hers, Elizabeth trembled at what she saw. The blue was as ice cold as his hands had been and as hard as the taut tension she had sensed in his strong body. Nick was angry. No, she realized, he was *enraged.* Was his rage at the driver who had caused such a senseless tragedy? Or was it at her for her lack of compassion? Her voice trembled as she whispered, "I'm sorry, Nick, I guess that sounds too uncharitable. I know that alcoholism is a disease, a terrible disease—"

"Yes," Nick interjected harshly, his voice as hard and uncompromising as his eyes. "Alcoholism is a terrible disease. But it should be a private one. If you're a drunk, you should spend every second of your life making certain that you give your disease to no one else—especially not to an innocent child. Don't waste any charity on drunks, Elizabeth, it's pure foolishness."

Pure foolishness. Nick's harsh words stabbed like the sharpest of knives. Elizabeth should have gotten even angrier. She should have told him what she thought of him and his condescending arrogance. But her anger vanished as quickly as it had come, taking its courageous energy with it, leaving her feeling empty . . . and a little lost . . . and terribly sad.

I'm so sorry I involved you in this! Nick thought as he gazed at her lovely stricken emerald eyes. I so desperately needed your talent and your courage and your hope. But now I've hurt you with my harshness.

But his harshness had come from the icy truths of his own heart, and if his cruelly honest words made Elizabeth think less of him then that was for the best— at least it was best for *her*.

"You don't need to wait," he said finally. "I'll stay. Thank you for operating with me."

Now he was dismissing her! Elizabeth felt the warm flickers of new anger, but she didn't allow them to burst into flame. What was the point? There was no point. She had wanted to talk to him—and had wanted him to talk to her—but it was obviously, so obviously, impossible.

After a moment, without another word, Elizabeth turned and left . . . as Nick had requested.

I hate you Nicholas Chase. The surprising thought came with such energy that for a startled moment Elizabeth's hasty retreat came to an abrupt halt. Was it true? Did she really hate him? Elizabeth tested the thought and the feeling of tranquility that could come with it. If she hated Nick, if he was deserving of her hatred, her heart could stop defending him and she could stop caring . . . and hurting.

But the tantalizingly peaceful thought of hating Nick didn't survive even the most superficial scrutiny. Elizabeth knew that what she felt about Nick was very far away from hatred. She didn't hate him, and never could. Which meant that she would simply—oh, not so simply!—have to keep caring . . . and hurting.

Elizabeth had started walking again and when she emerged from her thoughts and noticed where she was, she discovered that her steps had unerringly guided her to the quiet sanctuary of Stephen's research lab. She wouldn't share the sadness of this morning with her good friend, nor would she tell him what had happened with Nick; but just talking to Stephen and feeling the genuine warmth of his gentle dark brown eyes would make her feel better . . .

It was only when she turned the knob of his laboratory door and found it locked that Elizabeth remembered: Stephen was downtown discussing the final details of the Immunology Institute with the building's architect.

CHAPTER TEN

*W*hen the board of directors of the Pacific Heights Medical Center's future Immunology Institute selected architect Peter London's proposal from the many that had been submitted by architectural firms throughout the country, the selection was greeted with a mixture of enthusiasm and worry. Peter London's talent was indisputable, as was the thirty-six-year-old architect's reputation for quality and excellence. But Peter's fame had come from designing homes, hotels, commercial buildings, and resort complexes, not hospitals. And the San Francisco Bay Area already boasted one architecturally beautiful and award-winning hospital that was not quite as functional as it should have been—its corners a little too tight for stretchers to sweep through in one pass, its laboratories a bit too far away from where the specimens were actually obtained.

The board's enthusiasm for a building designed by the man whose trademark was accessible elegance eventually outweighed its worry. Still, to be absolutely certain that the expensive structure would be functional as well as elegant, the institute's future director, Dr. Stephen Sheridan, was given the task of working closely with the celebrated architect—to make sure that Peter understood the idiosyncrasies of a modern state-of-the-art medical facility.

Before meeting Peter, Stephen had been concerned that the famous architect might not be terribly receptive to his suggestions, caring far more for style than for function. But from the very beginning it was reassuringly apparent that Peter London was as committed to quality, excellence, and precision in his work as Stephen was committed to the same in his. With Stephen's technical advice and Peter's unfailing willingness to make changes until everything was exactly right, the end result was an efficient and functional work of art.

The structural blueprints had long since been completed. Now, with the celebration ball at the Fairmont just three weeks away, all that was left were finishing touches, the elegant embellishments and fine detailing that distinguished a Peter London creation from all others. Peter had surprised Stephen by wanting his opinions on those artistically—but not medically—important touches. After all, Peter had reminded him, the institute would be a second home to Stephen's patients. Peter hadn't added, although it was true, that he would never have solicited Stephen's artistic input had it not been very obvious that he and Stephen shared the same taste for understated elegance.

Only a few decisions were left to be made, and the purpose of today's meeting was to finish making them so that the scale model of the institute that would be on display at the ball would be as accurate as possible.

"I've had an eleventh-hour thought about the entrance," Peter said after the other decisions had all been made. "I think I can make it feel even lighter and more welcoming. If you have time, there's a boutique I'd like to show you—just about a block away—with an atrium similar to what I have in mind. What I would do in the institute would be less lavish than what I did at Sydney's, but the concept is essentially the same."

"You designed Sydney's?"

"Yes. Have you been there?"

"No, but I've certainly heard about it. I don't need to get back to the hospital for a while yet, so I'd be happy to go there with you now."

As Peter and Stephen made their way through the bustle of Union Square to Sydney's, Peter explained his relationship to Sydney and Walter Prescott. They were the Prescotts of Napa Valley's renowned Prescott Vineyards, and ten years before they had taken a chance with a bright young architect. The award-winning mansion at Prescott Vineyards had been one of Peter's first creations. Walter and Sydney had been so delighted with the mansion that they had commissioned Peter to design the bed-and-breakfast hotel they also owned in Napa as well as their hilltop home in Tiberon. And when, four years ago, the fashionable and energetic fifty-year-old Sydney Prescott announced that she had had it with traveling to New York and Paris to buy clothes and was going to bring the designs of the world to the women of San Francisco "or bust," she had asked Peter to design her elegant boutique.

Peter's obviously fond recounting of his relationship to the Prescotts finished just as he and Stephen arrived at Sydney's. Within moments of walking through the huge French doors into the rose-fragrant luxury, they were greeted by the glamorous Sydney herself.

"Peter!" Sydney smiled with obvious delight at the surprising yet very welcome appearance of her handsome and famous friend. "Don't tell me you're hand delivering the sketches for my Fifth Avenue boutique two weeks early?"

"No. But you will have them within two weeks," Peter assured. "Sydney, I'd like you to meet Doctor Stephen Sheridan. Stephen, this is Sydney Prescott."

"The Doctor Stephen Sheridan of immunology fame?" Sydney asked. Then, hesitating only a beat, she added knowingly, "Of Madolyn Mitchell fame?"

Stephen wasn't terribly surprised that Sydney had so swiftly and accurately made the connections. He had long since gotten the distinct impression from both Elizabeth and Madolyn that Sydney's was a sorority of sorts, a place where the regulars felt so relaxed and comfortable that they often shared tidbits from their personal lives. He was, apparently, a tidbit that had been shared.

"Guilty on both counts," he admitted, conveying with a warm smile and easy laugh that it didn't bother him that he had been discussed.

"Well, a lot of business has come my way because of both of those counts," Sydney said graciously. "Madolyn does all of her shopping here, and the boutique has become the unofficial supplier of evening gowns for the Immunology Institute ball. I have a feeling that most of San Francisco will be at the Fairmont that night. And why not? A celebration in honor of a building designed by the world's best architect and which will be home to the world's most brilliant immunologist is a pretty tough ticket to pass up."

"Well," Stephen countered with matching graciousness. "The reason everyone in San Francisco is buying their evening gowns here is because of you. Madolyn raves about the boutique, as does Elizabeth Jennings."

"Which must mean they rave about Christine," Sydney said. "I'm sure that

Christine would very much like to meet you, Stephen. If you would like to meet her too, why don't I see if she's free?"

"That would be nice. I would indeed like to meet the famous Christine."

"In the meantime, Stephen and I will be wandering through the atrium," Peter said.

"Be my guest." Sydney started to turn to leave to find Christine, but suddenly remembering, she turned back and asked, "How was your trip to New York, Peter? Did you find a model?"

"No." Peter frowned. "Not yet."

"Well, it hardly matters. *Promise* will sell itself." Looking to Stephen for confirmation and seeing only interested surprise, Sydney added, "I guess Peter hasn't mentioned his latest venture to you?"

"I guess not."

"Well. *Promise* is a perfume. The reason why Peter London, architect, is marketing a new perfume is, apparently, a long story—which he has never fully disclosed," Sydney explained, her voice filled with teasing fondness and not a trace of censure at Peter's secrecy. "However, the ending to the long and mysterious story is that *Promise* is sensational." Smiling at Peter she added, "I do hope that model or no model you're still planning to release it next spring."

"I am. Model or no model," Peter affirmed quietly. "So, Syd, we're going to look at the atrium."

"And I'm going to go find Christine."

Sydney and Christine had not appeared by the time Peter and Stephen had finished discussing a modified version of the atrium which, Stephen agreed, would make the institute even more warm and welcoming. Peter had to leave for a marketing meeting for *Promise* in Sausalito, but Stephen decided to wait a little longer—to meet the famous Christine.

But Stephen didn't need to meet the famous Christine. He had met her two years before. She hadn't been the famous Christine then. She had simply been the quietly courageous Mrs. Andrews.

Mrs. Andrews. That was how Stephen had always addressed her. He had called David by his first name, and David had called him Stephen, but there had always been the formality with David's wife—despite the hundreds of times that Mrs. Andrews and Dr. Sheridan had seen each other during that year, and despite the emotional intimacy of the many conversations they had had about her beloved husband's life . . . and death. Stephen had known her first name, of course. David had spoken it often, gently wrapping it in the tenderness of their extraordinary love. But David had never called his wife Christine. She had always been Christie, his lovely and so beloved Christie.

Now Mrs. Andrews . . . Christie . . . Christine was approaching him.

There was no surprise on Christine's face, of course, and there was even a soft smile of greeting in her luminous lavender eyes—but there was something else, too . . . a wariness.

"Hello, Doctor Sheridan. I'm Christine."

"Hello, Christine," Stephen said, understanding then the other message in the remarkable lavender—Christine wanted to conceal their previous acquaintance. He smiled, acknowledging her wish for privacy and his respect for same, and then to the shy and beautiful woman who had always called him Dr. Sheridan, but who now wanted to behave as if they were meeting for the first time, he said, "I'm Stephen."

As Stephen and Christine exchanged smiles, Sydney filled the silence with praises for both of them, as if they both were her prized pupils, Christine, the fashion genius, and Stephen, the miracle worker. Stephen murmured that he already knew that Christine was a fashion genius, and her lovely eyes eloquently told him that she already knew that he could work miracles.

Only moments after saying hello, Christine and Stephen said goodbye. Her two o'clock appointment arrived, ten minutes late and breathless, having raced to salvage as much of her appointment as possible because she knew full well that Christine would be booked solid as always for the rest of the day.

As Stephen drove back to the medical center, his mind filled with memories of the first time he had said hello to Christine Andrews . . . and the last time he had said goodbye.

"Hello, Mrs. Andrews."

"Hello, Doctor Sheridan. Can you help my husband live a little longer?" The question had been asked with quiet desperation, and it had been a plea neither for a lifetime nor a cure—just a little more precious time with the man she loved so much.

"Yes, Mrs. Andrews, I think I can."

LKC had given David Andrews twelve more months of life and love; eleven months of remarkable energy and health and a final month of deterioration and goodbye. During that year, every time David had received the life-prolonging yet potentially life-threatening infusions, Stephen had been at his bedside. In the beginning, both men had spent the hours in tense and expectant silence. But eventually, even though the risk of fatal anaphylaxis remained an ever-present concern, they had spent those long hours talking.

What David Andrews had talked about, all he had ever wanted to talk about in the final year of his life, was his beloved wife. He told Stephen a little about Christine's life before their love . . . and a great deal about the immense joy that that love had given him.

Christine had been the youngest daughter in a very large family. The fabric of her family had been loosely woven, not tightly knit, and the very shy Christine had been a forgotten thread left to fend for herself. David's voice had filled with bitterness when he had spoken of the family who had neglected Christine as a little girl and forgotten about her entirely—and forever—the day she left for college; but, David had admitted lovingly, his generous Christie had never felt any bitterness whatsoever. As a girl she had found her own joy making beautiful clothes for her hand-me-down dolls and bravely dreaming of the day when she would be a fashion designer.

It was because of shy Christine's bold dream that she and David had met . . . and then there had been the new and wondrous dream of their lifetime of love together. Eventually, Christine had encouraged David to pursue the dream that had lived in his own heart for so long, the dream of becoming an artist. Until Christine, he had been afraid to pursue that dream, afraid to fail, perhaps, or maybe simply reluctant even to struggle. But the shy and beautiful woman twenty years younger than he had made him believe with her quiet confidence and boundless love that all dreams were possible, and eventually he had left the safe cloistered world of academia to pursue his dream. For a long time they had had very little money, but they had had their wondrous love, and even the leanest years had never felt like a struggle at all. Finally, in the same year that would bring with it the diagnosis of lethal liver cancer, David Andrews had his first one-man show—at the prestigious Gallery in Ghirardelli Square.

David's voice had filled with bitterness when he had spoken of the family who had simply forgotten their shy and lovely daughter, but there had never been bitterness at all when he had talked about his own life-ending disease. And when he had spoken of his fears, there had never been mention of his own fear of dying—only his great fears for the young wife he would leave behind.

At least, David had told Stephen, she wouldn't be burdened with debts from his illness. Yes, the savings account that had just begun to grow would be largely depleted to pay the high deductibles, but they had an excellent health insurance policy and most of the enormous cost of his catastrophic illness would be covered. It had been Christie, David added softly, the always responsible Christie, who had insisted that they buy good health coverage when he left the university, even though the expense had cut sharply into their already modest income.

David had been spared the worry of leaving behind a destitute and indebted wife, but he had worried about her still. He wanted her life after his death to be a happy one, filled with love and laughter and all the dreams as yet unfulfilled . . . her brave girlhood dream of becoming a fashion designer . . . and her more recent and far more important dream of becoming a mother.

Just as David and Christine had decided that it was at last economically possible for them to begin having children, his cancer had been diagnosed. They had tried still, but as the doctors had warned it might, the toxic but necessary chemotherapy had poisoned the fragile sperm. During the final year of his life, they had made love to be as close as they could for as long as they could, but they had long since abandoned the hope that David could leave a part of himself with her. But, during that final year, David had received Stephen's innovative immunotherapy, not the toxic chemotherapy, and two months before his death, Christine had discovered that she was pregnant.

As he had received the last dose of LKC—because the miracle therapy had finally come to the end of its magic—David shared with Stephen the immense joy of Christine's pregnancy. It was a joy, not a sadness, because already the tiny life growing inside her filled Christine with great happiness. There would be some money left in their savings account after all the insurance deductibles had been paid, David explained, and Christine could make whatever additional money that she and the baby would need by working as a seamstress—work she loved and could do at home.

There had been a loving glow in David's dying eyes as he had told Stephen about the baby he would never see. The glow had always been there, of course, for Christine, because of Christine; just as her beautiful lavender eyes had always glowed when she was with David. Christine Andrews never permitted the man she loved so much to see anything but her love, her hope, and her joy. Her eyes had always glowed, and her voice had always been soft and musical, and the delicate hands that had touched David whenever they could had never been frantic nor possessive, just calm, just loving, just wanting to touch.

For David, Christine's loving eyes and voice and hands filled only with joyous hope; but in the private conversations she had with Stephen, the radiant lavender became stormy with anguished tears and the soft voice strained with heart-stopping fear and the delicate courageous hands trembled.

"David wants to die at home, Doctor Sheridan."

"Yes, I know. But how do you feel about that, Mrs. Andrews? I'll arrange for visiting nurses, of course, but still it may be very difficult for you."

"I want what David wants. It won't be difficult for me. And, please, don't arrange for anyone to come by. I won't need any help. We'll be all right, just the two of us."

Yes, but soon, Mrs. Andrews, very soon, David will leave you, and in that moment of his death, when his body is there but he is gone and you are alone . . . Stephen didn't speak that worry aloud to her, but he made her promise that she would call him when David died, no matter the time of day or night.

As he drove from Sydney's to the medical center, Stephen recalled the day that David had died, his frown deepening as he realized that the one-year anniversary of that death had been just a few days before. That Sunday afternoon in August had been quite glorious, the sky a brilliant sapphire, the summer sun a radiant gold, a day for celebrating—not for watching a most beloved husband die.

Stephen had been in his lab on that Sunday afternoon. Christine knew the phone number there, and that he often worked on weekends, but on the day her husband died, she did just what Stephen had told her to do: she dialed the number to his pager so that she wouldn't have to search for him.

Stephen heard apology in the quiet voice at the other end of the phone, as if Christine was sorry to have disturbed him on this splendid Sunday afternoon. But it was *he* who wanted to apologize to *her!* His immunotherapy was a breakthrough, a pioneering effort that might eventually light the way to a cure for cancer. But for David and Christine Andrews, the innovative therapy had not been a cure, only a stay.

Had David's illness simply come too soon? Stephen wondered. Or had his own bright mind simply missed some tiny clue years ago, a clue that might have led him to the revolutionary concept even sooner? Stephen didn't know, but still he thought, I'm so very sorry that I couldn't keep him alive for you forever, Mrs. Andrews.

Stephen's unspoken apology became a silent scream when Christine greeted him at the door of the modest house that she and David rented on Twin Peaks. She was dressed as she always dressed for David, in romantic pastels, her golden hair a cascade of glitter that gently framed her lovely face and spilled freely onto her shoulders. She looked beautiful, as she always looked for David, even for his death. Her spun-gold hair glittered, and the pastel dress sent a message of romance and love, but the glow was gone from her lavender eyes, and so was the fear—because what she had always feared most had finally happened. Her eyes were dark, almost gray, and her face was ashen, deathlike, as if she had died with her husband.

All the arrangements had been made in advance. Even before Stephen arrived, Christine had made the necessary call, and shortly after his arrival the two dark-suited men appeared to silently carry out their solemn task. Stephen needed to sign and date the death certificate, which he did, and then David was gone, and Stephen was alone with Christine.

David's parents were dead, Stephen knew, and Christine's family had forgotten her years ago, and no friends had ever visited David in the hospital. The world of David and Christine Andrews had been the very private world of two lovers, a world Stephen had witnessed perhaps more intimately than anyone else ever had. She was very much alone now, and Stephen very much wanted to stay with her, but it was abundantly obvious that she wanted him to leave. She seemed, in fact, almost desperate to have him go. She assured him that she was fine, and that some "very good friends" would come to be with her as soon as she called them. Stephen knew it was a lie and was amazed at how convincingly she spoke it, her gaze steady and unflickering.

There were no friends, Stephen knew: that was a lie. Christine was almost desperate in her wish to have him leave: that was the truth.

Before reluctantly acceding to her wish, Stephen promised, as much to David as to her, that he would call in a day or two to see how she was.

"No," she countered swiftly. Then, as if in apology for the swiftness of her refusal, she added softly, "Thank you."

For a terrifying moment, Stephen wondered if Christine wanted him to leave so that she could take her own life, an impulsive act of desperation, needing to be with David, knowing that she would not survive long without him anyway. How could she, with only half a heart? Stephen knew she would vehemently deny that intent if he asked her, and for a moment he considered simply staying anyway, forcing his unwanted presence on her, holding her, protecting her, comforting her.

But then he remembered. Christine was carrying David's baby. She would do nothing to harm the small precious part of David that lived within her.

So he left. And later that night he called her, even though she had told him not to, because he had been suddenly seized by an ominous and unshakable feeling that she was dying. Had she not answered the call, he would have gone to find her. But she did answer, and with a voice that was flat but clear, she told him that she was fine.

Stephen decided he wouldn't call her again. He was, after all, a grim reminder of David's death. But he did call, five days later, because he was so worried about her still . . . and because, he told himself, David would have wanted him to. Stephen heard a little more energy in her voice then, a little anger perhaps—and still the very clear message to stay away.

After that, he did stay away, never calling her, even though he thought about her often. With time, his worry changed to hope. He envisioned the same comforting image that had allowed David to die with such peace: the image of Christine and her baby. Stephen thought about the new life growing inside her, filling her with love and hope, and five months ago, when he finally figured out why he himself had been feeling so inexplicably happy and hopeful it was, astonishingly, because his subconscious mind had been envisioning Christine Andrews cradling her just-born infant.

But now Stephen had seen Christine again and all the comforting images had been instantly shattered. *There was no baby.* Madolyn had been raving about Christine for the entire six months that Stephen had known her, and she had even wondered, more than once, what she would do if Christine ever got pregnant and took a protracted maternity leave.

Had there ever been a baby? Stephen wondered. Or had that simply been a lie of love whispered gently and joyously so that David could die in peace? Yes, Stephen thought, as he remembered how courageously Christine had hidden her own fears from her husband. Yes, she would have given David that gift of love.

As he pulled into his parking space at the medical center, a dark frown crossed Stephen's handsome face. There was something more that Madolyn had said about her worry that Christine might become pregnant and leave, something that had made that possibility seem quite real. Christine worked very long hours, as if she were trying to earn as much money as she could—for a nest egg, Madolyn assumed.

There were other reasons why someone might work long hours at Sydney's, especially someone who was an aspiring fashion designer. The elegant boutique was an excellent place to establish a reputation for fashion and style, and Stephen had learned today that Peter London was designing a new boutique in Manhattan, in the heart of the fashion world . . .

But the woman Stephen had seen in Sydney's today didn't look like someone pursuing an exciting dream. Yes, Christine had been smiling and pleasant, and perhaps to anyone who hadn't known her before, she would have seemed perfectly fine. But Stephen knew how her lavender eyes looked when they were filled with hope and joy and love and dreams; and even though she had looked much better today than the last time he had seen her, Christine still looked to him like someone who had lost all of her dreams . . . not someone who was pursuing new and exciting ones.

Maybe she worked the long hours in the lovely rose-fragrant boutique simply to escape the terrible loneliness of her life without David. That was possible, Stephen thought. In fact, it was a very good reason and a very good place for her to be.

But what if, as Madolyn had presumed, Christine was working so hard because she needed money?

What if there had been other lies of love spoken to David so that he could die in peace?

CHAPTER ELEVEN

After thirty troubling yet illuminating minutes with the supervisor in hospital billing, Stephen went to medical records and requested all four volumes of David's medical file. The four thick charts, a compendium of all records from the referring hospital as well as the records kept during his year of care at the center, were in the archives, the basement room in a remote corner of the medical complex where the records of patients who had died were kept, because by law they had to be, but far away because the patients to whom they had once belonged would never again require further care. Medical records prided itself in being able to produce any active file in a matter of minutes; but trips to the archives were rarely made more than once a week, and never urgently.

Yes, Stephen told the surprised clerk, David Andrews was deceased. But, he added pleasantly but firmly, he needed the file right away anyway.

David was, and still is, my patient, Stephen thought. And there is more care that I need to provide for him.

Stephen extracted a promise from the clerk that she would go to the archives herself, as soon as the flurry of finding charts for the walk-in clinic subsided, then he left to wait in his office. As he walked, Stephen thought about the truth he had uncovered and the questions that lingered still. There was no baby. But had that promise of a new life, the great joy that part of David would be with Christine always, been simply a lie of love? Or had she really been pregnant, but so overwhelmed by the enormous debts after David's death that she had . . .

"Stephen?"

"Elizabeth," he answered as he turned in the direction of the familiar voice that had interrupted the deeply disturbing question. "Hi."

"Hi. You were about a million miles away." As she met his obviously troubled brown eyes, she asked softly, "Is something wrong?"

"Do you have time to talk?"

"Sure. In fact, I was on my way to your office to see if you'd returned yet from your meeting with the architect. Was there a problem with that?"

"No, no problem at all. Why don't we pick up a coffee and a tea in the cafeteria and go to my office?"

"Do you remember David Andrews?" Stephen asked when they were in his office and behind closed doors. "He was the patient who had hepatic cancer—"

"Of course I remember."

"Well, I just discovered that the Christine at Sydney's who you and Madolyn have been raving about all this time is his wife."

"Yes."

"*Yes?* You knew?"

"I've only known since Saturday."

"Were you going to tell me?"

Elizabeth stiffened slightly at the sharp demand, then met his frowning dark eyes directly and admitted quietly, "I honestly don't know, Stephen. I hadn't decided yet. Christine didn't know that you and I were friends—but she knew that we both worked here and she certainly knew about you and Madolyn—and she made the choice not to mention her past association with either you or the center."

"Until last Saturday."

"No. She only mentioned it then because of another coincidence. It's a long story, but as a result of that story, it came up quite naturally. Christine hasn't been trying to be secretive, Stephen. I think she's just very private, not at all the kind of person who would purposefully search for either attention or sympathy. It's been a year since David's death, after all, and she's obviously getting on with her life."

"But she's *not* getting on with it," Stephen countered. "She's spending every minute working as hard as she can to pay the hospital bills that should rightfully have been paid by her insurance company."

"What?" Elizabeth asked with obvious surprise and concern. "How did that happen?"

"Apparently when David was initially diagnosed, there was a question of whether he was predisposed to developing hepatic cancer because of a family history of hemochromatosis."

"A logical question to consider in anyone presenting with that type of cancer."

"Yes. And, in fact, there was even a cousin who had had what David thought might have been hepatic cancer. As it turned out the cousin had hepatic metastases, not primary liver cancer, and in the meantime all underlying risk factors including hemochromatosis had been categorically excluded anyway. But still, based on the initial suggestion of a possible family history of hemochromatosis, the insurance company refused to pay a penny for his care."

"The bills must be staggering," Elizabeth offered quietly. "Hadn't he been treated at another hospital for quite a while before being referred here?"

Stephen nodded solemnly. "He had a year of extremely aggressive—and very appropriate—chemotherapy, during which he had more than his share of catastrophic complications. By the time he was transferred here, his bills were already in excess of three hundred thousand, and once here, he was an inpatient on the oncology service—in the ICU for almost three weeks—before the decision was made to try LKC."

"At which point all his medical expenses were covered by your grant, weren't they?"

"Yes. Which is why I never had to fill out any insurance forms and had no idea of the truth." Stephen sighed softly. *The truth.* "I had no idea—and neither did David. Christine just quietly met with the supervisors in the billing offices here and at the other hospital and promised to pay all the bills in full, no matter how long it took her. David died believing that they had excellent coverage—which in fact they did—although the deductibles on the policy were higher than he had realized."

"But David must have been told that the studies showed that he didn't have hemochromatosis."

"I assume so, although I don't know for sure. That was all very ancient history by the time he was transferred here. My guess is that David did know the diagnosis had been excluded, but that he had no idea how important that knowledge was. He probably never even mentioned it to Christine, because it was a tiny detail that had no impact whatsoever on the outcome of his disease."

"But Christine knew the impact of that tiny detail on the insurance coverage, and yet apparently she never asked either David or his doctors about it. I wonder why not."

"Because," Stephen answered with quiet confidence, "she was afraid that David would find out that they didn't have insurance coverage after all. She knew that if he knew that his illness would leave her indebted for the rest of her life he would have refused further treatment."

Elizabeth became even more solemn as she thought about the gifts of love David and Christine Andrews had been so willing to give to each other. David would have died to spare his beloved wife financial hardship after his death, and Christine had committed her life to repaying the debts that had enabled her to spend as many precious moments as she could with her husband.

"I wonder why Christine waited this long after David's death before coming to you to confirm the diagnosis."

"Christine didn't come to me, Elizabeth. It turns out that Peter London designed Sydney's and since he wants to use a similar atrium for the institute the two of us stopped by the boutique this afternoon. I saw Christine, and we exchanged a brief hello as if we'd never met before, and after I left I started thinking about how hard Madolyn has always said she works. Madolyn's assumption has always been that the hard work was because she needed money, but I knew from David that she should have been fine financially. I got to worrying and stopped by hospital billing when I returned."

"And the supervisor told you that Christine had met with her and promised to pay all her bills in full."

"That, and that she could have declared bankruptcy, which is what the overwhelming majority of people with far less debt than this usually do." Stephen's voice softened as he added, "But that's not Christine. She's repaying the bills as promised, slowly but surely, sending as much money as she can every month and getting by on very little herself. I really hate the fact that she has struggled all this time . . . and that she was planning to struggle forever."

"Christine works very hard, Stephen, but I do think she enjoys what she does at Sydney's. She and Larisa met briefly in college—which is how this all came up last Saturday—and she had plans then to become a designer. Working at Sydney's isn't a bad stepping-stone for someone with that goal, and once the insurance fiasco is resolved, she can spend fewer hours in the boutique and do some designing, if that's what she wants."

Elizabeth had hoped that her truthful words would begin to reassure her friend. But in the midst of her reassurance, Stephen's expression grew even darker and more troubled—as if there had been something truly terrible about Christine having spent the past year working so hard at Sydney's.

"What are you thinking, Stephen?" she asked. Then, suddenly finding a possible answer to her own question, her gentleness vanished as she demanded, "Have you decided that Christine is a modern-day Cinderella who has spent the past year slaving away, dressing everyone else for the ball? Because, you know, if you have that casts me—and Madolyn, by the way—as the wicked stepsisters."

"Whoa!" Stephen commanded. "That wasn't what I was thinking at all." *I was thinking about the baby.* "It probably has been good for Christine to work at Sydney's, to spend time in such a happy upbeat place doing something for which she is obviously so appreciated and respected."

"Okay, well, sorry I bristled." Elizabeth smiled. Then, tilting her dark curls thoughtfully, she added, "Even though it wasn't what you were thinking, in one way, perhaps the most important way of all, Christine actually is a modern-day Cinderella."

"Oh?"

"Yes. She found her Prince Charming, and he found her. I remember your telling me about their relationship, how extraordinary it was, and hearing her talk about David last Saturday made me realize that she had truly lived the wonderful fairy tale about which most people only ever dream. Their love couldn't go on forever, but I imagine the memory of it will be enough to last Christine her entire lifetime."

"Yes," Stephen agreed softly. He had been a witness to the fairy-tale love of David and Christine, and even though David had confided in him his wish that Christine would find another love, it seemed impossible to Stephen that any other man could ever penetrate the wall of magnificent memories that surrounded her loving heart. Christine would never search for a new love, would never want or need to, but she had other dreams—and it was Stephen's hope to free her to follow them. "I've asked medical records to get David's files from the archives. Once I've got the pertinent lab reports in front of me, I'm going to call the insurance company and straighten this out."

"After first speaking with Christine."

"What? No, I hadn't planned to talk to her at all."

"I think you should, Stephen."

"Why? She surely wouldn't have any objection. She didn't choose to spend her life in debt. In fact, even though she and David had very little discretionary income, they made certain that they had good health coverage despite the fact that because they were self-employed the cost was very high. I'm simply correcting an error that was made a long time ago, Elizabeth. Any of David's doctors would have done the same had they known. I don't even particularly want Christine to know that I'm the one involved."

"I absolutely agree that the error should be corrected and that the insurance company should assume the debt. But I still think you should discuss it with Christine in advance. I can't explain why I think this, Stephen. It's just a feeling."

"And your feelings are usually right on target. Which worries me, because it hadn't even occurred to me to speak with her first."

"Well, I'm probably entirely wrong about this," Elizabeth said with a shrug. "My instincts about what's right—and wrong—to say have been very far off target today."

"Something with Larisa?"

"No. Something—or rather nothing—with your good friend Nick. As usual." Elizabeth gave a wobbly smile as she waved her slender hand in dismissal of the hopeless topic of Nicholas Chase. The four-hour-ago scene in the surgery lounge was still painfully fresh, but there was absolutely no point in discussing it with Stephen. He would be very annoyed at what Nick had done, as always, and, as always, she would only annoy him further by suddenly leaping to Nick's defense. Quickly finding a safe topic, she said, "Speaking of Larisa, though, she is at this very moment meeting with my brother to talk about her divorce from Julian. Hopefully it can happen soon. I don't think she'll really be better until all ties with Julian have been severed."

"Hello, Larisa." Mark greeted her warmly when he appeared at the doorway to his inner office only moments after his secretary had buzzed him to announce Larisa's arrival.

There was very little physical resemblance between Elizabeth and her blond-haired blue-eyed older brother. But now as Larisa met the smiling blue eyes, she realized that there were striking similarities between the Jennings siblings nonetheless, deep and important ones: kindness and generosity . . . and great strength of character.

"Hello, Mark."

"Please come in."

"Thank you."

Mark gestured toward a conversation area across his plushly carpeted office. As Larisa led the way, she hoped that her gait looked more graceful and confident than it felt. The stylishly loose-fitting silk harem pants that she wore still, a week after her desperate escape from Manhattan, gave the illusion of graceful elegance. She needed that illusion to cover her wobbliness just as she needed the pants to cover the fading-but-still-apparent bruises. The bruises were slowly fading, and the pain was gradually relenting, and her energy was returning in small unpredictable promises. Today, wanting to appear as strong and confident for Mark as possible, she had conserved her limited energy all day, hoping for a burst when she needed it.

When she reached her destination, Larisa paused in front of the window, smiling appreciatively at the spectacular view of the bridge and the bay. Then, swept by a sudden wave of weakness, she settled onto the nearby sofa and focused on the silver-framed portrait of Mark's two girls that sat on the coffee table.

"They're gorgeous, Mark," she said truthfully. "And so grown up."

"They grow up too quickly," Mark answered softly. "Wendy and I hope that you and Elizabeth will come to dinner sometime soon. We live in Atherton, which means we need to find a time when my little sister feels she can be that far away from the hospital."

"A feeling that has nothing to do with whether she's officially on call or not."

"So you've noticed." Mark smiled.

Larisa returned the smile and said quietly, "Last weekend she wanted to stay close by the hospital—to which she checked in frequently—because of Molly and Mary Ann. She made it sound like a special situation, but I had the distinct impression that there's always some patient she needs to be near."

"Always," Mark confirmed, his voice filling with a mixture of love and pride. "That's why, every so often, she has to be encouraged to leave town."

"I know she's really looking forward to Christmas in London." All the Jennings would be there and Elizabeth had already graciously invited Larisa to join them. "We'll take Harrod's by storm," she had teased. Larisa could think of nothing more wonderful than spending Christmas in England with the Jennings family, but it was a faraway dream. For now all her thoughts and energies had to be focused on trying to heal, trying to be stronger with each new golden sunrise than she had been the sunrise before. During the past five days, her thoughts and energies had had a very specific goal: to be as strong as possible for this all-important meeting with Mark. Mark . . . he seemed so warm, so welcoming. But, Larisa wondered with a shiver, when he learned the truths about her would he approve of his generous little sister's gracious offer that she join their family holiday?

"Christmas in London will be terrific," Mark agreed. "But, Larisa, maybe sometime you could convince Elizabeth to do something really frivolous like a pure vacation—something without family obligations or medical meetings or guest lectureships or cameo appearances in operating rooms."

"I'll give it my best shot," Larisa answered, amazed that this protective older brother who had once worried that she might lead his innocent little sister astray now wanted her help in orchestrating a frivolous adventure for her. It was a flattering request, but a most difficult one, because the once fearless and adventuresome Larisa Locksley who had existed at Berkeley existed no more. "I can't promise results, Mark. The truth is that Elizabeth is very happy working twenty-four hours a day."

"I know." Mark smiled. Then, because they had finished sharing their mutual love and concern for Elizabeth, he suggested, "So, Larisa, tell me."

"Why I want a divorce?"

"You don't need to tell me that if you don't want to," he assured her. "And the courts don't need to know anything more specific than irreconcilable differences."

"I guess that's good. Much more private."

"Yes." Mark hesitated briefly before adding, "Ideally, though, you and Julian should both know why the marriage is ending."

"Julian and I both do know, Mark," Larisa answered quietly. "But that doesn't mean that he isn't going to fight this. Julian doesn't like losing anything. He's going to be very angry when he learns that I want a divorce. In fact, I honestly don't think he'll permit it."

"You'll get your divorce, Larisa," Mark said confidently to the woman who had herself once glittered with limitless confidence but who now seemed so uncertain and fragile. "We'll—I'll—weather Julian's anger until he accepts the reality that the divorce will happen. So why don't you and I just discuss the settlement? Do you have a prenuptial agreement?"

"No. We had about a two-second discussion on the topic. I told Julian I wanted our love to last forever, and he said he wanted that too, and so we decided that the whole idea was too unromantic to pursue." Larisa shrugged softly at her own foolishness. "I know that everyone says a prenuptial agreement makes good sense, and everyone was definitely saying that six years ago, but . . . I don't have one."

"Don't be too hard on yourself, Larisa. The fact that you don't have a prenuptial agreement means that instead of getting ten, fifteen, or twenty-five million dollars, you're entitled to half of what Julian has earned or acquired while you were married. From what I know about Julian Chancellor, his empire is rock solid, not a house of cards built on a precarious foundation of volatile junk bonds or grandiose visions."

"That's right. Julian's empire is built on good old-fashioned cash and his instincts have always been pure gold. His empire isn't about to crumble." Larisa's blue eyes met Mark's as she said solemnly, "But I didn't marry Julian for his money and I don't care about it now. All I want is a divorce."

"You are legally entitled to millions, Larisa. In fact, I suppose that half of what Julian has made in the past six years could even entitle you to something in the billions."

"I don't care about any of it, Mark, not a penny," Larisa repeated softly. "And I can assure you that Julian will care. He hates to lose. He doesn't even know how to. In the six years I've known him, I know of only one instance in which he didn't get exactly what he wanted . . . and when it happened he was furious, enraged." A shiver of ice swept through her as she remembered that night and she was suddenly aware of the intense pain in her hands as her pale delicate fingers dug mercilessly and ever-deeper into her snow-white palms. Forcing her fingers to uncurl, at least a little, she continued, "No matter how bad our marriage has been, Julian is going to strongly resist the idea of a divorce. Attaching a price tag to that loss, making him part with even the tiniest piece of his empire, will make him only more determined to block the divorce. Really, Mark, just getting him to agree to a divorce would be a monumental triumph."

"Surely we can be more triumphant than that."

"No. All I want is the divorce—no money, no property, just my freedom." For a moment Larisa's eyes lit with a radiant hope, as if she could actually see that distant and wonderful dream. Then she returned to the present, tilted her shimmering firelit golden head thoughtfully and offered, "But that wouldn't make for much of a contingency, would it?"

"Contingency?" Mark echoed, feeling a sudden and powerful rush of anger as he realized that she was referring to his fee, *his* percent of the millions or billions. The surprising strength of the anger was because it came with old memories, reminders of the Larisa he once had known, the dazzling young woman who had so defiantly and contemptuously rejected his willingness to protect her as he had protected Elizabeth—as if Larisa didn't trust him. Her instant mistrust of him had been insulting and infuriating then, and now the implication that he would be disappointed if she didn't try to get as much as possible from Julian was insulting and infuriating once again. Mark struggled with his own emotions, finally subduing them by looking at the fragile woman who was seated across from him. Larisa had obviously been terribly hurt by Julian. Even without knowing the details, it seemed quite clear that she had loved and trusted her husband—and had been betrayed.

When he was calm enough to speak, Mark explained evenly, "I never work on contingency in divorce cases, Larisa. I made no contribution whatsoever to the marriage, so why in the world should I benefit from the divorce?" His voice became more gentle, more normal, as he added, "My fee for handling your divorce will be my usual fee for a family member—a smile, maybe?"

Mark hoped for a smile then, but Larisa's beautiful face remained solemn as she reminded softly, "You don't have a usual fee for family members, Mark. There has never been a divorce in the Jennings family, has there?"

Mark waved a dismissive hand. "If it will make you feel better, I'll keep track of my time and as part of the divorce agreement we'll let Julian pay all legal expenses. So," he continued swiftly, definitively, "I know you've said that you would be happy with just a divorce, but for the sake of argument, let's talk a little more about a financial settlement. You must have entered the marriage with a fair amount of money of your own. You were a top—*the* top?—fashion model when you met him, after all."

"My net worth when we married was about a million dollars. I was very rich by any standard in the world except Julian's—and I simply gave all my money to him. It wasn't a grand gesture, Mark. What I had was just a tiny drop in the vast ocean of Julian's wealth. He handled all our finances. I didn't have credit cards or a separate bank account, and I had no need for either. Julian has standing accounts at all the major boutiques, restaurants, and clubs in Manhattan, so with just my signature I could get whatever I wanted—and there was always cash at the penthouse for incidentals." Larisa shrugged softly at her confession, proof-positive of her own silly romanticism and so very contrary to the conventional wisdom of the eighties which strongly encouraged women to protect themselves financially. That important information had been communicated to the women of America through talk shows and national magazines. How ironic that so often it had been a photograph of supermodel Larisa Locksley that had induced women to buy those magazines. Her beautiful face had become a dazzling symbol of the strong yet feminine, romantic yet independent woman of the eighties; but Larisa herself had ignored all the sage advice and had given everything to Julian—her financial worth . . . and her self-worth. "Pretty foolish, huh?"

"No," Mark replied with quiet reassurance. "Even though I have to give legal advice about sensible strategies to protect oneself in the event that a marriage doesn't survive, I guess I still like to believe . . ."

"In the fairy tale."

"In the fairy tale," Mark echoed. "Yes."

"Well," Larisa said. "So much for happy endings. Where were we?"

"We'd established that you had about a million dollars when you entered the marriage."

"That was a gift freely given from me to Julian. I wouldn't expect to get it back, not that Julian would consider returning it anyway. I think he would view a million dollars as trivial compensation for six years of his life wasted in a failed marriage."

"All right. Tell me a little more about your life-style then. You've already said that your signature could buy anything you wanted."

"Yes. I was a princess living in a world of limitless luxury." Larisa's wry, sad smile eloquently conveyed the emptiness of that luxurious world. "It wasn't a life-style that I needed then . . . and it's certainly not a life-style I need now. I don't want—or need—support from Julian. Except for the six years of my marriage, I've worked virtually all my life. I'll find a way to support myself again."

"You hardly need to find a way to support yourself, Larisa. You'll go back to modeling, won't you? I got the impression from Elizabeth that you enjoyed it very much."

"I did. I loved it. But I think I'm a little past my prime as a model, don't you?" Larisa didn't pause long enough to allow Mark to answer. She knew his words would be far more gracious and encouraging than truthful. He was a Jennings, after all, and therefore much too kind to agree that yes, in fact, now that he really looked at her, it was obvious that she was past her prime. That truth hardly mattered anyway because . . . "Julian wouldn't permit me to model again anyway."

"Julian will have no say over what you do once you're no longer married, Larisa," Mark said calmly, even though he felt another powerful rush of anger. This time, at least, it was appropriately directed where it belonged: Julian.

"You don't know him, Mark. He has incredible power and influence. If it became known that he didn't like the idea of his ex-wife modeling again, no one would hire me. I'm not talking about anything criminal, of course. The only force Julian needs is the strength of his wealth. The simple truth is that no one—not the magazine publishers who would run the print ads, nor the fashion designers who might use me as a model, nor even the giant cosmetic companies—would risk Julian's disapproval."

"Okay," Mark agreed, despite his own powerful wish to go into an all-out battle with Julian Chancellor, to make him really pay for so obviously hurting Larisa. Mark subdued his own wish with the memory of the hopefulness in her brilliant blue eyes at just the thought of a divorce. Smiling, he said gently, "So, let me see if I have this right. What you would like is a nice, simple divorce."

"Nice, simple," Larisa echoed. "But impossible. Oh, Mark, I probably shouldn't even get you involved in this."

"Nonsense on both counts. First, it's not the least bit impossible, especially given that you're willing to forgo any settlement at all. And second, you've made me more than a little intrigued about Julian. I like challenges, Larisa. I'm looking forward to speaking with him."

"He can be very persuasive and very charming. He may say terrible things about me, Mark." Larisa frowned and confessed, "I've made mistakes, I don't deny that, but I'm sure that Julian will make them sound like horrendous crimes."

"Of course he will. That comes with the territory. I'm used to it, and, don't forget, I'm on your side." Mark smiled reassuringly and after a moment asked, "Just for the record, are there any mistakes that Julian's made that I should know about? A little ammunition I could use in return if I thought it was useful?"

"Julian knows what he's done," Larisa answered quietly. He knows what I've allowed him to do, she thought. But I can't tell you, Mark. I'm far too ashamed.

"Okay. I'll just weather the volleys, paying no attention to them whatsoever, and eventually Julian will have to talk to me about the divorce."

"I hope so."

"I know so," Mark countered firmly. "I suppose I could get Julian's telephone number from you?"

"Oh, sure."

As Larisa provided the number to the direct line to Julian's office and the name of his private secretary, Mark carefully recorded both on the yellow legal pad that had until that moment been quite untouched. Despite a memory that was almost as photographic as his little sister's, Mark always took comprehensive notes during meetings with clients. But he had taken none with Larisa. Her wish was simple and crystal clear. He wouldn't forget it.

"I'll call Julian first thing tomorrow morning," Mark said when he finished writing.

"Okay." Then, almost urgently, Larisa asked, "Julian doesn't need to know where I am, does he? I really don't want to talk to him . . . or see him . . . ever again."

"No, he doesn't need to know. But don't you think he might guess that you're with Elizabeth?"

"Yes, but as far as I know, he thinks she's still in Dallas."

"Oh. Good. He'll probably make the connection with my last name, though, so I'll plan to be up-front about the fact that I'm Elizabeth's brother and that you contacted me because you two were college roommates." Mark smiled. "I'll keep you posted on all relevant developments."

"All right."

"And remember, Larisa, nice and simple."

"Oh," she answered softly, "I hope so."

After speaking with Christine first. By her own admission Elizabeth's suggestion had been based on vague feelings, not a clear and logical reason. Still, because he respected and trusted her instincts—with the glaring exception of her inexplicable defense of Nicholas Chase—Stephen paused to reconsider her advice before calling the insurance company.

Elizabeth had an uncanny ability to sense the deepest layers of emotion with the minimum of clues. But, Stephen thought, this was a clear-cut issue of red tape, not an issue of deeply layered emotion. The error needed to be corrected, and it was his responsibility as David's doctor, as David's friend, to see that Christine not be encumbered for life by debts which were rightfully not hers to pay. This time, he decided, Elizabeth's instincts were wrong.

Stephen politely but firmly insisted on speaking with the insurance company's most senior available official. He knew that it would take a while to unravel the red tape, but starting at the top would surely make the unraveling process proceed more swiftly. And, as he pointed out when he finally had the right official on the line, surely the company itself, which in fact had an excellent reputation, would want a swift resolution as well. Stephen's approach was calm and collegial, a friend notifying a friend of an unwitting mistake, never implying even for a moment that the error might have been made intentionally to avoid paying the huge claim.

When the official pointed out that the case would need to be carefully and thoroughly investigated, Stephen readily agreed. But he did not allow the conversation to end until a definite time had been set for him to go over David's medical record with the claims adjustor to demonstrate exactly how the error had been made—and then to provide the documents that unequivocally proved that David Andrews's cancer had been simply a tragic whim of fate unrelated to any preexisting condition whatsoever.

CHAPTER TWELVE

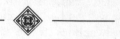

"We—Larisa, you and I—all know the truth about what really happened, Mr. Chancellor," Mark said quietly. "The question is, do you want the world to know?"

The silence at the other end of the phone told Mark that there was something, some dark secret truth that Julian had assumed Larisa would never disclose. Larisa *hadn't* disclosed the secret, of course, but Mark decided to try the bluff anyway. It was necessary, he had decided, because in the past five days, Julian hadn't budged at all from his initial position of no divorce. He hadn't budged, but he had been more than willing to talk. Julian wanted his wife . . . and Mark was his only link to her.

Julian was everything Larisa had promised he would be: arrogant, dogmatic, persuasive, confident. With the patient and almost-bored haughtiness of the very wealthy, he had explained over and over again that there *would be no divorce.* To which Mark had replied, over and over again, without haughtiness but with matching patience, that in fact there *would be.* Eventually Julian had taken the tack Larisa had predicted he would—a litany of her crimes. His approach was clever, his voice gentle not vituperative as he spoke of her cocaine abuse, her wantonness, her emotional instability. He was very willing to forgive everything, he said, because he loved her so much. And, because he loved her so much, he wanted to see that she got the professional help she so obviously needed. With almost convincing emotion, Julian told Mark that once Larisa got the help she needed and was truly better, he was confident that she would want to return to their wonderful love.

After five days with absolutely no headway, Mark decided to try the bluff, to let Julian believe that he knew the sordid secret and to further let him believe that Larisa was willing to make that secret public. And now, as the bluff was met with a silence that lingered a few beats longer than the carefully measured strategic pauses that had typified the past five days, Mark sensed victory—a first step toward victory—at last.

When Julian finally answered, the contempt in his elegant voice was unconcealed. "Larisa's life with me has always been luxurious, pampered, *perfect.* Whatever fantasy she has told you about any harm she might have suffered because of her marriage to me is purely a lie."

"Well. I was convinced," Mark replied with confident calm, even though he knew he was skating on the thinnest of ice. There was some specific secret, that was obvious now. But he seriously doubted that Larisa, who wouldn't even confess it privately to him, would be willing to reveal it publicly. Still, maybe all that mattered was that Julian believed she would. Mark repeated firmly, "I was convinced. I think most people would be."

"She's manipulating you, Mr. Jennings, just as she manipulated me."

"I don't feel the least bit manipulated, Mr. Chancellor."

In the resigned silence that followed, Mark sensed capitulation. He waited with restless patience, hoping that Julian's next words would be the ones he expected to hear.

The wait was worth it.

"I suppose Larisa is quite capable of manipulating the press." Julian sighed heavily. "All right. Larisa will get her divorce. But be warned. Just because I don't want her lies to become headlines in the scandal sheets doesn't mean that I'm going to roll over and play dead. Tell her for me that there are going to be some ground rules for this divorce."

"He's really willing to give me a divorce?" Larisa whispered with disbelieving joy when Mark called. "I can't believe it."

"We don't know the terms yet, Larisa," Mark reminded. "From now on I'll be dealing with Julian's attorney. Our initial conversation is scheduled for ten tomorrow morning."

"But the terms don't matter, Mark! I told you, I don't want anything from Julian but the divorce."

The terms did matter though, very much, because the first condition stipulated by Julian's attorney was simply impossible for Larisa to accept. Julian wanted them to live together again, for a period of six months, after which time, if it was what she still wanted, she could walk away with half of his fortune.

"I can't do it, Mark. I can't live with him again." She repeated with soft despair, "I just can't."

"I know. I already told his attorney that I doubted you would agree, but I promised I would discuss it with you anyway."

"The divorce isn't going to happen, is it?"

"Yes, Larisa, it is," Mark insisted with quiet and reassuring calm. He added lightly, "Don't worry. This kind of negotiation is all pretty typical. I'll call you back as soon as we're finished with the next round."

Mark calmly reassured his anxious client, but the truth was that the divorce between Julian and Larisa Chancellor wasn't typical at all. The bargaining chips in most divorces were money, property, and children; but the currency of the Chancellor divorce was quite different: emotion, control, power, and image. Mark had no idea how strong his—Larisa's—position was. There was obviously something quite specific that Julian did not want revealed. His own cocaine use, perhaps, or perhaps something else. But Julian had said from the outset that he wasn't going to roll over and play dead, and Mark sensed that he could be pushed only so far. Not that Mark was pushing. He had still asked for nothing except the divorce.

It was Julian himself who was doing the pushing. It was obvious that he wanted some concession, some proof of his power and control, and Mark feared that if Julian wasn't placated in some way that despite his intense distaste for scandal he would go to war in the arena of public opinion. And in that arena, Mark feared, Julian might well win. Larisa had herself admitted that her life-style had been that of a pampered princess, and surely Julian had many powerful and influential friends who would be very willing to confirm that Larisa Chancellor had been a most adored and treasured wife.

Larisa wanted nothing and Julian wanted something and Mark felt the pressure of time. They needed to come to closure soon, before Larisa's fragile hope became resigned defeat and before Julian's ever-diminishing patience disappeared altogether and he returned resolutely to his initial stance of no divorce.

It seemed like forever, but in fact only eight days had elapsed between Larisa's visit to his office and Mark's Friday afternoon phone call to present her with what he believed was the best he could do.

"Julian absolutely refuses a cash settlement of any kind."

"That's fine, Mark. That's what I expected. And as I told you, it doesn't matter. I don't want any of Julian's money."

"I know, but here's the interesting part: Julian wants to support you, in whatever life-style you choose, even a most lavish and luxurious one. He says that he will pay all of your expenses, every bill you send him, without questions or limits. I didn't ask for this, Larisa, and frankly it surprises me. But it seems to be something that Julian really wants to do."

Of course he wants to do it, Larisa thought. He knows that I couldn't bankrupt him—or even put the smallest dent in his vast wealth—no matter how hard I tried. This is just like when we were married. I had carte blanche, the wonderful illusion of freedom, but I was really always completely under his control. Julian wants that control still, watching me from a distance, knowing everything I do, every dress I buy, every salad I eat, every phone call I make. As if we were still married. . . .

Larisa felt the panicky breathlessness of suffocation as the invisible chains began to slowly tighten around her chest.

"Would I have to sign something requiring me to allow him to support me?" she asked finally, a rush of words that escaped in a gasp.

"No. In fact, Larisa, if you ever need any money, I would be very happy to—"

"Thank you, Mark," she interjected softly. "I'll be fine."

"Okay, well, just don't ever hesitate to ask if you need anything. So, let me tell you the rest of the terms. Julian wants both of you to agree never to disclose the details of the marriage or the divorce to anyone. He's obviously most concerned about revelations to the press—magazine articles, books, movies—but the language of the contract will read 'anyone,' so you need to know that that's what you're agreeing to."

"I agree to it. But the divorce documents will be filed with the courts, so won't they already be in the public domain?"

"No. Since this will be an uncontested divorce, the only documents filed with the court will be the signed dissolution papers proving that you both agree to the divorce. Everything else, the terms we're discussing and the contracts you'll sign agreeing to them, is strictly between you and Julian."

"I see. That's good. More private."

"Which doesn't mean there won't be interest in the divorce. Despite his distaste for publicity, Julian wants to meet it head-on by preparing a statement, preapproved by both of you, that will be released to the press as soon as the papers have been filed."

"Damage control. That's fine with me."

"Larisa," Mark cautioned quietly, "Julian's idea of putting a positive spin on the story is to make it appear as if it's he who is divorcing you. He also wants to give the clear impression that he feels so terrible about having fallen out of love with you that he has been immensely generous with the financial settlement. This really gravels me, but—"

"But I don't have a problem with it, Mark. Pride's an expensive luxury. Julian cares so much about image, and I couldn't care less."

"You're really amazing, you know."

"No. I just know what I want." *What's so very necessary for my survival.* She added softly, hopefully, "And it seems as if this is really going to happen . . . ?"

"There's just one final thing," Mark said very quietly. He wondered if it would be too much, a deal breaker even though they were so close, something she simply could not do. *Courage, Larisa.* "Julian wants a photograph to accompany the press release, a smiling picture of the two of you together once all the papers are signed."

"Oh, Mark," she whispered. "No."

"He wanted dinner in San Francisco, but I rejected that without even speaking to you, and also without revealing whether or not you're living anywhere near here. But, Larisa, I think the idea of getting this photograph is extremely important to Julian."

"Meaning if I say no, it might delay the divorce?"

"I honestly think it might," Mark answered solemnly. "With your permission, I'd like to suggest lunch in New York for the four of us—you, me, Julian, and his attorney."

"You would be there?"

"Every step of the way. I know this would be very difficult for you, but in addition to the fact that it will permit the divorce to progress without delay, I also think that the public interest will be greatly minimized if there's no hint of either scandal or bitterness. Going to New York will also give you—us—a chance to get whatever you left behind in the penthouse."

"There isn't anything in the penthouse that I want," Larisa said. "If possible, though, I'd like to have my clothes sent to Second Hand Rose. It's a shop that sells used designer clothes and gives the profits to charity."

"Done. So?"

"So, if we did have lunch in New York, when would we do it?"

"Two weeks from today. All the divorce documents and the press release will have been approved and signed in advance, so it would just be a matter of lunch and the photograph. We would arrive Thursday evening and plan to catch a flight back Friday afternoon."

"Two weeks from today," Larisa echoed. *I will see Julian again two weeks from today.* But how can I? *Because it's the only way you will ever be free.* "Okay."

"Good. And, Larisa, there's one final thing, a good thing, I think. The press release will include a statement from Julian expressing his support for the resumption of your modeling career, if that's what you decide you want to do."

"I can't believe Julian agreed to that." Larisa's grateful disbelief lasted only a few seconds before being harshly swept away by a crashing wave of reality. Julian could afford to be magnanimous about her career, because he knew what she knew: that no one would want her as a model again anyway. She and Julian both knew that truth, and Julian obviously assumed that she would never have the strength or courage or confidence to find something new. He fully believed that she would be dependent on him forever, bound to him by her own weakness, controlled by his immense power, as she had allowed herself to be controlled when they were married. And that was where Julian Chancellor was very wrong. "Did Julian agree to pay your legal fees?"

"You bet. And he will of course pay for our first-class trip to New York."

"How can I ever thank you, Mark?"

"You could give me that smile you owe me. I think I'd like to collect in two weeks. Let's say on our Friday evening flight back to San Francisco."

* * *

The thank-you smile for Mark would be easy, but the all-important smile for Julian's scandal-squelching photograph would be almost impossible. How could she smile a radiant, untroubled, convincing smile as she sat beside the man she once had loved and trusted but now hated and feared? Larisa didn't know. She only knew that somehow she had to find a way.

I will be able to smile that smile in two weeks, she promised herself. Somehow, for those necessary moments when the camera's eye winked at her, she would wear a radiant smile.

And, she decided, on that day she would also wear a new outfit, something that she—not Julian—had chosen, a brave symbol of her new life of freedom and choice. The bruises on her skin were almost gone, mere ghostly shadows of violence, and by next week they would have disappeared entirely. She would go to Sydney's then and amid the fragrance of roses and with Christine's talented help, she would find something lovely and hopeful to wear.

Larisa tried to envision her life beyond the lunch with Julian—where she would live, the kind of job she would try to find—but it was impossible. Until that important and terrifying event was behind her, until she had actually survived seeing him again, all thoughts and energies had to be focused on steeling herself for that day.

Still, she realized, she needed something, a small flicker of light at the end of the dark tunnel, a hopeful glimmer of proof that there would be life after seeing Julian again.

She would be seeing Julian in New York on Friday, and on the following night San Francisco would be celebrating its new Immunology Institute with a lavish black-tie ball at the Fairmont. What could be more hopeful than the celebration of a new building in which many lives would be saved and perhaps even cancer would be cured? Elizabeth had been encouraging her to accompany her to the fabulous ball, and it would be nice to meet Stephen at last, and maybe even the mysterious Nick.

I will go, Larisa decided. And I will wear the romantic, delicately beaded, flowing white silk gown that I wanted to wear on the eve of my marriage, but which Julian would not allow.

Her decision felt brave and triumphant, until she was suddenly swept by thoughts that stole her breath and made her tremble with icy fear. What if Julian had no intention whatsoever of allowing this divorce? What if this was all just a clever trap?

CHAPTER THIRTEEN

San Francisco
September 1991

Perfect, Madolyn mused approvingly as she gazed at the breathtaking reflection of herself. She was standing in front of a full-length mirror in one of the private dressing salons at Sydney's and she was wearing the gown designed by Christine for the Fairmont ball. The sapphire silk demurely yet alluringly draped her beautiful body, and there were tiny buttons, meticulously sewn, which Christine had added to enhance the exquisite detailing, but which privately delighted Madolyn for another reason altogether. She imagined Stephen's talented fingers struggling to undress her, wanting her so much, frustrated by the tiny buttons, and then wanting her all the more. Wanting her enough to ask her to marry him? *Yes*. That was part of her delicious fantasy—no, her plan—for the festive event that was now only eight nights away.

On that night of champagne and celebration, she would tell Stephen that she had decided to accept the network position in New York, and he would ask her to marry him, and for a while theirs would be the modern, sophisticated, bicoastal marriage of the very successful. Madolyn knew that Stephen would feel an obligation to remain in San Francisco until the construction of the institute was complete and a new director had been found. But then he could leave. His research could be done anywhere, after all, whereas she *had* to be in New York, the epicenter of network news.

Madolyn Mitchell had a history of getting exactly what she wanted, she made sure of it, and now she was about to get the two things she wanted most—a dream job in New York and a dream marriage to rich, sexy, brilliant Dr. Stephen Sheridan. Madolyn was quite confident that she didn't *need* the romantic gown Christine had designed for her for that special night. But, she thought with a soft seductive smile, looking this alluring couldn't hurt.

"It's wonderful, Christine," Madolyn gushed finally, remembering at last that Christine was there and had been quietly awaiting her assessment.

"I'm glad you're happy with it, Madolyn."

"I'm *delighted* with it, and Stephen will be too. In fact," she added as her beautiful violet eyes envisioned total triumph, "how would you like to design a wedding gown for me? We haven't set the date yet, and I suppose I should wait until I get Stephen's reaction to this gown. Oh, but I know he'll love it. I'd want you to do the entire wedding, of course—the gown for the rehearsal dinner, the bridesmaids' dresses, and maybe even a few especially romantic items for the honeymoon."

"I'd be very happy to," Christine murmured softly.

Christine was behind Madolyn, kneeling on the salon's plush carpet, making a minor adjustment in a silken fold. As a result, Madolyn didn't see the worry that filled Christine's lavender eyes at the mention of Stephen's name. Ever since their chance meeting two weeks before, Christine had worried that Stephen might have been offended that she had pretended not to recognize him—as if she was dismissing him . . . as if he hadn't mattered to her . . . as if she had somehow forgotten the most extraordinary gift he had given her, a gift no one else on earth could have given, one more year of love with her beloved David. Surely Stephen knew that she had forgotten nothing. Surely he understood that it simply made everything easier, more private, if her clients and coworkers didn't know about her loss . . .

Four hours later, as the city bus huffed and puffed its way from Union Square to the bus stop two blocks from her small rented house on Twin Peaks, Christine was worrying again about Stephen. She was still distracted by that worry when she arrived home and began to glance idly through the day's mail. Her attention became a little more focused, however, as her eyes fell on an envelope from a surprising source: the company from which she had purchased their health insurance. There had been no communications from the company for over three years, not since shortly after David's cancer had been diagnosed and coverage had been denied because of the preexisting condition.

Even though the envelope was marked "personal and confidential," Christine opened it unhurriedly. It was probably a form letter, urging her to renew her lapsed policy.

But the letter was, in fact, quite personal, too personal.

Dear Mrs. Andrews,

I am writing to inform you that a most regrettable error was made concerning your claim. Heretofore the expenses incurred during the illness of your husband, David Andrews, have not been covered because of the exclusion clause for preexisting illness. However, on August twenty-second, it was brought to my attention by Dr. Stephen Sheridan that the diagnosis of familial hemochromatosis as a preexisting condition for your husband's malignancy had in fact been ruled out.

Thus, in accord with the terms of your policy, we will assume responsibility for payment of medical expenses incurred in excess of the agreed-upon deductibles. I have contacted the hospitals regarding the payments that you have made to date, and having determined that the total amount remitted by you exceeds the required deductibles by $12,380, I am enclosing a reimbursement check for that amount.

Please be assured that the remainder of your husband's medical expenses will be paid promptly, and please accept my apologies for this error and for any hardship that this misunderstanding may have caused you. I assure you that the matter is being fully investigated . . .

Christine stopped thinking and simply began to act, compelled to action by powerful feelings she could neither define nor control. First the feelings willed her to walk to the kitchen drawer where she had kept the all-important notecard—and where it lay still. Stephen had given it to her the first time they met and on it he had written all of his phone numbers—office, lab, pager, home. The once so familiar numbers were indelibly etched in some quiet corner of her mind, but the powerful feelings that pulsed through her came with their own thunder, making the search for a quiet memory quite impossible.

It was ten-thirty Friday night. During the year in which David had been

Stephen's patient, Stephen had often been in his laboratory late at night, even on Fridays. Christine didn't know if Madolyn had been in Stephen's life then, but she did know that Madolyn had a newscast in thirty minutes, which meant that Stephen might logically be working late as well.

As Christine dialed the number to Stephen's lab, she realized that she had no idea why she was calling him, or what she was going to say. It doesn't matter! the powerful feelings thundered with astonishing confidence. We know why you're calling. We will give you the words to speak when it's time to speak them.

Stephen glanced from his watch to the silent telephone. In a moment, the phone would ring. The caller would be Madolyn, calling from her private dressing room at the station, the copy already written and rehearsed for her newscast, the final makeup check not due for a few minutes. She would be calling because it was Friday night, and she was off for the weekend, and that meant she wanted to see him. Madolyn would make her desires abundantly clear, her voice soft and sultry as she whispered her provocative suggestions . . . and promises.

Promises of passion were the only promises that he and Madolyn ever made to each other. Stephen frowned at the thought, amazed and vaguely troubled that their relationship had endured for this long on so little. But that was the relationship's appeal, of course. Its demands were physical not emotional, and its commitments were those made to pleasure, not to each other.

Stephen had never had a relationship like this. Always before there had been at least the hope of love. But with Madolyn there had never been that hope, not for either of them, not from the very beginning, and that had made it emotionally so very easy—and so very empty. Their relationship would be ending soon. Madolyn would surely get the network position in New York that she so obviously wanted. And that would be that.

It was an end, he realized, that he anticipated with as much relief as regret . . .

Stephen was still frowning when the telephone rang—right on cue.

"Hi," he answered distractedly.

"Doctor Sheridan? This is Christine Andrews."

"Hello, Mrs. Andrews," Stephen replied quietly, no longer distracted but frowning even more deeply as he realized that the informal first-name greetings of two weeks ago at Sydney's were apparently forgotten. They had regressed to their old roles of doctor and patient's wife, but her voice was very different from the soft courageous voice he had heard so often during the last year of David Andrews's life.

"Why did you contact the insurance company?" the new voice demanded, courageous still, but not at all soft.

"Because I believed it was wrong for you to pay for what should rightfully have been covered."

"But it was none of your business!"

"I'm sorry. I thought it was."

"Why?"

"Because David was my patient. I felt a responsibility to him and to his wishes. I knew he wouldn't have wanted you to spend your lifetime repaying his debts."

"But what about what I want?" The question came without warning, stunning and confusing, and suddenly the powerful feelings, with all their confident anger and indignation, simply vanished. Stephen was right. David had wanted her life after his death to be totally unencumbered, so that she was free to go on to new happiness and new dreams. But she had accepted the insurance company's decision without question, more than accepted—embraced. Why? Because she wanted a life committed to repaying his debts? Because then she would be living every day of her life for David still, feeling needed by him in his death as she had been so needed by him in his life? Because she would be so very safe, living forever in the memories of their love, never venturing beyond those wonderful memories, never being forced to find new dreams?

Because she was so terribly afraid?

"Mrs. Andrews?" Stephen's voice intruded very softly in the lingering silence. And then, even more softly, he asked, "Christine?"

"I have to go now," she whispered. "I'm sorry."

As she quietly replaced the receiver, hot tears began to spill from her stormy lavender eyes and violent sobs shook her slender body. The anguished grief might have flowed from her heart a year ago, the day that David had died, the same day that she had lost his baby. But the grief hadn't flowed then, she hadn't allowed it to, and she had kept David alive by devoting her life to repaying his debts.

But now there were no more debts to repay . . . and Christine cried tears of pure pain as she at last truly faced the irrevocable loss of her beloved David . . . and of his precious unborn child.

Elizabeth was right, Stephen thought sadly as he slowly replaced the receiver. I should have spoken to Christine before calling the insurance company.

But what was it that had bothered her so terribly? Was it his decision to invade her privacy? Or was it a decision she herself had made, an anguished decision about an unborn baby made because of the erroneous belief that she had a lifetime of debt ahead of her?

Stephen's hand rested on the receiver, reaching to her still. He wanted to go to her, to hold her and comfort her. But how could he? It was he, after all, who had caused her immense sadness.

When the phone rang, he answered it immediately, hoping it would be she . . .

"I tried to call a few minutes ago but your line was busy." Madolyn added with a seductive purr, "Don't tell me there's another woman."

Yes, Stephen thought. There is another woman. A lovely and loving woman whom I have unwittingly hurt. And all I want now is a little privacy in which to think about the unhappiness I have caused her.

PART THREE

CHAPTER FOURTEEN

𝒥ulian, his attorney, and the photographer who would take the picture of the amicably divorcing couple were standing outside Le Cirque when the limousine carrying Larisa and Mark arrived. At the sight of Julian, Larisa's already fluttering heart took flight, and the aching in her stomach became a gnawing pain, and there wasn't nearly enough air.

"Are you okay?" Mark asked as the limousine pulled to a gentle stop.

"No," Larisa confessed. "But I will be . . . in about three hours."

"We'll have a very nice flight home," Mark promised. "So, shall we?"

"I guess we shall."

Then they were standing on the sidewalk and polite introductions were being made and Julian was staring at her. His face wore the identical expression it had worn the first time they met—a charming and compelling blend of tenderness and seduction, desire and respect. Love at first sight, he had told her later, and it had been love at first sight for her too.

And now Julian was staring at her precisely as he had stared at her on that long-ago day, eloquently reminding her of a love that had once seemed so perfect.

Clever! her mind warned as all the pieces of her shattered heart began to tremble and scream with pain. How desperately she had needed to believe in Julian's wonderful love. How joyously and gratefully she had accepted it. You know what he's doing now, don't you? her mind demanded. Yes, of course I know, her heart replied. It's just that he does it so well. Which is why he is so very dangerous—still.

"Hello, Larisa," Julian said with the same soft wonder of their first meeting.

"Julian."

"Shall we go in?" he asked pleasantly, quite undaunted by the coolness of her greeting. "Daniel has prepared your favorite dishes and Sirio has made certain that we have our favorite table."

"Our favorite table?" Larisa echoed weakly. *Their* table was in a secluded corner, a rare place of privacy in the celebrated restaurant where the rich and famous came to see and be seen. Most of Le Cirque's clientele would be annoyed if they were not seated in the center of the room. But Julian was beyond such snobbery, above it. For the past six years, he and Larisa had always been seated at the very remote table for two.

"Have lunch with me, Larisa," Julian urged quietly, his dark eyes sending both a challenge and a plea: a challenge to her courage . . . and a plea to the heart that once had loved him so much that she would have died for him—perhaps had died for him. "Just the two of us, please."

"We agreed that we would all have lunch together," Mark reminded with quiet resolve, speaking the words to Julian as his eyes sent a silent message to Larisa, a confident reminder of his promise that he would stay with her.

"And we will, if that's what Larisa wants." Julian smiled tenderly and asked softly, "Larisa?"

"It's all right, Mark," Larisa said finally, bravely accepting the challenge to her courage, but not, not even for a moment, acquiescing to the plea. "I'll have lunch with Julian."

He knew I'd say yes, Larisa realized when they reached the table. The photographer was already there, positioning the flowers just so, and the sommelier hovered, waiting to pour the already chilled Dom Perignon into the crystal champagne flutes. Once seated, the champagne poured, Larisa and Julian raised their glasses, clinking gently and smiling, giving the photographer and the world a dazzling portrait of harmony.

"Aren't you going to drink any?" Julian asked after the photographer had left and Larisa had placed her still full glass of champagne on the pink tablecloth and returned her hands to her lap. "Just a sip to celebrate?"

"No. Thank you." Her mind needed to be alert and wary, and her memory needed to be very clear. "You go ahead."

"But I have nothing to celebrate. No, that's not true. I celebrate your well-deserved freedom from me." Julian's dark, seductive eyes smiled with solemn and wistful sadness. "I'm very serious, Larisa. I'm proud of you for leaving me, and I'm ashamed beyond words for what I did to you, not just that last night but for a long time. I have problems. We both know that. Your leaving me was the jolt I needed to seek professional help. I'm seeing someone now. It's just a beginning, but . . . maybe . . . I'll find some answers. And, maybe, someday you'll be able to forgive me."

"Don't ask me to forgive you, Julian. Not yet. Maybe not ever." Beneath the pink tablecloth, Larisa's tapered fingers dug deep, ever deeper, into her palms. "I am glad that you're getting help."

"So am I, I guess. I've spent a lot of time thinking I don't even deserve the chance to improve." He smiled a self-deprecating smile and confessed quietly, "I've also spent a lot of time thinking that it would have been best if you had just shot me."

Larisa's sharp nails journeyed even deeper. Until that moment, as Julian's words abruptly jarred the terrifying memory, she had completely forgotten that grim detail of the nightmarish night. But now she remembered that at one point in the midst of his brutal rage, she had managed to twist free and had crawled to the nightstand where she kept the small handgun Julian had given her. Julian hadn't tried to stop her frantic quest for the weapon, nor had he lunged for it when her trembling hands had pointed it directly at him. Instead, he had mocked her—just as years before another cruel and violent man had mocked her before raping her—laughing at her false and foolish bravery, taunting her to shoot him, knowing full well that she would never pull the trigger even to protect herself. She was so vulnerable, so desirable in her fragile courage, such a delicious victim.

Larisa had always been far too ashamed to tell Julian about the violent rape that had stolen her trusting innocence years before. He knew nothing about it, and yet, four weeks ago, he had eerily recreated that ancient scene, laughing at her . . . goading her to shoot him . . . brutally punishing her when she could not.

And now he was telling her that she should have shot him.

"I mean it, Larisa. I gave you that gun to protect yourself against anyone who might ever try to harm you. Maybe, even then, I knew that one day it might be me."

"I don't want to talk about this, Julian."

"Just a few more words. I want you to take the gun with you today. My attorney has it and the documents required by the airline in his briefcase. He'll give both to Mark before you go."

"I don't want the gun, Julian."

"Please take it, Larisa, so that I can know that you will be safe." Julian paused, smiled wryly, and added with menacing softness, "And so that I won't use it on myself."

"Julian . . ."

"Not fair, I'm sorry. But, please, just take the gun. And promise that if anyone ever tries to hurt you again, you'll pull the trigger."

"I'll take the gun," she agreed quietly, acceding to his wish, fighting the suffocating feeling in her chest as she did so. "Could we please talk about something else?"

"Sure."

For the remainder of the gourmet meal that was virtually untouched by either of them, Julian smoothly guided the conversation from one topic to the next, recounting amusing anecdotes with his effortless charm. Only over coffee at the end of the meal did he return the conversation to them.

"Where are you living, Larisa?"

"Oh," Larisa breathed, startled by the direct question and not certain that she wanted to answer it. But it was all right now, wasn't it? The divorce papers were already signed and in just a few more minutes she and Julian would part forever. "I'm living in San Francisco for now."

"That's good. The Bay Area is your home. I know how much you like it there—far better than the crowded chaos of Manhattan." He gazed at her, his handsome face solemn and thoughtful, and after an intense silence, he asked quietly, "May I call you?"

No! Never! her mind warned instantly. You see what he's doing, don't you? He's told you how despondent he feels, and how hard he's going to work to try to change, and now he's asking for your help—just an occasional transcontinental phone call. He's making it sound like such a small request . . . even though it is an enormous one.

"Julian, I . . ."

"It's too soon, isn't it? I know. I understand. It's too soon, too painful for me, too. But maybe in a month or two? May I call Mark then and ask him for your number, or at least your address? I could write the words I need to say, and you could tear up the letter unopened if you wanted . . ."

Julian seemed so humble, so contrite, so apologetic. But that's not the real Julian, her mind insisted. The *real* Julian is the one who is making you feel guilty for your apparent reluctance to help him. Yes. I know.

But Larisa also knew that the real Julian would persist, at least for a while, and she was very reluctant to put Mark in the middle. He had been there long enough.

"Let's leave Mark out of this, Julian. I'll give you my address and telephone number. But, please . . . it's really far too soon."

"Okay. Thank you." Julian waited in patient silence as Larisa wrote the information on a piece of paper she had withdrawn from her purse. Then, as she handed it to him, and their fingers touched briefly, his warm, hers icy, he asked, "It wasn't all bad, was it? Our love wasn't all bad. Didn't we have some happy times?"

The happiest times of my life, Larisa thought as she quickly withdrew her hand and then stood so abruptly that her untouched coffee splashed over the edge of the china cup. But the happy times were because *I* believed in *your* love. It was my foolish belief, my foolish illusion. You tricked me then, just as, I suppose, you think you're tricking me now. But you're not.

"Mark and I have to go now, Julian. There's going to be Friday afternoon traffic, and—"

"And you need to get away from me." Julian stood too and his dark eyes gazed at her with tender sadness. "I understand. I don't blame you. Goodbye, Larisa."

As the limousine made its way to the airport, Larisa realized that for the past month her focus had been on simple physical survival. Because her body had been so badly wounded she had concentrated all her energies on healing herself physically and had blocked entirely the immense emotional damage that Julian had caused as well.

But now, as her healed body traveled away from him and the deeply wounded heart that had been strangely silent for the past month began to scream its excruciating pain, Larisa wondered if this was a pain that she could survive. Would she ever be able to silence these screams? Or would the shrill and anguished cries be with her forever, relentlessly reminding her of Julian's brutal betrayal of her love . . . and reminding her, too, of her own betrayal of herself?

As Larisa made her way to the airport, serenaded by the piercing screams of her wounded heart, an elated Julian returned to his penthouse office high above Park Avenue and savored his triumph. One of Julian Chancellor's great talents was his ability to spot his opponent's weakness and prey on it; and that was what he had done today—*always*—with Larisa.

Julian regarded Larisa's willingness to help those who needed rescuing as a weakness, but now he was quite grateful for that weakness which he had always before held in such contempt. He would let Larisa rescue him, or believe that she had, and only when she had returned to him would she realize the truth.

Julian smiled as he remembered how she had looked today, so beautiful, so brave, so wonderfully fearful. She still wanted his love. That was abundantly obvious from the wistfulness he had seen in her beautiful expressive eyes.

Julian's smile faded and his lips tightened menacingly as he thought about what else he had seen in the bright shimmering blue. Somewhere, very deep, he had seen a courage, a strength, that he had never seen before. As if Larisa actually believed that she could simply walk out of his life.

He had been forced to give her the divorce. Not, as she had doubtless assumed, because of the fear that she would cry rape. He didn't give a damn if she told the entire world that he had raped her. Who would believe her word against his? No one. He would have made quite certain of that.

No, it wasn't the threat of the so easily trivialized cry of rape that had forced his hand. It was what else Larisa might have inadvertently said. In recounting the events of the night that had caused her to leave him, she might have mentioned that he had been enraged because of a real estate deal that he had lost . . . and Julian could not, would not, allow Peter London to know his immense anger at having been outsmarted by him.

Some day, when it suited Julian Chancellor, Peter London would pay very dearly for his cleverness; just as, some day, Larisa would pay very dearly for daring to leave him.

As Julian's thoughts shifted from Peter to Larisa, the cruel and dangerous smile returned to his lips. There had been such fragile yet defiant courage in her brilliant blue eyes today. Julian liked that delicate, hopeful bravery very much. It would make his conquest—and her punishment—all the more exciting.

Larisa actually believed that she could leave him.

In time she would learn how terribly mistaken she was.

CHAPTER FIFTEEN

"*How* are things going in there?" Larisa asked through the closed door of Elizabeth's bedroom just before eight Saturday night.

A limousine would be arriving soon to take them to the ball at the Fairmont. It was time now for last-minute inspections. Larisa had already inspected her own looks, briefly, just long enough to be certain that there were no major problems. The entire "look" was a problem, of course. She was dressed as she would have dressed, had Julian allowed it, on the most hopeful and joyous evening of her life. Then, as now, she would have worn her magnificent hair long and flowing, a shimmering cascade of firelit golden silk, and she would have worn the delicately beaded white gown that was so hopeful, so innocent, and so pure.

Who was she kidding?

"This may be as good as it gets," Elizabeth announced when she opened the bedroom door.

"As good as it gets is pretty gorgeous," Larisa said softly. "You look terrific, birthday girl."

"Thanks." Elizabeth smiled warmly at her best friend. "Likewise. I'm so glad you decided to come."

"Me too. I can't wait to meet the very nice Stephen Sheridan, not to mention the very infamous Nicholas Chase."

"You may not get to meet Nick."

"Really? From my reading of the admittedly complicated schedule posted by the phone in the kitchen, I'd concluded that the other transplant team is on call tonight and that neither you nor Nick is on call for trauma either."

"That's right. I assume Nick will be at the ball, but there will be so many people there." *And Nick isn't likely to seek me out.* As Elizabeth's thought continued, a wave of uneasiness swept through her. Nick wouldn't cross a crowded ballroom to say good evening to *her*, but he would most certainly make the journey to meet Larisa. Nick would be attracted to Larisa, and Larisa would be attracted to him, and . . .

Interpreting the sudden frown on her friend's face as concern that she might say something outrageous to Nick, Larisa assured quickly, "Don't worry. If I do happen to meet Nick, I will be very well behaved, I promise. I may casually try to spot the fatal flaw, however. I *know* you believe that such a flaw doesn't exist. But it does, Liz, it *must*. Nice men always like you. If Nicholas Chase doesn't, there must be something dreadfully wrong with him."

"What a good friend you are!"

"You're the good friend, Lizzie," Larisa said quietly. "I'm just speaking the truth."

The question of if, when, or how Larisa and Nick would meet was settled within moments of Elizabeth and Larisa's arrival at the Fairmont. Nick was standing alone in the middle of the elegant lobby, having also just arrived.

"That's Nick," Elizabeth said quietly as she realized the inevitability of the imminent meeting.

Nick had seen them arrive. Politeness demanded that he wait where he was until they reached him. But Nick did something even more polite. Instead of simply waiting, he walked to greet them.

"The iceman cometh," Larisa murmured softly as Nick approached.

Then he was there. He smiled politely as he said good evening to Elizabeth, and smiled still when he shifted his gaze to Larisa as Elizabeth made the introduction.

"Hello, Larisa."

"Hello, Doctor."

As her bright blue eyes met Nick's dark blue ones, Larisa realized that despite the fact that Elizabeth had told her about his reputation with women and his history of passionate yet meaningless affairs, she was still somehow unprepared for his compelling sensuality.

Are you one of those arrogant men whose looks have gotten you everything you have ever wanted, whenever you have wanted it? she wondered as she gazed at the devastatingly sexy black-haired blue-eyed surgeon. Has your pursuit of pleasure always been so easy that you've never had to make any effort whatsoever? Have you only pursued women who dazzle with the most superficial glamour—women like me—and never the truly beautiful ones, like Elizabeth? I suppose your seductive and arrogant dark blue eyes are simply too blind to see Elizabeth's extraordinary beauty. Well, it's your loss, Nicholas Chase. Because for some inexplicable reason, she actually likes you.

Really likes you, Larisa realized as she shifted her gaze from Nick to Elizabeth. Her friend's cheeks gave lovely and eloquent pink testimony to her discomfort in Nick's presence, even though her emerald eyes glowed with a deep shimmering radiance. Oh, Elizabeth, you have fallen in love with this stunningly handsome and stunningly arrogant man, haven't you? That's why you so defiantly defend him, despite his cruel indifference to you. A shiver of ice swept through her as Larisa thought, Oh, Elizabeth, how can you have fallen in love with someone like Julian?

"Well," Elizabeth murmured after the few moments of awkward silence during which Larisa's bright blue eyes had unflickeringly appraised Nick—and his dark blue ones had unflickeringly appraised her in return. "I should probably go find Stephen and Madolyn."

"I'll go with you," Larisa replied swiftly. She cast a final glance at Nick, a look of ice-blue contempt that both startled and intrigued him. "Goodbye, Nick."

"Goodbye, Larisa." Turning from the flashing bright blue to the radiant yet uncertain emerald, he added quietly, "Goodbye, Elizabeth."

*   *   *

What a contrast! Larisa thought moments later when Elizabeth introduced her to Stephen. True, as with Nick, she had been quite unprepared for Stephen's striking handsomeness—because, of course, when Elizabeth described people she described the important things: who they were not how they looked. Like Nick, Stephen was compellingly handsome and sexy, but when *his* sensual dark eyes greeted hers, Larisa felt kindness and warmth, not arrogance and ice.

This is the gorgeous man with whom Elizabeth should fall in love, she thought. But Stephen and Elizabeth were friends, and it was obvious from the genuinely untroubled smiles they gave to each other that neither was tormented by deep unrequited feelings. The only torment Larisa detected was the unconcealed disapproval in Madolyn Mitchell's indignant expression as Larisa gazed appreciatively at Stephen.

The conversation with Stephen and Madolyn was quite brief, interrupted first by someone who wanted to congratulate Stephen on the directorship of the institute—and to hear all about LKC—and moments later by someone else who wanted to meet the star anchorwoman.

Elizabeth and Larisa drifted away from Stephen and Madolyn, and for a while they tried to mingle together, but it quickly became apparent that it was impractical to do so. Finally, with a soft laugh, Larisa assured her friend that she was perfectly fine wandering by herself. Elizabeth didn't need to feel responsible for her. If she saw someone she wanted to meet, she assured, she would simply introduce herself.

Larisa had no wish to meet anyone. What she wanted was privacy—and champagne. The bubbly honey-colored liquid helped a lot. Larisa had forgotten how much. It was something she had learned during her marriage, a lesson in survival, even though in the past month, she hadn't had a drop to drink. She had needed her mind to be absolutely clear, to concentrate intently on willing her wounded body to heal; and besides, she had felt safe with Elizabeth—so safe so far away from Julian.

But now Julian was with her again, a vicious demon living deep inside her, clawing mercilessly at her wounded heart, relentlessly reminding her of all the betrayals and causing unremitting pain. In the past twenty-four hours, the screams of pain from her shattered heart had only become louder and more strident, wearing her down with their piercing shrillness, draining energy from her barely healed body. She needed escape, just for a little while, just long enough to regain the strength she needed to do battle with the pain.

The champagne worked wonderfully, magically, making her numb . . . and strong . . . and brave.

Privacy was impossible in the crowded ballroom, but Larisa finally found a place where she could stand forever with her back to the sea of rich and famous, turning only when she needed to lift another glass from the silver trays of golden champagne that wove like glittering threads through the colorful tapestry of silk tuxedos and satin gowns.

The private place was in front of the scale model of the soon-to-be-built Immunology Institute. Larisa had seen hundreds of models of grand buildings, pieces of Julian's vast empire. The model of this building might have triggered more unwanted memories of Julian, except that its style was so unlike anything Julian had ever chosen to build that the memories kept still.

Peter London, Architect, Larisa read as her eyes gazed at the engraved gold plaque beneath the model. Peter's name, like his distinctive architectural style, was quite unfamiliar to her. She was very certain that Julian had never commissioned Peter London to design any of his many buildings—even though he should have.

When installed in the lobby of the medical center on Monday morning, the model would surely be encased in clear acrylic. But tonight there was no protective covering over it, nor were velvet ropes draped around it preventing access. Larisa could get as close as she wanted . . . and she wanted to get very close . . . because it was like a wonderful dollhouse she had never had as a little girl. Someone had cared very much about even the most minute details of this dollhouse, just as she would have, had it been hers. Each tiny room was fully equipped with miniature state-of-the-art medical instruments, of course, but each was also painted and papered in the most unhospitallike springtime pastels and floral prints. There were dolls in the dollhouse, health care workers and their patients. Very nineties, Larisa decided, smiling softly at the discovery that about half of the tiny white-coated doctors were women.

As Larisa gazed at the model, she felt a wonderful sense of warmth and welcome. If one had to be sick, this would be a very comforting place to be. Beginning with the elegant white-pillared entrance with its chattering fountains and lush gardens of flowers, the building seemed to extend a most gracious greeting to all who visited it.

Larisa's soft smile faded abruptly as her blue eyes fell on two tiny dolls, a woman and a little girl. They were doubtless supposed to have been mother and daughter, but they weren't walking together. The mother was walking a bit ahead, and in her own weeping heart Larisa felt the little girl's panic as she desperately tried to keep up, so afraid of being left behind, so afraid of everything.

Larisa shifted the empty champagne flute from her right hand to her left and with her delicate fingers moved the little girl doll forward until she was beside her mother, their tiny hands touching. There. That was how it should be: the mother holding her daughter's hand, wanting to touch her, and protect her, and comfort her.

It had never been that way in Larisa's own life.

But that was how it should be.

Peter London stood nearby watching the astonishingly beautiful woman who gazed with such interest at the building he had designed. She was wholly absorbed in her task, and Peter was wholly absorbed in watching her, mesmerized by the play of the light of the crystal chandeliers on her fire-kissed golden hair, bewitched by her regal grace, and enchanted by the lovely innocence and purity of the gown she wore.

Peter had been drawn to her by her astonishing beauty; but what had intrigued and captivated him was the extraordinary vulnerability of her brilliant blue eyes and the softness of the smile that touched her lovely lips. He would have been quite content to simply watch her all night, never breaking the magical spell; but when her delicate fingers tenderly moved the small doll beside the larger one, Peter saw such sadness that all he wanted to do was rush to her and hold her until the immense sadness was banished from her sensitive heart forever.

Peter didn't rush, not wanting to startle her, but he did move closer, until he stood beside her facing the model as she did.

"What do you think?" he asked quietly.

Even though the deep voice was quiet, and strangely gentle, it startled Larisa nonetheless. She pulled herself from her faraway thoughts, and somehow remembering the hot mist of tears that blurred her vision, when she answered her words were spoken to the model, just as his had been.

"I think it's wonderful," she said softly. "Very beautiful and welcoming—and yet so functional."

"I take it you work at the medical center?"

It was safe to face him then, the mist had cleared, and when she did Larisa formed an instant and uneasy impression of elegance and power—an impression that came with an icy shiver as she thought, Like Julian.

Not exactly like Julian, she amended swiftly—and with surprising confidence. Perhaps it was the hair, the color of midnight's darkest shadows, beautifully cut but slightly too long for true blue-blood fashion. Or maybe it was the eyes. At first, Larisa had thought that they were the color of shadows, too; but as the light of the chandelier gently caressed them, she saw that they were green, not black, the dark, rich, inviting green of a forest at twilight. Inviting? For Larisa the image of a forest was an inviting one. As a little girl she had spent endless private hours in the wonderful dark green sanctuary of towering pines.

Larisa gazed at the seductive eyes, and for a trembling moment joyfully accepted their invitation for sanctuary from all her pain, wondering if she even saw in them a wisdom as solemn and ancient as the forest itself. But then the beckoning green became even more intense, and demanding—wanting something from her—and her mind warned suddenly, He's just like Julian!

Remembering his still unanswered question, and assuming that his asking meant that he did not work there, Larisa looked at him with proud defiance and said, "Yes, I work at the center. I'm a trauma surgeon."

Larisa didn't know if her lie came from the simple wish to be Elizabeth—and not herself—or if it was a challenge to this handsome and powerful man. I'm not just a beautiful woman, you see, not just a plaything for a man like you. I have my own worth, my own talent, my own power.

As soon as her lie was out, Larisa steeled herself for his reaction. A trauma surgeon? he would echo with obvious disbelief. And then as the seductive forest green suddenly became contemptuous and mocking, he would embellish, Not very likely. Forget the fact that you look frivolous and decorative—not serious and competent. There are other equally revealing clues to your lie. You simply don't seem strong enough emotionally. Your courage, such as it is, seems very fragile and very precarious. I seriously doubt that you could make important life-and-death decisions about your own life, much less about the lives of others.

Larisa waited for the taunting assault. But his eyes flickered with neither surprise nor disbelief. They simply gazed at her invitingly . . . *the woods are lovely, dark and deep*.

"Trauma surgery must be very difficult," he offered finally. "Emotionally as well as technically."

"Yes, it is," Larisa admitted as Elizabeth would have. Then, as her optimistic best friend would have done, she added, "But it is also very rewarding."

"I'm sure that's true." Peter smiled then, a gentle half smile, sexy and seductive. "As a trauma surgeon will you have much reason to go to the Immunology Institute?"

"Not at first. But eventually I will—if, when, emergency organ transplantation becomes standard care in acute trauma."

"That's going to happen?"

"I think so." At least, Larisa added silently, Elizabeth thinks so. "Trauma surgeons operate to control damage and to repair what can be repaired, but if there has been significant injury to a vital organ there's sometimes nothing that can be done."

"Trauma to the heart, for example?"

"Yes," Larisa answered softly, suddenly wondering if it was he who was the trauma surgeon and had just made the ominous discovery that the trauma to her own heart had been so massive that without a new one she herself would not survive. I will survive, Larisa told herself urgently; and then, with matching urgency, she told herself that she needed to get away from this dark handsome man. The dishonest conversation was suddenly becoming far too honest. She needed to escape before the searching forest green eyes—that so obviously wanted something from her still—discovered the truth. "Well. I really need to go check on a patient. There's an on-call team in the hospital, of course, but . . ."

"It's your patient and you want to be sure."

"Yes. Goodbye."

She vanished quickly, obviously as anxious to get away from him as to check on her patient. As he watched the glittering beacon of firelit hair disappear into the crowd, Peter felt an immense loss, an astonishing emptiness. She was rushing away from him, and all he wanted to do was follow her, and he might have . . . but then he saw her exchange smiles with Stephen Sheridan as she passed, and Peter knew that she wasn't lost to him forever. If he needed to know, if his heart compelled him to find out, he could learn from Stephen the name of the beautiful trauma surgeon whose lovely blue eyes had been filled with such sadness.

Larisa crossed the ballroom, acting out the charade that she was going to the lobby to make a phone call until she was far enough away from him that it was safe to change course toward the silver fountain of champagne beside the dance floor.

When she reached the fountain a soft smile touched her lips. She could stay here for a long time, listening to the romantic songs of love played by the band and marveling at the everchanging reflection of the crystal chandelier in the shimmering golden pond. And whenever she wanted she could get more champagne by simply holding her empty glass beneath one of the splashing waterfalls.

Perfect.

"Haven't you drowned it yet, Larisa?"

This time the invasion of her privacy came from directly behind her, and this time the male voice was familiar—and unwelcome.

"I beg your pardon?" she asked, her smile vanishing as she spun toward him.

"Haven't you yet drowned whatever it is you're trying to drown with champagne?" Nick clarified quietly.

"*Excuse* me? Have you been watching me?" *Just like Julian used to watch me?* "Have you been counting the number of glasses I've had?"

"I was counting," Nick replied calmly. "It was an interesting diversion for a while. However, quite frankly, I eventually lost both count and interest."

"But now you're suddenly interested again."

"I'm not interested in the amount—I know it's a lot—but yes I am interested in why you're drinking so much."

"I am not drunk, Doctor," Larisa announced coolly, her words clear and unslurred. She wasn't drunk. She was just a little high, high enough to float ever so slightly, unweighted by her pain for a brief wonderful time. Her graceful gait was steady, her words were clear, and her cheeks, until now, had been pale not pink. And the conversation with the forest-eyed stranger in which she had pretended to be Elizabeth? That wasn't a sign of intoxication either. During college, when she rarely ever drank, she had frequently, soberly made up new identities for herself. It had been a game then, a harmless and playful diversion. But tonight it hadn't been a game, Larisa knew. Tonight it had been a wish to be someone else, someone so much better . . . and yes, perhaps, the champagne had allowed that deep wonderful wish to float a little closer to the surface.

"I know you're not drunk," Nick answered solemnly. "That's the most worrisome part of all. It means that you're so accustomed to consuming large amounts of alcohol that you've become tolerant to the effects."

"I don't know about my tolerance to champagne, but I do know that my tolerance to this conversation is rapidly vanishing. No, let me correct that, it's completely gone." Larisa glared at him and added sarcastically, "Oh, I know what happened. I had an alcohol blackout and someone appointed you my guardian and I just don't remember. Right?"

"I appointed myself. I freely admit that you weren't involved in the decision."

"Well, you're off the case now, Doctor. I'm quite capable of monitoring my own alcohol consumption. Besides," she told the dark blue eyes that had watched her drink the necessary champagne but were far too blind to see her best friend's infinite beauty, "I have Elizabeth."

"Elizabeth?"

"Yes. And she's terrific, in case you hadn't noticed." Larisa paused to try to read the dark blue response to her pronouncement. But Nick's eyes would not be read. They were inscrutable as always. But, Larisa realized with surprise, they weren't cold. And were they perhaps even a little interested? When she continued, her voice filled with fondness for her friend, "If I did have a problem with alcohol, which I don't, living with Elizabeth would be like being at the best clinic in the world. In fact, during the past month while I've been staying with her, I haven't had a drop to drink."

"And you're still this tolerant after four weeks of abstinence? That's a very serious relationship with alcohol," Nick murmured quietly, worried about Larisa—and wondering about Elizabeth, what she really knew about alcoholism. Dr. Elizabeth Jennings knew all the medical complications and consequences, of course. But did she have any idea about why people drank? Had anyone ever told her about the desperate need to fill the gnawing emptiness or the frantic desire to silence the screaming pain? "Has Elizabeth actually been helping you?"

"Yes, of course she has."

"How?"

"By being there. By being Elizabeth. By being a wonderful friend."

Nick smiled softly as he thought about Elizabeth. She would help the only way she knew how, by being gentle and compassionate—and forgiving.

"If Elizabeth were really helping you, Larisa, she wouldn't have let you have anything to drink tonight."

"Oh, I see. Tough love, right? Well, that's not Elizabeth's style. She's emotionally very strong, of course, and inspirational and wonderful, but . . ." Larisa stopped abruptly. Why in the world was she trying to convince this arrogant man of how wonderful Elizabeth was? Why didn't she just walk away, run away to find Elizabeth and tell her gently but firmly that perhaps her idea of looking for a job elsewhere, as far away from Nicholas Chase as possible, was the best idea she'd ever had? Because, Larisa realized, there *was* something about Nick . . . something that wasn't all cruelty and arrogance . . . something that perhaps, when discovered, would reconcile her own diagnosis of deep flaws with Elizabeth's defiant conviction that he was sensitive—and wonderful. Maybe by talking to him a little longer and with a little less hostility, she might begin to discover what that something was. Smiling beautifully, she said softly, "I appreciate your concern, Nick, I really do. I probably have had too much champagne tonight, but it's just a one-time celebration."

"What are you celebrating?"

I want to talk about you, Nicholas Chase, not about me, Larisa thought. Tilting her golden red head coyly she teasingly countered his question with one of her own, "Have you ever been married, Nick?"

Larisa expected mock horror on the handsome face of the man famous for his midnight liaisons of passion—a mock horror swiftly embellished with an emphatic, "No, of course not!" Then, perhaps, she and Nick would discuss his views on the subject of marriage, and she would learn something more about him.

But there was neither mock horror nor a swift emphatic reply. Instead, the strong handsome face darkened with a troubled frown and there was a sudden storm in the dark blue eyes. When Nick finally answered her question, it was a soft and honest confession.

"Yes, I have been married, Larisa. Once. Very briefly."

"Are you divorced?" Larisa's voice was soft, too, as she suddenly became fearful that something tragic had happened to Nick's wife.

"Yes."

"Well, then maybe you'll understand. I signed my divorce papers yesterday. For me, that's a very good reason to celebrate."

It had been a reason, an excuse, for Nick to celebrate, too. He had done it with a weekend of Scotch.

"I have a great idea, Larisa," Nick said after a moment. "Why don't you try celebrating by dancing with me? It's much better for you than champagne."

"You really think so, Doctor?"

"Why don't we find out?"

Nick took the still full champagne glass from her hand and guided her to the nearby dance floor. There, as they swayed slowly to an evocative melody of love, Larisa made a discovery about Nicholas Chase: he was a wonderful dancer. Just as, she supposed, he was a wonderful lover. Nick had, it seemed, an instinctive understanding of how male and female bodies were supposed to move together.

"Let's talk about your marriage," Larisa suggested with a provocative smile.

"Let's not," Nick replied, smiling, too, the charming and disarming smile for which he was so well known. "Let's talk about yours."

"There's nothing to say about my marriage except that its end is a very good reason to celebrate."

Nick didn't want to talk about his marriage, and Larisa most certainly didn't want to talk about hers, and so they simply danced in slow sensual silence until Larisa spotted Stephen and Elizabeth dancing nearby.

"Stephen Sheridan is a very nice man, don't you think?"

Nick followed Larisa's gaze to Stephen and Elizabeth. After a long moment he answered, "Yes. He is."

"He obviously thinks Elizabeth is pretty terrific."

Nick nodded, his eyes thoughtful but not surprised.

What do *you* think about Elizabeth, Nick? Larisa wanted to ask. Had there been, she wondered, a flicker of envy when Nick's gaze had first fallen on Elizabeth dancing with Stephen?

Larisa didn't ask, knowing that Nick would never answer, but she reminded him quietly, "Of course, we've already established that Elizabeth *is* pretty terrific." After a brief pause, she suggested boldly, "I have a great idea. I would really like to dance with Stephen. He and I didn't have much of a chance to talk when we met earlier. And, Nick, I don't remember hearing you wish Elizabeth happy birthday."

"Today is Elizabeth's birthday?"

"Yes. So young, and yet so accomplished." Encouraged by his expression, which had seemed genuinely interested in discovering that personal detail about Elizabeth, Larisa urged softly, "So . . . why don't I dance with Stephen and you dance with Elizabeth?"

He wants to dance with Elizabeth, Larisa thought. Good.

"No."

"No? Come on, Nick! It's been wonderful dancing with you, really, so much better than champagne, but—"

"I said no, Larisa."

Why not? Larisa wondered. Why would Nick deprive himself of Elizabeth's wonderful warmth and goodness? Three years before, when Larisa herself had withdrawn from Elizabeth's friendship, it had been because of her own shame about what she had become, what she had *allowed* herself to become. She had wanted to shelter her lovely friend from the ugly truths about herself.

Could it possibly be the same for Nick?

Nick wanted to dance with Elizabeth, Larisa was sure of it. But his ice-blue eyes and the sudden steely tension in the lean body that touched hers told her with silent eloquence that he wasn't going to. And very soon, Larisa realized as she sensed his sudden restlessness, he was going to disappear. He wasn't going to spend another dance watching Stephen dance with Elizabeth. Which was fine, best, because for a deeply troubling moment Larisa had seen a flicker of doubt in Elizabeth's emerald eyes at the sight of her dancing with Nick.

Oh, Elizabeth! There's nothing between me and Nick! Yes, of course, he's gorgeous and seductive and sexy. And, yes, I think so little of myself and need so desperately to be touched by a man who doesn't want to own me that I could imagine spending a few hours learning from him the gentle and beautiful way that male and female bodies were meant to make love together. But don't you know that I never would?

I never would, Larisa vowed confidently. And, with matching confidence, she thought, Neither would Nick.

Nick moved his taut body away from Larisa as soon as the music stopped. But he didn't run away. Instead he waited patiently until her blue eyes met his. Then he offered quietly, "Call me, Larisa, if you ever need anything."

"Like a little tough . . ." Larisa stopped abruptly. Tough "love" was presumptuous. Tough "like"? Admittedly, right now, if pressed, Larisa would find herself defending Nicholas Chase against his critics. And yes, right now if pressed, she would confess that she actually liked him. But "like" seemed presumptuous as well. She needed to finish the sentence. Nick was waiting, politely, patiently, despite his restlessness to leave.

Finally, rescuing them both, Nick finished Larisa's sentence for her.

"Like a little tough love," he said quietly, acknowledging the presumptuousness with a gentle and almost uncertain smile. After a moment he added, "I mean it, Larisa. I'm available. I'm even a pretty good listener."

"Thank you, Nick. I mean that too."

CHAPTER SIXTEEN

"*I* have some news, Stephen," Madolyn purred when she and Stephen returned to her posh Nob Hill apartment following the Fairmont ball. "I've decided to accept the job in New York. They made me an offer I really couldn't refuse."

"I knew that they would. Congratulations. When do you start?"

"November first. My last day at the station here will be October first, so I'll have a month to find a place, get settled . . ." Plan a Christmas wedding, perhaps? Madolyn walked over to him, rested her perfectly manicured fingers delicately against his chest and looked up at his surprisingly solemn face. Was he worrying about her being so far away? Good, she thought. I'll help him arrive at a wonderful solution. Kissing his lips provocatively as she spoke, she whispered, "What are you thinking, Stephen?"

Stephen wasn't thinking, only feeling; and what he felt was relief that their intimate yet emotionally empty relationship would end so easily, so naturally . . . and so soon.

"Nothing."

"Well. Let's not think, then. Let's just *do*. Why don't you undress me? There are a hundred tiny buttons that need to be undone by your talented fingers. Of course," Madolyn whispered seductively as her own fingers drifted teasingly lower, "I'll be trying to undress you at the same time. It doesn't matter if you run out of patience, Stephen. Christine will just have to repair whatever damage occurs in the name of passion. I'll simply tell her that it was proof positive of how much you liked the gown."

"Christine?" Stephen asked, pulling away abruptly. *Christine*. It felt so strange to speak aloud the name that had been echoing in his mind and filling his heart ever since she had called him two nights before. "What about Christine?"

"She made this dress for me to wear to the ball. I told her how special tonight would be for you—for us."

"When did she make it?"

"She designed it weeks ago, of course, but she didn't actually finish the final detailing—she's such a perfectionist!—until late last night."

"Last night," Stephen echoed softly, frowning as he envisioned Christine working late into the night to finish this magnificent work of art—for him, to be enjoyed by him, despite the anguish he had caused her.

"Stephen! What's going on? I told Christine to make a gown that you would find absolutely irresistible, and I think she has. I'm not sure why you're resisting now. Stephen?"

Madolyn started to move toward him, to begin the seduction anew, but Stephen held up his hands to stop her.

"Let's not do this, Madolyn," he said quietly. "Let's just have it end with the memory of the last dance. That was very nice, didn't you think?"

"Yes. But it was a beginning, Stephen, not an end."

Stephen sighed. He didn't want a scene. He just wanted privacy to think about the lovely woman who had made Madolyn's beautiful evening gown . . . and he very much wanted to get away from the woman who so obviously regarded Christine as a servant—a Cinderella—after all.

"No, Madolyn. It was an end . . . the end."

"I don't understand what's happening!" Madolyn's violet eyes flashed with indignant anger. "Out of the blue, you've decided to end our relationship because I've taken a job in New York? Is my success so threatening to you, Stephen? Is this your latent sexism coming out of the closet? A wife who dabbled in local news was just fine, but—"

"A wife?" Stephen's mind spun. "We never talked about marriage, Madolyn. In fact, we never talked about us at all."

"Let's talk about us then! I love you, Stephen!"

"No. You don't. Please, Madolyn, let's not do this. Let's not change the rules at the last minute. I'm very sorry, terribly sorry, if I have misled you about my feelings. Until this moment, I honestly had no idea that you expected more than what we've had." *What little we've had.* "Believe what you must, but the truth is that this has nothing to do with your decision to move to New York. I think it's wonderful that you got the job. You've worked very hard and you certainly deserve it."

"But I don't deserve you? Is that it? How dare you patronize me!"

In her fury about the careful plans she had made and which were now destroyed, Madolyn needed something else to destroy. If they hadn't been in her apartment, surrounded by her prized crystal vases and delicate figurines, she might have reached for something to hurl at him. As it was, what Madolyn chose to destroy was the beautiful gown Christine had made for her. The gown was quite valueless to her now, and it had failed miserably in its mission to assist her in enticing a proposal of marriage.

In a frenzied rage, as if the soft satin had suddenly caught fire and was blazing against her fair skin, she tore it off. It happened in a flash, the magnificent sapphire gown shredded beyond repair before Stephen could even move to stop her. As he witnessed the willful and petulant destruction of something so painstakingly created, Stephen felt the immense and ominous power of his own rage . . . and he knew, an almost urgent knowledge, that he needed to get away from Madolyn—*fast.*

Stephen drove to the beach and stood at water's edge, listening to the thunder of crashing waves and staring into the vast darkness of the moonless autumn night.

And there, in the thundering darkness, Stephen thought about love.

He had no firsthand experience with it, of course. But he had had the extraordinary privilege of being an eyewitness to the extraordinary love of David and Christine, marveling at it, respecting its privacy . . . until three weeks ago when he had so unwittingly intruded.

Stephen had wanted to intrude again in the past two days, but he truly believed that it wouldn't help Christine to speak to him. It was he, after all, who had caused the harm. Stephen hadn't tried to speak to her; but he had called Sydney's each day to be very certain that she was there—that she was safe.

And now, in the middle of this moonless night, Stephen felt a powerfully compelling desire to go to her small house on Twin Peaks and intrude once again. He wanted to tell her how sorry he was for everything . . . for unraveling the insurance mix-up without speaking to her first . . . for Madolyn treating her like Cinderella . . . and, most of all, for his own failure to save her beloved David.

Stephen wanted to intrude once again.

But he didn't.

He had intruded far too much already.

A few miles away, Christine lay awake in the darkness of her Twin Peaks home, wondering if David's ghost might suddenly appear. Such a luminous vision would be only an illusion, she knew, its image merely a phantom created by her own fatigued mind, its words only the desperate wishes of her own aching heart.

David's ghost would not appear. It would not be driven by restlessness from the afterworld to speak words in death that David had been unable to speak in life.

Because there were no such unspoken words.

Because of Stephen Sheridan, she and David had had the chance to say all the words of love . . . and all the loving goodbyes. There was no need for David to return to her; but, Christine thought, he might return still, to speak again the words he had spoken with such loving urgency before he had died.

"Don't let the memory of our wonderful love fill the rest of your life with sadness, my Christie. Remember our love, my darling, and always be warmed with joy at that wondrous memory, but go on with your life. Promise me, please, that you will allow yourself to find new love, new happiness, new joy."

Christine had listened to David's impassioned plea and she had made promises to him that she knew she would never keep. She would never find a new love, and her happiness and joy would be remembered only, renewed every day of her life as she worked to pay his bills. She had been so grateful for the enormous debt. It had given her life purpose, a reason to live, the only reason to live after their baby died.

And until two days ago, when the letter from the insurance company arrived, she had been doing just fine, living entirely in past memories, quite oblivious to the present and without any fear of the future. The future, like the present, held no surprises, no demands, and no risks. It would be spent keeping the memories alive, keeping David alive, renewing with every payment she made her own deep gratitude to all those who had worked so tirelessly and compassionately to save him.

And now because of the doctor who had done the very most, but to whom she had never even owed any money, her life was hers again, with no purpose except what she chose to give it . . . and she felt so lost, so adrift, so scared.

Christine didn't know what she was going to do with the new life that had been given her; but she knew that she had to apologize to the man whose brilliance had given her a final year of love with David and whose concern for her had now given her a chance to begin again.

She had to apologize to Stephen . . . and she had to do it in person.

An icy tremble of fear swept through her as she thought about returning to Stephen's laboratory. Once she had gone there often, late at night after David had fallen asleep in his nearby room, and there she had confessed to Stephen all the fears and worries she had kept so carefully hidden from her beloved husband.

It would be very difficult to return to that place of such memories. But she had to—and would.

Christine wished that she had something more than an apology to give to Stephen Sheridan. Well, perhaps she did. She left her bed then, and in the predawn darkness of that moonless September night she began to sketch for Madolyn Mitchell a most beautiful and romantic wedding gown.

* * *

The following night, Christine caught the nine-thirty P.M. bus from Union Square to Pacific Heights, arriving at the medical center shortly after ten. It took eight more minutes to follow the once familiar route from the lobby to the research wing. Her footsteps slowed as she neared the corridor that led to the ward and stopped entirely when she reached it. As she stared at the long stretch of shining linoleum, Christine was transported back in time. If she walked down the corridor, beyond the nurses' station to the last room on the left, David would be there, waiting for her, healthy again after an infusion of Stephen's miracle therapy, so happy to see her . . .

Blinking back a sudden hot mist of tears, Christine made herself walk on, past the beckoning corridor to the other familiar one—the one that led to Stephen's laboratory.

The door was ajar, as it always had been, casting a golden beam of light into the shadowy hallway, inviting even the most timid of visitors to enter. How many wives and husbands had come here late at night to talk privately with their spouse's doctor? she wondered. Was that why Stephen worked so late at night and on weekends, to be available to them away from the daylight rush of rounds and conferences and clinic? Stephen did his important research during those quiet times, of course; but there were surely times when the research itself was quiet, when all tissue cultures were incubating and the new miracle therapies were being given a chance to work their magic without intervention. Was Stephen in his lab even during those times, like a teacher who holds office hours whether the students come or not, just in case there is a needy student who at last finds the courage to appear?

Christine had never encountered another anxious spouse on her late-night visits to Stephen's lab. But, she thought, if there's someone here tonight, someone whose loved one is still living—or still dying—I will leave, because it is so much more important for Stephen to talk to them than to me. She slowed her gait as she neared the golden beam and listened for the sound of voices coming from within, but there was only silence. And when she reached the open doorway, she saw him, quite alone, peering intently into his microscope. Looking for cancer? Looking to see if the cancer had vanished, vanquished or at least in retreat because of the therapy he had given it?

"Doctor Sheridan?"

"Mrs. Andrews. Hello." Stephen smiled softly as he stood and walked toward her. His greeting was as warm and welcoming as the golden beam of light. "Please come in."

"Thank you."

Without even thinking about it, Christine sat in the chair where she had always sat. And, as he always had, Stephen moved his stool until he was sitting directly in front of her. For a moment they were both a little lost in a bittersweet sense of déjà vu. Bittersweet, because there had been nights, especially in the beginning, when he had had such good news to give her. And then, in the end, when there had been only bad news to give, in quiet emotional conversations, the two of them had made the loving plans that would allow David to die the way he wanted to . . . at home with his Christie.

But this was a different time, and returning to the present at the same moment, they whispered in unison, "I'm sorry."

And then, in response to the other's apology, each offered gracious protests.

"It was so nice of you to check on the insurance."

"I should have checked with you first."

"No, you shouldn't have. It's just that . . . I guess it caught me by surprise."

"That's why I should have checked with you first."

"No, really."

"Yes." Stephen smiled and then added gently but firmly, "Really."

Christine's next protest was intercepted by a smile of her own, a soft answer to his, a silent acknowledgment that enough apologies had been given and received.

"Okay."

"Okay. And my name is Stephen, Christine."

"Okay, Stephen." After a moment she said bravely, "I wondered if you and Madolyn would like to have dinner at my house sometime. I know that you're both very busy, so it may not be possible to arrange, but . . ."

"Madolyn and I aren't seeing each other anymore," Stephen said quietly. Then, gazing intently at her surprised lavender eyes, he added, "However, I would very much like to have dinner with you. If that's okay."

"Oh," Christine whispered. "Yes. Of course it is."

"Good." Stephen smiled at the welcoming yet uncertain lavender. He felt uncertain, too; not about having dinner with her, he was *very* certain about that, but about the powerful, exhilarating, and dangerous feelings that suddenly pulsed through him. "Did you have a specific time in mind? I know you're busy, too."

"Well, as of today, I'll be less busy, at least I'll be spending fewer hours at the boutique." Christine shrugged, then confessed to the man to whom she had once confessed her deepest fears, "I decided that I need some time to think about what I'm going to do."

"Because someone, without checking with you first, suddenly changed all the plans you had made."

"In a good way," Christine assured softly. After a moment she repeated bravely, "This is good for me, Stephen. It will just take me a little time to adjust."

"Do you have any idea what you'll do? Designing, maybe? The gown you designed for Madolyn was magnificent, truly a work of art."

"Oh. Thank you. Well, yes, maybe a little designing, or at least a little bit more sewing. Anyway, I told Sydney that I'd like to work only every other weekend for a while."

"Is this weekend on or off?"

"Off."

"I'm off, too."

"Well, then, Saturday at seven?"

"That would be fine."

"Do you remember where I live?"

"Yes." *How could I ever forget?*

CHAPTER SEVENTEEN

"*I* gave your name to a number of women at the ball last Saturday," Madolyn told Christine when she arrived for her Thursday afternoon appointment at Sydney's. "I think you'll be getting more requests to design gowns."

"I already have been. Thank you very much for referring them to me."

"Well, the dress *was* a sensation. Stephen loved it, of course. He simply couldn't keep his hands off me! Would you like to hear a sad story, Christine?" Madolyn gave a dramatic sigh. Without waiting for Christine's reply, she elaborated, "I suppose it's the story of the nineties, the inevitable conflict between romance and career. I've just been offered a terrific—and very important—position with the network in New York. However, that great career triumph has had a huge price tag—my relationship with Stephen."

"Oh, Madolyn, I'm so sorry."

"I'm sorry, too, although not as sorry as Stephen is. I'd actually believed that he and I could have a modern, sophisticated marriage. I'd imagined we would simply commute for a while until he could join me in New York. Given his sense of responsibility to the institute that would have been next summer at the very earliest. I could have easily handled such a separation, but, unfortunately, Stephen couldn't. He wanted *much more* of me than that." Madolyn gave another dramatic sigh. "I thought we liberated the men, too, Christine, but it turns out that Stephen is really quite traditional. He showed his true not-so-nineties colors when he pleaded with me to stay here, not just until next summer, but forever."

But that's wonderful! Christine wanted to say. Isn't Stephen's love more important than anything else in the world? And isn't the work he does more important, too? Yes, he could move to New York, once the institute is built and they find a new director. But the move, no matter how smoothly and quickly it is done, would surely interfere with his research, wouldn't it? And mightn't that loss of a month, or a week, or even a day cost a month or a week or even a day in the life of some future patient?

"I'm afraid that what Doctor Stephen Sheridan wants is to have the little woman at home—or at least at the local television station." Madolyn shook her head as if still amazed by the revelation. "Poor Stephen. The truth is I just don't love him enough to sacrifice my career for him. I finally had to admit that to myself—and to him—even though it hurt him terribly. It seemed better, kinder in the long run, to simply make a clean break of it now. When he's recovered, he can go on, hopefully to someone more domesticated and less successful than I." After a moment, she added, "I certainly hope *your* husband is more modern than Stephen, Christine, because it's going to happen to you, too, you know. Someday a top fashion designer is going to discover you and convince you to move to the Big Apple. Frankly I hope it happens very soon, because in a month I'm going to need you in New York." An expression of mock horror touched her beautiful face as she exclaimed, "What am I going to do without you, Christine? Will you move to New York with me? *Please?* I know that Sydney is planning to open a boutique on Fifth Avenue. Maybe you should talk to her about transferring there."

"I'm really very happy in San Francisco, Madolyn." And you should be happy here, too, with Stephen, Christine thought as she felt a rush of emotions—a deep wish for Stephen to be loved and happy, and anger at Madolyn for her selfishness. Christine didn't want Stephen to be unhappy, ever . . . and yet something very powerful prevented her from bravely urging Madolyn to reconsider her decision to move.

"Oh? Well, I guess that means I'll just need to get the most out of your talent before I move. I'll need a whole new wardrobe, of course. I'd like to get started on selecting it as soon as possible. What openings do you have for this Saturday?"

"None, I'm afraid," Christine admitted quietly. "I actually won't be working at all this Saturday."

"Not at all?" Madolyn's disapproving expression clearly conveyed another question: Don't you understand that you are to be available to me *at all times*, Christine?

"No. Not at all." I'll be spending all day Saturday preparing dinner for Stephen. Not very nineties, Christine thought. Or maybe it was. Maybe the nineties would be the decade in which love and family became important again . . . and when the choices people made were choices of love.

"Good evening, Christine."

"Good evening, Stephen," she echoed softly. "Please come in."

"Thank you."

Stephen steeled his heart as he entered the small house. He had been here only once before, on the afternoon David died, and the somber memory of that death and its anguish had somehow forever shrouded the house in darkness. It would be even darker this evening, more dreary, because the scowling clouds that had hovered all day now wept cold soggy tears.

But Christine's house wasn't dreary at all. Not now, and, Stephen suddenly realized, not on the day of David's death either. How could it have been dreary? Christine had spent her marriage filling her husband's life with happiness and joy, and their home had always been a bright cheery symbol of that joyfulness.

The house smiled, and so did Christine, her beautiful face softly framed by the spun-gold silk that had been freed from its sedate chignon and now floated gently over her shoulders. Her smile was warm and welcoming, shy and brave, and there was something more in the lovely smiling lavender eyes.

What was it? Stephen wondered as she turned to hang his raincoat in the nearby closet. It looked almost like sympathy. For him? Was it actually possible that she might believe he was mourning the loss of Madolyn? Had Christine somehow imagined his relationship with Madolyn as comparable to hers with David? The thought was astonishing. And yet, perhaps, the shy and innocent girl who had fallen in love once and forever at age eighteen had grown into a woman who knew nothing at all about relationships that began without love and faltered for the same reason.

Stephen wanted to tell her not to worry—that his very intimate relationship

with Madolyn had meant *nothing*—but he had no wish to shatter her lovely innocence. He didn't tell her in words not to worry about him or his heart; but the
untroubled smile that greeted her when she turned back to him surely assured her
that he was fine.

"Do I hear a crackling fire?" he asked.

"Yes you do. In the living room. If you'd like to wait in there, I'll bring you
something to drink. I had thought white wine, because of what we're having for
dinner, but I do have other options."

"White wine would be nice. Shall I help you?"

"No. Thank you."

The living room seemed completely unchanged from the day David had died,
nothing moved, nothing added . . .

And nothing taken away, Stephen realized with relief as his gaze fell on the
magnificent portrait above the mantel. He had feared that it might be gone, sold to
help pay the bills, but it was still there, where it belonged, where David had always
wanted it to be.

Stephen had barely glanced at the portrait on the day of David's death. His
own tears on that day had been far too close to the surface to risk it. But now he
stood before the painting, admiring the talent and marveling anew at the extraordinary love. The portrait was of Christine, and it was stunning proof of David's artistic gift; but mostly it was stunning proof of their wondrous love. The painting was,
remarkably, a portrait of love as seen through the eyes of *both* lovers: the gifted
artist who had painted his beloved wife's beautiful face with such exquisite tenderness . . . and the lovely woman whose glowing lavender eyes spoke so eloquently of
her immense love for him.

"I couldn't sell it," Christine said quietly when she returned.

"David wouldn't have wanted you to."

"No," she agreed softly. "He wanted me to have something, some part of him,
always."

"Yes," Stephen said with matching softness. He vividly remembered David's
great happiness that he would be able to finish the portrait before he died. A gift of
love that Christine would have forever, he had said. Stephen also remembered how
that great happiness had paled in comparison to David's joy at the news of Christine's pregnancy. After a moment Stephen turned from the glowing lavender eyes
in the portrait to the solemn ones beside him and admitted quietly, "I know he did.
He told me."

"Oh." Christine's eyes widened briefly with surprise, then became very
thoughtful, as if she were debating saying something else, something that suddenly
filled the crystal-clear lavender with clouds as dark and stormy as the ones outside.

"Christine?"

She answered with a shake of her golden head; and, as if banished by the silky
sunshine, when her eyes met his again the clouds were gone and the lavender was
clear again and smiling.

"It seemed like such a blustery, soup kind of day, that I thought we'd begin the
meal with French onion soup," she explained as she finally handed him his wine.
"That's why I decided white wine beforehand seemed reasonable."

"This is wonderful wine," Stephen said after he took a sip.

"Oh, good." She tilted her head and asked, "Do you like French onion soup?
Not everyone does. I suppose I should have checked with you first."

"I love French onion soup," Stephen assured truthfully. "And I think it's awfully nice—and brave—of you to have made it. Admittedly, I don't cook much, but my limited experience with slicing onions has always been pretty disastrous from the standpoint of watery eyes."

"The trick is to keep your mouth closed while you're slicing."

"Really? That easy?"

"That easy."

Christine smiled a beautiful and untroubled smile, but still Stephen's mind filled with troubling images. This afternoon, as she had sliced the onions for the soup, Christine's lovely mouth had surely been closed, because she had been quite alone, without anyone to talk to or laugh with as she sliced. She had been alone, without companionship or laughter.

Had she been terribly lonely? he wondered. Had tears spilled from the beautiful lavender anyway?

Stop this, Stephen told himself. She's smiling now. She's not alone now . . .

Stephen had worried that he and Christine might have difficulty finding things to talk about. During the year that her husband had been his patient, they had, of course, spent many hours in quiet conversation; but those conversations had always been entirely focused on David.

But, Stephen discovered with relief, because of the honesty and emotions they had already shared, because they had already talked to each other about love and loss and joy and fear, they could talk about anything.

And they did, in a conversation that flowed like the gentlest of rivers, always in motion and yet unhurried, not rushing to its final destination because there were so many discoveries to be made along the way, a new one around every winding bend. Sometimes the discoveries were joyful, a cascade of soft laughter, and sometimes they were very solemn . . .

"What is it, Christine?" Stephen asked gently when the dark clouds that had been there earlier returned to her expressive eyes.

"Did David tell you that I was pregnant?"

"Yes."

"I lost the baby, Stephen," she said with quiet despair. "I miscarried."

As Stephen looked at the lovely lavender, gray now and so very empty, he realized that that was how it had looked the day David died. Her eyes had been gray then, and her face had been taut and ashen . . . and she had been almost desperate to have him leave.

"Oh, Christine," he whispered. "You lost the baby the day David died, didn't you?"

"Yes." She shook her golden head in soft disbelief still, after all this time. "The pain started just after he died, as if the baby had been destined to live only long enough to give him joy and peace at the time of his death." A smile of love touched her lips as she added, "And he did die peacefully."

Yes he did, Stephen thought as he looked at the extraordinary woman whose great love had protected her husband from truths that would have worried him and who even now, as she talked about a day when she herself had lost both that man and his unborn baby, was still focused on David, on his happiness and peace.

"But what about you, Christine?" he asked very gently.

"I suppose it was destiny for me not to know on the day my husband and my baby died that the insurance company's refusal to pay David's bills was simply a mix-up," she admitted quietly. "Having the bills to pay gave my life a purpose. I needed that purpose then, Stephen."

"And now that I've caused that purpose to be taken away?"

"Now I have to find something new." Christine smiled then, a brave smile intended to assure him that it was all right, that she was ready now to begin the courageous journey toward new dreams. "Actually, the something new is finding me. This week I agreed to design six more gowns . . ."

Stephen left the cheerful house on Twin Peaks shortly after three A.M. He hadn't wanted to leave, but he had early rounds and even though this was her weekend off Christine was meeting with a client to discuss the sketches she had done for a silver and gold silk chiffon evening gown.

Stephen hadn't wanted to leave Christine at three, or ever; and as he drove away he had to fight the powerful urge to simply turn the car around and return to her.

The urge was very powerful, and very wonderful, but so was the weapon Stephen had with which to fight it: the truth.

The hopeful truth . . . Christine is beginning her new life. The delicate butterfly is courageously emerging from her cocoon and in time she will soar gracefully to her dreams.

And the bitter truth . . . she is married.

CHAPTER EIGHTEEN

Sausalito, California
September 1991

*B*EAUTY AND THE BILLIONAIRE—The Fairy Tale Ends. It wasn't the headline on the cover of *People* magazine that caught the attention of Peter London's dark green eyes as he stood in the checkout line of Sausalito's Marina Grocery. It was the accompanying photograph of Julian and Larisa Chancellor, crystal champagne flutes raised in toast to their amicable divorce.

Peter reached for a copy of the magazine. Then, realizing that with the magazine he now had eleven items to purchase—not the ten that was the upper limit for the express lane in which he was standing—he moved to the end of another, much longer line. The wait didn't matter. After reading the brief article about Julian and Larisa, Peter was quite lost in thoughts and memories—thoughts of Larisa, who had bewitched him nine nights ago at the Fairmont ball . . . and memories of Julian, who was his most bitter enemy.

Peter never knew his mother, she died at his birth, but he knew and deeply loved his father. Thomas London was fifty-five-years-old when his son was born. He had been a carpenter for over forty of those fifty-five years, and he had been illiterate for all of them.

His father had dyslexia, Peter realized when he himself was older and well educated. And even though Thomas was a truly gifted artisan, his inability to read or write had always been a source of great frustration and shame, a bewildering and unconquerable flaw that had driven him from school at age twelve and had compelled him—until his marriage at age fifty—to live a mostly solitary life.

Peter sensed his father's shame and even as a young boy tried to teach Thomas to read. But it was impossible. The dyslexia was far too severe. Peter couldn't teach his father to read, but Thomas taught Peter about carpentry, sharing with his beloved son his love for his craft—and sharing too with Peter the dreams that he had for him. Thomas wanted Peter to have the luxury of choice that had never been his, a life whose opportunities and dreams were limited only by talent and desire, what one could do; not, as it had always been for Thomas, by what he couldn't.

"I'm going to be an architect, Pop," Peter announced at the beginning of his senior year in high school. It was Peter's own dream, what he truly wanted for his life, but it also was what Thomas would have been had he been able to read. "I'm going to go to Harvard and I'm going to become an architect."

Peter wanted to go to Harvard because of its academic excellence, of course, but mostly because it would keep him near the aging father he loved so much. Their home was in Concord, where Thomas had spent much of his life lovingly restoring the historic buildings of the Revolutionary War. Their life had been humble, and there had been times when they had truly struggled, but there was such happiness in their life, such a richness of spirit and a wealth of love that Peter had never felt the least bit deprived.

Father and son were a family of two, and Thomas was both father and grandfather, far older than the fathers of Peter's classmates, and magical, and wise. Despite his age, until he was stricken by arthritis, Thomas had had more energy than any of the other fathers. His mind remained lively, even after his art had been crippled, and on his seventy-third birthday, he joyfully celebrated Peter's acceptance to Harvard.

Peter arrived at Harvard as a young man eager to pursue his dreams—and to share that pursuit with his father. He knew college would offer new friendships and experiences, but still he had not anticipated a friendship with someone like Julian Chancellor. Peter had never known anyone like wealthy and privileged Julian, and he was surprised—and, yes, flattered—that Julian wanted the friendship. Peter didn't realize until much later, too late, that what Julian really wanted was his academic excellence.

Peter was both impressed and a little overwhelmed by his charming and confident new friend. Which was why, in the beginning, Peter chose to forgive the troubling things he noticed about Julian.

Julian Chancellor could buy anything he wanted. But he stole—no, Peter amended swiftly, he took. The clothes and books and albums and even money were always taken on the pretext of borrowing, but Julian never had any intention of returning them, nor was he ever apologetic when he didn't, as if his immense wealth and the privileges of his blue blood entitled him to whatever he wanted.

Carelessness, Peter decided. His wealthy friend was simply so accustomed to having everything without any effort at all that he just didn't understand the value of possessions that had been acquired through hard work. Peter justified and forgave Julian's carelessness, and he did the same for the laziness he saw. There was no doubt that Julian was very bright. But he couldn't be bothered to concentrate his intellect on his schoolwork. Always charmingly apologetic, having spent his days and nights partying instead of studying, Julian would appear on the eve of an exam to look at Peter's meticulous class notes.

Julian's carelessness and laziness were understandable, forgivable consequences of the effortlessness of his golden life. But Peter could neither understand nor forgive the way Julian treated Marcy. Marcy was Julian's girlfriend, and there were times when Julian seemed almost cruel to her, openly criticizing her, embarrassing her in front of others. Such unkindness was as foreign to Peter London as was the pampered life Julian Chancellor had lived; and as time went by Peter searched for a diplomatic way to discuss his deep concern with his friend.

Julian invited a small group of friends, including Peter, to spend the last weekend in April at a beach house at Cape Cod. They arrived at the twelve-room "bungalow" belonging to one of Julian's father's business associates late Friday evening, and on Saturday afternoon Julian insisted that they all accompany him to a twenty-five-acre estate located nearby.

"This is Innis Arden," Julian said as he drove his Mercedes through the massive stone pillars that marked the entrance. Then he drove in silence for a while, allowing his friends to marvel at the magnificence of the location, a secluded yet commanding site high above Nantucket Sound. Finally, when he was certain that they understood the significance and value of the breathtaking estate, he announced, "And it is rightfully mine."

"Yours?" one of the young men asked, not doubting, because he had learned never to doubt Julian, but amazed nonetheless.

"*Rightfully* mine," Julian repeated. "At the moment it's on loan to the people of Cape Cod, a gift from my mother's mother. It had been in her family for generations and when the dotty old bird died five years ago, she stipulated in her will that it would be open to the public for twenty years after her death. Which," Julian added as he scowled at an oncoming car, "as you can see, it is."

"And at the end of twenty years you inherit it?"

"No," Julian answered with obvious disgust, not at the question but at the grandmother who had chosen not to will the estate directly to her heirs. "I have to buy it when it goes on the auction block fifteen years from this August. The sale will be by a sealed bid, but I will be the highest bidder."

"How do you know?"

Julian arched a surprised eyebrow. "There are ways of knowing—and I'll know. And then, Innis Arden will be mine, as it should be, and I'll transform it into one of the world's most exclusive resorts. It will take a lot of work, of course, and a lot of money. The existing mansion will have to be completely demolished to make room for a luxury hotel, and there will be separate private bungalows over there where the meadow is now . . ."

Julian decided to begin the tour of the estate that would one day be his with the secluded cove—which, he assured his friends, would eventually rival the marina in Monte Carlo as a home for the greatest yachts of the world. The path to the cove was through the meadow.

And that was as far as Peter got. As the others continued on, he remained in the meadow, a most willing captive to the enchantment of color and fragrance that surrounded him.

The meadow was an extraordinary community of flowers—some cultivated, some wild—all crowded together and yet blooming in magnificent harmony, sharing the nurturing rays of the golden sun as if in mutual respect for the splendor of the other. Bright blue forget-me-nots delicately graced the elegant stalks of snow-queen irises; and lilies and lupines bloomed in a brilliant mosaic of sapphire, apricot, scarlet, and flame; and daffodils and daisies smiled their dazzling golden smiles at the dazzling golden sun.

The flowers bloomed in a magnificent harmony of color. And, Peter realized as he inhaled, there was a magnificent harmony of fragrance, too. Even the strongest of perfumes didn't overpower the delicate one of its neighbor. Lavender, and jasmine, and lilac, and violet all blended together, an intoxicating tapestry of fragrance into which were also gently woven the vibrant scents of forest and sea.

As Peter gazed at the astonishing beauty of the meadow and inhaled the flower-kissed air, he was swept with emotions that were at once powerful and empowering. Everything seemed possible here. All dreams . . . all hopes . . . all promises.

And Julian was going to destroy this paradise?

No!

Peter's impulsive "No!" became a solemn promise of love an hour later when he wandered through the mansion. Luxuriantly cloaked in lavender wisteria, the mansion was grand and elegant, lovingly built and impeccably maintained, a triumph of graciousness and style. The original structure was almost two centuries old, but there had been a more recent embellishment—a music room overlooking the enchanted meadow.

This was his father's work. Peter was certain of it. The obvious love of the wood—the joyful blending of different grains, the artistic use of knots and swirls to add texture, the meticulous detailing, the grace and majesty—were unmistakable.

"Hi, Pop."

"Peter!" A broad grin lit Thomas's unshaven face. Then, as he rubbed his arthritic hands over the stubble, his expression became a little sheepish, a silent confession that he no longer shaved every day, it was far too difficult. He shaved only when he expected to see his son, which was every other weekend. "I . . . I wasn't expecting you. I would've shaved if I'd known you were coming."

"It doesn't matter, Pop!" Peter exclaimed, keeping hidden from his loving voice the sudden rush of emotion, of sadness, he felt.

"I thought you were planning to spend this weekend at the Cape."

"I was there last night, but . . . Pop, did you ever work at Innis Arden? I was there this afternoon and to me the music room looked like something you would have created."

"It was." Thomas gave a slight shake of his head as the old memories swept through him. "My, my, it was over fifty years ago that I worked there. How did you happen to be in the mansion, Peter?"

"Innis Arden is open to the public now. We visited there because it used to belong to Julian's maternal grandmother."

"Ginny," Thomas said softly. "One of her daughters married a Chancellor, eh?"

"Yes, I guess. *Ginny?*"

"Virginia Alcott Forrester. She was the reason I got the job. She'd seen an alcove I had done in a house on Beacon Hill and trusted me to work on her beautiful home. Innis Arden was hers even then, a wedding present from her grandparents. Her husband was a financier who didn't like the remoteness of the Cape, so the estate became Ginny's private retreat when her husband was traveling and her children were off at the exclusive boarding schools they attended."

"It sounds as though you knew her quite well."

"She was forty and I was twenty, and she was wealthy and well educated and I was illiterate and poor. But she was very lonely, trapped in an unhappy marriage, and I could help her just by listening, and it didn't make my illiteracy seem so shameful. The only other woman I ever met who was as kind and as courageous as Ginny Forrester was your mother," Thomas said quietly. Then reading the silent question in his son's forest green eyes—Had his father had an affair with Julian's grandmother?—he smiled lovingly and elaborated, "Ginny and I felt a great fondness for each other—and yes, perhaps it was love—but we were worlds apart. Nothing ever happened between us, Peter."

"Did you maintain your friendship after you finished the music room?"

"No. That would have been very awkward for her. Impossible really. Shortly after your mother and I were married I heard on the radio that her husband had died. I remember thinking that she was free of him at last and I hoped that she would be able to live the rest of her life in peace at Innis Arden."

"I think that's exactly what she did, Pop." And, Peter thought, I bet she never became the dotty old bird her grandson described with such contempt. "She died about five years ago. In her will she stipulated that for twenty years following her death Innis Arden would belong to the people of Cape Cod."

"For weddings and picnics, I imagine," Thomas embellished with quiet confidence. "Ginny always believed that Innis Arden was a magical place that should be shared. She wanted to share its magic with her own family, but I don't think that either her husband or her children really ever appreciated it."

"They still don't. At least, her grandson doesn't. In fifteen years, when the estate is sold, Julian plans to buy it and convert it into a luxury resort. But, Pop, I think I'll buy it instead. I think it would be a very nice place for us to live, don't you?"

"A very nice place indeed, Peter," Thomas agreed lovingly. Thomas knew that he wouldn't be alive in fifteen years, but his eyes filled with hope as he imagined a future scene of joy. "A very nice place for my grandchildren to frolic."

Peter smiled at his father's allusion to grandchildren. Peter wanted his own family, some day, but that was a faraway dream. There were much more urgent dreams to pursue first. After a moment, he suggested, "Why don't we visit Innis Arden next weekend? Wouldn't you like to see it again?"

"Yes, Peter, I would. I would like that very much."

Ten days after Peter's first visit to Innis Arden, he discovered that Julian had paid another student to steal a copy of an exam that he was scheduled to take. Julian didn't attempt to conceal what he had done, nor did he express even a flicker of shame. He was Julian Chancellor after all, wealthy and privileged and fully entitled to have advantages over everyone else.

Peter knew it was time to confront his friend. At first, he earnestly implored Julian not to cheat simply because it was wrong to do so. And then, when it was obvious that Julian had no intention of altering his plans, Peter quietly warned that should Julian cheat, he would inform the administration of his flagrant violation of the honor code.

For several silent moments, the haughty dark eyes of the privileged heir met the solemn forest green ones of the carpenter's son. Finally, with an easy laugh, Julian relented, eventually even thanking Peter for showing him the error of his ways.

But even as he was expressing his heartfelt gratitude, Julian was plotting the destruction of the presumptuous Peter London. And Julian knew exactly how to get to Peter: through Marcy. It had been obvious for a while that Peter liked her. In fact, Julian thought with delight, whenever *he* was cruel to Marcy, it was *Peter* who seemed to suffer the most.

"I had to get away from Julian," Marcy whispered with soft despair when Peter opened his door to her timid knock at midnight. As the springtime moonlight illuminated her beautiful tear-glistening eyes, she cried, "I hate him, Peter! He's so cruel, so selfish, so . . . unlike you."

Marcy was lovely and sad and needy, and Peter was young and kind and gentle. He made love to her with tender passion, and afterward they fell asleep in each other's arms. When Peter awakened at dawn, Marcy was already dressed and getting ready to leave. She softened her abrupt goodbye with a lingering kiss and a promise to return again that night.

Within an hour of Marcy's departure, school officials hammered on Peter's door. They had received an anonymous "tip" that Peter had stolen copies of exams hidden in his room. The exams were found in his desk drawer; and there was money, too, far more than his academic scholarship had ever provided, tucked between the mattresses on the side of the bed where Marcy had slept.

Disciplinary committees were convened. They heard the testimony of Marcy, who resolutely denied the midnight visit during which she had planted the exams and money in Peter's room. And they heard Julian's testimony, his solemn admission that he had known about Peter's plan to cheat and had tried unsuccessfully to get him to change his mind; and his additional damning confession that yes, he had had a great deal of money stolen during the school year and had assumed that the thief had been Peter; and then his heartfelt wish that he had done more to help his poor troubled friend.

Two weeks before the completion of his freshman year at Harvard, Peter London was expelled.

"I'm still going to be an architect, Pop," Peter whispered hoarsely when he returned to Concord and was hugged tightly and lovingly by his father's crippled arms. "You'll see. It's too soon to try to get into another college yet. But I promise you, someday I will. I'll simply tell the truth, explain exactly what happened, and eventually I will find someone who believes me and is willing to give me another chance. In the meantime, Pop, I'm going to find work as a carpenter."

Thomas London knew that his son was neither a cheat nor a thief. But still, despite all Peter's hard work, his honesty and his talent, his dream had been stolen from him. And even though Peter promised to recapture his dream, their dream, the glow that had always lighted Thomas's aging eyes when he envisioned his son's bright future was gone . . . and almost overnight, his health began to fail.

Thomas lived less than a year after Peter's expulsion from Harvard, long enough to make many trips to Innis Arden with his son, but not long enough to see even the beginning of Peter's immense success.

Peter returned to Innis Arden three days after his father's death. It was late April, almost precisely a year since his first visit. The extraordinary meadow was in bountiful and fragrant bloom, having somehow triumphantly survived the icy cruelty of a most harsh winter. The delicate flowers had survived against all odds, defiant and brave in the face of all hardships, and now they reached joyfully for the golden sun.

In the enchanted meadow where all things were possible—all dreams, all promises, all hope—Peter inhaled the perfume of a thousand valiant flowers and whispered, "I will become an architect, Pop, and I will buy this magical place. I will never allow Julian to destroy this heaven. He has already destroyed so much." A rush of white hot rage swept through him, blurring the vivid colors of the meadow; but the shimmering heat did not blur in the least his determined vision of the future. "I promise, Pop. I *promise*."

It took several years and countless rejections but finally Peter was able to convince a small midwestern college to give him another chance. Within five years of his graduation, he was regarded as one of his alma mater's most distinguished graduates. From the very beginning of his career in architecture, Peter worked alone, selecting only projects in which his taste, his style, and his vision would not be compromised. Peter's uncompromising vision brought him fame—and wealth, more than enough to ensure that when the time came he would be able to make a most generous offer for the estate.

Over the years, Peter traveled to Innis Arden often, one of the estate's many springtime visitors, and with each journey he became more restless for the time when it would be his—to protect and treasure always.

But what if despite his own substantial wealth the magnificent estate went to Julian? Peter might still be able to save the mansion, or at least his father's music room. The wooden structure could easily be moved to another location. But what about the meadow? Its intoxicating fragrance was a rare gift of nature, an exquisite harmony of the scented whispers of flowers and forest and sea that was absolutely unique to that magical place.

If Innis Arden became Julian's, the extraordinary fragrance would be lost forever.

I won't let that happen, Peter vowed four years before the estate was to be sold. He found the best *parfumiers* in the world and sent them to the meadow in late April with all the other visitors. There they spent days inhaling the remarkable fragrance, memorizing its many layers and delicate nuances, finally returning to their laboratories to try to reproduce the evocative blend.

After three years, the scent was finally—and perfectly—recreated.

And Peter named the magical new perfume *Promise*.

Several months before the date in August when all sealed bids for Innis Arden would be opened, Peter had his own attorney contact the attorneys who would be handling the sale. He was delighted, but not surprised, to learn that the attorneys also represented the beneficiaries of the sale—Virginia Alcott Forrester's four grandchildren, Julian Chancellor and his three cousins. Julian would surely be able to "convince" one of his attorneys to "preview" the other sealed bids so that the bid he himself submitted would win—assuming Julian even cared about Innis Arden any longer.

It didn't matter to Peter whether or not Julian still cared about owning the estate. Peter's own reason for wanting the magnificent property had everything to do with dreams and promises . . . and nothing whatsoever to do with revenge.

Peter submitted a sealed bid in June. The amount he offered was well above the appraised value, much higher, he guessed, than any other interested parties, except Julian, would be willing to go. According to the rules of the auction, all sealed bids were to be received in the Manhattan office of the estate attorneys by noon on Wednesday August fourteenth. At eleven-forty-five on that August morning, Peter and his attorney personally delivered a new bid—an offer two hundred thousand dollars higher than Peter's previous one—and they remained in the office while all the bids were opened.

Peter's new bid was the highest. The next closest belonged to Julian and was an offer just ten thousand dollars above Peter's original bid. Proof positive, Peter decided, that Julian had cheated—or at least had tried to. Peter's own clever yet honest tactics had tricked Julian's dishonest ones—and honesty and Peter had triumphed.

Innis Arden was his. Peter celebrated the fulfillment of the solemn vow he had made by spending the hot August afternoon looking through photographs at both the Eileen Ford and Elite Modeling agencies. He was hoping to find a model for *Promise*. She had to be as extraordinary as the fragrance itself, delicate yet courageous, fragile yet valiant, hopeful against all odds. Peter knew that he might never find such a woman. He was resigned to that possibility and was fully prepared to market the perfume simply with the beautiful photographs of the meadow which he had had taken over the past four years.

At one A.M. on the humid August night that Innis Arden became his, Peter stood on the balcony of his suite at the Plaza remembering his first visit to the estate. "Innis Arden will be mine," Julian had confidently announced on that long-ago day.

What was Julian's reaction to his loss today? Peter wondered. He had bid on the property, and had even cheated to win, but Julian Chancellor had a vast real estate empire now. Did he really care whether Innis Arden was part of it? Or was the businessman in him quite content with his share of the profit from the sale?

Julian's reaction didn't matter, Peter reminded himself. It was just idle curiosity on his part.

But the truth was that had Peter known Julian's reaction and its consequences, it would have mattered to him very much. Because at the precise moment when Peter was idly wondering about that reaction, just a few blocks away his ancient enemy was savagely venting his immense rage at Peter's victory on his bewildered and terrified wife.

Julian's wife . . .

From the moment he had first seen the lovely woman with fire-caressed golden hair and vulnerable bright blue eyes, Peter's heart had raced with a sense of discovery. And when her delicate fingers had moved the tiny doll of the daughter to be beside her mother, he had known with absolute certainty that at last the extraordinary woman for whom he had been searching had been found. She knew about the promises of love. She would understand the meaning of *Promise*, the valiant hopefulness of flowers that survived the bleakest of winters to reach for the golden springtime sun . . . and the courage of human hearts to dream even when all the dreams had been shattered.

Peter had flown to Tokyo the morning after the Fairmont ball. During the past nine days, he had eagerly anticipated his return to San Francisco and the call he would make to Stephen Sheridan to learn the name of the lovely trauma surgeon. Now he had just returned, and hadn't yet called Stephen, and in the checkout line at the Marina Grocery in Sausalito he had learned her name himself: *Larisa Chancellor*.

According to *People*, Larisa would soon be the very wealthy ex-wife of the man who had once shattered Peter's dreams. But, the article asserted, despite the fortune that would be hers—a generous parting gift from the husband who no longer wanted her—Larisa had thoughts of perhaps resuming her modeling career.

Peter wanted the woman he had met at the Fairmont to be the model for *Promise*. But she was Larisa Chancellor. And, his mind warned, once before Julian had sent a beautiful and vulnerable woman to destroy his dreams.

It seemed impossible that Larisa had been at the ball to meet him. And yet, why had she been there? And why had she lied about who she was when she had known full well that in a matter of days the truth would appear on the cover of *People*? Had it all been a devious game orchestrated by Julian to bewitch, to intrigue, to seduce . . . and ultimately to destroy?

It seemed impossible.

And Peter needed her for *Promise*.

Which meant he would simply have to find out.

CHAPTER NINETEEN

*L*arisa stood at the living-room window of Elizabeth's apartment and gazed at the splendor of the autumn twilight. The brilliant blue sky had faded to pale pink, a soft pastel backdrop for a herd of plump lazy clouds that were bright white against the pale pink and haloed by a shimmering gold farewell kiss from the departing sun.

So beautiful, Larisa thought. And so peaceful.

Even as she was reflecting on the peacefulness, the tranquility was disrupted by the shrill wail of a nearby ambulance. Others might have heard the sirens as harbingers of tragedy, but neither Larisa's soft smile nor her sense of peace wavered at the strident sound. In the past few weeks, the frequent sirens had become symbols of safety and protection, comforting reminders that there were people out there, very close by, who were ready at all times to do battle with trauma and dedicated to doing whatever was humanly possible to conquer it. To Larisa the sirens had become symbols of Elizabeth . . . and like Elizabeth they were friends.

The sirens stopped abruptly, a silent signal that the ambulance had reached the medical center's emergency room. Almost immediately, a new strident sound filled the living room: the ringing telephone. Had she not just heard the siren, Larisa would have assumed that the caller would be Elizabeth.

It will be Elizabeth anyway, she decided as she walked toward the phone. Not all sirens signaled trauma, after all. Some signaled joy. Perhaps this ambulance had carried a soon-to-be new mother . . .

But the caller wasn't Elizabeth, and when Larisa heard his voice there was no more peace.

"Hello, Larisa."

No! her mind screamed, its silent scream more shrill and forboding than a thousand sirens, but in its silence totally futile. No trauma experts would be summoned to rescue her. She would be forced to endure this trauma alone. *You promised that if I gave you my phone number you wouldn't call for at least a month. It's only been ten days!*

"Julian," she answered finally.

"I know I said I wouldn't call for a while, but I haven't received any bills from you and I wanted to be certain that you understand that I expect to pay all your expenses."

"I do understand that."

"I know you took almost forty-four hundred dollars with you, but I would imagine that by now you're running a little low."

Almost forty-four hundred dollars. Did Julian know the exact amount she had taken? He had always acted so casual about the money in the penthouse, such a trivial amount for a man with his wealth. But, Larisa realized with an icy shiver, he had probably always known exactly how much she had taken—and when.

Julian's voice had shattered her fragile peace, and now his words sent the harsh and unnecessary reminder that she had almost depleted the money she had taken. The motel at JFK, the last-minute full-fare plane ticket to San Francisco, the bottles of iron and vitamins, the lovely dress she and Christine had selected for the lunch and photograph in New York . . . Soon, very soon, she would either have to accept Julian's support or find a way to support herself. Not that there was a choice: she would find a way to support herself. She had already decided that next week, when someone else's face was on the cover of *People*, she would begin the search. She had even thought about approaching Sydney regarding a job—as an assistant to Christine, perhaps?

"Don't you need money, Larisa?"

"No."

"All right," Julian said softly. "I understand. You want nothing from me, nothing to do with me. How can I blame you? But, darling, I want you to know this: I miss you and our love, and I'm spending every second of my life trying to face my flaws and correct them. Do you miss me at all, Larisa? Not the monster I became, but the man who fell in love with you?"

Are those really two different men, Julian? she wondered. Didn't the monster simply clothe himself in gentleness to seduce me into betraying every promise I had ever made to myself?

"Larisa?"

"I have to go, Julian."

"Okay," Julian agreed quietly, forcing subdued resignation in his voice despite the elation he felt at the fear he heard in hers. She was still very afraid of him and the power he had over her. Good, he thought. *Wonderful.* He added gently, "I understand. I'm sorry. I love you, Larisa. Goodbye."

* * *

What an illusion it had been to have believed she was actually getting stronger! What folly to have marveled at the peaceful sunset and imagined that such peace could ever be hers! Julian's voice had opened the floodgates of her pain, mercilessly drowning her foolish illusions in the brutal truth. She had not been loved. She had been only possessed and conquered and betrayed.

Larisa struggled to fight the gushing river of pain that flowed from her heart, to will it away with the magnificent sunset and memories of comforting sirens and promises she had made to herself about how much better everything would be to-morrow. But the sun was gone now. The pink and gold had faded to gray and the once plump and happy white clouds had been stretched into gaunt black lines, shredded like cotton candy torn apart by too greedy fingers.

The clouds were gone, and the comforting sirens were silent, and as the river of pain threatened to drown her, Larisa could not even imagine a tomorrow.

She needed to subdue the ever-rising waters, just a little, please. But she simply wasn't strong enough. She needed help. An army of trauma specialists, or . . .

A little alcohol? Yes, that would do nicely. If she could just escape for a while, just float far above the gushing river like a fleecy cloud. Larisa knew the eventual fate of that cloud, of course, but she needed to float now anyway, to bask for a moment in sun-kissed gold.

As she walked into the kitchen, it suddenly occurred to her that there might be no alcohol in Elizabeth's apartment. Oh, but surely there was! *There had to be.* A small supply for guests at least.

As her frantic search took her from one cupboard to the next without results, Larisa realized that she might actually have to leave the apartment to find a drink. Thanks to *People* and all the tabloids she would very likely be recognized. Well, she could smile, couldn't she, somehow, and say something clever about celebrating? Maybe, if she really had to—but was there really no alcohol here? Was this tough love from Elizabeth after all?

Just one drink, Lizzie, please. I promise I'll sip it very slowly.

Then, at last, in a cupboard above the refrigerator, Larisa found the treasure she had been so desperately seeking. The bottle of Courvoisier she had given Eliza-beth for her twenty-first birthday was there, scarcely touched, as were almost full bottles of bourbon, Scotch, and gin. Her slender fingers trembled as she hastily filled a glass with bourbon, and then the glass trembled as she raised it to her lips and took a large swallow.

And then another.

Magic, she thought, as she felt the wonderful warmth begin to fill her, a brave and able warrior in her battle against pain. The bourbon was softening the knife-sharp stabs to her badly wounded heart, blunting the effects of their violence, and in a few moments they would be all but forgotten. A smile began to curl her lips, but it stopped abruptly when she turned and looked at the kitchen. It looked like a disaster area, its drawers open and its cupboards ajar, gaping in silent and horrified testimony to her desperation.

She had been so desperate . . . in such pain . . . because of Julian. Because of Julian? a voice deep inside asked. Are you going to permit him to control you still? Are you going to betray yourself once again because of him?

But . . . you don't understand! her wounded heart cried. The pain is so great, too great. I'm not strong enough, not now, not yet.

But you have to be strong, and the strength has to begin right this minute. If you allow yourself to escape this way, even just for tonight, then Julian has won, hasn't he? *Hasn't he?*

There was no point in arguing with this voice. Larisa knew it spoke the truth. Of course, with another swallow of bourbon, or another glass, it might be muffled into silence. Or perhaps not. The voice was very strong and very determined. Did it truly come from within her? she wondered. From a tough loving place in her heart that believed in her still and trusted her still despite her own betrayals? Or was it a voice from the outside, the voice of a recent memory, a voice with dark blue eyes that seemed to understand.

What does Nicholas Chase know? the part of her that wanted to take another swallow of bourbon petulantly demanded.

"He knows a lot," Larisa whispered. He knows a lot about me, about things I don't want to face—but must.

Call me anytime, Larisa, Nick had said.

Larisa looked at the surgery call schedule posted on the corkboard beside the phone. Nick wasn't officially on call tonight, but would his pager be on anyway as Elizabeth's always was? From what Elizabeth said about him, Larisa guessed that it would be. And if not, she *could* dial the number penciled in beside his name, the unlisted home number given to Elizabeth but never used because it was too great— too bold—an invasion of Nick's privacy.

Larisa decided that she would page, but not call. If Nick didn't answer the page, then she would intrude no further.

"Daphne, the magical dragon, flew bravely toward the shimmering rainbow," Nick read quietly to his almost asleep son. Justin was on his lap, his small sleepy body curled close, Nick's lips gently caressing silky strands of golden hair as he read the bedtime story.

When Nick's pager sounded, Justin's blue eyes fluttered open, not with alarm but with interest.

"Oh, oh, Daddy. The hospital needs you."

"I guess so." Nick reached for the pager, but before looking at the lighted display himself, he showed it to his now wide-awake, very bright son. It was a fun game they always played. Justin would read his father's pager and then tell Nick who was paging him. It was far more than a game, of course. It was Nick's way of sharing with his son the hours of their lives when they were apart. Nick had never taken Justin to the hospital—his son was far too young and their life was far too private—but Nick had described it to him in great detail, and in Justin's imagination it was a happy place for his father to be. "Who needs me, Jussie?"

Justin knew by heart the telephone numbers of the places in the hospital to which Nick was most frequently paged. But the seven-digit sequence flashing on the pager now was quite unfamiliar to him.

"I don't know, Daddy," he said. "Who?"

"Well, let's see." It was a number that Nick recognized immediately, but one that Justin would never have seen. Pages to Elizabeth's home phone always came late at night, long after Justin was asleep. She would be on first call, and he would be on second call, and she would page him because she had just been notified about an incoming patient who would need them both. "It's Elizabeth."

"The nice lady doctor who works with you?"

"Yes. The nice lady doctor who works with me," Nick answered with an untroubled smile despite the fact that he was, in fact, a little concerned about the page. He had always told Elizabeth, and everyone else, to feel free to page him even when he was officially "off." Everyone else *had* always felt free—and paged him often—but Elizabeth never had . . . until now. "I'd better go call her. So, why don't I tuck you in, sleepy one?"

"Okay."

"Okay," Nick echoed softly as he lifted Justin from his lap and into the bed where Mr. Bear lay waiting. Nick tucked the billowy quilt around both boy and bear, lightly kissed Justin's cheek, and turned out the light before crossing the hallway to his own bedroom to answer Elizabeth's page.

"Larisa? This is Nick Chase. I'm answering Elizabeth's page."

"It wasn't Elizabeth's page, Nick, it was mine," Larisa confessed. "You made the mistake of telling me that if I ever needed to talk . . . but maybe this isn't a good time—"

"It wasn't a mistake, Larisa, and this is a good time," Nick assured. Then, very gently, he encouraged, "Tell me what's happening."

Larisa couldn't answer right away. She was suddenly swept with emotion, an overwhelming rush of gratitude and relief.

"Larisa?"

"Yes, I'm here." She took a soft breath. "What happened is that Julian called, and what's happening right this minute is that I'm staring at a few bottles of alcohol. So far, I've had a little bourbon, but I'm thinking about drinking all of it."

"But you don't want to. You believe that you need to, but you don't want to."

"Yes. That's right," Larisa answered quietly. "I need to, but I don't want to. I guess what I don't want most of all is to allow Julian to do this to me."

"Julian is forcing you to drink?"

"No," she admitted solemnly. "This isn't Julian's fault." *It's my fault for allowing him to do what he did, for trusting him more than I trusted myself, for being so blinded by my need to be loved that I betrayed myself in the process.* "I'm responsible. I'm to blame. Is that what I'm supposed to say?"

"Not if it isn't true."

"Well, it is true. It *is* my fault. I guess it's up to me to find a way out, huh?"

"Has the way out always been alcohol?"

"No! In fact, I rarely drank—really, almost never—before my marriage. It was always so important to me to be in control. Isn't that strange? I used to avoid alcohol for fear of losing control and now I'm turning to it." With soft bewilderment she asked, "Why am I doing that?"

"Because drinking is a kind of control. Because when you drink you can finally control the pain."

"You really do know, don't you, Nick?"

"What I know, Larisa, is that you're going to be okay."

"Really?" she countered sharply, upset that he had so swiftly rebuffed her question about him, her attempt to reach out to him as he was reaching out to her, but mostly terribly disappointed—and terribly afraid—that he had so quickly lost interest and was dismissing her by pronouncing her imminently curable when what she felt was mortally wounded. "That sounds awfully facile, Doctor. Awfully easy."

"It won't be easy, Larisa. I'm not implying that it will," Nick replied calmly. "But the truth is that you have a lot going for you. You don't have a lifetime pattern of drinking. You understand why you're drinking now. And, most importantly, you understand why you don't want to. Isn't that right?"

"Yes. But I hurt, Nick, I *hurt*. And what I want most of all is for the hurt to go away. How do I make that happen?"

"By trying to understand why you hurt."

"And that will magically make it go away?"

"There's no magic, Larisa. But understanding why you hurt will return to you some of the control that you've lost. It will allow you to make choices about your life. You know this. You've already told me as much. If you let the pain control you, then you will always be its victim. I seriously doubt that you are solely responsible for the pain you are feeling now, but you are—you can be—entirely responsible for how you choose to deal with it."

"Right now I want to deal with it by escaping from it. I want that desperately," she added quietly as she frowned at the gaping cupboards. "I don't want to feel this desperate . . . but I do. I can't think, or analyze, or try to understand when I feel like this. Something very powerful inside me is urging me to escape. How do I stop myself from succumbing to that urge, Nick? What do you do?"

Larisa regretted her second question the moment she asked it. This was about her, not him, and yet it was so obvious that what Nick knew—the secrets that she so desperately needed him to share with her—came from his own personal battles. For whatever reason, Nick had once been where she was now, and he had found a way to do what to her at this moment seemed quite impossible.

Larisa needed Nick's help, his expertise, his experience. But he had made it abundantly clear that he didn't want to talk about himself. And besides, she realized, she already knew how Nick found escape. Somewhere along the line, the gorgeous blue-eyed doctor had discovered that he could drown his own pain not in alcohol but in pleasure.

Nick hesitated before answering. His own situation had been so different from Larisa's. And, he thought, he had never himself followed the advice he had just given her. Oh, yes, he had explored the reasons for his own pain, and understood them perfectly, but despite that insight he had still chosen to drink. And it had been his choice to make because then he had been responsible to no one but himself.

Nick drank for himself, because he didn't care enough about himself not to, and when he had stopped drinking it had been because of the precious, wounded little boy who had needed everything he had to give. It had been so easy to stop drinking for Justin, an effortless decision of love; but it had been hard, too, because the tormenting pain hadn't abated, nor had the compelling and powerful wish to escape from it disappeared.

"I run, Larisa," he answered finally. "I run as fast as I can for as long as I can— and then a few miles farther, until I'm too exhausted to think or feel or even breathe. I'm not sure it would work for you, and I'm not recommending that you run through the streets of San Francisco in the middle of the night, but . . . ."

"I think it might work for me." Larisa's voice held a delicate whisper of hope. "I used to exercise all the time when I was modeling. After the most strenuous workouts, I remember feeling an almost blissful calm. That's a very helpful suggestion, Nick. Thank—what was that? Your pager?"

"Yes." It was a number Justin would have recognized instantly: the ICU. "I'd better answer it and call you back."

"You don't need to call me back, Nick," Larisa said bravely. "It's time for me to get to work."

"Are you sure?"

"Yes. As soon as we say goodbye, I'm going to run in place until I drop."

"Okay." Nick laughed softly, then said solemnly, "Call me anytime, Larisa."

"Thank you, Nick. You've really helped."

* * *

It sounded so easy when she was talking to Nick. His words were so wise and the calmness of his voice was so comforting. But now the lifeline was severed and she was alone in the kitchen where the open cupboards reminded her of her desperation and the bottles of liquor still stood defiantly on the counter beckoning to her. Fighting sudden panic, Larisa slowly and deliberately closed all the cupboards. Then, with a deep breath, she returned the bottles to their hiding place above the refrigerator.

There, she thought triumphantly as she washed the glass she had used. *Triumph*—except that the pain was back now in full force, screaming for relief and reminding her how terribly fragile she was. Larisa hastily dried the glass then abruptly left the kitchen for the spacious living room to exercise to exhaustion—and beyond.

She would exercise to music, she decided, as she pulled the curtains and crossed to Elizabeth's compact disk player. Although Elizabeth had made the modern transition from stereo to CD, she had not abandoned her—*their*—favorites from the past. All the oldies but goodies were there on the small shiny silver disks: the Beach Boys's sunny songs of summer, the songs of love by Streisand, the Beatles, and Patsy Cline, and the primal and energetic music of the Rolling Stones.

The Stones, Larisa decided. She selected a disk from the two-disk "Hot Rocks" collection, set the volume thoughtfully low, then moved to the center of the room and began to dance.

Dancing had always been a favorite form of exercise, but it had been a very long time since she had danced like this—or even exercised at all. The model thinness she had maintained throughout her marriage hadn't been the sleek healthy fitness of her modeling days. Instead, it had been an anxious thinness, the result of very little food and almost constant nervousness. Once her perfect body had been in perfect shape, and now? Now, quickly, so quickly, her lungs and muscles gasped with pain.

But that was good, she realized as she moved even faster. Because, just as Nick had promised, this new physical pain seemed to muffle the screams of her heart.

The phone rang midway through "Jumpin' Jack Flash." As she turned down the volume before answering, Larisa wondered if the caller would be a neighbor concerned about the noise. No, she told herself, the music wasn't loud to begin with and the apartment building was very well built.

The caller would be Elizabeth, or maybe Nick. It would *not* be Julian.

Whoever it was, she had to answer, because if it was Elizabeth and she didn't answer her friend would worry.

"Hello?"

"Larisa? It's Stephen."

"Oh . . . hi . . . Stephen."

"Hi. Are you all right? You sound a little out of breath."

"Out of shape to be exact." Larisa exhaled the words in a rush then gasped for more necessary air. "I've been exercising." Another necessary pause. "Elizabeth isn't here."

"I know. It's actually you I need to talk to. So why don't I do the talking while you listen and catch your breath? How does that sound?"

"Good!"

"Okay. Well, I just got a call from Peter London, the architect who designed the institute. He's planning to market a new perfume this spring and is looking for a model."

"An architect . . . marketing a perfume?"

"He says it's a long story, and I haven't heard it, but I can assure you from having worked closely with him on the design for the institute, Peter will have done his homework. He will have hired the best people to help him and will have insisted on quality and excellence at every turn."

Recalling the uncompromising impression of quality that had been obvious even in the scale model of the institute, Larisa offered, "Without compromise?"

"That would be my guess. So, anyway, he's looking for a model to represent the new fragrance and read in *People* that you might be resuming your career. Apparently he saw you at the ball, and noticed you and I exchanging smiles, so he called to see if I knew how to reach you. I wasn't sure you'd want me to give him your number, but I did tell him that I'd call you and have you call him if you're interested. If not, I can call him back and tell him that."

"Interested? In what?"

"In being the model for his perfume."

Larisa's breathing was calm now, as was her voice as she countered, "I can't believe that that's what he wants, Stephen. I'm sure he just wants to know if I know of someone who would be good."

"No. I'm very certain that who he wants is you."

And I'm very certain that he doesn't, she thought. He can't. He *won't*. Still, suddenly a little breathless again, she asked, "I get the impression that you like him?"

"Very much. So, shall I give you his number?"

"Okay. Yes. Thank you."

Before dialing Peter's number, Larisa thought about the architect who was so successful that he had the money to invest in launching a new perfume, an enterprise that she knew was both terribly expensive and terribly risky. She knew the reason for Peter London's success—she had seen the model for the institute after all—but she wondered if it was truly wise for him to take time away from his sketches to devote it to a project such as this. Did the world really need a new fragrance? Had Peter somehow discovered something so unique and so special that women would abandon their own signature scents to try it? Or would it simply go the way of most new perfumes, a flurry of energy and money and then nothing because the fragrance was ultimately so forgettable that it vanished into thin air?

Well, that was Peter London's problem. And it paled in comparison to her own. Peter had apparently seen her from a distance at the Fairmont, her face softly illuminated by the gentle light of crystal chandeliers, his own vision perhaps a little blurred by champagne. And he had seen the dazzling photographs of her in *People*, a collage of her most famous magazine covers and the photograph taken at Le Cirque in which she had managed to look almost radiant.

Once Larisa Locksley had been a talented actress. Once she had been able to light her brilliant blue eyes with shimmering optimism, as if she truly believed the world was filled with endless and wonderful possibilities. But not now. True, her perfect body was model thin, and she could still curl her magnificent lips into a provocative smile, but she could no longer force a look of glowing hopefulness into her blue eyes. It had taken her two weeks to prepare herself for the all-important photograph at Le Cirque, a command performance that had taken every ounce of energy and will, and it was an effort she could neither repeat nor sustain.

Peter London would see her haunted, vulnerable blue eyes, and he would be disappointed. But, because the famous architect was a man who could make a hospital a warm and welcoming place for its sick and needy visitors, he would conceal his disappointment and tell her with gentle tact that her "look," although sensational, wasn't quite right for his fragrance after all.

Unless . . . what if Julian was behind this? Peter was a gifted architect and Julian owned an empire of buildings. Larisa had never heard Julian mention Peter's name, nor if the new institute was any indication had Peter ever designed anything for Julian. But surely they knew each other.

Julian Chancellor had never commissioned Peter London to design a building, but had he hired him now to approach Larisa with the tantalizing possibility of a wonderful job? She wouldn't get the job, of course. On Julian's instruction, Peter would tactfully—or not so tactfully—reject her; and it would be Julian who was mocking her foolishness for even thinking about modeling again, shattering what little was left of her confidence in hopes of manipulating her into accepting his support after all.

Was Peter London friend or foe? Larisa wondered. Stephen obviously liked and respected Peter, which was an endorsement as strong as an endorsement from Elizabeth would have been, but . . .

Larisa sighed softly and promised herself that as soon as the call was over, no matter the outcome, she would dance again to exhaustion—and beyond.

"Mr. London? This is Larisa Locksley." Locksley, not Chancellor. She gave her maiden name advisedly. If Peter were in Julian's employ, it might cause a few beats of guilty silence.

"Hello, Larisa," Peter replied swiftly, without even the slightest pause, his voice as warm and welcoming as the hospital he designed had been. "It's Peter and thank you for returning my call. Did Stephen explain why I wanted to speak to you?"

"Something about a new perfume that you're planning to market."

"That's right. I'm looking for a model and read in this week's *People* that you might be resuming your modeling career. I wondered if we could meet to discuss the possibility of your appearing in the ads for the perfume."

"All right," she agreed cautiously.

"Good. When would be convenient for you?"

"I'm really quite free." Free? The word twisted and twirled in Larisa's mind. Free? Isn't the truth that you are completely trapped in a prison of memory and pain? She repeated quietly, "Quite free."

"Well, then, how about tomorrow? My architectural offices are in Union Square, but everything having to do with the fragrance is in my condominium in Sausalito."

Your condominium? Larisa echoed silently. An architect launching a new perfume was implausible enough, but to orchestrate that multimillion-dollar endeavor from a condominium? Still . . . Peter had Stephen's endorsement, and tomorrow would be a glorious day to drive across the bridge, and she had always loved Sausalito.

"Why don't we meet in Sausalito?" she suggested.

"Great. Shall I send a limousine for you and plan to have lunch here?"

"No . . . thank you . . . to both. I'll drive myself and there's really no need for you to feed me . . ."

After the conversation ended, Peter smiled softly as he thought about her. He had heard in her voice tonight the intriguing blend of courage and vulnerability that had enchanted him at the ball, the extraordinary combination of delicacy and strength that reminded him of the proud defiant flowers in the meadow at Innis Arden. Peter's smile faded as he thought about the trap he had laid for her by not telling her that they had already met. But it was necessary. He needed to know if she was genuinely surprised to see him . . . or if the surprise was feigned, because she had known who he was all along—because she had been sent by Julian to destroy his dreams.

Peter hoped, how he hoped, that Larisa would be genuinely surprised that it was he.

After the conversation ended, Larisa smiled softly as she allowed herself to indulge in the wonderful fantasy of modeling again. The fantasy was brief, as was the smile. Even if Peter London's interest in her was completely legitimate, he would be disappointed when he saw her and her tell-tale blue eyes at close range. And if Peter was working for Julian? The outcome would be the same. He would tell her that she wasn't right after all. At least she would be able to escape quickly, without lingering over an awkward lunch.

But what if it was a trap? What if Julian was waiting in the condominium for her?

The terrifying questions transported Larisa's mind instantly to the beckoning bottles of alcohol in the kitchen, and for three impulsive footsteps, her trembling body followed. But somehow she willed her mutinous feet to stop, and then to turn toward the disk player . . . and in moments she was dancing a breathless dance to "Satisfaction."

CHAPTER TWENTY

"Doctor Chase just called," Elizabeth's secretary announced when she returned to her office from the clinic. "I told him that I expected you back any minute."

"He wants me to call him?"

"Actually, he wants to see you. He'll be in his office for the next hour."

"Okay. I guess I'll go there now then."

"He said he could come here."

"No. That's all right. I'll go there."

Walking the one flight of stairs and three long corridors of linoleum that separated her office from Nick's was far better than anxiously waiting in her office for him to arrive. The walk gave her something to do, a chance to try to release a little of the nervous energy that pulsed through her. "Actually, he wants to see you," her secretary had said. Why would Nick need to *see* her? What couldn't simply be discussed over the phone?

Elizabeth knew at least one possible answer to that question—what had happened between them in the surgery lounge the day Danny had died. She had imagined their discussion about that morning a hundred times, a thousand. As she had rehearsed what she would say to him, Elizabeth had made the uneasy discovery that her own script changed with each rehearsal, sometimes indignant, sometimes apologetic. And as the days had become weeks, and it had become increasingly obvious she and Nick weren't ever going to discuss that morning at all, Elizabeth decided it was for the best.

Five weeks had passed, and in those weeks there had been other lives that she and Nick had fought to save—and some they could and some they could not; and they had operated in perfect wordless harmony as always; and as always Nick had been very polite yet very distant.

But now, after all this time, had Nick decided that they needed to discuss that morning after all? Would that discussion be a preamble to a discussion of what was so painfully apparent, that they simply didn't click and never would? Would he ask her if she had ever thought of finding a position elsewhere? Or would he be more subtle, casually mentioning a wonderful job he had just heard about and even graciously offering to call and recommend her?

"Hi."

"Oh, Elizabeth," Nick answered, standing up from his desk. "Hi."

"Jane said you wanted to see me?"

"Yes." Nick frowned. "I told her I could come to you."

"I know. I felt like walking." *I still feel like walking . . . running . . . because oh how I don't want to hear you politely suggest that I leave.*

Elizabeth didn't run. She simply stiffened, steeling herself as Nick left his desk and walked toward her, a neatly typed letter held in his hand. Was it from a colleague, somewhere on the East Coast, desperately seeking a surgeon uniquely trained in both trauma and transplantation?

Nick stopped in front of her, a polite distance away, and into the all-important space between them he extended the strong, lean, talented hand that held the letter. Elizabeth took the letter, but she didn't even glance at it. Instead her proud emerald eyes bravely sent a defiant message to his dark blue ones, *You tell me what it says, Nick.*

What's wrong, Elizabeth? he wondered as he gazed at her magnificent, yet almost fearful, green eyes. Whatever it was, the lingering silence seemed only to aggravate it, so he spoke.

"That arrived yesterday afternoon. It's an invitation to the International Congress on Transplantation Surgery that will be held in Paris in February. The planning committee for the congress wants the keynote address to be on living donor liver transplantation, and they also would like state-of-the-art presentations on both immunotherapy and renal transplantation. They asked me to give the keynote, and Stephen has agreed to do the immunotherapy talk, but I wondered if you would like to give the presentation on renal transplantation?" Nick stopped, was stopped, by a sudden and wonderful transformation. Elizabeth's fear was gone, replaced by soft surprise and luminous joy, and for a wonderful moment he was lost in the joyous radiance—lost, with no desire ever to be found. But, he reminded himself firmly, he had no right whatsoever to share her loveliness, even though she seemed to be offering it with such warmth and welcome. "You would need to review the literature, of course, as well as our experience here. It's a lot of work, but probably fairly interesting, and I think the congress itself is worth attending. They'll pay all expenses plus honorarium, of course."

Nick stopped speaking, and now it was her turn, but all that swirled in Elizabeth's swirling mind were completely unaskable questions. *You really want me to do this, Nick? You're really comfortable having me represent you and your transplant program at this prestigious meeting?*

Those questions were very important, and quite unaskable, but they paled by comparison to the question that made concentration almost impossible: *What were you thinking, Nick, when you paused to look at me? There was such softness in your eyes . . . it looked like tenderness . . . and for a wonderful moment I thought I saw longing too . . . and even dark blue desire.*

The look was gone now, the blue cool and polite as always as Nick waited patiently for her to speak.

"You said the meeting is in February?" she murmured finally.

"Yes. It begins with the keynote address on the evening of the sixteenth. That's a Sunday. The meeting itself will run until noon on Thursday the twentieth. I plan to return as soon as the meeting is over, but if you would like to spend additional time in Europe, I'd be happy to cover the service. Stephen is hoping to stay longer, to visit some of the major immunology centers, and I thought I overheard you say that your parents are on sabbatical in England."

"They are. I'll be visiting with them at Christmas, but it would be very nice to have a chance to see them again in February."

"Does that mean that you'd like to go to Paris? You don't need to give me an answer right now, of course, but I probably should let the planning committee know by early next week."

"I can give you my answer now, Nick." *I can easily give you the answer to your question . . . but how I wish I could know your answers to mine.* "I'd love to go to Paris. Thank you."

It was a glorious autumn day. Larisa wanted to feel the warm caresses of the breeze off the bay, so before beginning the drive across the Golden Gate Bridge to Sausalito, she rolled down all the windows of Elizabeth's car. She would repair her hair when she reached Sausalito, or maybe she would simply leave the magnificent golden red mane tangled and wind-tossed. That was the California girl look, after all, fresh and natural. Perhaps it was just the right look for what she assumed would be Peter London's fresh and breezy new fragrance.

The instructions Peter had given her guided her unerringly to a condominium building adjacent to the marina. After she parked, Larisa stood for a moment and simply admired the extraordinarily beautiful building. Obviously a Peter London creation, she decided—a triumph of grace and elegance and quality and style.

Everything she wasn't.

Peter's unit was the penthouse. Before entering the private elevator that would carry her there, Larisa looked at her reflection in one of the foyer's many mirrors. Her slender body and the wind-swirled golden red silk looked good, maybe even alluring. Perhaps, for his California girl fragrance, Peter London could be convinced to permit her to wear sunglasses to conceal her haunted and vulnerable blue eyes?

Wishful thinking!

Larisa sighed, pressed the button for the private elevator, and when it opened to more mirrors in the penthouse foyer, she walked to the door and rang the doorbell without so much as glancing at her reflection.

"Hello, Larisa."

"Oh," she whispered as she realized who he was. His forest green eyes were as dangerously inviting in the bright light of day as they had been in the glow of a crystal chandelier, and the very handsome man with hair the color of midnight shadows was as compellingly seductive and elegant dressed casually as he had been in a silk tuxedo. "You."

"Me," Peter confessed, immensely relieved to see surprise that was so obviously genuine. But Larisa's surprise lasted only a few seconds. Then it was replaced not with indignation, as it might well have been, but with sudden apprehension.

"I guess I shouldn't have pretended to be a trauma surgeon," Larisa offered quietly. "It wasn't a very plausible disguise, was it?"

"Yes, it was," Peter assured swiftly. "I was completely convinced. You certainly seemed to know what you were talking about."

"Well, my best friend is the real trauma surgeon."

"I see." Peter smiled his gentle and sexy half smile. "So, please come in. It's cluttered but . . . there's method in the madness."

Peter's penthouse was cluttered, but it was the energetic clutter of creative passion, not the careless consequence of indifferent laziness. Sketches were strewn everywhere, hastily scribbled memos of sudden inspiration, beautiful designs that one day might be given elegant and graceful life; and there were stacks and stacks of blueprints; and small models of buildings in progress; and framed and yet-to-be framed portraits of works of art that had already been built.

Peter's spectacular bay-view penthouse was so very different from the spectacular Fifth Avenue penthouse where Larisa and Julian Chancellor had lived. Julian had always been absolutely intolerant of clutter. Their impeccably designed surroundings had been lavish and luxurious, but nothing was ever moved even a millimeter from where it had been placed by the interior designer, and there was never any dust, not even a speck.

The stylish and inflexible sterility that Julian had insisted on in their home—in their life—was another reason that Larisa had stopped mourning her own sterility. How tolerant would Julian have been of the playful clutter of children? Not tolerant at all.

Unlike Peter, Larisa found herself thinking, quite unaware of the soft smile that touched her lips at the thought. For now it was obvious that Peter's buildings were his children, but it was somehow both very easy and very wonderful to imagine him with real little lives. He would so joyfully welcome their exuberant clutter. And, she decided with absolute confidence, he would proudly and lovingly display every finger painting and crayon drawing their small hands ever created.

"What are you thinking?" Peter asked gently, wanting very much to know what invisible image had touched her lips with such lovely happiness and had lighted her luminous blue eyes with a glow from very deep within.

"What? Oh," she murmured, "I guess I was thinking that I like the clutter."

"So do I."

The living room where they stood was brightly lighted by the golden autumn sunshine that smiled from outside. After a moment, Larisa looked directly at him, bravely raising her eyes to his, boldly providing him with the disappointing proof of too much unhappiness and too much betrayal. Larisa let her eyes be fully exposed, hiding nothing, not even trying to—because suddenly she wanted to get it over with. She wanted to put an end to the teasing fantasy that she could be even a tiny part of the wonderful creativity and passion that surrounded her.

Peter answered her direct gaze with a welcoming smile. Finally he said, "I really hope you're going to want to be the model for *Promise*."

"*Promise?*" Larisa echoed.

He teased gently, "You were expecting something more like California Dreamin' or Glitter Baby or Star?"

"I guess I was. But I like *Promise*." *I like the way your voice and eyes soften when you say it.*

Peter had planned to simply talk to her for a while, to make certain that his memory of her hadn't been playing tricks, but he already knew that it hadn't and he was very anxious to learn the answers to the all-important questions. Would Larisa like the fragrance? Would she understand it and believe in it as he did?

"Shall we see if you really do like *Promise?*" he asked as he removed a small glass vial from his shirt pocket and handed it to her.

Larisa's delicate fingers fumbled slightly with the glass stopper, but in moments she had it out and touched it to her wrists.

"Oh," she whispered as she inhaled the remarkable fragrance. "Oh, Peter, it's lovely."

Lovely and romantic and hopeful, she thought. Wonderful things that have nothing to do with me. I will buy this extraordinary perfume, and I will feel more hopeful just by wearing it, but I would be very wrong as its model. So very wrong, she thought as she lifted her eyes to meet the steady gaze of the man who didn't seem to share that knowledge—and should have, unless . . .

How much is Julian paying you, Peter? she wondered with a silent scream of pain. How many resorts has he promised you to look this wonderfully—and so convincingly—happy that I love *Promise*?

"Julian is behind this, isn't he?" she demanded accusingly.

"Julian?" Peter seemed genuinely startled by her accusation, startled not guilty, but there was something else, a deep dark shadow that Larisa couldn't interpret. "No. He is not."

"But you do know him."

"I knew him very briefly, fifteen years ago, when we were both freshmen at Harvard." Peter watched her reaction as intently as she watched his. Either she was a sensational actress or she knew absolutely nothing about the past history of Julian Chancellor and Peter London. Not that Julian should have shared that history with his wife. From Julian's standpoint it had all been quite trivial, another enemy conquered and forgotten. It had not been Julian's dreams, after all, that had been so cruelly destroyed. "I haven't spoken to Julian since college. And I assure you, Larisa, he had nothing to do with my decision to ask you to be the model for *Promise*."

"Then I don't understand why you want me," she murmured almost to herself. Then, as she found another possible reason, a thoughtful frown touched her lovely face. "Julian may not be behind it, but it's because of him, isn't it? Because I was his wife and that would attract attention?"

"No." *The fact that you were Julian's wife was a huge deterrent.* "Ever since the ball, I've been planning to call you to see if I could lure you from the OR long enough for a few photo sessions. The reason I want you to be the model for *Promise*, Larisa, is because of you."

"Old and withered *moi?*" she asked softly, disbelieving despite his smiling yet so serious gaze.

"Old and withered you, yes. You're mature, Larisa, and that's important, because this is a mature fragrance, don't you think? To me, *Promise* isn't wide-eyed and naive. It's a little wiser than that, fully aware of life's struggles and setbacks yet optimistic and hopeful still."

"Yes," Larisa agreed, that was *Promise*. But that wasn't her. Oh yes, she was very aware of life's struggles and setbacks. But couldn't Peter see that she was filled only with hopelessness and fear?

"I think you like the fragrance," Peter said. Then, seeing her confusion, he offered gently, "But you seem uncertain about something."

"You really think I'm the right model for *Promise?*"

"I know that you are."

She gave a bewildered shake of the golden silk that was kissed always by its own dazzling red fire but now glittered too with the fiery caresses of the autumn sun.

"I *know* that you are," Peter repeated with soft urgency, needing her for *Promise*, but needing even more that she not vanish from his life. "Do you have an agent I should call?"

"No."

"Well, then, shall we just talk about the terms of the contract right here and now?"

Larisa wanted so much to believe in whatever it was that the seductive dark green eyes saw in her, and she wanted so much, too, to accept the wonderful invitation to share with him the passion he obviously felt for his extraordinary fragrance.

"All right," she answered bravely, disbelieving still but unable—no, unwilling—to say no to either Peter or *Promise*.

"Good." Gesturing to a nearby chair, Peter suggested, "Why don't you make yourself comfortable and tell me what terms are important to you?"

"Okay." After they were both seated, she began haltingly, "Well . . . I'd like to be Larisa Locksley—not Larisa Chancellor."

"Done. I told you: I want you for you. So, Larisa Locksley, what else would you like?"

"Stephen said that you're planning to release *Promise* sometime next spring?"

"The last week of April."

"So, you will begin to run the print ads when?"

"That week." Peter guessed gently, "You'd like as much time as possible to elapse between the cover of *People* and your next appearance in a national magazine?"

"If you don't mind."

"I don't mind at all. At the risk of repeating myself, I want you for you. I'm quite happy to keep your participation entirely under wraps until that week if that's what you'd like."

"Yes." *Because if Julian doesn't know, then he can't interfere*. "Please."

"You got it." Peter smiled. "What else?"

"Well . . ." There was just one more issue, one that Peter probably hadn't even thought would be of much concern to her. Based on the *People* article, he undoubtedly believed that she had just signed divorce papers that would make her one of the richest women in America. Did that mean he thought she would be willing to model for free? No, Larisa assured herself, of course not. Smiling a beautiful untroubled smile, as if the question was merely idle curiosity, she asked lightly, "Were you planning to pay me, Mr. London?"

"Indeed I was, Ms. Locksley. Let's see. From the research that I've done, it's my understanding that top models get about ten thousand dollars a day."

"Yes," Larisa agreed bravely, even as she steeled her heart for the next words he would surely say: "Of course, you're not exactly a top model these days." She knew that somehow Peter London would find a gentle way to say the words; but she knew, too, that they had to be said. The truth was the truth, after all, and business was business.

"Is that okay?" Peter asked finally. "Is ten thousand a day all right with you?"

As Larisa realized that Peter wasn't going to say that of course she was no longer a top model, her carefully steeled heart began to race with disbelieving gratitude.

"Larisa?"

"Yes, that's fine," she answered finally, her voice astonishingly calm even though her mind now raced as rapidly as her heart. How many days would she need to work to free herself from Julian forever? "How many days of work did you have in mind, Peter?"

"I'm really not certain. All that I have lined up so far are the photo sessions for the print ads. They're scheduled for the third week in February." In response to Larisa's obvious surprise that the sessions had been scheduled so far in advance, Peter explained, "Even though I wasn't sure I'd ever find a model who was right for *Promise*, I knew that if I did I would want the photographs to be taken by Emily Rousseau Adamson. She's very eager to do them, but since she's expecting her first baby soon, we agreed on the dates in February—at her home in Los Angeles."

"Emily Rousseau Adamson?" Larisa knew the famous name, of course. She had seen the stunning celebrity portraits Emily had taken over the years, including most recently an extraordinary one of the Princess of Wales. "She's really the best."

"That's my plan for *Promise*, Larisa, only the best," Peter said quietly. Her cheeks flushed a beautiful pink at his obvious inclusion of her in that category—happy to be included, yet uncomfortable too. Rescuing her quickly, Peter returned to the issue they had been discussing. "Anyway, there will be at least five days of photo sessions for the print ads, more if we need them, and I may decide to do some television spots as well. So I guess that means somewhere between fifteen and twenty-five days of work."

"Would it be possible to agree on no less than twenty full days?"

"Sure. Does that mean that I could put you to work helping me brainstorm about marketing ideas if I can't keep you busy modeling for all twenty?"

"You can." After a moment of obvious uncertainty Larisa offered bravely, "I'd be happy to help you with the marketing ideas anyway, Peter."

"Terrific," he swiftly assured her. Smiling gently he added, "I will hold you to that, Larisa. In fact, if you have time today after we've finished our negotiating I could show you what we have so far."

"I'd like that."

"Good. So, let's finish our negotiating. Was there anything else you wanted to discuss?"

"No. That's it."

"Okay. Well, then, I have just one final detail. I'd like you to sign an exclusive agreement with me."

"What does that mean?" Larisa knew the answer of course: it meant that as nice and as wonderful as Peter London was, as different as he seemed from the men she had always attracted, he wanted to own her—as all men always had.

"It means that you would agree not to model for anyone else for the term of the contract," Peter answered, surprised by the question but mostly surprised and concerned by the sudden sharpness of her voice and the wariness of her flashing blue eyes. "I'd like to begin with a one-year agreement with an option to renew."

"Does it also mean that you have approval of my wardrobe for the entire year? And that I couldn't cut my hair or gain one single ounce?"

"No! It doesn't mean any of that. I'd like us to decide together the clothes for the ads, but what you wear the rest of the time is completely up to you. And it's your hair, and whatever length or style you prefer is fine with me, and given that you refused lunch today, I'd probably be in the position of wanting to force-feed you rather than the opposite." Peter paused, smiled gently, and said, "Here comes an understatement, Larisa: something bothers you about this. Please tell me what it is."

"It's the idea of being owned."

"Believe me, I hate the idea of being owned, too. I assure you that that is not my intention. I guess it's just that I feel that *Promise* is so unique that I want as its model someone who is uniquely associated with it." Peter paused, made the very difficult decision very quickly—because it wasn't so difficult after all—and then said, "But if it's important to you not to sign an exclusive deal, then we'll just do without it."

"No," Larisa said, having made her own difficult yet-not-so-difficult decision almost as quickly as he. "I would be very proud to be uniquely associated with *Promise*. I'd be happy to sign an exclusive contract."

"Are you sure?"

"I'm absolutely positive."

"Thank you," he said softly. "So, I'll have my attorney draw up a contract in which you will agree to model exclusively for *Promise* for a term of one year with an option to renew. It turns out that 1992 will be a leap year, so if we do a calendar year—something like October first to October first—the amount for the year would be three point six-six instead of three point six-five. Okay?"

"Three point six-six?"

"Three hundred sixty-six days at ten thousand dollars a day."

Three point six-six was three million six hundred sixty thousand dollars. He was going to pay her for every day of the year whether she worked or not. It was the kind of exclusive deal that top models signed, but . . .

"Larisa?"

"Yes, that's okay," she murmured finally. "That's fine."

"Do you have an attorney to whom I should send the contract?"

"Yes. His name is Mark Jennings. I think I may even have one of his cards in my purse. Peter, could you have your attorney put something in the contract stipulating in irrevocably etched-in-stone legalease that Mark gets ten percent of the total amount?"

"Sure." Then it was done. Larisa was going to be the model for *Promise*. "Would you like to see the marketing ideas now, Larisa? We can count this toward one of your twenty days, if you like."

"Oh, no, Peter, this one is on me. And I'd love to."

CHAPTER TWENTY-ONE

*T*he room in Peter's penthouse that housed the creative energy and passion that had been lavished on *Promise* was as large as the living room—and as cluttered. There was an invisible organization to the clutter, and Peter could have guided her on a very logical tour from concepts for marketing to sketches for the perfume bottle to backdrop photographs for the print ads; but as soon as Larisa walked into the room, she began to explore on her own, and Peter was quite willing to simply watch her make her own discoveries.

Willing . . . and anxious. Would she recognize the meadow at Innis Arden the moment she saw the photographs? he wondered. Had Julian ever shown her the magical place that he had once hoped to destroy? If he had, Larisa would surely recognize it, and then they would have to talk about Julian again, and Peter didn't want to—not yet. There had been such haunted vulnerability in her blue eyes when she had spoken Julian's name. Someday, Peter vowed, he would tell her his truths about Julian; and someday, he hoped, Larisa would share her own truths with him. But Peter hoped that it would not be today. He sensed that it was far too soon—and far too painful—for Larisa to talk yet about the husband who no longer wanted her.

Peter would know very soon whether or not Larisa recognized the meadow, because even though the photographs were on a table in the farthest corner of the room, that was where her graceful strides were taking her. She had seen the poster-sized blowups propped against the wall, and she wanted to get closer to that beauty. Peter followed, and almost immediately his worry was allayed, and he was left with the quiet joy of watching her gaze upon the magical meadow for the first time.

At first she simply looked, her blue eyes filling with astonished wonder. As she leaned down to get a closer look, a long strand of firelit golden silk fell across her beautiful face, veiling her eyes and obscuring her view. With a flicker of impatience, one slender hand captured the misbehaving strand while the other found its twin, and with deft graceful motions she knotted the two silken ropes together at the nape of her neck. Then, her eyes uncurtained once again and her hands free, her delicate fingers reached for the photograph to touch the beckoning flowers, gently, tenderly, with the trembling softness of whispered kisses.

It wasn't enough, Peter knew. Larisa wanted, needed, to get even closer to the meadow. And he wanted and needed to take her there. It was an astonishing realization because with it came a willingness to trust as he hadn't trusted for years, not since Julian; and with it came a willingness to *entrust*, to place the most important parts of himself—his heart, his secrets, and his dreams—in someone else's care.

I am very willing, Larisa, Peter thought. I am so ready and so willing. But I can see that you are wounded now, fragile and wary; and I know that it will be a while before you can allow yourself to trust again. But you can trust me, Larisa. I would never hurt you. *Trust me . . .*

Larisa turned toward him then, as if in response to the silent call of his heart, and for a wondrous moment she seemed to answer, I do trust you, Peter.

Then the hopefulness suddenly vanished, replaced by confusion, and she looked away from him, down at the photograph she held.

"Is this where *Promise* comes from?"

"Yes. It's a meadow on an estate in Cape Cod. It won't be in full bloom again until late April, so we'll use these photographs as backdrops for the pictures that will be taken of you."

"You don't need me," Larisa said quietly, her eyes still downcast, gazing at the meadow.

"Yes, I do." *Yes I do.* "Larisa?" *Look at me.*

"Yes?" she asked, finally looking up.

"Yes, I do need you."

There was another wondrous moment as the astonishing messages of his heart glimmered without shadows in his eyes—and the brilliant blue seemed to understand and to welcome the dark green invitation to share its desires and its dreams.

Then, in just a flutter of long beautiful lashes, the moment changed dramatically, her lovely blue eyes inexplicably losing their welcoming wonder and filling with sudden wariness and fear. *I do need you.* Peter's words had been spoken with such gentleness, and they had been eloquently embellished by desire, but nonetheless the words themselves had triggered in her memories of the cruel man whose need for her had been a controlling and destructive obsession.

As Peter gazed at the suddenly haunted and so fearful blue eyes, and sensed that in another moment she might simply turn and flee, his heart sent a powerful command. Don't leave, Larisa. Stay and share *Promise* with me. Stay and share all the promises and all the dreams.

Forcing reassuring calm into his voice, Peter said to the very wary woman before him, "Right now, Larisa, what I need are your thoughts about a designer for your wardrobe for the ads. I have a list of names—reputedly all top designers—but I'm not really sufficiently familiar with their styles to make an informed choice about who would be best for our needs. I imagine you've worked with all of them. Larisa?"

The worried gentleness registered first, and then the words, and as she met the gentle and worried green eyes, the reminder came: Peter London and Julian Chancellor are very different men. For whatever reason Peter believed that he needed her for *Promise,* and now he was asking for her opinion about a designer . . . and the green eyes told her quite clearly that he needed—and valued—that opinion.

"Actually, Peter, I do know someone who I think would be wonderful. Her name is Christine Andrews. She works in the city at a boutique called . . ." Larisa's mind filled with the warm, welcoming, fragrant images of Sydney's. "You designed Sydney's, didn't you?"

"Yes. That's where Christine works?"

"Yes, although she's going to be spending less time there and more time at her home designing and sewing. She's really very talented."

"So I should talk to her to see if she's interested," Peter said. Then, wanting Larisa to be as involved as possible, he asked, "Or would you like to ask her?"

"Yes," she answered with a soft smile. "I would like to very much."

"What?" Peter asked gently, wanting to know what had triggered the lovely smile.

"I actually met Christine years ago, in college. We shared the dream then that one day I would model dresses that she had designed. We talked about it when we saw each other again six weeks ago, but by then the dream seemed impossible."

"But now it's going to come true."

"Yes," Larisa answered softly. She looked at Peter for a thoughtful moment, and then, because his interested gaze was so very welcoming, she asked even more softly, "But that's what *Promise* is all about, isn't it? Impossible dreams becoming possible after all?"

"I hope so, Larisa." Peter wanted to say much more, but he had to be so careful with this lovely and wary woman. Finally he simply said, "Now that you've so easily solved the dress designer dilemma, how would you like to give me your opinion on the design for the perfume bottle? I've gotten as far as deciding to carve a single kind of flower in the crystal with its leaf as the stopper. Doing clusters of flowers didn't work—the detailing got lost—but since it is a meadow and the fragrance is a blend of many flowers, one possibility would be to have a number of different bottle designs. I guess that's what I'll do if I—you—can't decide that one flower is clearly the best." Peter gestured to a nearby overstuffed couch. "You'd better have a seat. There are sketches of every flower in the meadow, so this may take a little time."

Before Peter handed Larisa the sketches, she told herself that she would look through the entire stack once fairly quickly, for an overview and first impressions, and then she would carefully study them one by one.

But only five sketches into the first pass, she said, "Oh, dear. I'm afraid I'm going to have to disqualify myself as a judge. I should have known this was coming. I saw them in the photographs of course."

"Them?"

"The forget-me-nots."

"I assume this thing you have about forget-me-nots is a good thing?"

"I love them. They're so delicate and hopeful."

Larisa looked up then and Peter realized that the extraordinary bright blue of her eyes was the same extraordinary bright blue of the flowers that she loved so much. Peter sensed that Larisa herself had never made the connection—and, of course, the true bond between the lovely woman and the delicate and hopeful wild-flowers was so much deeper than the magnificent color they shared. It was a communion of spirit, a valiant courage to survive, to reach bravely for the golden sunshine despite the harshest of winters and against all odds.

"So, you're hopelessly prejudiced," Peter said softly to the beautiful forget-me-not.

"Hopelessly."

"What about the sketch itself? Do you think it's good of the flowers?"

"I think it's very good. Would they look like this etched into crystal?"

"Exactly like that." They *will* look exactly like that, Peter amended silently. The decision had been made. Forget-me-nots it would be.

When Elizabeth returned to her apartment at eleven that evening, she was greeted by a radiant Larisa and a glass-stoppered vial of perfume.

"Oh, Larisa," she whispered as soon as she inhaled the fragrance. "This is wonderful."

"Isn't it? It's called *Promise*, and for some completely unknown reason, Peter wants me to be its model—its spokesmodel, actually, because there may be television commercials in addition to the print ads."

"I can't imagine why he would want you," Elizabeth teased gently, then added with solemn candor, "I think you'll be wonderful, Lara."

"I hope so."

"I know so," Elizabeth said emphatically, her confident gaze holding her friend's not-so-confident one until Larisa answered with a brave smile.

"Thanks. Well, anyway, we'll know in April, when *Promise*—and the ads—are revealed." She tilted her golden red head thoughtfully and added quietly, "Peter has agreed to keep my role under wraps until then."

"Because of Julian."

"Yes, although I didn't specifically tell Peter that that was the reason. But it is, of course. If Julian doesn't know, then he can't interfere." Larisa shrugged. "Maybe it's not fair to think that he would interfere, but—"

"But this is yours, Lara, not Julian's," Elizabeth interjected firmly. "What you do is no longer any of his concern. So, tell me more."

"Well . . . I'm pretty sure that Christine is going to design the dresses that I'll wear in the ads. I called her earlier this evening and we're having lunch together tomorrow to talk it over." Larisa hesitated briefly, then added, "After which, I'm going to start looking for an apartment and a car."

"Whoa! You already have an apartment and a car. The drive you made to Sausalito today was the first real exercise—not counting short trips to Sydney's—that my car has had in weeks." Elizabeth's emerald eyes sparkled merrily as she embellished, "I really feel quite guilty that I don't let it out more often—to stretch its little wheels. And, speaking of guilt, I feel even guiltier about the second bedroom. Until you arrived, it had been ignored completely."

"But, Liz, don't you think I've imposed long enough?"

"If it had been an imposition to have you here, then I suppose it would have been long enough. But I love having you here, Lara. Please don't move out because of me. Move out because you want to, because you need more privacy or fewer sirens—you don't need to give me a reason—just don't move out because you think it's what I want."

Larisa didn't want to move out. The sirens had become her friends, and as for privacy . . . because of Elizabeth's busy schedule she really had more than enough privacy in which to wage her desperate battle against the painful memories. Absolute solitude would be an even greater test of her emotional strength, of course, but why test something she already knew was so fragile and precarious? It would be so wonderful to stay here, in the bedroom she would decorate with the photographs Peter had given her of the meadow, her own small safe world filled with *Promise*.

"But what about your privacy, Lizzie?"

"I promise I'll let you know if it begins to feel even the least bit invaded."

"Well, then, I'd love to stay—assuming you'll let me pay my half of everything."

"Whatever!"

"Okay."

"*Okay.*"

It was more than okay with both of them, and they told each other that with smiling eyes.

"I do think I'll buy a car though," Larisa said finally. "Exercise is one thing, but miles are another, and I may be doing a lot of driving back and forth to Sausalito. Peter says he would like me to attend the marketing meetings."

"I know Stephen likes Peter very much," Elizabeth said. "It sounds as though you do, too?"

"Yes. He's very nice." Nice, she mused with silent amazement. Nice men had always been attracted to Elizabeth, not to her. *Wait a minute! You think that the very nice, and very sexy, and very talented, and very wonderful Peter London is actually attracted to you?* a skeptical voice demanded. Well, no, I mean, he wants me to model for his fragrance. *For some unknown reason.* Yes, but, I thought, I wondered, it seemed to me that when he looked at me there was something more in his forest green eyes. *An invitation to join him in the lovely dark woods?* the voice taunted. *Dream on!*

"Speaking of nice," Elizabeth began.

"Yes?" Larisa encouraged swiftly, relieved to extricate herself from her own uncomfortable internal dialogue. "Speaking of nice?"

"Well, today that basically nice—not deeply flawed—Nicholas Chase asked me to give an important scientific presentation at a very prestigious meeting in Paris in February." Elizabeth shrugged softly. "I'm interpreting it as a vote of confidence."

"I'm sure that's the right interpretation, Liz." Just like I'm sure, too, that Nicholas Chase *is* nice—and deeply flawed. Not that even Nick's deepest flaws would deter lovely and generous Elizabeth. "Will Nick be going to romantic Paris, too?"

"He's giving the keynote address." Elizabeth smiled at her friend and admonished fondly, "Let's not get carried away, Lara."

As she lay in the darkness in the bedroom in which tomorrow she would hang the photographs of the magical meadow, Larisa thought about the three young women who had all been freshmen at Berkeley twelve years before. As her thoughts drifted to that distant time and its limitless dreams, Larisa felt whispers of hopefulness trying to find a home amid the raw wounds of her heart. There was a place there already for the girl whose emerald eyes had envisioned a wonderful dream of becoming a doctor—and of falling in love; and there was a place there too for the lavender-eyed girl who had shyly confessed her dream of becoming a designer.

Larisa felt great hope for the dreams of Elizabeth and Christine.

And what about for herself? Was there any hope for a happy ending to her own loveless and lonely life?

Maybe, Larisa thought bravely. Because, after all, making impossible dreams become possible was what *Promise* was all about.

PART FOUR

CHAPTER TWENTY-TWO

"*H*ere are the sketches I've done so far."

"Oh, Christine," Larisa whispered. "These are wonderful, so hopeful and romantic. I think they're just perfect and I know Peter will think so, too. In fact, why don't we show them to him right now? I'm pretty sure he's at his Union Square office all day today."

"You go, Larisa." Christine smiled. "As you can see from the stacks of fabric and sketches strewn all over the house, I have a few projects to do."

Christine's lavender eyes smiled, and she seemed so much more happy and serene than she had when Larisa had first seen her again in August, but still Larisa asked, "Is it all right that you're doing the dresses for *Promise*, Christine? You're not already overburdened, are you?"

"I'm fine! Overcommitted perhaps, but certainly not overburdened." Christine gestured to a stack of red and green felt, quite out of place amid the silks and satins that would eventually be transformed into elegant evening gowns. "I still have a few dresses to finish before the Christmas balls but at the moment my most pressing—and most important—deadline is the Christmas pageant at my local elementary school."

"How did that come about?"

"I saw a flyer for the school's Thanksgiving assembly, open to the public, and on an impulse I decided to go. I really enjoyed the assembly—the children were all so lively and excited!—but I couldn't help noticing their costumes. Pilgrims and Indians alike were all very ragged and missing such key items as hats and headdresses. The following week I met with the school principal—to offer to repair the costumes for next year—and she told me that the Christmas pageant costumes were even more worn."

"So you're recostuming the entire school?" Larisa asked with a gentle tease as she looked at the large stack of felt, the rolls of silver and gold rickrack, and the small plastic tubes filled with sequins and glitter.

"I guess it's fair to say that I'm the team leader, but I have lots of help from both mothers and teachers." Christine frowned slightly as she gazed at the unmade costumes. "Anyway, the pageant is on the twenty-first, a week from this Saturday, but the dress rehearsal is scheduled for the eighteenth. So, as you can see, I have my work cut out for me. You take the sketches to show Peter, Larisa, and I'll stay here and get to work on outfitting Santa's helpers . . ."

Christine Andrews was much better than she had been on that day in August. And, Larisa thought as she drove her car from Twin Peaks to Union Square, so am

I. So much better—because of Julian . . . and Nick . . . and Peter.

Julian's role had been passive since his phone call in September. She hadn't heard a word from him at all in the almost three months since that night, and Larisa was very grateful. Not that she needed Julian's voice to trigger memories of betrayal and pain. Those memories came anyway, sweeping through her without warning, contemptuous voices of thunder that drowned out the brave and delicate whispers of hope that came now, too, also without warning. At the most fragile moments, as she teetered on the edge of what felt almost like happiness, the memories would come crashing down on her like unwelcome waves on a sand castle, flooding her with pain—and urging her to seek escape.

But Larisa hadn't had one drop of alcohol since the night of Julian's call. She had battled the compelling urges with exercise, as Nick had suggested, and she had also found her own powerful weapon: *Promise*. At the times when she was the most raw, when every cell within her screamed for numbness and escape, she would go to her bedroom and gaze at the photographs of the magical meadow and breathe the remarkable fragrance—and the gentle and hopeful emotions evoked by the perfume would conquer the harsh and anguished ones. *Promise* was a magical potion, an invisible armor crafted by courageous flowers.

For the first few weeks following her frantic call, Nick had called quite often, always late at night, and always, Larisa realized, when he knew that Elizabeth was at the hospital. But as he had become increasingly convinced that she truly was better, not to mention very fit thanks to hours and hours of exhausting exercise, he called less often. Now it had been almost two weeks since Nick's last call, and perhaps she wouldn't hear from him again, and perhaps, Larisa thought, that was for the best. She sensed that he, like she, felt uncomfortable about the late-night conversations that took place in Elizabeth's apartment on Elizabeth's telephone . . . but so conspicuously and carefully without Elizabeth's knowledge. By unspoken agreement they had kept their "relationship" secret from Elizabeth; it was, after all, a relationship based on secrets. Larisa was strong enough now to want to share with Elizabeth her own secrets, her almost desperate need to drink and Nick's all-important role in helping her identify the problem and in dealing with it. But telling Elizabeth her story necessarily involved telling her what little she had learned about Nick—his never-discussed-again marriage and his never-discussed-at-all but obviously significant relationship with alcohol. Larisa knew that knowing Nick's secrets wouldn't change Elizabeth's feelings about him, not at all; but still, revealing them to Elizabeth would be a betrayal of Nick's trust—and Larisa owed him so much.

Larisa was better because Julian hadn't called . . . and because Nick had . . . but most of all, she was better because of Peter—and *Promise*, she amended swiftly, linking the two and firmly reminding herself that Peter's involvement with her was only because of *Promise*.

True, Peter had been wonderfully generous with her, allowing her to share his creativity and passion for the extraordinary fragrance; and he had seemed to truly value her opinions, calling her often to brainstorm about new ideas for the ad campaign, inviting her to the marketing meetings, encouraging her to call him anytime with her own ideas, or even to drop by his offices in Union Square if she happened to be at Sydney's.

Business, Larisa reminded herself as she rode the elevator to the penthouse offices of Peter London, Architect. *Promise* is very important to Peter, and I am the model for that very important project. It doesn't mean that I am important to Peter . . . even though sometimes, when his seductive dark green eyes gaze at me, he seems to be searching not for an angle or expression he wants to be sure to capture in the ads, but for something more, something deeper.

I know what's deeper, Peter, she thought. It was a grim thought, and surely one that would calm the heart that raced as always in anticipation of seeing him. I know what's deeper, Peter, and it's nothing that you would want to find.

"Larisa."

"Hi. You said I should drop by sometime." She shrugged softly and took a breath to provide oxygen to the heart that had been calmed briefly by her own sobering thoughts but now fluttered again in joyful response to the man who seemed so welcoming, so happy to see her even before she had given him her reason for being here. "Christine has finished the sketches, and they're so wonderful that I thought you would want to see them right away."

Peter and Larisa studied the sketches together, giving each work of art its full due, and when they had agreed that what Christine had created was all that they had hoped for and more, Peter said, "We need to celebrate, Larisa."

"We do? Because of the dresses?"

"Among other things. We never officially celebrated your willingness to be the model for *Promise*, nor the decision about etching forget-me-nots on the bottle, nor any of the other major decisions you've helped me make—any of which would have been reason enough for celebration. And now there's yet another reason. This weekend the meadow in Cape Cod becomes mine." Ours, he amended silently. "I signed the purchase agreement a few months ago, but it's taken this long to get all the paperwork resolved. The title officially transfers to me at midnight Saturday. So, Larisa, will you celebrate with me then?"

"Yes," she answered with quiet joy as her racing heart embellished, Of course I will.

Peter smiled his happiness at the forget-me-not blue eyes that seemed so happy, too, at the invitation, and after a thoughtful moment he suggested quietly, "I have a house at Lake Tahoe. Would you like to go there with me for the weekend?"

"Lake Tahoe?"

Peter's heart ached as he watched the glowing happiness fade from her lovely eyes, suddenly replaced by the fearful wariness he had seen in the beginning but which had recently been in hiding. He had so hoped that the wariness was gone forever, but now it was back—because, encouraged by the happiness he believed he had seen, he had broken his solemn vow to be so very careful with her . . . to move so very slowly.

"Oh, Larisa," he said softly. "It can't be a surprise to you to hear that I'm very attracted to you. But I honestly wasn't suggesting anything more than having a chance to spend some time together, to take walks in the snow, and read by roaring fires, and talk about ideas for *Promise* without being interrupted. I know it's too soon for you for anything more."

No, Peter, it's not too soon! her heart cried. But, as she thought about Tahoe and all the ghosts that haunted her still, her mind embellished sadly, It's not too soon . . . but it may be far too late.

"Let's forget about Tahoe," Peter said very gently. "But, Larisa, please know that no matter where we are, at noon in my office or alone at a lakeside house in Tahoe at midnight, you can always trust me. You never have a reason to be afraid of me."

I'm not afraid of you, Peter! *I'm afraid of Tahoe.*

"I do trust you, Peter," she said softly. Then, bravely fighting her fear, she added, even more softly, "And I would love to go to Tahoe with you this weekend."

Stephen stared thoughtfully at the two theater tickets that he had just removed from the desk in his lab. He hadn't need to remove them. He knew by heart all the information that was printed on them: *Nutcracker*, Union Square Theatre, December 21st, Eight P.M. The seat numbers engraved on the cobalt blue tickets were for the boxes at stage left, the same seats Stephen had had for the past five theater seasons.

Stephen hadn't been to any of the theater's performances since September. He had had absolutely no interest in finding a date to accompany him; and although he had no qualms about going alone, he decided that his solitude was far better spent in his lab trying to find answers—trying not to miss a tiny clue that might one day save someone's life . . . someone's husband's life.

Stephen's valuable season tickets hadn't been wasted. Elizabeth and Larisa had raved about the productions of *Cats, Phantom of the Opera,* and *Les Miserables* that they had seen in his stead. Elizabeth and Larisa wouldn't be able to use the tickets for the *Nutcracker* on the twenty-first—that was the Saturday evening that they were flying to England to spend the holidays in London with Elizabeth's family— and Stephen had another plan for that night anyway, a decision of the heart made long before it had become a conscious thought. And now the twenty-first was ten days away . . . and it was time to call her.

But, Stephen wondered, should he call, or should he simply leave her alone? He knew from Elizabeth that she was very busy designing beautiful gowns for the women of San Francisco as well as romantic dresses for Larisa to wear in the ads for *Promise.* And although Elizabeth herself didn't see Christine very often, Larisa did—and reported that she seemed quite happy pursuing her dream of becoming a designer.

Was Christine happy? Stephen hoped so. It was a hope that was with him constantly, just as lovely images of lavender and gold were with him too, always, drifting gently through his mind even when he was working. Now he was planning once again to intrude into Christine's life.

And if it was an unwelcome intrusion?

The lavender eyes that had always been able to tell him the most honest and important truths would let him know. He would make it very easy for her . . .

Christine shook her golden head slightly as she stared at the tiny drop of red blood that was forming at the tip of her index finger. She had pricked herself again, because again her thoughts had drifted while she sewed. At least this time the drift of her thoughts had been logical, wandering quite naturally from the elf costume on which she was sewing little bells to the Christmas pageant itself—and the invitation she had been thinking about making. But there had been other accidental needle pricks, lots of them, as her mind had filled with other not-so-logical questions. Was he pleased with the progress on the institute? Was he getting over the unhappiness caused by his breakup with Madolyn Mitchell? Had he found someone else, or did he spend every moment in his lab searching for ways to save others' lives and others' loves?

Christine hoped that Stephen was happy, and that the holiday season would be a joyous one for him, and she wondered if he might like to . . . that was when she had pricked herself, at the point when she was wondering if Stephen might like to go to the Christmas pageant. She would be backstage, of course, helping the excited children with their costume changes so that their proud and admiring parents could be in the audience. But Stephen could sit in the audience too, and it would all be very festive and happy, and it seemed like something that Stephen might enjoy.

But was she really going to find the courage to ask him? Or was she simply going to use her fingers as pin cushions for the next ten days?

"I was just thinking about you," she confessed when the phone rang five minutes later—and it was Stephen.

"You were?"

"Yes," she answered, so pleased that he seemed pleased. "I . . . Hi."

"Hi." Stephen drew a steadying breath, then simply told her why he had called, "I have tickets for the *Nutcracker* for the twenty-first—a week from Saturday—and I wondered if you would like to go with me?"

"Yes," she answered swiftly, then added softly, "And no. I'd like to go with you very much, Stephen, but I'm afraid I can't. There's a Christmas pageant at my local elementary school that night and I've made some of the costumes and have offered to help backstage during the performance. That's what I was thinking about when you called."

"And it had something to do with me?"

"Yes. I thought . . . I mean, it's an elementary school pageant, a far cry from the *Nutcracker*, but it will be festive and fun and . . ."

"And far better than the *Nutcracker*. So, if that was an invitation, I accept." After a slight pause, he asked, "Was it an invitation, Christine?"

"Yes, it was."

"Good." Stephen smiled in response to the lovely smile that somehow so eloquently and beautifully traveled through the phone lines. "I'm on call that night, but the holidays tend to be quiet."

CHAPTER TWENTY-THREE

Lake Tahoe
December 1991

$\mathcal{F}$rom the moment Peter and Larisa left her Pacific Heights apartment at noon Friday until they were within a few miles of Lake Tahoe, their conversation flowed easily and comfortably, punctuated occasionally with silences that were equally comfortable. But as they neared their destination, ascending into the snow-caressed world of the mountains—where the majestic evergreens were dressed in their laciest winter best and the streams had frozen into icicles that glittered like diamonds in the winter sun—the silence became tense; and the brilliant blue eyes that should have smiled at the splendor of the winter wonderland became fearful and apprehensive. Larisa sat very still, her taut slender body pressed against the seat, as if trying to push herself as far away as possible from whatever it was, yet knowing with a quiet fearful despair that it still wasn't far enough—she couldn't escape.

What was it? Peter wondered. What invisible monster has filled her with such dread? He wanted to help. But Larisa was somewhere far away, in a terrifying place where, perhaps, she even needed to be. So he simply drove in sympathetic silence, offering gentle smiles of reassurance to her unseeing blue eyes.

Larisa gazed straight ahead, her eyes fixed on an invisible image, the wariness in the forget-me-not blue increasing with each passing mile. Then, when they reached the outskirts of South Lake Tahoe, she turned her head, just a little, just enough to look at a motel, an unmenacing cluster of cheerful green and white cottages surrounded by an asphalt parking lot.

Peter had sensed that Larisa was going to turn her head even before it happened. He had felt her struggle, an increase in her already steely tension, as if she was trying to stop herself from looking, but knew full well that the struggle was ultimately useless. She had to look. She was compelled to by an unwelcome yet unconquerable magnet.

Then the motel was behind them.

Eventually her fists released the isometric clench that had imprisoned them for miles. But she was still very far away. Her gaze was no longer straight ahead but down, her firelit head bent by an immense invisible weight, her blue eyes veiled by a shimmering curtain of golden red silk.

"Here we are," Peter said quietly six minutes later when he brought his car to a gentle stop in the driveway of his lakeside house.

Larisa looked up at the sound of Peter's voice, startled by the voice itself, despite its gentleness, and even more startled to see that the image of the motel—the cottage—had been replaced by a magnificent creation of wood and stone.

"It's beautiful," she murmured.

If there had been such elegant lakeside houses here when she was a little girl, Larisa had never seen them. And she would have seen them, during one of her many joyous journeys along the shoreline. How she had loved the majesty of the lake, and how well she had come to know its many faces and moods. There had been days like this day, when the unrippled water was a perfect mirror of snow-kissed mountains and sapphire skies; and there had been other winter days, when the heavens glowered and the wind hissed and the lake roared with a vengeance of waves and spray. And there had been the days of autumn, when the mountain air was crisp and the leaves were red and gold; and the days of spring, when everything was so fresh and new; and the days of summer, when the gently lapping tranquility was disrupted by the noisy play of swimmers.

How she had loved this lake. How important it had been for her to be able to come here, along the trails in the woods known only to herself and the deer, and to stand at its shores. How important. How necessary . . .

"I think I'd like to go for a walk," she said impulsively. "If you don't mind. I won't be long."

"Of course I don't mind, Larisa," Peter said gently. "But please, first let me get you something warmer to wear."

With that, Peter got out of the car and went into the house. When he returned moments later—with an assortment of parkas, gloves, ski caps, and boots—Larisa was standing beside the car, gazing at the lake.

"It's a very long walk back to the motel, Larisa," he offered quietly. "And it's too dangerous to begin walking there now. Twilight will fall within the hour, and a storm front is supposed to be moving in by early evening. So, if you're planning to go there, why don't you take the car? Or let me drive you."

"I'd really just planned to walk along the lake." Even as she spoke Larisa realized that her steps might have taken her into the woods and along the trails she once had known so well, shortcuts from the lake back to town. She asked softly, "Was my reaction to the motel so obvious?"

Yes . . . to someone who loves you. "I just got the impression that it held memories—not very happy memories."

"No, not very happy memories at all."

Whatever the unhappy memories, Peter thought, they weren't memories of Julian. Had Larisa and Julian Chancellor ever been to Lake Tahoe together, they would have stayed in a penthouse suite at one of the grand hotels on the strip, not in the unprepossessing little motel on the outskirts of town.

A gust of wind swept off the lake, an icy whisper that promised soon, very soon, delicate snow-white crystals would begin to fall.

"Are the unhappy memories something you could think about right here? In front of a roaring fire?" Peter's deep voice was gentle and inviting. "With a mug of hot chocolate, maybe? The motel will still be there tomorrow morning, Larisa."

"I suppose I had hoped it wouldn't be there at all." She shrugged softly as she realized the futility of that hope. Even if the motel had been destroyed, completely leveled to make way for a high-rise hotel and casino, the memories would not have been demolished with it.

"How long has it been?"

"Since I was last here? Twelve years. But before that, for the first eighteen years of my life, this was home." Home? No, that was a wonderful word that held lovely meanings that Larisa had never known. Tahoe was simply where she had lived . . . and where so much of her had died.

Larisa shivered. From the icy wind that swirled her red and golden hair? Or from the icy ghosts that danced and swirled inside her?

"Let's go in the house," Peter urged gently. He wanted to urge so much more. *Tell me, Larisa. Trust me.*

"I called in an order to one of the local groceries before we left San Francisco," Peter explained when she found him in the kitchen unloading the cardboard boxes of just-delivered food.

It had been forty-five minutes since he had shown her to her bedroom—a wonderful second-floor room whose pine-framed windows overlooked the lake—then left to give her privacy to get settled. He had been worrying, and he saw that he had been right to worry; but now, at least, she was here.

Peter might have said more about the groceries, a casual allusion to the effect of the wonderful mountain air on the robustness of appetites. But Larisa had spent eighteen years of her life in this exhilarating air. And she was thin. And sometime in the past few months she had confessed to him that she had never eaten very much—not even, he realized now, during the years in which she had lived in this beautiful place that he loved . . . and she so obviously feared.

"Are you a gourmet cook, Peter?"

"Not gourmet," he answered, smiling as he gestured to a bag of spaghetti, proof positive of the truth of his statement. "I cook simple things."

"But good things," Larisa offered as she peered into the contents of the boxes.

"I hope so. Actually, I think so. That's not immodesty, because none of the recipes is actually mine. I'm simply a technician."

"Whose recipes are they?"

"My father's. My mother died when I was born, so it was just the two of us. For years he cooked and I watched. Then, when I was a teenager, he became quite crippled with arthritis and I became the cook for the family. But they were still his recipes. They still are."

Larisa smiled at the fondness she heard in Peter's voice as he spoke of his father; and then, because they were in Tahoe, in this place filled with so many of her own memories, her expression became thoughtful . . . and finally sad.

"Larisa?"

"I never learned how to cook at all."

It wasn't, Peter knew, the haughty pronouncement of an heiress whose meals had always been prepared by servants and who would have never wanted it any other way. It was, he decided, the wistful sadness of someone who had wanted to learn—and who most of all sensed how much she had missed by not having someone who had cared enough to take the time to teach her.

Oh, Larisa, please tell me.

"I promised you a roaring fire and a mug of hot chocolate," he said finally. "Or would you prefer something stronger?"

"No. Hot chocolate would be nice."

"Okay. Why don't I finish putting the groceries away and then I'll bring it to you? The fire is waiting for you in the living room, which is a straight shot through that door, and it should already be roaring."

The moment the kitchen door swung closed behind her, Larisa heard the beckoning sounds from the living room, the cheerful crackles of Peter's roaring fire; and when she reached the room she was greeted by a wonderfully welcoming red-orange glow. The fire provided enough light, and enough shadows, and Larisa needed the shadows, because she had decided to tell Peter about the icy ghosts that lived in Tahoe.

Larisa needed the shadows for her eyes—and for his . . . because she didn't want to see the wondrous dark green desire fade to disappointed disgust.

She was sitting on an antique wooden chair beside the fireplace when Peter joined her. It was a solitary place to sit, and although the collector's piece was eminently sturdy and functional, it was so much less comfortable than the overstuffed armchairs or the huge plush sofa. But Larisa had obviously chosen the hard and isolated chair by design—a stark lonely island in the red-orange sea.

"Shall I leave you?" Peter asked gently but reluctantly as he handed her a mug of hot chocolate.

"No, please," she answered, meeting his questioning green eyes briefly, then returning her gaze to the crackles and flames. "I'd like to tell you about the motel."

"Okay." *Good.*

Peter sat opposite her, on the other side of the huge stone fireplace. It felt far away, but at least he could see her profile in the shadows, and if she chose to look at him, he would be able to see her face.

"I guess I should just begin at the beginning. I was born here. My mother was a showgirl. I don't know who my father was. I don't think she knew either. I'm not sure why she had me. She told me often enough that having a baby—having me—was the greatest mistake of her life."

"A mistake that I for one am very glad she made."

Larisa looked at him, compelled by the unconcealed desire in his voice and compelled, too, by her own heart to send a silent warning. *You won't want me, Peter. Not when you know everything.*

Returning her gaze to the fire, she continued, "Anyway, because her pregnancy stole her body from her, she couldn't find work as a showgirl again. She became a cocktail waitress instead and later a blackjack dealer. There were always men, and I think some of them paid her with money or with drugs, but I'm sure she never considered herself a prostitute. Until I was eight, we never lived in the same place for more than a year. Sometimes we moved in with her boyfriends, and sometimes we lived with groups of people. It was the sixties, and even in Lake Tahoe there were communes and flower children." She stopped abruptly, suddenly flooded by emotions that preceded the conscious memory but which made her whisper, "And peace rallies."

"Tell me what happened at the peace rallies."

"I'd forgotten until just now." But now the memory had caught up with the emotions. "I was six. It was summertime. There were rock bands and sunshine and free love—and psychedelic paint. My mother's boyfriend made me take off my shirt and painted the slogan MAKE LOVE, NOT WAR on the front of my bare chest and a peace sign on the back. He wouldn't let me put my shirt back on, and neither would my mother. They paraded me around like that all day." Fire caressed fire as she gave a soft bewildered shake of her glimmering golden red head. "My first modeling experience. How strange. I loved modeling. I never felt at all compromised or embarrassed when I modeled. But I hated that day. I still hate it."

Oh, my darling, and I hate it for you. Peter hated that day . . . and all the days of her young innocent life when she should have been loved and so obviously hadn't been. Fighting his own anger, he reminded her gently, "You never let yourself be embarrassed or compromised during your career as a model, Larisa."

No, Larisa thought. I never did. Not in my career. But she had allowed embarrassment and compromise in her marriage. Julian had wanted her to wear provocative clothes, to display his magnificent prize to his friends, and she had acceded to his wish . . . and in private there had been even more humiliation.

"Until you were eight, you never lived in the same place for more than a year," Peter said finally. Larisa had withdrawn, her head bent in shame, her blue eyes veiled and hidden, and he was suddenly fearful that her story had ended, its retelling suddenly too painful, the anguished secrets of her lovely heart destined to live in shadows forever. Peter couldn't, wouldn't, let that happen. The episode at the peace rally was horrid, detestable, but Larisa had forgotten it altogether until now. It was a trivial memory of pain compared to the memories that lived in the motel. She needed to tell him about those memories. "Was that when you moved to the motel, Larisa?"

Peter held his breath and sent silent messages from his heart . . . and finally she lifted her head and bravely faced the dancing flames.

"Yes. My mother knew the manager and had learned from him that there was one cottage that was impossible to rent even during ski season. I suppose it was intended to be just a storage shack, not one of the rental units, because it was separate from all the others, located at the far end of the parking lot beside the trash cans. It's still there—I saw it today—but I couldn't tell if anyone was in it. Anyway, we were able to have it for almost nothing—no rent, just utilities and my help in cleaning the other cottages after school and on weekends."

"You were *eight?*"

"I didn't mind working, Peter," she said, turning to him, grateful for the indignation in his voice but wanting to reassure him that it wasn't necessary. "I've never minded working. And I liked the little cottage. It was so private compared to the other places we had lived and beyond the parking lot were the woods. I spent a lot of time there, wandering through the forest, finding trails that led to the lake. Sometimes I found small wounded animals in the woods and brought them back with me and took care of them until they were healed."

Peter saw the flickers of happiness in her eyes as she described the cottage from the viewpoint of the eight-year-old little girl who had so desperately needed privacy and had finally found it. But he remembered, too, her dread earlier when she had seen it again.

"So, for a while you were happy at the motel."

"For a while, yes, I was very happy there."

"And then?"

And then . . .

"I was twelve," she said as she returned her gaze to the fire. "One Saturday night a man came to the door. It was about midnight. I was asleep on my cot in the living room, and my mother was still at work at the casino. Her shift didn't end until two, but he told me that it was she who had sent him, so I let him in to wait for her. That wasn't unusual. There had always been men arriving at all hours, and as always I told him that there was beer in the refrigerator and a television in her bedroom."

Larisa stopped speaking then, and the room was silent except for the chatter of the fire, and when a smoldering ember suddenly burst into flames, adding its white light to the others, her lovely face was brightly illuminated.

And Peter saw such bewildered hopelessness.

He wanted to go to her, as he had been wanting to do from the very beginning. But she was on the stark lonely island where she wanted to be. So he reached out to her, the only way he could for now . . . with his heart.

"Larisa," he whispered with exquisite tenderness. "Please tell me."

"I was a very naive twelve-year-old. I guess I had begun to look less girlish and more womanly. I hadn't really noticed . . . but my mother had." Larisa drew a soft breath and when she spoke again it was a whisper of despair. "He had come for me, Peter, not for her. But she had sent him. She had given me to him in exchange for something—drugs or money or a debt that she owed."

"Let me hold you," he pleaded softly, and there was despair, too, in his gentle voice.

Larisa didn't turn toward him, but she frowned at the gentleness of his voice, a lovely frown of disbelief and hope. Then she shook her head decisively. *I have to tell you everything, Peter.*

"He told me he was a cop. I don't know if he was or not. He wasn't wearing a uniform." She added very quietly, "But he had a gun."

"I hope you killed him." Peter wanted to kill the man himself, wanted so desperately to travel back through time to that night of horror and prevent it from ever happening to her.

"No, I didn't kill him. He must have known that I wouldn't, couldn't, because when he saw me look at the gun he had put on the table, he let me escape from him to get it. I was so young, so foolish, so brave. The gun was very heavy and it wobbled as I aimed it at him. He laughed at me, goading me to pull the trigger, knowing that I wouldn't. When he raped me, he taunted me still, telling me that the reason I hadn't pulled the trigger was because I obviously wanted it . . . him." Larisa paused, then said in a faraway voice, "I've always wondered what my life would have been like if I'd had the courage to pull the trigger."

"It would have been a different kind of hell," Peter gently told the lovely woman who once had been a lovely little girl who had rescued animals, but hadn't rescued herself. And if she had pulled the trigger? She would have lived a lifetime of guilt. Either way, as a raped innocent or an innocent murderess, she was a victim of the most horrendous of crimes. "May I hold you, Larisa?"

"Peter . . ." She turned to him then, and Peter saw a brave flicker of hope drowned swiftly in a sea of sadness. "There's more."

"I know." Peter smiled tenderly and repeated softly, "May I hold you while you tell me?"

"No, Peter . . . I need to tell you everything . . . first."

"Okay." Then, guessing that the rest of the story had to do with revenge against the mother who had broken every promise a parent should make, he asked, "Did you call the police?"

"No. I told no one. I've never told anyone until now."

Even as his heart raced that she had trusted him and him alone with this anguished secret of betrayal, it cried, too, for all her lonely years of silent pain. "And your mother?"

"We never talked about it, but I think she understood what she had done, that she had gone too far. There must have been something in my eyes."

"Something that you saw as well."

"No. I never saw it. After that night, and for the next few years, whenever I looked in a mirror, all I saw was a shadowy blur. I had no idea what I looked like, except that with each passing year more people stared at me and wanted to be with me. The first time I saw a photograph of myself, really saw it, I was sixteen. I could tell that the girl in the photograph was quite beautiful, but I had no sense that she was me."

And you still don't, Peter thought. The article in *People* had described supermodel Larisa Locksley's remarkable ability to adapt her stunning beauty to whatever she was modeling. Whether the product was lipstick by Max Factor, or a gown by Scaasi, or jewels by Castille, she somehow sent the powerful and persuasive message that her extraordinary beauty was because of the rich color that adorned her lips, or the silk and satin that clung to her perfect body, or the rainbow of gemstones that encircled her graceful neck. She was a chameleon, ever-changing, always adapting.

Peter had read about Larisa's remarkable ability—and willingness—to lose herself in the product she was endorsing; and because of *Promise* he had witnessed it firsthand. Every discussion about the ads—the dresses she would wear or how she would wear her hair—had been entirely focused on what would be best for the fragrance, not on what would make her the most beautiful. And now Peter understood: Larisa had no sense of her own identity.

"But the beautiful girl in the photograph was you," he offered gently.

"Well, no, not really. She was just the coat of armor, the magnificent disguise that would enable me to go wherever I wanted to go. Where I wanted to go most of all then was away from here. I left the day I graduated from high school and never came back. My mother had already left Tahoe by then, five months before, to go to Las Vegas with a man she had met. I haven't heard from her since. I've thought that she's probably no longer alive, but if she is and has stayed away despite the allure of all the money I've had, then maybe she has a shred of decency in her after all."

"May I ask you a question? Now, when you look in the mirror, what do you see?"

"I don't spend a lot of time looking in the mirror."

"Well, you should. If you did, you would see a woman who is very lovely and very courageous. A woman I would very much like to hold."

"Oh, Peter," she whispered, wanting so much to be held by him. "There's more I need to tell you." *The most important truth of all.*

"All right." Peter steeled himself to hear about Julian, about Larisa's great love for the man he hated and her great anguish that Julian no longer wanted her.

But her quiet words weren't about Julian at all.

"Within a few days of the rape, I became quite ill. It was a pelvic infection, I know that now, but at the time I believed that I was being punished—and that I was going to die. Which was fine with me, I wanted to die, I waited for it. Eventually I realized that the pain and fever weren't going to be lethal and I started treating myself. My mother was a smoker so she had a medicine cabinet full of antibiotics that had been prescribed for attacks of bronchitis. She got a new prescription every time, three or four times a year, even though she never took the full course that was prescribed. I learned later, in health classes in high school, that the antibiotics I had taken—ampicillin, tetracycline and erythromycin—were the right ones for what I must have had. But I'd been sick for several months before taking anything, so even though the infection was eventually cured, the damage had already been done."

Larisa looked at the man who was gazing at her so tenderly, who had heard her painful secrets and had not turned away, whose dark green eyes told her that he wanted her still . . . the man whose home was now filled with the creative clutter of his genius but which one day would, should, be filled with the exuberant clutter of his children. She drew a steadying breath and then admitted to that man, "I'm not able to have children, Peter. There are new sophisticated techniques that might be tried, but the damage is so extensive . . ."

"You may not be able to give birth, Larisa, but you can have children. There are orphaned and abandoned children who desperately need mothers." Peter waited until her lovely blue eyes met his and then added very softly, "And you would be a wonderful mother, Larisa. I know because I was watching when you moved the figurine of the daughter to be beside her mother."

"You saw that?"

"Yes." *That was the moment I fell in love with you.* "May I hold you now? Please?"

Her answer came to him in the most hopeful color of forget-me-nots, and as he began to walk to her, she left her stark lonely island to meet him halfway.

And then she was in his arms, where she was supposed to be, and Peter simply held her.

Simply . . . it was an extraordinary joy. Until he sensed her sudden restlessness and felt her pulling away.

"Larisa?"

"Thank you for holding me, Peter," she answered quietly, with grateful disbelief, as if no one had ever really just held her before—and now she had pulled away because the wondrous comfort of being held had already lasted far longer than she deserved.

"I think we have a communication problem here," Peter said. "And it's my fault. When I asked if I could hold you I guess I should have made my intentions clear. I want to hold you, Larisa, just hold you—forever."

He drew her back into the gentle haven of his loving arms, and eventually they moved to the huge couch, and she lay against him, so safe and secure, her head resting on his chest as she listened to the strong and steady beat of his heart. She had never been held like this, by a man who wanted nothing from her, who wanted only to give her comfort, not to take from her perfect body the pleasures it could provide for him.

Larisa had never been held with the unselfish tenderness of love, and never before had it been she who made the first move for even more closeness—more intimacy—because always before such intimacy had led to the man's triumphant pleasure and her own humiliating conquest. But now the delicate whispers of desire that lived within her, but which never before had been allowed to speak, became very courageous. And when she bravely lifted her fire-caressed golden head and saw the tender desire in Peter's dark green eyes, the delicate whispers trembled with joyous hope.

Peter would have simply held her forever, marveling in that extraordinary joy and controlling with love his own immense desire for more of her, all of her. But now she was offering her lovely lips to him, wanting his kiss, and as his lips greeted hers and he discovered a kiss that he had never known before, never even imagined, the part of his swirling mind that was still tethered to thought sent a silent wish, If I could just kiss her like this forever . . .

There was such innocence to the kiss, such wonder at the magnificent discoveries they made together, such pure joy at the sharing of that magnificence. The kiss was innocent but so very intimate . . . and it was hungry but not possessive . . . and it was powerful but not conquering . . . and it was gentle and tender and filled with soft astonished sighs of desire.

And finally, when they both wanted more, when they wanted to share everything and give to each other all the gifts they had to give, it was Larisa who whispered the request of joy that she had never in her life whispered before.

"Make love to me, Peter. Please make love to me."

They made love in the four-postered bed in her bedroom overlooking the lake. Outside the snow danced, a wondrous swirl of delicate flakes illuminated by the porchlight below.

And inside there was such wondrous delicacy, too, as Peter's gentle lips and tender hands and caressing eyes lovingly nurtured her brave and hopeful desires. Somehow he heard their soft whispers, and he listened to their passionate secrets, and with infinite patience and exquisite care he encouraged them to speak, to blossom with unashamed beauty and courageous joy.

And when they both needed all of each other, when it was time to be as close as they could possibly be and to share all that could possibly be shared, his dark green eyes caressed her shimmering blue ones for a long moment that was beyond all words, and then their lips kissed again, and then their bodies did . . . but the most intimate caresses of all came from their hearts.

And after, he held her as unashamed tears spilled from her forget-me-not blue eyes, nourishing tears, like the gentle spring rain that enabled the delicate and hopeful roots of just-born flowers to find firm footing in the warm rich earth. Peter kissed the raindrops that spilled without shame from her beautiful blue eyes; and his kisses were as gentle and as nourishing as the tears; and both tears and kisses enabled the delicate roots of hope and love to find firm, courageous footing in the lovely warmth of her lovely heart.

When her tears finally stopped, Larisa wanted him to make love to her again. And this time, astonishingly, their loving was even more intimate, and more confident. And this time, after, there were no more tears, only gentle nourishing kisses until she drifted off to a deep and peaceful sleep.

As Larisa slept peacefully in his arms, Peter's not so peaceful thoughts drifted to Julian. His ancient enemy had been in his mind all evening, of course, in the unasked questions that had taunted and swirled as Larisa had told him about her childhood. She had never told anyone about the rape, which meant that she had not ever shared that very important truth with the man she had loved enough to marry.

Why not? Peter wondered. Because she loved Julian so much that she didn't want to disappoint him? Because she knew that his reaction would have been disdainful contempt for the sordidness, not compassion for the innocent girl who had been so brutally betrayed? Because, in her own shame, she feared that Julian might even have blamed her for seducing her own destruction?

And what about Larisa's inability to have children? Had that been an issue—the issue—that had ended her marriage? Peter couldn't imagine the Julian Chancellor he had known ever caring about children—ever caring about anyone but Julian. There were other Chancellors who could pass on the wealthy and privileged blue blood, after all, and as far as immortality, Julian's vast empire of buildings had already indelibly etched his signature for generations to come.

But what if Julian had wanted children? What if he and Larisa had tried without success to have them for the six years of their marriage? The Julian Chancellor who Peter had known would have doubtless blamed his wife for that failure; and since Larisa had never told him the truth about the rape or its consequences, he might have further blamed her infertility on the wild and wanton promiscuity of her modeling days. Peter knew that there had never been such days. Their loving tonight had been so wondrously innocent and so joyously pure that there never could have been.

But what if Julian had accused her of wanton promiscuity nonetheless? Peter already knew that Larisa hadn't offered in her defense the truth about the rape. Had she instead simply accepted Julian's condemnation and ultimately the loss of his love?

Larisa had been very deeply hurt by Julian. That had been abundantly obvious, so painfully clear, from the very beginning. Julian's cruelty to Larisa would have made Peter hate his bitter enemy even more—except that Larisa was here now, in his loving arms, where she belonged.

Where she belonged. It was such an astonishingly confident joy that Peter felt as if she had lived in his heart far longer than just the few months that it had been. Had their hearts, in fact, called to each other long before the night of the ball? Twelve years ago, when he had just been discovering Lake Tahoe, had Larisa, on that same glorious June day, been fleeing her own terrifying memories and vowing never to return? Had they passed on the winding mountain road? And had he felt an inexplicable rush of joy as she had passed, an enchanting yet undecipherable message as her fragile heart had sent a desperate call to his?

Perhaps, Peter thought. Perhaps.

Larisa was with him now, where she belonged, and he was going to spend his life making her happy, loving her as she always should have been loved. Peter knew that he had to be very careful still not to overwhelm her with his confidence in them—and in her. He was so very confident of her, her loveliness and worthiness, but Larisa needed to learn to love herself. She needed to know that it was safe to look in a mirror . . . and to smile with gentle joy at the image she saw.

For now, my lovely Larisa, I will be your mirror, he thought, his lips gently caressing the love-tangled fire-gold silk as she slept so peacefully in his arms. For now, I will reflect back to you with my loving eyes all the wonderful things about you that I know to be true. And someday you will believe those truths. And someday, my lovely forget-me-not, the children who we will find to love will frolic in the meadow at Innis Arden.

Chapter Twenty-four

*L*arisa and Peter awakened to a fairyland, a world that was dressed in pristine white and caressed by a golden sun that smiled gloriously from a brilliant sapphire sky.

Peter taught Larisa how to make pancakes, and she made one plump happy cloud for herself, and two such clouds and one snowman and a small forest of trees for Peter. And then they went for a walk. The snow was light, soft and fleecy, welcoming their footfalls as they walked along the lakeshore. After a mile, Larisa turned toward the forest, and following a trail that only she and the deer could see, she led the way toward town . . . and the motel.

Larisa wasn't certain how close she wanted to get to the tiny cottage, but as they neared the motel, Peter's dark green eyes journeyed solemnly to the place that had been her home, and her nightmare, and said quietly, "We could ask the manager if the cottage is vacant and maybe take a look inside." After a moment he added very gently, "We could spend the night there tonight, Larisa, if you would like to."

Larisa had spent six years of nights in the cottage after the rape, six years of remembered terror and imprisonment, and since leaving she had never imagined choosing to spend another night there. But with Peter, safe in Peter's arms, maybe it would be possible.

As Larisa was thinking about Peter's suggestion, the door to the tiny cottage opened—and suddenly all thoughts were forgotten and she and Peter simply stared, stunned by what, who, they saw emerge. The man was a police officer, in uniform and with a holstered gun, and the golden-haired girl was about the age Larisa had been when an evil man claiming to be a cop had knocked on the cottage door at midnight.

"Morning," the officer said when he and the girl reached Peter and Larisa. The officer was smiling, and the girl smiled too, her blue eyes as clear and untroubled as the sapphire sky and her smile as golden as the caressing sun. "Can I help you?"

"Has something happened, officer?" Peter asked.

"What? Oh, no. I live here. I'm in uniform now because I'm on my way to work. My wife and I manage the motel—actually she does—and my daughter and I were adjusting the television in one of the cottages."

"It works fine now," the girl added triumphantly.

"Shall we go find my wife? My name is Craig, and this is my daughter Melanie." Then, smiling warmly at the pretty blond woman who was now approaching them, he said, "I see that Darleen has found us."

After first-name introductions were made, Peter explained, "Larisa lived here when she was growing up. By 'here' I mean more than Tahoe, I mean the motel itself. In fact," he added, turning from Darleen to Craig, "she lived in the cottage from which you just appeared—which is why we were both staring at you."

"And now I'm the one who's doing the staring," Darleen said. "You're Larisa Locksley, aren't you? You and I were in high school together. We didn't actually know each other, but I recognize you, of course. I followed your career. We all did. I'd forgotten that you had lived here, at the motel. Maybe I never even knew it. Is this a sentimental journey?"

"I guess so," Larisa replied. It was a partial truth: this was a journey, although it was very far from a sentimental one. "I was wondering if it would be possible for Peter and me to take a look in the cottage?"

"You bet. We have people coming in later this morning—it's our only vacant unit—but you're more than welcome to take a look at it now."

At that moment, the amplified sound of a ringing telephone from the office called to Darleen, who was on desk duty, and Craig said that he really had to get to work. So it was Melanie who enthusiastically, and so fearlessly, led the way to the cottage that held such great fear for Larisa.

"This isn't our best cottage," Melanie explained with youthful candor. "I guess you know that. But Mom has completely redecorated it and Dad put in another window. Personally, I like it a lot. In fact, I think it should become my room the day I turn thirteen. That won't be for almost a year, but I'm already beginning to plant the idea."

The cottage was brighter and cheerier than Larisa had remembered—and so much smaller. She had lived in this tiny place until she was eighteen, but somehow her memory of its size had been the one made when she had first seen it, when she was only eight and it had seemed so spacious compared to the other places she had lived.

Melanie chattered happily about the cheerful new floral wallpaper and the new window that had already been added, and about the window boxes that could be added and the flowers that could be planted in them—all of which would help, she said, and all of which she would do when the cottage was hers. The happy chatter of a twelve-year-old girl who obviously loved and not feared the tiny cottage was definitely comforting.

But neither the happy chatter, nor the cottage's cheerful facelift, could truly exorcise the ghosts. They were still here. Larisa felt their sinister presence, dancing invisibly in the now brightly lighted corners and lurking beneath the pretty new wallpaper. The ghosts were still here. But, like the cottage itself, they seemed smaller than she had remembered, less monstrous and less menacing.

Why was that? she wondered.

Because of what you yourself have so bravely accomplished over the past few months, a voice answered. It was the same gentle, yet determined voice that had guided her away from Julian in August . . . and had compelled her to call Nick for help a month later . . . and which had, in the past few months, spoken soft encouragement as she had helped herself by facing her own pain, conquering it through understanding and resisting the powerful impulses that urged her to escape its merciless grip by floating far away.

The ghosts were smaller now because of her courageous journey into her own wounded heart. But the ghosts were still there. Because, Larisa knew, there was more gentle exploration still to be done. She needed to keep exploring and discovering until one day she could look into a mirror and see the woman she wanted to be—the woman who, inexplicably but so tenderly, Peter told her that he already saw.

"I'd better get going," Melanie announced with obvious reluctance. Brightening, she explained, "My friends and I are going skiing today."

"Thank you very much for showing us your cottage," Larisa said before Melanie dashed off to spend this glorious Saturday playing with her friends, not cleaning cottages.

"*Our* cottage. Mom used to show me your pictures on the covers of magazines." Melanie's fresh young cheeks flushed a lovely pink and she added, "I think it's really neat that you lived here when you were my age!"

"Shall I open some champagne? Admittedly the title doesn't officially transfer for another hour and a half, but we could toast things other than the meadow for a while."

Peter's dark green eyes told Larisa with tender desire that the "other things" he wanted to celebrate was them. Larisa wanted to celebrate that wondrous joy, too. But her heart already was celebrating, and the soaring giddiness she had felt in the past twenty-four hours was far beyond any place that alcohol had ever taken her. It would be safe to have a glass of champagne with Peter, but Larisa didn't need its euphoric effects—and she most certainly had no desire to float away from the magical feelings she felt so naturally just being with him.

"Would it be all right if I toasted . . . everything . . . with something soft?"

"Of course it would. Hot chocolate for two?"

They were already awake when the phone rang at six Sunday morning. They had made love and slept, and awakened and made love again, and now they were holding each other and talking.

"My answering service," Peter explained as he gently, and with obvious reluctance, uncurled himself from her and reached for the ringing telephone. "I always leave a number when I have projects under construction."

Peter's voice was calm, but Larisa saw the slight frown that touched his face as he spoke. He had projects under construction, yes, and problems routinely arose with such projects—but a call early Sunday morning was far from routine.

Peter's frown deepened and his handsome face grew darkly troubled as he listened in silence to the words of the caller. When he finally spoke, it was a question, "Was there damage to the music room?" The answer to that question caused a brief flicker of relief amid the worry, then there was pure worry again and finally a few succinct commands, "I want around-the-clock guards. I'm leaving tomorrow morning for Chicago and will plan to arrive in Boston on Thursday evening. Call me as soon as you learn anything about the cause."

Peter's hand lingered on the receiver for a solemn moment after he replaced it in its cradle. Then he turned to her and explained.

"That was my attorney in Boston, the one who handled the purchase of the estate on Cape Cod. Last night, shortly after midnight, there was a fire in the mansion."

"Oh, Peter."

"Fortunately, two teenagers were somewhere on the property at the time— young lovers who shouldn't have been there, and shouldn't have been doing what they were doing, but who nonetheless had the courage to do more than simply flee when they saw the blaze. They reported the fire immediately, and because of that most of the mansion was saved. If they hadn't called for help when they did, the wooden building would have been completely destroyed."

"I guess love makes one do courageous things," Larisa murmured softly.

"I guess so," Peter answered with matching softness.

For a moment the fire was forgotten, and they were lost in the silent hopes and promises of love, but eventually the shadows of worry flickered again and it was time to return to that troubling topic.

"Was there something about the music room, Peter? I heard you ask if it had been damaged."

"Until my father was crippled with the arthritis, he was a carpenter. The music room was one of his first creations—built over sixty-five years ago." Peter added with gratitude, "Thanks to those teenagers, it escaped the blaze entirely."

"I'm glad." The mansion had been saved, and the room created by the hands of the father he so obviously loved had been undamaged, but there was still such dark worry in his eyes. "What is it, Peter? What were you thinking?"

"I was wondering if it was arson."

"Arson?" Larisa echoed with surprise. "Do you think that's likely?"

"I don't know. Probably not." *I hope not*, Peter amended silently as he pulled Larisa back into his arms, nestled so close that she could no longer see his troubled face. She had seen and wondered about the dark worry in his eyes as he had been thinking about the question of arson. But there was an even darker worry that he did not want her to see. If the fire had been intentionally set, just moments after Innis Arden had become his, then there was only one person on earth who would have ordered that wanton destruction: Julian Chancellor, the destroyer of dreams. Peter had hoped that his enmity with Julian was past history, long since forgotten by Julian. But what if it was alive still, as hot and blazing as the flames that had engulfed the mansion?

Not once in this weekend of intimacies of the heart had Larisa mentioned Julian—or even alluded to her marriage or her divorce—and Peter hadn't pushed. He was in no hurry to hear about her great love for the man he hated. One day, when their own wonderful love had history and confidence, Larisa would tell him about her marriage, and he would tell her his own truths about Julian. But if the fire at Innis Arden had been arson, Peter knew that that day would come very soon. And if the inferno had been merely an accident?

Then Peter would tell Larisa everything in April, when they traveled together to the fragrant and enchanted meadow of *Promise*.

The beautiful bouquet of bright blue forget-me-nots arrived Tuesday evening. Peter had told her the evening before, when he had called from Chicago and they had talked for hours, that tonight he had a dinner meeting with clients and probably would be unable to call her. And so he had sent this lovely bouquet instead.

Larisa set the bouquet on the coffee table in the living room and for a very long time simply looked at it, marveling at the exquisite beauty of the delicate and hopeful little flowers. Finally, smiling softly in anticipation of reading his message, she reached for the small ivory card.

I will never forget you, Larisa. Forget me not. Julian.

No! her mind cried in swift silent protest. Julian had once known of her love of forget-me-nots, of course. In a grand romantic gesture, he had even permitted her to depart from tradition and carry a bouquet of them at their fairy-tale wedding. But since that day, he had apparently forgotten—or remembered but no longer needed the pretense of romance *because she was his*—and when he had given her flowers they had always been something else. Until now.

Now Julian had sent her the flowers she had always loved. But the message that accompanied the bouquet wasn't a message of love at all. It was, instead, a most ominous warning. She was not forgotten, Julian was telling her, and she never would be. And, even more ominously, she was *never* to forget him either.

Larisa had been so grateful that Julian had respected her wishes and hadn't called. She had even been hoping that he would never call again, that he had lost interest in her, that she was forgotten. But now she knew the foolishness of that hope, and now she trembled as she wondered, What if Julian has been having me watched? What if the forget-me-not bouquet is his sinister way of telling me that he knows all about *Promise*, including the closely guarded secret that the delicate flower I love so much will be etched on the crystal perfume bottles?

Larisa willed her swirling mind to focus on what it could mean if Julian knew that she was going to be the model for *Promise*. The answer was so simple, and so horrible: it meant that Julian could wield his immense power and influence to sabotage Peter's wonderful gift to the world. Because of her, *Promise* could be destroyed.

Larisa couldn't let that happen.

I need to speak with Julian, she told herself. I need to find out if he knows. And if he does know? Then I will have to say goodbye to *Promise* . . . and to Peter.

Oh, how her heart did not want her to dial the number to the penthouse on Fifth Avenue!

But it was that same loving heart that finally compelled her trembling fingers into action—for Peter, because of Peter.

"It's Larisa," she said quietly when Julian answered.

"I guess the flowers arrived. Are they all right?" he asked, his voice low and gentle. "The florist said it would take some doing to find forget-me-nots, but he assured me that they would be of top quality."

"They are." *The best that money can buy.*

"Good. I remembered how much you love them."

"Is that why you sent them?"

"What other reason could there be? Except, of course, the obvious one: that I hoped you would call." Julian added with loving concern, "I've been very worried about you, Larisa. You still haven't sent me any bills. You really must be almost out of money."

"I've found a way to replenish the money, Julian," she said as casually as possible. "I've found a job."

"A job? What job?"

Julian's voice lost its gentleness, and in its unconcealed harshness it unmasked all his apologies and promises for the lies that Larisa had always known them to be. But it wasn't the proof that she had been right not to trust the contrite and apologetic Julian that made Larisa's heart race with joyous relief. It was that he was genuinely surprised that she had found a job. She was *sure* of it.

But, she told herself, Julian is also very angry at the revelation. Which means I have to be very careful—and very convincing.

"I suppose it could be called free-lance fashion consulting. I give advice to women about clothes, accessories, hair, and makeup. Don't worry, Julian, everyone believes that I'm an immensely wealthy woman and that I'm doing this as a diversion, a lark."

"But you're getting paid for it."

"Of course I'm getting paid for it. In fact, I'm getting paid a lot. If my fees weren't high, my advice wouldn't be nearly as valued as it is." Larisa paused, and then bravely taunted the man who had so often and with such cruelty taunted her, "You taught me that, didn't you, Julian? The more people pay for something the more highly they value it?"

"What about other diversions, Larisa?" he demanded. "Are there other men in your life?"

"The answer is no," she replied evenly. Then, to further convince him, she added with icy indignation, "*Not* that that is any of your business. Our marriage is over, Julian. We aren't part of each other's lives any longer."

"You will always be part of my life, Larisa."

The words might have been a romantic promise of forever love, but from Julian's lips they were simply a warning. He was trying to terrify her, to control her again, to manipulate her with fear as he had always done.

But I'm stronger now, Julian, Larisa thought. There are no more invisible chains. I've cast them off. I am free of you at last.

"Leave me alone, Julian," she said with quiet calm. "It's over. Goodbye."

Oh no, my sweet, it is not over, Julian vowed with silent rage as she softly yet defiantly ended their conversation. It will never be over. But I still find this new courage of yours rather thrilling. I will leave you alone for a while longer, Larisa, just long enough for you to truly believe that I will permit you to live your life away from me. And then, my love, I will remind you, how I will remind you, of the only truth: that you are mine—and always will be.

CHAPTER TWENTY-FIVE

San Francisco
December 1991

On Saturday, December twenty-first, while Peter met with the fire inspector in Cape Cod, and Larisa and Elizabeth finished packing for their trip to England, and Christine ironed the small felt costumes that had gotten rumpled during the pageant's dress rehearsal, and Stephen tried to concentrate on his work but was distracted by images of golden hair and lavender eyes, Nicholas and Justin Chase joined the throngs of last-minute Christmas shoppers in Union Square.

Nick was on call for the transplant service, but it was very quiet. All the patients that could go home for the holidays were already there, and morning rounds on the ones who remained were finished by noon, and now they were shopping for Margaret's Christmas present from Justin. Nick's generous four-year-old son had "lots and lots" of ideas about presents for Margaret and he loved being in the midst of the holiday festivity of Union Square. He hummed happily to the carols that played in every store and paused frequently to gaze at the elaborately decorated windows. It was Justin not Nick who set the pace for the afternoon of shopping and singing and gazing; and Nick was infinitely patient, seeing through his son's shining blue eyes a joyful vision of Christmas that he himself had never seen as a child.

As they crossed Geary to get a closer look at the glittering tree in the center of the square, Nick heard the sound of rapidly approaching footsteps. At the sound, a quiver of anxiety rippled through him, followed swiftly by a powerful rush of adrenaline that sent his body on alert, ready to spring into action, like a soldier trained for battle. Nick's reflexive preparedness had been learned in the hospital, not on a battlefield, but like a soldier, he was instantly prepared for the worst—because people only ran in hospitals when it was a matter of life and death: the trauma team rushing to the ER to help an accident victim, the Code Blue team dashing to the ward in hopes of saving the life of a patient who had had a cardiac arrest. Nick's years of experience in hospitals had trained him to hear the sound of running footsteps as a signal of urgency.

But not here, his brain reminded his racing heart and suddenly taut body. Here, on this festive afternoon in Union Square, running footsteps surely only signaled frolicking excited children making a mad dash to see Santa Claus.

Except, his still tense body answered, these weren't the light footsteps of galloping children. These footfalls were heavy and purposeful—and getting closer. And, as Nick turned toward the sound, he saw at once that as in the hospital these racing steps carried ominous warnings.

There were two men, chasing each other, their faces filled with fierceness, their hands waving guns. Suddenly one of the guns was fired. And then, in the final moments of his life, the lethally wounded man went wild, firing his own weapon in a random rage. It all happened in a matter of seconds. Most of the crowd, although stunned and panicked by the gunfire, had been blissfully unaware of the danger as it had been unfolding. Like most of the crowd, Justin had been quite unaware. And even when the bullets began to fly, *and even when the dying man's gun was suddenly pointed directly at him*, Justin was confused by the commotion, but he saw neither the man nor the gun—and he felt no fear. All the fear belonged to Nick, who saw everything and who swooped down in front of Justin, shielding his beloved son's eyes from the horror and shielding Justin's small precious body with his own.

Nick prevented Justin from witnessing the terror, from being plagued by nightmares of it forever. All that Justin knew was that for some reason the father he loved and trusted suddenly pulled him close and tight against him—to a place that Justin was always quite willing to be. Nick shielded his son completely, his eyes, his body, the future memories of his young mind.

But neither Nick's lean strong body nor all of his love were impenetrable to the violence of a bullet.

Justin felt a soft surprising thud, not a piercing pain, as the bullet struck him, its velocity and impact blunted by its passage first through his father's chest. Then his father was lifting him and holding him even tighter than he had before—and that hurt, just a little—and then his father was running with him, away from the crowd that had formed a wall around the carnage.

Nick had no intention of waiting for the police or paramedics to arrive to methodically analyze what had happened. He knew all too well what had happened. He had felt the bullet strike his own chest, cracking his ribs and puncturing his lung as it traveled through him—and into his son's abdomen. Nick prayed a frantic useless prayer that the sudden hot blood in the place where their bodies touched—his left chest and Justin's right upper abdomen—was only his. But Dr. Nicholas Chase knew with instant, expert, and excruciating clarity that much of the blood was Justin's . . . and he knew, too, that Justin's wound was far more grave than his own.

As the crowd rushed toward the site of the shooting, Nick carried Justin away from the crush. In less than a block, he was able to flag down one of the many police cars that was converging on the scene and asked the surprised officer to drive them to Pacific Heights Medical Center.

"Why don't I call a medic unit?"

"My son needs far more than a medic unit can provide, and it will be much faster if you just drive us there. Please," Nick whispered with trembling emotion. "Please help us."

The police car traversed the streets between Union Square and Pacific Heights "Code Three"—light flashing, siren blaring, clearing traffic and ignoring stoplights. As he drove, the officer radioed dispatch, who in turn would notify the center's trauma team of their imminent arrival. "I have a four-year-old boy with a GSW to the abdomen. His dad's here, too. Apparently he's a doc at the med center—Doctor Nick Chase. He says to tell the trauma team that the boy is in shock, unconscious but breathing, and that he'll need immediate exploratory surgery. He says he thinks the bullet entered the boy's liver . . . ."

Within moments of the police car's arrival at the ER, Justin was in the trauma room. The trauma service chief Dr. Ed Moore examined him while other members of the highly trained trauma team inserted the necessary large bore intravenous lines into his small collapsed veins, placed the endotracheal tube in his throat, and drew the necessary tubes of blood.

Whenever a trauma patient, especially one with intraabdominal trauma, *could* be stabilized, it was desirable to get scans and X rays to assess organ damage in advance of going to the OR. But Justin's blood pressure was very precarious even with the aggressive fluid replacement and pressor therapy that had begun the moment the first line was in. It was abundantly, terrifyingly apparent that he was still bleeding—*briskly*—and even though everyone knew that the preop studies would have been desirable, they also knew that in this case there was simply no time. The age-old surgical adage applied: it was better to look and see than wait and see.

Perhaps it was already too late. The thought echoed silently in the minds of all those who worked on the small pale body. From the entry and exit wounds, it was obvious that the bullet had entered the liver and traveled through it. The liver was such a vascular organ, so easily shattered and so terribly difficult to repair.

"Okay. We're going to the OR in one minute," Ed said with quiet resolve less than five minutes after Justin arrived.

Ed spoke the words as an announcement to the entire team, so that they could all ready themselves for the next important step, but as he spoke, he looked at Nick. Ed and Nick were the same age, and both gifted surgeons, and they had spent hundreds of hours together—in the OR and at the executive meetings they attended as chiefs of their respective services. And since it was literally impossible for anyone to spend any time with Ed Moore without hearing about his own young son, Ed knew that Nick knew that he had a son. But Ed hadn't known until this tragic moment that Nick, like he, was a father—a father who was about to lose his son.

Do you want to be in the OR? Ed asked in solemn silence as his eyes met Nick's. Ed had no idea how he himself would have answered such an impossible question. Would it be better to be in the OR, to know without a doubt that everything had been done, even though everything wasn't enough? Or would it be best, in those moments, to simply be a father, waiting far away from the reality of the OR and praying for a miracle?

As Ed waited for Nick's answer to the impossible, his eyes left the tormented dark blue ones briefly, *they had to*; and in that emotional moment Ed's gaze fell from Nick's anguished face to his bloodied and still bleeding chest. And the impossible question became moot. Nick could not be in the OR. Ed had already learned from the tormented blue eyes that Nick's gravest injury, the one from which he might never recover, was the one to his heart; but he learned now, as his trained gaze quickly understood the solemn meaning of the rapid shallow breaths, that Nick's very survival was in jeopardy.

"We'll do our best, Nick," Ed promised quietly. Then, turning to his chief resident, he instructed, "Take care of Doctor Chase."

Nick was quite unaware of the small army of medical professionals who were working with swift, efficient competence to save his life; and he didn't feel the needles being put into him, nor the chest tube that was inserted between his shattered ribs, nor even the searing flames that ignited as each breath he took was an angry confrontation between his raw chest and his wounded lung. Nick was far away—in the OR with his son . . . and in Union Square, reliving those life-changing moments of terror.

He should have thrown Justin to the ground.

He should have thrown his son to the ground and then fallen on top of him. Yes, that would have hurt and stunned the little boy he had vowed never to hurt again, but it would have taken Justin completely out of harm's way. In those terrifying moments when he had realized that the gun was pointed at Justin, Nick had acted not by thought but by instinct, the deep instinct to protect his son even at the expense of his own life. Perhaps if he had ever been in the military and had been trained for war, he would have known to throw Justin to the ground, not just to shield the small body with his own. But the only war in which Nick had ever fought was an emotional one, doing battle with invisible phantoms and ghostly nightmares, and he had learned many things from his personal war—but not the right things—and now because his own experiences hadn't trained him to make the lifesaving move, his beloved son lay in the operating room with a wound that Nick knew to be lethal.

No! Nick's heart cried with silent despair. *Justin will be all right. The trajectory of the bullet will have been away from his liver, not into it. He will have been very lucky. Doesn't my precious boy deserve a little luck? Hasn't his young life been unlucky enough already?*

But there was to be no luck for Justin Chase.

"We were able to control the bleeding and he's stable now, but there was very little viable liver that we could save." Ed added with quiet emotion, "I'm so sorry, Nick."

Nick didn't seem to hear. Or perhaps, Ed thought, it was simply too painful to. As he waited, he watched the clouded faraway dark blue eyes become clear and focused.

"Were there other injuries, Ed?"

"No, none. Just the liver. With your permission, Nick, I would like to put Justin's name in the national transplant registry as soon as possible."

"That won't be necessary." *His precious son was lucky after all.* "You said Justin is stable now, Ed?"

"Yes." It was the truth, but both men knew it was a truth that would be short-lived. Justin would be stable for a while, deceptively normal, and then his body would realize that its liver was missing and he would begin to die. "We were able to stop all the bleeding and his pressure is fine off pressors. We're recovering him in the pediatric ICU. When I left him he was still asleep."

"I need to have you find Elizabeth for me, Ed. Please tell her that I'm sorry, I know she's supposed to leave in a few hours for England, but that I need her help."

"All right."

"Will you let me know as soon as you reach her?"

"Sure. Anything else?"

"I need to write some things down."

Ed answered by removing a pen and several unused note cards from the breast pocket of his white coat and handing them to Nick. "Here you go."

"Thanks."

As soon as Ed left to find Elizabeth, Nick felt the flood of hot tears in his eyes, tears that flowed from his weeping heart on a rushing river of pain and fear. For many moments he simply allowed the anguished tears to flow. Allowed? No, there was no way he could have held them back.

Finally he found control, such necessary control, and made his mind focus on what needed to be done. He began making the all important list.

At the top, in capital letters, he wrote the most important item of all: ELIZA-BETH.

* * *

"This is going to be such fun," Larisa enthused. She was sitting on Elizabeth's bed, watching her friend finish packing for their trip. Such fun, she thought, and a chance for us to talk, really talk.

"Lots of fun," Elizabeth agreed. She was about to embellish—a soft tease about taking Harrod's or Buckingham Palace or both by storm—when the phone started to ring. She smiled and predicted, "Peter."

"I hope so," Larisa answered as she moved to the phone. Yes, she assured herself. It will be Peter. He will be calling to let me know what the fire inspector said about the cause of the fire, and to wish me a good flight, and to promise to call me in London, and to remind me that we are spending New Year's Eve together. It will be Peter. It *won't* be Julian calling to tell me that even though *I* have told him that it's over, *he* won't allow it to be. "Hello?"

"This is Doctor Ed Moore calling for Doctor Jennings."

"Just a moment, please." Larisa covered the receiver. "It's a Doctor Moore. You didn't forget to sign out, did you?"

"No. I wonder what he wants." Elizabeth frowned briefly as she reached for the phone. "Hi, Ed."

Larisa couldn't see Elizabeth's face because as her friend listened to whatever it was Ed Moore had called to say, she walked to the window facing the medical center and stood there, very still, staring out.

"Please tell him that I will be there right away," she said finally, her voice as still and taut as her body. Then she replaced the receiver and when she turned Larisa saw the heart-stoppingly stricken emerald.

"What is it, Liz?"

"Nick has been shot," she answered quietly, and, even more quietly, she whispered, "And so has his son."

"His *son?*"

"He's four years old and badly injured. That's all I know, Lara. I have to go."

"I'm going with you."

CHAPTER TWENTY-SIX

"*E*d?" Elizabeth asked as she and Larisa came up behind him in the nurses' station in the ER.

"Oh, good. That was fast."

"We ran," Larisa said. "Please tell us what happened."

"This is my friend Larisa, Ed," Elizabeth explained. "She absolutely refuses to wait in the waiting room."

Ed heard the fondness amid the worry in Elizabeth's voice, and realized at once that she wanted her friend with her, and decided without a ripple of uncertainty that he wasn't going to get hung up on the ethics of discussing confidential medical details in front of Larisa. Besides, he knew, very soon the news media would have the story and all of San Francisco would know about the senseless Christmas tragedy involving the gorgeous and heroic doctor who had saved little Molly only months before—and yet had been unable to save his own beloved son.

"According to the police, what happened was that two armed men were chasing each other in Union Square—a drug deal gone sour apparently. One man shot the other and before the second one died he began firing random shots into a crowd which included Nick and his son Justin. And then what happened, what must have happened given their injuries, is that Nick moved between Justin and the gun, using his own body as a shield to protect his son." Ed felt a sudden rush of emotion as he imagined, *felt*, Nick's terror when he had realized that his son's life was in jeopardy. Unable to speak for a moment, Ed turned toward the nearby X-ray viewing box. When his voice was steady again, he gestured to the chest X rays that were illuminated on the box and said, "These are Nick's X rays. The gun was obviously very powerful. As you can see it shattered his ribs."

"What about his heart, Ed?" Elizabeth asked when she saw the massive trauma that had been done to Nick's left rib cage.

"Amazingly, the bullet missed his heart entirely." *Which doesn't mean that Nick's heart is going to survive what happened to his son.* "The bullet traveled through Nick's chest and into Justin's liver. There's a very small pedicle of viable liver left. It was all we could save, and it's not nearly enough to sustain life."

"Where is Nick now?"

"Still down here, in trauma room three. Justin is in the pediatric ICU, and Nick wants to be with him, but when I told him you were on your way he said he'd wait for you here. I'm not sure why he wanted me to find you, Elizabeth. He's been making a list of some sort, probably names of people who need to be notified. I assume he plans to give that list to you, and as soon as he does I hope that you'll convince him to accept some pain medication."

"He hasn't had anything yet?" Elizabeth asked, alarmed. She didn't look back at the chest X rays, she didn't need to. Her highly trained eyes had needed only a quick glance to assess the enormity of the injury and to imagine the pain.

"Not a thing. Maybe he wants to be clear for Justin." *So he can be awake and focused while he lovingly holds and comforts his son as he dies.* Ed sighed heavily. "But he's going to exhaust himself trying to fight the pain."

Elizabeth nodded solemnly. "I'll see what I can do."

"I'll be waiting right here for you, Liz," Larisa said. Then, looking up at Ed, she added, "If that's okay."

"Sure, Larisa. It's okay by me."

Elizabeth and Nick had been together in Trauma Room Three many, many times.

But never like this. Never with him lying motionless on a stretcher, his handsome face so pale and anguished, his damaged body so taut and still. Nick's dark blue eyes were closed, but the long black lashes glistened with the dampness of recent tears.

Oh, Nick. Elizabeth's heart wept for his immense sadness, and so did her emerald eyes. After a moment, she vanquished the tears, the ones that could be seen, and said very softly, "Nick?"

The eyes that opened held deep pain; but there was something else in the anguished blue, something that looked almost like hope.

"Thank you for coming, Elizabeth. I know you're supposed to be leaving for England tonight."

"It doesn't matter, Nick," she assured gently. Nothing matters but you—and whatever I can do to help you survive this immense loss. But what could she do? What could anyone do? "As of this moment, I'm officially on call for the holidays. That's a very small thing, Nick, nothing really. Please tell me if there's something else I can do to help you."

"I hadn't even thought about the service. That isn't why I need you, Elizabeth."

I need you, Elizabeth. In the midst of his anguish, as he spoke those four words, Nick's voice softened and filled with exquisite tenderness.

"No?" she asked softly.

"No," he echoed gently. "The reason I need you, Elizabeth, is to have you perform a living donor transplantation on my son—from me to my son."

"Nick . . ." *No.*

"I know you have a copy of the protocol in your office, but I've been writing it down anyway, point by point. I suppose mostly to keep my mind focused," he confessed, the emotional confession of a grieving father. It was a moment before he spoke again, but when he did his tone had shifted from personal to professional, from the emotional voice of a father to the calmly analytical one of gifted surgeon. "I think it's possible to get all the tests done and assemble the team and be in the operating room within six hours. Even though this surgery has never been done on an emergency basis before, I've always believed that emergency transplantation would someday have a major role in the acute management of trauma."

"I've always believed that, too," Elizabeth said to the gifted surgeon; and then, to that surgeon whose judgment had been so obviously blurred because he was also a father with a dying son, she reminded gently, "But, Nick, Justin is four years old."

Elizabeth didn't need to elaborate on her statement. The world's leading expert knew perfectly well that the extraordinary surgery he was proposing had only been done on infants. Elizabeth didn't need to tell Nick that, nor did she need to remind him why it was so: because there was only so much liver that could be safely donated from a living donor, enough for an infant's tiny liver but not nearly enough for a four-year-old who had lost virtually all of his own.

"Justin is an ideal candidate for transplantation, Elizabeth. He's a very healthy little boy." Nick's voice broke then, and he was a father, remembering the little boy who had only a short time ago been so happily humming Christmas carols, his bright blue eyes wide and laughing. So healthy, so happy. After a moment, Nick forced the emotion away and became the surgeon again, continuing firmly, "His excellent health makes him a better candidate than recipients who are transplanted because of severe underlying hepatic disorders. Justin's own liver is completely normal—it just needs time to regenerate. The transplantation will give it that necessary time."

"Yes, but . . ." But what about you, Nick? What about your survival? To give Justin enough tissue to sustain his life until his own liver could regenerate would mean taking . . .

"He can have all of my liver if he needs it, Elizabeth," Nick said in quiet reply to her unspoken worry. "I mean it."

The solemn dark blue eyes told Elizabeth with exquisite eloquence that Nick did mean it. Nicholas Chase had already proven once today his willingness to give his own life to save the life of his son. But that had been a moment of instinct, the reflexive action of a parent protecting his child. This gift, and Nick's willingness to give it, was far more calculated, but it was driven by the same instinct of limitless and immeasurable love.

"I can't do this, Nick." *I can't let* you *do this.*

"Of course you can. You're the best surgeon I've ever known." Nick saw a flicker of surprise and asked softly, "Didn't you know that?"

"No. But it doesn't matter." *Not now,* Elizabeth thought. Nothing mattered now except somehow convincing this intensely resolute man that what he was proposing was impossible—and somehow helping him accept the inevitable death of his precious son. She offered another gentle reminder, "You're very badly injured yourself, Nick."

It was the truth. His compromised respiratory status and extensive tissue trauma would make most surgeons quite reluctant to take him to the OR for even the most trivial of procedures.

"I have a few rib fractures," Nick answered dismissively. Then he searched her worried face for clues to the other serious medical concern about his own suitability as a liver donor. He had hoped that Larisa hadn't revealed his secrets to her friend; and, he decided as he gazed at Elizabeth, it was quite obvious that she hadn't. But now Nick had to reveal them himself. "Until three and a half years ago, I drank very heavily. I haven't had anything to drink since then, and as far as I know I've never had any hepatic damage as a result of my alcoholism, but you still need to know about it."

Elizabeth did need to know about it. The history of heavy alcohol consumption was very pertinent to her preparation for surgery. But, Elizabeth wondered, was Nick telling her so that she could prepare for the surgery? Or so that she could prepare for his death? *So that I won't blame myself if you die, Nick? So that I can blame your death on you and your drinking?*

On the morning when another four-year-old boy had died so tragically, and Nick wouldn't share with her the pain they were both feeling, an extraordinary thought had come to her as she had rushed away from him: *I hate you, Nick.* It hadn't been true then, of course. But as she felt the storm of emotions that swirled inside her, Elizabeth wondered if it was true now.

I hate you, Nick, for not ever trusting me before—and now trusting me with everything.

I hate you, Nick, for asking this of me—and giving me no choice.

She had no choice, because she saw so clearly that if his son died most of Nick would die with him. She had to operate for Nick, because of Nick, even though in trying to save the life of the son, Elizabeth might cause the death of the father.

The father. A man she hated?

Oh, no, her heart answered. *A man she loved. The only man she had ever loved.*

"Will you do the surgery, Elizabeth?"

"Yes," she whispered. "I will do it, Nick." *I will try to save your son—because that's what you so desperately want . . . and because I love you.* Then it was time for Elizabeth to focus, the doctor preparing for the surgery of her lifetime, and when she spoke again her voice was calmly professional. "May I see what you've written down?"

Elizabeth's expression remained calm, doctorlike, but her heart stumbled at the first word at the top of Nick's list: her own name in capital letters, traced and re-traced by Nick as he had waited anxiously to see if Ed had been able to reach her. *Her*, the best surgeon Nick had ever known. Doctorlike, Elizabeth moved on, reading the rest of what Nick had written, discovering that it was a verbatim replica of the detailed protocol—until the end, where, as at the beginning, there was a woman's name.

"Margaret?" Elizabeth asked.

"She needs to know," Nick answered almost to himself. "She needs to be told in person. After I see Jussie, I'll need to go tell her."

"Go? Where?"

"To my house."

"You don't seem to understand how badly injured you are, Nick."

"I'm okay . . . and the house is very close by."

"No," Nick's doctor said firmly. After a moment, she added gently, "I won't be able to leave until all the arrangements for the surgery are in the works, but maybe Ed could go, or Stephen, or . . . my friend Larisa is here, Nick. She's very gentle when someone is in need."

"Yes," Nick replied with surprising swiftness. "If Larisa is willing, would you ask her to tell Margaret?"

"I'm sure she'll be willing." Elizabeth paused. Nick had a hidden son. Did he have a hidden wife, too? Someone who had endured his notorious late-night liaisons of passion? She asked quietly, "Is Margaret Justin's mother?"

"No."

As Nick spoke, and a deep fear suddenly filled his blue eyes, Elizabeth felt waves of fear wash through her, too. Sometimes a patient had an ominous sense of doom, an uncanny anticipation of some impending physical catastrophe just before it struck. Was Nick sensing such a catastrophe now? Was his spleen sending a warning that it had been hit after all and was now on the verge of a swiftly lethal rupture? Or was the message from his heart, grazed by the bullet and just about to convulse into a rapidly fatal rhythm?

"Nick, what is it?"

"I was just thinking about Justin's mother," he answered distractedly. Then, focusing quickly, he said decisively, "We're divorced, but I'm going to need to talk to an attorney about what will happen to Justin in the event of my death."

"You're not going to die!"

Nick smiled gently, and after several moments offered softly, "Well, I need to talk to someone just in case. I need to be very sure that she doesn't get custody of him. There's always a lawyer on call for the hospital, isn't there?"

"Yes, for medically related legal issues, but . . . I'm going to call my brother. His specialty is divorce and I know he's in his office downtown this afternoon." Elizabeth saw both the hesitation and the sudden hope—and smilingly dismissed the hesitation. "It's no imposition, Nick. He's only minutes away, and he and his family aren't scheduled to leave for England until tomorrow evening."

"Thank you."

"You're welcome. So, I'd better go get things started. I guess I need your address to give to Larisa."

"Okay." When Nick finished giving it to her, he said, "In the top desk drawer in my study there's a large envelope with Justin's name on it. It contains the legal documents that your brother will need to see and also the immunologic studies that were done on both of us when Justin was born. The match is really quite extraordinary, Elizabeth. Stephen will be very pleased."

"Good. I'll make sure that Larisa brings the envelope back with her." Elizabeth would have left then, but she sensed that there was something more, something that came from the father, not the surgeon. "What, Nick?"

"Could you also have Larisa ask Margaret to bring Mr. Bear?" he whispered finally. *My little boy will need his Mr. Bear.*

Ed and Larisa hadn't moved very far from where Elizabeth had left them in the nurses' station.

"Nick wants me to transplant part of his liver to Justin," Elizabeth told them with quiet calm when she reached them.

"It can't be done, Elizabeth," Ed said firmly. "Justin has virtually no liver left, and even if he did, he's four years old. I'm not telling you anything you don't know, but maybe I didn't explain Justin's injury clearly enough to Nick. I guess I didn't see much point in going into great detail."

"Nick understands perfectly. He understands that Justin will die without the transplantation—and he understands the risks involved to himself."

"He understands that he could die? That, in fact, it's very *likely?*"

"Yes. Nick understands that." Her determined eyes met his skeptical ones with unflickering resolve. "I'm going to do the surgery, Ed. It will probably take about six hours to get all the tests and assemble the teams. Does Justin have that much time?"

"Six hours? Yes, I think so. But not a lot longer than that. Elizabeth . . ."

"This is possible, Ed. It's never been done but it *is* possible. Justin's own liver will regenerate, so I just need to give him enough of Nick's to buy him the necessary time. With the three-dimensional scans and Bill's expertise, I should know before I enter the OR exactly how much he needs."

"Who is Bill?" Larisa asked.

"Bill Barnes, the pediatric hepatologist."

"And will there be an adult hepatologist to tell you how much liver Nick needs to keep?"

"Yes. Her name is Rebecca Lansing." And, Elizabeth thought, Bill will tell me how much donated liver Justin will need, and Rebecca will tell me that it's far more than Nick can safely give . . . and somehow I will have to find a perfect balance—so that both father and son will survive.

Ed Moore knew that it was futile to argue further with the resolute Dr. Jennings, and he was a father with a young son of his own, so finally he simply said, "I'm here, Elizabeth. Hell, everyone on staff who hasn't already left town for the holidays will be here. There shouldn't be any problem assembling the two teams. In fact, if you like, I'll get working on that right away."

"That would be a big help, Ed. Thank you."

After Ed left, Elizabeth started to ask Larisa if she would be willing to go to Nick's house; but, because of the suddenly deeply troubled expression she saw on her friend's beautiful face, she asked instead, "What is it, Lara?"

"Did Nick tell you that he used to be an alcoholic?"

For a very long moment Elizabeth simply stared. Finally she answered quietly, "Yes. He did."

"Well, doesn't that make this all the more dangerous for him?"

"Yes." Elizabeth hesitated, not wanting to ask, not wanting to know, and yet needing to. "How did you know that about Nick?"

"On the night of the ball in September, I drank a lot of champagne, glasses and glasses with very little effect. Nick noticed and had a fairly blunt conversation with me about my obvious tolerance to alcohol and my potential for using it to escape from my problems. He offered to help me and I took him up on the offer ten nights later when Julian called."

"Nick came to the apartment?"

"No. In fact I haven't actually seen him since the night at the Fairmont. We've just talked on the phone a few times." Larisa gazed at the dear friend who had always been so generous with her—and now looked so betrayed—and assured, "There's absolutely nothing between me and Nick, Elizabeth."

"But you didn't tell me about this."

"I wanted to, but I sensed—although he never specifically said so—that Nick didn't want you to know about his drinking. But you need to know now because of the surgery, don't you? Even though I'm quite sure he doesn't drink anymore."

"Did you know about Justin?"

"No. I knew that Nick had been married briefly, and I got the impression that the marriage had been a disaster, but I had no idea until today that he had a son."

"Do you know who Margaret is?"

"Margaret? No."

"Do you know where Nick lives?"

"Liz, *Lizzie*, I know nothing!" Larisa pleaded with soft urgency. "Nick and I talked about me, not about him. He didn't want to talk about himself, not to me anyway. You were right about Nick, Elizabeth. He is sensitive and compassionate and kind. He helped me a lot and now I want to do whatever I can to help him—and you. Please?"

Elizabeth gave a bewildered shake of her luxuriant dark brown curls. "I'm sorry, Lara. There's just so much going on, so many revelations."

"And you can't even stop to think about any of them now because of what you have to do. I know, Liz. But please don't worry at all about this revelation. And please let me do whatever I can to help. Let me be the good friend to you that you've always been to me."

"You are a good friend, Lara," Elizabeth said softly. "And I do need your help. Nick wants Margaret, whoever she is, to be told in person about what happened to him and Justin. Would you be willing to go to his house and tell her?"

"Yes, of course I would."

Mark Jennings already knew about the violence that had happened many floors below his Union Square office. He had been drawn to his window by the screams of sirens and had seen from above the bloody aftermath. When his little sister called asking for his help for Nick, Mark told her without hesitation that he would be there soon.

Elizabeth's next call was to Stephen. As she dialed, she realized how glad she was that he was the immunologist on call today. Not, of course, that his partner wasn't fully capable; but it had been Stephen who had managed the intricacies of the immunosuppression for little Molly in August.

"Nick says that the tissue match between himself and Justin is astonishingly good," Elizabeth elaborated to the stunned silence that had fallen the moment she finished explaining why she was calling and what she was planning to do. "We're sending blood for emergency tissue typing anyway, of course, but Larisa is getting a copy of the apparently very extensive immunologic studies that were done when Justin was born."

"It's not the immunologic match that I'm worried about, Elizabeth. It's the surgeon."

"You don't think I can do this?"

"You know perfectly well that I'm not questioning your skill. But there's a limit to how much liver can be transplanted, and you just finished telling me that almost all of Justin's liver was destroyed."

"Yes, but apparently there's a viable broad-based pedicle onto which we can graft the donor tissue. And maybe when we get the scans, we'll find that Justin has more tissue mass left than Ed thought. You know how revealing the scans can be."

"What if the scans reveal that Justin has even less viable tissue than Ed thought? What then, Elizabeth?"

"I'm going to do this, Stephen, and I need your help." She paused, then added quietly, "And I need your support."

"You know you have that, Elizabeth. I'll be there soon."

"Oh, no," Christine's voice filled with sympathy and concern when Stephen called her moments later to explain why he wouldn't be able to go to the pageant with her after all. "How difficult for Elizabeth. Will you let me know what happens?"

"Of course. In fact, why don't you have me paged as soon as you're home from the pageant? The surgery will probably still be going on then, but I may have some news . . ."

CHAPTER TWENTY-SEVEN

"*E*lizabeth, this is Margaret."

"Hello, Margaret," Elizabeth said, smiling warmly at the attractive white-haired woman who appeared in the ER nurses' station with Larisa. Deep worry was abundantly apparent in Margaret's pale blue eyes and her slightly gnarled fingers tightly clutched the much-loved Mr. Bear.

"Hello, Elizabeth. I'm so relieved that you're here and I know how relieved Nick must be, too." Then, confident that father and son would be together, she asked, "Where are they?"

"In the pediatric ICU. It's on the sixth floor. I'd walk up with you but I'm waiting for my brother to arrive."

"Why don't I wait for Mark?" Larisa suggested. "You two go on up and we'll find you when he arrives."

Nicholas Chase should have been lying down in his hospital bed on 8 South, heavily medicated with Demerol, gathering strength for the assault on his already badly injured body that would begin again in just a few hours. But instead he sat bolt upright and drug-free in a chair that was positioned as close to Justin's ICU bed as possible. Nick's face was that of a loving father, except that it was terribly pale and the rippling muscles in his taut jaw sent silent signals of the physical pain that was compounding the emotional one. Nick wasn't dressed the way another father visiting his son would have been dressed, either. He wore a hospital gown and robe and a bracelet that identified him as a patient, not a visitor; and there were plastic tubes attached to his body—an intravenous line in his right arm and a much larger tube draining bloody fluid from the left side of his chest.

Nick gazed at his sleeping son, not wanting to awaken him because Justin's rest was so important, and needing more time himself anyway to find exactly the right words to say when he did. Nick wanted to say words to his beloved son that would endure beyond his own death, a comforting promise of love that would be with Justin forever; but he was so afraid of frightening Justin with his loving goodbye. Justin slept, and Nick ignored the crescendoing screams of pain from his own ever-weakening body and simply marveled at his son's wonderfully peaceful slumber, memorizing the moment, making a precious memory that would last for eternity.

Oh, my Justin, my beloved Jussie, how I love you.

Nick sensed movement behind him and turned to smile a silent greeting to Margaret and Elizabeth as they entered the small room.

"Daddy?"

"Hi, my little man," Nick whispered as he turned back to Justin. Then, extinguishing with love the sudden fire in his chest, he leaned forward and kissed his son gently on his cheek. "I'll bet your tummy hurts, doesn't it? You and I were in an accident together, and now we're at the hospital. Margaret is here, and Mr. Bear, and, Jussie, this is Elizabeth. Remember me telling you about Elizabeth?"

Justin nodded at Nick and then focused his clear blue eyes beyond his father and smiled his happy little boy smile at Margaret and Elizabeth and Mr. Bear.

"Remember the surgery that Elizabeth and I did last summer on Molly and Mary Ann? Well, Elizabeth is going to do that exact same surgery on you and me. She's going to put part of me inside you. And you need to remember, Jussie, that that part of me will be with you always, inside you, loving you." Nick stopped abruptly, stopped by his own shaky emotions and by the sudden flicker of worry in his son's blue eyes. "Anyway, we're very lucky that Elizabeth is here today because she's the best."

"I'll need to examine you a little later on, Justin," Elizabeth said quietly, sensing Nick's shakiness and rescuing him by distracting his suddenly apprehensive son. "Will that be okay with you?"

"Yes."

"Good. Right now, though," she added, looking back at Nick, "according to what the nurse said when Margaret and I arrived, they're ready for Justin in radiology."

"They need to take a picture of your liver," Nick explained gently to his son. "They'll be taking one of mine, too, so that Elizabeth can know all about the size and shape before the surgery. It's just a picture, nothing more, nothing that will hurt."

While Margaret accompanied Justin to radiology, Nick was officially signed in as a patient on 8 South. He needed to lie down, it was obvious even to him, although he still refused pain medication. His mind had to be clear and alert for his meeting with Elizabeth's brother.

Nick was lying flat in his hospital bed when Elizabeth and Mark arrived, but as they entered his room, he quickly sat up straight. The sudden movement triggered a burst of flames in his chest and a whirling in his head, and it took him a few moments to recover. He was so helpless. There was so much to be done—and he was *so helpless*.

"Thank you very much for coming, Mark."

"It's no problem at all, Nick. Elizabeth said that you have some concerns about the custody of your son?"

"Yes."

"I'll be in the ER, Mark," Elizabeth said as she started to leave to give them privacy.

"Will you stay, Elizabeth?" Nick asked. "You'll be caring for Justin so you need to know the truth." And, he thought, I also want you to know all the truths about me before I die. It will make my death easier for you.

I'll be caring for *both* of you, Elizabeth amended silently as she answered, "All right."

"Thank you." Nick returned his gaze to Mark and began his story. "Five years ago I became involved with a woman named Glenna Parker. We weren't in love, far from it, but nonetheless she wanted to make our relationship permanent and as a result intentionally became pregnant. We married, but it was obvious long before Justin was born that the marriage was a disaster and we agreed to a divorce that would become final after his birth. Glenna wanted sole custody of Justin—and a great deal of money for his support—and I gave both to her quite willingly. You need to know this, Mark, because if she charges that there was once a time when I chose to have nothing to do with my son, it is absolutely true."

"Okay," Mark said. "Was there a reason?"

"Yes. I was—I am—an alcoholic. Because of that, and other things that I had come to realize about myself, I believed that it was best for Justin if I never even tried to be a father to him." The soft breath Nick took caused a fire of pain, but it was trivial, so trivial, compared to the pain of the memory of his decision to let Justin live with Glenna. "When he was six months old, Glenna decided that she no longer wanted to care for him—not that she had ever really cared for him. She had obviously totally neglected him. He was terribly fearful and very quiet and withdrawn. He didn't seem to know anything about being safe or loved. You need to understand how Glenna treated Jussie when he was with her, Mark. You need to understand that he *cannot* be returned to her."

"And you think she'll try to claim him? Has she ever tried before?"

"I haven't heard a word from her in three and a half years. But if I die, and she'll know about my death because the news media is going to be very interested in this surgery, it will occur to her that Justin has no parent and a great deal of money. Money has always been very important to Glenna, and Justin will inherit far more even than the substantial earnings I've made over the past few years. I carry a two million life insurance policy of which Justin is the sole beneficiary, and Margaret has put most of her own personal wealth into a trust fund for him as well." Nick gestured to the large envelope that Larisa had brought from his house and which now lay on the nightstand. "I have a will, of course. It's in here, along with the divorce and custody papers. In it I've named Margaret as Justin's legal guardian."

"Excuse me, Nick," Mark interrupted. "But who is Margaret?"

"Margaret Reilly," Nick clarified. Then, as he clarified further, his voice filled with gentle fondness. "To Justin, to Justin's heart, Margaret is a combination mother and grandmother. But," he continued, the fondness giving way to concern, "she's not actually related to him. Margaret is the wife—the widow—of the surgeon who was my mentor during my residency. When Glenna brought Justin to me, I asked Margaret for help, and we've been a family ever since. Justin loves her and trusts her, and in the event of my death he should be with her. That's my will, and that's what's written down, but my fear is that the courts, not knowing the truth about Glenna, might give her custody, as Justin's biologic mother, rather than giving custody to a seventy-four-year-old woman who isn't a relative at all." Nick frowned, looked at Mark's solemn face, and asked, "Is that a legitimate fear?"

"I think so," Mark admitted with quiet candor. Then, smiling reassuringly, he added, "So, let's see how we can make absolutely sure that it won't happen. What does Justin know about Glenna?"

"Probably because of Margaret, he hasn't been terribly curious or concerned about Glenna's absence. When we have talked about her, I've told him that she and I weren't good enough friends to live together, and that I was very lucky to have been the one who got to live with him. He'll want to know more as he gets older, of course, and I've always planned to tell him everything when he was ready to hear it." The silent echo of his own words—*I've always planned*—stirred the immense sadness that Nick was fighting so hard to control. He wouldn't be the one to tell his son about his mother after all. Someone else would tell Justin. Margaret would tell him.

"May I look at the documents?" Mark asked.

"Of course."

During the silence in which Mark studied the divorce papers, the subsequent custody agreement, and Nick's will, Nick looked at Elizabeth for the first time since his story began.

Now you know all about me, Elizabeth, the apologetic dark blue eyes told the lovely emerald ones. *Now you know the kind of man I really am. Now you must understand why I have stayed so very far away from you.*

Nick hoped he would simply see comprehension—*Yes, Nick, I do understand, and you were very right to stay away from me.* But he steeled his heart for condemnation—*You abandoned your baby? You chose alcohol over your son?*

There *was* a message in the beautiful eyes that met his, but it was very pure, and very clear, and without any reservations whatsoever. *I love you, Nick.* The radiant emerald bravely told him that truth, and then lovingly encouraged him to reveal his own still-hidden truth, the most important one of all. And he did, he couldn't help it, because it was swept from his heart to his dark blue eyes on a joyous and powerful river of love. *I love you too, Elizabeth.*

For a few magnificent moments, Elizabeth and Nick were somewhere else, far away in a distant dream in an imaginary place where there were no dying fathers or dying sons ever, and where all the sins of the past were forgotten, and where even the deepest and most painful wounds were magically healed—a place where all things were possible . . . and where even their impossible love could flourish.

"This is interesting." Mark's voice broke the enchanted spell, returning them swiftly from the magnificence of the imaginary to the harsh truths of the real. "In addition to granting you sole custody of Justin, Glenna also signed papers that would enable your future wife to legally adopt Justin should you remarry. That's a little unusual, a little more final than the simple assignment of custody."

"So that should be helpful, shouldn't it, Mark?" Elizabeth asked. "Isn't that more proof that Glenna didn't want her son ever?"

"Yes, but . . ."

"But it's not really that helpful since I haven't remarried," Nick added quietly, correctly interpreting Mark's concern. Nick looked at Elizabeth then, and even though they were no longer in that wondrous imaginary place, and never could be, and even though the question was for Justin, and not for him, there was such soft hopefulness in Nick's voice as he gazed at her and asked, "Will you marry me, Elizabeth?"

"No."

The swift, harsh answer came from Mark, not from Elizabeth. Nick never saw Elizabeth's answer to his proposal because he looked so quickly to Mark, startled by the vehemence of his protest, yet quite unoffended by Mark's instinctive protectiveness of his little sister. Nick felt protective of Elizabeth, too. He had, after all, so very carefully protected her from his own love.

"The marriage could be annulled if I lived, Mark," Nick said quietly. "But if I died, Justin would legally have a mother, and that would effectively preempt any claim Glenna might make. From a practical standpoint, Justin would still live with Margaret."

"First of all, Glenna's lawyers would very easily establish that Elizabeth had no long-standing relationship with Justin." Mark drew a breath, trying to calm himself, then added as evenly as possible, "And second of all, Nick, I'm already concerned enough about the surgery that you're asking my sister to do."

"What do you mean?"

"I mean, I'm already worried that should you die, some self-appointed advocacy group will decide that what Elizabeth did was unethical and perhaps even bring criminal charges against her. If she were in any way a beneficiary of your death, I have no doubt that charges would be filed instantly."

"I'm not asking Elizabeth to do anything unethical, Mark. I'm asking her to use her incredible talent to save the life of an innocent little boy." Nick looked back at Elizabeth then, and with the same softness with which he had asked her to marry him, he asked, "Am I asking too much of you, Elizabeth?"

She hadn't even had a chance to answer, or recover from, Nick's question about marriage—and now there was this new one. But Elizabeth knew her answer to both questions, and it was the same for both: Yes.

Yes, Nick, I will marry you. Of course I will.

And . . . Yes, Nick, you are asking too much of me. You are asking me to watch you die.

But what Nicholas Chase was asking of Elizabeth Jennings was so very much less than what Nick was asking of himself. Nick was willing to die to save the life of his son, and he had not even for a moment questioned that immense decision of love.

And now Elizabeth didn't question the decision that she, too, had made for love.

"No, it's not too much, Nick," she softly told the man who, despite all he had to worry about, was now obviously concerned about her. Then, turning to her brother, she said, "It's not unethical, Mark. Just a little avant-garde."

"Nonetheless, you cannot appear to be a potential beneficiary. Legally, the best approach anyway is to have an affidavit taken today in which Nick openly admits to the charges that Glenna might use against him, and details her disinterest in Justin both while he was in her custody and over the intervening years, and then underscores that it is his will to have Margaret become Justin's legal guardian."

"That can be done now, today, before the surgery?"

"Sure. I can arrange that without any difficulty." Mark saw Nick's gratitude and relented a little on his personal stance about the man who he knew had caused his little sister such uncertainty ever since his arrival at the medical center. Whatever else Nick was, he was a loving father, as Mark himself was. "I promise you, Nick, I won't let Justin be given to Glenna. I'll keep the case tied up in legal red tape until he's fully grown, if necessary, and I won't touch a penny of his inheritance doing it."

After Mark left to make the arrangements for the affidavit, Elizabeth remained in Nick's room to update him on the progress of the impending surgery.

"We're scheduled to begin at eight and so far that seems a realistic time frame. Ed has agreed to first assist me in both rooms."

"Good."

"And . . ." Elizabeth told him by name every member of both teams. It was a reassuring list, the very best and most experienced, some of whom had not been officially on call on this holiday weekend but had been more than willing to come in.

"I should probably examine you now."

"Okay."

"Is there any additional history that I need to know?"

With a patient who wasn't a physician, Elizabeth would have gone through the comprehensive review of systems, the long list of questions designed to cover every aspect of the patient's past medical history, even the remote, long-forgotten childhood illnesses that could nonetheless be pertinent. But she didn't need to go through such a list with Nick, because he could tell her without prompting all the pertinent things she needed to know before taking him to the OR.

"I told you that I stopped drinking three and a half years ago, the day Glenna brought Justin to me, but I didn't tell you that I began drinking when I was eleven and that I drank very heavily, essentially daily, until the clinical years of medical school. After that I only drank when I could—whenever I could—when I wasn't in the hospital or on call." Nick paused for a moment to be certain that she, who was so dedicated to medicine and so responsible to her patients, had heard and understood that he had never violated that solemn trust either. Elizabeth's emerald eyes told Nick that she had heard; and the lovely green told him more: that it didn't surprise her. "As I mentioned earlier, as far as I know, I have never had any hepatic damage from the alcohol."

Elizabeth acknowledged his words with a thoughtful nod and then asked, "Is there any family history that I should know about?"

"I don't know much about my mother. She killed herself when I was three. I suppose it's possible, likely even, that she drank, too. My father was definitely an alcoholic, and also a very successful and highly respected trial attorney. He died six years ago from a combination of alcohol and barbituates that the coroner judged to have been an accidental overdose." Nick saw her sudden sympathy and said, "His death wasn't a tragedy for me, Elizabeth. He was never a father."

No, she thought sadly. The tragedy was that you never had either a father or a mother.

"I think that's all the pertinent history on me. As far as Justin is concerned, he's had all the usual childhood illnesses. Margaret can give you the dates. There's been nothing else, no previous hospitalizations. He's very healthy." Nick heard in his own determined voice what he had heard so often in frantic parents whose children had become innocent victims of senseless twists of fate. But he's so healthy! Just a few hours ago he was laughing and playing! Just a few precious hours ago, Justin had been frolicking in Union Square, his eyes gleaming with joy at all the festivity, his beautiful smile wide and bright as he talked excitedly about presents for Margaret. He will smile and frolic again, Nick told himself. I won't be there to see it, but my little boy will have a lifetime of happiness. "I guess that's all the history. Can you think of anything else?"

Yes! When we looked at each other, while Mark was reading the documents, I saw love in your eyes, didn't I? And when you asked me to marry you, even though it was to protect Justin from Glenna, there was much more, wasn't there?

Elizabeth knew that it wasn't the right time to ask such emotional questions. Later, when Nick and Justin were safe and well, then would be the time. Right now, she was a surgeon examining her patient for the most important operation of her lifetime—and his.

"No, I think that's all," she answered finally, removing her stethoscope from her white coat in silent signal that she was about to begin the physical examination.

Nick had been carefully examined in the ER, of course. The obvious trauma from the gunshot wound had been well documented and there had been compulsive and repetitive searches for other consequences of that injury—occult bleeding due to a splinter of bone that had punctured the spleen or arrhythmias from glancing trauma to the heart. Elizabeth needed to repeat the examination again, to be certain nothing had changed and to search for anything that might have been missed.

As Elizabeth's delicate fingers touched his skin, she felt icy coolness at the surface . . . but just beneath that there was heat, the fire she had felt before . . . and beneath that was his lean strength, steely taut now because of all his pain.

He's a patient, Elizabeth told herself as her slender hands traveled with expert and necessary boldness over his injured body. Just like any other patient.

But he wasn't just like any other patient.

He was Nick.

And he was a doctor, which meant that Elizabeth could examine him without words or instruction, in the same way that they always operated together, in perfect silent harmony. Elizabeth didn't need to tell Nick to stare at a place beyond her shoulder when she looked into the fundus of his dark blue eyes, or to take a breath each time her stethoscope touched his chest in a new spot. No words were necessary, and none were spoken at all until Elizabeth was midway through her examination of his heart. It was then, as she listened intently for soft rubs or whispered murmurs that might have been missed in the chaos of the ER, that Nick spoke.

"Elizabeth?"

"Yes?" she answered as she removed the stethoscope and looked at him.

There was so much more he could have said to her before he died. But all Nick said was, "Thank you."

And all that Elizabeth said, as she made a silent promise to her heart to tell him so much more when he and Justin were both safe and well, was, "You're very welcome."

CHAPTER TWENTY-EIGHT

*A*ll of San Francisco should have been holding its breath. All of its vibrant activity should have come to a shuddering and solemn halt.

But despite the tragedy that had befallen Nicholas and Justin Chase, the world continued to spin, and on that Saturday before Christmas, the staff of Pacific Heights Medical Center was kept exceptionally busy with a never-ending stream of new patients requiring care. Which meant that there was no one else available to do what Larisa was able to do, no one else without conflicting responsibilities. Larisa had only one responsibility: to do whatever she could do to help.

And in the six hours before the historic surgery began, Larisa had never felt more useful—or more trusted. She hadn't been given life or death tasks, of course; but still, during those important and frantic hours, she had been relied upon by Elizabeth, and by all the other doctors and nurses who had at first wondered how this beautiful woman was involved but eventually stopped questioning and simply relied upon her, too. Larisa kept a constant supply of fresh food and hot coffee in the first-floor conference room where the two teams assembled to discuss the minute details of the intricate surgery that they were about to perform; and she placed pages with the hospital operators and when the return calls came, relayed the important messages herself; and she made very certain that Elizabeth, Stephen, and the two hepatologists knew each bit of lab data the moment it became available.

The six hours passed with astonishing speed. It felt as if so much had been accomplished, but in fact it had simply been the compulsive and necessary preamble to the all-important task that lay ahead in the OR.

All-important, and impossible? Larisa had wondered as she had overheard the many conversations of the afternoon, some eager, some skeptical, and some, in whispers far away from Elizabeth, filled with the worry that neither father *nor* son would survive. Larisa had heard the conversations and she had seen the liver scans—Justin's, which showed in three dimensions just exactly how very little liver he had left, and Nick's, completely normal in size and without even a hint of the scarring that would indicate occult cirrhosis. And Larisa had been there, standing beside Elizabeth, when Bill Barnes had handed her a piece of cardboard that was his best estimate of the minimum amount of donated tissue that Justin would need to survive; and Larisa had seen, and surely Elizabeth had seen too, the grave expression of concern on Rebecca Lansing's face when that piece of cardboard was laid on top of Nick's scan. It was too much, Rebecca's expression said. *Far* too much.

Now the six hours were over. The two operating teams and their two patients were en route to the OR. There was nothing left for Larisa to do now but wait with Stephen and Margaret in the secluded waiting room. Larisa and Margaret and

Stephen would wait there, and Mark would wait at his home in Atherton with his wife and daughters, and six thousand miles away, Elizabeth's parents waited, too.

Just as Larisa was sitting down beside Margaret to begin their vigil, she heard her own name on the overhead paging system.

"It's probably the head of personnel wanting to hire you on the spot," Stephen said with a warm smile that told her again—even though he and the others had told her more than once before—how valuable she had been.

"It's probably the press," Larisa countered with a frown. Early on the head nurse in the ER had given her a white coat to wear, a pristine camouflage that made more easy and unquestioned her wanderings from radiology to ICU to clinical labs; but still, some of the many journalists assembled to cover the dramatic story had recognized her as the once-famous model and now even more famous ex-wife of Julian Chancellor. "Where's the nearest phone?"

"Halfway down the hall on your left. Have the page operator get a name first, Larisa," Stephen suggested. "If it's not someone you recognize, don't take the call."

But it was a name she recognized. She hadn't known where to reach him in Boston, and she wouldn't have had the time to try anyway. But now, exactly now, when she had time and she needed him so much, he was calling.

"Peter."

"Hi. I just turned on the eleven o'clock news and heard. The newscast said they've just gone to the operating room?"

"Yes, just."

"How does it look?"

"I don't know, Peter. I don't know. Elizabeth is so skilled, so talented, but there's a limit to what's possible."

"How are you?"

"I'm okay. Worried, but okay. I'm so proud of Elizabeth, and of Nick, but I guess I'm very afraid for both of them."

"Is anyone with you?"

"Yes. Stephen and a very lovely woman named Margaret."

"Good. I'll be there as soon as I can. It may be a while because it's snowing here and there are delays at Logan."

"You're coming back tonight?"

"Of course I am."

The tenderness in Peter's voice as he spoke the words enveloped her as if he were with her already, holding her in his strong and gentle arms. He was coming back to be with her and she wasn't even going to offer the slightest protest. Suddenly remembering why he was where he was, Larisa asked, "What did they decide about the fire?"

"There wasn't anything that specifically pointed to arson, so they're officially calling it accidental."

"Isn't that good, better, than if it had been intentionally set?"

"Yes, but the problem is that they aren't sure. There's nothing to point to arson, but they can't absolutely exclude it either."

"You sound discouraged, Peter," she said softly.

"I guess I am. I had hoped to have a definitive answer, and now I know I never will."

*　*　*

He lay before her, so pale, so still, and so totally powerless. He had relinquished his mind and his strength and his will to the anesthetic, and he had given the control of his heart and of his life to her.

We should have said more to each other, Nick! The thought came with a rush of panic as Elizabeth gazed at him and struggled against the heart-stopping impression that here, in this sterile room with its glaring lights, his pale motionless body looked almost dead. We should have said much more than "Thank you" and "You're very welcome." *I should have told you that I love you.* I should have said the words instead of simply hoping that you saw them in my eyes. I thought it wasn't the right time, I guess we both thought that, but . . . but what if it was the only time we were ever going to have?

We didn't say goodbye, Elizabeth reminded herself, calming herself with the memory. Nick and I didn't say goodbye—because we will see each other again and again.

"Are you ready, Elizabeth?" Ed asked, startling her.

But she needed to be startled out of her thoughts about the past and the future. She needed to focus all the concentration of her brilliant mind and all the gifts of her talented hands solely on the present.

Which is what she did.

"Yes. I'm ready, Ed."

She drew a soft breath, then made a straight and steady incision into Nick's abdominal wall. The strong, tautly disciplined muscles were relaxed now, paralyzed by the anesthetic, and the scalpel cut through them with deceptive ease.

Nick's liver appeared entirely normal, just as the high-tech scan had promised it would. That scan and Justin's smaller one were displayed on the view box a few feet away, and the autoclaved cardboard facsimile of the tissue that needed to be removed was lying on the sterile blue-green towels that draped Nick's badly wounded chest. The cardboard had been sterilized so that Elizabeth could safely touch it—but she had no need to. Her fingers already knew its size and shape, and in the past few hours, as her hands had memorized those two dimensions, her mind had imagined how she would make those two dimensions become three.

The piece of cardboard was a pattern, like the ones created by Christine to transform her magnificent two-dimensional sketches into flowing works of art. But there was a very critical difference. Even when the silken gowns caressed the bodies for which they had been expressly designed, adjustments could still be made, a tuck here, a seam easement there. But once Elizabeth had cut her piece from the extraordinary fabric of living tissue, there could be no adjustments, no fabric added or returned, no tucks, no easements, no embellishments—no matter how gifted a seamstress she was.

The incision Elizabeth would make could save two lives . . . or only one small one . . . or none at all.

She—they—had one chance and one chance only.

Elizabeth made the all-important incision with surprising confidence. She had known that she would be able to will her skilled fingers not to tremble, of course, but she hadn't expected the sudden inner confidence, the amazing certainty that had come just as she made the incision. But the confident certainty had come, a gift from somewhere, from Nick, perhaps, or from an even greater . . .

"He's in shock, Elizabeth," the anesthesiologist announced, his voice calm despite both the urgency and the disbelief that he felt. His brain and hands worked as he talked, increasing the rate of fluids in the intravenous lines from slow drops to wide open with quick flicks of his fingers, then reaching for the already prepared syringe of dopamine to chemically raise the blood pressure that had so mysteriously and precipitously vanished. "He was absolutely rock steady. There was no warning whatsoever, not even a trace of tachycardia, and now his heart rate's one-seventy and his pressure is sixty-palp. Something catastrophic has happened. He must be bleeding."

Had they missed an occult injury to the spleen after all? Or a tiny nick to the aorta, a pinprick from a splinter of shattered rib that had now caused the great artery to simply explode? Either of those catastrophes would have filled Nick's abdomen with blood, bright red and churning as his heart pumped frantically to try to counteract the sudden hypotension. But Nick wasn't bleeding, at least not in his abdomen. The ruptured vessel, if there was one, had to be in his chest; or perhaps the shock was an idiosyncratic reaction to the anesthetic; or perhaps she had taken too much tissue from him and all the cells in his body, sensing their imminent death, had just surrendered to the inevitable, collapsing all at once in astonished defeat.

Elizabeth didn't have time to either think about what had happened or to try to solve it. The rest of the team would have to find the answers that would save Nick. Right now, *right now*, she and Ed had to take the precious tissue that she had just so confidently removed to the little boy who lay motionless and pale in the adjacent operating room. Perhaps she had taken too many cells from Nick, maybe even only one too many, but the one cell that might have cost Nick his life could be the same one that would save the life of his son.

Elizabeth left, not knowing whether Nick would live or die and forcing herself not to think about it. Her mind and hands and heart had to be entirely focused on the delicate stitches that would embroider the precious tissue from the dying father to his dying son.

"Christine." Stephen stood as she walked into the surgery waiting room shortly after ten.

"Hi. I started to call you after the pageant, but I called a cab instead." After a hesitant moment, she confessed, "I guess I just wanted to be here."

"I'm very glad," Stephen said, his welcome at once warm and reassuring.

"I'm very glad, too," Larisa added as she joined them. "Peter is on his way back from Boston. Oh, Christine, this is Margaret."

Larisa didn't explain relationships. It simply wasn't necessary. They were all here because they cared, and that was all that mattered.

Two hours later, just after midnight, Elizabeth walked into the waiting room. She was clearly exhausted, but beneath the fatigue glowed a soft light of hope.

"They're okay," Larisa breathed.

"Well, they both survived the surgery. Justin sailed through it, without any complications whatsoever."

"And Nick?"

Frowning, Elizabeth said quietly, "Nick went into shock just after I removed the piece of liver."

"Anesthetic reaction," Stephen suggested swiftly, seeing at once her worry that it was the incision she had made that had caused the shock.

"I don't know. Maybe. That or the incision itself. No other reason was found."

"Is his pressure back up now?"

"Yes, and it's maintaining well off pressors. Both Nick and Justin are being transferred upstairs right now. Nick will be in the surgery ICU on the eighth floor and Justin will be back in the pediatric ICU on six. He's already awake, Margaret, awake but groggy, but he'll know that you're there."

"And Nick? Is he awake yet?"

"No," Elizabeth answered softly. "Nick's not awake yet. He was still quite deep when I left the OR to come here . . ."

CHAPTER TWENTY-NINE

"*D*addy's sleeping," Justin was told every time he asked about his father. The words were spoken by the nurses and Margaret and Elizabeth, all of whom spoke them with the most gentle of reassurance. Margaret had shared with those who needed to know what had happened in August, when Justin had been ill and had regressed to the fearful and withdrawn silence of the first six months of his life. Margaret wasn't sure how they could prevent such a regression now, especially as one day became two and then three.

But Justin's recovering body needed long hours of sleep, and that made him quite unaware of how much time had actually passed, and it made perfect sense to him anyway that his daddy was as sleepy as he . . . but it made no sense at all to the many medical experts who examined Nick in his ICU bed. He should have long since awakened. *But he hadn't*. Nicholas Chase was in a coma as mysterious and inexplicable as the shock that had developed so suddenly in the OR.

By the evening of the twenty-third, forty-eight hours after the historic surgery, Nick was no longer Elizabeth's patient. He didn't need to be. From a surgical standpoint, he was absolutely stable. Not a drop of blood had been lost from the hepatic incision site, and the perfectly straight abdominal wound that Elizabeth's scalpel had created was healing beautifully. Nick's care was transferred to a neurologist, who tried to make sense of his coma; and to a pulmonary specialist, who managed the chest tube and fractured ribs; and to Dr. Rebecca Lansing, who had been there from the beginning and was now monitoring Nick's lab values very carefully to determine if the amount of liver Elizabeth had left was enough to sustain his life until new tissue could grow.

Nick was no longer Elizabeth's patient, but she had other patients in the hospital now—including two new renal transplant recipients, patients for whom Nick would have performed the surgeries on the twenty-second and twenty-third, while she and Larisa had been taking Harrod's by storm, if only . . .

"Peter and I thought it would be nice for all of us to have Christmas Eve dinner together," Larisa said. "All of us" was Larisa and Peter and Stephen and Christine and Margaret and Elizabeth, and all except Elizabeth were in the ICU waiting room when Larisa made the suggestion.

"I think that's a wonderful idea, Larisa," Christine said.

"Oh, good, I'm glad." Larisa smiled at Christine and then turned to Margaret. "The apartment where Elizabeth and I live is very close, and I hoped that if we planned dinner for eight, when Justin is asleep, that you would come too."

"Well, I suppose, if Justin is asleep . . ."

"We'll hold dinner until he is."

"All right, Larisa," Margaret agreed. "Thank you."

"Would you like help with the meal?" Christine asked.

"Sure! We haven't planned much further than turkey and stuffing, which Peter's going to make from a recipe his father taught him. Any other specialties are more than welcome."

Christine cast a tentative glance toward Stephen just as he shifted his gaze to find hers. Their eyes met, and in answer to his silent question, she gave a slight nod and a beautiful smile.

"I happen to know that Christine makes sensational French onion soup."

"Really? Would you like to for tomorrow, Christine? You could prepare it right at the apartment if that would be easiest."

"I guess that would be easiest, and yes, I'd be very happy to." Tilting her golden head she said to Stephen, "Maybe I could show you how I slice the onions."

"I'll be there," Stephen promised. Then, reluctantly taking his eyes from the smiling lavender ones he suggested to Larisa, "Why don't I plan to pick up something from Just Desserts?"

"Wonderful." Larisa's expression changed from smiling to solemn as she added, "But, Stephen, there's something else I had hoped you would be responsible for bringing tomorrow."

"Okay. What's that?"

"Elizabeth," Larisa said quietly. Elizabeth, my dear friend who is working far too hard and being far too strong. Elizabeth, who needs to talk about her fears but won't . . . and who most of all needs to speak aloud her unspoken worry that it is she who caused Nick's shock and Nick's coma.

"I have to stop for a minute!" Christine exclaimed softly.

She turned to him then, lavender eyes glistening, cheeks flushed pink, a lovely smile on her lips. The tears in her eyes were sparkles of happiness, not raindrops of grief. As she had been slicing the onions for the soup, she had been talking almost breathlessly to Stephen, as if for the past three months she had been saving up things just to tell *him*—and now the words tumbled out in a rush, eager to be free and quite unwilling to hold back because of something as trivial as the imprudence of slicing onions and talking at the same time.

"Too much talking," she murmured.

Not enough talking, Stephen thought, his smiling gaze not wavering even when he felt a twisting ache deep inside as she delicately dabbed away the tears with her left hand—her wedding ring hand. The slender band glittered at him, a solid gold reminder of the truth, the warning: Christine is married. She will always be married to David. She is going on with her life—her dream of becoming a designer—and David would be so happy for her. This is what he had hoped for his beloved Christie.

They had been talking about her designs just before she had turned from the onions to him, and now, wanting to keep the conversation focused still on the dream that made her smile, Stephen said, "You clearly have the talent to design anything you want, but do you have favorites, dresses or outfits that you enjoy designing the most?"

"Oh." Christine's already flushed cheeks became a little rosier at his compliment, and then her beautiful face grew thoughtful as she considered his question. "I'd never really thought about it before. Making the costumes for the pageant and working with the children was wonderful, and designing Larisa's dresses for the *Promise* ad campaign has been very exciting. But, I suppose, if I had to limit myself, I would design dresses for romantic occasions—prom dresses and wedding dresses, something like that."

"Did you design your own?"

"Prom dress and wedding dress? No, neither. I didn't go to the prom, and David and I were married by a justice of the peace, just us and the two required witnesses, at the town hall in Berkeley." She hesitated a moment. Then, encouraged by his welcoming smile, she said, "As I was helping dress the girls in their costumes Saturday night, I was very tempted to make an offer then and there to sew their prom dresses for them when the time came, and their wedding dresses too, if they wanted me to."

"Like the man in New York who promised to pay for the college education of any and all the children in a certain elementary school class who graduated from high school?"

"Well, my offer isn't quite as significant as that."

"Oh, I don't know," Stephen replied quietly. "I think romance is probably pretty significant."

Christine answered with a smile of soft surprise, and, after a moment of slight confusion, turned back to the onions that still needed to be sliced.

Stephen watched in silence as she sliced, not prompting her with questions, because the questions that swirled in his mind now were ones that he had absolutely no right to ask.

What about romance in your life, Christine?

What about making prom dresses and wedding dresses for your own daughters?

Margaret arrived promptly at eight. Justin was asleep, she told them, and Nick was unchanged. By eight-fifteen, when Elizabeth had neither called nor appeared despite the promise exacted from her by both Larisa and Stephen that she *would* be there, Stephen quietly announced that he was going to the hospital to get her.

Stephen knew Elizabeth's patients very well. He was managing their immunosuppression after all. The patients who were officially in Elizabeth's care were completely stable. She wouldn't be with them, Stephen knew. She would be with a patient for whom she had already given everything she had to give. Stephen found her in the surgery ICU, standing outside Nick's room, staring at him through the plate glass.

"Time for dinner."

"Oh." She turned, obviously startled from a faraway thought. "Stephen. Is it time? I had no idea it was that late."

"Well it is, and I've come to personally escort you to the gourmet feast."

"I'll be there soon, Stephen, I promise. Please tell the others that I've gotten delayed and ask them to start without me. I'll be there, I will, but there's something I have to do first."

"Okay," Stephen agreed, relenting without an argument because the fatigued emerald eyes that met his were so very resolute.

Something I have to do first. Words I have to say to Nick. Elizabeth had talked to Nick often in the past few days, every time she visited. She had gazed at the handsome face that even in this deepest of sleeps seemed so very tormented; and she had told him how well Justin was doing; and she had pleaded softly with him to awaken, and sometimes she had even commanded him to. Elizabeth had spoken gentle words of reassurance, but there were other words, other truths, that remained unspoken.

Because he is going to wake up, she kept telling herself. And when he does we will both speak aloud the silent messages that were in our eyes before surgery.

But what if Nicholas Chase never woke up? Then she would never hear the secrets of his heart.

Maybe I will never hear the secrets of Nick's heart, Elizabeth thought as she entered the room and moved very close to him, to the bed where he lay. But at least, perhaps, please, he will hear the most important truths of mine.

"Hi, Nick. It's me, Elizabeth. I've just seen Jussie. He's fine, sleeping now, better and stronger with each passing minute, and very eager to see his daddy." Elizabeth's voice began to falter as she thought about the beloved little boy. Justin didn't know it was Christmas Eve, and they had decided not to tell him, to delay Christmas altogether until a time when he could celebrate with his father. Let him hear your love, not your fear. The words Nick had spoken to Danny's parents on that tragic day in August came back to her now, giving her strength as she confessed softly, "I love you, Nicholas Chase. I think you already know this. I suppose it's been obvious from the very beginning. And, Nick, I think that you love me, too. Maybe you thought I wouldn't love you if I knew about your drinking, or that once you believed it was best for Justin not to live with you. But I know both those things now, and I love you so much, Nick, so much."

Elizabeth had to stop then. Her voice was too shaky and tears filled her emerald eyes. She turned from Nick's bed and gazed out the window into the winter darkness. Nick had been given the room with the best view. Below was the courtyard, twinkling with cheerful white Christmas lights, and in the foreground lay the city, glittering like a crown of brilliant jewels in the clear winter air, and somewhere beyond, in the vast darkness, was the bay. Elizabeth didn't see the glittering lights, nor did she hear the Christmas carols that played softly in the distance. She saw only the vast darkness—and she shivered as she imagined its endless iciness and its endless silence.

"Elizabeth?"

For a moment she didn't believe the sound. It was a horrid hallucination— Nick's voice calling to her from the vast icy blackness.

But then she turned and saw his dark blue eyes. They were gazing at her, a wondrous expression of disbelief and hope, like someone who knew he must surely be dreaming . . . but was hopeful, so very hopeful, that the magnificent dream might possibly be real.

"Nick," she whispered as fresh tears began to spill. Her tears caused sudden fear on his face, but swiftly and so joyously she reassured, "Justin is fine, Nick."

"He is?" Justin is fine and I'm alive?

"Yes. In every way. The grafted tissue is already functioning very well, and emotionally, even though he keeps asking about you, he hasn't become withdrawn or fearful."

"How long has it been?"

"Three days, almost to the minute. It's eight-thirty, and it's Christmas Eve." After a moment she admitted, "Your surgery was a little more complicated than Justin's, Nick. Within seconds after I did the resection from your liver, you went into shock."

"Not because of the resection."

"Well, it was either because of that or because of the anesthetic. We don't have another explanation. Nor do we really have an explanation for why it took you so long to wake up."

"Maybe both were due to my alcohol use," Nick said quietly, solemnly reminding her of his deep flaws, gently shifting the responsibility from her, where it didn't belong, to him, where it did. Then he smiled, and reminding her of the astonishing truth for which she *was* responsible, he said very softly, "But I'm awake now, and Jussie is fine."

"And he's going to be so happy to see you."

"Not as happy as I will be to see him."

Elizabeth wanted that happiness now, as soon as possible, for both of them.

"Neither of you is officially my patient anymore, so before I start arranging father-son reunions, I'd better make some phone calls. I'll go do that right now. In the meantime, there's a phone call you could make."

"Oh?"

"Yes. There's a Christmas Eve dinner going on at my apartment. Larisa insisted on it and scheduled it for a time when she knew that Justin would be sleeping so Margaret could be there. I think I can say with extreme confidence that a phone call from you would really make Larisa's party."

"Okay," Nick agreed, smiling gently. After a moment the gentle smile faded and his handsome face grew very solemn. "Elizabeth?"

"Yes?"

"Thank you."

"You're very welcome."

Those were the words they had spoken to each other before the surgery—those words, and not goodbye . . . and not, either, the silent messages that had been in their eyes. And now the surgery was over, and both father and son had miraculously survived, and it would be safe at last to allow those silent joyous messages to return, and even to speak them aloud.

But there were no joyous messages of love in Nick's eyes now. The dark blue was only solemn—and troubled.

"What, Nick?"

It took a moment for him to answer, and when he did his voice was dangerously soft, and his words were a quiet warning. "Please don't care about me, Elizabeth. I have very little to offer, far too little."

It was amazing to Elizabeth how quickly—and with what clarity—she understood the devastating meaning of those quiet words. Perhaps he had heard her confession of love, or perhaps he was merely remembering the silent messages his own eyes had sent when he had believed he was going to die. But either way, Nicholas Chase wanted to set the record straight as soon as possible.

His exquisitely gentle and eloquent gazes of love had been his farewell gift to her, so that she could believe forever that her so-obvious love for him had been reciprocated after all. It was a most generous gift, but not a terribly risky one since he had fully believed that he was going to die.

But now Nick knew that he wasn't going to die after all, and now it was time for the real truth: *I know you love me, Elizabeth, but I don't really love you.* Nick didn't say it that way, of course. He was far too polite—and far too experienced in extricating himself from women who loved him—to be so brutally blunt. Instead he gallantly cast himself as the villain of the piece, placing responsibility for the love that couldn't be directly on himself, blaming himself just as he blamed himself and his alcohol use for every adverse event that had happened in the OR.

But Elizabeth knew the truth. It wasn't that Nick had far too little to offer. It was simply that he didn't want to offer what he had to *her.* His words and their meaning were as crystal clear as the cool winter night, and the emptiness she felt was as black and icy as the vastness beyond.

But somehow she smiled.

And somehow she spoke.

"I understand, Nick. And now I really want to get going on those phone calls."

When the phone rang at the apartment, Larisa assumed it would be Elizabeth, calling to say that she wasn't going to make the Christmas Eve dinner after all . . . so Larisa simply began issuing her gentle yet exasperated command the moment she lifted the receiver, "Elizabeth Jennings, you get over here right now! There's absolutely no reason for you to be there, and it's not even good for you to be. You have to let it go, Elizabeth, just for a little while."

"That sounds like some pretty tough love to me, Larisa."

"Nick?" she whispered. *"Nick."*

PART FIVE

CHAPTER THIRTY

*T*he nightmares were worse than all the ones that had come before. He dreamed about Justin, of course, relentlessly reliving the day of terror in Union Square, and he dreamed about Elizabeth. There were guns aimed at her, too, and he couldn't stop the bullets, even though he tried to so desperately. "I love you, Nick," Elizabeth called to him from the infinite abyss as she fell and fell and fell. He stood on the very edge of the abyss, watching her endless fall, and in answer to her dying pledge of love, he whispered a harsh warning of ice, "Don't care about me, Elizabeth!" And his words were more lethal than all her bloody wounds. He saw the hurt, the death in her emerald eyes, just before she vanished into the darkness forever.

The nightmares came every night, awakening him drenched and gasping after only a few moments of sleep. And even though his terribly weak body needed sleep so badly, Nick would leave his bed then and cross the hallway to Justin's room. There, he would try to calm himself by gazing at the very peaceful sleep of his very healthy son.

Six weeks had passed since the day in Union Square, and it had been almost five weeks since he and Justin had been discharged from the hospital. Justin was virtually well. The donated liver was functioning magnificently, and by now even if it was suddenly rejected, Justin's own liver had already regenerated enough to sustain him. Physically, his son was almost whole again, and emotionally, Justin was remarkably unscathed. He had neither nightmares about the day in Union Square, nor troubling memories of the events that had followed in the hospital. His only memory of the day in the square was a memory of love, the loving arms of his father curled tightly around him protecting him from a harm he never even saw; and his memories of the hospital were foggy, but not frightening. His daddy had been there, sleeping too, and Margaret and Elizabeth and Mr. Bear had been with him, and he had felt safe and loved.

Justin slept peacefully, as he always had, and Nick's sleep was more tormented than it had ever been before. Before . . . when his body had been strong and fit and he had been able to run in the midnight darkness until his exhaustion blurred the nightmares and muffled the screams of pain. Nick could have safely gone out into the darkness now, because Justin would not awaken, frightened, from his deep and peaceful sleep; but his once strong body was far too weak to run even a block much less the miles and miles he would need to run to vanquish the pain. He would need to run farther and faster than ever before, because the anguished cries of his heart, like his terrifying nightmares, were so very much worse than they had ever been; because, as with the nightmares, Nick's emotional pain now involved Elizabeth, loving her so much . . . and knowing that she loved him too . . . and knowing that their love was impossible . . . and remembering the hurt in her eyes when he had told her not to care about him. The emerald hurt had lasted only a flicker, but the memory of the immense pain that he had caused the woman he loved was indelibly etched in his waking mind and relived every night in his nightmares.

Nick had neither seen nor spoken to Elizabeth since the day that he and Justin were discharged. They had talked on that day, a painfully formal discussion of the plans for the transplant service while he was away. He would be on leave until the first of June, the minimum convalescence time that Rebecca Lansing would allow. During his five-month absence the two two-membered transplant teams would become one three-membered one, and Elizabeth would become acting service chief.

Nick hadn't seen her since that day. He might have seen her by accident had he kept his appointments in the hepatology clinic; but Nick couldn't risk seeing Elizabeth by accident, nor could he permit anyone to report to her how he looked. So he stayed away from the hospital entirely. Margaret drew the necessary weekly blood tests on him at home, and he and Rebecca discussed the results over the phone. The lab tests simply confirmed what Nick already knew from the oppressive weakness he lived with every second of every day: he wasn't getting any better. His liver wasn't regenerating the way it should have been by now.

His survival wasn't in jeopardy. He could live forever like this. This—being alive and having the extraordinary joy of watching his happy and healthy son grow up—was so much more than he had ever dared to hope. Justin's survival had been all that mattered. That had been gift enough, miracle enough, but he had been given even more—his own life—because of the talent and courage of the woman he loved so much . . . and had hurt so deeply.

Nick knew the sadness it would cause Elizabeth to see him this weak, as if she had failed, as if it was her fault that his liver wasn't regenerating—even though it was because of her that he was alive . . . and because of his own deep flaws, his past history of alcohol use, that he wasn't recovering as he should have been.

Nick couldn't let Elizabeth see him like this, and it was already February third, and in a few hours he would make the phone call he should have made weeks ago, but had kept putting off, hoping to be certain that he would be well enough to see her again by the fifteenth.

He was no better on this dark winter dawn, but he was going to make the call today anyway . . . and somehow, in the next twelve days, he was going to become well *for her*.

Elizabeth took a steadying breath before pressing the flashing button on her telephone which her secretary had just told her was a call from Nick.

"Hello, Nick. How are you?"

"Fine. Far better than my lab data might suggest," he said firmly. He didn't know if Elizabeth had been following his discouraging lab tests, but as a result of this phone call he knew that she soon would be. His voice softened, "I'm just fine, Elizabeth, and I have a very healthy little boy. How are you?"

"Everything's fine here, too," she said, answering his question as if it had been asked about the transplant service and not about her. "There are really no problems at all."

"I'm not surprised, but that's not why I'm calling."

"No?"

"No. I wondered if you would be willing to give the keynote address at the International Congress."

"You're not going to Paris after all?"

"Yes, I am going." *And somehow I will be well.* "But I thought that for the keynote address I would make an appearance as a specimen rather than as a speaker. A review of the world's experience with living donor liver transplantation would obviously be incomplete without a detailed account of what you did in December—and that's your surgery. I've already done a complete review of everything before then, and can get that information to you to use and restructure however you like, but the review is merely a preamble to what you did on Justin and me. That needs to be presented in great detail, Elizabeth. It was a very important surgery." Emotion touched his deep rich voice as he added, "I only know the stunning results—I'm living them—but I have no idea how you worked the magic."

As Elizabeth listened to Nick's words, and heard the surprised and gentle gratitude in his voice, she realized anew that he had had no expectation whatsoever that he would survive the surgery. He had convinced her to operate on him, fully believing that the incision she would make would be lethal. She felt a deep and powerful anger beginning to swell within her; but she subdued it, tranquilized it, with the icy memory of what Nick had said to her on Christmas Eve. *He doesn't want you to care about him—so don't!* Elizabeth subdued the anger with that memory, and then calmed it further by reminding herself of the most—the only—important truth: Nicholas Chase was alive. That was what mattered, all that mattered. The other wishes of her heart, that he could love her as she loved him, were quite trivial in comparison.

"Will you give the address, Elizabeth?" Nick asked into the lingering silence. "I realize that this is a last-minute request, and I would be happy to do the renal transplantation presentation if that would free some time for you to prepare the keynote."

"That talk is basically done. I can just give you all my notes."

"No. If you've already done the work, why don't you present it? Why don't you present them both?"

"All right," she agreed quietly, fighting the memory of her happiness the day that Nick had asked her to give just one of the presentations. A vote of confidence, she had decided joyfully. It had been wonderful, *enough*; but since then Nick had given her the greatest vote of confidence possible. He had entrusted to her care the life of his precious son—not to mention his own life. And after that she had wanted even more, something that wasn't hers to have: Nick's love. *Nicholas Chase is alive*, she reminded herself. *That's all that matters.* "Did you want to meet before we go to Paris, to go over what I'm planning to say?"

"It's not necessary. This is your show, Elizabeth."

Stephen smiled at the embellishment his secretary had playfully made on his appointment calendar at the top of today's date: a smiling red heart, complete with a feathery arrow.

Stephen needed no bright red reminders that today was Valentine's Day. He knew, and his own heart smiled as he thought about the evening that lay ahead. He and Christine were dining at the Top of the Mark, high above the glitter of the city, amid roses and candlelight and romantic music. Ever since Christmas they had seen each other often, usually making plans only from one date to the next. But candlelight dinner at the Top of the Mark on February fourteenth required advanced reservations; so he had invited her in advance, weeks ago, and she had accepted immediately, and they had decided together that they would dress formally for the special occasion.

Stephen smiled as he anticipated the evening ahead, but the smile faded a little as he thought about the sixteen days that would follow. Three months ago, when he had scheduled the visits to the major European centers of immunologic research, the itinerary he had been able to arrange had been quite thrilling. It still was—from a scientific standpoint. After attending the first two days of the congress in Paris, he would spend the following two weeks in Vienna, Edinburgh, Geneva, and Stockholm, learning, teaching, and sharing ideas with his colleagues. Three months ago, being away sixteen days had been a concern only from a professional standpoint—arranging coverage for his patients and making certain that his research was at a phase that could be ably managed by his research associates.

But now sixteen days away meant sixteen days away from Christine.

Stephen couldn't cancel the commitments he had made to his overseas colleagues, and it was a unique opportunity, but he hated the thought of being away from her for so long. He had even considered asking Christine to join him. She couldn't the first week, he knew. She and Peter and Larisa would be in Los Angeles, at the Bel Air home of Emily Rousseau Adamson, for the photo sessions for *Promise*. Larisa wanted Christine to be at the sessions, to make certain that the graceful folds of silk and the delicate whispers of lace on the magnificent dresses she had designed fell just so. And the second week? Christine would be busy, as always, designing the beautiful gowns that were in ever-increasing demand throughout the Bay Area.

But there was another reason Stephen had decided not to ask Christine to join him in Europe. He didn't want to overwhelm her. An entire week together would be a vast leap from what they had done since Christmas—evenings, many evenings; dinner, or dinner and the theater; and yes, more than once, talking until almost dawn. But that was all.

All? Stephen knew what those wonderful evenings of gentle laughter and quiet conversation and lovely lavender eyes meant to him—and what he wanted them to mean: the beginning of a lifetime together. And if that was an impossible wish? If Christine was married forever to David?

Then Stephen wanted to live his own magnificent delusion for as long as possible . . .

"I made myself a prom dress," Christine said, as she greeted him with a shy shrug and cheeks that flushed the same pale pink as the very romantic—yet demure and elegant—silk chiffon dress that she wore. It was a dress for a woman, but Christine had never gone to a prom, and even though the dress was womanly, her lavender eyes glowed with the hopeful innocence of a teenaged girl.

"It's beautiful." Stephen added softly, "You're beautiful."

"Oh!" Christine bravely met his appreciative gaze. "Thank you."

"You're welcome. I brought you some roses."

As Christine took the fragrant bouquet of exquisite cream-colored rosebuds from his hand, Stephen's heart nearly stopped.

She wasn't wearing her wedding ring.

Christine's eyes followed his eyes to the band of skin on her left ring finger that was even more pale than her delicate fairness. Then, lifting her beautiful face to his, she said quietly, "I decided it was time for me to take it off."

They caressed with soft smiles and gentle gazes across the flickering flames of pale pink candles; and they touched lightly but wondrously as they danced slowly to the most romantic songs of love; and when they stopped dancing their hands intertwined still . . . his right hand, which so carefully had administered to David the miraculous life-prolonging therapy . . . and her left hand, ringless now, its delicate fingertips tender from the needle pricks that had unceremoniously pulled her back from the astonishing, and terrifying, and sometimes terribly sad thoughts that had swirled in her mind since Christmas.

At midnight, when they stood on the secluded porch of her small house, quite hidden from all eyes but their own, Stephen kissed her. And Christine kissed him back.

It was a gentle hello greeted by a tender welcome . . . the joyous beginning of magnificent discoveries, of passionate warmth, and silent promises, and soft sighs of crescendoing desire. It was a shared and wondrous joy—until Christine pulled away.

Stephen saw desire still in the lovely lavender, but even as he watched, the shimmering desire was replaced by bewildered confusion.

"Christine?"

"Thank you for the lovely evening, Stephen."

"You're welcome," he said softly, wanting so much to help her but seeing so clearly that what she wanted was privacy.

Had his kiss overwhelmed her? Had its gentle but unconcealed passion somehow even frightened her? No, Stephen decided. Christine was confused, and troubled by her confusion, but she was not frightened. For a hopeful moment, he even thought that she was going to say something more, to try to articulate to him her bewildering emotions.

But then her eyes left his, and she fumbled to find the keys in her purse, and after she opened the door, she turned back to him very briefly and whispered, "Good night."

"Good night," Stephen echoed gently as she disappeared.

He didn't try to stop her. Her sudden wish for privacy was so obvious, and so compelling. But as he drove away, Stephen knew that he would speak with her in the morning, before he left for Paris—and the sixteen days that would be spent so very far away from her.

The tears began to spill the moment Christine pulled the door closed behind her, and as she walked even deeper into her house, *their* house, her vision became blurred with the hot dampness. But Christine didn't need her lavender eyes to see where she was going. Her footsteps were unerringly guided by her weeping heart.

And then she was there, standing before the magnificent portrait he had painted of her, and she whispered softly, "Oh, David. Oh, *David*."

Stephen waited until eight A.M. to call her. But there was no answer then, or at eight-fifteen, or at eight-thirty. Worried, he drove to her house.

Christine didn't answer his knock, but the porch light was off, and the flag on the mailbox was up—reassuring signals, Stephen decided, that she had long since awakened and left. Today was probably one of the rare Saturdays that she still worked at Sydney's, a long day dedicated to helping the many clients whose wardrobes depended still on her gift for fashion and style. This was obviously going to be such a day, and Christine had gone in early to prepare.

Sydney's didn't officially open its doors until ten, so Stephen returned to his apartment, put his luggage in his car, and arrived at the boutique just as the elegant French doors were being swung open.

Sydney herself greeted him.

"Stephen!"

"Hello, Sydney," he answered, a little surprised by the warmth of her welcome. He and Sydney had seen each other only twice before, in August when he had come to look at the atrium with Peter and a few weeks later at the Fairmont ball. Perhaps, he thought hopefully, Sydney's memory of him had been kept evergreen, and obviously warm, because of something Christine had said. "I'm looking for Christine."

"She's not here today, Stephen. I imagine that at this very moment she's having a power breakfast with Colin Gallagher."

"Colin Gallagher?"

"He just happens to be New York's hottest fashion designer."

"Yes, I know," Stephen said quietly. Christine had told him all about Colin Gallagher, how talented he was, how innovative and visionary. She had told Stephen about Colin Gallagher weeks ago, but she hadn't said a word about him last night. Stephen heard the disbelief in his own voice as he asked, "Christine is with Colin Gallagher this morning?"

"I assume so. I know she was with him all yesterday afternoon, and presumably they had a candlelight dinner together somewhere last night. He's wooing her, you see, trying to get her to move to New York to work with him." This was exciting news, but Sydney stopped abruptly when she saw that Stephen obviously didn't share her excitement. "All of which means that Christine isn't here this morning. Sheila is available, though, and I'm sure she'd be happy to help you."

"No, thank you, Sydney." Stephen forced a smile. "I just stopped by on impulse, and I actually have a plane to catch."

As he drove to the airport, Stephen realized that Sydney obviously knew nothing about his relationship with Christine. Why would she? he chided himself. *What relationship?*

Despite Christine's sudden confusion during their kiss, so very understandable given her immense love for David, last night had felt to Stephen like a joyous beginning, a brave and wonderful step toward happily ever after.

But, he wondered, had the evening that had felt to him like such a wondrous hello been in truth the gentlest of goodbyes? Even before their candlelit dinner, had Prince Charming already placed on Cinderella's delicate foot the glass slipper with which she would courageously journey ever closer to her own fairy-tale dreams?

As she walked to her preassigned seat in the first-class cabin, Elizabeth wondered if instructions had been given to the travel agency in Paris regarding who should sit next to whom. She already knew that she and Stephen had been assigned to sit together. And Nick? As she saw him take a window seat on the opposite side of the jet's expansive cabin, she decided, yes, such instructions had been given.

She and Nick had already spoken, of course, a brief polite greeting in the boarding area. Elizabeth would have walked on, but Margaret and Justin were there, and as she talked to them Nick had silently watched their animated conversation.

Elizabeth and Nick had scarcely spoken, but she had been so aware of him, how terribly pale he was, how dark circled his blue eyes, how uncertain his smile.

Elizabeth saw the uncertainty and pallor and fatigue, but she sensed, as always, the taut strength and smoldering fire in his lean and powerful body. The noble warrior had been badly wounded, but he was proud still, and strong, and disciplined.

Had it been sheer pride that had finally and so dramatically caused his lab tests to improve? she wondered. The improvement had begun six days ago, and it was so dramatic that Rebecca, hopeful yet disbelieving, had asked Margaret to draw additional blood samples yesterday—and the repeat blood work was even better still.

Had the incredibly disciplined Nick simply willed his own improvement because he had known that for the next five days he would be on display? Elizabeth herself had no intention of displaying him, of course, neither having him stand where he sat in the audience nor join her on the stage—surely he knew that; but most of the other surgeons attending the congress already knew what the famous Nicholas Chase looked like, and they would be looking at him now with renewed interest and curiosity.

Proud, and strong, and disciplined. The same adjectives could easily have been applied to her. She, too, looked very pale, and her emerald eyes were dark circled, too, from far too little sleep. The weeks between Christmas Eve and Valentine's Day had been frantically busy, handling the administrative responsibilities for the transplant service in Nick's absence and, at her insistence, taking call for both transplant and trauma as always. Elizabeth had kept herself very busy; but all the while, like Nick, she had been preparing herself to be on display—not for hundreds of eyes, as Nick would be, but just for the dark blue ones that didn't love her.

Elizabeth had hoped that the passing of time would make her better. But when it hadn't, she had done with her broken heart just what Nick had done with his broken body, simply willing it to heal—enough, at least, to send a proud and strong message to the sensuous dark blue: I'm fine, Nick. I'm just fine without you.

During the hectic weeks since Christmas, Elizabeth hadn't had one midnight chat, or even one late afternoon cup of tea, with Stephen. We can talk now, she thought as she settled into the seat beside the friend she had barely seen. We can talk from here to Paris, a nice, private conversation, muffled by the noise of the engines and thankfully very far away from Nick.

But from the moment she sat down, Elizabeth realized that Stephen, too, was very far away. She didn't intrude, not for miles and miles, but finally, when she could stand the sadness in his brooding dark eyes no longer, she asked softly, "What's wrong, Stephen?"

"Have you ever heard of Colin Gallagher?"

"Yes, of course. Why?"

"Did you know that Christine has a chance to work with him?"

Elizabeth stiffened at his almost accusatory tone, as if she had known and had intentionally withheld the information from him. It was a tone, Elizabeth realized, that she had heard once before—when Stephen had sharply demanded if she had been planning to share with him her discovery that Sydney's famous Christine was also Mrs. David Andrews. Both times the issue had been Christine; but this time Elizabeth had no hidden knowledge.

"No."

"He's in San Francisco, trying to convince her to move to New York even as we speak."

"I honestly didn't know, Stephen. I haven't even seen Christine since Christmas Eve. She and Larisa see each other quite frequently, but if Christine told Larisa about Colin Gallagher, Larisa didn't tell me." Elizabeth hesitated, then added gently, "I guess I also didn't know about you and Christine."

"Christine probably didn't mention that to Larisa, either. But why would she? There was obviously nothing to tell."

"We've talked before about how private Christine is, Stephen."

"Oh, yes, she's very private," he agreed bitterly. "She spent yesterday afternoon with Colin Gallagher and last evening with me, and she didn't say a word about the fact that he was in town."

"There could be *nonsinister* reasons for that."

"Really? I've been trying for hours to come up with one, just one, and so far I've come up empty."

"Well," Elizabeth began, but faltered quickly, at a loss, too, for a silver lining. "You'll just have to call Christine from Paris and find out."

Stephen had been thinking about calling her, of course, but it wasn't a conversation to have over the phone, and he had been thinking about taking the first flight out of Paris back to San Francisco, but . . .

"Aren't you going to call her, Stephen? Won't she be expecting you to?"

"I don't know if she expects me to call, Elizabeth, and I don't know if I'm going to. What's the point in confronting her with something she obviously didn't want me to know? I think she should accept the job with Gallagher, of course. I guess I had hoped it would have been something she would discuss with me."

"Because you would follow her to New York if she wanted you to, wouldn't you?"

"Yes, I would, Elizabeth. In a minute."

CHAPTER THIRTY-ONE

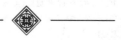

Paris
February 1992

$\mathcal{T}$he plane touched the tarmac at Charles de Gaulle at eight A.M. Paris time. The February morning was overcast, a gray cloudiness that matched the fogginess they all felt as they deplaned after the long flight through many time zones. Elizabeth, Stephen, and Nick shared a taxi to the Ritz; and then, because their lavish suites were all located on the same floor, they shared an elevator, too. Then they parted, to try to get some sleep in the ten hours that remained before Elizabeth's keynote address.

Elizabeth stood at the window of her elegant suite and gazed at the Tuilerie Gardens below, and the Seine beyond, and in the distance the Eiffel Tower. As tired as she was, she felt the invisible and almost irresistible pull of Paris beckoning to her, inviting her to discover its alluring mysteries.

I will, she promised herself. After I get a little sleep.

The keynote address was scheduled for eight P.M. in the hotel's grand ballroom. Elizabeth set her alarm for five, just in case, but she awakened refreshed and eager at one and spent the rest of the Sunday afternoon wandering through Paris, mentally rehearsing her talk as she battled the ever-crescendoing anxiety she felt because of it.

How many lectures have I given? she demanded of herself and her churning stomach as she walked briskly along the Champs-Elysees. The answer was simple: many. All had been compulsively prepared in advance, as this one had been; in fact, her meticulous preparation for the keynote far exceeded all the compulsiveness that had come before. She had written and memorized a precise outline of what she was going to say, in the order that she was going to say it; but, as always, she hadn't planned in advance the exact words she would use. She had learned from experience that finding the words just before she spoke them gave her presentations energy and spontaneity.

I always feel anxious before a lecture, she reminded her racing heart when she stood beneath the massive Arc de Triomphe. And often, the first few sentences of the lecture teetered precariously on a high wire of tightly strung nerves. But eventually the nerves relaxed and the butterflies flew away, and then she would actually enjoy herself—just as her audience enjoyed listening. She captivated her audiences with her energetic vivaciousness, and she intrigued them with her technique of presenting scientific information as if she were telling an interesting story, not simply reciting hard, dry data.

Nick has never heard me give a lecture! she realized with a rush of panic when she reached the charming Bagatelle in the Bois de Boulogne. Dr. Nicholas Chase probably wouldn't approve of her story-telling technique. But that was what she was planning to do tonight when she told the audience of distinguished surgeons the history of living donor liver transplantation. She was going to begin at the very beginning, when the technique was just an extraordinary concept to the visionaries, including Nick himself, and then she was going to reveal how the story unfolded, the triumphs and the failures, including the most recent chapter, written by her over Christmas weekend. It was the only interesting and coherent way to present the information.

But Nick might not agree, she thought as she wandered along rue de Longchamp toward the Grande Cascade. He might think she should have had more slides filled with data and fewer photographs of the people who had been involved. "It's your show," he had said. But still, he might not approve.

Which doesn't matter, remember? she asked herself as she gazed at the tumbling waterfall. Nick's approval doesn't matter anymore.

Long before the chairman officially convened the congress, every seat in the grand ballroom was already taken, and the adjacent meeting rooms, where the keynote address could be viewed over closed-circuit televisions, were already filled, too. As the chairman made his welcoming remarks and began his gracious introduction of the evening's special guest speaker, the butterflies that had been fluttering softly all day in Elizabeth's stomach suddenly became frantic.

Relax, she told herself. Almost without motion, she clenched her fists into tight balls, hoping to trap some of the nervous energy there, in the strong isometric contraction, and then letting it dissipate when she released. It was a technique that worked, Elizabeth knew, a most useful technique that she had learned from Stephen. He sat beside her now, sensing her tension, understanding it and smiling at her with reassuring calm. It helped that Stephen was beside her, and it helped, too, that Nick was far away, at the opposite end of the very long front row.

The sound of applause signaled the end of the chairman's introduction. On cue, Elizabeth rose, walked up the seven steps to the massive stage, positioned herself in front of the wooden podium and gazed at a distant place where the faces in the crowd were indistinct and blurred.

"It is a great pleasure for me to be here tonight," she began. They were rote words, mechanically uttered by all anxious speakers to test how much the nervous energy had affected their voices and to give some of the butterflies a chance to escape. She continued with more mechanical words, "If I may have the lights off and the first slide on, please."

The grand ballroom's glittering crystal chandeliers were dimmed in response to her request, shadowing the faces in the front row and casting all those beyond in total darkness. Elizabeth turned to the screen behind her to be certain that the slide that had been projected was the correct one and that it was right side up.

It was, and it was then that the keynote address really began, and after the first few sentences the butterflies flew away, and she was able to relax and simply share with the enraptured audience the fascinating story. Since the story did not involve Elizabeth until its very final chapter, she was able to recount the evolution of the extraordinary technique with reverence and awe, praising the talent and courage of those like Nick whose story it had truly been.

Elizabeth told that story for thirty effortless and enjoyable minutes, and then it was time for her own chapter, beginning with what happened on the festive December afternoon in Union Square.

Suddenly, with no warning whatsoever, all the emotions of that day came back, in powerful waves, flooding her eyes with a hot mist and filling her mind with a swirling torrent of memories that made her completely lose track of what it was she was supposed to say next. Not that she could speak anyway.

No! a coherent thought defiantly protested in the midst of the sudden chaos. This cannot be happening!

Elizabeth had always known how emotional—and sentimental and romantic—she was. There were television commercials that could make her cry, after all, not to mention weddings and novels and movies. And she had always cried for her patients, happy tears and sad ones. But she had always been able to control her emotions when they needed to be controlled—in the hospital, in the operating room, and, not that it had ever happened before, most assuredly during a scientific presentation.

This is a scientific presentation! she silently pleaded with the mind that swirled with images of Justin and Mr. Bear and the courageous and loving man who had been so willing to give his own life to save his son.

Finally an image—a memory—surfaced that enabled her to regain control. It was an image of troubled dark blue eyes and a memory of icy devastation. Don't care about me, Elizabeth.

Don't care, don't care . . . the shattering words echoed in her mind, a calming mantra of ice, and at last Elizabeth knew that she would be able to go on.

At last. How long had it been? To Elizabeth, the moments of silent emotion felt like an eternity. But in fact the pause had been quite brief, and to her rapt audience the moment of quiet reverence for the inexplicable tragedy that had befallen the happy four-year-old boy on that holiday afternoon had seemed quite appropriate. Most of the surgeons in the distinguished audience didn't know Elizabeth well enough to catch the sudden break in her voice, and they were too far away to see the slight tremble of her talented hands or the delicate misting of her suddenly confused emerald eyes.

Stephen knew what had happened. In her bewildering moments of helplessness, Elizabeth had looked to him and she had seen in the shadows his concern, but mostly his support, the reassuring smile that was a proud and confident reminder that she could do anything. Stephen knew what had happened, and what about the other man in the front row, the one who on that emotional day had seen in her eyes the deepest truths and secrets of her own loving heart? Nick was much farther away from the podium than Stephen. But still, if he had been looking, he would have been able to see her spotlighted face quite clearly, and if he had been listening, he would have heard the emotion in her voice.

Elizabeth didn't look at Nick during the eternity of emotion. She didn't dare. But when she finally spoke again, having calmed her voice and calmed, *iced*, her heart with the mantra of his devastating words, she cast a look of proud defiance at the shadowy place where she knew he sat—but into which she could not see. And later, as she described with dispassionate calm his alcohol abuse, his inexplicable shock and coma, and the markedly delayed recovery of his liver function, her proud green eyes traveled repeatedly to the shadows where he was hidden.

Elizabeth had filled her heart with ice not emotion, but to the admiring and enraptured audience her voice still held warmth and energy, and the final twenty minutes of the keynote address seemed as smoothly delivered and as compelling as the thirty minutes that had come before. Still, to Elizabeth, every second of those final twenty minutes was an ordeal—trying to concentrate on the speech, yet so wary of the heart that had betrayed her once already and without warning.

But there were no more betrayals, and at the conclusion of the speech, the entire audience stood and applauded until the chairman of the congress finally intervened and formally adjourned the evening's stunningly successful session. After that, the stage where Elizabeth still stood became crowded with doctors who wanted to both compliment her and ask her specific questions.

Normally, feeling relieved that a talk was over and a little euphoric that it had gone well, Elizabeth would have enjoyed the opportunity for informal dialogue with her colleagues. But now, even though this speech had been a success, she felt exhausted—and precarious. She needed privacy. And somehow she needed to get off the crowded stage and to the much-needed private place without encountering Nick. That was going to be difficult. Nick stood between her and escape, surrounded as she was by a wall of interested surgeons, but even across the distance that separated them, Elizabeth sensed the intense heat of the dark blue eyes that kept drifting to her, searching and demanding.

It was Stephen who rescued her.

"I'm sorry, Elizabeth, but we do have dinner reservations. We really should go now."

"Oh! We are late, aren't we?" she asked as she glanced at her watch. Then, smiling warmly but apologetically, she said truthfully to those who still had questions, "I'll be at the sessions for the next four days. We'll have more time to talk then."

Nick was still surrounded. Elizabeth felt his eyes follow her as she and Stephen whisked by, but she didn't turn to meet them.

They didn't have dinner reservations, of course, and Elizabeth could have perfectly well forgone food altogether and simply escaped to her suite or taken a long solitary walk through Paris. But Stephen insisted both on food and on his own nonthreatening and nonintrusive companionship.

"Your talk was wonderful," he said when they were seated in a cafe on Boulevard St. Germain in the Latin Quarter.

"If you choose to forget those unprofessional moments of pure emotion."

"Which most people didn't even know were happening, but which, if they did know, could only enhance their respect for you. Any surgeon who didn't understand the extraordinary emotion of that day—and who wouldn't have felt it too—shouldn't be practicing medicine."

"Spoken like a true internist. But you know surgeons, Stephen. I've probably set women, especially women surgeons, back two thousand years."

"At least two thousand," Stephen agreed with a smile.

"Do you think Nick realized what happened?"

"I don't know. I was looking at you, not at him."

"I know," Elizabeth answered softly, her voice filling with gratitude for his support. "Nick probably did realize what happened, and he's probably furious about it."

"Furious?"

"It was his keynote address, which he gave to me to give, and even though you and I believe that emotion is an acceptable ingredient for a doctor, the fact is that this was a very important scientific presentation."

"You think Nick could have talked about the gunshot wound to his son without a flicker of emotion?" Stephen asked. "You know I've never been Nick's greatest fan, Elizabeth, but I was there on that day in December and I don't for a second doubt his love for his son."

"No," Elizabeth admitted. "I don't think Nick could have talked with cool scientific detachment about that day. But he obviously knew that, Stephen. That, in addition to the fact that I was the one who had done the surgery, may have been why he asked me to give the speech." She sighed. "Well, anyway, what happened happened."

"What happened, Doctor Jennings, was a sensational keynote address."

The message light was blinking on the wall of her suite when Elizabeth returned from dinner with Stephen.

"Doctor Chase requests that you call him," the operator told her. "Extension seven sixteen. Shall I connect you?"

"No," Elizabeth replied swiftly. "No, merci."

She didn't want to talk to Nick no matter why he was calling—not if he was calling because he liked her talk, and most certainly not if he was calling to express his disappointment in her lack of professionalism.

"I think I'll take a nice long shower and go to bed," she announced to the hotel's elegant notepaper on which, as the operator had given her the message she had written, "Nick" and "716" and "No!"

"I love you, Justin."

"I love you, too, Daddy."

"I'll talk to you tomorrow, okay?"

"Okay."

"Good. May I speak to Margaret again for a minute?"

"Sure. 'Bye, Daddy."

" 'Bye, Jussie." A moment later, when Margaret was on the line again, Nick said, "He sounds fine."

"He is, Nick," Margaret assured. "We're doing just fine. Couldn't you tell?"

"Yes," Nick admitted. He had talked to his son for almost thirty minutes, a conversation in which Justin had excitedly told him the events of his day and during which Nick had detected no undue worry that he was far away. In the weeks before the trip, Nick had told Justin all about Paris, and they had found it on the map, and just as with the hospital and all the other cities to which Nick had needed to travel in the past few years, he had shared Paris with his son, making it seem close and familiar, not far away and unknown.

"How was Elizabeth's keynote address?"

Nick frowned as he remembered but answered truthfully, "It was wonderful."

"I'm not surprised." Margaret wanted to embellish—"Elizabeth is wonderful"—but she knew that that was nothing Nick didn't already know; and she knew also not to intrude on the very private decisions that he had made. "Well, you have a hungry son, so he and I are going to make something for dinner. Please give my best to Elizabeth."

Give my best to Elizabeth. Margaret's words echoed in Nick's mind after the call ended. He himself had given his best to Elizabeth: the gentle warning to her not to care about him.

That was the greatest gift he could give her, distance from him, so that she could find someone far better and far more whole to love, but this evening Nick had learned that Elizabeth hadn't heeded his gentle warning. And worse, she hadn't truly understood it. He had seen the hurt in her bewildered emerald eyes as she had struggled with her emotions. It was the same hurt that he had seen on Christmas Eve . . . and the same hurt he saw night after night in his nightmares— the anguished emerald belief that he didn't really love her.

Nick frowned at his watch. It was almost midnight. No blinking light signaled that Elizabeth had tried to return his call while he was talking to Justin. Perhaps she and Stephen were still strolling the streets of Paris. Needing to know, Nick dialed the operator. *Non, monsieur,* no messages for you, he was told. Ah, *mais oui, mademoiselle le docteur* did receive your message about an hour ago.

After her shower, Elizabeth dressed in her nightgown and robe, sat in a plush chair by the window, and gazed at the sparkling glitter of the City of Light as she thought about the evening—and about Nick's call. Her speech had, on balance, been very good. Stephen had convinced her of that and she herself knew that it was true. The turmoil had been inside her, hidden from everyone except Stephen, who knew her best. Nick probably hadn't even noticed. He was probably calling, as her boss, to tell her that she had done well.

Fine, Elizabeth thought, nonetheless pressing herself even deeper into the plush chair. Whatever it was, criticism or praise, Nick could tell her tomorrow morning. There would be many different scientific sessions running concurrently, but Elizabeth guessed that she and Nick would very likely attend the same ones, those most relevant to their shared areas of research and expertise.

Tomorrow she would run into Nick, and he would tell her, in the midst of a crush of surgeons, why he had called.

The ringing phone shattered Elizabeth's plan.

"It's Nick, Elizabeth. Did I waken you?" Dr. Nicholas Chase had awakened Dr. Elizabeth Jennings many times during the past year, when he and his patient needed her immense talent, and not once in all those late-night calls had he apologized for disturbing her. But those calls had been professional, and this call was personal, so now his voice held a soft note of apology for the intrusion.

"No. I'm awake."

"May I come see you?"

"Now?"

"Yes. I know it's late." Nick stopped abruptly, then continued, "And you're not alone. I'm very sorry to have—"

"I'm alone, Nick."

"Then, may I? We need to talk, Elizabeth."

His words sounded ominous . . . but his voice was so very gentle.

"All right."

"Thank you. I'm on my way."

Wait, I'm not dressed! The thought came after they had hung up and Nick was already on his way the short distance from his suite to hers. But this bulky bathrobe is far more modest than the pajamalike surgical scrubs he has seen me in so often. And the shower-damp dark curls and freshly scrubbed makeup-free face? It doesn't matter what I look like! Nick has seen me look as good as I possibly can look, and he has seen me after exhausting hours of grueling surgery and no sleep.

And, besides, it doesn't matter, remember?

CHAPTER THIRTY-TWO

$\mathcal{E}$lizabeth's luxurious suite had plush chairs and cozy conversation areas. But still, after opening the door to her midnight visitor and silently leading the way to the elegant living room, she didn't even offer a chair to him. Instead, she just stopped in the center of the room and turned to face him, her slender body stiff and wary beneath her bulky robe, her emerald eyes proud and defiant.

Nick stood a few feet away, a polite and careful distance, his body stiff and wary, too; but his troubled dark blue eyes were neither defiant nor proud . . . they were only very gentle.

"We need to talk about what happened tonight during your address, and about what happened on Christmas Eve."

"Christmas Eve?"

"When I told you not to care about me. You told me then that you understood why you shouldn't care—but, Elizabeth, I don't think that you do."

"Because you don't care about me," she whispered softly, bravely.

"But I do care about you."

"Because you don't love me," she said even more softly, and more bravely.

"Oh, but I do love you, Elizabeth."

I do love you, Elizabeth. The wondrous truth of his words was eloquently conveyed by the exquisite gentleness of his voice . . . and it was embellished even further by the tenderness in his loving blue eyes. Elizabeth's heart raced with pure joy as she whispered, "You really do love me."

"Yes, I really do love you. I have loved you for a very long time."

"And from very far away," she said quietly to the man who loved her, and had loved her for a very long time, but who had always kept such a careful distance from her—and who was keeping that distance still. "Why, Nick?"

"Because I knew that our love was impossible."

The tenderly spoken words were as devastating now as his troubled warning not to care about him had been on Christmas Eve. On that night, Elizabeth had quickly drawn her own shattering conclusion about the reason for his warning—that he didn't really love her—and had escaped swiftly from him. Tonight she would let Nick tell her the reason for his devastating words.

But she was trembling now, and she couldn't bare to watch his gentle yet so resolute dark blue eyes tell her why their love could not be—so she turned away from him, and, increasing the distance between them even more, she stood in the alcove where she had been sitting when he had called.

"Is it because of Justin?" she asked finally as she stared out into the glittering winter night.

"Because of Justin?" Nick echoed. Had Elizabeth been looking at him she would have seen his surprise—and his absolute confidence that she would have been a wonderful mother for the little boy who already loved her. "No, Elizabeth, not because of Justin. Because of me. I think you've somehow forgotten what you know about me, about my drinking . . . and that I once abandoned my son."

"I know that you used to drink, Nick," she countered softly. "And I know that you love Justin more than life itself."

Nick hadn't followed her into the shadows until then, but now he did, standing behind her, keeping a safe distance still, but one across which his words could be quiet and gentle.

"The alcoholism doesn't go away, Elizabeth, even if the alcohol does. I drank to escape from a pain and emptiness deep inside me. I'm not drinking anymore, but the pain and emptiness are there still."

"Because of your childhood."

"Yes. It's not a mystery. I don't know if I was ever loved as a child. If so, I have no memory of it. What I do know is that my mother slashed her wrists when I was three—and my demanding, perfectionistic, alcoholic father blamed me for her suicide."

She wanted to turn to him, to hold him and love him, but Elizabeth forced herself to gaze still at the winter sky. "But you couldn't have believed that, Nick!"

"I was three years old, Elizabeth, and he was my father. I spent my entire childhood being unloved and being told that I was undeserving of love—with my mother's suicide as vivid proof. I know now, of course, as an adult and a parent myself, that I was not to blame for her death. And I know that my father was a monster. But all the knowledge and insight in the world doesn't mean that I can change how that time was lived, or what happened because of it. The wounds will always be there . . . as will the emptiness. I didn't even know about the emptiness until Justin—and you—but now I understand what's been missing inside me for all these years."

"What's that, Nick?" Elizabeth spoke softly to the winter sky, even though her gentle question was really for Nick's deeply wounded heart. She knew he would have an answer to her question. It was obvious that what he was revealing to her now had been discovered by the bright mind which, in search of the truth about his own pain, had forced itself to make repeated journeys into those deep and anguished wounds. "What's missing?"

"A feeling of joyfulness," Nick answered with quiet and solemn confidence. "An inner core of happiness. You have it, Elizabeth, and somehow, despite the first six months of his life, Justin has it too. It had been almost lost when he came to me, but the ember was still there and with love and nurturing he became happy and hopeful. I suppose I was born with an innocent joyfulness, the potential for it anyway, but it was never nurtured—and now it's simply not there."

"But I see such joy and happiness when you're with Justin, Nick." *And, when you've permitted it, I've seen joy and happiness with me.*

"It's *his* joy and *his* happiness, Elizabeth. It all comes from him, but it spills over to me, filling the emptiness inside." *Just as, my beautiful Elizabeth, when I'm with you my emptiness is filled—overflowing.* "I have no joy or happiness of my own to give back. I have nothing to give—except unhappiness."

Like the moon, Elizabeth thought as she gazed at the golden-white ball in the winter sky. It looked like glittering fire, but it was all reflected light, its golden glow a brilliant kiss from the sparkling sun, its black scars and empty craters brightly lighted by the fiery star. Nick believed that he was like the moon, icy and black without the sun's reflected brilliance, but he was so very wrong!

"Justin isn't unhappy, Nick. You have given him so much love . . . and you would have given him your life."

"I've known what to give Justin—all the things that were missing from my childhood. He would be better off with another father, but he doesn't have that choice, and he's been very lucky to have had Margaret."

"He's been very lucky to have had you."

"Justin would be better off with someone else," Nick repeated softly. And then, even more softly, he said, "And, Elizabeth, so would you. That's what I came here to tell you tonight, to make sure that you understand."

"I do understand," she answered, turning at last, because at last she truly did understand. She gazed at the man who had made painful journeys into his own heart and knew a great deal about its wounds and its scars—but so very little else about the rest of it—and said bravely, "I understand that you love me . . . and that I love you . . . and that that's all that matters."

"No, Elizabeth," he whispered. "That's not all that matters."

"It's all that matters now, Nick. Right now, in this private place, it's all that matters."

Nick knew that he should have left. But how could he? He had wanted her so much for so long, and now her radiant emerald eyes told him that she had wanted him too, so much for so long. And they had almost lost each other once, almost lost the chance to ever share the truths of their hearts . . . and now they could show each other those joyful truths, sharing with each other all that they could share.

"Oh, Elizabeth." His hands touched her flushed cheeks then, and then tenderly, and with such loving wonder, cradled her beautiful face. "Do you know how much I have wanted to touch you, to feel your lovely softness, your wonderful warmth?"

"Nick," she whispered shakily, trembling from his words, from his touch, and from her own wondrous desires.

Her delicate trembling fingers reached for him then, touching his handsome face with the gentle caress of a whispered kiss, feeling even with that gossamer-gentle touch the strength that lay deep within him—and the fire. As she gazed at the dark blue eyes that smoldered with such passion and such desire—and such love—Elizabeth's heart sent a brave promise to his, *The ember of joyfulness, the deep golden glow of love is inside you, Nick. I can see it and feel it. It's there, and through our wonderful love you will discover it and believe in it too. I know you will.*

Long before this night of love, their talented fingers had danced together with graceful beauty. Now that magnificent dance of grace and beauty was joyously joined by their hearts and their bodies and their souls. And if the sensuous blue-eyed surgeon had an expert technique for making love, he didn't use it for loving Elizabeth. Theirs was a loving created just for each other, never rehearsed nor practiced before, created together from every gift each had to give, all joyful trust, all brave desire, all unashamed passion.

And when it was time for them to become one, the intense dark blue eyes held the gaze of the shimmering emerald ones as she welcomed him . . . and for a wondrous and astonishing moment neither of them could speak, or breathe, or move . . . and then, just before their crescendoing desires urgently commanded them to resume again their magnificent dance of love, they whispered, together, "I love you."

Elizabeth didn't want to sleep. She wanted to lie forever in his arms, feeling his heart beat against hers. But she needed to sleep, they both did, so finally she succumbed to the wonder of falling asleep in his strong and gentle arms.

Nick didn't want to sleep, even after he felt the change in her breathing that signaled she was asleep, perhaps even dreaming. Nick didn't want to leave this joyous wide-awake dream of holding her, not ever, and he most assuredly didn't want to leave it for the nightmares that he knew awaited him once his conscious mind relinquished its control to the slumbering demons that lived within.

But finally Nick fell asleep too, and on that night, after he had made love to Elizabeth and while he held her in his arms as together they slept, Nicholas Chase had no nightmares.

Elizabeth awakened first, and for a while she simply gazed at his beloved face. She saw such peace, a peace that hadn't been there before, not even when he had been in the deepest sleep of coma. The bedside clock told her that it was almost seven-thirty. She needed to get up, to gently and carefully free herself from his loving arms . . .

"Good morning," he whispered, his just-opened eyes already filled with love.

"Good morning," she echoed softly. "I was trying not to wake you. Stephen's talk is in an hour and I told him I would be there. He's leaving right afterward for Vienna."

"I'd like to hear his talk, too," Nick said, gently touching her cheek, a caress of wonder—and disbelief. He had awakened from a sleep without nightmares . . . and now once again he was living this magnificent dream. "I'll go shower and change and meet you downstairs."

* * *

Elizabeth arrived at the lecture hall before Nick, put her sweater on one chair and her notebook on the one beside it, then walked to the front of the hall to speak to Stephen.

"Hi. All set?"

"All set. Slides in order, podium lights figured out." Stephen stopped, stared at her, and asked, "What happened to you?"

"Happened?"

"You look . . ." As Stephen paused to search for the right description—radiantly beautiful, sparklingly joyous—he watched the radiant and sparkling emerald travel to Nick who had just entered the room. And then Stephen saw what perhaps no one in the world—except Elizabeth—had ever seen before: what pure happiness looked like on the handsome face of Nicholas Chase. Nick's progress toward them was stopped by a colleague from the Pasteur Institute who wanted to speak to him, so Stephen said quietly, "I guess I know what happened."

"Don't look so worried!"

"Just be careful, Elizabeth."

"I'm not afraid of Nick, Stephen. I never have been."

"I know. It's just that you—one—can be so easily fooled about love, misreading the other's feelings because you want so desperately to have them reflect your own." Remembering Nick's expression of pure happiness, Stephen admitted, "I'm obviously talking about myself, Elizabeth, not you. You know that I want this to work out for you."

"I know."

"Just be careful."

"I will," she promised, even though she knew it wasn't true.

It was far too late to be careful.

For the next three days and nights Elizabeth and Nick were together, sitting beside each other at all the scientific meetings, touching gently as they listened and took careful notes; and they wandered through Paris, discovering its romance and enchantment together; and Nick made his nightly calls to Justin from her suite; and then they went to bed, loving each other more and more every time.

Nick had willed himself to be just well enough—to *look* just well enough—to make an appearance at the congress in Paris. But in Paris, in love with Elizabeth, his strength truly and wondrously returned. His wounded body was finally healed and even his soul seemed stronger, because with her in his arms neither his nightmares nor the screams of pain that haunted him by day dared to intrude.

Nick was basking in the radiant glow of Elizabeth's sunshine, enveloped by the warm golden aura that shimmered around her. And the fountain of joy that danced deep within her overflowed to him, magically filling all the empty places in his heart with happiness, and there were even times when he felt surprising rushes that almost seemed to come from within *him*, as if a tiny ember of innocent joyfulness had defiantly survived the darkness of his childhood after all. But Nick knew that no such ember truly existed within him. It was just Elizabeth, *her* contagious happiness, *her* pervasive optimism and hope. She was giving, and he was taking, and . . .

On Thursday morning, a few hours before he would board the flight to San Francisco and she would make the brief over the channel voyage to spend a few days with her parents in London, Nick made love to Elizabeth for the last time. And she sensed in his fierce tenderness and the exquisiteness of his passion that it was a goodbye that was far more desperate and far-reaching than the brief separation that was about to begin. And when he whispered a final "I love you" before reluctantly separating himself from her, Elizabeth felt as if her heart had been torn in two.

She watched in silence as he dressed. When he was buttoning his shirt, and she feared he was about to leave, she sat up, clutching the covers to her, concealing the nakedness that had been so unashamed and so joyous for the wondrous days and nights of their loving.

"Nick?"

"I love you with all my heart . . . such as it is," he said quietly, not turning to face her as he spoke. "But I know it's not enough."

"But it is!" she cried with soft despair. And then, even more softly and with even more despair, she asked, "Or have you decided in the past three days that you don't really love me, after all?"

Nick turned to her then, and when her eyes met his, he issued an intensely solemn command. "Don't ever think that, Elizabeth."

"What else can I think, Nick?"

"What I told you on Christmas Eve and again on Sunday night—that I have nothing but unhappiness to give you." He gazed at eyes that were so unhappy now—proof of his words!—and yet seemed so defiantly disbelieving. After a moment he added quietly, "And what I told you the day Danny died—that alcoholism is a disease you don't give to anyone else. You keep it to yourself, where it belongs." The unhappy emerald was defiant, disbelieving, still. "Oh, Elizabeth, I thought you understood. It's too risky, too dangerous . . ."

"I do understand. I understand the danger and I'm willing to take the risk."

"But I'm not willing to let you take that risk."

The love and joy and desire that had filled the dark blue eyes for the past three days and nights of love were gone now, replaced by the once-so-familiar cool and distant politeness. Cool, distant, polite . . . and so resolute.

Nicholas Chase had made his decision.

"So what are we going to do, Nick?" Elizabeth asked, her words flowing on a sudden raging river of anger. "Operate together forever? Spend a few midnight hours of passion together once in a while?"

"I'm not going to return to the medical center," he answered quietly. "I'm going to find a position somewhere else."

"*No,*" Elizabeth countered swiftly. "If one of us is going to leave, I want it to be me. It's something I've been thinking about for quite a while anyway—because of you; and thanks to the historic surgery that you manipulated me into doing— because you knew how much I loved you—I'm really in great demand. It would be difficult for me to work in a place haunted by memories of you, but I imagine it wouldn't be the least bit difficult for you. You're the expert at sealing off your emotions and burying them deep beside all your other scars."

"Elizabeth . . ."

"I want to be the one who leaves, Nick," she said with sudden calm. Then, calm still, as if they were simply discussing the details of the on-call schedule, she asked, "Do you still anticipate that you'll be able to return to work on June first?"

"Yes."

"All right. Well, then, May thirty-first will be my last day." The calm evaporated then. It had been only an illusion, the deceptively tranquil eye of a raging storm. The anger was back, but now it dressed her voice in an unfamiliar cloak of flippancy and sarcasm. "This was *nice*, Nick! You're a terrific lover, just like everyone always said you were. Maybe we can do it again sometime. Our paths are bound to cross again and again at meetings. Of course, perhaps one day you will appear with a wife, having discovered that you aren't fatally flawed after all, that your famous dark side is just a shadowy illusion, easily vanquished by love. Or maybe I'll be the one who marries. Surely there's a man out there for me somewhere, someone with no secrets, no torments, no pain whatsoever. That's what you want for me, don't you? A teetotaler with rose-colored glasses, a cockeyed optimist just like me?"

"I want you to be happy, Elizabeth," Nick answered with quiet despair, loving her so much and so enraged with himself for hurting her. "You deserve happiness."

"Because I had a happy childhood? I'm not to blame for the luxury and privilege of having had a safe and loving childhood—just as you aren't to blame that yours was unspeakably awful." Elizabeth gave her head a soft bewildered shake and when she spoke again her voice was sad and thoughtful. "Because of your love, Justin's childhood will be as happy as mine was. In twenty or thirty years, when he falls in love with a woman who is troubled from something she didn't cause and can't change are you going to tell him to simply forget about her? To find someone who, through sheer luck, had a happy childhood too? I don't think that's the way love works, Nick." She paused, and then said very quietly, "It's certainly not the advice I plan to give our child."

"Our child?"

Elizabeth hadn't been careful, not with her heart or with her body, not with Nick; and Nick, who had always been so compulsive about birth control, hadn't been careful either, not with Elizabeth.

And now Elizabeth spoke the cruel words to hurt him, because he had hurt her so terribly, but when she saw his anguish, she assured quickly, and truthfully, "We haven't been using any protection, Nick, but I won't have gotten pregnant. My period is due to begin tomorrow and it will, I can already feel it."

As Nick stared at her, Elizabeth saw the full measure of the pain he had always hidden as carefully as he had hidden the love. She wanted to rush to him, to hold him and love him, but the icy blue eyes warned her away.

"I'm sorry, Elizabeth," he whispered finally, his voice hoarse with emotion. "I'm so very sorry."

Then Nick was gone, and Elizabeth didn't know whether he was sorry that they couldn't live their love forever . . . or that they had had even these few magical days and nights of love . . . or that she wouldn't be having his child.

Elizabeth didn't know very much when Nick left her. But the next evening in England, when she began to bleed right on cue, she knew that she was not carrying Nick's baby; and as she visited her own loving parents, she knew that she would try very hard to convince her broken heart that what Nick had done had been a noble gift of love, that he loved her deeply and truly believed it was best for her to live without him.

But with each passing moment, Elizabeth knew that her weeping heart would not be convinced. How could it be convinced of the gentle lie when it knew so clearly the painful truth? Nick simply had neither loved her enough, nor trusted her love enough, to have even wanted to try.

Elizabeth knew with certainty that her shattered heart would not be convinced . . . but she had no idea how it was going to survive the agonizing truth.

PART SIX

CHAPTER THIRTY-THREE

San Francisco
February 1992

Stephen drove directly from the airport to Christine's house on Twin Peaks. She wasn't expecting him, of course. He hadn't spoken to her in two weeks, not since their good-night kiss on Valentine's Day. Now it was the last Friday in February, and as far as she knew he wasn't due back from Europe until late Sunday. But from the moment of his arrival in Paris, Stephen had begun consolidating his schedule of commitments, fulfilling them all in two days less than originally planned.

Now he was back in San Francisco, and soon he would be with Christine again, listening as she told him the truth—whatever it was; and even though in the past two weeks he had been unable to find even one hopeful explanation for why she had hidden Colin Gallagher from him, Stephen's heart set a new pace in anticipation of seeing her again. But when he reached Twin Peaks and turned the final familiar corner onto City View Drive, his heart almost stopped.

In front of Christine's house was a large truck. He watched in stunned sadness as two men loaded Christine's bed—Christine and David's bed—into the van to join the rest of her furniture. Christine was leaving. Now. Today. If he had returned as scheduled on Sunday, she would have been long gone.

She's probably already gone, Stephen thought as the loaded van sputtered away. Still, he parked his car a short distance from the house and gazed at it through the mist of raindrops that now wept from the gray February sky. The front door of the house was closed, and even though the stormy afternoon had been quite dark before the rain began, there were no lights on inside.

Then he saw it—a glitter of gold in the shadowy darkness. Christine was there still. A final check of doors and windows, Stephen supposed, and the final closing of suitcases. And perhaps, a final goodbye to the house where she and David had lived the love that had been enough to last a lifetime . . .

Even though tears blurred Christine's vision as she wandered slowly through the small house for the last time, the memories she saw in each room were very clear. She lingered for a long time in each room, embracing the wonderful memories of love before bidding them a gentle farewell. And even though her journey was slow and lingering, eventually there was only one room left . . . the bedroom . . . where they had shared their hearts and their souls . . . and where they had created the precious new life . . . and where David had died . . . and where just a few hours later that precious new life had died, too, following David to his death as Christine herself had wanted so desperately to do. She had wanted to follow, but she had had debts to pay—and promises to keep. It was in the bedroom where David had held her tenderly before his death and made her promise to go on with her life, to find new happiness, new dreams, and new love. Christine had promised, gentle lies of love, but now, unbelievably, she was keeping those promises.

Christine finally bid farewell to the bedroom, and when she reached the front door, before opening and closing it for the last time, she whispered softly through her tears, "Goodbye, David. Goodbye, my love."

Then Christine Andrews left the protective cloak of memories and walked outside to begin her new life. A life, she discovered, that was going to begin in a torrential downpour. Had it been any other day, Christine would have dashed the two blocks to the sheltered bus stop, or simply gone back inside the house to wait for the cloudburst to pass. But today she could not return to the sanctuary of the place to which she had already said her loving goodbye, nor could she run away from it.

So she walked, slow deliberate steps, not a hasty retreat, amid raindrops and tears.

Stephen watched as Christine walked away from her house, her slender body straight and proud, her golden hair a bright glittering beacon in the storm-dark gray. She wore a raincoat, but carried only a purse and no luggage. The rest of her clothes and luggage were already elsewhere, Stephen assumed. The airport, probably, at the hotel where she would stay until her flight to New York.

Christine hadn't noticed his car, and now she was bravely and proudly walking away from him—and toward her dreams. But Stephen couldn't let her go without talking to her. Getting out of his car and into the rainstorm, his long graceful strides quickly brought him close enough to her to call to her.

"Christine?"

"Stephen," she whispered as she turned to him, startled, and then hopeful, and then aching. The thoughts from which his voice had pulled her had been thoughts about the courageous and hopeful choices she had made . . . and when she had turned she was suddenly face to face with the most courageous hope of all . . . and what she saw made her heart ache. Stephen was back two days early, but his dark eyes didn't send the joyous message that his early return had been because he had missed her.

"Let me drive you wherever you're going, Christine," he said quietly. "I'd like to talk to you."

They didn't talk at all during the three-mile drive from Twin Peaks to the destination Christine had given him—the corner of Lincoln and Twenty-first, across the street from Golden Gate Park. The Friday afternoon traffic was already heavy, and, because of the slick streets and pelting rain, it was also treacherous. Stephen needed to concentrate on his driving, and he forced himself to, even though he was so very aware of her tense body and the tense, awkward silence that traveled with them.

"It's that building there," Christine said, quietly breaking the silence as she gestured to a four-story red-brick apartment. "We can talk inside, if you like."

Stephen was able to park quite close to the building's entrance, but nonetheless their already damp hair got an extra layer of raindrops; and when they were inside the third-floor apartment to which Christine had a key and she reached to take his rain-drenched coat, she asked, "Would you like a towel for your hair?"

"Yes, I guess so. Thank you." He was only vaguely aware of the cold drops that spilled from his own rain-damp hair, but he was very aware of the ones that fell from the glistening spun gold onto her sad and lovely face, caressing it like dewdrops on roses.

Roses. As Christine disappeared to get the towels, Stephen looked at the unfamiliar surroundings—the white wicker furniture, the delicate porcelain lamps, the cheerful pastel pillows. Everything was unfamiliar *except* the bouquet of cream-colored roses on the white wicker coffee table. They were the rosebuds he had given her on Valentine's Day, fully opened now and beautiful still.

The roses he had given her were all that was familiar. The roses . . . and then Christine's shy smile, offered in hopeful response to the very gentle smile that greeted her when she returned with the two plush towels.

"Where are we, Christine?" he asked softly.

"In my new apartment. Well, it's not really new, and it's not really mine. I only have it as a sublet until the first week of May, but that will give me time to find someplace else."

"A place in New York."

"In New York? No . . ."

"You're not moving to New York to work with Colin Gallagher?"

"No." She tilted her damp golden head. "How did you know about that?"

"I stopped by the boutique the morning I left for Paris. Sydney told me. I've spent the past two weeks wondering why you didn't mention it to me." *Wondering, worrying, unable to find an explanation that wouldn't shatter my dreams.* Stephen looked gently at the lavender eyes that were going to save his wonderful dream after all and asked, "Why didn't you mention the job to me?"

"Because I knew I wasn't going to accept it. I told Colin that when he first called, but he insisted on flying out to try to get me to change my mind anyway."

"But he couldn't? It sounded like an extraordinary opportunity."

"Yes, but this," she said, gesturing gracefully to the new apartment, "is as much of a move as I want to make now." She looked up to his gentle brown eyes and asked bravely, "Why did you come to Sydney's that morning?"

"Because I wanted to see you again before I left. I wanted to talk to you about our kiss."

"Our kiss?"

"I wanted you to know that I understood your confusion and that there was no hurry."

"But you didn't regret kissing me?"

"Oh, no, Christine, I didn't regret kissing you. In fact, I've spent the past two weeks worrying that I would never get to kiss you again."

"And I've been worrying that you wouldn't want to."

"I want to. I will always want to," he added softly, searching for alarm and seeing only happiness—and raindrops.

He took the plush towels that she still held and gently dried her beautiful rain-damp face and glistening golden hair. And then, as he cradled her face in his hands, his dark eyes grew very solemn with desire, and he kissed her . . . and she kissed him back . . . and the kiss held all the wondrous promise of their first kiss, but it was warmer and hungrier and deeper than before, and more confident, and not at all confused.

Until Christine pulled away. In the startled instant before Stephen's eyes found hers, he felt a tremor of ice. But the lavender that greeted him glowed with pure and shimmering joy.

"Come to the bedroom, Stephen."

The bed was new, as were the quilted mauve comforter and lacy ivory pillows. There was nothing old or familiar in Christine's bedroom. Nothing at all, Stephen thought, realizing then that he hadn't seen it in the living room and in his subconscious mind had concluded that it would be in here.

But it wasn't.

"Where's the portrait?" he asked quietly.

Christine let go of his hand then and moved away from him, just a little, before answering.

"I gave it to the art museum. They were thrilled, of course, and I know their enthusiasm would have pleased David very much." A thoughtful frown touched her lovely face as she added softly, almost to herself, "And I think he would have understood."

"Understood?" Stephen echoed gently. He saw a flicker of confusion then, as if this wasn't something she had planned to discuss with him, as if she didn't think it had a place in their love. But it did. "I want to make love to you, Christine, you must know how much I want that. But we need to talk first. You've made some very important decisions—and changes—in the past two weeks."

"Yes. But they weren't impulsive decisions, Stephen, and I don't regret any of them." She looked bravely into his loving dark eyes. "I wanted us to have a place without memories, a place where we could make our own memories."

Oh, Christine. Stephen's heart wanted him to go to her now, to hold her and love her and begin to make their own wonderful memories—but his mind wouldn't allow it, not yet.

"But the memories are inside you," he said, wondering what was compelling him to force an issue for which there was no simple resolution. He didn't want Christine to forget David, of course, or to in any way diminish that extraordinary love. And yet . . . he was about to give her all of his heart—no, she already had it—and perhaps he needed to know how great a risk he was taking. "The memories of David will always be inside you."

"Yes," she agreed. Then, with surprise, she asked, "Are you afraid of my memories of David?"

"I guess I am."

"I'm afraid, too, but not of my memories." It was a small confession compared to the one she made next. "I'm afraid of losing you, Stephen, not of loving you."

"Oh, Christine." He couldn't promise that a tragedy wouldn't some day steal him from her, they both knew that, but there was one promise of love that Stephen could make. "I love you, Christine. I will always love you."

"And I will always love you, too, Stephen." And then, as he was about to begin a tender kiss that would take them to her romantic quilted bed and she saw a flicker of worry that told her he knew that she had never been with any man but David, Christine reminded him softly, "I'm not afraid of loving you."

There was no fear in their loving, only joy and tenderness and desire and love, and afterward Stephen held her lovely nakedness against him, his lips caressing her passion-tangled golden hair as he spoke.

"Did you say no to Colin Gallagher because you didn't think I would want to move to New York?"

"I knew from Madolyn that you had wanted her to stay here."

"*What?*"

"She told me that you loved her and—"

"I never loved Madolyn, Christine. I've never loved anyone but you." His lips found hers, and he told her again, showed her again, warmly, deeply, lingering far longer than he had intended to . . . because there were more words, important words, that needed to be said. Finally, reluctantly, he stopped the kiss and suggested, "Why don't you call Colin and tell him yes?"

"I want to stay here, Stephen. I don't care about being famous and I like having the freedom to design only the kind of dresses I want to design."

"Romantic dresses."

"Yes."

"Well," Stephen began softly, moving a golden strand from her eyes so that he could see the lovely lavender as he spoke. "The prom dress you made was wonderful, but I would very much like to see what you could do with a wedding dress."

"You would?"

"Only if you were the bride. Will you, Christine?" he asked gently of the eyes that had already given him their joyous answer. "Will you design a wedding dress and wear it at our wedding?"

"Oh, yes, Stephen. Of course I will."

CHAPTER THIRTY-FOUR

San Francisco
April 1992

"Nick, it's Larisa. I need to see you."

"Okay," Nick answered, surprised that she was calling, but detecting a note of urgency in her voice that made him agree to her request without questioning it. "When?"

"Now, if possible."

Now was ten P.M. on Wednesday, April twenty-second. Justin was asleep and Margaret was reading and Nick had been just about to leave for a run. He could run again now, and in the two months since he had left Elizabeth, his need to run had increased with each passing moment.

"Now is fine, Larisa. Where?"

"Can you come here?"

"To your apartment?" *To Elizabeth's apartment?*

"Yes. We'll be alone. Elizabeth just got called in for a major trauma. I guess you've never been here, have you? It's only about six blocks from your house . . ."

* * *

In Paris, when Elizabeth had told him about Larisa's love for Peter, she had also told him that she believed that Larisa had become even more beautiful with that love. And now, as Larisa opened the apartment door to him, Nick saw that it was true. She looked more beautiful than ever, radiant and hopeful, her cheeks flushed a rosy pink and her silky golden red hair caressed by the most brilliant of fires. There was fire, too, in her flashing bright blue eyes. Fire *and* ice.

"Come in, Nick. Would you like a drink? A little Scotch, perhaps?"

"No." *Yes.* "Would you?"

"No." Larisa could drink now, a glass of champagne to celebrate with Peter would be quite safe for her; but she didn't drink, not a drop, because it would not be safe for the magnificent miracle of love that was growing inside her. A lovely smile began to touch her lips as she thought about her baby, but Larisa blocked the wonderful thought and its smile and cast a brilliant ice-blue glare directly at Nick.

"What's wrong, Larisa?"

"What did you do to her?"

"I beg your pardon?"

"What did you do to my friend?"

"What did she tell you that I did?"

"Nothing!" Larisa exclaimed with obvious frustration. "Elizabeth says nothing happened, but I *know* that's not true. Something happened between the two of you in Paris, Nick, and whatever it was, it—*you*—hurt her terribly."

"I never wanted to hurt her."

"Well, you have. She won't admit it, of course. It turns out that when I get hurt—or betrayed—I get very weak and needy and look for ways to float far away from the pain. But when Elizabeth Jennings is hurt or betrayed she simply turns to steel. She's stronger than ever, working harder than ever. . . ." Larisa looked at the dark blue eyes that were obviously deeply troubled by what she was saying and repeated, more gently this time, "What did you do to her?"

"I told her the truth, Larisa. I told her that I loved her, and that I knew our love was impossible. She deserves far better than me."

"Oh, Nick."

"You know it's true, Larisa. You know enough about me to know—"

"That you're beyond redemption?"

"No," Nick answered quietly. "I was redeemed by my son."

And I have been redeemed by this hopeful innocent life inside me, Larisa thought, and by the wonderful love of my miracle baby's father. It was a joyous thought, and yet a shiver of ice suddenly passed through her, a twirl of an icy ghost that would not die, a reminder that she had loved and trusted before only to be brutally betrayed. But not this time. Go away, ghost! Peter would never betray me.

Larisa gazed for a long thoughtful moment at the man who was so nobly and so resolutely denying himself Elizabeth's wonderful love. Finally she said, "You know enough about me to know that I have some deep flaws, too, including the same one that you have—the uncanny ability to betray myself and my own happiness. Maybe I shouldn't be, but I'm trying again, giving myself another chance at love and happiness by trusting Peter . . . and myself." Larisa hesitated a moment then added with quiet urgency, "Elizabeth really loves you, Nick."

"And I really love Elizabeth, Larisa."

"You both turn to steel when you're wounded!" she exclaimed to the very cold and very resolute blue eyes. "I hate you for hurting her."

"I hate myself for hurting her, too, Larisa," Nick said quietly, calmly holding her icy glare. After many silent moments, a gentle smile touched his lips and he said softly, "But I'm very happy that you've fallen in love."

* * *

"Hi," Peter greeted her with loving surprise when Larisa called him twenty minutes later. "What happened?"

"Elizabeth had to go in for a case, so my plan to force her to talk to me tonight backfired. I did, however, get some information from Nick."

"From Nick?"

"On impulse, after Elizabeth left, I called him and asked him to come over. I wanted him to be here, in this place where she lives, so he could *feel* her sadness."

"I wish I'd known you were going to do that, Larisa," Peter said with obvious concern. "I would like to have been there, in case Nick became angry."

"Nick isn't dangerous, except to himself—and, I suppose, to the people who love him." Larisa paused, and then, to the man who made her feel so free and so safe, who loved her and protected her without possessing her, she added softly, "Thank you for wanting to protect me, Peter."

"You're very welcome. So . . . what did Nick say?"

"That he had told Elizabeth that he loved her, which he obviously does, and that he had also told her that their love was impossible because of what he perceives to be his own lethal flaws. It wasn't a line, Peter, it's what Nick really believes about himself."

"At least now you know what's been troubling Elizabeth. Are you still hoping to talk to her tonight?"

"No. From the description of the trauma that was coming in, she'll probably be there all night."

"Shall I come get you then?"

Larisa curled into the loving gentleness of his voice as if she were curled against him now, safe and warm and drifting off to wonderful dreams in his arms. But . . .

"I'm very tired, Peter." *And your baby and I need our sleep.* "I think I'd better just go to bed—soon—right here. I want to be well rested for our trip."

"All right. I'll be there to get you at nine tomorrow morning. Sleep well, my love."

"I will," Larisa promised. *We both will.*

As Larisa drifted off to sleep, she thought about the days that lay ahead. In just five days, on Monday, *Promise* would be released. At this very moment, the magnificent photographs Emily had taken of her against the backdrop of the meadow were being incorporated into major national magazines and the romantic forget-me-not crystal bottles filled with the enchanting fragrance were being shipped to boutiques and department stores across the country.

Everyone associated with *Promise* truly believed that once revealed the fragrance would sell itself; but Peter had decided he wanted television ads anyway, a celebration of the full-bloom springtime meadow if nothing else, a chance to share the extraordinary beauty of the place where the extraordinary fragrance had truly been created. The television ads were to be filmed next week, beginning Monday and finishing by Friday so that Larisa and Peter could return to San Francisco in time to attend Christine and Stephen's Saturday afternoon wedding.

The coming week would be exciting—and busy—but it was the private days that would come before that Larisa anticipated with the greatest excitement and joy. Tomorrow she and Peter would fly to Boston, and on Friday morning they would begin a leisurely sentimental journey to the places of Peter's childhood, ending up on Sunday at the estate on Cape Cod. Peter had told her that he wanted to share with her the places and memories of his childhood; and, he had added solemnly, there were some other very important things that he wanted to tell her.

There was just one very important thing that Larisa wanted to tell Peter, but it was the most important thing of all: the joyous news about the tiny miracle that lived inside her, the little life that had defied all odds, like the bravest of wildflowers. Larisa believed without question that her miracle baby was a little girl, and she decided that she would tell Peter about his tiny courageous daughter as they sat amid the courageous flowers in the magical meadow of *Promise*.

As Larisa drifted off to a most peaceful sleep, she envisioned Peter's immeasurable joy when she told him . . .

Peter had planned to drive Larisa to Concord on Friday and wander through Boston with her all day Saturday; but when he awakened Friday morning, so close to Innis Arden, Peter knew that that was where he wanted to take her first. Because it was there, in the meadow, that he would tell her the truth about his childhood dreams—and the man who had stolen them from him; and it was there that he would tell her the most important truth of all, that he loved her and wanted to spend his life with her.

Peter had already told Larisa a little about the father that he had loved so deeply, and during the drive to Cape Cod, he told her about the dyslexia that had crippled the dreams of the gifted carpenter long before the arthritis had crippled his art and about the wonderful dreams that the father and son had shared.

But it wasn't until Peter and Larisa were at Innis Arden, sitting on a sun-warmed patch of grass in the enchanted meadow amid the fragrance of *Promise*, that Peter told her what had happened to those dreams.

"I told you that I had known Julian briefly at Harvard," Peter began, his heart aching as he saw her lovely hopeful eyes cloud at the mention of Julian's name. Larisa had neither mentioned Julian nor even alluded to her marriage since the day in September when he had asked her to be the model for *Promise*; and Peter had hoped that with their love the painful memories would have long since faded. But as her beautiful blue eyes suddenly became very wary, Peter realized that she had not forgotten Julian Chancellor at all. "There's more to the story, Larisa. I'm sorry, but I think you need to hear it all." *And then, my darling, you can tell me about the pain he caused you too . . . and then, my love, we can both forget him forever and live our wonderful love.* "Okay?"

"Okay," she agreed quietly, barely able to breathe because the invisible chains from which she had so bravely freed herself were suddenly back, coiling tightly, ever more tightly, around her chest.

Peter told her the essential facts of his enmity with Julian as quickly as possible. But still, long before he had finished, her eyes had left his to gaze past the joyous flowers to the vast emptiness of the sea beyond.

"Larisa?" he asked when he had finished speaking. He had stopped the story with the day in August when Innis Arden had become his. There was more story he could have told, of course. He could have told her about his discovery that she was Julian's wife and his fleeting worry that she had been sent by Julian to enchant and seduce him as once Marcy had been; and he could have confessed that even if that had been the case, by then it was far too late, he was already hopelessly enchanted; and he could have spoken aloud his still tormenting worry that the fire that might have destroyed the mansion in December had been arranged by Julian. But Peter stopped the story with the day in August—because Larisa was already so terribly far away. "*Larisa?*"

"What was the date in August when you so cleverly tricked Julian?"

Peter didn't answer right away, not because he couldn't instantly remember the date, but because her voice terrified him. It was so hard and so cold.

"The fourteenth," he said finally. And then, because she wasn't going to look at him, he moved in front of her. And when he saw blue eyes that were as hard and as cold as her voice, he pleaded, "Larisa, talk to me!"

"You said you weren't sure if Julian even cared about Innis Arden any longer." Her icy voice spoke beyond the vast horizon to the memory of the night that Julian had lost the estate. "Well, Peter, you'll be pleased to hear that he was very upset indeed."

"What did he do to you?" Peter asked, as an ominous wave swept through him. Larisa didn't answer his question, not with words; but for just a flicker Peter saw in her forget-me-not blue eyes the same look of bewildered disbelief he had seen when she had told him what had happened to her when she was twelve. Controlling his rage enough to speak again, he asked with quiet despair, "He raped you, Larisa?"

"Don't sound so upset, Peter. Julian did what men—*all* men—have always done to me." She looked at him then with her hard and hopeless cloudy blue eyes and asked softly, "It's what you've done to me, too, isn't it?"

"Oh, Larisa," he whispered hoarsely. "How can you say that?"

"Wasn't using me as the model for *Promise*—with the meadow as the backdrop—all part of your plan to get back at Julian? 'Look, Julian, look what I've stolen from you now. Not only your precious meadow, but your wife too!' "

"Larisa, I *love* you. I brought you here to tell you what I believed you had to know about me and Julian and then to ask you to marry me. Here." Peter retrieved the velvet box from his jacket pocket and extended it to her. And then, because she wouldn't take it from him, he opened it himself. Inside was an engagement ring, *her* engagement ring, a flawless forget-me-not blue sapphire encircled by delicate petals of brilliant diamonds. "I had this made for you."

Larisa looked from the magnificent ring to Peter's loving, and so desperate, dark green eyes; and for a moment she remembered how much she had believed in his love and how nourished she had been by it. It was a wonderful memory, and how she wished she could live in it forever, but she forced it away, and then forced her eyes to leave the loving dark green ones and return to the glittering symbol he was offering her as proof of his love. She had been offered glittering yet meaningless symbols of love before—by the man whose empire Peter wanted to destroy.

"Oh no," she whispered as she realized the depth of Peter's betrayal of her trust and her love. "Having me model for *Promise*, flaunting me and the meadow together, was just a tiny part of your plan, wasn't it? This, your offer of marriage, was what it was really all about."

"There was no plan, Larisa. I fell in love with you."

"You believed that by marrying me, you would be marrying into half of Julian's fortune," she said, ignoring the loving softness of his eyes and his words, and ignoring too the heart that was crying to her, Listen to him! "Well, Peter, I'm afraid the only money I have is the money you've given me. I didn't want Julian's money, you see, I just desperately wanted to get away from him, to stop being owned by him. This is all such a terrible joke. I allowed myself to be owned by you so that I could stop being owned by Julian."

"I don't want Julian's money, Larisa. And I don't own you, nor do I ever want to own you." Peter's eyes searched hers, and when he spoke it wasn't to the icy surface he didn't know but to the uncertain flickers of love he saw still in the forget-me-not blue depths. "I just want to spend my life loving you."

"I trusted you, Peter," she pleaded softly. "I made a promise to myself that I would never trust again, but I trusted you."

"You *can* trust me. *I love you.*"

Listen to him! her heart cried. Listen to him! Trust him still. *Please.*

I want to trust him, but . . . she said very quietly, "You should have told me about your relationship with Julian."

"Yes, I should have," Peter agreed with matching quiet. "I know that now. But, Larisa, from the very beginning I sensed that you didn't want to talk about him, and frankly that was quite all right with me. All I knew about your divorce was what I read in *People*, and that article implied, more than implied, that it was Julian who had wanted the divorce. I've spent the past six months loving you, and wanting our love so much, but being afraid that you loved him still."

"Oh, no, Peter," Larisa whispered. "I never loved Julian, not really. It was all just an illusion." But your love for Peter, and Peter's love for you, is not an illusion, her loving heart defiantly reminded. Tell him that you know that! Reassure this wonderful man who loves you. Larisa looked at him, saw his gentleness and his torment, said very softly, "I know now that what I had with Julian was an illusion, a deception. I know that now, Peter, because of you."

"Oh, Larisa." It was a whisper of hope. "I love you."

"I love you, too, Peter." It was a wondrous truth, and a confident one, but there were other truths, terrifying ones—and they prevented her from curling into his loving arms. "You think Julian's responsible for the fire here in December, don't you?"

"I don't know. Maybe."

"Julian never forgives or forgets, we both know that. He's going to be enraged when he learns about me modeling for *Promise*, and if he ever knew about us . . ." Her eyes filled with immense fear and her voice lost its hope as she whispered, "Oh, Peter."

"Larisa, listen to me. Julian never needs to know—not about *Promise* and not about us. Why don't we go into the mansion right now and I'll make the calls that will stop the launch?"

"Most of the magazines have already gone to press, and even if they haven't by now more than one publisher will have told the media or perhaps Julian himself that I'm the model. *Promise* is already in the public domain. Julian is going to know, and he will do everything he can to destroy it and us."

"Then, after I get you settled in the mansion, I'll go to New York to see him."

"The damage has already been done, Peter. There's nothing you could offer him at this point that would appease him."

"My intention is *not* to appease Julian, Larisa," Peter said solemnly. "My intention is to warn him to stay away from you and us—forever."

"It's too late," Larisa said softly, speaking aloud the silent thought that had spun in her mind when Peter had asked her to spend the weekend with him at Lake Tahoe. Then, because he had believed she was still mourning the loss of Julian's love, he had gently suggested that perhaps it was too soon. Larisa had known it wasn't too soon, but a knowledge deep inside had warned her, even before their love began, that it was too late for her and Peter. She should have heeded that deep wisdom, but she hadn't—and now a precious and innocent life was involved. Larisa knew that Julian's immense fury about the loss of Innis Arden and even his anger when he discovered that she was the model for *Promise* would pale into insignificance when compared to his rage if ever he learned that she was carrying the baby of his ancient enemy. With sudden urgency she said, "I have to go, Peter. I have to go away now."

"We'll go away together, darling."

"No, Peter, that's not possible. Don't you see?"

"No, I don't see," Peter said with quiet calm, even though icy waves of fear washed through him. Peter London wasn't physically afraid of Julian Chancellor, of course, but there was fear nonetheless. Julian had stolen his dreams once before . . . and now the thief of dreams threatened to destroy the most important dream of all—his lifetime of love with Larisa. "We love each other, Larisa."

"Please, Peter, just let me go!"

Peter gazed at the woman he loved. Larisa was suddenly so desperate, and so fearful—as if she believed he would violently deny her soft plea for escape, as if she still put him in the same category as the evil men who had brutally betrayed her. Peter thought that they had gotten way beyond that—and back to their wondrous and trusting love—but now she was very far away again, and in another moment she might simply turn and run. The keys to the rental car were in his pocket, but he didn't want her driving, this upset, along the unfamiliar winding roads.

"Why don't I go to the mansion and call a cab for you?" he suggested finally, gently. "You can come with me or wait here until you see it arrive."

"Couldn't I make the call myself?"

"Of course. The mansion is open. The housekeeper's name is Ellen. If you like, I'll wait here until I see you leave." Peter's heart screamed with silent pain as the wary eyes told him that yes, that was what she wanted. He continued with great control, "After you leave, I'm going to stop the launch and then I'm going to New York to see Julian."

"Please don't tell him that you and I were lovers."

"All right, I won't. But, Larisa, we are far more than lovers. We *love* each other." After a moment he asked with quiet emotion, "Will you take the engagement ring with you?"

"No, Peter, I can't," she whispered. I *can't*. Let me go, Peter! But, she realized, Peter wasn't holding her. He was doing nothing to prevent her from leaving, nothing whatsoever to possess her against her will; but nonetheless Larisa felt the powerful call of his heart, wanting to hold her, pleading with her to stay forever with him and their love. The invisible bonds that had bound her to Julian had been punishing, suffocating, and dangerous; and the invisible bonds to Peter were wondrous bonds of love. But she had to flee those wondrous bonds as desperately as she had fled the destructive ones that had bound her to Julian—because now there was an innocent life inside her, a brave flower filled with hope and joy and promise, and she had to find a safe place for her precious little love. "I have to go, Peter. Goodbye."

After the cab that had come for Larisa pulled away from the mansion, Peter made the calls to abruptly stop whatever still could be stopped for the launch of *Promise*. Then he drove to Logan to catch a shuttle to New York. Larisa was at the airport, Peter knew. Ellen had overheard her make a reservation for the two-forty flight for San Francisco. Peter wanted to find her, but he forced himself to focus on what needed to be done, not on what had happened. We love each other, he reminded his aching heart. We will be together. This wondrous dream of love will not be destroyed.

Peter knew that Larisa needed time alone, and it was comforting to know that she would be in San Francisco, in her romantic bedroom filled with images of *Promise*. She would be safe there; and soon, very soon, he would be able to go to her, and cradle her in his arms as he assured her that they no longer needed to worry about the specter of Julian Chancellor.

But how could he ever truly give Larisa such a categorical assurance? Peter wondered as he made the brief flight from Logan to La Guardia. He planned to warn Julian to stay away from Larisa, from both of them, but what was the "or else"? He didn't have much ammunition—except for the fact that Julian was in essence a bully, and therefore, like all bullies, in essence merely a coward.

He wouldn't even offer an "or else," he decided. The threat would simply be implied by the icy resolve of his calm and unflickering gaze.

Icy? Calm? Peter's own ability to remain calm and cool in the presence of the man who had so brutally harmed his lovely Larisa was a worry far greater than what words of warning he would speak. How could he possibly control his rage? With love, he told himself. His love for Larisa would enable him to do whatever was necessary.

Whatever was necessary. When he was shown into Julian's office only moments after being announced and met his ancient enemy's mocking dark eyes, Peter's carefully suppressed rage burst into sudden flames. And in the brightness of that raging inferno, a thought presented itself with simple yet brilliant clarity: I will kill him. I will kill Julian Chancellor. Right now. Right this minute. With my bare hands.

Peter welcomed the glittering thought with a sense of great peace—and he let it go with great reluctance. It wasn't possible, of course, at least not practical, to murder Julian Chancellor in cold blood. The peaceful thought vanished, leaving Peter to fight the fires of rage that blazed within him even as he filled his eyes and his voice with the calm steadiness of ice.

"Peter. What a nice surprise."

"Is it a surprise, Julian?"

"You mean did I expect you to inform me in person about your new venture and my wife's role in it?" The smile on Julian's face was as dark and menacing as his eyes. Gesturing to a copy of one of the soon-to-be-published print ads for *Promise* that had been sent to him, he said, "As you can see, I already know."

"Your ex-wife."

"Ah, yes. And your mistress? Unfair question, although I assume that she is. She's really quite lovely, isn't she, Peter? So very willing to please, so happy to satisfy every imaginable sexual whim—"

"I'm here to warn you, Julian," Peter said, his voice icy still and his dark green eyes eloquently conveying their impractical—and yet so appealing—murderous wish. "I know what you did to Larisa. And I also know that you are responsible for the fire at Innis Arden."

"I don't know anything about a fire. And as for Larisa . . ." Julian stopped, smiled a charming conciliatory smile, and said, "Listen, Peter, it's obvious that we need to talk, to resolve some misunderstandings. I have a meeting I really must go to now, but why don't the three of us meet later? Let's say dinner at Le Cirque?"

"Not the three of us, Julian. And not dinner."

"Larisa's not with you?"

"Where and when, Julian."

"Right here. Nine o'clock. I'll have my secretary notify building security to be expecting you."

* * *

Something in Peter's solemn expression had given Julian the distinct impression that Larisa hadn't accompanied him to New York. But, quite obviously, Peter and Larisa had been together somewhere very recently, revealing their secrets to each other. At Innis Arden? Julian wondered. Yes, probably. And was Larisa there still, waiting for her lover to return with the triumphant announcement that he had warned Julian to stay away from her once and for all?

Because he paid people to keep him informed, Julian knew that there were guards at Innis Arden now, ever since the fire that had done far less damage than had been his hope; and he knew that in the past month a live-in housekeeper had been hired, as if Peter was planning to take up residence in the mansion; and he knew that the telephone number to the mansion had not yet been changed from the number it had been during the years that it had belonged to the people of Cape Cod.

Julian identified himself to the female voice that answered as Carlton Evans, a senior associate with the advertising firm that was handling the promotion campaign for *Promise*.

"I'm sorry, Mr. Evans, but Mr. London isn't here," Ellen replied.

"Well," Julian answered amiably. "It's actually Larisa to whom I need to speak most urgently. Is she there?"

"No. I'm sorry. She's not here either."

"Really? I had understood that both she and Peter were going to be there. I am reaching the mansion at Innis Arden, aren't I?"

"Yes, and they both were here, but they both left earlier today."

"I see." Julian sighed audibly. "This is a problem. I really do need to speak with Larisa as soon as possible. Did she by any chance tell you where she would be? A phone number perhaps?"

"No, no phone number. However, I did overhear her making reservations for an afternoon flight to San Francisco."

"Leaving at what time?"

"Two-forty. She left here shortly before noon, so I assume she was able to catch that flight."

"Wonderful," Julian said with genuine enthusiasm. It *was* wonderful, because it was only four-thirty now, and Peter was in New York planning to meet with him at nine, and Larisa was still en route to San Francisco, and *he* was in control. "I have Larisa's number in San Francisco, so I'll be able to reach her there. Thank you so very much for your help."

Before making the next calls, Julian removed a manila folder from a locked drawer in his desk. The folder contained financial data on Peter London—the detailed information required by the Chancellor family attorneys for the purchase of Innis Arden as well as various credit checks Julian himself had had done. Julian held in his hands extensive confidential information about his enemy; but all he withdrew from the folder now was the information that Peter himself would carry in his wallet—credit card names and numbers, driver's license, home address, and unlisted home phone.

The next two calls Julian made as Peter London. The first was to an airline to make a reservation—paid for in advance by credit card—for the six-fifty flight to San Francisco; and the second was to a car rental company, for which Peter had "express" privileges, which meant the car would be waiting, with no further paperwork required, when he reached San Francisco.

Then dark, handsome Julian Chancellor left his office to travel to San Francisco as dark, handsome Peter London. The casual clothes into which he changed were enough of a disguise. He wouldn't be recognized—his face simply wasn't that familiar to the general public—and, although he traveled extensively, it was always in his own jet, the same way the wealthy and powerful people who would have recognized him always traveled too.

And if the airline personnel had a vague memory of the dark, handsome man named Peter London who had been on the evening flight to San Francisco? Fine, wonderful, because they could help place Peter London in San Francisco at the time of the unspeakably brutal murder of Julian Chancellor's beautiful ex-wife.

"Oh, yes, Mr. London," the security guard greeted him when Peter returned to the Chancellor Building shortly before nine. "Unfortunately, Mr. Chancellor will be unable to meet with you after all. He phoned earlier to say that he had been called out of town on urgent business. He doesn't expect to return for several days, so he asked me to extend his apologies and offered to meet with you next week in San Francisco."

San Francisco. Peter's mind reeled. Was that where Julian was going now?

"Where is he?" Peter demanded sharply. "Where was the urgent business?"

"I don't know, sir. I'm sorry. He didn't say."

"Is there a phone here that I can use?"

"Of course. You can use this one."

Both the direct and nonstop flights to San Francisco stopped departing New York at about eight every night and didn't resume service again until six in the morning. But there were indirect routes on "red eyes," and Peter finally found one, involving two middle-of-the-night plane changes, that would depart New York at ten-thirty and have him in San Francisco by dawn. As soon as he made the reservation, Peter dialed Larisa's number in San Francisco. He knew she wouldn't be there yet—if on time, the two-forty flight from Boston should have been landing just about now—but maybe Elizabeth would be.

And what would his message to Elizabeth be? Peter wondered as the phone rang unanswered a continent away. That Julian might—*might*—be on his way to see Larisa? Surely he was overreacting, Peter told himself. His rationality and logic had been completely usurped by emotion, his immense love for Larisa and his almost equally immense hatred for Julian. Surely . . .

But still, he decided as he finally hung up the unanswered phone, he would keep calling until he reached her . . . and when he did he would tell her to stay where she was, in her very safe and very secure apartment.

CHAPTER THIRTY-FIVE

*L*arisa's flight from Boston should have arrived in San Francisco at six-ten Pacific time, but because of mechanical problems discovered during the scheduled stopover in Chicago, the original jet was grounded and its passengers were given seats on a flight that finally touched the tarmac in San Francisco at nine-forty—an hour and a half before Julian's flight from New York was due to arrive.

During that hour and a half, Larisa felt a strange sense of urgency, a restless and ominous feeling that despite her exhaustion, she needed to act tonight on the decision she had made instead of waiting until morning. At first Larisa fought the feeling. But with each passing moment the ominous restlessness crescendoed, and finally, just as Julian's flight was landing, she began to get ready to leave.

Larisa packed hurriedly, as she had once before, when she had desperately fled the Fifth Avenue penthouse. She packed most of the same old friends she had packed then—her jeans and sweatshirt from Berkeley, the tattered nightgown and robe; but one friend she left behind—the romantic beaded gown that Julian had refused to let her wear on the eve of their wedding, and which she had worn the night when she had first met Peter. The lovely romantic symbol of innocence and hope would stay behind this time . . . and in its place Larisa packed a symbol of hopelessness and violence: the gun that Julian had given her. Larisa reached for the box containing the lethal weapon with surprising confidence, even though she knew she would die before ever pulling the trigger.

Still, she packed it.

It was almost midnight, and Elizabeth wasn't home, and in answer to Larisa's call the page operator had told her that Dr. Jennings was scrubbed in the OR with a renal transplantation and would be for several more hours. So, Larisa left her best friend a note: *Dearest Liz, I have to go away for a while. Please don't worry about me. I'm okay. Love, Lara.* She hesitated a moment and then added, *I want you to be okay, too, Elizabeth Jennings!*

Larisa left the note in the kitchen, propped up against the ELIZABETH! CELEBRATE!! mug she had given her on her twenty-first birthday. Then she withdrew from her wallet the small card that Darlene Buchanan had given her in December and dialed the number to the motel in Lake Tahoe.

"Hello, Darlene? This is Larisa Locksley."

"Larisa! Hi."

"Hi. I didn't expect you to be answering the phones this late."

"I take the evening shift twice a week, when Craig is on duty. My night clerk will be arriving any moment, but I'm happy to be the one to have answered your call. Do you need a cottage?"

"Yes, if you have one. I'm in San Francisco and was hoping to drive up to-night."

"It's between ski and summer seasons, so we actually have several available—including, if you want it, the one where you used to live."

"Yes," Larisa answered quietly. "I would like that cottage, perhaps for quite a while if that's okay."

"Of course it is. Melanie will be so thrilled. Not," Darlene assured swiftly, "that she'll bother you."

"She would never bother me and I'm very much looking forward to seeing her again. Since I won't arrive until the middle of the night, I may sleep late in the morning. But please tell Melanie that when I awaken I'll open the curtains and would love to have her—and you, too, of course—come visit."

"Melanie will be there as soon as the curtains are open. Craig and I have a meeting in the morning with our accountant, so I won't see you until later on."

As soon as Larisa said goodbye to Darlene, it was time to say goodbye to the sanctuary of Elizabeth's apartment and her own bedroom of *Promise*. This time, she thought as she reached for her suitcase, she wasn't escaping to a safe haven where she would be rescued by the generosity of a kind friend. This time, *at last*, Larisa Locksley was going to rescue herself.

She would go to the tiny cottage and confront the icy ghosts that lurked there still. She would force them to come out of hiding from beneath the delicate floral wallpaper and she would stare at them bravely until she knew all their secrets and they were vanquished forever. And then, even more bravely, she would stand before the mirror and gaze with gentle love at the woman who had finally conquered her own ghosts . . . and who knew that her love for Peter had not been an illusion . . . and who was going to spend the rest of her life loving and protecting his beloved baby.

Julian had just brought the car rented to Peter London to a stop across the street from Larisa's apartment building when he saw her emerging from the gated underground garage. Julian might have ignored the car entirely—inexpensive, American-made, not acceptable for his wife—but the glow of a street lamp illuminated her magnificent hair, creating a brilliant beacon of fire that beckoned to him, and betrayed her.

Larisa didn't notice him, of course. He was a dark shadow inside one of many cars parked on the street. And even when he began to follow her, she didn't notice, because he drove without his headlights on until she turned onto Divisadero, brightly lighted and busy on this Friday at midnight.

Larisa drove cautiously, forcing her fatigued mind to concentrate on the long drive, abruptly stopping her thoughts whenever they began to drift with the wondrous reminder that she was carrying a most precious new little life inside her.

Julian followed, at first impatient with her cautiousness, wanting the speed and power of the car to match the pace and power of his racing thoughts; but finally he simply savored the slowness. There was a most delicious anticipation, a most wonderfully titillating tension as he leisurely imagined her terror and his triumph, her brutal murder and Peter's conviction for same.

Larisa was playing right into his plan, leading him to some remote place, perhaps known only to her and her lover; and, Julian decided, by now Peter himself was playing into his hand, too. He was doubtless already making his frantic journey from New York to San Francisco, having perhaps phoned Larisa first—when he discovered that Julian had no intention of meeting with him—telling her to flee and promising to join her as soon as possible. Wonderful, Julian thought. What could be more perfect than having Peter arrive to find his lover dead? He would rush to her savagely murdered body, covering himself with her blood, incriminating himself even further.

Julian's lips curled with lustful hunger as he imagined that bloody scene and his bitter enemy's anguished horror. How he wished he could witness it!

But he would be long gone by then, awaiting with more delicious anticipation the news of the brutal murder of the wife who, although he had eventually tired of her, the world knew he had always treated like a princess.

Julian watched from a distance as Larisa checked into the motel. His dark eyes followed her to the remote cottage and remained fixed there as she pulled the curtains and finally turned off the lights. Then Julian himself checked into a motel across the street, paying in cash this time and using neither Peter's name nor his own. He had no plans to sleep, of course. His energized body didn't need sleep, nor did he want to miss even a moment of the wonderful anticipation.

Julian could have made his move now, in the darkness of night; but the more he thought about it, the more likely it seemed that eventually Peter would appear. He would wait, he decided, at least long enough to give Peter time to return to San Francisco and begin the drive to Lake Tahoe. Besides, the idea of murdering Larisa in the morning was far more appealing than murdering her now, when she was too tired to plead and struggle the way he wanted her to; *and* she was always so beautiful in the morning, when she had just awakened and the memory of her dreams had left her blue eyes wide and hopeful . . . as if she truly believed that this new day would be better than the day before . . . as if in her dreams she had somehow forgotten the truth.

Julian could have murdered her now, but for many reasons, the morning held far more appeal. Perhaps the most appealing reason of all was that tonight the only weapon he had was his hands—and they were more than lethal enough; but in the morning he could go to the store he had noticed just a block away—with a boldly lettered sign proclaiming it to be a "hunter's paradise"—and he could buy a hunting knife . . . the kind with the jagged edge.

Peter's plane touched the tarmac in San Francisco just as the golden dawn was beginning to lighten the spring sky. As soon as he deplaned he found the nearest pay phone. He had called the apartment throughout the night, whenever he could, from the planes when they had phones, and from the ground as he had made his middle-of-the-night connections.

And always there had been no answer.

But she's there, he told himself. She's there. She's just not answering the phone.

This time the phone was answered.

"It's Peter, Elizabeth. I'm sorry to call so early but I need to speak to Larisa."

"She's not here, Peter."

"Not there?" An immense wave of pure ice stopped his heart and froze his breath.

"She was here," Elizabeth assured swiftly. "She left me a note, saying she needed to get away for a while and assuring me that she would be all right."

"Has Julian called?" he pressed, his heart beating again.

"Julian? No. This has something to do with Julian?"

"Yes," Peter admitted, breathing finally, exhaling the icy fear—and then inhaling pure frustration. Yes, he thought, this had something to do with Julian, whether or not he was anywhere near San Francisco. Larisa was fleeing from Julian—from *both* of them—both of the men whose bitter enmity had shattered her lovely hope for a safe and joyous love. "If he does call, please tell him nothing and let me know right away. I'll be at my place in Sausalito."

"Do you think that Larisa is there?"

"No," he answered with quiet—and anguished—confidence. "I don't know where she is, Elizabeth."

"What *happened*, Peter?"

"Julian and I go way back, a past history that I had hoped had long since been forgotten. I told Larisa about it yesterday . . . and it became obvious that Julian hadn't forgotten about the past at all." Rage washed through him as he thought about the proof that Julian hadn't forgotten, what he had done to Larisa on that August night.

"And that realization upset Larisa," Elizabeth offered into the suddenly charged silence.

"Yes." After a moment Peter asked, "Do you have any idea where she might have gone?"

"No, not offhand. I'd have to think about it."

"Well, if you do think of somewhere, will you let me know? And if you hear from her . . ."

"I'll tell her that you called, and that you're in Sausalito," Elizabeth promised. She could promise that, but even though she knew of Peter's great love for Larisa, and now heard his obvious immense worry, she couldn't promise that if she did think of where Larisa might be that she would tell him—not without checking with Larisa first. Because, as much as Elizabeth knew how much Larisa loved Peter, it was very clear that now, for some reason, she had run away from him. Putting a smile in her voice, because she very much hoped that the love of Larisa and Peter would survive, she said, "And Peter, if you hear from Larisa, please let me know. I'm on first call for trauma today so I'll most likely be at the hospital."

Maybe I already know where Larisa is, Peter thought just moments after his conversation with Elizabeth had ended. As he dialed Directory Assistance, and then the number to the motel at Lake Tahoe, he thought, maybe I already know where my lovely forget-me-not would go when her world has fallen apart—again.

"Yes, Ms. Locksley is here," the motel clerk said. "But the cottages don't have phones and we make a policy of not waking our guests this early in the morning— unless it's an emergency, of course. Is it?"

"No," Peter answered truthfully as the relief pulsed through him. It wasn't an emergency anymore. He knew where Larisa was now, and that she was safe. Julian knew nothing about the motel in Lake Tahoe. Larisa had gone to a place where Julian would never find her and where she knew—didn't she?—that Peter would. She was safe, and perhaps expecting him, but still something made Peter ask, "Did anyone else check in last night?"

"No, just her. Did you want to leave a message?"

"No. Thank you." *I will give her all the messages of love when I see her.*

* * *

Larisa had wondered if she would be able to sleep in the cottage surrounded by all the icy ghosts. But, in fact, she felt strangely safe in their midst. They were well known to her, after all, enemies and yet familiar companions. So she slept, a deep sleep without dreams or nightmares, awakening at nine and opening the curtains to a brilliant sapphire sky.

She showered, and dressed in her sweatshirt and jeans, and was just about to leave to get breakfast for herself and her baby when there was a knock on the door. Larisa smiled as she moved toward it.

It would be Melanie, the little girl she herself once had been. No, that was wrong. She had never been as safe or as loved as Melanie was. Melanie was the little girl who her own daughter was going to be, so safe, so protected, so very loved.

"Good morn—" Her smile vanished and her face filled with pure fear.

"Good morning," Julian answered, calmly stopping the door as she struggled to close it, surprised by Larisa's strength, but truly amazed by his own. He had never been so powerful, so *omnipotent*. He effortlessly stopped her from closing the door and then easily opened it wide and entered the tiny cottage.

"Get out, Julian."

"Sorry, Larisa. I'm afraid I just can't do that," he said, smiling charmingly, menacingly, and arching an approving eyebrow as the door locked automatically as it closed behind him.

"What do you want?"

"Let's see," Julian replied, thrilled by the sheer terror in her beautiful blue eyes. Then, as calmly as if he were in the midst of a negotiation for a piece of property, he explained, "What I want is to very slowly carve up your lovely flesh . . . and then let your lover pay for your murder." Julian extracted the just-purchased hunting knife from the pocket of his jacket and added softly, "And, Larisa, you know I always get what I want."

"Julian, *no!*"

"Larisa, *yes,*" he mocked. "I always get what I want, and I never wanted to let you go."

"Julian," she whispered to the man who was so obviously in control, and yet so obviously crazed with delusions of grandeur. She had seen glimpses of Julian's madness before, but now Larisa saw its full force: the wildly excited dark eyes, the menacingly seductive smile, the terrifying pleasure in his voice as he spoke so calmly about her murder. She fought her own terror, knowing that she could never overpower him, needing to keep him at bay, keep him talking, while her mind searched for a way to escape. She reminded him quietly, "But you gave me the divorce, Julian."

"I had to! I didn't want your *boyfriend* to know that I was upset about Innis Arden." Julian smiled conspiratorily and added, "I had plans, you see."

"The fire."

"The fire. Not an unqualified success, as you know. However, there would have been another fire, some time when Peter was in residence." Julian gave a dismissive gesture with the hand that held the gleaming hunting knife. "But this is better. *Much* better. Aren't you going to scream, Larisa?"

No, she thought in silent answer to his question. Larisa knew that a scream would cause more harm than good. The cottage was too remote for anyone to identify her scream—if they even heard it—as anything more than a vague sound. They would listen for the sound to repeat itself, to pinpoint its source; and when there was no second scream, because Julian's powerful hands would have clamped over her mouth, they would dismiss the sound they had heard as a cry of a bird, or a squeal of a tire, or the joyous shriek of a frolicking child.

A scream would accomplish nothing. It would only bring Julian closer to her, touching and confining her, and once that happened all was lost.

"You never did scream, my sweet," Julian continued when his question had been greeted with lingering silence. "I would have liked it very much if you had. Maybe I just didn't hurt you enough before. Maybe this time you will scream for me."

"I should never have divorced you," Larisa said suddenly, trying to get him to drop his guard, just for an instant, just long enough for her to dash past him and make her escape. It was her only hope. She continued softly, "I was very angry with you, Julian, but if I had understood how important Innis Arden was to you . . . I've been thinking about you, *us*, remembering what we had, what we still could have."

"There is nothing for you but death, *whore*."

Julian lunged at her then, the razor-sharp knife cutting through the sleeve of her sweatshirt as if it were gossamer silk and deeply slashing the delicate flesh beneath. Larisa felt no pain, only the hot dampness of her own blood; and then she felt the calm that had so bravely urged her to keep him talking while she plotted her escape evaporate into pure terror. There would be no escape. Julian's crazed eyes were now filled with a lustful desire that told her he would not stop until his hunger for her agonizing death and his triumphant revenge was fully and robustly satiated.

This is how it ends, Larisa realized with astonishing clarity. This is the full circle. I died here once before, a death of the heart and the spirit, and now I die here again . . . forever.

Julian obviously wanted her to fight him, to struggle valiantly but futilely to save her life. For a moment Larisa decided that her final victory—the only victory she would ever have—would be to deprive him of the pleasure of her struggle. She would simply give herself up to him, a willing victim, accepting her destiny with a sense almost of relief that both the foolish illusions and savage betrayals of her life were finally over.

But then something new filled Larisa, a power as strong as Julian's madness. She didn't know if it came from the heart that had solemnly and joyously promised to protect her baby *always* . . . or if it came from the small precious life herself, the courageous wildflower that had been so determined from the very beginning, putting brave delicate roots where no baby ever had dared to before because she wanted a chance to grow and live and laugh and fall in love.

So Larisa fought, stumbling away from Julian, twirling from the savage blows that became more and more vicious, and more and more calculated, as his pleasure increased. She was wounded, weak and bleeding, but still she fought. Julian liked her brave and foolish struggle, *he loved it*, and he wanted it to go on as long as possible, savoring her terror, marveling at the rich redness of her blood against the beautiful snow-white skin that became whiter and ever whiter as she lost more blood.

Julian let her twist away from him for a moment—it would be so wonderful to see a flicker of hope in her terrified blue eyes!—and watched with interest as she crawled across the small room. Her determined journey wasn't toward the door, a destination she knew he would not permit her to reach, but to her suitcase and to a box inside it. As soon as Julian recognized the box, he felt a rush of exhilaration, and he watched with eager anticipation as Larisa's pale trembling fingers removed the gun.

And then, as she so bravely pointed it at him, Julian laughed, as he had laughed in August and as another man had laughed in this same tiny room eighteen years before.

But Larisa wasn't that twelve-year-old girl anymore. She was a mother, keeping the most solemn of all promises of love—to protect her baby always . . . and to give that precious innocent life a chance for joy, for happiness, and for love.

Larisa was a mother, not the twelve-year-old girl anymore, but in her fading consciousness, she heard a little-girl voice cry, as it had cried all those years before, "Stop, *please*. I'll shoot you! Please *stop!*" Larisa knew her lips weren't actually whispering those brave and frantic words. Her mouth and lungs were fully engaged in the desperate battle to find air to supply her ever dwindling blood supply with oxygen, to keep her awake and conscious. The little-girl screams came from deep inside, from the innocent little girl she once had been . . . or from her own precious daughter.

Then Larisa Locksley did what she had never been able to do before, because before there had only been herself to save.

She aimed the gun at Julian's heart and pulled the trigger.

There was a sudden thunder in the tiny room, and Larisa saw the expression of stunned disbelief on Julian's face—and then the final look of anger. As his dying body fell heavily on top of her, he plunged the knife deep into her flesh . . . and plunged her world into soundless darkness.

CHAPTER THIRTY-SIX

$\mathcal{E}$lizabeth had never dialed Nick's unlisted home phone number. But she knew it *by heart*.

And now it was that heart that compelled her to dial.

"I need you, Nick."

"Elizabeth," he answered softly. *I need you too—so much.* He asked gently of her troubled voice, "What's wrong?"

"I just got a call from an emergency-room physician in Lake Tahoe." Elizabeth drew a breath to try to calm the rush of emotions, but her voice was still shaky as she whispered, "It's Larisa, Nick. She's been badly injured . . . stabbed."

Nick felt a sudden rush of shaky emotion, too, but he forced calm into his voice for Elizabeth, and with that calm sent a quiet reminder that she had called him many times to talk to him about badly injured trauma patients. "Tell me what happened, Elizabeth. Tell me everything. You said the call came from a doctor in Lake Tahoe?"

"Yes. She was at a motel there. I don't know why. She and Peter were supposed to be in Boston all this week, but she returned last night and left me a note saying that she needed to get away. Peter called me early this morning, obviously terribly worried about her. He told me then that he didn't know where she was, but he arrived at the motel just moments after she shot Julian."

"Larisa shot Julian?"

"It was self-defense, of course. He was trying to kill her. That's apparently quite obvious from her wounds, but there was also an eyewitness. The daughter of the couple who manage the motel had gone to the cottage to visit Larisa and saw through the window what was happening. The cottage door was locked so she ran to get the key and call her parents. She opened the door just moments before Larisa pulled the trigger. Peter and the girl's father—a police officer—arrived almost immediately after."

"Is Julian dead?"

"Yes."

"And Larisa?"

"She has lost a lot of blood, although there's no active bleeding now, but as Julian was dying he apparently stabbed her in the left upper quadrant of her abdomen. The physician who called says it's impossible for it not to have gone directly into her spleen. There's no clinical evidence of rupture yet but she needs to be explored. They're sending her here. The Flight for Life team is already on the way." She sighed softly and then simply confessed, "I can't do it alone, Nick. I can't operate again on someone I love—not without help . . . your help."

"I'm on my way."

"Thank you. Nick? There's something else."

"Tell me."

"Larisa is unconscious now, but earlier she was awake just long enough to whisper something about a baby. The physician who examined her in Tahoe thinks she's about four months pregnant. He also said that there are no knife wounds at all in her lower abdomen." Elizabeth drew yet another breath to combat yet another rush of emotion. "She must have kept twisting away to prevent Julian from stabbing her there."

"So the baby seems all right?"

"Yes." For now, Elizabeth amended silently, knowing that Nick was making the same silent amendment. The baby was fine . . . unless Larisa's spleen suddenly ruptured and caused catastrophic shock.

"I'm on my way, Elizabeth."

Larisa's lacerated spleen ruptured in the operating room, a violent and powerful explosion of tissue and blood. Had she been operating alone, or with anyone other than Nick, Elizabeth wasn't absolutely certain that she would have been able to act quickly and decisively enough to save her best friend's life.

But Elizabeth wasn't alone in the operating room, and her delicate and talented hands followed the confident lead of his, dancing their flawless graceful dance as always, calmly subduing the powerful gush of blood and carefully removing the irrevocably damaged tissue—but taking care, too, to leave some of the undamaged tissue behind to continue its important immunologic function of protecting Larisa against infection.

Together, Nick and Elizabeth saved Larisa's life, so swiftly that her unborn baby was never subjected to any of the adverse effects of shock; and after they had gently closed her abdomen, they left the operating room to find Peter.

Before they started the walk along the linoleum corridor to the private waiting room, Elizabeth turned to Nick, her beautiful face very thoughtful, and asked, "What did you think about Larisa's spleen, Nick?"

"That it had been previously injured," he said solemnly. "Why?"

"When Larisa came here last August, to escape from Julian and her marriage, she was very weak and very pale. She denied that it was anything more than exhaustion, but . . ."

"But it was an injury that probably saved her life," Nick gently assured, realizing that Elizabeth had been thinking about that time and wondering if she should have pressed Larisa further about her pallor and weakness. "It was the old scar tissue that contained the rupture until she got here. If the scarring hadn't been there the spleen would have ruptured much sooner."

"That's what I thought, too." She gave a bewildered shake of her dark curls and a soft smile touched her lovely lips.

"Why are you smiling?"

"Because Larisa has always accused me of being able to find the silver lining in even the darkest of clouds. I was just imagining her reaction to my telling her about the lifesaving silver lining to Julian's brutality."

As Elizabeth met the dark blue eyes that gazed at her with such gentleness, such pride in the lovely optimism that enabled her to always find the silver lining, her soft smile faded and the heart that had only survived for the past two months because she had resolutely wrapped it in steel suddenly broke free of its protective armor and cried with anguished despair, *I can't find a silver lining, Nick—not one troy ounce—in the loss of our love.*

"We'd better go find Peter," she said finally. Neither of them had had a chance to speak to Peter before the surgery. He hadn't been permitted to ride with Larisa in the Flight for Life helicopter and they were already in the OR when he arrived. "You've met him before, haven't you?"

"Yes." *Oh, my lovely Elizabeth, don't look so sad!* "I attended a number of board meetings about the institute and I spoke to him briefly again at the Fairmont ball."

Peter stood the moment Nick and Elizabeth appeared in the doorway of the waiting room, his exhausted dark green eyes haunted, anguished, and searching . . .

"She's going to be okay, Peter," Elizabeth reassured swiftly. "She did have a splenic laceration, but the rupture didn't happen until she was in the operating room and we were able to contain it. She'll have scars, of course. There were deep cuts on her arms and legs—"

"Scars don't matter," Peter said softly. Only Larisa matters. Larisa and . . . "And the baby, Elizabeth?"

"The baby is fine, too."

"Thank you," Peter whispered first to Elizabeth and then to Nick. Then he returned to Elizabeth, because he knew her the best, and asked quietly, "Where is she, Elizabeth? Can I see her?"

"She's on her way up to the Surgery ICU. The nurses will need time to get her settled in, and even though the anesthesia was kept quite light because of the baby, it will be a little while before she's fully awake."

"I'd very much like to be with her when she wakes up."

Elizabeth hesitated briefly before answering. "Let me talk to her first, Peter."

"To see if she wants to see me?" Peter saw the answer in Elizabeth's sympathetic yet resolute emerald eyes. And how could he blame her? Just a few hours ago he had asked her help in finding the woman who had so obviously fled from him.

"I'm sorry, Peter."

"I should have killed him."

"What?"

"I should have killed Julian."

"I thought you arrived at the motel after Larisa had already shot him."

"I did. I mean I should have killed him in New York."

"Peter . . ."

"Please tell Larisa that I love her, Elizabeth. Please tell her that."

"I will," Elizabeth promised gently. "And I'll come find you in the ICU waiting room as soon as I've spoken to her."

"Thank you. I think I'll go on up now." Peter smiled a soft smile of hope. "Maybe she'll awaken demanding to see me."

After Peter left, Nick and Elizabeth were alone in the small waiting room, and there was no rush to get to the ICU because Larisa was in very capable hands, and even though her heart still screamed with pain at the tenderness she had seen in his eyes moments ago—as if he had somehow forgotten that he didn't love her enough to even try—she had to bravely meet the dark blue just one last time.

And when she did, Elizabeth said, "Thank you very much for helping me, Nick."

"You're very welcome. Elizabeth?"

"Yes?"

"I would like to tell you about a nightmare that I've been having." After a moment he asked very gently, "May I?"

"Sure," she answered with a shrug. "Why not?"

The shrug was supposed to be light and casual, but how could it be when she was so weighted down with sadness? What was he going to tell her now? Yet another reason why their love was impossible? A stern reminder because he'd seen a flicker of hope in her eyes in response to the tenderness she had seen in his? The sadness was heavy, so very heavy, that it compelled Elizabeth to sit down on the couch.

"Tell me, Nick," she said, her gaze fixed on the floor. "Tell me about your nightmare."

"It's actually a nightmare that's with me all the time, day and night, whether I'm awake or not. And in it, Elizabeth, what I feel is the great emptiness of spending the rest of my life without you, never talking to you again, never touching you, never loving you . . ."

His voice was so gentle, so wondrously tender and loving that her vision of the floor became blurred with a sudden mist of hot tears. But still Elizabeth didn't look up. She simply steeled her weeping heart and waited to hear how the strong and disciplined Nicholas Chase was going to conquer this nightmare.

Then through the tears, he was there, kneeling before her, gently raising her chin until her glistening emerald eyes met his loving blue ones.

"Do I have to spend the rest of my life without you, Elizabeth?" he asked softly as he cradled her face in his talented and so gentle hands. And then, because the joyous answer glowed in her eyes before the emotion in her throat allowed her to speak, he whispered, "I love you, Elizabeth. I love you."

"Oh, Nick," she echoed finally. "I love you, too."

Nick tenderly touched the tears that spilled, such gloriously joyous tears, and then he kissed them, and then he kissed her lovely mouth, and finally, through whispered kisses, he asked, "Where are we going to live?"

Elizabeth pulled away and looked at him with uncomprehending surprise. "Larisa told me that your house was quite large. If you would be willing to share your bed with me . . ."

"Always, my love," Nick whispered, eloquently sealing the promise of his forever love with a gaze of dark blue desire. "But what I was wondering, Doctor Jennings, was where you've accepted a new job."

"Nowhere," Elizabeth confessed. "I haven't actually been looking."

"Because you sensed my nightmares?"

"No. I've tried very hard not to let myself even think that you would come back to me." She frowned and asked very quietly, "What would have happened if I hadn't called you today, Nick?"

"I would have called you. Well, first I would have tried to find out how you were. If you were fine, if you'd obviously put our love behind you, I would have left you alone."

"But you could tell just by seeing me today that I hadn't?"

"Yes, I could . . . but I already knew. Three nights ago your best friend gave me hell for hurting you so much."

"She did?"

"She did. And I've spent every second since then knowing I was going to talk to you—as soon as I could find a time when you weren't on call. According to the page operators that would have been tomorrow. I was going to call you then, Elizabeth, to tell you that I love you with all my heart."

"Such as it is," Elizabeth whispered softly, before Nick could. "It's a wonderful heart, Nick, and I'm going to take very good care of it."

"And, my love," he promised, "I'm going to spend my entire life taking very good care of yours."

"Peter?" Nick said from the doorway of the ICU waiting room.

"Nick," Peter answered, looking up and then standing up. "May I see Larisa now?"

"I haven't even seen her yet. The nurses have just gotten her settled. They say she's awake, though, and I'm on my way in right now. I only stopped to see if you knew that you were being paged."

Peter would never have heard his name being paged. He had been quite lost in imaginary—and wonderful—conversations with the woman he loved. "No, I didn't know."

"You can answer it on the phone by the couch. I'll be back, Peter, as soon as I've spoken to her."

"Nick."

"Hi." He smiled gently at the beautiful blue eyes that were so clearly very troubled, and didn't seem the least bit confused. Still Nick asked, "Are you alert and oriented, Larisa?"

"I know that it's Saturday, April twenty-fifth, and that I'm in the surgical ICU at the medical center, and that you and Elizabeth operated on me, and," her voice softened then and her troubled eyes filled briefly with deep gratitude, "I know that my baby is all right."

"Yes. And you probably also know that you hurt," Nick suggested gently. "You have a lot of very deep wounds."

Larisa shrugged. Oh yes, she hurt . . . but not one bit of the immense pain she felt was physical.

"What happened to Julian, Nick? I know that I shot him, but the nurses won't tell me what happened."

"He's dead, Larisa." Nick saw her eyes cloud then, but he decided not to pursue the topic, choosing instead, for now at least, to try to get her to look forward not back. "You have your work cut out for you. You're going to have to recover in record time because you have a few weddings to attend. Admittedly, Christine and Stephen's a week from today may be pushing it, but June isn't that far away either."

"June?"

"June," he confirmed, watching carefully the cloudy blue eyes that he was gently trying to lure out of the torment of the past and into the hopeful happiness of the future. "The wedding has to be in June, because Elizabeth's parents won't be back from England until then."

"Nick?" Larisa asked, focusing then, lured as Nick had hoped she would be by her love and hope—always—for her best friend.

"I know she wanted to tell you herself, but on our way here she was paged to the ER." *And I know she would understand why I'm doing this.* "Elizabeth has agreed to marry me, Larisa."

"Oh, Nick," Larisa said softly. "I'm so glad."

"I am, too. And I know that Elizabeth will want you to be her matron of honor."

"Matron of honor?"

"I imagine your wedding will happen before ours, Larisa."

"I won't be getting married, Nick."

"Why not?" he asked, even though he knew now, with certainty, because the bright blue had clouded once again—just as it had when she had learned that Julian was dead. "Oh, let me guess. Because you're a murderer?"

"Yes, Nick," Larisa answered quietly. "I *murdered* a man. I *am* a murderer."

"You shot a man who was trying to kill you. He damn near did kill you, by the way, and he absolutely would have if you hadn't shot him first."

"But I did shoot him."

"Yes, you did. For yourself, maybe, but mostly I think because of your baby. Isn't that right?"

"Yes, but . . ."

"Julian was going to *kill* your baby. You did the only thing a loving parent *could* do," Nick said definitively. After a moment he added softly, "You killed a man who deserved to die, Larisa. And now there's a man waiting outside who loves you very much . . . and who desperately wishes that he had been the one to kill Julian."

"Peter is here?"

"He's here, and he was at the motel. He arrived just moments after you shot Julian. Peter wants to see you, Larisa, and he wants to love you and his baby."

"You told Peter about the baby?"

"No. You regained consciousness briefly after the shooting and talked about the baby yourself."

"I can't see Peter."

For a very long time, Nick simply stared at her. And when he finally spoke his voice was dangerously quiet. "You *can* see him, but if you *won't*, Larisa, if you kill Peter's love because of some sense of unworthiness because of what you did to Julian, then, you truly are a murderer."

"Nick . . ."

"I'm going to go get him."

"*No!*"

"This is where the love begins to get really tough, Larisa. I'm your doctor—"

"Elizabeth is!"

"I'm your doctor and what I believe you need most right now is to see the man who loves you." Nick smiled then, and touched her cheek, and then, very gently, he assured, "It's going to be all right, honey, for both of us. It's going to be wonderful."

"Hi."

"Hi," she answered, looking briefly at his anguished dark green eyes before returning her own to her hands.

"You and I need to talk about a lot of things, Larisa," Peter said softly. "But right now you need to make a very important decision."

Larisa looked up again at his handsome—and so very solemn—face and asked, "What decision, Peter?"

"I just got a call from Craig Buchanan. Larisa, what do you remember about what happened in the cottage?"

"I remember everything."

"Then tell me, please," he said with gentle apology. "I'm sorry, Larisa. I know how difficult this is. But, darling, it's really important."

"All right," she agreed quietly, trusting him, *trusting* him.

"All right," Peter echoed gently. "First, tell me where you got the gun."

"Julian gave it to me when we were married. He insisted that I keep it after we were divorced."

"Okay. Now tell me what you remember just before you pulled the trigger."

Larisa gazed at Peter, drawing her strength from his as she relived the horror. "He laughed, mocking me, just like he had laughed in August, and just like that man had laughed years before when he had known that I wouldn't shoot him. I even heard my own voice—my voice when I was that little girl—pleading with him to stop, bravely telling him that I would shoot if he didn't. But he just laughed, and then I pulled the trigger, and there was a loud noise, and he looked so surprised . . . and so angry."

"Julian was very surprised, Larisa. He knew that the gun he had given you to protect yourself was filled with blanks."

"But I killed him, Peter."

"No, my darling, you didn't. Melanie killed him. She had gone to the cottage to visit you and when she saw what was happening she ran back to the motel office to get the master key, call her parents, and get Craig's gun. It was her voice you heard, Larisa, that was the little-girl voice that was pleading with Julian to stop. You must have both pulled the triggers at precisely the same instant because Craig and I were running to the cottage and we only heard one shot."

"Melanie killed Julian?"

"Yes."

Larisa frowned, then asked very softly, "Does she know, Peter?"

"No, not yet."

"Does she ever need to know?"

"Not necessarily. The police record will contain the truth, of course, but it can be sealed and the story that the press already has—that you shot him—could simply never be corrected."

Larisa knew now the decision she had to make.

And she made it with swift confidence.

And with that momentous decision she vanquished forever all the icy ghosts. Because it was a decision that conquered history. With it, she was permitting an innocent twelve-year-old girl to live her life without anguish. "A different kind of hell," Peter had said when she herself had wondered what her own life would have been like had she shot the man who raped her.

It was a hell that Larisa would not permit Melanie Buchanan to live.

"I don't want her ever to know the truth, Peter."

"I didn't think you would," Peter said gently. And then, because he had controlled his emotions for so long, and because he had almost lost this most precious of all dreams, he whispered, "I love you, Larisa."

"I love you, too, Peter. I had to get away because of Julian, because I knew that if he ever learned about the baby . . ."

"The baby," Peter echoed with soft joy. "May I touch her?"

"Of course," Larisa answered. "Her?"

"I just assume she's a little girl," Peter said softly as he gently laid his hand on Larisa's abdomen. "I just assume she's a little baby forget-me-not."

Then, as his hand still rested with loving wonder above the place where the tiny miracle, his infant daughter, was curled safe and warm deep inside, Peter gently kissed Larisa's brilliant tear-glistening blue eyes, and then her lovely trembling lips . . . and then, between tender kisses, he whispered to her all the joyous promises of love.

RAINBOWS

PROLOGUE

⊘he reporters clustered outside the main entrance of Memorial Hospital were an unusual blend—political commentators from Washington's elite press corps and entertainment editors from the major networks. Politically speaking, it was a "quiet" time in the nation's capital. The House, the Senate, and the Court were in recess for the holidays, and the President and First Lady were engaged in the charity galas of the Christmas season. But it wasn't the seasonal slowdown in political news that lured the suddenly-not-busy political reporters into a domain that should rightfully have fallen to their show business colleagues. They came because the story was Alexandra Taylor, and in this town of power, influence, and celebrity, Alexa was celebrated.

Alexa was an actress, not a Senator or Congresswoman. She held no elected political office in a city where politics was all. And yet, in a way, Alexa *had* been chosen by the people—by the millions of viewers whose love affair with her had made *Pennsylvania Avenue* the top-rated dramatic series for the past five years. Although some of Washington's political journalists felt obligated to make the occasional derisive remark about the sizzling prime-time drama of passion, power, and destiny in the nation's capital, none found fault with the show's talented and enchanting star. The press liked Alexa, just as her public did, and the somber faces of the reporters assembled in front of Memorial Hospital reflected genuine unscripted concern.

"We've been here all night, Joan, *hoping* for good news." Good Morning America's entertainment correspondent's wind-chilled and fatigued face provided vivid testimony to the all-night vigil, and her grim expression gave advance warning that the news wasn't good. "A hospital spokesperson met with us ten minutes ago and simply reiterated what we have known since shortly after midnight. Alexa Taylor is in critical condition. She survived last evening's emergency surgery for internal bleeding but she remains in a coma."

"Have you learned any details of the accident?" the show's hostess, Joan Lunden, queried from the studio in New York.

"The police have not yet issued an official statement, but we do have a few facts. Late yesterday afternoon, moments after receiving a mysterious phone call, Alexa left her secluded cottage overlooking Chesapeake Bay and began the drive down the winding road from the cottage to the Interstate. The road is a tortuous series of hairpin turns—a treacherous stretch that is, of course, very familiar to Alexa—and, although it is snowing now, at the time of the accident the roads were clear and dry. Despite her familiarity with the road and the safe driving conditions, however, for some reason Alexa failed to make one of the turns and her car plummeted over the cliff and exploded into flames on the beach below. Miraculously, she was thrown, or managed to jump, before the car became airborne."

"You said 'For some reason.' Do you have any idea what the reason was?"

"At this point there is only speculation. Judging from the distance travelled in air before landing on the beach below, the car must have been going very fast as it left the cliff. And yet, there were no skid marks, nothing to indicate that the brakes had been applied at all."

"Which means?"

"Which *seems* to mean that the brakes failed. An accidental mechanical failure . . . or an intentional one."

"The police suspect foul play?"

"As I said, the police have made no official statement. It is generally believed that the car has been so badly damaged that evidence of tampering would be impossible to detect."

"And what about the phone call?"

"Again, there is no information except that apparently it was immediately after receiving the call that Alexa began her ill-fated drive."

"So it is possible that she was upset—or distracted—by the call and as a result was driving too fast and lost control of the car?"

"Very possible. In fact, most likely. But, Joan, as you know in this town rumors travel faster than facts and a simple yet tragic accident can quickly become steeped in mystery and intrigue."

"Yes. Well. Thank you for this update. We'll be checking back with you later in the show, hoping for some positive word about Alexa's condition."

"I hope so. Oh! Wait a minute. I think I see Alexa's sister Catherine. The world-renowned concert pianist has been inside the hospital throughout the night, but now . . . Yes, this definitely is Catherine. And, oh, this is interesting, she is with Senator Robert McAllister. I wasn't aware of a connection between either Taylor sister and the dashing Senator from Virginia, but, like many Senators, he has probably served as a consultant for *Pennsylvania Avenue*. I don't know if Catherine will speak to the press, but perhaps the Senator will."

As Catherine grasped the sleeve of his overcoat, Robert instinctively placed his strong hand over her delicate and trembling one. He squinted beyond the bright glare of the television cameras to the limousine that was waiting in the distance to take them to the airport to meet her parents' plane. Between the hospital steps and the sanctuary of the limousine stood a wall of reporters. The wall parted, a narrow tunnel to enable Robert and Catherine to pass, but from both sides, in strident stereo, came the painful, unanswerable questions . . .

"Catherine, how is Alexa? Senator, can you tell us?"

"How significant are the injuries? Is she still in a coma? Do the doctors think she'll recover?"

"Ms. Taylor! We understand that you were in the cottage with your sister when the phone call came. Who called? What was the message? Is that the reason Alexa rushed out? Do the police suspect foul play?"

"The word from the doctors is that Alexa had internal bleeding and suffered traumatic shock to her kidneys. Have you donated blood for Alexa, Catherine? Would you be willing to donate a kidney if your sister's kidneys don't recover from the shock?"

Robert had warned Catherine that there would be a barrage of questions and had advised her to offer no answers during their journey to the limousine. Catherine knew what questions the reporters would ask—the same unanswerable questions that had tormented her all night. The same questions, except for that last one.

Would you be willing to donate?

Catherine's heart had a swift and confident answer to that question, "Yes, of course!" But with that answer came a silent anguished scream of pain. If Alexa needed my blood, my kidney, my heart, I would so willingly give it, but . . .

But what I could give would be no better than the gift of a stranger. Because Alexa, whom I love as my own sister, is not really my sister at all . . .

PART ONE

CHAPTER ONE

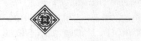

Kansas City, Kansas
May 1968

"My husband will be here soon," Jane Taylor told the pink-coated volunteer who had escorted her from her hospital room to the lobby. "I'll wait right here, in this unnecessary-but-hospital-policy wheelchair until he arrives. You needn't wait with me, really, I'll be perfectly fine."

The truth was that Alexander would *not* be arriving any moment. Jane hadn't even called to tell him that she had been discharged. And the truth was, too, that as soon as the volunteer disappeared Jane *was* going to get out of the wheelchair.

Jane didn't feel too guilty about lying. They—the doctors, nurses, and psychologists—had, after all, been lying to her. Their lies, like Jane's, were well-intentioned: what was best for her.

"We're going to transfer you to the General Medical Ward," the doctors had told her when she was well enough to leave the ICU.

The General Medical Ward—not Obstetrics—very far away from the new mothers whose babies had survived. As if seeing *their* joy would make *her* grief even greater! Jane knew that wouldn't happen, of course; her grief could not be greater than it already was. How astonishing to remember that only seven days ago her life had been pure joy.

Only seven days ago, on a glorious spring morning, Jane and Alexa and Alexander had driven from their home in rural Topeka to Kansas City, where Jane's exquisite pottery was to be displayed and sold at the prestigious Art Fair. It was their final adventure as a family of just three. Soon, very soon, they would joyfully welcome a new life into their circle of love. How excitedly six-year-old Alexa had chattered about *her* new baby, predicting, with her golden confidence, "A baby sister!"

The weeks of preparation for the fair had been easy for Jane, a creative pleasure not a stress; and Alexander, with Alexa's help, had loaded the van as a very healthy seven-months-pregnant Jane simply watched, laughing lovingly at the unnecessary pampering from her husband and daughter. There had been no stress, only joy and laughter, but still, inexplicably and horribly, just as they reached the outskirts of Kansas City, Jane went into labor. It began as a tearing pain and was followed quickly by a hot gush of blood.

Alexander sped to the nearest Emergency Room, and the doctors swiftly separated Jane from the baby that had been so safe inside her. Then there was an even greater separation, a permanent one, as Jane was taken by ambulance to the Intensive Care Unit at the Medical Center and her infant daughter was rushed, sirens blaring, to the Neonatal ICU at the Children's Hospital ten miles away.

Mother and infant received the best that medical science had to offer, but only Jane benefited. The daughter she was never to see died after five valiant days, and after Jane survived her own precarious battle with death she was transferred from the ICU to the General Medical Ward. The General Medical Ward, not Obstetrics, not Postpartum, just a somber place of sickness many slick linoleum corridors away from joyous new mothers and their babies.

This is best, Jane was told by the doctors, nurses, and staff psychologists. She was never told for whom it was best. For her? Or for the other mothers who might be made uncomfortable by her presence?

But the medical professionals were wrong! She should have been with the other mothers. She was a mother after all, Alexa's mother and the mother of the baby girl who had died. She should have been among the mothers, and she should have been allowed to visit the newborn nursery.

That was where Jane was going now, to see the babies in the nursery. She believed that seeing the babies would somehow give her the strength she needed to tell her golden-haired daughter about the baby sister who had died. Today, gently and together, Jane and Alexander would tell their precious Alexa the truth. And tomorrow, they would return to Topeka and tell the friends—who expected triumphant news of talented Jane's success at the Art Fair—the sad reality of their week in Kansas City.

When Jane reached the newborn nursery and gazed through the plate glass window at the infants cradled in pink and blue bassinets, she knew instantly that she had been right to come here. It helped to see the babies. Even though she had lost her baby and could have no more, seeing these tiny new lives filled Jane with hope.

A smile crossed Jane's lovely face, the first smile in a week, the gentle loving smile of a mother . . .

As Isabelle tenderly kissed the silky black hair of her infant daughter, her blue eyes swept down the corridor. Ahead lay the newborn nursery and behind, as always, lurked one of the men sent by Jean-Luc to follow her. Jean-Luc's men had been with her, constant menacing shadows, for over five months, throughout her pregnancy and still. They were less hidden now, and even more watchful, because now her baby had been born.

Isabelle lived in constant fear that the men would receive a lethal instruction from the madman who had hired them, an order to simply put an end to the innocent little life that threatened him so. That order would come one day, but for now Jean-Luc seemed content to torment her, a beast playing with its prey, confident of his complete control. She was trapped, he was telling her. There was no escape. Did she not understand?

Of course Isabelle understood. But she knew, too, that if she kept moving, as if ever hopeful that one day she would escape the men who shadowed her, Jean-Luc would keep his henchmen at a distance. As long as Jean-Luc believed it was Isabelle's naive and desperate hope for escape that compelled her restless journey, he would enjoy this tortured game of hide-and-seek. And that would give her more time . . .

Time to find the woman to whom she could entrust her precious daughter. In her months of searching, before the baby's birth and after, Isabelle had spoken to so many women—brief conversations under the watchful eyes of Jean-Luc's sinister shadows—and still her search continued. The woman existed, *she had to*, and when Isabelle found her she would know by a knowledge of the heart that was as deep and compelling and confident as the instinct that gave her the tireless energy to search until she found a safe and loving home for her baby.

For months Isabelle had roamed from city to city, always moving, always searching. And now her random yet purposeful wandering had brought her here, at this precise moment, to the nursery where a blond-haired woman with tear-damp emerald eyes gazed with such wistful gentleness at the newborn infants.

As she drew near, her heart began to quicken.

"Hello." Although French was her native language, Isabelle spoke so many languages flawlessly that her French accent was lost in the refined elegance of her speech.

"Hello." Jane smiled warmly at the beautiful woman with the soft regal voice. After a moment, her gaze fell on the baby girl wrapped in a plush blanket of pink cashmere. The woman's hair was blonde, and the infant's was lustrous black velvet, but the brilliant blue eyes left no doubt that they were mother and daughter. "What a beautiful little girl."

"Thank you. Is your baby here?"

"No." Jane gave a soft apologetic smile, remembering that she wasn't supposed to be here, among the happy new mothers and babies. But there was something in this mother's lovely blue eyes that made it seem all right for her to reveal her own sad truth. "I recently lost my baby girl. She was born prematurely and there were complications."

"I am so sorry. Surely you will have other babies."

"No. But I am already very blessed. I have a lovely six-year-old daughter. I had hoped to give her a baby sister, but . . ."

"Yes. I see," Isabelle murmured distractedly as she felt the intense gaze of the menacing figure twenty feet away, too far away to hear the words but staring at her with watchful eyes. The eyes would become more watchful, more interested, with each passing moment. "There is something I would like to discuss with you."

"Oh?" Jane asked, surprised at the suddenness of the request. She saw the soft plea in the brilliant blue eyes, a silent yet almost desperate cry for help, and added gently, "Yes. Of course."

"We can't talk here. Will you go to the Ladies Room in the main lobby, and wait for me there? It will be at least thirty minutes before I can join you."

Jane noticed the man hovering in the distance and guessed that he was the reason for the clandestine meeting. Jane's mind sent firm warnings to politely extricate herself from the situation, but all the warnings were quickly overridden by her kind and generous heart. She would help if she could.

"I'll wait for you."

"Thank you. Now will you please say good-bye, as if our conversation has ended and we have no plans to meet again?"

"Yes." Jane smiled, then glanced at her watch and exclaimed, raising her voice slightly, "Oh dear, look at the time! I'd better go. It was very nice talking to you. Good-bye."

After Jane left, Isabelle spoke unhurriedly to several other new mothers who arrived to gaze at their infants. After thirty minutes, she returned to the lobby, and, just as she was about to walk outside, as if the thought was sudden, she turned and asked the volunteer at the Information Desk for directions to the Ladies Room.

Thank God Jean-Luc had sent only men to trail her like bloodhounds! He would not have considered sending women to shadow her, of course, because he placed no value on women whatsoever—except when he wanted them for his pleasure. How ironic to find a silver lining to Jean-Luc's contempt for women! But there it was: Jean-Luc had sent no women to follow her, and that meant that she and her baby were safe, for a little while, in the Ladies Room.

"Thank you so much for agreeing to meet me," Isabelle murmured softly when she saw Jane.

"You're welcome."

"Are we alone?"

"Yes."

"Good." Isabelle looked from Jane to the small beloved face tenderly bundled in pink cashmere. Tears filled her eyes and her voice trembled as she asked, "Will you take her?"

"Of course." Jane saw the tears and heard the emotion, but nonetheless interpreted the question to be a simple request to hold the baby. A simple request . . . but it wasn't so simple for Jane. As she cradled the little girl in her arms, rushes of pain swept through her.

"I mean," Isabelle whispered softly but confidently as she saw the gentle loving way Jane held her baby, "will you take her and raise her as your own daughter?"

"Will I do what?" Jane asked, a whisper of hope and disbelief.

"She is not safe with me. I love her with all my heart—she *is* my heart— but . . ." Isabelle was swept by a sudden rush of rebellious emotions, voices from the heart that urged her to pretend that Jean-Luc and his men didn't exist. Fantasy! she reminded the defiant voices. Forcing herself to remember the reality, she continued with quiet calm, "You have lost your baby . . ."

"Yes, but you shouldn't lose yours," Jane answered softly as she waged her own private battle against emotions. *Yes, I will take her*, her heart had swiftly and joyfully answered Isabelle's stunning question. But Jane knew the pain of her own loss and believed, truly believed, that this mother and daughter should not be separated. She forced that belief, that island of rationality in the swirling sea of her own emotions, to speak, suggesting gently, "Maybe if you told me why it is you believe you can't keep her, together we could find a way that you could. Surely there is a way. Please, let me help you find it."

"I cannot tell you, and there is no other way." Her quiet, resigned voice and anguished blue eyes eloquently conveyed the truth of her words. She had searched tirelessly for other solutions and had found none. After a moment, she gave a trembling smile, and the anguished sapphire flickered with hope as she continued, "But you can help. All that I have prayed for from the moment I knew I could not keep her was that I would find a mother who would love her as I would have. I believe you are that mother."

It was a long moment before Jane could speak, a moment in which their glistening eyes met and held, and silent promises were made from the heart.

"I will love her," Jane whispered finally, unnecessarily, because her eyes had already made that promise.

"Yes. I know that you will." Isabelle's eyes held Jane's for a few moments longer, then she forced herself to turn away and focus on the other things that needed to be done before she left to begin the rest of her life without her daughter. She removed the large purse from her shoulder and withdrew a satchel made of plush blue velvet and bound by drawstrings of gold. Her delicate fingers opened the satchel and removed several of the many neatly folded pieces of tissue paper which, when unwrapped, revealed glittering diamonds, rubies, sapphires, and emeralds.

"She would have had great wealth," Isabelle explained. *She would have been a princess.* "I have converted some of her inheritance into precious gems. All are flawless and of the finest cut and color. The current wholesale value of the stones in this satchel is about twenty million dollars. I would suggest that you only sell the gems as you need them, because their value will surely increase over the coming years."

"I can't take these."

"I assure you they aren't stolen. They are rightfully hers."

"My husband and I aren't rich, and never will be, but our life is comfortable. We have worked very hard to save enough money to afford two children." Jane shrugged, not certain why she was refusing to take the gems, yet quite confident of the decision. Their life was modest, but so very happy. Jane had no wish to change it.

Jane's refusal to accept the life-changing fortune was more proof to Isabelle that she had found the woman with whom she could entrust her precious daughter. Isabelle had been very poor and then very rich, and she knew quite well that the only real treasure was love. This woman with the glistening emerald eyes knew that, too.

"Shall I tell you about myself and my husband?" Jane offered quietly.

"No, please don't. It is best if I know nothing about you and you know nothing about me . . . except this: she is my daughter, and she was conceived in the greatest of love. It is not safe for her to be with me, and it never will be." Isabelle's eyes filled with fresh tears as she heard the finality of her words. She thought she had prepared herself for this, steeled her heart, but now her breaking heart made a soft impulsive request, "Will you tell her, please, on her twenty-first birthday, about today? Will you tell her that I loved her, but that I had no choice?"

"Yes. Of course. What day was she born?" Jane asked, knowing that on that distant day, twenty-one years in the future, this mother, wherever she was, would send silent messages of love to the daughter who would just be learning the ancient truth.

"A week ago today. May twentieth."

"The twentieth," Jane echoed softly, as if memorizing the date. But that date was already etched in her heart—it was on that day that her own infant daughter had been born. "I will tell her then. Is there anything else I should tell her?"

"Please tell her not to try to find me. It would be impossible anyway, but there might be danger in the search." Isabelle frowned as another impulsive wish swept from her heart to her lips. "Her name is your decision, of course, and I wouldn't want it to be her first name, but . . ."

"Yes?"

"If one of her names, perhaps her middle name, could be Alexandra . . . ?"

Alexandra. After her father, Jane guessed, hearing the love in her voice as she asked the question. The baby girl's father's name was Alexander, and it was another astonishing coincidence, but she concealed her surprise, because the woman had said it was best if she knew nothing about them. So, Jane did not say, "My husband's name is Alexander," nor did she say, "My other daughter is Alexandra." She didn't speak that thought, but she heard her own unspoken words, My *other* daughter.

"Her middle name will be Alexandra."

"Thank you."

Isabelle forced herself to focus again on the important final details. After returning the blue velvet satchel to the large purse, she removed a small cloth diaper bag for Jane, a doll with dark black hair, and a blue-and-white checked cashmere blanket. Wordlessly and together, they removed the pink cashmere blanket from the baby. Then, as Isabelle tenderly wrapped her beloved infant in the blue-and-white checks, Jane clothed the doll in pink.

And then there was nothing left for Isabelle to do but say good-bye to her baby girl. Cradling her gently, she withdrew to a corner of the room, and as her lips caressed the soft cheeks and their sapphire eyes met, she whispered words of love, in French, as all the precious private words spoken to her daughter had always been.

"*Je t'aime, je t'aime, je t'aime,*" she whispered, over and over, as she had done so often. And then, kissing the small lovely face for the last time, she changed the tense from the present to the future—a future they would not share but in which her daughter would live in her heart always. "*Je t'aimerai toujours.*"

Then she turned, walked swiftly back to Jane, and gave her the beloved bundle. She slung the large purse over her shoulder, but before reaching for the doll, the decoy she would carry to lead Jean-Luc's men far away, and before leaving forever, she made a final impulsive decision. With trembling fingers, she unfastened the solid gold clasp of the necklace that had been, until then, hidden beneath her silk blouse.

The necklace was a strand of bright blue gems, from which was suspended a heart-shaped pendant made of more of the same brilliant blue stones. Jane saw at once that the brilliant blue precisely matched the remarkable eyes of the mother and daughter, but she had no idea that the glittering jewels were sapphires, or that that bright blue was for sapphires the most rare and precious color, or that the necklace was worth a fortune. She saw a different value for the magnificent necklace—a much greater one—in the emotion and love in Isabelle's eyes.

"Give this to her, please, on her twenty-first birthday. It was a gift from her father to me. We had one heart, her father and I, and now we give that heart to her." Isabelle frowned briefly, testing her own judgment in giving her baby the necklace, and then, confident that it was safe, she reassured Jane. "The necklace is lovely, breathtaking, but the design is quite traditional. It will not lead her to me."

Jane nodded as she took the stunning piece of jewelry.

"Well," Isabelle whispered as she felt the beginning of fresh tears in her eyes. She blocked the tears and the emotion in her throat with the vivid memory of the men who waited for her in the lobby. She spoke calmly, her voice strengthened by that ominous memory and the knowledge of what she must now do to insure her daughter's safety *forever.* "I must go. Please remain here another thirty minutes, or even longer if you can."

"I will love her," Jane whispered.

"Yes. I know that you will. Thank you. God bless you."

Then Isabelle was gone, to continue the journey that would lead Jean-Luc's men far away from Kansas City, and Jane was left to absorb the enormity of what had happened. It had taken place so quickly, and she had accepted it all so calmly, and now . . . now she knew that she had just lived through a miracle.

"Hello, precious little one," Jane whispered softly to the brilliant blue eyes that now looked to her for love, for answers, for the promise of a safe and happy life. "Hello, Catherine Alexandra. Do you like that name, my little love? I think it's perfect for you. And your sister will be so pleased, because it will make you two even closer. She is Alexandra Catherine, you see. Oh, little Catherine, how loved you will be, by me and your Daddy and your big sister. How very loved."

As you have been so very loved for the first week of your life, she thought, her joyful heart aching for the mother who had just given her this greatest of all gifts.

She made a silent promise to the sapphire eyes: *And, precious Catherine, if some-day your mother returns, because it is safe for her to have you with her, then, some-how, we will make that right, too.*

But, Jane realized with a mixture of sadness and relief, Catherine's mother would never be able to find them. They lived in Topeka, not Kansas City, and even though she had said that she'd recently lost her baby, she hadn't said when or where the baby had died. Her baby girl had died in a hospital across town, and in this hospital, where she herself had survived, Jane had been a patient on Medicine not OB. Unless Catherine's mother returned now, she would never be able to find them.

Please remain here for another thirty minutes, or longer if you can, Catherine's mother had asked. Jane remained for a full hour, ample time for Catherine's mother to get safely away—or to change her mind and return. Jane's heart stopped each time the door opened and then raced again when it was not the lovely woman with the sapphire eyes.

The baby girl born to her had died, but still Jane's breasts defiantly filled with rich nourishing milk. Even in the days in the ICU when she had needed all her strength just to survive herself, the milk was there, a painful symbol of her loss. And now, as the tiny hungry lips pulled eagerly at her welcoming nipples, Jane was surprised that she could feel even greater joy and love, but she could, and she did.

And later, when she removed a diaper from the bag Isabelle had left, there was another surprise: one hundred thousand dollars in large bills. Money to invest and give to Catherine on her twenty-first birthday, Jane decided. She and Alexander made enough money for the modest life they lived. But, Jane thought, perhaps we can use a little of this money, just a little, so that Alexander will need to give fewer music lessons at night and on weekends, and he can spend even more precious time with his daughters. His *daughters* . . .

"Alexander."

"Hello, darling," Alexander whispered with relief. He knew Jane had been discharged—*hours ago*—but he knew, too, that his wife might need a little private time. He imagined she might wander first to the newborn nursery, and then, perhaps, across the street to the park, to feel the warm May sun and see the flowers and try one more time to make sense of what had happened. It was an impossible task, he knew, because he had been trying, too. Alexander knew that his wife would need some private time, but as the minutes had turned to hours, he had become very worried. He asked gently, "Are you ready? Shall Alexa and I come get you?"

Jane's eyes misted at the tenderness in her husband's voice. How difficult this past week had been for Alexander, more difficult for him even than for her. He had spent sleepless days and nights commuting between the crosstown ICUs, believing for the first four days that he was about to lose both his wife and his baby, but lovingly concealing his heart-stopping fear. Alexander had been strong for all of them: for Jane, for the baby girl who had died, and for the golden-haired daughter who still did not know the truth about her baby sister.

And now would never need to know.

"Is Alexa right there?"

"She's in the other room, playing dolls with yet another new friend," Alexander's voice softened lovingly, ever-amazed, as Jane was, by their charming and extroverted daughter. Alexa had made lots of new friends this week, in hospital playrooms and at the motel. Alexa made friends easily, and that was wonderful, especially now, since she would never have a little sister. "Janie? Is there something—"

"Oh, Alexander . . . a miracle has happened."

As she sat in a phone booth in the park and cradled a contentedly sleeping Catherine, Jane told him about the miracle. She couldn't see the face of her beloved Alexander, the talented musician with the gentle soul of a poet, but she could imagine the sensitive eyes she knew so well and the range of emotions flickering through them—hope, fear, joy, disbelief . . . and worry.

"I haven't gone crazy, my love," Jane reassured him softly during a long silence. She knew Alexander's unspoken worry, and that he wouldn't utter it until he could hold her in his arms and protect her from the postpartum grief which had apparently become a psychosis and caused her to kidnap a baby.

"But Janie, it's just too . . . Why are you laughing?" he asked, his voice filling with even deeper concern as he heard her soft laugh.

"Because I forgot to tell you about the money and the jewels and the necklace."

She had told him the story, *three times*, but until that moment she had forgotten to tell him about either the fortune in jewels she had declined or the fortune in cash she had been given. The money and necklace were tangible proof that the miracle was true, but she had forgotten about them, because the only treasure that really mattered was sleeping happily in her arms.

"The money and jewels and necklace?"

Jane told him the story again, every detail, and she heard his soft worried protests fade into joyous disbelief until finally he whispered hoarsely, "We'll come get you now, darling. Alexa and I will come get you and Catherine."

"She's not my sister," Alexa announced with familiar Alexa confidence moments after first seeing the tiny infant cradled in her mother's arms.

"Yes, darling, she is your sister," Jane whispered softly after a stunned and worried moment. She reached for Alexa and as she lovingly stroked her daughter's silky blonde hair she explained gently, "Catherine's hair is dark, like Daddy's, not golden like yours and mine, and her eyes are blue, but she is your sister."

"*No.*"

"Alexa?"

"I don't want her to be my sister, Daddy. I don't like her."

"Alexa!"

"She's not my sister! I don't want her! Take her back to the hospital, *please*. Mommy! Daddy?"

For three weeks after whispering farewell to her beloved daughter, Isabelle tenderly cradled the doll and continued her restless journey. Somehow, she made her search appear as compelling as before, even though she was a mortally wounded creature, astonishingly still alive, roaming the earth without her heart.

She led Jean-Luc's men from Kansas City to New York, where, moments before boarding her flight to Nice, she approached one of the menacing shadows and handed him the pink cashmere bundle.

"I'm on my way to see Jean-Luc," she hissed softly in French. "I'll tell him you did your best but that he hired fools."

Isabelle had believed she would never return to L'île. But she was returning now, to confront the man who had so cruelly taken from her the immeasurable joy of living her life with her daughter. In Nice, she chartered a small plane to L'île des Arcs-en-ciel, and during the short flight from Nice to the Mediterranean island kingdom, her mind travelled to the time that had been the beginning of her loathing for Jean-Luc and the beginning of her love for Alexandre . . .

The year was 1948. The war that had claimed her entire family was over, but not—*never*—forgotten. Seventeen-year-old Isabelle had learned that in war no horror was beyond belief; and now, as hope began to find fragile footing in the remnants of despair, she chose to believe that in peace all dreams were possible. During the war, she had served the resistance in her native Paris with unwavering bravery. Now, in peace, as she pursued a dream, she wrote a bold letter to a Prince.

I have made a careful study of the designs of the jewelers in the Place Vendôme, Isabelle explained in her letter to Prince Alexandre Castille. She did not reveal that her "careful study" was simply made by peering into the glass showcases in the glittering boutiques of Cartier, Van Cleef and Arpels, and Castille. Of all the *joailliers*, it was Castille, she decided, that needed her creativity the most. The Castille designs were too baroque and not nearly *romantic* enough, she wrote bravely. She included sketches of her own innovative romantic designs and offered to journey to L'île to meet with the Prince, if that was his royal pleasure.

Alexandre laughed softly when he read Isabelle's letter, and then grew thoughtful. She was right, of course, this woman whose talents were so obvious from the sketches and whose boldness intrigued and enchanted him. Since the war, Alexandre had devoted himself to restoring the beauty of L'île, leaving his younger brother Jean-Luc to manage Castille Jewels. Jean-Luc had shrewdly handled the business end of their profitable, *if baroque*, jewelry empire, but there had been no innovations, no new art in their designs, for a very long time.

Alexandre made arrangements to travel to Paris to meet Isabelle. But on the eve of his departure, during his daily ride to watch the splendor of the rainbows for which his island kingdom was named, he was thrown from his horse and his leg was broken. Thus, it was Jean-Luc who journeyed to Paris to meet the young designer. And when he saw beautiful Isabelle, her golden hair and sapphire eyes and provocative lips, he knew that he must have her for himself.

Isabelle's years as an orphan of war had made her fearless. She taunted the evil men who had descended on Paris, insulting them and then fleeing to safety. She was street tough and courageous, because she had to be; but in her heart lived the delicate hope of an artist and the lovely visions of a romantic girl.

A romantic *girl*, a virgin until Jean-Luc raped her, his need for her an obsession, her desperate pleas only fueling his madness. As he brutally raped her, Jean-Luc whispered his love for her, and when it was over, he promised more: she would become his bride, his *princess*. Isabelle heard Jean-Luc's astonishing words, gazed bravely into his cruel eyes, and quietly whispered a solemn vow of eternal hatred.

On his return to L'île, Jean-Luc told his older brother that the girl had merely been toying with them. Her plan from the outset had been to work for Cartier. The news surprised and disappointed Alexandre. Six weeks later, when his leg had healed and he was in Paris, he himself paid an impulsive visit to the talented young designer.

Alexandre saw such terror in the beautiful blue eyes when she opened the door to him! The terror faded to confusion when Isabelle realized she was not looking at Jean-Luc. This man shared Jean-Luc's handsomeness, but he was older, and his expression was concerned and gentle, and there were no flickers of madness in his dark brown eyes.

Seventeen-year-old Isabelle and forty-year-old Alexandre fell in love, despite her hidden hatred for Jean-Luc, and despite the fact that the horror of Jean-Luc's brutal act lived within her still, a growing seed of evil that tainted her with sickness and unspeakable dread. She did not want to give birth to Jean-Luc's baby; but she could not bring herself to have an abortion. She simply, desperately, wished that the pregnancy would miscarry of its own accord. Then she fell in love with Alexandre, and her wishes became less desperate and more confident; surely the goodness that lived inside her now, because of Alexandre's love, would vanquish the growing evil.

Isabelle's wish came true at the beginning of the fourth month. Alexandre found her, unconscious from blood loss, and rushed her to a hospital. When she was well enough to speak again, Alexandre cradled her tenderly as she told him the truth about Jean-Luc.

Alexandre banished Jean-Luc, and married Isabelle, and they lived their wonderful love in the enchanted island kingdom in the sea. Jean-Luc was gone, but not forgotten. Alexandre and Isabelle wanted children, but in twenty years of loving it was not to be. The damage to her womb from the miscarriage had made it impossible, they decided sadly.

Alexandre and Isabelle wanted children as treasures of love, not as heirs to the kingdom, but there was that sadness, too. By the rules of royal succession that had governed L'île for centuries, the reigning monarch was always the firstborn of the firstborn. But if Alexandre had no children, then on his death Jean-Luc would inherit the throne, and thereafter it would be Jean-Luc's descendants who would become the rulers of L'île.

In September of 1967, Alexandre was diagnosed to have a rare and rapidly fatal form of leukemia. Isabelle and Alexandre spent very little time in the precious months they had left together discussing what would happen when he died. There was nothing to discuss. They both knew that Jean-Luc would make a swift and triumphant return to L'île. The only plans to be made were for Isabelle.

Alexandre moved his vast personal fortune in gems and money off L'île and placed it, in Isabelle's name, in bank vaults in New York, London, Paris, and Zurich. Then, in the time they had left together on earth, Alexandre and Isabelle simply loved each other, as they always had. And sometime in those tender nights of loving sixty-year-old Alexandre and thirty-seven-year-old Isabelle conceived a child. It was a joy Isabelle never shared with Alexandre. She knew it would not bring him happiness or peace, only fear at what might happen and rage at his own helplessness. Jean-Luc was too close to having the kingdom he so desperately wanted, just a dying heartbeat away. No matter what proclamations Alexandre made before his death about his unborn child, or how carefully he planned protection for Isabelle and the baby, the reality was that Jean-Luc would never allow Alexandre's baby to take L'île away from him.

Not that Isabelle wanted the island for their child of love! All she wanted, after she said farewell to her beloved Alexandre, was to spend the rest of her life loving their baby. Jean-Luc could have everything.

When Isabelle left L'île, shortly after Alexandre's funeral, Jean-Luc's men were already following her. Her pregnancy was still hidden then, but Jean-Luc's intentions were painfully, terrifyingly obvious: his evil obsession for her was alive, evergreen, still. Isabelle tried to escape Jean-Luc's men, but it was useless, and in time her pregnancy became apparent and their ominous vigilance only intensified.

All Isabelle wanted was freedom to spend her life loving her baby. But Jean-Luc intended no freedom for either mother or child, and only through her own cleverness was Isabelle able to trick him and find freedom for her precious little love.

And now, three weeks after saying farewell forever to her tiny infant, Isabelle was returning to L'île to tell the man who had taken her daughter from her how much she hated him . . .

The palace during Alexandre's reign had been like the entire island, a welcoming place of beauty, open to all who wished to view its graceful grandeur. But the palace gates were closed now, forbidding not welcoming, and heavily armed guards sent a solemn silent signal that Prince Jean-Luc was in residence. Despite the fortune he had taken with him when Alexandre banished him from L'île, during his years in exile Jean-Luc had discovered new ways, sinister ways, to amass even greater wealth and an even more intoxicating treasure—power. By the time of Alexandre's death, Jean-Luc was known throughout the world as a merchant of guns and drugs and terror.

L'île's new monarch was in residence now, and the elegant white marble palace had become a fortress, and a pall had fallen over the once joyful paradise. Even the birds are still, Isabelle thought sadly. And the warm air that had once been filled with the delicate perfume of a thousand flowers felt cold and stale. She wondered about the magnificent rainbows that filled the sky every evening after the nourishing tropical rain. Had they vanished, too, their dazzling brilliance faded to gray, an illusory memory of what had been and now was gone forever?

"Isabelle," Jean-Luc whispered when he saw her, his breath halted as always by the sight of her. His dark eyes were unrevealing and cold, even though his entire being filled with a powerful emotion that was beyond desire, a desperate need to possess her.

"You bastard."

"Isabelle . . ."

"How I hate you!"

"Don't hate me, *chérie*. A father does what he must for his children."

"You did it for yourself! You wanted L'île, and already you have contaminated it with your poison."

"Such anger, Isabelle. You are far too beautiful for anger."

As Jean-Luc spoke his eyes left hers and drifted to the wall behind her. Isabelle followed his gaze to a magnificent oil painting—of *her*. Before Alexandre's death, she had sent letters, diaries, portraits, and photographs—*all* the tangible symbols of their love—to her château in the Loire Valley.

But the portrait in oil that hung in Jean-Luc's private library in the palace was not a painting that had been left behind in error. It was a portrait he had commissioned himself, painted from the famous photograph of her taken twelve years before in the palace gardens at Monaco. She and Alexandre had been there, of course, to attend the wedding of their dear friends Rainier and Grace, the other Prince and Princess of an enchanted Mediterranean kingdom. The breathtaking photograph had appeared in *Life* magazine, a full page and in color, even though Princess Isabelle Castille was only a guest, not the fairytale bride. She looked like a bride, though, standing amidst the white gardenias, her lovely expression matching the romantic hopefulness of the day. And there was more romance in the photograph, private romance, because Isabelle had chosen on that romantic day to wear the sapphire necklace her beloved Alexandre had given her.

Over the years there had been hundreds of photographs of Isabelle and Alexandre, she so delicate and beautiful, he so strong and handsome. And in those photographs she had worn millions of dollars of jewelry designed by Castille—and yet it was *this* photograph, in which she had worn her most treasured jewels, from which Jean-Luc had commissioned a portrait for his own private viewing!

It angered Isabelle that Jean-Luc had the portrait, and it terrified her that in it she wore the necklace she had given her baby. Even if, twenty-one years from now, her daughter chose to search for her, it was beyond imagination that the sapphire necklace could lead to her. But Jean-Luc, using photographs of the necklace and beginning now *might* find the missing princess. What if he placed photographs of the necklace in American newspapers, captioned with an impassioned plea, ostensibly from her, searching for her daughter? What if the lovely woman with the emerald eyes read the plea and was tricked into coming forward?

What if? The unanswerable question came with such terror, until she remembered . . .

Jean-Luc doesn't know I gave her the necklace! He doesn't know, and it will be twenty-one years before my precious daughter even sees it. By then, if there is a God, Jean-Luc will be in hell. Before returning her gaze to Jean-Luc, Isabelle silently reminded herself, a calming mantra, She is safe. My baby girl is safe.

"How *dare* you have a portrait of me!" Isabelle accused when she turned, funneling all her emotions into anger, hiding her terror beneath layers of rage.

"I want far more than a portrait. I want *you*. I love you, Isabelle."

"You're mad."

"Mad with love. If we were together, your daughter could be with us."

Isabelle's heart missed a beat, a suspended moment of hope, but it was a cruel treachery. Jean-Luc might allow the little girl to live for a while, but one day there would be a tragic accident . . .

"I don't know where she is, Jean-Luc. She is hidden forever, even from me." Isabelle emphasized her words by issuing a challenge and a wish of hatred. "I hope you try to find her, Jean-Luc. I hope you squander your entire fortune in the search and spend the rest of your nights on earth tormented by the fear that she will appear. I hope it is that torment that kills you."

"Isabelle, Isabelle." Jean-Luc's soft mocking laugh could have been a loving tease in a normal man, but in him it was merely further evidence of his madness. Her hatred titillated him. "We are meant for each other, can you not see that? Marry me, my love. Be my Princess. I will show you love and passion that my older brother never could. It disgusts me when I imagine him making love to you in those months when his body was dying."

"It is you who are disgusting, Jean-Luc. You who are beneath contempt."

"You will learn to love me."

"You have a wife, Jean-Luc." Isabelle paused a beat, and even though her mind sent a warning, she whispered the taunt, "Or would you murder her as you murdered Geneviève?"

Geneviève was the lovely innocent girl who had fallen prey to Jean-Luc's wicked charms and married him. Isabelle would never have met her, because Jean-Luc had long since been banished from L'île; but one day, because L'île was the only place on earth that her monster husband could not follow, a desperate and frightened Geneviève appeared at the palace seeking sanctuary. Isabelle and Alexandre welcomed Geneviève, *and should never have allowed her to return to Jean-Luc*, but she was pregnant with the heir he wanted so much. She decided to return to him, to give him his child in exchange for her freedom. Geneviève gave Jean-Luc his son, but she was never free. A month after her son's birth, she was killed.

And now, even though her mind had sent a warning not to taunt him, Isabelle was accusing Jean-Luc of Geneviève's death. Surely this king of terrorists, this amoral madman, would not take offense at the accusation. But as she saw the sudden murderous rage in his dark eyes, she realized she had pushed too far, and the fearlessness she had always felt with Jean-Luc, her own immunity to harm because of his obsession for her, gave way to immobilizing fear. She was frozen, unable to flee. But then, as his powerful hands closed around her delicate neck, and she understood that she was going to die, the fear melted into an almost peaceful relief. She would die. The pain of her loss, her losses, would be over. She would be with Alexandre.

"Papa?"

At the sound of the young voice, the fingers that had been seconds away from crushing her slender throat released their grip. Jean-Luc's dark eyes flickered for a moment with bewildered horror at what he had almost done to the woman he loved. Then, as if nothing had happened, he smiled and turned in the direction of his ten-year-old son.

"Alain. Please come in and meet your Aunt Isabelle."

Alain. Somehow the realization settled in her swirling mind. *Geneviève's son.* But there was nothing in the serious yet calm young face to suggest that Alain had overheard her accusation about Geneviève, or even to indicate that he was aware of the violence his "Papa?" had interrupted.

"Bonjour, Tante Isabelle," Alain greeted her politely.

"Bonjour, Alain." Isabelle found a wobbly smile for the boy who would one day rule the island. In a different world, a world without Jean-Luc, would he and her daughter have been loving cousins? Or would Alain have resented being second in line to the throne *behind* his younger female cousin? Alain's genetic inheritance appeared to be all Castille, the dark handsomeness of Jean-Luc and Alexandre with none of Geneviève's fairness. Had this little boy inherited anything from his mother? Was there goodness in his veins, or was he pure evil like his father? The face was sweet now, a boy's face, and the dark eyes *seemed* sensitive. But the apparent sensitivity could be merely an illusion, she knew, like Jean-Luc's charm, a weapon to be used when it was expedient to do so. It didn't matter what kind of man this boy was to become. Whether it was his destiny to be good or evil, on this day Alain Castille had unwittingly saved her life.

"Well," she murmured after a moment, using Alain's appearance as a chance to make her escape. "I must go. Adieu, Alain."

Jean-Luc didn't try to stop her. He would have her followed, of course, perhaps forever. She didn't care. *Her* freedom, *her* safety, didn't matter any longer.

Her swift journey toward the palace gates halted in the midst of a marble courtyard. There, splashing her small fingers in a pond that swirled with colorful koi, was a beautiful little girl. She was Natalie, Isabelle assumed, Jean-Luc's four-year-old daughter and Alain's half sister. Isabelle's heart filled with more warmth for Natalie than it had for Alain, because she was a daughter, a princess, and because she smiled a lovely innocent smile at her aunt.

What kind of life could there be for children who lived in a world shadowed by Jean-Luc? Isabelle wondered as she left the palace forever. An unhappy life, she decided sadly. A life tainted by treachery and fear, not love and joy. For the first time in the weeks since she had been forced to give her daughter away, Isabelle felt a sense of peace. Her little girl was safe, and she would be loved.

Be happy, my precious little love, her heart whispered to her beloved baby in faraway Kansas.

Kansas . . . the home of the little girl who dreamed of enchanted places over the rainbow. Isabelle wondered if her daughter, like Dorothy, would dream such magical dreams. Of course she would—all little girls did. She would dream of enchanted magical places, but not even in her wildest dreams would she ever imagine the truth: that she was, and always would be, the Princess of the enchanted and magical L'île des Arcs-en-ciel . . . the Island of the Rainbows.

CHAPTER TWO

Manhattan
April 1989

Summoned by engraved gilt-edged invitation, New York's literati and glitterati assembled in the Plaza's Grand Ballroom for the annual Academy Award gala. Held on the Saturday evening following the presentation of the Oscars in Hollywood, the star-studded event was Manhattan's answer to super-agent Swifty Lazar's after-Oscar party at Spago. The guest list for both parties was similar—only the very rich, very famous, and very influential—but the sheer size of the Grand Ballroom permitted even greater lavishness. The *pièce de résistance* this year was a twelve-foot-tall ice sculpture of the famous Oscar. The glistening statue towered above a pond of vintage champagne, its icy surface tinted gold by the reflection of the expensive liquid that swirled at its feet.

Alexandra Taylor wove slowly through the bejeweled, couturied, and tuxedoed guests. She whispered gracious thank-yous to those who spoke their congratulations and smiled beautiful replies to those who simply raised crystal champagne flutes in silent toast. To the many appreciative and admiring eyes that watched her throughout the evening, Alexa seemed remarkably calm about her stunning triumph, greeting her victory with a regal dignity appropriate to the role for which she had just won the Oscar for Best Actress—Elizabeth I in *Majesty*, Lawrence Carlyle's stunning portrait of the magnificent queen.

Alexa's apparent calm was merely another demonstration of her remarkable talent. Beneath the tranquil facade her heart raced, *still*, even after six nights, a fluttering symbol of her immense joy. The joy was quite private, although she'd had very little privacy since the moment she had received the small golden statue. Very little privacy, and that was what was needed now, she decided, as she felt the invisible tug of the secluded moonlit terrace beyond the French doors. It was almost midnight, almost time to go home, but she needed a few moments of solitude in the shadows before beginning her smiling gracious journey back through the sea of rich and famous.

She would be alone on the terrace, she thought, a rare celebrity who preferred shadows to limelight. But she was not alone. Her immediate disappointment vanished quickly as she recognized the elegant tuxedoed silhouette and the midnight-black hair that shined in the moonlight.

"Bond," she purred softly as she approached him. "James Bond."

"I beg your pardon?"

"Oh! I beg *your* pardon," Alexa exclaimed when he turned to face her. "I thought you were Timothy."

"Timothy?"

"Dalton." As Alexa clarified she realized that her words did not enlighten the very dark, very seductive blue eyes. Whoever he was—*not* Timothy Dalton but certainly an acceptable Bond by any measure of elegant sensuality—he apparently was far enough removed from show business that he knew neither Timothy nor his role as the master spy. "You're not Timothy Dalton."

"No. I'm James Sterling."

"Oh. Hello," Alexa breathed softly.

She had heard of James Sterling, of course. *Who hadn't?* The stunningly successful attorney was at once phantom and legend in New York. *Phantom*, because although he donated generously to charities and the arts, he rarely bothered to appear at the galas; and *legend*, because although only thirty-four his skill as a negotiator made him the man chosen by the most powerful industrialists in the world to orchestrate their billion-dollar mergers, takeovers, and real estate deals.

The world's wealthiest chose James Sterling for their most important negotiations, although in truth it was James who did the choosing. From the moment of his birth, James had more than enough wealth to never need to work at all. But he had chosen to become an attorney, and a negotiator, and now he selected from the many projects offered to him only the ones that appealed, challenged, or intrigued.

The blood that flowed in James Sterling's veins was quite blue, quite patrician, and, his admirers embellished, it was as calm and cool as ice. It was the iciness, the unshakable cool under pressure, that made James the best at what he did. It was that same iciness, his detractors noted, that resulted in his notoriously short-lived liaisons with some of the world's most glamorous women.

Alexa was quite untroubled by James Sterling's reputation with women. He was a man, after all, completely within her control. A very handsome, very sexy man, Alexa realized as the seductive blue eyes met hers and she felt a wonderful rush of heat, like the tingling, giddy warmth of too hastily swallowed champagne. She acknowledged the moment with a demure smile. Then, because he seemed to be awaiting a follow-up to her obvious surprise in response to his name, she gave a beautiful provocative frown, as if his name triggered a distant but uncertain memory, and asked, "James Sterling, the attorney?"

"Yes." After a patient moment he asked, "So, who are you?"

Alexa blushed slightly at her own presumptuousness. She had assumed he would know her. She was practically the guest of honor at the gala. Did he really not recognize her? Or was he feigning uncertainty, *playing* as she had been?

"I'm Alexandra Taylor."

"Oh. Hello," James murmured softly, as surprised by her name as she had been by his. "Alexandra Taylor, the actress?"

"Yes. Alexa."

"Well, Alexa, you're the reason I'm here tonight. I wanted to tell you how magnificent I thought you were in *Majesty*."

"Thank you," she replied calmly, even though her mind swirled. James Sterling, the phantom whose everyday life was so dazzling that he rarely bothered with the glittering galas had come tonight *to meet her*? The revelation was astonishing and intriguing . . . until she detected something more than surprise on his handsome face. What was it? Alexa couldn't be sure, but she feared that it was the one thing she dreaded most—*disappointment*. She offered quietly, "I guess you expected someone a little more Elizabethan?"

"I guess so," James admitted.

It had only been four nights since he had seen *Majesty* on a rainy evening in Hong Kong, but in that time he had formed a clear image of the extraordinary actress. She would be British, of course, and although she had convincingly portrayed Elizabeth from seventeen to seventy, James guessed she would be about his age. He had envisioned a solemn and dedicated veteran of the London stage who had been lured to the silver screen by the gifted director Lawrence Carlyle. Her beauty would be sublime, as Elizabeth's had been, a magnificent richness of character. Her remarkable green eyes would be thoughtful, reflective, quite uncomfortable with the glitter of the party; and her red-gold hair, unattended by the stylists who were constant fixtures on the movie set, would be an unruly mane, a curly tangle unceremoniously snared with barrettes at the last minute, a small concession to fashion by a sensible woman who usually couldn't care less.

James had such complete confidence in his image of Alexandra Taylor that, as he had searched for her in the crowded ballroom, it had not occurred to him to ask someone to point her out. His eyes *had* lingered on the breathtakingly beautiful woman with the long golden hair and the sparkling emerald eyes, wondering who she was and if they should meet, but . . .

But now that dazzling and glamorous woman was here—claiming to be Alexandra Taylor. Was this really the woman who had so compellingly portrayed the many layers of the complicated and extraordinary queen that he had left the theater wishing he had known Elizabeth?

Yes, James realized as he saw the surprising flickers of uncertainty, clues to Alexa's own complexity, rippling through the remarkable emerald.

"The day after I won the award, I got a call asking if I would wear one of the Oscar-winning costumes and a red-gold wig for the party tonight," she murmured with a shrug, a soft apology to the man who had come tonight hoping to meet Elizabeth . . . and had found only Alexa.

"But you said no."

"It seemed a bit much."

"Because there are actresses here who didn't win?" James guessed quietly, hoping that was the reason, seeing at once in her surprised eyes that it was.

"I'm sort of an impostor."

"I see." He teased lightly, "Never done much acting?"

Only almost all of my life, Alexa mused. She never thought of her acting as a talent. It was and always had been simply survival.

"I've been a professional actress for the past eight years. Most of my work has been in television, although I have done a little theater. *Majesty* was my first feature film."

"Quite a debut."

"Quite a role."

But it wasn't just the role, James knew. Not many actresses, no matter how talented, could have portrayed Elizabeth as Alexa had. It hadn't *felt* like performance, and that had been the magic. There had been no distinction between the extraordinary queen and the extraordinary actress who had brought her to life. Alexa's Elizabeth was very personal and very intimate. As if Elizabeth was who Alexa was . . . or who Alexa wished to be.

"Tell me about Elizabeth," James urged quietly. Tell me about Alexa.

"Elizabeth was magnificent. I hadn't really known that before. I realized how terribly superficial my knowledge was when I began to research the role. In grade school, I remember learning about Sir Francis Drake gallantly throwing his cape across a mud puddle. I remember that mostly because it precipitated a flurry of similar gallantry among the boys in my class."

"Lots of muddy raincoats?"

"Lots. And then in high school . . . well, the issue of the Virgin Queen prompted quite a bit of extracurricular discussion as I recall."

"And remains unresolved in *Majesty*," James observed. Alexa's portrayal of Elizabeth had been of a sensual, passionate, bewitching woman, however the specific issue of the famous queen's virginity, or not, had not been addressed. "What did you decide from your reading?"

"I decided that Elizabeth had intimate relationships with men. Whether the relationships were sexual or not is trivial because the intimacy was so much deeper than that. I am very sure that Elizabeth was loved passionately for who she was, for her heart and spirit and soul."

"Which is what really matters? To be loved for who you are?"

"Yes. I guess," Alexa admitted softly, frowning slightly as she realized how personal the admission was and wondering why she had made it. "Weren't we talking about Elizabeth?"

"We were, but now we've shifted to you. We've already established that you consider sexual relationships—at least some sexual relationships—to be quite trivial."

"Yes," she agreed with a soft laugh. Then, with emerald eyes sparkling, she said firmly, "So, that's all we need to know about me. Let's shift to you. I wonder . . ."

"Yes?"

"Well," Alexa purred as her mind searched for clever, provocative questions to ask James Sterling. Her search was intercepted by a serious question, one for which she legitimately needed an answer. The question was serious, and important, but her tone remained soft, teasing. "I'm desperately seeking an attorney. Perhaps you could make a referral?"

"Of course. You'll need to tell me a little about the case."

"All right. Did you really not recognize me?"

"I really did not."

"Then you're probably not familiar with *Pennsylvania Avenue*, the television show, not the address."

James smiled. He had dined, more than once, at the address. And as for the show?

"I've heard about the show, but I've never seen it. That's not a value judgment by the way," he added swiftly. "I just don't watch much television. I never have. I do know, however, that it's the top-rated prime-time dramatic series. Are you the star?"

"It's an ensemble cast, but the character I play, Stephanie Winslow, is fairly high profile. She's a reporter—sexy, savvy, and intensely dedicated—and somehow she manages to be woven into almost all the major story lines."

Which means you *are* the star, he thought, realizing that, as with Elizabeth, Alexa somehow diminished her own talent by giving credit to the role. And, as with Elizabeth, James heard admiration in her voice as she spoke of Stephanie, as if she had nothing at all to do with Alexa.

"Why do you need an attorney?"

"Because it's contract time and I'm between agents."

"Why?"

"Why what?"

"Why are you between agents?"

"Why do you keep asking all these questions? The James Sterling that I've heard of does corporate work—you know, mergers and takeovers? But I feel like I'm on the witness stand!" Alexa's sparkling eyes narrowed as she added knowingly, "You're really another James Sterling, aren't you? James Sterling, the brilliant trial attorney."

"No. I really do my work in boardrooms, not courtrooms. But all attorneys, all good ones, ask the key questions."

"It's key to find out why I'm between agents?"

"Apparently. You seem to be resisting giving me an answer."

Alexa sighed, amazed that the conversation had become so personal, so quickly, *again*. She glowered at him, and he answered the glower with a laugh that was so soft, so gentle, so surprised that she gave a bewildered shake of her golden head and quietly told him something she had never told anyone ever before.

"I guess that my agent and I parted company because of artistic differences. When Lawrence Carlyle approached him to see if I would be interested in playing Elizabeth, he said no without even checking with me. That's part of an agent's job, of course, to screen projects. But he was supposed to turn down projects because they weren't worthy of me, *not* because he thought I wasn't worthy of them."

"But you were most worthy of playing Elizabeth," James reminded her. "Fortunately, somehow you and Lawrence Carlyle did get together."

"Yes. One day Lawrence simply appeared on the set of *P.A.* to talk to me directly. He had seen the series—it's very popular in England—and decided that Stephanie was a modern day Elizabeth."

"I see," James said, realizing that once again she had excluded herself from the equation. "So, not surprisingly, you and your agent parted company. You need a new agent."

"Yes, I do. But because of my success with *Majesty*, any agent worth his or her salt would be signing me to more movies."

"And that doesn't appeal?"

"Not until at least two years from now. *Pennsylvania Avenue* is in production from July through January, and so far I've filled every production hiatus with a major project. Next year, no matter what, I've promised myself the entire five months will be vacation."

"What are you doing now?"

"*Romeo and Juliet*—Juliet—on Broadway. I had promised myself this spring off, but . . ." But every time I remember the reason for the promise, that I need time away from the heroines I admire so much to be with myself—whom I don't admire?—I seem to find ways of breaking it. Alexa dismissed the disquieting thought with a soft shrug and continued, "Anyway, that's why I'm not looking for an agent. The only commitment I want to make now is to *Pennsylvania Avenue*. I already have a contract, of course, so all that needs to be negotiated is the new salary. I know exactly what I want, but I would prefer to have someone else do the talking. It would probably just be one simple call to Los Angeles. Is there someone you would recommend?"

"Sure. I'd recommend myself."

"No. I know a little about your reputation, James. This would be much too small for you."

"Really? Like you, Alexa, I have the wonderful luxury of being able to choose projects. I only choose ones that interest me—which this does. Besides, by remarkable coincidence, I'm flying to Chicago tomorrow, for two days, and then will be in Los Angeles until Friday. The meetings in L.A. are inconveniently spaced over several days. If I can fill the spaces by making phone calls for you I'll feel my time has been better spent."

"It would only be one phone call."

"No, it wouldn't. After I've read your existing contract and discussed with you what you want, I would need to do some research to see if your demands are reasonable." James saw the sudden flickers of worry in her beautiful eyes and guessed softly, "You were planning to have me make some unreasonable demands?"

"Can't I just tell you what I want and ask you to make the phone call?"

"You can, but I won't do it. I can promise you that I'll do my homework and get you a very fair deal." He smiled and added quietly, "And Alexa, I don't make promises I can't keep."

"I really just expected you to give me the name of someone else."

"I know. But in good conscience I have to recommend myself."

"Because you're the best at what you do."

"Just like you."

"Oh! Thank you. Well, if you really want . . ."

"I really want. So, let's see. Why don't you messenger a copy of your contract to my office Monday morning? They'll fax it to me and I'll review it and call you Monday night."

"All right." Alexa frowned as she thought about her already impossible Monday morning. But the contract negotiation was a top priority—which made getting the contract to James of utmost importance. She would simply have to shuffle her other commitments, unless . . . "My apartment is on Riverside Drive. I have a limousine outside and could go to my apartment, get a copy of the contract, and be back here in fifteen or twenty minutes. If you wouldn't mind waiting."

"I wouldn't mind. I would also be very happy to accompany you."

"Oh! Well, I . . ."

"Or would that put me in great danger of being challenged to a duel by the Earl of Leicester or some other suitor?"

"Jeremy—the good Earl—is quite married."

"And therefore off-limits?"

"Absolutely."

"And all the other suitors?"

"I'm here alone, James. But surely there's a lady-in-waiting nearby who would not be terribly pleased."

"I'm here alone, too," James said quietly. He added, even more quietly, "I told you, Alexandra Taylor. I only came tonight to meet you."

CHAPTER THREE

Alexa's apartment was on the third floor of a red-brick building on Riverside Drive. The building was old but solidly built, and the apartment had the kind of detailing that revealed the meticulous craftsmanship often missing in newer construction—vaulted ceilings, carved wainscoting, charming alcoves, and luxurious spaciousness. As James followed her from the foyer to the living room, he silently admired the floral wall coverings and soft pastel accents. He had been in many designer apartments, his own penthouse on Fifth Avenue included, and this felt quite different . . . homemade, comfortable, uncluttered.

There *was* clutter in the living room, he discovered, fragrant clutter from Alexa's recent triumph—hundreds of long-stemmed roses artfully arranged in an array of vases. James recognized some of the vases, the elegant carved crystal designs of Lalique and the delicate spring flowers of Limoges; but many of the vases were not china or crystal, but pottery, made by a talented artist whose work he had never seen. The same artist, he decided, who had crafted the beautiful hand-painted lamps that adorned the room.

"This is very nice, very homey. Are you the designer?"

"Yes. Thank you. It does feel like home."

"Which is where?"

"A farmhouse outside of Topeka. My father is a music teacher." Alexa gently touched one of the hand-painted vases and added, "And my mother is a potter."

"Talented family."

"Thank you," she murmured softly as she thought, And you haven't even heard about the most talented Taylor of all. The thought came with memories, bittersweet and unsettling. After a moment, Alexa shook the thought and looked up from the delicate hand-painted vase to him—only to be unsettled anew. Here he was, this devastatingly handsome, compellingly sensual stranger; and here they were, alone at midnight in her romantic rose-fragrant apartment. As his seductive dark blue eyes studied her, appraising and obviously approving, she felt once again the lovely rushes of delicious warmth; but she felt, too, tremors of uncertainty. When she'd told him that she was looking for an attorney it had been the truth, important, serious, and quite innocent. What if he thought it had all been merely a provocative ploy to lure him to her apartment?

James felt unsettled, too, struck anew by how beautiful, how alluring she was. She was even more appealing here than she'd been in moonlight; because here, in this charming place decorated by her, proudly and lovingly accented with home-made pottery, he saw even more enchanting glimpses of the lovely woman beneath the gold and emerald dazzle.

James knew very well that their chance encounter on the moonlit terrace might have led them here. They might have danced on the terrace, learning more about each other, leisurely affirming the attraction that had been so obvious from the first. They might have danced and smiled and sipped champagne, and eventually, the glowing emerald eyes might have invited him here. But, even though they both knew that might well have happened, that wasn't why he was here now. And he knew, and perhaps the uncertainty he saw in her eyes now meant that she *didn't* know, that the moment he had offered to represent her everything had changed.

Alexa was his client now. Which meant that for now, and for as long as she was, their relationship would be purely professional. James took his obligations to his career and to his personal code of ethics very seriously; just as, he knew, she did, too. He told her that now with his dark blue eyes. The eloquent blue told her everything: that his attraction to her hadn't vanished with the moonlight, *not at all*; and that he knew she took her career very seriously, as he did his; and that he was here, now, to help her with this contract that was obviously so important to her; and that, some other time, when she was no longer his client, he would very much like to be invited back to this romantic place.

His dark blue eyes sent all those messages with such clarity that the emerald ones understood perfectly and were both flattered and relieved; and they sent a clear and eloquent message in return, a sparkling promise that yes, if he wanted, there would be another time.

"Contract?" he asked finally, with a soft laugh.

"Contract," she echoed. "It's in the other room."

"Shall I follow you?"

Alexa smiled. "Sure."

She led the way to one of the apartment's two large bedroom suites. The two rooms, located at opposite extremes of the spacious apartment, were mirror images of each other, although for the moment only hers looked like a bedroom at all. The other, to which she led James, looked like the dance studio it once had been.

"As you can probably tell, the previous owner was a ballerina," Alexa explained. "I've been using this room as a combination gym, study, and storage room."

"But it looks as if it's about to be transformed," James observed as his gaze fell on the rolls of wallpaper, cans of paint, and drop cloths lying on the hardwood floor.

"Yes. The mirrors and ballet bar come out on Monday. After a little replastering and installation of chair rails, it will hopefully become a bedroom again. My little sister Cat is moving to New York in June. As you can see, I'm keeping with the Laura-Ashley-does-Kansas theme, although I've decided lilacs, not roses, for Cat." As she looked at the beautiful wallpaper, clusters of lilacs on ivory, Alexa's eyes filled with new uncertainty. She wanted the room to be like a bouquet, fresh and cheerful and romantic, and she had spent hours carefully selecting the floral wallcovering, and the perfect pastel green accent for the woodwork, and the matching fabric for the curtains and bedspread. But still she worried. After a reflective moment, she added quietly, "I hope she'll like it."

"Why wouldn't she?"

"Oh, I don't know," she answered with a soft shrug. It wasn't the bedroom she hoped Cat would like, of course, it was something so very much more important: I hope Cat will like *me*.

James watched as her lovely eyes became more thoughtful, and, just for a flicker, terribly sad. The moment passed quickly, but he was left with an indelible impression: there was something very important—and yet very troubling—about her little sister. And even though they were in this room to get the contract, and tonight was professional, not personal, he couldn't resist learning just a little more. "Her name is Cat?"

"Yes. Short for Catherine. She's a gifted musician, a pianist. Even though she'll only be twenty-one next month, she's already won both the Tchaikovsky and Van Cliburn competitions. Her professional career as a concert pianist could have started years ago, but she decided to go to college first. She's in her junior year at Oberlin now, although she's enough ahead on credits that she can graduate in December if she takes full course loads this summer and fall."

"So she's coming to New York to finish college?"

"Yes. At Juilliard. They're obviously quite happy to have her, if only for two terms. She needs to be here because the promoter wants an album to be released in time for her first professional concert tour, which debuts at the Opera House in San Francisco on New Year's Eve and then continues through North America and on to Europe."

"So she'll be going to school, learning new pieces for her concert tour, and recording an album? That seems like too much."

"Not for Cat. She'll handle it with ease."

"I guess so, if she's anything like her older sister."

"Like me?"

"Your nonstop award-winning career hasn't happened by accident. There must be a little discipline and drive sprinkled in with all that Taylor sister talent." James thought the observation was quite obvious, but it seemed to confuse her. Why? She had already admitted that she kept promising herself a little much needed time off, so she couldn't deny that she was driven. Was it possible that she doubted her own talent? "No? Not true?"

"I guess it's true. I just never think of Cat and me being at all alike." She frowned briefly, then shrugged. "Well. Let me get the contract, then we can go to the kitchen. There's a table there, paper and pencils if you need them, and good light. And I could make you some coffee or maybe something to drink?"

"Coffee would be fine." I have a contract to read, he thought. Tonight, we'll sit in the kitchen and drink coffee and talk about your contract. And next time, we'll sit in the rose-fragrant living room, and drink champagne, and, maybe, just maybe, you'll tell me why there is such lovely uncertainty in your emerald eyes when you speak of your talented little sister.

Alexa watched as James read the contract, his intelligent dark blue eyes focused, his handsome aristocratic features set in neutral and totally inscrutable. The master negotiator was at work now, and as she unabashedly studied him, she began to appreciate the reasons for his extraordinary success. There was the obvious—intelligence combined with the perfectionism of all successful people; and the subtle—his stunning sensuality. She imagined him at the negotiating table, disarming his opponents with his aristocratic elegance, his inscrutable calm, and the sensuous eyes that could appraise so intently, searching for truths, but which, unless he chose, would reveal nothing of the thoughts that lay in the dark blue depths. Women, if James Sterling ever even negotiated with women, would be distracted, unwittingly seduced by his compelling sexuality; and men would be distracted, too, envious perhaps, certainly admiring.

"OK," James said when he had finished his thorough reading of her contract. "Let's go point by point and you tell me what you had in mind."

"There really wasn't anything other than salary, assuming they don't want to undo other previous agreements."

"What about the residuals and royalties you get for reruns, syndication, and sales ex-U.S.?"

"I think the amounts in the existing contract are very standard."

James nodded, but then, as if "standard" was an unacceptable concept to the master negotiator, he penciled question marks next to the pertinent paragraphs.

"OK. So, what salary figure did you have in mind?"

"One million." Alexa had been silently rehearsing how to utter the large sum—twice what she had been paid last season—and rehearsing, too, the reasons she had used to convince herself that the amount was fair. High but fair.

If James had an objection, or even a reaction, he didn't show it. He simply jotted the numeral "1" above the five hundred thousand. Just a "1," without six zeroes, without any embellishment at all.

Just a "1," Alexa thought uneasily. It was probably the smallest number he ever wrote—just a million. Just a million was probably far less than his usual fee for any one of the many important deals he negotiated.

"Do you have a feeling for how that salary compares to other prime-time stars?" he asked.

"Just a feeling. Rumors, actually."

"I'll need to check. Could you give me some names?"

"Sure. Let's see, there's Joan Van Ark, and Susan Dey, and Dana Delany, and . . ." Alexa gave him the names of a number of actresses, as well as the series in which each appeared.

"There are no male stars on these shows?" James asked after he had recorded the names of the principal heroines and villainesses of *Dallas*, *L.A. Law*, *Knot's Landing*, and *China Beach*. "Ms. Taylor, don't you believe in comparable worth?"

"Yes, I do. Do you?"

"Of course. Does Hollywood?"

"I'm not sure."

"We'll find out. Give me some male names."

"OK. There's Larry Hagman—that's *Dallas*—and . . ."

James recorded the additional names, and the name and phone number of the executive producer in Hollywood with whom the negotiations would occur, and the numbers where he could reach Alexa both at her apartment and the theater where she was starring in *Romeo and Juliet*.

"I'll call you in a day or two, once I've had a chance to get what I need to determine what salary request we can reasonably make."

"Do you think you'll be able to learn about these other salaries?"

"Yes." James had no experience with negotiating individual contracts in Hollywood, but he had had business dealings—multibillion dollar takeovers—with a number of top industry executives. He had no doubt that he could very easily get what he needed. "That information will be of interest, of course, but most important will be gauging your value to *Pennsylvania Avenue* and *Pennsylvania Avenue's* value to the network."

"How will you do that?"

"Through a combination of informal conversations as well as getting specific data on advertising revenues generated by the show."

"This is going to be a lot of work, isn't it?"

"I don't think so. I'll call you when I have everything I need, and before I make the call to the executive producer. In the meantime, you should think about the deal breaker."

"Deal breaker?"

"The point at which we walk away." James saw her sudden confusion and clarified, "The salary amount that is so unacceptably low that there can never be a deal. Alexa?"

"There's no deal breaker, James. We don't ever walk away." She added quietly, "I would play Stephanie for free. No, I would *pay* for the privilege of playing her."

"You know the cardinal rule of successful negotiating?" he asked with a soft laugh. "You have to make the other guy believe you don't give a damn."

"But I do give a damn," Alexa countered swiftly. Earlier she had cast James Sterling as James Bond. Now as he was smiling his devastating smile and telling her that you have to not give a damn, her mind cast him in another famous role: Rhett leaving Scarlett. Frankly my dear . . .

Did she really want this man who didn't give a damn to negotiate this important contract for her?

"OK. No deal breakers, I promise. And I told you, I don't make promises I can't keep. Would you rather I didn't do this? Alexa? You've spent enough time in Washington to know how to extricate yourself from any situation."

"I have?"

"Sure. If you don't want me to represent you in this, Alexa, just say no."

During the silence that followed James had two distinct and opposite wishes. Just say no, Alexa, and I will give you the name of another good attorney, and you will no longer be my client, and we will abandon coffee for champagne, and dance amidst the roses, and begin to learn more about each other. That was one wish, undeniably selfish. But his other wish was even more selfish. Just say yes, Alexa. Trust me with this thing that is clearly so important to you. And then after, when you are no longer my client, we will begin . . .

"I would like you to represent me, James. You don't even need to check back with me once you've gathered the data. Just go for whatever amount you think is reasonable."

"You're sure?"

"Yes. I guess we should sign something. Most agents get fifteen percent."

"Agents get a percentage because they take an active part in managing your career. This is a straightforward contract negotiation. I will send you a bill for my time."

"The full usual amount."

"Absolutely," James promised as he stood to leave. "I'd better be going. I'll give you a call."

Then he was gone, and Alexa paced restlessly among the roses in her living room. Why hadn't she decided to forget about the contract and simply let him seduce her? Allowing him to negotiate his way into her bed would have been pure pleasure, and so very safe. In bed, she was in no danger from this man who made deals and broke hearts with equal icy ease. Her heart *could not* be broken, not even by the famous James Sterling, because a heart not given could not break.

Alexa never placed her heart in jeopardy, but still, somehow she had permitted him to wander off into the midnight darkness with something that was of immense value to her—the great joy of playing Stephanie Winslow, whom she admired. How could she have entrusted that very important part of herself to a man whose approach to negotiating was to not give a damn? Billionaires trusted James Sterling with their billion-dollar companies, but maybe to the billionaires, it was all a thrilling high-stakes game.

But this wasn't a game! At least not to her.

Alexa desperately hoped that it was not a game to James.

She should have remained in the rose-fragrant living room, or perhaps gone to her own bedroom to touch the small golden statue that was glittering proof of her success and worth. But, instead, compelled by some deep, self-destructive impulse she could not control, she walked to the bedroom that would be Cat's. As she frowned at the so carefully selected lilac wallpaper, she knew that even the enormous doubts she had about entrusting her career to James were quite trivial compared to the great doubts she had about her little sister.

The same April moon that had smiled a golden smile on the secluded terrace where Alexa and James had met now softly illuminated Catherine's path as she made her way across the Oberlin campus from Bailey House, the residence hall where she lived, to the practice rooms in the Conservatory's Robertson Hall. The beam of golden moonlight was lovely, but quite unnecessary. Even on a moonless night in the darkest of Ohio winters she would have found her way along the so familiar path; and even had she never traveled the path before, and even in a darkness darker than a moonless midnight, a deep instinct would have unerringly guided Catherine to a place where there was a piano.

It was midnight. The festive Saturday night noises of campus parties were beginning to fade, the raucous laughter softening as groups became couples and the large parties became private and intimate ones. Lost in thought, Catherine was oblivious to the sounds of love and gaiety around her; but had she heard them, she would have smiled an untroubled smile at the happiness of her classmates, quite unconcerned that she herself was alone on this Saturday night. She was, after all, precisely where she wanted to be, walking happily toward the piano she would joyfully play until dawn.

Catherine didn't hear the noises of parties, nor was she aware either of the chill of the brisk night wind. She felt very warm, warmed from within by the anticipated joy of playing soon and by the remembered joy of the day. It had been quite glorious; fresh and sunny and filled with all the hopeful promises of spring. She had spent the afternoon sitting cross-legged on a warm patch of grass in Tappan Square, reading *La Cousine Bette* by Balzac. She read the classic novel in its original French, and later, after the sun had fallen, taking its gentle warmth with it, she had returned to her room, and, also in French, she had carefully recorded impressions of what she'd read onto the colorful notecards she was compiling for the term paper she had to write.

She spent the evening with Balzac and just before midnight began the familiar walk to the Conservatory. She had been walking briskly, eagerly, but now as she neared Wilder Hall, the student union building, her footsteps slowed, and, on impulse, she veered from her path to the Conservatory to that building where the student mailboxes were housed. Why? she wondered as she tried to analyze the sudden and surprising impulse. Surely there would be no mail for her. It had only been two days since she'd received a letter from Topeka, and even though the long, happy, loving letters from her parents arrived frequently, just as her long, happy, loving ones to them arrived frequently in Topeka, there would not be another one from them so soon.

But something compelled her to check anyway, and as she neared her small mailbox and saw that it wasn't empty her heart fluttered with loving wonder at the remarkable telepathy between herself and her beloved parents. It had always been there, a wonderful, astonishing understanding that required no words. As her delicate virtuoso fingers spun the combination, Catherine noticed through the window that the letter was quite thin. It would be a brief newsy item that her mother had forgotten to include in her recent letter—good news about a neighbor, or about a pottery sale she'd made, or about her father's music. More than once, Catherine had done the same thing, remembering a detail she'd somehow forgotten and jotting it down on one of the beautiful postcards she had of Tappan Square in fall, ablaze with the magnificent colors of the turning leaves.

This was a postcard, Catherine discovered as she removed it. But it wasn't from Topeka. The pale blue card, on which was embossed an elegant white swan, was from Los Angeles, from the Hotel Bel-Air, from Alexa. And it read, in Alexa's sophisticated script: Cat, In all the excitement, I forgot to tell you how glad I am that you're moving to New York. Thank you again for the beautiful roses. A.

"All the excitement" had been the breathless conversation between the sisters on the morning after the Academy Awards. Alexa had called to thank Catherine for the lovely bouquet of Lady Di roses that had greeted her in her suite at the Hotel Bel-Air when, near dawn, she'd finally returned from the last Oscar party. Alexa had raved about the perfect, pale peach roses, how fragrant they were, how delicate and beautiful, how they were her favorite of all roses; and, at the same time, quietly, but like her older sister breathlessly, too, Catherine had told Alexa over and over how happy she was that she'd won. It had been a short conversation, because after the breathless gushes there had been awkward silence, and quickly, awkwardly, they'd said good-bye.

But, after the call ended, Alexa had obviously remembered other important words and had written the note. Catherine had had other important words to say, too; but she hadn't had the courage to say them, nor had she even bravely written them in a note. But she should have! She should have told Alexa how many times she'd seen *Majesty*, and how much she deserved to win the Oscar, and how proud she was of her, *always*, Oscar or no Oscar. And she should have told her older sister, too, how very excited she was about moving to New York. She should have said, or at least written, all those important things; but she hadn't; she had never had Alexa's effortless confidence.

After carefully putting the postcard in her coat pocket, Catherine returned to the moonlit midnight and very chilly night air. But she felt even warmer now than before, and her luminous sapphire eyes glowed from an inner joy. I forgot to tell you how glad I am that you're moving to New York, Alexa had written. Oh, how she hoped that was true! She loved and admired her older sister so much, and was so eager to be near her, and so hopeful that the delicate beginning friendship of the past eight years would take brave, firm roots, and then blossom and grow.

How she hoped Alexa would like her.

Without warning, the wonderful warmth vanished and an icy chill swept through her. It wasn't the brisk night wind, Catherine knew. It was instead the frigid shiver of an ancient ghost, a reminder that even though the recent memories were warm and hopeful, there had been a time—*most of her life*—when there had not been friendship between them. That painful time had been when they had lived together, under the same roof; a time when Alexa had had a chance to really know her little sister.

And she didn't like me then, Catherine reminded herself. What if, as she gets to know me now, she doesn't like me still?

All the warmth was gone, and she trembled with a deep, icy fear. And she began to walk even more briskly along the moonlit path to the place she now needed so desperately to be . . . to the piano . . . to her music . . . to that magnificent escape into peace.

CHAPTER FOUR

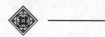

"*The* network has picked up *Pennsylvania Avenue* for two seasons," James told Alexa when he telephoned Tuesday evening.

"Two seasons? That's very unusual." She had been in show business long enough to know its whimsical nature. Commitments were always short-term—a season, *part* of a season—and cancellations could occur without warning.

"Yes, but it's happened. Obviously the network knows that after three seasons in the top slot *Pennsylvania Avenue* isn't about to lose its audience. The upshot is that they want to sign you to a two-year contract."

"That sounds encouraging, doesn't it?"

"You mean, evidence that they want you? I guess I should have begun with that—they want you, Alexa. Your role in the immense success of the show is critical. They're prepared to pay a substantial bonus, an incentive if you will, for signing the two-year deal."

"So you think we should go for it?"

"It's not 'we,' Alexa, it's you. There'll be plenty of money either way, so the issue should be what you want to do with your time and your career. You'd mentioned wanting to take some time off."

"Yes, but not time away from *Pennsylvania Avenue*. I'm very willing to make a two-year commitment, James."

"OK. I'll let you know when I think we're close to reasonable numbers. Did the mirrors come down all right?"

"What? Oh yes."

"The offer on the table, awaiting your approval, is six million for two years with an increase in your percentage for syndication and ex-U.S. sales to—"

"Six million?" Her voice came finally, interrupting him with a whispered gasp. He said the amount so casually—to him six million was probably just a "6"—but to her . . . "That's so much more than we talked about."

"The value of getting the facts, Alexa."

"They're comfortable paying me this amount?"

"Absolutely. The negotiations were very pleasant." He had been tough, of course, and he'd worn his elegant don't-give-a-damn demeanor to the negotiating table; but because as always he had armed himself with the necessary data, he was negotiating from a secure position of strength. His initial counter offer—ten million—had been purposefully high, just as the producer's initial proposal had been intentionally low. James fully expected to settle at five, and was surprised and delighted with six, although his dark blue eyes had greeted the amount with only calm approval. "I take it you're tempted to accept the offer?"

"Yes." Alexa laughed softly.

"All right. I think the paperwork on this will all happen very quickly. They want to get you signed, sealed, and delivered before someone tries to lure you back to the silver screen. I'll review the contract first, of course, and then forward it to you."

"Did I thank you?"

"No thanks are necessary, Alexa. This is what I do, what I *enjoy* doing." James paused. When he spoke again there was a softening of his voice, a shift from business to personal, as he quietly issued the one-word invitation. "So."

"So?" she echoed, welcomingly.

"So . . . would you like to have dinner with me?"

"Yes. But I should be inviting you to dinner."

"If that means a homecooked meal at your apartment sometime I accept. Are you a country cook?"

"Of course not!" Alexa answered swiftly. That's the other Taylor sister, she thought. With the thought came a wave of sadness as she remembered the joyful laughter that had come from the farmhouse's small kitchen as her mother had taught her little sister how to cook. She could have joined them, of course; but she had spent her girlhood as far away from Cat as possible, demeaning everything that was important to her by her own resolute unwillingness to participate. Alexa vanquished the unwelcome sadness by replacing it with the recent, hopeful memories of Cat. Then she was back to the present, to the incredible six-million-dollar contract and the incredibly attractive man who wanted to have dinner with her. "I don't cook, but I imagine I could get something from Le Cirque."

"You're proposing gourmet take-out?"

"Why not? Don't you think I could negotiate that?"

"I'm very sure you could. But, let me take you somewhere this time. How is this weekend for you?" When Alexa didn't answer right away, James assumed she was silently visualizing a combination of her performance schedule for *Romeo and Juliet* and her doubtless very full social calendar. He finally guessed, "Completely starcrossed?"

"No. In fact, the teenaged lovers have a Friday night appearance and then are off until Monday. The Shakespeare On Broadway company is presenting four plays this spring. *Richard III*, *Hamlet*, and *The Tempest* are holding down the fort for the weekend."

"But?"

"But I was planning to spend the weekend in Maryland."

"Where in Maryland?"

"About thirty miles due east of Washington. Until last November I lived in a townhouse in Georgetown while *Pennsylvania Avenue* was in production, but now I have a tiny secluded cottage perched on a cliff overlooking Chesapeake Bay. The cottage is wonderful, but it needs a little work."

"Along the Laura Ashley lines?"

"It did need work inside, but I was able to get that done over the winter. The inside rooms are in full bloom, but it's the outside flowers in the long-neglected garden that need attention. A team of gardeners from a local nursery has already done the hardest part, preparing the beds. All that's left is planting the roses that will be delivered on Friday."

"Which is what you're going to do this weekend?"

"Yes. It's my first garden. I like the idea of planting the flowers myself."

James heard the soft shrug in her voice and smiled. After a moment he said, "If your cottage is thirty miles due east of the capital and overlooks the bay, it must be near the Marlboro Marina."

"It is. Very near. You're familiar with the area?"

"My home—my parents' home—is five miles north of the Marina."

"Oh."

"My parents' home, and my sailboat. So . . ."

"So?"

"So, if I didn't have a date for dinner with you this weekend in New York, I would spend the weekend sailing in Maryland. If you like, we could drive down together, and I could sail while you plant, and then, if you're not too exhausted to move, we could have dinner at the Marlboro Hunt Club. Alexa, just say—"

"Yes."

"Good morning."

"Hi." She had decided, as she felt her heart quicken in anticipation of seeing him again, that her imagination had surely embellished the reality. He had been wearing a silk tuxedo that night, after all, and there had been moonlight and roses and . . .

But when James arrived Saturday morning, Alexa realized her mind had not been playing tricks. Even in the bright morning sun his eyes were as intensely dark blue as they had been in the moonlight, his smile as seductive, his hair as black and shining; and, in the case of James Sterling, the clothes did not make the man. Quite the opposite. In faded blue jeans, he was elegant still, his lean strength at once graceful and powerful.

"All set?" James asked after a moment. He, too, had needed a little time to adjust to seeing her again. He had almost convinced himself that the lovely vulnerability beneath the dazzling facade must have been an illusion. But no, it was there still, a soft whisper of turbulence beneath the sparkling emerald calm, beckoning and intriguing.

"All set."

"Is this all?" he asked as he reached for the small suitcase.

"Yes, just Cassini sequins for dinner tonight and a few how-to-plant roses books. I have extra jeans at the cottage."

"And a shovel?"

"The Marlboro Nursery has supposedly delivered everything I will need, including *their* planting and pruning instructions. I'm hoping that what Marlboro suggests will agree with at least one of the other books I've read."

"Which don't agree?"

"No!" Alexa laughed. "Minor discrepancies, admittedly, but apparently planting roses isn't an exact science. I hope that means, within limits, that it doesn't really matter."

"That's probably what it means. I think that roses tend to be very hardy. However, if you'd like yet another expert opinion we can stop at Inverness on the way to your cottage and examine the roses there."

"Inverness?"

"My parents' home. They have quite a few roses. I imagine the gardeners have done the spring pruning already, so it might be helpful."

"OK. Sure. Let's stop at Inverness."

* * *

"Choose a tape, if you like," James suggested once they were out of Manhattan and on the Interstate. "They're in the glove compartment."

Alexa examined James's tapes—Vivaldi, Mozart, Bach, Beethoven, Chopin—the most beautiful, most evocative works of the great composers, all so familiar to her, because of Cat; and, because of Cat all so able to stir memories and emotions . . . pride and guilt, hope and pain, hatred and love.

"No Prince? No Madonna? Not even Beatles or Beach Boys?" Alexa narrowed her sparkling emerald eyes and whispered with mock horror, "You're hopelessly classical, aren't you?"

"Not hopelessly." James smiled as he turned on the radio and pressed a button preset to a popular "soft rock" station. "I am, however, as of Thursday night, hopelessly addicted to *Pennsylvania Avenue.*"

"Thursday night's episode was the season-ending cliff-hanger," Alexa murmured softly, very flattered that he had made a point of watching. "The spring and summer reruns begin next week."

"Meaning I'll have to wait until mid-September to find out if Stephanie Winslow escapes the blaze?"

"Yes. Although you happen to have about six million clues that she does," she said, smiling, thanking him again. After a moment she teased, "Of course, if you were to be my agent, you would be allowed sneak previews of scripts and free access to even the closed sets as of July."

"I'm not going to be your agent. I'm quite happy to simply admire your work with the rest of the world. Besides," he added softly, "I don't want to run the risk of encountering artistic differences with you."

"Oh."

She smiled, and he smiled, and after a few moments of silence, he asked, "So, how is *Romeo and Juliet?*"

"The critics and audiences seem happy, but I keep wondering what could have possessed me to agree to play Juliet. I feel like such a fraud."

"Why?"

"Why? A love to die for? Moi?"

"Alexandra, do I detect a little cynicism about love?"

"Of course you do! More than a little. But don't tell me you're an incurable romantic, James," she said teasingly to the man who made deals and broke hearts with equal icy ease. She was quite confident that James Sterling did not believe in romantic notions such as falling in love.

"I admit to being skeptical, but not cynical."

"Meaning?"

James hesitated, wondering how much to reveal, reminding himself that he wanted *her* to reveal to *him* the truths that lay beneath the dazzling facade. Wasn't it fair for her to expect the same honesty from him? Yes . . . even though this truth sounded more like good-bye than hello. It was, in fact, what he told his lovers, gently, apologetically, when he said good-bye.

"Meaning that I'm probably not destined to have a consuming love. My life is already more than consumed by my two compelling passions—work and sailing—and I'm quite happy." James saw solemn comprehension, not disappointment, on her beautiful face, and realized that her admission that playing Juliet was a stretch had obviously been quite honest, not a flirtatious ploy designed to uncover his views on the subject. "Unlike cynical you, however, I do believe a *Romeo and Juliet* love is possible. I'm just skeptical that such a love will happen to me."

"You have a reputation as a breaker of hearts, you know," Alexa said quietly, thoughtfully, and without incrimination.

"Never on purpose, Alexa."

"No," she agreed softly. "They just expect too much. They expect more than you can give."

No, James thought. My lovers never expect more than I *can* give, only more than I *want* to give. For him it was simply a matter of choice. He was happy with his life—his privacy and his independence—and he had not yet met someone for whom he was willing to devote the time, energy, and emotion demanded by a consuming love. But it wasn't a choice for Alexa, he decided as he heard the softness of her words. Her lovers *had* expected more than she could give. But what did that mean? Why in the world would she believe that there was something about her, some essential ingredient, that limited her ability to love?

INVERNESS was chiseled in old English lettering into one of the two stone pillars at the entrance of the eighteen-acre estate. James turned onto the gravel drive, leaving the bright country road for the shadows of pines, but after a quarter of a mile the forest that provided a lush green wall of privacy from passersby opened to acres of manicured lawn and bountiful gardens. In the distance, on the bluff overlooking Chesapeake Bay, stood the mansion.

"Will your parents be here?"

"No. They're in Paris. My father is the Ambassador to France."

"Ah." Alexa gave her head a slight amazed shake. "And your mother?"

"She's a doctor, an obstetrician-gynecologist."

"Does she practice in Paris?"

"No. She stopped practicing even before my father accepted the ambassadorship, four years ago, on her seventieth birthday."

"She was forty when you were born?"

"Yes. I think she was a forerunner of the career women of the eighties. She was the only woman in her medical school class at Johns Hopkins and was one of the first to make full professor rank in the department. She and my father were thirty-nine when they met. Both had been intensely dedicated to their careers, with no plans of marriage, but . . ."

"Two skeptics taken by surprise?"

"Maybe." James smiled. "Anyway, they married and about a year later I came along."

"Another surprise?"

"I don't think so. If I was, I was a welcome one."

Alexa tilted her head thoughtfully at the sudden softness in his voice, a softness that revealed his gentle and genuine love for his parents.

"Do you see them much?"

"Often. My work takes me to Europe quite frequently, and, like all good Parisiens, my mother and father abandon Paris in August. However, instead of escaping to the Côte d'Azur, they come here."

James gave Alexa a tour of the mansion, finishing in the great room that overlooked a garden of recently pruned roses. After he led the way outside through the immense French doors, she knelt on the warm grass beside the beds intently studying the handiwork of Inverness's expert gardeners.

"This really was helpful," she said finally, standing, after she had fixed firmly in her mind the lengths and diameters of the remaining stems, and the angles and locations of the fresh cuts above the delicate new buds.

"I'm glad. So, are you desperate to start planting?"

"Don't I get to see your sailboat?"

"Of course. You have the choice of a bird's-eye view from the bluff or a close enough to touch view from the dock. The drawback of the close-up view is that the bay—and therefore the boat—is three steep flights of stairs down the bluff. Going down is easy, but coming back up is—"

"I want to touch it!" Alexa interjected swiftly. Three steep flights of stairs were not the slightest deterrent to her. She was healthy, fit, energetic. Besides, as James would discover soon, it was precisely three flights of carved granite stairs from where one parked the car to her cliff-top cottage.

"It's beautiful," Alexa whispered as she delicately touched the shiny teal blue hull of Night Wind, James's sleek, flawlessly maintained twelve-meter yawl.

"Thank you. Have you ever sailed?"

"A few times."

"And for some reason sailing doesn't appeal."

"I like to be able to leave when I've decided the party's over."

"Ah. Some heretic has lured you onto a sailboat in hopes of seducing you."

"Heretic?"

"I'm a sailing purist. Sailing is for sailing." James smiled. "There are other times for seduction."

"So I would be quite safe from seduction on Night Wind?"

"Absolutely."

But would I be safe from seduction at other times? Alexa wondered. She met his smiling sensual dark blue eyes and saw their eloquent answer, an answer she had very much hoped to see.

No, Alexa, you would not—will not—be safe at other times.

They climbed back up the three flights of red-brick steps from the bay to the mansion without breathlessness, and twenty minutes later, as they ascended the three flights of granite to her cottage, Alexa chattered effortlessly.

"Do you know, James," she began, the seriousness of her expression betrayed by her sparkling eyes, "is there a minimum size a place has to be before it can be named?"

"What are you talking about?"

"I think my little tiny cottage needs a grand name. Inverness Minor, or something."

"I see." He laughed, and would have started the search for whimsical suggestions, but they had reached the summit of their climb and all attention was necessarily focused on the dozens and dozens of pots filled with roses. "Alexa . . ."

"There's plenty of room for all of them!"

"Yes," James agreed as he gazed at the many freshly tilled beds. "And it's going to be spectacular, like living in the midst of a bouquet when they bloom, but, Alexa, I think I'd better help you with the planting."

"Oh, no, thank you. I can manage."

"Are you sure?"

"Oh, yes." Alexa turned from his smiling blue eyes and surveyed her tiny estate cluttered with potted roses. It was hopeless, of course, far beyond what she could accomplish by herself, but this was her first garden and she had been looking forward to carefully planning the design and puttering around in the warm, rich soil. When she turned back to him, she lifted her chin defiantly and affirmed with a soft laugh and bright eyes, "Quite sure!"

"OK."

"This does, of course, solve the mystery of why the owner of the nursery has suggested about a hundred times that I just put the roses exactly where I want them and let his crew plant them for me. I'd been wondering why he was so persistent about that."

"Do you think, many hours from now, that you might take him up on the suggestion?"

"Many hours and many sore muscles from now, yes, I think I just might."

"Well, I'll leave you then." His dark blue eyes studied her for a moment and then he added very softly. "There is, however, something about which I have been wondering."

"Oh?" she asked, her shining green eyes telling him that she knew what it was, and that she had been wondering, too.

"This," he whispered as his lips met hers.

"This," she echoed as she welcomed him.

They both had been wondering, and they both had been luxuriating in the gentle seduction, the playful teasing, the tingling anticipation. Both had imagined a warm, wonderful pleasure. *But neither had foreseen the fire.*

The kiss began with soft whispers, but very quickly no more words were possible. The powerful hot rushes of desire were all-consuming . . . demanding, consuming, demanding so very much more than a gently whispered hello.

It was James who stopped the kiss, finally and with great effort. As he pulled away his dark blue eyes met her suddenly surprised emerald ones, and he saw a magnificent desire that eloquently mirrored his own.

"Our dinner reservations are for eight-thirty, so I'll be back to get you at eight."

"You're leaving?"

"Yes. I'm going sailing, and you're planting your garden."

"You're playing with me."

"Oh no, Alexa," James said quietly. "I'm not playing with you."

Had he been playing, had she been any other woman, he would have taken her into her romantic bedroom in the charming cottage and made love to her right then, abandoning his own plans and vanquishing hers. The beautiful eyes that glistened with desire urged him so powerfully to do just that. But James had other memories of her eyes, sparkling with eagerness to create her garden of roses, and he knew how very important those plans were to her.

This afternoon they would pursue their private passions. And tonight, when they both chose, because they both chose, they would make leisurely discoveries about the astonishing passion that was theirs to share.

They dined by candlelight at the Hunt Club and danced on the terrace beneath the moon, seducing each other, savoring the seduction until finally it was she who whispered with a soft trembling laugh that they had to return to her cottage *now*.

The moonlight filtering through the lacy curtains cast her romantic bedroom in pale, misty gold. With another man, Alexa would have pulled the opaque layer of drapes and enveloped the room in protective darkness. But James's kiss and the talented hands that undressed her so gently swept away all thought, and she forgot to hide herself in the familiar shadows she preferred when making love. She was unashamed of her flawless body, of course. She knew well the silky, provocative perfection of her full breasts, her softly curving hips, her sleek flat stomach, and her long tapered legs.

The shadows weren't for her perfect body—they were for her eyes. Unshadowed, her eyes might reveal what she so often felt: *annoyance*, because she saw conquest blended with desire; *disappointment*, because the tingling sensations that quivered within her—soft, delicate whispers that teased and beckoned—were lost in the roaring thunder of her lover's passion; and finally *anger*, because her lovers, who knew nothing of her—and wouldn't love her if they did!—made breathless, impassioned confessions of love.

The whispers of desire awakened by James's tender touch made Alexa forget entirely about closing the drapes. He undressed her, lingering over each new discovery, kissing a tender hello to each new place until her soft laughter urged him to continue his sensual exploration and make even more intimate discoveries. James undressed Alexa, and then she undressed him, lingeringly and tenderly, too, until his soft sighs became as urgent for more intimacy as hers had been.

Then they were together, amidst a cool soft cotton rose garden designed by Laura Ashley, and . . .

"I need you."

"Yes," she whispered with quiet joy, needing him, wanting him, too.

James held her moonlit gaze as she welcomed him, and in the dark blue eyes she saw only desire, not conquest. And she heard, in his soft urgent whispers, only astonished truths about their passion not false promises of love. And she felt at last the magnificence of her own quivering desires, because they were not lost now, as they had always been lost before, but found, discovered, and nurtured so gently, so patiently by him.

"Alexa," he whispered when it was time, for both of them. *"Alexandra."*

"Hi." The moonlit tangle of silky gold was a wonderful symbol of their loving, but James gently parted it now because he wanted to see her eyes again.

"Hi."

"That was very nice," he whispered softly.

"Yes."

"Not trivial."

"No," Alexa agreed softly. Not trivial at all. "Very nice."

Nice, she mused, suddenly liking a word which had always before felt a little bland. If you can't say something nice, don't say anything, wise adults had always admonished; and since then pronouncing something "nice" had always seemed like damning with the faintest of praise. But "nice" sounded neither bland nor damning when whispered softly by James's talented lips. It sounded gentle and tender and special, and so much better than the falsehoods of love usually spoken to her in the awkward and disappointing moments after making love. Now, with James, those moments felt wonderful, so comfortable, so honest, so *nice* . . . until his handsome face became very serious.

Oh, James, don't trivialize this by telling me lies of love! Especially since we both know you don't even *believe* in it.

"What?" she demanded, surprising him with the sudden sharpness of her tone.

"You know the trouble with being seduced in your own bed, don't you?"

"No."

"It's the same as your problem with sailing. You can't leave when you decide the party's over."

"Oh," she whispered quietly as grateful relief swept through her. He wasn't going to tell her lies of love. He was simply, once again, giving her choices and placing value on what was important to her. He had been right to leave her to her garden this afternoon. And now . . . did James know that she always wanted her lovers to leave, preferring solitude to the paradoxical loneliness she felt when they stayed? Yes, he obviously knew that. Because he usually preferred solitude, too? Yes, she realized, but tonight was different . . . for both of them. Tonight he wasn't choosing to leave. He was asking to stay—if she wanted him to.

"I'm beginning to think that you're a very nice man," she said softly. Very nice, she thought, very gentle, very tender, very special.

"Just beginning? I decided that about you the moment we met."

Oh, no, James, I'm not nice! The thought came swiftly, by ancient reflex, an irrefutable truth. Should she share that truth with him? Should she warn him away? As she looked at the dark blue eyes that wanted to know why his words had caused her to frown, she realized that James Sterling needed no warning. He was in complete control, quite capable of making his own decisions, quite immune to love, and quite safe from being hurt, especially by her. James was in no danger. But she was in danger from him, from the compelling demands of their passion, and from the compelling demands of the blue eyes that somehow seduced her into telling truths about herself.

"Alexa?"

"I'd like you to stay."

"Good. I'd like to. Did you make a decision about the party?"

"The party?"

"Is it over?" James saw in her smiling emerald eyes that it wasn't over and gently drew her back to him.

"Not over," she whispered as her lips met his. The magnificent sensations rushed forward boldly now, eager and brave, because now there was a thrilling memory, not simply a trembling hope.

"RoseCliff."

"What did you . . .?"

"RoseCliff."

"Oh," she breathed with sudden comprehension. "The name for my tiny little estate. I like it."

"Just a suggestion. Something to think about," he murmured between hungry kisses, "some other time."

"Some other time, yes, but I like it," she murmured back. Then, just before her mouth acceded to the wonderful sensations that commanded her to stop speaking and just kiss him, she embellished softly, "It's very nice."

CHAPTER FIVE

*A*lexa's heart quickened in delicious anticipation as the elevator carried her in swift silence from the building's marble lobby to the Madison Avenue penthouse offices of James Sterling, Attorney at Law. He had been in Tokyo for the past twelve days, and the separation had been much more than just the disruption of their magnificent passion. The combination of their busy schedules and the time zone change conspired to prevent the luxury of the wonderful late-night phone calls that had become an important part of their relationship whenever he was away; the long, honest conversations that made them feel as if they had known and cared about each other forever . . . instead of for only seven weeks.

James had been back since noon, and now it was after six, but she had stayed away until now, knowing he needed time to work his way through the most important calls of the past twelve days, and wanting, when at last she saw him, to have him all to herself, his attention wholly concentrated on her.

She was so greedy for him! She wanted all of him, all at once, his eyes, his smile, his voice, his touch. She wanted to hear all the details of his successful negotiations in Japan, and she wanted to tell him, because he would want to know, the details of the last twelve days of her life, too. She wanted to laugh and talk and share . . .

But, she admitted to herself as she left the elevator and walked along the plush carpet toward his private office, right now what she wanted most was to see dark blue eyes that were happy to see her . . . and to feel talented fingers gently caress her skin . . . and to hear soft sighs of pleasure as he undressed her and discovered anew the silkiness of her perfect body.

The door to his office was ajar, for her. Without needing to open it further, she could see him seated at his desk. James sensed her presence immediately and rose to greet her.

"Hello there," he said softly, his voice full of welcome and promise.

"Hello." She leaned provocatively against the door jamb and whispered seductively, "Mr. Sterling, if you don't negotiate a swift, satisfying merger with me right now I'll—"

"Alexa," he interjected with a soft laugh. Then he had reached her, and opening the door to reveal more of the spacious office, he said, "I'd like you to meet Robert McAllister."

"Oh!" Had the man who had unwittingly overheard her seductive command been any other man on earth, Alexa could and would have artfully concealed her embarrassed surprise by smiling at him with an expression of pure innocence. But the man was Robert McAllister, and her cheeks flushed pink and her voice bristled instead of purred, "Senator McAllister."

"Ms. Taylor," Robert countered lightly, although he stiffened at her tone and at the magnificent emerald eyes that greeted him as if he had done something quite unforgivable . . . something far more serious than inadvertently preempting her passionate reunion with James.

"Robert tells me that you have never met," James said calmly, his dark blue eyes gazing questioningly at her.

"No. That's right. We haven't," Alexa replied.

Of course we haven't, she thought. Senator and Mrs. Robert McAllister had been conspicuously absent from "When You Wish Upon A Star"—the annual Christmas gala hosted by the producers and cast of *Pennsylvania Avenue*. In only three years, the celebrity gala benefitting children with cancer had become one of Washington's most successful fund-raisers. "When You Wish Upon A Star" received the enthusiastic support of the capital's brightest stars, political and otherwise. *All* the brightest stars, *except* the brightest one of all—Senator Robert McAllister.

The Senator from Virginia had been conspicuously absent from the Christmas gala, and he had been conspicuously absent, too, from the set of *Pennsylvania Avenue*. Virtually every other senator in Washington had dropped by the set at least once—to observe or kibitz or simply meet her—but Robert never had. Alexa believed, of course, that an elected official charged with the solemn task of running the government *should* have better things to do with his time than flirt with her. But that was not, she knew, the reason Robert McAllister had stayed away. No, he had stayed away from the set of *Pennsylvania Avenue* for the same reason he had never attended the celebrity gala—by careful design, to avoid her.

Now, as she felt the not-so-subtle heat of James's stare, she defiantly searched Robert's handsome face for proof that he had been assiduously avoiding her. But the dark brown eyes that met hers were steady, infuriatingly, *arrogantly* unflickering—his contempt for her quite hidden. Of course, she thought, Robert McAllister is a master politician, and therefore, perhaps even better at acting than I.

"Alexa, this is Robert," James spoke quietly, and for the first time ever she heard a few slivers of the famous Sterling ice.

"I'm delighted to meet you, Robert." She forced a soft purr into her voice and smiled a beautiful smile. "I didn't realize that you and James knew each other."

"We were in law school together."

"Oh, I see." Her beautiful smile held, even though the news was bad. She had assumed Robert had been seeing James on business, or politics. But this was worse. They were friends.

"My wife and I are in town for the weekend. We have a commitment for Saturday evening, but hoped that you and James would be able to join us for dinner tomorrow." Robert expected a swift yes. He had already learned from James that she didn't have a performance scheduled, and that James doubted she had made other plans for them. But Alexa didn't reply with a swift yes. Instead, she seemed at a loss, a little confused, as if searching for an excuse and finding none. As soon as he realized she was struggling, he helped her by offering quietly, "Of course, this is all very last minute. You probably have a conflict."

Just that I have no wish in the world to see your wife, Alexa thought. Was it possible that Robert really didn't know? Was it possible that the reason he never visited the set really was because he did have better things to do? It *was* possible, Alexa supposed, although she found it a bit surprising that Hillary would not have told her husband of their enmity. But, perhaps she hadn't. Perhaps she had simply made certain that she and Robert always had other "A-list" parties to attend on the evening of the Christmas gala.

How Alexa needed a party now, a legitimate excuse, or at least a gracious and convincing lie. But she had become less good at lying since James.

"My sister's twenty-first birthday is this weekend," she murmured finally. It was the truth, of course, but it sounded very feeble nonetheless.

"Let me give you a call later, Robert," James intervened quietly.

"OK. Good. I'd better be going. It was nice meeting you, Alexa."

"It was nice meeting you, too, Robert."

Alexa remained in the office while James walked Robert to the elevator. When he returned, he found her gazing out the window at the tangle of traffic thirty floors below. Her eyes were cast down, fixed on the snarl below, rather than straight ahead at the magnificent twilight. It was unlike Alexa to seek turmoil over beauty; but this time the turmoil had found her, an unwelcome visitor, and she was very far away. James waited for her to become aware that he had returned. When she didn't, he finally spoke, startling her even though his voice was quiet and controlled.

"I didn't realize you were so political, Alexa. And frankly if I'd had to guess about your politics, I would have imagined they would have been quite similar to Robert's."

"It has nothing to do with politics."

"You can't be annoyed that he overheard your remark."

"No," Alexa admitted softly. After a moment she found the courage to turn from the window to him. And when she did she saw what she had always feared the most . . . *disappointment*. She had behaved badly, rudely, to his friend, and James was disappointed in her.

"What then?"

"Robert's wife and I aren't terribly close."

"You've had a run-in with Hillary in Washington?" He could envision it happening, a clash of Hillary's patrician haughtiness and Alexa's intolerance of same, but it surprised him that such an encounter would bother Alexa for long. Wouldn't she simply dismiss it, and Hillary McAllister, with a defiant toss of her shimmering golden mane?

"A run-in, yes, but not in Washington. I haven't even seen Hillary for eight years, not since high school."

"It's hard for me to imagine how you and Hillary were at the same high school."

"We probably *shouldn't* have been—that was certainly Hillary Samantha Ballinger's view. But, for one glorious year, the poor country girl from Kansas and the rich daughter of the Governor of Texas were classmates. It was on her turf, in Dallas, and at Ballinger Academy. You've heard of Ballinger, haven't you? It's the exclusive, private school founded by Hillary's grandfather so that she and the heirs and heiresses of Dallas wouldn't have to mingle with the commoners."

"This is all about some high school rivalry?"

"It was deeper than that."

"But surely something you've long since outgrown," James offered quietly, although the bitterness in her voice and her lovely troubled eyes told him eloquently that the ancient enmity was far from over. It wasn't over, whatever it was, but it should be. They had been teenaged girls then, after all, and now they were grown women. "Alexa, Robert is a very good friend. I would like to have dinner with him and Hillary and you tomorrow night."

"Couldn't you go by yourself?"

"Not without a good reason."

"I thought I could always just say no."

"Not this time."

Alexa looked into the inscrutable blue eyes of the master negotiator, the man whose great success was in part his willingness to walk away from any deal if it didn't meet his high expectations.

"Is this the deal breaker, James?" she asked softly. If I don't go to dinner tomorrow night with my ancient enemy are we—whatever "we" are—over? Alexa didn't know what "they" were, but she knew she would miss him terribly if he suddenly vanished from her life. Would James miss me, too? she wondered. As she searched for the answer in his unrevealing eyes, and saw only more layers of the famous iciness, she thought sadly, Perhaps he really could simply walk away. Perhaps he could deliver the celebrated line without a flicker of regret, Frankly, my dear, I don't give a damn.

"Alexa," James began gently without answering her question. "Why don't you tell me about you and Hillary?"

About you and Hillary. As the words echoed in Alexa's mind, she realized that the story wasn't really about Hillary at all. It was about *her* . . . her failures, her unworthiness, her cruelty. Hillary had simply been a mirror, reflecting back with vivid clarity Alexa's own terrible flaws. Mirror, Mirror, on the wall, who's the cruelest of them all?

"Alexa?" James repeated softly, suddenly worried by the immense sadness in her eyes. Sadness and such uncertainty, as if she believed that if she allowed him this rare glimpse into a most private place in her heart, he wouldn't like what he saw. Didn't she know? He trusted his instincts about her, but she apparently didn't have the same faith in herself. "I need to speak with a client in San Francisco before I can call it a day. It's not confidential, so you needn't leave. Have a seat on the couch. Then, as soon as I'm done, why don't we go to your apartment and talk?"

It was a question, posed gently, but Alexa had already learned that this time she couldn't just say no. She would have to tell James the dark truths about herself, the "niceness" that wasn't really there at all, the awful emotions that had surfaced from beneath the glittering sunny gold almost twenty-one years ago, the moment she first saw her little sister . . .

"She's not my sister," she announced with familiar Alexa confidence as her eyes fell on the tiny infant so lovingly cradled in her mother's arms.

Her voice was confident, but already her small body trembled with bewildering emotions. The new and powerful emotions had begun the instant she had seen her parents gaze with loving wonder at Catherine, the same loving wonder with which they had only, and always before, gazed at her.

And now, as she made her pronouncement, there was something else in Jane and Alexander's eyes, something for her, something she had never seen before—worry, and then even worse, *disappointment.*

The disappointment lasted only a moment. But to six-year-old Alexa it felt like forever, never to be forgotten—and never, *please*, to be repeated—and in that moment the pure golden joy that had lived within her was irreparably tarnished. In her heart, she was changed forever, so wary, so wise, but the gifted actress she became on that day bravely acted the storm clouds away. She would be sunny and golden and charming again, *always*, because she so desperately needed to have whatever share of her parents' love could be hers. She needed so desperately never again to disappoint.

Alexa shone as brightly as before, but now the brilliance was artificial; and, like the glaring stage lights she would come to know so well, her brilliance was blinding, preventing with its stunning dazzle any glimpse into the darkness that lay beyond. She permitted no glimpses into the dark shadows of her young heart, but she knew very well what lurked there: bewildering monsters over which she had no control—jealousy, cruelty, hatred. The hatred for Catherine began the instant she saw her, and as her baby sister grew so did Alexa's hatred for her. Catherine was perfect, *perfect*, and Alexa knew only too well her own deep and disappointing flaws.

Even as a tiny baby, Catherine never cried; she just smiled an enchanting Mona Lisa smile. And her greatest joy, discovered long before she could walk or talk, was to sit on Alexander's lap as he played the piano, her huge blue eyes gazing intently as her father's talented fingers glided over the keys. She was completely mesmerized by the music her parents loved so much, but which had never held any allure for her older sister. Alexa had always been far too active to simply listen, preferring to dance and twirl and perform instead.

But Catherine, perfect Catherine, could quietly and joyfully listen to music forever.

"I hate you," Alexa whispered to her little sister. Even though Catherine was too young to understand the meaning of the words, a dark monster within Alexa compelled her to hiss them, a sinister mantra, over and over. The cruel words drew no response from Catherine, and Alexa *needed* a response. She needed proof that the baby wasn't perfect. If she could make Catherine cry . . .

Eight-year-old Alexa pinched herself first, finding a pinch that could make *her* cry and would surely bring tears of pain to a two-year-old. But when her fingers dug into Catherine's velvet soft forearm, not a tear welled in the sapphire blue eyes. The innocent eyes only widened, as if bewildered by what her older sister was doing, and then they softened with something that was even worse . . . *forgiveness*.

After that day, Alexa simply ignored Catherine altogether, as if she had no little sister at all.

Catherine Alexandra Taylor was three when she first touched her small fingers to the keys of her father's piano. From the very first moment, she *played*; and, from the very first moment, the complexity of what she played was limited only by the reach of her tiny fingers, not by the breadth of her talent.

Like her older sister, Catherine's talent was extraordinary; but unlike Alexa, who performed and dazzled for approval and admiration, she performed simply to share the gift for which she was as grateful and astonished as those who listened. She performed without nervousness, even in competition, happily lost in the evocative beauty of the music. Catherine performed to share, not to win, but, from the very beginning, she almost always won.

Catherine's extraordinary talent resulted in an extraordinary offer to her and her family when she was twelve. The world-renowned Conservatory in Dallas wanted her as a pupil. All expenses would be covered, including housing for the entire family; and Alexander, who had been Catherine's only music teacher, would be welcome to participate in the continued instruction of his gifted daughter, as well as the other students at the Conservatory; and eighteen-year-old Alexa would attend the prestigious Ballinger Academy for her final year of high school.

Alexa was immediately enthusiastic about the move. She had no nostalgia for Topeka, and no qualms whatsoever about being separated from her lifelong friends. Her "friends" were, and always had been, simply an entourage of admirers, not confidants. No friendships bound Alexa to Topeka, nor were there challenges still to be conquered. She had already won all there was to win—the admiration of her teachers and classmates . . . any and every boy she ever wanted . . . the leading role in all the school plays.

Alexa's enthusiasm swayed the three less enthusiastic Taylors. It would be good for Catherine to study at the Conservatory, of course, and the move wasn't irreversible. Since the Conservatory was providing housing, they didn't have to sell their small farmhouse in Topeka. They could return to Kansas whenever they chose.

Alexa decided that for her persona at elite Ballinger's she would be a surfer girl from Malibu, the wild daughter of a famous movie mogul who had been banished to the exclusive school for the rich and privileged because of some undisclosed—and deliciously daring—indiscretion. She created the new image because she was an actress—*and because it was better, always, not to be the real Alexa*—not because she was ashamed of her heritage. She was ashamed of herself, but never, ever, was she ashamed of her parents or her modest upbringing. She loved her parents deeply. It was *she* who had disappointed *them*, not the opposite. And who could blame them for cherishing the always perfect Catherine?

Alexa was proud of her musician father and artist mother, and it had never mattered at all that they weren't rich. She was proud, not ashamed.

Until Hillary Samantha Ballinger tried to make her feel ashamed.

Hillary discovered the truth about Alexa's real identity and promptly exposed her as a wanton liar. "I'm an actress!" Alexa countered defiantly, aching at the implication, so eloquently transmitted by the haughty arch of Hillary's patrician eyebrow, that she was obviously ashamed of her family. Who wouldn't be? Hillary's knowing look implied. Who wouldn't want to hide a past completely devoid of wealth, breeding, and class? Alexandra Taylor was very *very* common, Hillary warned her wellborn friends, and she should, therefore, be totally ignored.

But Hillary's warning to the other heirs and heiresses came too late. Alexa had instantly intrigued the other students, and now her undaunted dazzle in the face of Hillary's viciousness caused new rounds of admiration. Alexa glittered still, her confidence apparently unwavering, even though Hillary's words had wounded deeply.

Perfectly mimicking Hillary's well-bred Southern accent, Alexa artfully turned the tables on her, exposing the pretentious pettiness with wide, innocent, emerald eyes, until even those most loyal to Hillary were enchanted. The girls shifted allegiance cautiously, lured by Alexa's dazzle and courage but worried about betraying the powerful Hillary. The boys—including Hillary's longtime boyfriend—defected far more swiftly and without a flicker of fear. For years, Hillary had been a distant object of desire, a beautiful statue atop a marble pedestal, perched far above the admiring eyes; for years, her remoteness had given her a magical allure. But now here was Alexa. And, the boys discovered, Alexa wasn't remote at all, and they discovered too, her allure was even more magical. She was warm, not haughty, and she made them feel wonderful, special, *important* with just the caress of her beautiful smile.

Alexa was terribly popular, and terribly lonely. But, at long last, because of Hillary, the monsters that lurked in the shadows of her heart were allowed to come out to play; at long last, because of Hillary, she was finally able to free some of the hatefulness that dwelled within her.

Hillary Samantha Ballinger was a most worthy opponent. She was deserving of Alexa's monsters, of course, and she was well-armed with her own arsenal of unkind and hateful emotions. Hillary began the war, but Alexa promptly replied, and as the school year progressed the war raged on, bitter but fair.

Until, as in all wars, an innocent victim was claimed.

It was late April. Jane and Alexander had returned to Topeka to visit an ill friend, leaving Alexa in charge of her little sister. It was a simple task: twelve-year-old Catherine was entirely self-sufficient. What Catherine did after all—*all that she did*—was sit at her piano from dawn until dusk, happily lost in her magnificent music. Lost, and safe? Yes . . . unless her happy oblivion prevented her from noticing that the house was on fire or that an axe murderer had broken in and was towering over her, ready to strike.

Saturday came, and Jane and Alexander were still away, and Alexa wanted to go to the polo match between Ballinger and Highland Park. She didn't want her little sister to accompany her, but she couldn't leave Catherine alone because her parents had given her a solemn responsibility and *what if?* So, they went together, arriving at the polo field just as Hillary and three still loyal friends emerged from a silver BMW. Alexa sighed when she saw her enemy. In only six weeks, school would be out, the war would be over, and they would never see each other again. She had been hoping to simply avoid Hillary for these final six weeks. But now here they were, and because she knew Hillary wouldn't pass up the opportunity to say something derisive, Alexa began to summon the energy to cheerfully and cleverly counter whatever slur Hillary tossed her way.

"Well, well. If it isn't the white trash whore from Kansas."

For a stunned moment, Alexa simply stared. Hillary's stinging insult had far more venom than usual. She would have to dig very deep to find just the right reply. As she was searching, another voice broke the stunned silence.

"How dare you say that to my sister!" The brave words came from shy and timid Catherine. Catherine . . . who had been so happy to be included in the plans of the older sister she loved and admired *so much*, but to whom she had not found the courage to say one word during the long drive to the polo field.

As Hillary turned in the direction of the new voice, shifting her icy glare from Alexa to Catherine, her iciness melted into pleasure, perverse joy, as she gazed at the impossibly short hair, the impossibly earnest blue eyes, and the trembling young lips. Who was this unstylish little girl who was so obviously terrified of her own bravery? Was this vision in a rumpled sweatshirt and baggy blue jeans the virtuoso? Could this really be the gifted little sister who was the reason the very much hated Alexa Taylor had descended on her life?

"*What*—pardon me, who—is this?" Hillary queried, staring at Catherine and then glancing to her friends as if so bewildered that she was turning to them for enlightenment. Finally, she stared evenly at Alexa and ventured, "Your little brother? How embarrassing for you, Alexa. I honestly see no hope of this ugly duckling ever becoming a swan."

Alexa might have struck Hillary, might have strangled her, but she sensed the tremor of pain beside her as Hillary's cruel words found their mark deep inside her little sister. Alexa felt the pain and saw the tears in the magnificent sapphire eyes. Tears in Catherine's eyes! Catherine who never cried! Catherine who felt no pain! Catherine whom Alexa herself had once wanted to hurt . . .

Now Catherine *was* hurt, and it was Alexa's heart that screamed with pain. How could she have ever wanted to hurt the little sister who had so swiftly and so bravely come to her defense? Please, please, please, never know that I hated you. Please never remember that I tried to hurt you. Please forgive me . . . again.

As Alexa curled her arms around the little sister whom she had not touched for ten years, she felt Catherine's trembling pain and quivering fright. She tightened her grip and whispered softly, "C'mon, Cat, we're leaving. You are far too good to be anywhere near these people."

When they reached the car, they sat inside, facing each other, and talked for the first time in their lives.

"What she said wasn't true, Cat," Alexa said quietly.

"I know, but how could she have said it about you anyway?"

"Oh," Alexa answered with soft surprise. "I meant what she said about you wasn't true. Not a word of it. First of all, I'm very proud that you're my little sister. And second, there's no doubt in the world that you're a girl, not a boy. And third, there's also no doubt that you're very beautiful."

There was no doubt in Alexa's mind that Catherine was very beautiful. True, her hair was quite short, a shiny black velvet cap, but the functional style simply augmented her huge blue eyes. And true, she was a little plump, but, Alexa thought, the soft layer of luxuriant plumpness sent a rich bountiful message of radiant health. Catherine's life was her music. She had probably never even thought about her looks until now, as Hillary's cruel words forced her to. But the truth was that she was a very beautiful little girl. And one day, Alexa knew, whether Catherine thought about it or not, she would be a very beautiful woman.

"Oh, no, Alexa. You're the beautiful one," Catherine said with quiet pride for her older sister.

"Well, then, we both are. Everything Hillary said about you was a lie, Cat, and so was everything she said about me." Alexa wondered if her innocent little sister even knew the meaning of the word "whore." She hoped not. "White trash" was bad enough. And both, of course, were untrue. True, she hadn't been a virgin since a moonlit summer night in a cornfield in Kansas when she was sixteen; but even though she had enchanted the boys at Ballinger's, she had slept with none of them. She enchanted so artfully that she had yet to be accused even of being a tease, much less a *whore*. "Everything."

"I know," Catherine said. Then she dismissed Hillary Ballinger altogether and summoned the courage to talk to her big sister about something very important. "You called me Cat?"

"That's my nickname for you," Alexa admitted softly. The little sister she had ignored all these years nonetheless had a nickname. There was no affection associated with the name, quite the opposite; the girlhood discovery was a cloying reminder of their destiny. "It's your initials, of course, and mine are ACT. Mom and Dad must have known from the moment they named us that I would be an actress and you would be a kitten on the keys."

Alexa smiled, but her emotions swept her to all the sleepless nights, years before, that she had spent wondering how different her life might have been had she been Catherine Alexandra not Alexandra Catherine. Had she been CAT, would she have possessed the magical gifts of music so important to her parents?

"Cat," Catherine whispered, her sapphire eyes lighting with a deep joy, so happy that Alexa had a private nickname for her, so happy that Alexa had ever even *thought* about her.

"Do you like it?"

"Oh yes!"

Cat wasn't really right for Catherine, Jane and Alexander decided privately. The name would have been far better for sleek Alexa with her magnificent cat-like grace and appraising emerald eyes. But they embraced the nickname joyfully, because Cat did, and because while they had been away something wonderful had happened. How long they had waited, in silent helpless anguish, for their lovely daughters to become sisters.

Only six weeks remained until Alexa moved to New York, and the rest of the Taylor family returned to Topeka, but during those weeks the sisters spent as much time as they could together. It was the most fragile of beginnings, the delicate meeting of strangers who were bonded by little more than a wish from the heart to become friends. Alexa would invite Cat into her bedroom, and Cat would sit on the bed while Alexa roamed around, chattering on and on about nothing, and Cat would listen intently, mesmerized by her older sister's effortless flow of clever, lively, interesting words. Mostly Cat simply listened, but on rare occasions she conquered her shyness; and whenever she did, Alexa discovered, her little sister always spoke with unaffected and uncluttered honesty . . . and remarkable wisdom.

"I think we should forgive Hillary," she suggested quietly a week before school was over.

"You're kidding," Alexa said to the earnest sapphire eyes that never kidded. "No way, Cat. Never!"

"We should feel sorry for her, Alexa."

"Sorry?"

"Yes. Sorry that she needs to be so cruel. She must be very unhappy to be so cruel."

Alexa gazed at Cat, searching her solemn young face for some proof that her little sister was talking about *her*, forgiving *her*, not Hillary. But Alexa saw no hidden messages in the honest blue eyes. She wondered for a moment if she should confess anyway, You're right, Cat. Hillary must be very unhappy to be so cruel. Just as I was so terribly unhappy when I was cruel to you. Hillary and I are alike, you see. We need to be adored and admired. And when our domain is threatened dark monsters lunge up from our hearts to devour those who threaten us.

But Alexa didn't confess to Cat, nor did she ever forgive Hillary. She simply tried to forget all about Hillary Samantha Ballinger . . . because remembering her enemy, her most worthy opponent, was like remembering the ugliest part of herself, the part she wanted so desperately to believe no longer existed.

But now Hillary was married to a man who was James's very good friend. And Alexa realized that her reason for not wanting to see Hillary was simply fear that in seeing her ancient enemy she would see again her own cruel reflection.

Mirror, mirror . . .

But that old Alexa was gone, wasn't she? She hoped so, but she didn't know. She had spent so very little time with the real Alexa, immersing herself instead in roles of women to be admired and avoiding altogether the treacherous search for the monsters that might be lingering still in the shadowy places of her heart. Alexa didn't know if the monsters were gone, but since her friendship with James, she felt so hopeful. He knew her far better than she had ever before allowed herself to be known, and she was almost beginning to believe in the "niceness" he kept insisting she possessed.

James likes you because he doesn't know you! The harsh reminder came from nowhere, a breath of angry fire from a never-to-be-forgotten monster. Alexa sighed softly, a sad acceptance of her fate. She would have to tell him everything, and it might be more truth than he would want to know. But, a whisper of defiant hope argued, if you can confess to James, who is your friend, then maybe one day you can confess what you must—to banish the monsters forever—to your little sister.

James had watched Alexa while he made his business call to San Francisco, and he had seen the panorama of emotions that touched her beautiful face. When the call ended, he watched still, reluctant to interrupt her obviously so important emotional journey. But when she gave a soft resigned sigh, and he saw her lovely face fill with immense sadness and loss, he could bear watching no more. He hated her anguish, but he hated even more that it had been there all along, hidden, lurking, threatening. It would help her to tell him, wouldn't it?

He walked across the plush carpeting, and when she felt his shadow and she looked up into his gentle eyes, he said softly, "Let's go, sweetheart."

CHAPTER SIX

"*This* is new," James said quietly when he saw the Steinway baby grand piano in the living room of her apartment. His quiet words broke the silence that had travelled with them from his office.

"I thought it would be much safer for Cat to have a piano here. This way she won't have to go to the music rooms at Juilliard every time she wants to play." Alexa could imagine her little sister wandering around Manhattan at all hours, lured to a distant piano by the music she loved, oblivious of the sinister dangers of the city. "I'm assuming this apartment is so solidly built that she can play all night without disturbing anyone, but maybe you could help me test that sometime? If you could play 'Chopsticks' or something while I visit my neighbors?"

"Sure." After a moment, he added softly, "This is very nice of you."

Alexa gave an uncertain shrug and crossed the room to the piano. She ran her long tapered fingers over the polished wood surface and then onto the ivory and ebony keys, touching softly and evoking the rich clear tones.

"I haven't always been very nice to Cat," she confessed to the keyboard.

"But she's very important to you."

"Yes. She is."

"Tell me."

James extended a hand to her, an invitation to be in a safe place while she shared her darkest secrets. But Alexa didn't move to him. Instead, she sat on the piano bench, surprised by the unyielding hardness of the place Cat chose most often to be. Then she told him the story of the Taylor sisters, from the very beginning, the instant she first saw Cat, and with unyielding hardness toward herself, she confessed her flawed emotions and unforgivable crimes.

"Cat was a perfect baby. She was always so calm, so serene, so regal—just like a princess. She never even cried."

"Surely she cried," James countered gently, interrupting for the first time. He had wanted to interrupt Alexa's anguished words before, but he knew she wouldn't listen to his gentle reassurances until she had told him all the truths. He interrupted now because her breathless words of self-recrimination halted for a moment, and because he wanted to impose some reality on the too-perfect-to-be-real portrait she was painting of her baby sister. "All babies cry, Alexa."

"Not Cat. Really, James, she *never* cried." Alexa dug her long tapered fingers into her palms, a physical reminder of the pain she had once inflicted on her baby sister. "Even though I tried to make her cry."

"By telling her you hated her. But, Alexa, she was very young then, far too young to understand or remember."

"Oh, I hope that's true," Alexa whispered softly. How she wished she knew that Cat remembered nothing! Nothing, especially not . . . "I tried to hurt her once, physically, to make her cry. I guess I desperately needed proof that she wasn't perfect."

"How did you try to hurt her?" James asked calmly, even though a sudden worry swept through him as he gazed at her tormented face. Her emerald eyes were dark now, almost black, and the soft, intriguing ripples of vulnerability had become currents, strong, turbulent, disturbing. Until that moment it hadn't occurred to him that she might actually have done something truly unspeakable, a crime to match the grim anguish on her beautiful face. "Tell me, Alexa. How?"

"By pinching her. The pinch wasn't hard enough to leave marks, of course, but it should have made a two-year-old cry. I tested the pinch on myself, and it would have made me cry. But Cat didn't cry. She just stared at me with huge blue eyes, bewildered and yet forgiving."

Alexa stared at the hands knotted in her lap, unable to look at him, wondering if she would hear his footfalls on the plush carpet as he left. No, she wouldn't, because the thundering of the blood pulsing through her brain was far too loud. She wouldn't hear him leave, but when she found the courage, finally, to look up, he would be gone.

"That's all?" James asked gently, realizing that it was, and realizing, too, that to lovely Alexa it truly felt like a crime of immense proportion.

"*All?*" she echoed, startled into looking up then, and even more startled by what she saw in the dark blue eyes—gentleness, not disappointment. "Isn't that enough? Doesn't that seem unforgivably cruel?"

"It seems like sibling rivalry, probably a fairly mild case. You're going to have to tell me much more, Alexa, if you want to convince me that you were a cruel little girl."

"There isn't more. I simply ignored her after that."

"Did that bother her?"

"Oh, no, I don't think so. Why would it? Her life was bountiful, filled to overflowing with her music and our parents' love."

"So, once upon a time, you were very jealous of your baby sister. You were a little girl then, too, remember? And you had been an adored only child for six years. It makes perfect sense. Besides, Alexa, it feels like very old history to me. I don't hear jealousy or hatred when you talk about Cat now. I just hear pride and love." And such uncertainty.

"I am proud of Cat and I do love her . . . even though we barely know each other."

"Which means that somewhere along the line something changed?"

"Yes." Alexa gave a bewildered shake of her head as she remembered what—who—was responsible for the change.

"What happened?"

"Hillary Samantha Ballinger happened."

"Oh?"

"From the moment I arrived at Ballinger's Hillary made it abundantly clear to everyone that I wasn't good enough for her or her school."

"I see," James answered quietly. As a grown woman, and especially as Robert's wife, Hillary had learned to hide her disdain for those she considered to be beneath her. But he could well imagine the teenaged Hillary's unconcealed contempt for the beautiful and flamboyant country girl from Kansas; just as he could well imagine Alexa's hurt.

"I was definitely not good enough for Hillary, but her friends found me to be quite acceptable—including her boyfriend."

"You stole Hillary's boyfriend from her?"

"It wasn't grand theft, James! He came to me willingly, *enthusiastically*."

"And after you bewitched him away from Hillary? Was he a prize worth having?"

"Of course not. He had fallen for Hillary, after all, which meant his judgment and values were fatally flawed."

"So, it was just a game."

"No, James, it was just a war."

Alexa told him then about the Saturday afternoon in April at the polo field . . .

"Hillary really called you a 'white trash whore'?" he asked, beginning to truly comprehend the magnitude of the enmity between the heiress and the country girl.

"She really did. I don't know how much of it Cat understood, but she sprung to my defense like a tiny brave terrier against a tigress."

"And what did you do?"

"I put my arms around the little sister I hadn't touched for ten years and we went home."

"Why don't I put my arms around you now?" he suggested gently as he began to walk toward her. Alexa met him halfway, so grateful that he still wanted her in his arms.

"Thank you."

"My pleasure," he murmured into her silky golden hair. After a moment, he guided her to the couch and encouraged her to finish her story of the Taylor sisters. "And after that you and Cat became friends?"

"I don't know, James," she answered softly. "The beginning of friends, I think, at least that's my memory of the six weeks between that April afternoon and when I moved to New York. Since then we've seen very little of each other—brief visits at Christmas and holidays—and each time there have been so many changes in our lives since the last time that we never quite seem to catch up, much less go on. In the past eight years Cat has grown from a little girl to a young woman, and I . . ."

"You've become a superstar. Maybe Cat is a little star-struck."

"Oh, no. Why would she be? Her accomplishments are already so much greater than mine."

"How can you say that?"

"Because it's true! Admittedly, my career's higher profile, my successes more public, but . . . I told you about the competitions she's won, and the concert tour and album, and that she's being managed by Fordyce, the top performing arts agency. Cat's accomplishments *are* greater, James, but it's true, I guess, that it's my celebrity that has gotten in the way. During my trips home to Topeka, friends and neighbors are constantly dropping by and when I've tried to visit Cat at Oberlin, there's always been a steady stream of her classmates wanting to meet me."

"Which is why you're looking forward to her move to New York? Because celebrities are virtually ignored here?"

"Yes. That, and because for the first time in our lives I feel that Cat and I are the same age. During childhood, six years seems like a generation gap, but now we're both grown-up, away from home, pursuing our careers." When she spoke again her voice was filled with hope, "I have this fantasy that even though she'll be here, and I'll be in Washington, we'll make an effort to see each other. You know, I'll fly up for Sunday brunch at the Plaza, or she'll fly down for a weekend at Rose-Cliff, something like that." She shrugged softly. "Just a sisterly fantasy."

"But something that Cat obviously wants, too."

"No. Cat *needs* to be in New York, and it's logical for her to stay in my otherwise vacant apartment for the six months that she'll be here. That's all."

As James gazed at her hopeful, yet uncertain, emerald eyes, he wished he could reassure her that Cat was as eager to be sisters as she. But because he had no way of knowing, he knew such a reassurance would sound false.

"Is this Saturday really Cat's twenty-first birthday?" he asked finally, remembering Alexa's mumbled excuse to Robert.

"Yes."

"Are you braving the fans and visiting her at Oberlin?"

"No." Alexa frowned. "My parents are going, and although I'm trying not to put too paranoid an interpretation on this, when I suggested to my mother that I let my understudy do Juliet Saturday afternoon and fly to Oberlin to join them for dinner, I got the very distinct impression that I wasn't invited."

"Probably wise not to over interpret. So, why don't we do something special that night? Our own private celebration of Cat's birthday? And," he added tenderly, "why don't I just say no to dinner with Robert and Hillary for tomorrow night?"

"Really?"

"Really." James smiled and found her soft lips. "I've missed you."

"I've missed you, too."

"You mentioned something about a merger? A very friendly takeover maybe?"

As James led her to the bedroom where he would so slowly and expertly undress her, Alexa thought about how much she had missed him . . . and why. Because of their magnificent passion, yes, but because of something that was even more important—their magnificent friendship. That friendship had become even closer, even more important, in the past few hours. He had listened, and he had been so gentle, and he believed in her still; and maybe, someday, she would believe in herself. As Alexa thought about their wonderful friendship, she realized that there was another important friendship that had become quite lost, quite forgotten, because of her selfishness.

When they reached her romantic pink bedroom, James turned to face her. He circled her slender waist with his hands and waited to see the lovely anticipation and desire he knew so well. But when she looked up at him, he saw a frown, and very serious emerald eyes.

"What?" he asked gently.

"Robert is a very good friend, isn't he?"

"Yes."

"Like a brother?"

"I guess so."

"Including sibling rivalry? There wasn't an ugly battle between the two of you over Hillary was there?"

"No." James laughed softly. "No ugly battles about anything. We graduated first and second in our class from Harvard Law School—Robert was first—but even that wasn't the finish line of a three-year competition."

"It sounds strange to hear you being so calm about coming in second."

"Robert deserved to be first," James said quietly. "What do you know about him, Alexa, other than to whom he is married?"

"Not much. He's a major topic of conversation in Washington, of course, but because of Hillary I've usually tuned out whenever his name is mentioned. Despite that, though, I'm aware that virtually everyone—it almost seems to be a bipartisan vision—believes that he will be President."

"Yes."

"Which means, I suppose, that I *should* know about him." Alexa gave a theatrical sigh, and then smiled. "And who better to tell me than you?" With that, and a lingering kiss, she left him. She sat on the edge of her bed, and with the rapt attention of a child awaiting a favorite bedtime story, she said, "I'm listening."

As she waited for James to settle in a nearby chair and collect his thoughts about the story he was about to tell, Alexa began to imagine what the story would be. The tale of the handsome and dashing Senator would be a tale of wealth and privilege, the golden life of the golden boy, a life without struggle or torment. She was quite confident about what she would hear . . . and she could not have been more mistaken.

"Well. Let's see," James began. "He was born in rural Virginia. His father left when Robert was two, six months before his sister Brynne was born. The family was extremely poor, so from the time he was just a child, he worked to help support his mother and little sister. He's very bright—I told you how he did at Harvard Law School—but his grades in high school were just average."

"Because he spent so much time working to support his family?"

"I assume so. Anyway, he didn't qualify for a college scholarship, and he couldn't attend school and work enough hours to earn both his college tuition and help with the expenses at home, so he enlisted in the army."

"Why didn't he just work full-time for a few years and then go to college?"

"Because Robert's thirty-eight—four years older than I—and those were a very critical four years. He graduated from high school in the midst of the Vietnam War. At that time, any able-bodied eighteen-year-old not bound for college was likely to be drafted. He enlisted before being drafted, but it was only a matter of time. Being in the army provided a small but stable income for his mother and Brynne, and there was a little more money—combat pay—when he was sent to Vietnam."

"He went to Vietnam?" Alexa asked softly. She was younger than Vietnam, a different generation entirely, too young to remember the emotions and divisiveness as they actually occurred. Most of what she knew about Vietnam—what she'd seen and heard and read—was a blurry kaleidoscope of images, never in sharp focus, multifaceted and ever-changing still, even after all these years. Hollywood had begun to tell the stories now. But, she thought, it was a vision balanced more by politics than history. Most of what she knew about Vietnam remained a confusing blur, but there was one thing that was crystal clear: for the men who had fought in the war, their lives were irrevocably changed. "He *fought?*"

"He was a soldier, Alexa. He fought." James sighed softly, thinking, as he often did, especially since his friendship with Robert, how easy his own life had been, how privileged, how *lucky*. "Robert went straight from the battles of poverty in rural Virginia to the horror of war in Vietnam. That's entirely my editorializing, by the way. He never talks about either his childhood or Vietnam. What I know about his childhood, I've learned from Brynne, and what I know about his war record, I've learned from what I've read in articles that have been written about him."

"What do the articles say?"

"They mention the medals he received, of course, but most telling are the accounts of his leadership and bravery given by the men with whom he served."

"So he's a war hero."

"Yes, he is, although 'war hero' is not a label you'd ever hear him apply to himself. Anyway, by the time he returned from Vietnam, his mother had died and Brynne was a scholarship student at the University of Virginia. He enrolled at Virginia, too, on the GI bill, graduated from college with highest honors, and went on to a similar academic performance at Harvard. He could have joined any private firm in the country, of course, but even during law school he'd planned a career in public service. So, on graduation, he began with the District Attorney's office in Richmond. He dazzled as a prosecutor, and was clearly on track for election to DA, but the political powers came to him with an alternate plan—to bypass local politics altogether and make a bid for the Senate."

"Which he has done with such success that everyone thinks he'll be President some day," Alexa said quietly.

"That's right," James answered, quietly, too.

After a thoughtful silence, she tilted her golden head, smiled a mysterious smile, and said, "You still haven't told me the worst part."

"I haven't?"

"No. You haven't told me how the loving son and brother, war hero and patriot, brilliant attorney and dedicated public servant met the Wicked Witch of the West."

"Robert met gracious, charming, beautiful Hillary in Dallas while on a trip to discuss his Senate candidacy with her father, Sam Ballinger."

"And the ex-Governor promised to endorse him for the Senate, and eventually the White House, if he would marry his daughter?" Alexa teased softly. Then, forcing seriousness on her beautiful face, she continued analytically, "Sam doubtless knew that no man in his right mind would ever marry Hillary without such an incentive. All the oil money simply wasn't enough. He had to throw in a few votes, something, perhaps, like the entire state of Texas in the Presidential election?"

"Cute, but no. Robert McAllister is very much his own man. He met Hillary and chose to marry her."

"And what about Hillary? She's never been overly fond of us folk from humble beginnings. I suppose, however, that if marrying a dirt-poor country boy could provide a one-way ticket into Washington's most elite inner circle, not to mention the White House, she would deign to do it."

"Maybe, Alexa, Hillary recognized Robert's greatness."

Alexa drew a soft breath at his words, his tone, and the solemn expression in his dark blue eyes. "You really respect him, don't you?"

"Yes, I really do."

"And Hillary?"

"Hillary is Robert's wife."

Alexa sighed softly. She knew what she had to do, even though it scared her. But she would be with James, and that would make it easier.

"I think we should have dinner with Robert and Hillary tomorrow night."

"You do?"

"Assuming Hillary wants to. James, it's not by accident that I haven't run into the McAllisters in the three years I've been in Washington."

"I'm sure Robert has no idea that you and Hillary knew each other. He would have told me if he did."

"Well, maybe he doesn't know. But Hillary does, and she needs to be given a chance to say no to dinner."

"OK." James walked over to her then, and drew her up to him so that they were standing as they had been before the story began, his arms encircling her waist, her hands resting gently on his shoulders. "Are you sure you want to do this?"

"I'm positive," she replied, her confidence soaring as she saw a wonderful message in his dark blue eyes, something of immense value coming from him: he was proud of her. Feeling tinglingly giddy, and so safe, and knowing that very soon they would be making love, because there was such desire, too, in the seductive blue, she teased, "Of course, I won't be able to vote for Robert for President."

"No?"

"He has that same fatal flaw in judgment—falling for Hillary—that her high school boyfriend did. That kind of judgment problem worries me in a President."

"I see," he murmured, kissing her now, whispering between kisses. "That's why they don't let little children vote, Alexandra. You have to be a grown-up to vote."

"And I'm not?" she asked softly, sighing with pleasure as his talented lips began their journey down her neck and his talented hands found the buttons on her dress.

"Maybe you are," he whispered. "Why don't we see if we can think of something grown-up to do right now . . ."

CHAPTER SEVEN

"James will be bringing Alexa Taylor to dinner tonight," Robert told Hillary after speaking to James the following morning. "Apparently you know her?"

"Yes. James and Alexa?"

James had been vague about why Hillary needed to know, but now as he saw obvious displeasure on his wife's beautiful face, Robert asked, "Is that a problem for you, Hillary?"

"No, of course not," she answered, forcing a smile.

"Good."

As soon as Robert returned to the documents he had been reviewing when James called, Hillary's smile vanished. It was not a problem to see Alexa, she thought, but it was most definitely an annoyance. So far, she had masterfully avoided seeing her old nemesis. But with each passing year, as Alexa's name appeared on more and more of the important guest lists, it became increasingly difficult, and increasingly irritating. Did no one remember that she was merely an actress, playing a role, a faux celebrity with no *legitimate* claim to Washington society whatsoever?

Apparently not, and Hillary knew that it was only a matter of time.

And now the time was here.

As she adjusted to the inevitable, a slight smile touched her lips. They would see each other here, tonight, when Alexa was with James. And when they saw each other the next time, at some charity event in Washington, he would long since have tired of her, and she would delight in Alexa's obvious misery at her inability to hold the interest of rich, elegant, restless James Sterling.

She was perfectly dressed for the role of an adult, her flowing golden hair subdued into a sophisticated knot, her emerald silk sheath simple and elegant, her gold jewelry delicate and demure. And he had made a teasing but solemn promise not to leave her alone with Hillary, and she had made a teasing but solemn promise to be "incredibly nice," but as they neared La Côte Basque, Alexa felt sudden waves of panic. Did she really think she could behave as if nothing had ever happened between them? What if Hillary greeted her with "How very lovely to see you again"? She was just about to confess to James that she'd made a huge mistake, that with his gentle help she had *vastly* overestimated her maturity, when Robert and Hillary appeared from the other direction.

And then they were face to face, and it was Hillary who spoke.

"You probably hoped you'd never see me again, Alexa."

Alexa drew a stunned breath at the bluntness, and at the cool elegance with which Hillary spoke the words. It wasn't an apology, of course, nor was it an invitation for her to apologize, either. It was, simply, a way for them to go on. The *only* way, Alexa realized with a begrudging flicker of admiration.

"You probably felt the same about seeing me."

"Of course I did."

"Ancient history?"

"Ancient history."

Her memories of Hillary were so clear, so vivid, and yet, Alexa realized as she gazed across the candlelight at her old nemesis, the memories were dark amorphous emotions, uglinesses of the heart, not accurate portraits of Hillary herself. The memories were so monstrous and so ugly that Alexa had forgotten entirely how truly beautiful the sable-haired, sable-eyed Southern belle heiress really was.

Hillary was truly beautiful, and Robert was truly handsome, and the McAllisters were truly the perfect modern couple. He listened so attentively to her words, and she listened so attentively to his, and each greeted the other's thoughts with appreciative smiles of respect and approval.

The perfect modern couple, Alexa mused. Indeed, she thought, if Hollywood ever created a show about the First Couple of the Baby-Boomer era—short of casting a woman as President—the President would be a stunningly handsome Vietnam veteran, and the First Lady would be stunningly beautiful, and intelligent, and quite unafraid to express her own views. The President's sensitive eyes would give solemn testimony to the horrors he had seen, but they would smile, too, with proud admiration for the wife whose opinions he obviously valued so greatly.

In short, Hollywood would cast Robert and Hillary McAllister.

But Robert and Hillary weren't actors vying for a role. They were the real thing, the future occupants of the White House, and their act was stunning.

But an act! Alexa decided suddenly, surprised by her observation and certain that it must be wrong. The perfect couple *were* perfect, weren't they? Yes, of course, even though the perfectly scripted smiles of respect and admiration seemed to come more from the mind than the heart or the soul. And there seemed to be no spontaneous affection, no gentle surprised laughter, no swift knowing glances as some casual remark triggered an intimate memory.

Propriety, no doubt, she told herself. Appropriate, dignified, perfect First Couple behavior.

And what about the players themselves? Sincere, sensitive, thoughtful Robert McAllister was simply too good to be true. The Senator was definitely in contention for his own private Oscar, Alexa decided. His performance was quite convincing, of course, and most deserving of a small golden statue, but, unfortunately, the immensely talented actor had been given an impossible script. Whoever had written it—presumably Robert himself—had forgotten to sprinkle in even one tiny flaw, some small proof that the man was real.

Alexa wished she could believe the extraordinary and compelling sensitivity she saw in the sensuous dark eyes, but she couldn't. As the evening wore on, she found herself disliking him very much. How arrogant it was, she thought, to pretend to possess a sincerity and sensitivity that were so obviously contrived.

And what about the future First Lady? At least there was an honesty about Hillary. Now, just as eight years ago, the beautiful heiress did not even pretend to like Alexa. Of course, now Hillary's contempt was protected by layers and layers of impeccable manners, but even that downy comforter of graciousness was not enough to conceal the fact that she had not really changed at all. She was still very much the cruel little girl Alexa had known in Dallas . . .

"Tell us about your career, Alexa," Hillary suggested politely as they lingered over coffee. The evening had gone surprisingly well, a comfortable flow of neutral topics—until now. "You moved to New York after graduation?"

"That's right." Alexa smiled sweetly, even though she was quite certain that Hillary knew the details of her career and was laying a trap. "I studied at Juilliard for a year and then got my first role on television."

"A soap opera, wasn't it?"

"Yes," Alexa replied smoothly, despite the fact that Hillary had almost choked on the words "soap opera." Daytime soaps were apparently quite beneath her, incomprehensible to a patron of the fine arts such as she, almost as unimaginable as being raised in a farmhouse in Kansas. Alexa smiled beautifully and evoked a wincing smile from James as she calmly dropped a hand under the table and dug her fingernails into his thigh. "I was with *All My Children* until three years ago, when *Pennsylvania Avenue* began."

"Alexa has also worked in the theater, and, of course, has done the one movie," James added quietly, returning her hand to the table top, curled gently but firmly in his. He didn't elaborate on the "one movie," his words more meaningful by the understatement, his dark blue eyes sending an eloquent reminder of her astonishing performance.

"*Majesty* was your first movie?" Hillary asked. "I thought there might have been others along the way."

"You mean 'B' movies?" Alexa countered, realizing then what she should have known: the politely delivered soap opera slur was simply a warm-up. Hillary was cleverly drifting from the clean but not highbrow suds to the seamier and steamier aspects of show business—explicit sex and nudity. Surely the whore from Kansas had had no qualms about baring all along the way to her success. Alexa felt the instinctive rush of adrenaline, a soldier steeling for battle, and fought to keep her promise to be "incredibly nice." She was succeeding, calming herself, until she made the mistake of glancing at Robert.

For a wonderful, grateful moment, Alexa was actually convinced by, *seduced by*, the anguish and apology in the dark brown eyes. But, she reminded herself quickly, the sensitivity is simply pretense. He is neither wounded by, nor apologetic for, Hillary's sudden unkind attack.

If there was an authentic apology at all in the wounded dark eyes, she realized with sudden fury, it was an apology for *her* decadent morals, not for Hillary's assault on same. After all, *he*, the dirt-poor country boy, had managed to overcome all hardships with his integrity and honor completely intact; while *she*, the ill-bred country girl, had not been nearly so strong, succumbing to the most unfortunate compromises in an effort to advance in her déclassée career as an actress.

When she had told James the truth about the year at Ballinger, Alexa had shared the blame equally with Hillary for their war. But had Hillary, when she recounted the same story to Robert, confessed to either her own jealousy or cruelty? Of course not, Alexa thought. She had probably merely conveyed to her husband her lingering bewilderment that the administrators at Ballinger had permitted Alexa to roam its hallowed halls at all. Hillary had surely told Robert only *her* disdainful version of the saga of the white trash whore, and he had been able to add his own fuel to the fire of outrage by recounting Alexa's seductive remark in James's office.

And now Robert was gazing at her not with gentle apology for Hillary's cruelty, but rather with gentle apology for Alexa's own pathetic destiny—her decadent and unprincipled path from whore to actress, by way of nude movies.

How arrogant! How patronizing! How judgmental!

Alexa willed her voice not to reveal her trembling anger as she said very quietly to his arrogant dark eyes, "The wonderful thing about acting as a profession is that one needn't compromise his or her ethical standards. It's simply not required."

She paused, a carefully calculated moment of drama before delivering her next line, but Robert McAllister stole the line and the silence from her.

"Unlike politics?" he suggested softly.

Unlike politics was what Alexa had planned to say, of course, a silly taunt. And now Robert had intercepted the taunt, saving her and perhaps the entire evening, and making her dislike him all the more.

"Oh," she replied, recovering quickly and feigning confusion as she considered his suggestion. Finally, smiling beautifully, she added, "Well, yes, I suppose, now that you mention it, Robert . . . unlike politics."

"Sorry," Alexa whispered softly, an hour later, when she and James were alone in her apartment. As she freed the long golden silk that had been restrained in the sophisticated knot, she added, "So much for being grown-up."

"You were fine."

"But I let her get to me and I shouldn't have. Oh! I *really* don't like her."

"That's fair. I don't think she's crazy about you, either. No one is asking you to become best friends. You were fine. The evening was fine." James smiled reassuringly, but the emerald eyes remained troubled. "What, Alexa?"

"I really don't like either of them, James."

"You don't like Robert?" he asked, surprised.

"Not really."

"Because he intercepted your missile in midair?"

"I already didn't like him before that. He's so arrogant."

"Arrogant? Robert?"

"Yes, James, *arrogant*. You know, as in God's gift to We the People."

"You're wrong, Alexa," he told her with quiet confidence. "Robert McAllister is not arrogant."

"I can't believe you don't see it!"

"I don't see it, and I know Robert far better than you do."

Alexa gazed at his serious dark blue eyes and knew this was an argument she wouldn't win. "And what about Hillary?"

"I admit that Hillary isn't exactly my cup of tea."

"Well, that's at least a step in the right direction. So? Do we have to see them again? Another fun-filled evening?"

"No." James smiled enigmatically. "I had actually hoped that we'd be able to do a fun-filled weekend."

"You're kidding."

"No. Don't worry, there will be other people around."

"When? Where?"

"In August at Inverness. My parents will be home from Paris for a few weeks, for vacation and to host their annual garden party. The party is held on Sunday, and is a fairly major event, but there will be a small house party beginning the day before. Robert and Hillary will be there, and Brynne and her husband Stephen, and possibly Elliot Archer, another close family friend, and my parents and me. Even without Elliot that should provide ample buffer between you and Mrs. McAllister, shouldn't it?"

"You're inviting me to the house party?" Alexa asked softly. We're making plans for three months from now?

"Yes, and to the garden party, too, of course. You're invited, and, if you like, so is Cat."

"Please explain the point to me, Hillary." Robert's quiet words broke the silence that had travelled with them from the restaurant to their suite at the Plaza.

"The point, Robert?"

"The point of your unkindness to Alexa. You were taunting her, intentionally trying to demean her career. I think you hurt her feelings."

"Really?" Hillary smiled. "Good."

"Good?"

"I have known Alexa for a very long time, Robert. She's a tramp."

"I thought she seemed very nice."

"Nice? No, Alexa is not nice. I'm actually quite surprised that James is seeing her. She's really so far beneath him." She frowned briefly, then shrugged dismissively. "Well, she won't last long. None of James's women ever do, of course, and I imagine he'll tire of Alexa far more quickly than most."

Hillary turned, and began to walk to the bedroom, but she was stopped by his voice. It was quiet still, and edged with ice.

"I'm still waiting for you to explain to me, Hillary, the point of your unkindness to Alexa."

"Oh, Robert." Hillary sighed softly as she turned back toward him. "Let's not waste any more time talking about someone like Alexa Taylor. Trust me, she isn't worth it." Smiling seductively, she returned to him, and swaying gently against him, curled her perfectly manicured fingers under the lapel of his jacket, and whispered, "Come to bed."

Robert answered her by wrapping his fingers around her delicate wrists, and, with quiet strength, removing her hands from his chest. His dark, troubled eyes stared at her defiant, furious ones for a long moment, and then he said, "I'm going for a walk."

"A walk? In the middle of the night in Manhattan?"

"That's right."

"*Allô. Bonjour.*"

Alexa frowned at the greeting, even though she expected it. All calls to the French House on the Oberlin campus were answered in French; but, still, it always seemed a bit much. It was fine, *wonderful*, for the students who lived in the house to speak exclusively French within its walls, but she disliked being made an unwilling participant in the game whenever she called. Not that she participated, of course, never even so much as a *Merci beaucoup*.

Although it seemed a pretension to her for the students to impose their house rules on the outside world by answering the switchboard in French, Alexa didn't consider her little sister's fascination with French pretentious at all. From the first moment Cat had heard the elegant language, she had loved it; and now the melodic language of love flowed as flawlessly and as joyfully from her lips as music flowed from her talented fingers.

"Hello," Alexa replied in resolute but pleasant English. "Will you connect me to Cat Taylor's room, please?"

"*Certainement. Un moment, s'il vous plaît.*"

Catherine answered in English because the distinctive double ring signaled a call from outside.

"Hello?"

"Hi, Cat, it's Alexa. Happy Birthday."

"Alexa. Hi. Thank you."

"So, how does it feel to be twenty-one? Completely grown up?" Alexa frowned at the awkward triteness of her words. It was the kind of unimaginative question a virtual stranger might ask.

"Fine, I guess, not really different," Catherine mumbled, frowning, too, as she searched for words to speak to her older sister. "How is your play?"

"Good. Fun." *Fun?* A fun play about a love crazed teenager who kills herself? Alexa laughed nervously and added, "I mean, it's a fun cast and crew. When do Mom and Dad arrive?"

"They thought by mid-afternoon."

"That should be nice."

"Yes. It's nice of them to make the drive."

Alexa wondered if Cat knew that she had wanted to be there, too, but that their mother had quite firmly discouraged her plans to join them. She shook that memory, and the ancient feelings of rejection it triggered, and moved from the uneasinesses of the past to the hopefulness—hers anyway—for the future.

"Have you decided when you're coming to New York?"

"When would be convenient for you?"

"Any time is fine with me. *Pennsylvania Avenue* begins production bright and early on July third, so I'll need to be in Maryland by then, but I was hoping, depending on your schedule, that we might have a week or so together here at the end of June? I could show you around Manhattan."

"Oh, that would be wonderful."

"Good. So, when can you come?"

"My last exam is at eight A.M. on the twenty-third, and my term paper in French is due that afternoon, so . . ."

"So, that night or the next day you can hop a plane—fly into LaGuardia—and I'll be at the airport to meet you. OK?"

"Yes. OK. Thank you."

James appeared in the kitchen just as the conversation was ending. The soft uncertainty in Alexa's voice, and the telephone cord, tangled and twisted by her anxious fingers, told him quite eloquently that she had been speaking to her little sister.

"How's Cat?" he asked when she replaced the receiver and smiled up at him.

"Fine. Twenty-one. School's out on June twenty-third and she's planning to come right here."

"Good," James said, deciding on the spot that the end of June would be an ideal time for the long business trip to California he needed to make before August.

"You look as though you're about to leave."

"Guilty. I have a full day of work ahead of me. I'm not going to be able to make it to the play today."

"That's fine! I can't imagine being able to sit through *Romeo and Juliet* as many times as you have."

"It's not sitting through . . . it's enjoying. But, not today."

"Maybe we should defer our dinner plans," Alexa suggested, sensing his restlessness and knowing that he had not yet fully caught up from all the work that had accumulated during his trip to Tokyo.

"Defer our private celebration of Cat's birthday? Not a chance."

Alexa's graceful gait came to an abrupt halt as she neared the theater. There, in the line of people hoping to get a last-minute ticket to today's long since sold-out performance of *Romeo and Juliet*, was Senator Robert McAllister.

What is he doing here? Alexa wondered, and then, as emotions began to embellish the question, she thought, *How dare he?*

There was no doubt in her mind that Robert considered her acting career a totally useless and trivial pursuit. Fine, he had a right to his opinion. But couldn't he keep himself and his opinion far away from a place that was so important to her? Her career was terribly important to her, and so was this play, and she felt very much as though he was invading her privacy.

It's a free country, she thought wryly. And even though I don't want him here, Robert McAllister, patriot par excellence, is enjoying the hard-fought unalienable rights of free people to assemble where they choose and to appreciate the uncensored words of the world's great and gifted playwrights.

But, still, it felt as if Robert's *freedom* violated her *rights*. Just as Alexa's thoughts were drifting to the ACLU—does he really have the right to sit in arrogant judgment of my work?—reality, wonderful reality, quieted her angry emotions and a soft contented smile touched her lips.

Robert McAllister couldn't get in. Even if he were recognized, and by some unwritten rule of Senatorial privilege managed to advance from seventh place in line to first, the performance was sold out; and, if this Saturday matinee was typical of all the others in May, there wouldn't be any "no-shows."

As Alexa looked at the man who stood calmly in seventh place, she detected no impatience, no furtive or hopeful glances that he *would* be recognized, no concern even that his dark brown hair had been unceremoniously tousled by the wind.

Robert didn't look arrogant at all. In fact, she conceded begrudgingly, in this un-guarded wind-tossed moment, the darkly dashing Senator was terribly handsome, terribly sexy indeed.

But it wasn't an unguarded moment at all, Alexa reminded herself. Every stun-ningly handsome expression and mood was undoubtedly carefully rehearsed. She wondered what would happen when Robert discovered that he would not be able to get a ticket for today's performance. Would there be an unguarded rush of an-noyance that he had wasted his precious time standing in line? It was hard to imag-ine, of course, that he would actually be upset if he didn't see her play. Wouldn't spending an afternoon at the theater be for the important Senator an even greater waste?

Well, no matter. Robert would not be in today's matinee audience. The real-ization made Alexa feel much better . . . and then a little guilty. She had made a promise to James that she would be nice to his friend. And she would be! She would make no scene whatsoever. She would simply walk on, enter the theater through the side door not the front, and never tell a soul that she had seen him.

But then Robert looked up, right at her, and she saw such uncertainty in his dark eyes. *Practiced* uncertainty, she reminded herself swiftly, the sensitive-man-of-the-eighties look which was carefully calculated, she supposed, to appeal to the female vote. The look did nothing for Alexa, except to annoy, because now she could not escape. She walked over to him so that he wouldn't lose his useless place in line.

"Good afternoon, Robert."

"Good afternoon, Alexa."

"No Hillary?"

"No. She's shopping." Robert gazed at the eyes that from the first moment in James's office—and still—met his with beautiful emerald ice. After a thoughtful silence, he added quietly, "I wanted to see your play, but I get the impression you'd rather I didn't."

"Oh, no, Robert. I'm very flattered, of course," Alexa lied graciously. "I don't have extra tickets, but I can have a folding chair put in an aisle, or find you a place backstage. Neither is ideal, not terribly comfortable, and it wouldn't offend me in the least if you said no, but I'm quite certain there won't be any last-minute seats for this performance."

"I would really like to see the play—from any vantage point. Are you sure it's all right?"

"Sure."

Alexa had told James truthfully that playing Juliet was a major stretch for someone as cynical about love as she. But, from the very first performance, her Juliet had been convincing and magical. Every audience believed in the love of the star-crossed lovers, wanted it to last forever, and hoped against hope that, with apolo-gies to the Bard, the all too familiar tragic ending would be overthrown for a happily-ever-after one.

The lovers died, as always, on the Saturday afternoon that Robert McAllister watched from a folding chair in the aisle at stage right, but on that day Alexa's Juliet was more unforgettable than ever. There was a new emotion in the romantic heroine—*defiance*. The defiance was Alexa's, of course, as she eloquently showed the arrogant Senator the great value of her art; but the defiance came alive in Juliet, who, on that day, fought more courageously and passionately than ever to proudly defy the contrary stars.

Alexa couldn't see beyond the brightly glaring lights to know whether Robert had stood with the rest of the enraptured audience to applaud her remarkable performance, but she wondered vaguely as she took her curtain calls if he would come backstage to tell her what he thought. Not that she had invited him to, but no one would stop him if he tried. But, apparently, he didn't try. Nor was a note, not even a few words of praise hastily scribbled on a torn scrap of playbill, delivered to her. He had to get ready for the politically important black-tie reception followed by the politically important Governor's Ball, she knew, and he had thanked her, more than once, before the show, *but* he still might have found a quick and easy way to simply acknowledge her performance. She had been good today, especially good, but maybe that was too much for him to admit.

Not that it mattered what Robert McAllister thought of her, she repeatedly reminded herself as she sat in her dressing room, winding down from the performance, finding that it took far longer today than ever before. It couldn't, shouldn't, matter less; and yet, inexplicably and annoyingly, it bothered her very much that he had disappeared without a word.

When she left the theater at last, an hour and a half after the enthusiastic applause had finally stopped and the theater had emptied, her mind was still swirling with imaginary conversations with the arrogant Senator.

The arrogant Senator . . . who was waiting patiently outside the theater for her . . . and who did not look arrogant at all.

"Hi."

"Hi."

"I just wanted to tell you how magnificent you were."

"Oh," she breathed softly, all imaginary tirades suddenly quite lost. "Thank you. I didn't realize you were waiting. You should have come backstage."

"Oh, well, I . . ." Robert shrugged. "I didn't mind waiting."

"I usually leave the theater much sooner than this," she murmured. But, you see, I was so wound up, so angry with you. With *you?* she wondered as she met his gentle and uncertain dark eyes.

"I didn't mind waiting," Robert repeated quietly. And then, with a soft smile added, "But I'd probably better go now. You truly were magnificent, Alexa."

"Thank you, Robert."

And then he was gone, already quite late for his politically important reception, and she was left with the stunning truth. She had been very wrong about Robert McAllister. He wasn't arrogant at all. And there was no pretense.

He was simply, remarkably, the sensitive and thoughtful man that he appeared to be.

CHAPTER EIGHT

The Loire Valley, France
May 1989

*I*sabelle stood at a window in her seventeenth-century château. Her brilliant blue eyes gazed far beyond the magnificent vista of river and meadow, as if hoping to see the faraway place where, today, her beloved daughter would learn the truth about her birth. How astonishing that twenty-one years had already passed! The memories of the few precious days she had spent with her baby girl were so vivid, a journey traveled so often in the past two decades that, in many ways, those distant days seemed more bright and clear than all the years that had come between. And now, on this day, her little girl, a grown woman, would learn of those faraway days. But would she have any idea about the great love that had filled them?

"Isabelle? I brought you some tea."

Louis-Philippe's voice gently interrupted Isabelle's thoughts. At the sound of his voice, she withdrew her gaze from the panorama of the Loire Valley and turned to the kind man who had been her husband for the past ten years. Louis-Philippe had lost his much-loved wife, as Isabelle had lost her beloved Alexandre. Their relationship had begun with tender understanding of each other's loss and loneliness, and it had grown into the gentlest of loves.

Louis-Philippe knew Isabelle's secrets, and he had lived with her shadows—the men who had been sent by Jean-Luc to watch her always. At first, he had wanted to rid their life of the ever-watchful eyes, but his annoyance had faded as he came to realize how comforting their presence was to Isabelle. As long as the men were there, watching her and hoping she would lead them to her daughter, it could only mean that Jean-Luc's relentless search continued unrewarded. He had not found the missing princess. *She was safe.*

Then, six years ago, two weeks after the small plane carrying Jean-Luc and his second wife dove into the Mediterranean during the short flight from L'île to Nice, the shadows vanished. The plane crash was no accident, the news reports said, although the identity of the saboteur remained a mystery. Not that it mattered to Isabelle who among Jean-Luc's many enemies had chosen to murder him. What mattered was that the monster was dead . . . and the shadows were gone.

After fifteen years, the sinister watchdogs were gone. But what did their disappearance mean? she asked herself over and over. Why had Alain called them off? Was he, perhaps, unaware of their menacing mission? Or was the new monarch simply more cunning than his father? Had the boy who had unwittingly saved her from the powerful crush of Jean-Luc's hands grown into a man of even greater evil, more dangerous in his subtlety, more cruel in his deceit? Was it Alain Castille's plan to lure her into believing it was now safe to search, in hopes of following her to the princess who was such a threat to his kingdom?

Isabelle was so tempted, so very tempted . . . but she couldn't take the chance. Even when she heard that the new Prince had restored L'île to the magnificence of Alexandre's reign, a paradise of music and art and flowers, she forced herself to wonder if that, too, could be a clever deception. Alain was Jean-Luc's son, after all. He had spent his boyhood in a palace that had become a fortress. The lessons Alain had learned from his father had been lessons of power and greed and guns and terror, not ones of love and joy and music and poetry.

How she wanted to search for her daughter! But she could not take the risk. It would be virtually impossible to find her, of course. And, she told her pleading defiant heart, it wouldn't be fair.

Just as what's going to happen today isn't fair, she thought, as her trembling hands took the cup of tea Louis-Philippe brought for her. The delicate rattling of the Limoges china betrayed the emotions that swirled within her. Not that her husband didn't already know.

"What are you thinking, my love?"

"Just now, I was thinking how wrong it was for me to have asked that she be told the truth. It wasn't what I had planned, but when I gave her away and realized that she would never know of my love . . . such a selfish request, made for me, not for her. I would undo it if I could, but now I can only pray that the truth doesn't hurt her, and that she won't hate me. I have a memory of such love during the short time we had together . . ." Isabelle shrugged softly. Her memories of her daughter were treasures of immeasurable value. How she wanted to believe the memories were shared, mother and daughter, but that was nonsense! Her daughter would have no memory of her. And what would her reaction be when she learned the truth today? Anger? Betrayal? Sadness? Isabelle wanted no unhappiness, ever, for the daughter she loved so much; and yet, the realization that the now-grown little girl might well acknowledge the revelation with an indifferent shrug, a past history that was of no consequence, was devastating to her, too. She wished for something—a silent message of love from the faraway heart—but that was only more proof of her own sentimental foolishness.

"You're very confident that she will be told."

"Oh, yes." Isabelle knew the lovely woman with the emerald eyes would keep that promise, just as she had been comforted for the past twenty-one years with the knowledge that the woman would keep all the promises she had made, especially the most important one: *We will love her . . .*

"There's something that Dad and I need to tell you, darling." Jane spoke gently to the trusting and innocent sapphire eyes. It was time. The three of them had spent a lovely spring afternoon wandering around the Oberlin campus, and soon they were to leave for the birthday dinner at a nearby country inn, but they needed to tell her now, in the privacy of their motel room, because lovely, sensitive Catherine had already read the worry in their eyes.

"What is it?" she asked anxiously. The unspoken worry had now been acknowledged, and she was suddenly very fearful of what it could be. A serious illness, perhaps, in one of the parents she loved so much? Or in Alexa?

"It's something that happened a long time ago," Jane began quietly, looking from Catherine, whose lovely worried expression reminded her so vividly of the mother she had met twenty-one years before, to Alexander, who had agreed to help tell the story she had promised to tell on this day.

Jane and Alexander told the story together, one continuing when the other faltered, beginning where it began, on a glorious spring day and a trip to Kansas City. As Catherine heard about the sudden bleeding, the emergency delivery, the mother and daughter in ICUs in separate hospitals, she was amazed and saddened that her birth had been so terribly difficult for her mother—and a source of such worry for her father. It didn't surprise Catherine that her parents had never shared this with her before, but she wondered vaguely why they had chosen to tell her today.

"The baby died on the fifth day." Alexander's voice was gentle, and so quiet, but still the words thundered.

"Died?" Catherine echoed finally, not understanding, *not even beginning to understand*.

She waited, expecting to hear about a miracle. Had she been pronounced dead only to miraculously revive? Or was she a twin, undiscovered until after the sister had died, then suddenly announcing her appearance? A twin, yes, that was it. Catherine had read about twins, separated or lost at birth, and about how each sensed the loss of the missing half. She tried now to sense her distant twin, the baby girl who had died, but there was no sense of loss, *not for that sister*. There was only one sister she had missed, and she had spent her lifetime missing her desperately, but that sister was Alexa.

Alexa, who had sounded so eager to have her come to New York as soon as possible, *hadn't she?* Alexa, with whom, maybe, please, there had been delicate and precious whispers of friendship over the past eight years, *hadn't there?*

"I had a twin sister?"

"No, darling," Jane answered softly. Her emerald eyes brimmed with tears as she looked from Catherine to Alexander. But her husband could not tell this part of the story. Only she knew the words and emotions of the woman who had given them their beloved Catherine. "On the day that I was discharged from the hospital, I decided to go to the newborn nursery to see the babies before I left. I needed courage to face my loss, and courage to help Dad tell Alexa about the baby who had died. I went to the nursery looking for courage, Cat, and I found a miracle. I found you."

With loving wonder, Jane recounted the astonishing truths about that day. A distant corner of Catherine's mind heard the words and the emotion, and saved both to be remembered later, but only one truth swirled in her mind now, a thundering anguish, not an astonishing miracle . . .

"I'm not your daughter." It was a whisper, soft, delicate, tentative, like the deceptively gentle first breath of even the most devastating storm. *I'm not your daughter. And I'm not really Alexa's sister, even though I have spent my life missing her.*

"Yes, Cat, you are our daughter!" Alexander interjected, his gentle voice hoarse with emotion. "We aren't your biologic parents, darling, but you *are* our daughter."

Jane and Alexander had spoken the usual words to each other—"biologic," "birth," "natural," "real"—and rejected all but biologic and birth. They *were* Catherine's real parents, and to imply the relationship was anything but natural, *wonderful*, seemed so very wrong.

"You adopted me."

"Yes." Jane frowned and admitted quietly, "It wasn't an official adoption. Your mother didn't give me your birth certificate, and you were born on the same day as the baby who died, so . . ."

"So my birth certificate is hers? Her name was Catherine, too?"

"No, darling. Her name was Mary. She died before the name on the birth certificate was recorded—it just read 'Baby Girl'—so when we provided the correct name to the Bureau of Vital Statistics, we told them Catherine."

The name on the baby's death certificate was Mary, and Jane and Alexander had worried that the change might be discovered, but the registries of birth and death were quite separate, unlinked then by computers, and it had been a matter of simple paperwork. And it was safer than a formal legal adoption, they had decided, because there would be no trail that might lead whoever it was that Catherine's mother feared so much to Catherine.

The room fell silent. In the stillness, Jane and Alexander tried to reach the daughter with whom there was no genetic link, but with whom there had always been such deep and astonishing bonds. They were bonded by their love of music, of course, but bonded, too, by their quiet reserve, their serenity, and the important wordless messages of their hearts. Always before, from the very beginning, they had understood each other's silences. But now, as they tried to penetrate Catherine's silence, Jane and Alexander felt their emotions ricocheting back, blocked by a new invisible wall. And the eyes that had always been the brilliant, hopeful blue of a winter sky after a snowstorm were wintry still, but no longer hopeful, just the cold forboding blue of ice.

"Cat," Alexander whispered helplessly.

"Why are you telling me this now?" she asked, a soft demand and an even softer unspoken plea, *Why couldn't you have never told me?*

"Because I made a promise to . . . your mother . . . that I would tell you the truth on your twenty-first birthday."

"Why? So that I could know that she didn't want me?"

"Oh, no, darling, she wanted you. You must believe that. She loved you very much."

"But she was very young and very poor?"

"No," Jane admitted softly. "She was neither young nor poor. She told me it would be dangerous for you to be with her. I don't know why, darling, but I do know that she was being followed and that she was very fearful of the men who were watching her . . . and you."

"But what was her name? Who is she?" *Who am I?*

"I don't know her name, Cat. She told me nothing about herself, except that she was your mother and she loved you very much." Jane paused, and then added softly, "I think, although I'm not certain, that your father's name was Alexander. It seemed very important to her that your middle name be Alexandra."

But my middle name is Alexandra because of Dad! The thought came swiftly, a proud familiar truth that had been with her all her life. She had been named for her father, Alexander Taylor, the quiet, talented, wonderful man from whom she had inherited so many things, including her magical gift for music. She was named for him, and she shared that name with her sister, and it was all wonderful comforting proof of who she was—daughter, sister—and that she was where she belonged.

And now?

Now how she wished that this was all just a cruel joke! The incredible wish, because her parents were no more likely to play cruel jokes than was she, was suddenly so appealing. She could live with the discovery that there was a dark side to Jane and Alexander, some sinister twist in their minds that had made them tell her this. She could live with that if only she could have back everything she had believed to be true all her life.

But it wasn't a cruel joke, and as Catherine gazed at the mother and father she loved so much, something terrifying began to happen. She felt herself separating from them . . . drifting far, far away . . . and she couldn't make it stop!

Catherine tried to stop it, but as if she were in quicksand, the harder she strug-gled, the more quickly she suffocated. She was suffocating now, and she saw Jane and Alexander through a blurry fog, and they looked so different! No longer were they her mother and father, not really. Instead, they were the kind, generous, lov-ing people who had rescued an endangered orphan from some mysterious peril and had so lovingly welcomed that tiny helpless visitor into their lives. They had been so wonderful to their little guest, making her feel as if she truly belonged.

But she didn't belong! She was an impostor! She had been a guest in their home and in their hearts and in their lives, placed there by chance, not by the passionate union of a man and woman who had chosen to create a new life from their loving. Alexa was such a creation of Jane and Alexander's love, and so was Mary, the baby girl who had died, but she . . .

Catherine tried to stop the thoughts, but she was powerless against them. Like a raging river they swept through her, and then, engulfing her, they carried her swiftly away, downstream, so very far away from everything she had ever known. The past, that wonderful place where she had lived in such secure love, was a dis-tant memory, a lovely dream, vanquished forever by the truth.

The truth. She was not their daughter. She was the abandoned baby of a myste-rious woman and a man named Alexander. Had she been a creation of love? Or an unfortunate mistake? It hardly mattered, because there was the truth again: what-ever she had been to the man and woman who had created her, it wasn't enough. They had been able to give her away.

"They never tried to find me?" she asked softly.

"Not that we know, darling. I believe, although she didn't say this, that your father was no longer alive when you were born. It would have been almost impossi-ble for her to find you, Cat, and there was the danger."

"But what kind of danger? How can it be dangerous for a baby to be with her mother?"

"I don't know, my love," Jane answered gently. "But I truly believe the danger was real. She was very definitely being watched, and she took great care to be cer-tain that the man who was watching her didn't realize what was happening. That's why Dad and I have been so very careful, too, Cat. That's why we have told no one."

"But that's not true! You told Alexa! She has known all along!"

"No, darling, Alexa doesn't know."

Yes she does know! a voice from deep within her screamed. The voice had once been so familiar, a constant companion, but recently its relentless taunts had been silenced by hope. Now the unwelcome voice was back, harsh and clear, bring-ing with it all the ancient pain. She knows that I'm not really her little sister, and maybe that's why she has never liked me . . .

"Alexa doesn't know," Jane repeated quietly.

"Promise me that you will never tell her."

"I promise," Jane agreed softly, wishing she could add gently that it wouldn't matter to Alexa, but knowing that she couldn't confidently make such a reassur-ance. Yes, Alexa's voice filled with loving pride when she spoke of Cat now, but Jane would never forget the girls' first twelve years together, nor would she forget the astonishing pronouncement Alexa had made when she first saw Cat—"She is not my sister!"

*   *   *

Somehow Catherine survived the visit, hiding her pain, reassuring them that it was fine, she understood, it didn't matter. And then Jane and Alexander were gone, and she was alone, truly alone, with the truth and its glittering symbols: the magnificent sapphire necklace and the staggering fortune. Alexander had invested the one hundred thousand dollars very cautiously, but in the past twenty-one years even the most conservative investments had grown enormously. The trust he established for her, and which was now in her sole control, was valued at just over one million dollars.

She wanted none of it! She just wanted to go back to the time when she knew who she was and where she belonged.

But that time had vanished. No, worse, it had never even existed. As Catherine thought about who she had always believed herself to be, she realized how simple her identity had been. Catherine Alexandra Taylor was, *had been*, three important things: a daughter . . . a sister . . . and a musician. That was all, and it had been enough, *more* than enough. And now she was no longer either the daughter or the sister she had believed herself to be.

But she was still a musician. It was two weeks before Catherine summoned the courage to play again. She was so afraid of losing that final piece of herself, the gossamer thread that kept her tethered so precariously to her vanishing past.

She had always believed that her musical gift was part of her beloved father alive within her. But when she played again, and found that everything that had come before was only a whisper of her astonishing talent, she felt remarkable new relationships, compelling bonds to the great composers whose music she played. Her roots were centuries deep, a dominion beyond life, an inheritance of heart and spirit and soul. She had always marvelled at the genius of Mozart, Bach, and Beethoven; but now she felt their passion and emotion living within her, and now she understood their sadness, their isolation, and their pain. She played the familiar music as she had never played it before. And she played new music, too, breathtakingly poignant compositions that flowed from her own broken and bewildered heart.

Catherine clung ferociously to her music, the only part of her that hadn't vanished with the truth, and she tried desperately to adjust to her losses. She was not Jane and Alexander's daughter, not really, not in the way she had always believed herself to be. That truth was new for her, but it was not new for them. They had known always, and they had welcomed her and loved her *always*. She loved them too, so very much, but she still felt far away, and so awkward and unsure. In time, *please*, she would feel comfortable again with the parents she loved so deeply.

And what about Alexa? What about the much loved sister who was not a sister after all?

You're not her sister, the truth reminded her, an incessant chorus of pain.

But she doesn't know that! her desperate heart pleaded.

No, the truth conceded easily. But she'll find out soon enough, the instant she sees you. You feel so very different on the inside, can you possibly imagine that it doesn't show? It is as if you have a scarlet A—for Adopted—emblazoned over your heart! Alexa will know immediately . . . and she will be so relieved. She has never wanted you to be her sister, remember?

But she doesn't know, not yet, and what if I could keep my secret from her until some time when it is safe to tell her, some faraway time when it won't matter to her?

When will that faraway time be? When you and Alexa are good friends? Sheer fantasy!

But what if it isn't fantasy? What if Alexa and I could be friends? I have to find out. Somehow, *somehow*, I have to hide the truth until I know.

But how could she hide a truth that consumed every waking moment and surfaced in gasping nightmares during the rare times when she was able to sleep? Alexa would see the painful truth instantly in her exhausted, honest, troubled eyes.

As Catherine struggled for control over her turbulent emotions, a subconscious part of her found other ways to help her hide. Without making a specific decision, she allowed her always short hair to grow, until her sapphire eyes were veiled by soft, black-velvet curls. And she added a new layer to the plumpness that had always before been simply a rich and luxuriant symbol of her bountiful health. The new heavy shell, designed to protect and conceal her, was sallow and unhealthy, an eloquent symbol only of her immense pain.

How excited she had been about the move to New York, how happy that Alexa had wanted her to come as soon as possible, how hopeful that they could become friends. But now, in the few weeks left before she would see the sister who wasn't her sister after all, Catherine merely struggled to find the courage to make the most important journey of her life.

CHAPTER NINE

Manhattan
June 1989

"*H*i, Cat."

"Alexa."

"I was just calling to see what time your flight arrives Friday." Alexa spoke cheerfully even though she heard the flatness in Catherine's voice. She had heard the same flatness two weeks before, when she had called to see if her sister had made plane reservations yet, and the flatness was still there now, two days before she was scheduled to move to New York. "Cat?"

"I don't think I'll be able to come on Friday after all."

"Oh. No?"

"No. I haven't finished my French paper yet."

"Oh," Alexa replied calmly, despite her amazement. It was more than just another French paper; it was the major requirement for Cat's degree in French. And now that important paper wasn't finished? What possibly could have distracted her always disciplined little sister so much? "Have you been ill?"

"No. I guess I've just been concentrating on my other classes." It was true, although the concentration had only occurred in the past few days, an intense focus so that she could pass her final exams.

"So, when do you think you'll be arriving?"

"I'm not sure."

"Couldn't you finish writing the paper here?"

"Oh. Yes. I guess," Catherine answered hesitantly even though she knew that she would *have* to finish the paper in New York. She had many weeks of work yet to do on it, and her classes at Juilliard began in ten days. New York . . . ten days . . . it still seemed impossible. She spoke aloud something she had been thinking, a sad but sensible idea, and one that she could easily afford now that she was an heiress to a mysterious and unwanted fortune. "I was wondering if I should get my own apartment."

"Oh," Alexa whispered softly, trying to hide her disappointment. "Well, of course, if you want. But, Cat, this place really will be yours. In fact, it already is. I'm virtually all moved to Maryland."

"I just don't want to impose."

"It's no imposition! Really, it's a relief for me to have someone here. Besides . . . there's a piano here that needs to be played."

"A piano?"

"Yes. And the apartment is completely sound proof, so you can play any time you like without worrying about the neighbors—not that they'd mind hearing you. Why don't you stay here, Cat, at least in the beginning? If you don't like the apartment, you and the piano can always move."

"I'm sure I'll like the apartment. I just didn't want to impose."

"You won't be! So, when do you think you will be coming?"

"I really don't know."

"Well, why don't I send you a set of keys? That way you can arrive whenever you want. I'll send the keys by overnight mail, so you'll have them by Friday."

"I'm sure I won't be arriving until next week."

"That's fine. Whenever's convenient for you. I'll be at the cottage in Maryland."

After the conversation ended, Alexa fought her disappointment. How casually the ten days they had planned to spend together had been tossed away! The ten days *they* had planned to spend together? No, she admitted, the ten days *she* had planned. Cat obviously had no great desire to spend the time with her. *Why would she?*

The phone rang as Alexa was beginning to write a note to accompany the set of keys she would send by overnight mail to Oberlin. It was James, who had left yesterday for business in California that would keep him away for the next twelve days; James, who heard immediately the soft sadness in her voice.

"She seems very ambivalent about coming," Alexa told him.

"Maybe she's feeling nostalgic about college, or a little panicky about all the new projects she's undertaking, or a lot panicky about leaving the pastoral tranquillity of Oberlin for the chaotic energy of New York."

"No, it's none of those things. Those aren't the sort of things that would bother Cat."

"She's not bothered by normal human things?" James pressed gently, ever-amazed by the portrait Alexa drew of her perfect little sister.

"I think her ambivalence is about staying in my apartment."

"I think that's nonsense." His voice softened as he added, "I, for one, have no ambivalence about staying in your apartment whatsoever. It sounds to me as if you're now free this weekend?"

"Yes, but after your meeting Saturday morning you're sailing to Catalina."

"Unless I get a better offer." James waited for a moment, then asked lightly,

"So, *do* I get a better offer? I can be in either New York or Washington by about nine Saturday night."

"New York, I guess. Cat won't be arriving until next week." Alexa added softly, gratefully, "Did I ever tell you what a nice man you are?"

"I want your honest opinion," Alexa told him solemnly as they walked from the entry hall to the living room at ten P.M. Saturday night.

"Always."

The moment they reached the living room, James saw at once what honest opinion she was seeking. The sleek shiny piano had been adorned with an assortment of pastel satin ribbons, crowned with a colorful satin bow, and draped with a hand-painted sign, lettered in her beautiful script, WELCOME, CAT!

"Since I won't be here when she arrives," Alexa explained haltingly, "I thought . . . it's too much, isn't it? Too silly."

"I think it's very nice," he reassured gently as he smiled at the emerald eyes that were uncertain, as always, about her little sister. The beribboned piano *was* nice, of course, even though a bit young; but that was where the delicate relationship between the sisters had begun, and left off—when Alexa was eighteen and Cat was only twelve.

James looked at the gift-wrapped piano and wondered what Cat would think. Would she appreciate the sentiment, or simply dismiss the effort as silliness? He hoped the little sister who meant so much to Alexa would appreciate the loving welcome. He hoped that she was nice, and that she cared about being a sister to Alexa; but, as he thought about Cat, he realized he had formed no real image of her. How could he? What he knew about her, he had learned from Alexa, whose vision of her little sister was hopelessly blurred by her own complicated emotions— and from which cloudy yet rose-colored vision she had created a fanciful portrait of perfection.

James had heard about the perfect baby, the serene little princess who felt no pain and never cried, and about the extraordinarily gifted musician she had become, but he wondered about the reality of Cat Taylor. She would be beautiful, of course, like her big sister. Would her dazzling confidence be susceptible, as Alexa's was, to lovely vulnerabilities? Or would she be, as he feared, quite self-absorbed, believing herself to be what Alexa described—the *truly* talented sister— and dismissing, as Alexa herself did, her older sister's own immense gifts?

"What are you thinking?" Alexa asked, interrupting his thoughts, wondering at the sudden gentleness on his handsome face.

"I was thinking about your little sister." About how much I hope she doesn't hurt you, he thought, drawing her to him. As he kissed her, he added softly, "Actually, that's not quite true. I was thinking mostly about your little sister's big sister."

It felt like an impulse, at once self-destructive and alluring, and yet she had simply succumbed to the powerful magnet that had tugged at her ever since the conversation with Alexa on Wednesday evening. She finished her final exams, filled boxes to be shipped with clothes and books, and packed two suitcases with the essentials: her music, her term paper in French—now due in late August—and a few clothes. By Saturday evening, she was at the Cleveland airport waiting for her already much delayed flight to LaGuardia.

The flight was originally scheduled to arrive in New York at nine, but as it became clear that it would be more like midnight, Catherine was glad she hadn't called Alexa to tell her she was coming after all. Had she called, Alexa might have taken a shuttle from National to LaGuardia and would be waiting now, too. Catherine was glad she hadn't called. Tomorrow, when she was settled in the apartment, she would let Alexa know she had arrived.

Take a cab from LaGuardia. Give the driver the address—from memory, as if you've lived there all your life!—and tell him to take the bridge, Alexa had written in the long note that accompanied the keys sent by overnight mail. Have two dollars ready to give him for the toll. The total fare should be no more than twelve dollars. I usually tip fifteen percent.

Catherine knew the instructions in Alexa's letter by heart, but as the plane touched the tarmac fifteen minutes after midnight, she worried that she would have trouble finding a cab so late at night. No, she discovered quickly, her new city was quite awake at midnight on Saturday night. As they crossed the bridge, and she saw the brightly lighted silhouette of Manhattan, she felt a sudden and surprising eagerness for the life that lay ahead. In the next six months she would explore New York, and then, beginning in January, she would travel to other exciting and vibrant cities. And maybe, along the way, she would become very calm and very sophisticated about arriving in the world's most glamorous cities at midnight.

She had felt neither calm nor sophisticated when she had given the driver the address on Riverside Drive, nor when she had handed him the bridge toll right on cue; but when the cab pulled to a stop in front of the red-brick building and the fare was precisely what Alexa had written it should be, she tipped twenty percent in sophisticated appreciation of how smoothly it all had gone.

Alexa had clearly labelled each of the three keys necessary to gain access to the security building and to the double-locked apartment. There were lights on in the apartment, as she had promised there would be, set to a timer that magically sensed when the sun rose and fell. Catherine didn't need to look at the detailed floor plan of the apartment Alexa had drawn. Like the address, she knew it by heart. But, as she wandered from the foyer to the living room, along the plush-carpeted hallway lined with walls of springtime flowers, she discovered that the apartment was much larger than she had imagined it would be—and so bright and cheerful.

Catherine's sapphire eyes misted with emotion when she saw the pastel ribbons and words of welcome on the beautiful piano. She set down her suitcase and approached the magnificent instrument, her delicate fingers touching first the sign, and then the elaborate bow, and then the satiny veneer of the expensive wood.

She was exhausted, but she knew she would play tonight anyway. She had to. It had been two days, and her music was so necessary to her now. She would play, even though she was already exhausted, and even though she knew, too, that once started she might well play all night. First, she would unpack, and shower, and then . . .

As she crossed the living room to get her suitcase and find the hallway that led to her bedroom, her eyes fell on the coffee table. There, beside a vase of roses, was Alexa's purse, and, beside that, a man's wallet. Alexa was here, and she was not alone. She had unwittingly intruded on Alexa's privacy! Even though Alexa had said she would be in Maryland, she should have called to be sure.

So much for sophistication, Catherine thought miserably as she retreated swiftly to the beautiful bedroom of lilacs far away from where Alexa slept with her overnight guest.

* * *

As always, on their weekends together, James awakened long before Alexa. After he had showered and dressed, he stood over the bed, and, as she moved slightly, like a kitten stretching and then curling back into a cozy sleep, he tucked the covers over her beautiful naked body and kissed the smile that touched her lovely lips.

"It's the crack of dawn, isn't it?"

"A little past. I'll go get *The Times* and croissants and coffee, OK?"

"Hmmmmm," Alexa purred. She allowed herself this luxury once a week, a languid counterbalance to her high energy life, a dreamy lazy day in bed to recharge her batteries. As far as she could tell, James never recharged his extraordinarily high energy batteries, at least not with sleep. Sailing, not sleep, she decided, was the counterbalance to the relentless intensity of his life. James never slept late, not even on their weekends together, but he would return to her bed and . . . "Then you'll come back and wake me up properly?"

"You know I will."

His wallet was in the living room, but long before he reached the coffee table he had stopped his graceful stride. She was silhouetted by the pale golden rays of dawn that filtered through the lace curtains. Her hair was like his, midnight black and shining, and, like his, still damp from a recent shower. As she bent her head toward the keyboard, the glistening black spilled forward, obscuring his view of her profile with a veil of luxuriant curls. Her face was hidden, but her hands were fully exposed. Her delicate white fingers danced, touching the ivory keys with exquisite caresses—like whispered kisses—but not depressing them.

No sound came from the piano, but it hardly mattered. Simply watching the dance of her lovely fingers was mesmerizing . . . magical. James was quite content to watch in silence, and he did until the compelling need to see her face urged him on his legitimate mission across the living room to his wallet.

He wanted to see this black-haired Alexa, and he had invaded her privacy long enough without making his presence known. He crossed the room, expecting his movement to alert her, but she was lost in the magnificent music that surely swirled in her mind even though the room was silent. So he simply stood, staring at her boldly, content to wait until she sensed his stare, having no wish for that to happen soon because he was as happily lost in watching her as she was happily lost in her music.

He could see her face now, a wonderful view because the rich black curls that would have fallen into her eyes were held captive by a gold barrette, and he realized that the resemblance he had anticipated didn't exist at all. The Taylor sisters did not look alike; but there was a striking similarity nonetheless in the expression each wore as she so dazzlingly practiced her art—a bewitching mixture of determination and hope, concentration and dreams, perfectionism and magic. Like Alexa, Cat was at once performer and audience, focused on her performance, wanting to make it perfect, and yet lost, too, in the magnificence of the creation. Alexa gave life and spirit and soul to the beautifully scripted words she spoke. Cat quite obviously did the same for the notes she played.

So this was Alexa's little sister.

Catherine sensed his presence then and her graceful hands abruptly halted their delicate dance. *And it was as if the music had stopped.* The soundless room suddenly seemed more still. The magic vanished.

Until she looked up at him.

And then there was new, quite unexpected magic as he saw the bright blue eyes, dark-circled from lack of sleep, surprised, questioning, and so magnificently innocent.

Alexa had described Cat's eyes to him—the brilliant blue of a winter sky after a snowstorm—but he had discounted that description as he had discounted all the remarkable words she had used to describe her little sister. Now James gazed at the remarkable eyes and realized that Alexa's words were only the beginning of the image. The blue was indeed the brilliant blue of a winter sky; but there was more in the magnificent sapphire . . . a crystal clarity, a bright hopefulness, and, like her snow-white skin, an astonishing purity.

James remembered his worry that Alexa's sister would be self-absorbed, insensitive, dazzlingly confident. But she was none of those things. She was, as Alexa had tried to tell him, quite timid; and too, when it mattered, as it had that day at the polo field, she was quite brave. He saw both timidity and bravery now, because even though her bright-blue eyes courageously held his intense appraising gaze, her snow-white cheeks blushed a soft, timid pink.

"Hello. You must be Catherine," he said finally, deciding that she *should* be Catherine not Cat, but then wondering, "Or do you prefer Cat?"

"Catherine is fine," she replied, for the first time ever preferring her given name to Alexa's nickname, because of the way "Catherine" sounded when he spoke it.

"Good. I'm James."

"Hi." Catherine smiled a brave yet uncertain hello to the handsome man who gazed at her so intently.

She had never before met any of Alexa's "men." Whenever Alexa returned to Topeka, she always came alone, cheerfully explaining to the curious neighbors that whichever handsome leading man to whom she was currently romantically linked by the entertainment press was simply a good friend. "Nothing serious," she would announce with a laugh. "I'm still married to my career!"

Alexa never brought her lovers to Topeka, but now Catherine was in New York, in Alexa's apartment, and here was this most handsome man, gazing at her, and . . .

How she must look to him! Catherine remembered with dismay her wet hair, and the bangs unceremoniously restrained off her face, and her sweatshirt and jeans, and the extra pounds she now carried. Was the curiosity in his dark blue eyes simply amazement at the contrast between her—who he believed to be Alexa's sister—and the beautiful provocative woman with whom he had spent a night of passion? Should she confess everything? *I'm the ugly duckling, you see, but it doesn't reflect on Alexa at all, because she's not really my sister* . . .

Catherine might have blurted out that confession, or simply dashed out of the living room in mortification, but the powerful feelings that compelled her to stay overrode the impulses that urged her to hide, and all words remained very far from the surface, drowned deep in her overwhelming shyness. She neither ran away nor spoke; but somehow she willed her fingers to unclasp the barrette that held her bangs, freeing the black curls to partially curtain her so very exposed eyes. Then she just sat, quite still, even though her heart raced with sudden restless energy.

James's heart raced too. The racing had begun the moment her surprised blue eyes had first met his, and it had intensified as he had become so very aware of her embarrassment. Her embarrassment, and his own . . .

Alexa's lovely naked body was covered, of course, but she slept contentedly in the bedroom where they had made love, and where her clothes were scattered still, a flamboyant symbol of the urgency of their passion. James could not send this innocent young woman into Alexa's bedroom, and he even felt awkward about returning there himself to awaken her sleeping sister. Not that it wasn't abundantly obvious that he and Alexa were lovers, or that he saw anything but acceptance in the innocent blue eyes, but still . . .

"Alexa is sleeping," he said finally, after making a solemn vow that there would never again be a night when he made love with Alexa in one bedroom while Catherine slept in another. "I'm going out to get the paper, and fresh-ground coffee, and croissants. Come with me, Catherine."

It was a command, gently given. But even if James had posed it as a question, she would have gone with him; because all the warnings that reminded her of how she looked, and how impossible it would be for her to find words to say to him, would have been silenced by whatever it was that would have compelled her to answer "yes."

CHAPTER TEN

It wasn't yet seven A.M., but the June sun was already warm. Basking in the warmth of the light blue summer sky, the sometimes harsh and menacing city felt friendly and safe. The fragrance of freshly baked bread erased all memories of exhaust fumes and diesel, and the balmy air was alive with the songs of seagulls and the soft thud of jogging shoes on pavement.

They bought the Sunday *Times* from a corner newsstand, and croissants and fresh-ground coffee from a nearby bakery. Then, wanting to allow time for Alexa to awaken and make the discovery of Catherine's arrival before they returned, James suggested that they sit for a while on a bench by the river.

"Alexa will be so thrilled that you're here," he told her when they were seated.

"Do you think so?" she asked, the flicker of hope fading swiftly to doubt as she remembered that she had intruded on Alexa's intimate privacy with *him*. Surely that intrusion alone might make her very angry.

"I know so. Now you'll have some time together before she has to be in Washington and your classes begin at Juilliard."

"She told you about Juilliard?"

"About Juilliard, and the album you're recording, and your upcoming concert tour. You're going to be very busy."

Catherine shrugged, smiled a lovely embarrassed smile, then turned her eyes from him to the early morning activity of the river. Already a small fleet of brightly colored sailboats glided across the shimmering water.

"Are you a sailor?" James asked.

"No. Well, I don't know. I've never sailed."

"So you might be."

"I guess. It looks so peaceful."

"It is. Very."

"You're a sailor?" she asked bravely, turning once again to him.

"An avid one. Which means, when you're ready to give sailing a try, I should be the one to introduce you to it."

"Oh, no . . ."

"No?"

"Does Alexa like to sail?"

"Alexa *will* sail, although she gets a little restless. However, with you there to talk to that wouldn't be a problem." James paused as he saw the sapphire surprise at his confidence that her older sister's restlessness would be calmed by her presence. He smiled, underscoring that confidence, and asked, "So, would you like to give it a try sometime?"

"Yes, I would. Very much," Catherine answered softly.

"Good. Synchronizing schedules may be tricky, but, if we haven't found a time before August, there's a party then, to which you are invited, at my parents' home in Maryland. It will be the third weekend, the nineteenth and—"

"Cat!"

"Alexa," Catherine whispered. She turned in the direction of the familiar voice and stood as Alexa approached. "Hi."

"Hi." Alexa gave Catherine a brief hug and forced her smile not to wobble and her eyes not to reveal her concern. Something was terribly wrong! Cat's dark-circled eyes told of her sleeplessness, and there was heaviness now, a sallow, unhealthy, *troubled* layer where before there had been only soft, sensual, beautiful plumpness. What had happened to disrupt Cat's calm serenity so dramatically? Would Cat tell her? Alexa hoped so. She smiled reassuringly to the tired blue eyes hidden beneath the dark black curls. "I'm so glad you're here!"

"Me, too. The apartment is so beautiful, and my bedroom, and the piano . . . Thank you."

"You're welcome." Alexa turned to James, thanking him with a soft smile and then teasing lightly, "I had a feeling, when I awakened and discovered that Cat had arrived and you both were gone, that you might be watching the sailboats."

"It seemed like a good place to enjoy the morning sunshine."

"James is a sailing fanatic," Alexa explained to Catherine.

"She already knows that," James replied with a smile. Then, turning to Catherine, he added, "And, I hope, she's already accepted an invitation to go sailing—at the party at Inverness in August if not before."

"Yes," Catherine answered, a soft reply that was unwittingly embellished by a lovely smile and rosy-pink cheeks.

James returned to the apartment with them for a leisurely cup of coffee, then made the gracious exit he had been planning ever since Alexa had appeared at the river. He had known for weeks how important this time was for Alexa, and now he knew it was terribly important for Catherine, too. He had seen her reaction when Alexa had called her name—the sudden tension, the delicate hands curled into tight fists—and her grateful relief when her big sister had been so obviously happy to see her.

James knew one sister well, and the other sister hardly at all, but he wanted to reassure them both, "This will be fine, you'll see, because both of you want to be close." But he knew that wanting wasn't enough. And now he knew, too, that Catherine had secrets and doubts, just as Alexa did. Somehow they had to find a way through the treacherous emotional mine field of their past. Could it be navigated safely? James didn't know. He couldn't reassure. All he could do was leave them alone so that they could begin to try.

James left, and Alexa and Catherine were alone, and . . .

"This is so nice of you," Catherine murmured over and over as together they pored over the maps Alexa had made, personalized expressly for her little sister's new life in Manhattan. The safe, *safest*, routes to Juilliard and the recording studio were charted in vivid colors; and there were also safe, colorful paths to the best places to shop, or browse, or simply see the sights of the vibrant city.

So nice, Catherine whispered to the woman she loved and admired, and who seemed genuinely happy to see her. But would Alexa's warmth turn to ice if she knew that her gracious welcome was for a stranger, not a sister? The question spun in Catherine's mind, tormenting her, distracting her. She was so unused to deception, and here she was deceiving Alexa, of all people! But she couldn't tell Alexa the truth, not now, not yet. The conflict raged within her, depleting the energy she needed to find interesting *other* topics to discuss with Alexa and driving her even deeper into silence.

"What did you think of James?" Alexa asked, when she had said all she could think of to say about the maps she had made. She wanted to ask Cat what had happened to make her beautiful eyes so terribly troubled. Maybe someday she could ask such a question, and maybe someday her little sister would believe that she could trust her enough to tell her everything. But, Alexa reminded herself sadly, Cat has no reason to believe that now. So she found a safe topic to fill the lingering awkward silence: James, a recent memory shared by the Taylor sisters, warm, pleasant, and quite untarnished by the past.

"I think he's wonderful," Catherine answered swiftly, relieved to be able to speak an unequivocal truth.

"I think he's wonderful, too."

"You're in love with him," Catherine added softly. It was a statement not a question, because the affection between Alexa and James had been so obvious. They hadn't been physically affectionate in front of her at all, but their eyes and their smiles and the tenderness in their voices betrayed their true feelings. Alexa loved James, and James loved Alexa. And there was more: James's love for Alexa cast a magical net so wide that, at its very edges, there was even a gentle kindness in his dark blue eyes *for her*. "And he's in love with you."

For a moment, Alexa was taken aback, surprised by both the words and the honesty. But as she gazed at the eyes that met hers with solemn sapphire candor, she suddenly saw the twelve-year-old sister with whom there had been the fragile beginnings of friendship that distant spring. Cat had been so honest then, a little girl who had not yet learned the coy games that little girls learn and women perfect. The lovely unaffected honesty was there still, Alexa realized, because Cat had spent her life playing the music she loved, and she had never learned to play the social games at all.

"I had forgotten how direct you are, Cat," Alexa teased fondly. But even the obvious fondness didn't prevent sudden flickers of worry in Catherine's eyes.

"Oh, I'm sorry. I guess I shouldn't have—"

"Yes you *should* have," Alexa interjected emphatically. She added softly, "I want us to be able to talk about the important things in our lives, Cat."

"I want that, too."

"Do you? I'm so glad." Alexa smiled, somehow managing to hold the smile even though her confidence wavered as she thought about what she could say to Cat about James.

He *was* one of the very important things in her life, of course, but her little sister had announced with surprising certainty that she and James were "in love"; and Alexa knew they weren't. They were the skeptic and cynic, after all. Neither even *believed* in falling in love. Admittedly, she had already decided that one day her gentle, wonderful, skeptical friend *would* fall in love, and she had even privately wondered about the woman who would steal James's heart. One day, Alexa was very sure, James would find a consuming love. And what about her? Did her newfound belief in the possibility of love for skeptical James extend even to cynical her? No, not yet. And yet, *because of James*, she was beginning to believe in something she had never before imagined possible: herself, and her worthiness.

One day the skeptic, and perhaps even the cynic, might fall in love. But, even though they were wonderful friends and wonderful lovers, she and James were not *in love* with each other. But how did she explain that truth to the innocent blue eyes that gazed at her now? Alexa had no doubt that her little sister believed in love, and would find a perfect one; and she had no doubt either that Cat would make love only with the man who was that perfect and forever love.

But I'm not so perfect, Cat, Alexa thought. I never have been. And I have made a solemn vow to be honest with you, even though I know that the honest revelation of my flaws may disappoint.

"James is very important to me," she said finally to the earnest and attentive sapphire. "He is an important part of my life and always will be. I don't think that James and I will be together forever, Cat, but I do know that whatever happens between us, I will always care about him and his happiness."

"But that's love, isn't it?"

"Is it?"

"I think so. I think that when you love someone, you care about that person's happiness even if you're not destined to be together."

"Have you ever been in love, Cat?" Alexa asked, suddenly wondering if it could possibly have been a disastrous, and not perfect, love affair that had so dramatically disrupted the serenity of her sister's life.

"Me?" Catherine's eyes widened with surprise. "Oh, no . . ."

"Is everything all right?" Alexa pressed gently.

"It will be," Catherine answered quietly. *Please, please, please.* "I'm very glad to be here."

"And I'm very glad that you are. And so is James. Now that you've met him, I'll give you his unlisted phone numbers at work and at home. You really should feel free to call him any time. I know he'll be calling to check on you, too."

"No! Please don't ask James to call me. I know he's very busy, and I'll be fine. He doesn't need to worry about me."

"I wasn't going to ask him to call, Cat. But I know he will want to, without me asking."

"Then, would you please ask him *not* to?"

"All right, if that's what you'd prefer."

"Yes. Please."

"All right," Alexa assured again. After a thoughtful silence, she asked, "What about the party at his parents' home in Maryland?"

"I'd like to go to the party . . . if you're going."

"Of course I am. I have a promise etched in stone from the producer that I'm off for the entire weekend. Cat, you need to know that Hillary Ballinger will be there. She's married to Senator Robert McAllister now, and James and Robert are friends."

"Have you seen her?"

"I have, and it wasn't wonderful, but it was OK."

"Then it's OK with me, too."

"So?" James asked when he called from San Francisco Wednesday evening.

"So, we're having a nice time."

"Good. Am I interrupting?"

"No. I'm in my bedroom reading a script and she's practicing."

"Has she mastered Manhattan?"

"She will have, at least the necessary routes, by the time we go to Maryland. We're going to spend Saturday night at RoseCliff, then she'll return by herself and we'll both settle into our long, hot, busy summers."

"You know that I'm available if she needs anything. Will you tell her that?"

"I already have. She thinks you're wonderful, by the way . . ."

"But?"

"But she asked me to ask you not to call."

"Did she give a reason?"

"No. But I think she's a little—a lot—overwhelmed by you, and I think she's embarrassed about her appearance."

"Her appearance?"

"Her weight. She's planning to diet this summer in addition to everything else."

"I didn't notice that she was overweight," James said with quiet surprise. He believed that Catherine must truly be overweight, because Alexa's tone conveyed such loving concern; but he, the man whose lovers had been the most sleek and beautiful women in the world, hadn't noticed. What he had seen, what he remembered with vivid and enchanting clarity, were bright blue eyes, and snow white skin, and flushed pink cheeks, and black velvet hair, and delicate dancing hands, and brave-and-timid innocence. That was his memory of Catherine, and it was lovely and gentle. But, he realized, her memory of him was obviously uncomfortable and embarrassed. "Is she planning to come to the party at Inverness?"

"Yes. In fact, that weekend is the date by which all the major goals of her summer will have been met. Her French paper will be in the mail for Oberlin on that Friday, and a third of the new pieces she needs to learn for the tour will have been perfected, and her classes at Juilliard will be under control, and a sensible number of pounds will have been lost."

"It sounds as though you won't be seeing much of her this summer," James observed gently, even though he heard no disappointment in Alexa's voice.

"No. We may not actually see each other again until the weekend at Inverness, but we plan to spend some money on phone bills."

"Without the answered-in-French switchboard?"

"Without that." Alexa added softly, "And, I think, with a new closeness to the voice at the other end of the phone."

Even though she had never dieted before, Catherine knew how to do it sensibly. The nation's obsession with thinness, and concerns about the extremes to which teenaged girls would go to be thin, resulted in the addition of nutrition and proper diet techniques to the curricula of most high school health classes. Catherine knew how to diet sensibly, by eating small portions of nutritious food, and exercising, and modifying untoward behaviors; and that was how she dieted for the first week.

Then, even though she knew it was dangerous, she stopped eating altogether. The decision to diet incautiously—to lose as much weight as quickly as she could—matched the incautiousness of the decision to diet in the first place. She had always been plump, of course, and the plumpness itself prevented comparisons to slender Alexa. Would they be studied more closely for similarities if she was thin? What if the face that emerged from beneath the soft protective layers of flesh was so strikingly different from Alexa's that even Alexa herself began to wonder?

It was a terrifying worry, but a worry that was, remarkably, overridden by an even more compelling wish to look the best she possibly could. For herself, whoever *she* was. And for Alexa, who might be more proud of her. And . . . for James.

After two days without food, the gnawing hunger stopped and Catherine felt an astonishing clarity. All her senses were heightened. The world seemed brighter, more vivid, and her music rang with such purity, and the warm summer wind caressed her skin with such tingling delicacy, and sleep felt luxurious, and water tasted sweet, and . . .

Sometimes the clarity clouded slightly—a sudden breathlessness, a little dizziness on standing, a whisper of confusion or forgetfulness. Catherine knew the meaning of those clouds—signs that she needed food—and she begrudgingly obeyed the signs, providing a little necessary fuel for the body that had, for that blurry moment, needed more energy than was readily available from its stores.

She decided that had her demands for energy not been so high, she might have been able to fast entirely. But she needed energy for her classes, and the new pieces she was learning, and the French paper she was writing, and the frequent meetings with her manager at Fordyce who was arranging the concert tour. Her demands for energy were high, which meant that occasionally she had to eat; and yet, paradoxically, in the midst of days with little or no food, there came sudden, powerful, almost euphoric bursts of new energy. It was that omnipotent, euphoric energy that prompted her to agree to more and more appearances on the tour, until finally she was left with only a three week break between the end of her solidly booked North American tour in June and the beginning of her equally committed European tour in July.

Catherine's baggy clothes told her that she was losing weight, lots of it, and in the shower her hands soaped a new and different body. There were vestiges of her plump self, soft full breasts and curved hips, but mostly there was boniness and a very slender waist and thighs that no longer touched. She knew, from her baggy clothes and soapy hands, about the new body that was emerging as the fat melted away; but until ten days before the party at Inverness, she had no idea about her new face.

When she finally forced herself to sit before the mirrored antique vanity in her bedroom, Catherine saw the face of a woman—a *woman*—and a stranger. The woman bore no resemblance to Alexa, of course, nor did she look like the plump little girl who had gazed back at her on the rare occasions in the past twenty-one years that she had glanced at herself in a mirror. This woman with the rich black velvet hair and high aristocratic cheekbones and huge sapphire blue eyes and full provocative lips was a stranger—a hauntingly beautiful stranger who could turn heads and draw smiles, like the surprising appreciative smiles that had been following her around Manhattan for the past few weeks.

Catherine's initial appraisal of the strange and beautiful woman in the mirror was analytical. Then, quite suddenly, the appraisal became personal, and startling. *This is who I am.* Since May, she had known who she *wasn't*, neither the daughter nor the sister she had believed herself to be. Now, as she gazed at this new face, she wondered, for the first time, about the mother who had abandoned her.

Did you look like this? she silently asked the image in the mirror. On impulse, she removed the sapphire necklace from its hiding place in a remote corner of the vanity's top drawer and held it to her slender ivory neck. She stared at the reflection of the precious gems, an exact match of her own sapphire eyes, and wondered if this necklace, a gift from her father to her mother, had been created because the color was an exact match, too, of her mother's eyes.

As she gazed at her image in the mirror, her starved-for-days vision blurred, blurring the image, changing it, aging it slightly until . . . Was she looking at her mother? Did she have questions for that beautiful woman?

"Oh, yes, I have questions for you, Mother," she whispered. "What was wrong with me that you could so easily give me away? What was it about me that made you unable to love me enough to keep me? Do you know, Mother," she asked softly, "how much I hate you?"

"Truly an exquisite piece," the jeweller at Tiffany raved as he examined the sapphire necklace through his magnifying glass. "The stones all appear to be flawless. Are they?"

"I don't know."

"It would say on the appraisal." He saw her confusion and wondered for a moment if this beautiful woman dressed in baggy jeans was a cat burglar, a jewel thief who had come to Tiffany to sell this stolen work of art. He had assumed that she was the owner—a mistress, most likely, of one of Manhattan's wealthiest men— dressed waif-like as a disguise. He had assumed that the necklace was hers, and that she wanted to sell it, the affair over, or, perhaps, because she needed money for the cocaine that was possibly the only nourishment she provided her thin body.

"I don't have the appraisal. It was a gift."

"Yes. Of course. Did you wish to sell it?"

"No."

"To have it appraised then?"

"I just wanted to know if you recognized it. I had hoped to trace it to its original owner."

"Oh. Well, the design, the simple elegance of a heart pendant suspended on a strand of precious gems, is quite traditional. All the major jewellers would have similar pieces. The extraordinary quality and color of the sapphires might be a clue, depending on what records were kept by the designer."

"I have no idea who designed it," Catherine said quietly. Just as she had no idea why she was here. She only knew that something very powerful—surely anger, not sentiment—had compelled her to leave the mirrored vanity in her apartment moments after whispering to the blurry image and to come here to ask these questions.

"The designer I can tell you. All jewellers engrave their initials, usually on the clasp. Let me see."

Ever since she had begun to starve herself, Catherine's heart had set a new pace, fast and unhealthy. Now, as she waited to learn the name of the jeweller who had made the necklace, her already racing heart began to flutter, leaving her lightheaded and breathless. I will eat some sugar and some protein, she silently promised her swirling head and galloping heart, just as soon as I learn the name.

"This is probably not the original clasp," the jeweller said after several moments. "It looks very new."

"The necklace hasn't been worn for twenty-one years."

"Oh. Well, anyway, it must be a replacement clasp because I don't find any jeweller's initials. You know about the words that are engraved on the clasp?"

"Words? No. What do they say?"

"Something in French."

"May I look?"

Catherine held the magnifying glass in her hands, willing them to stop trembling just for a moment, just long enough for the tiny words engraved in gold to come into focus.

Then there they were: *Je t'aimerai toujours.* "I will love you always" engraved in the language that she, the little girl from Kansas, so inexplicably loved and spoke more fluently, more effortlessly, than she spoke English.

Je t'aimerai toujours. Was it a promise from her father to her mother? Yes, of course. It was surely *not* a promise from her mother to her. Or if it was a promise of forever love from her mother, it was a false one, *a lie.*

As Catherine left Tiffany to find something to calm her fluttering heart, she left with the certain knowledge that the sapphire necklace could never lead her to her mother. And that was just as well. In fact, it was quite comforting to have an answer—"It's no use!"—to future renegade impulses from her heart that might urge her again to search for someone she did not truly wish to find.

PART TWO

CHAPTER ELEVEN

"*Y*our parents are wonderful. You come by your niceness honestly," Alexa told James as he drove her back to RoseCliff following Sunday evening dinner with Arthur and Marion Sterling at Inverness. "Not to mention your good looks."

"Thank you. They liked you, too, of course. Why wouldn't they? Maybe we can do this again before the party."

"I'd like that. Speaking of the party, when I spoke to Cat last night she asked me what clothes to bring . . . and I wasn't sure."

James heard the uncertainty in her last words and gave her a quizzical glance.

"OK, I confess, I'm a country girl from Kansas and the only house parties I'm familiar with are in the movies. So, will this be like the picnic at Twelve Oaks in *Gone With The Wind?* You know, tightly-corseted women in hoop-skirted frocks who flirt outrageously, eat nothing, and retire for naps while the menfolk smoke cigars, drink brandy, and discuss politics? Or will it be like an Agatha Christie murder mystery in which a group of people with intertwining secrets arrive at a remote cliff-top mansion, sip champagne, and eye each other sinisterly as they wait for the drama to unfold?"

"Neither—although I have not yet exacted a promise from you that you won't eye Hillary sinisterly."

"You know I couldn't make such a promise, sugar," Alexa drawled, batting her long eyelashes as she mimicked Hillary's Southern accent perfectly.

"I think you'll be shamed into impeccable behavior because of Brynne, whom you will like very much, not to mention my parents and your little sister and—"

"I'm sure I will! So, how about some impeccable attire to match?"

"OK. The garden party on Sunday will be fairly dressy—like a formal summer wedding—but Saturday will be very casual. Sundresses, shorts, swimsuits, whatever."

"Swimsuits," Alexa mused provocatively, "I wonder how Hillary looks in a swimsuit these days."

"Sensational, I would imagine. Not as sensational as you, naturally, but sensational nonetheless. However, Hillary won't be appearing in a swimsuit."

"No? Why not? Improper First Lady attire?" Alexa's tease faded as she saw the seriousness in his handsome face and sensed that he was debating how much to say. After a thoughtful silence, she guessed softly, "It's something to do with Robert, isn't it? Because he has scars from Vietnam?"

"Yes."

"Oh." Alexa frowned softly, sympathetically. She hadn't planned to wear a swimsuit anyway, of course, because of Cat. Her little sister reported that her diet was going well, but even with a perfect body Alexa knew that timid Cat would not feel comfortable appearing in a swimsuit amongst strangers. She hadn't planned to wear a swimsuit because of Cat, and now, because of the dirt-poor country boy who had traded in the combat zone of his childhood for an even more horrible one, there was yet another important reason not to. "So, no swimsuits, snazzy for Sunday, casual for Saturday. That's easy. I'll tell Cat."

"How is she?"

"She sounds fine, peppy and positive. Her French paper is virtually done, her classes and new pieces are under control, and she says she's happy with her diet."

"Good. Oh, be sure to remind her—and yourself—to pack jeans, sweaters, and tennis shoes for our sail."

"Aye, aye, Captain."

Catherine would have liked to spend the Friday night before the party with Alexa at RoseCliff. She would have liked to see again the bountiful garden of roses, and she would have very much liked to have had an evening alone with Alexa.

But Catherine knew with absolute certainty that she didn't have the strength to climb the three flights of stairs to the clifftop cottage. So she flew to Washington on Saturday morning instead, arriving with only enough time to drive directly from National airport to Inverness. Alexa was already at the gate when the plane landed and the passengers began to disembark. She smiled admiringly at the stunningly beautiful woman who was approaching her . . . who was vaguely familiar . . . who was her baby sister!

"Cat! You're so *gorgeous*. But . . ."

"But what?" Catherine asked anxiously.

"But you've lost far too much weight in such a short period of time . . . haven't you?"

"No. I'm fine, really, Alexa."

"Well, you certainly look fine." Alexa tilted her golden head and carefully studied Cat's face, ignoring the flickers of sapphire worry. Finally, smiling, she said, "I hadn't realized it before, but you've got Mom's cheekbones—high, classically sculpted, incredibly patrician. I always secretly wished that I'd inherited them, but now I see that they look far better on you."

"Thank you," Catherine murmured softly, breathing finally, a breath of pure relief. But the wonderful relief was fleeting. As a sudden sternness subdued Alexa's smile, Catherine felt sharp claws of fear mercilessly clutch her ever-empty stomach. Had Alexa realized that her enthusiastic acceptance of her newly thin and dramatically changed little sister had been far too hasty? Was she about to declare that, on closer scrutiny, the lovely aristocratic cheekbones didn't really resemble Jane's after all? In fact, there was really nothing familiar looking about her, no family resemblance whatsoever.

But Alexa's sudden solemnity wasn't a prelude to a pronouncement that Catherine was an impostor. It was another worry altogether, a gentle, loving, sisterly one.

"You just stopped eating didn't you? Don't answer. I know you and your incredible discipline. But, Cat, you've lost enough weight now, haven't you?"

"I guess," Catherine replied, although she wasn't entirely certain. Losing weight had become so easy. Why not lose a few more pounds? She had lost all urge to eat, now eating only when breathlessness or weakness warned her that she must. And when she did eat the necessary nourishment, the uncomfortable fullness made food feel far more like medication than pleasure.

"*Yes.* Any more would be too much. You could not look more stunning, Cat. Wait until James sees you!"

"Hello, Alexa, dear," Marion Sterling said affectionately when they arrived at Inverness. Marion's welcoming smile and twinkling blue eyes first greeted the Taylor sister she already liked so much and then fell on her little sister. "And you must be Catherine. Welcome. We're absolutely delighted that you were able to join us this weekend."

"Thank you," Catherine whispered softly as she met James's mother. As with James, she instantly felt the warmth and kindness, a magical net of affection cast for Alexa but which captured her—a most willing captive—as well. "It's so nice of you to include me."

"It's our pleasure."

"Are we the last to arrive?" Alexa asked. "We ran into a bit more traffic than I had anticipated for a Saturday morning."

"You are the last to arrive, but you're not the least bit late. Luncheon won't be served for another hour. Why don't you get settled and then join the rest of us on the south veranda?"

Catherine and Alexa were led to their adjacent suites by one of the many staff brought in for the weekend of entertaining at Inverness. Alexa knew already that she would not be sharing her room in the mansion's east wing with James. On this weekend, at this house party in Maryland, only wedded couples were sharing beds. Alexa knew . . . and approved. Inverness was Marion and Arthur's home, after all, and, although her own parents were almost a generation younger than James's, it would have been the same in Topeka. Besides, having a room next to Cat's would be fun. Perhaps they would stay up until all hours discussing their impressions of the day.

Alexa unpacked her small suitcase quickly, brushed her long golden hair, gave herself a critical but ultimately approving glance in the full length mirror, and left her suite to find Cat. She was unpacking still, quite unaware of Alexa's sudden appearance in the open doorway. For several moments, Alexa simply watched, startled anew by the change in her little sister's appearance. The plump, luxuriant, sensuous beauty had given way to an even more beautiful one, slightly haunting, elegant and mysterious. Even the way Cat moved had changed. Her motions were slower now and ballerina graceful. Alexa had no idea that her sister's new gracefulness—so elegant and so regal—was simply a manifestation of her critically limited energy and her starving body's instinctive attempt to conserve whatever energy it could.

"Hi," Alexa said finally, when it became obvious that Cat wasn't about to sense her presence. "Aren't these rooms luxurious?"

"Hi." Catherine greeted Alexa and then responded softly to her question, "Oh, yes, very luxurious."

"Are you about ready to join the others?"

"I thought I'd change first."

"Really?" Alexa asked with surprise. Cat looked so beautiful in the simple elegance of the cream-colored silk blouse and blue linen skirt that it seemed a shame to change. "What you're wearing is fine . . . stunning."

"Thanks, but I think I'd like to change into a dress. Marion said luncheon wouldn't be for an hour, so there's time, isn't there?"

"Sure. Plenty of time."

"Then I will change," Catherine said decisively as she moved to the closet where she had hung her new clothes. How long it had taken her to select her wardrobe for this weekend! The selections had been hers, even though at each Fifth Avenue boutique the saleswomen had been very eager to help. More than one had shrewdly deduced, with knowing and appreciative smiles, that she must be Eileen Ford's newest discovery, and all had tried to dress her model-thin body in the latest fashions. Catherine looked stunning in the summer collections of Armani, Karan, and Klein, but, she explained with quiet apology, the ultra-chic clothes weren't really *her*. For her entire life, she had dressed of necessity, without a thought to fashion or style, but with her new shape came new attention to clothes. She had a definite preference, she discovered, and it was a preference for traditional elegance. She withdrew from the closet a very soft, very feminine, very demure floral print dress and held it for Alexa to see. "I thought this."

"That's beautiful." Alexa tugged at her lower lip, suddenly uncertain about what to do. Sisters undoubtedly dressed and undressed in front of each other all the time, but the Taylor sisters never had. "Should I go on ahead?"

"Oh, no," Catherine replied swiftly. "Would you mind waiting?"

"Not at all."

Alexa sat on the bed, determined neither to stare nor to avert her gaze entirely while her little sister changed. But, drawn by powerful magnets of concern and curiosity, it was virtually impossible to not to spend more time looking than not. It was concern that first drew Alexa's gaze, because as Cat shed the layers of silk and linen her true thinness was so abundantly obvious; and it was curiosity that held it, because her little sister's shape was so unlike her own. Alexa's sleek, perfect, golden body was made for scant bikinis and provocative gowns. There was no golden sleekness to Cat's new shape; but, Alexa thought, the snow white skin and curves that were softly rounded despite her thinness sent a message of pure femininity.

"Are you looking forward to the weekend?" Alexa asked impulsively, aware of the lingering silence and the intensity of her own stares.

"Oh, yes, of course. Have you already met everyone?"

"Everyone except Brynne—Robert's sister—and her husband Stephen. James says they both are very nice, although we may not really get to know Stephen. He's an architect in Richmond, where he and Brynne live, and he's in the midst of some project that will prevent him from arriving until the party tomorrow. So, today it will be Brynne, and the Sterlings—you'll like Arthur as much as Marion—and the McAllisters, and Elliot Archer."

"Elliot Archer?"

"I may not have mentioned Elliot before because James wasn't certain he'd be able to come. He's something like the nation's—which I think also means the world's—leading expert on terrorism. He's in his mid-fifties, although he looks much younger, never married, very dashing. I think he began his career as a secret agent, an authentic James Bond, and he still has that intriguing allure. I met him last week. He's very nice, too. I'm sure you'll like him." Alexa's description of Elliot stopped abruptly and she said quietly, "That dress is sensational on you."

"Thank you. I was wondering if . . .?"

"Yes?"

"Well, I've never worn make-up. I went to the cosmetic counters at some of the department stores but what they put on me seemed like too much. I thought maybe you could suggest something."

Catherine's voice trailed off, and for a moment Alexa was silent, moved by her little sister's uncertain request for her advice, and eager to be needed, but confronted with the truth: brilliant blue eyes framed by long midnight-black lashes, lovely pink cheeks, and full rosy lips. Finally, she said honestly, "You don't need make-up, Cat."

"I don't?"

"No. You have Mom's high aristocratic cheekbones, and like me you've inherited Dad's natural coloring."

"Here you are," Marion greeted Alexa and Catherine warmly when they appeared on the veranda. At the arrival of the beautiful Taylor sisters, conversations halted in mid-sentence and all attention focused on the house party's final two guests. "Now, let's see, who knows whom?"

"I know Alexa," the very handsome silver-haired man standing beside Marion admitted with a welcoming smile.

"Hello, Arthur," Alexa replied. "Arthur, I'd like you to meet my sister, Cat."

"Welcome, Cat."

"Thank you," Catherine answered softly to James's father. "Arthur."

"And this is Robert," Arthur said, gesturing to the man beside him, continuing the introductions as if they were in a reception line at a wedding.

"Hello, Robert."

"Hello, Cat." As Robert smiled warmly at Alexa's stunningly beautiful little sister, he wondered, not for the first time in the three months since he had last seen her, what reception he would get from Alexa herself. Until that afternoon, after her performance, she had always greeted him with magnificent emerald ice. But, for those brief moments, the ice had melted into something even more magnificent, a warm, welcoming emerald glow. Welcoming, and memorable. How well Robert remembered those moments, and how he had hoped that today the ice would be defrosted still. And now, as he left the luminous sapphire eyes and met the sparkling emerald ones, he saw quite eloquently, quite wonderfully, that they, too, remembered. "Hello, Alexa."

"Hello, Robert," she answered softly, luxuriating for a moment in the smiling dark eyes. Finally, she forced herself to leave that welcoming warmth to turn to his wife's always cool disdain, and, with carefully rehearsed off-handedness, she asked. "You remember Cat, don't you, Hillary?"

"Of course I do. How lovely to see you again, Cat."

"It's lovely to see you, too, Hillary," Catherine echoed politely, even though the sight of the senator's beautiful wife caused a pulsing thunder in her brain that made her far more dizzy than the lightheadedness which had been her constant companion since the third week of her diet. Catherine had been worried about seeing Alexa for fear that Alexa would guess she was not truly her little sister; and she had been worried about seeing James, worried yet eager, for reasons she could not define. But her greatest fear about today had been the fear of seeing Hillary again. What if the cruel girl from Dallas had grown into a cruel woman who would turn to the other guests, as she had turned to her teenaged friends at the polo field that day, and bluntly demand, "I ask you all, do these two look one tiny little bit like sisters? Isn't it obvious? They can't be. One of them is an impostor!" Amidst the dizzying thunder, Catherine bravely met Hillary's sable-colored eyes and felt the heat of her appraising patrician stare. Appraising and approving . . .

"My mother is in absolute heaven that you've agreed to spend a second week performing with the Dallas symphony this spring," Hillary gushed graciously. "Not that two weeks is enough, mind you, but at least it's better than just the one."

"Oh, good. I'm glad," Catherine murmured softly, quite unaware that she had agreed to a second week in Dallas. During her starvation-induced euphoria, she had simply empowered the Fordyce Agency to fill every second of her concert tour, and they had. She was unaware that she was scheduled to spend two weeks in Dallas next spring, but she was glad, *so very glad*, that Hillary had chosen to embrace her accomplishments and overlook her appearance.

"And this is my sister Brynne," Robert said after a moment. "Brynne, Alexa and Cat."

There could be no doubt that Brynne and Robert McAllister were brother and sister. They shared the same rich dark brown hair, and sensitive dark brown eyes, and elegantly sculptured features. But it was remarkable, Alexa thought, that the features that were so strong and handsome in Robert could soften into such delicate prettiness in Brynne. Brynne's dark eyes sparkled with radiant warmth, and there was such a generosity about her, such a glowing aura of kindness, that, as James had confidently predicted, Alexa found herself liking her *instantly*.

"Hello, Brynne."

"Hello, Alexa. Hello, Cat."

As Catherine, Alexa, and Brynne embellished their formal greeting with a brief discussion of Cat's impressions of New York, and unaffected praise from Brynne about both *Majesty* and *Pennsylvania Avenue*, and a few words about the exciting architectural project that, albeit exciting, would unfortunately keep Stephen in Richmond until tomorrow, Elliot Archer awaited his turn to be introduced.

Of the necessary skills that he had acquired during his many years of intelligence work, Elliot's ability to hide his emotions was, perhaps, his most valuable. More than once—*many times more than once*—his expertise at concealing his true feelings had saved both his own life and the lives of others. In the beginning, the skill had to be practiced; but now, after so many years, it was reflexive, a virtual instinct. Still, had any eyes been watching him when he first saw Catherine Taylor, they would have seen an instant of shock followed by unmistakable flickers of emotion—love, grief, and rage. But no eyes had been focused on Elliot at that precise moment, because all had been drawn to the stunning Taylor sisters; and he had swiftly vanquished all overt signs of the waves of emotion that swept through him, even though the powerful waves crashed and pounded still . . .

Because Catherine Taylor looked so very much like Princess Isabelle Castille. It had been over thirty years, but Elliot's memory of the lovely Princess who had given sanctuary to the woman he loved was still, always, exquisitely vivid. Isabelle's hair had been spun gold, and Catherine's beautiful face was framed in black velvet, but the remarkable sapphire eyes, the thoughtful tilt of the head, the soft smile and even softer voice were so astonishingly like Isabelle's. Had Isabelle and Alexandre had a daughter, she would surely have looked like Catherine Taylor. But, as Elliot knew only too well, the Prince and Princess of L'île had been childless. This beautiful young woman simply looked like Isabelle, and that remarkable resemblance simply triggered the waves of emotion that crashed still, even though by the time Alexa introduced her little sister to him, the handsome face of the dashing master spy was calm, smiling, inscrutable once again.

"It's nice to meet you, Cat."

"It's nice to meet you, too, Elliot." Catherine returned his pleasant smile until her restless heart, brave and timid, urged her on. There was one final hello, the greeting to the handsome man for whom it had somehow been so important for her to look her best. So that James would be proud, not embarrassed, by Alexa's little sister? And so that, perhaps, she would find the courage to speak to him? Because thin, beautiful women were always courageous and confident, *weren't they?*

"Hello, James," she said to the sensuous dark blue eyes that made all the dizzying breathlessness that had come before seem now to be the most stable of vital signs.

"Catherine," James answered softly, wanting to say a thousand things to her, some soft, some harsh, but finally simply asking gently, "Did you remember to bring jeans for our sail?"

"Yes."

"Good." After a long moment, he took his gaze from her and addressed the others. "I hope you all brought your jeans. Tonight should be ideal for sailing. The moon will be full and the breeze will be brisk and balmy."

It wasn't either the picnic at Twelve Oaks or a prelude to an Agatha Christie murder mystery, Alexa decided as the delightful afternoon drifted gently by. It was Christmas, a gathering of loved ones with no plot whatsoever and no purpose other than to be together. The others had been here before, many times, and now she and Cat had been included in this lovely gathering, and they had been made to feel so welcome. The afternoon was quite magical, as if Inverness had been showered with fairy dust, drenching everyone with pleasantness and joy. Of course, she mused wryly, the "magic" may simply be that I've been able to spend the entire afternoon floating from conversation to conversation without ever finding myself alone with Hillary . . .

"Did you visit L'île, Marion?" Hillary asked when they assembled in the formal dining room for dinner. "I remember your saying that you hoped to."

"Yes, we did."

"And? Is it really the romantic island paradise everyone says it is?"

"It truly is. Truly romantic." Marion cast an affectionate smile at Arthur. "And truly a paradise."

"L'île?" Brynne asked, her twinkling eyes communicating quite clearly, and without a flicker of embarrassment, that even if according to her sister-in-law "everyone" knew about the romantic island, *she* didn't.

Good for you, Brynne, Alexa thought, chiding herself slightly for her own hesitation in posing the same question. She had heard about a place called L'île, an island kingdom in the Mediterranean that was a favorite haunt of Europe's very rich, very famous, and often very royal. She wondered if this was the same L'île. If so, she was intrigued that Marion and Arthur had visited there and was quite eager to hear their impressions.

"The full name of the island is L'île des Arcs-en-ciel, the Island of the Rainbows," Marion explained. "L'île is located in the Mediterranean off the southern coast of France, and, like nearby Monaco, it's a principality. The royal family is Castille, as in Castille Jewels, although it is hard to imagine a more dazzling jewel than the island itself. The terrain varies from white sand beaches to luxuriant gardens to dense tropical forests, with each breathtaking spot linked to the next by paths of white marble lined with hedges of gardenias. Every vista would be a painter's delight, and I truly believe that in the flowers and sunsets on L'île I saw shades of plum and pink and gold that I've never seen before."

"You can tell Marion was impressed," Arthur offered lovingly as Marion paused for a breath. When she arched an eyebrow in response to his teasing, he admitted with a soft laugh, "And so was I."

"Tell them about Le Bijou, Arthur."

"All right. Well. Le Bijou is the hotel, the only one on the island. Like everything else, it's owned by the Castilles, and, like everything else, it is of impeccable quality and decorated with extraordinary taste—Persian rugs, jade statues, antique porcelains, and magnificent original art. Guests are made to feel quite special, and most welcome, as if there by personal invitation from the Prince and Princess. Marion and I agree that we've never stayed in a hotel as beautiful, or as luxurious, as Le Bijou."

"That's quite an endorsement," Robert said quietly, smiling slightly at the understatement. Marion and Arthur Sterling had stayed in the world's most celebrated hotels, and to be placed at the top of that elite list was quite an endorsement indeed.

As Elliot listened to the discussion of L'île, his face revealed only casual interest, even though his actual interest in the discussion was far from casual. He had never told Marion and Arthur about his great love, Geneviève Castille, or about the three enchanted weeks of love he had spent with her on the romantic island kingdom. He was glad now that he hadn't; because now he could ask, quite casually, about their impression of Alain Castille. Alain . . . the son of Jean-Luc, whom Elliot hated still, six years after his death . . . and the son of Geneviève, whom he loved still, over thirty years after Jean-Luc had murdered her.

"Did you meet the Prince?"

"Yes. We met both Alain and his half-sister Natalie. When Alain discovered we were staying at Le Bijou, he insisted that we move to the palace. Arthur's already told you that the hotel was palatial, but the palace was even more splendid. And Alain and Natalie could not have been more gracious hosts. They behaved as if there was nothing they would rather do than show us their beautiful island. They strolled with us along the white marble paths and told us all the wonderful myths and legends of L'île."

"Myths and legends?"

"There are a great many, but the most famous, of course, is the legend of the rainbows." Marion smiled mysteriously and then continued, "Every afternoon, just before tea time, the bright blue sky turns almost black as thunderclouds appear from nowhere. The sudden darkness is dramatic but cozy. The ambient temperature remains warm, and of course the rain is welcome because it nourishes the magnificent tropical flowers. The cloudburst lasts less than an hour, and when it's over the rainbows come out."

"More than one rainbow," Arthur embellished, wishing, as he knew Marion wished, that their words could even begin to convey the true splendor. "Sometimes five, six, even seven, all overlapping, blending together until the entire sky is filled with the brilliant colors."

"The rainbows begin in the sea and arch to the center of the island where they all converge in a huge cave." Marion elaborated. "The enormous cave was once completely filled with jewels—sapphires, rubies, emeralds, amethysts—which, according to legend, were in reality small glittering splinters of rainbow."

"What a lovely image," Catherine whispered.

"Yes, isn't it? On one of our walks, Alain and Natalie took us to the cave."

"And?"

"Not a jewel. There once *were* jewels in the cave, Alain explained. However, he admitted, the precious gems weren't crystallized bits of rainbows. Instead, because of L'île's strategic location along the ancient trade routes, it's most likely that roguish Castille ancestors intercepted jewel-bearing vessels, stole their precious cargoes, and hid the gems in the cave. At which point, in his telling of the true history of L'île, Alain Castille quoted Balzac." Marion looked questioningly at her extremely well-educated son and teased lightly, "Do you know the quote, James?"

"Hopefully I will at least recognize it," James countered amiably.

"Cat knows," Alexa murmured quietly. She had no intention of putting her little sister on the spot, of course, but asking Cat about something French was like asking her to play "Chopsticks" . . . very easy . . . second nature.

Catherine did know, although she apologized a little in advance, "Only yesterday I mailed my French term paper to Oberlin. There was quite a bit of Balzac in it. I think the quotation you mean is 'Behind every great fortune there is a crime.' "

"Yes."

"How gracious of Alain to admit to the crime," Elliot said quietly, even though his heart ached as he thought about the history of the Castilles—a history of great fortunes and even greater crimes.

"Alain is a very gracious young man."

"Is Alain the creative genius behind Castille Jewels?" Hillary asked.

"I imagine that it's Alain who insists, as he obviously insists with everything else on L'île, that the quality is impeccable. But I think Natalie is the talented designer. When we toured the design studio on the island and the jewelry boutique in the hotel, it was she who suddenly became the expert."

"Well," Hillary sighed softly as she extended her perfectly manicured left hand, "I would like to thank whoever is responsible for my wedding band. Other than Robert, that is."

"It's a Castille design?"

"Yes. Robert discovered it at the Castille boutique in Dallas two weeks before our wedding."

"It's very beautiful," Alexa said. She had noticed Hillary's ring during dinner at La Côte and had begrudgingly admired it then. The sparkling slivers of diamonds and emeralds imbedded into the shining gold were elegant, tasteful, and not, she imagined, terribly expensive—well within the means of the prosecutor Robert had been when Hillary had married him.

"Thank you, Alexa." Hillary's expression conveyed approval of, not gratitude for, Alexa's compliment. "I don't know when Robert and I will have time to visit L'île, but I would certainly like to send my thanks to Princess Natalie. Do you anticipate seeing her again, Marion?"

"Yes. Alain has invited us to spend Christmas at the palace. James plans to join us, beginning with a sail from Nice to L'île." A warm glow filled Marion's dark blue eyes as she gazed at the much loved faces around her. "I just had the most wonderful idea. Wouldn't it be marvelous if we all met on L'île sometime? I know it's probably impossible with everyone's busy schedules, but wouldn't it be lovely?"

CHAPTER TWELVE

"So," James said as the summer sky faded from blue to pink. "Time to go sailing. Alexa?"

"Oh, no, thank you," she sighed contentedly. "I'm much too mellow to move."

James got variations of the same answer from the others, including Arthur who was an avid sailor. James shrugged amiably with each refusal, and, smiling, finally announced to the brilliant blue eyes that had accepted his invitation weeks before, "I guess it's just us, Catherine."

"Oh. Well. Maybe . . ." Her words faltered quickly under his intense gaze.

"I'll wait here while you go change into your jeans," James said firmly as his eyes sent the same gentle command they had sent once before, *Come with me, Catherine*.

"OK," she agreed quietly, somehow hiding her sudden panic. She had wanted to go sailing tonight, of course. She had been looking forward to it for weeks. And this afternoon and evening had made her all the more eager. She had barely spoken a word all day, but it hadn't mattered. The others had chattered, and she had been part of the conversations with her attentive eyes and lovely smiles, and that was all that had been required of her. And it had been wonderful . . . magical. There had been even more magic—because, a few times, James had smiled at her, and she thought, yes, maybe, he approved of the way she looked.

How she had looked forward to the sail! James and Alexa would talk in their easy, clever way, and she would listen and smile, and . . . and now she and James were going to be alone! Catherine had already learned that her new appearance did not bring with it a new talent for lively, effortless conversation. If anything, she was even more shy with him now, because the dark blue eyes were far more intense than she had remembered.

Just borrow the clever line from Alexa, reason urged. Just tell him, with a soft purr if you can, that you're far too mellow to move, too.

That's what she should have done, but she didn't. And as she changed into her jeans with the slow graceful movements that were eloquent clues to her limited energy, she wondered with renewed panic how she would find the energy to think of words to say to him, and then the energy to speak them, all the while fighting to calm her racing heart.

Catherine wondered, but she had no answers. She only knew that she couldn't say no.

You can't do this! Her mind sent new and urgent warnings as she and James began the three flight descent from the cliff to the cove where *Night Wind* was moored. You can get down the stairs, but there is *no way* you can climb back up! Remember the reason you didn't spend last night with Alexa at RoseCliff?

I can do it! a defiant voice answered. I *will* do it.

When they reached the sailboat, Catherine sat in the cockpit while James cast off the lines and raised the sails. She marvelled at his graceful strength as he so effortlessly rigged the boat; and when he was out of her view she simply listened to the wonderful symphony of new sounds—ropes being coiled on varnished decks, sails unfurling in the night breeze, waves lapping gently against the hull. Once the sails were set and the lines were cast off, James joined her in the cockpit and expertly guided the sleek sailboat out of the cove and into moon-drenched Chesapeake Bay.

They sailed for a long time without any words at all, sharing with their soft smiles the wonder of the silent power as the boat glided swiftly through the dark water.

"So?" James asked finally. "First impressions?"

"I love it."

"So do I."

"Alexa says that sometime you are going to spend a year sailing around the world."

"I hope to." James smiled. "I think that sounds like a one-year prison sentence to your sister."

"Really?"

"I imagine it might sound that way to you, too."

"No," she answered softly. "Why?"

"It would mean a year away from your music. Or is your music always with you?" he asked, remembering the June morning when her delicate fingers had whispered soft kisses on the keys, and the room had been filled with passion and emotion even though there had been no sounds. "Do you hear it even when you aren't playing?"

"I guess," she answered slowly, "that my music is with me even when I'm not playing, but it's a feeling more than a sound."

"A peaceful feeling?"

"Oh yes." The greatest peace, she thought. The only peace, the only place where I know that I truly belong. "Is that what sailing is for you? Peaceful?"

"Very peaceful." Very peaceful and very private, he thought. At least, that was how it was when he sailed by himself. Whenever others joined him, the mood inevitably changed; the simple presence of another person disrupted the absolute peace and invaded—even if a friendly and welcome invasion—his privacy. The most exquisite tranquillity, James had discovered, could not be shared. Until now . . . with Catherine. He felt the extraordinary peacefulness now, with her; but there was a restlessness, too, because of her. The completely new and quite astonishing restlessness urged him, a powerful wonderful urge, to sail out of the bay and into the ocean and beyond—right now, with Catherine.

James gazed at the moonlit sapphire eyes, to see if they too felt the extraordinary peace—and just maybe, the enchanting restlessness—but in the lingering silence a frown had crossed her lovely face. She seemed to be searching, struggling.

"What are you thinking?" he asked gently.

That I can't think of what to say to you! I'm trying, but everything I think of seems so silly and naive. If only . . . Catherine finally answered his question with a question, her soft voice hopeful, "Do you speak French?"

"Not really. I had a year in high school and know some of the usual phrases, but that's about it. Why?"

"Because . . . I think I speak French better, more fluently, than I speak

English." Maybe, James, if I could speak to you in French I could be more clever. Clever at all, she amended miserably.

"You speak perfectly fluent English, but I think it's intriguing that you would speak French with even a matching fluency. Why do you?"

Because it's my heritage. The thought came swiftly, and with equal swiftness Catherine banished that agonizing truth and spoke a far less painful one. "For the past three school years I lived in a house where we spoke exclusively French. And I've been thinking in French still this summer because my term paper was written in French."

"Thinking in French?"

"Yes." She paused for a moment, thinking in French, and then explained slowly, "Whenever someone says something to me in English, I—automatically, I guess—translate it into French. And I always think about what I'm going to say in French first, and then translate it into English."

"Is that what you did just now?"

"Yes." Catherine sighed softly. "I feel, sometimes, that I lose something in the translation."

"Really? I don't think so, Catherine." James smiled at her until she smiled back, a slightly wobbly smile, but a very lovely one. Then, putting her at ease with his indisputably nonfluent French, and hoping it proved to her that it didn't matter, he asked, "*Voulez-vous* a mug of hot chocolate? You have to say yes—*oui*—because you haven't truly experienced night sailing without one."

"*Alors, oui, merci.*" Her eyes sparkled and the wobbliness of the smile magically vanished. "Shall I make it?"

"No. You steer."

"Me? How?"

"Come here."

James stood as he spoke and beckoned for her to take the place where he had been sitting. After she did, she curled her slender ivory fingers around the wooden spokes that were still warm from the heat of his strong hands.

"Now," he instructed softly as he looked at the ribbon of gold that rippled across the inky black water, "just follow the moonbeam."

The suggestion that they have hot chocolate had been intentionally casual, although James had been prepared to gently but firmly insist. He wanted to get some calories into her! He had watched, throughout the day, as she artfully pretended to eat, but in fact ate almost nothing. As he waited for the water to become piping hot, he considered preparing a platter from the fruit, cheeses, smoked salmon, and crackers that had been boarded for those among tomorrow's guests who chose to sail. He finally decided against the elaborate platter, worrying that it might only embarrass her. She would *have* to drink the mug of thick rich hot chocolate he made for her, and that would be a good start.

"My mother's recipe," he told her when he returned to the cockpit and handed her a mug. "It has a little cinnamon in it."

"Thank you," she said as she moved away from the helm, gratefully relinquishing it to him, and took the huge warm mug in her delicate hands. "Your mother, your parents are so nice."

"Thank you. I think so, too."

"You're very close to them, aren't you?"

"Yes. Very. How about you and your parents?" James knew the answer to his question, of course. He had learned from Alexa about the closeness of the quiet, talented parents and their quiet, talented youngest daughter. Alexa had shared with him the darkest secrets of her heart, secrets he had sworn never to reveal, especially, most especially, to Catherine. And he would never break that solemn vow. This question about her parents betrayed no trust; although, admittedly, he posed it because he already knew that its answer was one that Catherine could discuss easily, joyfully, with sparkling happy eyes. But as she considered the question, James saw no joy, only sadness, and a deep, deep pain. "Catherine?"

"My parents and I used to be very close," she admitted quietly.

"But something happened?"

"Yes. Something happened, and then I moved to New York, and . . ." And she hadn't spoken to Jane and Alexander since May. She had written, of course, because she didn't want them to worry. But the letters since May bore little resemblance to the long, exuberant ones she had always written before. The new letters were short, and free of emotion or embellishment, as if anything more might be an imposition on their time that she no longer had the right to make.

"And you miss them."

"Yes. I miss them very much."

"Do they know that?"

"I'm not sure. I've been thinking about calling to tell them, but somehow . . ."

"I think you should call them, Catherine. I think that is something they would very much like to hear."

They sailed until midnight. After James secured *Night Wind* to the wharf, explaining the knots to her because she wanted to know, they began the long climb back to the mansion.

You *can* do it, Catherine's mind, or perhaps her heart, sternly reminded her body. But quickly, very quickly, the body that had been betrayed by her, betrayed her in return. It was an overwhelming mutiny, every starved, rebellious cell screaming and gasping at once.

Her lungs gasped for air, but there wasn't enough! And her fluttering heart took flight, carrying her with it, floating, floating away!

"Catherine!" James's strong arms were around her in an instant, catching her before she fell and then holding her very close . . . so close that he could feel the terror of her heart—a frightened sparrow trying frantically to flee her chest—and the coolness of her skin and the fragile body that was so terribly light and thin. Light and thin, and soft and lovely. He held her very close, as if contact with his strong body would transfer desperately needed strength to her. But it didn't. He felt her becoming weaker not stronger. His lips brushed the silkiness of her hair as he spoke, "Come over here, to the bench, and sit."

He held her still, even when she was seated, and felt her frantic attempts to regain control of her heart and lungs. It seemed like forever, an eternity of silent prayers, but finally her gasping began to slow and she somehow found the energy to raise her spinning head and speak.

"I guess I'm a little out of shape."

"Dammit, Catherine, you're starving yourself!" Her voice had been soft and trembling, and now his voice trembled, too, with the sudden anger borne of immense fear.

"No," she countered softly, pulling away.

"Yes." James had known it the instant he saw her, and he had spent most of the day debating what to do. Should he speak to Alexa, or to Catherine? Alexa had asked him privately, "Doesn't Cat look stunning?"; but he had seen flickers of

emerald worry that suggested that she, too, knew her little sister's weight loss was far too rapid. James had decided he would discuss it with Alexa, gently encouraging her to speak aloud her worries to Catherine, but he hadn't yet had a chance. And now, because it was a matter of life and death, he was discussing it with Catherine directly.

Not discussing, *accusing*, he realized too late as he heard the harshness of his own voice and saw its effect on her lovely face. He had overwhelmed her again, as he had in June, but her embarrassment now went far beyond lovely flushed cheeks and a timid smile. Now he saw anguish on her hauntingly beautiful and terrifyingly pale face, and worse . . . because now the brilliant sapphire eyes glistened with tears.

Now he, who cared so very much about her, had done what only a cruel young Hillary had been able to do before: he had made Catherine cry.

"Catherine," he whispered softly. "You've lost a great deal of weight very quickly, perhaps too quickly."

"I'd never dieted before. Once I started, after the first few days, it was very easy."

"Easier and easier every day?"

"Yes," Catherine admitted quietly, miserably, an acknowledgment that she had permitted her starving brain to make irrational choices. It had been easy to permit those irrational choices, even though, deep inside, a voice had sent urgent warnings. She hadn't heeded the warnings and now her own gasping weakness truly terrified her. But that life-and-death terror was almost surpassed by her fear of what James thought of her. James, of all people. What if he believed that her incautious dieting was something more, something disturbed, pathologic, like anorexia or bulimia? "James, I'm not . . . I didn't do anything . . ."

"I know," he reassured gently. "You, Catherine Taylor, simply happen to share, with your older sister, extraordinary discipline and determination. Do you know what Alexa told me once, when she said she was going to spend an entire evening rehearsing her lines and I made an off-hand remark about practice makes perfect?"

"Yes, I know what she told you. She said, 'No, James. *Perfect* practice makes perfect.' "

"I have the feeling that may be a Taylor sister motto. And I think, maybe, you dieted a little too perfectly."

Catherine smiled a trembling and grateful smile. "I need to begin eating again, and when I'm stronger I need to exercise so that my body can become fit and healthy at this weight."

"It sounds as though you've read the books."

"Yes. I knew how to do it sensibly. I just got carried away. Thank you for catching me." Her voice became a soft whisper at the memory. It was a gasping fluttering memory of fear, but there was more to the memory: the feeling of his arms around her, the warm strength of his body, the delicate brush of his lips against her hair, the pounding of his heart. And there had been another breathlessness, exhilarating and so wonderful, that had nothing to do with starvation or terror.

"Of course," James answered softly, remembering too that oh-so-compelling, oh-so-lovely part of the memory. After a moment, he said gently but firmly, "Now I'm going to feed you. Another mug of hot chocolate and some food. We'll have a picnic right here, and then, eventually, we'll wander slowly up these stairs. OK?"

"Yes. OK. Thank you."

"You're more than welcome." James smiled. And then, before returning to *Night Wind* to prepare their midnight picnic, his handsome face became very solemn and he said quietly, "Promise me, Catherine, that you will start eating again."

"I promise."

James held her gaze, debating for five swift heartbeats. Then he simply told her.

"I'm not sure what made you decide to lose all the weight." His words stopped, suddenly distracted by the eloquent message of her moonlit blue eyes. The lovely eyes seemed to be telling him, with innocent candor, that *he* was the reason. After a moment, he continued shakily, "You are very beautiful now, of course, but you were very beautiful before, too."

There was more to say, a far more important truth. Your most magnificent beauty, Catherine, is who you are, deep inside.

But James didn't tell her that truth.

How could he?

Chapter Thirteen

*A*lexa was awakened by a soft tap on her bedroom door. The moonlight streaming through the open windows illuminated the bedside clock: twelve-thirty. Cat, probably, coming to tell her about sailing with James. Or, perhaps, James himself. No, Alexa decided as she sashed her emerald silk robe around her slender waist, James and I aren't furtive teenagers!

Besides, she remembered with a soft smile, last night, in her bed at RoseCliff, she and James had made up in advance for the next ten nights of separation. The garden party and James's responsibilities as host would last until late Sunday night, long after she had taken Cat to the airport and returned to RoseCliff. On Monday afternoon, James would leave for Denver for four days, followed by meetings in Chicago that he expected to last all weekend. They would be apart for at least ten nights; but still, Alexa knew, it would not be James at her bedroom door. No, her most welcome late night visitor would be her little sister, and they would stay up for hours chatting about the wonderful day.

But the visitor wasn't Cat. It was Brynne. But such a different Brynne from the woman with whom Alexa had spent so many pleasant hours during the day. Brynne's rosy cheeks were ashen now, her sparkling brown eyes cloudy and bewildered, her glowing radiance merely a memory. When Alexa had last seen her, three hours before, Brynne had announced with smiling apology that she was a little tired, contently so, and was going to bed early. She *had* gone to bed, her sleep-tousled brown hair proved it, but now she wore blue jeans and an incorrectly buttoned cotton shirt, not a nightgown and robe.

"Brynne? What's wrong?"

"I need Robert. I'm sorry, Alexa, I don't know which room he and Hillary are in."

"Well, I walked upstairs with them about an hour ago, so I know. Why don't you come in and wait here while I get him?"

"Oh. All right. Thank you."

Alexa walked hurriedly along the plush Oriental rugs that covered the shining hardwood floors. As she neared the door of Robert and Hillary's bedroom, she thought briefly about her bare feet, her clinging silk nightgown and robe, and her sleep-tangled golden hair.

It didn't matter how she looked! Nor did it matter that she might be intruding on a passionate interlude between the sexy politician and his patrician wife. All that mattered was that a little sister was in trouble. A little sister, Alexa realized, who turned instantly to her older brother when she needed help. Instantly and confidently, she thought, remembering Brynne's voice when she said, "I need Robert." Brynne needed Robert, and she knew without a trace of doubt that Robert would help her.

Alexa tapped firmly on the bedroom door, deciding she would tap louder in fifteen seconds and call Robert's name if need be. But she didn't need to repeat the knock. He opened the door in seconds. His dark hair was tousled, by passion or by sleep, and he wore a belted robe over his pajamas, and his feet, like hers, were bare.

"Hi." He smiled a quizzical smile.

"Brynne needs you. I don't know what's wrong but—"

"Where is she?" Robert's smile vanished and his dark eyes filled with worry.

"In my room."

Alexa led the way to her room, but stood aside at the doorway to allow Robert to enter first. He crossed the room to the chair where Brynne sat, on its very edge, and then knelt in front of her so that their dark brown eyes could meet.

"Honey?" he asked as he covered the small hands, curled in tight bloodless fists, with his larger ones.

"I'm miscarrying."

"Oh, Brynne. I didn't know."

"No one did. Not even Stephen. I had to try, Robert, just one more time. I know I said I wasn't going to, but I was so sure that this time . . . I just had to try." Her words ended in a soft sob and tears spilled down her stricken face.

"I know. It's OK, Brynne," he assured gently. "It's OK."

Alexa moved close enough for Robert to see her, and when the dark eyes that were so concerned for his little sister finally looked up and met hers, she asked softly, "Should I get Marion?"

"Brynne? Would you like Alexa to get Marion?"

"No. There's no need to bother Marion. I just have to go to the nearest hospital."

"I'm not sure where that is, Brynne. I'll need to find James and—"

"I know where the nearest hospital is," Alexa offered. "It's in Marlboro, about ten miles away. We can take my car and I'll drive."

"Thank you." Robert stood, still holding his sister's hands. "I'm going to get changed, Brynne. It will only take a few minutes."

After Robert left, Alexa quickly changed, too, into the outfit that she would have worn had she gone sailing with Catherine and James. As she was tying her tennis shoes, Brynne stood . . . and swayed.

"Brynne?" Alexa rushed to her and urged her back onto the chair.

"I was going to get my purse."

"I'll get it for you. Here. Just sit down. I'll be right back."

Alexa found Brynne's purse on the bedside table. She grabbed it, and then on impulse walked into the dressing room to search for a sweater or jacket. She drew a soft breath when she saw the nightgown and robe on the vanity in the dressing room. Both were blood-soaked, obviously ruined, and yet they had been so carefully folded, not tossed aside.

Because the bright red stains are memories of the tiny life Brynne so obviously treasures and now may be losing, or has already lost? Has already lost, Alexa decided sadly, as she remembered the expression of hopelessness on Brynne's beautiful face, as if she already knew, as if she had had experience with such a great loss before.

When they arrived at Marlboro Hospital, Brynne was taken immediately through the "Authorized Personnel Only" doors that led into the treatment area of the Emergency Room. Robert and Alexa waited in the waiting room adjacent to the ER, where, after forty-five minutes, Brynne's doctor appeared to give them the report.

"She has miscarried."

"I see," Robert replied with quiet emotion.

"The miscarriage appears to be 'complete', which means that a D and C will probably not be necessary. I want to keep her here, though, until I get the results of the blood work that has been drawn. Once those are back, assuming they're what I expect them to be, Brynne should be ready to go home. My guess is that will be in about two hours."

"All right. May I see her?"

"Sure. She wants to see you, too. I think it would be best for her if you made the visit fairly brief. She's exhausted, and I'm hoping she'll be able to sleep if she's left alone."

"OK." Robert turned to Alexa and asked, "Do you mind waiting a little longer?"

"No, Robert, of course I don't mind."

"Shall we go?" Robert asked when he returned from seeing Brynne.

"Go?"

"To Inverness, to take you back and pick up my car."

"To pick up your car . . . and Hillary."

"Hillary?" Robert echoed with soft surprise. After a moment, he said quietly, "No."

No? Alexa felt a sudden rush of anger for her ancient enemy. Robert was here for Brynne, helping her, supporting her, loving her; and even though this was obviously terribly emotional for him, too, he hid his own sadness to be strong for his little sister. He was here for Brynne, but who was here for Robert? Where was his loving wife? Was Hillary really so selfish and so vain that she would not forfeit even a few hours of her beauty sleep to help her husband? Did she have so little sympathy and compassion for Brynne's devastating loss? Or was, perhaps, the idea of sitting in a smoky, crowded waiting room simply *too* distasteful for her patrician sensibilities?

The waiting room *was* unappealing, of course. It was now filled, like most Emergency Rooms on a Saturday night, with a boisterous, predominantly intoxicated clientele that sought medical attention for bumps and bruises acquired during an evening of injudicious partying. The waiting room was not, at the moment, a place for quiet reflection about the loss of a much wanted baby. Brynne was protected from the noise, in a room far behind the heavy steel doors, but there would be no peace here for Robert.

And, Alexa thought as she gazed at his sensitive and so troubled eyes, he needs peace. Hillary may not be here for you, Robert, but I am. The thought was neutral enough . . . until it continued quite boldly, I *want* to be.

"I have an idea, Robert. My cottage is close by, much closer than Inverness and only a little farther away from Brynne than this noisy-and-not-so-tranquil waiting room. We can give the doctor the phone number and wait there, if you like." She smiled gently at the dark eyes that looked uncertain about imposing, and yet so very tempted. "This may sound terribly presumptuous of me, Robert, but I'm quite confident that the coffee served at RoseCliff is far better than what one can get from the coffee machines here."

"I'm sure it is, but Alexa . . ." his protest faltered because he didn't want to protest at all.

"Besides, Brynne will need a new nightgown," she said quietly. "And since I happen to be a bit of a pushover for nightgowns, especially the soft, fluffy, cozy kinds, I have a small collection of never-yet-worn ones at the cottage. I would very much like to give one of them to Brynne."

RoseCliff had been a light-hearted topic of conversation after dinner. True, her tiny cottage was far less grand than Inverness, Alexa had amiably admitted. And far less grand, too, than Clairmont, the famous Arlington estate that had been a wedding gift from Sam Ballinger to his daughter and son-in-law. But, she had added with a sparkling smile, like "Inverness"—and indeed in the same elegant script—"RoseCliff" was permanently chiseled into the granite boulders at the base of the stairs that led to the cottage. The engraving had been James's idea, and once he had her surprised yet eager approval, it was he who had commissioned the work.

"So this is RoseCliff," Robert said as he paused to admire the moonlit lettering.

"This is RoseCliff," Alexa echoed softly. She heard the attempt at a gentle tease in his voice, a valiant effort to lighten the mood, and she answered with a lovely smile that told the troubled dark eyes that the effort wasn't necessary for her, not at all, because she understood well the deep love for little sisters.

Alexa led the way up the stairs to her magnificent garden of roses and her tiny romantic cottage beyond. She made coffee, as promised, and, as promised, too, offered him the wonderful tranquillity of RoseCliff at night. They sat on the porch beneath a ceiling of stars, their faces softly illuminated by the full moon, listening to the songs of crickets, breathing the rose-fragrant night air, and talking, in quiet words punctuated by long comfortable silences, about the crickets and the roses and the moon and the stars.

Finally the words, or the silences, felt so comfortable that Robert said softly, "I want to tell you about Brynne."

"Yes," Alexa answered with matching softness. I want to hear about Brynne, Robert, she thought. And, Robert, I want to hear about you.

"Brynne and Stephen have been married for twelve years, and they've been trying for that long to have children."

"And she finally got pregnant? Only to lose the baby?"

"No. It's been more complicated, even more difficult, than that. Brynne has always been able to conceive, but for some reason her pregnancies invariably end in miscarriages."

"For some reason?"

"For some unknown reason. Brynne and Stephen have seen the best specialists and have had all the tests and procedures. Marion has made certain of that, of course, but even the best medical science has had to offer has not come up with an answer. That's why they've kept trying all these years, believing that someday . . ." Robert sighed softly. "Brynne has always been able to tell, almost immediately, when she becomes pregnant. She bonds instantly to the new life inside her, a bond of hope and joy, and when she loses the baby, it's a very great loss for her."

"Oh, Robert," Alexa whispered quietly. "Brynne would be such a wonderful mother."

"Yes. The best. And Stephen would be a wonderful father. Isn't it ironic that in an era when women can be whatever they want—when they aren't bound to spend their lives being mothers and when being a mother has even become devalued— that being a mother is all my very smart little sister wants, or has ever wanted?"

"Yes it is," Alexa agreed softly. "But, Robert, even if Brynne and Stephen can't have their own children, they can adopt, can't they?"

"They've tried. But because Brynne was always able to get pregnant, and be- cause she believed so strongly that eventually she *would* be able to carry a baby to term, they delayed pursuing the possibility of adopting for a long time. By the time they did, Stephen was almost forty, which put them in a low priority category with all the public agencies." A smile of gentle fondness touched his moonlit face as he continued, "I guess you've realized by now that in a way, in a very loving way, Brynne and I have ourselves been adopted by the Sterlings. Just as Marion made certain that Brynne and Stephen saw the best fertility specialists available, when the issue of adoption arose, James immediately volunteered to contact reputable attorneys throughout the country who were known to handle private adoptions."

"And that hasn't worked?"

"It almost has worked—twice. But both times—once within twenty-four hours of the baby's birth and the second time after the baby had been with them for almost six weeks—the biologic mother changed her mind."

"That can happen?"

"Absolutely. The era of closed adoptions, especially in the private arena, is rapidly vanishing. James felt terrible about what happened. He had met with both of the biologic mothers and truly believed they were confident of their decisions."

"And Brynne . . .?"

"It was terribly painful for her, of course, another loss, but she understood com- pletely that a mother would change her mind about giving up her baby. Anyway, the two attempts at adoption have made them very wary. I thought they'd decided to give up trying altogether, either for their own baby or adopting. It's taken such a toll on Brynne. The last time we talked about it, after she'd miscarried in March, she told me it was all over—everything, both the dream and the torment."

"But she had to try one last time."

"One last time." The crickets whirred gaily in the long silence that followed. When Robert finally spoke, his voice was very soft and his words were spoken to the twinkling stars, "I feel so helpless."

"Helpless, Robert?"

"I would do anything to put an end to Brynne's anguish, but I . . ."

"But there's nothing you can do," Alexa assured gently. "And you do help her, you know. You understand her sadness, and share it with her, and you are so gentle with her. Brynne obviously trusts you very much."

"I guess it's just that I spent so many years protecting Brynne when we were young, *trying* to protect her, and I want so very much to protect her from this pain. But I can't."

"No, you can't," she agreed quietly. And then, quite suddenly, Alexa felt it:

the immense power of the emotions that Robert kept so carefully hidden, buried so very deep inside. The immense power was quite invisible, and yet she felt it, and it was almost as if his frustration and helplessness and torment were inside her, too. After a moment, she said bravely, "This is taking a toll on you, too, Robert."

"Yes it is," he confessed, as he turned from the twinkling stars to her solemn and beautiful emerald eyes. Then, even more softly, he made another confession. "I don't usually admit such things."

And then, as their eyes met and held, there was another immense invisible power, buried deep and carefully hidden, too, by both of them, until now. Now, as the dark sensuous eyes gazed into the glowing emerald ones, the fluttering of their hearts fanned the powerful emotions out of hiding, and all the wondrous desire and longing came joyfully to the surface, dangerously brave, carelessly defiant.

"You don't usually admit such things, Robert?" Alexa echoed softly, breathlessly.

"No, Alexa, I don't."

The moon watched, and seemed to approve, because it enveloped them in a golden mist within which all was possible, and there were no thoughts of consequences, and it was safe, permissible, to share the deepest secrets and desires of their hearts. And in that golden mist, Alexa saw Robert's desire for her, an intense and wondrous desire that had begun long ago and reached far beyond this moment; and Robert saw, mirrored in the joyous moonlit emerald, a desire that was as intense, and wondrous, and far-reaching as his own.

Everything was safe, all secret desires permissible; and Alexa would have so joyfully welcomed the hands and lips that would have caressed her with the same exquisite tenderness as the dark eyes that were caressing her now . . .

But then the phone rang, and she left Robert and the magical golden mist for the too bright lights of the kitchen. Robert followed, and moments later, after sharing the news with him that Brynne was ready to be discharged, she left him again, to go to her bedroom, to get the nightgown for his little sister.

When Alexa returned to the kitchen, she found Robert drying the coffee mugs he had just finished washing.

"You didn't need to do that, Robert."

"I wanted to. Besides, it's habit."

"Habit?" From his impoverished and chore-laden childhood? she wondered. Or from his life as a soldier? He certainly did not, she assumed, nor did Hillary, wash dishes at Clairmont.

"I have a small, uninspired, unnamed apartment near Capitol Hill," Robert explained with a soft smile. "The drive to the house in Arlington is over ninety minutes, without traffic, and since I often have early morning and late night meetings, I frequently spend weeknights in town, in an apartment where I am solely responsible for washing my coffee mugs."

"I see," Alexa replied softly. And surely he would see, unless she bent her head and cast a golden veil across her emerald eyes, the dangerous wishes that leapt from her heart. There are nights, frequent nights, that you choose to spend away from Hillary? Perhaps, on one of those nights, you could come back here and we could talk again and . . . *What was she thinking?* Fortunately, she had bowed her golden head, and when she spoke finally, it was to the soft cotton garment she held in her hands. "Here is the nightgown for Brynne. I thought this one, with the roses, would be cheerful . . ."

Her words stopped at his touch, *they had to*, and she trembled as, with the exquisite tenderness she had imagined, he gently parted the curtain of silky gold. Robert trembled too, as he lifted her beautiful face to his and whispered softly, "Thank you."

"Thank you," Brynne echoed her brother's words an hour later.

They were in Brynne's bedroom at Inverness, and Robert had already bid them goodnight, and Alexa had stayed to be certain that Brynne was settled and comfortable. She was in the luxurious bed now, propped up against feather pillows, looking very young and very pretty in the soft fluffy nightgown Alexa had given her.

"You're welcome, Brynne." I wish there was more I could do for you, Alexa thought as she watched Brynne's dark brown eyes lapse quickly back into sadness after her gracious smiling thank you. "I'm so sorry."

"I know you are, Alexa," Brynne answered softly. "Thank you."

Alexa hesitated a moment, then, sensing that perhaps Brynne wanted to talk about it, she offered gently, carefully, "It just seems so terribly unfair. You would be such a wonderful mother."

"Oh, well, thank you." She frowned thoughtfully, and then confessed quietly, "I guess I do think it's terribly unfair. I guess I really do believe that Stephen and I have so much love to give." She gave her head a soft, bewildered shake. "But, for some reason, we weren't destined to have children."

"Whatever the reason is, it's a pretty faulty one." Alexa's voice was gentle, but her own annoyance at whatever unknown fate had caused this sadness for lovely Brynne was apparent.

"Yes it is, isn't it?" Brynne agreed swiftly, smiling at Alexa's bluntness, grateful to be able to acknowledge the injustice she herself sometimes felt, although rarely spoke of. "It's nice to be able to talk about this with someone other than Stephen or Robert, Alexa. It's been a source of such sadness for us all that it's been a very long time since we've simply glowered at the whimsical fates."

"I'd be happy to sit here and glower with you all night if you like." Alexa tilted her head thoughtfully at the eyes that clearly wanted to talk; and the face that so obviously needed rest. "Or, at least, for a few more minutes."

"Thank you. I would like to talk a little longer."

They talked, sharing quiet, important words and emotions, until finally, reluctantly, Brynne had to yield to the exhausted body that needed sleep.

"I'll come visit you tomorrow," Alexa promised.

"I'll be at the party."

"You will? Won't you need to stay in bed?"

"No. I'll be fine. I may do more sitting under pink umbrellas than wandering around the grounds, but I'll be OK. I don't plan to tell anyone else, not even Stephen, about the miscarriage. He didn't know I was pregnant, so . . . ."

"I understand," Alexa said quietly. She had learned tonight about Brynne's great love for her husband, and she understood the wish to spare Stephen further sadness. "I understand."

"Thank you for being here tonight, Alexa."

"You're very welcome, Brynne."

As Alexa crossed the hallway from Brynne's bedroom to hers, she looked at the closed door to Cat's room. She had imagined that on this evening she and her own little sister might have stayed up until all hours chatting. But, instead, tonight she had been with Robert's little sister, and she would hear another time about Cat's sail with James.

James. What would he say if, right now, she wandered stealthily to the other wing of the mansion and confessed everything to him? How would he respond to her memory of moonlit magic at RoseCliff, and the fact that her heart raced now, still, because of Robert? James, her wonderful friend, who was not in love with her, would simply explain to her, his dark blue eyes very gentle, that whatever she'd thought she had seen in Robert's sensuous dark eyes had been purely an illusion—that she had been, quite obviously, blinded by moonlight. That was what James would say, *wouldn't he?* He would not, surely not, be hurt, *would he?* Alexa thought not. She very much hoped not.

Still, she didn't wander to the other wing of the mansion to find James. But, she admitted to herself as she crossed instead to her own bedroom, it wasn't the fear of seeing hurt in the dark blue eyes that made her stay away, because she truly doubted that she would. It was, in fact, her reluctance to hear James tell her, however gently, that it had all been an illusion.

So, instead of finding James, Alexa went to her own bedroom, where, once inside, she was drawn to the window by a golden beam of light.

Hello, Moon, she greeted silently as her emerald eyes looked hopefully to the smiling witness to whatever it was that had happened at RoseCliff. Remember me? Could you tell me, please, did you happen to see the look in his dark brown eyes? I wasn't wrong, was I? Please? Oh, and Moon, since you're an expert on such things, and I'm merely a novice, could you tell me if these wonderful feelings that are swirling inside me still, these rushes of happiness and desire and joy, are these magnificent feelings what one feels when she's fallen in love? Yes? I thought so. And, Moon, there's just one more thing. Do you think, could you tell, was he feeling these wonderful feelings, too?

Washington's very most powerful people spent that Sunday at Inverness. They wandered among the prize-winning roses and through the elegant mansion, chatting about world-changing topics and trivial ones, sipping champagne, and sampling the endless array of gourmet delicacies presented to them on shining silver trays.

Senator and Mrs. Robert McAllister spent the day together, of course, and everyone wanted to talk to the future First Couple, and there were a great many people who wanted to meet Alexandra Taylor, too. Alexa and Robert never had a chance to speak to each other, not with words, but more than once, searching at the same moment as if by silent signal, their eyes met and smiled.

Alexa didn't speak to Robert, and Catherine didn't speak to James. She had planned to, to thank him again, but by the time she appeared for breakfast, he was already off helping Arthur make certain that the pink-umbrellaed tables were arranged just so on the emerald lawn, and that the tennis court got a final wash and the pool a final clean, and that the only slightly depleted larder on *Night Wind* was re-stocked. Before Catherine even saw him, much less found a private moment to speak to him, the guests began to arrive, and James assumed the role, with his parents, of gracious host. He was very busy after that. And, when the Secretary of State, a music afficianado, identified her as the beautiful womanly version of the teenaged Catherine Taylor he had seen win the Van Cliburn, she became very busy too.

"Guests are not obliged to give command performances at my parties," Marion intervened lightly but firmly when she overheard the Secretary's serious suggestion that Catherine give an impromptu recital on the rarely used but impeccably maintained Steinway. Marion smiled at the Secretary, a good friend for many years, and added, "No matter who makes the command."

"I wouldn't mind, Marion. Unless you'd prefer that I didn't."

"My dear Catherine," Marion answered with a twinkle. "It's taken an incredible amount of discipline for me not to ask you myself."

So Catherine played, sharing her gift, completely unruffled by her famous audience. The impromptu recital became an afternoon of music. At first, the guests who were drawn to the great room by her magic simply listened, mesmerized and enchanted. But eventually, in response to her offer to play whatever they wanted to hear, they began to make requests. Her repertoire was vast, and she delighted in playing all music, any music, from Bach and Chopin to Gershwin and rock 'n' roll.

Catherine played joyously, as always, and flawlessly, as always . . . until James appeared. Moments before, with a loving wink to his wife, the President had asked if she happened to know "I Fall to Pieces." She did, of course, and had just begun playing it when James walked in. How appropriate, she thought miserably, as she felt herself fall to pieces, *as always*, when his intense dark blue eyes fell on her. Her cheeks flushed pink, and there was the rapid fluttering of her heart that had nothing to do with starvation. She wasn't starving now, she knew, because she had eaten today, small frequent nibbles, and her body had responded with grateful, exuberant energy.

Catherine had become accustomed to the warm pink cheeks and racing heart that came without warning whenever James was near. But now, as she played, she felt even her extraordinary talent begin to fall to pieces. A delicate finger caressed the wrong key—once, then a second time! No one but she detected even the smallest stumble in the magnificent dance of her beautiful and graceful hands, of course.

But she noticed, and oh how she had wanted to play beautifully, fluently, flawlessly for him. But she couldn't. Nor could she look up and meet his eyes and smile hello and thank you. Oh, yes, she could smile a lovely smile at the President of the United States and bravely hold his admiring gaze and even talk to him while her fingers danced over the keyboard. But she *could not* look at James, not without stopping the music entirely. So she just played, her fingers dancing and stumbling, her eyes never meeting his.

James remained in the great room for only a very short time. He had agreed to take some of the guests for a dinner sail; and they were sailing still, a small blue and white speck in the distance, when Catherine and Alexa left the party.

"Mom?"

"Cat," Jane breathed. Her eyes filled with tears as her soft voice filled with joy. How patiently—and *desperately*—she and Alexander had waited for their beloved daughter to return to them. How they had wanted to rush to her and hold her in their loving arms and assure her over and over of their love. But Jane and Alexander knew it was Catherine's journey, not theirs, to make. And they knew, too, that even once begun, her journey home—to love—would be long and difficult. But now, at least, at last, the journey had started. Jane heard the delicate hope in her daughter's voice, and "Mom" itself was a huge brave step. Since May, Catherine's letters had begun with "Hello" and *"Bonjour,"* not with the so-familiar, so-taken-for-granted greetings of "Dear Mom and Dad" or, even, "Dearest Mommy and Daddy."

"Hi. Is Dad there?"

"He's on his way upstairs to the other phone."

They waited in silence until Alexander picked up the extension, and when he did Jane wondered if Catherine heard the trembling emotion in her father's quiet voice.

"How are you, Cat?"

"I'm fine, Dad. I just thought I'd call to say hi."

They talked for an hour, and there were times when Catherine's breathless descriptions of New York and the new pieces she was learning and the weekend she had just spent at Inverness felt wonderfully normal, wonderfully, hauntingly like the past. Hauntingly . . . a ghost from a past that didn't really exist. In the midst of the breathless descriptions, the painful memory of the truth would suddenly sweep through her, stopping her words mid-sentence. There would be silence then, and Jane and Alexander would wait with desperate prayers, but each time, Catherine finally spoke again.

Yes, she would send tapes of her new pieces, she promised. And, as soon as she got them from Marion, she would send the photographs of the President, First Lady, and Alexa leaning over the piano while she played. And, she promised softly, she would call again.

She would call again. That was the most wonderful promise of all. Because it meant that Catherine's brave journey back to her parents and their love had truly begun.

CHAPTER FOURTEEN

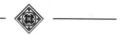

"*Y*ou have received substantial payments—*bribes*, Senator—for your recent votes on the defense contract proposals."

"That, Ms. Winslow, is a ridiculous, not to mention libelous accusation for which you most assuredly haven't a shred of proof."

"I have more than a shred, Senator—documents that you assumed had been shredded, but which are in fact now in the possession of the Senate Ethics Committee Chairman. I happen to have copies in my office, if you would care to see them."

"You won't get away with this kind of yellow journalism, Ms. Winslow."

"I'm not trying to get away with anything. You, however, did try. And now, thankfully, you've been caught."

Alexa's eyes—Stephanie Winslow's eyes—flashed at the startled and indignant face of the "Senator." She held the look, her beautiful eyes blazing, until the director called "Cut."

"Very nice," he embellished as the actors released their gazes of hostility and replaced them with satisfied smiles. "That's a print. Lunch time, everyone. Alexa, after lunch I'd like to begin blocking the scene that takes place in your office. Are you ready to do that?"

"Sure."

"Senator McAllister!" The reporters rushed to him, encircling him the moment he emerged from the Senate Intelligence Committee meeting. "We understand that one of the agenda items for today's meeting was the hostage situation. Have there been new developments?"

"You know I can't tell you anything," he admonished amiably.

The reporters did know that, of course, which was why many of their colleagues were following the other Senators who had attended the meeting. Sometimes Senators slipped up, accidentally revealing something that shouldn't have been revealed with an unguarded expression or an injudicious comment. Sometimes the "slips" weren't even accidental; they were intentional revelations, made for personal and partisan politics. Senator Robert McAllister was one of the newest members of the Intelligence Committee, yet he had never made an injudicious remark, either by accident or design. The reporters didn't expect carelessness or political gamesmanship from Robert. But they hoped that if there was anything that could legitimately be revealed about the behind closed doors Committee meeting, they could get a quote from him, because comments from the photogenic and respected Senator from Virginia always made the evening news.

A great deal had been discussed at the meeting, but, Robert felt, even making such a nonspecific observation would be an indefensible breech of security. Robert had been to war. He saw the shades of gray in issues that many of his colleagues chose to portray as black and white—miraculously right along party lines.

"Sorry," he said. His smile to the assembled reporters acknowledged that he knew they were only trying to do their jobs just as diligently as he was trying to do his.

Then he escaped to his office to spend the lunch hour returning calls, meeting with aides, reading the never ending stacks of documents that arrived on his desk every day, and trying, as he had been trying every second of the past five days, to forget about *her*.

But how could he? She had touched a part of him that had somehow survived the ravages of his past, a delicate and hopeful place in his heart that had miraculously escaped unscathed and unscarred. Robert knew very well about the thick, constricting scars in his heart, because it was he who had put them there, forcing the tough bloodless tissue over the tender wounds of his life, sealing those hurts and protecting himself from future pain.

He had believed, until now, until Alexa, that the only truly vulnerable place left in his heart was that very special place owned by his little sister. He had spent his boyhood protecting Brynne from the grim reality of their impoverished life, hiding his own tears and lovingly convincing her that *her* life could be filled with happiness long after he had privately given up all hope for his own.

Beginning as a very small boy, Robert was strong for Brynne. And as only an eighteen-year-old, he was strong for the men with whom he served in Vietnam, his mature calm lending a measure of sanity and control to a world he knew to be truly insane. He was heralded as a leader and a hero, and indeed he had courageously saved the lives and hearts and spirits of a great many men. But Robert knew the truth. His screams of pain at the horror he witnessed were silent to the men around him, but they thundered inside—until he silenced them, trapping them beneath thick scars, buried deep and forever.

Robert returned from Vietnam with an intense commitment to the vision of peace he saw for the world. He planned a quiet solitary life dedicated to public service and to the fulfillment of that vision. His heart was far too damaged, he knew, to ever fall in love, and until he met Hillary he had never even given serious thought to marriage. But beautiful, vivacious Hillary made it so very easy for him. She made it wonderfully, seductively, clear how much she wanted him; and, as a governor's daughter, she knew well the very public life a politician necessarily led, and seemed most eager and willing to share it; and, so it seemed, too, she truly believed in his important visions and his dreams. Theirs was a whirlwind romance, a glittering golden thread woven into the already vibrant tapestry of his campaign for the U.S. Senate.

Robert did not ask Hillary to marry him because she was the daughter of the very powerful Governor; it was not, *for him at least*, a marriage of political ambition. He simply wanted to marry the lovely, gracious, unselfish woman who had so enchantingly convinced him that he was not destined to live a solitary life after all. Admittedly, by their wedding day, he and Hillary had not had many truly private moments together; they had not, by that day, had a chance to share the very private intimacies of their hearts. Which was why, as he quietly spoke his solemn wedding vows to his alluring bride, he made a solemn private vow as well. He would share with her all of himself that he could. He would even, he vowed, expose his so carefully scarred wounds, enduring all that pain again, if she asked that of him.

But, as he discovered shortly after she became Mrs. Robert McAllister, Hillary couldn't care less about the boy who had been forced to become a man when he was only a frightened, starving little child. And she most certainly wanted to know *nothing* of the soldier's silent screams of horror. Her only interest, he learned, was in glittering symbols—the shining gold medals of the hero, not the thick ugly scars of the man.

Hillary did not want emotional intimacy, nor did she want any longer to be the warm, unselfish, loving woman he had courted. She reprised that enchanting role, of course, for the public appearances in which the world marvelled at their perfect marriage; and sometimes, especially in the beginning, she reprised the enchanting role just for him. Robert knew he had been tricked. But he felt a commitment to the vows he had made, and an even stronger commitment to the woman Hillary had been in the months of their dazzling whirlwind romance. He tried very hard to help her become that warm, lovely woman again—for him, for their marriage, *but mostly for herself*; but in time he finally realized that that woman was a phantom. She was neither who Hillary truly was, nor who she wanted to be. His wife was quite content, he discovered, to be the cold, vain, selfish woman she had always been.

Robert's heart was not further damaged by Hillary. She had never gotten that close. He might have lived his entire life without love, never really missing it, never knowing to search for more, never imagining that there could be *for him* the joy and happiness he had always promised Brynne. But now there was Alexa. He hadn't searched for her, hadn't known to, but now she was found, and he needed her. Oh, how he needed her.

And how much was the brilliant Senator, whose destiny it was to be President, willing to risk for this woman whose need for him could not possibly match his desperate need for her?

The answer was so simple.
Everything.

"Alexa, for you." The cameraman gestured with the telephone receiver he held in his hand.

"Oh, thanks." Alexa smiled as she walked to the backstage phone. "Hello?"

"Hi, Alexa. It's Robert."

"Hi," she whispered softly.

"I was wondering if . . ." He paused to recapture the breath that had left him when he heard the softness in her greeting. Softness, almost relief, as if she had been waiting for his call, but had not really dared to expect it.

"Yes."

"Yes?" he echoed softly, relieved, overjoyed. Alexa was saying yes to whatever it was he was about to propose. He hadn't even planned that far, but now his mind raced. It was Thursday, and he had a dinner meeting, and he had been planning to spend the night at his apartment in town. "Tonight? It would be almost eleven before I could get there."

"That's fine. Eleven."

Alexa met him on the moonlit path of roses. For a moment, they simply stared at each other, touching only with eyes that spoke so eloquently of their joy. Then his trembling hands gently touched her face, and her trembling fingers touched his, and then she was in his arms, and their lips found each other, greeting with welcoming wonder and astonishing need. He needed to touch her and hold her and kiss her and love her, and there were words, too, that he needed her to hear. The words came from the most delicate place in his heart, the brave, hopeful place that defiantly survived unscarred because it had known somehow, miraculously, that one day there would be Alexa.

"I have missed you, Alexa," he whispered between kisses. "All my life."

Their loving couldn't be leisurely. They needed each other, all of each other, far too much and far too urgently to make slow sensual discoveries. And when, swiftly, so swiftly, they were where they both needed so desperately to be, there was something even more extraordinary than their extraordinary passion; because, when they were together, when they were one, there was the most gentle peace, the most quiet joy, the most perfect happiness.

Alexa's delicate fingers tenderly touched the long wide scar that coursed down his abdomen, and moments later her soft lips followed, caressing lovingly, asking no questions, but welcoming anything he wanted to tell her.

"I have other scars, Alexa, much deeper ones."

"If you could show them to me, Robert, perhaps I could kiss them, too."

"Oh, my darling Alexa, you already have." Robert gently drew her to him and parted her love-tangled hair until he could see her emerald eyes. And when he could, he whispered softly, "I love you, Alexa."

"Oh, Robert, I love you, too." Her lips touched his, and in a moment they would need all of each other again, but now there was a question that needed to be asked and answered, for him, for them—so that he would know without doubt that her love for him was unconditional, no matter what secrets or horrors dwelled in his past. She asked gently, "Was there something about the war, Robert?"

"No, my love. Nothing specific, no shameful secret," he assured her truthfully. "I'm just like any other man who's been a soldier, that's all."

"I don't think, Robert McAllister," she answered softly, before losing herself again in the compelling desire of his sensuous eyes, "that you are just like any other man."

"Hello, James."

"Alexa."

"Is this a bad time to call?" It was six P.M. Chicago time on Saturday, and she had reached him in his suite at the Drake Hotel.

"No, not at all. My meetings are finished for the day." James frowned slightly as he reflected that it had been almost two hours since the day's meetings had adjourned. On any other Saturday in the five months he had known her, he would have long since caught a flight from O'Hare to National to spend the night with her at RoseCliff. But today, during the past two hours, he had simply stood at the window, gazing at the panoramic view of Lake Michigan and thinking—about Alexa, and about her little sister.

"So . . . can I come up?"

"Up?"

"I'm in the lobby."

"Hi."

"Hi. Come in."

"Thank you."

James watched with surprise and interest as, after a brief awkward smile and no lingering kiss, no kiss at all, she breezed past him and into the elegant living room of his spacious suite. Alexa quite clearly had an agenda.

"So?" he asked, when he had followed her into the living room and sat on the sofa across from the one she had chosen.

"James . . . something has happened."

"I can tell," he answered quietly. Then, as he gazed at her glowing yet uncertain emerald eyes, he added, "Something good, although you're not sure that I will think so."

"Yes," she whispered, marvelling at how well he could read her, and worried anew about what she had come to say and her ability to convince him of the one necessary lie.

"Do I guess? Frankly, I can't imagine what it could be."

"That's because it's the unimaginable. I've met someone, James, and we've fallen in love."

"Fallen in love?" he echoed softly. From a distant corner of his spinning mind spun the remarkable thought that he had so carefully suppressed all week, but which now twirled free and danced in jubilant defiance, *So have I.* "Love? Cynical you?"

"Cynical me. It's all your fault, of course," she said, as she had planned to say, speaking as many truths as possible. It *was* James's fault, for introducing her to Robert, but she knew that he was responsible for her love in a far more important way. And she wanted him to know that. She said softly, "You, James Sterling, made me believe in myself. You relentlessly told me that I was nice, not cruel, worthy of loving and being loved. I don't know if you really believe it. If not, you've created a deluded, love-crazed monster."

"You know damn well I believe it."

His solemn blue eyes told her that it was true. Alexa gazed at him, searching for other messages, but he was the master negotiator now, his stunningly handsome face set in neutral: controlled, inscrutable, cool. She had flown to Chicago to tell him, face to face, that their relationship was over, because she thought it was right to do so. She had not expected drama from James, nor had she wanted it, but there hadn't been even a dark blue flicker of regret. In fact, hadn't there been, at the moment he echoed "Fallen in love" something that might almost have been relief? Alexa didn't want James to be hurt, but still . . .

"What?" he asked with a soft laugh, unable to interpret the suddenly turbulent emerald stare.

"Dammit James! Does this matter to you, even a little bit? Did you care about our relationship at all? Maybe it's not fair for me to ask, but—"

"Alexa! *Of course* I cared about us. Do you really not know that?" James waited until her glare softened and her eyes confessed, Yes, I do know. Then he added gently, "I cared very much about us. And, Alexandra Taylor, I will care, *always*, about you and your happiness."

"Cat's definition of love," Alexa murmured softly.

"Oh?"

"Yes. She says that love is when you care about someone else's happiness always, forever, whether or not you are destined to be together. Which is the way I feel about you, too. So . . ."

"So?"

"So we love each other, even though we never told each other."

"Even though we never told each other before now," James amended softly. "Do I have to care about your forever happiness from a distance, or do we remain friends? We were wonderful lovers, Alexa, but we were—*are*, I hope—even better friends."

"Oh, James," she whispered, "I am so glad that you want to be my friend."

"Always." James sealed the promise with a gentle smile. Then, because it had been enough emotion for both of them, he teased lightly, "So, my friend Alexa, tell me about him."

"There isn't much to tell. We met on Thursday—two days ago!—and that was it. Love at first sight." Alexa spoke the necessary lie without a flicker, and even managed a sheepish smile when she confessed to a romantic notion she once had so defiantly scorned. The lie was necessary, she had decided. James could not know that her love was Robert. She hated the lie, but she hated her reason for it even more: *because James might not approve*. What if, despite his words of love and friendship, he believed that she was unworthy of Robert? Or, at least, that Robert's affair with her was not worth the risk to his important political career? The monsters that lurked in the shadows of her heart, symbols of her past failures and unworthiness, were there still, quieted by James's love and by Robert's; quieted, but not, perhaps never, silenced.

"Does he have a name?"

"Romeo. Appropriate, don't you think, since I've completely converted to belief in a *Romeo and Juliet* love? Besides, stealing a line from the young Ms. Capulet, 'What's in a name?' "

"This unsuccessful attempt at evasiveness means he's in one of your 'totally unsuitable' categories," James observed with a smile. Alexa had informed him once, half-teasing, half-serious, about the men who were, in her judgment, totally unsuitable for a serious romantic involvement should her cynicism toward love ever vanish. Actors were, naturally, impossible, as were, she had discovered in the past few years, politicians; the two shared, she said, an unappealing blend of supreme vanity, total self-absorption, and the unnerving ability to act their way out of any corner. Attorneys *had* been in the unsuitable category, on ill-defined "general principles," as had blue-bloods, but that was before James. Had her new love been an actor or politician or attorney or blue-blood, she would have tossed her golden mane, laughed merrily at her mistake, and confessed. But she didn't. Seeing apprehension in her lovely eyes, James guessed quietly, "He's married, isn't he?"

"Yes," Alexa admitted. She knew there were only so many lies she could tell him. She had told him the most important one—that she and her love had just met—and he had seemed to believe it. She didn't dare push her luck with less important ones.

"I thought marriage was an automatic deal breaker, Alexa."

"It used to be. But it isn't any longer. It can't be, not with him. I have to live this love for as long as I can, James, no matter what."

"It's dangerous."

"I know. Dangerous and foolish—not to mention *wrong*. That's a very deep, old-fashioned, country girl belief of mine."

"Old-fashioned, maybe, but very, *very* sound."

"Yes. But, James, I believe in my love for him more than I've ever believed in anything in my life. A consuming and compelling love wasn't going to happen to me, remember? But now it has."

"I can tell." It was so obvious. Alexa was radiant, more beautiful than ever, glowing from a deep and wondrous joy. "Just be careful, Alexa."

"I can't even promise that, James," she answered softly. She and Robert would be careful to keep their love hidden, of course; but she had no control any longer over what happened to her heart. It didn't belong to her any more.

She had given her heart to Robert. It was completely in his care.

Alexa declined James's invitation for dinner, pleading exhaustion, which was true, and a need to get back to Washington because they were filming in the morning, even though tomorrow was Sunday, which was also true. But mostly, she declined dinner because she feared that, given time and more questions and his ability to tease truths from her, he might begin to guess.

Alexa left, and James spent the evening, the entire sleepless night, thinking about Catherine. She had been with him all week, in enchanting thoughts that surfaced without warning—even, astonishingly, distracting him in the midst of the billion-dollar negotiations. The thoughts had been there, and he had rationed them as best he could, allowing brief enticing forays into a distant fantasy and then forcing them away, where they belonged. Eventually, when he had uninterrupted time, the lovely, renegade thoughts would be marched out, spoken to firmly, and then banished forever.

Banished forever, an act of love and will, because of Alexa, whom he loved and would never hurt. If he had met another woman and fallen instantly in love, as Alexa had, yes, then, of course, he would have gone to her and gently confessed, as she had to him, that the unimaginable had happened. And she would have been happy for him, as he had been for her.

But Catherine wasn't just another woman. She was the little sister whose birth had caused such chaos in Alexa's young life and with whom the relationship now was so important, so complicated, so fragile. James knew, with absolute certainty, that he would never have said, "I know, Alexa, that cynical you and skeptical me have never really believed in falling in love. But, you see, there is something so wonderful, so magical about your little sister . . ."

But now Alexa had found her own magical love.

And maybe, just maybe, it was the tenderness that he and Alexa had felt for each other that had opened their hearts to these even greater loves. Your fault, she had told him, a teasing grateful thank-you for convincing her of her own worthiness of love. But the truth was, in caring about Alexa, in loving her, James had made very important discoveries about himself. There had always been people he loved, of course—his parents, and Elliot, and Robert and Brynne. But, until Alexa, the "niceness" she had so quickly perceived hadn't in fact been there for any other lover. He simply hadn't cared before, not really, but he had really cared about Alexa. And because of caring about her, he had made wonderful discoveries about his own capacity for gentleness and tenderness and love.

"Your fault, Alexandra, that I am now able to fall in love with your little sister," he whispered softly to the glittering Chicago skyline. And then, even more softly, he added, "Thank you."

The wonderful thoughts of Catherine, now freed of restraint, danced in his mind, twirling and spinning and leaping with joy . . . until they crashed.

What about Catherine? a voice, perhaps the voice of reason, suddenly asked. Have you forgotten how young she is, how innocent? Don't you remember that every time—*every time*—you have been together you have caused her lovely cheeks to flush with embarrassment? You overwhelm her. Alexa told you that from the very beginning, and last weekend proved it's still true. In fact—how can you have overlooked this small point?—it was just a week ago tonight that you made Catherine cry. And don't you remember her reaction the following afternoon when you joined the others to hear her play? She couldn't even look at you!

Yes, Catherine is innocent, but I will be so gentle and so careful, his loving heart promised. And, yes, she is young, and yet not so young. There is sometimes such solemn wisdom in her lovely sapphire eyes, as if she has known sadnesses far beyond her years. And, yes, yes, I have embarrassed her, and I am so sorry for that. She *is* overwhelmed by me, I know that's true. But I am overwhelmed by her, too. And, perhaps, we are both simply overwhelmed by the magic. She feels it, too, I know she does. I see the wonder in her sparkling eyes and in her soft beautiful smile. And I think I know why she didn't look at me when she was playing the piano last Sunday afternoon. It's the same reason that I had to force thoughts of her from my mind while I worked this week. The distraction is so great, so enchanting, so compelling that it demands all attention.

You sound very confident of your feelings for Catherine, the voice of reason observed. But are you so very certain that this is what she wants?

I am very confident of my feelings. And, yes, I believe that this is what she wants, too. But, he vowed solemnly, if our love is not what Catherine wants, I promise I will leave her alone. We will do what she wants. The choices of the heart will be hers.

James wanted to go to her soon, *now*, but as a final begrudging concession to reason, he decided that there needed to be time between the end of his relationship with Alexa and the beginning of his love with her little sister.

Time . . . weeks . . . precious time away from precious Catherine.

CHAPTER FIFTEEN

Manhattan
October 1989

"*H*ello, Catherine? It's James."

"James."

"How are you?"

"I'm fine. Thank you." She could have embellished truthfully, "I'm truly fine, James, slender still, but strong and healthy and fit." But Catherine knew that he wasn't calling about her, not really. He was calling about Alexa. Even though Alexa had assured her, more than once, that his heart hadn't been broken, that obviously wasn't the case. And now he was calling to ask for her help.

"Good. I wondered if you'd like to go sailing with me on Saturday."

"Oh," she whispered softly, torn, as always, by conflicting answers when it came to James. Yes, because I want to see you. And no, because I have nothing to say that will help you. Alexa is very much in love.

"Or Sunday. Whichever is better for you."

"Saturday would be fine," she heard herself say, a brave and foolish answer from her heart.

"Good. I'm borrowing a boat from a friend. It's moored at the Southampton Club on Long Island. We should leave Manhattan about eleven. Is that OK?"

"Yes. That's fine."

"Hi."

"Hi." James smiled, so happy to see her, and for an enchanting moment he was lost in her bright blue eyes. Her eyes sparkled, so happy to see him, too, but surrounding the shimmering sapphire were dark circles and beneath them the always pink cheeks were ashen. "Catherine? What's wrong? Are you ill?"

"I'm fine. It's . . . nothing. What a glorious day for sailing! I just need to get a jacket from the closet, then I'll be ready to go."

"OK," he agreed uneasily, his impulse to press the issue intercepted by his reluctance to embarrass her—again. As she moved to the closet to get her jacket, he saw her slender body stiffen and her delicate fingers dig mercilessly into her snow white palms.

She's in pain, he realized. It was intermittent, he decided as her body relaxed just a little and her virtuoso fingers uncurled to reach for her jacket. Intermittent, coming in excruciating waves and then receding; but her pale drawn face and dark-circled eyes gave eloquent testimony to the fact that the pain had been with her all night.

"Catherine? Did you try to reach me to cancel? I was in my office this morning."

"No. I didn't try to reach you."

"Oh." Whatever it was, no matter the severity, she hadn't wanted to cancel their date. The realization filled him with both sadness and joy. "But maybe we should reschedule?"

"Yes. I guess we should." Catherine backed away from the closet, closed the door, and looked up bravely into his eyes. "Was there something you wanted to ask me about Alexa?"

"About Alexa?"

"Yes. About Alexa and . . ." She shrugged apologetically.

"About Alexa and her new love? No, not a thing. Why?"

"I thought that was why you called."

"No. I talk to your sister all the time. I have worries, as I'm sure you do, about the wisdom of what she's doing, but I'm delighted at how happy she is and hope her happiness will last forever." He gazed at her beautiful surprised eyes and added quietly, "The reason I asked you to go sailing with me, Catherine, is because I wanted to see you."

"Oh." Her reply began as a lovely breath of happiness, but it became a sharp gasp as a knife twisted deep inside her.

"Catherine, please, let me help you," James said softly. "Do you know what's wrong?"

"Yes. I know, and it will be gone in a few more hours." It should have been gone already! The severe cramping usually only lasted about eight hours, and it had already been nearly twelve. She had spent every pain-tossed moment of her sleepless night finding comfort in the certainty that it would all be over by morning, long before he arrived. She would be tired for their sail, but at least the cramps would have subsided. But they hadn't! The sharp claws dug into her still, first clutching and then, once their grip was deep and firm, twisting, causing even greater pain, stealing her breath and her strength.

"It's happened before?"

"Yes," she admitted, and, just for a heartbeat, her ashen cheeks flushed pink. "It's nothing, really, James. It's . . . I'm just having my period."

As the embarrassed blush vanished, sucked away by another wave of pain, he felt a most unusual mixture of helplessness and enchantment. Helplessness, because he wanted to stop her discomfort *now*; and enchantment, because it was the age of tampon ads on billboards and cocktail party conversations about PMS, but somehow that had passed her by. To lovely innocent Catherine, this was very private, very intimate.

"Hey, Catherine," he said gently when he sensed with grateful relief that the most recent wave of pain seemed to have retreated. "Remember my mother, the gynecologist? Admittedly, menstrual periods weren't frequent topics of conversation at the dinner table, but . . ." He paused, because his words had brought from her a trembling smile. Menstrual periods had *never* been dinner table conversation at Inverness, of course, and what he knew on the subject he had learned in vivid, uninhibited detail from women he had dated. But still . . . "I'm not embarrassed, Catherine. Please don't you be. Are your periods always this painful?"

"Yes, although it's lasting longer than usual this time. I think that might be because this is my first period since June. They stopped altogether while I was dieting."

"Have you seen anyone?"

"I saw a doctor at the student health center at Oberlin. She didn't think it was endometriosis, but she thought I should see a specialist when I got here and that I should probably start taking birth control pills."

"Did she give you the name of a specialist?"

"Yes, and I'll make an appointment for this week."

"Good. Now, what pain medications do you have?"

"Aspirin. It's not doing much, but I'm sure the cramps will stop soon."

"Have you had anything to drink?"

"To drink?"

"Vodka? Bourbon?"

"No. Why?"

James suppressed his surprise. He had known about the salutory effects of alcohol on menstrual cramps for years, probably since high school. But, apparently, Catherine hadn't learned this from her friends either in high school or college; nor had she learned it from her big sister, who, he knew, "treated" the mild to moderate cramps she had on the first day of her period with two glasses of Dom Pérignon.

"Alcohol seems to help," he explained, in answer to her question. Then, smiling gently, he offered quietly, "So, Catherine, shall I ply you with liquor?"

"OK. I don't know if there's even any . . ." She tilted her head, a thoughtful acknowledgment of what they both knew, that he was more familiar with Alexa's apartment than she. After a moment, she said softly, "I guess you do."

"Why don't you go into the living room, and I'll find some and bring it to you? Do you have a preference?"

"No. I've never really had more than a taste of anything."

"Oh. Well. Bourbon, then."

James knew there was bourbon here, his favorite brand, mild and rich and smooth. As soon as Catherine left to wait for him in the living room, he found the bourbon and a Saint Louis crystal highball glass and poured the drink undiluted and without ice.

"Here you go," he said when he joined her in the living room, where she was seated on the sofa, and handed her the glass. "Sip."

"Thank you. OK."

As Catherine sipped the expensive liquor under James's watchful gaze, she cast shy, apologetic smiles as if to say, Maybe I won't feel any effect. Maybe . . .

The bourbon hit her sleep-deprived and pain-exhausted body with a smooth rush of heat, filling her, bathing her, gently transporting her to a place where her mind floated, and there was no pain. The ferocious claws that had dug mercilessly into her for the past twelve hours magically withdrew, and into the tender wounds where the sharp claws had been, flowed a soothing, liquid warmth. She felt warm, and floating, and amazingly, wonderfully bold.

"Better?" James asked as he watched her eyes widen.

"Yes. I can't believe it. Thank you." She set the glass of bourbon down on the coffee tabled and announced, "I'm ready to go sailing."

He would love to have taken her sailing as planned. But James knew that the exhilarating rush from the alcohol, coupled with the euphoric relief that the pain was blocked, would soon give way to the legacy of fatigue from her sleepless night.

"I think bed would be better, don't you?"

For a magnificent moment her sapphire eyes filled with wonder, as if she thought he was suggesting that they go to bed together and welcomed the suggestion with desire and joy. It was only a moment, and when it was over, in a flutter of long black lashes and pink flushed cheeks, James wondered if it had only been a mirage. A mirage that made his heart race.

"Yes," she answered softly, finally. "I guess it would."

"Will you call me when you wake up, no matter what time?"

"OK. I don't have your number."

"Is that why you didn't call to cancel?"

"No. I didn't want to cancel."

"Because you thought I needed to talk to you about Alexa?"

"Yes." She lifted her eyes bravely to his and added softly, truthfully, "But mostly because I wanted to see you."

"Hi, James. It's Catherine. You told me to call no matter how late." It was after midnight, and she had just awakened, rested, refreshed, and free of pain.

"Yes. How are you?"

"Fine. I just woke up and I'm fine. Thank you."

"Good. I'm glad. Fine enough to have brunch with me tomorrow—no, today? I was going to suggest a sail, but the weather forecasters are talking fairly confidently about storms heading this way. So, how about trying Long Island's most famous champagne brunch? It happens to be in the Azalea Room at the Southampton Club, which means we could bring our sailing clothes, just in case, and sail after brunch if the weather looks clear when we get there . . ."

"I'd better not drink any of this," Catherine said with a soft smile as her delicate finger traced a line along the crystal champagne flute that had just been placed in front of her on the pink linen tablecloth.

"No champagne?"

"I discovered yesterday that alcohol makes me far too honest."

"Too honest?" James asked softly as he wondered which boldness from yesterday she decided had been too honest. Was it the soft confession that she had accepted his invitation to go sailing with him because she wanted to see him? Or the provocative sapphire wonder when he had suggested bed? And what as yet unspoken truth prevented her from drinking champagne today? Was it, perhaps, her version of the complicated history of the Taylor sisters? "Is it really possible to be too honest?"

"I think," she answered slowly, "there are some truths that need time before they can be told."

"Yes. I think so, too," he agreed gently. It was too soon, he knew, to tell her all the truths about his feelings for her. Some day, when she was ready, he would tell her those wonderful, joyous truths. And some day, he hoped, she would tell him the hidden truths which, unlike his joyous ones, were so obviously deeply troubling. Take all the time you need, lovely Catherine, but please know that you can trust me with all the secrets of your heart. "You really had very little alcohol yesterday, you know."

"I know."

Catherine knew it had taken only a few sips for the bourbon to work its magic on her pain. And what about the other magic, the warm, exhilarating rushes of pure joy, and the wonderful soft laughter that splashed merrily from a sparkling fountain of happiness deep within her? That magic, she knew, had nothing to do with alcohol. That magic was James. So gently, his dark blue eyes and warm smile lured her from her shyness, welcoming all her words, all her thoughts, all her truths.

But there were words she did not yet have the courage to speak to him. I'm adopted. My real mother didn't love me enough to keep me, you see. I'm not sure who I am, James, not yet, but each day I'm learning a little more. Catherine didn't have the courage to tell him that truth, not yet, or perhaps it was simply that she didn't have the courage to tell him the rest. There is something I have learned, James, about myself, a wonderful recent discovery. I have learned that when I am with you, I am everything I want to be.

Catherine didn't tell James her secrets on that stormy day. They talked instead of music and sailing, and raindrops and roses, and storm clouds and waves. And woven into the afternoon of soft smiles and softer laughter were invitations for future times to be together. Yes, she told him, she would love to see the Ring cycle at the Met, yes, all four operas. And she would love to dine with him at Manhattan's most famous restaurants, and view the Impressionist exhibit at the art museum, and . . .

Catherine answered yes to all his invitations, a joyous happy yes, and her beautiful honest eyes embellished, telling him the most important truth, the only truth he needed to know, Yes, James, I want to be with you.

CHAPTER SIXTEEN

Washington, D.C.
December 1989

"*A*ll weekend?" Alexa echoed softly.

It was the first Tuesday in December. In the three months of their love, she and Robert had never had a weekend together. Their loving had been on weeknights only, in rare, precious hours stolen from darkness. And in those cherished late-night hours, they shared an emotional intimacy that was exquisitely gentle and tender; and they shared, too, a breathless passion that was still as desperate, as urgent and as furtive, as it had been the first night.

Their desperate, furtive passion was a symbol, Alexa had decided, of what they both knew but neither said: their secret love could not endure. Their love was safe now, a secret easily kept because no one knew to search for it. The Washington press pursued Robert relentlessly in hopes of getting quotable quotes from the nation's brightest political star. But it would never have occurred to a single reporter, not even the most aggressive gossip columnist, to investigate the Senator's personal life. Why bother? Anyone in Washington who had ever seen them together, and virtually all the reporters had, knew that Robert and Hillary McAllister had a perfect marriage.

The secret love of Robert and Alexa would be quite safe—until Robert made his bid for the Presidency. Then, every detail of his life, no matter how personal, would be in the public domain. He would be pursued constantly, both by the political press and the legion of spies hired by the other party who had been given the virtually impossible task of finding even the tiniest chink in his impeccable armor. If Robert became the party's nominee for the 1996 election, which most political analysts predicted, their secret love was safe for at least four more years, perhaps almost five. And if he didn't run until the year 2000 . . .

Would she be willing to live this love of dark, desperate, stolen moments for four more years, or even eight? *Oh yes.* She would love him, whenever she could, for as long as she could.

And now he was telling her that beginning three days from now they would have a weekend together.

"All weekend," Robert whispered as his tender kisses wandered from her tear-dampened eyes to her kiss-dampened mouth. "All weekend, my love."

"Oh, no!"

"Darling?"

"I have to work on Saturday! We're filming on location at the Supreme Court. I have all of Friday off, but I have to work on Saturday."

"Then, on Friday, you make dinner for me. I'll be here in time for dinner, I promise," Robert replied, kissing away her frown. "And I'll make dinner for you on Saturday. And on Sunday, my love . . ."

All weekend, my love, he had promised, and her emerald eyes had filled with such lovely joy at the promise. How eagerly he awaited the moment when he could promise her, All of our lives, my love.

Maybe this weekend I will be able to make that promise, Robert thought, as, hours later, he held her in his arms as she slept. She was a portrait of peace and happiness, her golden hair haloing her beautiful face, a soft hopeful smile on her lips. As he gently touched the golden silk, her lovely smile grew, reaching to him from sleep, as if she had been dreaming about what he had been thinking—the time when, at last, they could be together always.

Robert had never discussed his joyous plans to spend his life with her—but, of course, she knew—and he wanted to make no specific promises until Hillary had agreed to a divorce. He had decided to wait until the Christmas holidays to approach Hillary. The Senate would be in recess then, and Alexa would be in Topeka; and, *if all went well*, Hillary could go to Dallas as always, to the lavish parties she loved, while he remained in Washington and moved out of the house. The decision to wait until the holidays had been a practical one, and not the least bit cruel. Christmas held no special sentiment for Senator and Mrs. McAllister, *no time did*.

But now, as Robert held the woman he loved and thought about the many Washington parties that he and Hillary would be expected to attend in the upcoming weeks, he made a new decision. He would talk to Hillary about the divorce very soon, this Thursday, the evening before she left for her weekend at the spa. He couldn't, wouldn't, live the public charade any longer.

It had always amazed Robert that no one could tell that the perfect script followed by the perfect First Couple-to-be was just a sham, a performance without heart or soul. He had survived it in the past, before Alexa, because his heart had been empty then, and the charade hadn't really mattered. But now his heart was filled, overflowing, with love for Alexa; and even if the sham hadn't been apparent in the past, it certainly should have been now, because he scarcely looked at Hillary any more; and yet, they were Washington's darlings, the picture perfect couple *still*.

It was time, now, for the charade to end; and, *if all went well*, it would. It was a very big "if". Robert knew that Hillary wouldn't "give" him a divorce. He would have to pay for it. The cost, he knew, might be quite high, because he wanted more than just a divorce: he wanted a quiet, private one. What he wanted had nothing to do with his political career, of course; it had only to do with Alexa. He knew that a highly publicized divorce, starring the talented actress in the real life role as "the other woman," would be devastating for her.

Robert knew that Hillary would have a price for what he wanted. He had to steel himself to weather her insults and her fury until she told him what it was; and then, for Alexa, for her protection and her happiness, he had to be prepared to pay.

"I love you," he whispered softly to his sleeping love. I love you, and, my darling, maybe this weekend I will have wonderful news for us.

Hillary always spent the first weekend in December at the Willows, the ultra-exclusive spa forty miles north of Savannah that catered to the South's richest women. She was a guest at the lavishly restored antebellum mansion at least four times a year, a tradition that had begun as a gift from her mother the day she turned sixteen. Hillary never really felt improved after her visits to the Willows. Indeed, the spa's many beauty, health, and fitness experts were hard pressed to find ways to enhance the perfect face, skin, nails, and body with which she always arrived. But she faithfully returned to the Willows nonetheless, because rich, beautiful, and influential women, like her, did such things.

Now, for the first time ever, Hillary had wondered if she should cancel her reservation for this booked-years-in-advance weekend before the all-important holiday social season began. She knew full well that if she spent the weekend at the Willows, Robert would spend it with Alexa at RoseCliff. And if she cancelled? Robert would spend the weekend at Clairmont working in his study, and when they shared their silent meals, she would see in his solemn eyes how much he longed to be with *her*. And she might even see something worse: the dark turbulence that made her fear that Robert was going to tell her about his affair.

As if she didn't already know! Months ago, she had followed him to the tiny cottage perched high on the cliffs. And, for months, she had churned with a hatred for Alexa that made all previous emotions about her long-time rival seem trivial; and she hated Robert, too, for doing this to *her*. She knew that their paltry affair would end, of course, *it had to*; but that would not put an end to Hillary's fury that Robert had risked scandal—risked the Presidency—for Alexa! How could he? How *dare* he?

Hillary had finally decided not to cancel her weekend at the Willows. The more Robert was with Alexa, she had reasoned, the sooner he would tire of her. And, she had wondered grimly as she gazed at her beautiful face in the mirror, were those really tiny little lines she saw now in her always flawless skin? Worry lines, *hatred* lines? Even more reasons to hate Alexa and Robert, she had decided; and more reasons, too, to spend a lavish rejuvenating weekend at the spa.

On Thursday evening, the night before her morning departure for Savannah, Hillary sat in the Florentine drawing room at Clairmont glancing through a stack of engraved, mostly gilt-edged, invitations. She expertly sorted the various soirées, receptions, galas, and black-tie charity balls in her mind, instantly recognizing the socially and politically important ones and dismissing the ones that weren't pure "A-list." And, as she sorted, she planned which ravishing designer gown she would wear to each, never needing to repeat, scowling as she imagined the conversation with Robert in which he would question her conspicuous extravagances and suggest yet again that, at the very least, she wear more American creations and fewer original designs of Givenchy, Chanel, and LaCroix.

Hillary's scowl at that imagined conversation—how dare he make any suggestions whatsoever?—deepened as she reached the engraved invitation to

Pennsylvania Avenue's "When You Wish Upon a Star" charity gala to be held on Saturday the sixteenth. She started to rip the invitation in half, on the way to a hundred tiny pieces, but she was stopped mid-ravage by a wonderful image.

Senator and Mrs. Robert McAllister would go to the gala this year. Alexa would be there, of course, wearing something trashy, tasteless crimson satin, perhaps, plunged to the navel. And she would be wearing her new gown of ivory silk, intricately sewn with the most delicate pearl and silver beads, like dewdrops on roses, endlessly pure, timelessly elegant. She would wear her sable-brown hair in a demure chignon, away from her beautiful face, to fully reveal her emerald earrings, the only jewelry she would wear, *except*, of course, the most important piece of all: the gold and emerald wedding band that would be a reminder to both her wandering husband and his brazen slut of precisely who and what she was.

Hillary's reverie was interrupted by the sound of approaching footsteps. Robert? At home on a Thursday night? Home, instead of RoseCliff? *Good*, she thought triumphantly. At last.

"Hello, Robert," she said, with cool surprise when he appeared in the doorway, not leaving the silk sofa to greet him, and, in fact, after a moment glancing back to the stack of invitations in her hands.

"Hello, Hillary. I'm here because I need to talk to you."

"Oh?"

"Do I have your attention?"

"Yes." She smiled prettily, disingenuously, as she looked up. "Of course."

"OK, then, the reason I've come here tonight is to tell you that I want a divorce."

"You're joking."

"No. You know that I'm not. And you know, too, that the joke is the marriage. We have both known that for a very long time."

"Do you honestly think I will give you a divorce, Robert?"

No, he thought. I know that you will not. But that's why I'm here, to learn your price for my freedom and Alexa's privacy. He said quietly, "You don't really have a choice, Hillary. I can file the papers just as easily as you can. I had hoped, I do hope, however, that we can reach an amicable agreement."

"There's someone else, isn't there?" she demanded suddenly, as if the horrifying thought had just occurred to her. "That's what this is *really* about, isn't it?"

"What this is really about, Hillary, is a marriage that exists in name only and needs to end. Yes, I have met someone, and I plan to marry her, but she is not the reason our marriage failed. It failed long ago, long before I ever met her."

"Who is she?"

"It doesn't matter who she is."

"Really? I sincerely doubt that the many reporters assigned to cover our very ugly and very public divorce would agree with you. My guess is that they would be most interested in every sordid detail about your mistress. Our divorce *would* be very ugly and very public, Robert, I promise you that. Your constituency has a right to know what kind of man you really are. As you know, womanizers aren't doing terribly well at the voting booths these days." Hillary stood up then and walked toward him slowly, allowing the effect of her threat to settle, reveling in her triumph. Finally she continued almost condescendingly to the man who had apparently, astonishingly, forgotten that he *could not* leave her, "Divorcing me, Senator McAllister, would cost you the Presidency."

Robert held her angry yet triumphant glare for several moments before replying very quietly, "Then so be it."

His quiet words instantly shattered both her confidence and her anger, leaving her only with trembling fear. He was really going to leave her, and she was powerless to stop him, *because* he was willing to give up everything—*everything*—to spend his life with her most bitter enemy.

She spun away from him, suddenly needing support for her trembling body, and finding it a few staggering feet away against the marble mantlepiece. Her eyes focused vaguely on the expensive adornments on the Italian marble—the Orrefors vase, the antique clock, the Boehm rose. How she wanted to hurl them at him! But, if she did, he would leave now, immediately and forever. He would waste no time in filing for the divorce, and all would be lost. She needed time to think, to plan, to somehow find a way to stop the divorce entirely.

Anger had never worked with Robert, nor had tears or threats, nor, not for a very long time, had seduction. But he was, she knew, a fair and reasonable man; and in the long, silent moments before she was steady enough to face him again, her spinning mind searched frantically for, and finally found, fair and reasonable appeals to make to her fair and reasonable husband.

"I don't want to fight with you," she said softly when, eventually, she turned back to him.

"I don't want to fight, either, Hillary."

"I will give you the divorce, uncontested and without a whisper of publicity, but I need time. Don't worry, I'm not talking about a reconciliation. I have a little pride, you know. I just need time to adjust, to decide what I'm going to do and if I'll even feel comfortable being in Washington any longer."

Robert's heart raced at "uncontested and without a whisper of publicity." Hillary had agreed, in principle, to the quiet divorce he wanted, and now she was beginning to tell him her price. He asked with amazing calm, "How much time did you have in mind?"

"Until the end of May."

"That's almost six months."

"I need that much time, Robert. And there is the celebration for my father's birthday in Dallas over Memorial Day weekend. You know what an important event that will be for him, and you've already agreed to give one of the major speeches. If we could just keep up appearances until Memorial Day, it would give me time to make plans and it would make that weekend untarnished for my father."

Robert reeled inwardly at "keeping up appearances." But, surely, the public charade would be more endurable once the private charade was over.

"Nothing is going to change between now and then, Hillary."

"I know that."

"Is there anything else you want?"

"Yes. Does anyone know about . . . her?"

"I don't think so. No."

"Then I have a final request. I would like to know that people aren't gossiping about me."

"You want me to stop seeing her until after we've separated."

"Yes."

Now he knew the full price for a quiet divorce: six months away from Alexa. *Six months*. It was a long time, but he knew it was not an unreasonable request. It would take Hillary a while to adjust. His vain, spoiled wife was quite unused to being denied anything, and even though this was not the loss of a love, for pretentious and ambitious Hillary it was a loss of great magnitude nonetheless. *Away from*

Alexa. Was that too high a price to pay? No, he decided, and he knew that Alexa would agree. "We've been waiting all our lives for each other, Robert," she would say softly as her emerald eyes filled with joy. "Can I wait six more months until our forever? Of course I can."

"I would need to see her one more time, Hillary, to explain."

"Of course."

"And if I agree to keep up appearances and stop seeing her, at the end of May you will give me a quiet, uncontested divorce," he said quietly, holding Hillary's eyes, searching for deceit, and seeing none.

"Yes, Robert," she answered with matching quiet and without a flicker. "I promise that I will."

Six months, Hillary thought as she paced restlessly in her bedroom. Six months with which to do what? *Nothing*, she realized miserably, except to hope that Robert would come to his senses, or that Alexa would become impatient with the wait and find a new love.

Hillary paced, and, as the winter night grew colder and darker, completely black, so too did her thoughts. Cold, and dark, and black, and suddenly quite hopeful. Maybe something terrible—terribly wonderful—would happen to Alexa.

Maybe Alexa would die.

Robert might have left the following morning without seeing Hillary, but, shortly before seven, as he was finishing a cup of coffee before beginning the long drive from Arlington to the capital, the phone rang, and, moments later, she appeared in the kitchen.

"Good morning, Robert."

"Good morning, Hillary."

"Did I hear the phone?"

"Yes. I have to go to Camp David for the weekend."

"Leaving now?"

"Leaving at two this afternoon. What time is your flight for Savannah?"

"At ten." But I won't be leaving this morning for a weekend at the Willows after all, she thought. She wasn't certain yet what she was going to do, but she felt quite confident that she had suddenly been presented with a chance to control her own destiny.

As soon as Robert left, Hillary made two phone calls. Then, after dressing elegantly, she drove from Arlington to the Washington studio where *Pennsylvania Avenue* was filmed, gave her name to the studio security guard and announced that Alexa was expecting her. She was, she explained truthfully, a co-hostess for a benefit for the homeless. Then, lying effortlessly, she further told him that Alexa had said she would be willing to appear at the event.

"There must be some mistake, ma'am. Ms. Taylor isn't scheduled to work today."

"You're kidding." Hillary's beautiful smile became a beautiful frown as she followed the guard's eyes to the schedule he held. She saw that Alexa had worked late last night, was off today, and if her quick glance at the much marked up schedule was correct, would be working most of tomorrow. Good . . . *perfect*. "I spoke to Alexa last week. Perhaps her schedule changed since then and she forgot to call me."

"Probably. Shall I tell her you were here?"

"No. Thank you. I'll reach her myself."

As Hillary sped along the interstate from Washington, D. C. toward Maryland, she caught sight of a police car hidden beside the road. Her eyes swept to the speedometer—sixty-eight!—and then to the rearview mirror as she pressed her suede pump to the brake. For ten breath-held seconds she waited for the police car to follow her, lights flashing, siren blaring, and steeled herself for a condescending "Now, Mrs. McAllister" lecture. But when the car didn't follow, she vowed to look frequently at the speedometer to be certain that her gold-tone Mercedes didn't fly toward RoseCliff as swiftly as her thoughts were flying.

Slow down, she told herself. And, as she slowed the car, gaining control, her thoughts came under control, too. She had raced to the studio because it seemed necessary to speak to Alexa before Robert did. But, she realized, it didn't matter.

By the time she began the three flight climb up the stairs to Alexa's secluded cottage, she felt amazingly calm. Why not? Even if her plan backfired she could lose no more than she had already lost—*everything*—and if it succeeded, her most bitter enemy might unwittingly become her greatest ally. As she climbed the stairs, Hillary noticed the roses. They were barren now, carefully draped in burlap for winter, their thorns hidden. You have to keep your thorns hidden, she reminded herself. You have to.

"Hillary."

"May I come in?" Hillary's calm stumbled briefly at the sight of Alexa, her golden hair tousled from sleep, her robe cinched tightly around her narrow waist; and there was a little more faltering when she left the colorless winter day behind and entered the romantic, pastel love nest.

"Of course. I'm surprised to see you."

"Wives and mistresses don't usually meet for coffee?" she asked, discovering to her relief that "mistress," spoken with glacial contempt, had a tranquilizing effect, helping her restore the necessary calm control. "No, I suppose not. Well, we can forgo the coffee."

"Hillary, I don't know what—"

"For heaven's sake, let's don't spend any time pretending it hasn't happened! I know all about you and Robert. He hasn't called you yet this morning, has he?" She paused, deliberately considering her own question, and then mused with a coy smile, "Or perhaps he *has* called and you still don't know what's happened. I guess that's the reason I'm here, Alexa. Robert may not tell you, and I want to make very certain that you know the truth."

"The truth," Alexa echoed numbly.

"Yes." Hillary smiled. She felt wonderful now, and oh-so-confident having the ever-confident Alexa at such a distinct disadvantage. Be careful, she warned herself. Don't overplay your hand. Be haughty and disdainful. "Did Robert ever happen to tell you why he chose you to have an affair with?"

"No." *Chose?* Neither of us chose! Our love happened because it was meant to happen.

"It wasn't by accident. Robert wanted to punish me, and I'd told him enough about our days at Ballinger for him to know that of all the women on earth it would hurt me the most to know that he had been unfaithful with you."

"Why would Robert want to hurt you?"

"Because I hurt him. He really told you none of this, did he? Of course not, because you might have been suspicious of his motives from the outset. Robert had an affair with you to get even with me—for the affair I've been having. I'm not the least bit proud of what I did. I was a little bored, I guess, and a little petulant about how hard he was working and how little time he had for me. And remember, Alexa, unlike you I didn't spend my past sleeping with everything in pants. So I allowed myself a foolish affair. I didn't even know Robert knew about it until last night." She sighed, softly, sadly, her dark sable eyes conveying deep regret for her own foolishness. "You can tell from the dark circles beneath my eyes that I didn't sleep, neither of us did, because we spent all night talking about what we had done, and what we want to do now. And what we want, after we've had a little time just to ourselves, is to begin our family. We've delayed because of Brynne, because she has desperately wanted children and has been unable to have them. Well, that's really none of your business. All that you need to know is that it's over, Alexa, not me and Robert, but *you* and Robert."

"But for some reason you don't think he'll tell me."

"He'll tell you something that will cause your affair to end, but it may not be the truth. He's very politic and probably more than a little embarrassed. He'll find a graceful way out. I'm very certain he won't admit that he used you, or that our marriage is stronger now than ever."

"But you're telling me."

"Yes. Because we have been at war for a long time, Alexa, and I want you to know that in this final and most important battle you have lost. It's a luxury for me to tell you, an indulgence, but not a great risk."

"You don't think I'll go public with this."

"No. I don't think so. I doubt you could destroy Robert's career even if you did. The other woman—the immoral seductress—is never a sympathetic role. You're a star, of course, but so is he, and he's also the great political hope for very many people. Destroying him, even attempting to, would ruin your career in the process. Maybe you don't care about that, or have so little pride that you might confess to a sordid affair in which you were the loser, but there's your sister to think about."

"What about Cat?"

"She'd defend you, I'm sure, as she did years ago, but I wonder if you want to drag her and her career through the shame? Your little sister is a lady. And you, Alexa, are a whore. You'll never be anything else."

"Get out."

"Well," Hillary continued smoothly, ignoring Alexa's trembling command but glancing at her diamond Chopard watch as if it might be nearing time for her to leave anyway. "I'd better be going. Robert's leaving work early today, at two, so that we can get to Dallas in time for a champagne and candlelight dinner. You look surprised, Alexa. Oh, that's right, this was going to be your weekend with Robert while I was at the spa. Well, plans have changed. We're spending the weekend in the bridal suite at the Mansion, the same hotel where we spent our wedding night. That was Robert's idea. Very romantic, don't you think?"

"Get out."

"Yes, we have the reservation," the desk clerk at Dallas' famous Mansion on Turtle Creek confirmed when Alexa called pretending she was Senator McAllister's secretary. "The bridal suite, as per the Senator's request."

"Thank you."

Her hands trembled as she returned the receiver to the cradle. She had believed Hillary's eyes and tone and confidence, but until that moment she hadn't believed her devastating words. *I still don't believe them.* And I won't, until I hear them from Robert. He will tell me the truth, whatever it is, I know he will.

In their months of love, Robert had never once mentioned Hillary or his marriage. Alexa had simply assumed, because of *their* desperate and passionate love, that his marriage was loveless; but, she had assumed, too, that in spite of its unhappiness, it would endure, would have to, because of his political career. And she had been willing, so very willing, to be Robert's hidden love, forever, because she believed so much in their love.

But what if he truly loved Hillary? What if he had come to her, as Hillary claimed, simply to hurt the wife who had hurt him so much? What if his desperate passion for her was really a disguised desperation for Hillary?

"No! I don't believe it!" Alexa cried defiantly to the gray sky, darkening now even though it was still before noon, an ominous black harbinger of a long cold winter. "Call me, Robert, please. And please, whatever the truth is, even if it's exactly as Hillary has said, please tell me."

Robert called at one-fifty. In the crush of compressing the obligations of his day so that he could leave for Camp David at two, he had been unable to find a private moment earlier in which to call her. His office phone had rung incessantly, including several aggravating crank calls from a caller who remained on the line but said nothing, and there had been a steady stream of people who needed his attention. It had been a frustratingly rushed day, but every time he had felt his sleep-deprived temper begin to fray, Robert had reminded himself of what Hillary had promised last night. He wanted to tell Alexa now, but there wasn't time; and, he thought, they were words that needed to be whispered softly, between kisses, as he held her for the last time before their six months apart.

As Robert dialed the number to RoseCliff, the warm joy of their love, the antidote to every frustration and every problem in his life, drifted over him.

His voice smiled, a gentle tender smile, when she answered.

"Hello, darling."

"Robert." Alexa curled her aching body in the tenderness of his voice and her mind banished the memory of Hillary. It hadn't happened. It was just a mirage, just a lie. "How is your day going? Do you still think you'll be able to get here for dinner?"

"Oh, Alexa, this weekend isn't going to happen."

"Why not?" No! Please, *no.*

"The President wants me at Camp David."

"Is it something top secret? No media coverage?" No way to prove or disprove?

"What? Oh, yes, I imagine so. Alexa? I'm very sorry," he said gently, surprised by the sudden edge in her voice. He had expected disappointment, but not the sudden disappearance of gentleness.

"So am I."

"Darling, I need to go now. The limousine is waiting. I should be back late Sunday night. I'll call you, if it's not too late. OK?"

"OK."

"I love you, Alexa."

I love you too.

CHAPTER SEVENTEEN

*T*he annoying crank calls to Robert's office had been made by Hillary. She recorded his voice, the polite "Hello" that, on repeated calls, degenerated into impatient demands "Hello? *Hello?* Who is this?" She made the recordings on a high quality hand-held recorder, one of many Robert kept around the house for dictation, and using another one made a careful single recording of two pleasant "Hellos" back to back, then a pause, then increasing annoyance, and in the background, she added her own voice, purring seductively, "Robert, who is it? Tell them to send us more champagne!"

Hillary made the recordings, packed a large suitcase, took a limousine to National, and by late afternoon was settled in the first class cabin of the flight to Dallas sipping champagne and silently toasting both the expensive empty seat beside her and whatever international crisis had taken Robert to Camp David. A few hours later, she was in the lavish lobby of the luxurious Mansion on Turtle Creek, preparing to casually murmur to the hotel receptionist that her husband was on a later flight. But no explanation was necessary. Apparently it was simply assumed that the important and busy Senator had been unavoidably delayed.

And then she was in the romantic bridal suite, her mission accomplished, and all that was left to do was reminisce about the exhilarating and triumphant day. She had moved with swift confidence from task to task, propelled by powerful bursts of adrenaline, and further energized by each successfully completed phase of her desperate plan. I, not Alexa, should have been an actress, she had decided after her performance at RoseCliff. Or a secret agent, she had mused as she listened to the tape she had made of Robert. Or a criminal, a rare and extraordinary criminal who is bright enough and clever enough to commit the perfect crime.

The wonderful exhilaration was with her as long as the adrenaline was, and the potent substance continued to spurt, in thrilling rushes, as long as there was yet another obstacle to conquer. But when she was safe in the bridal suite, all obstacles conquered, the adrenaline evaporated and took with it the sensation of euphoria.

Reality crashed quickly and mercilessly. Here she was, alone in a bridal suite because her husband did not want her, sipping Dom Pérignon, foolishly musing about how she had missed her calling as an actress, a secret agent, a criminal. Your calling, reality reminded her harshly, what you were bred to be from the moment you were born, is the wife of a powerful man like Robert McAllister. *And you have failed.* This desperate plan will not work. Perhaps you planted a seed of doubt in Alexa's mind, but beyond that all you have done is shown that you can make a few simple recordings on a tape recorder—idiot's work—on the vanishingly remote chance that Alexa will call. After performing that ridiculously simple and probably useless task, you bought and used two expensive airline tickets; and then, for your dazzling encore, you flew to Dallas and checked into a bridal suite with a phantom companion.

And here you are! Alone in a luxurious room, surrounded by flowers and champagne and caviar, with the silly tape recording strategically positioned by the phone. And you're even wearing a provocative silk negligee! For whom? For your phantom companion, of course . . .

Because Robert doesn't want you.

Robert only wants Alexa.

Hillary drank the champagne, trying to revive the wonderful feelings that had propelled her on her mission, but the alcohol made her far more sober than drunk, far more depressed than cheerful.

When she awakened the following morning, all the illusions were gone. She was no longer a talented actress. She was, instead, simply an understudy, destined never to get a chance to perform, reading her lines without heart. She ordered breakfast for two, Eggs Benedict and more Dom Pérignon, and as she picked at the elegant food, she glowered at the silk sheeted bed where she and Robert were supposed to be spending a weekend of passion.

Alexa, Alexa, how I hate you!

The telephone rang at four, startling her. The concierge? Calling to see if everything was satisfactory? Or Housekeeping wondering politely, discreetly, if the lovers wouldn't like new silk sheets, more plush towels, fresh terry cloth robes? No, Hillary told her racing heart. No one within the hotel would dare intrude on their privacy. The call had to be from outside the hotel.

And there was only one person it could be.

Her slender, perfectly manicured fingers became clumsy as she fumbled to activate the tape recorder's play button just as she lifted the receiver. She had set the volume soft, as if the phone were intruding on intimacy, and held it a slight distance from the receiver. As she listened to the wonderfully convincing recording of Robert answering the phone, and her own voice whispering seductively for more champagne, and heard nothing but the magnificent sound of silence on the other end, her heart began to race. And then, moments later, her heart became almost airborne, fluttering away, as she heard the even more magnificent sound of the silent caller hanging up, a quiet somber disconnect, long before the tape even ended.

Alexa. Oh, Alexa, did my perfect, desperate crime really work?

The adrenaline was back, celebrating her triumph with her, as she paced back and forth on the deep pile carpet. Hillary tempered her own euphoria, long before the adrelanine vanished, with a stern reminder that there was a scene to be played out that was completely beyond her control—the scene between Robert and Alexa. How she wished she could script that scene!

But she couldn't. She had done all she could do. Now, she just had to hope.

"Hi," Robert said when Alexa answered the phone *finally* at midnight Sunday night. She usually answered on the first ring, and as the phone rang and rang unanswered, fear began to creep into his mind, the heart-stopping fear that an obsessed fan had discovered the remote clifftop cottage where she felt so safe. "Were you asleep?"

"No." She had barely slept Friday night; and last night, after her call to the bridal suite at the Mansion, she had spent the entire night chiding herself, and the tears that would not stop, for her foolishness. Now some new masochistic urge made her ask, "How was your trip?"

"Successful, I think. Darling, I have something wonderful to tell you." Robert paused, expecting her to urge him to come over, even though it was quite late, but she was silent. "Alexa? Shall I come over?"

"No. I have a very early call tomorrow morning. Could you just tell me over the phone?"

"Alexa?"

"Please." Please, let's get this over with quickly! I can't possibly see you. I can't endure a gentle loving good-bye.

"OK. Well, my lovely Alexa, will you marry me?"

Yes, her heart answered instantly, but her fatigued mind intervened warily. "Marry?"

"Yes. Of course," he answered lovingly, surprised at her surprise and worried about whatever else it was—that edge again—that he heard in her voice.

"You're already married, Robert."

"Hillary has agreed to give me a divorce."

"When did she agree to that?"

"Thursday night."

"Did you tell her about me?"

"I told her I was in love with another woman."

"Did you tell her it was me?"

"No."

Lies! her mind screamed.

"And she agreed to a divorce, just like that?"

"No. She asked that she and I stay together until after Memorial Day. She wants time to plan what she's going to do, and there is a celebration for her father in Dallas that weekend. As soon as that's over, she has promised to give me a quiet divorce."

"I see. During which time we don't see each other?"

"She asked that."

So this was how he was going to do it. Did he actually believe her love for him was so fragile that in less than six months she would have found someone new? Or, perhaps, that simply because of this request she would cast him aside in an angry show of pique? Apparently, because this was how he planned to let *her* end their love: and it meant that he didn't know, must never have known, how much she loved him. She would wait six months, six years if need be, but somehow he had determined six months would be enough to drive her away. And what if she said, "Yes, of course I'll wait"? Would he call in May with a request for an extension? Or might there be a final call in which he confessed sadly that Hillary was pregnant— he had slept with her just one time, an idiotic mistake, because he missed *her* so much?

Alexa had believed the pain she had felt all weekend could get no worse, but now it did; because now the loss was far greater than simply the end of their love; now, whatever love there had been was brutally betrayed. It was cruel, so terribly cruel, for him to have asked her to marry him! From her anguish came a remarkable strength, defiant and proud. She would not let Senator Robert McAllister know of her foolishness. She was an actress, after all, and she was an expert at hiding her pain beneath dazzling layers of golden confidence.

"Oh, Robert," she purred softly, the bewitching yet menacing purr of a tigress luring her prey. "I'm so flattered by your offer of marriage."

"*Flattered?*"

"And embarrassed. It was a game, Robert, a game between me and Hillary. She and I have been rivals for a very long time. Didn't she tell you the story before we had dinner last spring? We were in high school together in Dallas, at Ballinger. She made me feel quite unwelcome there, and I retaliated by taking her friends, including her boyfriend, away from her. It may sound like a silly childish game, but I assure you, the emotions behind it weren't silly at all."

"What are you saying, Alexa? That you had an affair with me because of some rivalry with Hillary? That I was a pawn in some petty game?"

"I'm not proud of it, Robert, but I honestly didn't know it would go this far. If I'd had any idea at all that you were thinking about marriage . . ."

How could you *not* have known? he wondered, stunned. Wasn't it so passionately, and so desperately, obvious in every moment we had together that I wanted to spend my life with you? But those precious moments of love had been spent with Alexa, not with the stranger who was speaking to him now in the purring voice he had never heard before.

"Robert, please don't misunderstand," the strange voice continued. "Our affair was not a hardship for me. I enjoyed every minute I was with you. You're a wonderful man, but you're Hillary's kind of man, not mine. Please be assured that I care very much about your political career and would never do anything to harm you."

But you have harmed me very much. I love you, Alexa, oh, *how I love you*, and for you my love was all a game?

"Alexa," he whispered softly, the soft whisper of love that he had whispered to her in bed, a whisper of love to a woman who existed somewhere, didn't she? He needed desperately to reach that lovely, loving woman now. "*Alexa.*"

Oh, Robert, her loving heart answered in silent anguish. How she had loved the man who spoke to her so softly, his desperate need matching her own. How much she would need to believe, for the rest of her life, that that man had existed somewhere deep inside Senator Robert McAllister, a wonderful part of him that *had* loved her as she had loved him. Why couldn't *that* man have said a sad, loving, truthful farewell? She would never have betrayed him. Didn't he know that?

"I'm very sorry, Robert. Good-bye."

"It's over, Cat," Alexa told her little sister when she called the Riverside Drive apartment ten days later.

"Over?"

"Affairs with married men aren't destined to survive. I knew that going into it."

"Are you all right, Alexa?"

"Sure!" she answered brightly, even though with each passing day the bright cheeriness was more difficult to force, dimming despite her immense effort, and draining her energy so that now she actually felt ill. She was worse now than she had been ten days ago. The shock and numbness had faded, leaving her with pure, unrelenting pain. After a moment, she confessed softly, her voice flooded with tears, "No, Cat, I'm not all right. I'm very sad."

"Oh, Alexa. How can I help you?"

"You can simply remind me, whenever I begin to feel even the least bit sorry for myself, that I got precisely what I deserved."

"But I don't believe that!"

"I know," Alexa answered gratefully. From the very beginning of her affair, her little sister, like James, had cared only about her happiness.

"You loved him, Alexa, and love is right, not wrong. And . . . you never deserve to be sad."

"Thank you. It's just all so fresh. I guess what I need now is for a little—a lot of—time to pass." She sighed, and added, "And I need to get out of this town. I am very much looking forward to Christmas in Topeka."

"So am I."

"And then, beginning late next month, after we're done with *Pennsylvania Avenue* for another season, I may do something like wander around the world. I've thought about doing it before, but I've always had projects scheduled during the hiatus. Now I have no projects scheduled, and I even have an extra month off because we're not resuming production again until August. That gives me six months with nothing to do." *Nothing to do except what you've been promising yourself for years you were going to do: spend time getting to know Alexa.* She clamped down on a flicker of panic, the lazy yawn of a slumbering monster, and continued, "So, in six weeks I'll suddenly have plenty of time and space, both of which I need. But, right now, what I need most is James."

"James?" Catherine echoed softly. *But,* her heart began to protest until her brain intervened, *But what? But James is yours? Hardly! He has never even kissed you, remember? He has just made you feel wonderful and special and so very happy. But that's because he is so wonderful and special—a wonderful, special man who has been looking out for the naive little sister of the beautiful sophisticated woman he has always loved. And now Alexa is free, and she wants him again, and when confident dazzling Alexa beckons . . .* "You need James?"

"Yes. I need him to escort me to the 'When You Wish Upon a Star' gala," Alexa answered casually, even though her need was not casual at all. Senator and Mrs. Robert McAllister would be at the gala this year, she was sure of it. Hillary would *want* to be there this year, to gloat and parade her triumph, and Robert really could not afford to miss the important event for the fourth year in a row. "It's this Saturday evening. I can't remember when James is planning to fly to Paris."

Catherine knew James's plans. She knew that beginning later tonight, he would be in New Orleans for four days; and that he was returning on Saturday, in time for dinner with her; and that on Sunday he was flying to Paris to spend the holidays with Arthur and Marion on L'île; and that, after Saturday night, she would probably never see him again—because following Christmas with her family in Topeka, she would travel to San Francisco, where, on New Year's Eve at the Opera House, she would make her professional debut.

James had asked her, more than once, if she was going to give him a copy of the itinerary for her eleven month booked-solid concert tour of North America and Europe. And he had talked to her, more than once, *so often*, about meeting her for dinner wherever she was. But Catherine hadn't dared believe that that would ever happen. She had only bravely prepared her heart to say good-bye to him at dinner this Saturday. And now even the farewell dinner would never happen, because Saturday night was when Alexa needed him.

"You haven't spoken to him?"

"Not yet. We played telephone tag this morning, and I've been on location all afternoon. I assume he'll call me tonight."

"Yes, I'm sure he will."

* * *

She just wanted to say good-bye to him. Good-bye, and thank you. She realized, as she wove hurriedly through the rush hour crowd, that she had forgotten the scarf she had knitted for him, and forgotten, too, the copy of the itinerary she had made for him, finally, just today. But if she was to catch him before he left for the airport, and perhaps she was already too late, she couldn't take the time to go back for either. No matter! He wouldn't need the itinerary now, and the scarf was unimportant, too, a sentimental memory of their midnight sail last summer. Maybe, some faraway day, she would send the scarf to him accompanied by a letter that would thank him more eloquently than she would ever be able to do in person.

"I'm Catherine Taylor," she told the receptionist who was obviously just preparing to leave for the day. "I wondered if I could see Mr. Sterling, if he's still here?"

"One moment, please." The receptionist pressed the single button that connected her phone to the one in his private office. "Ms. Taylor is here. Oh. OK. I'll send her right back."

James assumed his visitor would be Alexa. Perhaps her attempts to reach him this morning had been to announce that she had a free evening and was flying to New York to toast the festive season with him as they drank hot buttered rum and watched the iceskaters glide to the sound of Christmas carols in Rockefeller Center. As he waited for her, he prepared himself for her exasperation when she learned that he was just about to leave for LaGuardia. But the beautiful woman who appeared in his doorway wasn't the one who had greeted him last spring with the confident, provocative proposal for a swift and satisfying merger.

It was her little sister, not so confident, but in that lovely uncertainty oh-so-provocative.

"Catherine," he said with soft surprise. Smiling welcomingly at the uncertain sapphire, he walked over to her, and as he helped her remove her coat, he gently added, "Hi."

"Hi. Thank you." She felt a wonderful rush of warmth at his smile, and at the surprised dark blue eyes that seemed so happy to see her. It wasn't until he left her to hang her coat that she brought herself to quietly ask, "Have you spoken to Alexa?"

"No. She called earlier, but we missed each other." James finished hanging the coat and returned to her. "Why?"

"Her relationship is over."

"Oh," he said with quiet sympathy. He knew how devastating this would be for Alexa. He saw a reflection of that immense loss in her little sister's lovely worried eyes. "How is she?"

"Very sad. James, she needs you."

"I think she probably needs both of us."

"She needs you to escort her to a gala in Washington this Saturday night."

James knew that Catherine had never told her older sister about any of their dates. Alexa would have mentioned it to him if she had. That was fine with him, more than fine, wonderful. He loved the privacy of their relationship and was very happy to share it with no one but Catherine. But now . . .

"Did you tell Alexa that I already have plans for Saturday?"

"No. I thought, James, if you want to cancel our dinner, it's fine. I understand."

"What do you understand, Catherine?"

"I understand about you and Alexa. Now that she's free again . . ."

"You think that Alexa and I will pick up where we left off, as if nothing has changed?" he asked softly, his heart racing as he saw the lovely hope in her beautiful eyes at his question. I think there are some truths that need time before they can be told, she had said on a stormy afternoon, and he had agreed. But now, lovely Catherine, it is time, isn't it? "Is that what you want?"

"No," she whispered the brave and confident truth to the man who had been so careful not to rush her, so careful to allow all the choices of the heart to be hers. But the dark blue eyes weren't careful now. They told her, quite eloquently, and quite urgently, of his desire and his love. "No, James, that's not what I want."

"That's not what I want either, Catherine," he said very quietly. "You see, I am completely enchanted by Alexa's little sister."

"You are?"

"You know I am."

Her full, soft lips had never kissed before, but they knew by a deep, wonderful instinct how to greet the lips of the man she loved. The greeting was soft at first, the most tender of hellos, and then, soft still, and tender, and so welcoming, the kiss became warmer and deeper. Her delicate snow white fingers caressed their own wondrous hello, greeting his face and weaving gently into his coal black hair, and, in touching James, her talented fingers discovered a joy, a gift, that was far more magnificent than her magnificent music.

Their lips kissed hello, and then their bodies did, in a kiss that began gently, too, but became closer and closer, until her heart pounded against his chest, triggering the terrifying memory of the only other time he had held her. On that August night, her fluttering heart had sent a frantic message of starvation, and even though what he felt now were surely just the strong, confident heartbeats of joy and desire, James pulled away, just a little, to look at her. And what he saw was glistening sapphire desire, and then a brief flicker of surprise and disappointment that he had stopped the kiss, and then pure desire and happiness again. Catherine was healthy and fit, as was he.

Although we are both starving, he thought, a most wonderful hunger—for each other.

"I have wanted to kiss you for a very long time, Catherine."

"I've wanted you to."

"Have you?"

"Yes. For a very long time." She looked up at him and smiled. Her smile was lovely, innocent, and yet so seductive in its unashamed messages of desire. She whispered softly, "I need to be kissed again, James. It's already been too long between kisses."

"Far too long," he agreed with a soft laugh as his lips touched hers.

Then he was lost again in her lovely eager warmth, and he had no wish ever to be found, but . . .

"Oh, darling," he sighed softly, holding her close, his lips kissing her silky black hair as he spoke. "I have a plane to catch. I can't even take a later flight because we're having a strategy meeting the moment I arrive. I'll call you from New Orleans, a thousand times, and I will see you Saturday night." He found her eyes then and asked, "OK?"

"OK to you leaving me now for New Orleans, and to calling me a thousand times," she answered with soft joy. Her lovely blue eyes became thoughtful as she added quietly, "But Alexa needs you Saturday night. Could you come for brunch at the apartment on Sunday before your flight to Paris?"

"Of course I can," he replied gently, not questioning her decision about Saturday night, seeing from her beautiful eyes that it was a generous decision of love—for the sister whose life was not so happy now. He had to leave for the airport, soon,

but he had to kiss her again, and he did, a good-bye kiss, reluctant and lingering, but a kiss that held the tender promise that soon, very soon, they would be kissing hello again. And then he really had to leave, but there was one last thing.
"Catherine?"
"Yes?"
"I love you."
"Oh, James, I love you, too."

CHAPTER EIGHTEEN

$\mathcal{A}$lexa had mentally rehearsed an angry tirade to deliver to James about the man for whom he had such great respect. But when he arrived at RoseCliff, and she saw his gentle concern, she just fell gratefully into his willingly offered arms. Because, more than anything, she needed to be held by someone who loved her.

"I'm so sorry, Alexa," he whispered as she curled against him.

"Me, too." She looked up at him, smiled a wobbly smile, and offered softly, "I won't say you didn't warn me."

"You know I hoped it would work out for you."

"I know." She lingered a moment longer in the luxurious shelter of his arms, and then with a sigh, dreading the evening that lay ahead, but knowing it was almost time to go, she pulled away. "Thank you for doing this tonight, James. I just don't have the energy to go by myself."

It was a quiet confession, but an enormous one, a symbol of how truly fragile she was. James knew she would dazzle at the gala, but now she was confessing to him what an effort it would be. Just to dazzle from a distance would require all of her precarious energy. She would have none left over to ward off all the men who would want to flirt with her. And men would want her tonight, perhaps more than ever, because on this night whose theme was "When You Wish Upon a Star," in her gown of soft emerald silk with her flowing golden hair, she was a romantic vision of dreams come true.

"I'll stick very close, Alexa."

"I was thinking . . ."

"Yes?"

"If you could hold my hand and not let go?"

"I can do that." James sealed the promise with a smile. Then, he asked gently, "Would you like to tell me about the bastard?"

"No. Thank you."

James kept his word. He held Alexa's hand and didn't let go. She drew strength from the strong hand that held hers as they wandered through the glittering sea of the famous and powerful, and she drew even more strength as they danced, their bodies moving together gracefully with chaste but intimate familiarity.

I can do this, Alexa thought. I can make it through tonight even if Robert is here. I'm sure of it.

"James? Alexa?"

The sound of Hillary's voice, and then the sight of Robert and Hillary slow dancing just a few feet away, instantly shattered her foolish confidence. But still, *somehow*, with her hand in James's, Alexa crossed the dance floor to greet Senator and Mrs. McAllister. And somehow, miraculously, when she spoke her voice sounded cheerful and gay.

"How lovely to see you, Hillary." She smiled pleasantly at Hillary and then, holding the smile, she turned to Robert. "Hello, Senator."

"Hello, Alexa," he replied quietly, even though his heart screamed with pain. There were no protective scars yet on the wound created by Alexa, and Robert wondered if there ever would be. After a moment, he shifted his gaze from the woman he loved to his friend. "Hello, James."

"Hello, Robert. Hillary."

"You finally made it to the gala," Alexa observed lightly. Then, like a gracious hostess, because after all this was *Pennsylvania Avenue's* charity ball, she added, "I'm so glad."

"So are we," Hillary answered with matching graciousness. "And it's so nice to see you, James. Are you still planning to join Marion and Arthur on L'île for the holidays?"

"That's the plan. I fly to Paris tomorrow and on Tuesday we'll set sail from Nice."

"Wonderful," Hillary murmured, although what was wonderful, she thought, was the way James held Alexa's hand, and the way they had been slow dancing together. The stunning couple had drawn stares, all admiring—except for Robert's, which had been a gaze of pure pain. After a moment, casually hiding her private hope of revealing even more evidence of Alexa's faithlessness, she asked, "Will you be going to L'île, too, Alexa?"

"No. I only have five days off. I'm going to spend Christmas in Topeka with my family."

"How nice. Well, James, please give Marion and Arthur our love. And," she added softly, "please remember to tell Princess Natalie how delighted I am with my romantic Castille wedding ring."

Hillary believed she had won. She believed it before the gala, and as she and Robert drove back to Arlington afterward, she believed it even more. His foolish affair with Alexa was over. Her plan had worked perfectly. She had won . . . and Robert looked as if he had lost everything. That would change, she assured herself. In time, this unfortunate episode in their marriage would be long forgotten, *assuming* that the pain in his dark eyes wasn't simply anguish that he and Alexa would be separated for five months.

"Robert?"

"Hmmmm?" he answered distractedly, even though he was a little relieved to be pulled away from the tormenting images of James and Alexa that had been blazing in his mind. Some of the images were simply scenes he had witnessed—Alexa teasing James, flirting with James, dancing with James. But there were other images, far worse—Alexa making love with James, last night, tonight, all the nights he hadn't been with her this fall. He had seen tonight, in his friend's steady untroubled gaze, that James had not known about their affair. Did that mean that, all this time, Alexa been playing with them both? "Did you say something, Hillary?"

"You're obviously suffering, Robert, and I can't stand watching it. If it's going to be this painful for you to be apart from whoever she is for the next five months, well . . . my father and I *will* survive."

"It's not a problem."

"No?"

"No. The affair is over."

"The married man was Robert?" James demanded angrily as he drove her back to RoseCliff shortly before midnight.

"What makes you say that?"

"Don't play with me, Alexa."

"Was it so terribly obvious?"

"No," he admitted, his tone softening as he heard the hopelessness in her question, as if now she had lost her ability as an actress in addition to losing everything else. "I don't think it would have been obvious to anyone who wasn't holding a hand that suddenly became ice. And then," he teased gently, "there was the small matter of fingernails that were digging for some mysterious treasure buried very deep in my palm."

"I'm sorry."

"I wish you'd told me."

"I was afraid you wouldn't approve."

"I might have questioned your motives, given your feelings about Hillary."

"I didn't have any motives," she said quietly. "I just loved him, that's all."

"And you still do."

"Yes, James, and I still do."

James warmed milk for her while she showered and changed into a new nightgown, fluffy, modest, never worn for a lover. He watched her drink the milk and then tucked her into her bed, gently refusing her half-hearted plea, a cry of loneliness far more than passion, that he join her.

After she fell asleep, he drove to Inverness.

I was afraid you wouldn't approve, Alexa had said in defense of not telling him about her affair with Robert. Would she approve of his love for her little sister? he wondered. Probably not, at least not right away. Alexa would worry about his restlessness, his need for challenges and privacy, his own admission that he doubted he could ever fall in love. In short, she would worry about Catherine's happiness.

You don't need to worry, he would assure her when the time came. No one cares more about Catherine's happiness than I. James wondered when he would speak those words to Alexa. It didn't matter. For now, for as long as Catherine wanted it to be that way, their love was secret, a private treasure to be shared with no one but each other.

"Did I awaken you, darling?" he asked softly, when he called her from Inverness, as he had told her he would, and as she had wanted him to, no matter how late.

"No. I was practicing. How was the evening?"

"It was OK. I'm glad you'll be together at Christmas. Right now, Alexa very much needs to be with people who love her. Especially her little sister." James expected a soft reply, but he only heard surprising silence, and finally asked gently, "Catherine?"

"Yes?"

"Do you know what I need?"

"No, what?"

"What I need, my love, is to see you as much as possible between our brunch tomorrow morning and the time I put you on your flight to Topeka Tuesday afternoon."

"James," she whispered with quiet disbelief and joy. "But . . ."

"It's just about breakfast time in Paris. I think I'll call my parents right now and arrange to meet them Wednesday on L'île instead of sailing with them from Nice."

"Do you think they'll mind?"

"Not at all." If they knew the reason, he thought lovingly, they would be overjoyed.

James and Catherine had presents for each other, gifts of love that had been in the making long before they had spoken their love aloud, because they had both known about their love for a very long time.

"Merry Christmas, darling," he said as he handed her a small gift-wrapped box. The beautiful wrapping, gold foil adorned with delicate satin ribbons in all the colors of a rainbow, signified a gift of jewels from Castille.

"Oh," she whispered when she saw the earrings, two perfectly matched sapphires the rare and precious color of her eyes. "James, they're beautiful."

James looked from the brilliant sapphires to the brilliant sapphire eyes and saw that the search he had commissioned Castille's Fifth Avenue jeweller to undertake had been worth it: the flawless gems perfectly matched her flawless eyes. As he smiled at her beautiful eyes, he saw a small but unmistakable ripple of uncertainty in the shimmering blue.

"Catherine?"

"They're magnificent. Thank you." Her eyes left his and fell for a thoughtful moment on the stunning earrings. She touched the precious stones with her delicate fingers; but instead of putting them on, she placed the small velvet box on the table and reached for the gift-wrapped package for him. Meeting his eyes again, and smiling softly, she said, "This is for you. It's not so magnificent . . ."

But the scarf Catherine had made was far more magnificent, James thought, and far more valuable than the sapphires. She had sketched the scene herself—*Night Wind* gliding across the sea on a shimmering moonbeam of gold; and then, the needles dancing in her delicate virtuoso fingers, she had knitted it.

"Catherine . . ." he faltered, truly at a loss for words.

"Do you like it?"

"I love it, darling. I love it."

"I'm so glad."

"But you, my love, are uncertain about the earrings," he said gently. "They are very returnable, Catherine. I'll take them back tomorrow."

"Oh, no, James. I'm not uncertain about the earrings at all. It's just . . ." She frowned, sighed softly, and admitted quietly, "It's just that there's something I need to tell you about me . . . and Alexa."

Good, James thought. At last, my lovely Catherine, you are going to trust me with the troubling secrets of your heart. "Tell me, darling."

"I will. In a moment. I have to get something from my bedroom first."

As he waited, James thought about what he would hear: Catherine's version of the history of the Taylor sisters. He didn't expect to be terribly surprised, he knew Alexa's version after all, but when Catherine returned from her bedroom, James was truly stunned. He watched in silent amazement as her trembling fingers positioned a dazzling sapphire necklace around the velvet box that still held the earrings he had given her. The necklace and earrings looked like a set, perfectly matched, made for each other, *made for Catherine*.

"This necklace belonged to my mother," she began, speaking first to the necklace she wished she had never seen. Then she looked bravely at him and said softly, "I never knew my mother, James. She gave me away when I was a week old. Alexa isn't really my sister."

Catherine told him the simple truths very quickly. And then, for the next hours, she told him about her complicated and confusing emotions: her bewildering pain, her frantic desperation as she felt herself being torn away from Jane and Alexander, her love for Alexa and her great fear of telling her the truth, and her deep bitterness toward the mother who had abandoned her.

"Oh, Catherine, I'm so sorry that this has caused you such sadness."

"I'm better now, James, much better. I felt so lost at first, and so alone and afraid. Do you remember when we were sailing that night and you told me I should call my parents to tell them I missed them?"

"I remember that you had been thinking about calling them anyway."

"Yes, well, but it helped me to hear that you thought they would want to know."

"And they did."

"Yes. I guess. I never actually told them I missed them, but I'm sure they know. We've talked quite a few times since then, and each time I feel closer. I haven't seen them since May."

"But you will in two days. And?"

"And I'm a little afraid." She paused, and then smiled a lovely smile of hope. "But mostly, I'm very excited."

"They love you," James said softly, confidently. "And so does Alexa."

"Oh, I hope so. But, James, it's still too soon for me to tell her the truth. I want to tell her, someday, but I need to wait until it feels more safe."

James nodded in silent agreement that she wait, but his concern was for Alexa, not Catherine. Alexa's love for Catherine wouldn't change, he knew, but Alexa was so very fragile now. She had just lost Robert, and even though the truth about Catherine shouldn't feel like a loss, he knew that right now to Alexa it would.

"I'm so glad you felt it was safe to tell me."

"Even though you thought you knew who I was and now . . . ?"

"I know who you are, Catherine. I have always known. You're the woman I love with all my heart."

"Oh, James . . ."

His lips found hers, as they had many times already on this snowy afternoon, but now the kiss was different, more tender, more passionate, and more deep . . . a kiss without secrets or shadows . . . a kiss of boundless forever love.

"Tomorrow, darling, I'll return the earrings," he whispered, finally pulling away from the kiss because suddenly kissing Catherine had become too much, *and not enough*.

"Oh, no, James."

She reached then for the velvet box and removed the magnificent earrings. They were designed for pierced ears, as hers were, but because of their great value, the tiny solid gold backings screwed, not slid, onto the posts.

"There," she said when her delicate fingers had finished fastening the brilliant gems. "I know I won't ever wear the necklace, James, but I'll wear my earrings always."

"They aren't actually for every day, do you think?" he teased gently.

"No," she admitted. "I guess not."

"I thought you could wear them for concerts."

"Yes. For concerts . . . and for kissing . . . and for making love," she said softly. "Make love to me, James."

"Oh, Catherine, there's no hurry. We've just discovered kissing. I think I could kiss you forever."

"Forever? Just kissing?"

"No," James confessed softly. "But . . ."

"We have these two precious, private days, James, and we love each other. Why wouldn't we spend this time sharing everything we can share, all our love, all our joy?"

"Why wouldn't we," he echoed gently as he smiled at her beautiful innocent eyes. So innocent . . .

"I've been on the pill for over two months," Catherine said, interpreting, incorrectly, the sudden worry on his handsome face.

"I wasn't thinking about that. It's just that I don't want to hurt you, not for an instant, and . . ."

"How could our loving possibly hurt me?"

It was all new for Catherine, and for James making love with the woman he loved was all new, too. They discovered each other with wondrous joy, treasuring each discovery, marveling at their desire and their love. Catherine trembled at the patient and gentle exploration of his loving hands and tender lips; and she gave everything to him, every gift she had to give, hiding no secrets of her lush and lovely snow white body, unashamed of her passion for him.

When it was time for both of them, when they needed to share all that could be shared, a loving frown of worry touched his handsome face. She greeted his frown with a soft smile, and then she greeted him, arching to him, welcoming him with confident joy.

"I love you, Catherine," he whispered. *Oh, I don't want to hurt you.*

"I love you, James." *How could our loving possibly hurt me?*

It didn't hurt. There wasn't pain, just a surprising tearing heat that was quickly, so quickly, forgotten, because then they were one, as close as they could be, and that was the greatest wonder of all.

For a timeless moment, neither moved, nor spoke, nor even breathed. They simply gazed at each other with silent, reverent wonder as their loving eyes eloquently acknowledged their joy.

They moved again finally, because they had to, urged on by their magnificent crescendoing desires . . . and they spoke, the most tender whispers of love . . . and they breathed, too . . . but soon, and over and over, James and Catherine were breathless again.

* * *

During those two days and nights of exquisite intimacy and passion, they loved, and made love, and made wonderful plans for their love. They poured over Catherine's intinerary, city by fabulous city, and city by city, they planned where they would dine, and the sights they would see, and the walks they would take. It seemed to Catherine that he planned to be with her in every city, every week, and when she mentioned that to him, a loving tease filled with hope, he promised that he would arrange his work so that he could be with her as often as possible.

"Maybe I should stop working altogether," he suggested softly, "and simply become a Catherine Taylor 'groupie.' "

"That would be wonderful."

"Yes, but as a 'groupie' I would expect to hear your performances. And," he added quietly, "the one time I heard you play, I thought my presence distracted you."

"Oh, yes, it did."

"Would it now?"

"I don't know. Shall we see?"

She played Mozart's "Sonata in C Major," one of the pieces she would perform on New Year's Eve in San Francisco. As he listened, James began to appreciate the true measure of her extraordinary gift. It is a gift, he realized, a gift that she so generously shares with her audience, graciously inviting whoever is listening to journey with her on her magnificent emotional voyage. He was traveling with her now, as first they paid a soft, delicate visit to hope, and then, in a cascading journey that felt like a waterfall, they spilled down to sadness, and then they flew, dancing, leaping, soaring to joy, and . . .

And suddenly the stunning journey stopped.

"Oh, Catherine," James whispered sadly, "it does distract you to have me listen."

"I think it's something I can conquer in a concert hall filled with hundreds of patrons. But today, James," she said softly, "if I'm over here playing, and you're over there listening, then I'm not where I should be."

"Then come to me, my love."

As Catherine left the piano to be in his loving arms, she realized the truly immense significance of what she had done. Today she was choosing James over her music. And she knew, without a doubt, without a fear, that given the choice between her music and James, she would choose James . . . always.

"I'm going out to get us some croissants," he announced at nine-thirty on Tuesday morning. He added lovingly, "I admit it's a fairly transparent excuse to get to wear my scarf."

"I see," Catherine laughed softly as she kissed him good-bye.

She wondered, as she closed the apartment door behind him, if the real reason he was leaving her, if only for fifteen minutes, was to begin to prepare them both for the almost two-week separation that would start at four this afternoon. They had already promised each other, over and over, that they would never spend another Christmas apart; but neither had suggested altering plans for this Christmas. This was a special and important Christmas for both of them—a private time alone with the parents they loved.

When the phone rang five minutes after James left, Catherine was certain it would be him, calling on the pretext of asking if she wanted cream cheese or raspberry croissants, but really calling to tell her something she felt too—that it had only been five minutes and already he missed her desperately.

"Hello?" she answered with a soft loving laugh.

"Is this Catherine Taylor?"

"Yes."

"Catherine, this is Elliot Archer. We met last summer at Inverness."

"Yes, of course. Hello, Elliot."

"I'm afraid I have some very bad news. About two hours ago, there was an explosion on the boat that the Sterlings were sailing from Nice to L'île."

"Oh, no."

"The explosion was probably caused by a leak in the gas line to the stove." Elliot paused briefly to fight the sudden rush of emotion that swept through him. "It would have been impossible for anyone to survive the blast. Robert McAllister suggested that we call you before notifying Alexa, in case you'd like to be with her when she is told about James."

"About James?"

"Arthur and Marion have been found. The divers are still searching for James, but as I said, it would have been impossible for anyone to survive the blast."

"James wasn't on the sailboat, Elliot."

"Robert saw him in Washington Saturday night and James told him then that he was leaving the next day for Paris."

"Yes, but he didn't leave then after all. He's still in New York. He was going to fly to Nice this afternoon."

"Are you sure?"

"Yes."

"Thank God." After a moment, Elliot continued quietly, "Well. I'd better let him know."

"I'll tell him, Elliot. I'll tell him and have him call you."

"Oh. All right, Catherine. I'll be in my office. He knows the number."

After the conversation ended, Elliot realized it had happened once again. Once again, Catherine Taylor had triggered his long-ago memories of Isabelle Castille. In August, the memories had been triggered by the astonishing physical resemblance, but now it was Catherine's great inner beauty that reminded him of Isabelle. It had been Princess Isabelle, after all, who had flown to London to tell him of Geneviève's death. She hadn't needed to, of course, but she had, because she knew how devastating the news would be for him, and she had wanted to help him with his grief, if she possibly could.

And now Elliot heard in Catherine's soft voice the same gentle wish, a wish to help James, if she could.

"Oh, James."

"What's the matter, darling?"

"It's your parents. Oh, James, there was an explosion on the sailboat."

"Catherine?"

"They were killed," she said very softly, very gently. She saw his shock, and even though he didn't ask the questions, she knew he needed to hear more words, as she had needed to, more proof. She explained quietly, "Elliot says it was probably the gas stove. He called here, thinking you were with them, wanting me to fly to Washington to be there when Alexa was told. Oh, my love, I'm so sorry."

Catherine's lovely eyes glistened with tears, and as the numbing waves of shock began to ebb, James felt moist heat in his own eyes. Tears were so unfamiliar to him that he couldn't remember how long it had been since he had felt them; and so unfamiliar, too, that his first impulse was to hide them.

Hide his tears from the woman he loved?

No, he thought as the tears spilled freely. I do not need to hide my tears from Catherine.

"Mother was probably making her famous hot chocolate," he said quietly an hour later.

Catherine answered as she had answered all his words and tears—with love. She had held him, and she had tenderly kissed his tear-dampened cheeks, and now she smiled softly, as he did, as they remembered lovely Marion.

It was another hour before James called Elliot. Both men focused on details, not emotion; a brief review of the facts that Elliot knew, and a brief discussion, too, of the plans for the memorial service that would be held two days before Christmas. The arrangements for the service, and for the reception to follow, were already being made by the ever-efficient Office of Protocol.

"I'll fly to Washington sometime after four this afternoon, Elliot. I'll call you when I arrive."

"After four?" Catherine asked as soon as he replaced the receiver.

"After I put you on the flight to Topeka."

"I'm going with you to Washington."

"No."

"Yes!"

"No. Catherine, listen to me. You need to be with your parents." His words were stopped by a rush of emotion. How he wished he had told his own parents his reason for not sailing with them to L'île! If he had told them, then perhaps, as his mother had been making the hot chocolate, they might have been joyfully speculating about their black-haired, blue-eyed grandchildren laughing and frolicking at Inverness. James had planned to tell Marion and Arthur about his love for Catherine when he saw them. But now it was too late, and his voice was hoarse with impassioned emotion as he continued, "Darling, being with your parents is more important now than ever, don't you think?"

"I will be with them, James, in a few days. Maybe we both will be," she added softly. "But right now I need to be with you."

"You are with me, Catherine. You are always with me. All I need is to be able to talk to you, darling, and I will call you every night. That's all I need, or want." James smiled at her worried sapphire eyes. "Besides, even though I need no more than to be able to talk to you, Elliot will be there, and Robert and Brynne."

"And Alexa."

"She needs to be in Topeka, too."

"She will be, but not until the twenty-fourth."

Three hours after James kissed her good-bye, Catherine saw the beloved parents she hadn't seen since May. She had such vivid memories of them, a lifetime of seeing their loving faces. But now, even from a distance, they looked different, less vivid than she had remembered, and a little faded and worn.

Was it that they were older? Had the past seven months aged them so? she wondered sadly. No, she realized as she drew closer. The difference she saw wasn't age at all. It was the expression of uncertainty in their gentle eyes.

Uncertainty? About her? About her love?

Catherine rushed to Jane and Alexander then, and as she did she soared over the deep abyss that had separated her from her parents for so long. By the time she reached them, she was far far beyond the treacherous abyss, and she whispered over and over as she hugged them, "Oh, Mom, oh Daddy, I love you both so very much."

CHAPTER NINETEEN

The memorial service and reception were over, and only those closest to James remained at Inverness. They—Alexa and Elliot, and Robert and Hillary, and Brynne and Stephen—sat in the elegant great room with him; and on this sad day, all petty wars and all bitter betrayals were put aside, and all eyes filled only with honest emotional messages of grief for the loss of Marion and Arthur.

"There's something you all need to know," Elliot said.

"What is it?" James asked tiredly. He was exhausted. He had uttered a thousand gracious thank-yous to those who had come to offer their condolences, and all he wanted now was to call Catherine. He had missed her terribly in the past few days, but he had not for one moment wished that she had been in Washington during this time of such sadness.

"The explosion on the sailboat wasn't caused by a leak in the gas line, James. It was caused by a bomb."

For a stunned moment, no one spoke, but the thoughts that suddenly swirled in their minds were remarkably the same. Marion and Arthur's death hadn't been simply an accident, an inexplicable tragedy caused by some unknown and whimsical fate.

Someone had known that Marion and Arthur would die.

Someone had wanted it.

Someone had caused it.

"A bomb?" Brynne echoed finally.

"How long have you known, Elliot?" Robert asked.

"A few hours. We're going to have to let the press know tomorrow, so I wanted you all to know tonight."

"Has anyone claimed responsibility?"

"No. Not yet."

"What *do* you know, Elliot?"

"Very little, James."

"Because the trail is cold now."

"No. The explosion was investigated as possible sabotage from the very beginning. The best agents in Europe have been working on it. So far, we have nothing. The sailboat had been moored in one of the busiest marinas on the Côte d'Azur, lots of traffic, lots of tourists, many people with potential access."

The room fell silent again, and again the thoughts of the assembled group were remarkably the same, drifting to the summer evening only four months before when Marion had raved about L'île. How eagerly she had anticipated her return visit to the romantic island of rainbows, and how her dark blue eyes had sparkled as she had wished aloud that some day, despite the busy schedules of their successful lives, they could all find time to meet for a holiday on L'île.

But now Marion's wish would never come true.

Because someone had decided it was time for Marion Sterling to die.

"I think you all should go now," James said quietly. In the silence, he had stood up and walked to the windows, and now his quiet words were spoken to the dark gray winter sky. After a moment, he added, "It's getting dark and the wind seems very strong. There may be a storm on the way."

"Maybe we should all stay here tonight, James," Brynne offered.

"No. Thank you," he whispered tightly. "No."

James's need for privacy was so obvious that eventually they all complied. Alexa was the last to leave, kissing him softly on the cheek before she returned to RoseCliff to finish packing for her early morning flight to Topeka.

The winds were too strong and too dangerous, and the vast blackness of the winter night was broken only by a thin sliver of moon, but still he sailed. And as he guided *Night Wind* through the treacherous darkness, he struggled, too, with the dark and treacherous emotions that swirled within him. The emotions were new and very powerful. Without even a whisper of mercy, they violently trampled all the gentler emotions of his heart, crushing them, proclaiming them gone forever—they had to be!—because everything had changed.

James wore the beautiful scarf Catherine had made for him, and as *Night Wind* raced across the inky sea, he reached to touch the soft wool, as if reaching to touch her, needing her soft warmth. But he couldn't feel the softness or the warmth. His fingers were numb, chilled to ghostly whiteness by the icy wind, the delicate nerve-endings unable to feel anything but frigid pain.

His most gentle emotions were crushed by powerful new ones . . . and warmth and softness seemed far beyond his reach . . . and a deep ominous voice shouted above the howling winter wind that his greatest loss was yet to come.

"I know about the bomb, James," Catherine said gently when he called, finally, five hours after she had learned the devastating news from Alexa. She had tried during those five hours to reach him, but there had been no answer at Inverness. "Were you sailing?"

"Yes."

"James?" she asked softly, urging him to talk to her as he had every other night, sharing his emotions, his sadness, his loss.

"I won't be able to be in San Francisco for your debut after all, Catherine."

"It's too soon to know that for sure, isn't it?" she asked quietly, fighting ominous ripples of panic as she felt him pulling away from her. She fought the ripples, and very bravely she began to fight *for him*. She continued softly, "In the meantime, I'm coming to Washington. My visit with my parents has been wonderful but—"

"No," he interjected harshly. Then, hearing his own harshness, he added gently, "No, darling. Elliot and I will be going to France."

He was going, that was decided, although he knew he needed Elliot's help if his trip was going to have any value.

"Oh! When?"

"Hopefully tomorrow."

"Oh." He was already so very far away. She reached for him with a whisper of love, "James . . ."

"Oh, Catherine," he answered softly. "I need to go to France. I'm not sure when I'll be back, but my love, no matter what, I will call you in your suite at the Fairmont after your dazzling debut. At midnight on New Year's Eve, OK?"

"OK. James?"

"Yes?"

"Somehow, this will be all right, won't it?"

James heard the uncertainty in her voice, and he knew that what she was really asking was if *they* would be all right, if their gentle love would survive the ravages of his rage.

He knew his lovely Catherine was asking for a promise.

And James didn't make promises he couldn't keep.

"I'll call you, darling, on New Year's Eve."

"I'm going to France with you," James said as he entered Elliot's office, unannounced, at eight the following morning.

"I'm not going to France, James."

"*What?*"

"I told you last night. The best agents in Europe are investigating."

"You're an expert—*the* expert—on terrorism."

"And I promise you that once we have any data, even the slightest clue, I will become intimately involved. But there's nothing yet. You know—at least you *should* know because I loved your parents very much—that if my participation in the field would help I would have been on a plane long ago."

"Yes, I do know that, Elliot," James replied quietly. "So, all we can do is wait?"

"Wait for what, James?" Elliot knew the answer to his question. He knew the wishes that swirled in James's heart; and he knew, too, that James might not speak them. So he spoke them for him. "Wait until the terrorists are found and then murder them in cold blood?"

"Right now that sounds very good," James admitted quietly, deeply troubled by his own bloodthirstiness and very relieved that Elliot seemed to understand.

"Right now it sounds very good to me, too. But I know about the intoxication of revenge. You become convinced somehow that there will be pleasure in it. And, perhaps even worse, you begin to believe that everything will be better after. But nothing is better, and that makes the emptiness even greater." Elliot sighed softly. "Revenge changes nothing, James. Your loss is still the same, still as great, still as irrevocable. Revenge doesn't help the pain, and it can cause great harm by tainting the memory of those you loved with hatred and rage."

As James listened to Elliot's quiet and impassioned words, he realized how little he really knew him. James had always known *how* Elliot had chosen to spend his life—never marrying, in constant danger, risking life and defying death with casual calm—but now, for the first time, he realized there must have been an intensely personal and emotional reason *why* he had made such a choice.

"Elliot?"

"I know whereof I speak, James." Elliot quietly acknowledged the existence of a reason, but the finality of his tone closed the subject.

"I have to do something, Elliot. I have to be involved."

"I don't need more agents, and even if I did I sure as hell wouldn't let you anywhere near this investigation." Elliot held up his hand, stopping James's protest. "I'm not going to license you to kill, James, but I—this country—could use your help."

"My help?"

"Your knowledge of international law coupled with your skill and finesse in negotiating would make your services very valuable to the State Department."

"Was there something specific you had in mind?"

"If it were entirely up to me, I'd send you to Central America with the team that's going back down in the middle of January. The cease-fire dialogue has reached an impasse—again—and I think we need a new face at the negotiating table. However, there are any number of equally critical cease-fire and treaty negotiations, not to mention the hostage situation, on-going throughout the world, and it might be decided that you'd be of greater value elsewhere."

"You seem quite confident that this is something I could do."

"I am *absolutely* confident that it is. Except for the modestness of the surroundings, and the relatively small amount you would be paid as a government consultant, I don't think you'd notice a great difference between this and the work you've always done. The principles that govern negotiations between nations, James, are virtually identical to those governing negotiations among billion-dollar corporations."

"Money, territory, and power?"

"Yes. Money, territory, and power. We use those three as currency—we have to—but in so doing we hope to secure far more elusive and far more valuable treasures."

"Like peace and freedom," James offered quietly.

"Like peace and freedom," Elliot echoed with matching quiet.

The idea of working as a negotiator for the government appealed to James very much. If there was really something that he could do that might curb terrorism and insure a world in which loving couples could always sail in complete safety to paradise islands, he would gladly do it. And there was something else, far less valiant, that appealed, too. He and Elliot would be working together, and Elliot would keep him informed about the investigation into his parents' murder, and someday he would look into the evil eyes of whoever had willed their death, and if this bloodthirstiness still churned within him . . .

"I'm very interested, Elliot."

"Good. This really hadn't occurred to you before, had it?"

"No. Why?"

"I had always assumed that your work, especially since it so frequently has involved international conglomerates, was part of a very smart plan to prepare you to be Secretary of State when Robert becomes President. Your parents didn't think it was, and I guess they were right."

"You discussed this with them?"

"With them, and with the people who have asked me repeatedly when I was planning to recruit you."

"But you said nothing to me."

"No, because there's another rather critical difference between this work and what you've done in boardrooms, James. This can be extremely dangerous. You can, and will be, face to face with some of world's most volatile people; and you will be on their turf, in some of the world's most unstable places."

"So you were protecting me. And my parents," James added softly. *And now it is they who have been murdered.* The thought swept him swiftly back to the unspeakable crime itself, and he asked, almost urgently, "Do you really have no idea who is responsible for the bomb, Elliot?"

"None. Calls claiming responsibility will start pouring in as soon as word gets out that it was a bomb, but those late calls are usually simply opportunistic. Any legitimate claim should have come in by now." He frowned, then added quietly, "I don't know, James, somehow this feels personal."

"Personal?"

"Yes. An attack intended to make a political statement against the United States would have been staged in Paris, in or near the embassy, not while your father was on vacation, and especially not with your mother on board. This feels more like a vendetta to me, very personal, something like a disgruntled—and psychopathic—embassy employee."

"I was supposed to be on board, too, Elliot," James reminded him, his words causing a new anguish. *What if . . .* "What if I was the intended target?"

"That's something you and I need to discuss, although I think it's extremely unlikely. You're so accessible here. Why assume the unnecessary risk of planting a bomb in a busy marina halfway around the world? I honestly don't think that you were the target. However, I still need to know what negotiations you've handled over the last couple of years, and, more importantly, your current projects."

"There's nothing current. I wrapped up a deal last Saturday in New Orleans and have a stack of proposals on my desk that I was going to look at in January." James frowned as he remembered how he had planned to screen the proposals. He would have looked for those that were challenging, of course, but he would have had Catherine's concert tour itinerary on his desk and would have made decisions that would have permitted him to be with her as often as possible.

The memory came with great pain, because James knew now, already, that all the wonderful plans he and Catherine had made for their love would never happen. He knew now, already, that he had to say good-bye to her and their magical love. Her world was, and always should be, a gentle world of love and joy; and for now, and perhaps forever, the world in which he was compelled to live was an angry world of murder and terror and revenge; and his ugly world belonged nowhere near her lovely one. And for now, and perhaps forever, he had to devote his time and energy to that harsh and tormented world, not to creating a quiet and gentle life of love with Catherine.

"James?"

"Sorry," he answered, apologizing for his distracted silence. Remembering what they had been discussing, he observed quietly, "You didn't mention last night that you would be needing information about my work."

"I knew you would be here this morning."

James nodded solemnly. "Yes. I am here, Elliot. And I have no outstanding projects. So, I'm available to go to Central America, or wherever, in January."

"I think this might be a very good time to take that sailing trip around the world you've always talked about."

"You know I can't do that. You know I have to do something."

"Yes," Elliot answered softly. "I know. OK. I need to talk to a few people. As soon as I've done that, I'll give you a call."

"Good. In the meantime, I'll get the information you need from my office."

"OK. Oh, and James, we need to see the letters of condolence you receive. The ones from Europe are obviously of greatest interest, but I'd like to have all of them screened."

"All right."

"Has anything arrived yet from Prince Alain?"

"I honestly don't know. I haven't looked."

Catherine sat by the telephone in her suite at the Fairmont, waiting for his midnight call, watching the hands of her clock move so slowly toward twelve. The knock on the door didn't register at first, and when it did, she moved to open it reluctantly. It would be a bouquet of winter roses and a brief message of apology . . .

But it was the man she loved, his blue eyes dark-circled, his beloved face pale and drawn. James was here, now, but Catherine was very certain that he hadn't been in the audience at her concert this evening. She would have known, and she would have left the stage, in the middle of her dazzling performance, to go to him. He must have known that. That must have been why he had stayed away.

"Oh," she breathed as she gently touched the taut skin beneath his eyes with her delicate and loving fingers. "Oh, you're here."

Catherine led him into her suite and into her bed, and James followed, so willingly, as she led him to the magical place of peace and joy that was their love. He had believed that that gentle, fragile place was gone, trampled by the monstrous emotions that raged within him now. But for one night of exquisite intimacy and passion, the monsters were still, the nightmares were banished, and the churning restlessness was calmed . . . and there was only the gentle tenderness of their love.

"Good morning," she said softly when she walked into the living room of her suite and found him standing by the window.

"Good morning," he answered gently, turning away from the bright blue splendor of the first day of the New Year to the far more magnificent bright blue splendor of her eyes.

"Are you leaving so soon?" He was fully dressed, and she was in her robe, her silky black hair softly tangled from their night of love.

"Yes. Darling, I only came to say good-bye."

"Good-bye?" Catherine echoed softly, even though part of her had sensed, in the intense emotion of his loving, that that was what he had been telling her.

"Yes. Good-bye," James answered quietly. Then he began to explain, slowly, gently, wanting her to understand, as he did, why he *had* to say good-bye to her and their love. "Their death—their murder—has changed me, Catherine. I'm angry, and restless, and consumed by ugly yet very powerful thoughts and emotions. I don't know if I could conquer my rage even if I tried, but the truth is, my love, that as painful—and even terrifying—as the emotions are, I don't want to force them away. I don't want to ever feel calm or complacent about what was done to my parents."

"I don't want to ever feel complacent about what was done to them either, James. Their death has changed me, too. I'm angry, too."

"Do you want to find whoever killed them and point a gun at his heart and pull the trigger and watch him die?"

"No," she answered softly. "And I can't believe that's what you want, not really."

"It is what I want, Catherine. Really. Believe it," James said quietly. It was the truth, such an ugly truth. Surely now he would see sad comprehension on her beautiful face. Surely now she would understand that his monstrous thoughts and emotions—and, perhaps, someday his deeds—had no place in her gentle lovely world. But James didn't see comprehension. He only saw love.

"Is that where you're going, James? To find whoever planted the bomb?"

"No. That's Elliot's job, although he has promised to keep me informed. In the meantime, I'm going to work as a negotiator for the State Department. Maybe there's something I can do that will help prevent a similar tragedy from occurring to someone else. My intentions aren't terribly noble, Catherine, I just have to do something. It's my need as much as anything."

"I understand why you have to do that, James," she said softly, and then, more softly, "But I don't understand why you're saying good-bye."

"Because, Catherine, I'm no longer the man I want to be for you, or for our love. All my gentleness is gone."

"Your gentleness wasn't gone last night."

"No, but I wonder if I was only borrowing from you. Maybe, my darling, if I clung to you the restless rage would be quieted for a while. But it would come back eventually, and eventually my bitterness and anger would consume us both. I love you far too much, Catherine, to let that happen."

"You can't love someone too much."

"Oh, yes, darling, you can. I want your life to be filled with joy, not with nightmares and hatred and rage. I don't want this unhappiness for you, Catherine. Don't you understand?"

As she gazed at the man she would always love with all her heart, she tried to understand. But she couldn't. How could this be a reason to end their love?

"And would you leave me, James, if you were dying? To spare me that unhappiness?"

"I'm not dying, Catherine."

Yes you are! her heart cried. You are dying—your gentle loving heart is dying—and you have decided not to share that pain and sadness with me. Because you want only joy and happiness for me, but . . .

"But what about what I want, James?" she asked suddenly, urgently. "Doesn't that matter?"

Once he had vowed, a most solemn promise of love, to do only and always what Catherine wanted. All the choices of the heart would be hers, he had promised. She wanted their love still, despite everything. But it was not what he wanted for her. And now, very softly, very quietly, James broke his solemn vow.

"No, Catherine, it doesn't matter."

There had been confusion and uncertainty on Catherine's beautiful face when she had asked her urgent question. But now, as she heard his quiet and resolute answer, the confusion and uncertainty vanished, and he saw comprehension . . . *at last*.

"I trusted you with all my secrets, James, all my anger and all my pain, but you don't trust my love enough to share your sadness with me."

"It's not a matter of trust."

"No," she agreed softly, sadly. "It's a matter of love. You never really loved me."

"Oh, Catherine, I loved you. I will always love you."

* * *

I will always love you. The words echoed in her mind long after James was gone. How well she knew those false promises of love! *I will always love you. Je t'aimerai toujours.*

Long ago, she had been abandoned by someone who claimed to have loved her, but didn't. Now, once again, she had been left in the name of love. And now, once again, she had not really been abandoned because there had been *too much* love, but because there had not been enough.

CHAPTER TWENTY

Inverness Estate, Maryland
February 1990

"*E*lliot? This is Alexa Taylor."

"Hello, Alexa."

"I was calling about James." It had been almost six weeks since the bitter cold January night when he had said good-bye. At first his good-bye had frightened her. It had sounded so ominous, so permanent, as if he wasn't certain he would ever return. James had reassured her quickly, scolding her for being melodramatic. And yet, still, on that night, he had reminded her very gently that he loved her, and he had told her even more gently that Robert McAllister was a fool to have ever let her go. "Is he all right, Elliot?"

"Yes. He's fine, Alexa."

"Oh, good. Would it be possible for me to get in touch with him?"

"Can you tell me why?"

"No. Well. Would it matter?"

"Maybe. How urgently do you need him? I expect him back in less than two weeks. Can whatever it is wait until then?"

"Yes," she answered, although *it* wasn't waiting. The tiny new life inside her was growing every day. "If you speak to him in the meantime, though, will you tell him that I'm at Inverness?"

James had given her a set of keys to the mansion, and the code for the alarm, and he had told her that she should feel free to go to Inverness whenever she needed time away from the love nest that held such bittersweet memories of Robert. Alexa was there when James called three days after her conversation with Elliot.

"You're answering my phone with a British accent?"

"Well, yes, I am. Hi."

"Hi. Elliot said you called?"

"Yes. I need some legal help."

"*Alexa.* You called Elliot because you want me to negotiate a contract for you?"

"No. It's something else. Something very important. I'm not trying to be coy, James. It's just something I need to discuss with you in person. I called Elliot because I needed to know if you would be back in the foreseeable future."

"I will be."

"Victorious as always?" Alexa teased, a gentle tease that suddenly transported them both back to the happy, uncomplicated time when they had been lovers.

"Victories don't come so easily in this arena," James admitted quietly. "The name of the game is patience and compromise."

"Not two of your favorites."

"No. But I'm learning."

In fact, he had already been proclaimed a master by the State Department veterans. His cool was, as it always had been, absolutely unshakable. He was an elegant sculpture of ice that never melted, not even in the sweltering jungle heat, and not even when agreements that seemed *so close* suddenly dissolved like mirages in the desert. The consensus was that they were making progress, astonishing progress, and in a month they would return and try again. James was learning patience and compromise. And he was learning, too, the stark truth about the hope for world peace. It could happen only as long as one understood that for each small painstaking step forward, there might be a giant step back, and that then one had to be willing to begin the patient, steady, tireless march all over again.

"Robert's baby?" James asked abruptly when he saw Alexa and her very obvious pregnancy ten days later.

"Yes. Of course."

"How did it happen?"

"The usual way."

"*Not* the usual way, Alexandra. You were always so fanatically careful. Or was this planned?"

"*No.* You know that nothing except abstinence is one hundred percent effective. I wasn't careless, James," she said quietly, truthfully. "It just happened."

"OK," he said, his voice softening finally as he looked at Alexa, who he loved and was so vulnerable now, so fragile, so very much in need of his help. But how could he help her, when his own emotions were so raw and frayed? Somehow a little gentleness surfaced as he asked, "So . . . now what?"

"Now I need you to handle the adoption for me."

"The adoption?"

"I want Brynne and Stephen to have the baby, James. I know how desperately they have wanted children, and been unable to, and I know what wonderful, loving parents they would be."

"That's all very true, Alexa, but don't you think you should discuss this with Robert?"

"With Robert? He didn't want me, remember? There's no reason for him to ever know about the baby." Besides, she thought, as she had thought so often in the past weeks, I think Robert would want this, too, for his little sister, and for the tiny, precious treasure of love that is growing inside me. "This is my decision to make, James."

"Then I think you should think about it."

"I *have* thought about it. I have thought about nothing else since the moment I learned I was pregnant. I've made the decision that I believe is the best one for the baby. Being with Brynne is being with family, after all, and with Brynne and Stephen the baby's life will be so happy, so filled with love—and so untouched by questions or uncertainties about its absentee father."

"But what about the uncertainties of being adopted?"

"The uncertainties of being adopted?" Alexa echoed with a thoughtful frown. "I guess there could be uncertainties for Brynne and Stephen, but can't you eliminate them by making it a closed adoption? Isn't there a legal way to have the documents sealed forever? I want you to be able to assure Brynne and Stephen that there is no way that their baby can ever be taken away from them."

"I can do the legal paperwork, yes, but Alexa, I can't assure them that the baby won't ever be taken away."

"You can't?"

"No, darling," James said gently to the obviously confused emerald. He reminded even more gently, "Because the baby's mother, *you*, will know where her baby is."

"Oh, yes, but I would never . . . In August, while you and Cat were sailing, Brynne had a miscarriage. I was with her. I watched as she realized that her dream was over, it had to be, because the pain was simply too great. I will never try to take this baby away from Brynne, James," Alexa promised quietly, a solemn promise from the heart. "You just have to believe it."

As he gazed at her lovely thoughtful eyes, James knew that Alexa would keep her sacred vow, no matter what, not even at the cost of great anguish to herself. He could truthfully assure Brynne and Stephen that the baby's mother would never appear to claim her child, but did that confident knowledge mean that the secret was completely safe?

"Who else knows about the baby, Alexa?"

"No one else knows, James, and no one, except for the doctor, ever will. I haven't even looked for a doctor yet. I thought you might know someone?"

"Yes, I do," he answered, thinking immediately of Dr. Lawton, one of his mother's closest and most respected colleagues, and a longtime friend of the Sterling family. Family . . . "You're not planning to tell your parents or Catherine?"

"No. I've decided it would be best not to. I hate the lie, but . . ." Alexa gave a soft shrug. "My parents and Cat think that as of four weeks ago I'm on a six-month jaunt around the world. And, thanks to Barbara Walters, as of Academy Award night in late March, most of America will think so, too."

"Barbara Walters?"

"For her Oscar Special this year, she's doing interviews with Meryl Streep and Jessica Lange and me. My interview was taped on the set in late January, just before we finished filming for the season. The pregnancy was quite hidden then, even though I had all sorts of precarious emotions floating very near the surface. But still, I suppose because it was so important, I managed not to cry at all during the interview and spent a great deal of time raving about my upcoming around-the-world adventure. I supposedly left on Valentine's Day, which is when I moved here. My mail has been held since then, and all my bills have been paid in advance, and the Marlboro Nursery will take care of my roses. I bought a first class around-the-world airplane ticket, with unlimited stopovers, and I withdrew seventy-five thousand dollars in cash from my bank."

"Why did you do that?"

"So that if anyone ever tried to prove where I'd been, I could just say I'd paid for everything in cash and that's why there was no trail of credit card receipts."

"Why *would* anyone try to prove where you'd been, Alexa? Did someone else know about your affair with Robert?"

"I'm just being careful for the baby's sake, that's all," she answered without answering. Then she lifted her face to him and asked softly, hopefully, "Will you help me with this, James?"

James hesitated, torn by conflicting emotions. He believed her decision was confident and firm, a solemn and generous decision of love. And he knew, as she did, that with Brynne and Stephen the baby's life would be filled, overflowing, with happiness and love. And what great joy this would bring to Brynne and Stephen, and even to Robert. *But. . .*

"James?"

"Yes, Alexa," he answered finally. "I will help you."

I will help you because Catherine, for whom this would cause such immense sadness, will never know.

"What exotic place are you in now?" Catherine asked when Alexa reached her in her suite at the Four Seasons Hotel in Seattle in April.

"No exotic place," Alexa confessed softly. She had been debating telling her sister the truth for weeks. The debate had been silent, never involving James, an emotional struggle between her vow to be honest with Cat and her almost lifelong habit of hiding her flaws from those she loved because of her great fear of disappointing them. But for her baby sister, this would not be the revelation of new flaws. Surely Cat already believed that it would be best for a baby to have a mother other than Alexa. "I'm in Maryland. I've been here all the time. Cat, I'm pregnant."

"Pregnant?"

"The baby's due in June." Alexa paused briefly and added quietly, "And will be adopted."

"Adopted? Oh, Alexa, no." *No!* "Why?"

"Because it's best for the baby."

"Best for the baby?"

"Yes." She reminded softly, "I wouldn't be a very good mother."

"You would be a wonderful mother, Alexa!"

"Oh, no, Cat," Alexa countered swiftly, her emerald eyes filling with tears at her little sister's surprising confidence in her. "I wouldn't be. And it would be best for the baby to have a mother and father, and—"

"Best for the baby, or best for you? Because it would be a bother for you to raise a baby?"

"A bother? *No.*"

"Then keep her, Alexa, or let Mom and Dad raise her. I know they would welcome her and love her."

"Her?"

"The baby."

"No, Cat. I can't ask that of them. And, please, I don't want them to know. I just wanted you to know . . ." *I just wanted you to know, and to understand, and to love me still.*

"And now that I know, Alexa, I will help you. I'll cancel the rest of my tour, right away, and move into RoseCliff with you, and after the baby's born I can help you take care of it."

"Oh, Cat, thank you, but no. The way you can help me is by understanding that this is what I truly believe is best for the baby."

"But I don't understand, Alexa."

"Will you try?" she asked softly as fresh tears flooded her eyes. This had been such a foolish mistake. The love and confidence had vanished from Cat's voice, and all Alexa heard now was disappointment. "Will you think about it and call me back? I'm at Inverness."

"Inverness?"

"Yes. I'm quite hidden. The doctor, a friend of Marion's, even comes here to see me." Alexa paused, and then, because she knew her little sister had always thought he was wonderful, she added quietly, "James is going to handle the adoption for me."

"James?" It was a whisper of pain. James is going to handle the adoption? James is with you? "I thought James was out of the country."

"He got back about three weeks ago. He's leaving again at the end of next week, but he should be back by the middle of May, several weeks before the baby is due."

Every day, every second of every day and every night, Catherine had missed him, and wondered about him, and worried about him. Her desperate longing came alive in her music, stunning her audiences more than ever before, as they journeyed with her from the joyous ecstasy of her remembered love to the anguished sadness of that love's loss. Recently, in the breathtaking voyages, there had been something new, a delicate, trembling hopefulness as Catherine courageously dared to believe that her precious love would return to her.

I will always love you, James had promised. At the time, his promise of love had only been a haunting reminder of the mother who had abandoned her. But, in soft, defiant whispers, Catherine's loving heart had convinced her to believe that he would return. She herself had once been swept away from those she loved by powerful emotions she could not control. She had needed time apart from Jane and Alexander then, but finally, because her love for them was strong and deep and real, she had made the journey back to their love.

It will be the same for James, she had so bravely decided. He will find his way back to our love. He will trust me and allow me to help him with his anguish.

But now James had returned to Alexa, to help her, as he always did when she needed him. James was helping Alexa. And, the most painful realization of all, by being with her in the private hours they spent together at Inverness, James was allowing Alexa to help him as well.

"Cat?" Alexa asked into the long silence that had fallen.

"It's wrong, Alexa. It's wrong for you to give your baby away." And it's so very wrong for James to help you!

"Cat, please!"

"I'm sorry, but that's what I believe."

"Cat . . ."

"I have to go."

"Why did you tell her?" James demanded angrily.

"Because she's my sister and I wanted to be honest with her and I foolishly believed . . ." Alexa sighed softly. "It was a mistake."

"Maybe the mistake is what you're planning to do, Alexa."

"No." She met his intense gaze with clear emerald eyes that didn't flicker. "No."

Alexa's eyes had been clear and unflickering from the beginning, her decision firm and resolute. James had suggested that they wait, perhaps until after the baby was born, before mentioning anything to Brynne and Stephen, but she had been adamant that he tell them right away. And so he had, and now, sometimes, Alexa even referred to the baby as Brynne's. But did she really not hear the new gentle softness in her own voice? James wondered. Was she truly unaware of the bond of love between herself and the tiny life inside her? Whenever he tried to tell her, her magnificent green eyes turned to ice, as they did now, warning him away.

"We're going for a long walk, James. You're not invited because you're glowering and that bothers the baby."

He was glowering; but, after Alexa left, his expression softened to loving concern for Catherine. How terribly upset she must be. How painfully torn between her love for Alexa and the secrets of her own gentle heart. How sad she must be, how confused, how alone.

James wanted to go to her. He wanted to hold her and kiss her and love away her sadness. But he didn't trust himself to go to Catherine. He didn't trust himself not to succumb to his desperate need for her—a need that would, he knew, ultimately only drown her, as he was drowning, still, more and more every day, in the tormented depths of his rage.

James knew he couldn't, shouldn't, go to Catherine. But he could talk to her, couldn't he? He could try to help her understand. Alexa hadn't told him where she was, but James had her itinerary in his dresser drawer beneath the carefully folded scarf she had made for him. He took neither the scarf nor the itinerary with him on his treacherous travels, of course. He carried no symbols of Catherine or their love with him at all, because, should he be taken hostage, he wanted no links of danger to her.

Catherine was in Seattle, James discovered. Before dialing the number of the Four Seasons Hotel, his mind drifted to the wonderful plans they had made for their love in the Emerald City. They would go to the top of the Space Needle, of course, and wander through Pike Place Market, and take a wind-blown ferry boat ride, and visit the Locks, followed by lunch at Hiram's, and . . .

The strident sound of the telephone didn't startle her. Indeed, for several moments it simply blended into the strident thoughts that had screamed in her mind ever since her conversation with Alexa. When she finally realized that it was the phone, she quickly realized even more: it would be James, and he would keep calling until she answered.

"Hello."

"Hello, Catherine. I want to help you understand."

"I'm fine, James," she answered swiftly, wanting, *needing*, to stop the gentleness in his voice, because it caused such pain. "I do understand."

"It's her decision, darling, and hers alone. It has to be. She can't make it based on what you—"

"Did you tell her about me?"

"No, of course not. Of course I didn't tell her. You know that." *Don't* you know that, Catherine? Don't you know, my love, that I would never betray your precious secret? He was about to ask her, to be certain, but Catherine spoke first, a soft, devastating question.

"Is it your baby, James?" Oh, how she hadn't wanted to ask that! But it had been there from the beginning, one of the very first screams, and it had only grown louder, more taunting and demanding, as the minutes passed.

"No, Catherine, how could it be?" James asked with an astonished ache. When Alexa's baby was conceived, you and I were in love, remember?

"But it could be—once could have been—yours." Catherine no longer recognized the voice that was speaking. But it was a voice she would come to know very well. It was her new voice, the one that would be with her for the rest of her life, the voice that no longer held any hope for the love of Catherine and James. The strange voice continued calmly, "If you pretended this baby was yours, James, no one would ever guess that it wasn't. Maybe Alexa is afraid of raising the baby by herself and if . . ." Even the new voice, empty of all hope, couldn't finish the sentence.

Catherine couldn't finish the sentence, but James knew what the words would have been. After many silent moments, he asked very quietly, "Is that what you want, Catherine? Do you want me to marry Alexa?"

Oh, no, James, her defiant heart cried. That's not what I want. But what I want, I cannot have. I want you, and you are gone. I can't have that wish, but I have another wish, a desperate wish for Alexa's baby to be with her mother, where she should be, and if this is a way that that can happen . . .

"Yes, James. That's what I want."

CHAPTER TWENTY-ONE

Dallas
May 1990

"*R*obert?" Hillary asked when she walked into their bedroom suite in her parents' mansion in Highland Park and found her husband packing his suitcase. It was the Sunday of Memorial Day weekend. The festivities celebrating Sam Ballinger's sixty-fifth birthday had been flawless, capped with an eloquent speech given last evening by his son-in-law. The public celebration was over, but Hillary had assumed they would stay in Dallas another day. The Senate wasn't scheduled to reconvene until Tuesday, after all, and the Gorbachevs weren't due to arrive in Washington until Wednesday evening. "What are you doing?"

Robert looked up at her with surprise.

"The celebration is over, so I'm leaving, as we agreed. I should be completely moved out of the house in Arlington by tomorrow night."

"Moved out?"

"Don't do this, Hillary," Robert said, his voice quiet but edged with icy warning. He had survived the past six months, *barely*, living for this day when he would be free at last of his loveless marriage, and free at last to mourn the loss of his beloved Alexa in private. "Don't pretend, not even for a moment, that you thought we weren't getting divorced after all."

"You told me your affair was over!"

"Yes, and I also told you from the very beginning that our marriage was a travesty and that it had failed long before I met her. The fact that you may believe, or can even pretend to believe, that there is any marriage left after the past six months simply proves how very little we ever had."

"It was all a lie, wasn't it, Robert?" Hillary demanded, her sable eyes flashing with indignant rage. "She *has* been waiting for you, hasn't she? Maybe not even waiting. Maybe you've been seeing her still all this time even though you promised you wouldn't. If you've broken your promise to me Robert —"

"I haven't broken any promises, Hillary. No one is waiting for me."

"Then, Robert . . ."

"Stop," he commanded, startling her into sudden silence. "Let it go, Hillary, just let it go gracefully. I'm sure that you would prefer to file the divorce papers, and that's acceptable to me, but please do it soon. I don't want anything, of course." Except my freedom, he thought. *Beginning right now.* "Good-bye, Hillary."

"Robert!" she cried, but he was gone, racing away from her, with no destination other than *not* to be with her. *Because of Alexa.* Alexa was gone from his life, but still Robert preferred to be alone, with only the memories of his lost love, than to spend another minute with her.

"How I hate you, Alexa!" Hillary hissed as she hurled a crystal decanter across the room, shattering an antique mirror into hundreds of sharp glittering pieces. "How I hate you!"

Robert didn't breathe comfortably until the plane left the tarmac at the Dallas–Fort Worth airport. He took a deep breath then, and wondered as he did if it was the first unconstricted breath he had taken since December.

The bright May sunshine streamed through the airplane window, glinting off his scuffed gold wedding ring. Robert stared at the ring, as if noticing it for the first time. He hadn't, he realized now, thought about it at all when he and Alexa had been together, because for him, for so very long, it had been a symbol of nothing.

But had Alexa noticed? Had it bothered her? Should he have taken the ring off before their nights together? Robert stopped the questions abruptly. They were, after all, questions about the Alexa who had never really existed—the lovely vulnerable woman whom he had loved so desperately. The real Alexa, the clever confident woman who had simply been playing with him, would not have been bothered by his wedding ring. Indeed, she would probably have enjoyed seeing the ring on the hand that caressed her so urgently, a golden symbol of her triumph over Hillary.

Robert removed the ring and forced his thoughts away from the past and into the future . . . to his most welcome privacy and solitude . . . to the work in which he believed so strongly . . . and to the wonderful joy that would soon be coming into his life. Soon, very soon, Brynne's baby would arrive.

A soft smile touched his handsome face as he anticipated that great happiness, wavering slightly as worry crept in. James had assured them all that the mother's decision was firm, and that once the baby was given to Brynne and Stephen there would be no way for her to ever to find her adopted child, but still . . .

It will be fine, Robert decided firmly. It *has* to be. Brynne has suffered enough losses. We all have.

"Alexa?" James tapped on the door of her bathroom as he called her name. It was two A.M. and her lights were on and he had heard water running. Neither the lights nor the water had awakened him in his own room two spacious bedrooms away. He was awake already, driven gasping from sleep by the tormenting nightmares that had been his constant companions since December—except for the one magnificent night when they had been banished by Catherine's love. As he had gazed out his bedroom window, he'd seen the golden beam of light from

Alexa's room. She was awake, too, and probably restless. Perhaps, she'd like to play a little backgammon.

"James? I'll be out in a minute. I've already called Dr. Lawton. He's going to meet us at the hospital."

"You're in labor?"

"The real thing," she replied as she opened the bathroom door. "So, how do I look? Doctor Lawton said that this kind of hair dye—it will wash out in six washes—is safe, and it makes a good disguise, don't you think? I have some horn-rimmed glasses for you to wear, a very scholarly look. James?"

James didn't answer, he couldn't, because he was too stunned by her midnight black hair, still damp from the dying, her blackened eyebrows and lashes, and her eyes, tinted sapphire blue by contact lenses.

"I'd never really seen the resemblance before either," Alexa said quietly, correctly interpreting his astonished impression that it was Catherine not Alexa who stood before him. She had never seen the resemblance before, but as she had gazed at herself in the mirror, checking her disguise, Alexa had seen very clearly the little sister with whom her impulsive decision to reveal the truth had caused such irreparable harm.

"Nor had I," James whispered finally. He knew full well that any resemblance—beyond the Taylor sister look of determination—should not have been there. And it never had been, until tonight. But tonight Alexa looked like Catherine, and James was left with the horrifying feeling that it was Catherine not Alexa he was taking to the hospital to have the baby she would give up for adoption.

"So, shall we go?" Alexa asked, her voice now quite matter-of-fact and quite empty of emotion. "Doctor Lawton has notified the hospital that we'll be arriving. We're the Smiths, by the way, James and Juliet."

They hadn't discussed James's role, other than to accompany her to the hospital and then take the baby to Brynne and Stephen in Richmond. But, as he had done in December when Alexa needed him, he had taken her hand and not let go. And, as in December, at some point in the night her fingers began to dig deep into his palm. But James didn't even notice. Tonight he was witnessing a miracle—the miracle his mother had described so often and always with such great awe.

"A healthy girl," Dr. Lawton announced quietly moments after the baby was born. He and Alexa had agreed in advance that he would tell her the sex and health of her infant, and nothing more.

"A beautiful little girl," the delivery room nurse embellished enthusiastically.

Dr. Lawton grimaced slightly at the nurse's words. He hadn't told her that the baby was to be adopted, because he hadn't wanted to draw any special attention to Alexa. Not that Alexa was recognizable, not at all; and even James was quite transformed by the glasses.

The baby cried then, an announcement that her voyage from the warm cave where she had lived for nine months had been made safely. An announcement, and a question. Where was the other comforting heartbeat she knew so well?

"May I see her?" Alexa asked softly, all the softnesses that had touched her voice all spring now combining in the gentlest of sounds.

"Of course," the nurse answered warmly. "Let me just get her ready."

In a few moments, the little girl, clean and dry and wrapped in a pre-warmed blanket, was cradled gently in her mother's arms. As James watched Alexa's trembling fingers touch her daughter's soft cheeks, and saw all the love Alexa had so defiantly denied, he began to plan the very difficult words he would speak to Brynne and Stephen and Robert. Brynne's heart would be broken, again, and Stephen's and Robert's. But there would be joy for Alexa, and for Catherine. Hearts would break . . . and, perhaps, hearts would mend.

But even as James thought about the words he would say, he saw the subtle change in Alexa's expression. A moment later, she touched her lips to her daughter's forehead, an exquisitely tender kiss of love, and then looked at the nurse and whispered, as she handed the baby to her, "Thank you."

"She'll be waiting for you in the newborn nursery."

Alexa nodded absently, but her eyes followed the nurse and her baby until they left the delivery room. Then they were alone, the three people who knew the truth, Dr. Lawton, Alexa, and James.

"Will I be able to leave tonight, Doctor?" Alexa asked. The plan, assuming all went well, had been that she would return to Inverness as soon as the delivery was over.

"Yes."

"Why don't you stay here with the baby, Alexa?" James suggested quietly.

"Don't call me Alexa!" she warned urgently.

"It's just the three of us—"

"—just the two of you," Dr. Lawton interjected. "I'm going to give you a little privacy."

"Alexa," James continued after the doctor left, firmly repeating her name as a reminder of who she was. Alexa, not Juliet, a mother who had just given birth to her baby—*her* baby—not a romantic heroine performing a carefully scripted role to perfection. "Alexa . . ."

"I haven't changed my mind, James, and I'm not going to." Even though my heart wants me to! Her heart wanted her to, but it was a battle Alexa allowed her logical mind, once again, to win—for her baby. It's wrong, Cat had said, and Alexa knew now that her little sister had been right, at least partially. It *was* wrong for her, for her heart; but it was right, *best*, for her daughter. Wasn't it? Yes. *Yes*. "Please call Brynne and Stephen right now."

"No."

"Damn you." Her tinted sapphire eyes filled with tears and she whispered, "Please don't do this to me, James."

"I want you to spend the night here and see her again."

"No. It's too risky for me to be here. Someone might recognize me."

"OK. I'll bring her to Inverness tomorrow as soon as she's been discharged. You need to see her again. Alexa, you need to think about this!"

"I don't need to see her again." The memory of the moments she had touched and kissed and smiled hello to the lovely little girl who had been conceived in such love would live in her heart . . . always. "And I *have* thought about it."

"You've thought about all the reasons to give her to Brynne. But, Alexa, I don't think you've thought about all the reasons not to."

"Very selfish reasons, James, and very emotional ones."

"Maybe if we got married . . ." He hadn't asked her before. He was convinced it would not have changed her decision, and he had his own reasons—selfish and emotional—for not wanting to spend his life as Catherine's brother-in-law. "Will you marry me, Alexa?"

"Oh, you're such a nice man," she whispered as she gazed through tears at her beloved friend. James was so tormented, battling his own demons, but he had still found the energy and emotion to help her. For a moment—a lovely dream—Alexa considered his proposal. *I could spend my life loving my daughter*. But then she forced the dream away. It was such a selfish dream, and so unfair, to everyone but her. Could she really ask James to spend his life pretending to be the father of his best friend's baby? Could she really ask him to live his life with her, and deprive him of a chance at the kind of love she had felt with Robert? It was unfair to ask that of him, even though he was offering, but it was most unfair to her baby. The best life for her daughter, the most happiness, would be to live with parents who loved each other as deeply as she had loved Robert. And that was far more than anything she could offer, either with James or without him.

"Please call Brynne and Stephen, James. I'm not going to change my mind."

"Please tell me," Alexa said thirty-six hours later when James returned from Richmond.

"Why are you doing this?"

"I want to know that Brynne and Stephen were happy."

"They were happy beyond words," James answered truthfully. The look in Brynne's eyes had been astonishingly close to the look he had seen in Alexa's eyes when she held her baby daughter—as if Brynne had spent the past months bonding with the baby girl, too. And of course she had. Brynne knew very well what it felt like to have a new life growing inside her. "Beyond words."

"Have they picked a name?"

"Dammit, Alexa!" James growled, and then felt instantly guilty. Alexa looked like death. After two washings, the midnight black hair had faded only to dirty gray, and her eyes, thankfully no longer sapphire, were gray-green, the emerald now filled with dark clouds of grief. He wondered, as he had been wondering, if he should have been more forceful about her seeing the baby another time, or if he should have insisted that she marry him. He repeated, very softly, "Dammit, Alexa."

"Just tell me, James, and then I'll never ask another question about her. I know that because of your friendship with Brynne and Robert you will watch her grow. I promise that I won't spend our lifetime asking you to be my spy." It was a solemn promise to them all, to James, to Brynne, to her baby, and to herself. "Just tell me her name. Please."

James gave a soft sigh and said gently, "They named her Kathryn, after Stephen's mother. It's spelled with a K and a Y."

"Are they going to call her Kat?"

"No. They're going to call her Katie."

For a long time Alexa said nothing. She just gazed out the window to the rose garden and far far beyond, her lovely eyes envisioning a distant dream. As he watched, James witnessed an act of will that consumed every ounce of energy left in her soul. When she finally looked back at him, her emerald eyes were sad but very clear.

"Will you take me for a sail, James?"

"Of course I will."

"This Tuesday, Elliot?"

"Yes. We need to be in Damascus by Thursday, so we should leave Tuesday." Elliot heard James's hesitation and added quietly, "You don't have to do this, James. In fact, maybe it's time for you to return to private life."

Private life? James mused. No. Those memories were far too painful. He felt much less pain when he was in places steeped in hatred, not in places that reminded him of love. He needed to work, needed to look into the eyes of the kind of people who might have ordered the death of his parents, and with those evil people he needed to make slow determined negotiations toward peace. He was restless, eager to flee the memories, but it had only been a week since Alexa's delivery, and even though she was valiantly fighting her sadness, she was still so very fragile.

"Let me call you back, Elliot."

"Sure."

James replaced the receiver and looked up to see Alexa. She had been outside, lying in the warm June sun, hoping to turn her pale white skin into glowing gold. In the six weeks remaining before *Pennsylvania Avenue* resumed production, she needed to lose weight—an easy task because she had no hunger; and—an impossible task—she needed to become the relaxed, confident, carefree woman who had spent the past six months traipsing around the world. Alexa had been dutifully lying in the sun when Elliot called, but she had been drawn from the rose-fragrant veranda by the sound of the telephone and the hope that it was Cat, calling at last.

But Cat wasn't going to call.

"Elliot?" Alexa said, chastising herself for her foolish hope that she and her sister would ever reconcile. "Word about your parents?"

"No. Still absolutely nothing."

"He needs you?"

"Yes. But . . ."

"But you're worried about me." She smiled bravely. "I think it's time for me to return to RoseCliff."

"If anyone saw you . . ."

"No one will. If you could just buy food to last me about three weeks, I should be very presentable after that."

James knew Catherine was in Denver. Tomorrow she would give the final concert of her North American tour, and in three weeks she would begin her tour in Europe. What wonderful plans they had made for these next three weeks. A few days in romantic, charming Aspen, they had decided, and then . . .

James stopped the distant memory of love, but he did not stop the decision to call her.

"It's James, Catherine."

"James."

"Alexa had her baby—a baby girl—a week ago, and she has been adopted by very loving parents." He paused, sighed softly, and said quietly, "Alexa needs you, Catherine. Alexa needs her sister."

"Is she at Inverness?" *With you?* If I go to see Alexa—and, oh, how I have thought about calling her!—will I see you, too?

"No. She's at RoseCliff."

The knock at her cottage door startled and then terrified her. What if it was Hillary? *What if it was Robert?*

Alexa cowered in the kitchen, out of sight. She was unable to see the intruder at the door, but she would be able to catch a glimpse when whoever it was began to leave.

Go away, whoever you are!

"Alexa? Are you here? Alexa?"

"Cat?" she whispered as she rushed to the door. "Cat."

"Hi." Catherine's heart wept when she saw the haunted emerald eyes. Oh, Alexa, I should have been here a long time ago! "May I come in?"

"Of course." As she opened the door to her small cottage, Alexa said softly, "Cat, there's no one else here. I had a baby girl . . . and I gave her away."

"I know. Alexa, I've come to apologize. I should have accepted your decision and supported you."

"How *could* you have supported me, Cat?"

Alexa's tone was sad and bewildered, but the words cut through Catherine like the sharpest of knives, plunging with surgical precision into an already bleeding wound in her loving heart. Was it true? Had James revealed to Alexa the secret of her own adoption? Had he broken that solemn promise of love?

"What do you mean?"

"I mean that somehow you knew what I was doing was wrong. Somehow you knew how difficult it would be for me. How did you know that, Cat? You have always been so wise."

"I'm not wise, Alexa."

"But you knew, without ever having been a mother yourself, that giving away a baby is . . ." Alexa softly shook her head. There were no words, only emotions. "Somehow you knew."

"No," Catherine whispered. I never knew about the mother's pain, only the baby's. But now, as she heard Alexa's anguish and saw her haunted eyes, she wondered, Did my own mother suffer like this? Is it possible that she really did love me?

"Cat?" Alexa asked softly, as the sapphire eyes she had seen cry only once before suddenly filled with tears.

"I never knew until now about the mother's loss. I only knew about the baby's." She turned away from Alexa then and moved to the nearby picture window that gave a breathtaking view of roses and sky and sea. Catherine didn't see the view, her eyes were blurred with fresh tears, and she barely heard her own words above the thundering of her heart. "I knew how the baby felt because I'm adopted. I'm not really your sister, Alexa."

"Yes you are! I was there, Cat. I was in Kansas City when you were born. I saw you the moment you were released from the hospital." How vividly she remembered that day. How vividly, too, she remembered her own desperate words, She's not my sister! I don't want her! And now, on this day, even more desperately, Alexa's heart cried, I want her to be my sister, please, *please!* She whispered softly, pleadingly, lovingly, "You're my baby sister, Cat."

At the softness in her voice, Catherine turned back to Alexa and confessed bravely, "No, Alexa, I'm not. I've only wanted to be. Your real baby sister died."

"No," Alexa protested quietly.

"Yes," Catherine countered gently, her heart swelling with hope as Alexa greeted the revelation with sadness and defiance, not even a flicker of the relief she had always feared. "On the day she was discharged, Mom visited the newborn nursery. She was looking for the courage to tell you what had happened, and instead . . ."

Catherine told Alexa everything she knew about that day. It was the same story she had told James, the identical story told by Jane to her. But now, as she spoke of the mother who had claimed to love her but had given her away because of some mysterious danger, Catherine's voice was soft, not bitter. And now, there were bewildering questions in her heart where before there had only been the confident answer: she didn't really love me.

"Do you know how often I've wondered if *I* was adopted?" Alexa asked softly when Catherine's story had finished.

"You?"

"Yes. I was the misfit in the family. You and Mom and Dad were so alike, so gifted and talented, and I—"

"Oh, but Alexa, you were everything! You were very talented too, of course, and you were also beautiful and confident and vivacious. I was always so proud of you!"

"Were you? Oh, Cat, and I was so jealous of you."

"Jealous? Of me?"

"Of course. And," Alexa confessed softly, fearfully, "I guess because I was so jealous, I was also very cruel to you. I didn't want you to be my sister. Don't you remember?"

Catherine heard both Alexa's fear that she would remember, and her great hope that she wouldn't. She wanted to assure, No, Alexa, I don't remember. But today, beginning today and forever, there could be no more lies, not even the most gentle lies of love.

"I remember, Alexa," she admitted, continuing swiftly, lovingly, "But I understood. I was so quiet and so shy. I thought it was embarrassing for you to be my sister."

"Embarrassing? Oh, Cat, no, never. I always thought you were perfect, a serene, perfect, beautiful princess." Alexa gave a wry trembling smile of pain. "You must have been relieved to learn that you weren't truly related to me."

"No!"

"No?" *Even now?* Alexa wondered, but was afraid to ask. Instead, very quietly, she tried to explain what she had done and why. "I love my baby, Cat. I will always love her. I gave her away because I believed it was best for her, even though it wasn't best for me. I gave her away, and it feels as though I have given away my heart."

Hot tears spilled from Catherine's eyes as she listened to Alexa's words. They were familiar words, engraved in gold on the clasp of a sapphire necklace given by another mother to her baby girl: *Je t'aimerai toujours*. And there were other words, forgotten—dismissed as false!—until now, the words her mother had spoken to Jane when she had given her the necklace: "We had one heart, her father and I, and now we give that heart to her."

"I'm comforted," Alexa continued quietly, "by the knowledge that her life will be safe and happy and filled with love. She'll probably never even know I existed. The adoption was closed, all records sealed, and her parents may choose never to tell her she was adopted."

"Does that matter to you?"

"When I held her, I had a sudden impulse to request that she be told. I wanted her to know that I loved her and that I believed with all my heart that what I was doing was best for her. I didn't make the request, and I think it's better that I didn't . . . because now she can never hate me."

Or love you. The thought came to Catherine without warning, an astonishing thought trembling with emotion.

"You hate your mother, don't you, Cat?"

"I guess I did, but . . ." But now, she thought, I wish, somehow, I could let her know that I understand. I wish I could reassure her that my life has been happy, as she hoped it would be, and that I have been safe and loved.

"Cat, if you can, forgive her," Alexa said softly, and, even more softly, she implored, "And, then, if it is possible, please forgive me."

"Forgive *you*, Alexa? I'm the one who needs to be forgiven. I'm the one who always wanted to be your sister, and yet I wasn't a very good sister when you needed me."

"But you are my sister," Alexa whispered, a soft statement, not a question, just a most gentle whisper of love. "You *are* my sister."

PART THREE

CHAPTER TWENTY-TWO

"*W*here next?" James asked Elliot as they dined together in Elliot's hotel room.

It was a celebration of sorts. They had finally accomplished all they could have reasonably hoped to accomplish, a small hopeful step. It had taken a month and every ounce of James's energy to maintain his famous cool, and now, already, he was asking about the next project.

"How about a sailing voyage around the world?" Elliot offered quietly.

"No. This is good for me, Elliot."

"I'm not sure of that, James," Elliot replied truthfully. Every day he saw more of himself in James—the fearlessness of a man who, having already lost everything, has nothing more to lose.

"*I'm* sure."

"Well. It sure as hell is good for the future of the free world."

"Good. So, where next?"

"Colombia, but not until late August. There's nothing until then, and the Colombia effort will probably consume all fall, so how about a one-month sailing voyage in the meantime?"

"I probably won't sail, but maybe I will stay over here—Europe—for a while."

"That sounds good."

"I thought I'd visit L'île."

"You won't find anything there, James." Elliot's smile faded. "I thought we had an agreement that I would keep you informed, and that you would stay away from the investigation. I know it's been seven months, and we still don't have a damned thing, but—"

"Elliot," James interjected. "My reason for going to L'île is purely sentimental, because they loved the island so much. I guess it should have occurred to me, but hadn't, that the bomb might have been connected to their intended visit. It obviously has occurred to you, though. Why, Elliot? Something more than the simple reason that L'île was their destination?"

"Yes, although nothing more specific than the bloody history of the damned place."

"The bloody history of L'île? Mother and Father described it as a paradise."

"L'île is a paradise, but from time to time the island's tranquil beauty has been shattered by its rulers. There have been benevolent Castilles, of course, but there have also been treacherous ones."

"Alain?" James asked with surprise. He remembered how gracious his parents had found the Prince to be. And he remembered, too, the thoughtful letter of condolence he had received from Alain after their death.

"As far as the intelligence community of the free world is concerned, no, Alain Castille is not treacherous."

"But the intelligence community has made a point of finding out. Why?"

"Because of Jean-Luc, Alain's father. Jean-Luc was banished from L'île by his older brother, Alexandre, and during his years of exile on the French Riviera, he created an empire of power and terror. When he returned to L'île—as monarch, because Alexandre died without an heir—Jean-Luc's enormous power became even stronger and more dangerous. As L'île's head of state, the terrorist Jean-Luc enjoyed diplomatic immunity and protection. We couldn't assassinate him. We could only watch and hope like hell that he didn't arm one of the most strategically important islands in the Mediterranean with nuclear warheads. We couldn't assassinate him, but, fortunately, someone did. We still don't know the identity of the assassin, but Jean-Luc had plenty of enemies, including former 'friends' whom he had betrayed. Anyway, he was killed, seven years ago, when his sabotaged plane dove into the sea."

"And?"

"And Alain Castille assumed the throne and the criminal activities appeared to vanish."

"Appeared to."

"That was the question seven years ago. Jean-Luc never concealed what he was doing. That was part of his megalomania. He flaunted his power and corruption and delighted in the fact that the civilized world was powerless to stop him. When Alain assumed the throne, the question was had the criminal activities truly ceased, or was Alain simply far more subtle, and therefore far more dangerous, than Jean-Luc? Alain has been watched very carefully, and there is no evidence whatsoever that he is continuing Jean-Luc's menace."

"But you're telling me this."

"Because I don't want you to hear about it and think you've made an important discovery. The treachery of selected members of L'île's royal family is old news."

"Have you ever met Alain, Elliot?"

"No."

"But you've been to L'île?"

"Yes. Many, many years ago. Before Jean-Luc."

"Why don't you come with me?" James suggested. As he watched Elliot's reaction to his suggestion, he saw the well-trained eyes of the master spy cloud ever so slightly and felt a sense of déjà vu. He had seen the same look when Elliot had spoken with quiet emotion about the emptiness of revenge. There had been something personal then, a distant yet still so painful loss, and there was something very personal and very painful now—something to do with L'île. "Elliot?"

"The difference between consultant negotiators and paid civil servants is that we have to show up on a regular basis," Elliot countered lightly. "You go, James. I think you will find it very peaceful."

Peaceful? James wondered. His memories of peace were far, far away. He churned with angry energy still, although in recent months his monstrous emotions raged a little less, as if battered by frustration, and they had given way, in small begrudging growls, to an emptiness which felt almost worse than the restless rage— less vital somehow, less alive. The thundering emotions had subsided slightly, and in the relative quiet he had begun to hear the soft voices of his gentler emotions, trampled but miraculously still alive, a resilient chorus of remembered joy that urged him to go to her.

Go to Catherine, the soft voices sang. Go to your love.

But James knew that he had nothing to offer her. He had even less now, more emptiness, less life, than he had had on the morning he said good-bye. He wondered if, as Elliot suggested, he could perhaps find a little peace on L'île—peace *at least* for the soft voices of love.

And if the voices weren't quiet? If the romantic island paradise simply made the gentle memories of love sing with greater confidence? James had no answer for those questions. But he knew—and the resilient chorus *knew* that he knew— where Catherine was. She had been in Paris last week, and next week she would perform for the Princess of Wales at the Royal Albert Hall, and this week she was in Vienna . . .

The vision in Alain Castille's long-lashed dark brown eyes was perfect, and from the box seats reserved for royalty at the Staatsoper in Vienna he had a perfect view of the stage; but still, after willing his hand not to tremble, the Prince of L'île des Arcs-en-ciel gestured for the opera glasses that rested in his Natalie's lap.

Natalie always brought opera glasses. Playfully, yet discreetly, she would eye the jewels of the other patrons, casting scowls of mock petulance at her half brother when she spotted a design that wasn't Castille. Natalie didn't share Alain's great passion for music, but she very much enjoyed accompanying him on his frequent excursions to attend concerts throughout Europe.

She handed the opera glasses to Alain and watched with surprise and curiosity as he focused on the beautiful pianist who was dazzling the audience with her stunningly emotional performance of the "Mephisto Waltz." As Natalie watched, Alain's darkly handsome features settled into a somber grimness. His aristocratic profile resembled that of an ancient Greek statue, she thought, the solemn marble face of a general preparing to lead his men into a battle from which they might never return, committed to that path because there was no noble choice other than to defend the homeland.

It cannot be! Alain's mind protested defiantly. It cannot be!

But it was. An almost identical face, framed in spun gold not black velvet, had been indelibly etched in his mind for over twenty years. How vividly Alain remembered the moment when he had overheard Isabelle accuse Jean-Luc of murdering his mother. Jean-Luc's massive hands would have crushed Isabelle's slender throat had he run—and he had wanted to, far away and forever!—but he could not let Isabelle die at Jean-Luc's hands as, apparently, his own mother had. He had feigned innocence, interrupting them as if he had only just arrived and overheard nothing, even though his own small heart was filled with a loathing for Jean-Luc that far exceeded all the hatred that had come before.

After Isabelle left, Jean-Luc had told him the story of the missing princess. On that day, and on so many other days, he had been forced to stand in front of the portrait of Isabelle and listen to Jean-Luc's obsessive madness about her and her missing yet so menacing daughter. Each time Jean-Luc told the entire story anew— as if Alain had never heard it before—a ritual repetition that felt almost religious, a terrifying pagan religion in which Isabelle was both goddess and sorceress.

"Isabelle deserves to die," Jean-Luc had whispered, his voice always trembling with pleasure and then fading to a wistful sadness, because it was a pleasure to be postponed, like that of lovers unable yet to share their passion. "But, until the missing princess is found, Isabelle must live. She will lead us to her daughter and then they both must die."

As they had stood before the portrait of Isabelle, Jean-Luc had commanded solemn promises from the boy who would one day be Prince of L'île. "You must make it your mission, Alain, to find the princess and see that she is destroyed. L'île belongs to you, my son, and to your little sister. Natalie need never know the threat exists. You must protect L'île, and you must protect her. It is your duty. Swear to me that you will."

Alain had made the promises, knowing full well the only vow he would ever keep was to protect his half sister, and he spent the next six years tormented by the eventual consequences of his lies. Surely the blatant lies to his father would doom him to hell, and he would spend eternity with the man he hated.

When he was sixteen, Alain—Alain's soul—escaped the torment; because, when he was sixteen, he discovered that he was not Jean-Luc's son. It was an assignment to be completed over the Christmas holidays, while he was home from the exclusive boarding school in Switzerland where he spent the school year with other sons of princes and kings. He was to make a diagram of his royal pedigree, with eye and hair color, and handedness, and blood types, if available. His mother's blood type existed somewhere, kept because she was the mother of the future monarch, although he did not dare ask Jean-Luc's permission to search for it. But he did learn Jean-Luc's blood type: O. There was no doubt. Only a month before, Jean-Luc had been shot, a nonlethal wound from a now dead enemy, and he had required blood transfusions. Jean-Luc's blood type was O; and, as Alain already knew from class, repeating the test twice because it was so rare, his own blood type was AB. Which meant that Jean-Luc could not be his father.

Alain returned to Switzerland with a falsified pedigree, assigning type A to Jean-Luc and type B to his mother. Ten years later, when one of Jean-Luc's enemies finally succeeded in killing him and Alain returned to L'île as Prince, he found his mother's medical records and discovered that at least part of the pedigree had been true: Geneviève Castille's blood type had been B. Alain unsealed a second set of medical records, desperately hoping to learn that he wasn't an impostor prince after all, but instead the son of Alexandre, the older brother of the missing princess, and hence L'île's most legitimate heir. How joyfully he would search for his missing little sister then! But Alexandre's blood type, typed repeatedly because of all the transfusions he had received as he was dying of leukemia, was O, like Jean-Luc's.

There was not a drop of Castille blood in Alain's veins. He was neither half brother to Natalie nor cousin to the missing princess. He was an impostor. He should have told Natalie; but she was only seventeen when Jean-Luc died, too young and innocent to deal with the empire of terror that was her father's legacy. And he should have told Isabelle and offered to help her in her search for L'île's legitimate monarch; but he only told the men Jean-Luc had assigned to shadow her to cease their ominous vigil.

Alain told no one. He only waited, and with each passing day he grew more confident that his secret would be safe forever. It was his destiny, he decided to believe, to rule the island he loved so much. He was the rightful owner, even though an impostor prince, because it was he who had lovingly restored L'île after Jean-Luc's reign of destruction, he who had enabled the island's beauty to bloom anew, like a hopeful spring flower awakening from the harshest of winters.

In the seven years of his reign, Alain had come to believe that L'île was truly his kingdom.

And now he was looking at the woman who could take it all away from him. Alain was certain it was she. She had Isabelle's lovely face and her brilliant blue eyes, and, most telling of all, she wore the same sapphire necklace that Isabelle had worn in the portrait. Jean-Luc had obviously not known that Isabelle had given the necklace to her daughter, but nonetheless, he had spent hours raving about the fortune Alexandre had spent finding the perfect gems. What foolishness! he had scoffed. What silly romanticism for a woman who should have been—as all women should be—simply a possession, to have, to use, but never to treasure. This was the same necklace, Alain had no doubt. His trained eyes appreciated the rare color and quality of the precious stones even through the opera glasses. And there were earrings, too, never mentioned by Jean-Luc, but quite obviously designed as companions to the necklace.

Alain knew other details about Isabelle's daughter: her age, her date of birth in a Chicago hospital, her disappearance sometime in the next four weeks along a path that meandered between Chicago and New York. He glanced at the program, a final desperate hope, but the brief biography of the gifted twenty-two-year-old from Kansas only confirmed what he already knew. It was she, the woman who could take from him all that he loved, and who could, as her father had done to Jean-Luc, banish him from L'île forever.

Catherine Taylor obviously did not know of her birthright. Perhaps she did not even know of her adoption. Would she stumble on the truth as she traveled throughout Europe, dazzling the most dazzling royalty with her great gift? Would Rainier, perhaps, be struck by her similarity to Isabelle and even give a frowning glance to the necklace? Yes, but her lovely face and the extraordinary necklace would evoke only fleeting ripples of emotion, vague bittersweet feelings that would vanish long before they became thoughts. And even if a thought formed—How much she looks like Isabelle Castille!—it would go no farther than an intriguing impression. Because no one, Alain was quite certain, knew that Alexandre and Isabelle had had a child. And what about Isabelle herself? What if *she* happened to see this daughter who was so obviously her own? But Isabelle lived a quiet life in the country, with her husband, almost never venturing from her secluded Loire Valley château.

You are safe, Alain assured himself. Catherine Taylor does not know who she is, and there is no one but you who can tell her.

Twenty-two years before, when ten-year-old Alain had sensed danger for Isabelle, he had vanquished his own fear and bravely intervened. Now all the danger was for him, and it was wise, and not uncourageous, to quietly flee.

But Alain was drawn to Catherine. He needed to meet his beautiful enemy.

"Do you remember where the reception is?" Alain asked Natalie as the applause following Catherine's second encore finally began to fade.

"At the Imperial Hotel. Why, Alain, are you thinking we should go?"

"You sound so surprised."

"Just because my older brother's aversion to such things, unless protocol mandates, is legendary?" she teased.

Alain conceded her point with a fond smile. It was quite true that, although just as legendary were his regal graciousness and elegant charm, he almost always greatly preferred privacy to lavish galas; he almost always chose a quiet dinner by himself, or with his little sister, over mingling with strangers. But tonight was an exception, because of the black-haired, blue-eyed stranger who wasn't really a stranger at all.

"I'd like to meet Catherine Taylor," he explained calmly to Natalie's smiling, interested eyes.

"She's really gifted, isn't she?"

"Yes."

"And very beautiful."

"I suppose she is. I thought I might ask her to join us for a late supper after the reception."

"But surely she will already have plans for this evening."

"Yes. Well, tomorrow then," Alain said quietly with a small smile, a gentle apology, although most of his handsome face was set in stony resolve. He had not forgotten that he and Natalie were scheduled to fly to Paris in the morning to meet with the jewellers at the Castille boutique in the Place Vendôme, but his dark eyes sent a clear message that this was more important. "I would like to hear her play again anyway."

"You and your music, Alain!" Natalie replied with a soft tease. She teased because she knew quite well that a pout would not change Alain's mind, nothing would, and she had no wish to annoy him. "*Bien!* But I'm going on to Paris as scheduled. The designers are expecting us—"

"—you—"

"They like to see you."

"I'll come the day after tomorrow."

"Saturday?"

"We'll make a special trip next month. *D'accord?*"

"*D'accord.*"

The reception celebrating Catherine Taylor's debut performance in Vienna was held in the Grande Salon of the Imperial Hotel. The guest list boasted the rich, the famous, the noble, and the royal; an elite assembly of people whose love of music was as authentic as the original designer gowns and glittering flawless gems they wore. They had come to honor Catherine, because these elegant patrons of the arts were authentically grateful that she had honored them with her great gift.

By the time Natalie and Alain arrived, Catherine was already surrounded by admirers. She smiled softly, graciously, at the lavish words of praise, receiving each new compliment with almost surprised gratitude. *Like the true princess she is*, Alain thought uneasily, observing her demure graciousness from a short distance away as he and Natalie politely waited for an opportunity to approach her. Catherine stood with quiet, regal dignity, straight and proud in a long gown of pale blue silk, her midnight black hair swirled atop her head in rich, luxuriant curls. The legitimate princess of L'île des Arcs-en-ciel didn't wear a crown of jewels, of course, only the stunning sapphires at her neck and ears; but as the chandelier's golden light filtered through its crystal prisms, the luminous gold was transformed into brilliant colors that fell on her shining black hair like a glittering crown of rainbows.

Alain and Natalie would have politely awaited their turn to meet the virtuoso. But when the reception's hostess, a baroness, spotted them, her aristocratic face registered such pure delight that they had come that the other guests surrounding Catherine followed her delighted gaze, and, also recognizing the Prince and Princess allowed them to approach at once.

Catherine watched with appreciative interest as Alain and Natalie drew near. Such a stunning couple, she thought. He, tall, dark, and handsome, and so elegant in the black silk tuxedo; and she, an auburn-haired vision of grace and beauty in her flowing gown of spun-gold chiffon.

"May I introduce Princess Natalie," the baroness beamed happily.

"Hello." Catherine smiled warmly at the remarkable gold-flecked brown eyes that smiled warmly in return.

"And Prince Alain," the baroness added.

"Oh." Catherine's voice filled with soft surprise when she heard his name. "Natalie" by itself hadn't triggered any memories, but combined with "Alain" it certainly did. "From L'île des Arcs-en-ciel?"

"Yes," Alain replied quietly, even though his heart pounded uneasily at the sudden sadness in her sapphire eyes. It was sadness, not possessiveness, he thought, but quite clearly L'île meant something to Catherine Taylor, something he needed to find out, something, perhaps, that Natalie should not hear. Alain immediately abandoned plans to even ask about a late supper tonight. He and Catherine would dine together, sometime. He would stay in Vienna until they did.

Alain and Natalie and Catherine talked for a while, about her performance, about Vienna, about the priceless tapestries that lined the salon walls. Finally, because he knew that there were others waiting patiently to meet her, Alain asked Catherine if she would like to have dinner with him the following night.

Yes, she told him without hesitation. Catherine knew Alain had sensed something in her reaction to L'île, and that it had worried him, and that she needed to explain about Marion and Arthur. And she knew, too, that it needed to be done quietly and in private, not in the midst of this festive gala. Her performance for the following day would be in the afternoon, so they agreed that Alain would call for her at her hotel at eight.

They chatted a little longer, and then Alain and Natalie were gone, and Catherine met a hundred more dazzling people; and it was only much later, in the privacy of her suite, that she had a chance to reflect on the fact that she had made plans to dine with a handsome prince. In the past six months, as she touched all corners of North America with her breathtaking talent, Catherine had been wined and dined by the very rich and very famous, and she had become quite expert at communicating with beautiful gracious smiles and very few words.

But did that mean she was now the sophisticated woman she had imagined herself becoming as she had gazed for the first time at the midnight glitter of Manhattan? Yes, perhaps she was that woman, at least on the surface. She was quite fearless now, unafraid of glamorous new cities and glamorous new people—even the most handsome of princes. Her cheeks didn't flush pink with sudden embarrassment any more, and the wide-eyed innocence had long since vanished from her sapphire eyes, and the rich black curls that had once been a necessary veil for those timid blue eyes were pulled bravely off her face and twirled into lustrous knots of black silk on top of her head. That elegant calm gave her the look, the *illusion*, of sophistication, she supposed. But, of course, she knew the truth. The look of unblushing serenity came simply, painfully, from the loss of her love.

A truly sophisticated woman wouldn't love, *still*, a man who didn't love her, would she? No, absolutely not. Nor would she unknot the elegant chignons, allowing the long black hair to cascade over her shoulders and be caressed by the wind, *as if she were sailing*, as she walked for hours on end trying to soothe the emotional wounds that were reopened every time she played her music.

Catherine knew she wasn't sophisticated, not really, but still it was now possible for her to conceal her shyness and her fear beneath the elegant calm and to dine with a handsome prince. She needed to see Alain again, to explain that she had known Marion and Arthur; but, astonishingly, she was looking forward to their dinner. Why was dining with Alain suddenly more appealing than the long solitary walk that had become almost necessary after each emotionally exhausting performance? Why? Because, astonishingly, almost immediately, she had felt comfortable with him.

But why? . . . *Mais pourquoi?*

And then she knew: because the so very comfortable conversation with Alain Castille had been in French. The baroness's introduction had been in English, she was certain of that. But, at some point, they had shifted to French. Which one of them, Alain or she, had spoken the first word in the beautiful language of love? Catherine couldn't remember. But why hadn't Alain remarked on her flawless French? Surely it must have been a surprise to hear such fluency from a country girl from Kansas.

Perhaps, Catherine mused, Alain hadn't realized, as she hadn't, until after. She wondered if he, like she, had been struck by how wonderfully comfortable their conversation had been.

Catherine frowned slightly, a frown of surprise not worry, when she entered her elegant suite at seven the following evening. The heavy brocade drapes were drawn, blocking out the summer twilight and the view of the gardens below. On previous evenings, the maids had left the drapes open, and she had stood by the windows and watched the drama of the sky fade from blue to pink to gray. Now the room was dark and shadowy. Well, she couldn't have lingered tonight anyway, and the drapes needed to be drawn while she got ready for her dinner with Alain.

As Catherine crossed the suite toward the dressing room, one of the shadows came alive, leaping at her as she passed. She sensed the soundless motion, but before she could turn toward it she was trapped by strong arms, restraining her and holding a rag tightly—too tightly, she couldn't breathe!—over her nose and mouth.

Just before she was enveloped by darkness, Catherine saw the faces of the people she loved, and in her mind she called to them, I love you, Mom. I love you, Dad. I love you, Alexa.

I love you, James.

"Catherine!" She was in a dream from which she could not awaken. Above her, beyond the dream, voices were calling to her, anxious voices, and one that was more calm, and vaguely familiar, a comforting voice that spoke to her in French.

"Alain," she whispered as her heavy lids opened, finally, to his beckoning voice.

"Are you all right, Catherine?"

"Yes. I guess. What happened . . . ?" As she asked the question, she felt a strange hot dampness on her neck and reached to touch it—blood! And there was even more blood, she realized as she stared at her delicate fingers, because there were cuts on them as well.

"A burglar," the hotel's security chief answered, his voice filled with relief that she had awakened and deep chagrin at what had happened. Catherine Taylor was not the only victim of theft this evening. The burglar had stolen a passkey from a maid; and while the maid had frantically searched for it, thinking she had simply carelessly misplaced it, he had entered several suites, all uninhabited except Catherine's, and stolen money, gems, and watches. The chief continued in French, because that was the language the beautiful woman spoke to the Prince, "Mademoiselle Taylor, je suis désolé."

As the ether that had caused her swift unconsciousness began to wear off, Catherine's understanding of what had happened to her became crystal clear. She had surprised the burglar, who, after subduing her with ether and a knife had stolen the sapphire necklace that she had only just started wearing, a symbol of a love that might have existed after all. Now the necklace was gone, and gone, too, were the sapphire earrings, another symbol from another love. Her earlobes were unhurt, without blood or pain. The burglar had obviously been familiar with expensive gems and their settings and had taken the time to carefully unscrew the gold backings from their delicate posts.

"I would like to take her to the hospital now," the hotel's doctor said. "Thankfully, the knife wounds are superficial, but they need to be cleaned and sutured. And even though it appears that her unconsciousness was due to the ether, not a blow to the head, I would like to observe her overnight in the hospital."

"May I come in?"

"Alain. Yes, of course." It had been hours since she had been taken by ambulance from the hotel to the hospital, hours that she had spent, until now, attended by a careful and thorough team of doctors and nurses. Had Alain been waiting all this time?

"How are you, Catherine?"

"I'm fine. I think this night in the hospital is quite unnecessary, but . . ."

"Better to be safe."

"Yes. I guess." Her smile faded slightly as she followed his concerned dark brown eyes to her bandaged hands. "The cuts weren't deep, no damage to nerves or tendons, but the doctors say it will be several weeks before I can play again."

"Will you return to the States?"

"I'm not sure. I haven't thought that far ahead yet."

"Well, then, may I suggest that you spend at least part—and hopefully all—of your convalescence on L'île?"

"On L'île?"

"The tranquil beauty of the island can cure the deepest of wounds. Do you know about L'île, Catherine? Not everyone does, but I got the impression when we met that you had some special knowledge." *What do you know, Princess Catherine, about your magical kingdom of rainbows?*

"Not a special knowledge, Alain. It's just that I knew Marion and Arthur Sterling."

"Oh," Alain whispered softly. "How?"

"My sister Alexa and their son James are very close. Last summer, I spent a weekend at Arthur and Marion's home in Maryland. They were such wonderful people."

"Yes, they were. Their death was a great tragedy." Alain's expression grew solemn and reflective, adding strength and detracting nothing from his handsomeness. After a moment he asked gently, "Does the remembered sadness of their death make you reluctant to visit L'île, Catherine?"

"No, just the opposite, Alain. I would very much like to see the paradise Arthur and Marion loved so much."

CHAPTER TWENTY-THREE

L'île des Arcs-en-ciel
July 1990

"*The* Prince is in Vienna until tomorrow," James was told when his call was connected to Alain's private secretary. The secretary recognized James's name, of course, and immediately extended the gracious welcome that Alain had promised in his letter of condolence. "But the Princess is in residence, *monsieur*, and she will be so pleased to receive you today."

When James arrived at the palace an hour later, he was escorted from the main entrance through a marble courtyard ablaze with bougainvillea and into a private sitting room overlooking the sea. The vista was a tableau of brilliant shades of shimmering blue—as the bright azure sky kissed the sunlit sapphire sea. Breathtakingly beautiful, James thought, a thought he had had a hundred times during the three days he had already spent wandering around L'île. Truly a paradise . . .

"Monsieur Sterling?"

James turned from the breathtaking natural beauty to yet another of L'île's extraordinary treasures—Princess Natalie Castille. There was indeed a great richness about her, the beautiful light brown eyes flecked with gold, the aristocratic features that were at once delicate and sensuous, the luxuriant mane of auburn hair that glittered with all the colors of fire.

"Your Highness."

"Please call me Natalie."

"I'm James."

"How terrible we—my brother Alain and I—feel about your parents, James. They were such very lovely people." Natalie spoke softly and emotionally. Her voice was elegant, accented only with the accent of impeccable education, and her English was flawless, although, because she spoke it so infrequently, slightly formal. "We anticipated their visit, and yours, last Christmas with much joy. How fortunate that you weren't with them on the sailboat."

As Natalie spoke the last words, her expression was both sympathetic and wise—as if she well knew that there had been times in the tormented months of rage since his parents' murder that James had wondered if he had truly been fortunate to have escaped death himself. After a solemn moment, she freed her beautiful face of all sadness and asked, "Have you just arrived? Alain and I hope that you will stay here, at the palace, during your visit."

"I actually arrived a few days ago. I have a magnificent room at the hotel."

"A few days ago. Have you spent those days exploring the island?"

"Yes. I think I've walked along every beautiful path."

"Searching for clues?" Natalie asked softly, without censure.

"Clues?"

"Our father was a very evil man, James," she said quietly. "Alain and I know that. We lived with his madness, after all. We understand the scrutiny that must be given us as his children. It is part of his legacy to us. Although Alain and I never speak of it, I know we have both searched our own souls fearing that we will find some trace of Jean-Luc's evil within us." Smiling softly, she added, "I believe that we have both escaped his madness. Our true inheritance is this tranquil island, not our father's treachery. My half brother is not a terrorist, James. You will see that at once when you meet him. So, you have searched for clues and found nothing sinister. But, has anyone given you a guided tour?"

"No."

"Then it shall be my pleasure to tell you the stories that accompany the mystical beauty of our island. Alain will not be back until noon tomorrow. If you like, since you have already walked all the paths, in the morning we can sail and you can view the island from the sea."

For the rest of the afternoon and during an elegant dinner that evening at the palace, Natalie told James the enchanting myths and legends of L'île. The following morning, as he expertly guided Alain's sleek sailboat across the shimmering sea, she told him about the not-so-enchanting childhood of the children of Jean-Luc Castille.

"The palace was like a fortress under siege. There were heavily armed guards everywhere, in every room, at every corner, behind every door."

"And now there are no armed guards at all."

"No. No guards for the palace and no bodyguards for Alain or me. It's an obvious reaction to a childhood in which there was so very little freedom. Alain and I enjoy great freedom now, but we are careful, of course, because our wealth makes us targets for kidnapping. We avoid excessive publicity, and whenever we leave L'île, we always travel in our own jets."

"More than one jet?"

"Yes," Natalie admitted with a sparkling smile. "We each have one. Alain and I like to travel together, but there are times—such as now—when he wanted to remain in Vienna and I needed to go to Paris on business. We began the trip in his jet but had to call for mine."

"It sounds as though you and Alain are very good friends."

"Yes, we are. I suppose we're like soldiers bonded by war. And yet," she added thoughtfully, "although Alain and I had similar childhoods, we didn't actually *share* the experience. Alain is six years older than I. From an early age, he was sent off to schools for princes and kings. We had almost nothing to do with each other until I was a teenager. I was in boarding school by then, too, and I was considered quite wild. My wildness was really little more than normal teenage behavior, but was nonetheless regarded as unbecoming a princess."

"More infringement on normal freedoms."

"Yes. I was rebelling, I suppose, and trying, too, to get attention. No one here even noticed, except, to my great surprise, my older quite proper and quite princely brother. Alain and I became friends then, even though my wildness didn't instantly vanish. More than once Alain had to ride in on his white charger and prevent me from a foolish and defiant marriage. He still protects me, although I'm long since grown and not the least bit wild any more."

"Not about to plunge into an unwise marriage?"

"Oh no." Natalie smiled an untroubled smile. "Not about to plunge into any marriage. I'm only twenty-six, so there's no rush, but I'm not sure I ever will marry.

My vision of marriage is far from appealing. Alain's mother died shortly after his birth—and Jean-Luc forbade anyone to mention her name—and the relationship between my mother and Jean-Luc was turbulent at best. There is, of course, historical precedent for daughters of such tyrannical monarchs as Henry the Eighth never choosing to marry."

"Indeed. And what about Alain? Will he ever marry?"

"Eventually he will, he *must*, to father L'île's next ruler. But I don't think it will be for a very long time. Alain was engaged to be married once."

"Oh?"

"Yes. Her name was Monique. She was with French intelligence, a beautiful secret agent sent to investigate Alain shortly after Jean-Luc died."

"Alain knew that?"

"Not before he fell in love with her."

"And he was furious when he discovered her true identity?"

"Furious? No. Alain never gets furious."

"Did you ride in on your white charger and put an end to his foolishness?"

"Oh, no. I was thrilled about Monique. She was very lovely and very much in love with Alain. It would have been a perfect marriage. Monique told Alain the truth, and they planned to marry, but . . ." Natalie's beautiful face clouded with sadness. "She and Alain were driving from Saint Paul de Vence to Monte Carlo. There was a terrible car accident and Monique died."

"Was Alain injured?"

"No. He and Monique were driving in separate cars. They had planned to return one of the cars to the airport in Nice en route to Monaco. Alain was following her when the accident occurred. He was merely a helpless witness to the horrible tragedy." She shook her head softly at the devastating image. "Alain will marry someday, to give L'île its next monarch, but I am quite certain that he will never again plan to marry for love."

"Natalie is sailing," Alain said, gesturing toward the boat in the distance as they drove from the landing strip to the palace. "Do you sail, Catherine?"

"Yes." At least I used to, she amended silently. I used to sail with the man I love . . . *loved*. She banished the memory, or maybe it was simply banished for her, because as she turned her eyes to the beauty of the island, Catherine felt the most amazing sense of peace. She whispered softly, "Alain."

"I knew that you would like it."

Throughout the breathtaking drive and as he showed her the elegant marble palace, Catherine simply whispered, over and over, Alain, *Oh, Alain*, as she marvelled at the splendor.

"And this, Catherine, is the music room. You can practice here once your fingers begin to heal."

"*C'est magnifique.*"

"*Oui. D'accord.* It is my favorite room in the palace. From here, while you're sitting at the piano, you can see the rainbows. They are right there, close enough to touch, and they fill this entire window."

"And where is the cave? Marion said there was a cave that was once filled with precious jewels—glittering splinters from the rainbows."

"It's just beyond that hill. If you like, I'll take you there."

"Oh, yes, I would like that."

"Marion told you the legend of the rainbows, Catherine, but did she tell you the truth about the treasure trove of jewels?"

"Yes, she did. But now that I'm here on this magical island, Alain, I think I believe that the wonderful legend is really true," she answered softly. After a moment, she returned her gaze to the azure sky which, in just a few hours, would suddenly scowl with dark storm clouds, and then would cry warm, nourishing tears, and then, the tempest over, would smile again, the brilliant azure now gift-wrapped with rainbows.

As Alain saw Catherine's obvious enchantment with the island—*her* island—he remembered the confession he had made to Marion Sterling, borrowing from Balzac, "Behind every great fortune there is a crime." There had been many thieves in L'île des Arcs-en-ciel's royal family. There were the ancient Castilles, who plundered the tiny vessels laden with treasure chests of gold and gems as they made their dangerous voyages along the trade routes from the Orient. And there was the modern Castille, Jean-Luc, who had plundered hope and dreams and beauty and peace.

But now, even though no Castille blood flowed in his veins, it was he, Alain, who proved to be the greatest thief of them all. Because it was he, the impostor prince, who had stolen by far the most precious treasure—the magnificent island itself.

"Alain!"

Alain smiled with relief as Natalie's voice interrupted his troubling thoughts. Catherine smiled too in anticipation of seeing Alain's sister again. But as she turned her smile faltered.

"James."

"Hello, Catherine," James replied softly, as startled as she. Natalie had mentioned that Alain might be returning from Vienna with a guest, but . . .

Now here was Catherine. She was so beautiful still, so very beautiful, but in the almost seven months since he had said good-bye to their love, she had changed. Her blushing innocence was gone, and her sapphire eyes seemed so wary and watchful, as if on alert for someone who might hurt her. *Oh, Catherine, I never meant to hurt you!* James wanted her to see that message in his eyes, but she wouldn't hold his gaze. Finally, reluctantly, his own troubled blue eyes fell, and when they did there was a new worry. The white gauze bandage on her neck had been hidden by the black velvet hair which, much longer now, tumbled in a luxuriant cascade of soft curls almost to her breasts. But as she had tilted her head, *shying away from him*, he saw a corner of the bandage.

"What happened?"

"I . . . Oh, James, you haven't met Alain."

The two men greeted each other with polite formality, and Alain offered sympathetic words about Marion and Arthur, and then the conversation returned to Catherine's wounds.

"A burglar entered Catherine's suite at her hotel in Vienna and stole her jewels from her," Alain explained quietly.

"Oh, no," Natalie whispered.

"I'm not badly hurt," Catherine assured. "The burglar used ether, but he had a knife, too, and I must have struggled before the drug took effect. The cuts on my neck and fingers aren't deep, everything will heal, but it will be a few weeks before I can resume the concert tour."

"And will you spend those weeks here, with us, I hope."

"Thank you, Natalie. Alain, too, has made that very generous offer." Catherine had accepted Alain's offer for "a few days only," although until James had appeared she had already been wondering if she would ever want to leave this beautiful, peaceful place. But now the peace was shattered, and she wanted, needed, to get away from the dark blue eyes that were staring at her with such gentle concern.

"What was stolen, Catherine?" Natalie asked. Then, frowning, she added, "Not that magnificent necklace you wore at the concert, I hope. I noticed it, of course. The color and quality of the sapphires were exquisite."

"Yes. The sapphire necklace was stolen, as were a pair of sapphire earrings." Catherine looked at James then, a brave look of proud defiance. Yes, James, I wore the earrings still. I didn't wear them because of some foolish hope that you would return to me, but as a memory of a love that meant so very much to me . . . even though it did not have the same meaning for you.

"You must let us replace the stolen jewels," Natalie said. "I have a memory of the necklace and with your memory, too, I should be able to sketch it. And the earrings—"

"Thank you, Natalie, but no," Catherine replied, her refusal polite yet firm, just as it had been when Alain had made the same gracious offer. "I don't plan to replace either of them. Both the necklace and the earrings were symbols of distant memories . . . and I think the time has come to let those memories go."

"Then you must let me design something else for you," Natalie offered. "A symbol of a new memory—your first visit to L'île—created from all the colors of the rainbow."

Following the lavish luncheon in the palace's summer dining room, Natalie and Alain retreated to his study for a brief but necessary discussion of her trip to the Castille boutique in Paris, leaving Catherine and James alone. After a few moments of silence, in which sapphire met dark blue briefly and then fell, Catherine turned away from him and walked to the window overlooking the sea. She tried to find peace in the tranquil beauty, but it was impossible, because she was so aware of him, across the room . . . and then standing behind her.

"I'm going to leave as soon as Natalie and Alain return," James said quietly. "I just wanted to say good-bye."

"Good-bye," she whispered, without turning to face him, as her heart cried, How many times must we say good-bye, James?

"Catherine?"

She had to turn then, because she had always been compelled to follow the soft commands of his voice, and when she did she met dark blue eyes that were filled with concern.

"May I look?" he asked gently as he gestured to the bandages on her neck.

How she ached at his gentleness, for his gentleness. Oh, James, please go away! But Catherine knew that he wouldn't leave until she had complied with his request, so she began to reach for the tape that secured the white gauze to her snow white skin. But her delicate fingers were clumsy now, wrapped in bulky bandages themselves, and trembling, because of him; and finally it was his strong and tender fingers, trembling, too, that gently peeled back the gauze.

James saw that the wound was superficial, just as she had said it was. The burglar's razor sharp knife had made a thin straight incision, almost surgical, across the right side of her lovely neck. In time, the scar would be almost invisible, a slender white thread the color of her skin; but now the wound was dark red, a vivid reminder of the recent violence. As James looked at the wounds, he felt powerful rushes of anger at whoever had harmed her, and an even more powerful—but impossible—wish to be with her and to protect her always.

"I had the impression earlier, as you were describing what happened, that you didn't remember struggling with the knife," he said finally.

"No, I don't remember struggling—I don't even have a clear memory of the knife—but I must have struggled." As she answered, Catherine pulled away from the oh-so-painful tenderness of his touch and firmly pressed the tape back onto her neck.

"You have to be so careful," he said softly.

"I *am* careful, James," she countered swiftly, amazed at the swiftness and effortlessness of her lie. She wasn't careful at all, of course. She wandered the dark streets of unknown cities at all hours of the night, oblivious to her surroundings and the lurking dangers, wholly absorbed in the impossible task of trying to free her heart from the memories of love, of him.

"Good. I'm glad," he said gently, wanting impossible wishes, but knowing the truth, that he had to leave soon, *now*, for himself, for his heart, and, as was so painfully clear from the wary sapphire eyes, *for her*. "Well. I'd better go. I'll find Alain's study and say good-bye to them on my way out."

"James?"

"Yes?"

"Thank you for calling me about Alexa. I went to see her—I suppose you've talked to her and already know that." Catherine fought yet another wave of pain as his blue eyes told her, gently, apologetically, that yes, he did already know. "Anyway, we're close now, very close, and I just wanted to thank you."

"You're welcome."

"And James?"

"Yes?"

"Thank you for helping her. I should have been there for her and I wasn't . . . but you were. I'm very sorry that I was angry with you about that."

As he gazed at the woman he would always love, James wondered if she had other regrets. Did she regret her suggestion that he marry Alexa? Did she regret that their love was just a memory whose time had come to be forgotten? The questions were self-indulgent *and* self-destructive, because he already knew the answers. From the first moment she had seen him again, Catherine's beautiful sapphire eyes had quite eloquently conveyed their wariness of him, and it had been very obvious that she was far, far away from their love.

Which is where she should be, James reminded himself sternly. I have nothing to offer her. And even though I will never forget it, will never want to, it is best for lovely Catherine that she is able to forget our magical love.

After a moment he whispered softly, "Good-bye, Catherine."

"I think, Catherine, that Alexa was not the only sister who was very close to James Sterling," Alain suggested quietly a week later.

They were sitting on the cliff above the sea watching the splendor of the rainbows. They had come here every afternoon, while the sun was still golden in the azure sky, and when the storm clouds gathered and the rain began to fall, they sought shelter in the nearby gazebo. They weathered the storm there, warm and dry in the midst of nature's torrential drama. As soon as the rain relented, they returned to the cliff's very edge, as close as they could be to the rainbows that were born in the sapphire sea and arched above them, a canopy of the most brilliant colors, as they reached to the legendary cave of glittering gems at the center of L'île's tropical emerald forest.

Every afternoon Alain and Catherine had come here to share the splendor of the rainbows; and to share, too, quiet words and gentle smiles. Catherine felt so comfortable with Alain, and so wonderfully safe—a safety and comfort which, she knew, went far beyond the simple, effortless joy of speaking to him in French. Alain was like L'île itself, she had decided. Warm, and welcoming, and possessed with wondrous powers of healing. Here, on this enchanted island of rainbows, her knife wounds were healing far more quickly than the doctors had predicted; and here, too, even her broken heart was finally beginning to mend. All her wounds were healing here, because of the wondrous healing powers of the island, and the wondrous healing powers of its gentle Prince.

They had shared the splendor of the rainbows, and quiet words and gentle smiles. And now, quietly and gently, Alain was asking her about the secret love that had been known only to herself, and to James. Would she share that painful secret of her heart with Alain? Yes, she thought as she drew her sapphire eyes from the shimmering rainbows to him. I will share that secret, and perhaps others, with you, Alain. But what of *your* troubling secrets, gentle Prince? I know you have them, and that they torment you, even though you artfully conceal them in the shadows of your dark eyes. Will you, in time, trust me enough to tell me? I hope so. And, in the meantime, I will trust you.

"You are right, Alain," she began softly. "Alexa was not the only sister who was close to James. I was once very much in love with him myself . . ."

CHAPTER TWENTY-FOUR

Washington, D.C.
September 1990

𝒯he days were unusually warm for mid-September in Washington, but on either side of daylight the crisp air sent whispers of autumn, promises of rust-colored leaves, golden harvest moons, cozy woolen scarves, and bright rosy cheeks. For Robert, as he jogged along the Potomac and inhaled the cool dawn air, the unmistakable taste of autumn triggered memories of love. He had spent last autumn loving Alexa, and he had been with her on glorious mornings like this, tenderly and reluctantly kissing her good-bye as the sun began to lighten the autumn sky.

Robert didn't need the autumn air to remind him of Alexa, of course. She was with him always. But now, as he inhaled, he felt himself succumbing to the restless urgings he had battled all summer. He needed to talk to her, if she would agree. He needed her to show him the woman she had claimed to be, the woman for whom their love had been simply a game.

Robert needed to be shown that woman, because still, no matter how hard he tried, whenever he conjured up images of Alexa, he only saw visions of love.

* * *

A long night of filming lay ahead for the cast and crew of *Pennsylvania Avenue*, which was why, the director announced, they would take a full hour for the dinner break. The break was only ten minutes old when the stage manager knocked on the door of Alexa's dressing room.

"Senator Robert McAllister is here to see you," he announced with obvious enthusiasm when she opened the door.

"Senator McAllister?" Alexa echoed weakly.

"That's right! I think this is the first time he's ever stopped by."

Yes, Alexa thought, this is the first time the distinguished Senator from Virginia has ever visited the set of *Pennsylvania Avenue*. But why is he here now? Was he coming to tell her the truth at last? Or did he want to resume where they had left off, his marriage to Hillary rocky again, or perhaps so unshakably stable that he needed a little diversion?

If either of those was the reason, Alexa had no wish to see him. It was far too late to hear the truth she already knew, and even though she had once been so willing to spend her entire life loving him only in precious stolen moments, if that was all they could ever have, and even though she loved him still, resuming her affair with him was impossible. She had given her heart once to Robert, and it had been completely in his care. But now that fragile and broken thing, whose only signs of life were piercing quivers of pain, was hers again; and Alexa knew she had to protect it from further harm.

But what if Robert had somehow found out about Katie? What if his visit had something to do with her daughter's happiness? That terrifying worry made her own immense pain at seeing him again quite inconsequential.

"So, shall I tell him you'll see him?"

"Yes. I will see him."

In the few minutes before Robert knocked on her dressing room door, Alexa summoned all her talent and let her memory travel to the time before love when her emerald eyes had been able to flash with confident icy contempt at his arrogance.

But he didn't look arrogant now! His tired brown eyes looked only uncertain and sad. And the emerald ice, such a thin fragile layer, was melted instantly by the warmth inside her, the defiant embers of love that would not die.

"Hello, Alexa."

"Hello, Robert."

"I wondered," he began softly. "I wondered if, sometime, we could talk."

"Talk about what, Robert?"

"About us."

His voice was so gentle, but the words felt like the heaviest of weights, pressing down on her delicate shoulders and slender legs until she knew she could no longer bear the oppressive weight while standing. Somehow she willed her wobbly legs to move, away from him and to the nearby couch. But even when she was seated the weight was still there, bending her head, casting a most welcome curtain of golden silk across her face. Oh, Robert, I don't have the strength to talk about us. Once I prayed that no matter what the truth, you would tell me, as proof of our love and our trust, but now it's far too late. Just seeing you causes so much pain, too much.

After a moment, Robert moved beside her, and, after another moment, he very tenderly parted the silky gold. The gesture was painfully familiar to both of them, because this most gentle caress of love had been made so often after their passionate loving, when he needed once again to see her glowing emerald eyes. "Alexa?"

"Don't! Please." As she lifted her head in proud defiance, her gaze fell on the hand that had touched her. "You're not wearing your wedding ring."

Oh, Alexa, his heart cried. He had come to see the woman who had been playing with him, a woman who, had she even noticed the ring, would certainly never have cared. But that woman wasn't here. Only Alexa, the lovely, vulnerable woman whom he loved so desperately, was here.

"Oh, Alexa," he whispered softly. "Did it bother you that I wore the ring last fall? I didn't even think about it, darling. I should have. I'm very sorry."

"No, it didn't bother me," she truthfully told the so very worried, *so very beloved,* sensitive dark eyes. "But please, Robert, tell me why you're not wearing it now."

"You know why," he said gently, as delicate whispers of hope began to tremble deep within him. He gazed at her beautiful, confused face and said quietly, "Hillary and I are getting divorced. I told you that in December, darling, the night I returned from Camp David . . . the night I asked you to marry me."

"But it wasn't true!" *It can't be true!* the protest came from the heart that had suffered enough pain already; a heart that could not possibly endure learning that her precious daughter had been lost because of . . . *No!* She reminded him urgently, "You weren't at Camp David that weekend. You were in Dallas, with Hillary, in the bridal suite at the Mansion on Turtle Creek. Robert, I heard your voice!"

"No, my love. I was at Camp David, somehow keeping my mind on my work, but filled with such joy because Hillary had agreed to give me a quiet divorce." Robert's dark eyes were soft as he spoke of that remembered joy. But they hardened, as did his voice, when he spoke again. "Tell me what she did." *Tell me how Hillary destroyed that magnificent joy.*

"She came to RoseCliff on that Friday morning. She said that you had told her about our affair, and that you'd told her, too, that you'd only slept with me because of an affair she'd had that had hurt you deeply. She said you'd reconciled and were going to spend the weekend in Dallas, a second honeymoon, and I called . . ." Alexa couldn't continue, because his dark, angry eyes told her so painfully, so eloquently, that all Hillary's words had been lies.

"She must have recorded my voice," Robert said with quiet rage as he remembered. "Before I left for Camp David, there were repeated calls to my office in which the caller never spoke, but remained on the line." He paused, fighting the rage, amazed by its strength and its power, but needing now to say soft, gentle words to his love. "My marriage to Hillary was never really a marriage. I should have told you that, and that I was going to divorce her, but it never occurred to me that you didn't already know. I've never loved anyone but you, Alexa. I've never, not for one second, my darling, stopped loving you, and, I guess, I've never stopped dreaming that somehow, someday, you would agree to spend your life with me."

Robert drew a soft, shaky breath as he watched the golden curtain of silk fall once again across her beautiful face, intentionally cast as she bowed her head in response to his impassioned words of love. Was it too late? his heart cried. Had she stopped loving him? Had Hillary won after all? He believed he had seen love in the beautiful emerald eyes, but now . . . Now she was in hiding, where she wanted to be, and this time he couldn't part the silky curtain. This time, all he could do was wait until she was ready to tell him her decision.

I still love you, Robert. Oh, how I love you! The fragile, broken heart that had for so long been filled with pain cried now to be filled once again with love, only with love. But there were other emotions, powerful and dangerous and damaging, that vied for space in her delicate heart: rage, hatred, and bitterness toward Hillary, whose cruel trickery and deceit had cost her the loss of her daughter. Now as Alexa felt the rage and hatred and bitterness fight aggressively to establish firm footing in her fragile heart, some deep instinct, perhaps that wounded heart's deepest instinct for survival, warned her not to let those ravaging emotions in; because all the hatred and rage in the world would not change the truth: she had made a solemn promise of love never to reclaim Katie, and she would not ever break that solemn vow.

Alexa's damaged heart cried desperately to be filled only with the most gentle and joyous of love, and that was what she wanted, too. But how, *how*, could she possibly conquer the rage and hatred and bitterness that so boldly and so powerfully demanded their rightful place? Vanquishing the powerful and so damaging emotions seemed an impossible task, and she felt her gentle life of love with Robert becoming just a lovely dream very far beyond her reach . . .

But then, quite suddenly, Alexa was touched by a distant memory of love. The image of her twelve-year-old sister and her earnest sapphire eyes and her soft voice was clear and bright and so powerful that Alexa felt the angry emotions begin to miraculously melt away. She waited for many disbelieving moments, fearing that they would return with a vengeance, but they didn't; and finally she looked up to the man she loved.

"I think we should forgive Hillary," she said quietly, using the same words Cat had spoken to her so many years ago. Smiling lovingly at Robert's surprised and skeptical brown eyes, she continued, "That's advice my very wise little sister once gave me. She said that we should forgive Hillary, and that we should feel sorry for her, because she must be very unhappy to be so cruel. I want to forgive her, Robert. I need to. And, I guess, I do feel sorry for her, because she will never know the kind of happiness that we have. I've never been in love with anyone but you. James was, and is, my wonderful friend, but there has been nothing more than friendship since I fell in love with you. He was with me at the gala that night because I didn't have the strength to be there alone, knowing that I would see you with Hillary." She smiled at the dark eyes that now filled with such desire and such joy and said softly, "I've never stopped loving you either, Robert, not for a second."

"Oh, Alexa, I love you," he whispered emotionally as his tender hands cupped her beautiful face. His dark eyes met her emerald ones, joyfully mirroring her happiness and her love, and vanquishing all flickers of rage. Their eyes should have been exact mirror images, but, Robert realized, there was something else in Alexa's beautiful eyes, something that shouldn't have been there. He had seen it—the deep, deep pain—the moment he had first seen her again; but it should have been conquered now, by their wondrous love and joy, and yet it lingered, a ripple of pain and sadness very deep, but very real, in the glistening emerald. Lovely, generous Alexa could forgive, but there was obviously something she could not forget. He would love her, with every ounce of his soul, and someday she would share the sadness with him, and they would conquer it together or perhaps it would simply be loved away. But, until the pain vanished from the beloved emerald, he would never forgive Hillary for this unknown harm she had done to his lovely Alexa. He smiled at his beautiful love, wanting to love away all sadness, and whispered again, "I love you."

"Oh, Robert, I love you, too."

Their lips met and kissed the gentlest of hellos, a tender welcome home, my love, and a promise of forever. After a few loving moments, the kiss ended and she simply curled against him, where she needed to be, nestling as close as she could, safe in his strong and gentle arms. And, as her golden head rested softly against his chest, she heard the joyous songs of his heart, *Welcome home*.

Robert didn't speak for a while, swept by the immeasurable joy of the moment, holding her again, knowing it would be forever. Finally, when he was able to speak, he shared with her the new joy that would be a part of that wondrous forever happiness.

"In June, Brynne and Stephen adopted a baby girl. Did James tell you?"

"No," Alexa answered softly, because somehow her swirling mind remembered that James would never have revealed such a confidence. And then, she heard herself say, "How wonderful for them."

"So wonderful," Robert echoed, his lips gently caressing the golden head curled under his chin. "Oh, Alexa, wait until you meet little Katie. This summer, when I missed you so much, and I wondered how I would survive, I would drive to Richmond for the weekend, or even just for the day, and seeing that lovely little girl was an island of such peace and happiness."

There is so much love in Robert's gentle voice for his baby daughter! her heart cried. Alexa feared he might feel her trembling, but she couldn't pull away, not even a little, because then he might search for the eyes he must not see.

"Did I ever tell you, my darling Alexa, that I never believed my commitment to the vision of peace I have for the world could have become stronger or deeper than it was—but that it did the moment I fell in love with you?"

"No," she whispered, almost finding the courage to look up at him then, because those gentle words of love were more than enough to explain the tears that spilled so freely. But she didn't look up, and it was very lucky that she didn't, because of what he would have seen in the glistening emerald had he been gazing at her as he said the next . . .

"Well, it did. And after that, I was certain it would get no stronger. But it did, Alexa, the moment I first held Katie. She is so innocent, a joyous treasure of hope and promise. The first time I held her, I made a solemn promise that I would do whatever I could to make this world a peaceful, lovely place for her to spend her precious life."

Oh, Robert, I made solemn promises, too, to Katie, and to Brynne, and to my heart, and to you.

The dinner break ended far too quickly. But, he teased lovingly before leaving her dressing room, if she hadn't had to return to work, he would never have let her go, and then he wouldn't have been able to go to his apartment and get all his things so that they could begin tonight, at RoseCliff, to spend the rest of their lives together.

Robert needed to get his things, and he needed to talk to Hillary. He had hidden his rage, for Alexa; but as he remembered the anguished sadness in her eyes, the painful symbol of some unknown wound that was still unhealed despite the wondrous joy of their rediscovered love, the rage came back in dizzying waves, so strongly that he abandoned his plan to drive to Arlington. He would call her instead. He had no wish to see Hillary ever again, and, as the powerful waves swept through him, he became even a little afraid of what might happen if he did.

"I have to hand it to you, Hillary."

"Robert?" Hillary recognized his voice . . . barely. The usually rich voice was just a skeleton now, ice-cold and stripped of all warmth or compassion.

"I knew very well, from firsthand experience, how deceitful you could be, and how vain and selfish and spoiled you were. But I truly underestimated the extent to which you would go in order to get what you wanted."

"I *know* I haven't filed for the divorce yet, Robert! I should have, and I will. I promise."

"No, Hillary, *I* will file, as soon as possible," he said with the omniously quiet control of the most icy rage. "But let me make a promise to you, and believe me, it is a promise I will keep. The moment we are divorced, the moment I am finally free of you, I will marry Alexa, who I love with all my heart."

"Thompson!" Robert called to the man walking twenty feet ahead of him.

At the sound of his name, Thompson Hall turned around, and when he saw that the greeting had come from the party's favorite son, a warm, welcoming smile crossed his face. Robert was the shining star, the great hope, and as one of the party's top political strategists, Thompson was going to help make it happen. *Not*, he well knew, that Robert McAllister would need much help. Thompson would just be going along for the dazzling ride of power and prestige.

"Good morning, Robert."

"Good morning. Do you have a minute?"

"For you? Always."

They walked together to the privacy of Robert's office, chatting about nothing of consequence until the heavy oak door was closed securely behind them. Then Robert got right to the point.

"Hillary and I are getting divorced, Tom. My attorney will file the divorce papers at the Arlington courthouse either late this afternoon or first thing tomorrow morning. I imagine that the court reporters will notice the filing, so I wanted you and the PR people to know in advance. I doubt there will be more than a few ripples of curiosity, but it seems prudent to have an answer prepared."

"An answer? What possible answer can there be?"

"How about the truth? Hillary and I made the decision to divorce almost ten months ago. We stayed together until late May, in large part because of the celebration for Sam, and have been living apart since then."

"Robert, you really must rethink this."

"That's the truth, and frankly it's already far more than anyone really needs to know."

"No, I meant you need to rethink the divorce."

"I beg your pardon?"

"Divorcing Hillary is politically very unwise. Are you sure you can't come up with some arrangement short of divorce?"

"The reason I am telling you this, Tom, is to advise you. I am not asking for your advice. Hillary and I are getting divorced. Period. Marriages fail. The country is grown-up enough to accept that, and if not—"

"If not?"

"If not, there are many ways that I can help realize the visions we all share for the nation, and for the world, that do not require election to public office."

"You can't be serious."

"I am . . . absolutely." Robert gave a dismissive gesture, the subject closed, and then continued with an easy smile, "I probably should tell you now, to give you time to adjust since these revelations are clearly difficult for you, that I am planning to marry Alexa Taylor as soon as the divorce is final."

"Alexa Taylor? As in the star of *Pennsylvania Avenue?*"

"Yes." Robert paused, steadying his eyes and voice before speaking the next. He disliked the lie, any lie, but this had seemed so very important to Alexa that he had quickly and gently agreed to it. "Our relationship began this summer, after Hillary and I had already separated, and shortly after Alexa's return from her trip around the world. We've managed to keep our love quite private, and that's how we would like it to remain for as long as possible."

Thompson Hall staggered out of Robert's office as if he had been struck a close-to-lethal blow. The entire political party *had* been struck, of course, and for Thompson the blow was personal as well. As an advisor to the President he would wield enormous power, but if Robert McAllister's career was sabotaged by an unwise marriage . . .

Something had to be done. Thompson considered having the party's most influential leaders discuss the matter with Robert. Divorcing Hillary was bad enough, they would tell him, as Thompson had, but marrying Alexa Taylor was political suicide. Yes, of course, Alexa was a celebrity in her own right and immensely popular. And yes, there was the very recent precedent of a First Lady who had been an actress—not to mention her actor husband—but the Reagans had come from a different era in Hollywood altogether. An actress Alexa's age, Thompson knew, did not conform to the nation's image of a First Lady. But Thompson hadn't dared voice his own concerns about Alexa's suitability as a wife, and he guessed other party members might be equally reluctant.

The only hope, he realized, was Robert's fiancée herself. Alexa had to be approached carefully, diplomatically, he knew, and it was he who had to do it . . .

Alexa was just about to leave the studio when Thompson called. She had never met him, but she was well aware of his important role in the party, and well aware, too, that Robert had planned to tell him about both his divorce and their marriage. When Thompson said he needed to meet with her privately, Alexa told him that Robert wouldn't be home until very late and gave him directions to Rose-Cliff.

"This country needs Robert McAllister, Ms. Taylor."

"I know that, Mr. Hall."

"I hoped you did. That makes my mission a little easier."

"Your mission?" Alexa echoed uneasily.

"I need to ask you to reconsider your plans to marry Robert."

"I see. You believe that I'm a political liability?"

"I'm afraid that you are. You're an actress, Ms. Taylor. Although your lifestyle may be fascinating and glamorous to middle America . . ."

"It is not a lifestyle becoming a First Lady? A little too much sex and cocaine?"

"Alexa," Thompson soothed patiently, his voice gratingly condescending. "When Robert runs for President, the other party—the bad guys—will spare no expense to find out every detail of your life. They know that uncovering some distant scandal about you—nude photos taken when you were a starving young actress, an episode of experimentation with drugs—is their only hope of defeating Robert. They know they won't find skeletons in Robert's closet, so they'll make an exhaustively detailed search of yours."

"And they will find no skeletons, Thompson," Alexa soothed patiently in return, addressing him by his first name, as he had addressed her, and perfectly matching his tone of condescension. "I don't use drugs, and I never have. I was very lucky with my career. I never starved. I never had to make compromises."

"So every moment of your entire life could be replayed before the America public? Because it will be."

"Every moment. Yes."

"Well, great, that's an immense relief." He smiled broadly, but it was a political smile, not a genuine one, and it didn't diminish in the least as he added, "Then you won't mind at all that I'm having you investigated."

"You're *what?*"

"Having you investigated." Thompson's smile vanished as he observed with quiet menace, "And, apparently, you do mind. That suggests to me that there is something to be found."

"No. I very much resent, however, the invasion of my privacy, and I'm sure Robert won't stand for it."

"Robert would be annoyed as hell, but he *would* stand for it. Admittedly, I had hoped to keep this between the two of us, but if you want him to know, I can very easily defend my reason for having it done. As I told you, it's going to happen some-day, and it's just smart politics for us to find out in advance if there's something— perhaps an incident you've completely forgotten—that might be twisted in a way that could cause great harm. If we know in advance, we can control the damage and make sure the proper spin is put on the story. Robert would think it's premature for me to be doing this now, and he would be furious that I believe if we discover something truly damaging you should reconsider your marriage plans, but he knows full well it will be done eventually. So, Ms. Taylor, I can defend my reason for investigating you, but what is your defense for not wanting it done?"

"It annoys me, just as it would annoy Robert. Nothing more." Alexa gave a soft shrug, as if it couldn't matter less. "So, go ahead, have me investigated."

"Are you planning to tell Robert?"

"I guess not, as long as you agree to come to me first if you find anything at all that troubles you."

"I will come to you, providing you promise that if there is something which, in my judgment, would harm Robert's career, you will give your marriage plans serious reconsideration."

"That's an easy promise for me to make, Mr. Hall, because I know you will find nothing."

"Then I will be the first to wish you all the best in your marriage."

"Thank you." Alexa smiled, and after a moment asked very casually, "How long will the investigation take?"

"A few months. It should certainly be completed by Christmas."

You really want to find something, don't you, Thompson Hall? Alexa thought as she heard him leave, his car roaring away, and then screeching and skidding as he took the first treacherous curve far too fast.

As masterful as he was politically, his eyes had betrayed him when he vowed that he would be the first to wish her all the best should the investigation uncover nothing of concern. Alexa knew that he disapproved of her, and always would, but in a strange way she found his enmity very comforting. Thompson would have her investigated as an enemy would, meticulously searching for flaws, overlooking nothing, pursuing all clues. If her so carefully hidden secret could be discovered, his compulsive investigation would find it. But, if her precious secret remained hidden, she could put that tormenting worry to rest forever. She would know that Katie was safe, and always would be; and safe, too, would be her own life and love with Robert.

Thompson had told her that the investigation would be completed by Christmas. But, would she have already learned, long before Christmas, that she had to leave Robert and their love? In three weeks they were spending the weekend in Richmond with Brynne and Stephen and Katie. Would she learn, on that weekend, that she would have to say good-bye to Robert to protect herself from the anguish of being forever merely just a visitor in her beloved daughter's life?

CHAPTER TWENTY-FIVE

"*W*elcome!" Brynne's dark brown eyes sparkled as she greeted Robert and Alexa. "Stephen and I are so thrilled about you two!"

"Thank you, Brynne. I feel very lucky," Alexa answered softly, trying to focus on Brynne but so very distracted by the knowledge that a precious little girl was somewhere quite near. She kept her hands buried deep in her coat pockets, far away from Robert's. Her fingers had betrayed her before, by turning to ice and digging deeply into a man's palms, and she knew that they would have betrayed her now, a trembling clutch of joy and fear, had Robert held them.

"I'm the lucky one," Robert said quietly.

"Yes you are, Robert," Brynne concurred with a loving sisterly tease. "And don't you forget it!"

"I won't. Not ever, not for a second." He spoke the last, very softly, to Alexa. "We seem to be missing a husband and a daughter. My guess is that they're together somewhere."

"Naturally. They're in Katie's room."

"As you'll soon see, Alexa, from all the toys and blankets and pillows, the description 'Katie's room' applies to every single room in this house," Robert explained with a gentle smile.

"True enough," Brynne admitted with a soft laugh. "But right now, she's in her very own bedroom. She and her Daddy, who doesn't have the wonderful luxury of being able to be with her all day every day, have been playing since dawn, without a nap. Now he's trying to convince her that just a little nap might be a good idea. He's been up there quite a while, which means it may not be working, even though Katie's very sleepy."

"So sleepy that her big brown eyes have finally fluttered closed, despite her very strong will," Stephen said as he appeared in the foyer and smiled warm welcomes to Robert and Alexa. "I promised her that when she awakened she'd see her Uncle Robert and meet her Aunt Alexa. She fell asleep quite happy."

"There is a one hundred percent likelihood that Stephen and I will spend every minute between now and the time Katie joins us talking about her," Brynne confessed lovingly.

"There's nothing wrong with that," Robert said.

"No, I know there isn't. But we really do want to hear about the two of you and your plans."

"Our plans are very simple, and very wonderful. Alexa and I are going to spend the rest of our lives together. We're planning to be married on Valentine's Day."

"Very romantic." Brynne smiled, then added quietly, "And probably more sensible than your original plan of getting married the second the divorce is final."

"Yes," Robert agreed, as he had agreed when Alexa had said the same thing, between tender kisses, two weeks before. Getting married the moment the divorce was final would draw the kind of attention they had so far managed to completely avoid, she had said; and by February, *Pennsylvania Avenue* would be through filming for the season and she could spend every moment being his *wife*; and, besides, she had added softly, the divorce of Robert and Hillary McAllister was final on December nineteenth, the anniversary of Marion and Arthur Sterling's death.

"How is your sister?" Brynne asked Alexa an hour later. The men were out, buying wine for dinner, and they were in the kitchen, Brynne rolling pie crust, Alexa watching.

"She's fine," Alexa answered softly as the words "your sister" created waves of emotion. The waves were gentle, the emotion loving, because of Cat's visit to RoseCliff in June and the many transatlantic conversations they had had since then. Alexa had told her little sister the truth about Robert, that he had been her secret love and was the father of her baby; and Cat had accepted that difficult revelation with love, and empathy, and a wish, as always, for Alexa's happiness. "I think Cat's in love, too. I think she's fallen in love with Alain Castille."

"The Prince of L'île? Really?"

"Yes, really. She's on tour in Europe now, and it seems that Alain manages to attend virtually every concert, and on the rare days that she's not performing, she's at the palace." Alexa smiled. "She sounds very happy, and I think the relationship is quite serious."

"I remember how much Marion and Arthur liked Alain, how gracious and charming they thought he was. They would probably think this was wonderful."

"Yes, I think they would," Alexa agreed quietly. Frowning, she added, "But I've been a little uncertain about telling James about Cat and Alain, because I'm sure that any mention of L'île would trigger memories of the tragedy."

"So you haven't told him?"

"No, but I haven't actually had a chance to. He's been away for months, working on some very important negotiations in Colombia. He doesn't even know about Robert and me yet."

"Will that be a problem? You and James—"

"No, it won't be a problem. James and I are very good friends. We haven't been more than that for a long time."

"How is he, Alexa?" Brynne asked suddenly. "I used to feel close to him, but since Arthur and Marion's death, he's been so far away, both literally and emotionally. I'm sure Robert told you that it was James who handled Katie's adoption for us, and it was even he who brought her here to us." She sighed softly. "James has done *so much* for Stephen and me. I wish there was something we could do for him. What do you think? Is there something?"

"I don't know, Brynne. He's always been very private, and since Marion and Arthur's death, he's been even more—" Alexa was stopped mid-sentence by the almost imperceptible sound, a sound only a mother could hear, a sound heard by both Alexa and Brynne.

"Did you hear her, too?" Brynne asked, surprised. Even Stephen didn't always hear the very first noises Katie made when she awakened and wondered where her parents were.

"I guess so."

"She's just awakening, still finding her baby bearings. I like to get to her before she's fully awake, so she won't be upset. Not," Brynne added with a soft smile, "that I've ever delayed getting to her long enough to know if she even gets upset."

Brynne was midway through the lattice on the top of the cherry pie, but she simply left that unimportant project and began to cross the kitchen to quickly wash the flour off her hands before going to Katie.

"I'd be happy to go get her," Alexa offered softly. "Unless you think it might upset her."

"Oh, thank you. No, it won't upset her. She seems to know right away when she meets someone who loves her. And," Brynne added, her soft voice filled pride and love, "I'm pretty sure you're going to love our little girl."

"I'm pretty sure I will, too."

"OK, so I'll finish with the pie crust while you get Katie. Her room is upstairs, the second door on the left."

Katie was cooing soft hellos to her room as she floated from her happy dreams to the reality of her safe and happy life. Alexa stood in the doorway for a moment, listening to her daughter's happy sounds, then walked with legs as unsteady as her trembling emotions to the pink and white crib.

Oh, you're so very pretty, aren't you? Alexa asked silently as she gazed through a blur of tears at the smiling little girl. She saw Robert in Katie's pretty face, Robert and Brynne, and although others would have seen her own delicate features had they known to look, Alexa saw no resemblance to herself at all.

So very pretty, and so very happy, she thought as Katie's dark brown eyes sparkled a curious untroubled welcome to the new face that smiled at her with such love. Alexa's face was quite unfamiliar to Katie, of course. Even if the tiny infant had been able to make a memory of the face that had gazed so lovingly at her in those few moments after her birth, she would have remembered a face with black hair and blue eyes, not the one she saw now. This face, with golden hair and glistening green eyes, was a face that Katie could greet with a curious untroubled smile.

No troubles for you, my darling, Alexa thought, a wish and a promise. Only happiness for you, my little love. Then, whispering softly, she spoke for the first time, "Hello, little Katie."

Alexa's whisper was filled with the same softness with which she had spoken to her daughter in the months before Katie's birth and for those few precious moments they had together after Katie was born. At the sound of Alexa's soft loving voice, a flicker of confusion crossed Katie's face and her big brown eyes strained to focus more clearly on the unfamiliar face hovering over her.

Oh, is it possible? Does she recognize my voice? Alexa wondered as a fresh flood of hot tears spilled down her cheeks. And then gently, so very gently, she lifted her daughter out of the crib and curled her into her arms. Katie's eyes remained intently focused on Alexa's face and now her tiny hands reached eagerly for the tear-dampened cheeks, touching, patting softly, searching.

"Oh, Katie, Katie," Alexa whispered. But her loving voice only caused more confusion. *Confusion*, not happiness, not joy. *I must say no more words*, she told herself. *I want no worries for Katie, no confusion, no sadness, not even for a moment, even if . . .*

Did this mean she would have to say good-bye to Robert and their love after all? Before today Alexa had wondered if she might have to leave him to protect herself. But she knew now, already, that that wouldn't be necessary. The great joy of seeing Katie *far* outweighed the immense loss.

But, from the moment she had first learned of her pregnancy, every decision Alexa had made had been made for her baby's happiness. Would it be best for Katie never to hear her voice again? Would there always be, for Katie, something troubling and confusing about her Aunt Alexa?

Alexa said no more words. She just cuddled Katie close to her, softly kissing her dark curls as she rocked her gently and memorized the precious moment—Katie's soft warmth, her delicate sweetness—as she battled the fear that it would be their last.

That was how Brynne found them many minutes later, the pie crust long since finished. Neither Alexa nor Katie sensed her appearance in the open doorway; so, for a while, Brynne simply watched, smiling softly at the exquisite tenderness and love that she saw.

How lovely and loving Alexa is, Brynne thought as she watched the gentle scene and remembered Alexa's kindness to her on a most sad August night. *How lucky Robert is to have found her. What happiness there will be now, at last, for my beloved brother.*

As Brynne gazed from Alexa to the precious bundle she cradled so gently, her thoughts flowed from Robert and Alexa's happiness to her own. *How blessed she was.* The miracle of Katie was a bountiful joy beyond words. And yet, as if that immense joy weren't enough, more than enough, there was now another little miracle, a tiny new life, living, flourishing, within her.

Brynne had told no one about the tiny new life—except Katie. "Oh, Katie, Katie," she would say. "You're going to have a little sister or brother. A little sister, you think? Yes, I think so too. And I think, also, my precious little miracle," she would add with soft wonder, "that, somehow, this new baby is here because of you. Maybe she hears how much fun we're having, and feels all the love inside me because of you, and maybe, my Katie, that's why she's decided to grow big and strong."

Brynne's baby was eighteen weeks old, exactly Katie's age, a treasure of love created the night Katie was born, after James called, because she and Stephen had forgotten, on that night of immense joy, to take the precautions they had so carefully taken to prevent the sadness of future losses. This baby had already survived six weeks longer than the babies they had lost, and the doctor was very optimistic, but Brynne hadn't yet told Stephen. She wouldn't, not until she was sure, and that would probably be long before he even began to guess, because the little life inside her was curled, safe and protected, very low in her welcoming pelvis.

For now she would only share the secret with the beloved bundle cradled so gently in Alexa's arms; the beloved little girl who, now, Brynne needed very much to cuddle herself.

"I don't hear a fussy baby," she said softly.

As Brynne's voice broke the magical spell, there was, for Alexa, who had lost all sense of time, a moment of confusion. But there was no confusion for Katie. At the sound of Brynne's voice, her brown eyes sparkled with joy—her whole pretty face sparkled!—and she turned excitedly toward the soft, loving voice she knew so well: the voice of her mother.

"Not a fussy baby at all," Alexa agreed quietly, focusing quickly and watching Katie carefully as she spoke. One delicate dark brown eyebrow furrowed, just a little, the smallest ripple, but Katie's eager attention remained on Brynne. Whatever had been vaguely troubling about her own voice seemed quite forgotten in the memories of pure joy that were evoked by Brynne's.

"She's never a fussy baby," Brynne said as she reached for her excited daughter. When she held Katie in her arms, the two pairs of happy brown eyes met, and noses rubbed softly, as she asked, "How's my baby girl? Did you have a nice nap? Oh, Katie-Kate, look at your pink sleepy cheeks! You needed a good rest, because you and your Daddy had such fun, didn't you?"

Brynne exchanged gleeful greetings with Katie for several moments before looking back at Alexa. But when she finally did look, a thoughtful frown touched her pretty face.

"Have you been crying, Alexa?"

"Happy tears, Brynne. I'm so happy for you and Stephen . . . and Katie."

"Thank you," Brynne whispered as her own eyes misted. "I still don't really believe it's happened. My heart stops every time the telephone rings."

"But I thought the adoption was closed. I thought James had made certain the biologic mother could never find her."

"Yes, that's right, he did. But still . . ."

"She's your daughter, Brynne," Alexa said with quiet confidence. I made a promise of love, and I will never break that solemn vow. She was speaking in a normal voice now, not the special voice that was just for her baby girl, and she saw with exhilarating relief that this voice triggered for Katie no confusing memories at all. Her heart raced with joy as she repeated, in the voice that meant she didn't have to say good-bye to Katie, "She's your daughter."

James returned from Colombia on November first. The only mail of interest waiting for him at Inverness was a hand-delivered note dated two weeks before: *James, I have wonderful news. Call me. Love, Alexa.* She would not reveal her news over the phone to him, but thirty minutes after his call to RoseCliff, she was at the door of his mansion.

"Oh, James, how can I help you?" she asked when she saw him. He looked so exhausted, his handsome face so drawn, his dark blue eyes drained of color until they were almost gray.

"Help me?"

"You've helped me so much and I . . ."

"I'm OK, Alexa. I'm just very tired." He tried smiling, and failed, because it had been so long since he had smiled, but he said truthfully, "Actually, the negotiations are really going quite well. We're going to regroup for a couple of weeks and then return to give a final push. Hopefully, we'll have a signed agreement before Christmas."

"Oh, good. It would be nice if you were here at Christmas."

"So . . . tell me your wonderful news."

"My wonderful news is that Robert and I are going to be married on Valentine's Day. We want you to be the best man, of course, and Cat and Brynne will be—"

"Does he know?"

"No, James, he doesn't know. And I'm never going to tell him."

"He needs to know, Alexa."

"I can't tell him. I thought I might be able to, but two weeks ago we drove to Richmond to see Katie. Robert loves her *so much*, and she loves him. It's almost as if they both somehow know. But they don't know, and they never will, and this way it can always be a wonderful, joyous, untroubled love. If Robert knew the truth, it would cause him such terrible sadness." Alexa shrugged softly, as if her next words might make no sense to James, and then continued quietly, "I love Robert far too much to tell him, James. I would say good-bye to him forever before I would cause him such pain."

Alexa had shrugged, as if he might not understand, but of course James understood perfectly. Oh, yes, Alexa, I know all about loving someone too much to want to cause them sadness or pain. That's the reason I said good-bye to Catherine, who I loved, *love*, so very much.

"Oh, Alexa," he sighed softly.

"What, James?"

"I have this vague memory of a time when everything seemed uncomplicated and happy. The memory is so distant, I wonder if the time every truly existed."

"It did exist, and it will exist again. Everything is going to be better, James, for both of us. It *has* to be," she said firmly. Then, smiling a beautiful dreamy smile, she predicted with quiet confidence, "Everything will be much better by Christmas."

"That's the second time you've mentioned Christmas, Alexa. Is there a reason?"

"Yes, in fact there are several reasons. First of all, you'll be here, having returned triumphant from Colombia. And Cat will be here, because she's going to perform at the traditional White House Christmas Concert. And my parents will be here. I'd very much like you to meet them."

"And I'd very much like to."

"Good. I'm glad. Let's see, there are more reasons. Oh, yes, Robert's divorce will be final." Alexa smiled happily and forced herself to hold the radiant smile as she casually said the next, "And, by Christmas, as much as he hates to admit it, and probably *won't* admit it to me, Thompson Hall will have discovered that I'm an entirely suitable spouse for Robert."

"What does that mean?"

"You know who Thompson Hall is, don't you?"

"Yes, of course."

"Well. He's having me investigated, to see if I'm really future First Lady material. It made me angry at first, but it's something that would be done eventually by someone, and it will be the most wonderful Christmas present of all to know without a flicker of doubt that no one can find out about Katie—*ever*."

"But we already know that. Aside from Dr. Lawton, whose ethics are without question, the only people who knew about your pregnancy are people who love you very much. And the same is true for the people who knew about your affair with Robert." James's dark blue eyes searched her emerald ones, and when the emerald faltered under the intense blue gaze, he asked sharply, "Alexa?"

"Hillary knew about our affair."

"What?"

"In fact, it was cruel and clever Hillary who orchestrated our break-up."

"She knew before the evening at the gala?"

"Yes. She's a terrific actress, isn't she? Maybe if you'd been holding *her* hand that night, you would have felt it turn to ice." Alexa added lightly, trying to soften his angry blue glare, "Of course, Hillary's hands are probably always icy."

"This changes everything, Alexa."

"No, it doesn't. Hillary knows nothing about the baby. She believed she had successfully ended our affair. And you know as well as I that she wasn't prowling around here last spring. Besides, James, if Hillary knew anything she would have long since used the information."

"Really? Have you forgotten so quickly about your longtime enemy? I think, and this is based on what *you* told me about Hillary as a teenager, that it's quite possible she would hold onto the information, savoring it until just the perfect moment. Like the eve of your marriage, maybe? Or, perhaps, the day of Robert's nomination for the Presidency? Or the moment just before his inauguration? Do you have any reason to believe that Hillary would balk at destroying Brynne, Stephen, and Katie along with you and Robert?"

"Hillary doesn't know!"

"You don't know that. Dammit, Alexa, have you forgotten why you gave Katie to Brynne and Stephen? So she would be safe, and happy, and untouched by scandal or uncertainty, remember? Do you want her to become known as the little girl who cost her father the Presidency?"

"*No!* That will never happen, James. I won't let it happen," she said softly, solemnly. "If Hillary knows—and I truly believe that she doesn't—she will tell Thompson Hall or me. I *do* know Hillary, and I'm very sure that I'm the only one she would really want to hurt. I also have no doubt that what would give her the greatest pleasure would be to prevent my marriage to Robert. If Hillary knows, she'll tell Thompson or me, and she'll do it fairly soon, *before* the divorce is final."

"And?"

"And if she goes to Thompson instead of coming to me, he'll tell me. He agreed that if he uncovered anything worrisome, he would come to me first, to try to convince me not to marry Robert."

"*And?*"

"If Thompson Hall discovers anything that could even remotely lead to Katie, I will tell Robert good-bye."

James knew it was true. He saw in the beautiful emerald a look he had seen once before, on the day she had asked him to handle Katie's adoption; a look that said, quite eloquently, that she would keep the solemn promise from her heart, no matter what, even at the cost of great anguish to herself.

CHAPTER TWENTY-SIX

Alain and Catherine sat at their special place on the cliff above the sea watching the brilliant rainbows fade gently into the pink winter twilight. They sat in silence, as they often did, as they shared the magnificence before them. But, on this warm winter evening, the silence wasn't comfortable as always; it was troubled, a trouble to match the dark worry Catherine saw on Alain's handsome face. In less than an hour his private jet would carry her swiftly to Paris, and from there she would fly to Washington. They would be apart for ten days, the longest separation since their gentle love began. It could be their impending separation that was troubling him, she supposed, but she sensed it was something more. Something he would tell her, Catherine knew, because in their love there were no secrets that weren't shared.

"Alain?" she asked softly.

"There's something I'd like you to think about while you're away, Catherine."

"All right," she agreed as she saw uncertainty in his dark eyes. The uncertainty didn't need to be there. Alain could tell her anything. Smiling, she urged gently, "What is it?"

"I was wondering," Alain said very quietly to her welcoming sapphire eyes, "if, while you're away, you'd think about marrying me."

"Oh, Alain," she whispered, her surprised blue eyes sparkling with happiness, giving him his answer before she spoke it aloud. "I don't need ten days to think about it. Yes, I will marry you."

"Yes?"

"Of course I will," she repeated softly as he drew her gently into his arms. "I love you, Alain."

"And I love you, Catherine," he whispered as his lips tenderly caressed her silky black hair. After a moment, he found her shimmering blue eyes. "I love you, and for the next ten days I shall miss you very much."

"And I'll miss you," she admitted softly. Then, smiling, she reminded lovingly, "But you'll be very busy spending time with the friends you've ignored all fall because you've been with me."

"True, and you'll have a wonderful time visiting with Alexa and your parents." Alain smiled, and added softly, "But this will be the last Christmas we spend apart."

Alain's promise was tender and loving, but Catherine suddenly felt a tremor of ice, the chilly stirring of almost forgotten ghosts. Just a year ago, *on this same Sunday in December*, James had made the same loving promise to her.

"Yes, our last Christmas spent apart," she echoed quietly, still chilled by the icy ghosts of the love of Catherine and James. Their wonderful, private love had been so secret that when it died only they knew it had ever even existed. Such secrecy scared her now, as if hidden loves could not survive, and Catherine wanted this warm, gentle love with Alain to last forever. "May I tell Alexa and my parents that we plan to marry?"

"Of course. And may I tell Natalie? She'll be so thrilled. Already she thinks of you as a sister."

"Oh, yes, please tell her."

"She'll want to be involved in the design of your engagement ring."

"Yes, she will, won't she?" Catherine asked with a soft laugh of fondness for her future sister-in-law. Natalie was a gifted designer, bold and innovative. She could design a breathtaking engagement ring, a true work of art, but . . .

"But, Catherine, the ring should be what you want," Alain quietly addressed her unspoken worry that what Natalie might design would be magnificent, but not her, not *them*.

"And what you want."

"I was thinking, perhaps, a bouquet of emeralds and rubies."

"I love you," she said softly in response to the gentle tease. A bouquet of emeralds and rubies would be a disaster, of course, but Alain was simply suggesting something as far removed as possible from the obvious: exquisite blue sapphires to match her exquisite blue eyes. She had told him about the sapphires she had received before in the name of love, from her mother and from James, and she knew his tease was his gentle way of telling her that he would never give her gems that would recall those other sadnesses.

"I love you, too, Catherine." Alain took her slender left hand in his and after a moment admitted quietly, "I actually have been thinking about your engagement ring."

"Yes?"

"I thought a diamond, simple and elegant, a flawless brilliant cut solitaire in a delicate setting of white and yellow gold."

"Oh, Alain, that would be lovely."

"Is there no respect whatsoever for days on which divorces are final?" Alexa demanded with an exasperated laugh as she replaced the receiver of the phone and turned to Catherine, with whom, until the telephone rang, she had been enjoying a leisurely breakfast in RoseCliff's cheery kitchen.

"What horrible thing is happening?" Catherine asked.

"They want me to work today! Cat, did I or did I not return after eleven o'-clock last night with a solemn promise from the director that in exchange for the late shoot I would have today off?"

"Yes, you did. But now they need you?"

"Just until mid-afternoon, they claim. And—I guess I should get this in writing!—they are now saying that if we can finish the scene they want to shoot today, they won't need me again this week, which means I'll be off until after Christmas."

"That sounds good."

"It sounds very good, doesn't it? Much too good to pass up. So, I guess I'll need to have you drop me off on your way to the White House, and when I'm finished I'll get a ride or take a taxi home."

"I should be done with the rehearsal by noon, Alexa. Why don't I just plan to go back to the studio and wait for you?"

"Oh, no, Cat, if you don't mind, you'll need to meet James."

"James?" she echoed softly.

"Yes. He called me yesterday afternoon at the studio. Whatever it was he was negotiating in Colombia is finished, triumphantly, and he's arriving home today. His flight is scheduled to land at Dulles at one-fifteen, and I told him I'd be there to meet him."

"Do you usually meet him?"

"No. But it was just a year ago today that his parents were killed, and I thought . . ." Alexa shrugged. "I didn't say that to him, of course, and I don't know if he'll be even more sad about them today than any other day, but . . ."

"But what?" Catherine asked quietly.

"But he didn't tell me not to meet him. No matter what, it's Christmas and James is alone. I'm hoping he'll join us for Christmas dinner. I thought I'd invite him when I saw him today, but maybe you could? Cat, can you meet him? Do you mind?"

"No, of course I don't mind."

"Great. Thanks. Invite him for dinner tonight, too, if you like. Robert thought he'd be able to get here by six."

They had talked, when they had made the wonderful plans for their love, about how terribly romantic it was going to be greeting each other at airports. They would never be apart for more than a week, they had promised, and at the time each had wondered privately if even a week would be far too long to endure.

And now Catherine hadn't seen James since they had said good-bye on L'île in July . . . and it had been precisely a year to the day since the wonderful plans for their secret love had begun to die.

But when James walked off the plane and saw her waiting for him, it was as if the past year had never happened and their joyous, magical love was alive, *flourishing*, still. He hadn't expected her to be there, of course, and in the unguarded moment of surprise, his defiant heart responded before his mind, sending its bold and illogical wishes with swift joy to his dark blue eyes, filling them with unconcealed desire and love. And, in that same moment, even though she had given it fair warning that she would be seeing him, Catherine's heart answered with its own bold and defiant joy, sending messages to her sparkling sapphire eyes that precisely mirrored the wonderful wishes and desires in his.

The magnificent moment couldn't last. Quickly, *too* quickly, their minds intervened, subduing their fluttering joyous hearts with stern reminders of the truth, and by the time James reached her, they each acknowledged the wonderful and wondrous moment, *that should never have happened*, with smiles that were apologetic, and very, very gentle.

"Hello, Catherine," he said softly.

"Hi. Alexa had to work after all."

They talked a little, and filled the silences with more gentle smiles, and soon Catherine was slowing the car to a stop in front of the mansion at Inverness. She hadn't invited James for Christmas dinner with her family yet, much less for dinner with Robert and Alexa at RoseCliff tonight. Nor had she told him the news that would surely be mentioned at both gatherings . . .

"James?"

"Yes?"

"Alain has asked me to marry him, and I've told him yes."

"Alain? Alain Castille?"

"Yes." Catherine frowned. "I guess Alexa hadn't mentioned to you that Alain and I have been seeing each other?"

"No."

"Oh." She looked bravely into his surprised blue eyes. "I think you're supposed to wish me all the best."

"Catherine . . ."

"Yes?"

"How well do you know him?"

"I know him very well, James," she assured softly, with a grateful smile for his gentle concern.

"Good." James hesitated a moment and then asked quietly, "Do you know about his father?"

"Yes, I know about Jean-Luc. I know all about his treachery and his madness. But how do you know about Jean-Luc, James? Oh, no," she whispered as she found an answer to her own question. "Is that why you were on L'île in July? To investigate Alain?"

"No. Elliot told me a little of L'île's history before I visited, that's all." James hesitated again, knowing he had very little right to pry and yet remembering so clearly what Natalie had told him that morning as they had sailed: *Alain will marry someday, to give L'île its next monarch, but I am quite certain that he will never again plan to marry for love.* After a moment he said gently, "Actually, it was Natalie who told me about Alain. Catherine, she told me that he had been engaged once before."

As the meaning of James's words settled, Catherine was swept by waves of emotion; powerful, unfamiliar rushes of anger, and the more familiar, more delicate whispers of sadness. The emotions swirled together, battling to be heard. The more powerful, anger, spoke first.

"And that he loved Monique very much? And that when she died so tragically, while he watched in helpless horror, that he was quite confident he would never fall in love again? Oh, yes, I know that." As Catherine paused, the anger washed away as swiftly as it had appeared, and when she spoke again it was with a soft, bewildered voice of sadness. "Is it so impossible for you to imagine, James, that someone could truly love me? Just because you couldn't—"

"I loved you, Catherine. You know that."

"I suppose I believed you did," she answered, her voice still soft and sad. But then it was anger's turn to speak again, and it rushed back with a vengeance, crushing all delicacy and bringing with it the aching memories of how hurt she had been when he left her. James had hurt her, *so much*, and now she heard herself speaking hurtful words to him, words that flowed with astonishing effortlessness from her heart to her lips on a gushing river of pain, "But I was so naive then, James. I didn't really know about love when we were together. But now I do. I've learned the truth about love from Alain. He knows everything about me, *everything*, and I know all his secrets, too. His life has been filled with terrible tragedies, but, unlike you, he is not afraid to share even his darkest emotions. Alain trusts me and our love enough to share both his joy and his pain. You only wanted to share the joy, James, and now I know that that's not really love."

"Oh, Catherine."

"Be happy for me, James!" she defiantly commanded the stricken blue eyes. "You wouldn't let me love you when you needed my love and I was so willing to give it, remember? Alain loves me as you never did. He wouldn't send me away if he were dying. He would allow me to love him."

"I loved you, Catherine," James whispered softly. "How can you believe that I didn't?"

"It doesn't really matter now, does it?"

Yes, his heart screamed. Yes it matters! I loved you . . . I love you . . . I will always love you.

"No," he answered quietly before turning to get out of the car. "I guess not."

Alexa was at RoseCliff, puttering in the kitchen, when Catherine returned from Inverness.

"How is he?"

"Fine."

"Is he coming for dinner?"

"No. Not tonight, and I forgot to ask him about Christmas."

"Are you OK, Cat?"

"Sure. I think I need a long hot shower."

"Be my guest. Is it getting cold outside?"

"Oh, yes, I guess." Catherine felt chilled, but the icy shivers which swept through her had nothing to do with the rapidly darkening sky or the frigid winter wind. The shivers were simply the restless and tormented swirlings of the ghosts of a dead love. The icy ghosts had been sleeping, but they were awake now, wide awake, and they were very upset.

"They're predicting snow tonight. It's not supposed to start until after midnight, but if it comes earlier it might be best for Robert to spend the night here."

"He can spend the night here anyway, Alexa. Really, it wouldn't bother me at all." It only bothered me when it was James in your bed, she thought. James, James . . .

Catherine took a long shower and dressed for dinner. The outside world might be preparing for a winter snowstorm, but RoseCliff was warm and cozy, as always, and Catherine knew she would be quite comfortable in silk.

"Gorgeous dress," Alexa said when Catherine reappeared. She smiled questioningly, because her little sister had been in her bedroom for almost an hour, but Catherine simply returned the smile.

"Thank you."

"I'm having tea. Would you like some?"

"Sure. I'll get it. Shall I get some more for you?"

"Yes. Thanks."

Catherine poured the tea, and they sat in the romantic living room and gazed at the swirling gray drama unfolding over Chesapeake Bay. The snow was still a long way off, but the storm clouds already stretched ominous dark fingers across the sky.

The telephone rang as Catherine and Alexa were discussing the plans for their parents' visit which was to begin early the next morning. Jane and Alexander would tour the set of *Pennsylvania Avenue*, of course, and Robert would show them the sights on Capitol Hill, and after Catherine's concert at the White House they were all dining with the President and First Lady . . .

"Your Prince or mine?" Alexa teased gaily when their conversation was interrupted by the ringing telephone.

"I'll answer it," Catherine said, hoping, indeed, that it would be her Prince. She needed Alain's warmth to melt the icy ghosts. She needed to be reminded of a safe gentle love . . . not a dangerous and magical one. "Hello?"

"Once upon a time there was a beautiful little girl whose mother didn't want her."

"Who is this?"

"If you want to know what became of the abandoned baby come to the Marlboro Marina now."

"Who . . ." Catherine began again, but stopped because the voice was gone, the message delivered, the connection severed.

"Cat? Who was it?" Alexa asked as waves of fear washed through her. Thompson Hall? Hillary? For months, every time the phone had rung, her heart had raced, and she had said a silent prayer before answering it—just as, she supposed, Brynne always did, too. As if the silent prayer could change the message of the ringing phone! But Alexa had forgotten this time, because Robert's divorce was final today, and surely she would have heard by now if Thompson had found anything, and it was almost Christmas, and everything was going to be fine . . . "Cat?"

"Oh, Alexa."

Catherine took a soft breath and told her exactly what the caller had said. As she watched Alexa's emerald eyes, she saw first the loss of hope, the *end* of hope; and then, after only a moment, she saw familiar Alexa determination.

"I'm going to the Marina."

"I'm going with you." Catherine underscored her words by handing Alexa one of the two winter coats that hung on the antique coat hook and putting the other one on herself.

"No, Cat," Alexa said quietly. "Please stay here. Please stay here and call James and tell him what has happened."

"James, but not Robert?"

"No, not Robert. I've never told him about the baby, Cat. I can't tell him."

"Because she's Katie?" Catherine asked gently. It was a guess, of course, but . . . "Robert talked about her so much at dinner Monday night, and you'd never even mentioned Brynne's adopted daughter to me, so I wondered if maybe she was your baby."

"Yes, Cat, she is," Alexa admitted softly. "Katie is our little girl. I haven't told Robert. I can't. It would hurt him too much."

"But Alexa . . ."

"I have to go. Please, Cat, will you stay here and call James?"

"What can James do?"

"I don't know. But, please, just call him. I have to go now. Where are the car keys?"

"In my purse. Here." As Catherine gave Alexa the keys, she said, "Alexa, this will be all right, you'll see."

"No, Cat," Alexa answered quietly. "I don't think it will be."

CHAPTER TWENTY-SEVEN

*A*s soon as Alexa disappeared down the stairs and out of sight, Catherine dialed the once-familiar number to Inverness.

"James?"

"Catherine, I—"

"Alexa needs your help. She just got a call from someone who knows about the baby."

"Let me speak to her, please."

"She's gone. The message was for her to go to the Marlboro Marina."

"And she did?"

"I couldn't stop her, James. She . . ." Whatever Catherine had been about to say was swept away by a sudden overwhelming fear. She didn't remember hearing a sound, but there must have been one, because as she was trying to decipher her immense and inexplicable fear, she heard the crash. "No!"

"Catherine? What is it?"

"It was . . . a crash. Oh, James, *no.*"

"I'm on my way. I'll call the paramedics and the police from my car phone." James wanted her to wait at RoseCliff, but he knew she wouldn't, so he whispered softly, "Catherine, darling, be careful."

Catherine wasn't careful. When she reached the foot of the stairs, she dashed across the parking area and directly onto the winding road, running down the middle because it was the shortest route to Alexa.

But there was no Alexa, just an ominous plume of gray-black smoke, darker even than the stormy winter sky, a sinister flare that rose from the car burning on the beach below. Catherine reached the edge of the cliff and would have found a way down the treacherous granite wall—even though there was none—but Alexa wasn't in the inferno on the beach. Her motionless body lay just six feet away, on a ledge beneath where Catherine stood. After quickly removing her coat and tossing it onto the pavement as a marker for James and the paramedics, she scrambled down the cliff to Alexa.

"Alexa," she whispered to the face that was already ashen from internal blood loss. She was unconscious, but alive. Her chest lifted and fell in rapid shallow gasps, and her pulse beat frantically in her neck. Catherine was careful not to move her, but gently, so gently, she touched her warm cheek to Alexa's cold one and whispered, "I love you, Alexa. Help is on the way, so please fight as hard as you can. Oh, Alexa, I love you. Please fight. *Please.*"

The paramedics from Marlboro arrived within five minutes. By the time James arrived, having made the twenty-minute drive from Inverness in thirteen, Alexa's dangerously low blood pressure was being supported by intravenous fluids and pressors, her neck and back had been stabilized, and the Trauma Team at Memorial Hospital, having been notified that she obviously had internal bleeding, had communicated in return that there would be surgeons and an OR waiting for her.

Alexa was still on the ledge when James arrived, and Catherine was still there, too, kneeling on the cold hard granite as close to Alexa as she could be without interfering in the lifesaving efforts of the paramedics. Catherine didn't interfere, but her delicate hand found a way through the wall of backs to gently touch Alexa's golden hair.

The small ledge had become even smaller with the addition of paramedics and their equipment. James wanted to climb down, to be with Alexa and Catherine, but there was no room; and he would have been stopped, anyway, because there was a police lieutenant who had been awaiting his arrival with interest.

"Are you the one who called?"

"Yes. I'm James Sterling."

"Lieutenant Ed Baker. How did you know to call, Mr. Sterling?"

"I was talking to Alexa's sister Catherine on the phone when she heard the crash."

"That's Catherine on the ledge?"

"Yes."

"Good. I'll need to talk to her. I've only been here about five minutes, but already there are some things that bother me a whole lot about this accident."

"Like what?"

"Like the fact that there are no skid marks on the pavement, and the tracks of the wheels indicate that the car went straight off the cliff."

"Meaning?"

"Meaning, did Alexa Taylor drive off the cliff on purpose?"

"No."

"You sound confident."

"I am confident. I know Alexa very well. She would not take her own life." Or would she? James wondered. Had the call signaled an end—*the* end—to her? I will tell Robert good-bye, she had vowed, if her precious secret was ever discovered. Was this her good-bye? Good-bye to Robert and Katie, and good-bye to her own anguish? A *love to die for, James?* Alexa had teased a million years ago, long before either she or James had believed in love. Now, to protect the man she loved and his precious daughter had she given her own life? No, James thought. Please, *no.* "She would not."

"Well, good. I'm glad to hear that. I'm a real fan of hers, and I'd hate to think she was so unhappy. Still, something happened. Something made her drive like a bat out of hell and lose control of her car. Maybe her sister knows what it was."

"Maybe," James agreed quietly. But maybe, he thought, if I can talk to Catherine first, she won't tell you what it was. "May I speak with Catherine first, Lieutenant? She may be in shock, and I would like to explain to her why you need to talk to her."

"Sure."

At that moment, the paramedics stood, ready to move Alexa off the ledge and into the waiting ambulance. Catherine stood, too, and as she did, Lieutenant Baker and James both moved forward, as if to stop her, even though she was far away from them. The movement was instinctive, protective, because they saw how precariously near the edge she was. She had been safe, kneeling on the granite, but now her trembling body wavered, and if she stepped back at all, even an inch to give the paramedics more room to maneuver, the fall would be instantly lethal.

But even though her eyes remained focused on Alexa, Catherine seemed to know her own proximity to disaster, and she didn't step back. She stood her ground and, very softly, asked the paramedics if she would be able to ride in the ambulance with Alexa. No, they told her, a police officer would drive her if she needed a ride. Catherine touched Alexa for as long as she could, and then the physical bond was broken, and moments later Alexa was gone, her departure signalled by the harsh sound of blaring sirens.

Alexa was gone, but Catherine hadn't moved from her precarious perch on the ledge. James climbed down to her, and, as he approached, he saw the immense despair in her bewildered blue eyes. She looked so lost, and so fragile. Her delicate slender body, clothed only in sheer silk, shivered from the winter wind, and from the even greater chills of shock and grief. James wanted to rush to her, but she was still one terrifying step from eternity, and he was afraid of startling her, afraid even that she might back away at the sight of him. *Why wouldn't she?*

"Catherine?" he asked softly.

She didn't back away. She hesitated only a moment and then fell into his arms, allowing him to cradle her trembling body against his strong warmth.

"Oh, Catherine," he whispered into her wind-tossed, silky black hair. "She's going to be fine, darling."

"She has to be, James."

"She will be." It was a wish, not a promise, because he had seen Alexa's deathly paleness before the ambulance left.

James didn't want to let Catherine go, not ever, not ever again. But her shivering body needed even more than his loving warmth could provide. And he knew, soon and together, they would have to make a very important decision. He released her from his arms reluctantly and helped her into the coat she had tossed as a marker for the paramedics. After gently buttoning the buttons for her, he cupped her cold lovely face in his warm hands. His voice was soft, because he was speaking to Catherine, not because he worried that his important words would be overheard. The police were far away, talking among themselves, and even their loud voices were muffled by the winter wind.

"Darling, the police lieutenant needs to speak with you about what happened just before Alexa left RoseCliff."

"Oh." After a thoughtful moment, she added, "I see."

She *did* see, he realized. He had been worried that her shock and grief might make her unable to truly understand. But she understood, without further words from him, and as he watched, James witnessed an act of love—for Alexa. Her brilliant blue eyes told him, even before she spoke, that she had willed the shock from her mind.

"I know about Katie, James. Alexa told me just before . . ." She fought the rush of emotion and continued quietly, "I'm going to protect her secret. I have to."

"OK. I agree. After you talk to Lieutenant Baker, I'll drive you to the hospital. We'll make a brief stop at Marlboro Marina on the way."

"Yes." She smiled softly, grateful that perhaps in this small way, by simply protecting her precious secret, she was helping Alexa. "OK."

Lieutenant Baker was waiting by his car. He smiled sympathetically as Catherine and James approached.

"I just have a few questions, Ms. Taylor. I'm sorry, but they're necessary."

"I understand."

"OK. Now, it's obvious from the physical evidence—the distance the car traveled in the air before landing on the beach—that your sister was driving very fast.

I'm trying to figure out why. You were with her right before she left the cottage?"

"Yes."

"Had she been drinking?"

"Drinking? No. Well, she and I were having tea."

"Did she, had she, taken any drugs? Cocaine or something?"

"No. Alexa doesn't ever use drugs, and she rarely drinks."

"You were having tea and then she suddenly left, driving very fast. Why?"

"Alexa received a phone call just before she left the cottage," Catherine answered, realizing she needed to provide some explanation.

"Do you have any idea who the caller was or what was said?"

"No."

"But the call upset her?"

"Yes."

"Was she on her way to meet the caller?"

"I think so."

"Do you know where?"

"No."

"Had she been getting calls, do you know? Perhaps there was an obsessed fan?"

"I don't know. I've only been visiting with her for the past three days. She didn't mention anything that was worrying her."

"But she got a call, out of the blue, that upset her enough to make her dash out of the cottage and drive so recklessly that she . . . I'm sorry, Ms. Taylor."

"Does it really matter what the caller said?"

"Probably not," Lieutenant Baker agreed easily. Then his expression changed, very slightly, even though his calm tone still sent the message that his questions were simply routine. "I just need to ask you about the car, Ms. Taylor."

"The car?"

"Do you know when Alexa last drove it?"

"Alexa? Last night. She returned from the studio about eleven."

"And as far as you know the car was working fine then?"

"Yes. And it was working fine all day today."

"Today?"

"Yes. I had it today."

"Oh. I see. What time did you return to the cottage?"

"Just before three."

"And the call came?"

"At four."

"OK. That's all for now. I know you want to get to the hospital. If you think of anything else, here's my card. Please give me a call."

James had no fear of who would be waiting in the parking lot at the Marlboro Marina. It would be Hillary, he imagined, or perhaps Thompson Hall. He planned a very brief conversation with whoever it was, just long enough to say he knew all about the blackmail call.

But the parking lot at the Marlboro Marina was quite deserted.

Had Hillary or Thompson heard the scream of sirens on the nearby road to RoseCliff and fled upon realizing that the call intended merely to blackmail Alexa out of her marriage to Robert had in fact precipitated a horrible tragedy? he wondered. Yes, perhaps, *probably*. But, as James surveyed the empty parking lot, Lieutenant Baker's words came back to him, taking on new meaning, a meaning that matched the police officer's somber expression as he had asked so seemingly casually about the car. There were no skid marks, he had said, *as if Alexa hadn't even attempted to stop,* and the tire tracks were straight, *as if she hadn't even tried to swerve away from the lethal cliff.*

James had assumed that Alexa had neither braked nor swerved because by the time her distracted mind realized the car was out of control she somehow knew her only hope was to jump. But what if she had tried to brake or swerve, and *couldn't?* What if the reason that no one was waiting here for Alexa was that the caller *knew* she would not survive the drive down the winding road from RoseCliff to the Marina? It seemed unimaginable—it *was*—and yet clearly the astute Lieutenant Baker had been considering the possibility from the very beginning.

"What, James?" Catherine asked softly, pulled from her own desperate thoughts as she sensed his sudden tension.

"Catherine, we need to tell Lieutenant Baker the caller wanted Alexa to come here."

"Why?"

"Because the police need to get fingerprints from the pay phone." Even as he said it, James knew what a futile exercise it was likely to be: a call from a murderer, made simply to lure Alexa into a drive of death, would surely *not* have been made from here. Dusting for prints seemed futile, but James was unwilling to take the chance that he might be wrong.

"I thought we decided that we didn't want the police to know the details of the call. If they find the person who called, James, they will find out about Katie."

"Yes, but Catherine . . ." James sighed softly. "Darling, what I believe is that Alexa was upset, and driving carelessly, and that what happened was a terrible accident."

"That's what I believe, too."

"But, Catherine, we have to consider the possibility that whoever made the call may have also tampered with her car."

"No, James," she whispered, a soft plea from her heart. One year ago today, their world had been torn apart by an act of unspeakable brutality. It couldn't be happening again. *Please.*

"I don't think the police need to know what the caller said, but I think you should tell Lieutenant Baker that you now remember Alexa mentioning that she was coming here," James continued quietly, resolutely, even though all he really wanted to do was to hold her and reassure her. But he couldn't, so he urged gently, "Help me with this, Catherine. Doesn't that seem like what we should do? Doesn't that seem best, safest, for Alexa while we're waiting to know for certain that it was an accident?"

"Yes, I guess, it does," she said finally. "Yes. All right. I agree."

"OK. Good. Was the caller a man or a woman?"

"It was a whisper." Catherine frowned, searching for a clue, an impression, something. But there was nothing. "I don't know. I can't even guess."

"Did you notice if anyone was following you when you left me at Inverness?"

"No," she answered softly. "I didn't notice anything. I was just thinking about what we—I—had said. James, I'm sorry."

"I'm sorry, too, Catherine."

CHAPTER TWENTY-EIGHT

$\mathcal{M}$emorial Hospital's eighth-floor Intensive Care Unit waiting room was indistinguishable from the one on the first floor adjacent to the Operating Room. Both rooms were windowless and sparsely furnished with well-worn vinyl couches, institutional clocks, and coffee tables littered with frequently clutched but rarely read magazines. The two waiting rooms were essentially identical. But, nonetheless, when Catherine, Robert, and James received word, just after midnight, that they would be continuing their vigil in the bland room eight floors up, they greeted the news with unconcealed tears of joy.

Alexa had survived her first hurdle.

"We're closing now," the trauma chief told them. Even if they hadn't understood the surgical jargon, they would have known from the surgeon's fatigued but triumphant face that the report was good. "Alexa was terribly lucky. The internal bleeding was very significant, but we were able to oversew the hepatic and splenic lacerations, so no removal of organs was necessary."

The trauma chief was the first in a series of physicians to appear throughout the long night and give reports on Alexa's progress.

"She has multiple rib fractures," the pulmonary specialist informed them at one A.M. "The lung tissue beneath the fractures is injured, which means we will keep her on the ventilator for a while. This will insure adequate ventilation to the damaged areas, and in addition, because the ventilator will do the breathing for her, it will allow her to conserve energy."

"The period of hypotension—low blood pressure—due to blood loss, coupled with the traumatic injury to muscles, has caused her kidneys to shut down," the renal specialist explained at three-thirty. "We see this quite commonly following severe injuries. Very often, and we hope this will be true for Alexa, the kidneys overcome the shock and recover completely. We will support her until that happens with careful fluid and electrolyte management, and with emergency hemodialysis if necessary."

"She's in a coma," the neurologist said at dawn, shortly before Catherine and Robert left for the airport to meet Alexander and Jane. "I've examined her very thoroughly, and an MRI scan has already been done. There's no evidence of intracranial bleeding and no indication of any permanent neurologic damage."

"So she'll wake up?" Catherine asked softly.

"Yes. She'll wake up. I can't tell you how soon. I can tell you, though, that I've taken care of many patients who have awakened from a coma and remembered the words that had been spoken to them while they were unconscious. So, talk to her. Tell Alexa what you need her to hear."

* * *

They all—her parents, her sister, the man she loved, and the man who was her friend—had emotional words of love they needed their beloved Alexa to hear; and each spent precious moments at her bedside telling her those most important words.

Catherine told Alexa of her love, and then—because what if in Alexa's silent darkness there was the tormenting worry?—she spoke words to reassure. Catherine hoped that Alexa heard her soft, private reassurance, and that the words gave her sister peace.

"James and I decided that the police didn't need to know what the caller said. I told them that it was you, not me, who answered the phone. So don't worry, Alexa, your precious secret is safe." Catherine smiled softly and continued, "James is going to find out where both Hillary and Thompson Hall were at four o'clock yesterday afternoon. Neither of them was at the Marina after your accident, but whichever one it was probably left at the sound of the sirens. The call and the clandestine meeting seem like cloak and dagger theatrics, but remember how we were sitting in the living room discussing plans for Mom and Dad's visit just before the call? Hillary or Thompson must have come to the cottage, heard our voices, and then arranged the meeting at the Marina to speak to you in private. Anyway, somehow James is going to find out where each of them was at the time of the call." She paused, and after a thoughtful moment, she added a quiet truth, "He'll be able to find out, you know he will. He's always been there when you needed him."

Robert gazed through tears at his beloved Alexa. She looked like a porcelain marionette, motionless now, because the strings attached to her pale delicate body—the intravenous lines and monitor leads—had yet to bring her to life. How he wanted to curl her broken body in his arms and carry her away . . . to RoseCliff . . . to their wonderful love.

But Robert couldn't take her away, not yet. He could only hold her lifeless hand in his and touch his warm cheek to her cool one as he spoke.

"My darling love," he whispered. "It's been almost twenty-four hours since your accident, twenty-four miraculous hours. Your kidneys are already recovering from the shock, and your hematocrit is stable, and your lungs beneath the rib fractures are expanding far better than was hoped. Everything is healing miraculously. You just need to wake up, Alexa, that's all."

Robert paused to fight a wave of trembling emotion. He didn't want her to hear his fear, only his confident love. Finally he began again, "I just spoke to Brynne. She sends her love, of course, and even though I told her that given your miraculous recovery we'll very likely spend New Year's with them as planned, she insists on coming here to visit you anyway. They'll drive up tomorrow, assuming the roads are clear and Stephen can get away early enough. She thinks they'll arrive too late to visit tomorrow night, but says she'll be here bright and early the following morning."

And you'll be wide awake by then, won't you, my darling? he pleaded silently, pausing again as his voice threatened to falter. He fought the emotion with the memory of his conversation with Brynne, her obvious love for Alexa, her confident insistence that Alexa would be fine, and the happy images Brynne had wanted him to share with her. "Brynne wanted me to tell you that Katie is absolutely enraptured by the bright lights of Christmas, especially the twinkling lights on the tree. She says she's taking thousands of pictures, so we'll be able to see her joy for ourselves."

The happy images of Katie's sparkling eyes laughing with glee at twinkling

Christmas lights swept Robert swiftly, emotionally, to other happy images, future ones, magnificent dreams. "Did I tell you how much I like your parents? I know I did, a thousand times already, but in case you weren't listening before, they're wonderful, my darling. What wonderful grandparents they will be for our babies. Oh Alexa, Alexa, think of our love, our life, our babies . . ."

We have a baby, Robert! We have a beautiful little girl who is enraptured by the twinkling lights of Christmas. Alexa's emerald eyes fluttered open then, and with complete consciousness came an acute awareness of all the sensations that had previously been only a vague part of the dream world in which she had been living. She was instantly aware of the fire in her chest, and every muscle in her body felt as if she had exerted it far beyond endurance. But Alexa ignored the fire and firmly instructed her muscles to endure just a little more—for Robert.

And then, for the tear-filled dark eyes she loved so very much, Alexa found a beautiful smile.

"She's awake," Robert said emotionally when he returned to the ICU waiting room ten minutes later and gave the wonderful news to her family.

"Awake?" Jane echoed.

"Oh, Robert . . ."

"She's awake, although I think she's about to drift off to sleep. She awakened a little while ago, and I guess I should have come out the second she opened her eyes, but I couldn't bear to leave her."

"That's all right," Alexander whispered hoarsely. "Do you think she recognized you?"

"Oh, yes, I know she did," Robert answered quietly. "And I'm sure that very soon, she'll be insisting that they remove the endotracheal tube so she can talk to us."

Robert's loving face revealed neither the urgency he felt about hearing what Alexa would say, nor the guilt. He had known, ever since he had first seen her again, that there was a deep, painful, hidden sadness. He had hoped to love it away, and in the past few months, there had been wonderful, breathtaking moments when her emerald eyes had glowed with pure joy; but, so quickly and always, the sad, painful flickers would return. And when gently, so very gently, he had urged her to tell him what troubled her so, she resolutely denied anything was wrong at all. But Robert had proof, in the beautiful eyes he knew so well; and in their loving, *her* loving, a loving that was as desperate and furtive as it had been before—as if she still did not believe their wonderful love would last. He had urged her to tell him, many times, but sometimes even his gentle questions caused whispers of emerald fear, and, instead of pushing further, he just held her.

But I should have pushed her! The tormenting thought had echoed and reechoed in his mind ever since the accident. If I *had*, might she never have taken the nearly lethal drive? Oh, did my beloved Alexa almost die to protect a secret she kept from me?

"I'm sorry to interrupt." The words came from the ICU clerk who now stood in the open doorway of the waiting room. "There's an overseas call for Catherine at the nurses' station."

"Oh. Thank you."

It would be Alain, Catherine knew. As she walked from the waiting room to the nurses' station, she realized that it had been twenty-four hours, almost precisely to the minute, since she had reached for the ringing phone at RoseCliff hoping the caller would be Alain. She had needed his gentle warmth then to melt the icy ghosts that had frolicked within her after the angry, hurtful words she had spoken to James. But yesterday afternoon, the caller had been the whispering messenger of tragedy, not Alain, and since that sinister call, she and James had been gently bonded by their love for Alexa and by the precious secret they kept for her. Catherine's angry and hurtful words had long since been forgotten, perhaps even forgiven; but still, now, twenty-four hours later, the icy ghosts lingered—because, she had discovered, it was so terribly difficult to be this close to James . . . and yet so far away.

Now, twenty-four hours later, Catherine needed the warmth of Alain's gentle love still, perhaps even more now than she had needed it yesterday afternoon.

"Alain?"

"*Oui*, Catherine. How is she, *chérie*, how is Alexa?"

"Oh, Alain, she's better. She had been in a coma, but just a few minutes ago, she woke up."

"I'm so glad, darling. And I'm so sorry I wasn't with you. I only just heard the news. Have you been trying to reach me?"

"No. Your itinerary and all the phone numbers you gave me are at RoseCliff, and I've been here since the accident. I knew you'd call as soon as you heard."

"It was Natalie who heard. She just phoned me."

"You're not together?"

"No. She went to Gstaad the evening before last, as scheduled, and I decided to spend one more day in Paris. I was at Versailles all day yesterday, and although I'm sure that the radio and television carried reports of Alexa's accident last night, I spent the evening reading—and calling you. Now I know why there was no answer at RoseCliff. I'm so sorry I haven't been with you all this time, darling, but I will be there very soon, and Natalie is coming too."

"Oh, no, Alain, you don't need to come."

"I want to be with you, Catherine."

Alain's warm words didn't melt the icy ghosts. *Indeed* they only triggered more chilling memories of the other love; memories of the time of great tragedy when Catherine had wanted desperately to be with James—to love him, to help him— and James had not allowed her to be. Was she doing that now with Alain? No, not at all. Just the opposite.

"I would want you to be with me if Alexa weren't better, Alain," she said softly, truthfully. "But she *is* better. She's going to be fine."

"Cat and I were having tea, discussing plans for our parents' visit, when the phone rang." Alexa narrowed her beautiful green eyes, searching for the precise memory, and after a moment continued, "I said something like 'Your Prince or mine?' and . . ."

"And?" Lieutenant Baker urged.

"And then darkness. It was a silent darkness—and so very black—but finally it became gray and was filled with familiar voices that were calling to me. I wanted to answer them, to reassure them, but there was such heaviness." Alexa frowned at the almost desperate memory of hearing the voices of those she loved and wanting to cry out to them—Yes, I hear you, I love you, *I love you!*—but unable even to open her eyes. She shook away the memory and smiled. "And then I woke up."

"You don't remember what the caller said."

"No. My memory stops just before I answered the phone."

"You don't remember the accident at all?"

"No. Lieutenant, I'm very sorry. I remember nothing except blackness from the moment I asked 'Your Prince or mine?' until I was here in the ICU. Nothing. I'm sorry. I want to remember, but I can't."

Alexa couldn't remember, and according to the neurologist who had been caring for her, she never would.

"It's called retrograde amnesia," the doctor explained. "It means loss of memory for the event and for a period of time prior to it. It's very common in serious head injuries."

"Will she ever remember those lost minutes?"

"No. She never will."

Alexa's retrograde amnesia meant that the police investigation would close, officially ruled an accident. The car had been destroyed beyond any hope of finding evidence of tampering, had there been any, and with neither that evidence nor Alexa's clear memory of a mechanical failure, the "case" could not be pursued. *Case?* Lieutenant Baker asked himself as he signed the final page of the report. *What case? Who the hell would want to murder Alexa Taylor?*

Alexa's retrograde amnesia meant that the police investigation was closed, and it meant, too, that Catherine and James would need to tell her about the telephone call she could not remember. They decided to tell her together, while Robert was spending a few necessary hours in his office and while Jane and Alexander were resting in their nearby hotel.

"James and I know what the caller said, Alexa."

"So do I, Cat."

"You remember?"

"Yes. I remember the call. And I remember your telling me what you had told the police and why." She added softly, gratefully, "Thank you. Thank you both."

"You're welcome."

"Do you remember the accident, Alexa?" James asked.

She softly shook her golden head, still bewildered that, despite how hard she tried to remember, those monumental moments remained hidden, and always would. "What I told Lieutenant Baker about the blackness is true, but it began a few minutes later, just as I left the cottage. Did you find out who made the call, James?"

"No. I only found out that it couldn't have been made by either Thompson or Hillary."

"It couldn't have?"

"No. I spoke with Thompson myself. He was quite surprised by my visit, and seemed uncomfortable that I knew about his investigation of you, but he said that the investigation was completed weeks ago, before Thanksgiving, and that it turned up nothing of consequence." As James recalled the meeting with Thompson, his memory affirmed what he had concluded then: that Thompson Hall was telling the truth. James had obviously caught him off guard, and in those unguarded moments there had been barely concealed disappointment that he had found nothing to prevent the marriage, but not a flicker of guilt or deceit. "I believe him, Alexa. And, he has a fairly airtight alibi for the time of the call. He was with Robert."

"Oh. So it *has* to be Hillary."

"But it wasn't. She's in Dallas now, apparently enjoying her role as the spurned wife, or at least capitalizing on it. Anyway, because I didn't want to leave Washington, I had someone who Elliot recommended check up on her. It turns out that on the day of the accident, she was actually in Savannah at the Willows. As part of the tranquil environment of the spa, guests at the Willows don't have phones in their rooms. There's just one phone, in the main office, and Hillary didn't use it at all during her three day stay." James paused, and then added slowly, "She didn't personally make the call at four Wednesday afternoon. But, Alexa, that doesn't mean she didn't have someone make it for her, and it doesn't mean she didn't hire someone to tamper with your car."

"No one tampered with my car, James! I was upset. I was driving too fast and lost control. Fortunately, I had the sense to jump clear."

"But you don't remember that."

"No, but that's what happened. I'm sure of it. No one I know is capable of murder, James," Alexa whispered softly, wanting to believe it, no, *believing* it, because it was too horrible to believe anything else. She added with a trembling smile, "Not even Hillary. Besides, Hillary could have very easily achieved what she wanted—the end of my plans to marry Robert—by simply letting me know that she knew about the baby. She didn't need any treachery beyond words. I think, had she known, she would have told me in person, reveling in that final victory." Alexa paused, sighed softly, and continued quietly, "But someone knows, someone from the hospital, I suppose. It hardly matters who knows, or even if they know anything more than that I had a baby girl I gave away. What matters is that someone knows something, and whatever it is, it's enough . . . too much."

As Catherine heard the resignation in Alexa's voice and saw the hopelessness as the emerald eyes envisioned a life without Robert, she realized that Alexa was still planning to say good-bye to her love.

"You have to tell Robert, Alexa." Catherine's voice was soft, as always, but it was laced with urgency. "He needs to know."

"Oh, Cat, how can I tell him? The truth would cause him such sadness, such pain. I love him far too much to tell him."

"But that's wrong, Alexa, don't you see? Yes, of course, this truth will cause Robert great sadness, but not too much, not more than you yourself live with every minute of every day. And maybe if you and Robert shared the sadness, the pain would be less for both of you." Catherine sighed softly, so very aware of the intense dark blue eyes that gazed at her. You may not believe this, James, but I do! "Robert loves you *so much*, Alexa. I know you want to protect him, because you love him, but isn't that terribly unfair to him, and to your love?" She took a breath, and her sapphire eyes didn't look at his dark blue ones, they couldn't, as she added quietly, "Maybe all loves aren't strong enough to survive both joy and sadness, but surely the love you have with Robert is."

As Alexa listened to Catherine's soft, impassioned words, she began to feel something that felt miraculously, wonderfully, like hope.

"My wise little sister," she whispered gently.

"I'm not wise, Alexa."

"Well, I think you are. You always have been. You're right, Cat. I do need to tell Robert." I need to, she thought, but can I? Yes, I can, I *will*. Alexa made the silent promise to her hopeful heart, and then she sealed it bravely by saying aloud, "I'll tell him tonight, while you're at the White House. Are you going to Cat's concert, James?"

The question startled him, because he had been so lost in memories, but he recovered quickly and answered with an easy smile, "No. I actually have quite a bit of work I need to do. Elliot likes to have an unofficial record of my overall impressions of the negotiations—and the negotiators—and I need to get going on that while my memories are still fresh."

And besides, he thought, Catherine hasn't invited me to attend her concert.

But it would be safe now, wouldn't it, Catherine? There would be no risk, now, that you would stop playing and leave the stage to be with me, where you belong, would there? James knew the painful answers to his questions without even looking at the beloved sapphire eyes. Yes, it would be quite safe. She had a new love now, a love that she so obviously believed was far deeper and far stronger than their magical love had ever been.

CHAPTER TWENTY-NINE

After James and Catherine left, Alexa refused all the afternoon's scheduled pain medications. The frequent demerol shots made her groggy, permitting her trying-to-heal body to fall easily into necessary—and almost constant—sleep; and she needed to be wide awake when she told Robert the truth. The demerol was for pain, too, the doctors said, but Alexa had already decided, even though she had never used drugs, that she must have an innate tolerance. She was receiving lots of demerol, and although it made her sleepy, it did very little to numb the pain.

Or so she thought. As the afternoon wore on, and the demerol wore off, Alexa realized that the fire in her chest had simply been a smoldering ember, prevented from flaming by the narcotic, and the immense aching in her muscles had been nothing—the ache of a weekend athlete who has overexerted—compared to the bone-deep pain she felt when the drug was withdrawn. And she had been completely unaware, under the constant influence of demerol, of the recent surgical incision in her abdomen.

Now the screams of her damaged bones and nerves and muscles and skin were unmuzzled, loud and piercing, keeping her very wide awake, even though her unnumbed battle against pain expended her precious and limited energy.

She was very wide awake when Robert arrived. Her beautiful pale face was haloed by shining gold, washed and brushed by a generous nurse, and she was propped up, positioned among pillows that, without the demerol, had lost their softness against her bruised and ravaged body.

"Hello, darling." Robert greeted her lips with a gentle kiss.

"Hello," she whispered. She wanted the gentle kiss to last forever, but she knew her energy was limited, and she had made promises to her heart. "Robert?"

"Yes, my love?"

"I know what the call was about."

"Tell me, darling," he urged softly. And then, because he saw such fear in her beautiful eyes, he assured gently, "Whatever it is, Alexa, our love is stronger."

Oh, Robert, how I hope that is true! She took a soft breath, and waited for the fiery flames in her chest to fade, and then she looked into his loving eyes and said very quietly, "The call was about a beautiful baby girl who was abandoned by her mother."

"Alexa?"

"She's our daughter, Robert. Katie is our baby."

"Oh, no." It was a long, slow whisper of pain. "Oh, Alexa."

As she gazed at him through the blur of her own tears, the screams of pain from her heart drowned out even the deafening screams of pain from all the unnumbed nerves in her badly battered body. Oh, Robert, how this has hurt you! her heart cried as she saw his stricken eyes, tear-filled, too, and so very wounded. I should have said good-bye to you, my love, instead of telling you, she thought. And then, as she watched his immense pain, Alexa was suddenly swept by a new fear. Have I caused you this anguish in vain? Will we say good-bye, after all, because this is far too great a truth for you to understand or forgive?

"Oh, Robert, I'm so sorry," she whispered softly, helplessly, as she tried desperately to reach the dark eyes that were so very dark now, so very turbulent, so very far away. "When I made the decision, I believed it was the best for Katie, for her happiness. And she is happy, Robert, and so very loved."

As Robert heard the hopelessness in Alexa's voice, he pulled himself from his swirling emotions and looked at the woman he would always love with all his heart. And when he saw her despair, and her fear, he echoed gently, "Yes, so very loved, Alexa. Katie is the most loved little girl in the world."

"Brynne's little girl, Robert?"

Robert knew what his beloved Alexa was asking with her trembling question. She was asking him to live this devastating secret with her and to conquer the immense sadness and loss with their love.

No! his heart cried in swift protest. Katie is *our* baby, *our* precious little girl. She loves us, and we love her. From the very first moment I held her, and every time since, there has been something so extraordinary, a joy beyond all words; and, my darling, whenever you and Katie are together, you're in your own special world, shared by just the two of you, a secret place of love. I've seen your special love for Katie, and hers for you, and now I understand it. Oh, Alexa, Katie is our little girl!

The protests came swiftly and powerfully. *But there were other places in Robert's loving heart.* And now it was their turn to speak, reminding him of his great love for Brynne, and of all her losses, and of his vow to protect her always. The gentle voices came with images—Brynne and Stephen and Katie together—and those were such joyous, such happy images, too, of love. The voices that spoke to Robert from the place in his heart where his love for Brynne lived were gentle and very compelling, but even they might not have persuaded him to abandon his wish to claim Katie as his own.

But then another voice spoke, a gentle, quiet voice that called to him from the greatest love of all, his love for Alexa. She had made this most generous decision of love, for Katie, for Brynne, and, even, Robert realized, for him; and she had lived with the excruciating pain of that decision every second of every day, hiding it, protecting them all. Now his beloved Alexa was asking him to live that painful secret with her. And Robert knew that he would, for her, because of her; and he knew, too, that he would never, not for an instant, allow her to doubt the decision of love that she had made.

"Brynne's little girl," he echoed finally, smiling a trembling, but so confident smile of love to her lovely, tearful emerald eyes. "I love you, Alexa. I love you."

He held her then, cradling her very gently, but she pressed closer and closer, and he held her ever more tightly, until they were so close, so tight, that there was no room between them for secrets, not ever again. And even though he held her bruised and ravaged body so tightly against his own, somehow, magically, there was no physical pain . . . and even the screams of pain from her heart were silenced now by his love.

"Robert? Alexa?"

At first Brynne's soft voice was simply part of the images that swirled in their minds, because, as they held each other, vowing to keep Alexa's promise of love, the images they both saw were images of Brynne: her hopelessness and anguish at the loss of yet another small beloved life, and her radiant joy as she loved her little Katie.

But after a moment, they both realized that the soft familiar voice wasn't part of the images at all. It was real. She was here.

"Brynne," Robert whispered as he opened his eyes and gazed beyond Alexa's golden head to the smiling, slightly apologetic face of his little sister.

"I'm intruding."

"No," Alexa assured quickly, recovering far more quickly than Robert, because she had lived this secret for so long, and because she knew that now, especially now, everything had to seem quite normal—and normally, she and Robert wouldn't have considered it an intrusion at all for the sister they both loved to have found them embracing, especially not after Brynne had just made the trip from Richmond because of her love for them. Alexa found a beautiful, welcoming smile and said, "Hi, Brynne. Come in."

"Are you sure? I know I said I thought we'd arrive too late tonight to be able to visit, but Stephen was able to get away early after all . . ."

"Come in," Robert echoed, trying to sound as calm as Alexa, but having no idea whether he succeeded because his racing heart pumped sounds of thunder to his brain.

"Well . . . OK." Brynne smiled. "Thank you. How are you doing, Alexa?"

"I'm fine, Brynne." I will be fine, Alexa thought. Until now, she had been using her determined mind to try to convince her wounded body to heal. But, she realized now, it wasn't mind over matter that would work, it was heart over matter. She would heal quickly now, her heart would see to it, so that she could be home with Robert. "I'm just fine."

"Good. I'm glad." Brynne knew she had intruded on something important. Maybe it had something to do with why she was here, and maybe not. At any other time, she would have gracefully withdrawn, but tonight she had her own important words to say, in private, to Alexa; and for her own heart, and for Alexa, she needed to say them now. And so, with an uncharacteristic and almost sassy smile, she looked at her older brother and asked, "Could I talk to Alexa alone, please, just for a little while?"

Normally, Robert would have teased her about "girl talk." But he couldn't be normal, not now, not yet. Now he very much welcomed the chance for a little privacy—assuming Alexa was comfortable. I'm fine, Robert, her emerald eyes lovingly told him, I love you.

"OK," he agreed. He gestured to the briefcase he always brought with him, work to do during the long hours while Alexa slept, but when he stayed anyway to be near her, and added, "I have plenty to do. I'll be in the waiting room."

After Robert left, Brynne removed the bulky winter coat she had been wearing, and, as she did, Alexa saw that not all of the bulk was the down-filled coat.

"Brynne," she whispered as she saw her future sister-in-law's very pregnant shape.

"She's a little girl, Alexa, a very healthy, very lively little girl," Brynne said softly, her brown eyes misting at what was still an almost unbelievable joy. "I'm already seven months along and the doctors say everything is going perfectly."

"Seven months?" Alexa echoed, frowning slightly as she recalled the last time she had seen Brynne. It had been less than a month ago, at Thanksgiving. Alexa had many joyous memories of that holiday weekend in Richmond, and she had a very clear memory of Brynne, how radiant she had been, how rosy her cheeks, how glowing—joyful signs of pregnancy, even though her body had been slender as always.

"It seems I have the kind of pelvis that allows the baby to grow, healthy but almost invisible, until quite late in the pregnancy."

Alexa nodded softly, fighting a deep ache as she thought, So do I.

Brynne crossed the small room and sat in the chair by the bed, pulling it as close to Alexa as she could be. Then she began, very softly, "She was conceived the night that Katie was born, sometime very shortly after James called to tell us." The pink in Brynne's rosy cheeks deepened slightly at the intimate admission, but it was necessary, part of the words she had come to say. "Stephen and I had decided to never try again, and that night it was quite unplanned, a symbol of our joy, I guess, at the miracle of Katie. And then Katie arrived, and somehow all the happiness and love that came with her made it possible for this tiny new life to grow and flourish inside me. I truly believe that, Alexa. I truly believe that this healthy little girl, this miracle inside me, is because of the miracle of Katie." Brynne drew a soft breath, preparing her own heart, and then said very gently, "Because of Katie, and, Alexa, because of you. She's your baby girl, isn't she?"

The sudden tears in the emerald eyes gave Brynne her answer, even though it was a while before Alexa could speak, or even nod her golden head. She nodded finally, slowly, to the dark brown eyes that were tear-filled, too, and, after a few more moments, she whispered, "How did you know?"

"I didn't know, not for sure, until this moment. And it didn't even occur to me, not consciously at least, until your accident. Robert told me about the mysterious phone call that was clearly so upsetting to you, and about his own fear that there had always been a secret you'd kept from him. It all came together then, at a conscious level, even though my memory had been recording images of you and Katie together for a long time, especially that first day, when I watched you holding her and you didn't know I was there. I know you tried to hide it, and if it weren't for the accident I don't know when or if I would have realized, but now I do." Brynne paused, because even though she and Stephen had discussed it over and over, and had agreed, and even though it was what her own loving heart wanted and believed, it was still so terribly difficult. "Now I do know, Alexa, and what I want, and what Stephen wants, is for Katie to be with you."

"Oh, Brynne," she whispered, a whisper of tears and joy and disbelief. "Oh, Brynne."

"Robert loves Katie," Brynne continued, speaking more of the words she had planned to say, to convince Alexa, even though the emerald eyes needed no convincing. "It won't matter to him, not at all, who her father was. He will love her as his own."

"Robert is Katie's father," Alexa said quietly.

"Oh," Brynne breathed with a rush of emotion. With Stephen's gentle help, she had carefully prepared her heart, as much as was possible, for this conversation with Alexa. But this revelation was completely unanticipated. She had believed, because they had both told her so convincingly, that their love had begun just last summer, after Robert's separation from Hillary and two months after Katie had been born. Now, as Brynne learned this new truth, her heart and her eyes flooded with fresh tears. "Does he know?"

"I told him just before you arrived."

"And you'd decided never to tell me, hadn't you?" Brynne asked softly.

Alexa's soft shrug gave her the answer, and in the next moments of silence, as they gazed at each other through the blur of even more tears, both realized the gifts of love that each had been so willing to give, and the secrets of love that each would have been so willing to keep. In those silent moments, Brynne realized that Alexa and Robert had decided never to tell the truth about Katie, and that they would have kept that solemn vow; and, in those silent moments, Alexa realized that once Brynne had guessed the truth, even if she hadn't been blessed with the miracle that lived within her now, she would have come to her and spoken the words she had spoken tonight.

"I love you," Alexa whispered finally.

"I love you, too," Brynne answered quietly. Then, with a soft smile, she stood and announced decisively, "Well. Why don't I go get Robert? We have plans to make."

Brynne found her brother alone in the small, windowless waiting room. Robert hadn't opened his briefcase, of course. He had spent the private moments sitting with his elbows on his knees and his head in his hands, absolutely motionless, even though his heart pounded and his thoughts whirled.

"Robert?"

"Brynne," he said, looking up, his eyes unfocused at first, but focusing quickly as he saw her pregnancy. "Brynne?"

Brynne gazed at the brother who had spent his lifetime protecting her, and would have protected her still, keeping this painful secret, and said softly, lovingly, "I'm having a baby girl, a cousin for Katie."

She saw the joyous comprehension in his dark eyes, and for the first time in her life she saw tears. Always before, even as a little boy, Robert had hidden his tears from her, bravely protecting her from all the sadnesses he knew so well. But now he didn't hide his tears, these tears of joy, not sadness, and as they moved to hug each other she whispered, "Oh, Robert, what loving cousins our daughters will be."

After the White House concert, and after dining with the President and First Lady, Jane, Alexander, and Catherine returned to their hotel, located directly across the street from Memorial Hospital. Catherine stopped briefly in her parents' room, long enough for Alexander to call the hospital to make certain that Alexa was all right, and, upon learning that she was, she kissed them good night.

But Catherine didn't go to her room down the hall. Instead, still wearing the long green velvet skirt and ivory silk blouse beneath her winter coat, she walked into the chilly midnight air and across the street to the hospital. Alexa was out of the ICU now, and on the ward, where visiting hours were more strictly enforced. The evening visiting hours had long since ended, of course; but it was Christmastime, when any patient who could be home was home, and Catherine knew that the rules had softened for those who had to remain. After waving at the nurses, and receiving friendly conspiratorial waves in return, she walked quietly to Alexa's room.

The door was ajar. Catherine drew a soft breath before looking in, a hopeful wish that she would find Alexa sleeping peacefully. That was what she hoped to find, but she had come tonight in case Alexa was still awake, unable to fall into a peaceful sleep because of tormenting memories of telling Robert the truth. Her heart skipped a sad, sympathetic beat when she saw that Alexa was awake, propped up against pillows, gazing outside at the midnight darkness. But, as she neared, Catherine saw a soft smile, dreamy and most peaceful, on Alexa's beautiful face.

"Alexa?"

"Hi," Alexa answered, turning to her with a smile of surprise and welcome. "I'm so glad you're here. I was going to ask them to bring in a phone so I could call you." Her emerald eyes misted as she said softly, "Katie is coming home to us, Cat."

"Oh, Alexa. How . . .?"

Alexa told her in a breathless rush of joy and tears, completely ignoring, as she had ignored for hours, the flames in her chest as she drew the deep necessary breaths at the end of each rush.

"Brynne and Stephen and Katie are across the street, in the same hotel as you, and they've said you're welcome to meet your niece whenever you want."

"Really? You're sure that it's all right?"

"Yes. This is difficult for Brynne and Stephen, of course," Alexa said quietly. "But they are being so wonderful, so generous. They're going to stay here until I'm ready to be discharged, and then Katie and Robert and I will begin our life together at RoseCliff." Their life together would begin at RoseCliff, and, someday they would move into a larger home; but they would never live in the White House. It didn't matter, Robert had reminded her gently. She mattered and Katie mattered. And, he had told her between tender kisses, even though he would leave public office, he would never leave public service, nor would his commitment to helping insure a joyous and peaceful world for his wife and daughter ever waver. Alexa smiled at those loving memories, and her emerald eyes sparkled as she told Catherine the rest of the plans they had made. "Robert and I will be married as soon as it can be arranged, definitely before I leave the hospital and before you and Mom and Dad leave."

"I don't have to leave on the twenty-sixth, Alexa, and even though Dad has performances scheduled with the symphony, I'm sure they could get an alternate and—"

"Oh, no, Cat. I'm going to be ready for discharge by the twenty-sixth, or the twenty-seventh at the very latest. In fact, I was just informing my body of that when you arrived." She smiled, remembering the silent instructions she had been issuing, the joyous commands of heart over matter. She would heal, in record time, for her daughter and her husband. "And once I'm discharged, and Katie and Robert and I are at RoseCliff . . ."

"You'll be the family of three that you want to be," Catherine gently finished the thought. "And that's all you'll want or need."

"Yes," Alexa answered softly, grateful that Cat understood. "I think we need time alone together."

"I think so, too. OK. We'll all leave as scheduled on the twenty-sixth, but I'll be back, whenever you're ready for visitors, and I know that Mom and Dad will be counting the days . . ." Catherine stopped abruptly as she saw the sudden look of doubt in Alexa's face. "Alexa?"

"Oh, Cat, I'm so afraid to tell them about Katie."

"What?" Catherine asked, not questioning the reality of Alexa's fear, because she saw the sudden emerald uncertainty, but amazed, astonished, that it would exist. "Afraid, Alexa? Why?"

"Because I know they'll be so disappointed—not about Katie, of course—but in me, because I gave her away."

"No, Alexa, they won't be disappointed. They'll understand perfectly why you did what you did. I know they will."

Alexa softly shook her golden head. She knew very well that she was going to once again disappoint the parents she loved so much—even though she saw such confidence in her little sister's eyes. Oh, those wise sapphire eyes. How Alexa wished she could believe them this time! But this time, Cat, she thought sadly, I know that you are wrong.

"Alexa . . ."

"Could you tell them for me, Cat?" she asked suddenly, on impulse, her voice soft, uncertain, almost desperate. Alexa knew the great love, the extraordinary closeness, between her parents and Cat. Maybe . . . "Maybe, if you explained to them they *would* understand. You know everything about why I made the decision that I made, and we were planning to tell them this visit that I knew you were adopted, remember? So, maybe, you could tell them about that, and how close we are now, and how it was because of what I did that you told me?"

Catherine knew Alexa was wrong. Their loving parents would not be disappointed. But, she wondered as she listened to Alexa's soft impassioned plea, what if *she* was wrong? She wanted to spare Alexa that sadness, all sadnesses.

"All right, Alexa," she agreed gently. "I'll tell them."

"We just met our beautiful granddaughter," Jane said, her voice filled with love and wonder as she greeted her golden-haired daughter the next morning.

"She's very lovely," Alexander added with quiet emotion.

Alexa looked at them, and even though she saw love, and not a flicker of disappointment, she whispered softly, "I'm sorry."

"Sorry, my darling. *Why?*" Jane asked, genuinely incredulous, even though she was a little prepared. After Catherine had told them everything—and they hadn't been disappointed, not for a second, only sad and concerned about the silent anguish Alexa had endured—she had told them, too, about Alexa's worry. She repeated softly, "Why, Alexa?"

"I thought you'd be disappointed that I gave her away."

"No, darling. We understand. It was a courageous choice made from the deepest of love." Jane gently touched her daughter's silky golden hair, just as she had on that distant day in the park when she had tried to gently reassure Alexa about her new little sister. "We've never been disappointed in you, Alexa."

"Oh, but you were, don't you remember? You were so terribly disappointed in me when I first saw Cat and didn't want her to be my sister. Don't you remember?"

"We'll never forget those moments, Alexa," Alexander answered softly. "We weren't disappointed in you, darling, not at all. We were stunned that you so confidently announced that she wasn't your little sister, and that it upset you so, and I think we were both suddenly very worried that what we thought was truly a miracle was going to be a terrible mistake."

"We lost a little of you that day, Alexa," Jane added quietly. "You were always our happy, confident, golden girl, and after that . . ." She sighed softly. They had lost a little of their precious daughter that day, and, as desperately as they had tried, they had never, not in all these years of loving her, been able to rediscover that missing piece. Looking lovingly at the emerald eyes, so very much like her own, Jane whispered gently, "We love you so much, Alexa. You've never disappointed us, you never could."

Alexa listened to their wonderful words and wanted so much to believe them. But she had such a clear memory of that distant day. There *had* been disappointment then, she knew it. But, she wondered now, had the disappointment been her own, deep inside her, terrible disappointment at the discovery of the dark, ugly monsters that dwelled in her own heart? Yes, perhaps, *yes*. There had been ugly monsters within her, lurking in the shadows of her heart; but all those monsters were gone now, never to return, conquered and vanquished by love.

"It was truly a miracle. I love my little sister so very much," she said softly, her eyes lighted from within by a deep golden glow. Then she added, even more softly, as tears fell from the luminous emerald, "And Mom? Daddy? I love you so much, too."

Tears filled all eyes, and for a moment neither Jane nor Alexander could speak, because they saw in their beloved daughter's sparkling eyes the immeasurable joy of knowing, truly knowing, that she was loved completely, unconditionally, always. At last, oh at last, the Alexa they had lost was finally found! They hadn't seen this magnificent look of pure and confident happiness on her beautiful face for such a very long time, not since . . .

"You look exactly the way you looked on that morning in May when we were driving to Kansas City," Jane began emotionally; and when she faltered, Alexander gently and emotionally, too, finished his wife's thought, "Exactly the way you looked when you announced, with your unshakable confidence, that you were going to have a baby sister."

CHAPTER THIRTY

*R*obert and Alexa were married on Christmas Day, a wedding joyfully witnessed by little sisters and parents, but not by James. He was invited, of course, but it was easier for him, for his heart, to stay away. He spent Christmas alone at Inverness, sailing until the winter twilight. He sailed all day the following day, too, and then worked late into the night completing the meticulous notes that he presented to Elliot in his office at eight on the morning of the twenty-seventh.

"I didn't expect these so soon," Elliot said. "This must mean all is well with Alexa?"

"All is very well. In fact, she's going home today."

"Is her family still here?"

"No. They left yesterday, her parents to Topeka, and Catherine to L'île."

"To L'île," Elliot murmured thoughtfully.

James watched Elliot's expression drift to the one he had seen before, when Elliot had spoken of the beautiful island paradise, and after a moment he offered quietly, "There's something about you and L'île."

"Yes, James, there is," Elliot admitted. He had been thinking about telling James sometime—as a gentle warning perhaps—because with each passing day he saw James becoming more and more like himself. Perhaps now was the time. "It's very old history, thirty two years old to be exact, but it's the reason I am who I am today. Back then, I was a graduate student. I had won a two year scholarship to study philosophy at Oxford and had planned, eventually, to spend an idyllic and scholarly life as a professor at an Ivy League school. Anyway, during a summer holiday, I travelled to L'île, where I met, and fell in love with, Jean-Luc's first wife, Geneviève. Jean-Luc was in exile then in the south of France, and Geneviève had fled from him, seeking sanctuary on L'île because she knew he could not follow her there."

"And she was given asylum?"

"Oh, yes. Alexandre and his wife Isabelle welcomed Geneviève." Elliot smiled with fond remembrance as he added, "They welcomed both of us actually, and gave us privacy for our love. Geneviève and I had only three weeks then, but we knew we would spend our lives together. I had to return to England, and with Alexandre's help, Geneviève was going to end her marriage to Jean-Luc and join me. But shortly after I left L'île, Geneviève discovered she was already pregnant with Jean-Luc's child, the heir he wanted so desperately. She decided to return to him, to give him his heir in exchange for her freedom." Elliot sighed heavily, a sigh weighted with bitterness and regret. "I was so naive then. I had spent my life in the cloistered world of academia. And even Alexandre had underestimated Jean-Luc's evil. But how was he to know his brother's true treachery? Geneviève was the first of the many people Jean-Luc was destined to murder."

"Jean-Luc murdered Geneviève?" James asked softly, emotionally, realizing that it must have been that brutal death that had transformed Elliot from would-be college professor to master spy; just as his own parents' brutal murder had dramatically and irrevocably changed the course of his life, and of his love.

"It was never proven, but there's no doubt. A month after Geneviève gave birth to Alain, she was shot to death in Nice, twenty miles from the villa in which she lived with Jean-Luc. Alain was with her, and I've always wondered if, on that day, she was trying to escape, taking her infant son with her after all, because she couldn't bear the thought of leaving him with Jean-Luc."

"Oh, Elliot, I'm so sorry."

"So am I, James, still, after all these years." Elliot looked thoughtfully at James, knowing he didn't need to point out the obvious: that James was travelling down the same dangerous, solitary path. It was a useful path, of course, and undeniably challenging, but the path started in the name of love inevitably led to a life without any love at all. James knew. Elliot didn't need to tell him. After a moment, Elliot smiled, and, believing he was returning to a happier topic, he asked casually, "Is Catherine giving a concert on L'île?"

"No, Elliot, Catherine is in love with Alain," James answered with quiet apology. *Alain . . . the man because of whom, perhaps, your beloved Geneviève lost her life.* "They plan to marry."

James expected a wince of pain, a bittersweet acknowledgment of the irony, *something* other than what he saw on Elliott's handsome face—a gentle and approving smile.

"That seems appropriate."

"Appropriate?" James echoed with amazement. For some reason, Elliot seemed quite willing to accept the marriage of Catherine and Alain; just as he himself *should* have accepted it. She had obviously found great happiness with Alain, and James wanted happiness, only happiness, for her always; but still, to him, it felt so terribly wrong. "Appropriate, Elliot? Why?"

"Because Catherine looks so astonishingly like Isabelle Castille."

"Isabelle? Alexandre's wife?" James asked, and as he did he suddenly felt a sense of ominous urgency; a feeling that was not yet tethered to conscious thought, but was nonetheless both terrifying and foreboding.

"Yes."

"I remember your telling me in Damascus that Jean-Luc became monarch because Alexandre had no children," James said quietly, as his bright mind began to decipher the ever more urgent, ever more terrifying feelings. "When was that? When did Jean-Luc assume the throne? Do you know?"

"I know everything there is to know about Jean-Luc Castille," Elliot answered softly. "He assumed the throne on January seventh nineteen sixty-eight. Why, James?"

James didn't answer right away. He couldn't. It was impossible, and yet, if it was true . . .

"James?"

"Catherine was born that same year, five months later, in May. Her mother had blond hair and bright blue eyes, just like Catherine's, and she told Jane Taylor, to whom she gave her infant daughter, that it was too dangerous for her baby to stay with her. Catherine's mother offered Jane a velvet satchel filled with jewels, which Jane didn't take, but she did accept, to give to Catherine on her twenty-first birthday, a sapphire necklace. Jane got the feeling that Catherine's father was dead; but because her mother asked that Alexandra be Catherine's middle name, she believed that his name had been Alexander."

As Elliot listened to James's words, his expression changed from polite yet skeptical to alert, concerned, and very interested. As soon as James stopped speaking, Elliot took a small key from the top drawer of his desk and, after inserting it into a side drawer, removed the large battered envelope that contained the only tangible memories of the love that had been so brutally taken from him—a few treasured letters and a few precious photographs.

Elliot kept the envelope in his desk, an unnecessary reminder of why he did what he did, but in truth it had been years since he had opened it. Seven years, to be exact. The envelope of memories had been last opened, and then closed, perhaps forever, when he learned of Jean-Luc's death. Elliott knew there was at least one small black and white photograph of Isabelle, but, until he looked, he had forgotten entirely about the photograph from *Life* magazine. As he unfolded the magnificent picture of the Princess, he realized that his memory hadn't been playing tricks at all about Catherine's remarkable resemblance to her.

"This is Isabelle," Elliot said as he handed the *Life* photograph to James. "It was taken in the palace garden at Monaco the day that Prince Rainier married Princess Grace."

"Elliot, you know this is Catherine," James whispered. "And . . . this is the necklace she was given on her twenty-first birthday. Oh my God."

"What?"

"Last summer, when Catherine was performing in Vienna, her necklace—*this* necklace, Elliot—was stolen. It wasn't the only theft in the hotel that night, but the others were probably done to cast suspicion far away."

"Far away from whom?"

"From Alain. Elliot, we need to get to Catherine—*now*. She's in very great danger. As Alexandre's daughter she, not Alain, is the legitimate heir to L'île, isn't she?"

"Yes, James, but as far as we know, Alexandre and Isabelle Castille never had a child."

"*Haven't you been listening?* They did, *Isabelle* did, after Alexandre died. Isabelle had to give Catherine away because she knew Jean-Luc would never allow her to take the throne from him."

"Even if that's true—and in a moment I will make a call to learn if it is true—there is no reason to assume that Alain knows."

"But Alain *does* know. Catherine told me herself that he knows everything about her." How well his aching heart remembered her words: Alain knows everything about me, James, *everything,* and I know all his secrets, too. "And she believes Alain has been honest with her, too, but in reality he has simply charmed her with lies. She's his *cousin,* after all, and he's told her none of this."

"You're painting Alain Castille to be a very evil man, James."

"Just like his father, Elliot. Alain is Jean-Luc's son, remember? He is the son of the man who murdered the woman you loved. Oh, that's it, isn't it? You're blinded to Alain's evil because he's Geneviève's son as well."

"Perhaps," Elliot admitted softly. "But, James, I've never been the one to make decisions about Alain Castille. I've purposefully stayed very far away from the investigations and allowed others to interpret the findings without my influence. I guess I have always hoped that Geneviève's son would have more of her goodness than Jean-Luc's evil, but, James, that has always seemed to be the truth."

"Until now."

Elliot didn't answer. His answer would have been simply a wish, and what he needed to do now was begin the search for the truth. He dialed an overseas number that he knew by heart—InterPol. After a brief conversation, and a short silent wait while computers at the other end whirred, Elliot had the telephone number to the château in the Loire Valley.

Louis-Philippe's two children and five grandchildren spent every other Christmas with Isabelle and Louis in their château. The grandchildren were there this holiday, scampering around the vast estate, filling the silent halls with gleeful laughter. When Elliot's call came, all five grandchildren were in the kitchen helping their mothers and Isabelle prepare dinner.

Louis-Philippe answered the transatlantic call in his study. Isabelle had told him about Elliot and Geneviève, so he recognized Elliot's name at once. The solemnness in Elliot's tone made Louis-Philippe lure Isabelle from the kitchen with just a gentle smile, waiting to tell her it was Elliot until they neared the quiet study.

"Elliot Archer?" she echoed softly when Louis told her. How long had it been? Isabelle knew the answer without thinking. Elliot had called her in late December, shortly before Alexandre's death, a gentle call of sympathy and love. She had almost told him then about her pregnancy. She might have told him, and asked for his help in hiding her, had she imagined that Jean-Luc would begin following her the instant Alexandre died. And now Elliot was calling, *almost precisely* twenty-two years later to the day, and her voice trembled just a little as she spoke into the phone, "Elliot?"

"Hello, Isabelle. I need to ask you something. I'll just ask it bluntly and if the answer is no, we'll talk of other things."

"What, Elliot?"

"I need to know, Isabelle, if you and Alexandre had a daughter."

"Oh, Elliot," she breathed, eloquently answering his question with emotion. "Have you found her? Is she well? Is she safe? Elliot!"

"Did you give her to a woman in a hospital in Kansas City, Isabelle? Did you give her the sapphire necklace?"

"Yes! *Yes!* Elliot, where is she? Please tell me!"

"She is well, Isabelle," he answered quietly. And was Catherine safe? Elliot didn't know, but he would do everything in his power to see that she was. "She is very lovely. She is very much like you."

"Elliot, I have to see her."

"You will. I'll call you back within the hour."

After he hung up, Elliot stared at the silent phone for several moments before looking at James. Finally he said quietly, a soft astonished sigh, "OK. Catherine is the Princess of L'île. I'm not sure how to proceed."

"Get her the hell away from Alain."

"As far as we know, Alain has done nothing wrong. A necklace stolen on a night when other jewels were taken from other hotel guests does *not* suggest that Alain is responsible. And, James, it is *not* a crime to marry a cousin, assuming Alain even has any idea that that's what he's planning to do."

"He knows."

"We have no evidence that any crimes have been committed, James, no reason to think that Catherine is in any danger whatsoever." Even as Elliot spoke, he frowned slightly, taunted by another ghost from L'île's past.

"What, Elliot? Something is worrying you."

"I was thinking about Alexa's accident."

"*Why?*"

"I got the impression from the interviews I saw with Lieutenant Baker that he was worried about foul play."

"He considered the possibility because there was nothing to indicate that Alexa had tried to avert the accident. The investigation went nowhere because the car was completely destroyed and Alexa has no memory of the moments immediately preceding the crash. *Why*, Elliot?"

"I was thinking about a woman named Monique."

"The French intelligence agent who was sent to investigate Alain and ended up falling in love with him."

"Yes. I don't remember telling you about her."

"You didn't. Natalie did."

"Did she tell you how Monique died?"

"A car accident," James whispered as a tremor of pure fear swept through him.

"Monique was an expert driver, very comfortable with the hairpin turns of the roads along the cliffs of the French Riviera. It was never really clear what made her lose control of her car that day. Alain was following in his car and was an eyewitness to what happened. He said she made no attempt to stop or swerve before the car left the cliffs, as if, perhaps, she had passed out at the wheel. The car was completely destroyed, and the police had no choice but to conclude it was an accident."

"It was Catherine, not Alexa, who answered the phone at RoseCliff," James said with quiet horror. "The message, about a beautiful little girl whose mother had abandoned her, could have been for Alexa, but it also could have been for Catherine. And it was Catherine who was driving Alexa's car that day. Alain Castille is a murderer, Elliot. He murdered Monique, and he tried to murder Catherine."

And she's with him now, halfway around the world, his mind spun with restless horror. I should never have let her go. I should have told her that I love her. I should have asked her if we could try again.

"OK," Elliot said calmly, even though his heart raced, too. "You use the phone in the outer office. Get us on the afternoon Concorde. That will put us in Nice by midnight. Then call Isabelle, have her meet us in Nice, but don't let her know that our eventual destination is L'île. I don't want her going on ahead of us. As of this moment, Alain is a suspect in an attempted murder. That means I can, and immediately will, put in place a team of agents who will watch him and Catherine. He's a suspect, James, that's all. We haven't a shred of proof that any crime has been committed, and we can't move until we do. I mean it. He's like any other free man—presumed innocent until proven otherwise."

"I understand. But you're going to get the proof. You're going to find out that Alain Castille was in Washington on the day of Alexa's accident."

"I'm going to get people working on that right away. But James, if Alain was in Europe on that day, then what we're left with is the delicate issue of an innocent man who believes himself to be the legitimate monarch of L'île, and who has already lost one love, and who has, by extraordinary coincidence, fallen in love with his cousin."

"I don't think we're going to have to worry about delicacy with Alain Castille. I'm very sure he knows everything. Elliot, do you promise me that Catherine will be safe?"

"We have people on L'île, and I'll try to get someone into the palace," Elliot answered. It wasn't a promise. It was simply the best he could do. In the hours it would take to determine Alain's whereabouts on the day of Alexa's accident, he had to hope that Catherine herself would be vigilant.

At Isabelle's gentle but firm insistence, Louis-Philippe remained at the château with his children and grandchildren. I'll bring my daughter back, she told her husband. Isabelle made that brave promise, but in fact, her wishes were far less grand.

If she could just see her daughter, even from a distance, that would be so wonderful. And if somehow she could get close enough to see that there was joy in the blue eyes, proof that her baby's life had been happy, that would be a dream come true.

Isabelle's logical mind didn't dare wish for more, but her loving heart bravely did. What if they could meet and talk and touch? What if, for one precious moment, she could see love in the eyes she feared had hated her ever since they learned the truth?

When Isabelle met James Sterling at midnight in Nice, her heart began to believe in *its* wishes. This handsome man, who so obviously loved her daughter, was going to make all the wishes come true.

It wasn't until they were in their adjacent suites at Le Bijou on L'île that Elliot and James told Isabelle about the potential danger. She understood the danger perfectly, of course. She had known Jean-Luc, after all, and even though she, like Elliot, had hoped that Alain had escaped the madness, she knew it was quite likely that the little boy who had saved her life had not been able to save himself from his father's evil. She understood, and with regal dignity, she hid her heart-stopping fear.

The call for which they had been waiting, *waiting*, finally came. It was a definitive call, and it left them quite stunned.

"Alain was at Versailles all day and in his suite at the Ritz all evening. He didn't make a point of being seen, but he is recognized in Europe, especially in France, and he was definitely seen by many independent observers. There is absolutely no doubt about it, James," Elliot told the skeptical dark blue eyes. "Alain was not in Washington on the day of Alexa's accident."

"Well. That's wonderful," James said evenly. He knew, they both did, that Alain could have hired an assassin, as Jean-Luc often did. But that might take forever to uncover and he wanted to go to Catherine now. "So, it's just that delicate issue, isn't it? I'm sure I'll think of a way to handle that."

"You're going to the palace now?"

"You know I am." James stared evenly at Elliot and then, with a soft smile, turned to Isabelle. "I'm going to tell her that you're here, Isabelle. I'm going to bring her back with me."

"Oh, James. Thank you."

"Why don't you wait a little longer, James," Elliot suggested quietly.

"I thought you said Alain was in the clear."

"Yes, but there are some other things I'm having checked. I should know in about an hour."

"I'll look forward to hearing whatever it is when I get back."

Elliot gave a half-smile. The final details were the most farfetched of all. "OK. Just be careful."

"There's no danger, remember?"

Catherine finished playing Chopin's "Fantasy Impromptu" and smiled softly at Alain.

"*Magnifique*, Catherine."

"*Merci.*" She left the piano bench and joined him at the window overlooking the cove. She saw worry in his dark eyes and asked gently, "Alain?"

"There is something you need to know about me, Catherine."

"All right," she answered, a little surprised that with all they had shared, all their honesty, there was a secret, obviously very important, that Alain kept from her still. It didn't matter what it was, of course, but . . . "Tell me."

"I thought we could walk to the cave." *Where centuries ago the rogue Castilles hid their stolen treasures, and where now you will learn about the greatest thief of them all.* "We can go now, if you like."

"All right. I'll go change my shoes and get a sweater." Catherine smiled at his worried handsome face, and before leaving him, she kissed him very gently on the lips. "Wait for me here. I'll be right back."

CHAPTER THIRTY-ONE

Catherine frowned as she entered her suite of rooms in the east wing of the palace. Someone had drawn the heavy curtains, obscuring the lovely view and creating dark shadows. She felt the fear before her mind told her why; but eventually the memory came: the shadowy suite in Vienna.

Catherine shook off the memory as she crossed the darkened living room to the pink and cream bedroom with its satin and lace canopied bed. She saw the painting immediately, its elegantly carved gold frame propped up against the pink satin; but the magnificent painting's many meanings, and their significance, came more slowly, in layers. At first, she just saw the beauty, not even realizing for a few moments that the beauty was *hers*, a mirror image of her lovely face, framed in spun gold not black velvet. That realization was just beginning to dawn when she suddenly saw the horror.

The beauty and the horror were so out of place together . . . like carnage in paradise . . . like violence at a garden wedding . . . like a bomb on a sailboat at Christmas.

The throat of the beautiful woman in the portrait had been slashed. Fresh, glistening, bright red drops—of paint? of blood?—rolled down the painting, flowing from the slash over the sapphire necklace painted in oil and onto the real sapphire necklace—*hers*—that lay, with her sapphire earrings, on the cream-colored carpet.

"No!" the protest escaped her lips, a soft anguished scream, even though she had not yet begun to comprehend the meaning of what she saw. Catherine didn't comprehend, not yet, but she knew instinctively that it was a truth she would not want to know. It was yet another truth, she feared, that would tear her away from those she loved.

"Catherine? I thought I heard you scream," Natalie said as she rushed into the bedroom. As her eyes followed Catherine's to the portrait, she whispered softly, "Oh, no."

"Natalie? What does it mean? Do you know?"

"Oh, yes, Catherine. I know. It means our beloved Alain has gone mad," she whispered sadly. Very gently, Natalie guided Catherine away from the mutilated portrait and urged her to sit in one of the plush silk chairs. "Sit here for a moment, I think we have a moment, and I will tell you. You don't know about your real mother, do you, or about your connection to L'île?"

"No," Catherine answered shakily.

"The woman in the portrait is your mother."

"My mother?" Catherine echoed softly, starting to rise, to move, to rush back to the portrait. My *mother*.

Catherine started to rise, but she was gently yet firmly stopped by Natalie. "No, Catherine, please don't go back to look at it. I promise, when this is over, I will find you far happier portraits of her."

"Who is she, Natalie?" Catherine asked. Who is she? *Who am I?*

"Her name is Isabelle. She was married to my uncle, Alexandre. You are their daughter, Catherine, which makes you our cousin." Natalie paused a moment before quietly finishing the astonishing revelation to the stunned sapphire eyes. "And that makes you, not Alain, the legitimate monarch of L'île."

No, Catherine's heart answered defiantly, understanding before her swirling mind the painful implications of Natalie's remarkable words. If Natalie knows this, then surely Alain . . . *No,* it can't be. He would have told me. Finally, fearfully, she asked softly, "Alain knows this?"

"Yes. Of course he knows," Natalie answered with gentle sympathy. "Catherine, I know how difficult this is for you, how shocking, and I'm sorry that I have to tell you everything at once, and so quickly. But I must. We have so little time. All right?"

"Yes," Catherine herself agreed, even though, with each passing second, she became more and more confident that these were truths she did not want to hear. *But she had to.* She drew a deep breath and added bravely, "All right. Tell me."

"L'île is Alain's obsession. He loves his island more than anything in the world. Everything he has done has been done to protect this paradise. He hated what our father did to the island, making it a haven for criminals and terrorists not the rendezvous for poets and lovers that it was meant to be. That is why," she explained as softly, as gently, as was possible for the words she had to speak, "when he could stand the desecration no longer, Alain murdered Jean-Luc."

"No!" Catherine countered swiftly in instant defense of the man she loved. But who was the man she loved? Where was he? Did that gentle, loving man even really exist? She had just learned that Alain had betrayed their love, in which their trust had meant so very much, by concealing from her the most important secret of all; and now Natalie was telling her, her beautiful dark eyes solemn and sorrowful, that he was a murderer. Catherine knew that her Alain, the man she had loved, was not. But, she realized, she was learning now about an Alain she didn't know. "Murdered, Natalie?"

"Yes," she replied sadly. "Alain murdered Jean-Luc, and, although I'm certain it was unintentional, because she rarely accompanied Jean-Luc on his trips, he murdered my mother, too. Unlike Jean-Luc, Alain derives no pleasure from murder. Every murder he has committed has been of necessity, necessary deaths so that L'île would flourish under his loving rule."

"Every murder?" Catherine echoed with crescendoing horror, horror at the brutal facts themselves, and horror that she was beginning to believe them.

"Alain also had to kill Monique. He loved her deeply, as I know he truly loves you, Catherine." Natalie sighed softly. "But, I suppose, he feared she would discover that it was he who had assassinated Jean-Luc. Alain fears losing L'île, and it is a fear far greater than the fear of losing his own life. He fears losing L'île, and that, dearest cousin, is why he tried to murder you last Wednesday in Washington. Oh, Catherine, I'm so sorry. I should have known when Alain insisted so firmly that I go ahead to Gstaad while he remained in Paris for another day."

Natalie softly shook her fire-lit auburn hair and then made a confession laced with apology and love, "I am a little blinded by my love for my brother. You yourself know that there is such gentleness in Alain, such goodness—it is not his fault that he is condemned to suffer our father's madness! I have known of his madness, and denied it, praying it would vanish. But now the madness is out in the open, the portrait proves it. Alain's intent to murder you is clear. I fear he may have already murdered Isabelle."

"Oh, no," Catherine whispered, a soft whisper of despair.

"I don't know that he has killed her, Catherine," Natalie added swiftly. "The portrait only makes me think so. But I promise you, when all this is behind us, if Isabelle is alive, you and I will find her. Right now, my cousin, you must leave L'île."

"We both must leave, Natalie," Catherine said, her voice suddenly quite decisive and calm. She was accepting the truths now. She had to. The proof was here, in this lovely bedroom. And there was more proof echoing in her mind—the whispered message about the beautiful baby girl who had been abandoned by her mother. The message had been for her, not Alexa, and it had been delivered to her because Alain recognized her voice.

"No, Catherine. I must stay with Alain. Even though his madness is now full-blown, I know that my brother will not harm me. I can subdue him, I'm sure of it. Perhaps this overt sign of his madness is a desperate plea to have it over with at last. If he could spend his days in an asylum where he could see flowers and listen to music . . . well, I don't know if it is possible, but Catherine, please try to forgive him. He cannot help his madness."

"I'll stay, too, then. We'll subdue him together."

"No, it's not safe for you here. You must believe that, and you must leave now. Later, when it is safe, you can return to claim the island that is rightfully yours, and if you will allow it, I will remain here, too, and we will be cousins, and I hope we will be friends." Natalie smiled softly, a smile of hope, then her beautiful face became focused and solemn. "You must leave, Catherine, now. Take the speedboat. It's very easy to handle. Head due north—there's a compass beside the steering wheel—and you will arrive in Nice. Wait here while I get the keys for you. Lock the door behind me and only open it when you know it's me. Bien?"

"Oui, Natalie, bien. Merci."

She should have waited for Natalie in the living room of her suite, but after throwing the dead bolt lock, Catherine returned to the bedroom and stood before the slashed portrait of her mother.

"Please be alive," she whispered. "Please be alive so that I can tell you I understand what you did, and that I love you."

Catherine gazed at the unseeing sapphire eyes in the portrait, smiling, joyous, hopeful eyes, and when she could no longer see the face because of the blur of her own tears, she knelt on the floor and carefully gathered the red-splattered gems. The red was ink, not blood, she discovered as she wrapped the necklace and earrings in a lace handkerchief and put them in her pocket.

While Catherine waited in the shadowy room that was so like her shadowy suite in Vienna, her thoughts drifted to that night, and to the knife wounds that had been intentionally superficial, not lethal. Why hadn't Alain killed her then? she wondered. What sinister madness had made him need to toy with her, luring her to his kingdom only to charm her into his web of treachery and deceit? She had survived that night in Vienna, because Alain had permitted her to survive. But what if she wasn't so lucky this time? What if, in the next moments a living shadow leapt from the darkness, and the knife sliced deeper, mortally wounding?

If she died here today would there be words of love she should have spoken to those she loved, and hadn't? "Mom, Daddy, I love you," she had said those words over and over in the past year, and she would call her parents again, as soon as she was safe in Nice and tell them again. And if she didn't make it to Nice? Catherine knew that, if she died, there would not be words of love left unspoken to Alexander and Jane. And what about the words of love to Alexa? No, Alexa too knew of her deep love. But, still, how Catherine wanted to speak again with her big sister . . .

She smiled softly as she imagined that future conversation. First she would say, with quiet apology, that it should have been she, not Alexa, who made the almost lethal drive. "Nonsense!" Alexa would exclaim, dismissing Catherine's worry with a loving smile and a graceful wave of her hand. Then, after waiting patiently until she saw that Catherine's worry was indeed vanquished, her emerald eyes would suddenly sparkle and she would announce, "I always *knew* you were a princess, Cat!" To which Catherine herself would reply, very softly, "Yes, Alexa, but have I told you, directly enough, that all I ever wanted to be was your little sister?"

She and Alexa would have that conversation, *please*, but even if she never escaped from L'île, Catherine knew that Alexa knew all the truths about her love.

If she died now, today, there would only be one beloved person to whom the honest words of love had not been spoken.

I must live. I must live so that I can go to him and gaze bravely into the dark blue eyes that filled with such joy at the airport that day and tell him of my love, still, always, forever . . .

Please let me live so I can tell James how much I love him.

"James Sterling?" Alain echoed with surprise when he was informed that James was in the marble foyer awaiting a response to his request to speak with the Prince. "Yes, of course I will see him. Please show him in."

As he waited, Alain was swept with waves of fear and worry. There could only be one reason that James was here: Catherine. Had James come to tell Catherine that he loved her still? And if he did, would she go away with him? *No*, Alain answered in silent defiance. *Catherine will not leave me.*

"Hello, Alain."

"Hello, James."

"I've come to invite Catherine, and you of course, to dine with me and Catherine's mother this evening at the hotel."

"Jane is here? At the hotel? I don't understand."

"Not Jane, Alain . . . Isabelle." James saw surprise, but not confusion, in Alain's dark eyes, and after a moment he continued with quiet rage, "You knew. You bastard."

"Yes, James, I knew," Alain answered with matching quiet, but unlike James's, his voice filled with sadness not anger.

"And you weren't ever going to tell her, were you?"

"I was planning to tell her everything this evening, James."

"What a remarkable coincidence. I don't believe that for one second, of course, but it doesn't matter. I know the truth now, and I will make very certain that Catherine knows it, too."

"You don't know the truth, James."

"Don't I? Why don't I tell you what I know, Alain? I know that you and Catherine are cousins. I know that she is L'île's legitimate monarch. And I know that you are an impostor."

"You are partially right, James, and partially wrong." Alain sighed softly. He knew that he would have to tell James the truth; it was the only possible way he could convince him to leave. "Catherine is L'île's legitimate monarch, and indeed I am an impostor. But I am a far greater pretender than you imagine. Where you are wrong is in your belief that Catherine and I are cousins. We are not. Catherine is Alexandre's daughter, but I am not Jean-Luc's son. I'm not a Castille. I am not related to Catherine at all."

"Who are you?"

"I don't know. I only know the science. My blood type is AB. My mother was type B, which means my father had to be A or AB. Jean-Luc—and Alexandre—were both type O. I'm an impostor prince, James, but there is no pretense in my love for Catherine. I love her with all my heart, and she loves me. I believe she will love me still, and will choose to marry me still, after she has learned all the truths."

Yes, James thought, lovely, generous Catherine will be able to hear your truths and forgive them all.

But there are other truths she needs to hear.

"I don't think you understand, James, about Catherine's ability to love," Alain continued quietly in response to the frown on James's face. "She loved you very deeply once, but you didn't trust her love as I do. You hurt her terribly, far more, I think, than you will ever know."

"I know I hurt her, Alain. I did it in the name of love, but I realize now how foolish that was. I still love her. I still want our love. Catherine doesn't know that, not yet, but after you tell her your truths, I am going to tell her mine."

"So be it," Alain replied softly. "The choice, all the choices, will be Catherine's."

"And I choose Alain," Catherine announced as she walked into the music room. The shortest route from her suite to the cove was along a hallway beyond the music room. She could have passed swiftly and safely, unobserved by Alain, but her stealthy dash had stopped abruptly when she had heard James's voice. She had heard his voice, the sound before the words, and as she approached she had heard the words, *I still love her. I still want our love. Catherine doesn't know that . . .* And now I know, James, and it is what I want, too. But for now I must pretend that our love doesn't matter to me. She repeated softly, speaking to the dark brown eyes of the madman, afraid even to glance at the dark blue ones for fear of revealing her heart, "I choose Alain."

As Catherine walked to Alain, she saw love, not madness, in his eyes. Love, and hope, and a soft, wistful sadness. She wondered at the gentle sadness, and then she realized with a rush of compassion, Alain knows his own madness. It is beyond him, a demon he cannot control, and perhaps, as Natalie suggested, he simply wishes his torment were over. It's almost over, Alain, Catherine promised as she smiled lovingly into his dark eyes. It's almost over.

"I think, Alain, that I need a few moments with James. I would like to explain to him privately about our feelings for each other. Will you wait here while he and I walk to the cove and back?"

"Please don't leave with James, Catherine," Alain whispered with such soft desperation that her heart ached for him.

"Just to the cove and back, Alain."

"There are things I need to tell you, Catherine."

"Yes, I know. I will return very soon to hear them."

"You need to hear them from me, not from James. Catherine, please, let James go now. Meet him later, if you must."

Catherine saw sudden turbulence in Alain's dark brown eyes and feared further provoking his barely controlled madness.

"All right, Alain. I will stay." James will escape now, she thought, and later, after Natalie and I together have helped you, I will join him. "I will stay."

"No, you will go, Catherine." The words, a quiet yet powerful command, came from Natalie. "You and James will take the speedboat and go now."

Natalie stood in the doorway of the music room. In the minutes since giving Catherine the keys to the speedboat, she had changed into a long white satin gown and had adorned her beautiful auburn hair with flowers. She looks like a bride, Catherine thought. She has created a tranquil and soothing vision for Alain.

But like the beautiful portrait in Catherine's suite, the image was confused, and there was unexpected horror mixed in with the tranquil beauty. Because, in her delicate hand, Natalie Castille held a gun. Beauty and violence . . . half-warrior, half-bride.

"James can go now, Natalie," Catherine answered softly. "I will stay with you to help Alain."

"Help me?" Alain asked, taking his worried eyes for a moment from the terrifyingly powerful semi-automatic weapon and looking questioningly to Catherine. "What help do I need, Catherine?"

"I know what you've done, Alain," Catherine replied gently. "Natalie told me everything. It isn't your fault. It is a madness you inherited from Jean-Luc. You love L'île so much. I know, Alain, and I understand."

"What do you know, Catherine?"

"She knows that she is the missing princess," Natalie explained softly.

"I had no idea that you even knew of her existence, Natalie," Alain said quietly, returning his gaze to Natalie and the gun.

"Oh, yes, Alain. Of course I knew. I heard Jean-Luc tell you the story a hundred times."

"Then isn't it wonderful, Natalie, that we have found our cousin?" Alain asked softly as he moved toward her, just a few steps, just enough to put himself between the gun and Catherine. The gun was from Jean-Luc's arsenal, he assumed, hidden by Natalie before he himself had given the command that all weapons be destroyed. What else had Natalie saved from Jean-Luc's reign of terror? More guns? Grenades? *Plastique?*

"Wonderful? Oh, no, Alain. It isn't wonderful at all. L'île is yours. I gave it to you because I knew how you loved it. Catherine can't have L'île, and she can't have you."

"You gave me L'île, Natalie? How?"

"By getting rid of Jean-Luc." Natalie made the announcement with childlike pride, her crazed eyes suddenly innocent and expectant, as if awaiting well-deserved praise for the gift she had given. When no praise came from Alain for the murder of her own father, she explained, using the simple and terrifying logic of her own madness, "I knew that as long as Jean-Luc was alive you would stay away from L'île, and from me. I gave L'île to you, Alain, and I would have given myself, but I knew, since we shared the same father, that you would never touch me. And that was fine, enough!" Natalie's voice aged then, maturing in instants from a disappointed child to a jilted lover, and her eyes flashed as she demanded, "Why couldn't it have been enough for you? Why did you have to fall in love with Monique?"

"Oh, Natalie," Alain whispered softly as he realized that it had been his own blindness to Natalie's madness that had cost the life of the woman he had loved so much. He had been quite blind to Natalie's fatal obsession with him, and he should have been so aware! His own boyhood had been spent witnessing Jean-Luc's obsession with Isabelle. But Natalie had inherited Jean-Luc's cleverness and charm, as well as his madness, and Alain hadn't seen it. "Oh, Natalie."

"Monique had to die, Alain," Natalie said simply, without remorse, but with a slight trace of impatience at his surprise at a death that was so obviously necessary. "Everything was better after that, remember? We were together again, with no intrusions on our privacy."

"I remember," Alain answered quietly as he recalled the immense grief that had kept him on L'île, a grief that had seemed, for a very long time, refractory even to the island's miraculous healing powers.

"But it didn't last. You got restless. You needed to travel to hear your precious music again, and you even started welcoming visitors into our home." She sighed softly, like a long suffering wife, and her dark eyes narrowed as she scolded gently, "Oh, Alain, you should never have invited the Sterlings to spend Christmas here."

"Oh my God," Alain breathed. He wanted to turn to James, to utter his apology to James's face, but he didn't dare take his eyes from Natalie or turn his back to the finger clutched around the trigger of the lethal weapon. His eyes remained on Natalie—who was smiling triumphantly now as she recalled how successfully she had prevented the Christmas visit of Arthur and Marion Sterling—but he whispered to James, a whisper of grief and guilt, as if he were responsible for Natalie's madness, "I'm so sorry."

"Alain?" Natalie was pleading now, a desperate lover. "I love you. Everything I've done has been for you. Don't you see?"

"Yes, Natalie. I see."

"Then let James and Catherine go. Let them take the speedboat and leave us here, together. Alain, please!"

"All right," Alain agreed. Then, reconsidering almost instantly, he suggested gently, "I have a better idea, chérie. Why don't you and I take the boat?"

"Oh. Yes. Why don't we, Alain," she answered softly. "Catherine has the keys."

Alain turned to Catherine and took the keys from her delicate hand. There were words he wanted to say to her, such important words, but it was far too dangerous to speak them aloud, so he sent the silent message of love with his eyes. *I love you, Princess. You must always believe that. Be happy, my precious love.*

He smiled a trembling smile, a forever good-bye to the lovely and yet so bewildered sapphire; and then he looked to James, who had moved closer, ready to shield Catherine, as he himself had in case Natalie's madness suddenly erupted, and he asked, "Will you tell her, please, everything that I told you? It is the truth, James, every word of it, and I want her to know."

"Yes, Alain, I will tell her," James promised quietly.

"Thank you," Alain said softly before leaving them and crossing the room to Natalie. He extended his hands to her as he neared, hoping she would relinquish the lethal weapon, but she only took one of his hands and maintained her expert grasp of the gun. Alain had wondered if he would be able to get the gun and overpower her, but he realized at once that the danger would be too great. It didn't matter. All that mattered was that he get Natalie away from Catherine . . . forever.

Alain and Natalie left through the French doors that opened from the music room into the garden, and in a few moments they were visible beneath the window, walking hand in hand down the white marble path to the cove. As James saw them disappearing in the distance, his worry that Natalie might still harm Catherine subsided, and a new worry took its place. What was happening? It didn't make sense. Surely Alain could not believe they would escape. The speedboat was fast, a powerful state-of-the-art inboard, but still a piece was missing.

And then James knew. The boat was taking Natalie and Alain to a place that had nothing to do with speed . . . a place Natalie had wanted to send Catherine . . . a place where, in her madness, she was quite willing to go, as long as her beloved Alain would be there with her . . . forever.

"Oh my God."

"What is it, James?"

"I have to stop them."

He didn't explain. There wasn't time. He simply moved with graceful speed out the French doors and onto the white marble garden path. Catherine started to follow, but before she reached the French doors there was commotion behind her as a group of heavily armed men, led by Elliot Archer, burst into the music room.

"Elliot! It was Natalie. She—"

"Yes, I know. I just received word that she was in Washington last Wednesday. Where is she?"

"Down there, in the cove. Alain has convinced her to go away with him, but there's something else, something James just realized. He's down there, too."

"There must be a bomb in the boat," Elliot whispered.

"Oh, no!"

"Alain, don't do this!" James yelled when he reached the wharf.

"It is done, James. Let us go. Please."

James saw at once that he had no choice. Natalie still clutched the gun and there was wild fury in her eyes at his intrusion. He stopped but stood his ground as Natalie and Alain boarded the speedboat. Natalie boarded first, moving swiftly and decisively to what James assumed was the lethal ignition switch. She inserted the key and turned it; but the twist of her slender wrist caused a purr not an explosion. The bomb was connected to something else, James realized, just as it had been on the sailboat that had killed his parents. Something set to explode away from port— the throttle, perhaps, a certain lethal speed.

Alain cast off the ropes and looked to Natalie. Her hand was extended to him, a bride to a groom, a graceful invitation to join her in a forever love, and her eyes, crazed now, completely mad, glistened with rapturous anticipation. Alain moved to her with regal dignity, a monarch accepting all blame, even though none was his, quite willing to forfeit his own life to put an end to her madness.

As Alain moved toward Natalie, and the boat moved away from the wharf, James leapt onto the stern. When the boat rocked, signaling that he had boarded, Alain's eyes filled with sad surprise, and Natalie's glared with determined rage. As Alain turned toward James to urge him, or throw him, away from the boat, Natalie's hand grasped the throttle, moving it forward, closer and closer to eternity.

The boat lurched from the sudden acceleration . . . and then it exploded, a burst of fire erupting from the sapphire sea. The red-orange flames reached toward the sky, an orphan sun seeking its parent, and above the flames, like the dark thunderclouds that heralded the appearance of L'île's rainbows, were billowing mountains of ash and smoke.

There were flames and smoke in the azure sky.

And there were rainbows, too, thousands of them, in all the glistening places where the gasoline kissed the sea. The watery rainbows rose and fell with the waves, and they encircled the blazing inferno . . . a sea of rainbows around an island of fire.

CHAPTER THIRTY-TWO

James came up gasping, his starving lungs finding more smoke and fumes than fresh salt air. He surfaced in smoke, not fire, and as his eyes strained to focus through the smoky veil, he saw a vision of white satin—a bride, floating amidst the rainbows and shrouded by the flowers that had adorned her auburn hair. James saw at once that Natalie was dead. And, he thought, like Ophelia, she looked so innocent in death, at peace at last, her madness finally conquered.

James did not see Alain, nor did Alain answer his frantic calls. James heard voices, of course, shouts from the wharf and closer ones, as men swam toward the fiery scene, but he ignored those voices. The only voice he wanted to hear was the voice of the man who had been so willing to give his life to save Catherine. And who *has* given his life, he thought grimly as his repeated calls to Alain were answered only by ominous silence.

Then James saw it, a red much darker than the red of the floating rainbows, a dark, dark red that beaded in small round drops on the surface of slick sheen of the gasoline. *Blood.* His? Natalie's? Or Alain's?

James dove beneath the hot toxic surface into the cool blue depths of the sea. The depths were cool, but they weren't blue. They were red, vividly colored by the blood that flowed freely from the badly wounded body of Alain. James wrapped his arms around Alain's lifeless body and carried it to the surface. The body was lifeless, deathly still, but he felt the frantic pumping of Alain's young healthy heart. The pumping was frantic, the fight for survival desperate and brave; and yet, with each powerful stroke, the hope for survival was critically undermined, because with every valiant heartbeat, Alain lost a little more precious blood into the sea.

This time when James surfaced, there were other swimmers nearby, strong uninjured men who took Alain's wounded body from his grasp and began to transport the Prince swiftly to the wharf. James waved off help for himself—he was quite alive, and Alain might not be much longer.

The men carrying Alain led the processional through the watery rainbows to the wharf. James followed, flanked by two men who swam nearby ready to assist him if he faltered. And behind them, at a somber distance, were the men carrying the white satin body of the Princess.

Elliot had arrived at the palace with a team of agents and had summoned medical backup the moment he realized there might be a bomb on the boat. The royal physician, as well as doctors and nurses from the clinic near the hotel, were waiting on the wharf. All the medical professionals began to attend to Alain the instant he was pulled from the water. But, as it became clear that there was more than enough help, one of the doctors left Alain to meet James when he arrived.

"I'm OK," James assured the doctor quickly, although he was surprised, as he followed the physician's worried gaze, at the extent of his own wounds. Some of his many cuts were quite deep, and there were burns, too. And they hurt, he realized, aware for the first time of the deep searing pain of gasoline and salt on his raw, torn flesh. Still, he repeated, "I'm OK."

"OK, yes, *monsieur*, with proper cleansing and dressing of these wounds. The gasoline will continue to cause damage to the tissues until we wash it away. I would like to take you to the clinic now."

"All right. Thank you. In a moment."

James needed to talk to Catherine. She stood close by, her eyes filled with worry, and Elliot, worried, too, stood beside her. James smiled at the doctor, a smile of gratitude and a promise to return soon, and then walked over to Catherine and Elliot.

"I'm fine," he assured them, too. He looked around briefly, to be certain there was complete privacy for his next words. There was. The activity on the wharf was focused on the frantic efforts to save Alain's life. Even James's doctor had returned to the wall of humanity that surrounded the wounded Prince. Confident that his words would not be overheard, James returned his gaze to the worried blue eyes and whispered softly, "I'm fine, Catherine, but Alain is very badly injured. He needs you."

James saw uncertainty in her eyes, the confusing and conflicting emotions about Alain, whom she loved, but who she believed had so cruelly deceived her.

"Catherine, listen to me. Alain's deception was not what you think. He's not your cousin. He's not related to you at all."

"He's not?"

"No. Alain is not Jean-Luc's son. He was going to tell you everything this evening. He was worried about telling you, but his fear was fear of losing you, not L'île." James stopped, seeing that these new truths merely added to the lovely sapphire confusion. After a moment, he told her a truth she already knew, the most important one, and one that she had once, so angrily, hurled at him. Very quietly, he said, "Alain loves you very much. Catherine?"

"Yes?"

"When Alain realized there was a bomb on the boat, he stopped us from leaving and chose to go himself. He knew that he would die, but he knew, too, that you would be safe. That was all that mattered to him. Do you understand that, Catherine? Do you understand what he did?"

"Yes, James," she answered softly to the man who seemed to have forgotten his own heroism. The moment James realized there was a bomb, he too had made courageous and compassionate choices. He could not stand by and watch an innocent man die. And, she wondered, even though James had once so coldly told her of his wish to fire a bullet into the heart of whoever had murdered his parents, perhaps, after all, he could not even stand by and watch Natalie die. "I understand what you both did."

Her brilliant sapphire eyes—brave and lovely and welcoming—met his, and for a magnificent moment James allowed himself to be lost in the magic. James knew he was lost, and, as always, he had no wish ever to be found, but . . .

"Alain needs you, Catherine," he whispered softly, breaking the magnificent magic spell. "He loves you, and he may be dying, and he needs your love."

"Yes," she answered quietly. Alain loves me, and he may be dying, and he needs my love. Catherine wondered if James heard his own words, and if he remembered that there had once been a time when he was dying too, a death of the heart and the soul, and had refused her love even though he needed it so desperately. She would go to Alain now, of course, and she would be with him for as long as he needed her to be, but the words James had spoken such a short time ago still sang joyously inside her, *I still love her. I still want our love.* But Catherine didn't see that message of love now in the faraway dark blue eyes. Had his loving words only been spoken to lure her away from the madman he had believed Alain to be? Were James's words of love as false as her own *I choose Alain* had been? It didn't matter now, because now she needed to be with Alain, but someday she would find out. She would see James again, *she had to*, because, no matter what, she would bravely keep the wish that she had wished for so desperately as she waited for Natalie to return to the shadowy suite, *Please let me live so I can tell James how much I love him.* I will tell him, she silently promised her loving heart. Then she said very softly to the faraway eyes, "Yes, James, Alain needs me now, and I will go to him."

James watched as Catherine crossed the wharf, and, with only the softest of words, she caused the wall of humanity to part so that she could be near Alain, touching him and whispering words of love. Once Catherine was gone from sight, James joined Elliot, who stood nearby at the edge of the wharf, his eyes fixed on the smoldering sea.

"You were right, Elliot. The motive for my parents' murder was completely personal. Natalie simply killed them because she was annoyed that they were intruding on her Christmas with Alain. And she killed her own parents, and Monique, and she tried to murder Catherine. And do you know what I feel about her death? Nothing. Not a whisper of relief." James paused, collecting his thoughts and emotions, preparing to say more words to Elliot. I even felt a little sad for her, Elliot, isn't that strange? And if I had been able to get the gun from her I would never have turned it on her, *never*. You were so right, Elliot, about the emptiness of revenge. James wanted to make those confessions to Elliot, to his face, but as James looked at him, trying to draw the other man's eyes from the sea, he saw pure emotion on the face of the master spy. "Elliot?"

"I overheard you tell Catherine that Alain is not Jean-Luc's son."

"Oh, Elliot," James breathed softly. That final revelation would have occurred to him, of course, quite soon, once he had any time at all to reflect on the afternoon of astonishing revelations. And now, as he realized, he very gently told Elliot what he knew, "Alain told me that his blood type is AB. Genevieve's was B and Jean-Luc's was O."

"And mine is AB." Elliot's eyes blurred with tears and he whispered emotionally, "He's my son, James. Alain is my son."

He had to be with him! He had to hold his son and tell him of his love for him. Please, *please*, before Alain . . .

But Elliot couldn't kneel beside Alain's wounded body and gently cradle his head as Catherine did. Elliot was in charge, and now there were questions to be answered about transporting Alain off the island. He was alive still, barely, the royal physician informed Elliot. Alain had many wounds and burns, like the nonlethal ones that James had, but he had one wound that could kill him quickly. It was quite simple, a deep knife-like laceration to his thigh, so deep that it severed a large artery through which a great amount of blood had been pumped into the sea. The bleeding was stopped now, by a probably too tight tourniquet, but they feared loosening the bind, even a little, because they knew that the loss of even one more drop of blood might cost Alain his life.

The emergency vascular surgery Alain so critically needed was unavailable on L'île. In moments the decision was made to fly him immediately to Nice. He would be flown in his own jet, accompanied by the necessary medical personnel but no extra passengers; not Catherine, who had spent the last few minutes telling him of her love; and not Elliot, who might never be able to tell his son of his.

Natalie's jet and pilot were in Paris, delivering gems to the Castille boutique, so it was decided that Catherine and Elliot would fly to Nice in one of the many seaplanes used to transport hotel guests from the Côte d'Azur to L'île. Elliot asked Catherine to wait on the wharf while he made the quick trip to the landing strip with the doctors and Alain. It was Elliot's responsibility to see that Alain made it safely off the island, of course. And even though it was impossible for him to whisper his love to Alain, he was able to see the face he had never seen, and as he helped carry the stretcher up the steep path to the palace, Elliot was able to tenderly touch his son's lifeless hand.

Elliot had asked her to remain at the hotel, but the moment she heard the explosion, Isabelle had rushed to the palace, along with almost everyone else on the island, guided by the ominous plume of smoke and fire. She had been in the crowd that had assembled on shore but was kept off the wharf while Alain was there. When Alain was taken away, the crowd followed in somber procession behind their Prince, and Isabelle walked slowly, tremblingly, toward her daughter.

Catherine stood alone at the edge of the wharf, gazing at the sea, awaiting the arrival of the seaplane. There was no reason for her to take her eyes from the sea, no reason to turn at all.

But she felt herself turning, as if drawn by a most powerful magnet. And then there she was . . . the beautiful woman in the portrait, and for a breath-held moment of pain Catherine thought she must surely be a mirage, a wonderful and yet so cruel trick of her mind. But the cruelty—"I fear that Isabelle is dead"—had been Natalie's, spoken simply as a final tormenting sadness for the woman who had stolen Alain from her.

She wasn't a mirage, Catherine realized with wondrous joy. She was alive, and her sapphire eyes were crying and smiling and filled with such hope that the baby she had loved enough to give away would come to her now.

Catherine made the first trembling step, and then Isabelle moved too, and in only a moment they were close enough to touch. With brave and delicate wonder, Isabelle's trembling hands touched Catherine's tear-dampened cheeks, and she smiled the same loving smile that had joyfully caressed her baby girl so very many years before, and then her precious daughter was in her arms again, and Isabelle cradled her gently and whispered softly, "Catherine."

The mother and baby were together again, but Isabelle's baby girl was a grown woman now; and now, for the first time in her life, her beloved daughter spoke to her. And when she did, Catherine spoke in French, the beautiful language in which Isabelle had told her tiny infant over and over and over of her love.

"*Maman.*" And then, because Catherine wanted Isabelle to know everything all at once—that she understood, and that her life *had* been filled with happiness and love, as Isabelle had prayed it would be—she softly whispered the greatest reassurance of all, the same promise of love Isabelle had given her, engraved in gold, "*Je t'aimerai toujours, Maman.*"

* * *

The vascular surgeons in Nice expertly repaired the severed artery in Alain's leg, and as for the blood he so desperately needed, there were most willing volunteers. A rare and perfect match, the hematologists marvelled when they tested Elliot's blood and found that it was AB, just like the Prince's. Alain could receive any blood type, they knew, since his own AB made him a "universal recipient"; but it was wonderful that some of the new blood circulating in his healing body would be such a perfect match.

Elliot willingly, gratefully, donated his perfectly matched blood, and Isabelle donated, too; and, for the first time in Alain's life there truly was royal blood, Castille blood—Catherine's—flowing in his veins.

His severed artery was repaired, and his blood volume was replenished, but still Alain remained delirious for almost thirty-six hours. The delirium, the doctors explained, was due to a combination of factors—his prolonged shock, his near drowning, the aftereffects of the anesthesia, and the "toxic" effects of the gasoline and sea water that had seeped into his system through his deep open wounds.

Only Catherine was with Alain during his wakeful hours of delirium. She sat with him, softly trying to reassure the wild yet unseeing eyes. What terrifying images does he see? she wondered. Alain was obviously hallucinating, and it was obvious, too, that the distorted images of his delirious mind were quite horrifying; but, at least, when his terror-stricken eyes fell on her, even though there was no recognition, there was neither, for Catherine, any fear.

Elliot stayed away from his son's bedside during Alain's delirious wakefulness. He was a stranger to Alain, after all, and he didn't want his image to confuse Alain, nor to become in his son's hallucinating mind the disturbing image of a monster. But there were times when Alain was sleeping that Elliot was at his bedside, tenderly mopping the brow that became damp as, even in sleep, the images frightened and tormented still.

"Do you think that Geneviève knew Alain was my son, Isabelle?"

The doctors were with Alain, making their frequent rounds on the Prince, and Elliot, Catherine, and Isabelle were alone in the nearby waiting room.

"Oh, no, Elliot, I think not. Her pregnancy was apparent to her so soon after you left L'île that it seemed impossible that the baby could have been yours."

"But Alain was with her when she was killed."

"Yes. I think, as you wondered at the time, that she was trying to take her with him when she escaped. But, Elliot, she may have known only that she could not leave her son with Jean-Luc." She added quietly, "It's a certainty that Jean-Luc never knew the truth."

"No," Elliot agreed softly. "He would not have permitted Alain to live if he had."

Catherine listened in silence to the quiet and emotional conversation between her mother and Alain's father. It was a discussion to which she had nothing to add except her lovely expressions of gentle sympathy, expressions that were so very like Isabelle's.

Catherine had no words to add to Isabelle and Elliot's emotional reminiscence about L'île's long ago past . . . but she had a few very important words to say about L'île's future. And, when their conversation had ended, and the room had fallen silent, she spoke them.

"No one else ever needs to know the truth about Alain."

"Catherine?"

"No one else ever needs to know the truth about Alain, or about me."

They were just a few words, spoken with quiet confidence, but they were monumental words . . . a royal command . . . the first and last royal command Princess Catherine would ever give. The Princess of L'île had spoken, and her face had been solemn and regal as she did. Her beautiful face was regal still, after her quiet proclamation, but now once again there was the soft, lovely, uncertain smile of Catherine Taylor, not the confident princessly smile of Catherine Castille. And then she was a daughter again as she asked Isabelle hopefully, "Would my father have approved, Maman?"

"Oh, yes, my darling." Isabelle gently moved a long strand of black silky hair away from her daughter's beautiful face, a gesture of love between mothers and their babies, even when the precious small faces were fully grown. Catherine didn't pull away from the loving touch, as grown daughters sometimes did. Her sapphire eyes simply filled with joy. After a moment, Isabelle continued softly, "He would most definitely have approved. Because, above all, your father believed in love. He knew very well that the bonds of love are far stronger, and far more important, than the bonds of blood." Isabelle smiled, and as she drew her daughter to her, she whispered, "Oh, he would have been so very proud of you, Catherine."

"*Bonjour*, Catherine."

"Oh, Alain, you have returned to us," Catherine answered softly. When she had left him at midnight, she had thought that his sleep had seemed deeper and less troubled, and now, seven hours later, his mind at last was clear. "*Bonjour.*"

Catherine kissed him gently on the cheek and then looked very carefully at his handsome face. She saw in the gentle dark eyes she knew so well that Alain was searching, trying to remember. He would, she knew, be completely unaware of everything that had happened after the explosion, but had he also lost some of the memory of the events that had come before? Did Alain, like Alexa, have retrograde amnesia? It would be best if he did, Catherine decided. She could very gently tell him the truth about Natalie, but she could spare him the details of her confessions in the music room, when her mad and fatal obsession for him had been so horrifyingly revealed.

"Alain?"

"I remember James following us to the cove. He jumped onto the boat just as we were leaving. I turned to him, to try to stop him, but it was too late." Alain closed his eyes briefly, as if trying to block out the next image; but it was there, and always would be, whether his eyes were open or closed. "Oh, Catherine, I remember the look on Natalie's face so well. Her eyes were wild and enraged, and yet, at the same time, so full of love for me, and she had a smile of such triumph. She looked like a beautiful little girl whose dream had finally come true." Alain sighed softly and asked quietly, "What happened?"

"Natalie died in the explosion, Alain. She was killed instantly."

Alain nodded. His pale handsome face conveyed sadness and grief; and the solemn recognition, too, that Natalie's death had been a blessing.

"And James?" he asked suddenly.

"James is fine."

"Oh, good. Is he here?"

"No. He has called, of course, to check on you. He returned to Washington late yesterday."

"Did he tell you the truth about me, Catherine?"

"Yes, Alain. He told me that you are not my cousin, and that you had planned to tell me everything that night, and . . ." *And that you love me very much.*

"Catherine . . ."

"I think that all the people who need to know that you are not Jean-Luc's son already know, Alain, and the same is true about the people who know the truth about me."

"What are you saying?"

"That L'île is yours and always will be."

"Oh, no, Catherine."

"Oh, *yes*, Alain." Catherine smiled lovingly at his disbelieving, and yet so hopeful, dark eyes. "You are the Prince and monarch of L'île des Arcs-en-ciel. It is right, Alain, and it is best. Isabelle says that Alexandre would have very much approved."

Alain gazed at the sapphire eyes he knew so well, and loved so much, and he saw, in the shimmering confident blue, that she had made her generous decision of love and was happy with it.

"Catherine," he whispered softly, emotionally. "Thank you."

"You're most welcome."

Many moments passed before Alain was able to speak again. They spent the moments together, fingers intertwined, eyes tear-misted and loving, smiles gentle and trembling.

Catherine had given him L'île, a treasure of immeasurable value, the second greatest gift she had to give. Alain knew that her greatest gift—herself, her love— belonged to someone else. He had known that the moment James told him of his love, still, for Catherine. And now, when he could finally speak again, he searched for gentle words that would make it very easy for lovely Catherine to say good-bye to him.

"James told you my truths, Catherine, and did he tell you his?"

"No. We haven't spoken since just after the explosion." We haven't spoken since he told me to go to you, because you were dying and needed my love, she thought. And even when he has called the hospital to check on you, his calls have been for Elliot.

"But you heard what he said just before you walked into the music room."

"Yes, but I'm not that certain he meant it."

"Oh, Catherine," Alain assured lovingly, "he meant it. I saw his eyes when he spoke of his love for you. James loves you very much."

"Well," she answered with a soft uncertain shrug. "I'm not sure. But, Alain, I need to find out."

"And you will find that he loves you with all his heart," Alain predicted gently. "How could he not?"

"Oh, Alain, I . . ."

"I understand about your love for James, Catherine. You told me all about it, remember?"

"Yes." I told you, Alain, because of your kindness and your warmth and your gentleness, and because . . . "I love you, Alain."

"I know that, and I love you, too." Alain smiled softly. "Go now, darling. I will be fine."

Oh, yes, Alain, you will be fine, Catherine thought as she met his gentle eyes. She saw his sadness at the loss of her love, but she saw, too, such hopefulness. No longer was he the impostor Prince of L'île, and no longer either would his loves be threatened by Natalie's madness. All the storm clouds have vanished, Alain, and there has been the most nourishing rain, and from now on, for you, there will be only the most brilliant rainbows. She smiled softly as she thought about his future happiness, and about the great happiness that would be his very soon . . .

"I will go now, Alain." Catherine kissed him gently and then said quietly, "There is someone waiting outside who wants to see you."

"Hello, Alain. My name is Elliot Archer."

"Monsieur Archer," Alain replied with polite surprise. "At last we meet. I have heard of you, of course. I know that it is you who have had me watched for all these years in a relentless search for treachery on L'île."

"Alain . . ."

"I resented the vigil, Monsieur Archer, but now I know that you were right to search."

"I'm not here to talk to you about the treachery on L'île, Alain," Elliot said softly. "I'm here to talk to you about the love."

"The love?" Alain echoed with matching softness as he saw what looked like tears in the dark brown eyes that were so very much like his own.

"Yes. The love. I want to tell you about your mother, Alain, and about your father . . ."

"Maman?" Catherine asked as she looked at the airplane ticket Isabelle had just handed her.

"For this afternoon's Concorde to Washington."

"But I'm going to the château with you to meet Louis-Philippe and his children and grandchildren."

"I think it is far more important for you to go to Washington. Didn't James tell Elliot that he would be leaving very soon to spend the next few months sailing in the Caribbean? You could search the Caribbean for him—and I think that is what you have quietly planned to do—but it seems more sensible to go to him now."

"But we've had so little time together."

"We have our lifetime, Catherine. Now that you are found, my precious love, I will never lose you again," Isabelle promised. "And Louis-Philippe and I will definitely be in Topeka in February."

"Oh, good. I'm so glad."

"I am, too," Isabelle said, smiling softly as she thought about the joyous family gathering, to which she had been invited, that would happen on Valentine's Day. It wouldn't be a wedding celebration, because Alexa's wedding had already taken place; it would just be a joyous celebration of fathers and mothers and daughters and love. She would try once again, on that visit to Topeka, to thank Jane for loving her precious baby. She had tried a thank-you two days before, when she and Jane had spoken on the phone, but, for both of them, the words had been too quickly flooded by tears. But, Isabelle thought, Jane knew, because, from the very beginning, they had communicated through the silent messages of the heart; and two days ago, those silent messages of love had journeyed quite clearly and quite eloquently back and forth across the ocean. Isabelle gazed at the daughter who had been raised with such love and urged again gently, "We will be in Topeka in February. So, my darling, go to James now. Go to that wonderful man who loves you so very much."

CHAPTER THIRTY-THREE

Inverness Estate, Maryland
December 1990

Catherine arrived at Inverness an hour before twilight. Snow fell softly from the pale gray sky, but the winter wind held its breath and the pure white world was very still. As she gazed at the unlighted mansion, a shadowy unsmiling silhouette, she realized that James wouldn't be inside; and she wondered, as she walked swiftly through the barren rose garden and across the lawn to the edge of the cliff above the bay, if he was already gone.

No, she saw with relief when she reached the ledge. *Night Wind* was still there, rocking gently in its moorings, and there were cheery golden lights on inside. James was obviously there, preparing his boat for its long winter sail.

As she looked at the sailboat three flights below, Catherine remembered the only other time she had made the journey down the cliff to the bay. Her mind had sent such urgent warnings on that warm August night. You can't do this! You can get down the stairs but you cannot climb back up.

But then she had gone with James anyway, because she had to.

Just as she had to go to him now.

And now, even though her fit slender body could so effortlessly ascend the steep brick stairway, her heart told her bravely, You won't need to climb back up. James will want you to stay.

On that warm August night, Catherine Alexandra Taylor had known very little about who she really was. And now, on this snowy winter day, she knew everything, all the truths, and she was so very blessed with such wonderful love.

Catherine knew all the truths now, but there was a most important truth she had learned long ago, on that summer night . . .

When I am with you, James, I am everything I want to be.

James was on the wharf, securing a new rope to a cleat. He wore the scarf she had made for him, the soft and beautiful memory of the moonlit night when they had fallen in love.

James wore the gift of love she had given him a year ago, and Catherine wore the gift he had given her then, too, the brilliant sapphire earrings to be worn for concerts, for kissing . . . and for making love. Catherine wore the magnificent earrings, and she wore even more magnificent symbols of their magical love—her sparkling sapphire eyes, her flushed pink cheeks, and even the hopeful innocence that had been in hiding for so long.

"Catherine," James whispered with quiet joy when he saw her. "You're here."

"Yes," she answered bravely to the dark blue eyes that filled now with such hope, such happiness, and such love.

She had come today to say the words she had promised her heart that she would say. But he spoke first, because there were truths that he, too, had promised his heart he would speak.

"I was so very wrong, my darling. I should never have left our love. I didn't want to, Catherine, but I truly believed that I had to, and that it was best. But it wasn't best," he confessed softly. "At least, my love, it wasn't best for me."

"It wasn't best for me, either, James."

"Oh, Catherine, I'm so sorry I hurt you. I have only and always wanted to love you." His trembling hands touched her cheeks then, and as he cupped her beautiful face, the winter wind blew the softest of kisses, lifting her silky black hair and revealing the sapphire earrings she wore, symbols of love that had been violently stolen and now were found. Just like our magical love, he thought, as he whispered tenderly, "I love you, Catherine. I love you with all my heart."

"Oh, James," she echoed joyfully. "I love you, too."

As James touched his beloved Catherine again, all the gentle voices of his heart began to sing with joy; and as Catherine touched her beloved James again, her delicate fingers learned anew that touching him was a wondrous gift far greater than all her magnificent talent.

They touched, and kissed, and later, on that snowy evening, in their joyous and tender loving, James and Catherine discovered the most beautiful music of all.

PROLOGUE

❖

New York City
February 16, 1987

*B*rooke sat bolt upright. Her heart raced and her breath came in shallow gasps. The dial of the bedside clock glowed ten-thirty. Brooke frowned at the clock. She had only been in bed for fifteen minutes; it was hardly enough time to fall asleep much less to dream! But something—it *must* have been a nightmare—had forced her violently back into wakefulness.

Only later would Brooke recall that she was already reaching for the phone when it rang . . .

"Hello," she breathed uneasily as her mind frantically tried to reassure her anxious heart.

It will be Andrew, Brooke told herself. He will be calling to discuss one final detail, one final *twist*, of the State of New York versus Jeffrey Martin. Andrew was the deputy district attorney. He and Brooke represented the State of New York. Together they planned to put a legal end to the renegade career of Manhattan's most successful cocaine dealer.

Logically, the late-night phone call would be from Andrew. But illogically, and fueled with a knowledge that defied logic, Brooke's heart resolutely pumped dread through her body.

"*Brooke!*" The voice was filled with sheer terror.

"Melanie! What's—"

"He tried to kill me. Brooke, help me!" The terror was strong and pervasive. But the voice wasn't. It was the voice of a body that was badly injured. In shock, maybe dying . . .

It was the voice of Brooke's sister, Brooke's *twin*.

"Melanie," Brooke spoke urgently, "where are you?"

"My apartment," Melanie answered slowly, as if bewildered that something so horrible could have happened in that sanctuary.

"Is he gone?"

"Yes. Brooke it was *him*. The Manhattan . . ."

The Manhattan Ripper. That was the news media's name for the knife-wielding psychopath who had terrorized Manhattan, brutally murdering its young women for the past ten months. The police knew the Ripper was a man because his victims were raped. No one had ever seen him. The Ripper didn't leave witnesses, only victims.

But now Melanie had seen him. And, miraculously, she was alive. *Still.*

"Are you hurt?"

"So much blood," Melanie murmured dreamily. "So much blood."

Melanie was badly hurt. Her voice faded in and out of reality, drifting away. . . .

"Melanie," Brooke spoke sternly She had to make Melanie focus on the present—if it was possible, if Melanie hadn't already lost too much blood.

"Yes, Brooke," Melanie answered in a little-girl voice, surprised that her older sister was talking to her so harshly. What had she done wrong?

"Melanie," Brooke continued softly. There had been so much harshness between them, so much for so long. It hadn't always been that way; it couldn't be that way now. Brooke added gently, her voice choked with emotion, "Mellie."

Mellie . . . It was Brooke's special name for Melanie when they were little girls. *Mellie*. The name recalled such happy memories of laughter and love between sisters—twin sisters—still bound by the unique closeness born in their mother's womb, before the realities of life drove a wedge between them . . .

Brooke shook the memories that flooded her mind. She needed to tell Melanie those lovely memories were with her still, despite the bitter ones. She *would* tell her. But not now. Now she, *they*, had to save Melanie's life.

"Mellie, have you called the police?" Brooke asked, knowing the answer, but hoping.

"I called you!" The voice said clearly, *I called you because you are my sister—my older sister—and I know you will save me*.

"I'm glad you called me, honey. It was the right thing to do. Now listen carefully, Melanie. You have to hang up the phone so I can call the paramedics and the police. As soon as I've done that I will call you right back and we'll talk until they arrive. OK?"

No answer.

"*Melanie*."

"Uh-huh." The answer came weakly as if from a small child who had answered by nodding her head instead of speaking. Was she getting too weak? Or was she just drifting, too, to the memories of the two happy little girls?

"OK, Mellie. Hang up now. I'll call you right back."

An almost unbearable emptiness swept through Brooke as she heard the phone disconnect. It felt like an end. An ending. The end.

No! Brook shook the thought away angrily as she hurriedly dialed the emergency police number.

"This is," Brooke began urgently, then forced control in her voice and assumed her usual professional tone, "this is assistant district attorney Brooke Chandler. I need a medic unit dispatched to . . ."

Brooke provided the necessary information in a matter of moments. Just before the call ended, she added authoritatively, "Have the police department contact Lieutenant Nick Adrian. He needs to be there."

"Will do, Ms. Chandler," the dispatcher replied with respect. The police, the emergency unit dispatchers, the paramedics, and the district attorney's office were all coconspirators in the war against crime in New York City. They were on the same team. The dispatcher had no idea that the assistant district attorney's call was more than good teamwork. There was nothing in Brooke Chandler's tone that sounded like emotion. "I'll let Lieutenant Adrian know you think he needs to be there."

The Manhattan Ripper case was Nick Adrian's special project, his special nightmare. Nick knew more about the psychopath than anyone else. He had seen every morbid bit of horror the killer left in his wake of death. Nick knew more than anyone else. But Nick knew—and it tormented him night after sleepless night—that despite ten months of searching and four savage murders they still had no idea who the killer was. They were at his mercy, waiting for him to strike again, hoping he would make a mistake and leave even the smallest clue.

Nick needs to be there, Brooke thought as her trembling fingers dialed Melanie's number. He *has* to be. It wasn't because the Manhattan Ripper was Nick's case. Nick needed to be there because he would help Melanie. Melanie . . .

As Brooke listened to Melanie's phone ring, unanswered, her frantic thoughts darted to the other people who needed to know.

Five rings.

Her parents. How could she tell them what horror had befallen their golden angel? Would they blame *her* for allowing this to happen to Melanie? New York was Brooke's city. It was her fault. She should have protected Melanie . . .

Brooke would call her parents from the hospital, as soon as she knew that Melanie was all right.

Ten rings. Pick up the phone, Melanie. Mellie. Please.

Adam Drake needed to know. The society pages of yesterday's—*yesterdays*—Sunday *Times* featured a color photograph of Melanie and Adam taken at *Fashion* magazine's gala Valentine's Day party. Melanie and Adam stood in front of an ice sculpture of Cupid, the perfect backdrop for their fairytale romance. Distinguished elegant Adam and dazzling golden Melanie, smiling, happy, in *love*.

Adam Drake was the reason Melanie left Charles Sinclair. It was so obvious. Why did Melanie deny it? The celebrated breakup of super-model Melanie Chandler and handsome, powerful magazine editor Charles Sinclair occurred months ago, but the emotions lingered. Even at the Valentine's Day party, according to the article that accompanied the photograph, there had been a "scene" between Melanie and Charles. . . .

Charles, Brooke's mind whirled. *How can I tell Charles about this? How can anyone tell him?*

Fifteen rings. Melanie, come *on.*

But Charles needed to know, and Jason needed to know. Charles and Jason, the *other* twins.

Twenty rings. Answer the—

The ringing stopped. So, for a moment, did Brooke's heart. Someone had taken the phone off the hook. Melanie? The Ripper? The paramedics? Nick?

"Melanie?" Brooke whispered.

Silence.

"Mellie, honey," Brooke spoke lovingly to the silence, "I called the paramedics. They'll be there any moment. Hold on, darling. Please. And Nick. He's a police officer. You can trust him, Mellie. He'll take care of you."

Brooke paused, blinking back tears, hoping to hear something, the smallest sound, from her twin. Brooke heard nothing. But she *felt* a presence. Brooke knew Melanie was there, and Melanie would hear her words.

"Mellie. Don't try to talk, just listen. We'll talk when you're better." Tears streamed down Brooke's cheeks. She closed her eyes and saw a little girl with sun-gold hair and bright-blue eyes frolicking on a white sand beach. Brooke could almost hear the laughter. "I love you, Mellie, I always have. We need to talk about the things that have come between us. We *will* talk. Remember the summer we spent at the beach when we were five, Mellie? Remember what fun we had. . . ."

Suddenly there was noise—commotion—at the other end. Brooke held her breath. She heard pounding. It lasted only a few seconds. Then Brooke heard a crash as the door gave way.

"*Christ.*"

Brooke felt the paramedic's horror as he saw her twin sister.

Help her. Please.

"Is she . . . ?" another voice asked.

"I don't know," the voice, now close to the phone, close to Melanie, answered. "Let me find her carotid."

Please. Please. Please.

Depthless, immobilizing fear settled in Brooke's heart as she silently prayed for the other heart; the other heart that once had been so close.

"OK, Joe, let's get to work," the paramedic breathed finally. "She's still alive. . . ."

PART ONE

CHAPTER ONE

"*S*o it's true."

"Charles," Brooke breathed with surprise. What was Charles Sinclair doing *here*? Why would Charles Sinclair leave the luxurious air-conditioned offices of Sinclair Publishing and journey through the midday heat and humidity and humanity of downtown Manhattan to the district attorney's office? "What—"

"I had to see for myself if Brooke Chandler, attorney extraordinaire, had really forsaken Perkins, Crane, and Marks—not to mention Sinclair Publishing—for . . ." Charles paused. His dark-brown eyes calmly surveyed Brooke's tiny office. The walls wore peeling yellow-gray paint and the linoleum floor was a spiderweb of cracks. A portable fan noisily recirculated the stifling summer heat.

What is he thinking, Brooke wondered.

It was impossible to tell. Whatever Charles *really* thought of her stuffy, dingy office was artfully concealed beneath layers of impeccable manners and aristocratic politeness. At least that was what Brooke chose to believe. But there were other ways to interpret the behavior of the handsome and fashionable editor-in-chief of Sinclair Publishing Company. The polite, pleasant veneer *could* be masking the worst form of arrogant contempt—*indifference*.

Charles's critics proclaimed that the blue blood flowing through his veins, carrying with it a heritage of wealth and power and privilege, was as cold as ice. Witness, they argued, the never-ending series of love affairs begun by Charles and, when he became bored, ended by him. Charles Sinclair's passion was spent on his magazines. There was nothing human . . .

"The glamour of the DA's office?" Brooke finally finished Charles's sentence. "I haven't forsaken Sinclair Publishing. I could still do work for you, assuming—"

"Assuming we would want you? Of course we would. Or, did you mean, assuming you have time? Because—" Charles smiled wryly at the stacks of depositions, police records, and court documents cluttering Brooke's office—"you won't."

"I could make time," Brooke answered swiftly.

Brooke had always planned to work in the district attorney's office after graduation from law school. But during school she clerked for Perkins, Crane, and Marks, the prestigious Manhattan law firm retained by Sinclair Publishing Company. Brooke met Charles and almost changed her plans because of him. She *almost* accepted the position-that-would-lead-to-partnership at Perkins, Crane, and Marks. Because then she would see Charles, work with Charles, be with Charles.

But to what end? Brooke's logical mind finally demanded. There was nothing *personal* between them. There never would be. Brooke Chandler was not Charles Sinclair's type. Brooke was not one of New York's most beautiful, talented, and glamorous women.

It would be easier to stay with the plan to work in the DA's office, Brooke decided. Easier not to see him.

But now Charles was *here*, his brown eyes friendly and polite, and she was telling him she would find time to do legal work for Sinclair Publishing.

"It would keep me sane. A nice clean advertising contract, once in a while, to offset the felonies." Brooke smiled, tilted her head, and added quietly, "I meant, assuming I pass the bar."

"You probably have quite a track record of failing examinations," Charles teased. It had come up once—John Perkins was reciting the accomplishments of his star law clerk—that Brooke graduated summa cum laude from Harvard and was first in her class at Columbia Law School.

Brooke shrugged, her blue eyes frowning for an uncertain moment. She admitted, awkwardly, as if compelled to confess, "I'm a worrier."

"It's probably why you're so good," Charles observed. Then, surprised by the rush of pink that filled Brooke's cheeks, he added, "That's a compliment, Brooke."

"Oh, Brooke, you're back from court. Andrew—" Jean Fletcher, a second-year law student who was clerking at the DA's office, burst into Brooke's office. "Oh! Sorry. I didn't realize."

Jean stopped abruptly and stared with unconcealed amazement at Charles.

"You were saying something about Andrew?" Brooke asked after making introductions.

"Yes." Jean forced her attention away from Charles. "He wants to have a strategy meeting about the Norris case at two."

"Fine." Brooke explained to Charles, "Andrew Parker. He's the deputy DA and a brilliant litigator."

"I've heard of him."

"Oh, Brooke, I almost forgot," Jean interjected. "I was working in your office while you were in court and answered a call on your direct line. It was your sister. She said she told them Yes after all."

"*Yes?*"

"That's what she said." Jean waited a moment, but Brooke was lost in thought. Jean shrugged, cast a final appreciative glance at Charles, and withdrew.

"You have a sister." Charles finally broke the silence that followed Jean's departure.

"Oh. Yes." Brooke frowned slightly. More than a sister, Charles. A *twin*. It was important personal information. Except there was nothing personal. . . . "Melanie. She's a model. Apparently she just agreed to sign with Drake Modelling Agency."

"*Agreed* to? Did she actually consider turning them down?" Drake Modelling Agency handled only top models, only a few, only the *very best*.

"I thought she *would* turn them down," Brooke murmured.

"No one says No to Adam Drake," Charles said flatly.

Charles knew Adam well. Drake models appeared frequently in all three of Sinclair Publishing's magazines. Because Drake models were the best. Just as the magazines—*Images*, *Fashion*, and *Spinnaker*—were the best. Charles Sinclair and Adam Drake were alike, handsome and powerful and wealthy. Both were used to saying No. But neither was used to hearing it.

"You don't know Melanie," Brooke whispered softly.

But Charles *will* know her, Brooke realized.

Melanie would make Charles's spectacular magazines even more magnificent. Brooke could imagine the high-gloss photographs of Melanie, elegant and glamorous in designer gowns and glittering jewels, that would appear in *Fashion*. And the natural shots—Melanie's golden hair wind-tossed and her long tanned legs stretched over the varnished decks of a sleek sailboat—perfect for *Spinnaker*. And the soft romantic watercolors visually enhancing the wonderful literature that filled the pages of *Images*.

Photographs of Melanie would appear in Charles's magazines. And Melanie would dazzle and sparkle at the fabulous parties Brooke read about. Melanie would mingle—because she would *belong*—with the powerbrokers and celebrities of fashion and publishing and art and theater. People like Charles.

Melanie was Charles's type. Melanie was like the beautiful women with whom Charles had affairs.

Except Melanie was more beautiful. And Melanie was *Melanie*. No one said No to Melanie.

"She wasn't sure she wanted to leave California," Brooke continued, trying unsuccessfully to shake the inevitable image of Charles and Melanie together.

"Then why did she contact Drake?" Charles asked. He knew how irritated Adam Drake would be by a fickle model. It surprised Charles that Adam hadn't simply cancelled further negotiations at the first sign of hesitation.

"She didn't. They contacted *her*."

"Oh." Charles wondered if Adam had ever done that before. "Is she an older or younger sister?"

"Younger," Brooke answered carefully. Another confession. "Twenty minutes younger. We're twins . . . too."

"I didn't know that," Charles murmured distantly, frowning briefly. Then, smiling, he asked, "Are you identical?"

Brooke stared at him for a long, bewildered moment. An aristocrat with impeccable manners wouldn't ask such a question. It was worse than indifferent, worse than ice-cold. It was *cruel*.

Brooke's blue eyes flashed hurt, then anger. Charles's eyes answered with surprise and concern.

He couldn't have asked that *seriously*, could he? Brooke's mind whirled as she looked into the serious, concerned brown eyes.

"No," Brooke breathed finally. *Of course not.* "She's blonde, like Jason." Like your golden twin.

"Oh." Charles nodded. Then he glanced at his watch and added, "I had better be going."

"Thanks for stopping by." *Why did you stop by? Will you ever stop by again?*"

"Don't work too hard, Brooke." Charles gave a parting shot to the stacks of work in Brooke's office, smiled at her, and left.

Jean appeared in Brooke's doorway seconds after Charles left.

"That was *Charles Sinclair*."

"I know. I introduced you."

"How do you know him, Brooke?"

"I don't really know him. I did some work—"

"He just happened to be in the neighborhood? He just *happened* to wander all the way from Park Avenue in the midday heat?" Jean pressed.

"Charles wanders. He works out ideas for the magazines by pacing around Manhattan."

"But you don't know him."

"No," Brooke repeated firmly. It wasn't information Brooke learned from Charles. John Perkins had told her. John described it as a restless prowling, like an animal, driven to search, compelled to keep moving.

"But Charles *is* the creative genius behind *Images*, isn't he?" Jean pushed. "*Images* is his vision—his *fantasy*—isn't it?"

"I think Charles and Jason create *Images* together." Brooke smiled. "You're going to make a good lawyer, Jean."

"It seems impossible that *Images* is a joint effort. Especially between Charles and Jason Sinclair. They seem so different," Jean mused. "Of course, they *are* twins. One mind, one heart. Or don't you buy that? You should know."

Brooke shrugged, suddenly uneasy. There was a time when she and Melanie communicated in perfect, wordless harmony. There was a time when they knew, instinctively, the other's thoughts and dreams. But that was years and years ago. As they grew, the differences became more important than the closeness.

"Well," Jean continued quickly, sensing Brooke's discomfort, "end of cross-examination. I'll see you at two in Andrew's office."

After Jean left, Brooke sat at her desk and tried to concentrate on the legal brief she was writing. But it was impossible. Charles's visit—now a confusing memory—and the startling news that Melanie was moving to New York haunted her.

Brooke sighed, finally permitting the swirling thoughts and emotions to surface. She had to face them. She had to face the facts.

Charles. Charles was a midday mirage. He would never be a part of her life. She would never really know him. But Melanie would . . .

Melanie. Melanie was moving to New York. Fine. Brooke had her own identity now. She was happy with who she was. She was doing what she wanted to do. Melanie wasn't a threat. That was all ancient history.

Good, Brooke told herself calmly, I can handle it.

Then the emotions took over.

Why was Melanie *really* doing this? She had everything in California. Wasn't it enough?

No. Of course it wasn't enough. Having everything had never been enough for Melanie. . . .

A continent away Melanie grabbed her car keys and dashed out of her Westwood apartment into the warmth of the perfect California summer day.

She drove the pale-blue Mercedes sports coupe west along San Vicente Boulevard to the ocean. The traffic heading east toward the maze of freeways was heavy. *They* were going inland to the smog and heat and stagnation. *She* was going to the beach.

Melanie hummed softly to the music on the radio, her fingers tapping rhythmically to the beat, and smiled contentedly as the fresh ocean breeze swirled her long golden hair.

Will I miss this? she wondered. The California lifestyle with its easy sunny freedom and the year-round songs of summer was all she had known for twenty-five years. The warm sparkling sunshine and limitless blue Pacific and gentle ocean breezes still made her tingle with joy. Her body was sleek and healthy and golden, and her spirit was joyous and free.

Melanie was like what Southern California used to be, before the crowds and the smog and the too fast pace and the drugs and the crime and the glitter that was false. Before all that there was *real* glitter, the natural glitter of a golden sun smiling on the endless pristine seascape and luxuriant tropical foliage. Melanie flourished in Southern California. This was *her* lush green land, *her* vibrant exciting town, *her* sapphire-blue ocean, *her* snow-white beach. Life was easy. Melanie was in control and unafraid.

What would it be like to live on the East Coast? Would she fit in? Would she feel comfortable? Brooke had moved to the East Coast right after high school and never returned. She lived in Boston, attending Harvard University, for four years. Then she moved to New York City—to *Manhattan*—for law school.

If Brooke can do it, so can I, Melanie told herself with bravado. She knew it wasn't true.

She *couldn't* do what Brooke could do. Brooke earned her many successes through hard work. If Brooke put her bright, logical, disciplined mind to something—anything—she could achieve it.

Melanie's successes were *handed* to her. All she had to do was smile and dazzle and *perform*. She just had to be what everyone *expected* Melanie to be: beautiful and happy and charming and slender and sexy and fashionable and radiant.

It was so easy.

And it was so hard.

Melanie sighed softly as she eased the Mercedes sports coupe into an oceanside parking space. She tossed her car keys under the front seat, shed her light cotton windbreaker and her sunglasses, and scampered gracefully down the narrow gravel path to the beach.

Usually when Melanie jogged she could downshift her mind into neutral. Usually she could breathe the salt air and feel her strong, athletic body pumping against the wind and the sand. Usually she didn't think, she just *felt*.

But not today. Not since she said Yes to Adam Drake. Ever since then a constant taunting dialogue echoed in her brain.

Why are you moving to New York? You have everything you want right here. Isn't it enough?

Yes, of course.

So, why are you moving, Melanie? To impress Brooke?

No.

Good. Because Brooke won't be impressed even if you are the top model in the world. It's just too easy.

Maybe I want to be friends with Brooke.

You think that's possible? After all these years?

Yes. Sure. It has to be.

So you're moving to New York to be friends with Brooke? It has nothing to do with the fact that Drake is the best agency—

Of course that matters. I love modelling. If I really want to make the most of my career I have to move to New York.

It really might show Brooke if you become the best in the world. It's hard to stop competing after all these years. . . .

I don't want to compete with Brooke anymore.

Oh?

I feel empty. Part of me is empty.

The twin thing.

Something.

So, move.

I am.

But, remember, Brooke may not feel the same way. Why should she?

I know.

Melanie stopped, panting, at the end of the beach. The jog had turned into a full run. Everything ached. Her arms, her legs, her rib cage, her *lungs*.

But there was a deeper ache, a painful clue to how empty she would feel if she moved to New York and she and Brooke grew even further apart. It was fear of that pain that almost made her say No to Adam Drake.

Brooke doesn't really like you, remember?

I remember. But she doesn't know me. It's been so many years.

It's a very big risk.

Yes. But I have to try.

CHAPTER TWO

Pasadena, California
September 1963

"*What* have we here?" The preschool teacher eagerly hurried across the classroom toward Ellen Chandler and her identically dressed four-year-old daughters. "*Twins.*"

By the time the teacher reached them, Melanie and Brooke had removed their matching blue-hooded jackets, revealing Melanie's straight sun-gold locks and Brooke's dark-brown curls.

"Oh!" the teacher exclaimed. A little disappointed she added, "They aren't identical."

"No," Ellen murmured, almost apologetically.

"Well, it actually makes it easier for us if they aren't." The teacher recovered quickly. "We can tell them apart. And they can't play as many tricks on us."

The teacher looked down at the two sets of blue eyes—one dark, one light—that gazed earnestly in return. She smiled a knowing smile. "I bet you two have your share of tricks." Then she looked at Ellen and added, as if Melanie and Brooke weren't there, "I don't envy you having twins. Twice the work. I'm sure you're just as glad it's time for them to start school."

Ellen frowned, lifted her chin, and said firmly, "I think it will be good for them to meet other children. But I will miss them very much."

Ellen knelt down in front of her daughters, wrapped an arm around each one and pulled them close. "Be good, my little ladies."

"We will, Mommy," Brooke and Melanie answered in unison.

That night, in the bedroom they shared even though they could each have had their own, Melanie and Brooke talked about the events of their first day of school.

"We were the only twins." Melanie frowned. "Everyone else was alone."

"We're lucky."

"But, Brooke, what if . . ."

"What if what?"

"What if," Melanie whispered, "what if everyone starts out as twins and one twin always dies?"

"Mellie."

"What if that's the way it's supposed to be?"

"It's not."

"How do you know?"

"I know."

Melanie was silent for a moment. Then she said urgently, "Brooke, promise me if I die I can be your shadow."

"I'm not going to talk to you if you say things like that."

"*Promise* me."

"I promise."

They chewed thoughtfully on chocolate-chip cookies for several minutes. Then, at the same instant they had the same worry, another troublesome memory from this baffling, disruptive day. Brooke started the question and Melanie finished it.

"Do you think Mommy . . ."

". . . wishes she didn't have us?"

"Twice the work."

"But we *help* her."

"Maybe we should help more."

"We should."

"We will," they agreed together, nodding solemnly.

After several moments, Melanie asked, "Brooke, what's identical?"

"Mommy says it means exactly alike."

"But the teacher said we *weren't* identical. And we are," Melanie said firmly.

Brooke and Melanie didn't look in mirrors. For the first four years of their lives, and the nine months before they were born, the other was always there. The same size. The same shape. With the same thoughts and ideas. They brushed each other's hair and stared in each other's eyes and *assumed* they were looking at reflections of themselves.

Brooke had made the discovery they didn't look exactly alike six months before, staring in disbelief at the very different little girls she saw reflected in a plate-glass window. It worried and upset her. But she didn't tell Melanie, because she knew it would upset Melanie, too.

"No. We are exactly alike *inside*," Brooke explained earnestly. "But we look different. That way people can tell us apart."

Melanie followed Brooke skeptically toward the full-length mirror in their parents' bedroom.

"See?" Brooke asked when they stood in front of the mirror. "Your hair is yellow and mine is brown."

Melanie shrugged. "But that's all."

"Your eyes are a different color blue," Brooke persisted. She had suffered alone with this for six months. It was a relief, finally, to share it with Melanie.

Melanie stared in the mirror at her own pale-blue eyes. They were the color of a summer day sky. Melanie had never seen these eyes before. The eyes she knew so well, Brooke's eyes, *were* different. Brooke's eyes were deep dark blue—ocean blue, not sky blue. Melanie stared, mesmerized by her own eyes, half hating them, half intrigued by the pretty color. The more she stared, the more Melanie liked the soft pale blue that stared back at her. And the halo of gold that framed her face.

Finally Melanie said, a pronouncement, "Maybe it's better not to be identical after all."

* * *

As little girls, Brooke and Melanie were The Twins. The similarities were more important than the differences. Melanie and Brooke had a combined identity—the Chandler Twins—not two distinct ones. They were inseparable and indivisible.

As they grew, their unique identities emerged. But, because they were twins, they couldn't be simply Brooke and Melanie. The twin unit still existed. Instead of being indivisible, each formed a complementary and opposite half of the whole. They were the *golden* twin and the *dark* twin, the *smart* twin and the *athletic* twin, the *fun* twin and the *compulsive* twin, the *happy* twin and the *serious* twin, the *beautiful* twin. . . .

The labels—assigned carelessly and even whimsically—came from teachers and friends and family. Throughout grade school, Melanie and Brooke paid little attention to the labels. They knew they were identical *inside*. They shared everything, understood each other perfectly and wordlessly, and were best friends.

Then, one day, in sixth grade, Melanie didn't select Brooke to be on her hopscotch team.

"Melanie, why didn't you choose me?" Brooke's deep-blue eyes glistened with tears.

"You aren't any good at hopscotch. You're not *athletic*," Melanie answered simply, amazed by Brooke's reaction.

"But, I'm . . . we're . . . *twins*," Brooke sputtered.

"Brooke, you're being silly. If you were captain of the spelling team, would you choose *me?*"

"Yes! Of course!"

"That would be *stupid*, Brooke," Melanie insisted flatly. "You wouldn't win if you picked me."

"*Still.*"

"It would be stupid. And you're not stupid."

As tears spilled onto Brooke's cheeks, Melanie's eyes flooded with tears, too; because then, still, they shared everything. Then, still, the other's sadness made her twin ache.

"Brooke!" Melanie cried, throwing her arms around her sister and holding tight. "Please don't cry. I'm sorry. Let's go do something else. I don't feel like playing hopscotch anyway—it's a dumb game!"

During the summer of their thirteenth year, something happened that neither girl could change or control or stop or alter. It was a label that couldn't be ignored, and it drove them apart.

That thirteenth summer Melanie became beautiful. Her little-girl golden prettiness transformed into breathtaking, heart-stopping, head-spinning beauty. Heads spun when they—until Brooke could no longer stand being the ugly companion—walked by, and mouths murmured *oohs* and *aahs* and smiled appreciative, dazzled smiles.

Melanie smiled a flawless, happy, radiant smile in return. This was *fun!* Why was Brooke being such a sad sack? Brooke, smile!

But Brooke couldn't smile. It hurt too much. Sometimes Melanie's admirers had cameras and they not so graciously asked Brooke if she would step aside, out of the picture. . . .

Brooke stepped aside and completely out of the picture. She retreated into *her* labels—bright, scholarly, capable, competent, serious, compulsive Brooke—and shunned all that was Melanie. Melanie, momentarily surprised and hurt that

Brooke abandoned her, rebounded quickly, finding solace in the wonderful *high* of being the stunningly beautiful, happy, *popular* twin.

Brooke and Melanie were no longer a unit and they were no longer two halves of a whole. Now they were sisters and siblings competing as sibs and sisters did. But their competition was all the worse because there were important yet-to-be-assigned labels. The *best* twin, the *favorite* twin. . . .

Ellen and Douglas Chandler watched their twin daughters grow with a mixture of pride and wonder and concern. Each girl was so *special*; each had her own unique talents and personality. But the twin bond was special, too. The twins' parents marvelled at their perfect communication; words and giggles and ideas would begin in one and finish, without dropping a beat, in the other. Brooke and Melanie's unspoken communication was free-flowing and effortless and wondrous.

Ellen and Douglas's wonder shifted to helpless concern as they watched their teenage daughters emphatically deny the bond. Each twin tried desperately and forcefully to prove that she was no part of the other. There were *no* similarities, *nothing* in common. They shared no friends, no hobbies, no laughter. They didn't even celebrate their birthday together anymore.

As her daughters transformed from little girls to little women, Ellen wondered if she knew them at all. What kind of women would they be? *Controlled* women, Ellen decided. *Controlled, driven, private* women.

Ellen's heart ached as she watched Brooke struggle with Melanie's sudden beauty. At first, Brooke sought comfort in food. Her dark lovely face and slender young body became heavy, ugly symbols of her great unhappiness and pain. Eventually, Brooke reversed it all. She stopped eating and became thin, even thinner than Melanie. Rigidly and with unfailing resolve, Brooke discovered the self-discipline and control that would enable her to survive any pain and achieve any goal. After that, Brooke escaped into her goals and her achievements.

"Honey," Ellen lovingly stroked Brooke's short-cropped dark-brown hair, the antithesis of Melanie's long flowing gold, "when you are older, in college, you will be very beautiful."

Ellen knew it was true. Brooke would mature into a dark, seductive, sultry beauty. It would happen whether Brooke *allowed* it or not. Right now, at age fifteen, Brooke denied herself any attention to her appearance. Her clothes—somber blues and browns and grays—and her looks were neat and orderly and functional. But Brooke *would* be beautiful.

"It's not *important*, Mother," Brooke answered sternly, pulling away.

Oh, my darling, Ellen thought. I wish I could help you.

But Ellen couldn't. Brooke wouldn't talk about her pain; it was private.

In Melanie, in her golden daughter, hidden deep beneath the sunny surface, Ellen saw the same control and drive and privacy. Melanie radiated pure sunshine; the sun never went behind a cloud, and it never set. But *that* was Melanie's control. Melanie might suffer and struggle and hurt and ache. But it would be private; she would never let it show.

Melanie had to be all and always happy and shining just as much as Brooke had to be all and always serious and competent. Each girl demanded it of herself, because *they*—the twins who vehemently denied their relationship—demanded it of each other.

And all Douglas and Ellen could do was hope it would pass. The vigorous denial of the twin bond gave their daughters almost limitless energy; it was much stronger than the gentle, loving advice of a mother or father. . . .

During high school, on the rare occasions when the family ate dinner together, the conversation rapidly degenerated into a litany of each twin's accomplishments, designed as a challenge to the other to push even harder and achieve even more. Brooke and Melanie shared nothing but the all-consuming desire to be the best. Or, at least, to be better than the other. Each excelled in her own sphere, and each belittled what her twin considered to be important.

"Debating is just arguing for argument's sake, isn't it?" Melanie asked one evening. Brooke captained the school's debate team and won local, state, and national competitions. Melanie tossed her golden hair as she dismissed the value of Brooke's achievements. "It seems so pointless."

"But not *mindless*," Brooke countered with contempt. Melanie was the head cheerleader and had just won the lead in the school play. Brooke's blue eyes icily reminded Melanie what she thought of cheerleading and acting.

Brooke studied constantly, won top honors, had few friends, and didn't date. Melanie studied when necessary, earned all B's, and was constantly surrounded by an admiring entourage of friends of both sexes.

Brooke spent her free time curled on her uncluttered bed in her perfectly ordered, silent bedroom, reading books on law and writing essays in her journal. Melanie never had a moment of free time. Her life was a golden collage of dances and parties and music and laughter. Her graceful, sleek body frolicked in the sapphire ocean and galloped horses bareback on the white sand beach and sent seductive, tantalizing messages of vitality and joy.

Brooke's favorite classes were history and English. Melanie's favorite classes were home economics and study hall. During study hall, Melanie eagerly sketched designs for clothes, and during home economics she sewed them. The clothes Melanie wore—her own designs—were daring and vivid and innovative.

Melanie enjoyed designing outfits for herself, but her favorite activity was creating new "looks" for her friends. They flocked to her bedroom—a colorful clutter of clothes and fabric tossed carelessly amid books and shoes and scarves and ribbons—and emerged, giggling and thrilled, as vivid, sexy "fashion statements."

Melanie's eye for color and design and fashion and style was instinctive. And it was more than an *eye*; it was a talent.

"Melanie, I can't wear bright red with my coloring!" a friend protested.

"Oh, but you can," Melanie countered confidently as she expertly cuffed the bright red sleeves, knotted the shirttails, and stood back to admire the surprising stylish effect.

"I can," the friend breathed. "Wow."

Brooke steadfastly ignored the laughter and music and gaiety that flowed from her sister's bedroom-boutique and rigidly battled the uneasy thoughts that plagued her.

Why can't I look like Melanie? Brooke's heart cried. Why can't I *be* like Melanie? I want—

No you *don't*, Brooke reminded herself sternly, as she fastened her neatly pleated navy-blue skirt and buttoned her wrinkle-free white blouse.

If only Brooke would let me help her with her clothes, Melanie thought wistfully a thousand times. Then Melanie would remember the haughty disdain in Brooke's cold blue eyes and low deep, somber voice. Brooke doesn't like me. I will never be good enough for Brooke. Why should I care if she looks drab and dowdy? I shouldn't care. I *don't*.

At the end of their senior year in high school, Brooke, the class valedictorian, was voted Most Likely To Be President. Melanie, the prom queen all three years for a prom to which her twin was never invited, was chosen Most Likely To Be Miss America.

Brooke won a full scholarship to Harvard. She moved to Boston a week after graduation from high school. Melanie enrolled at UCLA and worked at a florist in Westwood to help offset the cost of her education.

Divided by a continent and away from the expectations of the other, Brooke and Melanie began to make discoveries about themselves. Brooke's dormitory room, adjacent to Harvard Square, was a maze of unfolded clothes and scattered record albums and term papers in progress and unshelved romance novels. During her freshman year, Brooke added tweeds to her wardrobe of brown and navy and gray. By her sophomore year—after months of secretly and eagerly trying different combinations in the privacy of her room—Brooke started to wear colorful sweaters and embroidered blouses and bell-bottom jeans. She let her hair grow and casually gathered the unruly brown curls in brightly colored scarves and ribbons.

Brooke and her girlfriends danced to Beach Boys music and talked about the "men" who asked her—*her*—for dates. Those "men" gazed into Brooke's deep blue eyes and whispered hoarsely how pretty she was and how much they wanted to hold her and kiss her and . . .

Brooke returned their gazes in wide-eyed disbelief. But they showed her they meant it, and Brooke stayed out long past curfew, giggling breathless explanations to the dormitory supervisor about why she was so late.

Brooke's life suddenly overflowed with laughter and friendship and joy. She discovered a happy, warm, lively, loving Brooke. But what about the other Brooke, the self-disciplined, driven Brooke? Where was she? Still there, Brooke realized. That Brooke was part of who she really was, too. The new, happy Brooke was still going to graduate at the top of her class at Harvard and attend Columbia Law School. She was still going to be the best lawyer she could be.

Melanie's dormitory room, overlooking the tennis courts and Pauley Pavilion, was impeccably neat and ordered. Her books were shelved alphabetically and her clothes were carefully folded. Melanie studied diligently and earned A's. Late at night, in the peaceful privacy of her tidy room, Melanie sat cross-legged on the floor in her baggy gray sweats and sketched designs for beautiful clothes.

In college, with Brooke no longer watching, Melanie shed her colorful plumage and her entourage of admirers. She wore bland, colorless clothes, little makeup, and unadorned hair; but still she was not anonymous. It was impossible to shed the conversation-halting-I-don't-care-if-it's-rude-to-stare beauty. By the end of her freshman year, everyone knew Melanie Chandler, the stunningly beautiful but aloof coed who preferred studying to dating. She must have a boyfriend somewhere else. . . .

Melanie studied and sketched and sewed. Every morning, at dawn, she jogged along San Vicente Boulevard to the beach at Santa Monica. She loved the feel of the soft white sand and the gentle lapping sound of the ocean and the graceful freedom of the seagulls and the taste of the cool salt air. Her sky-blue eyes marvelled at the pale-yellow dawn and she felt great peace.

In her junior year, the term project for Melanie's class in fashion design was to design and sew three outfits. Each student was to submit the completed designs. Melanie did even more; she included photographs of herself modelling her outfits.

A week after the term project was submitted, Melanie's instructor stopped her before class.

"I showed the photographs to a friend who works for Malibu Sportswear and he showed them to the owner." The teacher smiled. "Who would like to see you."

"Really?" Melanie couldn't believe it! It was her dream—her private, secret dream—to be a designer. . . .

But when Melanie met with Grant O'Connell, she learned that it was *her* beauty, not her beautiful innovative designs, that Grant wanted.

"You have the look we want, Melanie. Healthy California, natural and athletic. You are an athlete, aren't you?"

The *athletic* twin. Melanie didn't participate in team sports at UCLA. But she kept fit, running on the beach, horseback riding, surfing . . . private sports.

"I guess." *What did you think of my designs? Did you even look at them?*

"We'll need to do a formal photo session, of course. Swimsuits, shorts, sundresses—the entire Malibu Sportswear line. But I think you're exactly the model we've been searching for."

Malibu Sportswear *had* been searching. They had received hundreds of applications, but none had been quite right. Until Melanie Chandler. And she hadn't even applied.

"Model," Melanie murmured. *I want to design clothes for models to wear. I don't want to be a model.*

But Melanie loved modelling. She loved the beautiful clothes. She loved the photographs they took of her. She didn't dwell on the fact that the beautiful woman in the photographs was *her*. Her artistic, fashion-conscious eye simply appreciated the beauty.

Melanie didn't forget her dream to be a designer—someday. For now, modelling was fun and exciting. And it was something she could do well.

With modelling, and her instant success, came celebrity. Melanie was in the limelight again. But this time she was doing it for herself, not Brooke. She could set her own limits. This time she could, *would*, protect the private, peaceful, quiet moments of her life that meant so much to her.

On the rare but necessary occasions—Christmas, holidays, their parents' twenty-fifth wedding anniversary—when Brooke and Melanie saw each other during college, they lapsed into the uncomfortable long-since-abandoned labels. Melanie glittered and dazzled. Brooke retrieved her old navy skirts from the back of her closet, forsook her colorful ribbons, and forced a now unfamiliar somberness on her lips. Both hated the charade and were grateful when the visits were over.

Between the requisite family visits, Brooke and Melanie had no contact. Then, one spring day during their senior year, Melanie impulsively reached for the black rotary phone in her dorm room, called Directory Assistance in Cambridge, Massachusetts, and moments later dialed Brooke's number.

Brooke lifted the receiver of her peacock-blue Princess phone on the first ring. "Hello."

"Brooke?"

"Melanie. I can't believe it."

"Can't believe what?"

"I was just about to call you."

"Really. Why?"

"I have no idea. I just . . ."

". . . wanted to talk to you."

"Yes."

They wanted to talk. But they couldn't. The painfully awkward attempt at conversation sputtered and finally died. Stupid. Dumb. What made them think they had anything to say to each other?

They lapsed into silence for another three years.

Until one day, seven years after Brooke left Pasadena to get away from her twin and find herself, Melanie called to tell Brooke that Adam Drake had flown to California because he wanted Melanie to move to New York. . . .

CHAPTER THREE

New York City
July 1985

"*M*argot, you look very happy," Charles observed as Margot Harper, fiction editor of *Images*, walked into his office.

"I have the five finalists for the fiction contest."

"And?"

"They are all very good." Margot stopped abruptly.

"But? But one is sensational?" Charles guessed.

"One is sensational."

"You all *agree?*"

Usually Margot and the other editors were not unanimous in their decision of the winner of the *Images* fiction contest. The annual contest was so important to the winner. It frequently launched a career for an unknown-but-destined-to-be-great writer. The editors were supposed to select on the merit of the story. But in the back of their minds they were making a prediction about the future success of the author. Usually it was a difficult decision; the *Images* fiction contest always attracted entries of exceptional quality.

"Is it because the others weren't good?" Charles asked.

"No. Any might have won another year. Of course—" Margot shrugged—"you may not agree with our choice."

As editor-in-chief it was ultimately Charles's decision. But he valued the judgment and opinions of his editors. Of the hundreds of entries, Charles only read the five selected by the editors. Charles smiled. "You're not going to give me any clues, are you?"

"No," Margot said firmly as she handed him the stack of manuscripts. "Here they are. In alphabetical order."

Margot hesitated. Charles eyed her quizzically "Yes?"

"One was handwritten. We had it typed. But we gave you the original also."

"*Handwritten?*"

"The author lives in Africa. I don't think she had access to a typewriter."

Margot tried to say it casually; but, of course, it was a dead giveaway. Charles knew instantly that the handwritten story by the writer who lived in Africa must be his editors' unanimous choice. Charles smiled reassuringly at Margot. It didn't matter that he knew. It wouldn't influence him. He would choose the story he thought was best.

* * *

That night, in the elegantly and expensively decorated pastel-and-cream living room of his penthouse overlooking Central Park, Charles read the stories. He read them slowly and carefully and in alphabetical order. The handwritten one was the fourth. Charles almost decided to read it last. No, he could be objective.

Charles looked at the handwritten copy. It was quite legible, written with a dark blue fountain pen in elegant script. He decided to read the original. His eyes drifted from the title, "Emerald," to the author's name: Galen Elizabeth Spencer.

"Galen," he whispered. *"Galen."*

As Charles stared at the pages of notebook paper he held in his hands, he remembered a lovely, innocent fifteen-year-old girl writing in a crimson notebook in the dim light of a kerosene lamp. It was a foggy, dreamy memory of red-gold hair and huge green eyes that shyly and bravely told him, No, Charles, you can't read what I'm writing.

Finally I get to read those precious secret words, Galen.

Charles's hands trembled slightly as he turned to the first page . . .

. . . by the time he finished Galen's story, Charles's heart was pounding with quick, uneasy energy. Charles paced around his penthouse trying to subdue his heart and focus his thoughts. He swallowed a glass of bourbon—his mouth was so dry—and stood for timeless minutes gazing at the sparkling glitter of the Manhattan skyline.

Finally he dialed the number to Jason's apartment on Riverside Drive. The phone rang, unanswered, twenty times. Charles glanced impatiently at the Tiffany chime clock on the white marble mantel. It was eleven o'clock on Friday night. Jason could be anywhere.

Charles put down the receiver. Then, without thinking, without specifically trying to recall the number he had not dialed for over eleven years, Charles's fingers pushed the sequence of buttons that would connect him to the estate in Southampton. Charles guessed that Jason spent time there. But they never discussed it.

As Charles listened to the distinctive ring of the Southampton exchange, uneasy feelings flooded him; ancient painful feelings that reminded him of a part of his life that was over but would be with him always.

Answer the phone, Jason, goddammit.

Jason stared for a moment at the always-silent phone. How could it be ringing? No one had the number, not even any one of the many caretakers or gardeners or housekeepers. Jason needed the phone to *make* calls. But it hadn't rung, literally, for years.

Jason laid down his paintbrush and wiped the paint from his hands with a turpentine-soaked rag as he moved slowly toward the phone.

"Hello?"

"Jason," Charles breathed. He had almost hung up. He had almost needed to stop hearing that ring. "Am I interrupting—"

"No, Charles," Jason answered swiftly. Of course Charles had the number. It had been his home, his telephone number, once. *Too.* "Is something . . . ?"

"Everything is fine. I just finished reading the entries for the fiction contest." Charles stopped abruptly. He realized then that he had never even read the fifth story. He *would* read it. But it wouldn't make a difference.

"Oh?"

"There's one, Jason," Charles began, his voice gaining pace and energy and enthusiasm as he spoke. "It's so good. I've never read anything like it. It's romance and adventure and passion and strength and beauty."

Charles took a breath. After a moment he continued, his voice low and soft,

"And with the art, Jason . . . it's our vision of what *Images* should be."

Our vision, Jason mused. It was true. *Images* was their creation. Together they had transformed *Images* into Elliott's dream for his beloved magazine—a harmonious, sensual, graceful blend of art and literature. Charles and Jason created each splendid issue together, but only Charles knew if the final product met their vision. Only Charles could read the words.

Charles and Jason together wove the art and literature in *Images* into a beautiful, intricate, compelling tapestry. Charles spent long, patient hours telling Jason about the words. Jason listened carefully and translated the passion and emotion of the words into art.

And either Charles told him perfectly or Jason understood perfectly, because the art and the words always blended. *Perfectly.* As if a single heart and mind had carefully and lovingly chosen both.

"Tell me about 'Emerald,' Charles."

As Jason listened to the story of Emerald—the captivating love story of a naive young girl and a dashing, experienced adventurer set in turn-of-the-century Africa—his mind formed clear, vivid images of the scenes Charles described. And of the beautiful, innocent, passionate heroine.

"So?" Charles asked when he was through. Charles didn't say, because he never would, *If you could read it, Jason! It reads like poetry.*

"More than one picture." Jason was thinking out loud. "Probably three. Watercolors, I think. The mood needs to be soft and romantic."

"Yes," Charles agreed. "Even though 'Emerald' has danger and adventure in it, it is, above all, a love story."

"I think Fran should be the model for the art," Jason continued seriously. "Fran should be Emerald."

Even if Charles and Jason were in the habit of friendly, brotherly, *twin* teases and taunts, Charles would not have observed lightly that Fran just happened to be Jason's lover. Because Jason's decision was a professional one. And it was the right one. Fran Jeffries would make a perfect Emerald.

"I'll speak with Adam on Monday," Charles said. Fran was a Drake model. "Jason, I think we should offer her—Galen—a contract for four stories to be published over the next year."

"*Really?*" Jason's surprise was obvious. There were a few authors, *established* authors, whose work was published repeatedly in *Images*. But never an unknown. And never four times in a year.

"It's that good."

"All right."

Jason's permission was necessary. *Images* was Jason's magazine. Just as *Fashion* and *Spinnaker*—all of Sinclair Publishing—belonged to Jason, not Charles. Jason's signature would secure the four-story contract with Galen Elizabeth Spencer. Jason's signature. Jason's money. Jason's profit.

But *their* vision.

After he hung up, Charles realized he hadn't told Jason that he knew Galen; or had known, barely, a teenage girl named Galen in Kenya. Maybe Galen wouldn't even remember. His name on the letter he would send her—congratulating her and inviting her, as all winners were invited, to spend a week at Sinclair's expense in New York City—would mean nothing to her. She had known him only as Charles, the Peace Corps worker with malaria who wanted to read her stories.

* * *

"God, she is beautiful," Steve Barnes whistled under his breath as he sifted through the photographs of Melanie Chandler modelling Malibu Sportswear. It was because Adam Drake had seen *these* photographs that he decided to fly to Los Angeles to see *her*.

"These don't begin to do her justice. They were taken to sell the clothes—which they did—not Melanie. But you"—Adam levelled his blue-gray eyes at the man he considered the best fashion photographer in the business—"you will be able to make her the top model in, I would guess, under six months."

"Is she a bitch?" Steve asked, tossing the photographs onto Adam's carved oak desk.

Adam grimaced slightly. Steve's contempt for the models annoyed Adam. But Steve was the best and Adam had never heard a word of complaint.

"She's lovely," Adam answered firmly, remembering the sky-blue eyes and sensuous lips that smiled coyly, disbelieving, when he told her how much money he would give her just to sign a contract with Drake. And when he told her how much money—it was a conservative estimate—she would make in the first year, Melanie tossed her sun-gold hair and laughed merrily. As if she didn't *care*. As if it didn't *matter*.

But something did matter to those sparkling eyes and beckoning lips. They became serious and thoughtful as she told him honestly how much she loved her life in California. She would have to think about it. She would have to *think* about moving to New York and becoming the top model in the world.

It just might not be that important.

A week later Melanie called and told him, Yes, she would come. And there was something in the soft, sexy voice that made Adam decide *some* part of it was very important after all.

"She's unspoiled," Adam continued, his eyes sending a message to Steve: *Be gentle with her.* "Natural. Unpretentious—"

"It will be interesting to see what fame and fortune do to that," Steve suggested knowingly. He knew what would happen. He spent his life dealing with vain, selfish, beautiful women.

"I hope," Adam murmured, "that it does nothing."

Steve shrugged and turned to leave.

"Oh," Adam said. "I almost forgot. Charles Sinclair called. They want Fran to model for the art for the *Images* fiction winner. December issue. Something set in Africa. I'll have Alice schedule an appointment with Charles and Jason to see what they have in mind."

"Like taking the shots in Africa?"

Adam smiled. Charles and Jason might want that. The cost never mattered, only the quality.

"Fran, huh?"

"They need dark brown eyes and hair."

"She's Jason Sinclair's, uh, *girlfriend*."

"I know. And *you* know that Fran doesn't need connections to get jobs," Adam added hotly.

Fran's silky brown hair blew into Jason's face as she curled against him. Jason cradled her in one arm and steered the sailboat with the other. The late-afternoon summer breeze glided the sailboat briskly and silently across the white-capped waters of Peconic Bay.

"This is heaven," Fran purred against Jason's strong neck.

"I love it." Jason tilted his head skyward toward the lingering warmth of the afternoon sun. He closed his light-blue eyes and felt the wind, strong and powerful, caress his cheeks. He inhaled the clean salt air and sighed. He loved to sail. He loved the energy and the silence and the peace. It was a passion he had shared with Elliott, a passion they still shared. Part of Elliott was always with him when he sailed.

"You sail with your eyes closed?"

Jason smiled. He opened his eyes and gazed into the lovely brown ones.

"I could sail Peconic Bay with my eyes closed. If there were no other boats. . . ."

"Did you live near here when you were a boy?"

Jason nodded. He narrowed his eyes against the setting sun and looked toward shore. In the distance he could see the perfectly manicured emerald-green lawns of Windermere sweeping from the red-brick Georgian mansion to the white sand beach. Windermere was Jason's boyhood home and his home, his private retreat away from Manhattan, *still*.

Jason loved Windermere, despite the bittersweet memories and the haunting, unanswered secrets. Jason wondered—a tormented, helpless wonder—if some of the answers lay in Elliott's journals. Was there something there—emotions and secrets of his beloved father—that Jason should know? Or never know?

Jason sighed heavily. The journals were in Elliott's desk, as they had been since the day Elliott had died. But Jason couldn't read the words. And there was no one Jason could trust to read them to him. . . .

"Jason?" Fran touched her slender ivory finger to his cheek.

Jason caught her hand and pulled it to his lips.

"Yes." He pressed his lips against her hand and smiled gently into her soft fawn eyes. Fran, I don't know if I will ever be able to share Windermere with you, Jason thought. What we have is wonderful. You make me feel wonderful. But . . . maybe it's just too soon for me to be certain. And I have to be certain. So certain. "I grew up in Southampton. Charles and I grew up here."

CHAPTER FOUR

Southampton, New York
August 1952

". . . *tomorrow they would greet the dawn together.*" Elliott Sinclair stopped reading and gazed at his beautiful, pregnant wife. Meredith was lost somewhere—in the story he had just read to her, in the picture she was painting, in gentle dreams of their unborn child. Elliott waited in silence. He was in no hurry to interrupt this moment. He could spend his life watching Meredith.

Finally she turned toward him, her pale-blue eyes shining. "That was lovely. A beautiful story. If . . ."

"If?"

"If there could be art to go with it," she said softly.

At her request—a shy, quiet request—Elliott had read every word of the latest issue of *Images* to her while she painted.

"There *is* art in *Images*."

"I know. But it's separate from the literature. If the words and art could blend, so that together they created an image . . ."

Elliott considered Meredith's suggestion. Her idea was innovative and exciting. Done right, with great care and thought and painstaking, loving attention to detail, every issue of *Images* could be a work of art.

"Yes," Elliott whispered finally. "*Yes.*"

Meredith smiled, but her lips trembled slightly, uncertain and hesitant. His thoughtful, sensitive wife had more to say. Elliott urged gently, "What else, Merry?"

"*Images* should be for everyone, not just the wealthy."

Elliott smiled at the pale-blue eyes he loved so much. *Tell me, Meredith.*

"You already have two magazines for the aristocracy. *Fashion* is for elegant, bejewelled, glamorous women and *Spinnaker* is for their yacht-loving husbands."

"His-and-her magazines?" Elliott laughed softly.

"Yes. His-and-her magazines for your friends." Meredith shrugged. "Which is fine. The magazines are magnificent."

"But?"

"But *Images* should be for everyone. I don't mean the price. People are willing to pay for quality. I mean the *vision.* Poetry and literature and art should be for everyone. Like sunsets and roses and . . ."

Meredith shrugged again.

"Your nose is red," Elliott said softly, moving toward her.

"I'm a little embarrassed. I mean, you do have a magazine empire. You know what—"

"It's fuschia, actually." Elliott wiped the smudge of paint from her nose, then kissed the spot where the paint had been. "I love you, Meredith. And you're right about *Images.* And sunsets. And roses. If you help me, if you remind me of the vision, if we do it together . . ."

"You and I and Charles," Meredith murmured, gently touching the bulge under her painter's smock. In three months she would have Elliott's child. It filled her with such joy. *Charles* was Elliott's choice for a boy's name.

"You and I and Jason," Elliott countered lightly with Meredith's choice.

"Jason, if he's blond like me. But Charles, if he's dark like you. And Rebecca, if she's a she." It was what they had agreed.

"And you and I and Jason or Charles or Rebecca will make *Images* a thing of beauty for everyone." Elliott wrapped his arms around her.

"Yes, darling, we will."

Meredith went into labor at six A.M. on November eleventh, twelve hours before she gave birth to a healthy golden-haired baby boy with pale-blue eyes. It was all easy. Elliott was with her—touching her, stroking her damp blond hair—the entire time. Thirty minutes after the delivery Meredith was back in her hospital room holding her beautiful baby, herself cradled in her husband's arms.

"He looks just like you," Elliott whispered lovingly.

"All babies . . . No, you're right. He *does* look like me," Meredith said, smiling, nuzzling the brand-new silky blond hair. "I guess he's Jason."

"He's Jason."

"Our next son will be Charles, all right? No matter what or who he looks like."

"Our next son? Are you ready to do this again?" Elliott teased.

Meredith didn't answer in words, but she pressed closer and nodded her head against his lips.

"I love you, Meredith."

"I love you, Elliott."

Elliott held her and their son for several silent, tender moments. Suddenly, abruptly, Meredith pulled away and searched for Elliott's eyes.

"Meredith?" Elliott saw fear in her pale-blue eyes. *Why fear?* "*Merry?*"

"Promise me something, Elliott." Her voice was urgent.

"Anything darling." *What was wrong?*

"Promise me that you will love him, cherish him, protect him. *Always.*"

"Of course I promise that. But we will do that together. *Forever.*"

"But if anything ever happens to me," Meredith persisted as tears spilled inexplicably onto her cheeks.

"Nothing is ever going to happen to you," Elliott said firmly, trying to conceal the worry in his voice. "Meredith, what's wrong?"

"I don't know," she answered truthfully, forcing a smile. Her lips trembled. "Just emotions catching up with me, I guess. Seeing our precious baby, our precious Jason."

But it was *more*. A deep sense of dread and emptiness pulsed through her. Something was terribly wrong.

Elliott pulled her close again, kissing her and the baby, feeling her tremble.

Then the pain came. Cramping, tearing, excruciating pain that caught her breath and held it.

"*Elliott,*" she gasped. "Get the doctor, *please.*"

As Elliott rushed out of the room he saw the blood that had already begun to seep through the bedding. Meredith closed her arms around Jason and pressed her lips against his warm soft forehead, trying to find strength, trying to breathe.

Elliott returned almost immediately with two doctors and a nurse.

Meredith smiled at him, a distant, dreamy, loving smile. She handed Jason to him and said, "Love him always, Elliott. And know that I love you. Always."

It wasn't possible to control the bleeding in time to save Meredith's life. As the doctors battled frantically but futilely to save her, they discovered the cause of Meredith's bleeding. Retained products of conception . . . a second placenta . . . another life.

The second baby, the twin, was tiny and undernourished. Surely he was too weak, too tiny, to survive. Still, he was breathing. And his heart pounded. They moved him quickly into an incubator in the newborn nursery.

"Doctor, have you spoken to him?" The head nurse of the newborn nursery glanced meaningfully at the incubator labelled *Baby Boy Sinclair*. "It's been almost two weeks."

"I know." The doctor grimaced.

"Maybe it's hard for him to come back here, because of his wife. But that's his *son* fighting for his life!"

"*I know.*"

The doctor moved beside the Baby Boy Sinclair incubator and looked at the tiny, fragile infant. He was so small, so helpless, so alone. His little perfect arms and legs struggled against the air. Or maybe they were reaching, desperately trying to find some sign of life and warmth in his cold, lonely world.

The doctor put his finger into the incubator beside the small hand. The reaction was instant and instinctive. The tiny fingers wrapped around his, holding tight, unwilling to release the grasp.

The doctor blinked back tears. Who is going to love you, little man? Who is going to care for you the way your mother would have?

Not your father, the doctor thought angrily. Could Elliott Sinclair actually blame this helpless baby for his wife's death? The doctor was afraid that that was exactly what Elliott was doing. It was just grief. Surely it would pass.

But the doctor wondered, his jaw muscles rippling as he recalled the conversation with Elliott, once Elliott had finally agreed to speak with him. The doctor eagerly told him of the remarkable progress his son was making, what a *fighter* he was. He asked Elliott what he wanted to name him. And all Elliott said was, *If he lives, call him Charles.*

Charles Sinclair was released from the hospital when he was two months old. A nursery, away from Elliott's bedroom where Jason slept, had been prepared, and the nurses, nannies, and staff of housekeepers had been notified that there would be another infant at Windermere.

When Charles arrived home, in the arms of the chauffeur, Jason was playing with Elliott in the great room. The chauffeur had been instructed to take Charles to his room, away from Elliott and Jason. But the moment Charles entered the house, Jason became distracted, frowning, anxious. He wriggled in Elliott's arms in the direction of the entry hall.

Elliott spoke to him lovingly, but Jason's restlessness increased and tears threatened. Elliott carried him to the window, to the panoramic view of the gray-green wintry Atlantic Ocean. Usually Jason loved that, as if he *felt* the beauty even though his young eyes couldn't really see the vastness. But not today. Today Jason just kept turning, now almost frantically, toward the entry hall.

Finally, reluctantly, Elliott gave in to Jason's urgent demands. The chauffeur and Charles's nurse were preparing to take Charles upstairs to his remote isolated nursery. Even before Elliott and Jason appeared, Charles became animated, his thin, quiet body suddenly energized and eager.

And when Charles saw his twin, the first smile of his short lonely life erupted on his face and the first sound he ever uttered flowed—a squeal of joy—from his frail lips. Jason squealed in return. And smiled and giggled and wriggled, commanding Elliott to carry him even closer.

Finally the twins were close enough to touch, again, as they had for nine months of their lives. Jason's plump, soft, dimpled hands grasped Charles's lean, undernourished arms. Small fingers explored eyes and noses and mouths. And all the time they were talking—a language of coos and gurgles—and laughing.

Charles and Jason spent the afternoon, the afternoon of their reunion, playing on a soft blue blanket on the floor of the great room. Elliott watched with amazement and concern. His happy, charming, beloved Jason was even happier now.

Jason wants to be with Charles, Elliott thought as he gazed at his sleeping sons, curled together, each sucking his twin's thumb as if it were his own, a portrait of peace and harmony. I can't separate them if Jason wants to be with Charles.

Elliott couldn't separate Charles and Jason. But *he* could ignore Charles. When Elliott returned late at night from work he would go to their crib, his voice gentle and loving as he spoke Jason's name. Elliott would lift his golden-haired son from the crib and leave the room, taking Jason with him and leaving Charles, his small arms stretching frantically toward the loving voice of his father as it faded in the darkness.

Charles was left alone for endless hours in the dark silence. And as he grew, Charles understood that even though he and Jason were close, and even though he *wanted* his father's love as much as Jason did, Jason was the only one who would be loved.

There was something wonderful about Jason. Something that made Jason loved.

And there was something wrong with Charles. Something that made him *not* loved.

Charles's happy times were with Jason. They had a hundred games—a *thousand*. They shifted from one game to the next without pause, one moment patiently taking turns filling a red plastic bucket with sand, the next moment impatiently chasing each other on the grass, the next moment pulling each other's hair and laughing.

One afternoon, when they were two, Elliott witnessed the twins' game of tug-of-war. Standing on sturdy two-year-old legs that had just learned to walk with some degree of confidence, each had hold of a corner of a silk pillow. This day it was Charles who let go first. Jason, the would-be victor, toppled backward clutching the pillow. His head hit the floor with a thud, and in the stunned moment in which Jason had to decide if he should laugh because he won the game or cry because the thud surprised him, Elliott rushed beside him to make sure he was all right.

That wasn't part of the game. And it got worse. As soon as Elliott was certain that Jason was all right, he lunged at Charles, grabbing him violently.

"You are a bad, bad boy," Elliott scolded as he spanked Charles over and over, harder and harder. "A horrible boy."

"Do, do, do!" Jason screamed his version of *no*. He toddled toward Elliott, his small arms flailing. When he reached Elliott his pale-blue eyes were flooded with tears, and his face twisted with horror as he saw what his father was doing to Charles. Jason's small hands wrapped around Elliott's strong forearm. *"Do!"*

Elliott stopped spanking Charles the instant he saw the look in Jason's eyes. It was as if Elliott was punishing *Jason*, not Charles. As if hurting Charles caused pain to Jason.

"Jason, don't cry," Elliott whispered, releasing his rough grasp on Charles and scooping Jason into his arms. Charles fell to the ground, sobbing large gulps of pain and sadness as Elliott held Jason, talking softly to him, reassuring him.

The spanking was the first and only time Elliott Sinclair ever touched Charles. He didn't scold Charles again—he only neglected him—until Charles and Jason were four and a half. That June, while Jason was taking a sailing class for children at the Peconic Bay Yacht Club, Elliott called Charles into his study.

"The language between you and Jason has to stop." Elliott glowered at Charles. "Sir?"

"Jason doesn't speak English. Not one word. And it's your fault."

Charles blinked back tears. It was true that Jason didn't speak a language anyone but Charles could understand. He and Jason had their own private language. As Charles learned the language of their nannies and their books and their *father*, Jason fidgeted and seemed disinterested. Jason understood English. But he didn't speak it. He seemed quite content to have Charles translate for him.

Father, it is not *my* fault that Jason doesn't speak. Please don't blame me.

"As long as you and Jason continue your own silly language, Jason will never learn to speak properly. If you don't stop it at once I will send you away. You are a bad influence on Jason. He would be better off without you."

"No, please, Father." Charles felt the darkness and silence closing in. His heart pounded with panic. He sputtered, "I'll make sure that Jason learns to speak."

It was a painful, emotional struggle. Jason didn't understand. He felt betrayed. Why didn't Charles want them to be special anymore?

"Charles, tell me why," Jason pleaded in *their* special twin language.

Charles ignored him, his heart aching, drenched in fear. What if Jason couldn't speak any other language? What if Father sent him away? *Try, Jason, please try.*

Jason did try. By their fifth birthday Jason was speaking fluently, if reluctantly. Charles taught him the meaning of all the words he knew. He taught his twin how to speak perfectly. It took great effort and care and patience.

But no amount of effort and care and patience could teach Jason how to read.

"Your son has a form—a severe and somewhat atypical form—of what is called dyslexia," the specialist told Elliott a year later. He added, unnecessarily, because it was the reason that Elliott had sought help, "He can't read."

"Atypical?" Elliott asked hopefully. Maybe that was good. Although the specialist had said *severe*.

"He is quiet, not terribly verbal. But unlike most dyslexics who are reluctant to speak, Jason *can* speak fluently. Perfect syntax. His vocabulary is truly exceptional for a six-year-old. You have done very well—"

"Can he be taught to read?" Elliott interjected, realizing that it was *Charles* who had done very well, *Charles* who had taught Jason to speak. Against all odds.

"I really don't know. His block is very severe. We can try, of course. It will be a frustrating and difficult struggle for him. And it may never work."

"Never?"

"It doesn't mean that Jason can't learn. He retains and assimilates the spoken word beautifully. I wonder if we should just focus on that and work *around* the dyslexia." The specialist was thinking out loud. He continued, "Jason has the verbal equivalent of a photographic memory. It's really quite remarkable. He is very bright. There is nothing he can't learn. He just has to hear it, not read it. Of course your other son is also very bright. His ability to read and write is way beyond that of a six-year—"

"We're talking about Jason," Elliott interrupted impatiently. He didn't want to hear about Charles's brilliance.

"Yes, well, there are special schools. Not many, admittedly. There is one in California. Or you could hire tutors. Jason can be told—and will remember—everything another child would learn through formal schooling. He could probably even attend a regular school if someone read the assignments to him and if he could take oral examinations."

"I'll hire tutors," Elliott decided without hesitation.

Elliott didn't want Jason to go away to school. He loved him too much to be apart from him. Jason was so much like Meredith. He was so generous, so loving, so kind, so happy. Even the dyslexia, Elliott realized, was like Meredith. Meredith *could* read, but she rarely did. In the evenings, she would paint and Elliott would read aloud to her. Elliott couldn't remember seeing Meredith read a book or even a newspaper. But he remembered vividly the way her soft blue eyes concentrated as he read to her or as she listened to the news on the radio.

Meredith had dyslexia, too. It hadn't been as severe for her as it was for Jason.

But it was one more thing that his beloved son had inherited from his beloved Meredith. It made Elliott love Jason even more.

Elliott hired the best tutors. Until they were twelve, Charles and Jason both had all their schooling at Windermere. Charles was Jason's best and most devoted tutor. Charles read to him and told him stories. Jason listened eagerly as Charles told him about Robin Hood and Tom Sawyer and Huckleberry Finn.

Sometimes they would pretend the dense wood surrounding Windermere was Sherwood Forest or the Atlantic Ocean was really the mighty Mississippi. Charles and Jason enjoyed living the fictional adventures Charles read about, but, even more, they loved to create their own stories, imagining scenes together, sharing visions. . . .

Charles read about twins. He told Jason some of the stories, but not others. Charles didn't tell Jason about the biblical twins, Esau and Jacob, who tricked and connived and competed for their birthright. And he didn't tell Jason about Romulus and Remus, the twin sons of Mars whose bitter quarrel over the location for their city on the Tiber River ended in Remus' death at the hands of his twin.

Charles chose not to tell Jason about Esau or Jacob or Romulus or Remus. But Charles told Jason—and they shared the story again and again as they sat on the beach and searched for *their* constellation in the star-glittered sky—about Castor and Pollux, the Gemini.

"Castor and Pollux were the twin sons of Zeus and Leda. They loved each other . . ." Charles began.

". . . and Neptune rewarded their brotherly love by giving them power over the wind and waves," Jason continued enthusiastically. He especially loved the story because already he shared Elliott's passion for sailing and Castor and Pollux were the special guardians of all seafarers. "And he gave them St. Elmo's Fire, the mysterious light that guides lost sailors to safety."

"When Castor died in battle," Charles spoke quietly, "Pollux was so upset that he begged Zeus to allow him to join his twin."

"Zeus said Yes and they became the Gemini," Jason finished the story solemnly.

The pattern of Charles's life established before his birth continued throughout his childhood. The lovely, warm, secure moments—his mother's womb, curled against Jason in their crib, laughing and playing with Jason—were so fragile. Without warning, the happy moment would suddenly be disrupted and he would be alone again. It happened whenever Elliott came home.

At first, when he was old enough to follow, Charles would go with Elliott and Jason. But it soon became too painful to be with Elliott and Jason, watching their love and being *excluded* from it. So whenever Jason was with Elliott, Charles retreated to the wood-panelled library at Windermere and read. Eventually he read every book in the vast library.

Charles read every book in Elliott's library, and he read every issue of *Images*, *Fashion*, and *Spinnaker*. Charles dreamed of being an editor and publisher like Elliott. He would make Elliott so proud of him! Someday, Elliott would love him, too.

When Charles was twelve, the terrible loneliness and isolation that had punctuated his boyhood became permanent. Without warning or explanation, Charles was sent to Morehead, an expensive, exclusive boys' school in Pennsylvania. The cost didn't matter to Elliott. He just wanted Charles away from Jason, away from Windermere, and away from *him*.

Jason stayed at Windermere, surrounded by a constant stream of well-paid and enthusiastic tutors who taught him English and history and mathematics and science and geography and literature and current events. The tutors weren't told that Jason had dyslexia. Elliott *implied* there was something wrong with the beautiful pale-blue eyes that watched them so attentively and were so appreciative of *their* hard work for him. Jason's eagerness to learn seemed tireless. And his tutors matched his energy and enthusiasm with their own. They all cared about the happy, charming boy with the white-blond hair and rosy cheeks and ready smile. He was so special.

Jason didn't understand why Charles had gone away. But Jason guessed it was because Charles was so bright. Charles needed to get away. It held him back, encumbered his learning, to be at Windermere with Jason who could learn nothing on his own. It was *nice* that Charles had been willing to stay for twelve years. He might have left sooner. Jason missed Charles so much! Even with his father, and all the tutors, Jason felt terribly lonely. But he would never tell Charles. He would never make Charles feel guilty for having finally left. . . .

Without Jason, without the hope of wonderful moments to offset the lonely, isolated ones, Charles somberly accepted his fate. He was meant to be alone and unloved. There was something about him—something wrong with him—that made a solitary life his destiny. In a small corner of his heart he felt relief to be away from Elliott and the constant reminder that his father didn't love him.

In broad daylight, in the middle of his English class, Charles accepted the realization calmly. But at night, tossing and turning in his bed in his dormitory room, Charles dreamed of a day when Elliott *would* love him, when the nightmare would end and he and Elliott and Jason would be a family.

Charles's dreams gave him hope. He wrote long, loving letters to Jason and Elliott. Charles mailed the letters to Jason in care of Elliott. Elliott could read them to Jason.

Charles wrote to Jason about his life at Morehead. Charles made it sound like a wonderful, exciting adventure he wanted to share with his twin through his letters. Charles didn't tell Jason the truth—how sad and lonely he was—because he didn't want to make Jason sad. But sometimes, because he couldn't help it, because he hurt so much, Charles told Jason how desperately he missed him.

I want to be like you, Father, Charles wrote bravely to Elliott. He would never have had the courage to *tell* Elliott. But he could write it. And Elliott could see how hard he was trying to achieve his dream. . . .

Charles's grades were the highest in his class. An essay he had written had been entered in a national contest, and the short story he sent to Elliott would be published in the town paper, and he was elected to the editorial board of Morehead's literary magazine even though it was only his first year and . . .

Charles's letters to Jason and Elliott were never acknowledged, much less answered. Jason could call, couldn't he? Couldn't he have one of the tutors dial the number for him? And Elliott . . .

But Charles heard nothing. Still, he eagerly awaited the Thanksgiving break, forgetting his destiny, forgetting that Windermere was not his home.

No one came to get him. At eight o'clock on the Wednesday night before Thanksgiving Day, the headmaster at Morehead placed a call to Windermere.

"Mr. Sinclair is away for the holiday," the chauffeur explained.

"What about his son?" the headmaster demanded, relieved he had told Charles to wait *outside* his office.

"His son is with him."

"His *other* son."

"Oh." The chauffeur's voice softened. It was *he* who had brought the tiny, frail two-month-old Charles home from the hospital twelve years before. The chauffeur knew, he had seen it, the silent agony of the serious, unloved little boy. "Oh, dear. May I speak with him?"

"Hello?" Charles asked eagerly moments later. Jason's voice. *Elliott's* voice.

"They are away, Charles. Sailing in the Islands. I will get in the car right now to come fetch you."

"Oh. No, thank you. I have schoolwork to do." Charles blinked back tears. And the familiar aching.

"Yes, well." Then the chauffeur asked quietly, vowing to himself that he would be responsible, "When does Christmas break begin?"

For the next six years, whenever Charles returned home he felt like a visitor. He felt like a friend of Jason who was spending the holidays with Jason's family. A *friend*. It was an awkward friendship at best. Jason never mentioned the letters Charles wrote to him, although he always seemed happy to see Charles.

During summers and holidays Charles and Jason tried without success to recapture the familiar closeness. They were both changing so quickly. They were boys becoming young men, making discoveries, learning, wondering. The brief moments together weren't enough. Too much happened during the long, silent gaps between visits. They drifted apart, friendly and polite, but separate.

Most of the time Elliott paid little attention to Charles. But sometimes—a few horrible times that Charles would never forget—he caught his father staring at him. And what Charles saw then, in the dark eyes of the man whose love he wanted so desperately, was hatred.

"I want to go to college, Father," Jason told Elliott a week after Charles returned to Morehead for his senior year.

"Where?" Elliott asked cautiously. Charles had decided on Princeton, Elliott's *alma mater*. What if . . .

Jason shrugged. He didn't know much about colleges. It would be nice to be at Princeton with Charles. But that wouldn't be fair to Charles. Charles would worry about him, wondering if Jason could survive outside the protected, cloistered world of Windermere, assuming the burden if Jason *couldn't*. Jason said quietly, "Not Princeton."

Relief pulsed through Elliott. *Good.*

"I should be on my own," Jason continued tentatively. He thought about it all the time. It scared him and excited him. He had to *try*.

Elliott smiled at the earnest pale-blue eyes of his beloved son. Then he tousled the white-blond hair and said gently, his voice begrudging but full of love, "All right. But don't go so far away that you can't come home for the regattas."

"No," Jason agreed. "I won't."

Elliott and Jason decided on Harvard. Elliott made a few calls. It was easier to grant Elliott Sinclair's son an interview than to explain why Jason was not really a suitable applicant. . . .

The admissions interviewers were instantly charmed by the quiet, intelligent boy with the pale-blue eyes—he had an eye problem?— and gentle, polite manner. They decided to give him the SAT examination orally. Jason answered question after question, effortlessly and accurately.

Charles had told him how easy the SAT examination was, but that was *Charles*. Still, the examination was easy for him, too! Jason wanted desperately to tell Charles, but Jason didn't know how to use a phone.

Harvard University was pleased to offer Jason Sinclair a place in the entering freshman class of 1970. The dean of students agreed to serve as the liaison with faculty and tutors. With Jason's remarkable memory he could major in any subject. Did he have any idea what he wanted to do?

Jason had a precise idea of what he wanted to do, even though he had never articulated it. What was the point? What he wanted was impossible. Jason wanted to be able to read. He wanted to be like Elliott and Charles. He wanted to be able to run Sinclair Publishing the way Elliott did. He wanted those impossible things.

And he wanted something else. He wanted to be independent, to find something that was his, to learn how to survive without help.

When the dean of students asked Jason to declare a major, Jason answered swiftly and confidently, even though he had never thought about it before, "Art history."

CHAPTER FIVE

*D*uring spring semester of his senior year at Morehead, Charles made an important decision. This summer he would find the courage to ask Elliott if he could spend time with him at Sinclair Publishing. Nothing was more important to Charles. He would happily abandon the carefree summertime activities of Southampton—flirting with girls at the pool at Shinnecock and playing tennis and swimming—in favor of working with Elliott in Manhattan.

Charles knew that Elliott was grooming Jason, the beloved son, to run the company. That was fair. Jason was the eldest. But Jason couldn't read and Charles *loved* to. Surely there would be room for both sons in the company. . . .

This summer Charles would tell Elliott how much he wanted to be a part—however small—of Sinclair Publishing. Did he need to reassure Elliott that he wouldn't compete with Jason for control of the company? Charles would never compete with Jason. But Jason would need help. Jason would need someone to do what he, Jason, could never do.

Charles would do that willingly, *eagerly*. It was what he dreamed about. Jason could have the control and the power. All Charles wanted was a chance do what he loved to do and *could* do. . . .

Elliott telephoned Charles's dormitory room at Morehead two days before graduation.

"Father?" Charles's heart leapt. Maybe Elliott had decided to come to the graduation ceremony to watch Charles receive top honors after all!

"I need to discuss some business matters with you, Charles," Elliott said flatly.

"When?"

"When will you be done with school?"

I'm done now. I graduate day after tomorrow. Why don't you come?

"The day after tomorrow."

"When are you planning to come here?" Elliott asked. He did not ask, When are you planning to come home?

"By midafternoon Saturday." Charles's heart ached. His father sounded so serious and distant. What was happening?

"All right. We'll meet here at three on Saturday," Elliott said.

An appointment with his father? In his own home?

Charles felt his dreams begin to die.

"You're disowning me," Charles whispered in disbelief after he listened to his father's words. They were in the great room in the mansion at Windermere. Charles sat facing the tall French doors that opened onto the colorful rose gardens already magnificent in early June.

"I am providing you with a substantial trust fund. A lot of money, Charles. You will never have to work. And I am giving you a penthouse on Central Park West." Elliott firmly reiterated what he had already told Charles.

"But I have no part of Sinclair Publishing," Charles said quietly. "I never will have."

"No."

"You're disowning me," Charles repeated.

Elliott shrugged.

"Why?" Charles asked. He wasn't thinking clearly. But how could he? He needed to know what he had done wrong. He needed to understand.

Elliott looked at him. And the look, a little surprised, full of hatred, asked, Don't you know?

"Your things have been moved to the penthouse," Elliott continued, ignoring Charles's question and avoiding his son's hurt bewildered brown eyes. "You can go there now. On Monday you will meet with the attorneys. There are some papers to sign."

"Guaranteeing that I will never fight this?" Charles asked. Some things were clear. Even in the midst of this unreal nightmare, the message from his father, the bottom line, was clear.

Charles was no longer part of the Sinclair family.

"What about Jason? Can I say good-bye to my own brother?" My own twin?

"Jason is sailing. He won't be back for hours."

"Am I permitted to see him or to speak to him? Or do I sign something about that, too?"

"Of course you can," Elliott answered easily.

Charles and Jason's closeness had suffered from disuse and separation over the past six years. This would separate them further. Jason's love for his father was strong and unshakable. Just like the unfailing, unwavering love Elliott felt for Jason.

Charles decided he would call Jason in a day or two. He knew Jason wouldn't call him. Someone—Elliott—would have to dial the number for him. Charles wondered how Elliott would explain this to Jason. Maybe Jason knew the reason. Maybe Jason *agreed* with Elliott.

Maybe Charles wouldn't call Jason after all.

Charles drove down the long gravel drive, away from the house that had never been his home, his eyes stinging with tears. He felt the empty loneliness that had been woven through the happy moments of his life now settling firmly and irrevocably in his heart. It was part of him. It was who he was and who he would always be.

John Perkins stared with amazement at Charles Sinclair. As he and Elliott had drawn up the legal papers over the past few months, John assumed Elliott must have a compelling reason to disown his son, however generously. John expected a rebel. He expected long hair, drug-glazed eyes, obvious contempt for the life and dreams of his father, *something*.

But all John Perkins saw two days after Elliott banished Charles from Windermere was a polite, bewildered, sensitive young man who appeared, in every way, to be a young version of the father who was washing his hands of him. The physical resemblance between Charles and Elliott was striking—dark, handsome aristocracy laced with a slightly mean, slightly threatening sensuality. The resemblance between father and son ran far deeper than looks. In both men John Perkins saw great pain; a somber, persistent grief for a loss of immeasurable magnitude.

Why? John wondered. He realized that the young, dark eyes staring at him, as if *he* were the executioner, were asking the same question.

"I don't know, Charles." John answered the unspoken query. He had to clear the air before he offered the next, "But if I can help."

"Your firm could manage the . . ." Charles didn't even know the words. Trusts? Assets? Funds? All he knew was that his father had given him millions of dollars to be rid of him forever.

"Everything. If you want us to." At least until Elliott comes to his senses and takes you back. But Elliott won't do that, John realized sadly.

"Yes. Thank you."

Six months later, in a luxury apartment on Fifth Avenue, a beautiful young woman watched as Elliott dressed in the darkness. It was three in the morning and he was leaving her, as he always did, to return to his apartment on Park Avenue or to make the long drive to his forbidden-to-her retreat on Long Island. Now, fortified by champagne and an unusually passionate evening of love-making, she urged herself to ask the question she had never before had the courage to ask.

She had never asked before because there was something a little frightening about Elliott Sinclair. And she had never asked before because she knew, if the well-publicized history of the past fifteen years of Elliott Sinclair's love life meant anything, that she was just the latest in an endless series of meaningless affairs.

But could he make love like that and not really care? Wasn't she, finally, the special woman in Elliott Sinclair's life?

"Elliott? What am I to you?"

"What?" His voice was harsh.

"You have been with me for almost six months." Even though you have never spent the night with me. She shook the thought. "We see each other almost every night." Except when your precious son is home from Harvard.

"You're my mistress," Elliott answered impatiently.

"How can I be your *mistress*? You don't even have a wife!"

In the dark shadows she saw the anger in Elliott's eyes. She shivered involuntarily, suddenly afraid he might harm her. But Elliott didn't move toward her. He did just the opposite. In a silent rage, he finished dressing and left.

She knew that she would never see him again.

* * *

Sixty miles away, in Princeton . . .

"Do you want some more dope?" The pretty coed with strawberry-blond curls held a half-smoked joint to Charles's mouth.

"Mmm." Charles inhaled slowly, expertly filling his lungs with the smoky heat and holding his breath.

"Do you want some more of me?" she cooed, pressing her soft nakedness against him and slowly curling her fingers in his shoulder-length brown hair.

"I have to go," Charles said as he exhaled.

"You always leave, Charles. Why don't you spend the night?"

Charles didn't answer. Instead, he stood up from the bed, his handsome, naked body silhouetted by candlelight, and pulled on his faded jeans.

"Don't you like making love with me?"

"Yes," Charles answered truthfully. "We just did it. *Twice.*"

"But you never hold me afterward. And you don't stay." She pouted and whispered carefully, "Sometimes I think you don't care, Charles. Sometimes I think you don't love me."

Of course I don't *care*, Charles thought as he smiled a seductive smile. And I don't *love*.

Charles left Princeton two weeks before the end of his freshman year. By spring he had become restless with the drug-blur of his life. In fall and winter the drugs and the girls had provided a warm, seductive, foggy escape from his shattered dreams. He missed class after class in favor of the endless, purposeless pleasure of drugs and sex. He convinced himself that the dreams didn't matter anymore. Nothing mattered, not literature or reading or writing or . . .

But Charles bought every issue of *Images*. And he imagined wonderful conversations with Elliott. He would tell Elliott what was wrong with *Images* and Elliott would listen carefully and his dark eyes would glisten proudly at his son.

If there could be art to go with the literature, Father.

What do you mean?

If the words and art could blend, so that together they created an image. . . .

Yes. What else?

Images should be for everyone, not just the wealthy.

You're right, Charles, Elliott would say. Then smiling, he would urge, *Come back, son. Come help me make* Images *all it can be.*

"It's not going to happen, you idiot!" Charles yelled aloud in his dormitory room one spring evening. "*Face it.*"

It took all of April for Charles to wean himself off the mind-numbing drugs and to force himself back into the painful reality of his life. On May first he dialed the Madison Avenue law offices of Perkins, Crane, and Marks.

"Mr. Perkins, this is Charles Sinclair."

"Yes, Charles. How is Princeton?" Charles sounded fine. John imagined a robust, handsome Ivy League look. In fact, Charles now looked the way John had expected the disowned son of Elliott Sinclair to look last summer. Charles's body was thin and sallow, his hair was long and tousled, and his dark eyes were vacant and glassy.

"Fine, sir. But I have decided to take some time away."

"Oh?"

"Yes. I have joined the Peace Corps. I'll be leaving for Kenya in a week?"

"And returning?"

"It will be at least two years. I wanted to give you my address."

"Good idea. We will undoubtedly need to reach you about some of the investments."

"Oh. That doesn't matter. Do whatever you think is best," Charles murmured. "I just wanted you to know where I will be."

In case something happens to Jason or Elliott.

"You're early." Jason was already smiling as he responded to the light knock on his dormitory-room door. The confident, charming smile for his date dissolved into a thoughtful, tentative one for his twin. *"Charles."*

"You're expecting someone."

"In a while."

Charles and Jason hadn't seen each other or spoken to each other in over a year, not since *before* Charles had left Windermere forever. Charles had never made the call to say good-bye.

"How are you, Jason?"

"Fine."

Jason looked fine, as if the new environment—Cambridge, Harvard, the stately red-brick dormitory—suited him more than terrified him. Charles had worried that it would be overwhelming for Jason. But the pale-blue eyes were relaxed. Jason wore a cream-colored sweater with a crimson H—a letterman's sweater.

"What's that for?" Charles asked, gesturing toward the letter, wondering if Jason had any idea what the crimson shape meant.

"Yachting?" Jason looked at Charles, and a thousand questions bombarded his mind. What's wrong, Charles? Why did you leave? What happened between you and Father? Why didn't you even say good-bye? Why are your eyes so empty?

Jason started to speak, but stopped. As carefully and patiently and lovingly as Charles and Elliott and all the tutors taught him how to speak, the language was still foreign. He couldn't use it to express his feelings or emotions. It didn't belong to him. It wasn't part of him.

Their language—the private, special language he and Charles had shared until Charles wouldn't share it anymore—had been different. How he wished he could tell Charles, in their special language, how he felt.

Instead he asked politely, "How are you, Charles?"

"I'm good. I guess I need a haircut. I'm going away for a while. I wanted you to know. . . ."

In Kenya, Charles learned to be comfortable with his isolation and solitude. The physical exhaustion of his daily work—construction work under the blazing equatorial sun—numbed his mind without clouding it. He found peace in the wild, vast beauty of Africa. The haunting pain that had driven him into hedonistic hiding during his year at Princeton subsided, and he could be alone without feeling the empty ache of loneliness.

Charles kept a polite, acceptable distance from the other volunteers. He worked beside them during the day, but withdrew in the evening, preferring a solitary walk on the savanna to fireside reminiscences of home and college and family.

At the end of the second year in Kenya, Charles and his team were joined by an anthropologist.

"Are you here to study *us?*" Charles asked one evening when he unexpectedly found the man on *his* grassy knoll.

"Spectacular sunset, isn't it? Please sit down. What did you ask? . . . Oh, yes. . . . No, although studying Peace Corps communities might be interesting. Actually, I'm studying beliefs and customs about twins in different parts of Africa. I'm just using this as base camp for a few weeks."

"Twins?"

"Yes. Of course the highest twinning rate in the world is in Nigeria. I have been there for the past year."

"What sort of beliefs and customs are there about twins?"

"Basically whether the tribe fears or reveres them. Some tribes welcome twins, celebrating them as symbols of fertility and good harvest. Other tribes reject—and even kill—them."

"Kill? *Why?*"

"Animals, not *humans*, typically have multiple offspring. So, for some tribes, a human twin birth means that the mother consorted with evil spirits. In other tribes, two children equal two fathers. Thus, the twins are a symbol of the mother's infidelity. Sometimes the mother *and* the twins are killed."

A pang of sadness and loss swept through Charles for the mother he had never known. He knew so little about her; Elliott never told them, *him* anyway, about her. *Meredith Sinclair.* Her signature was on the beautiful paintings at Windermere. But who was Meredith Sinclair? All Charles knew was that his mother was a wonderful, talented artist. . . .

"Awful."

"It's natural to fear something so different. Actually, most tribes revere twins."

"I'm a twin," Charles admitted slowly. "I have a brother. We're not identical."

"Really? So you must already know all this."

"No. I know about the mythological twins like Castor and Pollux. . . ."

"The belief that twins have supernatural power—good and bad—over weather is quite universal. Twins have been credited with both horrible droughts and desperately needed rainfall. Some mythical twins ascend to earth on lightning bolts and argue in claps of thunder." The anthropologist smiled. He asked lightly, "Do you and your brother have much control over weather?"

Charles laughed softly and shook his head. "I'm afraid not."

"Being a twin is such a unique experience," the anthropologist continued seriously. "To be that close, that much a part of another human . . . I've really become intrigued since doing this study. Do you mind if I pry?"

Charles shrugged.

"Do you know each other's thoughts?"

"No," Charles answered swiftly. After a moment he added, "When we were very young, we did. We had our own language."

"Are you terribly competitive?"

"No. Not at all. We've never competed." The only prize was Elliott's love. And that belonged to Jason. It always had and always would.

"That's unusual."

"We haven't really been together for nine years."

"Who is the firstborn? Not that that is a big issue in American culture. Critical in the Bible, of course, and in the royal families. The heir apparent and so on."

"He is?" Jason, firstborn and heir to the empire.

"In parts of Africa," the anthropologist explained, "the secondborn is the important twin. He is the eldest and strongest and heir. He sends his younger brother into the world to announce his impending birth and to make certain the world is a fit place for him."

That night Charles sat awake in his tent and carefully transcribed what the anthropologist had told him into his journal. Someday, Charles hoped, he would share what he had learned with Jason.

During the middle of his third year in Kenya, Charles acquired malaria. He was transported, with high fever and delirium, to a small clinic sixty miles away.

"You need to stay with him, Galen," Elise Spencer told her daughter. "I have to attend a delivery in the village."

"Yes, Mummy," Galen answered uneasily. She knew there was no choice. Her father was away for three weeks, providing much-needed medical care to the most remote villages. Sometimes Galen accompanied him, but this trip she stayed behind to help her mother at the clinic. To *help* but now she was being left alone! And the new patient looked so sick, so pale. She asked weakly, "What does he have?"

"It's *Falciparum* malaria, dear, so he's going to be delirious. I've given him his first dose of chloroquine." Elise smiled at her shy fifteen-year-old daughter. "You just need to make sure he doesn't crawl off the cot in his delirium. If he gets too hot, sponge him down. And, Galen?"

"Yes?"

"If he goes into coma . . ."

Galen looked at her sick charge. Underneath the pallor of sickness lay strong sinewy muscles and youth and health. "He *won't*."

At first she was part of his dreams, a lovely vision with red-gold hair and green eyes who blended with images of Jason and Elliott. But as his mind cleared, as he remembered what was *real* about Elliott and Jason, she was still there, smiling at him, whispering softly to him.

"You'll be all right, Charles," the British accent reassured, over and over. "You're getting better, stronger."

"Who are you?" he asked one day. Her words were becoming a reality. He *was* getting better and stronger.

"Galen. Galen Elizabeth Spencer. Mummy and Daddy are doctors for the clinic here."

"And you're a nurse?" Charles asked the wide young green eyes. "And a writer?"

"No." Her cheeks flushed pink. *"No."*

"No? You're not just writing my vital signs in those notebooks, are you?" Charles gestured toward the crimson notebook in her lap. As he gestured, lifting his arm from the cot, Charles realized how weak he still was. He had been just about to ask her to take a walk with him along the river. But it was much too soon.

"No," she admitted.

"Then what?"

"Just stories." Her voice was barely audible, and she tilted her head, throwing a curtain of red-gold between herself and Charles.

"Let me read one."

"No."

"Tell me then."

"No, Charles. I can't do that, either."

"OK, scaredy cat. Then tell me about Galen Elizabeth Spencer."

"I'll tell you about the places I've lived. Would that be OK?"

"That would be very OK."

Charles remained at the clinic for two weeks. By the end of the first week, he was strong enough to take slow walks along the riverbank and on the savanna. Galen accompanied him when she could. The hours they spent together were mostly silent, but they were *together*, sharing the magnificence of a brilliant purple-pink sunset or the splendor of a gazelle bounding across the high grass or the peaceful, melodic chirping of the spectacular tropical birds.

Four days before Charles was scheduled to leave, Elise Spencer announced that she needed to go to Nairobi. The clinic supplies had dwindled and had to be replenished. Elise had hoped to wait until her husband returned, but she couldn't. And now was a good time to be away. There were no patients lying in the cots in the makeshift hospital and no babies were due. The sickest patient, Charles, was virtually well.

Charles, Elise mused. The strong, silent Peace Corps worker made her timid daughter feel safe and confident. It would be best to take the necessary trip before Charles was gone.

Three hours after Elise left for Nairobi, a pregnant woman who was visiting from a distant village went into labor. The woman's frantic sister found Galen and Charles sitting by the river's edge, watching a baby hippo's clumsy antics in the warm, muddy water.

"No," Galen told the woman, "she's in Nairobi, but—"

"But Galen's here," Charles finished confidently. "And I'm here to help her. Please tell your sister that we're on the way. We just have to pick up, uh, the medical bag."

"Charles," Galen whispered as the woman left. The fear in her emerald eyes matched the panic in her voice. "Do you know how to deliver a baby?"

"No." He smiled at her. "But you do. You told me you've watched."

"Yes, I've watched!" Galen paused, catching her breath, searching her memory for deliveries she had witnessed. "Sometimes, there is almost nothing to do, because everything is fine. But, Charles, there can be complications, horrible ones. Mummy needs to be here. We have to go after her!"

Charles saw the fear in Galen's eyes and knew it was rational fear based on knowledge. Galen knew what could go wrong. She had seen it. As an ice-cold shiver of terror pulsed through him, Charles realized that he had knowledge about childbirth, too. He had never watched a baby being born, but he knew about a woman who had died giving birth to her twin sons. . . .

Still, they had no choice.

"Galen." Charles was amazed that his voice could sound so strong and calm. "We can send someone after your mother, but it can't be you. You know how to deliver babies. I'll help you. Tell me what we need to do."

Galen frowned briefly, then her eyes met his and she smiled a shy, brave smile.

"All right." Her voice still trembled, but the pace of her words was slow and controlled. "We need to stop by the clinic and get Mummy's medical bag and sterile forceps and a scalpel and string."

Galen calmly spoke the medical terms, but could she *really* apply forceps to a tiny, fragile skull?

Charles saw the doubt and panic begin to return to her eyes and said quickly, refocusing her on the mechanics, "The scalpel and string are for an, uh . . ."

"Episiotomy," Galen supplied the correct term. "No. We'd need a suture set for that." Galen frowned. She *couldn't* perform an episiotomy, even though she had seen it done. *No*. She forced her thoughts away from that worry and told Charles something she could do, would *have* to do, "That scalpel and string are for tying the umbilical cord."

"Oh." Charles looked surprised.

"It *does* happen naturally, of course. The vessels clamp down on their own. But if you tie it off, you can separate the baby, and hold it and care for it, immediately."

"I see. How do you do it?"

"You tie the cord in two places and cut in the middle. You just have to be sure," Galen continued, giving firm instructions to herself, "that the string nearest the baby is tied very tight."

"Uh-huh," Charles agreed uneasily.

As Galen spoke, the reality of what he was about to witness and the horrible knowledge that his own mother had died giving birth increased Charles's sense of dread. But as Charles's inner terror crescendoed, Galen became visibly calm. By the time they reached the small mud hut in the village, Galen had vanquished, or banished for the time being, her fears.

As Galen entered the hut, she transformed into her mother, mimicking the calm, reassuring manner she knew so well. Galen had seen Elise deliver many.babies. Galen had heard the words and the tone and had seen the soft, caring, compassionate smile on her mother's lips.

"How are you?" Galen took the woman's clammy hand and squeezed gently. "This is Charles. He's here to help. Not that we will need much help." Galen smiled comfortingly. "Babies deliver themselves, you know."

The woman shook her head vehemently.

"Yes," Galen spoke softly. "Yes they do. Let me see."

Galen walked to the foot of the cot and lifted the woven blankets that covered the woman's legs and abdomen. Charles stood motionless near the doorway of the small hut, watching Galen, waiting for her instructions, hoping, hoping . . .

Charles watched her suppress a gasp, then her emerald-green eyes, glistening with tears, found his.

"It's almost born," she whispered. "Charles, I need the clean towels and the string and scalpel, please."

Charles moved beside her and watched in speechless wonder as Galen gently, but confidently, eased the baby, a little girl, from the birth canal. Charles's hands trembled as he cut two twelve-inch pieces of string, and Galen's hands trembled as she tied the string around the umbilical cord.

"Do you think it's tight enough?" she asked in a whisper.

Charles didn't know. It looked tight. He whispered back, "I think so."

Slowly, carefully, breath held, Galen cut the umbilical cord. The knots were tight enough! She hesitated for a moment, then wrapped the now squirming baby in a clean towel and carried the precious bundle to her mother.

"You should rest," Galen told the new mother. "We've sent for Mummy. She'll check on you as soon as she returns."

The woman nodded as grateful tears spilled down her cheeks.

The moment Galen said "Mummy," the moment the ordeal was over, her braveness vanished and she was a shy fifteen-year-old girl again. Charles took her hand and led her out of the hut and away from the village. When he stopped, finally, and turned to face her, Charles saw liquid, astonished eyes and trembling lips.

"Hey." Charles touched her cheek gently. "You were terrific."

Galen couldn't speak. Her words were blocked by a sob.

"Galen." Charles wrapped his strong arms around her shaking body and held her tight. "Galen."

After many moments Galen finally spoke. She buried her red-gold head into Charles's chest and whispered, "It was a miracle, Charles . . . a miracle."

Four days later, Charles returned to the Peace Corps village.

"Good luck with your writing, Galen," he teased carefully.

"Good luck with your buildings, Charles," she teased in return.

Galen realized, as Charles left, how much she knew about *what* he was—kind and gentle and sensitive—and how little she knew about *who* he was. Charles told her he did construction work for the Peace Corps and that he was American. Charles never told Galen his last name. And the other names—Jason and Father— that he called desperately when he was delirious he never mentioned at all when he was well.

A week before the end of his third year in Kenya, Charles felt a sudden, urgent need to return home. *Home?* Where was that? The posh penthouse on Central Park West? The dorm room at Princeton that probably still smelled of marijuana? Certainly not to Windermere . . .

Charles didn't know, but the feeling was strong. It had something to do with Jason. Jason needed him. Jason was in trouble. Charles had to go *now*.

A week later Charles sat in his elegant penthouse overlooking Central Park immersed in culture shock but feeling inexplicably *comfortable*. The urgency had dissipated. *This* was where he was supposed to be, at this moment, as the dark, ominous storm clouds gathered to the northeast over the Atlantic Ocean and moved swiftly toward Long Island.

CHAPTER SIX

Southampton, Long Island
June 1974

*J*ason completed his studies at Harvard two weeks before the other graduating seniors. At the end of his courses he was given oral examinations. As Jason made the trip from Cambridge to Southampton, already a Harvard graduate, his classmates were just beginning Reading Week.

The route from Jason's dormitory at Harvard to the mansion at Windermere was a now familiar one. The most direct way, which Elliott taught Jason during his freshman year, was to take a taxi to Logan Airport, a plane to La Guardia, and a limousine to Windermere. Jason needed only to pay the taxi driver, find his way to the appropriate departure gate at the airport, and provide the limousine driver in New York with the Sinclair Publishing Company account number.

Paying the taxi driver was easy. With Elliott's help, Jason memorized the faces on bills—Washington, Lincoln, Hamilton, Jackson, and Grant—and the monetary value assigned to each face. Since Jason had no trouble doing mathematics in his head, determining appropriate cab fare, plus tip, was simple.

Negotiating Logan Airport was trickier. Elliott made certain that Jason had an ample supply of prepurchased airline tickets. Jason always flew on the same carrier and quickly became familiar with the terminal and the usual departure gate. When the departure gate changed, Jason would have to ask directions, his pale-blue eyes offering sincere apologies for being a bother to his fellow travelers and airport personnel.

Once Jason was on the plane, heading for La Guardia, he was home free. He could always get a limousine, even if it meant a wait, and he never faltered as he recited the perfectly memorized Sinclair Publishing Company account number to the driver.

Jason was almost home now, and he couldn't wait. He had such wonderful, exciting news to share with Elliott!

I'm an *artist*, Father. Look at my paintings. Do you like them? I think the style is like my mother's. . . .

Jason loved the wonderful, vivid pictures, painted by Meredith, that adorned the walls of the mansion. He had no idea he had inherited her marvelous talent. What if his art appreciation course at Harvard hadn't included studio time? What if he hadn't been forced to put a paintbrush in the hands that hadn't held a pen or a pencil in eighteen years?

But it *did* and he *had* and he might tell Elliott how his painting made him feel—Father, it makes me feel so free!—or he might keep that small part private.

In his art, in his own remarkable talent, Jason found a release for the turbulent feelings that churned beneath the always calm, always cheerful exterior. For twenty-two years Jason felt like a puppet, a charming, intelligent creation of a hundred dedicated tutors. Jason was *grateful* to all of them. The tutors didn't treat him like a machine, but that was how he felt. He was so dependent on them all.

Before his painting, there was nothing that was uniquely Jason; there was nothing private or personal. Jason was everyone else's creation and he was a masterpiece. But who was *he*?

With the discovery that he was an artist, Jason discovered himself. At last he was more than a bright, pleasant, meticulously trained and impeccably educated *specimen*. At last it really *didn't* matter whether he could read or write. That wasn't what Jason Sinclair was meant to do. He was meant to translate emotion and passion into rich, beautiful images.

Jason's art professor at Harvard tried to convince him to stay at Harvard for an additional year for formal training. The professor was confident that Jason's talent was marketable; Jason could be a *major* artist. His work—even in its embryonic, untrained form—was vital and powerful and unique.

But Jason didn't care about sharing his talent with the world. Jason didn't care about fame or success. It was enough that he had found something that gave him such peace and joy. Jason didn't need to make a career of his art. His career was with Sinclair Publishing. And even that—something he wanted to do because of Elliott but feared because how could it ever be *his* if he couldn't read?—suddenly became less frightening. Jason's talent made him believe in himself.

It was raining hard as the limousine pulled into the long drive at Windermere. A sudden June storm had brought cold rain and strong gusts of wind. Before the limousine pulled away, the driver helped Jason carry his luggage and his paintings, curled dry and secure in a black plastic tube, to the marbled foyer inside the mansion.

Father isn't here, Jason realized, a little disappointed.

Of course, Elliott wasn't expecting him home so soon. It was all part of Jason's surprise for Elliott; the paintings *and* his early arrival home.

It would be a wonderful summer. On weekdays, he and Elliott would live and work in town. They would spend the weekends in Southampton, sailing, playing tennis, dining at Shinnecock Golf Club, and enjoying the peace and quiet of Windermere. While Elliott read manuscripts Jason would paint. There was so much Jason wanted to paint. He would continue what Meredith had begun—the permanent commemoration of their magnificent home.

It would be a perfect summer. Perfect, except that, for the fourth summer in a row, Charles would not be there.

Jason had no idea what happened between Charles and Elliott four years before. When he arrived home from sailing the day Charles moved out, Elliott unemotionally told him that Charles was gone and that it was for the best. And when Charles came to his dormitory at Harvard a year later, Charles didn't mention it at all.

It angered Jason that neither Elliott nor Charles offered an explanation. But Jason didn't let his anger show. Charles and Elliott had always protected him, as if his inability to read was an *illness*. As if, despite how bright he was, there were things he couldn't understand.

Jason didn't push. Because then, before he discovered that he could paint and that it didn't matter that he would never be able to critically review a manuscript, a large tormented part of Jason believed that there *was* something wrong with him. Not an illness, but something that didn't give him the right to push Elliott or Charles on issues they didn't choose to share with him.

Last Christmas, when Elliott had told him that Charles would never inherit any part of Sinclair Publishing and wanted Jason to agree that he would never give any of his shares to Charles, Jason didn't ask his father *why*.

But now life was different. Jason had something that Elliott and Charles didn't have. It gave him power and confidence. This summer he would find out what had happened between Elliott and Charles.

By five-thirty in the afternoon Elliott still had not returned and the storm had worsened. The gray-green water of the Atlantic Ocean swirled angrily in the distance, meeting the torrents of rain with its own windswept salty spray. It was a dramatic scene, almost colorless, a picture in a hundred shades of gray. On another day Jason would have found great peace in sitting at his easel and translating this powerful rage of nature onto canvas.

But today Jason was too restless, too anxious. Where was Elliott? He was in Southampton, somewhere, because the house had been opened for the weekend and a used coffee mug sat on the kitchen counter. But where? Elliott usually preferred to stay at Windermere. He only left to go to the club to play tennis or to dine.

Or to sail. But Elliott wouldn't be sailing today, as much as he enjoyed the challenge, because today there was no challenge, only danger. No one would sail today. But what if Elliott had left before the storm hit? What if, before it was a true storm, it had been a gusty, exhilarating day? A perfect day for sailing . . .

Jason didn't know how or when the storm began. The weather had been clear until they reached Long Island.

Jason wanted to call the Peconic Bay Yacht Club and the club house at Shinnecock and even Elliott's office in Manhattan, in case, discouraged by the inclement weather, Elliott had returned to work. But Jason couldn't read a telephone book. He had no idea how to use a telephone. His remarkable memory enabled him to easily and accurately memorize a sequence of numbers, but could he match the symbols on the phone with the numbers in his mind?

Jason believed he could. In the past few months, perhaps bolstered by the confidence his painting gave him, Jason began to notice numbers—on the money he carried, on signs along the road, over the departure gates at the airport, on cash registers and receipts—and the numbers made sense! Jason needed someone to check him, to make sure he was right. Elliott would help him. This summer, he would learn to use numbers, to dial a telephone. . . .

If only I could drive, Jason thought. I would drive to the yacht club *and* Shinnecock *and* Manhattan, and I would find him.

Jason couldn't drive, but it was another plan for this summer. If he could read numbers, he could read the speed limit signs and the car speedometer. And he had already learned the meaning, by observation, of a red octagonal sign and a yellow triangular one and . . . if someone read him the rules, and if he was allowed to take an oral examination, he could drive, *couldn't* he?

This summer, maybe, but not today, not *now*. Now, Jason couldn't dial a phone, and he couldn't drive. He could only wait—desperate and frustrated and trapped—miserably consumed by the familiar feelings of helplessness and dependence.

Jason heard the sound of sirens in the distance. He opened the front door of the mansion. His heart pounded uneasily. As he walked down the brick stairs Jason saw the police cars. The sirens hadn't been distant at all; they had been on the private drive leading from the entrance of Windermere to the mansion. The whistling of the wind and the pelting of the rain and the roar of his own blood pulsing in his head had merely muffled the sound.

There was no need for sirens, no need to rush. The news was forever. The sirens simply matched the harsh turbulence of the day, strident and punishing. The sirens were a warning and a signal.

A warning of something unspeakable.

A signal that something wonderful was over.

The officers had sounded their sirens in angry protest against the raging storm and what it had done to a man they all knew and respected; a man whose life had not been entirely happy and whose greatest happiness after the tragic loss of his beautiful wife was his beloved son Jason.

Jason was away at college. He wouldn't be at home. He would not hear the sirens. He *should* not hear the sirens.

But Jason was there. And the officers told him, in the rain, their own tears mixing with the cold raindrops, that his father was dead. Elliott had been sailing and was caught by the unexpected storm. He drowned in the violent sea. They had just recovered the body. Elliott had been wearing a life preserver.

"If he was wearing a life preserver," Jason protested swiftly.

"He was probably hit in the head and thrown from the boat," the officer explained gently. He knew it was true. He had seen the body. And the head injury.

Jason stared at them all for many moments, his eyes registering disbelief and terror. They stood facing each other, the officers, the bearers of the horrible tragic news, and Jason, the beloved son, the innocent victim. The *other* innocent victim of the punishing storm. As they stood, immobile, silent, the rain fell even harder, drenching them, chilling them with an outer coldness that matched the chill within.

* * *

As Charles drove through the walls of rain toward Windermere, he forced his concentration on the dangerous rain-slick winding road and didn't think about why he was in Southampton. Charles didn't *know* why. The same urgent feeling that made him leave Kenya dragged him from the warm luxury of his Manhattan penthouse into the violent summer storm and forced him to drive *too fast* toward Windermere and Elliott and Jason. . . .

Charles saw the nest of Southampton police cars as he approached the brick pillars at the entrance of Windermere. He parked his car at a distance and darted into the woods, running along the now overgrown paths where he and Jason spent wonderful hours sharing make-believe adventures. By the time Charles emerged from the woods onto the emerald green lawn his clothes were rain-soaked and branch-torn and his face and hands were scratched.

Charles narrowed his eyes against the pelting rain and looked across the expanse of manicured lawn toward the Georgian mansion. There were more police cars in the drive in front of the mansion. Standing on the porch in the rain, in the middle of a huddle of police officers, was Jason.

"Son." The officer touched Jason on the shoulder. "Let's go inside. There must be someone we should call . . ."

"My brother is in Africa," Jason murmured numbly.

Oh, yes, the officer remembered, there *was* another son. But *that* son, the dark twin, had vanished from Windermere. No one in Southampton knew why, but there was speculation that Charles must have done something terrible.

The officer looked at Jason, the beloved son. Jason was in shock, and the only family he had left in the world was in Africa. The officer tried to guide Jason into the mansion. But Jason resisted, spinning free, and inexplicably faced the woods. In the distance, blurred by sheets of rain . . .

"Charles," Jason whispered.

"We'll try to reach him, son," the officer said sympathetically. "It may take a few days."

"*Charles.*" Jason ran to meet the approaching figure. The officer followed.

"Jason," Charles panted when they met at the edge of the red brick drive. "What happened?"

"It's Father . . ."

"*What?*"

"He's dead, Charles."

"No. God, no."

The police officer watched with interest, his well-trained mind entertaining a series of questions and theories. Wasn't it peculiar that the estranged son miraculously appeared—from *Africa*—moments after Elliott's death? Why were Charles's clothes drenched and torn? Why were there scratches on his face? Why did he come through the woods? Where had he been earlier in the afternoon, say, for example, at the moment of the lethal blow to Elliott Sinclair's head?

Charles's shock looked genuine, and his horror matched that of his twin. Still, they would have to check. They could begin checking this afternoon. In a day or two, if necessary, they would ask the questions of Charles. For now, until there was reason to suspect guilt, Charles was an innocent young man grieving the tragic death of his father.

Charles and Jason went inside the mansion, and the police retreated to the pillared entrance of Windermere to protect the bereaved twins from the inevitable onslaught of the press. It was the least they could do.

* * *

Charles and Jason sat in numb silence at opposite ends of the sofa in the great room. Twilight fell, shrouding the mansion in darkness.

"Why did you come here today?" Jason's voice finally broke the silence.

"I don't know." *I had a feeling you needed me.* "I just had to."

"But did you know about . . . did you know what happened before you arrived?"

"No."

The darkness cast shadows across their faces, hiding their eyes.

Jason's blurred, grief-stricken mind whirled. He didn't know his twin anymore. They hadn't been close for so many years. And now, in this intimate, tragic, private moment, Charles had miraculously reappeared. Why? Why had Charles left? Why had he returned? Jason needed to know.

"What happened between you and Father?" Jason asked quietly.

"When?"

Four hours ago, Jason thought and shuddered. *No, I can't even think that.*

"When you left, four years ago."

"Nothing. I don't know why he made me leave."

"Father wouldn't have *made* you leave!" Jason protested. *Don't lie to me, Charles, please.*

"Nothing *happened*, Jason."

Jason heard the edge in Charles's voice, but he couldn't see his face. Was Charles angry because Jason had struck a nerve? Or was he angry, as Jason was angry, at the nonsensical tragedy of Elliott's death? Or was Charles angry because Jason was taunting him instead of trying to find the closeness they needed now, so desperately?

I have to trust him, Jason thought. *Even though he won't tell me why Father disowned him or why he is here today. I will trust him.*

"Why did he have to die, Charles?" Jason's voice broke.

Charles didn't answer, but the words of the anthropologist he met in Kenya swirled uneasily in his mind: *Twins have supernatural power—good and bad—over weather. Do you and your brother . . .*

"Where was St. Elmo's fire?" Jason demanded bitterly, his thoughts drifting with his twin's to the fabled Gemini, guardians of all sailors. Why wasn't Elliott guided to safety in the storm?

"*Myth,*" Charles hissed hoarsely. He added softly, "It's just a myth, Jason."

Charles started to shiver, chilled from his rain-soaked clothes and the icy horror of Elliott's death.

"We should get changed and eat something," Charles murmured between clenched teeth.

"What about the magazines?" Jason's voice was shaky, too, quivering from cold and emotion and panic. What about Elliott's beloved company and his wonderful magazines?

"What about them?"

"Father said he gave you your entire inheritance four years ago and that you would never own any part of Sinclair Publishing."

"Unless I buy it."

"He told me," Jason said slowly, "that I was never to give or sell you any part of Sinclair Publishing."

Charles drew a breath. Why did Elliott hate him so much? In Kenya Charles had found peace with his solitude. But now, being in this house where he couldn't be loved, the depthless pain rushed back, reminding him that there was something terribly wrong with him.

"I guess I'm going to inherit the entire company," Jason continued carefully.

"I guess so."

"I can't run the company without someone I trust, someone who knows about *me*, someone who has Father's instincts as editor-in-chief."

"No, of course you can't. But Sinclair Publishing has the best editors in the business. There are probably three or four who could step into that position tomorrow . . ."

A long silence followed. Finally Charles stood up.

"Could you do it?" Jason asked quietly in the darkness.

"Do what?"

"Be editor-in-chief."

"*Me?*"

"I thought that was what you wanted to do."

"Yes. Someday." It was his dream, *still*. After Elliott had disowned *him*, Charles tried desperately to disown the *dream*. But he couldn't. It was who he was.

"Could you do it now?"

"Are you asking me to?" Sudden warmth pulsed through Charles's shivering body.

"Yes. I need your help." Jason spoke confidently, but fear seized him. Could he really trust Charles? Jason didn't know, but he had no choice. It was the only way he could save Elliott's dreams.

"Then, yes," Charles whispered, "I'll do it."

Six months after Elliott's death, Jason knocked on the door of Charles's adjoining office at Sinclair Publishing.

"Come in. Oh, Jason, hello."

Charles forced a smile for his twin. Charles was exhausted. Running Sinclair Publishing Company had been a monumental task for *Elliott*, despite his uncanny business instincts, years of experience, and respect of the entire publishing world. And now he, Charles, inexperienced and with unproven instincts, was trying to take Elliott's place. The powerbrokers of publishing and the press and the fashion barons hovered like skeptical, hungry vultures, waiting for the estranged son—how dare he?—to fail.

The support within the company was strong; but it was support for Elliott's memory and for Jason, the loved son. Charles had no idea how long the support would last or if there would ever be support for *him*. He was just a visitor, as he always had been, but the future of Sinclair Publishing Company was riding on his shoulders.

Charles owned no part of the company. He could have been an employee— Jason told him to name his salary—but Charles would accept no money. Sinclair Publishing was his heritage and his dream. . . .

"You need help, Charles." Jason looked apologetically at his tired, overworked twin.

Charles shrugged. He couldn't ask for help. Everyone was watching, and there was the secret—Jason's dyslexia—to protect.

"I think I can help. I majored in art history at Harvard. I have an eye for color and design." Jason paused. He could tell Charles he was a talented artist, but he didn't. "Would it help if I handled the art for the magazines?"

"Yes. It's the biggest struggle for me," Charles admitted gratefully. If Jason could really do this . . .

"Good. Then, that's settled." Jason hesitated. The next was personal. It was so important to him—it would give him such a feeling of independence—but he had to be certain he was right. Someone, *Charles*, had to tell him. Jason sighed softly, then continued, his voice tentative, "There's something . . . I need your help."

"Yes?"

"You know I can do mathematics in my head."

Charles nodded. He knew that. He discussed all of the company's financial issues with Jason, and Jason understood perfectly.

"Well, I *think* I can read and write numbers."

"Really?"

"I need to have you check me to be sure."

"Of course." Charles paused. He asked carefully, "Is it happening with letters also?"

"No." Jason smiled wryly. "And I don't think anything's *happening*. I think I always could have done numbers."

By the first anniversary of Elliott Sinclair's death, it was obvious that Sinclair Publishing Company wasn't going to fail. *Fashion* and *Images* and *Spinnaker* flourished, rejuvenated by the energy and talent and vision of the Sinclair twins.

"I want to make changes in *Images*," Charles told Jason fourteen months after Elliott died.

"What changes?" Jason asked swiftly, worried. *Images* was Elliott's legacy.

"I would like the art and literature in *Images* to blend, so that together they create an image."

Jason listened to Charles in stunned silence. Charles was describing Elliott's dream! It was a dream Elliott had shared with Jason a hundred times. It had seemed so private, something just between them. Now Jason heard the words, the same words, from his twin.

"Did you and Father discuss this?" Jason asked finally.

"No." Only in my fantasy conversations. Charles added wistfully, "We never talked about the magazines."

"It's what Father dreamed *Images* would be."

"Then we'll do it? Together? I'll tell you the stories . . ."

Jason nodded solemnly. *Spinnaker* will be mine, *Fashion* will be yours, and *Images* will be ours.

As *Spinnaker*, *Fashion*, and *Images*—the new *Images*—soared in popularity and prestige, the world wanted to know all about the handsome, powerful, and wealthy Sinclair twins. The press obliged willingly, and Charles and Jason cooperated politely and easily, as if there was nothing to hide.

Jason and Charles Sinclair made such good copy! Charming, pleasant, golden Jason, and dark, seductive, restless Charles.

Jason was an expert yachtsman, preferring the vast, wind-tossed sea to the glitter and glamour of Manhattan. Jason's love affairs lasted months or years, and they were *almost* private. Someday Jason would find the right woman and they would have happy, golden, beautiful children. Everyone would celebrate the day he found his true love, because everyone wished happiness for Jason Sinclair.

Charles was like Manhattan: fast-paced, energetic, dazzling, and a little menacing. Did Charles Sinclair ever sleep? His seductive elegance graced all the important parties—they would be devastated if Charles Sinclair didn't appear—and all the major fashion shows in New York and Europe. Charles's love affairs with New York's most glamorous women were high profile, well publicized, and short-lived. Charles Sinclair would probably never marry or have children, and that was almost certainly for the best.

The press and public were happy with their profiles of the Sinclair twins. Jason was the perfect symbol of *his* magazine, *Spinnaker*: healthy and natural and pure. And Charles was the perfect symbol of *Fashion*: sexy and risky and elegant. But which twin was responsible for Sinclair Publishing's greatest triumph, *Images*?

No one knew Charles and Jason created each issue of *Images* together. No one knew, because no one asked. Charles and Jason would willingly have told them. It wasn't a secret, they would say, smiling, as if there were no secrets.

But, of course, there *was* that one astounding secret: the terribly interesting and potentially devastating fact that Charles Sinclair, editor-in-chief of Sinclair Publishing, worked for no money to help his dyslexic twin run the company his father had vowed he would never own . . .

CHAPTER SEVEN

New York City
September 1985

"*B*rooke, it's for you, line three. It's about the Cassandra case."

"Thanks." Brooke depressed the blinking button. "This is Brooke Chandler."

"This is Nick Adrian, NYPD."

"Yes?"

"I hear the DA's office is dropping half the charges against Cassandra before you even go to trial. Do you know anything about that?"

Of course Brooke knew about Cassandra. The case had monopolized her summer. It virtually prohibited her from studying for the Bar. And now, finally, the trial was scheduled to begin—*tomorrow*—the day Melanie was moving to New York. Of course she knew about Cassandra.

"Yes, I know about that." It was so hot in her office! Mid-September and still humid.

"Tell me why."

"Because we don't have enough evidence to convict on all the counts."

"We *sent* you enough evidence. Did you lose it? The DA's office has been known to misplace evidence before. Especially if it's too much of a nuisance to prosecute." The voice was deep and cool.

Who the hell did he think he was? How dare he say that about the DA's office?

"We weren't too happy with the way NYPD collected the evidence."

"Want to spell that out?" The voice turned to ice.

"I don't really have time." Brooke's iciness matched his. He was wasting her time.

"Well, you've told me enough. For example, if I were Cassandra's attorney I would be one happy man right about now."

"Oh, my God," Brooke whispered. What had she done? She held her breath.

"I'm not," Nick said after a long silence. "I'm who I said I was. Let me tell you who you are. You're a recent law school graduate. You probably made *Law Review*. You took the Bar four weeks ago and are on pins and needles waiting to hear if you passed. During law school you clerked at a prestigious law firm with a Madison Avenue address. Then, in the eleventh hour, you felt a pang of guilt, an urge to serve the people, so you signed up with the DA's office. How am I doing?"

"I always planned to do trials," Brooke interjected defiantly. But it was a weak protest. Except for her motives for joining the DA's office, his description of her was entirely accurate.

"Well, that's a little original. I like it when attorneys don't even *pretend* to be altruistic."

"Who are you? Why are you doing this?"

"I told you who I am. I really called to find out why the hell the charges were dropped. But, 'tis the season."

"Meaning?"

"There's a new kid, like you, every year. They don't stay—you won't—because there are greener, cushier pastures in, say, Westchester County."

"I'm going to stay."

"If you stay will you promise to stop ignoring the evidence we so carefully and *legally* collect?"

"Sure," she breathed.

"Good. It was nice talking to you, Brooke."

Brooke listened to the dead line and tried to regain her composure. She had almost made a critical mistake. She *had* made a critical mistake, but fortunately it was to someone who was on the same side of the law. Even though he wasn't on her side. Or was he? What he'd done was a cheap lesson for her. Dirt cheap. All it cost her was a little pride.

"Who in the world is Nick Adrian?" Brooke asked as she walked into the open office.

She got a few confounding answers.

"He's the best narcotics detective in the city."

"He's an arrogant sonofabitch."

"He is absolutely gorgeous."

"Probably impotent."

"I don't think so."

"Sounds like you know."

"I hear he's being transferred to Homicide."

"Is that a demotion?" Brooke asked hopefully.

"No way. Brooke, the guy is the best. What did he do to you anyway?"

What did Nick Adrian do? He probably saved her career in the DA's office. Brooke would have to thank him if they ever met. Maybe they wouldn't.

"Nothing," she said.

Of course they would meet. She was planning to stay.

* * *

Nick returned to his small apartment at eleven P.M. The heat of the day still hung over Manhattan, heavy and suffocating and oppressive. Nick collected his mail as he passed through the foyer. There were two pieces: the electricity bill—he would open that tomorrow or the next day—and *The New Yorker*, badly damaged from being unceremoniously wedged into the too-small mailbox.

Nick swore under his breath and frowned at the torn and wrinkled magazine. Wanton destruction annoyed him. More than *annoyed*, it enraged him. Maybe that was why his war against crime was so impassioned. That was what crime was— wanton, senseless, careless destruction of property and lives and minds and hope.

Nick glowered at the mutilated magazine and admitted the other reason he felt so emotional about *The New Yorker*. It had been a month since he submitted his short story, "Manhattan Beat," to the magazine. He hadn't heard back. Nick wondered what it meant. It could be a *good* sign—they were considering accepting it. Or a *neutral* sign—no one had even looked at it. Or a *bad* sign—it lay in the Reject pile awaiting return to its presumptuous author when time permitted. Returning rejected material could not be a top priority, could it?

Nick had been away from his apartment—tying the "red-tape" around a perfectly orchestrated midnight drug bust—for almost twenty-four hours. In his absence the apartment had accumulated all the day's heat and allowed none to escape. Nick's first breath drew in a moist warmth which settled, heavy and tenacious, in his chest. Nick opened the windows even though he knew there was no breeze. He turned on the portable fan—unopened electricity bill be damned— poured himself a glass of Scotch, and filled his bathtub with cold water.

Nick felt the tension drain out of his body as the cool water drenched his tired muscles, and the warmth of the Scotch drenched his exhausted mind. His thoughts drifted to the events of the past twenty-four hours—the late-night phone call, the textbook drug bust, the meeting with the Chief of Police about his transfer to Homicide as soon as he finished his testimony in the Cassandra case. . . .

The Cassandra case. This time they ought to stop Cassandra once and for all.

Except the DA's office was waffling, playing it safe. The DA's office . . . Brooke Chandler. What does she look like, Nick mused as the last swallow of Scotch took hold. She *sounded* efficient and haughty and ice-cold.

Ice-cold, with a soft, sexy voice.

Charles and Jason stood in the Concorde reception area. Galen's flight from Paris's Charles de Gaulle Airport had just arrived. The passengers were clearing customs.

"Do you think she'll recognize you?" Jason asked.

"I don't know," Charles answered distantly. There was nothing in the correspondence with Galen over the past two months to suggest she knew that Charles Sinclair, editor-in-chief of *Images*, and Charles, the Peace Corps volunteer stricken with malaria, were the same. "Probably not."

Charles and Jason watched as the Concorde passengers, the ritual of customs and immigration behind them, rushed through the exit door into the bustling international terminal at JFK toward their waiting limousines. These were purposeful, important, wealthy men and women who commuted across the Atlantic as routinely as they crossed town. It was many moments after the transatlantic powerbrokers vanished from the reception area that Galen emerged.

She wore an old-fashioned—*tattered*—floor-length pink-and-purple gingham dress with a crocheted white shawl draped over her shoulders. She clutched a bright red duffle bag to her chest. Neither perfectly tailored twin noticed Galen's archaic clothes or the clash of the torn duffle bag. What caught their attention were her astonished green eyes squinting against the brilliance of New York, as if she were Dorothy arriving at the Emerald City of Oz.

"Galen?" Charles spoke gently.

Charles and Jason walked toward her, as if drawn by instinct to protect her. Protect her from what? From the startling foreign glamour of which the Sinclair twins were the most dazzling symbols?

"Charles?" Galen whispered. As she stared into his brown eyes, her full lips spread slowly into a shy smile. "Charles without a beard."

"I wasn't sure you would remember. That's why I didn't tell you in the letters."

The green eyes flickered amazement. Not remember? Galen started to answer, but she couldn't find the words and simply shook her head, frowning slightly.

"Galen," Charles rescued her quickly, "this is—"

"Jason," Galen said quietly. She found a shy smile for Charles's golden twin.

"Did I . . . ?" Charles began. He didn't remember telling Galen about Jason. But of course she knew the name of the owner and publisher of *Images*. . . .

"You called his name when you were delirious." Galen's eyes held Charles's for a moment, sealing the memory. Of course I remember.

"Let me take this," Jason interjected, reaching for the bulging red duffle bag. It dropped slightly—it was heavier than he expected—as he took it. Jason recovered instantly, swinging it effortlessly over his shoulder.

"My stories," Galen explained apologetically to Jason. Turning to Charles she added, "You wrote that you might want to publish more, so I brought them with me."

"Good. Let's get you to your hotel. You must be exhausted."

"Your letter said something about dinner tonight?"

"Jason and I would like to take you to dinner at Le Cirque. It's—" Charles was stopped by the sudden look of apprehension. Galen Elizabeth Spencer did not want to have dinner at one of Manhattan's trendiest restaurants.

"I brought stories instead of clothes," she mumbled, gesturing weakly at the red duffle bag.

Charles started to offer to buy her a dress—*ten* dresses, a hundred—but he thought better of it. He didn't want to embarrass her. He suggested gently, "Why don't we just have a casual dinner at my place tonight?"

Charles arched an eyebrow at Jason, who nodded agreement.

"Perhaps Fran could join us?" Charles suggested to Jason.

"She's in Bermuda."

Charles and Jason silently searched their respective lists of female friends, silently rejecting one after another as too stunning, too self-absorbed, too glamorous.

"How about Brooke?"

Jason nodded and added confidently, smiling at the green eyes he had just met, "You'll like Brooke, Galen. She's very nice."

"Brooke, Charles Sinclair called," her secretary told her when she returned from court.

"Charles Sinclair?" Brooke repeated quietly.

"Yes. There was no message, except to have you call him."

"All right." Brooke's heart set a new pace. Why was Charles calling? It couldn't be that he had legal work he wanted her to do. Despite her offer, Brooke knew Charles would never ask her to moonlight for Sinclair Publishing.

"This is Brooke Chandler returning Charles Sinclair's call."

"Oh, yes. He is in a meeting. But he asked that you speak with Jason Sinclair."

"Fine." Maybe it *was* work for Sinclair Publishing, Brooke thought, a little deflated.

"Brooke?"

"Hi, Jason. Charles—"

"Brooke, Charles and I are having a very small, very informal, very last-minute dinner party tonight. It's in honor of Galen Spencer, this year's winner of the fiction contest. We hoped you could join us."

"How nice," Brooke answered mechanically, wondering why *her*, why at the last minute. Brooke suddenly remembered why she couldn't. "But, my sister is arriving this evening."

"Melanie?"

"Yes, how . . . ?"

"Fran mentioned it. In fact—" Jason laughed easily—"she mentions it constantly. Your sister is *the* topic of conversation among Drake models. Something about their jobs."

They're afraid that once Melanie arrives their modelling careers may be in jeopardy, Brooke mused.

"Oh, well." Brooke fumbled awkwardly. She couldn't tell Jason it was a silly worry.

"Is she an older or younger sister?" Jason asked the same question Charles had asked two months before. Apparently Charles hadn't told *his* twin about the Chandler twins.

"We're twins. Not, of course, identical. We're golden and dark, like you and Charles." Golden and dark. Sunny and stormy. Open and secretive.

After a moment's silence Jason said, "Melanie is invited to the dinner party, too. We would love to have both of you."

Brooke spent the afternoon in court. She listened attentively to Cassandra's attorney's opening statements and nodded at Andrew Parker as he jotted down precedents raised by opposing counsel that she would need to check. Brooke forced thoughts of Melanie's arrival and the dinner with Charles and Jason to the back of her mind. It took great discipline, but that was her specialty.

At the end of the day, as Brooke rushed from the courthouse to her tiny apartment on West Fifty-seventh Street to dress for the evening, the carefully suppressed worries, now unrestrained, flooded her mind. She was anxious *enough* about seeing Melanie. And now she would be seeing Charles, introducing Melanie to Charles. . . .

Brooke scowled at the dresses in her closet. They were all so soft and colorful and pretty and feminine! Brooke didn't wear plain, drab, dowdy clothes anymore. That wasn't who she was *now*. She had long since left the vestiges of high school behind her. The new Brooke, the real Brooke, was happy and stylish. The new Brooke liked her silky chestnut curls and deep-blue eyes and full sensuous lips. . . .

But next to Melanie, she would always be plain and drab, wouldn't she?

Brooke sighed. Then, with firm resolve, she chose her most feminine dress, swept her curls softly off her face, and artfully accented her huge blue eyes with shadow and mascara.

This is it, Brooke thought, critically examining the finished product. This is who I am.

Brooke arrived at La Guardia by taxi ten minutes before Melanie's flight landed.

"Brooke!" Melanie touched her cheek briefly, awkwardly, to Brooke's. "You look terrific."

"So do you."

Melanie looked fresh and *refreshed* from the transcontinental flight. In sharp contrast to her fellow travelers, Melanie appeared rested and wrinkle-free and cool and full of energy. It was all illusion, all part of the perfect golden image. Melanie had spent the flight—stomach knotted and fists clenched—wondering why she had made this foolish decision and if it was too late to turn back. *Mr. Drake, I'm sorry. I wasn't thinking clearly. I don't belong in New York. You see, I have a twin sister and we've been apart for so long and I thought . . . .*

"Charles and Jason Sinclair invited us to dinner tonight. I said Yes. I hope that's OK."

"Charles and Jason Sinclair? As in *Images?*"

"Yes." It surprised Brooke that Melanie made the association with *Images* rather than *Fashion*.

"It's fine, *wonderful*," Melanie lied graciously. She had mentally prepared herself for a quiet dinner with Brooke; that would be hard enough. But this . . . she would have to dig deep to find the energy.

"I thought you'd like to drop your luggage off at your apartment."

"And change."

"You look fine." Melanie wore a straight white linen skirt—miraculously unwrinkled—with front and back slits tastefully exposing her long tanned legs, a turquoise cotton blouse, and a simple gold necklace. She was the picture of understated elegance. "It's casual."

"I'd feel better if I changed. I *am* eager to see the apartment."

A luxury, decorator-furnished, all-expenses-paid apartment on Central Park East was included in Melanie's contract with Drake Modelling Agency.

"This is nice," Brooke said forty-five minutes later as they walked from room to room of Melanie's apartment.

"It is," Melanie breathed with relief. It *was* nice. It felt peaceful and quiet and she had a lovely view of the park.

"Charles, I'm sorry we're late," Brooke said apologetically when they finally arrived at Charles's penthouse.

"You're not. Jason and Galen aren't here yet. Come in."

"Oh. Good. Thank you." Brooke took a deep breath. Then, with a calm that amazed her, she said, "Charles, this is Melanie."

"Welcome to New York, Melanie." Charles's dark eyes smiled at the magnificent sky-blue ones. At, not into. Melanie's eyes resisted penetration; like perfect tranquil ponds they reflected the world but revealed nothing of the pale-blue depths.

So handsome, Melanie mused as she smiled at Charles. "Charles, what a wonderful place!"

Adam Drake has discovered pure gold, Charles thought as he watched Melanie flow gracefully into his tasteful, elegant living room. Melanie nodded appreciatively, as if *her* approval of his taste would somehow make him happy. Pure, egocentric, impossible gold.

"Charles," Melanie purred, "I love this Monet. I can't believe it isn't hanging in the Louvre."

"You mean the Jeu de Paume." Charles quietly reminded her that the major Impressionist works were housed in the Jeu de Paume, not the Louvre. "It used to be."

"The Jeu de Paume." Melanie's eyes sparkled, acknowledging Charles's victory. Touché, Charles. What fun it will be to spar with you! But I have to be on my toes, don't I? "Of course. Silly of me."

Undaunted, Melanie swept across the living room to the window overlooking Central Park. Her apartment was almost directly across from his, on a lower floor, blocked from view by the trees.

"Lovely," she murmured. When she turned away from the spectacular view, her eyes fell on an Orrefors crystal vase of roses standing beside the marble fireplace. "Oh!"

Melanie moved to the vase of roses and gently traced the delicate lavender petals with her finger.

"Sterling Silver," she spoke to the prize-winning rose by name.

"That's very good," Charles observed. How the hell did *she* know the species of that rose?

Melanie smiled a proud, dazzling, defiant smile. Take that, Charles Sinclair.

The sound of quiet conversation in the marbled foyer signalled the arrival of Galen and Jason. Charles's attention shifted from roses and Melanie to Galen. Melanie and Jason introduced themselves as Charles protectively shepherded Galen toward Brooke.

"Hello, Galen. Welcome." Brooke smiled warmly. She looks like a small, frightened bird, Brooke thought, desperate to fly away and be free. Don't worry, Galen, no one here will hurt you.

"Hello Brooke." She's so beautiful, Galen thought. She seems nice. "Thank you."

"And this," Charles said as Jason and Melanie, now introduced, joined them, "is Melanie."

Prepare yourself, Galen, Charles thought.

"Hello Galen." Melanie smiled. Then she tilted her head, narrowed her pale-blue eyes and added quietly, "You have the most beautiful hair I have ever seen."

Melanie emphasized the sincerity of her words by impatiently running her long fingers through her own spun-gold locks, as if the shiny gold had suddenly turned to gilt.

Galen frowned slightly at the earnest sky-blue eyes. Then she touched a strand of the waist-length red-gold silk that was as much a part of her as her shyness or her need to write or her old tattered clothes and whispered, "No."

"Yes!" Melanie countered emphatically. It was not a debatable point. "Have you ever twisted it in coils and piled it on top of your head? Stuck a few wild flowers in it?"

"No." A soft laugh.

"*No?* Galen, I'll have to show you how to do that. How long will you be in New York?"

"For a while," Galen answered quietly. She spoke to Melanie, but her eyes drifted for a questioning moment to Charles and for a brief flicker to Jason. "I thought it might be good for me, for my career, to live in New York for a while."

"Then you and I have moved here on the same day for the same reason." Melanie smiled conspiratorially at Galen. Now they had something much more important in common than long beautiful hair.

"This calls for a toast," Jason said. He helped Charles pour chilled champagne into crystal glasses.

"To successful careers in New York." Charles raised his glass to Galen and Melanie. Then, turning to Brooke, he added, "To all of you."

The evening flowed easily and effortlessly. Melanie's energy kept the conversation light and flowing, and she filled the rare silences with her happy, golden laughter.

Melanie is making it fun and easy for everyone, Brooke thought, marvelling at Melanie's confidence and energy. Melanie, the *fun* twin. It wouldn't have been the same evening without Melanie. *She* could never have made Galen feel so comfortable.

What does Charles think of Melanie? Brooke wondered. But she knew the answer. Charles was charmed and enchanted by Melanie, just like everyone was. How could he not be?

"Tell us about your stories, Galen," Melanie urged during dinner.

"They're just stories about Africa."

"*Just*," Charles teased gently.

"What are they about? Galen? Charles? *Jason?*" Melanie pushed.

Melanie looked to the golden, sunny Sinclair twin for an answer. But, for a fleeting moment, the sun had gone behind a cloud. Doesn't Jason like Galen's writing? Melanie wondered.

"They—'Emerald,' at least, Galen hasn't shown me any others yet—are wonderful literary journeys into love." Charles spoke, rescuing Jason. Charles's voice softened as he said *love*.

The conversation halted for a moment.

Why did you frown when Melanie asked *you* about my story, Jason? Galen wondered.

Love, Brooke mused. The way Charles said it . . .

I haven't read it, Galen. I can't. I'm so *sorry*.

Fabulous theatrics, Charles, Melanie thought. The inflection on "love" was perfect—*so* seductive. Charles Sinclair, the great lover. Melanie wondered if he was. Probably. She guessed Charles did everything spectacularly well.

" 'Emerald,' " Melanie mused, looking at Galen's eyes. "Is it autobiographical?"

"No." Galen blushed.

"Emerald, the heroine, has dark-brown eyes and hair," Jason explained. See, Galen, I know *that* about your story.

"Are all your stories love stories?" Brooke asked.

"No. Only four are. The others are about life in Kenya."

"So, you're the Isak Dinesen of the nineteen eighties," Melanie suggested.

Charles arched an eyebrow at Melanie. Then he remembered. There had just been a movie about Isak Dinesen. Charles was a little surprised Melanie hadn't said Galen was the *Meryl Streep*. . . .

"She's one of my favorite authors," Melanie continued, staring defiantly at Charles. You are so handsome, Charles, but so arrogant.

"Mine, too," Galen agreed.

Mine, too, Brooke thought. But when had *Melanie* read Isak Dinesen?

"Are you planning to publish all your stories, Galen?"

"If they're publishable. Charles wrote something about—"

"They'll be publishable," Charles predicted confidently. It was a safe prediction, if "Emerald" was any indication of Galen's talent. "Maybe we could publish all four love stories in *Images* and arrange a book deal for the others."

"A book?" Galen whispered.

"Sure. We don't do book publishing, but I can make some phone calls to people who do."

"Really?"

"Of course."

"It sounds like you may need an attorney to look at some contracts, Galen. My fee is an autographed copy of your first book," Brooke offered.

"Thank you, Brooke."

"All your stories are set in Africa?" Jason asked. He wanted the emerald eyes to know he was interested in her work.

"Most of them. I have a few about India. We lived there when I was young." Galen paused. Then she added, hoping it would please these four magnificent people who were being so kind to her, "Beginning tomorrow I'll write about Manhattan. I would like to do a collection of stories about twins."

The reaction was immediate. They all spoke at once.

"You wouldn't want to do that."

"There's nothing special, *really*."

"Better to stick with love stories."

"It's too confusing."

Galen drew a sharp breath. They weren't pleased. The emotion, the common thread that suddenly bound the two sets of twins, was fear.

CHAPTER EIGHT

New York City
October 1985

*A*t nine-thirty in the morning on the second Tuesday in October, Andrew Parker queried the group of lawyers in the DA's office.

"Does it surprise anyone here that Brooke Chandler passed the Bar?"

"*What?*" Brooke asked.

"It doesn't surprise me," someone said.

"No, not a bit," another added.

"How . . . ?" Brooke whispered weakly.

"I have my spies at the courthouse." Andrew flashed his confident, charming, I-rest-my-case smile. "The list was posted at nine A.M."

"Are you sure?" Brooke had been planning to go to the courthouse at noon. The results were always posted a day or two before the notice arrived by mail.

"Of course I'm sure. But I had him jot down your candidate number, just in case there is *another* Brooke Chandler." Andrew handed her a scrap of paper with a number, *her* number, on it.

"There isn't another Brooke Chandler. There never could be," someone added amiably.

"But how does he know I passed?"

"They don't post the names of the losers, Brooke. So, what does everyone think, a celebration lunch for Brooke?"

"Sure, where?"

"Somewhere near the courthouse, I'm afraid. I think Ms. Chandler wants to see the fine print herself. Am I right, Brooke?" Andrew teased.

Brooke nodded sheepishly. She wanted to see her name on the list. But it would be there. She had done it. She had passed the Bar!

Not that there should have been any doubt. Brooke passed—more than *passed*—every exam she had ever taken. But she worried about them all, especially the important ones. What if . . .

Relief pulsed through her, relief and elation.

"Brooke, sorry to interrupt, you have a call on line three."

"Oh. Thank you. I'll take it in my office."

Twenty seconds later she spoke into the phone, "This is Brooke Chandler."

"Congratulations, counselor."

"Who . . ." Brooke began. The voice was vaguely familiar. It was a pleasant, seductive, easy voice. But the memory it evoked wasn't pleasant; she had heard the pleasantness turn to ice. "Lieutenant Adrian."

"Very good."

"I don't deserve the congratulations, *you* do," Brooke said lightly.

"What?" How did she know?

"I heard it was your testimony that really sealed the verdict on Cassandra."

"Oh," Nick said. Oh, *that*. "You weren't there?"

Nick had decided, as he was giving his testimony, that Brooke Chandler was not there. There was no face in the DA's entourage that could possibly match the voice.

"No. I missed it. I was in the library researching a very old precedent." Brooke was sorry that she had missed Nick's testimony. Everyone said he was so good—so *cool*—on the stand. "I don't really deserve any congratulations for what happened to Cassandra."

"That wasn't what I was calling about."

"Oh?"

"I heard you passed the Bar."

"That's *very* recent information."

"I'm a very good detective. So, now you can start looking for a million-dollar practice in Westchester."

"No way, Lieutenant Adrian."

"No? Maybe I'll see you then. Maybe we'll do a homicide case together sometime."

"I'm looking forward to it," Brooke answered gaily. Maybe it wouldn't be so hard to thank him after all, if she ever saw him.

After Nick hung up he wondered, what would Brooke Chandler think if she knew "Manhattan Beat" was going to be published in *The New Yorker*? That was *his* exciting news. It had come in yesterday's mail. Nick hadn't told anyone, but he had almost told Brooke Chandler. Whoever she was.

"Galen." The voice—one of her housemates—called through the door of her room. "You have a phone call."

"Yes?" Galen rushed to the door. "Who is it?"

"Some man. He said his name, but I didn't catch it."

Charles. It had to be Charles. She'd been waiting to hear from him. She had given him her duffle bag of stories. He told her he would call after he finished reading them all.

Galen's hands trembled as she lifted the receiver of the communal phone on the battered wooden table in the entry hall of the brownstone on Spring Street in Greenwich Village. Her housemates, like her co-workers at the Champs-Elysées coffee house on Washington Square, were aspiring actors and actresses, dancers and musicians, poets and writers, artists and comedians. The phone was the link to their dreams. It had brought luck recently; last week a housemate made the chorus line of *Cats*. . . .

"Hello? Charles?"

"They're all sensational, Galen."

"Really?"

"Really." Sensational was an understatement.

"You want to publish them?"

"*Yes*. Galen, I'd love to publish every one, one at a time, for the next few years. But it's better for you to publish a book."

"I thought you wanted to publish 'Emerald' and three others." Galen spoke quietly. Charles didn't really like them after all! He was her friend, and he was being kind; but his kindness didn't extend to publishing her stories in *Images* in the name of friendship. . . .

"I do. I would like to publish 'Emerald' in December, as scheduled. Then 'Sapphire' in March and 'Jade' in June and 'Garnet' in September. If that's not too tight a schedule for you."

"For *me*? The stories are already written."

"But the revisions."

"*Revisions?*"

"Minor fine-tuning. The sort of changes you made yourself along the way."

"I didn't make changes."

"From draft to draft." Somehow they weren't communicating.

"There weren't drafts. I just wrote them."

In the silence that followed, Charles remembered the teenage girl beside his cot, staring in the distance, focused on something only she could see, mesmerized. Occasionally she would smile, fill her blue-ink fountain pen and write in slow, confident strokes, perfectly translating the image of her mind's eye into words.

One draft, the way she wanted it.

"Galen," Charles continued patiently "Your stories are sensational, but they can be *better*."

"How?"

Charles heard skepticism mixed with fear.

"I've written some suggestions. You don't *have* to follow them. I will publish your stories as is if you insist."

"I insist," she told him bravely.

"Galen." Charles's patience was faltering. "Most writers welcome feedback from editors. Don't take this personally."

"How do you *expect* me to take it, Charles?"

Charles sighed. He answered flatly, "Professionally."

"Oh," she breathed. *Oh.* Her stomach churned.

"Why don't we get together tonight and discuss—"

"I'm working."

"I will send my suggestions to you by courier, then."

* * *

At midnight the following night, Galen dialed the unlisted telephone number Charles had given her to his penthouse.

"Charles, you were right," she began as soon as he answered.

"Galen?"

"Your suggestions, Charles. My stories can, will, be better. Thank you."

"It's what editors do."

"Yes, but—"

"It's my job, Galen."

"Still . . . these were so sensitive, so . . ."

"Good." Charles laughed softly, then, changing the subject, said, "I am glad you called. I've found three major book publishers who are very interested in publishing the collection of African stories."

A long silence followed.

"Galen?"

"Why are you doing this, Charles?" she asked quietly.

Charles didn't answer. He didn't *have* an answer.

"Happy Birthday, Brooke! Trick or treat?"

"Likewise, Melanie. Treat. Come in."

Halloween babies *and* twins. For the first twelve years it had been so much fun. They celebrated their Halloween birthdays by dressing up in wonderful costumes, sometimes identical, sometimes complementary. They hadn't celebrated a birthday together since seventh grade. It was Melanie's suggestion, just as window-shopping along Fifth Avenue or brunch at the Tavern on the Green or seeing the sights of New York, together, was initiated by Melanie.

Brooke accepted Melanie's suggestion of birthday dinner politely, as she accepted all of Melanie's ideas, and even offered her apartment. In the six weeks since Melanie had moved to New York, she had never been in Brooke's apartment. Always before they met in public, amid the amusing distractions of Manhattan. Sometimes Galen joined them.

But tonight, on their twenty-sixth birthday, Brooke and Melanie were alone and private. They sat in Brooke's small, immaculate living room thoughtfully eating carrot sticks and searching their minds for safe neutral topics. Noticing the recent issues of *Images* and *Fashion* neatly arranged on the dust-free coffee table, Melanie offered eagerly, "I can't wait to read Galen's story."

"The December issue, isn't it?" Brooke asked, then blushed. It was a stupid question, fueled by nervousness and the desperate desire to keep the conversation alive. They both knew "Emerald" would appear in the December issue. Galen was their friend and *she* was Galen's attorney. Brooke knew the precise date of publication of all Galen's stories in *Images*.

"Her next one, 'Sapphire,' will be published in the March issue," Brooke continued quickly, providing new information. "And Charles has spoken with several book publishers who want to publish her stories about Africa. Galen and I are meeting with them to discuss terms next week. It's so nice of Charles—"

"Good old Charles." The cynicism in Melanie's voice was lost in the crunch of a carrot stick.

"Do you see him much?" Brooke asked carefully.

"All the time. He's at the fashion shows, of course. And we seem to be on all the same guest lists."

"How is he?" Brooke hadn't seen Charles since the dinner for Galen at his penthouse, but she had discussed the details of Galen's contracts with him over the phone.

"Fine, I suppose."

Even though Melanie *saw* Charles frequently, they didn't speak. After the first few parties, after awkward attempts at light banter deteriorated quickly into unveiled taunts, Charles and Melanie avoided each other. Melanie didn't *like* Charles. It was an easy decision to defend. Charles Sinclair viewed the world with such arrogance and disdain!

But it bothered Melanie that Charles didn't like *her*. She wasn't used to being disliked; only in high school, only Brooke . . . Melanie shook off the painful memory. Charles didn't even know her. It was more proof that there was something wrong with *him*. Melanie added wryly, "Vintage Charles Sinclair."

The timer on the oven sounded with a startling buzz.

"Time to make the sauce." Brooke stood up.

"Can I help?"

"No. Thanks. The kitchen's too small. It will just be a few minutes." Brooke added gaily, "Make yourself at home!"

Left alone, Melanie's nervous energy drove her to pace in the tiny living room, and that done in a matter of moments and taking Brooke literally, she explored the rest of her sister's apartment.

There wasn't much to explore—only two closed doors. The first was a small bathroom with ancient wallpaper and a chipped mirror. Behind the second door was Brooke's bedroom. Melanie opened the door and gasped.

"Brooke!" she shrieked. "Come *quickly!*"

"Melanie? What's wrong?"

"Brooke," Melanie exclaimed in mock horror as Brooke rushed into the bedroom. "Your room is a *mess!* The bed is barely made. There are mounds of clothes and piles of books and . . ."

Melanie suppressed a giggle with great effort and found a stern face. "Brooke. This is serious. You are the *neat* twin. Someone has been in your bedroom and almost destroyed it!"

Melanie couldn't contain herself any longer and the giggles won out and were contagious, and in moments Brooke and Melanie, weak with laughter, flopped helplessly onto Brooke's haphazardly made bed.

"I can't believe it, Brooke." Melanie tossed a pair of jeans that lay on the bed onto an already clothes-cluttered chair.

"So they were wrong." Brooke shrugged. "We're both messy."

"No. I'm *neat*. I," Melanie hesitated. She continued slowly, suddenly serious, "I hated living in a messy room all those years."

Melanie lay on her twin's bed and stared at the ceiling, avoiding Brooke's eyes; Melanie felt as if she had made a monumental confession. It was monumental, or *could* be. It *could* be the beginning of telling each other the truth.

"And I," Brooke whispered, staring at her own piece of cracked plaster ceiling, "hated wearing all those drab clothes."

Melanie sat up and turned to look at Brooke. "Bright colors really do suit you. Which reminds me, I got you something."

Melanie left the room.

"Here." Melanie handed the gift-wrapped package to Brooke when she returned. They hadn't given each other presents for years. The package was small. It fit, completely hidden, in her purse. She could have left with it, if it hadn't felt right to give Brooke a present. Melanie added awkwardly, "Happy Halloween."

"Thank you." Brooke opened the package and withdrew a beautiful silk scarf. "Oh, Melanie."

"There's one shade of blue . . . here"—Melanie pointed to a dark-blue piece of the silk—"I thought it exactly matched your eyes. Let's see."

Melanie turned and led the way to the bathroom.

"It *does*," Brooke agreed moments later as they stood side by side in front of the mirror. "Exactly."

"Your eyes, Brooke. I remember . . ." Melanie frowned.

"What?"

"I remember when I learned we weren't identical." Melanie spoke to Brooke's image in the mirror. "I remember looking in the mirror and thinking how pretty *my* blue eyes were. Like the sky."

"They are." Brooke answered Melanie in the mirror.

"But your eyes are so dark. So interesting."

Brooke and Melanie watched the faces in the mirror for a long silent moment. As they watched, the faces became solemn and thoughtful, transformed by bittersweet memories and worrisome questions. What *else* did you hate? What else of mine did you want?

"If only you had my eyes, Melanie Chandler," Brooke's tease had an uneasy twist, "you *might* have a shot at a really big modelling career."

"Eyes half closed, Melanie. The breeze is stroking you and it feels so good." Steve's voice was low and seductive and mean. He crouched in front of her, taking shot after shot, moving around her, making her move, coaxing her. . . .

Melanie arched her neck and breathed the forced air from the portable fan. The photo session was in one of the studios at Drake, but Melanie could pretend the hot lights were the warm California sun and the fan-fueled air was a fresh sea breeze. That wonderful memory made her smile. She didn't need Steve's vulgar words. . . .

"Spread your legs, Melanie. Wider. *Wider*. Open your mouth. Wet your lips. Now think about my cock. It's big and hard. Think about where you want it. Your mouth."

Melanie froze. Her pale blue eyes flashed with anger. "How *dare* you?"

"How dare I what?"

"Speak to me like that."

"Like what? Like you're a whore? It's what you are, you know," Steve snarled.

"How can you say that?"

"You *sell* your body, Melanie. You *sell* sex. Just because no one touches you doesn't mean—" Steve's voice was ugly. "What do you think men do when they see your pictures? How do you think they *use* your pictures?"

"You have a filthy mind," Melanie hissed.

"I'm just being honest with you."

"The truth is," Melanie said icily, her body trembling with rage and fear, "my pictures sell beautiful clothes and beautiful jewels and—"

"The truth is you're a whore."

"*No.*"

Melanie rushed out of the studio and into the dressing room. Once inside the door she drew deep breaths. It didn't help. She couldn't breathe, the knot in her stomach tightened, and her body trembled.

"Melanie?"

"Fran."

"Melanie, sit down." As Fran spoke she put her hands on Melanie's quivering shoulders and pushed her firmly onto a hard wooden chair in front of a makeup mirror. "What happened?"

"Steve," Melanie squeezed her eyes shut against the memory.

"Oh."

"Oh?"

"He made some suggestive comments to you during a session?" Fran guessed.

"Yes," Melanie breathed. At least she could breathe now. "And he said that I was a whore, selling my body."

"That sounds like Steve," Fran murmured. "I don't think he's too fond of women, at least not beautiful ones."

"He's done this to you?"

"To everyone."

"Has anyone told Mr. Drake?"

"Are you kidding?"

"Adam Drake is a fine man. He would fire Steve instantly if he knew."

"Melanie, let's do a little reality testing. Steve is probably the best fashion photographer in the world. He may hate us, but he makes us look wonderful. And we all—you, me, Steve, Mr. Drake—make a lot of money."

"The pimps and the whores," Melanie whispered.

"I don't believe that and neither do you," Fran countered impatiently.

"No," Melanie agreed quietly, frowning slightly. "But I think Mr. Drake—"

"Melanie, ten years from now, when you and I are *history* in the modelling business, Steve will still be the top photographer around and Drake will still be the number-one agency. We are commodities with short shelf lives—"

"What a happy thought!" Melanie laughed, tossing her golden hair and with it the unpleasantness with Steve. She wasn't going to let Steve Barnes ruin this for her. She could tolerate his vulgarity if she had to. "Ten years?"

"If we're lucky. Maybe only five." Fran looked at their reflections under the harsh lights of the makeup mirrors. Flawless beauty now, but it wouldn't last. "What are you going to do after our fling with fame is over, Melanie? Where will you be in ten years?"

"In ten years," Melanie mused distantly, "I'll be living with my husband and children in Malibu. We'll have horses and a white sand beach and rose gardens. In my spare time, when the children are in school, I'll design clothes."

"Oh, my God."

"What?"

"I kind of imagined that *you* of all the models in the history of Drake would be the one to end up with Adam. But that would put you in a penthouse in Manhattan for life. And he *had* his children two marriages ago."

"He probably has no intention of remarrying anyway."

"He almost got married last summer. To Dr. Jane Tucker, a neurosurgeon who works at Cornell. I met her once. She was very impressive. So, anyway, how many children?"

"Two, I think." Melanie frowned briefly What if she had twins? "How about you ten years from now?"

"In ten years—hopefully long before that—I will be Mrs. Jason Sinclair."

"Really?"

"It's all I want." Fran sighed. She glanced at her watch and added, "In fact, I am on my way to see him now to cancel our lunch date because of the Tiffany shoot. See you later, Melanie, you homebody whore."

Fran cast a playful smile at Melanie as she left.

Melanie sat in the silence of the dressing room for a long time, staring at herself in the mirror and thinking. Finally she walked down the hall to the studio. Steve was preparing for another session.

"If you treat me like that again," Melanie began solemnly. . . . She saw Steve's back stiffen in response to her words. "I will tell Mr. Drake."

"Mr. Drake?" Steve taunted. "*Adam* will laugh at you. He might even fire you."

"I don't care," Melanie answered calmly, truthfully. It was what she had decided. She loved modelling because it was so beautiful. But Steve was tainting it. She would rather give it up than have it tainted. "But, Steve, he might fire *you.*"

"No."

"There's an easy way to find out." Melanie's voice was strong and confident. She believed she *would* win. Adam Drake loved beauty, too.

"You wouldn't tell him." It sounded like a threat. Steve spun and faced her. His dark eyes were hidden in shadows, but Melanie still saw the rage. And the fear.

Steve was afraid.

"Try me."

CHAPTER NINE

*G*alen left Charles's office just as Jason emerged from his.

"Galen! Hello."

"Hello, Jason." She blushed.

"How are you?"

"Fine." Give me a minute, Jason. I have to think what to say. . . . She felt him pulling away. The words burst out, awkward and unrehearsed. "Charles just showed me the art for 'Emerald.' He said you chose it. It's . . . Jason . . . so beautiful. Perfect."

"I'm glad you like it. If you have a moment there's someone in my office you might enjoy meeting."

Galen followed Jason into his office. A woman stood by the picture window overlooking Manhattan.

"Fran." Jason's voice drew her attention away from the gray-black clouds that threatened to drench all of Manhattan.

Fran turned gracefully and elegantly and smiled a beautiful smile.

"Galen, this is Fran Jeffries. Fran was the model for 'Emerald.' "

Galen stared at the lovely brown eyes and rich dark hair and breathtaking beauty. The art Galen had just seen in Charles's office captured the innocence of the character Galen had created. But this woman was so confident, so experienced, so beguiling. She wasn't Emerald, was she? Galen didn't know and it confused her.

Galen knew Emerald so well. So much of Emerald *was* Galen. So much of what was inside.

Galen smiled politely at Fran and wondered if she and Fran had anything in common. There was certainly nothing on the surface, and probably nothing inside. Fran. Emerald. Galen. What was real and what was art?

"It's nice to meet you, Fran."

"It's nice to meet you. I can't wait to read your story. Jason keeps raving about it."

Really? Galen looked shyly to Jason for confirmation—a smile, a nod—but Jason's pale-blue eyes avoided hers.

"Jason, I have to go," Fran said. "I'm sorry about lunch, but Tiffany calls. See you tonight. Good-bye, Galen."

Galen moved to the window as Fran and Jason kissed good-bye. It was a brief kiss, nothing more. But it was enough, too much.

"She's very beautiful," Galen said after Fran left. She spoke to the thunder-clouds.

"You look hungry." Jason ignored Galen's comment about Fran. Maybe he hadn't heard it.

"What?" Galen spun to look at him, to see if his pale-blue eyes were serious. They were.

"You look like you've lost weight."

Embarrassed, Galen folded her arms around her thin body. It was true. She *had* lost weight. Sometimes she got so involved in her writing she forgot to eat. She was thin to begin with and now Jason—*Jason*—noticed that she looked even thinner, even gawkier. Galen reached for her handwoven cloth purse. "I'd better go."

"Have lunch with me." Jason blocked her exit. "Fran just cancelled and I have reservations for two at La Lumière. Will you join me?"

La Lumière. Galen had heard of it. It was expensive, exclusive, and elegant. Most people couldn't even *get* reservations. One had to be *known*.

"I'm not dressed . . ." Galen looked at the utilitarian wool coat she had bought—secondhand—when the Indian summer suddenly gave way to an early frost. Underneath she wore an old cotton dress. She didn't own any clothes suitable for lunch at La Lumière.

"Who cares?" Jason asked.

You care, Jason. I'm sure you care. You're just much too polite, much too well bred, to let it show.

Later that night, as Galen thought about the lunch at La Lumière with Jason, she couldn't remember if she even touched her gourmet meal. And she couldn't re-member if there was anyone else in the restaurant, or the color of the tablecloth, or the name of the waiter, or the kind of flowers on the tables, or the art that hung on the walls. Galen couldn't remember any of the things that everyone else considered so memorable about the restaurant.

All Galen could remember was the way he made her feel, the way he laughed, the way his eyes looked at her, the way he leaned toward her until they almost touched.

And when Jason thought about it later that night, before he and Fran made love, and after, and even during, he wondered if it had all been a dream. Surely it had been just an illusion, just a moment of fiction wedged between the realities of life.

Because for two and a half hours there had been magic. Jason had never felt such joy and enchantment, never before in his life, not even for a minute.

It wasn't real. It *couldn't* be.

Galen waited—restless, anxious, eager, waiting—for one week.

Maybe Jason doesn't know how to reach me, her heart suggested with each passing day.

Of course he does, her mind answered. He just isn't calling. He isn't going to. Why would he? He has Fran . . . Emerald. . . .

At the end of the week, Galen decided to send him a thank-you note. It was appropriate, wasn't it? *Polite.*

A busboy at the Champs-Elysées agreed to hand-deliver it for Galen at noon. Galen wrote Jason's name and the word *Personal* on the envelope.

The busboy reported that Jason's secretary was at lunch. He asked the receptionist to put it on Jason's desk.

Jason noticed the pale-pink envelope on his desk the instant he entered his office. It was so out of place. Jason's office was cluttered with photographs and sketches and layouts and designs. But not *words.* There were no letters or memos or appointment calendars or manuscripts or telephone directories in Jason Sinclair's office.

Jason gazed at the pale-pink envelope and the beautiful design drawn in blue fountain pen. Jason's artistic eye recognized the lovely, delicate design, and knew who drew it, but he couldn't know its meaning.

Jason closed his eyes. Feelings of helplessness flooded him, bringing with them ancient anguish. He was *dependent* again, destined to know only what someone else chose to share with him, unable to know it on his own. As the horrible memory of the day of Elliott's death—the day of his greatest helplessness—began to surface, Jason quickly opened his eyes.

Jason put the unopened envelope in his suit pocket and walked, coatless and desperate, into the winter chill.

Why didn't he just ask Charles to read it to him? Charles did all the reading for the Sinclair twins.

Because this was different. *Private.* Charles didn't need to know.

I don't *want* Charles to know, Jason realized as he walked along Park Avenue, his cheeks numbing quickly in the icy November wind. There was so much Charles had never shared with him.

Despite the bitter cold, Jason wasn't alone. The streets of Manhattan were crowded with purposeful people rushing swiftly to warm destinations. Jason was surrounded by humanity, *literate* humanity. He was surrounded by people who could read the precious note in his pocket. But Jason was recognizable. He had to be careful who he asked.

After several blocks, Jason turned off Park Avenue onto a side street and headed east. The humanity changed: less purposeful, even colder, and without warm destinations. These people wouldn't recognize him. The first two people Jason spoke to were like him—they couldn't read.

Three blocks east of Park Avenue the street ended in a schoolyard. Groups of teenagers huddled in defiant celebration of recess despite the winter cold. Jason approached a boy who huddled by himself.

"Can you read?"

"What d'ya mean?"

"Can you read?" Jason repeated.

" 'Course I can."

Jason wondered if it was bravado.

"Would you read this for me?" Jason took the envelope from his pocket. "I'll give you twenty dollars."

The boy eyed him skeptically.

"Twenty-five," Jason offered. Or fifty. Or a hundred. Or a *million*.

"Somethin' wrong with your eyes, mister?"

Jason shrugged. "OK?"

The boy nodded, eagerly shoved the money into his jeans pocket, and took the note.

"OK. This here says," he began, scowling at the envelope, *"Jason. And Per . . . son . . . al. Personal.* You want me to read what's inside?"

"Yes. Please." No. But do I have a choice?

"Dear Jason. Thank you for lunch. No, it's more." The boy frowned, struggling. *"Lunch . . . eee . . . on."*

"Luncheon," Jason breathed. Very British. Very Galen. "Go on."

"Luncheon last week. It was . . . lovely. I have thought of little else." The boy stopped. "There's one more word. It's strange. I'll spell it to you."

Jason listened to the letters that had no meaning.

"Could the word be *Galen?"*

The boy wrinkled his nose, studied the pink notepaper, and nodded energetically. "Yup. That's what it is. *Galen.* Funny. Is it a name?"

"Oh, yes." Jason retrieved the notepaper from the boy's hand. "Thank you."

"Sure."

Jason hesitated. "You probably won't believe this, but, it's so important. You should learn to read as well as you possibly can."

"Sure." The boy shrugged. "I will."

I have thought of little else. The words echoed in Jason's mind. Neither have I, Galen. But it wasn't real. It was just a lovely fantasy. If we see each other again it will only be disappointing, won't it?

Still, as Jason thought about her, the magical feelings swirled inside him. He walked faster and faster in the bitter cold, beyond Park Avenue toward Greenwich Village and Galen.

By the time Jason reached the Champs-Elysées coffee house his lips were blue with cold and his cheeks had faded from rosy red to ashen. As soon as he saw her, Jason tried to turn his numb lips into a smile for her. It must have worked, or Galen just smiled anyway, and in moments Jason's cold body was pulsing with a magical warmth that was Galen.

"Jason."

"Hi."

"Hi."

"I got . . . Thank you . . . it was nice. . . ."

"Oh." She blushed. "Yes . . . it was nice."

They stood in the entrance of the Champs-Elysées fumbling to find words, but eloquently communicating with their eyes and their smiles. Galen was an artist with words, but her art was in writing not speaking. Her emotions and feelings flowed articulately from her heart to paper. But speaking the words—*saying* what was important—was foreign to her.

Saying what was important was as foreign to Jason as it was to Galen. Jason spoke the language that Charles, Elliott, and the tutors taught him—their language, not his—because he had to. But the words weren't his. Jason couldn't use them to express his feelings. Jason painted his feelings, and he shared his paintings with no one.

Until now he had never wanted to.

"When do you . . ."

"In an hour."

"Are you free?"

"Yes."

Jason and Galen spent the next two weeks falling quietly and confidently in love. They dined in Greenwich Village, in dark secluded restaurants where no one recognized *him* and where *she* felt at home in her long calico dresses. Jason felt at home in the Village, too. He loved the music and the theater and the art and the people. They were people like him: quiet, talented, passionate artists.

Jason belonged in the Village and he belonged with Galen. He smiled at her and held her hand and desperately hoped that she knew. Galen smiled back with glistening emerald eyes and hoped that he knew, too.

Late at night, after Jason left her at the door of the dilapidated brownstone on Spring Street, Galen lighted her hyacinth-scented candles, drew ink into her fountain pen, and wrote letters to him telling him how she felt.

At the end of the second week Jason suggested they spend Thanksgiving weekend in Southhampton at Windermere.

"Will Charles be there?" Galen asked.

"No. Charles doesn't live there. No one else would be there. We would be alone." The sizable staff required to maintain Windermere did their work on weekdays and vanished on weekends when Jason was in residence. It had been that way ever since Elliott's death.

Jason watched her struggling, searching for words, her lovely eyes flickering with worry.

"Don't you want to be alone with me?" he asked gently, bewildered.

"Yes."

"No?"

"Yes. It's just," Galen faltered. Then she remembered. She had written it all down already. When she told him he would understand. Her eyes met his bravely, "You read 'Emerald,' Jason. That's who I am."

Jason shrugged slightly, unable to hold her gaze. Of course he knew the story. He sensed the mood and passion from what Charles told him. But Jason didn't *know* Emerald; he didn't know that when Emerald fell in love, when she gave herself to love, it was forever.

Jason doesn't feel the same way, Galen realized. She had exposed herself entirely by telling him about Emerald. And now Jason was telling her he couldn't promise anything.

"I haven't—" Jason gazed into her tear-damp emerald eyes and he knew he had to tell her—"I haven't read 'Emerald.' "

"Why not?" Galen's voice trembled. Foolish, innocent, silly Emerald. Silly *Galen*.

"Because," Jason spoke hesitantly. He had never told anyone before. Only Charles knew. Jason reached for her hand. "Because I can't read."

"Can't read?"

Jason told her. Jason told her in the language that had never been his; it was a story without emotion. Jason didn't tell Galen about the anger and frustration and helplessness. He didn't know how to.

"Is it dyslexia?" Galen asked when the pause was so long that she decided he had finished.

"I guess so."

"There's so much work with that now. Have you—"

"I'm adjusted. I almost forget about it until there's a story I want to read or until I get a note on pale-pink stationery."

"Who read it to you?" Galen asked. "Charles?"

"No one who knows you or me."

"Oh."

"Galen? What's wrong?"

"Writing. It's how I communicate."

"Not the only way."

"I've written you a letter every night."

"You have? Will you read them to me?"

Galen started to shake her head, but Jason seemed so pleased about the letters. Maybe she *could* read them to him—this weekend, at Windermere, when they were alone.

"Jason, I . . . Emerald . . . I am inexperienced."

"There's no hurry, Galen. About anything." We have forever.

"Jason," Galen breathed as they walked, hand in hand, through the mansion at Windermere.

"I love it here." I love sharing Windermere with you.

"Does your art ever appear in *Images?*" Galen asked.

"What?"

"Your paintings, Jason. They're magnificent."

What Galen had been noticing and admiring and loving, even more than the panoramic views of the sea or the rich splendor of the mansion, were Jason's wonderful paintings. Jason had never told Galen about his painting, but she didn't seem surprised. It was just one more marvelous discovery about the man she loved.

"Some are my mother's."

"Yes." Galen hesitated. "The signatures . . ."

"Oh." Jason smiled. "Of course."

"Hers are wonderful, too," Galen added quickly.

"The style is similar."

"Yes. But yours are stronger and more vivid." More emotional. "Have you ever done a show?"

"No." Jason's painting was for him and for Windermere; and, now, for Galen. He continued gently, "I would love to do a painting of you."

"Oh, I wouldn't be a very good model." Galen's cheeks flushed pale pink.

Jason touched her warm cheeks and smiled into her eyes.

"You are beautiful, Galen, so beautiful."

Jason kissed her full, soft lips. He felt her tremble.

"Galen?"

"I've never . . ." She looked down, too shy to meet his eyes.

"Made love. I know. Galen, I won't push you. Kissing doesn't mean—"

"I've never *kissed.* . . ."

"No?" His voice was so gentle. "Do you want to?"

"Yes, Jason. I just . . . if I do something wrong."

"You can't do anything wrong. Nothing is wrong. We'll do this together, learn together. OK?"

Galen answered him with her lips, kissing his cheek, then finding his lips. Jason held her face in his hands and laced his strong fingers through her fine shiny hair.

How long had it been since he had just kissed someone? *Just*, Jason mused as the thrill of kissing her, the wonder of sharing that warmth and closeness with her pulsed through him, filling him with joy and desire. *Just*, he thought, as she opened her mouth, inviting him, wanting more of him, more closeness, more warmth, more discovery.

We'll learn together. Jason was learning that he could do this—kiss his beloved Galen—forever. He could spend forever in the tangle of red-gold silk that covered them both as the passion of their kisses grew. They kissed for a half an hour, then an hour, then two as the great room fell dark and cold in the early winter twilight.

Between kisses they gazed at each other, smiling, tracing gentle lines around the other's eyes and lips and face and neck. They kissed lips and mouths and cheeks and eyes and necks and hair and hands. Again and again.

Sometimes the kiss was a long, slow, leisurely dream. And sometimes it was deep and urgent and eager.

That night Jason and Galen walked hand in hand to her cheerful pink-and-cream bedroom overlooking the courtyard and rose gardens. Jason kissed her good night in the hallway.

"Sleep well, Galen."

An hour later Jason heard a soft knock on his door. He was awake, lying in the darkness, thinking about her, unable to sleep.

Galen stood in the hallway, barefooted, wearing a tattered paisley bathrobe over a modest flannel nightgown.

"I couldn't sleep."

"Me neither."

Jason waited. He needed to know what she wanted. There weren't any rules. They were learning together. But this had to be her decision. He smiled at her, encouraging her to tell him.

Galen smiled in response to his smile, then frowned.

"What, Galen?"

"Do you think we could sleep together? I mean, literally, sleep. It's too soon, but . . . being this near you without being with you. Would that be unfair to you? Would it be wrong?"

"Nothing is wrong." Jason led her by the hand to his bed.

Galen took off her robe and crawled in beside him. Jason wrapped his arms around her and held her close. Within moments they were both asleep, their restlessness vanquished by the peace and joy of being together.

CHAPTER TEN

"*How's* the law-and-order business?" He leaned against the doorjamb of her office just as he had six months before. Then, the sweltering heat of summer collected in her office. Now, two days before Christmas, she kept herself warm with endless mugs of overbrewed coffee.

"Charles." Brooke smiled. She tilted her head to the pages and pages of legal briefs stacked in precarious piles on the floor and table and said, "Disorderly. But legal."

"It was nice of you to make time to help Galen."

"She's my friend."

"You negotiated quite a deal for her." Galen had told Charles the details of the two-book contract. She would be well paid for her stories about Africa *and* for another yet-to-be-written collection.

"It was fair. Who is it that says, Quality is always worth the price?"

Charles looked embarrassed for a fleeting moment. He recovered quickly, guessing lightly, "Brooke Chandler?"

"Charles Sinclair."

The conversation came to a shuddering halt. The realization that she had been teasing Charles caught up with her. Who did she think she was? Melanie?

"I sent 'Sapphire' to Mitchell Altman in Hollywood." Charles's voice was suddenly all business. "He's interested in making a movie from the story. He'll fly out in mid-January to meet with Galen and her attorney to talk about the rights, who'll do the screenplay, that sort of thing."

"Is Sinclair Publishing becoming Sinclair Productions?"

"Jason and I will be the executive producers."

"Sounds like fun."

"Do you really have time?" Charles gestured to the mounds of work in her office.

"Yes," Brooke answered truthfully. Nights. Weekends. Every night. Every weekend. She wasn't dating. She had offers, but she said No. There was no one. Brooke added another truth, "I enjoy it."

"Maybe enough to someday give up the life of crime and come to work at Sinclair?"

"Maybe." Brooke smiled. Maybe.

The five beats of silence that followed felt to Brooke and her pounding heart like a hundred.

"Are you going away for the holidays?" Charles asked finally.

"Yes, to see my parents in California. Melanie can't go. Adam wants her here for his New Year's Eve party. Something about her celebrity image and keeping a high profile at the right events."

Charles nodded. "Very effective marketing. Adam's New Year's Eve party is the grand finale of the season."

"I was invited," Brooke said carefully. What if an unguarded look of horror crossed his handsome face at the news? Brooke, you don't understand, Adam Drake's party is for the Beautiful People. Brooke explained quickly, "Actually, Andrew Parker was invited. He's married, of course, but his wife will be away. Andrew thought I should go." Brooke smiled. "Effective marketing for the DA's office, I guess."

"But you won't be back in time?"

"No."

"That's too bad." The dark eyes were serious.

"I'm really sorry I can't go to the party," Brooke told Andrew that evening. She added hopefully, "Maybe your wife will return in time."

They were at Giorgio's on Fifth Avenue, sipping hot buttered rum as frenzied, last-minute, holiday shoppers rushed past on the street outside. Brooke had accepted Andrew's invitation—a holiday drink after work—reluctantly. Andrew was her mentor, her role model, the kind of brilliant, insightful, articulate trial attorney she wanted to be. Brooke was in awe of Andrew. Going for a drink with him . . .

But the hot buttered rum and spirited holiday crowds and glitter of Fifth Avenue made her feel warm and festive and confident.

"Allison won't return in time." Andrew's voice was low. He sighed and explained, "She's in an institution, Brooke."

"An institution?" Brooke could barely hear her own words above the laughter and gaiety of the crowd at Giorgio's.

"She's ill. It's a kind of depression." Andrew's dark eyes stared thoughtfully at his gold wedding band and then at Brooke.

"Andrew, I'm so sorry." Brooke had an image of Andrew's wife—strong and beautiful and talented—a perfect match for confident, handsome, brilliant Andrew. Andrew hid the sadness so well. Brooke's deep-blue eyes told him, again, how sorry she was.

"Brooke, I'm all right," Andrew reassured her swiftly. "I shouldn't have mentioned it."

"Yes, you should have," Brooke spoke softly.

Andrew smiled a half-smile. "There are times—months—when Allison is fine. Then, without warning . . ."

"It must be very difficult." All the more difficult, Brooke realized, because Andrew loves her so much.

Andrew nodded briefly. Then, purposefully shifting the topic and the mood, he urged, "Tell me about California, Brooke. What will you do while you're home?"

What you should be doing, Andrew, Brooke thought sadly, celebrating the holidays with people I love.

"You see before you an unemployed waitress." Galen laughed softly. "They found a replacement today."

"You're probably the first employee in the history of the Champs-Elysées to give notice."

"They've been so nice to me. It's the least I could do."

"Let's go to Windermere now and stay through New Year's Day," Jason suggested.

"You have the Drake party."

Jason had planned to make a brief, dutiful appearance at Adam Drake's New Year's Eve party while Galen was working. Now she was free. They could go to the party together, but Jason knew it would overwhelm her.

"Not anymore."

"Shouldn't—?"

"No." I should be with you and we should be at Windermere.

Jason and Galen arrived at Windermere just as the first snowflake fell from the wintry gray sky. Jason built a fire in the great room and they settled into their peaceful ritual, Jason painting, Galen writing, both pausing as if by a silent signal to gaze together at the spectacular views of the winter sea.

"What are you reading?" Jason asked when he looked up from his easel.

Usually Galen wrote, curled in the huge sofa, surrounded by candles scented with lilac and wild rose and hyacinth and French vanilla, her fountain pen resting between her lips while she planned the next sentence, word perfect, before writing it down. Jason loved watching her write, absorbed, thoughtful, sometimes smiling, sometimes frowning, *living* the moments with her characters.

But today Galen was reading. And her concentration was intense.

"It's a book about dyslexia." Galen watched Jason carefully as she spoke. She didn't want to make him angry. If Jason could *be* angry.

He smiled.

"So, do I have it?" he asked idly.

"Well, you're male and you told me that your mother may have been dyslexic. That fits."

"Really?" Galen had his attention.

"You don't know much about it, do you?"

Only how it feels, Jason thought.

"No. Tell me." Jason put down his paintbrush.

"It was first recognized in the late eighteen hundreds. It was called word blindness."

"That's apt," Jason murmured. He added thoughtfully, "I see the letters, but I am blind to the words they form."

Galen waited a moment before continuing. "In some people it's just words. In others it's words and numbers."

"I learned mathematics in my head. It wasn't until . . ." Jason paused, his eyes narrowing as he recalled his helplessness that horrible stormy afternoon. He blinked, clearing the pain, and continued. "It wasn't until after my father died that I discovered I could read and write numbers."

That discovery had given him such freedom!

"And you can write your name," Galen reminded him carefully. Surely he could read and write letters, too. It might be a struggle, but . . . "Your signature is on your paintings and on contracts. . . ."

"My art teacher at Harvard taught me. It's really his signature. I see it as a design, not a sequence of letters. I don't know where *Jason* ends and *Sinclair* begins."

"Oh." Galen was beginning to appreciate the magnitude of Jason's dyslexia and how frustrating it must be. She continued, changing direction, "The experts used to be divided about whether dyslexics could be artists."

"Why?"

"Because sometimes they have difficulty with spatial relationships."

"We do?" Jason asked, for the first time in his life identifying himself with all the others who were like him. He wondered who they were, how they had adapted to their lives, if they were as lucky as he. He looked at Galen and felt so lucky.

"Sometimes. But there have been talented artists. Even before you," Galen added lovingly. "Artists and engineers and architects and doctors and lawyers and poets and writers and—"

"Writers?"

"It is believed that Hans Christian Andersen was dyslexic. They've analyzed the original copies of his work, the way he wrote and spelled. . . ."

"He must have been able to write well enough. It must not have been so severe."

Galen was silent for a long moment. Then she began quietly, "There are ways, Jason, to teach—"

"Galen," Jason sighed. That was where this was leading. She wanted him to try. "Oh, Galen. I would give anything to be able to read. But I can't. I can't even read a stop sign. I've tried, honey. After I discovered I could read numbers I had such hope. But . . ."

Jason shrugged.

Galen had read the horrible case studies of people with dyslexia who died because they couldn't read warning signs: Stop; Railroad Crossing; Danger; High Voltage. She shuddered. She also had learned that even when people with dyslexia were taught to read so that they could function safely and independently, they rarely read for pleasure. It was always a struggle.

Galen remembered then, for the first time *feeling* what it must be like for Jason, the terror she herself had felt as a little girl in a remote part of India. The written language bore no resemblance—because the symbols weren't letters, they were uninterpretable, nonsensical lines and curls—to anything she knew. She remembered spending fruitless hours staring at the signs on street corners and in the markets, trying to make sense of them, but unable to.

She was so *afraid* of getting lost and being unable to find her way back to her parents! Galen remembered the horrible frustration and isolation and fear.

"I'm sorry, Jason," she whispered.

"Don't be." Jason moved beside her because it had been too long, an hour, since he had kissed her.

When they awakened the next morning their entire world, the magnificent acres of Windermere, was white and pristine and pure. Virginal.

"Jason," Galen breathed as they gazed out Jason's bedroom window across the soft white blanket and delicately snow-etched trees toward the gray-green sea. "Will you paint this?"

Jason stood behind her, his arms wrapped around her over the modest flannel nightgown.

"If you want me to." He kissed the top of her head, nuzzling his lips in the red-gold tangle.

Galen was still for a moment. Then she turned in his arms and softly touched his handsome cheeks with her slender white fingers.

"I want . . ."

Jason waited. Her eyes told him she wanted much more than a painting of Windermere in snowy splendor.

"Make love to me, Jason."

Jason didn't ask her if she was sure. If she wasn't, if he sensed uncertainty as he was loving her, he would stop. If he could. Could he? He wanted her so much. Holding her warm, lovely softness against him night after night had been such pleasure. And such torment.

Could he stop? *Yes.* If he had to. If her eyes or her body sent a message of doubt he would stop. His love for her would stop him.

But all the green eyes told him was that they wanted him. It was time. And all the softness underneath the flannel nightgown told him, as she pressed against him, moving in a rhythm of passion and desire, was to hurry please, and to be gentle.

"I love you, Galen," Jason whispered as his lips found hers.

They kissed in front of the window in the pale morning light as the snow fell silently outside. Finally Galen eased away, and, her eyes searching his and finding love, she lifted her nightgown over her head.

Jason had never seen her naked. He knew her lovely round cream-colored breasts from feel and taste, but not from sight. And he had imagined the rest.

But she was even more beautiful than he had imagined. Her round, soft womanliness was modestly draped by her long red-gold hair. Jason thought of Botticelli's "The Birth of Venus." It was a distant image, because his mind and his senses were consumed by his desire for her.

Jason removed his pajamas and they stood gazing at each other, not touching or speaking or moving. Then, at the same instant, they smiled, gentle, loving, knowing smiles.

Jason lowered her onto the bed and their naked bodies met in joyous discovery.

She was so soft and warm and lovely!

Oh, Jason, *Jason.*

I want you, Galen. All of you.

Jason searched her eyes as he loved her, searching for doubt and finding none as he touched her breasts, her hips, her thighs . . .

"Galen," he whispered hoarsely, when he could barely wait a moment longer and he thought it was time for her, too.

"Jason." Her eyes glowed, welcoming and confident, as she moved her hips under him.

Her smile didn't waver and her eyes squeezed tight—it hurt a little—for only a moment. Then they were together. They paused for a moment, acknowledging the wonder of the union with loving smiles and shining eyes. Then Jason had to move again, quickly, and their lips kissed and their eyes closed and their arms and legs held tight and the rhythm of their loving was *I love you, I love you, I love you.*

CHAPTER ELEVEN

"*Hello*, Charles." Melanie smiled a beautiful, sexy smile. It was almost midnight, almost time to greet the New Year.

"Hello Melanie." Charles smiled in return, matching Melanie's smile in sexiness and adding a curve of danger.

Viveca Sanders, New Orleans belle turned Rona Barrett of Manhattan, stood nearby watching the exchange between Melanie and Charles with great interest. Viveca's nightly television show, *Viveca's View*, entertained its faithful fans with intimate details and tantalizing gossip about New York City's Beautiful People.

That's right, Viveca, Melanie mused, casting a conspiratorial smile her way. You just witnessed the first conversation between Charles Sinclair and Melanie Chandler in almost three months.

It *had* become conspicuous. Charles saw Melanie at all the fashion shows. Charles watched from a seat of honor—reserved for him as editor-in-chief of *Fashion*—at the end of the runway as Melanie modelled the stunning, elegant, avant garde, and chic collections of Lauren and Blass and Ellis and Miller and Klein. Charles saw Melanie at the shows, and he saw her at the fabulous lavish parties attended by New York's most famous and wealthy and powerful.

Melanie Chandler's meteoric rise in the world of fashion *should* have at least piqued the interest of Charles Sinclair. Yet he seemed singularly unintrigued by the newest and most glamorous star in the galaxy of Manhattan celebrities.

And now Charles and Melanie were talking and smiling and everyone was watching.

"This month's *Images* was wonderful," Melanie purred honestly. It was true. Of course, she was complimenting the wrong twin. *Images* was pure Jason—passionate, sensitive, imaginative—it *had* to be.

"Did you like 'Emerald'?"

Wonderful performance, Charles, Melanie thought. You actually seem interested in what I thought of the story.

"Galen is very talented, isn't she?"

"Very. Wait until you read 'Sapphire.' " Charles hesitated a moment, frowned slightly, then asked, "Do you think you could sit on a horse in Central Park in mid-January and pretend it was equatorial Africa?"

The dark eyes were serious. What was he asking? Did he want her to model for the art for one of Galen's stories? The watercolors of Fran for "Emerald" had been breathtaking.

"Yes," Melanie answered quietly. She completely forgot about their audience. "I know I could."

Maybe Jason is right, Charles mused, as he looked at Melanie and tried to be objective. Jason wanted Melanie to model for the art for "Sapphire." It was Jason's decision, but he had sensed Charles's reluctance and they hadn't yet arranged it with Adam.

Jason *is* right, Charles decided. She may be blinded by her own brilliance, but her beauty is flawless. Melanie will make a perfect Sapphire; the artist won't capture her personality.

"OK."

"What does that mean?" Melanie pushed. The dark eyes became aloof, impenetrable walls. Charles was dismissing her.

"I will speak with Adam."

"Speak with *me*."

Before Charles could reply, cheers of "Happy New Year" and strains of "Auld Lang Syne" flooded the room. Adam Drake's rich and famous guests were greeting the New Year with kisses and hugs all around. No one was watching Charles and Melanie anymore.

"Happy New Year, Melanie."

Melanie's sky-blue eyes met his and beckoned, taunting but intrigued. Charles Sinclair was going to kiss her. He *had* to, it was the New Year. The idea was a little exciting. Melanie lifted her chin slightly, tilted her head, and smiled.

Charles returned the smile, but he didn't kiss her. Instead, he turned and kissed someone else, *anyone else*.

"You bastard," Melanie hissed.

She watched his back stiffen. A deep instinct warned her too late that it might be dangerous to anger Charles Sinclair.

Charles turned to face her. His dark brown eyes sent an ice-cold message of arrogant contempt. Even though Charles didn't move toward her, even though there was no physical threat, Melanie stepped back. Charles watched with astonishment. She was afraid of him. *Why?*

Charles started to follow her, but Melanie was already in the embrace of Russ Collins, Publisher of *Style* magazine, and Viveca Sanders's mauve sunset lips had found Charles's, and the New Year had begun.

"Maybe I shouldn't go."

"Yes, you should, darling." Galen kissed the frown away from his handsome forehead. She continued gently. "And if they want you to crew for the Cup, you should do that, too."

They *did* want Jason to crew for the America's Cup. Last week, the captains of both *Shooting Star* and *Westwind* had asked him. Two months ago, when he was with Fran, Jason would have accepted eagerly. He had always dreamed of racing in the America's Cup.

But now . . . Jason couldn't imagine being away from Galen. Even if she was with him in Australia for the six months, he would see very little of her. Just being away for a week, as he was planning to now, seemed too long. But Alan Forrest wanted Jason's advice about a new rigging for *Shooting Star*, and Alan was an old friend.

"I'm not going to crew."

"But if Dennis Conner wants you to crew for *Stars and Stripes*, Jason . . ."

"No. I do plan to be in Fremantle next January to watch Dennis bring the Cup back home. That is, if you'll come with me?"

"Oh, yes."

"This is such a bad time for me to be away." Jason's frown returned. "I should be at Melanie's photo session *and* at the meeting with Mitchell Altman."

"Adam knows what you want," Galen reassured him. "And Charles will be there."

Yes, Jason thought, Charles will be there, helping and protecting Galen. For the hundredth time Jason almost decided not to go.

"And the *author* will be there," Jason added lovingly. "But will she tell them if they're doing it wrong?"

"Of course," Galen answered bravely. She was brave with Jason; his love gave her courage and confidence. "It will be good practice for the movie."

"I'm going to miss you." Jason wrapped his arms around her.

"And I will miss you." Galen sighed. "But I'm going to get a lot of work done. I *have* to start on the revisions for 'Jade.' And I'm having dinner with Brooke and Melanie Friday night."

"That's nice."

"Yes. I haven't really seen them since . . . since you."

"Since *us*," Jason corrected quietly. "Since us."

"Galen, it's wonderful to see you. You look," Brooke hesitated, searching for the right word. Beautiful? Yes. Radiant? Yes. *Womanly*. Brooke needed to fill the pause that was becoming awkward . . . "Terrific."

"Thanks, so do you."

"Hi, Galen." Melanie joined them. "You know Fran Jeffries, don't you?"

"Fran, yes, how are you?" Galen managed to keep strength in her voice.

What was Fran doing here? Galen's pounding heart demanded. Fran was a logical guest, she realized, forcing calm. Fran and Melanie worked together. They were friends. And Fran was free on Friday nights now that her boyfriend—make yourself say it, Galen, her *lover*—had found someone new.

"I'm fine," Fran responded mechanically, but the flatness in her voice betrayed her. She hadn't been fine since Jason left her.

"Galen," Melanie began eagerly. "Are you ready for tomorrow's shoot? You know, if I freeze to death in the name of art . . ."

"Melanie, you shouldn't do this if—" Galen interjected, worried.

"I'm teasing. I can't wait."

"It's going to be an *event*, Galen." Brooke smiled, but she fought uneasy memories of Melanie in her favorite role as center of attention. She continued, "Quite an audience. Adam, Charles, you, me. Even Mitchell Altman has decided to watch. Fran, would you like to come along?"

"Jason won't be there." Fran's tone made it clear that Jason's presence—or absence—was all that mattered.

How does Fran know that? Galen's mind whirled.

"Oh?" Melanie asked.

"I spoke with him yesterday." Fran's voice brightened slightly as she remembered. They had talked for ten minutes. Jason's voice was kind and gentle. Even if his words—what they meant—were not. "He's sailing for a week, checking out the rigging for one of the America's Cup entries."

"Fran and Jason used to be together," Melanie explained to Galen.

I know, Melanie. I *know*. But why did Fran and Jason talk *yesterday*?

"Fran and Jason are *still* together," Fran corrected swiftly. "He'll get over her, whoever the hell she is. He'll realize how special what we had really was."

No, Fran, *no*.

"You don't know who she is?" Brooke asked.

"No. No one seems to. Jason never liked the parties, but he—we—went to the few really important ones." Fran sighed. "This year he even missed Adam's New Year's Eve party."

"Maybe the woman is married," Brooke offered.

"Maybe he's ashamed of her." Fran smiled hopefully.

"Maybe, since we have the author of the most romantic stories ever written right here, we should ask Galen." Melanie's wasn't a serious suggestion. She merely made it to shift away from her one friend's relentless preoccupation with Jason and to include her ever-shy *other* friend.

But Galen had retreated, a little frightened bird, to a far corner of the living room.

The hair stylist swirled Melanie's silky golden hair into soft curls on top of her head and wove blue satin ribbons into the gold. The dresser adjusted the one-of-a-kind Miguel Cruz ivory lace wedding dress while the makeup artist put the finishing touches on the *look*. Melanie entered the trailer in Central Park wearing high-heeled leather boots, skintight designer jeans with matching denim jacket, and a mink Cossack hat. An hour later she emerged, a breathtaking ethereal portrait of femininity and innocence and grace.

"What, no sidesaddle?" Melanie teased gaily as she climbed a small step ladder to mount the prize-winning palomino. Once settled into the English saddle she smiled radiantly at her audience as the dresser and Steve's assistant adjusted the layers of lace. Melanie held the reins loosely as the trainer led the horse.

Brooke and Galen and Charles and Adam and Mitchell Altman watched in silence as Steve, expert and professional, and Melanie, expert and professional, created and photographed perfect pose after perfect pose. During the necessary breaks, when Melanie's muscles finally protested or she began to shake from the winter wind or the horse became restless, Melanie didn't speak. She was an actress still in character.

"I think that's plenty," Steve announced finally. He smiled at Melanie as if they were dear friends instead of the bitter enemies they had become since Melanie declared war that day last October. When he was alone with her, Steve did nothing to conceal his animosity; but the vulgar remarks ended. In public, he and Melanie were exemplary professionals, working together harmoniously and artistically to create the beautiful pictures that made both of them so rich and famous.

"OK." Melanie smiled in return. "Thanks, Steve."

As the trainer started to lead Melanie back toward the step ladder, she collected the reins and pulled the horse's head away from him.

"Galen, is this"—Melanie gestured to herself and the exquisite look of fragile feminity—"really Sapphire? Or is Sapphire like Emerald? Strong and passionate."

"She's like Emerald," Galen answered quietly.

It bothered her from the moment Melanie emerged from the trailer. If only Jason were here. Why didn't Charles say something? Charles knew Sapphire. Galen looked to Charles, but he was strangely detached, barely watching the photo session, speaking occasionally to Adam or Mitchell.

"All right. Steve?" Melanie asked sweetly. Dear friend? "Would you mind taking just a few more shots?"

Melanie swung her right leg over the front of the saddle and slid to the ground.

She took the saddle off the horse and instructed the trainer to change the expensive silver-and-leather bridle to the hemp halter. She slipped off her white satin slippers and stood barefooted on the frozen grass until the trainer made a stirrup with his hands and helped her onto the bareback palomino.

Melanie had everyone's attention now, including Charles's. Her eyes met his, seducing him, daring him to watch as she loosened the curls, and her long beautiful hair fell in ropes of golden silk and pale-blue satin.

"I won't charge you for this, Charles." Not money anyway. But there's a price—your arrogance. I can make you want me. And when you do, when you want me desperately, I'll show how I really feel.

Melanie took the hemp rope, pulled the horse's head, pressed her bare feet into its belly and galloped away.

"Brooke," Galen whispered anxiously.

Brooke had been watching Charles. Melanie was doing this for Charles, flirting with him, teasing him, making him want her. *And it wasn't working.*

He's not impressed, Melanie, Brooke realized with amazement. Adam was impressed. And the trainer. And the hair stylist and dresser and makeup artist and Galen and Mitchell And even Steve, as he unpacked his camera and prepared to take the best shots of the day.

Everyone was impressed. Except Charles.

"Don't worry, Galen," Brooke answered. "Melanie knows what she's doing."

Melanie knows what she's doing, and it's not working.

"She's very good," Galen murmured.

"She's sensational," Adam agreed. Then he teased his friend, "Come on, Charles, *smile*. Apparently I'm not charging you."

"If she lames the horse on this damned frozen ground," Charles growled.

"She won't, Charles," Brooke assured him. A deep instinct told Brooke confidently that Melanie would never harm an animal. A human being, yes—a sister, yes—but not an animal.

As if sensing Charles's concern, or her twin's confidence, Melanie slowed the gait to a gentle rocking canter. She circled the field twice, then loped back toward the group. She pulled up near Steve, her chest heaving from the exercise, her cheeks flushed, her hair a wild damp tangle of gold.

"Now," she whispered to Steve as she caught her breath. Her eyes swept toward Charles for a moment, but he had turned away, bored and uninterested in *her*, to talk to Mitchell.

You bastard, Melanie thought.

"You're glowering, Melanie," Steve observed cheerfully, looking at her through the lens of his camera. "Give me one of your Good-Day Sunshine looks, please."

"Do you think she can act?" Mitchell asked Charles and Adam after the photo session was over.

"Sure," Adam answered confidently.

"Why?" Charles asked quickly.

"Because she's perfect. I'm not a big believer in models becoming actresses. Usually they're stiff or their voices aren't good. But Melanie's flawless."

Flawless, Charles mused. That had been his initial impression of her, too.

"I wonder how easy it would be to direct her," Charles said.

"Easy," Adam assured him. "She's not temperamental. She's tireless, energetic, professional. . . ."

"What do you think, Charles? This is really your decision. You and Jason *are* the executive producers."

"What am I deciding?"

"Whether to ask Melanie if she's interested in playing Sapphire in the movie. It's not really much of a risk. Melanie Chandler will be big box office, even if she can't act. My bet is she'll be sensational."

"Brooke and Galen and Mitchell and I are dining at La Côte tonight, Adam," Charles answered without answering. "Why don't you and Melanie join us?"

Of course I can act, Melanie thought later that evening when Mitchell posed the question to her. I've been acting all my life. What did you think of my performance with Steve today? Or with Charles? Or even now . . .

"It would be fun to try," Melanie purred prettily.

Why the false modesty, Brooke wondered. Melanie played the lead in all the productions in high school, and she was very good.

"So you'll do it?" Galen asked. Melanie had made Sapphire come alive today. Working with Melanie would be so comfortable and so much fun!

"It's up to Charles, isn't it?" Melanie tilted her head and threw a pale-blue dare: Tell me I can't have the role, Charles. Tell me in front of all of them.

"It's up to Charles and Jason," Charles responded evenly. "And then there's the contract. You might not like the terms."

"Which are . . .?"

"We'll draw it up. I've just made the decision for Jason." Charles smiled a handsome, aristocratic smile at Melanie. Then he turned to Brooke and the smile became human. "You should go over it with a good attorney."

Quality is always worth the price. That was Charles Sinclair's motto. I don't want to know the price you put on my twin, Charles, Brooke thought. I don't want to know how much you're willing to pay for a few months of Melanie Chandler's golden life.

Brooke thought those troublesome thoughts, but her blue eyes sparkled at Charles.

Brooke actually likes him, Melanie realized with amazement. So does Galen. Don't they see it? Don't they see that the only person Charles Sinclair cares about is Charles Sinclair?

But it's not *true*, a renegade part of her mind argued. Charles does care about Brooke and Galen. He asks Brooke's opinion and listens carefully and thoughtfully to what she says. Charles respects Brooke, and he is helping Galen realize her dreams.

Charles just doesn't care about *you*, Melanie.

"What's the time frame?" Adam asked.

"Galen," Mitchell's voice softened, as all voices softened when they looked into the timid-trying-to-be-brave emerald eyes, "says she'll have the screenplay done by May. The plot and chronology can go as is. It's just a matter of translating the emotion and romance of the prose into dialogue. The characters need to speak their feelings instead of thinking them."

Just, Galen trembled at the word. That's *just* exactly what I've never been able to do. But with Jason's help, and Charles's . . .

"And then revisions in June and July," Galen added boldly. *Revisions* was a word she could say now. The *revised* version of "Sapphire" was better than the original. "So, in August or September we go to Kenya."

"Oh-oh." Melanie looked at Adam.

"We've already made commitments to the major couturiers and jewelers in France and Italy for August and September."

"You'll be in Europe for two months?"

"That's what the boss tells me." When Adam told her about it a week ago, Melanie was thrilled. She and four other models would spend two months showing the fabulous clothes and jewels of Dior, Lacroix, Van Cleef and Arpels, Chanel, Gucci, Saint Laurent, de la Renta, Tiel . . .

Between the photo sessions and shows they would explore Paris and Cannes and Monte Carlo and Rome and Milan and Naples and Florence.

"How about mid-October to mid-December?" Mitchell suggested.

"Fine with me." Melanie smiled amiably.

"And me," Galen agreed. "Charles?"

"I guess. I'm trying to remember when Jason will be away for the America's Cup trials."

He won't be, Galen thought.

"Jason will want to be there, too?" Mitchell asked.

"Yes," Charles answered. "We'll both want to go."

"Who will run Sinclair Publishing?" Brooke teased.

"Is that an offer, Brooke? Because if it is you've got it."

Brooke blushed, laughed softly, and shook her dark brown curls.

"Mitchell," Melanie's voice was low and seductive, "have you thought about who you will cast as Jeremy?"

Jeremy was Sapphire's roguish, sexy, daring lover; the man who unleashed her hidden passion.

"I don't know, Melanie." Anyone you want.

CHAPTER TWELVE

New York City
February 1986

"$\mathcal{I}$t will take me all night to finish the revisions for 'Jade.' I promised I would have them to Charles before he leaves for Paris."

"And you will."

"If I work all night. I feel guilty that I didn't get them to him sooner. But," Galen's voice softened lovingly, "that's your fault."

"It's your fault for making me need you every minute. Can't you finish them over here?" Jason was in his apartment on Riverside Drive. Galen was in her tiny room in the brownstone in Greenwich Village.

"Not if you're there."

"I won't bother you."

"I would want you to."

"Come over when you're done. Whenever."

"It will take me all night."

"I won't throw the dead bolt, just in case."

"Jason."

"You're really not coming over?"

"No," she sighed wistfully. "I'm really not."

When his doorbell rang at eleven o'clock that night, Jason assumed it would be Galen. She had her own key, but maybe her arms were full of a not-quite-revised manuscript, hyacinth-scented candles, and fountain pens. Jason was already smiling as he opened the door.

"*Fran.*" The smile faded quickly.

"Is she here?"

"No."

"May I come in?"

Jason frowned. "Fran . . .

"Jason, please, just for a minute." The dark-brown eyes were liquid and her lips trembled.

Reluctantly, Jason opened the door wide and stood aside as she entered. This was pointless and painful, but she was so upset.

"Who is she, Jason? I have a right to know."

"It doesn't matter who she is," Jason said firmly. No one knew. Galen and Jason hadn't even told Charles, yet. It was still too precious to share.

"It matters to me."

"Fran, we've gone over this."

Jason told Fran in November, the day after Galen sent the pale-pink note, that he couldn't see her anymore. It was difficult for both of them; they were good together. Jason had almost decided he was in love with her.

But that was because Jason didn't know what love was. He didn't know until Galen.

"You're still seeing her, aren't you?"

"Yes."

Jason told Fran his new love was forever when she called him in early December. And he told her again when she called in January.

"You're going to marry her?"

"Yes." Jason and Galen had never talked about marriage, but he knew. They both knew.

Fran began to cry.

"I'm sorry, Jason," she whispered, impatiently wiping tears that wouldn't stop. "I miss you so much. I really thought what we had was good."

"It *was* good," Jason said gently. He cared about Fran. He was sorry he hurt her. It was an honest mistake. If he had known there could be magic, he would never have gotten so involved with Fran. But he hadn't known.

"Hold me, Jason," she pleaded.

Jason moved beside her and wrapped his arms around the lovely body he had known so intimately. Jason felt no rush of desire; he only felt sorry that Fran had been hurt.

After a few minutes she pulled free.

"Will you just talk to me for a while, Jason? Not about her or us."

They sat in the living room and drank bourbon and talked about safe, neutral topics that had nothing to do with either of them. Fran inadvertently stumbled onto the most personal topic of all.

" 'Emerald' was wonderful. Galen's next story will appear in the March issue, is that right?"

"Yes," Jason replied evenly. He didn't want Fran to know about Galen. He could imagine Fran confronting Galen, trying to convince her, as Fran had tried to convince him in December and January, that she and Jason belonged together.

"When I first read about naive, innocent, trusting Emerald, I wondered how you could have chosen me for the art—*You* of all people." Fran's provocative brown eyes reminded him of their not-so-innocent lovemaking until Jason's eyes reminded her that it was over. She sighed and continued thoughtfully, "Sorry. Anyway, I was like Emerald, once upon a time. Maybe there's a part of Emerald in everyone."

"Maybe."

"I had dinner with Galen—and Brooke and Melanie—last month. Galen is so quiet. I guess the passion is deep inside her."

"I guess so." Jason's mind spun. Why hadn't Galen told him about dinner with Fran? It must have bothered her. Why hadn't she shared it with him?

"So," Fran began carefully. She didn't want to make Jason angry. "It's two in the morning. You're not spending the night with her tonight whoever she—"

"No."

"Let me stay, Jason."

"No."

"Just let me fall asleep in your arms one last time. I don't want you to make love with me. Just hold me."

"*No.*"

"It won't hurt you," Fran pleaded as tears filled her eyes. "And it will help me."

"How?"

"It will make it seem more real. Talking to you has helped. You don't look at me the way you used to." Her voice was so sad. "And being in bed with you without making love to you . . . well, that never would have happened, would it?"

"It's not going to happen."

"I *know*. I won't try to seduce you. It would be too humiliating."

Jason shook his head slightly and sighed. Fran was unhappy and exhausted and it was late. She'd had too much to drink. If it would help her, he could let her fall asleep in his arms.

Jason took her hand and led her into the bedroom. He didn't bother to clear the empty crystal glasses from the table. And he didn't remember to throw the dead bolt.

Charles is going to like this, Galen decided as she read the final page of her revised version of "Jade."

It was five A.M. Galen looked out her small window into the predawn darkness of the cold February morning. She wanted to be with Jason. She reached for the phone to tell him to release the dead bolt, but she didn't dial.

Jason had probably forgotten to throw it anyway. He usually forgot. Jason didn't worry about the daily robberies that plagued the wealthy inhabitants of Manhattan. Maybe he didn't even know about them. Jason couldn't read the newspaper, and that sort of crime rarely made the television or radio news. There were worse crimes to report in Manhattan.

Galen smiled. She would surprise him, awakening him with gentle kisses . . .

Galen let herself in with her key. The hall light was on. Funny. Jason usually turned it off. Maybe he was expecting her.

Galen pulled up abruptly when she saw a coat, a woman's coat, on the chair.

As she noticed the two empty highball glasses on the table a sense of dread washed through her.

No. It isn't possible. It can't be.

Galen's heart pounded and her stomach churned as she forced herself to walk toward Jason's bedroom. She didn't want to know, but she had to.

The bedroom door was open. The soft light from the hall illuminated the room. Galen only looked for an instant, but her mind made a memory she would never forget, its every detail perfectly and indelibly preserved.

Fran's clothes were tossed carelessly—because their passion couldn't wait?—on the floor. She wore Jason's pajamas; at least, his pajama *top*. Fran's arms draped across Jason's chest and her head lay in the crook of his arm. The rest of her body was hidden beneath the covers with his. Jason slept peacefully, his strong arms casually encircling her. His tousled golden hair glowed in the darkness.

It was a beautiful tranquil picture—the perfect portrait of lovers satiated from a night of passion.

I hate you, Jason, Galen's heart screamed as she ran through the dark, cold, dangerous streets of Manhattan. I will always hate you. I hate you for doing this to us. I hate you for doing this to love.

I hate you for doing this to Emerald . . .

Emerald. Jason lay in bed with Fran, the woman whose lovely image appeared next to her words; the real Emerald. The Emerald Jason *really* loved.

Galen telephoned Charles at ten.

"I'll send the revisions over by courier this morning."

"Fine. Are you happy with them?"

Happy? Galen mused.

"Yes. Of course. Have a nice trip, Charles."

Galen hung up before Charles could answer.

Charles waited ten minutes before calling her back. Maybe she was just exhausted; emotionally exhausted from immersing herself in her story and physically exhausted from staying up all night.

But Galen's voice hadn't sounded like exhaustion. It had sounded like despair.

"What's wrong?" Charles asked directly when she answered the phone.

"I—" Her voice broke. "I can't talk about it."

Charles waited without speaking for several moments.

"Why don't I come over?" he suggested finally.

"No, Charles, thank you. I'll be fine, really. I just need some time." Time. How much time? Would any amount of time lessen the pain? Galen added flatly, "I just need to grow up."

But it had nothing to do with growing up, Galen realized. It had to do with abandoning everything she believed. She had always believed—it was simply faith until she met Jason—in love. She believed in it with all her being. Her stories celebrated the wonder and magic of love.

Now she knew the truth. It was all a myth.

"I'm available, Galen. At least, until about two."

"Then off to Paris."

"You can reach me there, too. My secretary has my itinerary. Galen?"

"Yes. Thank you, Charles. I'm all right. Really. Good-bye."

Five minutes after Charles's second conversation with Galen, Jason appeared at his door.

"Good morning."

"Jason."

"Did Galen get the revisions for 'Jade' to you?" Jason asked casually. He had expected to hear from her by now. He didn't want to waken her if she was asleep.

"She called. She's sending them over."

"Oh." Jason concealed his disappointment. He hoped she would bring them over herself. He wanted to see her. He wanted her in his arms. Nothing had happened with Fran, *of course*, but it felt so wrong. There was only one woman who belonged in his arms or in his bed or in his life.

Galen was probably asleep now. He would wait until early afternoon before calling.

The revisions for "Jade" arrived by courier at eleven-thirty. As Charles put them in his briefcase, he thought about his trip to Paris and about Galen. The trip to Paris was business. It was part of his responsibility, as editor-in-chief of *Fashion*, to view the spring collections of the major couturiers of Europe. It was a responsibility Charles enjoyed. The fashion shows were exciting, and there were other pleasures, like Monique.

But the hedonistic pleasures were easily expendable if Galen needed him . . .

"Galen?"

"Charles. They should be there any minute." The lifeless voice spoke with great effort.

"They're here. That's not why I'm calling."

"Oh."

"Have you ever been to Paris, not counting the airport?"

"No."

"Why don't you come with me? It sounds like you need to get away."

"Run away," Galen breathed. She was suddenly tempted, *so* tempted.

No, Charles thought. Paris is getting away. St. Barts is running away. . . . In three months, in May, he would run away—for a while—to St. Barts.

"I'll be at the shows all day. You could join me or wander around Paris or stay in the hotel and work on your screenplay or take luxurious bubble baths . . ."

Charles thought he heard a soft laugh. I'm your friend, Galen, let me help you.

"I wouldn't be very good company."

"I'm not looking for company, Galen." I wasn't very good company for you once, either, when I was delirious, but you never left my side. And that was *before* we were friends.

Jason telephoned Galen at one-thirty. He had waited long enough.

"Hi." He was relieved to hear her voice. "Were you sleeping?"

"No," she answered flatly, her heart pounding.

Galen didn't want to talk to Jason, but she had to. It had to be behind her. She hadn't decided by the time Jason called if she would tell him she had seen him with Fran. What if he tried to make an excuse or offer an explanation? It would be so humiliating.

No excuses or explanations, Galen decided impulsively. And I don't have to explain, either.

"I'm not sleeping. I'm packing. I'm going on a trip."

"*What?*" The sound of her flat, lifeless voice worried him as much as her words.

"I'm going to Paris with Charles."

"Charles," Jason breathed in disbelief.

"Charles sensed I needed to get away. He offered to take me with him."

"Why do you need to get away?" Jason asked carefully. She must know about Fran. *Somehow*. I have to explain.

"I just do."

"I didn't throw the dead bolt last night. I thought you might come over."

"I told you I wouldn't."

"And you didn't?"

"I told you I wouldn't," Galen repeated. "Why?"

"Because I want to be certain we don't have our signals crossed." Jason was going to tell her, when his arms were around her, about the *nothing* that had happened with Fran and how *terrible* it made him feel. He wouldn't tell her now, over the phone, unless the flatness in her voice was because of Fran.

But it wasn't because of Fran. Galen hadn't come over. So what had happened? It had to be Charles. . . .

"I don't think we have our signals crossed, Jason."

"Then what has changed since last night?"

The tears came then, washing away the anger and the control, drenching her in sadness. She couldn't speak. She didn't want him to hear the tears. She didn't want him to know how much he had hurt her.

"Galen?" His voice was so gentle.

Galen forced herself to remember what she had seen in his bedroom. With the vivid, painful memory came the emotion: I hate you.

"It's over."

"Over? How can it be over?"

"You know about love, Jason, it's all a fiction anyway."

"I *don't* know that."

Well, I do, thanks to you.

"I have to go. Good-bye, Jason."

Jason held the receiver in his hand long after the line had disconnected.

Charles. He had always been there, part of Galen's life. Maybe Charles and Galen had loved each other, years before, in Africa. Maybe they found that love again. In spite of what Galen felt for Jason, her feelings for his twin were stronger. It explained why Galen wanted to keep *their* love private, hidden from the world and from Charles. All this time, Galen had been struggling to make a choice. And now she had made it.

It isn't possible, Jason's mind screamed. But it was. Galen was going away with Charles. She had chosen Charles.

Jason walked out of his office and into his brother's. He needed to know.

I need to know if Charles has taken away someone *else* I love. Jason shuddered at the unsummoned thought and the hatred that churned inside him.

Charles wasn't in his office. He had already left.

Jason took a taxi to the brownstone on Spring Street. The young bearded man who answered the door told him that Galen had gone on a trip. She would be away for one week.

CHAPTER THIRTEEN

She is devastated, Charles thought. Whatever it is, it's tearing her apart.

Galen didn't speak during the taxi ride from Spring Street to JFK, except to acknowledge Charles and his kindness—briefly and awkwardly—with a trembling smile and eyes that threatened to cry, *again*.

When Charles handed the first-class tickets to the agent, Galen murmured, almost to herself, "I don't have money with me. I'll have to pay you back."

Galen had money in the bank. She had been paid substantial advances for the four short stories that would appear in *Images*, for her book, *Songs of the Savanna*, and the screenplay for "Sapphire." The advances were payments for *promises*; Galen wondered now if they were promises she could keep. Her mind was so foggy and her heart ached. What if she had lost the clarity and peace so necessary to her writing?

Charles got the boarding passes and touched her briefly on the shoulder, indicating the way toward the first-class lounge on the concourse. Before they reached the lounge, when they were away from the crush of passengers in the main terminal, he stopped and faced her.

"It's on me."

"What?"

"You're not paying for any of this. You're my guest."

"Charles, I . . ." Tears spilled down her cheeks. "Thank you."

She was so raw and so fragile. Whatever it was, *whomever* it was had taken her life and smashed it into a thousand pieces. If he could undo it for her, he would.

But he couldn't. He could only be her friend.

Charles put his arm around her small, thin shoulders. So fragile . . .

They stayed in adjacent suites in the Hotel Meurice on the Place Vendôme. The first night, during a gourmet dinner Galen barely touched, Charles tried to pique her interest in the City of Light.

"The Meurice is centrally located. You can walk, safely, to the Louvre, the Jeu de Paume, the Rodin Museum, Sainte-Chapelle, Notre-Dame, and the Left Bank. It's a long but interesting walk along the Champs-Elysées to the Arc de Triomphe. You should probably take the Métro—it's very easy, Galen—if you want to go to the Eiffel Tower or Montmartre. Of course, you're welcome to come see the collections with me. Tomorrow morning I'll be at Chanel." Charles looked at the sad distant eyes glistening in candlelight and asked gently, "Galen?"

"Yes?" She almost jumped. Her mind had been so far away. "Charles, I'm sorry. Not very good company . . ."

"It's OK, honey."

"You're so nice to me."

That evening, before saying good night and withdrawing to their separate suites, Charles and Galen made arrangements to meet for lunch at Charles's favorite sidewalk cafe in the Latin Quarter. Charles circled the location on the pocket map of Paris he bought for her.

The next day, after viewing the fabulous Chanel spring collection and murmuring apologies to Monique, France's most glamorous model, Charles rushed to the Latin Quarter. He arrived ten minutes late. It didn't matter; Galen wasn't there. Charles waited for two hours, until it was time, past time, for him to be at Yves St. Laurent.

Where the hell was she?

Probably blissfully lost in the wonders of the Louvre, Charles tried to reassure himself. It happened to him in the Louvre or in front of the rose window in Saint-Chapelle or gazing across the Seine at the flying buttresses of Notre-Dame. Charles often lost track of time in Paris.

But Galen wasn't a happy tourist discovering the limitless joys of Paris. She was despondent and distracted. What if she wandered in front of a speeding car, or into the Seine . . .

As the magnificent St. Laurent spring collection paraded past on some of the world's most breathtaking models, Charles's anxiety increased.

You should be out looking for her. You shouldn't have left her alone. You shouldn't have brought her with you if you couldn't take care of her.

Charles wanted to leave, but he couldn't. It would be impossible—physically *or* politely—to extricate himself from his chair of honor at the end of the runway.

Finally, mercifully, it was over.

Charles checked for messages with the concierge in the mirror and marble lobby of the Meurice. There were none. But there was a note on the door to his suite: *Charles, I'm sorry, Galen.*

Charles knocked on the door of her suite.

"Galen?" Please be all right.

The door opened slowly. Her pale, drawn face and her dark-circled emerald eyes told him it had been a sleepless night and a tormented day.

Galen hadn't been blissfully lost in the treasures of the Louvre.

"Are you all right?"

"I forgot about our lunch, Charles. I'm sorry."

"You've been here all day, haven't you?"

She nodded, head bent.

"Come here." Charles guided her gently to the silk chaise lounge near the window that overlooked the Tuileries and the Seine. Charles sat beside her, holding her hands. "Look at me, Galen."

The red-gold head lifted slowly.

"Tell me."

"Charles, no, I can't."

Her head started to drop again, but he caught her chin, lifting it, making her eyes meet his.

"Tell me."

Galen's eyes filled with tears and she tried to look away. But he wouldn't let her.

"Galen."

"I . . . I loved him so much, Charles," she whispered through the tears.

"What happened?"

"He never loved me." That was all Galen could say that night. The tears came and she didn't have the energy to fight them.

Charles held her against him until her silent sobs subsided, finally vanquished by exhaustion. He carried her into the bedroom, gently tucked her into bed, and stayed until she fell asleep.

Galen spent the following day at the Louvre. That night Charles dined at the Tour d'Argent with the *joailliers* from Van Cleef and Arpels. Galen remained at the Meurice and went to bed early. The next evening Charles made reservations for them at *Taillevent*, but, at the last minute, he and Galen decided to dine in his suite.

"I think I'll go to Versailles the day after tomorrow. Could you join me?"

"No." Charles watched her reaction. She was going to go anyway. *Good.* "I wish I could. Be sure to walk to Le Petit Trianon."

"Marie Antoinette's hunting lodge? I will." Galen tilted her head and gazed at him thoughtfully. "You think I'll survive this?"

"You already are."

"Not really. You're protecting me."

"I'm not."

Galen smiled a soft, wistful smile. *Yes, you are.*

"I've always had someone protecting me. Until I moved to New York, it was my parents. Then it was you. Then it was—"

"Him."

"Him," Galen repeated quietly. *Your brother. Your twin.*

"And you were in love with him," Charles said carefully. Galen had told him nothing more since the night she cried in his arms.

"Love." Galen's voice was distant, because love was a distant memory, a blurry dream. "Do you believe in love, Charles?"

"For some people, yes. For people like you, people like Jason—"

"But not for you?" Galen asked swiftly. Her mind reeled at Jason's name. *No, Charles, love isn't for people like Jason.*

"No," Charles answered easily. It *was* easy if he didn't think about the reason—the inexplicable, impenetrable hatred of the father whose love he wanted so desperately. "I'm not meant to love." *Or to be loved.*

"What about Viveca?"

"*Viveca?*" Charles's surprise was genuine. He and Viveca had been "dating" since early January. Charles liked Viveca. He liked the sultry, inquisitive sensuality that smoldered beneath the frilly Southern belle fluff. But *love?*

"Yes. You—" Galen blushed.

She is so naive and innocent, Charles thought, suddenly feeling great anger toward the unknown man who had hurt her so deeply.

"You sleep with her, don't you, Charles?" Galen asked bravely. *See I'm not so naive or innocent any more.*

"It may be my fate not to love, but I'm not doomed to loneliness." Charles smiled as he spoke, but his words made her sad eyes even sadder. "Galen?"

"I want you to be happy, Charles."

"Galen, I *am* happy. I'm living my life exactly the way I want to," Charles told her truthfully. *I am living my dream.* "Even if there isn't love, there are wonderful, warm moments to share."

"Sharing warm, wonderful moments," Galen mused. "That's far better than living the illusion of love."

"Did it feel like an illusion when you were with him, Galen?"

"No," she sighed softly. "But he—"

"He made a big mistake."

"Make love to me, Charles."

It was their final night in Paris. They were in Charles's suite, drinking champagne. The golden lights of Paris twinkled below.

"Galen."

"Share a warm, wonderful moment with me."

"Honey, this isn't the answer." Charles spoke gently to the lovely emerald eyes.

"I'm not looking for answers."

"You are looking for ways to be strong and independent."

"This is a way." *I need to know how it feels to make love with someone I don't love. I need to know how it felt for Jason every time he made love with me. That knowledge will give me strength.*

"No." Charles touched her hot, flushed cheek with his strong cool fingers.

"Don't you like me, Charles?"

"You know I do." *I like you too much to do this, even though I want to. . . .*

"Charles."

Galen's soft lips, tentative and trembling, found his.

"Galen," Charles whispered. His lips brushed lightly against hers. Then he wrapped his strong arms around her and drew her close.

Galen's kiss became confident and demanding. She opened her soft mouth to welcome him. Charles responded; his deep, intimate kiss betrayed his desire and passion. Galen's mind spun. The tender lips that kissed her, the gentle, experienced hands that explored her, the sensual, sleek body that wanted her didn't belong to an unknown lover. They belonged to Charles, her dear friend with the dark seductive eyes and hidden passions and lips that . . .

Lips that were kissing her naked breasts and making her tremble with deep, warm, tingling sensations.

You don't need to be so careful, Charles! I'm not that fragile. I know how to do this. I want *to do this with you.*

Galen awakened at eight A.M. She was alone in the bed, Charles's bed. She closed her eyes briefly, remembering the tenderness of the night. He had been so gentle! They had shared a warm, wonderful moment of their lives. It hadn't felt awkward or wrong, and she had learned what she needed to know. It was possible to make love without being *in* love. Jason had made love with her even though he was in love with Fran. And she had made love with Charles even though she was in love with . . .

She had proven it. The knowledge gave her strength, even though it was more proof—devastating proof—of her own foolish naiveté.

As Galen lay in Charles's bed, remembering the tender intimacy of their loving, a wave of panic swept through her. How could she face him? What did Charles think of her? Galen didn't have answers, but she knew that she couldn't put it off. She had to see him, face him, and leave.

Galen frowned, sighed, and got out of bed. Her hands trembled as she dressed and hurriedly brushed her red-blond tangles. She took a deep breath and opened the bedroom door. Charles sat in the living room, fully dressed, reading the *International Tribune*. He stood up when she appeared.

"Good morning."

Galen couldn't meet his inquisitive, probing eyes. She had *made love* with him! And she felt naked still.

"I have to go," Galen whispered.

"Go?"

"Go pack. When is our plane . . . ?"

"We leave the hotel at noon."

"All right." Galen started to move toward the door. Charles caught up with her and blocked her path.

"Galen, what we did last night was nice. I don't know if we'll ever do it again— we both have to think about it—but it was *nice*. It didn't hurt us and it didn't hurt our friendship." Charles made her look at him. "Did it?"

"No." Galen smiled a shy smile. She added courageously, "And it was nice."

"Good. Then how about some tea and croissants?"

"No, thank you. I really do have to pack." And I have to think about what happened last night. And, Galen realized with dread, I have to prepare to return to New York and my life without Jason.

Galen spent the next two weeks in her tiny room on Spring Street. She made a few false starts toward the outside world, but they always ended just inside the front door of the brownstone. She couldn't go outside. Jason was out there, somewhere, and he was with Fran.

Galen needed to write. She had promised the screenplay of "Sapphire" by May and the revisions for "Garnet" by June. But now that she knew the truth, how could she perpetuate the myth? She couldn't write about love anymore. Love—the wonderful, magical love of Emerald and Sapphire and Jade and Garnet—didn't exist.

Galen couldn't write about the fantasy, and she couldn't write about the *reality*; the shattered dream was too close and too painful. And who would want to read about it anyway?

Night after sleepless night, in darkness illuminated by her candles and warmly scented with French vanilla and hyacinth and lilac, Galen grieved for what she had lost. She grieved for the dream, and for the man.

She missed Jason so much!

Galen missed Jason, and she missed Charles. She wanted to talk to Charles, but she couldn't find the energy to call him.

Two weeks after she and Charles returned from Paris a package arrived in the afternoon mail.

"Oh," Galen breathed as she carefully removed the lilac silk and ivory lace dress from the neatly folded tissue paper. It was so beautiful. Beneath the dress were two gold barrettes and a small cream-colored envelope. Galen opened the envelope slowly. What if it was from Jason? What would she do?

The card read, *Galen, this seemed like you. Melanie.*

"This is Melanie." Melanie answered her call in the models' dressing room.

"Melanie, it's Galen. Am I interrupting?"

"No. They're setting up the studio for the next session."

"Thank you so much."

"Oh, it arrived already?"

"Yes. It's lovely. I've never . . ." I've never seen such a beautiful dress.

"Worn lilac? But does it work? I thought *that* shade, and *your* hair, might."

Galen hadn't thought about how the dress would look on *her*. She would never wear something so beautiful. But now, in response to Melanie's question, Galen stood in front of the cracked mirror on the wall and held the dress against her. Strands of her red-gold hair fell across the fabric. The effect was stunning.

"It's perfect," Galen whispered truthfully.

"And it fits all right?"

"Oh." She should have tried it on before calling, but it hadn't occurred to her. "Yes."

"Good. I have an image of you wearing it with your hair in swirls dotted with small sprays of pink and white lilacs." It was more than an image; it was how Melanie sketched it when she designed the dress for Galen.

"Sounds lovely."

"However, failing lilacs, I included those gold barrettes. I thought if you swept your hair off your face—a soft sweep, the way Brooke does her hair—it would look nice."

"Oh, yes, I see," Galen murmured.

"Are you OK, Galen? You sound—"

"I'm fine, Melanie. I'm just overwhelmed. It's so beautiful."

"I'm glad you like it. Oh-oh. They're calling for me. I have to go. Galen, let's get together soon, all right?"

"Yes, sure, I'd like that."

After Melanie hung up, Galen tried on the dress. It fit perfectly. The soft hues of the dress and her hair and her eyes blended into a harmonious bouquet of color. It was as if the lilac-and-ivory dress had been made especially for her. Galen wondered where Melanie found it. There was no label.

Her spirits lifted by the beautiful dress and Melanie's thoughtfulness, Galen impulsively dialed the number to the private line in Charles's office.

"Hello."

"Hello." Charles was relieved to hear her voice. He knew she needed time and she would call when she was ready, but still he worried. "How are you?"

"Not making great strides."

"I would try for baby steps. Are you writing?"

"Can't."

"I'm not a big believer in writer's block."

"I'm too unfocused."

"Maybe writing would help you focus."

"Maybe. You're not really a very sympathetic sort, are you?" Her voice had a slight lilt, a little tease. She knew Charles was her friend. She knew, too, that sometimes he helped her most by pushing her.

"I don't think you need sympathy. You probably need dinner, though, knowing the way you tend not to eat. How about tomorrow night? La Lumière?"

La Lumière. She and Jason—*she*—had fallen in love at La Lumière. She couldn't go back there; but she *had* to. La Lumirè was exactly where she needed to go. She even had a beautiful dress to wear.

"That would be nice." Nice. Making love had been *nice*. But she couldn't do that again, not now, not yet, maybe not ever. "Charles?"

"Just dinner?"

"Is that OK?"

"Of course. I told you it was something we would have to think about." Charles added easily, "And you have."

But what about you, Galen wondered. Have you thought about it? What do you want?

"I'll be by at eight," Charles said.

"Why don't I just meet you at the restaurant? I know where it is."

All right, Charles thought. If it makes you feel strong and independent.

"*Galen.*"

"Hello, Charles." She blushed. "New dress."

Before Charles could reply, Henri, the maitre d', offered to seat them. Henri was not in the habit of keeping the Sinclairs waiting. Henri looked at Galen and silently admired Charles's taste, as he always did. All of Charles Sinclair's women were magnificent, but this woman was so different from Charles's usual companions. Hers was a serene, timeless beauty, not a confident, glamorous, contemporary one. Henri approved, and so did Charles.

"I like your hair that way," Charles told Galen after they were seated and had ordered champagne cocktails.

"Melanie said I should make swirls of hair and lilacs. This is a compromise."

"Melanie? Did she help you find the dress?"

"She sent it to me."

"Out of the blue?"

"Yes. When I called to thank her she made it sound like nothing."

It wasn't *nothing*, Charles knew. The dress—a terribly expensive original design—looked as if it had been made especially for Galen. To have seen the dress and known how perfect it would be for Galen took a very special eye, not to mention time and effort and care.

Melanie?

"Did she say where she got it?" Charles couldn't guess at the label. He knew the work of the major designers; it wasn't one of them. It was a new, innovative talent, someone whose designs would become familiar to him and who he might someday feature in the pages of *Fashion*.

"No, but I wonder." Galen shook her head. It seemed impossible. But . . . there was no label, so much had been sewn by hand, and it was exactly the right size. Clothes were never the right size for her; she always had to make alterations.

"What?"

"I wonder if Melanie made it."

"No," Charles said definitively. "No."

Jason entered the restaurant just as Charles and Galen were leaving. He was alone. Jason's motive for dining at La Lumière was the same as Galen's; it was part of saying good-bye to the dream.

"Galen!"

"*Jason.*"

"Hello, Jason." Charles smiled at his twin. The smile was untainted, neither apology nor gloat.

Jason had seen very little of Charles in the past two weeks; he hadn't wanted to. He realized now, as his eyes met his twin's, that Charles had no idea that he and Galen had ever been together.

Galen never told Charles about us, Jason thought sadly. We weren't that important to her. All that mattered—her top priority—was that she didn't hurt the only man she really loved, *Charles*.

Jason didn't want to look at her, but he couldn't help it. How she had blossomed—proud and beautiful—nurtured by Charles's love!

Galen didn't want to look at Jason; but she couldn't help it, either. She made herself think about Fran as her eyes met his.

I am going to survive this, Jason.

PART TWO

CHAPTER FOURTEEN

New York City
March 1986

It was dark, and he was warm and strong, and his lips were soft and gentle, and he wanted her. The demanding sensations swirling inside her wanted her to let him love her. It would be so easy. He wanted her so much and her mind was playing wonderful tricks, pretending he was Charles . . .

Brooke pulled away.

"Andrew."

"Brooke?" Andrew had dark, seductive eyes, like Charles.

"I can't. This is wrong. Your wife . . ."

Allison Parker had been home and "normal" since early January. But last night, Andrew told Brooke over cocktails at the Hunt Club, he had to face the agony of taking Allison back to the sanitarium. Andrew spoke softly, sensitively, and the intimacy of the conversation flowed so easily into the intimacy of the kiss . . .

"Let me worry about Allison."

But you love her, Andrew, Brooke thought. Not that what drove Brooke and Andrew into each other's arms was *love*. It was much simpler than that—just unfulfilled sexual desire and loneliness.

"I can't anyway, Andrew." Even though it would be so easy.

Andrew touched Brooke's flushed cheek gently and smiled.

"Friends?"

"Of course."

Their hands touched the book at exactly the same moment.

"Oh!" she exclaimed, looking up into the face. It was a strong, handsome face, framed in dark black curls and highlighted, a subtle, understated highlight, with steel-gray eyes.

"Sorry." He took his hand from the book. "Ladies first."

"What about tie goes to the runner?"

"I think 'ladies first' wins over everything."

"Well," she said hopefully, but unconvincingly, "there must be another copy."

"There will be on Monday."

It was Saturday. The book, a collection of short stories entitled *Reflections* was released on Thursday and sold quickly. More copies, hastily reordered, would arrive on Monday. At that moment she held the only unsold copy in Manhattan.

"Were you planning your weekend around this book?" she asked. *She* had been. She was going to hide in her apartment, away from the late-winter snow, and escape into the book the critics hailed as the best collection of short stories in a decade.

"It was going to be my Saturday night," he answered. "I have to work this afternoon."

"Well,"—she had a briefcase of work—"I don't *have* to have it this evening. I can read it this afternoon and you can have it tonight."

"Really?"

"Sure," she agreed as they walked to the cash register. He started to withdraw some bills from his wallet, but she held up her hand. "I'll buy it. Ladies first."

They walked into the cold March morning. The snow was falling lightly adding a clean fresh layer to the foot that already blanketed the city.

"I should have written my address for you while we were still inside." Her gloveless hands started to search in her purse for a pen and paper.

"Just tell it to me."

He listened, nodding slightly when she finished.

"And what's your name?"

"Brooke."

His lips curved into a slow, knowing smile and his gray eyes twinkled.

"Why? What's yours?"

"Nick." He watched her ocean-blue eyes widen.

"Lieutenant." She laughed softly, extended a cold hand to him, and felt the warmth and strength of his handshake.

"Counselor. At last we meet."

"Yes," she murmured. The thank-you that she had been dreading for seven months suddenly seemed easy. "What you did last September . . . It was a gentle way for me to learn a hard lesson. Thank you."

Nick shrugged. "So, when shall I come by to get the book? What time are you leaving for the evening?"

"I'm not leaving. Any time is fine."

"You don't have plans?"

"No."

"How about seven?"

"That's fine."

"I'll see you then, Brooke."

"I'm sorry," Nick apologized as soon as Brooke opened the door. He was an hour late. "We were interviewing a suspect. I couldn't even get away to call."

"It's no problem. *Interviewing?*"

"Interrogating." Nick grinned.

"Someone I know?"

"Someone you may get to know. We need a little more evidence before we can make a charge that will stick."

"And you know how *we* are about evidence!"

"Indeed."

"Anyway, you couldn't have called to let me know. My telephone number is unlisted."

"You don't think that's really an obstacle, do you?" Nick teased. He could get any number for any address in the city in a matter of minutes, for police business. But this—Brooke—was personal.

"Oh." Her cheeks pinkened slightly. Another just-out-of-law-school remark. Brooke had been with the DA's office for nine months. She was beginning to feel comfortable, but there was something about Nick's casual confidence that made her uncertain about herself and all the things she didn't know.

"How is the book?"

"Wonderful. I haven't—"

"Finished? That's good. At least I hope it means each story is so good that you want to linger over it—live with it—for a while before going on to the next."

"That's what it means." Brooke handed him the book.

"Well, don't worry. I'll return it to you bright and early tomorrow morning."

"That's OK. I can linger over the ones I've read until Monday."

"That good?"

"Yes."

They stood in the entry area of her small apartment. Nick's hand still rested on the doorknob, poised to leave as soon as he got the book. Now he had it, but he hesitated. Brooke said she didn't have plans. What the hell . . .

"Have you eaten?"

"No. I've been reading and lingering."

"And I've been interrogating since noon. Would you like to go somewhere?"

It was Brooke's turn to hesitate.

"No?" he asked pleasantly.

"I don't know." She had taken the afternoon off to read *Reflections*. She had planned to spend the evening with the contents of her bulging briefcase.

"When do you think you'll know?" Nick asked easily. "I'm famished."

"I know now." Brooke decided impulsively. "Sure, I'd like to."

They walked to an Italian restaurant nearby and ordered pizza.

"Are you Italian?"

"Nickolai Adriani?"

"Greek."

"Abbreviated Greek. Born in Brooklyn." Nick thought, And raised on street fights and poverty in the deadly shadow of crime.

"Did you always want to be a cop?"

"Did you always want to be a lawyer?"

"Who do you think is the better, er, interviewer?"

"Do you want to try to find out?"

"No!" Brooke exclaimed. You would win, her sparkling blue eyes told the calm gray ones. She added seriously, "I would like to know why you always wanted to be a cop, if you did."

Nick started to counter, to continue the playful banter, but he stopped. He would tell her. What the hell . . .

"I did. Something about believing the streets should be safe for children and that innocent people should be free from harm." Nick spoke quietly.

Brooke wondered if Nick had been harmed, or if someone he loved had been. Was Nick's a personal vendetta against crime? Or did he just, simply, *care?* Brooke couldn't tell, but, whatever the reason, it was very important to him.

"That's," Brooke searched for the right word. *Wonderful? Impressive? Moving? Inspirational?* She finished weakly, "Nice."

"It's just the way it is. You probably wonder why I didn't go to law school."

Brooke thought for a moment before answering.

"I guess that being a lawyer would be too removed for you. I think you want to catch the criminals *in flag*—" Brooke stopped abruptly. It was a legal term.

"*In flagrante delicto?*" Nick smiled.

"Yes." In the very act of committing the offense.

"There *is* something clean about catching someone with two hundred thousand dollars worth of coke he's trying to sell to an undercover agent."

"Until we muddy it up with technicalities? I bet you're not very tolerant of mistakes," Brooke mused. Why would she say that? There was nothing in the tranquil gray eyes to suggest intolerance. But Nick was good. He did his job well and he cared. And if you were good and cared, you didn't tolerate mistakes; not from yourself or from others.

"I bet you're not, either."

They ate pizza in silence for several bites. Then Nick said, "I'm a little surprised you don't have a boyfriend."

"Lieutenant Adrian, you are making deductions without enough facts." Why wasn't she offended by his remark? Of course he was right. . . .

I *could* have a lover, Lieutenant, Brooke mused. Yes, you know him. You may even know the tragic story about his wife.

"Ah-ha," Nick continued. "He does exist, but for some reason he is unavailable on Saturday night. Let's see, he flies the Concorde and is at this moment touching down in Paris."

"No."

"He's a doctor on duty for the night. Or he's starring in an off-Broadway show and you're going to meet him later. But why wouldn't you be at the theater, admiring him? Or he's married. No, that doesn't seem like you."

No, it doesn't seem like me; and it isn't happening.

"Maybe he's a cop on an all-night stakeout," Brooke suggested, swiftly shifting away from the married man guess.

"That doesn't seem like you, either," Nick said evenly. "I give up."

"You were right to begin with. No boyfriend."

"Don't tell me you're married to your career. . . ."

"Would that be so bad?" She was, and it wasn't so bad, for now, until . . .

Nick didn't answer.

"Do you mind if we stop?" Nick asked as they passed a newsstand on the way back to Brooke's apartment. "I want to buy the new issue of *Images.*"

"Here it is, sir." The vendor handed the magazine to Nick. "March issue. Hot off the press."

"I used to subscribe," Nick explained to Brooke as they continued the short walk back to her apartment. "But my mailbox is too small. Magazines get damaged. So, I pay newsstand prices. More profit for the Sinclair twins."

"I'm sure if Charles and Jason knew they would make some arrangement. . . ."

"Charles and Jason? You know them?"

"Yes. Not *well.* Through legal work."

Brooke invited Nick into her apartment for coffee. She had an ulterior motive; she wanted to see the art for "Sapphire."

"May I? Galen Spencer has a story in this month's issue. I've read it, but I just want to see how the art turned out."

"You've read it?" Nick wanted to see the art, too. Like everyone in New York, Nick knew who had been the model for Galen Spencer's latest romantic heroine.

"She's a friend." Brooke smiled a wry smile. "And client."

"Any more surprises?"

The smile faded as Brooke reached for the magazine—just that one *other* surprise. "I have a subscription, but it always arrives about three days after everyone else's in town."

"You should really talk to Charles and Jason about that."

"Cute."

Nick noticed the recent issue of *Fashion* on Brooke's coffee table and leafed through it while Brooke looked at *Images*. Nick had never opened an issue of *Fashion* before. Why would he? But, as he turned page after page, his interest increased. *Fashion* was more than a random series of high fashion photographs. Like *Images*, it was a carefully, lovingly crafted work of art.

Nick and Brooke sat across from each other engrossed in the magazines. Finally Nick looked up, expecting to attract Brooke's attention with his eyes, but unable to. She was totally absorbed.

Nick watched, captivated and intrigued. There was something in the photographs that evoked in Brooke a bittersweet mixture of pride and pain. Her head tilted thoughtfully, her lips smiled a soft smile, but her lovely dark blue eyes were stormy.

"She's your sister, isn't she?" Nick spoke quietly. In the hushed silence of the tiny apartment his voice sounded loud.

Brooke looked up at him. "What did you say?"

"Melanie Chandler is your sister." Nick changed his question to a statement.

"Yes," Brooke whispered. Not that it was a secret, but, so far, it had escaped even the watchful ever-curious eye of Viveca Sanders. It would not have been big news; just a small, embarrassing item: *Model Melanie's Mousy Twin*. "Very good detective work."

"I'm a very good detective."

"How did you know?"

Nick shrugged. It had something to do with the eyes that gazed—sky blue or ocean blue—at the world with such determination.

"We're twins."

"That's interesting." Nick meant it. It was *very* interesting. He realized too late he shouldn't have told Brooke.

"It is?" Brooke's voice was icy.

Nick walked across to her and retrieved his issue of *Images*.

"If you point me in the direction of the coffee, I'll make it." Nick's smiling gray eyes finally defrosted the dark-blue ones.

CHAPTER FIFTEEN

$\mathcal{G}$alen tried to write. She put words on paper, but they didn't make sense. Always before the words had flowed, clear and sure, like a crystal-blue river flowing from a pure mountain lake. But now the words and ideas and feelings came from different directions, forming tortuous, crisscrossing paths that started nowhere and travelled aimlessly.

For a solid month, urged by Charles through careful phone calls and occasional necessary meals, Galen tried to write. But what once had been so easy, and had given such pleasure, was impossible. Every day brought more anger, frustration, and exhaustion.

Finally, she made herself sick.

Galen couldn't eat, even though something inside told her she must. The same *something* told her she needed to see a doctor.

Eight weeks after she and Charles returned from Paris, Galen waited in the cheerful office of Sara Rockwell, M.D. Dr. Rockwell specialized in obstetrics and gynecology. Galen made an appointment with Dr. Rockwell because *that* was what worried her the most. Other potential causes of her symptoms—leukemia, tuberculosis, kala-azar—seemed less urgent than the one Dr. Rockwell was trained to diagnose.

Galen decided to wait for the test the doctor said would only take an hour.

"The test is positive. You're pregnant." Sara Rockwell smiled.

And Galen sighed. Dr. Rockwell had already told her, during the pelvic examination, that if she was pregnant it was very early. Her uterus was small. She was eight, nine, maybe ten weeks along. It was difficult to be more precise than that on physical examination, especially this early. As Galen waited, knowing the test would be positive, she thought, Eight weeks means it's Charles's baby; nine or ten weeks means it's Jason's.

"I can't have the baby," Galen told Dr. Rockwell.

"Oh?"

"No. I guess I need to have an abortion," she whispered in a voice that wasn't hers. Someone else was speaking, someone who had slept with two men—*brothers* —and was pregnant by one of them. She added, "I don't have a choice."

"You do have a choice, Galen," Sara countered swiftly. "That's the whole point. You can choose not to have the baby. Or you can choose to *have* it."

Galen stared at her. "You don't understand."

"Tell me what I don't understand," Sara urged gently, warning herself, Stay neutral.

"I don't know who the father is," Galen confessed quietly, embarrassed.

"I guess that's important if you think the potential father might have a genetic disorder that should be screened prenatally," Sara offered, chiding herself a little. She knew about Galen Elizabeth Spencer. Sara had read "Emerald" and "Sapphire." She knew Galen could care for her child, would love her child, and might never forgive herself for making an impulsive emotional decision.

It was the same approach Sara took with all her patients, not just the Galen Spencers of the world. She wanted her patients to make the right choice, whatever it was. It had to be carefully considered.

"There's nothing genetically wrong with the father. It's one of two men," Galen admitted a little defiantly. If Sara Rockwell was surprised or shocked at Galen's admission—she was neither—it didn't show. "They both are healthy."

"And you are healthy."

"Yes." I am carrying a healthy, genetically sound baby.

"Why do you want an abortion, Galen?"

"I'm unmarried. I don't know who the father is. Not that it matters anyway," Galen started to explain, then stopped. It was true. It wasn't relevant. If she knew Jason was the baby's father, would she tell him? No. And if Charles was the father? Maybe . . .

"So, its socially a little awkward . . ."

Galen frowned at Sara.

"I'm not trying to make your decision for you, Galen. I just want to be sure that you really consider it. Just because the procedure is small doesn't mean the decision is."

"You think I should keep the baby?"

"I can't possibly make that decision for you, but I can provide you with literature and telephone numbers. As I'm sure you are aware, abortion is an emotionally charged issue on both sides."

"How soon do I need to decide?"

"You have time. Weeks. The risk goes up with time, so it's a balance between having enough time to be certain and not waiting too long."

Galen nodded.

"Shall I get the literature and phone numbers for you?"

"No. The only one I need to talk to is myself. I'll let you know."

"That's fine. And if you have any questions, please call."

Galen called Sara the following day.

"I'm going to have the baby."

"OK." *Good.*

"I need to ask you some questions."

"Go ahead."

"Well, due to the social, uh, awkwardness of this," Galen began, trying to sound confident, "I need to move away."

"I'll be happy to refer you to another obstetrician. Do you know where you are going?"

"I'm not sure, but I need to move before I begin to show. When will that be?"

"It varies. Certainly by the fifth month. In the meantime I should see you soon. We need to talk about diet and nutrition. I want you to start gaining weight. You seem a little frail."

"No, I'm strong," Galen said bravely. *Strong and independent.* "I always have been thin. Is that a problem?"

"You just don't have any reserves for yourself, much less for the baby. Are you eating?"

"I'm quite nauseated. Not just in the morning."

"You need to force yourself to eat."

"OK," Galen agreed vaguely. She had more questions, pressing questions. "Will there ever be a way to know who the father is?"

"Probably not before the baby is born, not by uterine size anyway. A two-week difference in gestational age can be subtle."

"And you can't guess when it would have been possible for me to get pregnant?"

"Not with your history of irregular cycles."

"And after the baby is born?"

"Blood-typing might help. It doesn't prove paternity, but it can exclude it. But that all depends on their blood types and yours."

"I'm type B. One of them is type O." Galen knew that Jason was type O because she had read the contents of his wallet, including his blood donor card, to him one day. "I don't know about the other, but they are twins."

"Twins?" Then Sara made an educated guess about the identity of the potential fathers. Sara hadn't even told Galen that she knew who *she* was. It wasn't pertinent. Now Galen had unwittingly told her that Jason or Charles Sinclair had fathered her child. *That* wasn't pertinent, either, except to the unborn child who was heir to an enormous publishing empire.

"Not identical."

"Then the other's blood type could be any of the four, depending on what his parents were. Obviously if he's O, like his brother, or B, like you, it won't help. But if he's A or AB . . ."

"A or AB," Galen repeated.

"*And* the baby is A," Sara added. She continued, "Beyond simple blood typing there are more sophisticated genetic tests. With twins—even fraternal—there might be such genetic similarity that it would be impossible to be certain. Those tests would require carefully collected samples of the father's blood."

"It's probably better not to know," Galen murmured.

But three nights later when Charles called, because he hadn't heard from her for almost ten days, Galen asked him.

"What's your blood type?" Galen made the question sound impulsive. In fact, she had been waiting for most of the conversation, hoping to make it seem like an unimportant afterthought.

"Why? Don't tell me you're shifting to murder mysteries."

"No, I just read an article about the percentages of each type in the population. I'm B, which is a little unusual."

"I'm O. Very mundane."

"Oh. O," Galen repeated. Then I'll never know. . . .

"You sound disappointed."

"No. Just in search of an A, I guess."

"So, are you writing?" Charles asked after a brief silence.

"Yes." Galen was forcing herself to write. She needed money, and a career, to support her unborn child. "I should finish the revisions of 'Garnet' by next week."

"That's ahead of schedule. How's the screenplay?" It was due in three weeks.

Galen sighed. She had rehearsed this. She was going to call *him* when she had her speech exactly right. But now he was asking.

"I'd like to postpone filming the movie until next spring." Galen held her breath.

"Why?" Charles asked evenly.

"I'm having trouble writing about love." It was true, even if it wasn't the *real* reason. But she couldn't tell Charles why she couldn't be in Kenya with him and Jason in the fall. She couldn't tell him that her baby —her baby and his or his twin's—was due in early November. "My rose-colored glasses are shattered."

"I thought you were fixing them."

"I need time, Charles." The truth. "I'm sure that Melanie—"

"Melanie is hired help."

"Charles, please."

"Galen, you signed a contract."

"I can't do it, Charles." Tears filled her eyes and her voice broke. Since the night she found Jason with Fran, Galen's emotions had been only skin deep. Now, with her pregnancy, they were right at the surface, raw and exposed and fragile.

"Yes you can."

"You won't let me change the contract?" Galen felt betrayed. Charles, you're my friend, *please*.

"It's not my decision." Charles and Jason were executive producers, but . . .

"The signatures on the contract are yours and Jason's. You can ask him."

No I *can't.*

Five days later Galen awoke with lower abdominal cramps. It felt like the beginning of a menstrual period.

But I shouldn't be having a period!

Galen lay quietly, willing the cramps away. After several minutes they were gone, an uneasy early-morning memory. Galen waited for fifteen minutes, thinking about her baby—happy thoughts—before getting up.

As she finished dressing the pain came again. This time it was so severe that it knotted her stomach and paralyzed her lungs. And this time the pain was accompanied by a hot dampness on her thighs.

Blood. No.

Doubled over with pain and fear Galen staggered to the phone in her room. Galen had gotten the private phone, because of Jason. She had been meaning to have it disconnected. With trembling fingers she dialed the number to Dr. Rockwell's office.

"Galen. Take a few deep breaths. Calm down."

"What is happening?"

"I can't be certain over the phone, but I can get an idea. I need to ask you some questions. All right?"

"Yes." Galen straightened slightly. She wasn't more calm, but the pain had eased a little.

"Is there a lot of blood?"

A lot? There shouldn't be *any,* should there? Any amount is too much.

"No."

"Have you passed clots or tissue?"

"*Tissue?* No. Just red blood."

"Is the pain in the middle or on the side?" Sara was asking questions that would help her decide whether Galen could come to the office or needed to go directly, possibly by ambulance, to the emergency room. Now she was asking about a possible ectopic—tubal—pregnancy. Ectopic pregnancies were life-threatening.

From everything Sara knew about Galen, it was unlikely that she would have an ectopic pregnancy. Galen had only been sexually active since late December. She—they—had used no birth control. Sara remembered the surprise in Galen's eyes when she asked the question. Of course they used no birth control. They were in love—always and forever—and if she got pregnant it would be wonderful. The look of surprise, and the brief memory of the lovely dream, had faded quickly, dissolving into what looked like despair.

Galen was a low risk for ectopic pregnancy—virtual monogamy, no history of pelvic inflammatory disease, no previous pregnancies, no known tubal damage—but Sara had to exclude it.

"The pain is in the middle. Like a period. Only worse."

"How does it feel now?"

"The pain is less—it did that earlier, too—and the bleeding has slowed," Galen answered hopefully. Maybe she was overreacting.

"Call a cab and come, now, to my office. If it gets worse on the way over, go to . . ." Sara gave Galen the name of two hospitals. "OK?"

"Yes. Am I losing the baby?"

"Not necessarily, Galen. I'll know more when I see you."

* * *

"The internal cervical os is closed," Sara told Galen after she completed the examination forty-five minutes later. "And you haven't passed tissue. That means you're having what is called a threatened abortion."

"Threatened?"

"That's what it's called."

"What does it mean?"

"It means that you haven't lost the baby," Sara explained carefully.

"But I may."

"Yes. We'll know in the next few days. The pain and bleeding may stop and everything may be fine. Or it may increase and you may miscarry."

"What can I do?"

"First, you can understand that none of this is your fault. Many women miscarry in the first trimester. Often it is because there is something wrong with the fetus. Even the things I am going to tell you to do now don't necessarily change the outcome. But I want you to do them because they are safe and sensible for you and the baby. OK?"

Galen nodded.

"Strict bed rest." Sara hesitated. Then she continued, even though it didn't seem applicable, but was a usual recommendation, "Pelvic rest."

"What?"

"No intercourse."

"Oh."

"How's your weight?"

"I've gained a pound!"

"That's not much."

"I've really been trying." Tears threatened. It was a struggle for Galen not to lose weight. To have *gained* a pound, despite the nausea, was a major accomplishment. But it hadn't been enough! What if that was why she was losing the baby?

"Babies are very tough," Sara said, correctly reading Galen's self-recrimination. "You must know that from all the time you've spent in underdeveloped countries."

Galen did know that. She had seen it.

"You know who I am."

"Of course. What I don't know is whether you have a living situation that can ensure strict bed rest and nutritious food and someone who can watch you for the next few days." In other words, what I don't know is, Do you have a friend?

Galen thought about her living situation in the brownstone. Her third-floor room, the main-floor kitchen, and the housemates who changed too frequently to become friends did not meet Dr. Rockwell's requirements. Galen had friends—Charles and Brooke and Melanie—but none of them could know about her pregnancy.

"Not really."

"I think it would be best to put you in the hospital. We don't usually do that for threatened abortions, but . . ." Sara paused, thinking, But most women have husbands or lovers or families or friends or *someone*. Most women, but not Galen. Sara continued, "But given your weight, a few days of enforced nutrition seems sensible. Is that all right?"

"Whatever is best for my baby."

CHAPTER SIXTEEN

Galen was hospitalized in a small community hospital north of New York City. The pain and bleeding subsided after four days, but she remained hospitalized for three more days, to be safe, to be *sure*. They made great progress with her nutrition. She gained weight and the anemia improved with iron and her electrolytes were back to normal. Even her cheeks had a soft pink glow of health.

"You look good," Sara told Galen on the morning of her release from the hospital.

"I feel good. Happy. Lucky."

"Ease back into things slowly...."

"I thought we were out of danger."

"I believe you are, from the standpoint of the threatened abortion. I think the baby plans to go the whole nine months." Sara smiled. "I'm more worried about you—your strength—than the baby. So take it easy. Eat."

"I will. I promise. I really feel better than I have in a long time."

It was true. Galen felt better physically and better emotionally. During the week in the hospital, during the long hours of waiting and hoping and praying the baby would survive, the blur of the past two and a half months came into clear, sharp focus. She had to take charge of her life. She had to make decisions for herself and her baby.

First and foremost, Galen had to sever all ties—personal and professional—with the Sinclair twins. The tie with Jason was already broken—everywhere but in your *heart*, a voice taunted—because he betrayed her and them and everything she believed in.

And Charles, her dear friend . . .

Galen didn't dwell on whether it was *fair*. None of it was fair to any of them.

"Brooke? It's Galen, are you busy?"

"*Galen*. Where are you?"

"At the brownstone." She had been back, home from the hospital, for an hour. "Why?"

"I tried to reach you all last week."

"Oh. I was away. Was there something?"

"No." *Yes*. Charles had called because he was worried about Galen. He wondered if Brooke had heard from her. "I just called to say hi. Are you all right?"

"Yes. Fine." Galen wished she could tell Brooke. It would help explain the question she was about to ask. But no one could know. Galen sighed and continued, "Brooke, how difficult would it be for me to get out of the contract for the screenplay?"

Charles had asked the same question! Brooke told Galen what she had told Charles three days before.

"It wouldn't be difficult at all, *legally*."

"Really?"

"No. I wrote it that way. You would have to refund the advance."

"Of course."

"Galen, what about *Songs of the Savanna* and *Spring Street Stories?*" Brooke had negotiated a two-book contract for Galen. The completed manuscript for *Songs of the Savanna*—the stories about Kenya—had been promised for September. *Spring Street Stories*—stories about life and people in Greenwich Village—was due next spring.

"I will complete them as scheduled." Galen paused. She asked quietly, "Brooke, could you just send something in writing cancelling the screenplay contract?"

"I *could* Galen, but . . ."

"I have to tell them myself, don't I?" She would have to see Jason and Charles one last time.

"Galen, let's have lunch," Brooke suggested. "Are you free today?"

"No, not today. But we will, Brooke, before I leave."

"Leave?"

"I'll explain later. I have to go now. Thank you, Brooke."

Galen's next call was to the executive offices of Sinclair Publishing Company. She scheduled an appointment with Charles and Jason at ten the following morning. That done, she sat on the lumpy mattress in her room and gazed at herself in the mirror.

Hopelessly out of date and naive, she thought as she looked critically at her waist-length red-gold hair and her unstylish clothes. I can't look like this anymore. It isn't how I feel inside. I'm not a wide-eyed virgin full of hope and dreams. I'm a twenty-six-year-old woman who is about to have a child. I *know* what's on the other side of the dream. I've been there. It's where I'm going to live.

Time to step into the eighties, Galen Elizabeth Spencer. Not with wide eyes . . . but with your eyes wide open.

It didn't scare her. Nothing was as frightening as learning that everything you believed in was just a mirage. And she was beyond that now; she had faced it and accepted it. Galen wasn't afraid anymore. She wasn't afraid and she wasn't alone. There was a new life—a life that wanted to live—growing inside her. How she would love that precious little life! She already did. Despite everything, Galen still believed in her own ability to love, deeply, unselfishly, and forever.

"Cut it all off," Galen told the hair stylist two hours later.

"Are you sure? This is the most beautiful hair. . . ."

"I'm sure."

"Do you want us to make a fall for you?"

"No. Do you want to buy it from me?" Galen suggested, remembering "The Gift of the Magi." But that was a different century. Maybe they didn't buy hair, real hair, in the nineteen eighties.

But they did. Galen and the owner of the salon settled on a price that included the haircut *and* styling *and* cash.

"We're going to cut it pretty short," he warned. "On the other hand, that's the style—*a* style—and with your eyes . . ."

The result was dramatic. Galen's remarkable emerald eyes, no longer hidden by the red-gold veil, commanded attention. The lovely eyes attracted the attention, but they were only part of the effect; the fine, straight nose, the healthy pink cheeks, the full, sensuous lips. . . .

Galen wasn't old-fashioned pretty any longer. Now she was modern and stunning and beautiful.

Beautiful, Galen mused as she sat in her room that evening, hemming, desmocking, and modernizing one of her dresses. *You are so beautiful, Galen.* Jason's words, whispered gently, as he kissed her and made love . . .

Galen pricked her finger with the sewing needle, distracted by the memory of Jason. Go away, *dream*, she told herself with annoyance, Go *away*.

Charles noticed Galen's name in his appointment book with a combination of relief and apprehension. She was *back* from wherever it was she had been for the past week. Good. But why had she scheduled an appointment? Why did she want to meet with him and Jason together? Was it just about delaying the filming of "Sapphire"?

Galen appeared in Jason's office at precisely ten A.M. Charles and Jason were already there. They stood up and drew silent breaths when they saw her. She looked so different! Her hair, her eyes, her face, her dress—somehow vaguely familiar—radiated confidence.

Strong and beautiful and independent, Charles thought, relieved. Good for her.

But as he watched Galen closely, as she smiled, as she extended her hand first to Jason and then to him, he saw her lips tremble slightly and her eyes flicker with uncertainty.

She's trying so hard, Charles realized. And she'll make it. We'll help her.

Darling Galen, Jason's heart cried. He wanted her, missed her, so much. He wanted the old Galen or the new one, it didn't matter. He had never really known her anyway. What he thought they had—a love forever—never existed. The "love" vanished overnight, but still Jason wanted her.

Jason wondered why Charles looked so surprised by Galen's appearance. It was as if Charles and Galen hadn't seen each other for a while, as if something had happened between them in the weeks since Jason had seen them at La Lumière. Was it already over between Charles and Galen? Was Galen just another of Charles's women?

"You look wonderful, Galen." Charles smiled, encouraging her.

"I needed a change." Galen looked at her hands for a moment, collecting her thoughts and calming her racing heart. Then she raised her proud head and added, "I need some other changes, too."

"Yes?"

"Ten days ago, I spoke with Charles about delaying the deadline for the screenplay." Galen paused. "Well, I've changed my mind."

"Good," Charles said, but the look in her eyes worried him.

"I've decided to cancel the contract," Galen continued bravely. "I'm not going to write the screenplay at all. I've brought a check in the amount of the advance."

"You want someone else to write it?"

"No. I hold the copyright. I don't want a movie made from 'Sapphire'. Ever."

"Why not, Galen?" Charles demanded, suddenly angry. He was worried about her tears—she was so fragile—but he couldn't let her get away with this. It made absolutely no sense.

"You know why." Her glistening emerald eyes met his for a moment.

"Galen, you had a love affair that didn't work out the way you wanted. It happens." Charles forced gentleness into his voice. "But you go on. You don't run away, especially not from *us*."

As Charles spoke the last words, he saw what looked like hatred in her lovely eyes.

Charles drew a sharp breath. What have I ever done but care about you, Galen?

Jason watched and listened. *A love affair that didn't work out the way you wanted.* Galen loved Charles, but Charles didn't love her. It was over with Charles, and still Galen hadn't come back to *him*.

She was leaving both of them because it was too painful to be near Charles. . . .

What had happened between Galen and Charles to make her want him out of her life forever? What had happened between Elliott and Charles to make Elliott want Charles out of *his* life forever?

"Keep the advance," Jason whispered.

"*Jesus Christ!*" Charles hissed as he stormed out of Jason's office.

"I'm sorry that something happened to hurt you this much," Jason told Galen after Charles was gone. His voice was so gentle, so loving.

Galen couldn't speak. Her astonished emerald eyes met his for a bewildered moment before she left.

"She asked me if she could break the contract. I told her yes." Just like I told you when you asked, Brooke thought.

"Why the hell did you write that escape clause into the contract?"

"Because I always try to do what's best for my client," Brooke spoke quietly into the phone. He sounded so angry, and he was blaming *her*. "Don't you think, no matter what . . . you couldn't force her to write it."

Brooke wondered if Charles was still there. She wondered if the polite aristocratic eyes matched the icy voice.

"And she didn't give you any reason?" Charles finally broke the silence.

"No," Brooke whispered.

"It doesn't make any sense."

"I know. I'm sorry, Charles."

"For what?" A slight tease, a little softness. "For being such a damned good attorney?"

"Is Melanie Chandler available? I'm a friend." Galen had remembered her friend, and the fabulous leading role that would never happen, in the middle of the night. As soon as the ordeal of telling Charles and Jason was over, Galen walked along Park Avenue to Drake Modelling Agency. Galen wondered if Melanie would be as angry as Charles had been; Melanie had every right to be.

The receptionist at Drake assumed Galen was herself a model and directed her to the models' dressing room. The dressing room door opened before Galen had a chance to knock.

"*Fran.*"

Fran looked at her quizzically and without recognition.

"I'm Galen Spencer. We met . . ." In Jason's office and at Brooke's apartment. And I saw you—you were asleep—in Jason's arms. Don't you know me? I'm the mystery woman who wasn't really a threat to your love after all.

"Galen. I didn't recognize you."

"Galen?" Melanie overheard the conversation and joined them. "Wow."

Galen shrugged. "A new look."

"Sensational," Fran murmured. "I have to go. It was nice seeing you again, Galen."

Galen nodded politely. It wasn't so nice. . . .

"How are you, Galen?" Melanie asked cheerfully. She wanted to *demand* of her troubled emerald eyes, Tell me what is wrong.

"Fine." Galen frowned. "Melanie, I've decided I don't want a movie to be made from 'Sapphire' after all."

"Oh?" Why did Galen look so worried? Because of *her*? "That's OK, at least with me."

"Really?"

"*Really*. It's probably best for me not to take a break from my modelling career anyway." Melanie waved it away with her long, graceful hands. She hadn't really been looking forward to spending two months in Kenya with Charles Sinclair. "No big deal."

Relief flickered across Galen's face, but a deeper sadness lingered.

"What's wrong, Galen?" Melanie asked gently.

"I'll be all right."

"Don't you want to talk about it?" Galen *hadn't* wanted to talk about it, Melanie realized. That was why for the past two months Galen had graciously, but firmly, declined Brooke and Melanie's invitations to get together. Maybe now . . .

Yes, Melanie, but I can't.

"No."

"Maybe in a week or two?"

"I'm leaving New York."

"Where are you going?"

"I'm not sure. I'll let you know." Galen moved to the door to leave. "Thank you for not being angry about the movie, Melanie."

Galen didn't know where she would go when she left New York. It would be easy—safe and easy and her parents would protect her and her baby—to go back to Kenya. But that would be going *back*, and she had to move ahead. At the beauty salon she had browsed through the current issue of *Unique Homes*; there was a photograph of a charming stone-and-cedar gatehouse in Lake Forest, Illinois.

Galen dialed the number of the real estate agency listed in *Unique Homes* underneath the photo ad for the gatehouse in Lake Forest. The gatehouse, situated on two acres of parklike property, had a view of Lake Michigan, a private inner courtyard surrounded by a six-foot brick wall, two fireplaces, a wood-panelled study, a country kitchen. . . .

The pace of the agent's voice increased as she described the property. Did Galen know Lake Forest? No? Well, it was one of Chicago's most prestigious north shore suburbs—old money and elegance and privacy and charm. The asking price was a little high, the agent admitted, but Galen could probably get it for right at half a million.

"Are you interested?" the agent asked.

"It sounds lovely," Galen murmured, reeling at the price, wondering if she should just apologize and hang up. "Perfect. Do you think they would consider renting it?"

There was a long silence.

"*Renting?*" It was almost a gasp. Homes in Lake Forest weren't usually rented. The agent sputtered finally, "I don't know."

"Do you think they might be?"

The agent hesitated. They *might* be. The owners lived in the mansion on the property. They didn't really like the idea of subdividing the property—it had been in the family forever—but they didn't like the gatehouse sitting vacant, either. One would never list a house in Lake Forest as a rental. Still . . . the agent wondered about the woman with the soft British accent from New York. The owners might rent to the right person.

"Why don't you give me your name and number and I'll get back to you?"

Charles called her at ten that night.

"Why, Galen?" he demanded as soon as she answered.

"I had to."

"Really. *Why?*"

"I just did. You're the one who kept telling me to resolve the past and get on with my life."

"I didn't expect you to do something crazy like tossing away everything and everyone that happened to be around during the great tragedy of your unsuccessful love affair."

"I wish you could just believe that I know what I'm doing. I wish you could understand how I feel."

"Let me tell you how I feel, Galen. I feel betrayed."

"Betrayed," Galen breathed. *She* felt betrayed. "If the movie had done well . . ."

"Do you think I'm talking about *money?*"

"No," she admitted softly. I know the kind of betrayal you mean. I know about the betrayal of love and friendship.

A long silence followed.

"I thought we were friends," Charles began again finally. His voice was gentle. He wanted to understand. "I thought we talked to each other and told each other the truth."

Tears filled her eyes. She wished she could lessen the hurt in Charles's voice. But what could she say? If she even hinted that there was something more, something that didn't make what she was doing seem so crazy, Charles would push until he found out.

"Was it because we made love? Did that really change everything after all?"

It wasn't because we made love, Charles. That was lovely, but. . . . If Charles knew I was carrying his baby he would probably want to marry me, Galen realized suddenly. She allowed herself to think about it for a moment, and the vision was pleasant. She and Charles cared about each other. They could make a gentle, loving life together with their child.

But Galen didn't *know* the baby was his.

And Charles was Jason's brother. She couldn't spend the rest of her life seeing Jason, she with Charles and Jason with Fran. Galen could never see Jason again. Seeing him today hurt too much, because, today, more of her wanted him than hated him.

"No. It wasn't because we made love," Galen answered finally, part truth, part lie. She added sadly, she would miss him, it wasn't fair, "It just has to end. That's all."

Good-bye, Charles.

CHAPTER SEVENTEEN

New York City
May 1986

𝓜elanie stood at the edge of a rose garden in Central Park, her arm stretched toward the rain-wet petals of a pale-pink rose. It was six-thirty in the morning. The spring dawn was soft yellow and the air was clean and fresh following the midnight rain.

A restlessness had driven Melanie from her warm bed into the cold, still dawn. Restlessness for what? Melanie didn't know. Now, as she touched the velvety petals, warm tears spilled inexplicably onto her cold cheeks. What was *wrong?* Why was she crying?

The sound of approaching footsteps pulled her from her thoughts. The menacing intruder hovered close behind.

Please go away. Melanie's body stiffened with fear. *Please.*

"Melanie?"

Melanie spun and looked through a blur of tears at familiar brown eyes. But not so familiar, because now they weren't taunting; now they looked concerned.

"Are you all right?" He had never seen her like this. She wore a pale-gray sweat suit, bland, baggy, colorless, and no makeup. She was unadorned, and her eyes glistened with tears, but she was so beautiful. And so sad.

"Yes. I'm fine. Thank you, Charles. Just looking at the roses." Melanie impatiently wiped the tears from her cheeks. But then there were new tears; they wouldn't stop. *Why?*

"Here." Charles withdrew a monogrammed handkerchief from his pocket.

"Thank you." Melanie accepted the offered handkerchief mechanically and held it in her hand, staring at it, as if its use was unknown to her.

"Speaking of raindrops on roses," Charles murmured as he retrieved the handkerchief and gently dried her tear-damp cheeks. She watched him with startled blue eyes which, for the moment, had stopped weeping.

"So. What's wrong?" The dark-brown eyes wanted to know.

"I don't know. These lovely roses remind me of—" Melanie stopped, suddenly confused. It was her heart speaking to Charles Sinclair.

"Of home? Are you homesick?" Charles asked gently. He knew about homesickness. He had been homesick all his life. He had never had a home.

"Maybe, except we didn't have roses." She smiled distantly. The roses didn't remind her of home. They reminded her of her dreams. In the life she would have someday, there were gardens and gardens of roses. "Sometimes I feel like a withered leaf. Every time I try to pause for even a moment a gust of wind comes and whirls me away."

"The price of success and celebrity. You have no privacy, and there's nothing constant but whim and change. That's why I escape to St. Barts—" Charles stopped abruptly. He was telling Melanie Chandler something private and important. Of course St. Barts was on his mind, he was going there in less than a week, but still. . . .

"I haven't taken a vacation," Melanie mused. Not a vacation or a holiday or even a moment to breathe since September. Without looking back, without skipping a beat, she had arrived in New York and soared right to the top. "Do you suppose a vacation would help?"

"Maybe. But maybe it's more. You need to decide if this is what you really want. It's a roller coaster, Melanie, and you haven't even gotten to the steep part." It might have been a warning except his voice was soft.

"Why are you so wise?"

"I'm not. And you are not a withered leaf. You have a good shot at becoming an icicle, however. Do you want my coat?"

Melanie realized then that Charles was dressed in a three-quarter-length camel's hair coat over his perfectly tailored suit. It was six-thirty in the morning, and Charles Sinclair—Manhattan's dashing and dapper playboy—was on his way to work.

"No. I'm fine." *Better* thanks to you. Melanie took the handkerchief from his hand. "I'll return this to you."

"OK."

"I'd better go. Thanks."

"I like your jogging outfit."

Melanie felt a rush of adrenaline pump through her, and suddenly she was a soldier preparing for battle. It was going to end badly with Charles Sinclair after all. He couldn't resist the one final taunt, the few words that would prove all the other words had been false. Melanie's eyes narrowed as they met his.

But the dark-brown eyes weren't taunting. They were telling the truth. He liked her drab, baggy gray sweats.

"So do I," she whispered.

Melanie watched the honey-colored drops splash into the pool of champagne at the base of the ice sculpture fountain. She smiled slightly as she tried to remember *which* extravaganza this was. Let's see, if it's Friday it must be the *Cosmo* party. The dazzling, glamorous parties were part of the whirring blur of her life. The gowns and coiffures and jewels and partners varied from night to night, but the ice sculptures and champagne fountains and gourmet hors d'oeuvres and mountains of caviar and beautiful and handsome faces were the same.

And the conversation was the same.

"Melanie, the cover of *Vogue*. Really the best cover in years."

"Melanie, twelve pages of Dior's spring collection, *all* modelled by you. Unbelievable."

"Melanie Chandler, probably the sexiest voice in television commercials *ever*. X-rated, really."

"You must be terribly disappointed about 'Sapphire'."

And Melanie smiled her flawless smile, her sky-blue eyes sparkling, as her sexy voice answered softly, "It was a lucky shot."

"Dior designed a long blond look this season. It just worked out."

"Not that sexy."

"No. I'm sure Galen made the right decision."

Melanie gazed into the golden pond of champagne. Her reflection glittered back at her in soft honey ripples. Her reflection and another.

"Do you know the legend of Narcissus?"

It was a taunt, a not-so-subtle reminder of her own vanity. Those kind, gentle, early-morning moments in the park were a mirage.

"I'm not admiring myself."

"Neither was Narcissus. He was a twin. He and his sister looked very much alike. When she died he spent endless hours gazing at his reflection because it reminded him of her."

"I always thought . . . something about a wood nymph named Echo . . ." Melanie narrowed her eyes, trying to remember.

"There are two versions of the myth. The mythologists are divided to this day." Charles smiled.

"Poor Narcissus. What a bad rap. Hard enough to be a twin," Melanie mused. Then blushed. She was telling Charles Sinclair the truth again.

"Hard enough," he agreed.

Melanie reached into her Gucci evening bag and retrieved Charles's washed, ironed, and carefully folded handkerchief. "I thought I might see you tonight."

"Thank you." Charles raised the handkerchief to his nose. "*First*. What you always wear."

"I guess the scent is in my evening bag," Melanie apologized, embarrassed, shaken. She always did wear First. It was her favorite perfume. Charles had noticed.

"I could wash it—"

"I like it."

"Charles." Viveca Sanders joined them and slipped her perfectly manicured fingers around Charles's arm. She flashed a well-trained—trained not to use the muscles that would lead too soon to wrinkles—television camera smile at Melanie. "Melanie, I just saw the Tiffany ad. I never gave a hoot about diamonds until now. When are you coming on my show?"

"Viveca, always working," Charles teased lightly.

But they were all working. That was why they were here.

"*Sometime*, Viveca," Melanie promised gaily. She would have to appear on *Viveca's View*. It was part of her job, part of the celebrity expectations. She would put it off until Adam told her that she *had* to.

"I love these firm commitments." Viveca turned her attention to Charles, her fingers squeezing possessively. She spoke softly, "Charles, I have to find out why George Phelps is here alone. I'll be back."

Viveca cast a seductive glance at Charles and a territorial one at Melanie.

Don't *worry*, Viveca.

"Would you like to dance?" Charles asked as Viveca disappeared among the forest of designer dresses and silk tuxedos.

Melanie nodded without looking at him and turned toward the dance floor. Charles guided her through the crowd, his hand strong and warm on her bare back. Melanie paused when they reached the edge of the dance floor. Charles took her hand and led her to a dark, secluded corner.

They began to dance, awkwardly assuming the formal ballroom position. They danced that way—stiff and distant—for a few moments.

Then Charles laughed softly, and in one fluid motion lifted both her arms around his neck and wrapped his arms, strong and gentle, around her back and waist.

"Melanie," he whispered, pulling her close.

She rested her forehead gently against his chest and shook her head, unable to speak, suddenly overwhelmed. The closeness felt so wonderful, and the soft, seductive way he spoke her name . . .

"What?" Charles asked quietly, lifting her chin, gazing into her eyes.

"You," she breathed.

"You," he whispered in return.

Take me away, Charles. Take me to a private place where we can dance forever.

"What are you doing later tonight?" The sensuous brown eyes wondered.

Making love with you. Melanie's mind spun. Somewhere in the spinning images she saw Russ Collins, who she had met at Adam's New Year's Eve party and had been dating since March. Russ was probably looking for her. Russ knew how Melanie felt about Charles; he would be surprised to find them dancing together. Russ would be even more surprised to learn that Melanie wanted Charles, desperately.

"Seeing you." Melanie heard a voice, her voice, answer.

"One o'clock?"

She nodded.

"Tell me where you live.?

One. One-fifteen. One-thirty. One *forty-five*.

As the minutes passed, slow, heavy minutes, the eager anticipation that had carried her through the rest of the evening vanished. In its place was a deep aching fear that this was what Charles Sinclair had planned all along. He wanted to show her her own foolishness. She didn't really believe he wanted her, did she? She couldn't really think that after all the animosity everything would magically change, could she?

Months before Melanie had laid—tried to—the same trap for him. But Charles hadn't taken the bait. Now the tables were turned, and she had fallen for the ruse.

Damn you, Charles. *Damn* you.

Numbly, Melanie removed the strand of flawless diamonds from around her neck and replaced it, to be returned Monday, in the peacock-blue box labelled Tiffany and Co. Then she replaced the diamond-and-sapphire earrings and the diamond bracelet . . .

The buzzer sounded. Melanie's heart pounded with renewed energy and excitement; anticipation flooded through her in warm, tingling, frightening waves.

"Yes?" she spoke into the intercom linking her apartment to the building's main entrance.

"I'm sorry."

Melanie pressed the button to release the front-door lock. It would take him two minutes to reach her apartment. As Melanie paced impatiently, she caught her reflection in the hall mirror. I look naked without the jewels, she mused, gazing at her bare arms and long, graceful neck. That's OK, isn't it? Isn't that what this is all about? Is it? Damn you, Charles. It was almost easier when I thought you weren't going to come. Easier to hate you . . .

The doorbell rang.

"Hi."

"Hi."

His just-washed dark hair was still slightly damp. His silk tuxedo had been exchanged for khaki slacks, an oxford shirt, and a cashmere V-neck sweater.

He went home to change, Melanie realized. After he took Viveca home. After he. . . . What if Charles had made love to Viveca before coming here? What if that was why he was so late?

Charles touched her face with his hands and Melanie stopped thinking. He held her face as his lips hungrily explored hers. Melanie returned his deep, searching kisses and her hands found his damp, strong back beneath the cashmere and cotton. Charles pulled her close, wrapping his arms around her, enveloping her in warmth and strength and desire.

But the breathless embrace and the warm deep kisses weren't enough. Their bodies urgently demanded more; they had to be even closer, *now*.

"Where is the bedroom?"

Melanie's blue eyes told him to follow her.

They undressed each other quickly There was nothing gentle or leisurely, no pretense of wondrous discovery, no careful, lingering kisses, no slow exploration in search of pleasure. . . .

As soon as they were naked Charles was inside her; it was what they both wanted and needed. They shared the urgency, and now, as their strong, healthy bodies moved together—consumed with desire and passion—they shared the ecstasy.

Afterward, they held each other tight and close, unwilling to let distance intrude again. This was how they wanted to be, this close, *joined*. At first, even though they lay very still, there wasn't silence. Their hearts—each heard both hearts—pounded noisily and their lungs recovered in gasps from the breathless moments of their loving.

Finally there was only the soft rhythm of quiet breathing and the strong, slow beats of their athletic hearts and the wonderful warmth of their still-joined bodies.

"You," Charles whispered.

"You," Melanie breathed into his chest.

She lifted her chin and found his lips. Charles took her lower lip gently in his teeth.

"Is it possible to do that again?" she asked between kisses.

"Possible?" Charles laughed softly. "Yes."

"Now?" Melanie knew the answer. It was already happening.

"Maybe more slowly this time," Charles spoke into her mouth. "I needed you so much."

I still do, he thought, as he felt the same urgent need and desire. He couldn't control it.

"Maybe more slowly next time." I need you, Charles, just the same way, *please*.

"The time *after* this time."

"I should go."

"Go?"

"It's five-thirty," Charles answered simply. But he didn't move. Melanie felt his hesitation.

Tell him not to go, Melanie. But what if he *wants* to? Then you'll be humiliated. Then you'll know.

"You're welcome to stay." Forever.

Charles stayed. They slept in each other's arms and were awakened by desire—their bodies already moving in a rhythm of love—once in the morning and once in the afternoon. Twelve hours after he said it the first time, Charles said it again.

"Now I really should go."

"There *is* food here." Melanie smiled. "Well, there's lettuce and lemon juice and sprouts."

"Aren't you going to the Tony Awards?" Charles asked. "I can't imagine Russ would miss them."

Russ. Russ was before *you.* Last night I said good-bye to Russ, because of you . . .

"Melanie?"

"Russ is going. I'm not." She forced gaiety in her voice. She added firmly, as if it was her first choice, "I need a quiet night."

It *was* quiet in Melanie's apartment that night, but it wasn't the peaceful quiet she treasured. Tonight the quiet wasn't interrupted by the soft, comforting swishing of pencils as she sketched. Tonight the silence was absolute; except for the strident thoughts that echoed and reechoed in her brain.

What a fool she was! Charles Sinclair had promised nothing. They spent a night and a day of passion. That was all. She had shared meaningless moments of pleasure before, but last night with Charles felt so different. Even before it happened she knew it would be different; that was why she told Russ Collins good-bye.

"I think we should stop seeing each other, Russ," she had purred, her blue eyes sorrowful.

"What? Melanie, *why?*"

"It's me, Russ, not you. I'm not really a very nice person. I'm self-centered and petulant. You're better off without me."

These words had worked in high school and college and even after. Melanie delivered them with great sincerity when she felt, as she inevitably did, suffocated by a relationship. They were her escape when she was tired of being coddled and admired, and when she yearned for her precious privacy

"Melanie, that's nonsense," Russ replied calmly. "Tell me the real reason."

Russ had almost startled her into telling the truth; but, fortunately, she hadn't. After their secret night and day of passion, Charles returned to Viveca, to be with Viveca under the bright lights and watchful eye of Manhattan. And Melanie sat in her twilight-darkened apartment and felt as if her heart had been torn from her.

Charles called at ten. Melanie answered the phone in the darkness.

"I couldn't cancel this evening with Viveca. Not the Tonys. It was too important to her."

"Charles."

"Yes. Do you understand that, Melanie?"

"Yes." Maybe.

"May I come over later?"

"Charles, I . . ." Yes. *Please.* Oh, later? You mean after you've tucked Viveca into bed? "No."

"How about tomorrow? We could go riding in the park."

"You ride?"

"Just a little better than you."

"Oh?"

"I'll show you."

"Brooke and I are going to Boston tomorrow." It was Brooke's idea. She offered to show Melanie the historical, charming city where she had spent four years of her life. Melanie was thrilled at Brooke's suggestion, because, mostly, still, when she and Brooke got together, it was *her* idea.

Melanie wanted to be with Charles, but it was important—too important—to spend time with Brooke.

"For the day?" Charles asked.

"Uh-huh."

"How about Monday evening?"

"Adam wants me to . . ."

"Do you want to see me again, Melanie?"

"Yes," she breathed. Come over tonight, Charles, even if you've been with Viveca, even if we only have an hour or two before I leave for Boston. "Very much."

Charles hesitated. He *had* to see her. It had only been five hours since he left her and already he ached for her.

"Come to St. Barts with me then. We leave Tuesday morning and return Sunday."

We. Charles and Melanie.

"I have sessions booked all week." But I don't care. I could just cancel them, couldn't I?

"You were talking about a vacation." If you can't come with me, I'll stay here, to be with you.

"Yes, but, Adam . . ."

"I'll talk to him. He's here tonight."

"No. I'll talk—*tell*—him."

"So, yes? We're going?"

"We're going."

Brooke and Melanie walked along the Freedom Trail, ate clam chowder in a restaurant overlooking Boston Harbor, toured Harvard and Bunker Hill and Faneuil Hall, and strolled among the picnickers in the Commons. Next trip, they decided, exhausted but excited by their fascinating journey into history, they would go to Concord and Lexington.

It was a wonderful day. Brooke and Melanie could have fun as long as the history and lives they explored belonged to someone else. They could be amiable, easy companions as long as the topics were neutral and impersonal.

At least we're not enemies, Melanie thought, searching for a glimmer of hope in the slow, difficult struggle to become Brooke's friend.

The animosity, the contempt for all that the other held important, had vanished. Of course, by unspoken mutual truce, Brooke and Melanie had long since stopped taunting each other with their accomplishments. Melanie didn't tell Brooke that she was already among the highest paid models in the world, and Brooke didn't tell Melanie that she was about to be appointed the youngest assistant district attorney in the country.

Brooke and Melanie didn't talk about their work, and they didn't talk about their personal lives. On that Sunday afternoon in Boston, Melanie didn't tell Brooke about Charles or the trip she was going take with him to St. Barts.

CHAPTER EIGHTEEN

*M*elanie finally gave up on sleep at four Tuesday morning. The mental pacing that kept her awake all night became physical as she nervously and aimlessly moved from room to room in her apartment.

What was she doing? She didn't even know him. Until recently she had disliked him as intensely as she had ever disliked anyone. What would she *say* to him? The taunts had come easily, fueled by contempt, but now . . .

Brooke was able to talk to him. Brooke and Charles talked about business and law and contracts and stories. Charles *listened* to Brooke, respected Brooke's opinion, valued her intelligence. Brooke could talk to Charles and hold his interest, but could *she*?

Melanie sighed as she inspected the contents of her neatly packed suitcase for the fifth time. It was a colorful collage of shorts and halter tops and sundresses and swimsuits. On the top lay her sketchpad and her plastic box of colored pencils. Melanie's hand rested for a thoughtful moment on the sketchpad. Then she removed it and the pencils and returned them to their place in her sewing room. She wouldn't sketch in front of Charles; it was much too silly and trivial.

But wasn't *she* too silly and trivial for Charles? What did she have to offer?

The answer came with a hard, painful jolt.

What do you *think* you have to offer? Your flawless, perfect, beautiful body and your flawless, perfect, beautiful face. Charles Sinclair may be terribly scholarly and intelligent, but he is also a sexual, passionate man. When it comes to you, Melanie Chandler, Charles doesn't *care* about the story, just the art.

Charles arrived at seven.

"Hi. All set? Do you have your passport?"

"Hi. Yes." Melanie's answer sounded like, *Yes, of course,* even though she had only remembered the passport at six-thirty.

The limousine glided away from Manhattan and the already heavy crush of early-morning traffic.

"How was Boston?" Charles asked when they reached the bridge.

"Wonderful. Such history. Everything is so old."

"Spoken like a true Californian." Charles smiled.

Melanie returned the smile, but her stomach ached. Brooke would never have said something so silly. Brooke would have told Charles—and he would have listened with such interest—the intriguing details of the Boston Tea Party.

"Have you been to Europe?" Charles asked.

Melanie shook her head. Her passport was only two weeks old. "But I'll be there in August and September."

"I know."

Of course Charles knew. Melanie remembered his unconcealed annoyance when they had to delay the filming schedule of "Sapphire" until October because of her trip to Europe. But that was a different Charles Sinclair, wasn't it? This one was smiling at her and his eyes were gentle.

"I've never been out of the country before," Melanie admitted softly. So if you want the limousine to turn around and take me back. . . . Even the cover is a fake, Charles. I'm not really the worldly, sophisticated woman pictured in my photographs. It's only an illusion, just trick photography.

Charles answered the worry in her eyes by reaching for her hand.

Charles kept hold of her hand, releasing for the brief necessary moments of check-in and security clearance, until they settled into their seats in the first-class cabin.

"No breakfast?" Charles asked when Melanie shook her head in response to the stewardess's request for entrée selection.

"This," Melanie answered lifting the glass of champagne, "is plenty."

"You probably don't eat much."

"Not much." *That's why I have the perfect, beautiful, flawless body you want. . . .*

Their conversation was interrupted by a communication from the pilot describing the flight plan. By the time the pilot's message was over, Melanie had taken a thick paperback book from her purse and finished the glass of champagne. Charles retrieved a manuscript from his briefcase, accepted an offer of more champagne for both of them, and began to read.

Melanie stared at the page of her book, but she couldn't read. Shouldn't they be talking and laughing and getting to know one another in a way other than *that*? The champagne made her warm, but it didn't give her the courage to talk to him. Where was the endless, effortless stream of gay flirtation that was her trademark? Where was the Melanie Chandler *charm*?

"That must be quite a passage," Charles observed thirty minutes later. In those thirty minutes Melanie hadn't turned a page.

"Riveting."

"Why don't you read this?" Charles handed her the manuscript he had been reading—"Garnet" by Galen Elizabeth Spencer.

"Oh. The final gem."

Charles smiled. If anyone could tease Galen about the names of her stories, and their heroines, it would be Melanie. Perhaps Galen had told Melanie something about why she left.

"It arrived yesterday. The return address is a post office box in Lake Forest, Illinois."

Melanie nodded. She knew where Galen was. She also knew the address and telephone number of the gatehouse on Mayflower Lane. Apparently Galen didn't want Charles to know; maybe Charles was part of the mystery Galen steadfastly refused to reveal.

"You knew she was in Lake Forest?"

"Yes. Brooke and I saw her off at the train station when she left."

"Train?"

"Galen said she wanted to see the countryside." Melanie frowned briefly. "But I also think she didn't want to fly."

"Do you . . ."

Know why she left? Know why she cancelled "Sapphire"?

Melanie looked into his serious brown eyes and shook her head.

"I have no idea, Charles. *Something* happened, but she never told me what it was. I thought you would know. You and Galen seemed so close."

"I know that she was in love and it ended badly. But . . ."

"It doesn't really explain everything."

"No."

Melanie read "Garnet" twice, losing herself in it, forgetting, for a moment, that she was flying to St. Barts with Charles.

"What did you think?" he asked when Melanie finished reading.

"Wonderful."

"Like the other gems."

Melanie frowned slightly.

"What?" he urged.

"It's not as hopeful or joyous as the others."

"No."

"It's a little sad and wistful, like . . ."

"Like?"

"Like Galen was when she left."

Melanie chewed thoughtfully on her lower lip.

"I do think it's wonderful, Charles. It's bittersweet, but that's more realistic, more the way love really is." Melanie blushed. She was telling Charles Sinclair, editor-in-chief of *Images*, about the quality of a short story; and she was telling Charles Sinclair, the man, about love.

"You're right, Melanie." His voice was gentle and seductive.

Right about *what?*

An hour after their jet landed in Martinique, Charles and Melanie boarded the Windward Air nineteen-passenger Twin Otter STOL that would take them to St. Barts. Melanie gazed out the window during the fifteen-minute flight mesmerized by the sparkling blue Caribbean. As the small plane swooped through a narrow passage that miraculously appeared in the volcanic terrain and came to a sudden stop a few feet short of the white-capped sea, Melanie gasped and clutched Charles's arm. Her pale-blue eyes shimmered with fear.

Charles curled his strong, confident hand over her cool anxious one.

"Melanie, I'm sorry. I should have warned you."

Charles didn't even think about it anymore. The tourist books and travel magazines made much of the precipitous descent into St. Barts: *Not for the weak at heart!* But for Charles it was all so familiar; it was all part of the wonderful feeling of being on St. Barts.

Charles had discovered St. Barts two years after Elliott's death. Since then he returned as often as he could.

St. Barts was peace and paradise and privacy.

Charles drove the rented Mini-Moke along the narrow, winding road from Baie de St. Jean east toward Lorient. At every turn they were greeted by a breathtaking vista of turquoise water and snow white sand and lush tropical foliage and azure sky.

"Lovely," Melanie whispered into the warm, fragrant breeze that welcomed her to the tropics.

"We're staying at a villa," Charles explained when they reached the Anse de Cayes.

Melanie nodded into the wind. She hadn't known that. She had imagined a hotel.

"Have you stayed there before?" Charles seemed to know where he was going.

"Yes. It's my favorite."

It would be my favorite, too, Melanie thought when they reached the villa. It was perched on a cliff above the Anse and hidden in a bountiful bouquet of apricot and pink and violet bougainvillea. Walls of flowers provided impenetrable privacy for the pool and veranda. No one could see them, but they could see a sparkling blue forever of sea and sky.

"Oh," Melanie breathed appreciatively as she followed Charles through the beautifully decorated interior to the veranda. When she saw the view and the white sand beach below, she whispered again, "*Oh.*"

"The villa has its own beach." Charles gestured to the gate in the forest-green wrought-iron fence surrounding the veranda. The gate opened to a white gravel path. "This is the only way to get there, except by boat."

"Lovely." Melanie turned to the dark, handsome stranger who had brought her to paradise.

"Come here." The seductive eyes wanted her. Melanie obeyed their command. "Did I tell you how glad I am that you're here?"

"No." Tell me. No, she thought as rushes of desire pulsed through her, *show me.*

Charles made love to her on the veranda in the fading golden rays of the tropical sun. The soft fragrant breeze caressed their naked flesh and the seagulls cooed and the ocean hummed.

Their lovemaking could have followed the leisurely rhythm of the tropics. It could have been slow and soft and lingering.

But it wasn't; they needed each other too much.

"I was wrong about you." Melanie lay beside him on the sand in the secluded cove carved out of volcanic cliffs.

"Oh?"

"I thought"—Melanie gently kissed his lips between words—"you were so arrogant."

"But I'm not?" Charles returned her kisses.

"No." Not at all.

"Neither are you. I was wrong, too."

Charles kissed a gentle path from her lovely warm mouth to her soft, round breasts. Melanie didn't wear a bathing suit top. There was no need. No one could see her but Charles. Her perfect breasts belonged to him. All of her, every inch of her golden body, belonged to Charles. Charles wanted her and she gave him all that she could give.

Charles and Melanie spent most of their idyllic week on St. Barts in the intimate privacy of the villa. They made brief excursions to shop in the charming villages and to dine at the island's gourmet French restaurants. They saw familiar faces— wealthy, famous, celebrity faces like theirs—but acknowledged them only with silent, knowing nods. Respect for privacy; that was the rule on St. Barts. That was why the rich and famous escaped there to mourn losses, rediscover themselves, and fall in love.

"One more fabric shop." Melanie's sky-blue eyes sparkled as she tugged playfully at his hand. This would be the fourth fabric shop they had visited. Melanie didn't explain her fascination with the shops, and Charles didn't ask. They gave her pleasure, that was enough. Charles watched amiably, his brown eyes amused and loving, as she enthusiastically touched and admired the wonderful bold colors and the exotic floral prints.

"You're insatiable."

"So are you," she answered seductively.

"Only with you." I can't get enough of you.

The conversation began as a tease outside a fabric shop in Lorient, but suddenly became serious and tender. They acknowledged the moment by wrapping their arms around each other and holding tight. The hug lingered, as it always did, and they let go reluctantly after Charles gently kissed her temple and whispered softly, "One more fabric shop."

The day before they left St. Barts, Charles made a trip to the village by himself.

"You'll see," he answered the surprised blue eyes that asked, Why?

When Charles returned three hours later, he found her on the veranda, gazing at the sapphire ocean, lost in thought. Melanie spent the hours missing him and realizing that tomorrow this wonderful perfect dream would be over. *Over*, or just different?

Melanie didn't know. She knew Charles's passion and desire, but she didn't know how he felt about *her*. He never told her. Charles never spoke the words all the other men had always spoken; he never even told her she was beautiful. But Charles held her and kissed her and smiled into her eyes; and Charles made desperate, breathless love to her.

Why was their loving so desperate? Melanie wondered. It was desperate—an urgent need driven by consuming desire—for both of them. As if a deep instinct warned them that it couldn't last. What if tomorrow it was over?

When Charles found her on the veranda, Melanie's fists were clenched and her body was rigid with fear.

"Hi." Charles kissed the back of her neck and felt the tension. "Are you *cold?*"

"No," she whispered, arching her lovely neck against his lips and not turning to face him until the tears vanished. "How was your trip?"

"Successful, I think. You have to tell me." Charles handed her a square white envelope-size box. "The shop doesn't go in for silk-lined velvet, but they had what I wanted."

What Charles wanted, what he left the villa to find, was a long strand of flawless pearls. Charles's discriminating eye knew quality. He would not buy Melanie anything but the best. Charles searched patiently until he found exactly what he wanted. While the delighted jeweller processed the sale of the best strand of pearls in the Caribbean, Charles held them in his hand, admiring the rich luster and imagining them around her lovely neck. He hoped she liked them.

"*Charles.*" Melanie had just vanquished sad, frightened tears. Now new tears—happy, joyous ones—filled her eyes. Her hands trembled as she tried to fasten the eighteen-carat gold clasp. "Help me."

Charles helped her on with the perfect pearl necklace, and he helped her off with her clothes.

It wasn't over when they returned to Manhattan, but it was different. There were so many hours of each day when they were apart; their busy, successful careers demanded it. They spent the free moments, *all* the free moments, together. They preferred to be alone—they longed for the luxurious privacy of St. Barts—but made the necessary appearances at the required parties, galas, and *events* together.

No one knew when Charles Sinclair and Melanie Chandler fell in love, but everyone knew they *had*. It was so obvious. The New York press, who had followed Charles and his notorious affairs for years, and Charles's friends, who had watched with head-shaking amazement as he ended yet another dazzling liaison, were unanimous in proclaiming this new love to be very special indeed.

"They are *always* holding hands, for God's sake."

"They're in *love*."

"I never knew what *happy* looked like on Charles."

"The way they look at each other!"

"Melanie seems a little subdued. Where are the famous golden cascades of joy?"

"Who needs cascades of joy when you have radiance? She's more beautiful than ever."

"Do you think he gave her that fabulous pearl necklace? She wears it all the time. So much for diamonds. . . ."

"I'll be back in a few hours." Melanie sealed the promise with a lingering kiss.

"Good," Charles whispered, touching her lips. "Give my regards to Brooke."

Melanie hadn't seen Brooke since their trip to Boston four weeks before. The moments she had with Charles were so precious; Melanie begrudged every minute they spent apart.

But she had to see Brooke.

Not that Brooke had to see *her*. . . . Brooke hadn't called; at least, there were no messages from Brooke on Melanie's newly installed—she spent every night at Charles's penthouse—answering machine. Brooke might refuse to leave a message on a machine, but Brooke *knew* where Melanie was. Everyone in Manhattan knew that Charles and Melanie were together. If Brooke wanted or needed to reach Melanie, she could.

At the end of the fourth week, Melanie called Brooke and suggested Sunday brunch at the Plaza. Melanie and Brooke often met for meals, in the diverting crush of noise and humanity, even though neither ate enough to justify the expense. They nibbled on fruit and drank pots of black coffee and the silences were filled by the bustling activity of the restaurant.

Brooke agreed to meet Melanie for brunch; but, Melanie thought, Brooke sounded reluctant. Maybe it was just Melanie's imagination—her guilt—overreacting. Besides, why should *she* feel guilty? Brooke could have called *her*.

Brooke doesn't care if she sees you or not, an uneasy voice reminded her. The "Save the Chandler Twin" campaign is your project, not Brooke's.

"How are you?" Melanie asked as soon as she and Brooke were seated in the Palm Court at the Plaza.

"Fine," Brooke answered mechanically. "How's Charles?"

Brooke didn't want to ask the question, and she *really* didn't want to hear its answer. But she couldn't help it, and she had to. Charles and Melanie had *happened*, and she had to face it. Brooke tried to desensitize herself by compulsively reading every article about them. She became a habitual watcher of *Viveca's View*. Brooke learned everything the press knew about Manhattan's hottest romance.

Now she was going to hear about it firsthand.

"Charles is fine. He says to say hello." Melanie smiled at her twin. Brooke's depthless blue eyes were dark and serious. Brooke, what's the matter?

"I didn't think you liked Charles."

Melanie drew a breath. Brooke's voice was so stern; it was as if Brooke was informing her silly little sister that one could not go from disliking someone to loving him.

"I didn't really know him."

"And now you do?"

"Yes." *No, Brooke, I don't know Charles, but I love him! We're learning about each other slowly and carefully. He has secrets, I have secrets. . . . Why are you cross-examining me?*

Melanie searched her twin's eyes and found the icecold answer: Brooke didn't approve. Brooke had *never* approved of what was important to Melanie. But how could Brooke not approve of Charles? Brooke liked and respected Charles, didn't she? Weren't Brooke and Charles—so alike in their brilliant accomplishments— *friends?*

Oh, no, Melanie's heart ached as she understood what the ocean-blue eyes were telling her. It wasn't disapproval of Charles; it was disapproval of *her.*

I've never been good enough for you, have I, Brooke? And now you believe I'm not good enough for Charles, either. . . .

Melanie believed it, too; it was her greatest fear.

"I want to show you something." Charles led her by the hand from his bedroom onto the huge terrace overlooking Manhattan. Dark, rich soil filled the previously empty red-bricked garden wells.

"Dirt." Melanie squinted in the early-morning June sun.

"Topsoil. Ready to be planted. I thought you might like to choose the flowers."

Charles sounded tentative; maybe he had guessed wrong.

"Yes!" Melanie's lips found his and explored for a long, soft moment. Finally she asked, "Do you think roses would grow here?"

"Sure. The drainage is good. We'll probably have to wrap burlap around them in winter. It's so unprotected. . . ."

"You really do know, don't you?"

Charles shrugged, but he did know. He loved the rose gardens at Windermere. As a little boy he had helped the gardeners.

Melanie watched a flicker of sadness darken his eyes. *Tell me what makes you so sad, Charles. I see the deep, painful secrets you try so hard to conceal. Can't you tell me? There is nothing you could tell me that would change the way I feel. . . .*

"There's a nursery in Southampton that specializes in roses," Charles said without answering her question.

"Let's go."

Charles laughed and tightened his arms around her. "OK."

"We need to swing by my place on the way back to get some shorts. Do you have a shovel and trowel—and . . ."

"Whoa. I thought we'd just choose the flowers. I was going to have someone come out next week to plant them."

"Oh."

"You *want* to plant them?" Charles was pleased. He hoped Melanie would like the idea of a flower garden, and she more than liked it.

"*Yes.*"

* * *

Six hours later Melanie sat cross-legged on the red-brick terrace surrounded by pots of roses and azaleas. She wore UCLA gym shorts and a pale-yellow blouse knotted under her naked breasts. She was sketching a design of the garden.

"I made you some iced tea," Charles said as he emerged onto the terrace. "How's it coming?"

Melanie told him an hour ago, when he suggested that he begin digging, that it would be at least an hour before she was ready.

"We bought too many Sterling Silvers."

"I seem to remember a pair of earnest blue eyes telling me with the greatest confidence that one could never have too many Sterling Silvers." Charles rested his hand gently on top of her golden head.

"Well, that *is* right. We just didn't buy enough Garden Partys."

"Ah. Let me see what you're doing." Charles felt a little resistance as he took the sketchpad from Melanie's hands.

"Just drawing a picture of how it will look," she explained quickly. "Trying to get the colors to blend."

Charles looked for an amazed moment at the sketch of the garden. It was very good. Curious, he started to flip to the beginning of the sketchpad.

"Charles, don't."

He stopped. "Why? What is it?"

"It's just sketches of designs for clothes. Silly." Melanie reached for her sketchbook.

"Not silly. But I won't look if you don't want me to."

"Thanks," she said as he handed it back to her. She turned away from him and faced the colorful pots of roses. "I guess we should start digging."

"Melanie." Charles spoke quietly. "The dress you gave Galen. She wondered if you made it. Did you?"

Melanie gave a slight nod.

"I never planned to be a model. I wanted to be a designer." Melanie spoke softly as she told Charles her secret dream. "But when I had photographs taken of me wearing my designs, it was me, not the clothes, that was marketable."

"Just because you *are* doesn't mean your designs *aren't*. The dress for Galen would have been. You must know that. You model clothes with designer labels that aren't nearly as beautiful."

Charles looked in her blue eyes and discovered that Melanie *didn't* know. He urged gently, extending his hand toward her. "Let me take a look."

Melanie sat beside him on the chaise lounge as he slowly, studying each page with great care, looked through her sketchbook. The half-finished sketch on the last page of designs was a dress made of a fabric they had seen on St. Barts.

"Melanie . . ."

"It's just a silly hobby . . . how I relax."

"They're wonderful."

Melanie shrugged.

"I mean it."

"Thank you."

"Are you going to do something with these?"

"No. Maybe next life . . ."

Charles didn't push. For some reason Melanie seemed shy and uncertain about her talent.

"You don't design clothes for yourself, or, at least, there are no sketches of blondes."

"That's true."

"I wonder why."

"I don't know." Melanie tilted her golden head thoughtfully. "I guess it's more fun to design clothes for Brooke and Galen and Fran. I close my eyes and picture them in one of my designs."

"Maybe when you close your eyes and picture yourself what you see—your happiest vision—is a pale-gray sweat suit."

"Maybe." The lovely blue eyes looked a little sad.

"Maybe," Charles whispered gently as he pulled her close to him, "you're a butterfly in search of a cocoon."

CHAPTER NINETEEN

New York City
June 1986

"*A*nd is it your testimony, Mr. Jones, that you were in Atlantic City and not New York on the night of October fifteenth, nineteen eighty-five?" Brooke stood near the jurors. When the witness answered her questions—looking at her because her blue eyes demanded it—he spoke to the jury as well.

"Yes."

"And is it further your testimony, Mr. Jones, that despite the accounts of four other witnesses who saw you in Manhattan—"

"*Objection.*" The defense attorney stood up. "The credibility of the witnesses who *allegedly* saw Mr. Jones—"

"Ms. Chandler?" The judge raised an eyebrow at Brooke.

"If opposing counsel would like a *voire dire* to determine the credibility of the four witnesses." Brooke looked earnestly at the judge.

"Mr. Hansen?" the judge queried.

"No, Your Honor."

"Objection overruled. You may proceed, Ms. Chandler."

Brooke cast a glance of carefully suppressed triumph at Andrew. He answered with a smile that told her, *You've got him now, Brooke.*

"Raise your chin, Melanie," Steve commanded.

"It's *raised.*" Melanie stood up straight, breaking the pose that Steve had been setting and resetting for the past half an hour. Melanie slowly moved her head through a range of motion, relaxing the taut, fatigued neck muscles.

"Christ," Steve hissed.

"I don't know why this is so difficult."

"Do you want me to tell you?"

"Yes."

"And you won't go crying to Adam?"

"I won't."

"You look terrible."

"*What?*"

"I'm trying to find an angle that won't reflect off the goddamned dark circles under your eyes. They glow *through* your makeup."

"I . . ."

"You've taken your whoring a little too far, Melanie. You're wearing it on your face. As if the whole world doesn't already know you spend all night every night screwing Charles Sinclair."

"You have no right . . ."

"I'm telling you the truth, Melanie. I always tell you the truth. You just don't want to hear it."

Melanie glowered at him, but she didn't move to leave.

"I'll tell you one more thing. It won't last. He'll leave you just like he's left every other woman in this town. You may think you're special, Melanie, but you're not. You're just the only one he's never had before. You could throw away your whole modelling career—you will if you don't get some rest—because of him. Don't do it, Melanie, because it won't last with Charles Sinclair. That's the truth."

"Brooke, you were terrific. What a victory." Andrew raved as he and Brooke walked from the courthouse back to the DA's office.

"Thank you. It feels good."

"It always feels good to win."

"Well, when you *know* the other guy is a criminal." Brooke smiled at Andrew. Andrew played to win. He didn't spend a lot of time dwelling on guilt or innocence. "This win feels good."

"Good enough to have dinner with me, Brooke, to celebrate your first single-handed conviction?"

"Andrew, I can't." *We* can't.

The past four months had been as if the night in March never happened. Andrew didn't mention Allison, nor did he ask Brooke out. Their relationship was as it had been before; the comfortable, professional relationship of respected colleagues.

"Just dinner, Brooke."

"No, thank you."

"Do you have someone?"

"No," Brooke answered truthfully.

"I worry about you."

I worry about you, too, Andrew. I'm sorry your life isn't happy. Brooke met his concerned thoughtful brown eyes and almost relented. Dinner would be nice, but . . .

"I'm *fine*, Andrew."

"So, that's a firm No?" Andrew teased.

"A firm, but flattered No." Brooke laughed softly and shook her head.

"Lieutenant Adrian, please," Brooke said twenty minutes later to the voice that answered the phone in Homicide.

It was a full minute before she heard Nick's voice.

"Nick Adrian."

"The author?"

In the past four months, Brooke had spoken to Nick over the phone several times about homicide cases they were preparing to prosecute, but she hadn't seen him since the night in March. *Reflections* had been returned to her in the day's official correspondence from the police department the following Monday. There had been a note: *Enjoyed the book. And dinner. And coffee. Nick.*

Yesterday's mail brought *The New Yorker*, with a short story entitled "Manhattan Beat" by Nick Adrian. It was a powerful, gripping, sensitive story. Brooke called to tell him how much she enjoyed it, but suddenly she felt awkward. She didn't know Nick. If he had wanted her to know he could have told her that night, while they were *discussing* short stories.

He chose *not* to tell me, Brooke realized as she waited for him to answer her question. Why am I doing this?

"Yes," Nick answered after a long pause.

"It's a wonderful story, Nick." There. Good-bye.

"Thanks."

Who was going to say good-bye first?

"Why didn't you tell me?"

"Let's see . . . Jason and Charles and Galen and Melanie."

"We spent a lot of time talking about short stories before their names came up. It seems like a conspicuous omission."

"The first time you call me about something other than the strictest of business is after you discover I am published in *The New Yorker*. What does *that* seem like to you, Counselor?"

"You're interrogating me."

"I think it's a pertinent question. To which you know the answer even though you may not admit it."

"What's the answer?" Brooke asked, knowing it, hoping Nick had a different answer.

"The answer is, Nick is suddenly worthwhile. Nick is more than *just* a cop. He's only *slumming* as a cop because that's the sort of thing serious writers do. You know, *living* the material. How am I doing?"

Brooke didn't answer, but her mind reeled. How much of what Nick said was true? Part of it, she realized, hating her own pretension, Part of it.

"You're a goddamned snob, Brooke," Nick whispered angrily just before hanging up the phone.

Nobody said good-bye.

"I made reservations for eight o'clock at Le Cirque. I told Jacques you might splurge and have four asparagus spears."

"A splurge would be three." Melanie smiled.

"So, shall I come by about seven?"

"I can't do Le Cirque tonight, Charles."

"Oh?"

"I need an early night. I'm getting dark circles under my eyes." *That* part of what Steve said was true; but not the rest, even though it was her greatest fear.

"Oh. All right."

"It's OK? I thought I'd try to go to bed about seven-thirty." So if you come by at seven.

"It's fine. I'll call you tomorrow."

No, wait, Charles. Don't be angry. I didn't mean we wouldn't be together tonight.
"OK."
"Good night, Melanie."
"Good night, Charles."
Melanie sat by the phone for twenty minutes. Charles had misunderstood. She wanted to see him. She wanted him in bed with her. Couldn't they just hold each other and fall asleep? But what if it was *she* who had misunderstood? What if Charles didn't want to be with her unless they could spend the night making love, having sex, *screwing*.

"No," she whispered. They had fallen asleep in each other's arms every night since St. Barts. Very late, *after* they had made love, yes, of course, *but* . . .

Melanie reached for the phone and dialed his penthouse. She had to talk to him. She needed to know.

The line was busy. He's calling Viveca, Melanie's fatigued mind taunted. Viveca, or any one of a hundred other women. Maybe even Brooke. *No.* He's probably just talking to Jason.

Melanie made herself wait for ten minutes before redialing. When she did there was no answer.

Charles was gone.

"This is Brooke Chandler from the DA's office. Is Lieutenant Adrian there?" Brooke placed the call—to apologize—at nine A.M. The night had been almost sleepless; he was right, and she had to tell him.

"No. He's out on a case. Can someone else help?"

"No. Would you please tell him that I called?"

Melanie had never been to Charles's office. They never tried to see each other during their busy workdays. Even now she only had an hour between photo sessions. It was barely enough time, but she had to see him.

Melanie walked along the marble corridors oblivious to the splendor of her surroundings. Some other time—please let there be other times—Charles could give her a tour of the fabulous building.

"My name is Melanie Chandler. I wondered if I could see Charles Sinclair." Melanie's words were unnecessary. The receptionist recognized her instantly and, given another instant, would have guessed what she wanted. *Everyone* knew about Charles and Melanie. "Let me see if he's free."

Two minutes later Charles appeared on the plush carpeted circular staircase at the far end of the reception area. The staircase led to the private executive offices of Charles and Jason and their editors.

"Hi."

"Come to my office."

They didn't speak again until they were inside Charles's magnificent office and the heavy door was closed and locked behind them.

"How are you? Your dark circles look better."

"Yours don't," Melanie whispered, and gently touched the blue-black shadows beneath his dark eyes. Despite her anxiety about their misunderstanding, and what it might mean, Melanie had slept; it was a testimony to how desperately she needed the sleep. But Charles looked as though he had been up all night . . .

"I guess I don't sleep well without you."

"I never wanted you to."

"No?"

"I thought I could go to bed early and you could join me." Melanie shrugged, acknowledging that it was a silly sentimental idea.

"How about if we both go to bed early? Should we try that tonight?"

Melanie answered him with a kiss that would have led to much more if she hadn't miraculously remembered her photo session. She pulled away reluctantly.

"I have to go." As Melanie turned toward the door, her gaze fell on the framed photograph on the wall. Steve must have taken it during the photo session in Central park last winter. Melanie hadn't seen it before now. It was a picture of *her* but not as Melanie Chandler, sophisticated high fashion model. Instead, it was a provocative, seductive portrait of a beguiling temptress. "Oh."

"Steve took that just after you said, 'I won't charge you for this, Charles.' "

"I didn't think you were paying attention."

"Always."

Nick returned Brooke's call at ten o'clock that night.

"You got my unlisted number."

"I thought you were calling about business. I wasn't able to return the call until now." The message had said *from the DA's office.*

"It wasn't business. I called to apologize."

"Not necessary." Nick sounded tired and defeated. "I was putting my words in your mouth, voicing my own paranoia about the value of what I do for a living."

"Nick, what's wrong?" Brooke decided the flatness in Nick's voice had nothing to do with their conversation yesterday. Something had happened; something *important* and terribly disturbing.

"Bad, bad murder today. Last night, actually." Nick had been at the scene, in her nice secure apartment, all night and most of the day. "It will be on the eleven o'clock news."

"What?"

"A young woman—twenty-seven, beautiful, a very successful broker with a big firm on Wall Street—murdered," Nick answered heavily. The woman had been raped and then knifed to death. Nick didn't tell Brooke that. "Her name is, was, Pamela Rhodes."

"I've heard of her. She did stock market commentary on the morning news shows."

"Yes."

Brooke could feel Nick's horror. He must have seen something unspeakably terrible. It shook him, and it enraged him.

"Do you know who did it?"

"No. Probably someone she knew, or thought she knew. It happened in her apartment. There was no sign of forced entry and she was dressed up." At least she had been, before . . .

"You'll find him soon." Brooke wanted to encourage him. She hated the tone—the tonelessness—of his voice.

"I hope so. I hope like hell this isn't the first victim of some crazy."

"Why do you think it might be?"

"Just a hunch. It was so brutal, and not one clue. Not a print to be found. We'll get a blood type from the semen, but other than that . . ." Nick sighed. "It just seems like more than a spurned lover. A little too, uh, professional, *meaning* psychopathic."

"Oh."

"Be careful, will you, Brooke?" Nick asked suddenly, the energy returning for a moment to his voice. Then he had to go. The police pathologist who had just completed the autopsy on Pamela Rhodes walked into his office. "I'll talk to you later. Thanks for calling."

So much BLOOD—too much. It will be less MESSY next time. Next time? Of course! There will be a bloody ETERNITY of next times until SHE understands. She CANNOT treat me this way!!! When she does, someone has to PAY. . . .

He looked at the words he had scribbled into his journal two nights before—only hours after he had brutally murdered Pamela Rhodes—and he smiled at the exciting memory.

CHAPTER TWENTY

*T*he July Fourth sun shone brightly on the Liberty Weekend celebration in New York Harbor. The unveiling of the revitalized Statue of Liberty the night before had been spectacular. Today's festivities—the parade of boats and the tall ships—would climax in a phenomenal fireworks display.

"Jason, this is such a thrill!" Brooke exclaimed as she boarded the one-hundred-twenty-foot yacht at the New York Yacht Club. "Thank you for including me."

"I'm glad you could come." Jason smiled graciously.

Brooke hadn't seen Jason for months. *He looks a little sad,* Brooke thought. His golden, sunny smile had lost some of its shine. Impulsively Brooke gave Jason a brief hug.

"Make yourself at home, Brooke. I'd show you around, but I have to stay here until we cast off."

Brooke wandered among the crowd on the yacht, smiling in recognition at face after famous face. It was after she smiled a familiar hello to the handsome if controversial network news anchorman—and he smiled in return—that Brooke realized with embarrassed horror she was behaving as if she knew them. She did know who they were. She watched them perform on television and film and stage, she listened to their music, and she admired the fabulous clothes they designed. They were recognizable, but she wasn't.

Still, they returned her smiles.

Because I must be someone, *Brooke realized. I wouldn't be on this yacht on this special day with these special people if I weren't. They just can't place me.*

"Brooke!"

"Hello, Adam." A truly familiar face.

"This is kind of exciting, isn't it?"

"A perfect day."

"Let me introduce you to some people," Adam offered.

Brooke and Adam retraced her steps. He introduced her to some of the faces with whom she had already exchanged smiles. Adam introduced her as Brooke Chandler; sometimes he added that she worked in the DA's office. Adam never mentioned that she was Melanie Chandler's *twin* sister.

Brooke hadn't seen or spoken to Melanie since their brunch at the Plaza. She followed Charles and Melanie's golden love affair in the press and wondered when it would end. What if it never did? What if, as the papers and magazines and television proclaimed, their joyous, blissful love was forever?

When Jason called a week ago to invite Brooke to join the Independence Day cruise, she accepted because she needed to see Charles and Melanie together. Brooke needed to find out for herself.

Charles loves her, Brooke decided as twilight fell over Manhattan. Brooke had never imagined such softness or such happiness in the dark-brown eyes. Charles loved Melanie; it was obvious. And there was something new—something serene—about Melanie.

"Anything on the Pamela Rhodes murder, Brooke?" the anchorman asked after dinner. Charles, Melanie, Adam, Jason, the anchorman, and Brooke sat on the aft deck, sipping after-dinner drinks in the twilight, waiting for darkness and the spectacular fireworks display to begin. He added pleasantly, "Off the record."

The question surprised Brooke. Then she remembered that Adam had mentioned the DA's office when he introduced them.

"On or off," Brooke replied. "It doesn't matter. I don't know anything."

Except the way Nick Adrian sounded, and his *off-the-record* fear that it was just the beginning.

"You knew her, didn't you, Charles?" Adam asked.

"One of Charles's many—" Jason began, but he saw Melanie's pale-blue eyes widen and stopped mid-sentence.

Charles reacted as if he'd been struck.

Jason, what is wrong? Charles wondered as he recoiled from the bitterness in his brother's voice. There had been an edge to Jason's polite reserve for months. Charles stared at his twin—what is it, Jason?—for a long bewildered moment. Then he answered heavily, "I knew Pamela."

An awkward silence ensued as they all frantically searched their minds for new, safe topics.

"That Jones conviction, Brooke," the anchorman finally murmured. "Really impressive."

"Oh, well . . ." He *does* know who I am, Brooke realized with amazement.

"Andrew Parker had better watch out."

"Oh, no. Andrew's the best. He's taught me everything I know."

"He may have taught you too much."

The last words were lost in the burst of light and color in the balmy July night as a galaxy of dazzling fireworks exploded overhead. Drawn by the magnificent spectacle appearing over the Manhattan skyline, they moved to the shiny brass railing on the leeward side of the yacht.

Only Charles and Melanie lingered behind.

"Melanie?" Charles held her hands in his and spoke softly.

"Why didn't you tell me that you knew Pamela Rhodes?" The light of the sky rockets danced off her pale-blue eyes.

"I knew her before I met you."

"But . . ."

"Darling, it doesn't have anything to do with us."

"Still . . ."

Charles stopped Melanie's lips with his own, and they convinced her, softly and tenderly, not to worry. As they kissed, their passionate faces were illuminated by brilliant rainbows of color in the summer sky. Jason and Brooke witnessed their twins' kiss. . . .

A rush of tingling, excited feelings flooded Brooke, as if Charles were kissing *her*. Brooke extinguished the surprising, wonderful sensations quickly, angry at her own reaction. Face it, Brooke.

Did he kiss Galen like that? Jason wondered with a mixture of sadness and rage. Did Charles seduce Galen as he is seducing Melanie? Of course he did. That was Charles's specialty; he lured his victims into a warm, secure web of love. Then, once trapped, he abandoned them. Jason's knowledge was firsthand. Charles had left him, without warning or explanation or apology, when they were twelve; and he did it again when they were eighteen.

Melanie steadfastly refused to think about her trip to Europe. It wasn't a thrilling adventure any longer. It meant being away from Charles. Each day Melanie's confidence in herself and their love grew stronger; but it was still delicate and fragile and precious. There were secrets they hadn't shared, and their lovemaking still had the desperate urgency of lovers fated to share stolen moments of passion, not a forever-and-always love.

Ten days before she was scheduled to leave, Adam gave her a final copy of her itinerary. There was one weekend, maybe two, that she could fly back to New York to see Charles. Maybe he would join her, maybe he could find a week or two. . . .

Melanie lay awake, safe in his arms, her mind racing, trying to visualize a way to give them a week. She would do photo sessions night and day. She could do that; somehow there wouldn't be dark circles. It seemed, Melanie thought, recalling the schedule that was neatly folded in her purse in Charles's living room, that there was one day with only a two-hour session planned in Rome at Gucci . . .

Melanie gently lifted the arms that held her and slid out of bed. Charles moved, but he didn't waken. When Melanie returned a half hour later—it *was* possible, she would talk to Adam in the morning—Charles was on the opposite side of the bed. Melanie crawled in carefully.

He felt so far away. Maybe he would wake up, find that she was not in his arms, and pull her close, the way they were supposed to be.

Tell me Father, please. I need to understand.

Elliott laughed a mean laugh.

You don't deserve an explanation.

Please.

The sailboat lurched in the heavy sea. Charles's heart ached with the familiar emptiness.

You don't deserve my love, Elliott hissed. Do you want to know why?

Yes, please. And I want you to love me, Charles added quietly.

I'll never love you. No one ever will. You're evil, Charles.

No.

Yes.

Elliott's dark eyes glistened with hatred. There was a sudden deafening crash followed by a frenetic swirl into darkness . . .

After it was over, Elliott lay on the deck. Bright-red blood gushed from his head and his dark eyes no longer glistened. Instead, his eyes clouded and his lips turned into a mean smile just before he died.

No, Charles pleaded.

"No!" Charles sat upright in bed. His naked chest heaved, and he held his head with his hands.

"Charles?" Melanie touched his damp, cold back.

But Charles didn't seem to hear her or feel her touch. Wordlessly, without looking at her, he left the bed and the bedroom. After a stunned moment Melanie followed.

Charles was on the terrace in the rose garden they loved so much. His hands were clenched tight at his sides. His handsome face was a tormented shadow in the pale moonlight.

"Charles."

He looked at her slowly and without recognition. Melanie gasped when she saw the pain in his dark eyes. She put her arms around him.

"Charles, tell me," she whispered. It was something more than a nightmare; it didn't go away when he awakened. It was what had been there all along, making their love so desperate and so fragile. Tell me, *please.*

Charles pulled away violently. Anger and confusion merged with the pain.

"I need to be alone, Melanie."

"Charles . . ."

He turned away from her. "I mean it."

Melanie retreated to the bedroom. She paced in the darkness, taunted by her own fears.

You don't know him, Melanie. And he doesn't want you to know him. He doesn't care enough to share himself with you. You're no different from all the others. This is how it ends with Charles Sinclair.

After an hour Melanie got dressed. She was stopped by his voice as she walked through the living room. Sometime in the past hour he had come in from the rose-scented air.

"Where are you going?"

"I guess I need to be alone, too, Charles."

Melanie looked toward him, but his dark eyes were hidden in shadows.

Stop me, Charles. Don't let this happen.

But Charles didn't stop her, and she left.

"I don't know if you realize this, *dear,* but we're leaving in five days for the most important modelling dates of your career."

"I know that." Five days. It had been five days since she left Charles's penthouse in the middle of the night. In five more days she would leave for Europe.

"So do you plan to look like death warmed over for Yves and Christian and Oscar?"

"I look fine."

"You look like shit," Steve corrected swiftly. Then a mean smile curled on his face. "Oh, God, it *happened,* didn't it? He dumped you."

"None of your business."

"This is a new record, Melanie. What was it, less than three months? Even vacuous Viveca kept his attention for longer than that."

Melanie trembled with rage as Steve continued his cruel harangue.

"Are you frigid, Melanie? I've always . . ."

"That's *it*, Steve. I warned you."

Melanie rushed out of the studio and up the flight of stairs to Adam's office.

"Is he in?" Melanie demanded of Adam's secretary. Tears threatened. Stay angry, she told herself.

"Yes. But . . ."

Adam's office door was ajar. Melanie walked in talking.

"I don't have to take it, Adam. If you let him treat me that way anymore I'll leave." Melanie stopped abruptly. Adam wasn't alone.

Charles. What was he doing here?

Business, of course; business as usual. Charles and Adam were seated at a table studying photographs. They both stood up and both moved toward her when she entered.

"Melanie, what's wrong?" Adam demanded, worried.

At that moment Steve burst in, panting, his eyes wild with rage.

Melanie glowered at Steve, then turned back to Adam.

"Him or me, Adam, you choose."

Don't look at Charles, Melanie's mind warned. But she couldn't help it. Her eyes flooded with hot tears. The exhaustion of five sleepless nights and the nervous energy of five days without food converged in a sudden ice-cold shiver. Miraculously, Melanie willed her trembling body to move out of Adam's office and away from *him*.

"Bitch," Steve hissed under his breath. Steve's anger turned to fear as he saw Charles moving toward him.

But Charles rushed past him to follow Melanie.

He found her in an alcove, pressed against a wall, trembling. Charles put his arms around her and held her tight.

"Melanie," Charles whispered softly, his lips lightly brushing her golden hair. "Darling."

Melanie felt his wonderful warmth and strength. Hold me, Charles, don't ever let me go.

He already *has* let you go, a voice reminded her. With great effort Melanie controlled her trembling and pulled free.

"Tell me about Steve. What did he do to you?"

"Nothing." Don't look at me as if you care, Charles. "I'm a little raw, that's all."

"I don't want him going to Europe with you. I'm going to speak to Adam."

"No, Charles, really. It's nothing."

They stood, close, but not touching, for several silent moments. When Melanie spoke, it was about *them*; what happened with Steve was so trivial by comparison.

"I'm sorry, Charles." Melanie forced a smile, but her lips quivered.

"I'm sorry, Melanie. I . . ."

"No." She held up a thin trembling hand. "I shouldn't have pushed you. There's no reason you should tell me."

"You were trying to help." Charles gently moved a strand of tear soaked gold away from her sky-blue eyes. His touch made the tears begin anew.

"Yes, but—" Melanie shook her head helplessly. The tears and emotional exhaustion had won again.

I would tell you, darling Melanie, if only I knew. But I don't know, and it has hurt you terribly. I have to let you go. Somehow I will find a way to live my life without you. I have to, but not yet. I can't leave you like this.

Charles cupped her damp cheeks in his hands and smiled.

"You owe me a dinner at Le Cirque. I'll pick you up at seven-thirty."

After Charles left, Melanie returned to Adam's office. Adam stood by the window and Steve sat in dark brooding silence by the door

"I apologize." Melanie addressed her apology to Adam, not Steve.

Adam looked surprised. Melanie wasn't temperamental. It seemed unlikely that the fireworks with Steve had been *her* fault. But the beautiful blue eyes were accepting the blame, or, at least, the responsibility.

Melanie did accept responsibility for what happened. She had let her raw, fragile emotions affect her work; it wasn't professional.

"All right." Adam smiled at her. Then he looked sternly at Steve. Steve had provoked Melanie; there was no other explanation. Adam issued the warning to Steve, "If anything like this happens again, I am going to demand the facts."

Melanie and Charles didn't dine at Le Cirque that night. They spent the evening—and the night and the next day and every minute until Melanie left for Paris—in Charles's penthouse, loving each other, silently and passionately saying good-bye.

"Siena was founded by Remus. It may even have been his choice for their great city."

"But Romulus preferred Rome, and killed Remus because of it."

"You should go to Siena anyway." Charles smiled and held her closer. "The buildings are made of white-and-black marble, and the view of the countryside from the *campanile* is magnificent. The Paolo, the famous horse race through the town, is held in August."

Charles didn't talk to Melanie about the relationship they both knew was ending. Instead, he told her, as he held her in his arms on their rose-fragrant terrace in Manhattan, about his favorite places in Europe.

He's sharing them with me now, because he won't be with me. Why, Charles? Melanie's heart cried in silent anguish. *I love you so much. And if you don't love me, why are your eyes so sad?*

"You'll love the roses in the Borghese Gardens in Rome. And there's a small hunting lodge with statues by Bellini in the courtyard. It's a little hard to find, I just stumbled onto it as I was wandering—"

"Why don't you show it to me?" Melanie regretted her question the moment she asked it. The sudden pain in his dark eyes matched the depthless ache in her heart. *I'm sorry, Charles, I just don't understand.*

"Jason is going to the America's Cup trials in Australia. He'll be away from August to November. . . ." Charles couldn't finish the lie. They both knew he *could* get away—they had all planned to spend two months in Kenya filming "Sapphire," hadn't they?—he just wasn't going to.

* * *

Charles took Melanie to the airport. They held hands in a distant corner of the Air France first-class lounge until her flight had been called for the final time.

"*Au revoir* Charles." Until we meet again.

"Good-bye, darling." It's over.

Melanie sat on a park bench in the Tuileries under the hot late-August sun. The Champs-Elysées swarmed with tourists, but the Parisians had vanished, as Charles said they would, escaping to the Riviera for the final month of summer.

Charles. In three and a half weeks, the pain hadn't diminished and the hope hadn't died. It wasn't really good-bye; it was just sadness about the two-month separation. I'll hear from him. There will be a message waiting for me at the Bristol.

But there were no messages at the hotel from Charles.

Melanie looked at the postcards that lay beside her on the bench and thoughtfully fingered the magnificent pearl necklace Charles had given her.

She sighed softly, picked up a postcard, and wrote,

Dear Charles,
Greetings from the Jeu de Paume and apologies to your Monet for once placing it at the Louvre instead of this magnificent spot!

Stupid, Melanie thought. She ripped the postcard in half and tried again.

Dearest Charles,
I love you so much.

No, she couldn't tell him that, even though it was true. Charles had never told her he loved her. Of course he hadn't! Because he *didn't*.

Melanie wasted three more postcards of Impressionist paintings before writing,

Charles,
I miss you.
                         Melanie

Melanie carried the postcard with her for a week before addressing it, applying the correct postage—now Italian because they were in Rome—and mailing it.

Adam watched Melanie's torment with helpless concern. He resisted asking her— it wasn't his business anyway—because she was trying so hard not to let it show. Adam noticed the change, because he had known her before. He knew there used to be a natural golden joy, a happiness that glowed from a radiant soul. The gazelle-like spring had vanished from her stride, and her flawless smile came with effort.

Adam noticed, because he had known the unspoiled, confident, dazzling California surfer girl. But the couturiers of Paris and Rome, who didn't know the old Melanie, marvelled at the new one. They gasped in breath-held admiration at the proud, bewitching, haunted eyes, the austere aristocratic face, and the graceful elegance. They proclaimed her—the Americans were right!—the most beautiful model in the world.

In her suffering, Melanie Chandler had become even more beautiful.

*   *   *

Adam finally decided to speak with her at the beginning of the fifth week. If she didn't want to talk, fine. He just wanted her to know he was available, and he cared.

"Do you have the energy to walk back to the hotel?" Adam asked.

"Sure." Melanie had spent the afternoon being photographed modelling the exquisite, creative jewels of Bulgari. The mental strain of holding pose after pose matched the physical rigors of a fast-paced, high-pressure fashion show; both were exhausting, but after a photo session a brisk walk felt good.

"Are you enjoying Rome?" Adam asked after they had travelled for a block and a half along via Condotti.

"Oh, yes. The roses in the Borghese Gardens—" Melanie began, then stopped. She had only seen Charles's favorite places; she hadn't visited the Colosseum or the Forum or the Pantheon or the catacombs. "Yes."

"Good." Adam waited until they had successfully crossed the chaos of the via Veneto before continuing carefully, "I sort of expected Charles would join you over here."

Melanie smiled a wistful smile.

"It's over, Adam." Melanie needed to speak the words aloud. It made them seem more real, and they were real. Her love affair—her *affair*—with Charles Sinclair was really over.

"I'm sorry."

"You know Charles—he doesn't have long-lasting relationships."

Adam and Melanie walked in silence toward the Eden Hotel. As they approached, Adam said, "I've known Charles for many years, Melanie. What he had with you . . . did you end it?"

"*No.*"

"Then I don't understand."

"Charles just didn't want me anymore," Melanie whispered softly. He never wanted *me*. He only wanted my beautiful body, and once he owned it he quickly became bored.

Adam looked in her lovely sad eyes and thought, How could he not want you? How could anyone not want you?

Adam and Melanie didn't talk about Charles again, but Adam became her friend. Slowly and patiently he tried to resurrect the joy he knew lay buried beneath the unhappiness.

"Adam!"

"What?"

"You're trying to make me laugh!"

Adam had been teasing her as they strolled through the yacht basin in Monte Carlo. He had finally resorted to pretending he was going to push her into the sparkling blue Mediterranean.

"Is that so bad?"

"*Why?*"

"Because I love the way you laugh."

Melanie didn't laugh then. Her blue eyes became soft and thoughtful and she whispered, "Thank you."

Melanie laughed later, and it was a little golden and almost joyous, at the antics of the octopus in Jacques Cousteau's Oceanographic Museum. Adam wanted to acknowledge her laugh with a kiss, but he resisted, settling for gently draping his arm around her as they walked back to the splendid Hermitage Hotel.

* * *

"Off with the old and on with the new, eh, Melanie?"

"What?"

Steve gestured for her to lift her chin a little higher before answering. They had driven to Cap d'Antibes for a photo session at the Hotel du Cap. "Charles for Adam."

"You're wrong."

"I'm never wrong," Steve snarled. "Which one is the better lover, Melanie? Or do you ever let anyone actually touch your perfect body? Maybe that's why Charles finished with you so quickly."

"Stop it," Melanie warned.

"You prefer to touch yourself, is that it? Or, I've got it, you and Fran have always seemed close—"

"That's it," Melanie spoke calmly.

"That's it? You and Fran?"

"No, that's *it*. I warned you."

Melanie took a taxi from Cap d'Antibes back to Monte Carlo. Adam was working in his suite when she arrived.

"That was in *October?* Why didn't you tell me then?"

"I thought I could handle it. I *did* handle it. It was all right—not pleasant, but all right—until about three months ago."

"OK." Adam frowned briefly then smiled. "You're having dinner with me—that is, watching *me* eat—at seven."

"I am?"

"Yes. We have reservations at Gabriella's."

Four hours later, as Adam and Melanie dined at the most romantic restaurant in the principality of Monaco, Steve Barnes drove at breakneck speed toward the airport at Nice. Steve was returning to New York; Adam had just fired him.

"It seems too extreme," Melanie murmured.

"Not extreme enough," Adam corrected swiftly. "There's no excuse for what Steve did."

"Maybe it's me." Melanie frowned.

"You weren't the only one. I made some calls before I met with Steve. He's been doing this kind of thing for years."

"Fran did say he did it to her."

"Why in God's name didn't anyone tell me?"

"Afraid, I guess." Melanie tilted her golden head.

"Hey"—Adam reached between the pale-pink candles and touched her flushed cheeks—"never be afraid to tell me anything, OK?"

Melanie's eyes answered with a sparkling, happy flash of blue: "Never?"

"Never."

Melanie laughed softly and cupped his hand in both of hers.

"You're a kind man, Adam Drake."

Charles stood just inside the door The concierge at the Hermitage told him that mademoiselle and monsieur were dining at Gabriella's. Charles could have waited until she returned, but . . .

He was desperate to see her. He made the trip on impulse, urged by his aching desire and loneliness; he missed her so much! Maybe, if he told her about himself, as much as he *knew*, and she was willing to take the risk, they could try.

Charles was desperate to see Melanie, and in his desperation he had created a fantasy. As he watched her, laughing and happy as she flirted with Adam, the dream dissolved into bitter reality.

You can't guarantee her happiness, a voice deep within reminded him. There is something terribly wrong with you. Let her *go*. You have no right.

Charles turned to leave, but Adam's voice stopped him.

"Charles!"

"*Charles*," Melanie breathed. Without looking at Adam, Melanie left the table and quickly wove through the tables to Charles.

"Hi." *I got your postcard. I miss you, too. I love you.* "I was in the neighborhood. I just . . . my plane leaves in two hours."

A hush had fallen over the restaurant; interested eyes watched the celebrated couple and ears strained to hear.

"Let's get out of here."

Gabriella's was perched on a steep cliff. Narrow paths wound through terraced gardens. Moments after leaving the restaurant, Charles and Melanie disappeared into the dense green maze.

"Tell me why you came." Melanie spoke quietly when they stopped finally safely out of sight. "You weren't just in the neighborhood."

"No. I came to see you." *To tell you about a wonderful fantasy I had.* Charles sighed. "I came to explain why it—*we*—will never work."

"Why?" *No, don't tell me, Charles. I don't want to hear it.*

"I'm no good for you, Melanie. Seeing you with Adam—"

"There's nothing between me and Adam! Charles, you can't believe there is."

"No," Charles answered truthfully. "But Adam, or someone like Adam, can give you the happiness you deserve."

"And you can't?"

"I haven't, have I?"

"Yes."

"No. I've hurt you. I didn't mean to, but I did. It's me, Melanie. I have deep flaws . . . " *And you are flawless.*

"I can't believe it!" Melanie's eyes flashed with anger "That's *my* line, 'You'll be better off without me.' Can't you do better than that?"

"No, it's the truth." Charles hated the anger and pain in her eyes; he hated himself for causing it.

"Why did you really come, Charles? Just to twist the knife?"

"*Melanie.*"

"So, *twist* it. Tell me the truth. 'You're not good enough for me, Melanie. I'm *bored* with you, Melanie.' " Her eyes filled with hot tears and she had to get away from him.

"*No,*" he whispered as she disappeared into the green maze.

Charles started to follow her, but he stopped. Would it help her? She didn't believe the truth, and she *couldn't* believe what she said about herself. She was *too* good for him; he could spend forever with her and never feel a second of boredom. She knew that, didn't she?

Of course she did. The angry words—full of contempt for his foolishness—made it easier for her to hate him, easier for her to forget him, easier for her to get on with her life.

Charles didn't follow Melanie. There was nothing more to say.

CHAPTER TWENTY-ONE

"*F*ireworks in Monte Carlo! Good evening, I'm Viveca Sanders and this is *Viveca's View*." The camera zoomed in to Viveca's face. "Yesterday, a blow-up between top model Melanie Chandler and celebrated fashion photographer Steve Barnes led to the photographer's precipitous departure from the Cote d'Azur. Only hours after severing her successful business relationship with Mr. Barnes, Ms. Chandler ended the romance that has captivated Manhattan since May."

A photograph of the yacht-cluttered harbor in Monte Carlo appeared on the television screen.

"Last evening," Viveca continued, "Charles Sinclair arrived in Monte Carlo only to discover super-model Melanie Chandler enjoying an intimate dinner with model-mogul Adam Drake. Melanie and Charles vanished for an out-of-view confrontation following which Charles promptly left Monte Carlo."

Viveca's face reappeared on the screen. Her eyes sparkled and her full lips turned into a slight smile.

"Both men returned to New York today. However, neither Charles Sinclair nor Steve Barnes is talking. Meanwhile, on the French Riviera, a new photographer is marvelling at the opportunity to photograph the world's premier model. And perhaps tonight Adam and Melanie's romantic repast will not be interrupted . . ."

"Goddamned bitch," Steve hissed at the television as the camera faded from Viveca's smug face to a commercial.

Across Manhattan, Charles swore at the same face, angrily turned off the television, and stormed out of his penthouse.

Oh, Melanie, Brooke thought. How could you do that to Charles? He cared so much. . . .

The phone rang. It was Andrew, calling to discuss the most effective order of witnesses in the State versus Fortner trial.

"Allison is ill again, Brooke," Andrew said softly after he and Brooke had plotted their legal strategy.

"Andrew, I'm sorry."

"Brooke, if I could just see you. I could use a friend."

Brooke smiled as she thought about her handsome, persuasive friend.

"You're a married man with political aspirations. Even a hint of scandal could ruin your future."

"Let me worry about that. Besides, Brooke, the marriage is no good. As soon as Allison is well enough, I am going to end it."

Brooke knew it was Andrew's frustration talking, not his heart. Andrew would never leave Allison. Maybe Andrew didn't hear the softness in his voice whenever he spoke Allison's name, but Brooke did.

Brooke wondered if Andrew would even be interested in her if he were free. Now she was forbidden fruit and a challenge. The Deputy DA loved challenges and risks, and he loved to win. We're not Edmund Rochester and Jane Eyre, Brooke mused. Ours isn't a passionate, desperate love foiled by a mad wife.

"I have some depositions to read, Andrew, especially now that we've changed the order of witnesses."

"Brooke . . ."

"I can't," Brooke said apologetically. She wasn't rejecting him, she was rejecting the situation. She hoped he knew and understood.

"All right." Andrew laughed softly, easily. "I'll see you in court."

"Yes." Good, he *did* know. Brooke added quietly, "Goodnight, Andrew."

Brooke heard the sirens in the distance. It was almost midnight. Distant sirens and midnight and the too-hot humid September weather went together.

But now these sirens were close. Brooke looked out the window and saw NYPD squad cars, two ambulances, and a medic unit arriving at her apartment building. She watched as uniformed men rushed inside.

Brooke quickly changed out of her robe into jeans, a light cotton blouse, and tennis shoes. The hallway outside her apartment was cluttered with other tenants; some rushed to the scene, and others walked slowly, not wanting to go, but unable to resist.

By the time Brooke reached the apartment, two floors below, she had heard one word—whispered, gasped, and shrieked—over and over: *Murder*.

The door to the apartment was ajar, but the view inside was completely obstructed by police officers. Brooke knew the woman who lived there. Belinda Cousins was only a few years older than Brooke. She owned and ran a well-known Madison Avenue advertising agency. Belinda and Brooke did their laundry at the same time—eleven o'clock on Friday night. Where were the good men? they laughingly asked each other. They talked about how it was safer to live here, in an inexpensive, low security apartment building, than in a glamorous penthouse on Fifth Avenue. Not that Brooke had a choice, but Belinda did.

Brooke approached one of the officers.

"I'm Brooke Chandler from the district attorney's office." Brooke smiled, remembering her faded jeans and tousled hair, and explained, "I live here. May I go in?"

"If you want to, ma'am, Ms. Chandler." The officer stepped aside.

"Don't let her in!"

"Nick," Brooke whispered. She recognized his voice and saw him, his back, hunched over something.

Instinctively, Brooke walked toward him.

"Get out of here, Brooke," Nick hissed over his shoulder. He didn't turn to face her.

"Nick, I—" Brooke gasped.

Nick's warning came too late. Brooke was already in the middle of the blood-splattered room. And even though Nick tried to protect her from seeing what he saw, using his body to block her view of the mutilated body of her *friend*, Brooke saw enough.

"Oh, my God," Brooke breathed, reflexively covering her face with her hands.

Nick couldn't go to her. He couldn't let her see the face, what had been the face. Nick couldn't even turn around; he could only listen to Brooke's horror behind him.

"*Nick!*"

"Go back to your apartment, Brooke," Nick whispered hoarsely. "Please."

"I know her, Nick. You can help her, can't you?"

"Jesus Christ, would someone please get her out of here?" Nick yelled angrily over his shoulder.

It was three hours before Nick could leave the murder scene. He had to see it all and think about it all while it was fresh. Nick had to search for clues amidst the carnage. And he had to deal with his own reaction before seeing Brooke.

Nick saw the slit of light under Brooke's door. Of course she wouldn't be able to sleep. Who could? Nick wondered if she was expecting him. . . .

"Brooke," he called softly without knocking.

"Nick?"

"Yes."

Brooke opened the door hesitantly. She was scared. As soon as she saw him, she opened it wide.

"Nick," she whispered. Tears filled her dark-blue eyes.

Nick felt almost as helpless now, two feet away from her, as he felt three hours ago when he couldn't move because he wouldn't let her see the rest of Belinda Cousins' body. Then Nick extended his arms, and Brooke fell against him gratefully. As he held her tight, the helpless feeling vanished. Brooke curled against him, resting her head in the curve of his neck, and cried. Nick stroked her fine chestnut hair, comforting her, wishing he could erase the gruesome image from her brain.

When Brooke finally pulled free, Nick missed her warmth and softness immediately. He needed comforting, too. She had given it to him without even knowing it.

"It was him, wasn't it? The psychopath you were afraid was out there."

"I think so," Nick said. He was sure of it. "What makes you ask?"

Brooke hesitated.

"The way you sounded when Pamela Rhodes was killed. It was as if you had seen something unspeakably horrible. Like this."

"It was the same," Nick said. Come back to my arms, Brooke. Let me hold you.

"I made some coffee."

"It's three in the morning. Aren't you going to work pretty soon? Like in four or five hours?"

"I made enough coffee to last for four or five hours. I made enough for both of us," Brooke answered quietly.

She didn't want to be alone.

Brooke and Nick talked until just past dawn and it was time to get ready to face the day.

After Nick got her to promise that she would have a peephole installed in the door—he expected the apartment manager was already working on it—and a dead bolt lock, they didn't talk about the murder or crime or the law or their jobs. Instead they talked about his writing, about the short story that was published and the new one he had started, and books and plays and movies and songs. And, in little bits, they talked about their lives.

Just before the autumn sun cast a yellow hue over Manhattan, as tears spilled, and she was too tired to care, and she needed to say it out loud to someone, and they were bonded forever by the sight of the dead woman, Brooke told Nick how angry she was at her vain, self-centered, insensitive twin for hurting Charles Sinclair.

You wouldn't care so much about Melanie ending a love affair, Brooke, Nick thought, if you didn't care so *very* much about her lover.

There was less BLOOD this time. I'm getting better—practice makes PERFECT. This one pleaded so frantically!!! I patiently explained to her that it wasn't my FAULT. I had no choice! Another WOMAN had signed her DEATH warrant. I don't think she believed me. At least, this time, there was less BLOOD.

He finished writing and closed the blue leather journal. He carefully washed the bloodstained knife in the sink, dried the shiny blade on a soft cloth, removed the whetstone from his desk drawer, and began to sharpen the lethal weapon for the next time.

There *would* be a next time, he thought with a smile. Unless something happened to stop him—it was up to *her*—he would kill again in precisely one month.

Melanie returned from Europe on October first. She waited until the seventeenth, two weeks before their birthday, to call Brooke. Melanie didn't know if she and Brooke could try again. The progress they had made, the fragile beginnings of friendship, had been shattered in one stroke by Melanie's relationship with Charles. Brooke's disapproval, Brooke's obvious disdain for Melanie's foolishness, made it impossible for them to be together. Except for Liberty Weekend, when they kept a cool, polite distance, Brooke and Melanie hadn't seen each other since the disastrous brunch at the Plaza.

Now Melanie's relationship with Charles had ended, as Brooke knew it would. Brooke was right. Brooke was always right. Melanie didn't know if she and Brooke could begin again, but if Brooke was willing . . .

Why wouldn't Brooke be willing, Melanie wondered as she dialed the phone. After all, Brooke had lost nothing. It was she, Melanie, who had lost everything, including her pride.

"Hello, Brooke. It's . . ."

"Melanie." Brooke asked dutifully, "How was Europe?"

"Fine." Awful. "How is your work?"

"Fine. Busy."

"Are you involved in the Manhattan Ripper investigation?"

"The what?"

"The man who killed Pamela Rhodes," Melanie began. Pamela Rhodes was one of Charles's women; like her, a name on Charles Sinclair's long list. "Last night, he murdered Ryan Gentry, the actress. Apparently he killed someone else in September. I'm surprised—"

"Last night? Oh, no," Brooke murmured. She hadn't heard. She had been in the archives of the law library at Columbia all day and hadn't even watched the evening news. "Who is calling him the Manhattan Ripper?"

Brooke knew it wasn't Nick. In fact, it probably infuriated him.

"I don't know. The news media, I guess."

"Oh." Brooke's mind's eye recalled the horrible image of Belinda Cousins. A psychopath was brutally murdering Manhattan's beautiful, successful young women. And he chose as his targets women like Melanie, her *sister*, her *twin*. Brooke felt a sudden rush of emotion. If anything ever happened to Melanie . . .

"I wondered if you'd like to come here for our birthday," Melanie suggested tentatively.

"Yes, Melanie. I'd like to very much."

"Brooke, It's Nick."

"I just heard. I'm sorry."

"I'd like to talk to you about the case. I need to bounce my ideas off someone." Nick's tone was matter-of-fact and businesslike. This *was* their business. The tone softened as he added, "You."

"OK," Brooke agreed uneasily.

"Brooke, I'm not going to show you pictures, for God's sake." The softness was suddenly gone. He was so tired—too tired—and his emotions were raw; but he was taking his fury out on her of all people. "Sorry. Maybe this wasn't such a good idea."

"Here's what I was just about to make for dinner—cheese and crackers. There's plenty for both of us."

"Sounds good."

"OK, so?"

"Thirty minutes. Thank you, Brooke."

Nick arrived thirty-five minutes later. He had stopped, it took five minutes, to buy a bottle of champagne.

"I like the peephole and the locks." Nick hadn't been at her apartment, and hadn't seen her, since the last murder.

"You look really tired." The dark circles and cloudy gray eyes told a tale of many sleepless nights.

Brooke knew Nick had been busy. In the past month he had made a few brief calls to her at work. He wanted to see if she was all right. Was she still sleeping with the lights on? Brooke told him, Yes, she was sleeping with the lights on, but she *was* sleeping.

Which was more than she could say for him.

"The unusually hot, humid summer left its share of unsolved murders," Nick explained with a shrug. Brooke's thoughtful dark-blue eyes continued to stare. Nick smiled. "Go ahead, say it, you look terrible, Nick."

Brooke frowned slightly. That wasn't what she had been thinking. She had been thinking, You are so handsome, Nick. It was what everyone said about him; gorgeous, sexy, seductive Nick Adrian, the lieutenant with the bedroom eyes. Brooke had never thought about it before. After all, counting tonight, she had only seen him four times.

"You look hungry, Nick."

They ate cheese and crackers and drank champagne and talked about the case.

"Are they really calling him that?" Nick's annoyance at the Manhattan Ripper label was obvious.

"Yes." Before Nick arrived Brooke had watched the news. Every station used it. Tomorrow "Manhattan Ripper" would be a newspaper headline.

"What *is* there about glorifying criminals? There is no glory in what this man does. He is evil, unbelievably evil." Nick felt his rage surfacing.

"Like when they talk about terrorists *masterminding* a hijacking or a bombing," Brooke said quietly.

"That drives me crazy, too." Nick smiled and the rage retreated.

"Ryan Gentry," Brooke spoke the name of the murdered woman quietly. "I read a review about her in last Sunday's *Times*."

Nick nodded. "Broadway's most enchanting actress."

"They've all been so special, haven't they? Young and talented and successful."

"Yes. Just like—"

"My sister."

"Just like *you*. New York's newest and youngest assistant district attorney."

Brooke smiled. "I hadn't even thought about *me*. I'm not like those women."

"Yes you are." Nick's gray eyes were concerned and serious. "You have to be very careful, Brooke."

"I am," she assured him, but it wasn't true. She could wander around Manhattan so totally preoccupied with a case that she was oblivious to her surroundings. She would have to be more careful, even though it had nothing to do with the Manhattan Ripper murders. Brooke added, "These women weren't murdered at random in the streets. They were in their apartments."

"Yes. There was no forced entry and they were all dressed up for the evening."

"So it had to be someone—some man—they all knew."

"If he's there, we can't find him. There doesn't seem to be a personal link between the three."

"OK, then someone they all knew *of* and had no reason to fear. Someone well known, someone you and I . . ." Brooke's voice trailed off.

That was what scared him. The dead women were smart, savvy, and sophisticated; they weren't easily fooled. Yet they had permitted, *welcomed*, this lunatic into their homes. And for all Brooke's success, for as bright and discerning and astute as she was professionally, there was a trusting innocence about her.

"That's one possibility. He could be someone we all would recognize. Who else?"

"Someone with a plausible line."

"Such as?"

"Someone writing a book on career women of the eighties. That's *in* right now."

"OK. So the man is either just famous, and they'd like to meet him, or he approaches them through what matters most to them—their work."

"It seems hopeless, Nick. Where do you start?"

"It's not hopeless, Brooke. It's just going to take time," Nick answered quietly. And it may cost a few more lives, he thought, feeling a rush of ice-cold fear.

Three days later, when Brooke walked into Andrew's office, Nick and Andrew were sitting at the desk staring intently at several eight-by-twelve-inch photographs. Their handsome faces were somber.

"Andrew? Nick?"

"Brooke!"

Andrew and Nick quickly gathered the photographs and covered the stack with a folder.

"What's . . . ?" What were the pictures? Their faces told her it was something she didn't want to see.

"The chief of police and the district attorney have decided the DA's office has to become involved *now* with the Manhattan Ripper investigation."

"Manhattan Ripper? Is that what *we're* calling it . . . him . . . *it*?"

"Afraid so."

"How can the DA's office help with the investigation?" Brooke asked, frowning.

"You can't. At least, not yet, not until we get a lead or a suspect." For now it was Nick's investigation. He could handle it. "This is pure P.R.—I keep Andrew informed and we present a unified front to the press—that sort of thing."

"But Andrew doesn't have to go to the scene of the crime," Brooke said flatly. It was bad enough that Nick had to be there, and Andrew had enough worries of his own.

"No." Andrew smiled reassuringly at her concerned blue eyes. "I don't. Nick will call me right away, so that I know."

"Why did you look at the photographs?" That was what Nick and Andrew had been doing when she walked in, studying pictures of the Manhattan Ripper's victims.

"I thought I should," Andrew answered evenly, but he frowned. "Probably a bad idea."

Brooke nodded in somber agreement.

"I worry about you, Brooke," Andrew spoke to Brooke as if Nick wasn't there. His voice was gentle and concerned. "Being alone . . ."

Brooke shrugged away a shiver of fear.

"I'm *fine*, Andrew."

The intercom on Andrew's desk sounded.

"Yes?"

"There's a call for Ms. Chandler from Charles Sinclair," the muffled voice spoke from the desk. "Shall I take a message or . . ."

"I'll take it in my office." Brooke's cheeks flushed pink. "Andrew, I'll be back. Good-bye, Nick."

A half a minute later Brooke depressed the blinking button on the phone in her office.

"Charles?"

"Hello, Brooke. How are you?"

"Fine." How are *you?*

"Good. I wondered if you could have lunch with me one day this week."

"Yes." *Why?* Brooke consulted her appointment book. Wednesday and Thursday she would be in court; she and Andrew would spend the lunch recess planning strategy. Assuming the case ended when they anticipated, she should be free on Friday. "Is Friday all right?"

"Friday's fine."

Charles told Brooke he would meet her at the Court Jester, a restaurant located near the DA's office. He said good-bye without ever telling her why he wanted to see her.

She would find out on Friday. As Brooke penciled the initials *C.S.* into her appointment book, she realized that Friday was Halloween; her birthday, *their* birthday. On Friday Brooke would have birthday lunch with Charles and birthday dinner with Melanie . . .

"I want to ask you something, Brooke," Charles began after they ordered lunch. "But I don't want you to feel under any pressure."

Please don't ask me to convince Melanie to come back to you, Charles. I see the sadness—the great loss—in your dark eyes. I see how much she hurt you. But . . .

"OK." Brooke's heart pounded. *Please.*

"We really need an attorney full time at Sinclair. I've spoken to John Perkins and he agrees. He can provide us with someone from the firm. That would be fine"—Charles smiled at her—"but it wouldn't be as good as you."

"Me?" Brooke wondered if Charles could hear her. She couldn't hear anything except the roar of blood pounding through her brain. *Me?*

"Of course you. Before we agree to anyone else, Jason and I want to know if you would consider it. I didn't know if you planned to do trials and criminals always or . . ."

Brooke shook her head and breathed, "I don't know."

"You might consider it?"

"Yes. I'd need to think about it."

"Of course. Let me know whenever."

Charles and Brooke spent the rest of lunch talking about her work, and his, and books and theater and even the abrupt wintry end of the long, balmy fall. Charles and Brooke covered many topics, but neither mentioned Melanie.

That evening Brooke gazed in amazement at her twin sister. Melanie looked so tired. Her face was thin and drawn and the bright blue eyes were gray and lifeless.

"Are you ill?" Brooke asked the moment Melanie opened the door.

"No. I'm just a little tired. I've been doing extra work." The demand for Melanie Chandler was virtually limitless. Melanie urged Adam to keep her as busy as possible. She wanted to be too tired to think. She could resurrect beauty and energy and dazzle from her exhausted face if she *tried*. Tonight, for a birthday celebration with Brooke of all people, Melanie had forgotten to try.

"Did you get sick in Europe?" Brooke pressed.

"No. I'm not sick, really." Melanie forced a twinkle into her sparkleless blue eyes.

Melanie led the way into the apricot-and-cream living room in her apartment. A platter of celery and carrot sticks, neatly arranged in orange-and-green rays around a bowl of crab dip, lay on the glass-top table.

"Have you seen Charles, Brooke?" Melanie asked after they sat down.

"Yes." Why do you want to know? Does it give you *pleasure* to know how much pain you can cause? Is that a measure of your own magnificence? Brooke felt her anger surfacing.

"How is he?"

"How do you *think* he is?"

"Fine, I guess." Why was Brooke scowling at her?

"You really amaze me, Melanie. You have to have everything and everyone, and it's still not enough. It's not enough until you throw them away."

"Brooke, what are you talking about?"

"*Charles*. It wasn't enough just to hurt him. You had to humiliate him publicly."

"*What?* Charles left *me*." Melanie's eyes filled with tears. "I wasn't good enough for him."

"Not good enough? Perfect, golden, beautiful Melanie not good enough?" Brooke stood up. Her dark-blue eyes narrowed at her twin. "What game are you playing now?"

"I'm not playing any game! I've never been good enough for you, Brooke. And from the beginning you made it clear you didn't think I was good enough for Charles."

Brooke paused for a startled moment. What was Melanie talking about? *Nothing.* She was simply trying to shift the blame. It wasn't going to work. When Brooke spoke, her voice was ice, "The whole world knows what happened. Why would you *lie?*"

"I'm not lying, Brooke!"

"You *are!*"

Brooke and Melanie stared at each other, glowering and bewildered. In just a few words, years of resentment and bitterness and anger had been revealed. They had finally spoken the painful truths hidden in their hearts. Now they had reached an impasse and neither knew how to find a way beyond it.

"Why couldn't you just stay in California?" Brooke finally broke the tense silence. Without waiting for an answer, she turned and left.

"Brooke," Melanie whispered. "Brooke."

They both cried that night. And they both remembered—and it was probably an omen—they had forgotten to wish each other Happy Birthday.

CHAPTER TWENTY-TWO

Lake Forest, Illinois
November 11, 1986

"*C*hicagoland" awakened to snow. It was an early snow and a heavy one, blanketing the entire area with a soft, fleecy layer of pristine whiteness. The snow surprised the weather forecasters and annoyed the commuters. It sent shoppers rushing to the grocery to buy food for pantries and rock salt for walkways and candles in case the electricity went out.

Almost everyone had a reaction to the unexpected heavy snowfall. Most resented it; a too-early harbinger of the hard cold winter that lay ahead. A few ignored it, taking it in stride. And fewer still—the children—enjoyed it.

The children enjoyed it, and Galen enjoyed it. Everything was so beautiful. A cottony-soft fairyland, she thought, gazing out her window across the expanse of untrodden snow toward the lake. The trees, barren for weeks of their leaves, were alive again, dressed in lacy white, decorated for winter.

It was on a day such as this—silent, peaceful, virginal—that she and Jason first made love . . .

Galen sighed. She should work, on this day of all days, on "Sonja." "Sonja" was the story she had to write, the story that told the truth about love. "Sonja" exposed the fantasy of love and the bitter reality of betrayal.

Galen had to write "Sonja," even though it was a painful journey through the memories of Jason.

She had to set the record straight. She had to let her readers know. They trusted her. Their letters were mailed to Sinclair Publishing and forwarded to her post office box in Lake Forest. They believed in the lovely portrait of love Galen painted for them. And now Galen knew the portrait was false. She had an obligation to let her readers know.

But today Galen couldn't make herself carve the painful words from her heart. Today was a day to sit before a crackling fire and watch the snow fall and feel the wonder of the small life that was inside her still.

Still. With each passing day it became more likely that the baby's father was Charles, not Jason.

"I wish you could see this day, little one," Galen whispered softly to her unborn child. "But there will be so many days like this for us to share."

At three in the afternoon, the white-bright sky turned black, bringing with it an early nightfall and a violent winter storm. Snow fell in thick opaque walls, tossed and swirled by the cold, angry wind. Galen watched the awesome drama unfold. Such turbulent beauty! Galen felt serene and content; she was warm and safe and cozy in her gatehouse in the midst of a raging flurry of snowflakes.

The first pain came at three-thirty. Its significance didn't register right away. It was a squeeze, strong and warm, more than a pain. Then the next came, stronger, warmer, bringing with it a little more discomfort. Then the next. Then it was five o'clock and she had had three contractions in thirty minutes.

I have to get to the hospital, Galen realized. I have to call a cab or an ambulance.

But the phone line was dead! Galen depressed the disconnect button again and again. There was no dial tone. The telephone lines were above ground. Perhaps a tree had fallen. They would fix it soon, they *had* to.

The telephone was her only link. Galen didn't own a car—she didn't know how to drive—and walking in this storm would be dangerous if not impossible. The snow was dense and deep. The nearest house, the owners' mansion on the lake, was lost in a whirl of white. The path and trees that could serve as guideposts had vanished in the blinding blizzard.

Galen didn't want to think about what might happen if the phone wasn't restored quickly, but she had to. She needed to make preparations, in case....

Galen gathered blankets and towels and candles and matches. She found scissors and string, carefully cut two pieces of string, and put the string and the scissors in her pocket. As she moved around the gatehouse, gathering items and placing them near the fire, Galen stopped six times because of contractions. And she paused fifty times to lift the receiver of the phone. Hoping, *hoping*, for a dial tone.

The outdoor lights on the barren rose stems cast spiny, twisted shadows on the brick. A frosty wind blew across the terrace, chilling his face and numbing his hands.

Why did you put this off so long? Charles chided himself as he carefully tied the protective layer of burlap over the pruned-for-winter roses. Were you waiting to do it with *her?*

Charles pricked his thumb on a frozen thorn and swore softly. Don't let yourself think about her.

Charles thought instead about her dark-haired twin.

Brooke had called today. She remembered it was his birthday and wished him a happy one. Then she told him she had decided, Yes, she would become the attorney for Sinclair Publishing Company.

"Really, Brooke. That's wonderful."

"I think so, too."

"When?"

"As soon as I can find the courage to tell Andrew, plus about three months."

"He'll be upset?" Of course he would; losing Brooke would be a great loss for the DA's office.

"Yes." Brooke smiled slightly. Andrew wouldn't understand. He loved the courtroom battles and the strategy. Andrew enjoyed the game and relished the triumphant victories. You're so good, Brooke, he would tell her. How can you throw it away? I have to, Andrew, she would reply. I don't love it. I can't make it feel like a game.

"I won't tell anyone except Jason until you give me the word."

"Thank you." Brooke frowned slightly. It didn't matter, except Belinda had been her friend, and she and Nick and Andrew were a team of sorts. . . . Brooke added quietly, "I would sort of like to see this Manhattan Ripper business through."

"I didn't realize you were close."

"Wishful thinking."

"To you." Adam raised his champagne glass and smiled. "Belated Happy Birthday."

"Thank you," Melanie whispered. *Her* birthday had been a disaster. Now it was Charles's birthday and she was dining with Adam at Lutèce. She added, forcing enthusiasm, "I think the shoot went well today."

"Very well."

Melanie chewed her lower lip thoughtfully, considering whether to say the next. She had to.

"Adam, I greatly prefer photo sessions and commercials to shows. Do you think—"

"I *think* the truth is that Charles is at the shows," Adam suggested gently.

"Yes." That was why she hated doing shows. She hated his intense dark eyes appraising her as she walked down the runway. You've seen this body before, Charles, you've *owned* it, her mind would scream as she felt his gaze. I gave it all to you, and you didn't want it. Stop looking at me!

"Can't you forget about him, honey?" Adam's blue-gray eyes were concerned and gentle. Adam didn't care if Melanie ever set foot on another runway. He just wanted her to be happy and confident again. The sad sky-blue eyes were proud and determined, as always, but the confidence had vanished. Charles Sinclair had done so much damage. . . .

"I'm trying, Adam." Melanie smiled bravely.

"Try very hard right now. Viveca Sanders is heading our way." Adam stood up when it was clear that Viveca's destination was their table. "Viveca. How nice to see you."

"Adam," Viveca purred. "And Melanie. We've missed you at the parties, Melanie."

"My fault, Viveca," Adam interjected. "Melanie's schedule hasn't permitted it."

"I'll be at the holiday parties." Melanie smiled as if she couldn't wait.

"Oh, good. You really do add such sparkle." Viveca looked as if she was about to leave, but she hesitated. Then, on impulse, she asked, "Melanie, come with me for a moment, will you?"

Melanie sent a plea for help to Adam. His eyes told her it was easier not to resist Viveca; *resisting* Viveca made her suspicious. Without a word, Melanie nodded and followed Viveca into the lavish pink-and-white marble ladies' room.

"I'm not even going to ask you about Adam," Viveca began as she arranged a lock of hair that had fallen out of place.

"Good. There's nothing—"

"I just want you to know that I really admire what you did to Charles. It took guts."

"What?"

"Dumping him."

"But I—"

"I think everyone that's ever been with Charles vowed to end it before he did. But they—*we*—were all addicted. The sex was too good and he was handsome and powerful and irresistible. It's hard not to get hooked on leisurely expert sex, isn't it?" Viveca sighed, took a breath, and continued, "We all overlooked, or forgave, the fact that the bastard never spent the night or held us or gave one small damn. He was quite happy to share his perfect body, but nothing else."

Melanie's mind whirled. *Leisurely expert sex.* It had never been like that with Charles. They were always so desperate for each other, as if it was the first time—and the last time—every time.

The bastard never spent the night. They spent almost every night together, falling asleep in each other's arms and awakening that way, holding each other, reluctant to let go.

He never gave one small damn. No, that was true, he never did.

But Charles was the one who ended it, just as Charles did with all his women. It was the same for her as it had been for the others. Wasn't it?

"Charles has hurt a lot of people." Viveca's voice was solemn, laced with bitterness. "Maybe now he knows how it feels."

"I don't think—"

"Charles comes to the parties, but he comes alone and leaves early."

"Really, Viveca—"

"Is Adam even better? Is that how you could do it?" Viveca held up her hands. "No, I promised, no questions about Adam. You still haven't been on my show, but we can't do anything until this is all ancient history. The viewers would expect questions about Charles and Adam, and I have a feeling you just wouldn't answer."

I would tell the truth, Melanie thought. Even though no one seems to believe it.

At nine o'clock, Galen's gatehouse lost electricity, and, with it, light and heat. Galen lit her scented candles and pulled a layer of blankets over her. The fire had long since died and the heat dissipated quickly.

The labor pains were frequent now, and painful. They pulled her breath from her. But she pulled it back, breathing the way she knew to. She did know. She had seen many babies born, in mud huts of Kenya and on sun-parched fields in central India. She had seen it, and she had helped, once. She and Charles . . .

And now it was *her* baby—and maybe it was theirs, hers and Charles's—and she needed his help. He had helped so much that time. His dark, smiling eyes had given her such confidence. Galen closed her eyes, remembering Charles and the strength he had given her.

This is Charles. He's here to help. Not that we will need much help. Babies deliver themselves, you know. She had spoken those words then, smiling reassurance to the frantic mother-to-be.

Help me now, Charles, *please.*

Galen felt her fingers becoming cold—what if they were too numb to tie the string?—and fought her own resistance to push. You have to push, Galen. You know you have to.

The baby was born at ten. Galen forced herself to push. She felt resistance for a moment, and then none.

And then her baby spoke to her, as if in answer to all the gentle words Galen had whispered to her—to *her*—for all those months. It wasn't a cry or a wail. It was a hello.

Galen gazed at her precious little girl, covered with blood, breathing, moving, silhouetted by candlelight. Galen wanted desperately to cuddle her, but an ancient instinct stopped her. There was one more thing to do first. The most important thing. *You tie the cord in two places and cut in the middle*, she had explained to Charles. *You have to be sure that the string nearest the baby is tied very tight.*

With hands trembling but miraculously nimble, Galen tied the string around the umbilical cord. Then she took the scissors and cut the cord. Galen held her breath. A little blood oozed from her side, the placenta side, but the baby's side was tight and secure.

Then, as her warm tears spilled on the naked head of her baby girl, Galen held her and kissed her. *It was a miracle, Charles . . . a miracle.*

Galen wrapped them both, together, in blankets. Then they talked. Mother to daughter. And daughter, in small coos, to mother. Finally, they fell asleep.

They were awakened at midnight by sudden light, the electricity restored, and the promise of heat. Galen walked to the window, carrying her baby in her arms, and gazed at the aftermath of the storm. It was a fairyland again. Huge, amorphous snowdrifts, like harmless soft monsters, glistened beneath the porch light. The world was still and peaceful and beautiful again.

"What a day this was, my darling," Galen whispered.

Something tugged at the back of her mind about this day. What was it? Oh, yes, today was Jason's birthday. Today was Charles's birthday. And now it was his—*whose?*—daughter's birthday.

Happy Birthday, precious little one.

"Brooke?"

"Hello Charles. Cheers." It was December twenty-third.

"You don't sound very cheery."

"I just told Andrew." She had been *hinting* about it for the past six weeks, but today she told him outright that she was going to leave the DA's office and join Sinclair Publishing.

"He wasn't happy."

"At first, he was furious." The memory of Andrew's reaction still bewildered her. She had expected he would tell her she was throwing away a brilliant career in criminal law, not to mention the political opportunities she was squandering. She expected Andrew might even say she wasn't tough enough after all. Brooke had expected anger, but she hadn't expected him to take it personally.

But he had; it was if she were abandoning him, *too*. It must have been a bad time. Perhaps Allison was ill again for the holidays. Andrew's personal reaction was immediate, and it was short-lived. He recovered quickly, teasing her about the expected things, and finally wishing her well.

"At first?" Charles asked.

"Yes. Then it was fine. But—"

"But you're having second thoughts?"

"Not really. I guess—" Brooke stopped. Why had she called Charles? "Tell me I'm doing the right thing."

"From my very selfish standpoint, you're doing a terrific thing. But you have to decide."

"I have decided. I told Andrew I would leave the DA's office sometime in March."

"You'll have the Manhattan Ripper convicted by then?"

"I've decided he's gone. It's been two months. He was just a horrible nightmare."

"I hope so," Charles agreed quietly.

When she saw him, Melanie stepped in front of the Renoir, blocking his view. Jason smiled, turned off the tape player, and removed the headphones.

"Melanie. How nice to see you."

"You, too, Jason. Back from Australia?"

"Yes, for the moment. I'm going back to Fremantle in a few weeks to watch the finals."

"You realize that everyone else in Manhattan is doing last-minute Christmas shopping?"

"Which leaves this fabulous Impressionist exhibit just for us." Jason gestured to the virtually empty gallery.

Melanie nodded. It was why she had come. It was peaceful here, away from the frantic festive holiday crowds.

"I've never known anyone who rented one of those." Melanie's eyes sparkled at the tape player in Jason's hand. "Does it really tell you more than the guidebook?"

"Probably not," Jason replied easily.

They walked together for a while, admiring the fabulous paintings and talking.

"How is Charles?" Melanie asked finally.

"Fine. I was sorry—"

"Me, too." You don't *look* sorry, Jason. You're probably tired of exchanging the end-of-relationship platitudes with Charles's women.

"How's Brooke?"

"Fine." How do I know? I wonder if she hurts the way I do? "Everyone is so consumed with this Manhattan Ripper business."

Jason nodded thoughtfully. At least Galen was away from that fear. She used to wander Greenwich Village as if it were a wild, wonderful, *safe* African savanna. Jason was glad Galen was away from the horrors of Manhattan; he was glad she was away from Charles.

This will be the MANHATTAN RIPPER'S little Christmas present to this wonderful town. THE MANHATTAN RIPPER! What a fabulous name! Viva La Press! I love NEW YORK.

The Manhattan Ripper laughed a low, mean laugh. Then his dark eyes narrowed and he wrote angrily,

More will DIE. It is NECESSARY. Tonight, the distinguished DOCTOR. Even the ivory tower of academia isn't safe from the MANHATTAN RIPPER. This will be an important LESSON. This will make her understand. It will be the Ripper's formal

WARNING *before he plunges the knife into the* GOLDEN HEART *and slashes the lovely* GOLDEN NECK.

"Melanie." Viveca clutched Melanie's forearm tightly.

"Viveca?" Viveca's rosy cheeks were ashen.

"I need to speak with you."

Melanie followed Viveca to a far corner of the crowded room. The *Vogue* holiday open house was still in full swing. *Everyone* was here, or had been. Melanie and Adam arrived early and planned to stay late. They had to; *Vogue* was a valued client, and Melanie was the prestigious holiday issue cover. Charles had come, and gone, alone, hours ago. He and Melanie didn't speak, but she felt his dark eyes watching her. He started toward her once, but Melanie quickly turned away.

"Viveca, what's wrong?"

"I just arrived. On the way over I heard a special bulletin on the radio. The Manhattan Ripper . . ." Viveca paused for a breath.

"*What,* Viveca?" *Is it Brooke?* No, please, if anything ever happened to Brooke.

" . . . murdered Jane Tucker."

"Jane Tucker," Melanie repeated softly as relief pulsed through her. Jane Tucker, the name was familiar, why?

"Adam and Jane were once engaged to be married. It didn't work out, but . . . Melanie, you have to get him out of here before everyone finds out about it."

Melanie nodded and left to find Adam.

He went with her, without question, as she had gone with Viveca. Adam saw the sadness and terror in her pale-blue eyes. When they were alone in his car, Melanie told him.

"Oh, my God, *no.*"

"Adam, I'm so sorry."

"When are they going to find the bastard?" Adam demanded, his handsome face twisted with rage and anguish. "When are they going to put an end to this insanity?"

Brooke watched the eleven o'clock news as she got ready for bed.

"The Manhattan Ripper has claimed a fourth victim. Earlier this evening the body of Dr. Jane Tucker, associate professor of neurosurgery at . . ."

Brooke watched the television screen. The cameras panned to the apartment building where the dead woman had lived. Brooke knew that Nick was inside searching the blood-splattered apartment for clues. She knew he was churning with rage. Brooke wanted to talk to him. She would. Nick would call, as he had before.

Brooke hoped Nick knew he could call anytime, even in the middle of the night.

Nick didn't call that night. And he didn't call the next day. It was Christmas Eve, but the city offices were open. Nick could call her at work or at home.

But he didn't call.

At three in the afternoon on Christmas Day Brooke telephoned Nick's precinct headquarters. She asked for him without identifying herself.

"Lieutenant Adrian."

"Hi. It's Brooke."

"Brooke," he breathed. He wanted to talk to her, but he wasn't going to. He would call her *sometime.* Some other time. He would call her sometime when there hadn't been a murder and they didn't have a case to discuss. He would ask if she wanted to go for a walk or to dinner or for a ferryboat ride. Nick had been thinking about calling Brooke on December twenty-third. But then the call came about Dr. Jane Tucker. "Merry Christmas."

"Same to you."

"Uh, why . . ."

"I was wondering," Brooke began. I was wondering why you didn't call me. She continued, "How do you hear about the murders? You seem to know the same night."

Very sharp, Brooke. Nick had told Andrew—as DA's office liaison Andrew needed to know everything—but Nick hadn't told her. The press hadn't tumbled to it yet. But the press had only been involved—really involved—since the October murder. Now it was a cause célèbre. "Famous" cases of serial killers were featured in the local papers and on television: Ted Bundy and the Hillside Strangler and the Green River Killer. Would the Manhattan Ripper be the next psychopath to elude the police for months, even years, leaving in his wake terror and death? What was the NYPD doing? Didn't they need a task force instead of just the usual investigation team? Was Lieutenant Nick Adrian really doing enough?

"He calls." Nick's voice was low, the information clearly confidential. It was not even widely known throughout the precinct.

"*He* calls? Have you spoken to him?"

"I did this time," Nick said heavily, remembering the disguised voice and its gruesome purpose. "Now that he knows I'm in charge of the investigation. Before he just left a message."

"What message?"

"Each time he says we should get to the address he gives as soon as possible. Then he hangs up. It's much too quick to trace. This time it sounded as if he was calling from a phone booth."

"As soon as possible," Brooke repeated. "Are they alive when he leaves them?"

"No." There was no question, no possibility, of that.

"Has he called at other times?"

"No. He doesn't seem interested in playing psychological cat-and-mouse with the police. Beyond what he is already doing." Nick sighed. "I really don't know why he calls, Brooke, but he calls within half an hour of the murder."

"Maybe he can't stand the thought of them just lying there," Brooke said quietly, shivering. *She* couldn't stand the thought. It was a normal reaction. But was any part of this man, this maniacal murderer, *normal?*

"Is this how you usually spend Christmas? Calling your local PD?" Nick asked suddenly, pulling them both away from the grisly subject of the murders.

"No."

"Are you having dinner with Melanie?"

"No." We tried a birthday dinner together. She repeated softly, "No."

"Do you want to have dinner with me?"

"Yes, I'd like to."

"One ground rule. We don't talk about the murders. We don't talk about murder at all. Or crime. Or law. Or work."

"Then what can we talk about?" Brooke teased. After a moment, she continued seriously, "I know. We can talk about your short stories."

"We can talk about why it makes you so sad that you aren't having Christmas dinner with Melanie," Nick countered carefully. He heard the sadness. He imagined a storm in her dark-blue eyes.

"No," Brooke whispered, "we can't talk about that."

CHAPTER TWENTY-THREE

New York City
February 1987

"*H*appy Valentine's Day, Galen."

"Melanie! How nice to hear from you. I was going to call you. The cover of *Fashion* is sensational."

"Thanks." The only problem with the fabulous photograph of Melanie on the February issue of *Fashion* was it meant that she had to attend Sinclair's Valentine's Day party at the Essex House. Adam insisted; he would escort her, of course. "How are you?"

"Fine." *I have Elise and she is joy.* Galen laughed softly, "Except the editors for my next book think my feature story, 'Sonja,' is unpublishable."

"Oh, *that*," Melanie answered gaily. "Isn't the book due to be released next month?"

"That's *Songs of the Savanna*—the stories I wrote about Kenya, minus the *gems*. My next book, the one I'm working on now, is called *Spring Street Stories*. It's about life in the Village."

"What's the problem with 'Sonja'?"

" 'A too bitter portrait of love,' they said."

"Sounds right up my alley," Melanie murmured. She added with genuine enthusiasm, "I'd really like to read it. I may not be an editor, but I certainly am a fan."

"And a friend. Thanks. I'm going to rework it for a while, then maybe I'll send it to you."

"Great. Perhaps I should come there. Lake Forest sounds enchanting."

"It is," Galen agreed. But you can't come here. Galen felt a pang of sadness as she realized she would probably never see Melanie again. Her dear friends could never know about Elise. They would have to remain long-distance voices. Melanie and . . . "How's Brooke?"

"Fine. I guess."

"Looking forward to her new job," Galen suggested carefully.

"New job?"

"At Sinclair Publishing." *Working with Elise's father, whoever he is.*

"Oh." Brooke working with Charles!

"You haven't talked to her, have you?"

"We had an argument."

"I know. Brooke told me almost two months ago."

"What did she say?"

"Nothing. She sounded sad, just like you do. Melanie, can't you two work it out?"

"I don't know," Melanie spoke softly. *I want to.* Then why don't you just pick up the phone and call her? Because I *can't.* Besides, *she* could call *me.*

* * *

"What in the world is the assistant DA doing in my office on Saturday afternoon?"

"What are you doing here?"

"Paperwork." Nick gestured at stacks of reports. "And it *is* my office."

"I'm escaping from Jeffrey Martin."

"Ah, but can he escape from *you?*"

"I hope not. I really think it's airtight."

"When do you go to trial?"

"Early this week. Probably Tuesday."

"Well," Nick said after a few beats of silence, "I think it's nice you decided to escape here."

Brooke tilted her head slightly, and her blue eyes became thoughtful. "Actually, I'm here to make a confession."

"Really? Should I recite *Miranda* to you? You have the right to remain silent—"

"No I don't." Brooke sighed quietly. "I should have told you this a long time ago."

"What, Brooke?"

Don't be angry, Nick.

"I'm leaving the DA's office. As soon as the Jeffrey Martin trial is over. I'm—" Brooke stopped. Nick was smiling at her; *smiling,* not gloating or glowering.

"Going to work for Sinclair Publishing," Nick finished her sentence. *Going to work for Charles Sinclair.*

"You knew."

"Andrew told me in December." Nick frowned as he remembered why he had seen Andrew on Christmas Eve; Nick had to give him the details of Dr. Jane Tucker's bloody death.

"Oh." *Oh.* That meant Nick knew when they had dinner together on Christmas Day. "Why didn't you . . ."

"Why didn't I *what?*"

"I don't know. Call me up and say 'I told you so' or point out that I can't save the world by negotiating advertising contracts."

I don't have the right to do that to you, Brooke. And you have the right . . . the right to be with Charles Sinclair if you want to.

"You make choices," Nick answered seriously. He had been thinking about getting out. He was tired of seeing mutilated bodies. He'd been wondering if he could write a novel. He added, "You've probably made a good one."

Brooke smiled. *Thank you, Nick, for making this so easy.*

"How's Melanie?" Nick asked. He hoped the problem Brooke wouldn't talk about at Christmas was resolved. The sudden storm in her eyes told him it wasn't.

"I don't know."

"You make choices," Nick reminded her quietly.

"Yes." *And I don't* choose *this. Then why don't you just pick up the phone and call her? Because I* can't. *Besides, she could call me.* Brooke shrugged, suddenly restless. "I guess I'd better go."

Nick felt her pulling away. He had no right, but . . . "Do you think you'll feel like escaping again in, say, about three hours? For dinner?" *To celebrate Valentine's Day?*

Brooke hesitated. "Escaping, yes. But no more confessions."

Nick nodded. *Enough confessions for one day.*

* * *

Melanie smiled wryly at the ice-sculpture cupid. His love-drenched arrow aimed ominously at a mountain of caviar.

"Whoever invented Valentine's Day?"

"No cynicism tonight," Adam teased. He touched her cheek lightly with his finger and smiled into her bright blue eyes.

"OK," she agreed easily. Everything was easy with Adam. He made her feel warm and secure and calm. "Do you think it's safe to eat the caviar?"

Adam laughed. "Oh, I see. It might be tainted with love and passion and romance. Would that be so bad?"

Melanie started to speak, then her eyes sparkled at his and she bit her lip. She smiled coyly and said, "I just edited a terribly cynical remark."

Adam and Melanie smiled at each other and a nearby camera flashed, capturing the happy, sparkling moment. The Sinclair Valentine's Day party was the event of the weekend; it was being well photographed for the society pages of tomorrow's *Times*.

It was Charles's party, but, miraculously, Melanie managed to avoid him. She was aware of his presence, dark and handsome and menacing, but she successfully avoided his eyes and artfully kept herself at a safe distance. There was no point in speaking to him; it was almost too painful just seeing him.

Toward the end of the evening, Melanie walked through the elegant French doors onto the terrace. It was cool, but Melanie needed a private moment. The winter moon was full and the dark sky glittered with stars. The roses were wrapped, snug and safe, in burlap.

"Melanie?"

Melanie stiffened at the sound of his voice. It was soft and seductive; the familiar voice of the dark stranger who had taken her to paradise, and back. Go *away*.

Charles moved closer.

"Melanie, I'm glad you came to the party."

Silence.

"You look happy, Melanie. You and Adam look happy."

"I wonder"—the ice in her voice matched the winter cold—"what happened to our roses."

"I covered them with burlap."

Warm tears spilled onto her cold cheeks as she remembered the sunny, happy day they planted the roses, and the pleasure they had sitting in the fragrant, colorful garden. But that was Charles; he took pleasure in beautiful things, like her.

But he didn't care. *He never gave a small damn.*

"I'm surprised." Melanie didn't recognize her own voice. It was empty—a shell without substance—just like she was in his eyes.

"Why?" Charles moved in front of her.

"Because . . ." Her blue eyes met his and she was suddenly consumed with anger. When she spoke again she still didn't recognize the voice, but it was no longer empty. Now it was full, overflowing, with hatred. "I thought you enjoyed watching beautiful things die."

"*Melanie.*"

"You're no better than the Manhattan Ripper, Charles. *Worse*, because your victims survive even though you've torn out their hearts."

Her words caused such pain! His dark eyes became wild with anguish. Melanie had seen the same tormented look the night on the terrace after his nightmare.

I cared then, Charles. I cared so much. But now I'm like you. I don't care.

It wasn't true. As she turned to leave, her heart pleaded, *Stop me, Charles.*

But he didn't move, and she walked away from him, back through the French doors to his fabulous party, and into the curious eyes of Viveca Sanders.

"Melanie?" Viveca looked beyond Melanie to the terrace. She recognized the shadowy silhouette. She was witnessing the aftermath of another off-stage fight between Charles Sinclair and Melanie Chandler. Was he trying, as he had without success in Monte Carlo, to convince her to come back to him? "Melanie?"

Flashbulbs sparkled in Melanie's eyes, and everyone was asking questions. Still bewildered and shaken by the hateful venom of her own words, Melanie stood stiff and mute. Finally Adam was by her side and she whispered, "Get me out of here, Adam. Please."

Adam wrapped a strong arm around her and swiftly guided her through the curious crowd.

"I could kill him for what he did to you," Adam whispered hoarsely when they were finally alone. "For what he's still doing . . ."

"I hate this," Melanie told Adam when he called the following morning. Melanie glowered at the Sunday *Times*. A radiant picture of her with Adam—"The Happy Couple"—smiled back.

"What do you hate?" Did she hate the fact that *they* had been portrayed as a loving couple? Or did she only hate that the accompanying article described Charles as the twice-spurned lover and strongly implied that they had argued about her love affair with Adam?

"All of it. It's all false."

Yes, Adam thought. But I wish it weren't. Adam wished his lovely golden-haired friend *would* become his lover.

"I'm going to call Viveca."

"Viveca! Why?"

"I have to clear the air, Adam."

"You need to tell the world that Charles Sinclair left you?"

"Yes." What if Charles thought *she* was spreading the lies. It doesn't matter what Charles thinks, she reminded herself. Still, it wasn't *true*.

"Melanie, think about it."

"I have."

"Do some more thinking."

"Adam . . ."

"I'll call you from Paris and we'll discuss it. If you still have to do it, let's carefully select the right way. I'm not sure a live, on-camera interview is the answer. OK?"

"OK. You'll call?"

"You know I will. Nothing rash in the meantime, *d'accord?*"

"*D'accord.*" Agreed.

He reached her by telephone in the models' dressing room at Drake two days after the Valentine's Day party.

"This is Melanie."

"Ms. Chandler." He spoke with a slight British accent. "This is Robin Shepard. I write a column . . ."

"Yes, I know." Robin Shepard wrote a celebrity gossip column, "Profiles," for the *Times*.

"I would like to do a piece on you."

"All right." Melanie smiled. Adam must have decided she was right after all. "Profiles" was the perfect forum.

"Where shall we meet? I find interviews in the person's home often the most comfortable."

"That would be fine."

"How would this evening suit you? It's short notice."

"Tonight would be fine." Melanie knew that Robin Shepard was doing a favor for Adam which was really a favor for her. Robin Shepard was too much a gentleman to mention that Adam had arranged it. Melanie almost told him that she knew. "Perfect."

"Ten o'clock? I have a dinner I must attend first."

"Ten o'clock," Melanie agreed and gave him her address.

He arrived promptly at ten and spoke to her through the security intercom.

"Ms. Chandler. It's Robin Shepard."

Melanie pressed the button to release the front-door lock of the building. Somewhere in the back of her mind it registered: his accent was gone. But it was in the back of her mind. In the forefront stood the hope that the interview would go well.

When her doorbell rang two minutes later, Melanie didn't even look through the peephole.

She just opened the door and realized, too late, who she was letting in.

PART THREE

CHAPTER TWENTY-FOUR

*B*rooke sat bolt upright. Her heart raced and her breath came in shallow gasps. The dial of the bedside clock glowed ten-thirty. Brooke frowned at the clock. She had only been in bed for fifteen minutes; it was hardly enough time to fall asleep, much less to dream! But something—it *must* have been a nightmare—had forced her violently back into wakefulness.

Only later would Brooke recall that she was already reaching for the phone when it rang. . . .

"Hello," she breathed uneasily as her mind frantically tried to reassure her anxious heart.

It will be Andrew, Brooke told herself. He will be calling to discuss one final detail, one final twist, of the Jeffrey Martin case. Logically, the late-night phone call would be from Andrew. But illogically, and fueled with a knowledge that defied logic, Brooke's heart resolutely pumped dread through her body.

"Brooke!" Sheer terror.

"Melanie! What's—"

"He tried to kill me. Brooke, help me!" The terror was strong and pervasive. But the voice wasn't. It was the voice of a body that was badly injured, in shock, maybe dying. . . .

"Melanie," Brooke spoke urgently, "where are you?"

"My apartment," Melanie answered slowly, as if bewildered that something so horrible could have happened in that sanctuary.

"Is he gone?"

"Yes. Brooke it was *him*. The Manhattan . . ."

The Manhattan Ripper. The Ripper didn't leave witnesses, only victims. But Melanie had seen him. And, miraculously, she was alive. *Still.*

"Are you hurt?"

"So much blood," Melanie murmured dreamily "So much blood."

Melanie was badly hurt. Her voice faded in and out of reality, drifting away. . . .

"Melanie." Brooke spoke sternly. She had to make Melanie focus on the present—if it was possible, if Melanie hadn't already lost too much blood.

"Yes, Brooke," Melanie answered in a little-girl voice, surprised that her older sister was talking to her so harshly. What had she done wrong?

"Melanie," Brooke continued softly. There had been so much harshness between them, so much for so long. It hadn't always been that way; it couldn't be that way now. Brooke added gently, her voice choked with emotion, "Mellie."

Mellie . . . It was Brooke's special name for Melanie when they were little girls. *Mellie.* The name recalled such happy memories of laughter and love between sisters—twin sisters—still bound by the unique closeness born in their mother's womb, before the realities of life drove a wedge between them. . . .

Brooke shook the memories that flooded her mind. She needed to tell Melanie those lovely memories were with her still, despite the bitter ones. Brooke *would* tell her, but not now. Now she, *they*, had to save Melanie's life.

"Mellie, have you called the police?" Brooke asked, knowing the answer, but hoping.

"I called you!" The voice said clearly, *I called you because you are my sister—my older sister—and I know you will save me.*

"I'm glad you called me, honey. It was the right thing to do. Now listen carefully, Melanie. You have to hang up the phone so I can call the paramedics and the police. As soon as I've done that I will call you right back and we'll talk until they arrive. OK?"

No answer.

"Melanie."

"Uh-huh." The answer came weakly as if from a small child who had answered by nodding her head instead of speaking. Was she getting too weak? Or was she just drifting, too, to the memories of the two happy little girls?

"OK, Mellie. Hang up now. I'll call you right back."

An almost unbearable emptiness swept through Brooke as she heard the phone disconnect. It felt like an end. An ending. The end.

No! Brooke shook the thought angrily as she hurriedly dialed the emergency police number.

"This is," Brooke began urgently, then forced control in her voice and assumed her usual professional tone, "This is assistant district attorney Brooke Chandler. I need a medic unit dispatched to . . ."

Brooke provided the necessary information in a matter of moments. Just before the call ended she added authoritatively, "Have the police department contact Lieutenant Nick Adrian. He needs to be there."

"Will do, Ms. Chandler," the dispatcher replied with respect. The police, the emergency unit dispatchers, the paramedics, and the district attorney's office were all coconspirators in the war against crime in New York City. They were on the same team. The dispatcher had no idea that the assistant district attorney's call was more than good teamwork. There was nothing in Brooke Chandler's tone that sounded like emotion. "I'll let Lieutenant Adrian know you think he needs to be there."

Nick needs to be there, Brooke thought as her trembling fingers dialed Melanie's number. He *has* to be. It wasn't because the Manhattan Ripper was Nick's case. Nick needed to be there because he would help Melanie. Melanie . . .

As Brooke listened to Melanie's phone ring, unanswered, her frantic thoughts darted to other people who needed to know.

Five rings.

Her parents. How could she tell them what horror had befallen their golden angel? Would they blame *her* for allowing this to happen to Melanie? New York was Brooke's city. She should have protected Melanie . . .

Brooke would call her parents from the hospital, as soon as she knew that Melanie was all right.

Ten rings. Pick up the phone, Melanie. Mellie. Please.

Adam needed to know. The society pages of yesterday's—*yesterday's*—Sunday *Times* featured a color photograph of Melanie and Adam taken at *Fashion* magazine's gala Valentine's Day party. Melanie and Adam stood in front of an ice sculpture of Cupid, the perfect backdrop for their fairytale romance. Distinguished, elegant Adam and dazzling golden Melanie, smiling, happy, in *love*.

Adam was the reason Melanie left Charles. It was so obvious. Why did Melanie deny it? Even at the Valentine's Day party, according to the article that accompanied the photograph, there had been a "scene" between Melanie and Charles. . . .

Charles, Brooke's mind whirled. How can I tell Charles about this? How can anyone tell him?

Fifteen rings. Melanie, come *on*.

But Charles needed to know, and Jason needed to know. Charles and Jason, the *other* twins.

Twenty rings. Answer the—

The ringing stopped. So, for a moment, did Brooke's heart. Someone had taken the phone off the hook. Melanie? The Ripper? The paramedics? Nick?

"Melanie?" Brooke whispered.

Silence.

"Mellie, honey," Brooke spoke lovingly to the silence, "I called the paramedics. They'll be there any moment. Hold on, darling. Please. And Nick. He's a police officer. You can trust him, Mellie. He'll take care of you."

Brooke paused, blinking back tears, hoping to hear something, the smallest sound, from her twin. Brooke heard nothing, but she *felt* a presence. Brooke knew Melanie was there, and Melanie would hear her words.

"Mellie. Don't try to talk, just listen. We'll talk when you're better." Tears streamed down Brooke's cheeks. She closed her eyes and saw a little girl with sungold hair and bright blue eyes frolicking on a white sand beach. Brooke could almost hear the laughter. "I love you, Mellie, I always have. We need to talk about the things that have come between us. We *will* talk. Remember the summer we spent at the beach when we were five, Mellie? Remember what fun we had?"

Suddenly there was noise—commotion—at the other end. Brooke held her breath. She heard pounding. It lasted only a few seconds. Then Brooke heard a crash as the door gave way.

"Christ."

Brooke felt the paramedic's horror as he saw her twin sister.

Help her. *Please*.

"Is she . . . ?" another voice asked.

"I don't know," the voice, now close to the phone, close to Melanie, answered. "Let me find her carotid."

Please. Please. Please.

Depthless immobilizing fear settled in Brooke's heart as she silently prayed for the other heart; the other heart that once had been so close.

"OK, Joe, let's get to work," the paramedic breathed finally. "She's still alive. . . ."

Brooke strained to hear, but the voices were distant and muffled. The receiver of the phone must have rolled over into the deep pile carpet in Melanie's apartment. Brooke heard bits.

"Can you get a fourteen-gauge needle in her?"

"—so clamped down. Try a femoral or a jugular—"

"—needs to be intubated—"

"—it's a pneumo, not a tension, but she'll need a chest tube—"

Then a familiar voice, worried, asked, "How is she?"

"As stable as we can get her here. We're about to roll."

"What's with the phone?" Nick asked, lifting it with a handkerchief to protect prints—not that there would be any.

"She was holding it when we arrived, *clinging* to it. It took some strength to pull her fingers away." The voice faded as the medics rushed out of the apartment with Melanie.

"Hello." Nick spoke into the receiver.

"Nick. Thank God you got there so quickly."

"We were on our way when your call came."

Of course, Brooke thought, the Ripper always calls to tell them where to find the victim. But Melanie was *alive.*

"Nick?"

"I don't know, Brooke," Nick answered gently. I don't know if she will live. Melanie was badly, horribly injured, but not as badly as the others. The Ripper had left before making the final, instantly lethal cuts Nick knew so well. Something had stopped him, or interrupted him. "Did you call her?"

"No." Tears blurred her eyes. I *wanted* to call her. I was *going* to, *sometime.* "She called me after he left."

"You spoke to her?"

"Yes. She told me that it was *him,"* Brooke whispered. She added urgently, "Nick, I have to go now. I have to be at the hospital with her."

Nick could envision Brooke running across Manhattan in the middle of the night. She was trying to sound calm and in control, but he knew better. Nick looked at the blood-splattered room and made a decision.

"I'll be there in five minutes to take you to the hospital."

"But you have to be *there."* You have to be in Melanie's apartment, at the scene of the crime, finding out who did this to her.

"I have to be here. And I have to be at the hospital to talk to Melanie," Nick said firmly. He knew it would be hours before he could talk to Melanie, assuming she lived. It was a very big assumption.

Mostly, Brooke, Nick thought, I have to be with you. He repeated, "I'll be at your apartment in five minutes."

Before leaving Melanie's apartment, Nick ordered the officers to collect prints and photographs and samples, but not to disturb anything. He would return in a few hours.

Brooke opened the door as soon as Nick knocked and was halfway into the hallway when he put his hand on the door to prevent her from pulling it shut. Brooke's hair was tousled, her cheeks were damp, and her dark-blue eyes glistened with fear. She wore jeans and a light cotton blouse buttoned incorrectly.

"Just a minute." Nick guided her gently back into her apartment.

Then, carefully, Nick unbuttoned and rebuttoned her blouse and parted her tousled hair with his hands.

"I don't care how I look, Nick!" But she didn't resist.

"I know." *And you look so beautiful.* "OK. Now, sweater and coat and then we can go."

Brooke pressed against the far door of the squad car, her body rigid with fear. Nick felt her despair and fear as he drove quickly through the treacherous rainslick streets. He wanted to help her, but he had to concentrate on his driving.

Finally he extended his hand to her. She took it gratefully, wrapping both of her hands, cold and small, around his strong, warm one. When they reached the hospital, when he moved to get out of the car, she moved with him. Unwilling or unable to release his hand she slid across the seat and followed him out on the driver's side.

The emergency room was brightly lighted, noisy and busy. Nick passed through the Authorized Personnel Only signs toward the trauma room. Brooke still held his hand and he felt her hesitation. She was so afraid of what might be behind those electronic steel doors.

What *were* they going to find beyond the impersonal steel doors, Nick wondered. He should have left her in the waiting area. But would she have agreed to stay behind? *Could* she have released his hand? Nick didn't know, because he didn't try, and now it was too late.

"Nick." Frank Thomas, one of the hospital's trauma surgeons, greeted him. Frank and Nick had worked together on a number of cases.

"Frank. How's—?"

"Chandler? She's in the OR now. She's carved up pretty badly, although some of the wounds are superficial and ugly but not life-threatening. She has one chest wound. If we're—if she's—lucky it will be above the liver. And she has several abdominal wounds, probably deep. She's in shock so the best guess is that she's bleeding into her belly. They're exploring her now," Frank explained quickly, looking at Nick. Only toward the end did he shift his gaze to the woman who clung to Nick and whose face radiated such fear. Frank frowned.

"This is Brooke Chandler, Melanie's sister." Nick realized grimly that his impulse to leave Brooke outside had been correct.

Frank shot Nick a glance that said, Christ, Nick, why didn't you warn me? He could—and would—give the same facts to a family member, but he would use different words.

"We are concerned," Frank began again, speaking to Brooke, trying to compensate for *carved up pretty badly* and *bleeding into her belly* and *best guess*. Nick should not have brought her back here, not without checking. What if Melanie was lying, dead, in the room with the plate-glass windows behind him? Frank could tell from Nick's expression that he knew that. And Frank could tell from the way Brooke held Nick's hand and pressed close to him that this was not a *usual* case. Rules were going to be broken.

Frank continued, speaking to the frightened blue eyes, "We are worried that her spleen or her kidneys may have been injured. They are quite vascular—they bleed easily. Melanie is in the operating room now so they can look for a bleeding site and stop it."

Brooke nodded. She knew not to ask about chances.

"Where can we wait, Frank?" Nick asked. "I want to keep Brooke away from the press."

Nick didn't want the Manhattan Ripper to know, if he didn't already know, that Brooke—Melanie's twin—existed. Nick especially didn't want it known that Melanie had called Brooke after the attack.

Frank led them to a small waiting area near the operating room.

"Will others be coming?" Frank asked.

"Are there people we should call, Brooke?" Nick paraphrased Frank's question.

Brooke nodded, but offered no names. Yes, but how can we? How can we tell them?

"I'll let you know, Frank," Nick said. Then, before Frank left, he added, "Thanks."

Nick held her for a long time, his arms wrapped around her, feeling her silent sobs and the deep, horrible fear that shook her body. Finally Brooke pulled free.

"Adam needs to know." It was so difficult to *think*. All thoughts led to Melanie. "And Charles and Jason. And my parents. We should wait before calling them—they can't get a plane before morning anyway."

"I'm going to ask an officer to reach Adam and the Sinclairs. And I have to call Andrew."

Panic flickered across Brooke's eyes at the thought of Nick leaving. Then, with great effort, Brooke subdued the panic and nodded.

"We reached them all," Nick told her when he returned twenty minutes later. "Adam is in Paris. He'll take the first plane. Jason is coming from Southampton. Charles and Andrew should be here soon."

"Thank you."

Andrew was the first to arrive.

"Brooke," Andrew spoke her name as he entered the tiny waiting room. He put his arms around her gently and whispered, "I am so sorry, darling."

Brooke succumbed gratefully to Andrew's comforting strength and warmth. He held her tight, was still holding her, when Charles arrived moments later.

Nick watched as Charles entered the room. The dark, aristocratic eyes sent a message of deep, unfocused, heart-stopping fear. It was the same look Nick had seen in Brooke's eyes, the look he still saw despite her brave attempts to stay rational.

Nick started to move toward Charles, to help him because Charles Sinclair needed help, but before Nick reached him, Charles spoke. "Brooke?"

"Charles." Brooke pulled free from Andrew and moved to Charles. Her trembling hands briefly touched his handsome, worried face. Oh, Charles.

"How is she?" His voice was hoarse with fear.

"We don't know. She's in surgery." *We*. Brooke realized as she spoke that Charles didn't know Andrew or Nick. "Charles, this is Andrew Parker, and this is Nick Adrian."

Brooke didn't identify Nick and Andrew with their titles. She couldn't say words to Charles like "homicide" or "Manhattan Ripper case."

Charles shook hands with Nick and Andrew. The men nodded solemn greetings, and then there was nothing more to say. All they could do, now, was wait. Brooke retreated to a pale-green vinyl couch. Andrew sat beside her. Charles and Nick pressed against paint-chipped walls on opposite sides of the small, sterile room.

One hour after Charles arrived, a doctor appeared. He wore green surgical scrubs and a turquoise surgical mask. They all stood at attention when the doctor entered the room.

"We have more surgery to do, but we've finished the exploration."

"And you found?" Nick queried.

"Bleeding from the spleen. We've stopped that. Her liver and kidneys are fine."

"And everything else is fine?" Charles asked.

"Well, no. There *are* other knife wounds." The doctor saw the anguish in Charles's eyes. He added reassuringly, "But the abdominal wounds were potentially the most serious, and we have those under control."

"So she is going to live," Charles spoke softly.

"It's too soon to know. I'll keep you posted." The doctor waited a moment before returning to the operating room, but there were no more questions. They had all heard the answer to *the* question. *It's too soon to know*.

"Tell me what happened." Charles turned his dark eyes to Nick. The muscles in his strong jaw rippled. Charles wasn't asking. He was *commanding* with his bigger-than-life power.

"We don't know, Charles." It was Brooke who spoke. "All we know is she was able to call me after he left."

"She called you," Charles breathed.

I wish you hadn't told him that, Brooke, Nick thought. I didn't want anyone, even her friends, even *your* friends to know that Melanie talked to you after she saw the killer.

"Yes." Brooke's eyes filled with fresh tears as she remembered the terror in Melanie's voice.

"What did she say?" Charles demanded.

Why does Charles Sinclair have to know? Nick wondered uneasily. It *could* be a normal reaction for someone who cared very much and was trying to understand, trying to make sense of something that was senseless. But Charles seemed so desperate.

"She told me that it was him, the—" Brooke paused. She wouldn't say it. "She told me she needed help."

"That's all?"

"That's all." Brooke's voice was barely audible.

"I'm going to leave for a while, Brooke," Nick said, purposefully shifting the conversation.

"You're going to her apartment." Brooke's eyes met his.

Nick nodded solemnly. He could leave her now. She wasn't alone. Nick wanted to hold her and promise her that it would be all right. But he couldn't hold her, and he could make no promises.

"Nick, should I?" Andrew was torn. Maybe he should go with Nick—as the DA's office liaison in the investigation—but if he could help Brooke.

"There's no need for you to come, Andrew." Nick shifted his gaze from Brooke to Andrew. Be here for Brooke, Andrew, in case. "Thanks."

"OK," Andrew agreed easily.

As Nick left, he caught a brief but suppressed movement from Charles. He wants to come with me, Nick thought. *Why*. To prove to himself that this nightmare has really happened? To force himself to admit it?

Or is there another reason?

CHAPTER TWENTY-FIVE

$\mathcal{N}$ick returned to the hospital just before dawn. His long and careful search of Melanie's apartment yielded no clues. Nick stopped in the trauma area before rejoining the others.

"Any word, Frank?"

"I heard ten minutes ago that they're about to move her to the Intensive Care unit."

"Great," Nick breathed. She was still alive. "How is she?"

"So far so good. They took part of her spleen and the lower lobe of her right lung. She's very lucky. It could have been much worse."

"What about the skin lacerations?" Nick knew the medical term—*lacerations*—and used it, even though it didn't adequately describe the wounds. What Nick had seen were deep, jagged *gashes* where the assailant's knife had viciously ripped her lovely flesh.

"The plastic surgeons closed them all as soon as they knew she would survive surgery. She'll have scars, but . . ."

She's alive, Nick thought. And for some reason the Manhattan Ripper stopped before inflicting the final, lethal wounds to her face and throat. There was something else the Ripper always did to his victims. Nick asked, "Was she sexually assaulted?"

"I don't know. I saw Sara Rockwell arrive about thirty minutes ago. I assume she's in there now, collecting evidence while Melanie is still under anesthesia."

Moments before Nick entered the waiting room, Brooke and Charles and Andrew and Jason, who had arrived from Southampton, had been told that Melanie was about to be moved to Intensive Care. Nick found Brooke's eyes and saw a glimmer of hope amid the fear and fatigue. The hope was fragile, no one was offering guarantees, but . . .

"Nick, have you heard?" Brooke smiled a trembling smile.

Nick returned a smile and wanted to hold her.

"Good news."

"Did you find anything?"

"Working on it, Brooke." He had found nothing. But even *that* was confidential police information. He might tell Brooke, but not the others.

Before Brooke could press further a woman entered the room. She wore a dark-blue surgical scrub dress covered by a long white coat. Above the left breast pocket of the white coat, embroidered in emerald-green thread, was the name Dr. Sara Rockwell.

"Lieutenant Adrian?" Sara scanned the group and settled on Nick. His was the only face—male or female—that Sara didn't instantly recognize. She had seen the others on television and read about them in newspapers and magazines. Andrew Parker, Manhattan's brilliant deputy DA. Brooke Chandler, Andrew's able and impressive assistant, and—Sara had read somewhere—Melanie Chandler's twin sister. And the handsome and powerful Sinclair twins, one of whom was the father of Galen Spencer's baby.

Which one, Sara wondered. Which twin had Galen loved? Or had she loved both? And which twin, or both, had loved her? And was either involved with the beautiful woman she had just examined?

One of them is, Sara concluded as she observed their worried faces. One of them is *very* involved.

"Dr. Rockwell." Nick moved toward her.

"May I . . . shall we . . ." Sara gestured toward the door.

The information was police business, for Nick only.

"Has something happened?" Brooke asked anxiously.

"This is Brooke Chandler, Melanie's sister," Nick explained. "Brooke, Dr. Rockwell just examined Melanie to see if she was assaulted, uh, sexually."

"*Raped*," Brooke whispered. The others—the other victims—had been raped. Brooke knew that. "She was, wasn't she?"

Sara looked at Nick with a glance that asked, Do you want the answer in front of all of them?

Nick shrugged. Why not? They were all involved, himself included, even though he shouldn't be.

"No," Sara answered definitively. She cast a sympathetic glance at Brooke and then beyond Brooke to the very concerned Sinclair. "No, she wasn't raped."

"No?" Brooke repeated weakly. Relief swept through her. It made a difference. As violated as Melanie already had been, it still made a difference that *that* hadn't happened.

"No."

What made him stop? Nick wondered for the hundredth time that night. Melanie would tell him. . . .

No visitors until noon, the doctors said. By then the anesthetic should have worn off and Melanie would be awake.

Brooke and Charles and Andrew and Nick waited in the ICU visitors' lounge. Adam arrived at ten.

"She's going to be all right, Adam." Brooke greeted him with that reassurance. Even though no one reassured Brooke—they couldn't—*that* was what she was going to believe.

"Thank God," Adam breathed.

"She's resting. We can see her at noon." *We*. The doctors had said family only. But Adam was the man Melanie loved, surely he would be allowed. . . .

Adam's tired eyes smiled at Brooke and relief softened the strain on his face. Then he looked beyond Brooke, at Charles, and his face hardened with rage.

"What the hell are you doing here?"

"Adam," Brooke whispered to Adam's back as he moved, fists clenched, toward Charles. "Charles cares about Melanie."

"*Cares?*"

"Yes." Charles's dark eyes blazed at Adam.

"She really loved you, Charles. Christ only knows why. It almost destroyed her when you left her. You should be lying in there, not her, not Melanie."

"Adam!"

"Mr. Drake, I'm Nick Adrian with the NYPD." Nick casually positioned himself between Charles and Adam. "This really isn't helping."

Adam looked at Nick. "You're a cop? Good. You can get a restraining order. I know Melanie wouldn't want him here."

"I can't do that." Nick's voice was calm and firm.

"Can you, Andrew?" Adam turned to the man who was such a celebrity in his own sphere that his name appeared on important guest lists, such as Adam's exclusive New Year's Eve party.

"Adam." Andrew's calm matched Nick's. "We have to have cause. If Charles wants to be here—"

"He does." Charles held Adam's gaze until Adam looked away. Then Charles turned to Brooke to gratefully acknowledge her support.

But Brooke was distracted, lost in thought. *She really loved you, Charles,* Adam had said. *It almost destroyed her when you left her.* Charles left Melanie? Melanie had tried to tell her that—"I'm not lying, Brooke!"—and Brooke had refused to believe her. But it was true. Brooke saw it in Charles's eyes, and he didn't deny Adam's accusation. Charles had left Melanie.

But there was more in Charles's tormented dark eyes. Charles left Melanie, but he loved her, *still.*

Melanie didn't awaken by noon. She didn't awaken at all that day, or the next. The doctors couldn't explain it. There had been no head injury. They did brain scans and CAT scans and EEGs; all the high technology only confirmed what they already knew. Melanie Chandler should be awake.

But she wasn't.

Brooke and her parents and Adam kept vigil at Melanie's bedside. They talked to her and touched her and held her lifeless hands and pleaded with her to wake up.

Melanie heard Brooke's voice, but she couldn't open her eyes. The lids were so heavy and there was so much pain.

"Mellie," Brooke whispered softly to her pale, unresponsive twin. An ancient promise haunted her.

Brooke, promise me if I die I can be your shadow.

I'm not going to talk to you if you say things like that.

Promise me.

I promise.

No, I don't promise, Mellie. You aren't going to die.

I'm dying, Brooke. Am I already dead? I can't see you. I can't make my eyes open. I can't talk. There is something in my throat. Help me. *Brooke.*

Brooke gently touched Melanie's forehead above the tape that held the nasotracheal tube through which a ventilator breathed oxygenated air into her twin.

"There's a tube to help you breathe," Brooke answered Melanie's thought. "I'm sure it's uncomfortable. As soon as you wake up they can take it out. You're going to be fine. Oh, Mellie, can you hear me?"

Yes, Brooke, I can hear you! Keep talking to me, Brooke. Don't give up. I can hear you. Please don't leave me. I am so afraid.

"I won't leave you, honey. I never will. We'll be friends again—so close—like we used to be. OK?"

Yes! I want to be your friend. I've always wanted to be.

"Today is Wednesday, February eighteenth. You've been asleep for two days.

We're all here. Mom and Dad. And Adam. And," Brooke hesitated. She stroked Melanie's blond hair thoughtfully. *She really loved you, Charles. It almost destroyed her when you left her.* Maybe, maybe . . . "And Charles is here."

The long, golden lashes flickered.

Charles is here? Where?

"He's been here the whole time." Brooke watched Melanie's pale eyelids. There was life behind them for the first time in two days! "He hasn't been in because he's not family, but . . ."

Was it her imagination or did Melanie's brow furrow slightly? To hell with the *rules*, Brooke decided impulsively. "I'm going to get him, Mellie. He wants to see you."

Charles had been there almost continually, resolutely keeping his own private vigil in a far corner of the waiting room. Charles was there, even though there was no hope that he would be able to see her, and even though Adam glowered at him and Melanie's parents eyed him skeptically. Only Brooke, when she wasn't in Melanie's room, sat beside Charles.

"Charles?"

Charles stood up. "Is she . . .?" A spark of hope flickered in the tired brown eyes.

"No. She's not awake, but I want you to talk to her."

Brooke and Charles walked into the ICU. Brooke cast a defiant glance at the nurses. He's my long-lost brother, her blue eyes told them. He only *looks* like Charles Sinclair. No one stopped them.

"This is all right with Lieutenant Adrian," Brooke lied to the guard outside Melanie's room. It *would* be all right. The guard was there in case the Manhattan Ripper tried to finish what he had started. That had nothing to do with Charles.

Brooke led the way into Melanie's room. She and her parents and Adam had adjusted to the sight of the frail, lifeless body of their beloved Melanie, but for Charles it was a heart-stopping shock.

I thought you enjoyed watching beautiful things die. God, why had Melanie said that? Had she somehow known?

Charles took Melanie's pale, cool hand in his and stared at it for a moment. Plastic tubing flowed into a purple vein. It was taped securely, but there were dried bloodstains between her fingers. Did they have to try again and again to find a vein? Had they hurt her?

Charles wanted to take her away.

His lips touched her temple as he whispered, "I love you, Melanie. You have to know that, darling. I believed your life would be happier without me, but I never stopped loving you. Come back to me, Melanie."

She was dreaming and it was a lovely, wonderful dream. His soft, gentle, loving voice spoke words he had never spoken to her before, words she had dreamed he would speak. It was such a wonderful dream. Oh, *Charles.*

Charles felt pressure in his hand and his heart leapt. "Melanie, I love you so much. . . ."

The pale-blue eyes fluttered open and focused slowly on his handsome face. He was so close and so worried. Don't *worry*, Charles.

"Hello, darling," Charles whispered.

Hello, Charles. I thought I was dreaming, but you're here. Did you really say I love you?

"How are you?" Charles smiled through tears of joy.

Melanie began to search her memory for answers. The details didn't come, but there were vague images of something horrible. Her eyes narrowed, trying to make the memory come into focus.

"Hey." Charles gently kissed her cheek. "Don't think about it now. It's over. Just concentrate on getting well. OK?"

Melanie frowned. The foggy memory troubled her. Don't think about *what?* And why couldn't she talk? What was in her mouth?

"Melanie." Charles smiled lovingly at her. "Remember the morning I found you in the rose garden in the park? I wanted to hold you so much. Did I ever tell you that?"

The frown vanished and her face transformed as Charles pulled her away from ugly memories to lovely ones. The lovely memories of Melanie and Charles.

Brooke withdrew quietly from Melanie's room. She didn't belong there, witnessing their private, intimate reunion. Melanie was awake; that was all she needed to know.

Nick was outside Melanie's room, glowering at the guard, when Brooke appeared.

"Its my fault, Nick. I told him it was all right with you."

"*Why?*"

"She needed to hear his voice, Nick. The rest of us, as much as we love her," Brooke's voice faded. Then her eyes narrowed and she asked defiantly, "Why do *you* care if Charles sees her anyway? It may be an ICU rule, but it has nothing to do with the police investigation."

The gray eyes told her nothing.

"Nick?"

"You just shouldn't have done it, Brooke," Nick said evenly. There was something about Charles Sinclair, the intensity of his concern, Adam Drake's vehemence that Charles not be allowed near her. . . .

"Yes I should have," Brooke answered quietly. Her dark-blue eyes glistened. "She's awake because of him. . . ."

Because of how much he loves her.

"She's *awake?*"

Brooke nodded and impatiently brushed away a warm tear.

"Brooke, I'm sorry. I shouldn't have gotten angry. . . ."

The following morning the anesthesiologist removed the nasotracheal tube. Melanie coughed as the tube was withdrawn. Then she gasped for breath. Then she groaned in pain as the deep breath of the gasp caused fire in the right side of her chest where the knife had entered and the surfaces were raw and inflamed. She took a smaller breath and it hurt, but not as much. Then, as the doctors watched, prepared to reintubate her if she was too weak or in too much pain to breathe on her own, Melanie began to breathe.

And talk.

"Oh," she whispered, her voice hoarse from the lingering irritation of the tube. "Oh."

"How are you doing, Melanie?" the anesthesiologist asked. He needed more than one syllable.

"OK," she uttered, then forced a smile. "Better. On balance. Better. I think."

"Is it the chest pain that's bothering you?"

Melanie nodded. It had been there, part of the painful aching of her entire body, before. But now, because of the deep breath she had taken, it was the worst pain.

"Is it better with shallower breaths?"

"Better," she admitted. "But not perfect."

"Let's give her some Demerol," the pulmonary specialist said. They couldn't give her Demerol before extubation because it might have depressed her breathing or her energy. But now they could. She was breathing on her own. "This will block the pain, Melanie, and enable you to take deeper breaths."

"I like these shallow breaths."

"I know. But the lung needs to expand to prevent complications."

"Oh."

An hour after Melanie was extubated, after she had received enough Demerol to diminish the pain without blocking her respiratory drive, Nick was allowed to interview her. Only for a few minutes, the doctors said. She will fatigue easily and she needs her strength.

But Melanie's strength held up well. She made it hold up; she needed to talk about it. Melanie remembered everything in vivid detail. Maybe talking about it would help purge the horror. Until now, she couldn't talk. She had been trapped in a world of choking tubes and puffing ventilators and the sometimes regular, sometimes erratic beeping noises that almost drove her crazy.

"I want Brooke to be here," Melanie told Nick when he asked. "If she wants to be."

Brooke wanted to be. At first, Nick said No, for Brooke's protection.

"Nick, if Melanie knows something, the killer will assume I know it, too. If there *is* something, it's safer for me to know."

Nick had to agree; it was safer. Still, it was ultimately Melanie's decision, and Melanie wanted Brooke to be there.

Brooke held her twin's hand while Nick and Melanie talked.

"Do you have any idea who did it?" Nick asked. If he only had a short time, because of Melanie's energy, he would start with the bottom line.

"I know exactly who did it," Melanie answered simply. "It was Robin Shepard."

"What?"

"Robin Shepard," Melanie repeated. "He said he wanted to put something about me in 'Profiles.' I thought Adam had arranged it. . . ."

Melanie's blue eyes clouded briefly as she remembered *why* Adam would have arranged it. She blinked away the horrible memory of the bitter, venomous words she had hurled at Charles. There were enough horrible memories.

"What did he look like?" Nick asked gently.

"I didn't see his face or his hands. He wore a dark stocking over his head, and he wore gloves."

"What about his eyes?"

"They were dark brown. His hair was dark, too. I saw some of it at the edge of the stocking."

"Height?"

"Taller than me with my heels on. Six feet, I guess."

"Weight?"

"I don't know. Slender, but not thin. Strong." Melanie shuddered involuntarily.

"You OK?" Nick was pushing her, and she was doing well; except for the name, it was helpful information.

"Nick, why don't you just go get him? Melanie told you who he is," Brooke urged.

"Brooke." Nick's voice was gentle. Brooke wanted it to be easy for her sister.

The attorney part of Brooke knew he needed more than a name, and Brooke didn't know the name Melanie had given him was useless.

"I'm OK, Nick," Melanie said. "Go on."

Nick waited a moment before asking the next question. He knew it would startle her. He asked it softly.

"Melanie, was he someone you knew?"

"I told you who he was—Robin Shepard. I'd never met him before."

"Forget who he said he was, Melanie. Was the man who assaulted you—the strong, slender man who was six feet tall with dark hair and eyes—someone that you knew?"

Nick watched Melanie carefully as she considered his question; it worried her. She hadn't thought about it before, and now that she did, it scared her. Was there something?

Finally she shook her head. No, it wasn't possible. No one she knew would do such a thing to her. No.

"Did you recognize the voice?" Nick pressed. Her head shake hadn't been an emphatic No. There was a trace of doubt.

"No, but it was probably always disguised. Even in my apartment it sounded strange, unnatural."

"And the eyes?" Eyes were so personal. If they were eyes she knew well . . .

"I couldn't see the entire eye. The holes were small. I could just see the color, not the shape."

She had seen enough to make her worry about a man she knew with dark-brown eyes, Nick decided. And not enough to reassure herself it wasn't him.

"Keep thinking about that, Melanie. If it could possibly be someone you know, I need to hear about it," Nick said firmly, sensing that she was worried, a little, and guessing that she wouldn't tell him. That was all right. He could think of a man she knew who fit the description, a man whose name she would never give him.

Melanie nodded.

"Do you want to talk about what happened?" Nick asked gently.

"Yes," Melanie answered, but she sighed. She was suddenly so tired. She wanted to tell it all. She *could* tell it all. She remembered every brutal second of the horror, how it felt and what she was thinking. She had to tell it all, but not now. "Sometime."

"OK. Do you have the energy for two more questions?"

"Nick," Brooke murmured.

"It's OK, Brooke."

"Do you remember what he said in your apartment?"

"Yes. He said, *I have to do this. There is no other way. You understand.*" Melanie frowned. "What could that mean? I *don't* understand."

It could mean that it was someone you know, Nick thought uneasily. Someone with whom there had been love and hate and passion and bitterness. . . .

Nick shrugged and smiled at her.

"All right, final question for now," Nick continued. It was, in some ways, *the* question. "Something must have happened to make him leave. He—"

Nick stopped.

"Didn't kill me," Melanie whispered softly. "I don't know why he didn't."

"Did you say anything?"

"I pleaded with him." Melanie shuddered. "I called for help."

Nick was certain that all the Manhattan Ripper's victims had pleaded and called for help. It hadn't stopped the killer before.

"Called for help. Who did you call?"

"I called for Brooke." Melanie's voice was soft. *I called for the people I love.* She added, even more softly, "And I called for Charles."

Charles, Nick mused.

"Did he stop suddenly?"

Melanie considered Nick's question for a moment. "Yes, I guess he did. He stopped and stared at me. He looked startled and then confused."

"After that he left?"

"Yes." Melanie's energy was visibly fading.

"Brooke?" Melanie asked dreamily, her eyes fluttering.

"Yes?"

"It didn't hurt when he stabbed me. It just felt like pressure, but I *heard* it. It was like . . . remember when we got our ears pierced? Remember how afraid we were that it would hurt?"

"But it didn't." It had been an exciting and scary adventure; they braved it together, half anxious, half giggling. Of course she remembered.

"No. But the sound . . . do you remember what we decided it sounded like?"

"I remember, Mellie," Brooke answered gently. She had been remembering the giggles, but now she remembered the sound of the sharp needle puncturing cartilage. "It was a crunching sound. Like celery."

"Uh-huh," Melanie whispered as her eyes closed. "Like celery."

CHAPTER TWENTY-SIX

"Would you like to come with me to see Robin Shepard? Or do you have to go to court?" Nick asked as they left the ICU.

"Andrew is single-handedly waging war against Jeffrey Martin."

"Andrew can handle it."

"Andrew has been so helpful," Brooke mused. "He has been such a friend throughout all this."

"Andrew's a nice man," Nick observed carefully.

Brooke nodded thoughtfully. "Yes."

She doesn't see it, Nick thought. *Brooke has no idea how much Andrew cares about her. But that is Brooke's specialty. . . .*

They walked in silence for fifty feet before Brooke said suddenly, "You wouldn't let me come with you to see Robin Shepard unless you knew he had nothing to do with it."

"That's right. But do you want to come anyway?"

"Yes."

They walked through the maze of shiny narrow corridors in the recently renovated building that housed New York City's largest newspaper. Robin Shepard's office was in a remote corner on the fourth floor facing the East River. The door to Robin Shepard's inner office was closed.

"May I help you?" a secretary in the small outer office asked.

"I am Lieutenant Adrian, NYPD. I would like to speak with Robin." Nick showed her his badge.

"One moment please." The secretary retreated behind the inner office door and returned moments later. "Please come in."

Robin Shepard was not the Manhattan Ripper. Robin Shepard was five feet five inches tall with shoulder-length auburn hair, green eyes, and a lovely figure. She was a very attractive woman who smiled warmly at Nick.

"Nick, how nice to see you."

"Hello, Robin. Robin, this is Brooke Chandler."

Robin recognized Brooke and, of course, knew the connection with Melanie; it had been common knowledge since the Liberty Weekend celebration.

"I am so sorry about your sister. How is she?"

"She's OK."

"Good. This is an official visit, isn't it?"

"Yes," Nick replied. He told Robin Melanie's assailant had used her name as his passport into her apartment. Nick also gave Robin Melanie's description of the man.

"Terrific," Robin said grimly.

"He must not know you are a woman," Brooke suggested.

"Not necessarily," Nick said. "He could know very well. He only had to count on the fact that Melanie didn't know. And if she did know, and called him on it, he could have admitted the joke or hung up. It wasn't a big risk."

"I've been reading 'Profiles' for four years and I always assumed you were a man." Brooke smiled at Robin.

"Has anyone ever noticed that it's the *women* who always assume that the other successful career person is a *man?*" Nick asked lightly.

"Touché."

"I wonder if he's used my name each time?" Robin asked, frowning.

"Possibly. All the women would recognize it."

"And welcome me with open arms," Robin observed solemnly.

"It's pretty scary," Nick agreed.

"You can't hide from life because of one crazy," Robin said defiantly. Then she teased, "Besides, do you know how angry *you* would be if some woman you needed to interview told you to come by her office the next day after she checked on your badge number?"

Robin was talking about *them*, how they had met. It had been in her apartment late one night when Nick needed information for a case.

"Police business."

"A great cover."

"Do you have any idea who it *could* be?" Brooke interrupted the repartee. "Someone on your staff?"

"Just because this maniac used my name doesn't mean he is, or ever was, associated with me or the paper." Robin stated the obvious. "The physical description includes more men than it *excludes*. The blue eyes and green eyes and gray eyes may be off the hook, but . . ."

Robin looked at Nick when she said gray eyes.

"So we're back at ground zero," Brooke murmured.

"No, not at all," Nick countered confidently. "We have a description plus an

MO. I'm going to hold a press conference this afternoon."

"You're going to get a lot of calls. Everyone in the city will know at least one possible suspect."

"That's OK. Someone out there really *does* know him, has seen him, works next to him. And revealing his MO may make women even more cautious."

"I don't know if you've noticed, Nick, but this town is already totally panicked about this psychopath. Describing his MO—and I agree you must—will put an end to meaningful male-female intercourse," Robin paused, smiling, "as we know it."

"I have to tell the press he used your name," Nick continued firmly, ignoring her innuendo. "And why we know it's not you."

"I have never pretended to be a man. In fact I've been pushing the editor for a picture beside my byline for years. This may do it."

"Good." Nick made a move to leave. "Thanks, Robin. If you think of anyone . . ."

"I'll let you know right away. Oh, Nick, I've been thinking about doing a profile on you. Cop and author, something like that. I wanted to do it soon, but now I'm wondering if I should wait until you solve this Manhattan Ripper business, write the book about it, and win the Pulitzer Prize."

"That will be a very long wait," Nick said. Not that he wanted a column written about him *ever*. "I plan to solve the case right away, but I would never write a book about it."

"Nick, why not? Someone is going to. It might as well be the man who knows more about it than anyone else *and* is a fine writer." Robin smiled.

"All I care about is getting him," Nick said seriously. It wasn't entirely true; all Nick cared about was getting him *before* he hurt someone else—someone like Brooke or Robin. "You be careful, Robin. You're one of *them*, you know."

"*Them?*"

"Yes. The successful women, his targets."

As Nick and Brooke left Robin's office, Brooke winked conspiratorially at the undercover agent who was assigned to protect her.

"When are you going to give that poor man his freedom?"

"Maybe after the press conference," Nick answered vaguely. Maybe never. He couldn't really justify continued police protection for Brooke any more than for any other young woman in Manhattan.

"But the killer knows that Melanie doesn't know who he is. And, therefore, I don't."

"I'm not taking the protection off Melanie until we get him."

"Melanie's an eyewitness. There really isn't a reason to protect me."

"Except that you are so damned trusting."

"Not anymore," Brooke told him solemnly. "If anyone needs protection it's Robin. She *may* know him. Don't you think it's likely that he worked for her or the paper at some time?"

Nick shrugged. Of course he thought it was likely. Of course Robin needed protection. That was why he arranged for it when he made the call to schedule the press conference.

"She's pretty fond of you."

"Fond?" Nick asked, surprised, his eyes twinkling.

"Pretty interested in you."

"We're friends."

"I'm surprised you're not married."

"Married? To Robin?"

"To anyone."

Nick didn't answer, but later, as he drove Brooke back to the hospital, he said, "I was married once."

"It didn't work out?"

"No. We met in college. I was a nice, safe English major. After we graduated and were married and I was teaching high school English and thinking about getting a Ph.D., I decided to become a cop. It was a childhood fantasy. I even told her about it before we were married, but I don't think either of us really believed I would do it. Anyway, I did, and it was awful for her."

"Why?"

"Any time I was five minutes late getting home she assumed I'd been killed. And every time the phone rang and I wasn't there she was certain it was bad news. She wasn't being paranoid. Cops do get killed, especially in this town. It was awful for her."

"Was it awful for you?"

"She didn't make it awful. She kept her fear hidden for a long time. But I wanted kids, we both did, and . . ."

"You couldn't."

"She wouldn't," Nick corrected. "Not as long as I was a cop. That's when—how—I learned how much she hated what I was doing. And while I was considering giving it up, she fell in love with someone else. By the time she told me how much she hated the way I was spending my life it was already way too late to save the marriage. So, we divorced and she remarried and has three kids and lives in the suburbs."

"And you're still a cop."

"Still a cop."

"And you would still like to have kids," Brooke added quietly after a few moments.

Nick didn't answer. He didn't have to. They had reached the hospital.

"I'm fine, Adam," Melanie told him two days after the tube in her throat had been removed. "You really need to be in Europe."

"I think I need to be here."

"I have plenty of company, and I sleep most the time anyway."

"Still."

"Go." Melanie smiled through the fire that smoldered, threatening to burst into flames of pain, in her chest and abdomen. She was overdue on her Demerol shot, but she wanted to be awake, and not groggy, for her talk with Adam.

Adam frowned briefly. He would go—she was right—but there was something he had to tell her first.

"Melanie, don't let him hurt you again. I know he's here now." Adam paused. *He* didn't want to hurt her.

"Because of the crisis." Melanie sighed softly. There was a foggy memory of soft, lovely words—Charles's words—*I love you, Melanie.* Was it a memory, or a dream? A *dream*, she told herself firmly. She couldn't allow herself to think it was real. "I know, Adam."

"I don't trust him, Melanie."

"Adam, Charles is your friend!"

Not anymore, Adam thought, remembering their angry exchange and the iciness that lingered.

"I don't trust him when it comes to you."

* * *

Adam returned to Paris. A day later, at Melanie's insistence, Ellen and Douglas Chandler returned to Pasadena. She was *fine*, Melanie told them lovingly. And Brooke was here, and Charles . . .

Charles spent most of every day at her bedside, reading manuscripts while she slept and talking gently to her, holding her hand, when she awakened. In the evening, when Brooke arrived after a day of battling Jeffrey Martin in the courtroom, Charles left. Charles sensed that Brooke needed private time with Melanie as much as he did. They each had secrets and confessions to share with their precious Melanie.

Brooke and Charles needed to tell Melanie *now*, in the rare moments when her trying-to-heal body allowed her to awaken and the narcotics released their foggy grip. They knew she might not hear, or understand, but they had to tell her. They would tell her again later, too, when her body was strong and her mind was clear.

"It's a nightmare, Melanie, but it feels so real."

"Charles, you don't have to . . ."

"Yes, darling, I do." Charles sighed softly. He had to tell her about more than the nightmare. He had to tell her about an unloved little boy and the man he had become. He *would* tell her all of it when she was well. For now, he would tell her little, important bits. "The nightmare is about my father. There was always something . . ."

Charles paused. How could he explain something he didn't understand? Charles made it simple. "I was never good enough to earn his love."

I was never good enough for Brooke, either, or for you, Melanie mused dreamily. Her thoughts began to drift to the bittersweet memories of her past, carried by the blurry warmth of Demerol and fatigue, but Charles's loving brown eyes pulled her back. Melanie fought to stay awake, focused on Charles, and the present, and these precious moments with him. "You were saying . . . your father . . . the nightmare . . ."

"In the nightmare, my father and I argue." I plead for his love. Charles frowned, remembering. "There's a violent storm, and a sudden crash, and he dies."

"How awful," Melanie whispered softly just before the narcotics won and she succumbed begrudgingly to necessary sleep.

"I wanted so much to be you," Brooke told Melanie.

"*Me?*"

"Yes. I was jealous." Brooke smiled thoughtfully and stroked the golden hair. "I guess I still am."

"Jealous," Melanie murmured. "Of me?"

"Yes." Brooke laughed softly. "That surprises you?"

"I wished I could be like you." But I was never jealous.

"*Why?*"

"You did important things. You still do." Melanie's voice faded, then found a final burst of strength. "I am so proud of you, Brooke."

"Oh, Melanie, I am so proud of *you*. I always have been."

One evening, Melanie awakened to find Brooke and Nick and Charles at her bedside.

No, she realized as her just-wakening eyes sharpened their focus, it isn't Charles, but he is vaguely familiar. . . .

"Melanie, this is Andrew Parker."

Of course, the deputy DA! Melanie had seen his picture on television and in the papers.

"Hello, Andrew."

"Hello, Melanie. How are you?"

"Fine, thank you. How's Jeffrey Martin?"

"I think we're closing in." Andrew smiled confidently.

"Good." Melanie returned the smile, then frowned. There was something she meant to tell Nick. What was it? Oh, yes. "Nick, you told me to let you know if I thought of who he might be."

"Yes?"

Nick and Brooke and Andrew waited in breath-held silence.

"Steve Barnes."

"Who is he?" Andrew asked.

"The photographer Adam fired in Monte Carlo," Melanie answered. "Because of me."

"Have you seen or heard from him since?" Nick asked.

"No. I've heard *of* him. He's working, but it's not the same for him. He's not at the top anymore."

"Sounds like a motive."

"And there's something else. Jane Tucker and Adam were once engaged to be married."

Eight days after Melanie arrived at the hospital—bloody and wounded and dying— she awakened to an almost familiar feeling of strength and energy. The feeling had awakened with her, a glimmer of hope, and it hadn't faded. Melanie eagerly told the doctors that she wanted to sit in a chair and maybe even walk a little. . . .

"Why are you smiling?" she asked, stopping, breathless in the midst of her requests.

"Because you've turned the corner," the attending physician replied. "You're ready to be well again."

"Yes, I am. *Finally.*"

"Not finally, Melanie. Your whole recovery has been remarkable. Your will to be well is ahead of your body's ability to recover. Your injuries are serious and major. Even though you are in excellent health and very fit, it will take a long time before you are fully recovered."

"So don't get discouraged?" she teased happily. It was such a relief to know that her strength and energy would return. She had worried—a foggy, drugged, fatigued worry—that she would never feel good again. "I won't. So I can sit in a chair?"

"Sure. With *help*. Slow and easy. OK?"

"OK," Melanie agreed readily, but her mind spun with wonderful plans. She would sit, then walk, then take a long hot shower . . . Surely the wounds, carefully hidden by sterile dressings, must be healed by *now*.

That was something else she needed to do. She needed to look under the bandages and see for herself what the doctors and nurses examined with such interest every day. Melanie hadn't seen the wounds. She was lying down when they examined her—she was *always* lying down, but not anymore—and it hurt too much to flex her neck to look, and besides, she had been too tired to care.

But now she cared, again, about everything.

Don't get discouraged, she reminded herself later that night as she lay awake—she could stay awake for hours now—reflecting on her accomplishments of the day. The accomplishments seemed so small when she remembered how much effort and energy they had required.

She sat in a chair three times, each time remaining a little longer, ten minutes, fifteen minutes, *twenty* minutes. Each time she was forced to stop because the weakness would come and her heart would race and her mind would blur and she couldn't think or breathe. The weakness was worse than the pain, but the pain was there, too. The fragile healing fibers of the deep knife wounds pulled and stretched and finally sent hot, searing messages of angry protest.

Why was there so much pain, Melanie wondered. She still hadn't looked at her wounds. Her courage waned because of the pain; so much pain meant they couldn't be healed. She would look at them tomorrow, or the next day.

It was too soon for a real shower, but her doctors approved the nurses' plan to wash their favorite patient's long golden hair in the morning.

Melanie fell asleep, smiling, thinking about her hair being clean and shiny again.

When Charles arrived at eleven the next morning he found Melanie sitting at the edge of her bed, her head bent, her shoulders hunched, her face obscured by a mane of slightly damp golden hair.

"Melanie?" He had knocked, hadn't heard an answer, and now peered in, expecting her to be asleep. At the sound of his voice she looked up. Her pale-blue eyes glistened with tears. "Darling, what's wrong?"

"I can't even brush my own hair." She stared at the brush in her useless hands.

After the nurses washed her hair and towelled it almost dry, they offered to brush it for her. But Melanie said No. She wanted to do it; she wanted to do that one *normal* thing.

But the moment Melanie raised her arm above her head, the pain from the stretched and rebelling wounds became severe. Still she didn't stop. She was getting used to pain. Pain was better than the fogginess of Demerol. But after two strokes her arm became heavy, weak, *useless*. There was nothing she could do. She could fight the pain, but not the weakness. She had to stop.

Without a word Charles took the brush from her hand and very gently began to brush the golden silk.

Melanie trembled at his touch and her mind drifted to memories of last summer. Charles loved to brush her hair, but his strong hands always became too gentle. When Charles found a tangle, she would take the brush and pull impatiently at the snarl of silk. And his hands, suddenly free, would find her face, her neck, her breasts, her thighs; and they would make love, and the gold would be tangled again.

Melanie sighed.

"What a sigh," Charles murmured as he brushed gently, so gently.

"I want to be well, Charles." I want more than that. I want to go back to those lovely memories.

"You will be. You look well now. The doctors are thinking about—what is it they said?—oh, yes, writing you up as a case report of a miraculous recovery."

"But I can't *do* anything. I am so weak." Melanie told him about the weakness, but not the pain. She didn't want to tell Charles about the pain.

"That will pass."

Charles brushed in silence for several moments.

Tell him, Melanie. Even if he already knows it you need to tell him.

"Charles?"

"Hmm?"

"I am so sorry for what I said to you at the Valentine's Day party."

Charles stopped brushing and knelt in front of her. He peered under the curtain of gold until he found her eyes.

"I am so sorry for hurting you. For all the hurt," Charles said heavily, as if weighted down by every pain she had ever suffered, including the horror of the Manhattan Ripper.

"It's OK. I'm OK." *Now, because you're here. But when I get well and you are gone again . . . I can't think about that.*

Charles took her hands in his.

"May I have this dance?" *May I have this life, this love?*

"Yes."

Charles stood up and pulled her gently to him. He folded her arms against his chest, because he sensed that she couldn't lift them to his neck. Then he wrapped his arms around her and held her tight, providing support, as they swayed gently together.

"Am I hurting you?" His lips brushed her clean gold hair.

"No," she whispered into his chest. It all hurt, her whole body hurt. But beyond the pain was something so wonderful. Beyond the pain was Charles. His hands, his arms, his lips, his body, his warmth, his strength. *Charles.* Nothing else mattered.

If only this moment could last forever.

But it couldn't. The weakness came suddenly and without warning, drenching her in overwhelming fatigue that, unlike the pain, she couldn't fight or control. She could conquer the pain, but not the weakness. It won every time.

Charles sensed it immediately; her body shuddered and became limp. Quickly, carrying her easily, Charles laid her on the bed.

"Are you OK?" he asked anxiously. "Should I get the doctor?"

"No, Charles," Melanie reassured the concerned brown eyes. "This happens all the time."

"I shouldn't have—"

"Yes, you should have." Melanie forced her eyes to stay open a little longer. It was a small conquest over the fatigue that was demanding she go to sleep *now*. She looked at him and whispered, "Thank you."

Melanie didn't know if it was just a lovely wish or the beginning of a happy dream or if it was real. It *felt* real. It felt like the touch of his lips, so soft, so tender, pressing lightly against hers as she fell asleep.

Melanie awakened two hours later. Charles was gone. But the memory filled her with warmth and joy and hope. *Maybe.* She would be out of the hospital soon. Maybe they could begin again. . . .

Melanie got out of bed and walked to the sink, above which hung a small mirror. Melanie needed to see how soon it would be. *Surely* the wounds were almost healed. . . .

Melanie pulled the paper tape that held the edge of a large bandage over her left breast. The bandage fell free, exposing a thick pink-purple scar that puckered her skin and redefined the shape of a breast that *used* to be perfect and round and firm and proud. Now it was misshapen, stretched and twisted into a new, ugly shape by the gruesome scar.

Melanie gazed in horror.

No. *No.*

Melanie felt her dreams die. She and Charles could never begin again.

It was over.

CHAPTER TWENTY-SEVEN

*W*hen Brooke arrived at six o'clock that evening she found Melanie staring trancelike at her hands.

"Melanie?"

"Oh, Brooke. Hi." Melanie's voice was flat.

"You look great."

Brooke noticed the shiny golden hair at once. As she moved closer she saw the tears.

"Mellie?" Brooke asked gently. "What's wrong?"

The softness of Brooke's voice made the tears spill faster. Melanie shook her head, unable to speak. Brooke sat on the bed beside her, touched her hands to Melanie's shoulders, and waited.

Finally Melanie spoke.

"Brooke, I saw what I look like today," she whispered bitterly. "I looked under the bandages. You have no idea. . . ."

"I do know, Melanie. I was here one day when they changed the dressings. You were half asleep."

"So you know how ugly."

"They are just beginning to heal. The doctors say they will become fine white lines."

"Fine white lines all over my breasts and abdomen," Melanie murmured. Then her eyes flashed, "And you know they won't be fine, Brooke. You've seen them. They'll be thick and ugly *always.*"

"So you won't model swimsuits anymore," Brooke suggested carefully.

Melanie looked at her twin with surprise. She hadn't even thought about her modelling career. It was over, too. She could still model clothes that covered her torso, but she *wouldn't.* She wasn't beautiful anymore. She no longer had a beautiful body to wear under the beautiful clothes.

"No, I won't model," her voice faded. *And I won't be with the man I love.*

"You'll have a few scars, Melanie." More than a few, Brooke knew. And they *would* be horrible and disfiguring. She added truthfully, "But you can model if you want. And . . ."

Brooke couldn't say it. She couldn't say with certainty that it wouldn't matter to Charles. Brooke *believed* it wouldn't, because she had always believed in Charles. But what if she was wrong? What if the blood in his aristocratic veins really was ice-cold after all? Charles had hurt Melanie before.

Brooke knew Charles loved Melanie; she only hoped he loved her twin *enough*. . . .

Melanie awoke the following morning with the certain knowledge that she had to get out of the hospital as soon as possible. She had to begin her new life. The doctors agreed that with a visiting nurse and careful follow-up, she could, in keeping with her miraculous recovery, leave in two days.

Usually Charles arrived at the hospital by midmorning, but not today. By the middle of the afternoon she still hadn't seen him. Maybe he knew; maybe he had felt the scars, the ugliness, beneath the sterile dressings as he held her against him. Like the princess and the pea, Melanie mused. The prince and scars.

It was just as well, she decided. It would be easiest if Charles made the decision to stay away.

Jason arrived at three o'clock.

"Jason, how nice of you to visit." Melanie hadn't seen Jason since the day in the art museum before Christmas.

"You look good, Melanie." Jason smiled. "Charles asked me to tell you he'll be over this evening. There was a problem with the copy for *Images*. . . .''

"I know he's very busy, Jason. Tell him there's no need to visit every day. I'm getting much better. In fact, I'll be leaving soon."

"Leaving soon?" Nick echoed her last two words as he entered the room. "Hello, Jason. Leaving soon, Melanie?"

"Oh-oh," Melanie explained pleasantly to Jason. "Here comes trouble. Nick has a fantasy about stashing me away in a safe house until You Know Who is caught."

"Not a fantasy, my dear eyewitness," Nick replied with matching pleasantness.

"See? He's not about to let me wander the streets of Manhattan. Safe house is a euphemism for jail."

"Have you already found a place?" Jason asked.

"No," Nick answered. "This is the first I've heard about leaving soon."

"I have an estate in Southampton. The house has a state-of-the-art alarm system. Guards placed at a few strategic locations would make it virtually impenetrable. I assume Melanie's safety is the major concern."

"Yes."

"I think she'd be safe there. And it's beautiful and peaceful. You're welcome to it." Jason made the offer first to the steel-gray eyes and then to the pale-blue ones.

"Jason, that is so generous," Melanie breathed.

"It's very generous, Jason," Nick agreed.

"Does that mean . . . Nick?" Melanie asked eagerly.

"I need to go look at it, arrange for guards, make sure it's safe."

"I know it will be," Melanie said confidently. "Jason, I can't believe this. It's so nice of you."

"It's really nothing." Jason was happy to help.

"Jason, I just thought of something." Melanie's blue eyes sparkled. "There's probably a beach, isn't there? Somewhere nearby. Maybe I could go for drives in a squad car to see the beach?"

"The house is on the beach, Melanie. Lots and lots of beach."

*   *   *

Nick agreed to Southampton because it would be nice for Melanie. She had been through so much already. This way she could be near Brooke, and Charles.

Charles. Nick would feel better if he could find Charles even something *close* to an alibi. Nick had been trying to do it without actually asking him, but he was coming up empty. No one seemed to know where Charles Sinclair was on the nights of the Manhattan Ripper's brutal attacks.

Yesterday Nick had received the report from the Southampton police on the death of Elliott Sinclair. The death was ruled an accident. Note was made of the fact that Charles Sinclair, the estranged son who was working with the Peace Corps in Africa, had mysteriously appeared moments after news of Elliott's death. It was regarded as an interesting, but not troublesome, coincidence. The report did not include interviews with anyone at the Peconic Bay Yacht Club who might have been able to tell them if Elliott Sinclair was alone when he sailed into the storm. . . .

After Nick received the report, he made some calls. He spoke with the Southampton police officers who interviewed Charles at the time. They told him that Charles was distraught, *naturally.* Charles's explanation for his mysterious reappearance, they recalled, was that he "just had a feeling" Jason needed him. Nick next spoke with John Perkins who was unable to shed light on the estrangement of Charles and Elliott Sinclair. Nick planned to speak with the harbormaster at Peconic Bay Yacht Club—the man who might know if Elliott sailed to his death alone—upon his return from vacation next week.

Nick would feel better when he had at least one airtight alibi for Charles Sinclair for a night that the Ripper attacked. He also wanted convincing evidence that there really was no mystery about Elliott's death. Best of all would be if one of the hundreds of daily "tips" called in regarding the identity of the Manhattan Ripper paid off.

Until then Charles Sinclair was a suspect, but Nick couldn't prevent him from seeing Melanie.

"You'll be staying at Windermere?" Charles asked when she told him four hours later.

"Yes." *Why does that bother you, Charles?*

"You could stay at the penthouse. It would be much easier to guard than Windermere. I'm going to talk to Nick—"

"No," Melanie said swiftly. *I can't stay with you, darling. I can't be with you. I can't ever let you see the way I look.*

His dark eyes—loving, questioning, bewildered—met hers.

"Being at the beach . . . in the country . . ." Melanie fumbled. *None of that would have mattered if she hadn't seen the scars. All she would have cared about was being with Charles.*

Charles started to speak, but at that moment Brooke and Nick arrived. The four of them talked about Melanie, how well she looked; and about Windermere, how wonderful that would be; and about the Jeffrey Martin trial, how well it was going.

After thirty minutes, Nick stood up to leave.

"I'd better go," Nick said. He added, as if it were an afterthought, "Charles, I wonder if you would let me know where you were on the nights—"

"*What?*" Charles stood up and faced Nick. His dark eyes flashed with anger.

"I need to know," Nick said evenly.

"Nick, you can't possibly—" Brooke began.

"Think I'm a suspect?" Charles finished Brooke's sentence. His voice was low. "That's exactly what Nick thinks."

"No," Melanie whispered.

"It's routine. Charles matches the description," Nick explained, carefully watching Charles's reaction.

"It's not routine," Charles hissed. "You aren't collecting alibis from every man fitting the description who knew Melanie or the others."

"I would appreciate your cooperation in this, Charles." Nick's gray eyes sent a challenge.

"You have no right, Nick. And it's more than insulting to even suggest—"

"Do you know the dates?"

"No I don't."

"June nineteenth, September seventeenth, October seventeenth, December twenty-third, and February sixteenth."

February sixteenth. That night Melanie had been the victim.

Charles forced the anger for Nick from his eyes and looked, gently questioning, at Melanie.

Do you believe I could have done that to you, Melanie? Is that why you don't want to stay at the penthouse?

"Charles," Melanie whispered.

"Don't you know," Charles began. His voice was hoarse, a tenuous balance between tenderness and rage.

Yes, I know, Charles, I know.

Charles turned back to Nick. When he spoke his voice was ice. "You had no right to ask me in front of them."

Charles held Nick's eyes for several angry moments. Then he left.

Brooke and Melanie stared at Nick in stunned silence.

"This is a murder investigation," Nick said finally, firmly, first to the sky-blue eyes and then to the ocean-blue ones. He repeated before he, too, left, "Murder."

"I'll be back, Melanie." Brooke followed Nick out of the room.

"Nick."

Nick turned and waited.

"How dare you?"

"How *dare* I?"

"How dare you imply that Charles—"

Nick took Brooke by the arm and guided her out of the bright lights of the hospital corridor into a dimly lit supply room.

"Brooke. I know what I'm doing."

"Then tell me. Make me understand why you would do that."

"I've told Andrew. You know he's the contact in the DA's office."

"Tell *me*."

"You're too personally involved." Nick found her dark-blue eyes in the shadows. *Just like I'm too personally involved, only you don't know it.*

"Melanie's my sister, but—"

"And you're in love with Charles." Nick spoke softly.

Brooke's eyes became thoughtful and serious. *Maybe once I was, or thought I was,* she mused. *But not now.*

Finally she smiled a soft wistful smile and said, "I'm not in love with him, Nick. I care about him. I care about him and Melanie. I admit that. But I'm a professional, too, Nick. You can trust me with whatever you have."

Nick decided to trust her. He wanted to trust her, and he wanted to believe her.

"Charles fits the physical description. His blood-type is O, and he is right-handed."

"Right-handed?"

"Andrew really hasn't told you anything, has he?"

"I guess not."

"We know the Ripper is right-handed. At least he—"

"Uses a knife with his right hand," Brooke completed the sentence. *I'm not that fragile, Nick,* she thought bravely as an ice-cold shiver pulsed through her.

"Yes. And I can't find an alibi for Charles for any of the five nights."

"He must have been at a party or a theater opening or . . ."

"I've really checked, Brooke. He was at a party on December twenty-third, but he left early, and alone. That's why I had to ask him."

"In front of—"

"If he has nothing to hide, it's just an insult from a lowly cop. But . . ."

"He was very angry," Brooke whispered. "But that doesn't mean guilt. Charles is very proud."

"An expensive luxury."

"What about Steve?" Brooke asked suddenly. "Have you followed up on him? He has reason to want to harm Melanie and Adam. . . ."

"Of course I have followed up. Steve isn't the Manhattan Ripper." Nick paused. *Hear this, Brooke.* "Steve Barnes is left-handed. His blood type is B. He was in Tokyo on the night of the attack in October."

"He knew two of the victims. . . ." Brooke protested weakly.

"So did Charles, *at least* two." *Charles was* involved *with two; and he knew, or certainly had met, Jane Tucker when she and Adam were together.* Nick watched Brooke's face in the shadows.

Brooke frowned and shook her head slightly. *It's not possible.*

"You knew that, didn't you?" Nick asked. "You knew that Charles and Pamela Rhodes were lovers."

"Yes, but . . ." *There had to be more. There was still something Nick hadn't told her.* "What else, Nick?"

Nick sighed. Brooke said she wasn't in love with Charles, but she was blinded to the facts of the case. Her logical, incisive mind was cluttered and confused by emotion. Maybe if he told her everything. . . . She needed to be aware. She needed to be careful.

"Thirteen years ago Charles's father died in a yachting accident. He was killed by a severe blow to the head. It happened during a storm. The police report says he was hit by the boom of the sailboat."

"So?" Brooke heard the defiance in her voice. Nick was about to tell her something that might make Charles Sinclair's blood type and physical description and righthandedness and lack of alibis suddenly more than circumstantial, and she didn't want to hear it.

"Less than an hour after Elliott's body was found, Charles arrived at the family estate. His clothes were torn and dirty and soaking wet."

"So?"

"Charles had been away—in Africa—for three years. Until that moment no one knew he had returned."

"Coincidence. He missed his father and twin—"

"Elliott disowned Charles four years before."

"Why?" Brooke knew it was true. It explained why Jason, not Charles, signed all the contracts for Sinclair Publishing. She repeated softly, "Why?"

"No one seems to know."

"Charles must have had a reason for why he returned *then* from Africa."

"He told the Southampton police he 'had a feeling' Jason needed him." Nick paused. Then he added skeptically, "Charles began his journey home from Kenya a week before Elliott's death and arrived in New York the day before Elliott died."

Brooke retreated deeper into the shadows of the supply room.

"Brooke?"

"When Melanie and I were fourteen I signed up for an overnight camping trip in Yosemite Park with my science class." Brooke's voice was distant with the memory. "It wasn't the sort of thing I usually did. Melanie was the outdoors one, the athlete. But, sometimes, I pretended I was Melanie."

Sometimes I wanted so much to be Melanie. Brooke sighed.

"Anyway, I guess I was pretending I was her, because I left the group and climbed a steep rocky hill. I scampered up it like a mountain goat, just like Melanie would have. When I got to the top, where it was flat and safe, I was clumsy Brooke again and I tripped on a tree root and badly sprained my ankle. I couldn't walk. I had wandered too far for anyone to hear my calls for help.

"When they discovered I was missing they began a search. My parents and Melanie drove up from Pasadena. Moments after Melanie arrived she started urging the rangers to climb the steep, rocky hill. Naturally the search was centered in the opposite direction toward the flat, dense forest. No one would expect *me* to climb the hill. They would have ignored anyone else, but even then Melanie was beautiful and charming and persuasive.

"Apparently she finally threatened to search by herself. That convinced a ranger to go with her. When they found me it was pitch-black. I didn't even hear them coming." Brooke's voice choked with emotion as she remembered how she and Melanie had downplayed it at the time. *It was just a lucky coincidence! She was no part of Melanie and Melanie was no part of her. There was nothing special about them; it wasn't because they were twins and there was a bond.* "Melanie knew where I was. She knew I needed her. Something told her. . . ."

Nick moved into the darkness until he was very close to her.

"Brooke, Charles left Africa seven days before a completely unexpected storm hit Long Island. There was no way. . . ."

Brooke spun and faced him. Her blue eyes flashed. "I don't *care* if it makes sense, Nick. It can *happen!"*

The moment Brooke returned to Melanie's hospital room, Melanie asked, "What did Nick say, Brooke? He doesn't really think that Charles—"

"He has to pursue every possibility no matter how remote," Brooke answered vaguely. Then, purposefully shifting the conversation, she said, "Galen called today. She just found out. She wants to talk with you, but she doesn't want to disturb you."

Melanie smiled. *Shy, thoughtful Galen.*

"I'll give her a call in the morning."

Brooke and Melanie talked about Galen for a while. Before Brooke left, she asked, offhandedly, "Do you know anything about Charles and Jason's father?"

Why, Brooke? Does it have something to do with why Nick suspects Charles?

"Not really." *Just that Charles has a nightmare about an argument with him, during which his father dies, and the nightmare is so real that it awakens him, gasping and fright-ened and tormented. . . .*

"How is 'Sonja'?" Melanie asked Galen after she had assured and reassured Galen that she was fine.

"Still unpublishable. I can't change it." *I can't even try.*

"Send it to me," Melanie urged eagerly.

"Oh, no . . ."

"*Yes.* I need some good reading. . . ."

"This isn't good." Galen hesitated. "But I'll send you 'Sonja' and the rest of *Spring Street Stories* and the bound galleys for *Songs of the Savanna.* Hopefully, the others will offset 'Sonja.' "

"What a wonderful care package!"

"Shall I send it to the hospital?"

"No." Melanie would be leaving for Windermere in the morning. Nick told her to tell no one when or where she was going. "Could you send it to Brooke?"

After Melanie finished talking to Galen she studied the 1986 calendar the nurses had found for her. Perhaps *she* could provide an alibi for Charles. Last June they had been together almost every night. *Almost.*

June nineteenth. Melanie's heart raced and her stomach ached as the realization settled. June nineteenth was the night she had gone to bed early and alone. She had called Charles back and reached a line that was at first busy and then unanswered. Melanie had no idea how Charles spent the night of June nineteenth. Except that, perhaps, he was angry with *her* . . .

September seventeenth. On September sixteenth, Charles arrived in Monte Carlo to say good-bye, again, forever. By the night of the seventeenth, Charles was back in New York. Melanie remembered her angry question—"Why did you really come, Charles? Just to twist the knife?"—and shuddered.

October seventeenth. Melanie had no idea where Charles was that night. He wasn't a part of her life then, anymore, even though he was still a part of her heart. Melanie knew she missed him that night, as she missed him every night.

December twenty-third. Melanie's heart leapt. She had seen Charles at the *Vogue* holiday open house. She had seen him from a distance. He was alone. He had started toward her—perhaps to speak with her—but she had turned away. Melanie remembered seeing Charles leave, several hours before Viveca told her that Jane Tucker had been murdered.

February sixteenth. Melanie could not give Charles an alibi for that night, except he was *not* with her. The wild, dark eyes and strong, lean body and brutal, savage hands belonged to someone else. They belonged to a stranger who stopped his merciless assault when she called Charles's name. . . .

Melanie tossed the calendar aside. She had come up empty, worse than empty. Exhausted, Melanie sought refuge in sleep. But her dreams were confusing, horrible scenes of Charles and Nick and Brooke. Nick's wounded head spurted bright red blood as Charles laughed. Or was it *she* who was laughing? And why did Brooke have that knife?

When Melanie awoke, gasping, it was dark outside. She had spent her last day in the hospital thinking about him and dreaming about him. But she didn't see him that day. Charles didn't visit. And he didn't call.

CHAPTER TWENTY-EIGHT

$\mathcal{M}$elanie left the hospital by ambulance at six-thirty the following morning. The ambulance provided an excellent cover, and, despite her strong will, there was no good evidence that Melanie could sit up in a car all the way to Southampton.

Since no one expected Melanie to be well enough to leave the hospital for at least another week, it would be days before the discovery was made by the press. Then, and only then, would Nick issue a statement that she had been moved to a safe house in another part of the state.

The guards, off-duty police officers, were already in position by the time Melanie arrived. Nick had spent the previous afternoon at Windermere with Jason making all the arrangements. Before leaving, Nick gave Jason three automatic telephone dialing machines and asked Jason to program the machines with numbers Nick gave him to the Southampton police, Nick's office, and Nick's apartment. Jason nodded. He would see to it that it was done, even though, because he couldn't read the instructions, he couldn't do it himself. Maybe one of the guards wouldn't mind.

"Jason," Melanie breathed after the ambulance left and she was settled in the spacious charming first-floor bedroom that had once housed the live-in cook. Cheerful flowery paper adorned the walls, and yellow-and-white lace curtains framed the window. Melanie gazed out the window toward the emerald lawn and beyond to the white sand beach and gray-green sea. "This is wonderful."

"I thought it would be best for you to be on the first floor. The kitchen is nearby, and it's a short walk to the great room and library."

"But you chose this room because of the view, didn't you?"

"You did mention something about beach." Jason smiled. "Although most of the rooms have views. You'll see. When you're rested we can take a tour."

"I'm rested."

"I meant in a few days."

"Let's see how far we can get today," Melanie urged, standing, encouraged by the legs that supported her and seemed willing to move.

"OK," Jason agreed and offered his arm.

Melanie curled her hand around his forearm and they walked slowly into the huge entry hall. Melanie paused a moment, marvelling at the white marble floor, the huge crystal chandelier, the rich, colorful Oriental rugs, the shiny brass planters filled with luxuriant jade plants, and the lovely, bright paintings that hung on the natural wood walls. She frowned slightly as her eye fell on something that was distinctly out of place.

"What are those?" she asked, gesturing to a stack of boxes.

"Automatic telephone dialing machines. Nick wants one at your bedside, one in the entry hall, and one in my bedroom, all programmed to reach him and the local police."

"Did you explain to him that the high tech look really clashes with the overall tranquillity of the place?"

"No," Jason answered, frowning slightly.

"Jason?"

"Would you be willing to program them?"

"Sure. That's just the kind of project I need."

Melanie didn't ask why. Maybe Charles had already told her, but Jason doubted it.

"Melanie, do you know why I asked you to program the machines?"

"No. Probably because it will be one less game of backgammon you have to play with me to keep me amused," she guessed lightly. Then, watching his face, seeing uncharacteristic doubt in his confident handsomeness, she added quietly, "No. Why?"

"Because I can't read. That's something you probably should know." For your safety.

Can't read? What did that mean?

"You mean you don't read well." Melanie's mind searched for facts. She had never seen Jason read anything. But why would she? Then she remembered the day in the art museum when she teased him about listening to the recorded tour. *Teased* him.

"I don't read at all. I only write my name."

"It must be so frustrating," Melanie spoke softly, almost to herself.

"It's a little frustrating," Jason admitted.

"Understatement of the year?"

"Understatement of the first twenty-two years of my life." *Until I discovered my painting.* "Now I almost forget about it until something comes up like programming automatic dialing machines."

"Consider them programmed, *after* my tour."

Melanie smiled and nodded appreciatively as Jason led her through the elegant mansion. Each room was a masterpiece of style and art and exquisite taste. Throughout, on wall after wall, hung magnificent paintings.

Finally, because she had been silently admiring them, Melanie moved to one of the paintings for a closer inspection. The scene was dramatic, a violent storm painted in shades of gray. Melanie felt the force of the tormented angry sea battling the raging turbulent sky. Melanie gazed at the painting for many moments before her eyes drifted to the signature.

"You did this?"

"Yes."

"No wonder it's only a *little* frustrating being unable to read. What talent, Jason!"

"Thank you."

"You're welcome! Who is Meredith?" The painting next to Jason's, a lovely, colorful, full-bloom garden of roses, was signed *Meredith Sinclair*.

"My mother. Our style is similar. Her paintings are a little more pastel, a little softer than mine," Jason answered thoughtfully. There was a reason for the difference in style. Meredith's eye didn't see violence and death and tragedy in a summer storm the way his did. . . .

"Your mother. Is this—Did you and Charles grow up at Windermere?"

Melanie turned to face him. As she turned, the weakness hit her, sudden, unexpected, and overwhelming, as always. *"Oh."*

Jason guided her swiftly to the sofa and helped her lie down.

"Talk about a little frustrating," Melanie said after the fogginess in her brain cleared slightly. "It comes without warning."

"I think it's because you push to the absolute limit," Jason observed mildly. "Do you want to settle in here for a while? I can get a comforter for you."

Charles telephoned Windermere just as the winter sun was setting.

"She's fine." Jason smiled at Melanie. "She keeps looking wistfully at the beach and talking about jogging. How's . . ."

Melanie watched as Jason discussed the business of Sinclair Publishing Company with his twin. After fifteen minutes Jason said, "She's right here."

Jason handed the receiver to Melanie and quietly withdrew from the great room.

"Hello, Charles."

"Are you all right?"

"Yes." Are *you?* "It's so lovely here."

"Uh-huh. I just spoke with Brooke. She has an express mail package for you from Lake Forest."

"From Galen."

"Brooke says she and Andrew have to spend tomorrow working on the trial so she won't be able to visit until Sunday."

"Brooke should rest. I'm *fine.*"

"I thought I could bring the package out tomorrow."

"Oh." Yes, *do,* so I can tell you that I believe in you and trust you and love you. *No.* The image of her horrible wounds became vivid. Don't come. There is no point.

"Is that a Yes?" Charles's voice was quiet and tentative. And hopeful. Trust me, Melanie.

"Yes," she whispered.

The police-appointed visiting nurse arrived at Windermere at nine Saturday morning. After removing the sterile dressings and carefully inspecting the wounds, she announced, "You don't really need all these dressings anymore."

"I don't?" Melanie asked, surprised. Wouldn't it be best to keep the scars covered *forever?* Wouldn't it be best to hide the ugliness *always?*

"No. Except for the abdominal surgical incision, which should be covered until I remove the sutures on Monday, you don't need the dressings. The wounds are healing beautifully. There's no evidence of infection."

Melanie had stopped listening. The words *healing beautifully* were swirling in her brain. What could the nurse possibly be *thinking?* Of course, maybe from a professional standpoint, there was something wonderful about the way the mutilated tissue had formed a clean, tight mesh. Perhaps it did make a statement about the remarkable recuperative properties of the human body, but from a personal standpoint . . .

"So what do you say? Shall I just re-dress the abdomen?"

Melanie nodded absently. Then she asked, searching for a glimmer of hope, "Does this mean I can take a shower?"

"Are you strong enough?"

"Yes," Melanie answered confidently. If she could take a nice long shower and wash her hair before Charles's visit . . .

Wait a minute, a voice told her. Do you want him to brush your hair again? Do you want him to dance with you? Have you forgotten?

No, she told the nagging voice of reality. I haven't forgotten. The shower is for *me*.

"All right, but keep the abdominal wound as dry as possible. Shower with the dressing on and re-dress it afterward. I'll leave extra dressings in case it gets wet." The nurse smiled. The abdominal wound was virtually healed. A little water wouldn't hurt, and the benefit of letting Melanie take a shower was worth it. "Shall I stay while you take your shower?"

"No, thank you. I'll be fine. I'll see you Monday."

Melanie *was* fine, until the end. Then it came, as it always did, without warning. She felt herself falling. She fell against the tile wall of the shower stall and slid, her fall broken slightly by her outstretched arms, to the tile floor. Her whole body trembled with pain; every previously injured and still raw nerve fiber screamed out against the sudden violent motion. It was all old pain—a vivid reminder that she was not yet healed. There was no new injury.

It was minutes—five, ten, she didn't know—before she could find the strength to reach above her head and turn off the water. The movement triggered a new round of pain. Sharp shooting tremors ricocheted from one side of her body to the other. Melanie suppressed a scream. The weakness hadn't subsided and the pain was almost beyond her control. She needed help.

No, she told herself firmly. This is just weakness, which will pass, and pain, which you can control. You can help yourself. You *have* to.

Twenty minutes later, still curled on the tile floor of the shower stall, Melanie began to shiver from the cold. She crawled out of the shower onto the plush, carpeted bathroom floor. Her strength surprised her. *This is just weakness. It will pass.* It was passing, gone until the next unexpected moment. The pain was less, or she had more strength to control it.

Melanie pulled herself up from her knees by clinging to the marble vanity. She gasped as she saw the reflection of her naked body in the mirror above the vanity. Melanie had made no effort to see all her wounds—the glimpse, in the hospital, of the purple scar on her breast had been enough—but she tormented herself with how ugly and disfiguring they might be. Now she removed the one remaining dressing, completely saturated with water anyway, and saw the full measure of the destruction. It was even *worse* than she had imagined. She had to force herself to face it.

This is me, Melanie thought. This is how I look. This is how I will always look.

Tears spilled from her pale-blue eyes as she gazed in horror and disbelief at the purple-and-pink tracks that lined her once lovely breasts and now bony rib cage and the abdomen that used to be so flat and the hips that used to curve into a smooth roundness. The scars were *more* than ugly, uneven, discolored markings, more than superficial graffiti, more than skin deep. The scars took away her shape. They destroyed the soft, lovely contours and permanently dimpled and distorted the firm smoothness.

Carved, she thought, shuddering. I've been carved. He took my beautiful body and carved a new, grotesque one.

Melanie was filled then, for the first time, with an unspeakable hatred for the man who had done this to her. Until now she had thought little about *him*. He was not part of her life. He had only been part of her life for those few terrible minutes. But now Melanie realized that he—and that night—would be with her always. She hated him for what he had done to her. Every time she looked at herself she would be reminded of that hatred.

I just won't look, she decided firmly, reaching for a clean silk nightgown and robe.

Why should she look? It wasn't her body anymore. It didn't belong to her. She could keep it covered—and keep her distance from anyone who might want to know what lay beneath—and no one would ever know. Her face was still hers. Her lovely face and . . .

Neck. Melanie drew in a breath as she saw that one scar tracked above her clavicle toward the angle of her jaw. It had been covered until today by the pristine white dressings. But now its purple-pink tentacles were exposed, reaching defiantly above the collar of her robe.

After I dry my hair and brush it I can pull it forward, she thought. It will cover the scar. And I can buy blouses that will cover it enough.

But for today the hair will do. Charles will never notice. She didn't want Charles to know about the ugliness. She didn't want him to know what she had become.

A familiar aching consumed Charles as he approached the brick pillars that marked the entrance to Windermere. He hadn't been here since Elliott's funeral, three days after Elliott's death. Even after Elliott was gone, even when he might have lived here with his brother, Windermere was not his home.

Charles was stopped by police guards at the entrance of the estate. They checked his identification, confirmed his name and photograph on their list, called the house to notify Jason, and let Charles pass. As Charles drove along the red-brick drive, he noticed that the white ash and sugar maples were taller and the emerald forest seemed more dense.

Jason met Charles on the porch, a gracious host greeting his guest. It had always been that way.

Melanie appeared in the entry hall just as Charles and Jason walked inside.

"Should you be up?" Charles asked, concerned. He moved toward her. The package from Galen was tucked under his arm.

"You can't keep her down," Jason explained.

"Until she falls down," Melanie added.

She glanced at Charles and saw desire—familiar, desperate desire for *her*—in his eyes. *No, Charles. You wouldn't want me if you knew. We had our chance.*

"My goal for today is to make it to the day room," Melanie announced gaily, avoiding Charles's eyes.

Charles smiled, and Jason frowned for a moment. It wasn't a big frown or a persistent one. It was just a brief, passing worry, something about the day room.

Melanie accepted the offer of a strong arm from each twin. They strolled from the foyer through the great room and beyond to a long hallway lined with paintings.

The mansion was brighter, more cheerful and colorful, than Charles remembered. It was the paintings, Charles decided. There had never been this many before. But they were Meredith's; he recognized the style. Charles wondered where they had been all the years he lived at Windermere.

Melanie felt Jason's pace slow slightly, a final moment of hesitation, as they approached the day room. . . .

The day room was light and cheery, a bouquet of soft pastel pillows, white wicker chairs, and delicate porcelain lamps. Bay windows provided panoramic views of the sea and the gardens and the woods. A single painting—a breathtaking portrait of Galen—hung in the room.

Charles froze when he saw the painting. After a stunned moment he turned to Jason with a look of utter incomprehension. Jason didn't meet his gaze; his eyes were focused on the portrait.

Melanie marvelled at the magnificent painting. Galen's lovely emerald eyes sparkled courageously, sending messages that were at once naive and seductive. Jason had perfectly portrayed the magic of a girl becoming a woman, capturing the precise moment when innocent hopes and dreams become confident knowledge, and there is no longer any fear.

It was a portrait, Melanie realized, that could only have been painted by a man who knew Galen well and loved her deeply.

"It's lovely, Jason," Melanie whispered.

"Jason?" Charles's eyes fell to the signature on the painting. "*You* painted this?"

Melanie stared from one twin to the other. Charles didn't know that Jason could paint? How was that possible? How long had it been since Charles had been here?

"Yes," Jason answered flatly, defiantly.

"When?" Charles pressed.

"I finished it about a month ago."

"Have you seen her?"

"No. I did it from memory."

There was a long, tense silence. Charles and Jason were lost—caught—somewhere in a tangle of the past and its secrets.

"Why didn't you tell me?" Charles asked finally. *Why didn't you tell me about your painting? Why didn't you tell me about Galen?*

Jason answered his twin with an icy stare. His pale-blue eyes sent their own set of questions to the dark ones. *Why haven't you ever told me why Father disowned you? Why did you mysteriously return on the day he died? Why didn't you tell me about you and Galen? Galen. I loved her, and she loved you, and you hurt her so much she left both of us.*

Melanie watched, horrified by the sudden anger in their eyes. Charles and Jason were always so polite with each other, so civil, so unemotional. There was emotion now—deep and angry and disturbing.

The ringing telephone shattered the tense silence. Jason retreated to a distant room.

"You'd better sit down." Charles guided Melanie to a white wicker couch with green and mauve cushions.

"So had you."

Charles smiled briefly. "Too many surprises."

"It must have been Jason," Melanie whispered.

"Yes," Charles breathed. *Why hadn't Galen told him? Why hadn't Jason told him?*

"I wonder," Melanie mused as she remembered the title of Galen's short story. "Charles, would you open the package for me?"

Charles tried for a moment, but was unable to easily tear the sealing tape with his fingers. He withdrew a small jackknife from his pocket. At the sight of it Melanie shivered involuntarily.

"Oh, Melanie," Charles whispered softly as he realized what had happened. He quickly returned the knife to his pocket and put his arms around her. "I'm sorry."

"It's OK." She pulled free and tossed the mane of golden hair courageously. "I have to—"

Melanie stopped because Charles wasn't listening. He was staring at her ivory neck and the purple-pink scar revealed by the toss of her head. Instinctively, Melanie reached for her neck, covering the ugliness with her lovely, tapered hand.

Charles looked at her for a minute, then took her hand away. He bent toward her and gently traced a path along the scar with his lips. At his touch, his *kiss*, she trembled. Oh, Charles.

No. I'm not the woman you remember. Your body won't want mine as desperately as it used to. This ugliness is only the tip of the iceberg.

Alone the scar on her neck could be tolerable, a pastel-pink badge of courage, a grim novelty of sorts. But it was only the tiny tail, a small tentacle, of a large ugly monster.

"Charles, don't."

"Melanie."

"Please," she began. She found some control—the image of herself in the mirror could stop the pounding of her heart and the trembling and the desire—and said firmly, "Please open the package, with your knife."

"I can—"

"No."

This time the cold chill inside her when she saw the knife again—it was a trivial knife compared to what *he* had used—didn't erupt into a shiver. She wouldn't let it. She found control, amazing control. Charles opened the package quickly. His hands were efficient and expert with the knife. He closed the knife and returned it to his pocket before handing her the manuscript.

Melanie read the title page: "Sonja."

"Galen said her story—it's a story about a love that didn't last—is unpublishable." Melanie handed the manuscript to Charles. "Tell me if it's about Jason."

Charles stared at the title. Of course it was about Jason. It was written by someone who knew all about him. Someone Jason trusted enough to tell his greatest secret.

"What do you think?" Charles asked carefully.

"I think it's the way someone with dyslexia might see the word Jason," Melanie answered. Jason. Sonja. The same letters, but in a different order. Melanie watched Charles's reaction to the news that she knew about Jason's dyslexia. It *hurt* him. "He had to tell me, Charles. Nick left some automatic dialing machines. Obviously Jason couldn't program them. He had to tell me."

"Too many surprises," Charles repeated heavily.

"Too many secrets," she added softly.

Charles and Melanie fell silent, each reflecting on their own surprises and secrets, each wishing there were none and that there wouldn't have to be more, each knowing that there always would be.

He can never know about my scars, she thought.

I have to tell her everything I know about myself, and what I don't know, so that we can go on. . . .

Jason's return to the day room interrupted the silence. Jason's handsome face was calm, free of emotion. Jason's anger toward his twin was apparently vanquished, or, at least, hidden beneath a polite veneer.

"That was Nick," Jason said. "He's at the police station in Southampton. He'll be by in about twenty minutes."

"The police station in Southampton," Charles breathed. What the hell was Nick doing there? *"Why?"*

Jason shrugged. "Probably making sure the weekend shift knows that Melanie is here."

"What other reason could there be?" Melanie asked quietly. Her pale-blue eyes searched Charles's for the answer. But she couldn't find answers in the darkness. She only saw secrets and torment and pain. Charles, what is it?

"None," Charles replied flatly. "Melanie, you don't believe . . ."

"No, Charles, I don't." Their eyes met for a moment. The intensity of his seductive dark eyes became too great—he wanted her and she knew it could never be—and her eyelids fell, casting doubt.

Charles watched her for a moment in stunned silence. Then he stood up.

"I'd better go."

Charles touched Melanie's cheek lightly with his hand before he left. He tried to look at Jason, but it was only a sidelong glance accompanied by a barely civil smile.

"He doesn't want to see Nick," Melanie explained after Charles left. "Damn Nick."

"Why?" Jason asked.

"Because Nick is treating him like a suspect, Jason. How—"

The look in Jason's eyes stopped her.

.Oh, my God, her mind screamed. Jason believes his twin *could* be the Manhattan Ripper.

CHAPTER TWENTY-NINE

$\mathcal{M}$elanie read and reread Galen's short story. Not that "Sonja" was good. Another reader would put it down. In its present form "Sonja" probably was unpublishable. But Melanie read it because it was the story of two people she cared about. It was the story of Galen and Jason.

After she finished reading the manuscript Melanie lay awake, troubled by what she had read; it didn't make sense. Galen had written of love and betrayal and disillusionment. She had written about a man who deceived her, a man who had never truly loved her. Melanie had seen the just-completed portrait; it was painted by a man who was deeply in love, *still*. Melanie remembered the look in Jason's pale-blue eyes. He seemed more betrayed than betrayer.

A piece was missing.

The next morning, after a few hours of fitful sleep, Melanie found Jason at his easel in the great room.

"Good morning." Jason paused to smile at her.

"Good morning." Melanie smiled in return. Then, before she could change her mind, she asked abruptly, "What happened between you and Galen?"

"What?" Jason looked up in surprise. "What do you mean?"

"Why did you fall out of love?" Melanie asked boldly, making assumptions, but convinced they were correct. As she watched his pale-blue eyes Melanie knew she was right. Jason *had* loved Galen. He still did.

"I didn't," Jason answered quietly. "She did."

Melanie thought for a moment. Could Galen have written the story in reverse? The letters in his name were jumbled to make the heroine's name. Was she really telling the story from *his* perspective? No, Melanie decided. Galen's words were too personal, the hurt too visceral, the pain too intimate. Galen believed that Jason had betrayed her.

And Jason believed the same of Galen.

"Are you sure?"

"Yes. She was in love with someone else the entire time."

"How do you know?"

"Because I know who he was." Jason sighed and added flatly, "Galen was in love with Charles. And when that didn't work out, *because* it didn't work out, she left."

"No."

"*No?*"

"Galen and Charles were never in love."

"Melanie, you can't know that. You weren't even—"

"I *do* know, Jason. Charles told me Galen was devastated by a love that didn't last. He thinks that's why she cancelled the film contract for 'Sapphire' and left New York."

"The love that didn't last was with Charles."

"It's not true, Jason."

Melanie watched Jason's eyes narrow, searching the painful memories, trying to find a different explanation. He wanted to believe her.

"Galen thinks you betrayed her, Jason."

"How . . ." he began weakly. There were too many questions. How do you know? How could Galen believe *that*? And there was the exhilarating hope that what Melanie was saying might be true.

"I just read a short story she wrote. It's called 'Sonja,' " Melanie said meaningfully.

Jason shrugged. It meant nothing to him. Of course it doesn't, Melanie realized, Jason wouldn't know that Sonja was an anagram of Jason.

She told him.

"The story is about me and Galen?"

"Yes. Your identities are concealed of course," Melanie said. Galen's anger apparently did not extend to revealing one of publishing's best-kept secrets—that Jason Sinclair couldn't read. "It's about a talented musician, Sonja, who falls in love with a poet who is deaf. So . . ."

"So he can't ever know her talent because he can't hear," Jason finished softly, remembering how much he wanted to be able to read Galen's words, the words that sprang from her soul, words she could write but was afraid to speak. They spoke to each other with their eyes and their hearts; they found their own language of love. "But they learn to communicate."

"The beginning of the story, as they fall in love, is magical. . . ."

"What happens?" Jason asked urgently. He needed to know. If only he could read the words himself. He was dependent again—dependent on Melanie—but she wanted him to know. Melanie seemed to care.

"He betrays her."

"How?"

"She discovers he is in love with another woman. He always has been. The mood shifts from wonder and magic to pain and rage and disillusionment and bitterness."

"How does she learn about the other woman?"

"She is scheduled to give a concert at Carnegie." Melanie knew the details of the betrayal wouldn't be exactly what had happened between Jason and Galen, but there might be bits of fact that would help Jason understand. "They come to New York for the week. She returns to the hotel early one night—the conductor has become ill and the rehearsal is cancelled—and sees him leaving their room with the other woman, a woman from his past. They are embracing, smiling, gazing at each other, obviously in love."

"And she never tells him she saw them," Jason whispered.

"No. She doesn't want to hear his lies."

Jason held his head in his paint-spattered hands. Finally he looked up and stared out the bay window toward the gray-green sea. But Jason wasn't staring at the sea; he was staring at a distant memory.

"I asked her if she came over that night." Jason spoke softly to the memory. And Galen didn't answer, he remembered suddenly. She had *avoided* answering.

Melanie watched the emotion and pain in Jason's unfocused eyes.

"So it was true," Melanie breathed finally. Jason *had* betrayed Galen.

"No."

"But she might have seen something that looked obvious?"

"Yes." Jason's voice was bitter. If Galen had seen him with Fran why didn't she tell him about it? Because, like Sonja, Galen didn't want to hear lies, Jason realized. Galen knew what she had seen and could find no explanation in her heart, or in her experience, that could make it less than it appeared. "Fran came over one night."

"But you weren't in love with Fran." Melanie knew that.

"No. I was in love only, always, with Galen."

They sat in silence for a moment. Jason, lost in his memories, and Melanie, thinking about "Sonja" and about Galen and Jason . . .

"Go to her, Jason," Melanie urged suddenly, startling him. "Tell her what happened."

"What makes you think she'll listen? You just told me the story ended with rage and disillusionment and bitterness."

"Yes, but it doesn't ring true. No matter how hard Galen tries to tell the reader that love is a myth, that there never was love between them, that she hates him, you, it's unconvincing. She doesn't really believe it herself. Galen has never stopped loving you, either."

"Do you know where she is?"

Melanie answered by telling him the telephone number and address for the gatehouse on Mayflower Lane. Jason memorized them instantly.

"When are you going to go?" Melanie asked eagerly.

"After this business is all over." Jason used "this business" as the euphemism for the Manhattan Ripper.

"No, Jason, go now. Don't stay here because of me! I'm fine, and you are a dear man to keep me company and let me stay in this lovely place, but you don't need to be here. You know I'm safe. Even though we don't see them we are surrounded by guards. I'll tell Nick that you'll be away and if he wants to have one of the guards stay inside the house that's fine."

"You're serious, aren't you?"

"I'm an incurable romantic just like everyone else. If you and Galen could work this out . . ." Melanie's eyes sparkled. "Bring her back with you, Jason."

Jason's eyes sparkled in return. If only it were possible.

"I'll go in the morning," Jason breathed. He couldn't lose any more than he had already lost.

Jason rehearsed it, what he would say to Galen, a thousand times. He rehearsed it last night in his bed, *their* bed; and on the plane from La Guardia to O'Hare; and in the limousine as it sped north along the tollway, exiting after thirty minutes at Lake Forest; and, one last time—he sensed they were near—as they passed green-and-white signs he couldn't read labelled Deerpath and Onwentsia and Sheridan and, finally, Mayflower Lane.

The rehearsals were all for naught. When Jason saw her beloved, bewildered emerald eyes, he couldn't speak.

"Jason."

He extended his arms toward her, but she backed away.

"Galen." Jason's arms fell, heavily, to his side.

"Why are you here?" she asked helplessly. Don't look at me like that, Jason, not like that. I used to believe that look was love.

"Because I love you."

"No." Galen said swiftly.

"Melanie told me you wrote a story about us."

"Yes." Galen lifted her chin defiantly. "About how you betrayed . . ."

"I never betrayed you, Galen."

"You *did.*" The eyes flashed with emerald anger.

"No."

"Jason, I *saw* you in bed with her." The pain of the memory washed through her, leaving in its wake the familiar, horrible ache.

Jason grimaced. Galen had seen them in bed together! No wonder . . .

"Galen, may I come in?"

"No." Galen frowned and her eyes filled with fear.

Galen, don't be afraid of me, Jason's heart cried. She was so far away.

"Please let me tell you what happened."

Galen shrugged, but she didn't close the door.

Please listen to me, Galen.

"Fran came over that night, uninvited. She was upset. I had explained to her that it was over, but she didn't accept it. We talked and drank bourbon, she much more than I, until very late. Then she asked if she could stay." Jason sighed. He should have said No; if only he had said No.

"She said she needed to know that I could be in the same bed with her without wanting to make love to her," he continued heavily. "Somehow that would help her believe, finally, that it was over. She was exhausted, upset, a little drunk. I said Yes. We slept. If you saw us you would know we were both wearing pajamas. Nothing happened, Galen, *nothing.*"

He watched the lovely eyes struggling, trying to understand, wanting to.

"Why didn't you tell me?" Galen asked finally.

"I was going to. Even though nothing happened, and even though I wasn't sure you would understand, I was going to tell you." Jason shook his head. "In the light of day it felt so wrong. Even though—"

"But you didn't tell me."

"I never had a *chance*. You told me you were going away with Charles. You told me our relationship was over."

"But you must have known it was because I had seen you with Fran!"

"I *asked* you," Jason reminded her gently. "And there was always something special between you and Charles."

"You thought I was in love with Charles?"

"What other reason could there have been?"

"You never even tried to explain. It seemed like more proof that you had never cared about me or us."

"You were never in love with Charles?"

"No, Jason." Tears spilled from her eyes and her lips trembled. "I was never in love with anyone but you."

Jason extended his arms again and this time she came to him.

"Galen," he whispered hoarsely. "My darling Galen. I love you so much."

"Jason, I love—"

Galen stopped abruptly and stiffened slightly. It was a sound that only Galen heard, or maybe she only sensed it. It was their way of talking, mother and daughter. Elise rarely cried. When she awoke, when she wanted her mother, she made soft, cooing sounds.

"Galen?" Jason asked.

Galen stared at him for a long moment. *Oh, Jason, there is so much more . . .*

Jason smiled at her, reassuring her, caressing her with loving eyes. *Galen, tell me . . .*

Galen sighed softly. Then she took his hand and led him into the gatehouse, across the living room, up the carpeted stairs to her bedroom. At the bedroom door she released Jason's hand and entered ahead of him, smiling at the huge blue eyes that sparkled when they saw her.

The cooing increased—happy, excited talking.

Galen lifted Elise gently from her crib and kissed her soft sleep-flushed cheek. Elise's tiny dimpled hands touched her mother's face in delighted welcome.

"Are you hungry? Yes? Of course you are." Galen sat on the bed and unbuttoned her blouse. Only after Elise was tugging contentedly at her breast did Galen raise her glistening eyes to Jason's.

"Galen, is she," Jason's own emotion, and something in Galen's new tears, made him stop.

She shook her head slightly. "I don't know, Jason. She could be yours. I want her to be yours. She was born on your birthday." Galen's smile quivered.

"Then she is mine. She has my eyes." Jason moved closer and ever so gently touched Elise's rosy cheek with his finger.

It was true. Elise had beautiful pale-blue eyes, Jason's eyes. And she had dark curly hair. Neither her hair nor her eyes were inherited from Galen.

Galen sighed. She had to tell him the truth—all of it. It had been a terrible mistake not to tell Jason she had seen him with Fran. Because she hadn't told him *that* truth there had been so much pain. . . .

And now, when there was a chance that they might be able to find the love again—the love that had been, simply, misplaced—the truth could destroy it all. How could she tell him? How could she *not*?

"Galen," Jason urged gently, watching her struggle. "Tell me."

"She has your eyes, my darling, and she has Charles's hair."

She felt the shock of her words hit his body like a punch. After a few moments he lifted her chin, so gently, and made her look into his watery eyes.

"You said . . ."

"I didn't love him. I slept with him once, because I needed to know how it felt to make love with someone you didn't love. I needed to understand how you could have made love with me all those times and been in love with Fran."

"But that didn't happen."

"I know that now."

"But you did make love with Charles. What did you learn?"

"I learned it was possible, but that I still loved you. And, I learned again—I had always known it—that Charles is sensitive and kind." Galen frowned. "That's something I don't think you know."

Jason avoided her eyes. It was true; Jason *didn't* know that. And Galen didn't know about Nick Adrian's suspicion about Charles, or about what happened between Charles and Elliott.

"Does Charles know?"

"About Elise? No. No one does."

"Elise," Jason spoke softly. "That's beautiful."

"It's my mother's name. Her middle name is Meredith, for your mother. Elise Meredith. She is such a joy." Galen idly weaved her fingers through the dark-brown curls as Elise nursed.

Jason stroked the dark curls thoughtfully for a moment. Then he walked across the room and stared out the window toward Lake Michigan.

Galen watched helplessly.

What if he decided that *her* betrayal was too great? What if he decided, now that he had learned the truth, that it really was over? What if he couldn't live with the fact that she had made love with Charles? What if he could never forgive her for that? And what about Elise? What if he could never love her as long as the uncertainty persisted about whose baby she really was?

"There's something I need to know." Finally Jason spoke, and, when he did, he turned to face her.

"Yes?" *Please don't say good-bye Jason. Please give me another chance. . . .*

"I need to know how you feel about me—*us*—now."

"I love you, Jason," she whispered.

Jason nodded seriously.

"How do you feel, Jason?" She held her breath. *Please.*

"I love you more than anything in the world, Galen. I will love Elise, no matter what. Is there any way . . . ?"

"Oh, Jason, I have caused you so much pain." Galen gazed at the pale-blue eyes that desperately wanted to know that the precious little girl was really his.

"So much joy," Jason corrected quickly, lovingly. His question was still unanswered.

"You and Charles have the same blood type." Galen answered the question he had begun: Is there any way to know whose daughter she is? "There are more sophisticated genetic tests. I never looked into them because they would require samples of your blood and Charles's."

"We'll need to do that."

Galen started to answer but was stopped by Elise, who wriggled away from Galen's breast, now fully awake and no longer hungry. Elise gurgled happily and strained to focus in the direction of the strange, deep voice that was speaking to her mother. Her pale-blue eyes met Jason's and her face erupted into a gleeful smile.

Jason moved to her, arms extended, and looked questioningly at Galen.

"Of course you can hold her, Jason." Galen carefully transferred the eager bundle from her arms to his.

Elise knew very few people aside from her mother. The doctor, of course, for routine checkups, and the faces at the post office and grocery who smiled at her but didn't touch.

Few people, aside from Galen, had ever held her.

But Elise went to Jason without a flicker of uncertainty. She boldly studied his big blue eyes and patted his chin with her soft hands and tugged at his collar and cooed. Jason held her tightly. Too tightly, Galen thought, but Elise didn't seem to mind the constraint. She didn't struggle to be away from him. She only pressed closer, intrigued by his mouth and his smile and his eyes and his warmth.

Galen saw the happiness in Jason's eyes, as he naturally and unselfconsciously cuddled Elise. She has to be his, Galen thought. She has to be.

After a while Galen and Jason took Elise downstairs. They spread a soft pastel blanket on the living-room floor and Elise played between them, her blue eyes flashing with delight, her soft laugh almost constant. Galen and Jason watched the baby—*their* baby—but once their hands fell on the same toy together and the touch lingered and their fingers entwined.

Elise fought the sleepiness that overcame her for as long as she could. They watched her gallant struggle to keep her eyelids open and smiled gently and lovingly.

"Don't be afraid, little one," Jason whispered, cradling Elise as she finally succumbed to the happy exhaustion. "We'll be here when you awaken. And we'll play again. Over and over."

Jason kissed the sleepy face and looked at Galen. "Shall I take her upstairs?"

"She can sleep down here." Galen arranged a soft protected bed out of the cushions on the sofa.

Jason slowly lowered the sleeping baby into the bed Galen had made. Elise stretched when he removed his hands, then curled, contented, safe into the familiar feel of her blanket and the sofa.

Galen and Jason watched the sleeping baby for a few moments. Then Jason turned to her and smiled.

"Galen." He touched his hands to her face and gently laced his strong fingers into her silky hair. She trembled at his touch. Or was it only his own trembling that he felt "How are you?"

"Oh, Jason," she whispered. "I am so afraid."

"Of what?" he asked carefully, pulling her close, hiding his own fear, showing her that *she* had nothing to fear.

"Of waking up from this dream," she murmured as her lips met his.

CHAPTER THIRTY

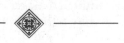

"*C*harles?"

"Melanie."

They hadn't spoken for four days; not since Melanie couldn't hold his gaze when he asked if she believed he could be the Manhattan Ripper. Now she was calling him, and he sounded so sad.

"Hi." That *wasn't* why I couldn't stand to look in your eyes, Charles.

"Hi." His voice was gentle, gentle and sad and far away.

"Do you know the follow-up on 'Sonja'? Have you spoken with Jason?"

"No." Jason hadn't been in the office all week. Charles assumed he was staying in Windermere with Melanie. There had been no pressing business, no reason to call Jason.

"Oh." Melanie frowned. Charles needed to know. "Jason believed that Galen left him for you."

"For *me?*"

"She didn't, did she?" Melanie asked quietly.

"No. I told you last summer . . ." Charles's tone softened as he said *last summer*. "Galen believed he never loved her."

"But he did." Melanie paused. She didn't want to talk to Charles about love. "Anyway, the reason Galen left New York, the reason she couldn't be filming in Kenya in November, was because she was carrying Jason's baby."

"*What?*"

"She was pregnant. She had their baby—Elise, isn't that a lovely name?—in November. On his, your, birthday."

Charles's mind whirled. November. He and Galen had made love in February. Jason's baby or his?

"How do you know all this?"

"Jason went to Lake Forest. They're coming home tonight. They plan to be married next week."

A long silence followed. Melanie had finished her reason—her *excuse*—for calling. She called under the pretext of giving Charles some good, happy news, but she really called because she wanted to hear his voice. And she wanted him to know that she believed in him.

"How are you, Melanie?" Charles asked finally.

"I want this all to be over."

"So do I, darling." *So do I.*

"Are you confident you'll get a guilty verdict, Ms. Chandler?"

A crush of reporters swarmed around Andrew and Brooke as they emerged from the courthouse. The closing arguments were over and the jury had retired to deliberate on Jeffrey Martin's guilt or innocence.

"I'm confident that we *should*," Brooke spoke to a television camera. Then she tossed her head toward Andrew and smiled.

Brooke felt wonderful. The trial had been faultless. She and Andrew had worked so well together. It was a perfect ending; as soon as the jury returned its verdict her job as assistant district attorney would be over. By this time next week she would be sitting in her office at Sinclair Publishing reviewing advertising contracts.

"Are you really leaving the DA's office?" another reporter asked.

"Not if I can help it," Andrew answered amiably, smiling his gorgeous, confident smile.

"Yes." Brooke's blue eyes sparkled at Andrew. "Yes, I am."

Charles arrived at Windermere an hour after twilight. He hadn't planned to return to Windermere at all. As much as he wanted to see Melanie, he had to stay away for now. Charles wouldn't push her, and he couldn't stand the doubt in her eyes.

Charles hadn't planned to return to Windermere, but he needed to see Galen. He needed to see Galen's *baby*.

The house was surprisingly dark. Charles walked toward the kitchen, guided by a yellow beam of light.

Charles paused a moment, his heart pounding, when he saw the red-gold head bent lovingly over the dark brown one cradled in her arms. Charles walked across the kitchen. Galen didn't hear him above the whistling of the teapot and the cooing of her baby. Charles touched her gently on the shoulder and said quietly, "Welcome home."

"Charles!" Galen smiled, happy to see her dear friend. After a moment she could no longer hold his intense gaze; the serious dark eyes were asking questions that demanded answers.

"Your tea is ready," Charles observed. Instead of moving to the stove to remove the hissing teapot, he extended his arms to Elise.

Galen watched her precious baby girl go to Charles as easily, as eagerly, as she had gone to Jason. Elise laughed and nuzzled her dark head against his, her curls intermingling, an exact match, with his. Elise wrapped her tiny hands in Charles's hair as he whispered to her.

Elise didn't go to strangers. Even with Melanie, Elise kept a careful eye on Galen and Jason. But Elise went, without worry, to Jason, and now to Charles. A deep, confident instinct told Elise that she had nothing to fear; she was where she *belonged*.

Galen had convinced herself—because they wanted it so desperately and because of how Elise responded to Jason—that Jason was Elise's father. The sophisticated genetic tests were hardly necessary, or *were* they? Galen wondered helplessly as she watched her daughter with Charles, and Charles with Elise.

Galen's hands trembled as she poured the hot water over a tea bag.

"Would you like something, Charles? Tea? Coffee?"

"No, thank you, and yes. I would like to know," Charles spoke with great control, "if she is mine."

"I don't know, Charles." Galen forced herself to find his eyes. "I don't know."

"I need to know."

"We all need to. There are some tests. They may not be conclusive since you and Jason are twins, so genetically alike, but . . ." Galen stopped and gazed, startled, beyond Charles toward the kitchen door. Galen whispered, "Melanie."

Charles spun, catching Melanie's eyes before she could change the look. Melanie knew; she had heard it all.

"Hello, I'm sorry, I'm interrupting," Melanie mumbled, backing away.

"No," Charles and Galen said in unison. For different reasons they wanted the conversation to be over.

"No," Galen repeated. "In fact I was just about to leave. It's time to give Elise her bath and get her ready for bed."

Galen took Elise from Charles and left quickly, her tea still brewing on the kitchen counter.

"Hi." Charles smiled gently at Melanie. "How are you?"

"I'm better. Stronger." *Why did you lie to me about you and Galen? How many other lies have you told me?*

"We were never in love," Charles said quietly as he moved close to her.

"What?" Melanie breathed weakly. They *had* been in love; in her fantasies and her dreams and her lovely memories of last summer. She had even dared to hope. . . . But then she looked at herself in the mirror and she knew it was over. Why did he have to tell her it had never existed at all?

"Galen and I were never in love."

"Oh." *It didn't matter.*

"We made love once. We weren't in love. There were other reasons."

Melanie understood other reasons. Other reasons were all she knew before she fell in love with Charles.

"I understand. And I understand that you need to know if you are Elise's father."

"I've never been—" Charles stopped before he said the rest, *in love with anyone but you.* He stopped because he promised himself he wouldn't push her.

"You need to know," Melanie repeated quietly.

"I need a drink. Will you join me?"

"You, not the drink."

"Something else? Hot chocolate?"

"No, I'm fine."

"Shall we go to the library?"

"Sure."

Melanie sat curled in a huge leather chair in the wood-panelled library and watched Charles pour himself a large glass of undiluted bourbon.

"How about a roaring fire?" Charles asked before he sat down. The kindling was already laid. Charles added two logs and lighted the paper beneath the grill. The dry wood caught instantly; red-orange flames danced, sending light and warmth and cheerful crackling into the room.

Charles settled in a leather chair facing Melanie. Charles started to say something to her, but the library door opened and his attention was drawn away. Charles stood up.

"Hello, Jason," Charles said flatly.

"Hello, Charles. I wanted to be the one to tell you about Elise."

Jason doesn't know I'm here, Melanie realized suddenly.

Jason was behind her, and she was completely obscured by the enormous leather chair, her legs curled beneath her, her head a full foot beneath the top. Melanie looked at Charles, but his dark eyes were focused on his twin.

"Why? It's none of your business. It's between me and Galen." The bitterness was deep.

"It's between all of us. It has to do with that precious little girl's life."

"Yes. And her fortune," Charles whispered. "It's too bad it's between us—the three of us—because we're not a very responsible group."

"Meaning?"

"I'm disgusted with you and Galen and myself. Disgusted and disappointed. None of us behaved even like trusted friends, much less like brothers or—"

"*Trust?*" Jason interjected angrily. "That's a funny word to come from your lips. You certainly don't know what it means. Next you'll be talking about brotherly love and honesty. Go ahead, it will make the sham complete."

"What the hell are you talking about? My God, Jason, when have I ever betrayed your trust? *Ever?* When have I ever been dishonest with you?" Charles demanded, incredulous.

"When? I'll tell you. When it was most important for us to be brothers, to love each other and care about each other and trust each other. That's when. You set the ground rules of mistrust and dishonesty, not me."

"I don't know what you're talking about, Jason," Charles whispered. "When? Tell me."

"When Father died. You wouldn't tell me why he disowned you."

"I told you I don't know why."

"*That's* the lie."

"It's not a lie."

"I don't believe you. But you believe this, Charles, if Elise is yours, I will fight for her." Jason's voice turned ice-cold and threatening. "I will do whatever I can to get her away from you. I may not have to do anything. Nick seems a little worried about your mysterious reappearance the day Father died. . . ."

"You can't believe," Charles breathed. His eyes met his twin's and he saw hatred. "Oh, my God, you do."

"Yes, Charles, I do."

Jason stared at Charles, his pale-blue eyes unrelenting. Finally, without speaking, he turned and left.

Charles fell heavily into the chair and held his head in his hands. Melanie watched the torment stiffen his body then send shudders of rage and hopelessness through it. How could she help him? She would offer him her love, but she *couldn't.* Besides, Charles had forgotten she was there. It would be best if she just left, quietly, before he remembered.

Melanie stood up to leave, but the voice that told her legs to move toward the door wasn't as loud as the commands of her heart. She walked over to him and gently touched his shoulder. Charles looked up, startled, his face white, his eyes wild. He forced control into his eyes, found a look of concern just for her, and took her hands in his.

"I am so sorry you witnessed that."

"It doesn't matter," Melanie told him truthfully. *I believe in you, Charles.*

It was a terrible MISTAKE not to murder her. I let SENTIMENTALITY obscure my MISSION. It won't happen again! This time there will be enough BLOOD for two murders. This time there will be TWIN BLOOD!!!

The Manhattan Ripper frowned briefly. He wondered if he had ever murdered a twin before. . . .

* * *

"You're the second person to ask me that this morning," the harbormaster at Peconic Bay replied.

"Really? Who was the other?" Nick asked. Charles?

"Jason Sinclair was here bright and early."

"What did you tell him?"

"The same thing I'm going to tell you—the truth. Elliott Sinclair sailed into that killer storm alone."

"You're sure?"

"Yes," the harbormaster answered a little impatiently. Jason Sinclair had pushed him, too. "I saw him arrive. I helped him load the boat. We talked about the storm clouds in the distance. I cast him off and watched him sail away."

With the last words, his voice softened, as if he should have known to prevent Elliott from making that fateful sail.

"What's this all about?"

"We just wondered if someone had been with him."

"Well, no one was. Besides, anyone with him would have been killed, too. There was almost nothing left of the boat."

Nick knew that. He had seen the pictures. Nick had seen pictures of the boat, and pictures of Elliott Sinclair.

"So Jason was here," Nick mused.

"He's a fine sailor, like his father was. Of course he mostly sails out of New York Yacht Club these days . . ."

"How about the other son, Charles?"

"Not a yachtsman."

"He didn't spend much time here?"

"None."

"Would you recognize him?"

"Of course. He looks exactly like Elliott."

As he drove from Southampton to Manhattan, Nick decided that the Southampton police were right; Elliott Sinclair died alone in a violent storm. Charles's reappearance was simply coincidence; and even if it was something more, some mystical precognition, it was still far from a crime.

And maybe the wild torment in Charles's dark eyes the night Melanie was attacked, and his rage when Nick suggested that *he* might have done it, were not signs of guilt, either. Maybe they were only the emotions of a passionate man who was deeply and desperately in love.

I need to talk to him, Nick thought.

On impulse, Nick decided to go to Charles's office. Nick was able to see Charles within ten minutes of his arrival.

"I haven't received your alibis," Nick said.

"That's because I don't have any."

"No?"

"Except for December twenty-third, when I was at the *Vogue* party for a short time I was alone each night for the entire evening."

"Isn't that a little unusual for you?"

"No."

"What did you do those nights by yourself?"

"I don't know. Took a long walk, read, drank. I don't know."

"That's not very specific."

"I don't need to be." Charles glared at Nick. "Is that all?"

"Guess so."

"Are you done investigating my father's death?"

"Yes."

"And?"

"His death was accidental. He died alone in a storm."

"I wish you would tell my brother that," Charles murmured under his breath.

"Jason knows."

"Oh?" It hardly mattered. Jason had believed it was possible that Charles had murdered Elliott; *that* was what mattered.

"Yes." Nick looked for a moment at Charles before leaving. I hope like hell you aren't the Ripper. I hope it for you and Jason and Melanie. And Brooke . . .

I hope it, Nick thought as he walked down the circular staircase from the executive suites, but I don't know it . . .

"I really believed Charles might have been on the boat," Jason told Galen.

"And that he killed your father?"

"I don't know." Jason had never allowed the worry to mature. His mind had placed Elliott and Charles together on the yacht a thousand times, but after that . . . "Maybe an accident."

"But Charles *wasn't* with him. You believe that now, don't you?"

"Yes."

"I don't understand, Jason. What would even make you think it? Why would Charles . . ."

Without answering, Jason led Galen past the room where Elise lay sleeping to Elliott's study. He removed a small brass key from the top drawer of Elliott's carved-oak desk.

"My father's personal papers are locked in these drawers. I know there are letters and I think there is a journal." Jason had looked through the desk, once, a year after Elliott's death, hoping he could find an answer. But if an answer was there, it lay in words he couldn't read. Jason had relocked the desk, wondering if its secrets would ever be revealed. Now, twelve years later, he was handing the key to Galen. "Will you read through them, Galen?"

"Oh, Jason." No.

"I need to know about Charles. We both need to, because of Elise."

Galen nodded slowly. If there was something about Charles, something that made gentle, loving Jason believe his twin capable of murder, they needed to know it.

Elise cooed softly in the distance.

"I'll go," Jason whispered.

Galen nodded again. It would be easiest to go through the papers without Jason watching. It would be difficult enough to do alone. It was such an invasion of privacy, and what if she learned something *terrible*?

Galen sighed softly and gingerly unlocked the top right-hand drawer of the carved-oak desk.

"Jury's coming back, Brooke."

"Really? So soon?"

"It has to be good news." Andrew smiled confidently.

"I hope so." Brooke grabbed her briefcase and coat and glanced at her watch: one-fifteen. If the case was really over, if she and Andrew had won the conviction, this would be her last afternoon in the DA's office. It wouldn't take long to empty her desk; she could do it before she left work tonight. Brooke smiled at Andrew. "Okay, let's go."

CHAPTER THIRTY-ONE

"Nick, there's a woman here to see you. She says it's about the Ripper."

Nick looked up from his cluttered desk and cocked his head at the detective. There was a steady stream of people coming to the precinct with information about the Ripper. So far none had paid off. Usually Nick didn't even get involved. The fact that the detective was bringing the woman to him might mean something.

"You think she's got something?"

"I don't know. She won't talk to anyone but you."

Nick grimaced; it was one of the many drawbacks of the publicity that the Manhattan Ripper was *his* case. "Where is she?"

"Sitting just beyond Larry's desk."

Nick stood up and looked through the bulletproof plateglass window surrounding his office. All he could see was her softly curled chestnut hair and her head tilted the way she tilted it when she was thinking.

Nick smiled. It was Brooke, paying a surprise visit. Maybe she wanted to tell him about the Jeffrey Martin verdict. Nick had just heard; he could pretend he didn't know.

"I'll see her."

Nick's smile faded as he approached. A swirl of dark smoke hovered above her chestnut hair and her clothes were plain and drab. She wasn't Brooke.

Nick stopped a few feet away from her.

"Hello. I'm Lieutenant Adrian."

She turned her head slowly. Nick drew a breath when the dark-blue eyes met his. She had Brooke's eyes, Brooke's *face*. Nick thought, She is an older, haggard version of Brooke. Once this woman had been beautiful; once she had looked very much like Brooke. Who *was* she?

She stood up, transferred her cigarette into her left hand, and extended her thin right hand to Nick. He noticed a fine tremor.

"Lieutenant Adrian." Her voice was rich and deep. "I know who he is. I will need your protection."

Nick nodded and gestured toward his bulletproof, soundproof office. He waited as she gathered her purse and a dark-blue leather folder. The purse was frail and battered—like she was—but the leather folder was new, expensive, and elegant.

Nick didn't know who she was, but instinct told him that she held the clue to the identity of the Manhattan Ripper.

It scared him to death that she looked so much like Brooke. . . .

She didn't speak again until they were inside his office and he had closed the blinds. Then she told him her name.

"You're his . . . ?" Nick asked as his mind whirled. Oh, my God. . . .

"I'm his wife. I'm not as old as I look." She smiled wistfully. It was a beautiful smile, Brooke's smile.

"Why do you think it's him?"

"I don't think it, I know it." She paused and reached into her purse.

Another cigarette? Nick wondered impatiently. Talk to me. If it's true, I need to do something *now*.

But she didn't withdraw a cigarette; she withdrew a whetstone.

"I didn't find a knife, and I didn't find bloodstained clothes, but I found this."

Nick took the whetstone. Even if there were traces of blood, it proved nothing. He needed much more. Nick didn't even know if this strange woman with the bewitching face was who she said she was; it seemed unlikely.

As if reading Nick's mind, she handed him a photograph. It was a wedding picture—their wedding picture—and she was young and lovely and her ocean-blue eyes sparkled with joy and she *was* Brooke.

"What else," Nick breathed. He needed more, legally. He fought the strong urge to reach for the phone and have him arrested; *just cause* be damned!

"His journal." She handed him the blue leather folder. "It was locked in the desk in his study—so was the whetstone—but I broke the lock. It's all legal, all admissible. It's my house, too. I was an attorney once. . . ."

Nick was vaguely aware of her words. He had opened to the first page of the journal and was reading the entry:

So much BLOOD—*too much. It will be less MESSY next time. Next time? Of course!*

In the back of his mind he thought, This is a lot of evidence, but no *proof.* What if this woman, who Nick wanted to believe because she looked like Brooke, was crazy? The woman looked a little crazy. What if she was trying to *frame* her husband?

Nick needed a handwriting analysis of the journal, and he needed a search warrant. It would all take time, and, if she was telling the truth—if *he* was crazy and *she* was sane—there was no time to waste.

"Why did you break into his desk?" *What made you suspect your husband of a crime so heinous?*

"I saw Brooke Chandler on television this morning. She was interviewed as she left court yesterday. I used to look like her. I used to be smart and bright and beautiful like her. And he wanted me desperately." She sighed and the blue eyes clouded. When she spoke again her voice was low and haunting. "He wanted me so much he murdered my roommate."

"What?"

"I didn't know it until I read his journal today. I guess, over the years, I have wondered. We met at Princeton. He was obsessed with me. He hid the obsession well beneath his easy charm and confidence. I was flattered, but I was happy with my life and my plans for a career in law. I liked him, but I didn't need him."

She paused. Her dark-blue eyes narrowed as the horrible distant memory came into vivid focus. "So, he made me need him."

"How?"

"My roommate was murdered. She was raped and stabbed to death. It happened in our room. I was the one who found her . . ." Her voice faltered. She took a deep breath. "Anyway, after that, I was devastated, and he was strong and supportive. He convinced me—and I believed it—that I needed him."

"And now?"

"Now I have nothing left. Little by little he has taken everything away. I was a good attorney, but it was too threatening to him. He convinced me—he can be very persuasive—that a good wife doesn't work. I used to be very close to my family, but he drove a wedge between us. He stripped me of everything until he had complete control. *Almost* complete." She smiled wryly. "Every so often, to escape, I spend a month or two in a sanitarium. It makes him angry; he feels abandoned."

"But you're not crazy." *He is.*

"Isn't it crazy not to have left him? Isn't it crazy to have allowed this to happen?"

"Why didn't you leave him?"

"Fear, I guess. I am nothing—I have no identity anymore—without him."

"But . . ." *That's nonsense.*

"I know I still exist somewhere, buried deep, but it is so hard to dig out." The exhaustion in her voice betrayed years of emotional chaos. "And he is still obsessed. He still tells me of his desperate, endless love. In his warped mind, I am still young and strong and beautiful, like . . ."

Brooke. Nick had heard enough; he believed her. He needed to do a lot of things all at once, but the only one that mattered was making certain Brooke was safe.

She *is* safe, he tried to convince himself. Brooke is the one woman in the world he won't harm.

Except, an uneasy voice warned, Brooke isn't behaving as he wants her to. Brooke remained strong and independent, even when his victim was her *twin*.

And Brooke is making changes that might anger and provoke him very much. . . .

The mansion at Windermere was silent and somber, as if grief-stricken by the argument between Jason and Charles. Melanie spent most of the day in her bright-yellow first-floor bedroom. Jason and Galen and Elise kept to themselves in their distant, private wing of the mansion.

Jason played with Elise in front of the fire in the bedroom. As he played with the precious little girl who might be his daughter, Jason's mind drifted to Galen and the solemn task he had given her. What was she learning? Were there answers? After two hours, Jason gathered Elise and returned to Elliott's study.

Galen was sitting on the floor. The contents of the desk—letters in shoeboxes and a leatherbound journal—surrounded her; they were pieces of a puzzle whose answer horrified her.

"Galen?"

She looked up from the journal. Jason could tell that she had been crying.

I am so sorry I made you do this, Jason thought, his own helplessness haunting him.

"It doesn't seem possible," Galen whispered. *How did Charles survive? Did* he survive? And who could blame Charles for anything he might do?

"What, darling?"

"Your father held Charles responsible for your mother's death. He never forgave Charles, and he never even tried to love him."

"But my mother died when we were born."

"Yes. But you were born first. And"—Elliott had described the scene with Meredith in her hospital room after the birth of their beloved Jason—"your mother seemed fine. No one knew she was carrying twins. She started to hemorrhage. They discovered the second baby—*Charles*—while they were unsuccessfully trying to save her life."

"I never knew that." Jason frowned. He added firmly, "It doesn't make sense anyway. She died because she was carrying twins. It had nothing to do with *which* twin."

"To your father it did. He never wanted Charles to live. Charles spent the first two months of his life in the hospital. Did you know that?"

Jason shook his head. He sat down on the floor beside Galen and whispered softly, "Tell me everything."

Elliott's journal was a detailed, eloquent, beautifully written chronicle of the birth and lives of his twin sons. The pages were filled with emotion and passion; his great love for Jason, and his hatred for Charles. Elliott was a brilliant, insightful, critical man. He recognized that his hatred of his youngest son was irrational. Elliott despised himself for hating Charles. Elliott knew what harm he inflicted on the little boy with the bewildered brown eyes. Elliott knew, but he couldn't help it, and he couldn't stop.

"Did you and Charles have your own language?" Galen asked. She bypassed the twins' infancy and early childhood. Jason wouldn't remember it, and she couldn't tell Jason about the long, dark, lonely nights Charles spent in his crib while Jason played with his loving father. It filled Galen with such rage. How could anyone do that to a helpless, innocent child?

"Yes, we did, until Charles decided he didn't want to speak it anymore."

"Elliott made him."

"No."

"Elliott threatened to send Charles away unless you started to speak English." Galen blinked back tears. This was so difficult. Jason needed to know the cruel dark side of the father he loved so dearly; it was the only way that he and Charles could go on. Galen hated to shatter the memory of Elliott's love for Jason—that was real, too—but Jason had to understand how much damage Elliott had done to his twin. Galen continued, emotionally, "Jason, Charles was only four and a half! Elliott threatened to send him away."

"No. He never would have."

"Yes, Jason, he *would*. Elliott sent Charles away when he was twelve, didn't he?"

"Charles wanted to go. He was bored being with me. Charles was so bright; it slowed him down to be here, learning at my pace. . . ."

"No. Charles pleaded with Elliott not to send him away."

"When Charles came home at vacations, he seemed restless and distant. We weren't as close."

"Maybe that's because you never answered any of his letters." Galen spoke softly.

"His letters?"

"Charles wrote to you every week for the first few years. Later, the letters weren't as frequent. They are all here, in order by postmark, unopened." Galen gestured to the shoeboxes that lay on the carpet.

"No." Tears filled Jason's eyes and his voice broke. His hand trembled as he reached for the nearest shoebox. He removed a letter and stared at it with unseeing eyes. "What does it say?"

"The envelope reads, 'Master Jason Sinclair, Esquire.' " Galen smiled thoughtfully at the large, boyish handwriting and the little-boy humor. Charles and Jason had been good friends, once. They could have been such good friends if Elliott . . . "It was mailed in care of Elliott."

"Will you open it and read it to me?"

Galen opened the envelope. It had been sealed for over twenty-three years. It was the first letter Charles had written. He wrote it the day after he arrived at Morehead. Charles wrote enthusiastically about his new school. He told his twin about the ancient haunted buildings and about the headmaster, "straight out of *Oliver Twist.*" Galen read the letter with enthusiasm, as it had been written; but they both felt Charles's loneliness. Charles was trying to sound happy for his twin, to share this *adventure* with him, but he missed Jason so much!

"I can't . . ." Jason held up his hand. *I can't hear anymore.*

Galen and Jason sat in silence. Elise cooed softly on a blanket on the floor between them. She had been quiet, as if she understood that she was learning something very important and very sad about her father. Whoever he was.

Jason leaned over and kissed her velvety-soft cheek and idly stroked her dark-brown curls.

"And he disowned him because?" Jason began finally.

"Because Charles was eighteen and no longer needed a legal guardian."

"Did he ever tell Charles why?" *I told you I don't know why. It's not a lie.* Jason held his breath.

"No." Elliott had meticulously described Charles's reaction to the news; bewildered, uncomprehending, deeply hurt. After all the years of rejection, until that moment, there had still been hope and love in his son's sensitive brown eyes. "Charles never knew."

"How he must have hated Father."

"Oh, no, Jason. Charles loved him. There are letters here from Charles to Elliott. They were unopened, too, but I read some. Charles desperately wanted Elliott's love. Everything Charles did was to please Elliott."

"How could he love him?"

Galen shrugged. "Charles didn't know what Elliott was doing, or why. And he saw how much Elliott loved you, how loving Elliott could be."

"I should have told Charles about the papers in the desk years ago. But I didn't trust him. I was sure that Charles had done something. . . ."

"How could you know? How could you even begin to guess?"

"I have to tell him now. He needs to know."

Their eyes fell on Elise. If she were Charles's daughter . . . There was nothing wrong with Charles; there was no reason for her to be kept from Charles.

"What are you doing?"

"Packing." Brooke had been gradually moving out of her tiny office. Today, her last day, only a small boxload of items remained.

"I can't believe you're leaving. After today . . . wasn't it exhilarating to win?"

Brooke smiled. "It was a perfect swan song."

"Stay."

"Andrew, we've discussed this. This isn't for me, even though I've loved working with you. I want to go to Sinclair. It's my choice."

"You are throwing away a brilliant career."

"I'm doing what I want to do."

"How can you *choose* to work for a man who is the prime suspect in the Manhattan Ripper case?"

"Prime suspect?" Was there something—*evidence*—that Nick and Andrew hadn't shared with her? Was there something more than loosely connected circumstance? "There isn't anything."

"I talked with Nick this morning. Charles doesn't have one goddamned alibi. Don't you think that's a little suspicious for Manhattan's most high-profile bachelor?"

"Charles doesn't *need* alibis."

"Brooke, it scares me so much that you trust him."

"I *do* trust him, Andrew."

"Charles already attacked Melanie. How much closer does he have to get?"

"He *didn't*."

"You're blind, Brooke, why can't you see?"

"Stop it, Andrew."

Brooke's eyes flashed with anger. *Leave me alone. I'm going, and I'm going to work for Charles.*

"Brooke, I care about you." Andrew's voice was gentle.

"Well, *don't*. I don't need your concern. Just leave me alone, *please*." Brooke stared down at her hands; they were trembling.

"I don't want it to end this way," Andrew whispered softly.

"But this is the way it is going to end, Andrew." Brooke's eyes met his defiantly. "It's over."

Andrew held her gaze for several moments. His brown eyes met the ocean-blue ice with soft concern, but the ice didn't melt. Finally, reluctantly, Andrew left her tiny, almost empty office.

As soon as Andrew left, the trembling that Brooke had controlled with great effort erupted into a cold shiver. On impulse, she reached for the phone and dialed the number for Sinclair Publishing Company.

She had to speak with Charles. Why? For reassurance? *Charles, tell me that you're not a psychopathic murderer. Charles, look again at your calendar, find an alibi. Surely there must be a beautiful woman—an* alive *beautiful woman—who spent one of those nights in your arms.* . . .

"Charles Sinclair, please. This is Brooke Chandler calling."

"One moment please."

Hang up, Brooke, a voice told her.

"Brooke."

"Charles." He didn't sound like a psychopathic killer.

"Hi."

"Hi. I called to tell you that Jeffrey Martin is over—we won—and I'll be able to start work on Monday."

"Terrific. But you don't sound terrific."

"I just had an argument with Andrew."

"About?"

"My brilliant career." *About you.*

"Are you having second thoughts?" Charles didn't want to force her; Brooke had to be certain.

"*No*," Brooke answered firmly. *I* know *you're not the Ripper.* "Of course not."

"Because if you are—"

"I'm *not*. It was silly of me to call. I'll talk to you later." Brooke hung up quickly. Afterward she thought of safe topics she could have discussed with him.

Are you going to Windermere this weekend, Charles? Have you seen Galen and her baby? Are you going to see Melanie, the woman you love, the woman Nick and Andrew think you brutally attacked?

Brooke sighed. There weren't safe topics. When was this going to *end*?

Melanie finally emerged from her room in the late afternoon. Dark-gray storm clouds were gathering outside, and the mansion was still strangely silent. Melanie walked into the great room and felt a sudden cold breeze. The French door leading into the rose garden was open.

As Melanie moved to close it, she saw Jason. He stood in the garden, coatless in the bitter cold air, staring at the sea.

"Jason, hello." Melanie joined him. "You left the door ajar."

"I wanted to hear the phone." Jason spoke into the wind. "I'm waiting for a call from Charles."

Charles usually returned Jason's calls promptly, but not today, not after last night. If Jason didn't hear from Charles soon he would drive into town. Jason had to find Charles and tell him everything.

"Oh."

"Have you spoken with him today?"

"No." Melanie hesitated. She had to clear the air. "I was in the library last night, Jason, when you and Charles argued."

"I know some things I didn't know last night. I need to tell him, apologize to him—"

Jason stopped abruptly because Melanie suddenly shivered.

"You're cold, let's go in."

"No." Melanie frowned. "Jason, I . . ."

"What, Melanie?"

"I feel as if Brooke is in great danger." Melanie's voice was distant and eerie. "I need to reach her and warn her."

As Melanie spoke, a clap of thunder sounded off shore. She shivered again. Jason stared at the dark, turbulent sky and the storm that was rapidly approaching. Jason remembered a storm like this, coming out of the blue, bringing with it death and destruction.

"Let's go call Brooke and Charles," Jason said firmly. Jason was suddenly all the more determined to speak with *his* twin, because, as if Melanie's premonition were contagious, Jason sensed danger for Charles.

The lamplight flickered as they made their calls.

Melanie called Brooke at work and was told Brooke had left. Melanie dialed the number to Brooke's apartment and there was no answer.

"I guess she's on her way home," Melanie murmured as she handed the receiver to Jason.

"Didn't you give him my messages?" Jason demanded with uncharacteristic annoyance moments later as Charles's secretary told him that Charles had gone for the day.

"Yes, I gave him all of them."

Jason depressed the disconnect button and started to dial the number to Charles's penthouse. Halfway through, the line went dead.

CHAPTER THIRTY-TWO

"*B*rooke left about five minutes ago, Lieutenant Adrian."

"Was she alone?"

"Yes."

"Where did she go?"

"Home, I guess. She was carrying a small box. It was her last day here." The clerk paused. "Is there someone else who could help you?"

"No." Brooke's last day. "Yes. Let me speak with Andrew Parker."

"Oh, dear. He's gone, too."

"All right. Thank you."

Nick dialed the number to Brooke's apartment. There was no answer.

If the officer he had just assigned to follow her and protect her had gotten to the DA's office in time . . . Nick looked at his watch. In five minutes he would try her apartment again, and if she wasn't there he would find her.

Brooke walked briskly. The wind was cold, and large raindrops had started to fall. Gray-black clouds hovered in the distance over Long Island. The wind was invigorating and the raindrops felt cleansing. Brooke decided to stop at her apartment, leave the box, change, and go for a long walk.

Brooke pulled on her jeans and found a wool plaid scarf in the back of her closet. She opened her apartment door just as the doorbell sounded.

"Oh!" she exclaimed. "Hi. I'm glad you came over. It was stupid."

"Can we talk?"

"Sure. Come in." Brooke turned and led the way into her small living room.

"I need to have you with me." His voice was a whisper.

"What?" She spun, smiling, but the smile faded quickly when she saw his wild dark eyes. Brooke repeated, her voice barely audible, "What?"

"You just don't understand."

"No." *Yes.* Brooke's heart raced. Could she get to the door? Could she dash past him?

"Maybe if Melanie hadn't lived." His voice was so strange. "Maybe then it would have been enough."

"But she lived, and I'm so glad." Brooke didn't know how to talk to him. He was no one she knew, no one she *cared* about. When he wasn't like this—when he wasn't insane—she could cajole him. "It's so wonderful that Melanie didn't die."

"She called your name. That was the only thing that saved her."

"Good," Brooke whispered. She started to edge toward the door, but he blocked her path.

"But nothing can save you."

The shiny, menacing hunting knife looked incongruous in the hands of a man wearing a perfectly tailored three-piece gray suit. But the lethal weapon was *real*, and was going to kill her.

"Why?"

From the hallway, as he approached Brooke's apartment, he heard their voices. The door was ajar. He tapped lightly, waited only a moment, then pushed the door open wide.

"You really don't know?" He gave a short, ugly laugh. "I was so patient with you, Brooke, *too* patient. We could have been so good together. I would have taken such good care of you. He doesn't even love you. He loves your sister!"

"Why don't we try?" Brooke was pleading for her life.

"It's too late. You betrayed me."

He raised the knife above his right shoulder.

"Please," Brooke whispered. "Please don't."

As the razor-sharp blade plunged at its target, Charles grabbed him from behind, startling him, and averting the lethal blow.

"*Charles.*"

"Run, Brooke."

Charles should have had the advantage; he attacked Andrew from behind. Charles was strong, but Andrew's madness gave him extraordinary strength. Andrew twisted out of Charles's grip and spun to face him. He stared at the man who in his deranged mind had become his greatest enemy. Charles had stolen Brooke from him!

"*You,*" Andrew hissed.

Andrew slashed with the knife, and Charles spun away. Andrew slashed again and again, relentless in his madness. His lips turned into a half-smile and his brown eyes were wild and blazing. Charles repeatedly dodged the blade, but he was fatiguing. The sight of blood—his blood—on the knife blade told him Andrew was winning.

"*Nick.*" Charles heard Brooke's voice from the hallway. "In there, please hurry!"

Nick ran past Brooke into her apartment with his gun drawn. Brooke followed.

"Drop it, Andrew." Nick pointed his gun at Andrew's heart.

Andrew smiled a half-smile and stood up straight.

"This is quite a party, isn't it?" Andrew glanced from Charles to Nick to Brooke. "All the boyfriends, or should I say *lovers?* Of course, that doesn't apply to me. But you, Charles. And you, Nick."

Andrew's voice had an eerie singsong quality; he was mesmerizing them with his madness.

"It's over, Andrew. Drop the knife."

"You won't shoot me, Nick. You *can't*. We both know the rules."

"I will shoot you, Andrew. Look at Charles, he's bleeding. I had to shoot you to stop you from killing him. *Look* at him," Nick commanded. Nick didn't think it would work. Andrew knew that he hadn't gravely injured Charles, but if Nick could make him look—drop his guard—for even a fraction of a second . . .

Andrew didn't turn his face or body, but he let his eyes dart briefly toward Charles. It was enough. Nick dropped his gun and grabbed Andrew's right arm at the wrist. Nick's hands held tight, cutting off circulation, and his strong fingers worked to pry the knife away.

The knife fell to the floor. Nick released his grip on Andrew's wrist and tried to find a new hold that would subdue him. But Andrew spun free, laughing, and backed away from Nick.

Andrew backed away, stepping into the small box that Brooke had brought home from the office. He lost his balance and fell backward. As he twisted to break the fall, Andrew's right temple struck the metal radiator.

The blow—the full weight of his strong body against the metal—was instantly lethal. Andrew's lifeless body slumped down the wall and onto the floor. His head, propped against the wall, faced them. Bright red blood pulsed from his temple into his dark-brown hair and spilled onto his cheeks like crimson tears. The bleeding stopped quickly; there was no heartbeat to sustain it.

Andrew's dark-brown eyes, now clouded and bewildered, stared at them.

Nick solemnly retrieved his gun and made a call to the precinct to arrange for the homicide squad and the coroner. Brooke followed Nick away from Andrew. Brooke expected Charles to follow, too, but when she turned around she found that Charles hadn't moved.

He still stood in front of Andrew, his eyes staring into the dead dark eyes, unable to move. Charles didn't see Andrew, the psychopathic murderer. Charles saw Elliott—the Elliott of his nightmares—with his taunting dead eyes and his head crushed from the strength of the storm.

"Charles?" Brooke moved beside Charles and touched him lightly on the forearm. It was wet where she touched, wet with Charles's blood! "Charles, are you hurt?"

Charles didn't seem to hear her. He was mesmerized, transfixed, lost in a private horror. Brooke looked to Nick for help. He was still on the phone.

". . . No, I'll tell Mrs. Parker myself." Allison was safe, under police protection, in a room at the Excelsior; now she was safe and *free*. Nick hung up the phone and crossed the room to Charles and Brooke. He spoke firmly, "Charles, what is it?"

Charles squeezed his eyes shut and pressed his strong, trembling fingers against his forehead.

"What, Charles?" Nick pressed. Charles was in some form of shock, but why?

"My father." Charles's voice was heavy. "The way he died. It must have been like that. He must have looked like that."

No, he didn't look like that, Nick thought. Nick had seen Elliott Sinclair's head injury, and Charles *hadn't*. It was more proof—unnecessary now—that Charles was innocent. Charles was innocent of all crimes.

"Let's drive into town," Melanie suggested after forty-five minutes had elapsed and the phone line was still dead.

"There are probably trees across the road. That's why the phone is out. There might be power lines down, too," Jason explained calmly. Jason didn't feel clam. A sense of dread pulsed through him for his twin, and he kept remembering a storm like this thirteen years ago.

"The power lines aren't down," Melanie protested weakly. The lights had flickered but, so far, the electricity had held.

"Why don't I turn on the television for local news? Maybe we can find out about the roads," Galen suggested. Not that Melanie could leave Windermere anyway: It was her *safe* house.

As the television picture came into focus, Melanie whispered, "That's Brooke's apartment building."

It was a special bulletin. The camera crew was positioned outside, in the

waning twilight and pouring rain. The building's entrance was cluttered with police cars, medic units, the coroner's van, and numerous police officers.

"The information is unconfirmed—we are waiting for the appearance of Lieutenant Nick Adrian or Deputy District Attorney Andrew Parker, the two authorized spokesmen of the Manhattan Ripper investigation—but we understand that
the Manhattan Ripper is dead. We know that this is the apartment building of
Brooke Chandler, assistant DA and twin sister of the only surviving Manhattan
Ripper victim, super-model Melanie Chandler. Unconfirmed sources report that
Brooke Chandler, Nick Adrian, and Andrew Parker—as well as magazine mogul
and sometimes companion of Melanie Chandler, Charles Sinclair—all entered the
building in the past hour and a half. It is possible that a trap was set by the PD
working with the DA's office. It appears, if so, that the trap was successful. That's
all we have now, Burt, but we'll stay here until we have all the answers. Back to you
in the studio . . ."

"They are all right," Jason whispered unconvincingly.

"You know they're *not*, Jason," Melanie countered. "We have to go to them."

"We have to wait here. There is nothing we can do. We have to wait." Jason's
heart fluttered with fear. He had waited here once before, helpless in a violent
storm, until the sirens brought news of death.

By the time the first news crew arrived outside Brooke's apartment building on
West Fifty-seventh Street, Nick and Charles and Brooke were already in Nick's
office at the precinct.

"The phone lines are down to all of east Long Island. I'll have dispatch radio
the guards at the estate and tell them that you are safe."

"Thank you." Brooke smiled at Nick then touched Charles's bloodied sleeve.
"Maybe a doctor . . ."

"It's a flesh wound, Brooke. It's nothing." It's nothing compared to what he
must have done to Melanie, or what he was planning to do to you.

"Why did you come to my apartment, Charles?"

"I didn't like the way you sounded when you called. I didn't think I'd heard the
whole story."

"You hadn't." Brooke closed her eyes briefly. "Andrew had just made a point of
reminding me that *you* were a suspect."

Charles sighed and looked from Brooke to Nick.

"I'm sorry, Charles. I never *wanted* it to be you." Nick shook his head slowly.
"God, I was so wrong. I never even considered him."

"Why should you have considered him, Nick?" Brooke asked swiftly. She had
never considered Andrew, either, but she had spent many tormented hours
convincing herself that it couldn't possibly be Charles. "He didn't even know
Melanie. . . ."

Brooke frowned. She suddenly recalled the crazy words Andrew had spoken
before he lunged at her with the knife. Andrew didn't know Melanie, but he knew
her. Andrew wanted *her*. Was it her fault?

"Why did you come over, Nick?"

Nick told them about Allison Parker. There was no way Nick could tell the
story without mentioning Brooke's resemblance to Allison.

"Andrew loved Allison," Brooke said softly. "But sometimes he felt betrayed
and abandoned by her."

"All Andrew's emotions about Allison were disturbed. She was his obsession.

Andrew murdered her roommate at Princeton to scare Allison into needing him."

"And he was doing that with me? Oh, *no.*"

"Brooke, this is not your fault. You happened to look like Allison, that's all."

"He wanted me!"

"I think he wanted Allison—young, strong, beautiful Allison—back again. You said he felt she was abandoning him." Nick spoke the next very quietly, "Brooke, Andrew tried to *murder* you."

"*Still* . . . What he did to those women, and Melanie!" Brooke's horrified blue eyes looked at Charles.

"It's not your fault." The brown eyes tried to reassure her.

"He was crazy, Brooke."

Nick's phone rang. "Ten minutes. All right. Sure. Thanks." He hung up the phone. "Press conference in ten minutes."

"You don't need us for that, do you?" Charles asked. "I want to get changed and drive to Windermere. I can bring Melanie home now, can't I?"

Home, Brooke mused.

"Yes. Of course."

"Brooke, do you want to come?"

"Oh, I . . ." Brooke faltered.

"I could use your help tonight, Brooke," Nick interjected swiftly.

Brooke nodded. Somehow it was right for her to be here, with Nick, as they wrapped up the Manhattan Ripper case. She had imagined a night like this, when it was over, when she and Nick and Andrew—

Andrew. Brooke's blue eyes grew dark and thoughtful.

"Brooke," Nick continued firmly. *Don't think about it now, Brooke. It's too fresh. Focus those beautiful eyes and that bright mind on the mechanics. There's a lot of work left to be done, even though he's dead.* "I need to check on a few things before the press conference. I'll meet you downstairs in ten minutes. OK?"

His words, *check on a few things,* jarred her legal mind.

"Was his blood type O?" she asked quietly. Brooke knew Andrew was right-handed with dark eyes and dark hair, and she knew that he intended to kill *her.* But was Andrew Parker the Manhattan Ripper? They had to be certain before they told Manhattan to breathe a sigh of relief.

"Yes." Good, she was with him. "I'm going to check with the handwriting expert now. If he hasn't finished comparing the journal entries with the samples of Andrew's handwriting I got from the DA's office, we'll wait."

"We need to go over all the evidence."

Nick smiled. He already had. More evidence was being collected at Andrew's apartment. In a remote corner of a closet the officers had already found something Allison Parker had missed—a blood-splattered black stocking with eyeholes.

"We will." Nick turned to Charles. Nick had two messages for Charles; both were important, and both were emotional. "Thank you, Charles, for saving Brooke's life. And I'm so sorry about—"

"You were doing your job. I fit the description. Melanie and I had our share of well-publicized problems."

"That's gracious of you."

"I'm just glad it's over. I was afraid . . ." Charles faltered.

"We couldn't have pressed charges."

"You already had," Charles replied flatly as his dark eyes found Brooke. *You already had with the people who counted.*

"I'm sorry," Nick repeated hoarsely before he left his office. Nick knew that even his *suspicion* of Charles had done damage to Charles with the people he loved—Melanie and Jason and Brooke.

After Nick left, Brooke moved closer to Charles. "Charles, I never . . ."

"But it worried you." It worried you, and it worried Melanie. And *Jason*; Jason *believed* it was possible.

"I just wanted it to be over, too." Brooke sighed softly. She needed to tell him; if they were going to work together, and if he and she and Melanie . . . "Charles, what Andrew said about you and me . . ."

"Andrew was crazy, Brooke. Nothing he said—" Charles caught the look in her eyes and stopped abruptly. He smiled gently and touched her flushed cheek with his finger. "Not so crazy?"

"I remember a wide-eyed law clerk who was pretty enchanted," Brooke admitted shyly.

"Brooke." Charles lifted her chin slightly and gazed into her eyes. "I'm very flattered."

The brown eyes told her it was the truth; Charles meant it.

"I'm flattered that you're flattered." Brooke laughed softly, and her heart didn't ache. Charles could be her dear, beloved friend. Brooke continued easily, so easily, "Next life. This life is with Melanie."

"Yes," Charles whispered quietly.

Brooke smiled. "Give her my love."

CHAPTER THIRTY-THREE

Charles drove along the rain-slick roads toward Southampton. The driving was treacherous. Branches cluttered the roadway and the wind swirled and the rain pelted. It would have been smarter to wait until morning. . .

But Charles could not wait to be with Melanie. If only he could avoid seeing Jason. Maybe Melanie would be alone in her cheery yellow bedroom, or in the library, and they could leave unnoticed.

"Andrew visited me in the hospital," Melanie breathed in amazement after they watched the latest special bulletin.

The electricity had held, despite the storm, but the phone line was still dead. Melanie wanted to speak with Brooke, but she was reassured to see her—safe and calm—at the press conference. Melanie looked for Charles, hailed by Nick as the hero of the piece. Brooke gave Charles *and* Nick equal credit for saving her life. Melanie looked for Charles, but she didn't see him.

"He *visited* you?" Galen asked.

"Yes. It was probably a test to see if I could recognize him. But I looked into his eyes and told him how much I believed it was Steve Barnes." Melanie shivered.

"Thank God it's over," Jason said. He wished it was all over. He wished he already had spoken to Charles and somehow everything would be all right. Restless, even after the special bulletins told them Brooke and Charles were safe, Jason reached repeatedly for the still-dead phone.

When they heard the front door open, they all stood up. They listened in silence as he tapped softly on the door to the yellow bedroom and called her name.

"*Charles.*" Melanie crossed the great room toward the foyer. Jason and Galen followed.

Charles appeared, his dark hair darker from the pelting rain, and his face cold from the bitter wind. Charles didn't look at Jason or Galen. "Melanie, it's over, let's—"

"Charles, I've been trying to reach you," Jason interjected. "Didn't you get my messages?"

The soft, loving look for Melanie vanished as Charles turned toward Jason.

"I don't think we have anything—" he stopped abruptly when he saw the look of worry in Jason's eyes; Jason's eyes and Galen's eyes. Charles breathed, "Oh, my God, is it Elise? Has something happened?"

"No," Galen answered swiftly. That precious child is well, sleeping peacefully in a home where another child suffered horribly. Oh, *Charles*. Galen blinked back tears.

"What is it?" Charles pressed. He looked to Melanie for the answer, but she didn't know. Galen and Jason hadn't told her.

"Charles," Jason spoke softly. "This afternoon I asked Galen to go through Father's desk. I knew there were letters and a journal."

"Yes?" Why hadn't he ever known that?

"We know why he disowned you."

"Tell me." Charles's voice was barely audible.

"Maybe I should leave," Melanie suggested quietly. She had already been an unwitting witness to the argument between Charles and Jason.

"No." Charles looked at her with surprise. There can't be secrets between us, Melanie, not anymore. Charles knew he was taking a risk; Melanie might learn something that would turn her against him. But it—whatever it was—had already separated them once. Charles sighed. "You need to hear this." Whatever it is.

They walked into the great room. The fire crackled cheerfully. Elliott's journal lay on the marble end table. Jason moved toward it, glowering at the words he couldn't read written by the man he once had loved. *Once.*

"Father blamed you for our mother's death." The pain of his words and their meaning flickered in Jason's pale-blue eyes.

"What?" Charles didn't understand.

"She died while you were being born," Jason said heavily. "And he blamed you for it."

"No." Charles shook his head.

"Yes."

Galen saw the look of bewilderment and hurt and sadness in the beautiful brown eyes. Galen recognized the look. Elliott had described it so well; when he left Charles alone in his crib, when he spanked him viciously, when he openly loved Jason and neglected Charles, and finally, the last time, when Elliott disowned him.

"Your father was a mean and irrational man," Galen said emotionally. She hated the man she had never known.

"No." It was Charles who spoke, defending the man whose love he had wanted so desperately and who had treated him so cruelly. "No."

"I didn't know until today that you had ever written letters to me, Charles," Jason told him apologetically. Believe it, Charles. Our father was a man who deserved hatred, not love.

"So many letters," Charles breathed. He closed his eyes for a moment and felt the pain of a young boy—his pain—whose loving letters had never been acknowledged. But still he wrote, sharing the secrets of his heart and soul with his twin. "He never . . ."

"No."

The impact of what Charles had just learned suddenly hit him. Emotions swirled within him. He needed to be alone with this; he had to try to make sense of it. Charles clenched his fists and felt a warm wetness on his forearm where the knife wound had reopened and started to bleed.

"I . . ." Charles couldn't speak. He had to get away. Charles saw concern, and love, in the three sets of eyes; hurt they couldn't help him, not now. Charles shook his head slightly, then crossed the great room to the French doors that led to the rose garden and the sea beyond.

After a moment Galen took the leather journal from the marble end table and rushed after Charles into the storm.

"Charles, wait."

Galen didn't know if he heard her voice above the wind. He moved swiftly into the storm and the darkness.

"*Please.*"

Charles stopped, but he didn't turn around. "Galen, I need to be alone."

"Yes, I know." She stood close behind him. "But you need to read this. You need to read his words."

Charles turned and stared at her with wild brown eyes wet with rain or tears or both. "*Why?*"

"It will help." Galen forced Elliott's journal into his hands. Galen didn't know Elliott, but she hated him. Charles had known him and loved him. Charles had called to him desperately as he lay alone and delirious and maybe dying in Africa. Charles needed to know how Elliott really felt, how torn he had been, how much it had hurt him to treat Charles the way he did. Charles needed to know how much Elliott really had loved him and how much Elliott hated himself for being unable to show Charles that love. "Please read it, Charles."

Numbly Charles took the leather journal and slipped it under his windbreaker. Then he turned and disappeared in the darkness toward the angry sea.

What if he doesn't stop at water's edge, Galen wondered. What if he walks into the sea to die as Elliott had died in a storm-tossed watery grave?

Galen sighed. Charles was his own man; but somewhere in the emotions that tossed and turned within him was a deep love for Melanie. Galen had seen it in his eyes. Charles would remember Melanie and it would save him.

"Where is he?" Melanie asked anxiously when Galen reappeared at the French doors.

"He went for a walk toward the sea."

"He'll probably go to the beach house. There's light there and protection from the rain." Jason moved to the bay window as he spoke. He thought he saw a dark figure on the lawn; but it was a night of dark shadows. Jason couldn't be sure. A few moments later he saw his twin's figure on the lighted porch of the beach house.

Charles stood, motionless, and faced the endless darkness of the night and the sea. Then he sat, bent over, and started to read. "He's there now."

Sometimes I want to love him so much, but I can't. I look at him and I remember Meredith and it makes me hate him all over again.

Charles read Elliott's words and knew why Galen had given him the journal. Buried deep beneath the hatred, between the careful, horrible chronicles of abuse, were glimmers of love.

I read one of his stories today, the headmaster sent it to the office. God, Charles is talented! He is so bright and creative and sensitive. I should tell him how proud I am.

Why didn't you tell me, Father? Just *once . . .*

Oh, those bewildered brown eyes when I told him to leave. He doesn't understand, but his life will be happier away from me forever. Charles will begin his own magazine, and it will be far better than Images *ever was.*

I wish him happiness, now. I hope someday Charles will find someone to love.

After Charles read every word—the hatred and the love—he held his head in his hands and cried.

"Go to him, Jason," Galen urged gently.

They were in their bedroom. She was nursing Elise, and Jason stared out the window at the beach house. After Charles left the great room, they had disbanded in silence; Melanie went to her bedroom, and Galen and Jason went to theirs.

"I have to wait until he comes back to the house. Charles needs this time alone."

Jason watched as Charles finished reading and held his head in his hands. Eventually, Charles got up and walked off the protected porch. But he was still there, facing the angry sea.

Jason's view was of the beach house and the sea beyond. The lawn and gardens directly below were obscured by the structure of the mansion. Jason didn't see Melanie as she walked—her golden hair whipped by the wind, her slender body wavering like a young tree—along the white stone path toward the beach house. Had he been watching, had anyone been watching, he would have noticed her slow, determined path and admired her courage.

And he would have seen her fall.

It came like all the other times—but it hadn't happened in almost a week, it wasn't supposed to happen anymore!—the sudden unexpected weakness that commanded her to lie down, *quickly*. She couldn't lie down in the middle of the path in the heavy rain and the bitter-cold wind. She couldn't and *wouldn't*. This time she wasn't going to let the weakness stop her; she was going to be with Charles. Melanie could see him in the distance, his back to her, gazing at the sea.

This time she would conquer the weakness, she decided defiantly.

But her body betrayed her. She had pushed too hard. Her arms wouldn't even reach out to break her fall. She screamed with pain as she fell on the stone path. Her fall was heavy, unbroken, and hurled by the angry wind. Her scream was a reflex; it was a scream from a pain that was the *sum* of all pain that had come before.

Breathe, her mind told her. But the pain stopped her from breathing. In a moment it would stop her heart. The pain was within her, surrounding her heart and her lungs and her brain; and the pain was on the surface, relentlessly battered by the wind and rain. All of her, every cell of her, was a raw, gaping wound. Every nerve root, *almost* mended, was torn again and angry and screaming at the insult.

Melanie forced a breath, and another. She was breathing. Melanie knew because each breath made her chest sear with white-hot pain. She couldn't move. She couldn't even raise her head off the ground. She felt sharp pieces of stone digging into her cheeks, but her head was too heavy to lift. Her whole body began to shake, chilled from her drenched clothes and the bitter cold, and the trembling made it all hurt even more.

How could it hurt even more? But it did.

Then he was there, bending over her.

"Melanie," he whispered.

Charles cradled her in his arms and caused a new round of pain as he pulled her against him. He had heard the scream, a heart-stopping human wail, above the noises of the storm. At first he hadn't seen her in the darkness; the direction of the scream, tossed by the swirling wind, had been vague. Finally he saw the shimmer of gold and he ran to her.

"Charles." Her lips formed the word, but there was no sound. When she opened her eyes, Charles saw the disbelieving glaze of pain and a faint flicker of happiness for him.

Charles lifted her shaking body in his arms, suddenly aware that he had caused her more pain. He hesitated. Putting her down would hurt her more, again. He already had her in his arms. He would carry her to the house, to warmth and safety. Charles walked on the grass beside the path; maybe it would be less jarring.

As he neared the veranda Charles saw another figure. Jason had seen Charles's sudden dash from the beach house and went to the great room to meet him. Jason assumed that Charles was dashing against the storm, dashing for the cover of the house. But Charles was carrying Melanie. . . .

"Charles, is she all right?"

"Jason, thank God. I didn't know how I would open the doors without—" Charles stopped. Without putting her down and hurting her more. "We'll need lots of warm towels, and scissors to cut her out of her clothes."

Jason led the way, holding doors, helping Charles take Melanie to her bedroom. Charles set her gently on top of the bed. Jason brought a stack of plush dry towels and a pair of scissors.

"How is she?" Jason asked.

Melanie opened her eyes and nodded slightly.

"I think that means she's OK," Charles answered gently, looking in the sky-blue eyes for confirmation. Melanie smiled a shaky smile. "I'm going to get her dry and into bed."

"Do you need help?"

"No. I think we can manage."

"I'll be in the kitchen if you need me."

"Thank you," Charles said. "Thank you, Jason."

Charles talked to her, like a father talking to a child who would understand but was too young to answer. He didn't want her to try to talk, but he wanted her to know what he was doing.

"I'm going to dry your hair a little then wrap it in a towel," Charles explained as he did just that. When he finished he said, "I think it will hurt the least if I cut your clothes off."

Melanie's eyes opened and Charles saw fear. He remembered her fear when he used his knife to open the manuscript from Galen.

"Oh, Melanie darling. He's dead. He can't hurt you. And I would never hurt you. Don't you know that?"

Melanie didn't answer and closed her eyes.

Carefully, pulling the wet cloth away from her skin, protecting her from the touch of cold steel with his warm fingers, Charles cut away the cashmere sweater and the cotton shirt beneath it. As the wet clothes fell away, until all she wore above her waist was the rain-soaked bra, Melanie began to tremble.

She was afraid to open her eyes. She couldn't bear to see the expression on his face—his horror and revulsion at her scarred grotesque torso. She felt his hands, warm and gentle, as they removed her bra and dried her with a soft fluffy towel.

"Hey," he said softly. "What do you want to put on?"

"There's a nightgown in the top dresser drawer." Melanie was surprised by the strength in her voice. The pain was subsiding. The startling, breathtaking hot stabs of pain had muted into a constant dull throb and her strength was returning. But it was all too late; Charles had seen her scars. "I'm better now. If you can just hand me the nightgown, I can do the rest."

She heard him open the dresser drawer.

"Is the light too bright?" Charles asked when he returned. It wasn't bright at all. The room was softly illuminated by the light from the bathroom. It was just a gentle glow. Still, her eyes were closed.

"No." Melanie forced them open. It was all right as long as she didn't look at him.

"Can you sit up? Just for a moment. I'll help you. Then I can slip this over your head."

Charles put his arms around her to help her and met resistance. She pushed herself against the bed; her body stiffened with pain.

"Melanie?"

"I'm all right, Charles, really. I'm warm now. The pain is less. I can get dressed and undressed on my own. Thank you." She took the nightgown and covered her breasts.

"I want to stay here—with you—tonight. I can sleep in the chair." *I want to be with you, Melanie. What I have just learned—as difficult as it was—has set me free. I can love you. There is no reason—*

"No." Melanie looked at him then. She saw his surprise and concern; she read it as pity "No, Charles. Please, just go away."

"Melanie."

"Please."

Charles watched her for a moment, but her eyes wouldn't meet his again. Finally he kissed her on the cheek and left the room.

After Charles left, Melanie touched the spot where he had kissed her. Then she warmed her still-cold face with her own hot tears.

Good-bye, darling Charles. Good-bye, not au revoir.

Charles went to the kitchen. He needed a cup of coffee before beginning his drive back to Manhattan. He was exhausted, but he couldn't stay at Windermere unless he was with Melanie. He would return in the morning to get her.

Melanie would come with him, wouldn't she? The doubts were behind them now, weren't they? His doubt about himself, about what was wrong with him, no longer existed. And if she had ever doubted him, ever believed that he could have been the Manhattan Ripper . . .

It was over. And she had braved the angry storm to be with him. And even though just now she had asked him to leave . . . Charles frowned slightly.

Charles's frown deepened when he entered the kitchen. He had forgotten that Jason would be there. Jason sat at the kitchen table drinking coffee.

"How is she?" Jason asked.

"Tired. Hurt. Discouraged," Charles answered. He was describing himself, too.

Jason nodded and poured a cup of coffee for Charles. They sat at opposite ends of the table.

"I didn't even know Melanie had gone out," Jason said after several silent minutes "I was watching you. When you left the beach house I went to meet you."

Charles stared vacantly at Jason. I can't talk about it now, Jason.

"There is something I am going to do as soon as possible."

"Oh?" Charles asked without curiosity.

"I'm going to give you half of everything. Sinclair Publishing, Windermere, everything."

"What?"

"It's your rightful half. If I'd known the reason that Father disowned you . . ."

"He made you promise never to let me have it," Charles reminded him.

"A promise to a man like that!" Jason's voice was bitter.

"Oh, Jason," Charles sighed. "Don't hate him."

"How can you say that?"

"He loved you, Jason, very much." Charles smiled slightly. "And he loved me, too."

Jason frowned.

"He did, deep down, but he never really recovered from our mother's death."

"How can you be so forgiving?"

Charles shrugged. "Maybe it is just such a relief to know, finally, there is nothing wrong with *me*."

They sat in silence for a moment.

"Charles, about last night, about accusing you of Father's death, I . . ."

"Nick said you spoke with the harbormaster. You know I wasn't there." Charles's voice was edgy.

"I know you weren't there anyway." Jason's eyes met his twin's. "Tonight, before you went to Brooke's apartment, I sensed that you were in great danger. I tried to reach you, to warn you. . . ."

Charles nodded. Jason was trying, and he *would* try. If they could free themselves of the secrets, maybe they could be close again. *If* . . . there was one more secret, and it was the most important, the most precious. . . .

"I need to know if she's mine, Jason," Charles whispered finally.

"I know."

"I don't even know what I will do if she is. I know she belongs with Galen and I know Galen belongs with you. But if she's my daughter, if she's part of me . . ."

Jason looked at his brother—the twin who had been deprived of so much that should have been his—and Jason understood, then, how much it meant to Charles. It wasn't that Charles wanted Elise to be his daughter—they all knew it would be best if she were Jason's—but, if she were, Charles wanted to know. Charles wanted to love her the way a father should love his child.

"You know what I've been thinking about all night?" Jason asked as he made a vow to himself that if Elise were Charles's daughter they would work it out. He and Charles and Galen would make it work. They had enough love, more than enough, for the little girl and for each other.

"What?"

"All those hours you used to read to me when we were little boys. Those were such happy times." Jason's voice broke.

Charles smiled, his dark eyes suddenly moist. "Those were happy times for me, too."

* * *

Melanie lay in her bed, her entire body throbbing, unable to sleep. Finally she forced herself out of bed to the window overlooking the drive. Charles's car was still there. It was one-thirty in the morning. Charles was probably planning to spend the night.

I can't see him. It was a knowledge that surpassed all the pain. She could not see Charles Sinclair again, *ever.* Charles had seen her wounds; he knew what she had become. She couldn't face him; she didn't want to see his pity or his contempt.

Melanie squinted as she looked into the driveway and realized that the brightness was the full moon. The storm had passed. The night was crisp and clear and still and bright. Maybe . . .

Melanie moved slowly, her pace limited by pain, toward the bedside table and the telephone. She held her breath as she lifted the receiver.

There was a dial tone! Someone could come to take her away. She could be gone before morning. Melanie pressed the button that automatically dialed Brooke's apartment. There was no answer.

Of course Brooke wouldn't be there. Her apartment was the scene of a crime. There would be blood. . . . Melanie wondered about her own luxury apartment. Had someone—Adam, Brooke, the landlord, the police, *who* handled that sort of thing?—removed *her* bloodstains from the furniture and replaced the expensive wool carpet and washed the walls?

Melanie pressed the button that automatically dialed the direct line to Nick's office.

"Adrian," he answered. Melanie heard the fatigue in his voice.

"Nick? It's Melanie."

"Hi. You made it into town?"

"What? No, I'm at Windermere. It's all right for me to leave, isn't it?"

"Sure." Nick frowned. "Didn't Charles drive out this evening?"

"Yes. He's spending the night. I sort of hoped I could leave now." Melanie's voice faltered. She didn't want to explain why. She just wanted to leave.

"Well, we do run a round-trip service for our safehouse guests," Nick said easily, but he was worried about her. What was going on? "I've already turned the guards loose, but I'll find someone. When will you be ready?"

Nick guessed her answer before he heard her relieved grateful voice whisper, "I'm ready now, Nick."

"Realistically, it will be thirty minutes. Would you like to talk to Brooke?"

"*Yes.* Is she there?"

Nick didn't answer, but he handed the phone to Brooke.

"Melanie?"

"Brooke, are you all right?"

"Yes." Melanie's question recalled the horror of Andrew's attack. For the past six hours Brooke had forced objectivity, helping Nick with the legal details. Now she shuddered, remembering her own fear and thinking how very much worse it had been for her twin. "Are you?"

"Sure," Melanie answered swiftly and unconvincingly. "Brooke, do you know if my apartment is . . ."

"Yes. It's fine."

"Good. Why don't you plan to stay there until yours is fixed?" Melanie didn't ask, Why don't you plan to stay there, *too?* She knew she would only be in her apartment long enough to pack.

"Thank you."

"Nick is sending someone to get me now."

"I'll be here, at the precinct, when you arrive and then we can go to your apartment." Brooke frowned. "Melanie?"

"Yes?"

"It was because of me." Brooke knew that Charles wouldn't have told her. It was something the press didn't need to know, but Melanie did. Brooke had to tell her.

"What was?"

"Andrew was trying to frighten *me*."

"Tonight?"

"No. From the beginning. That was why he killed. That was why he attacked you."

Melanie's hand tightened around the receiver and she tugged at her lower lip with her teeth. It was because of Brooke? There was a *reason* in Andrew's warped violent mind? No, it wasn't possible. . . .

"He stopped when I called your name," Melanie whispered finally. It was possible. It was true.

"Oh, Melanie, I am so *sorry*."

"Brooke," Melanie said softly. She *felt* the pain of her twin's guilt. "It's not your fault. I would never blame you. . . ."

Melanie said it again when she embraced Brooke in Nick's office three hours later; and she repeated it an hour later when they arrived at her apartment. Each time Melanie said it with finality, as if it was absurd for Brooke to even *imagine* that she would blame her. Brooke would believe it for a while; until she looked at Melanie, stiff and pale from pain, and saw the deep sadness in her sky-blue eyes. Then Brooke's eyes would fill with sorrow again; and Melanie would notice and remind her anew that it wasn't her fault.

Melanie entered her apartment hesitantly. She was glad Brooke was with her.

"It looks, uh, *normal*, doesn't it?" Melanie asked with relief. Not that anything was normal anymore. She had to find a new setting for normal. "You're welcome to stay here, even after your apartment is all right. I'll be away for at least two months."

"*Away?*"

"Yes." Melanie looked at Brooke and told her the truth. "I'm changed. I need to find out who I am *now*, what I want, where I'm going."

"I know you do. I hoped I could help."

"You have. You can. I need you to be my friend."

"I am. You know I am."

"Yes." Melanie smiled at her twin. "Brooke, first I have to go away for a while." Brooke nodded. "Where are you going?"

Melanie shook her head slightly. "I can't tell you, but I'll be safe. I'll call you, and Mom and Dad. I don't want you to worry."

"You found me once, when I was lost on top of a remote mountain."

"You don't need to try to find me, Brooke. I won't be lost."

"OK. When do you leave?"

"The plane departs at nine." It was true. The plane Melanie planned to take, tomorrow or the next day or whenever she was strong enough and had made all the travel arrangements, departed daily at nine. She wouldn't be on the plane today. It would take all her strength to pack and take a taxi to an airport motel where, hopefully, no one would recognize her under her hooded jacket. She would rest and recover there until she was fit to travel. "I'd better start packing."

Brooke watched Melanie pack turtleneck shirts and jeans and scarves and tennis shoes. Brooke watched her sift through her drawers of carefully folded colorful clothes and select the few that were drab and old and colorless. Brooke shuddered inside as Melanie slid her graceful hands under the layers of designer swimsuits she would never wear again and retrieved a neatly folded pair of gray sweat pants and a matching sweat shirt.

Once Melanie had finished packing the clothes in the small suitcase, she added two sketchpads, a container of colored pencils, a pincushion silvery with pin heads, a large pair of scissors and a box of needles and thread.

"Remember how much I enjoyed sewing and drawing clothes designs in high school?" Melanie asked offhandedly by way of answer to Brooke's obvious curiosity.

"Not really." *We weren't friends, then.*

"It's a hobby." Melanie hoped it could be something more. She had always hoped it. Now she would find out. Now it was all she had left.

Melanie insisted that Brooke not accompany her to the airport, and Brooke acquiesced. Melanie didn't want her to have any idea where she was going.

Melanie doesn't want me to know where she is going because she doesn't want Charles to find out, Brooke decided. *Why? Charles had gone to Windermere to bring her "home." What had happened?*

"What about Charles?" Brooke asked finally as she walked Melanie to the waiting taxi cab.

Melanie's blue eyes glistened as she met Brooke's.

"Take care of him, Brooke," Melanie said quietly. *Love him.*

CHAPTER THIRTY-FOUR

"She's gone, Brooke?" Charles asked, incredulous, when he called Melanie's apartment three hours after Melanie took the taxi to the airport.

Charles had awakened early—he had barely slept—and taken a long walk on the storm-tossed beach and finally, at ten, tapped gently on her bedroom door. Melanie left a note, thanking Jason for his kindness in offering her refuge at Windermere and saying good-bye to Galen and Elise; but that was all. There was no note, no message, for Charles.

"Yes."

"Why?" It was a soft whisper of despair.

"I don't know, Charles." *Don't you know?* Brooke assumed that something had happened with Charles. Melanie's urgent departure, and the deep pain in her eyes, could only have been because of Charles.

"Where did she go?"

"I don't know."

"How was she when you saw her?"

"She looked tired." *And so sad. Melanie looked the way you sound, Charles. What happened?* Brooke added hopefully, "Maybe getting away will be good for her."

The Manhattan Ripper was dead; and Melanie Chandler vanished; and Brooke Chandler joined Sinclair Publishing Company; and Jason Sinclair and Galen Elizabeth Spencer were married; and Lieutenant Nick Adrian refused numerous offers to write a book about the psychopath, as did Allison Parker, who, it was rumored, was going to resume her career in law; and Charles Sinclair was no longer at the parties; and then there was nothing more to say.

The press left them alone to get on with their lives.

Three weeks after Galen spent a somber afternoon reading the journal of Elliott Sinclair, she and Elise and Jason and Charles went together to the office of the geneticist who would tell them which twin was Elise's father. Elise squirmed in her mother's arms as they sat in tense silence in the doctor's waiting room.

"Elise," Galen whispered to the wriggling child. Galen thought about it for a brief moment, then she handed her lively, happy daughter to Charles. Galen smiled softly at the surprised brown eyes. "Entertain her, will you, Charles?"

Charles didn't need to entertain Elise. Just being in his strong arms, patting his cheeks, and hearing his deep gentle voice was entertainment enough. Elise cooed contentedly and was no longer restless.

After Galen gave Elise to Charles, she reached for Jason's hand. Her fingers touched his gold wedding band, new and shiny and matching hers.

This is going to be all right, Galen reminded her fluttering heart. No matter what, we will make it all right.

Jason still held Galen's hand, and Charles still held Elise, when they sat in the doctor's office and heard the results.

"You are genetically very close." The doctor looked from one twin to the other. Physically, they were so different, but genetically . . . "However, there are two markers that are quite distinct. Elise has them, and Galen doesn't, and Jason does."

Galen and Jason greeted the wonderful news with silent tears of joy and an even tighter squeeze of the hands that already held so tight. Galen looked through her blur of tears toward Charles, but she couldn't see his reaction. His face was hidden, nuzzled in Elise's dark-brown curls. When he looked up finally, his eyes were dry.

Charles carried Elise—neither Galen nor Jason made a move to take her from him—until they reached the hospital lobby.

"I think I'll walk back." Charles broke the silence that had been with them since leaving the doctor's office. Charles gave Elise to Jason, met his twin's eyes, and smiled a shaky smile.

Jason returned the smile, and the thoughtful pale-blue eyes sent a message.

Tomorrow, or the day after, or the day after that, Charles, when this is behind us, we need to begin again.

We will, Jason, Charles pledged, perfectly understanding Jason's thought. I just need a little more time.

* * *

Three hours later, when Brooke walked into Charles's office to discuss a contract, she found him staring at the provocative, seductive photograph of Melanie as Sapphire. In the three weeks since Melanie left, Charles hadn't mentioned her. But Brooke knew he thought about her, missed her, every minute. Brooke saw the depthless, silent sadness.

Take care of him, Brooke, Melanie had said.

How can I? Brooke wondered. He is so private.

Now, in this rare, unguarded moment, as Charles gazed at the picture of the woman he loved, Brooke saw his immeasurable sorrow. Charles didn't know she was there; she was intruding. Brooke turned to leave, but her movement drew his attention.

"Brooke."

"Charles, I'm sorry." *I'm sorry to have disturbed you, I'm sorry about Melanie. How can I help you?*

"Have you spoken to her, Brooke?"

"Yes." Brooke smiled wistfully at his hopeful brown eyes. *She doesn't talk about you, Charles, but I feel her pain.* "I don't know where she is. If I knew, Charles, I would tell you."

Charles nodded gratefully. Brooke would help if she could.

"How is she?"

"I think she's better," Brooke answered truthfully. Sometimes Brooke heard a slight lilt in the long-distance voice.

"Does she still plan to be away for two months?"

"Yes." Brooke didn't tell Charles the rest; it was only a guess. I don't think Melanie is ever coming back, not here, not to New York, not to you.

"Is Lieutenant Adrian in?" Brooke asked the receptionist at the precinct. Brooke could see Nick's office but the blinds were closed.

"Oh, Ms. Chandler, how nice to see you! Yes, he's in."

"Is he alone?"

"Yes. Go on in."

Brooke hadn't seen Nick or spoken to him for over five weeks, not since they spent the night wrapping up the Manhattan Ripper case and she left at dawn with Melanie.

"Nick?" Brooke tapped softly on the door that was ajar.

"Brooke." Nick opened the door and smiled. "How are you?"

"Fine. And you?"

"Consumed with paperwork, as usual. Come in."

Nick shut the door, and they were alone in his blind-darkened office, and Brooke suddenly felt anxious and shy. She had come for a *reason*—another confession to Nick Adrian—but she might not find the courage to tell him. There was the reason, that might leave, unspoken, with her; and there was the *excuse.* . . .

"I thought of a name for your book—*In Flagrante Delicto.*"

"My book?"

"About, uh, the case."

"I'm not going to write a book about it."

"I read that in Robin's column, but—"

"I'm not going to."

"Why not?"

"Because," Nick spoke solemnly to the ocean blue eyes, "of the innocent victims."

There were the innocent victims who had died. And there were the innocent victims who had survived: Melanie and Charles and Allison and Adam and *her.* Nick refused the lucrative book offers because of all of them; but, mostly, he refused because of Brooke.

"Nick . . ." Thank you.

"Besides I'm writing a novel."

"About?"

"About life." *About love. About you.* Nick shrugged. "So, how's your new job?"

"It's good. It was the right decision." Brooke frowned slightly.

But something isn't the way she hoped it would be, Nick mused. Some*one* isn't what she had hoped. Was Brooke here to tell him, her good friend Nick, about the love that wasn't happening with Charles? If so, Nick thought impatiently, let's get it over with.

"How is Charles?"

"Charles?" Brooke sighed softly. "Charles is so sad. I don't think Melanie is coming back to him."

"And that's bad?"

Brooke looked at Nick with surprise. "Yes. For both of them."

"But that isn't why you frowned when I asked you about your job?"

Brooke shook her head slowly and her cheeks flushed pink.

"What then?" Nick asked gently. Maybe . . .

"No homicides."

"Which means?" The seductive, inquisitive gray eyes wanted to know the real reason she was here; they demanded it. "Brooke?"

"Which means," Brooke whispered, "I don't see you."

"Brooke." Nick touched her face and felt her tremble Then he kissed her. "Brooke."

"Nick."

They spoke between long, deep, tender kisses.

"I have wanted you."

"Yes?"

"So much."

"Yes." *So much.*

Charles noticed Adam Drake's name on his appointment calendar and frowned. Tomorrow you go away—*run away*—to St. Barts, Charles told himself. Get it all behind you before you leave.

"I'm here to apologize, and it's long overdue."

Charles had never seen doubt in Adam's blue-gray eyes, but he saw it now.

"There's no need to apologize, Adam. It was an emotional time for all of us."

"I was wrong," Adam insisted.

"No, you were right. I hurt her terribly." So much that even though I am finally free of the secrets that made me unable to trust myself with her love, she can't trust me enough to try again. "I hurt her too much."

Charles sighed.

"Besides, Adam, you were involved—"

"No, we weren't. I think I was the only man Melanie even *saw* after you, Charles, but we weren't lovers."

Melanie had been faithful to him? For a moment Charles's heart pounded with hope. He had been faithful to her and the wonderful memory of their love. Had she been faithful to that memory too?

No, Charles decided sadly. Melanie's aversion to new relationships wasn't fidelity; she was merely afraid of getting hurt again.

"That explains why you returned to Paris."

"Yes. Didn't Melanie tell you that there was nothing between us?" Why not? Adam wondered. Revealing that truth had been so important to Melanie. It was all she cared about the day before she was attacked by the Manhattan Ripper.

"In Monte Carlo, but not since." Charles frowned. Melanie and Adam may not have been lovers, but they were friends. Maybe . . . "Have you talked to her, Adam? Do you know where she is?"

"She called last week." Adam heard the quiet desperation in Charles's voice; it matched the emptiness in hers. If Adam knew where Melanie was, he would tell Charles. *I don't trust him when it comes to you,* Adam had told her once. It wasn't true any longer. Adam sighed. "I'm sorry, Charles, I don't know where she is."

"Why did she call?"

"To tell me she was never going to model again. She doesn't think she is beautiful anymore."

Doesn't she know that her magnificent looks are just a tiny part of her true beauty? Charles closed his eyes briefly, his mind tormented by the question. *Oh, darling Melanie, where are you?*

Charles finished packing and gazed at the sapphire-blue Caribbean. His week on St. Barts was over.

Charles had come to the lovely tropical paradise—where the rich and famous go to mourn losses, and rediscover themselves, and fall in love—to say good-bye to the memory. Charles hadn't been able to rent *their* villa on such short notice; it was already taken. Maybe it was just as well; it had been painful enough here, a mile away.

"Monsieur is leaving today?" the housekeeper asked as she emerged from the just-swept living room onto the terrace.

"*Oui.*"

"*Dommage.* Your friend is staying for two more weeks."

Charles spun around. "My friend?"

The housekeeper look confused. She had taken care of the villa when Charles and Melanie were there a year ago. She had assumed . . .

"My friend?" Charles repeated.

"With the long golden hair."

"Where is she?" Charles could barely speak.

"At the villa where you usually stay. Perhaps I shouldn't have told you. . . ." The housekeeper frowned.

"Oh, yes, you should have. Thank you."

Hopeful, wonderful thoughts swirled in his mind as Charles drove the mini-Moke toward the villa. Melanie had chosen to come here, to the place where they had fallen in love. . . .

Charles knocked softly on the villa door. He didn't want to frighten her. There was no answer. Melanie still didn't answer as the energy of his knocking increased. She must be on the terrace or in the cove.

On impulse, Charles turned the doorknob. It was open! Doors were left unlocked on St. Barts. There was nothing to fear. But there had been such horrible, unwelcome intrusions in her life. Charles was glad, despite everything, Melanie felt safe here.

Charles called her name as he walked through the familiar villa. Everything was familiar but the living room. It had been transformed into a designer's workshop. Melanie was designing clothes from the wonderful, vivid tropical fabrics of St. Barts. Some of the fabrics lay neatly folded; others had already been sewn into breathtakingly beautiful creations. Sketches of designs lay on the table beside orderly rows of colorful thread.

Charles blinked away a rush of emotion, then walked beyond the living room onto the terrace. Melanie wasn't there; she had to be at the beach in the private cove. Charles's hands trembled as he opened the forest-green wrought-iron gate.

Melanie sat on the white sand at water's edge. She could be naked here—she had been naked, always, with him—but now she wore a modest white cotton cover-up. She didn't hear his footfalls on the soft sand, but something made her turn toward him as he approached.

"*Charles.*"

"Hi." He knelt on the sand beside her.

"How . . .

"I didn't know. I never even thought to look for you here."

"Look for me?" *Why would you look for me?*

"Yes, of course." Charles frowned briefly, then asked softly, lovingly, "How are you?"

"I'm fine." Melanie looked at him for a moment then spoke to the water and sky. "I'm much stronger."

It was true. Her body was strong again. She jogged and swam and the pain was almost gone and the weakness was vanquished. Her body *felt* fit, but she avoided looking at it. One day she caught her reflection in the mirror and noticed that a once dark-purple scar had faded into a pastel pink. Maybe, as promised, eventually the scars would all be fine white lines; it didn't matter.

"I saw your designs. They're wonderful."

"Thank you." Melanie smiled slightly. "I've even sold some at the boutique in Lorient."

"Melanie Chandler, New York's hottest fashion designer," Charles suggested carefully.

"Not Melanie Chandler." *And not New York.*

"No?" Melanie Sinclair?

"I don't want my success—if I have success—to be because of who I was."

"Who you *are,*" Charles corrected swiftly. *Melanie, look at me.* "So, what label?"

Melanie smiled wistfully at a distant memory that lay beyond the azure horizon.

"I thought of it because of what you said once."

"Yes?"

Melanie nodded and whispered the name of the label that already appeared on the designs she had sold in St. Barts, "Cocoon."

"Melanie."

The softness of his voice filled her eyes with tears. Charles wanted to hold her and kiss away the sadness, but she was so far away.

"Melanie, I know I hurt you terribly And I know you wondered if—"

"No." She turned and spoke to the dark-brown eyes. "No, Charles, I never wondered that."

I never wondered if you were the Manhattan Ripper. I always believed in you, Melanie thought as she returned her gaze to the sea. I always loved you.

"I thought you wanted to try again." His voice was so gentle.

"Yes," she whispered just above the soft sea breeze.

"Then what happened, darling? Why did you leave?" *Tell me, please.*

Don't you know, Charles? Of course, you know. Why are you asking?

"Remember what you told me in Monte Carlo, that I would be better off without you?"

"Yes. I believed it then."

"Because you had deep flaws."

"Yes, and because I loved you so much."

"But you didn't really have deep flaws." Melanie smiled sadly "And now I really do."

"I don't understand."

"Charles, you've seen what I look like."

Hot tears spilled onto her cheeks. Charles moved in front of her, cupped her lovely, sad face in his strong hands, and made her eyes meet his.

Why are you looking at me like that, Charles? Why are you smiling? How can there be desire in your eyes?

"Melanie, is that all?"

"*All?*"

"Darling, I love *you*. I hate what he did to you, because he hurt you and frightened you, but it doesn't *matter*."

"Charles, I . . ." Melanie's voice broke.

Charles rescued her with a kiss.

"I love you, Melanie," Charles whispered as his lips brushed against hers.

"I love you, Charles."

They made love on the white sand beach in their private cove on St. Barts. The tropical sun caressed their naked bodies with a gentle warmth and the sapphire-blue water lapped softly at their feet. They made love slowly and tenderly, leisurely savoring the magnificent joy of being together. This time their loving wasn't desperate.

This time they knew they had forever.

A NOTE ABOUT THE AUTHOR

Before writing her bestselling novels *Love Songs*, *Bel Air*, *The Carlton Club*, *Room-mates*, and *Illusions*, KATHERINE STONE practiced medicine, specializing in internal medicine and infectious diseases. She lives with her husband in the Pacific Northwest and is currently at work on her next novel.

marks noted
pg 139, 321
8-21-98 ay

Fiction St719n
5-98
Stone, Katherine, 1949-

A new collection of
 three complete novels /

ALBANY COUNTY
PUBLIC LIBRARY
LARAMIE, WYOMING

DEMCO